I0763505

RIXON RAIDERS

SPECIAL EDITION COLLECTION

L A COTTON

RIXON RAIDERS
Special Edition

Edited by Andie M Long
Back Cover Art by Dily Iola Designs

THE TROUBLE WITH YOU

To anyone struggling to balance what you think you should be doing with what you want to do...

We only get one life.

Live it.

1

Hailee

"SON OF A BITCH." I slammed my dresser drawer shut and stomped into the bathroom adjoining my room. The one I grudgingly shared with my step-brother.

"Jason!" I yelled, rooting through the laundry hamper, clothes flying everywhere. My breath came in short, sharp bursts. "Jason, I swear to God, I'm going to—"

"Problem, sweetheart?" Mom's head appeared around the door. She caught a flying tee and balled it up, looking at me like I'd lost my freaking mind.

"Jason stole all my bras."

"Hailee Raine, I'm sure he did no such thing." Her expression slipped, her filler-smooth forehead cracking as much as it could. "Are you sure they aren't just all in there?" She motioned to the hamper; the one I was still rummaging through like a crazy person.

My brow rose as I ground out, "He took them. I'll kill him."

"Sweetheart." She let out weary sigh. "Can you and Jason please try to get along this year? It's senior year, you're practically adults. These silly little pranks you two play on—"

"Denise, have you seen my wallet?"

"I think you had it by the coffeemaker," Mom shouted down to her new husband, my step-dad, Kent. "I'd better go help him and then I need to scoot, or I'll be late for the gym, but, baby?" She paused, peering back into the bathroom. "Please try, for me."

"Sure thing, Mom, see you later," I said through gritted teeth, the lie rolling off my tongue easily. She smiled, wishing me a good first day before disappearing down the hall.

I'd learned a long time ago not to expect Mom to intervene in one of mine and Jason's wars. But it didn't matter; I hadn't needed her to fight my battles for a long time.

"Jason," I yelled, storming into his bedroom. I didn't even bother knocking, walking straight inside. Lucky for me, he was just pulling on his jeans. Although it wouldn't have been the first time I'd seen him butt naked.

"Good morning to you too," he said drolly, running a hand through his bed hair.

"Where are they?"

"*They*?" His brows crinkled but his mask of innocence wasn't fooling me.

"My bras, jackass. I know you took them."

"If I wanted to steal bras, I could think of more creative ways." His eyes danced with amusement and I narrowed my gaze, cutting him with a hard look.

"It's the first day of school. I need a bra." No way could I survive a whole day without one. I wasn't one of those girls with a washboard stomach and flat chest. I had curves, more than I cared for at times; especially in gym class when Mr. Tinney made us play dodgeball or volleyball.

"Give me one back," I said. "And we'll forget this whole thing ever happened."

"I have no idea what you're—"

"You want war?" I hissed feeling a ripple of irritation spread through me. "Fine, but don't expect me to go easy on you."

"Ooh, I'm running scared. What are you going to do? Cut me with those?" Jason smirked, dropping his eyes to my chest, where my nipples had hardened with the cool air. I threw my hands around myself, anger bubbling beneath my veins.

Hate was a strong word, but it was the only noun to accurately describe what I felt for my step-brother. He chuckled, throwing random items into his backpack. I was surprised he was even bothering. Senior year was basically a formality for the Rixon Raiders. They would spend more time on the football field this semester than sitting in class. Because their performance on the field was far more important than any test score, *obviously*.

Rolling my eyes, I bit out, "This is really how you want to play it?" I gave him one more chance to concede, but I should have known he wouldn't. Jason Ford might have been my step-brother, but he was still an asshole of epic proportions.

"Like I said, *Hailee Raine*..." He looked so smug, knowing how much I hated when my mom called me that. "I have no idea what you're talking about."

"Fine, but don't say I didn't warn you." I flipped him off before stomping out of there, his smug laughter rolling off my shoulders.

When I finally padded downstairs fifteen minutes later, Kent frowned at me, or rather, my outfit. "Don't ask," I said, in no mood for one of his lame attempts at a joke.

"Wasn't going to say a thing," he replied around a half-smile, as I grabbed the Pop-Tart box from the cabinet and shoved one in the toaster.

"Those things will rot your teeth."

"Does this face look like it cares?"

"Let's be honest." Jason breezed into the room. "No one's going to be looking at your face today."

"Fuck you," I mouthed.

"I heard that," Kent grumbled earning me a snicker from Jason.

They were as bad as each other. *Like father, like son.* Jason had his dad's good looks: unruly brown hair, ice blue eyes framed by long lashes, and a smile that could charm even the most prudish girl to drop her panties. But it was more than that. Jason came from a long line of football players. Rumor around town was Kent had been headed straight to the NFL before a senior-year injury ended his successful college career with the Penn Quakers. It must have been a bitter pill to swallow, but now Jason was set to follow in his footsteps. And the whole town couldn't be prouder. *Someone pass me the bucket.*

The toaster popped, and I pulled off a piece of paper towel, using it as a glove to retrieve the Pop-Tart. "That's me, bye," I said. "Try not to break a leg." I winked at Jason before leaving the house.

My best friend Felicity—or Flick as I tended to call her—was already waiting for me at the end of the driveway in her sunflower yellow Beetle. "That's an *interesting* look you have going on there." She smothered a laugh as I climbed inside.

"Ugh, don't." I shoved my glasses onto my head to keep my hair from my face as I bit into the Pop-Tart, letting the sugary overload tamp down some of my anger. "Jason stole all my bras."

I'd had to improvise and wear a bikini top. It had a little padding, but it was obvious to anyone who knew me I didn't have my usual *support.* With the weather still warm though, it wasn't like I could wear anything other than a t-shirt. Not unless I wanted to spend the day sweating *and* unsupported.

Flick snickered as she drove off. "You'd really think he has more important things to do with his life given it's senior year."

"Oh no, Jason still has more than enough time to make my life hell. But don't worry." I flashed her a secretive smile. "I'm plotting his demise as we speak."

She grimaced. "Not that I haven't enjoyed you putting him in his place a time or two over the last few years, but don't you think you should maybe... back off? He was bad last year but this year he'll be..." She shuddered, not finishing her thought.

Flick was right.

Ever since Jason and I were forced upon one another in sixth grade, when his dad and my mom announced they were moving in together, we'd been at war. Jason didn't want a sister and I had no time for a brother. Especially one as annoying and conceited as Jason. We were polar opposites —him: popular and athletic; and me: artsy and free-spirited. Jason lived and breathed football, like most of Rixon. But not me. I barely even knew the rules of play. Needless to say, as we got older, the rift between us only grew.

He loved nothing more than to piss me the hell off and I loved nothing more than spending my days plotting my sweet revenge.

"Just because everyone else thinks the sun shines out of his ass, doesn't mean I have to lie down at his feet and take his shit."

Flick's brow shot up. "He does have a rather fine ass though."

"Take that back." I almost choked on a mouthful of Pop-Tart. "Take that back, right now."

"What?" Her soft laughter filled the car. "I'd never sample the goods, but it doesn't hurt to look."

"Oh my god, I can't listen to this. Not first thing on a Monday morning." I jammed my fingers in my ears, but she wouldn't shut up.

"Don't tell me you've never had a sneak peek at the guys when they're over? You must have checked out Asher or Cameron's—"

"Felicity Giles, who are you and what have you done with my best friend?"

"What?" She grinned. "I'm just saying, I'm all for hating on the football team, but it doesn't mean we can't appreciate their physical—"

"Stop." I leaned over clapping my hand over her mouth. "Would you just stop, already?"

I didn't want to think about Jason and his friends that way. *Especially* not Cameron Chase. He had reveled in making my life miserable as much as my step-brother ever since we started junior high together. Granted, it hadn't always been that way. When we'd first moved in with Jason and his dad, Cameron had been a buffer to his best friend's open-hostility toward me. For the last five months of sixth grade I'd foolishly believed we might become friends. But then the summer before junior high happened and everything changed.

Everything.

And I realized Cameron Chase was a douchebag just like my new step-brother.

Rixon High School came into view and Flick pulled into the parking lot, her vintage yellow Beetle sticking out like a sore thumb next to all the shiny new Hondas and Fords. Like me, my best friend didn't conform to the masses. We climbed out and made our way toward the school building, and all my earlier anger dissolved at the prospect of getting back in the studio. Unlike most of my classmates who were excited to be back amongst their friends, reliving memories of their summer escapades, I was itching to get back to class, notably art class.

"Breathe it all in." Flick inhaled deeply as we reached the doors. "Our last first day at high school. We'll never start a new year here again. Next year, we'll be freshmen."

I grabbed the door handle and glanced back at her. "We'd better make it count then." I smiled. A genuine honest-to-god smile. Because she was right.

One year.

I only had to survive one more year. Of this town and its beloved football team; of my step-brother and his asshole friends.

Then I'd be free.

But despite my excitement at what the future held—far far away from Rixon, if I had anything to do with it—it was senior year, and I intended on making the most of it.

Then a familiar voice washed over me, a cruel reminder from the Universe that while I still roamed the halls of Rixon High, there was no escaping *them*.

"Looking good, Sunshine."

My eyes snapped up to find Cameron Chase, Rixon Raiders star wide receiver and my step-brother's best friend, smirking at me. "You know I don't like being called that," I said calmly, schooling my irritation.

"I know," he replied with an air of indifference, his shoulders lifting in a shrug. "Nice ti... *t-shirt*." His gaze dropped to my chest before lifting slowly to my face again, amusement dancing in his murky blue eyes. "Is it cold in here or are just happy to see me?"

Cameron winked, before slipping around me and Flick. He shoved my hand off the door handle and I jerked back, caught off-guard by the tiny bolts of electricity shooting through me. He paused for a second, looking at his hand, before shaking his head and ducking inside the building, letting the door slam closed behind him... and right in my face.

With a heavy sigh, I yanked it open and slipped inside, Flick trailing after me. "Just look at that ass," she whispered, leaning in close, watching Cameron's retreating form as kids tripped over themselves to move out of his way. But I wasn't looking at his ass. My eyes were burning into the back of his head, imagining all the painful ways I could hurt him. He glanced over his shoulder, our eyes locking, and I let out a frustrated groan.

I knew that look.

I'd seen it enough over the years. But I'd never seen it from Cameron before. Sure, he went along with Jason's pranks and efforts to find new ways to piss me off. But he'd never been so blatant about it.

I glared back, willing him to look away. But to my surprise—and irritation—he turned around fully, walking backward, his eyes still set right on me. My stomach knotted, the intensity in his gaze disarming. He looked like he either wanted to kill me or devour me, and knowing Cameron the way I did, I knew it wasn't the latter.

Shit, what had him so worked up?

Except for the wedding, I'd avoided the three of them as much as possible over the summer. They had been gone a lot: attending football camps, and then summer practice, and Mr. Bennet had let them vacation at his place in The Hamptons as a pre-birthday treat for Asher. On the rare occasion they were over at the house, I made myself scarce, locking myself away in my bedroom. But from the way Cameron was looking at me, anyone would think I'd killed his puppy and he wanted slow, painful revenge.

"Hmm, Hails, what is happening right now?" Flick's voice pulled me from my thoughts, but it wasn't enough to save me from the trap he'd ensnared me in. "Why is Cameron looking at you like that?" She looped her arm through mine, but before I could respond, Jason appeared out of nowhere and slammed into Cameron, the two of them doing that awkward guy hug thing. I finally shook off the lingering feel of his eyes and went to my locker.

"That was weird," Flick added.

"Probably just enjoying the show." My eyes dropped to my chest and rather obvious nipple situation.

"Maybe," she mused, unconvinced.

I wasn't convinced either. Because I'm pretty sure Cameron had been sending me a message.

And it looked a lot like *game on.*

2

Cameron

"FUCK YEAH, SENIOR YEAR," Asher waggled his brows as he casually leaned against his locker. Most of the kids had already made their way to class, but not our little group. We were in no rush. It wasn't like anyone was going to tell us to move it along.

"Shit, man, did you get a look at Hailee?" Joel Mackey, a sophomore, and our new tight end, grinned. "Can we thank you for that, Jase?"

My eyes wandered absently to where she was just disappearing down the hall with her best friend. I didn't linger though, sliding my gaze to Jason who shrugged with indifference. He liked to play with Hailee, but he wasn't one to brag about it; not outside of our trio anyway.

"Well, I for one, enjoyed the show."

Before I knew what was happening, my hand collided with Joel, slapping him upside the head. He yelped like a little bitch, his smile replaced with a grimace. "Show some damn respect, that's your QB's sister."

"*Step*-sister," Jason corrected me, shooting me a funny look.

"Sorry, Jase, I was only messing around," Joel mumbled, rubbing away my hand print from his skin.

I hadn't meant to hit him, but hearing him talk like that about Hailee didn't sit right with me. Besides, the idea the little fucker had been looking at her at all... The only people allowed to mess with her... to look at her... to *talk* to her... were Jason, Asher, and me.

"Hey Jason, Cam." Khloe Stemson, head cheerleader and total pain in the ass, approached us. "Looking good." Her eyes grazed past Jason and landed on me, and she licked her lips like the viper she was. "I was thinking we should probably get together to talk about the pep rally—"

"Not now, Khloe. We have to get to class." Jason pushed past her, flicking his head for us to follow. Her eyes fixed on me again, glittering lust and desperation, but if she thought I was going to save her, she was barking up the wrong tree. Khloe wasn't the kind of girl you saved. She was the kind of girl you fucked and then moved on.

Swiftly on.

"Are we really going to class?" Asher asked as we made our way down the deserted hall.

"What do you think?" Jason grumbled. "I can't believe we're stuck with Khloe all year."

"Like you haven't already banged that." Asher elbowed Jase who levelled him with a hard look.

"Exactly," he ground out. "And I'm not looking for a repeat. Ever." Contempt dripped from his words, as if the idea of being with a girl more than once was crazy. But then, when girls threw themselves at you the way they did Jason, I couldn't blame him.

Being a Rixon Raider came with a certain set of privileges. We were treated like gods in the halls at school; and outside the school gates, around town, wasn't much different. It was easy to get swept up in it all. The girls. The attention. The respect. But being the team's star quarterback was a whole other deal. Jason Ford wasn't just a Rixon Raider—he was *the* Rixon Raider. The guy legends were made of, and we all knew he had a one-way ticket straight to the NFL.

"So, what's the plan?" Joel said and Jason's head whipped around as if he'd totally forgotten he was with us.

"You should get to class."

"But—"

"Later, Mackey." I shoved him toward the stairs, and he walked away, shoulders slumped, dejection burning in his eyes.

"Little fucker's got balls talking about Hailee like that," Asher said, and my spine straightened.

"Hailee would eat him alive. But no one will touch her," Jase grunted. "Everyone knows she's off-limits."

Thank fuck.

"Anyone would think you want her, the way you act all—"

"What the fuck did you just say?" Jason had Asher pinned up against the wall before he knew what had hit him.

"Easy, man." Asher's eyes were wide, his hands up by his sides in surrender, as I watched on.

Jason and Hailee's games of push and pull were nothing more than sibling rivalry gone bad. Really fucking bad. Me and Asher had been around long enough to know how it was between them, so why Asher was pushing the issue now was an interesting development.

"I'm just yanking your chain," he choked out. "I didn't mean anything by it."

"So don't fucking be saying that shit." He relaxed his hold and Asher slumped down the wall, rubbing his throat. "You know I can barely tolerate her ass and don't even get me started on Denise. I swear I should have figured out a way to sabotage the wedding before they went through with it. I can't believe my dad married that smug bitch."

It was no secret Jason had issues. I would have liked to say his dad's recent nuptials with Hailee's mom was the reason for his anger, but he'd always been that way. Ever since we were kids, he'd had giant chip on his shoulder, angry at the world and everyone in it.

"I don't know," Asher said. "She's always been nice when we come over. Offering us cookies and milk, batting her come-fuck-me-eyes in my direction. Hey, if you need me to help throw a wrench in their post-wedding bliss, I'm more than willing to take one for the team." He grinned, quirking his brows, and Jase tackle hugged him, the two of them falling into the wall again but this time with smiles on their faces.

"Mr. Ford, Mr. Chase, and Mr. Bennet, what a surprise." Principal Finnigan appeared, hands clasped behind his back, disapproval etched into his expression as he watched my two best friends untangle themselves.

"Good morning, Sir." Jason swept a hand through his messy hair, laying it on thick. "How are you today?"

"All the better for seeing you." He deadpanned. "I trust I can expect nothing but hard work and a mature approach to your school experience this semester?"

"Of course, Sir."

"Glad to hear it. It would be a shame to find yourself on the bench in your senior year." The principal gave us a scathing look before going about his business.

"Motherfucker..." Asher muttered under his breath. "Like he can actually do that."

"He's just pissed the school board overruled him last year." There had been an incident with our rivals Rixon East High. Our names all got cleared in the end, but Principal Finnigan had made it his mission to see that the reputation of the football team be *cleaned up*, whatever the fuck that meant.

Finnigan didn't get it. An out-of-town transfer last year, he didn't understand what it was like to live in Rixon, to play football in Rixon. He didn't understand people looked the other way if they saw you up to no good, even if they recognized you as a Raider. Because Rixon, Pennsylvania, was a football town. And it just so happened to have one of the longest standing rivalries in the history of high school football. A rivalry that spilled off the field and into people's lives. A rivalry so embedded into the history of the town, people accepted it as readily as they accepted Fourth of July or Thanksgiving.

"Coach warned us he could be a problem this year, so we need to try to keep our noses clean." Jason shouldered the door to the athletics field, and we cut across the grass to the gym.

"Screw that," Asher said. "Thatcher will be looking to get payback after what you did to Aim..." He backtracked when Jase levelled him with a hard look. "My bad. I'm just saying, after what went down, he'll be gunning for blood."

"He can bring it." Jase growled. "If they come onto our territory, then that's on them. Finnigan can't pin anything on us if it's got their fingerprints all over it."

"So that's it? We just roll over and let them come at us?" Asher threw Jase an incredulous look. But Jase's eyes darkened, a wicked glint in his narrowed gaze as he said, "Who said anything about rolling over?"

"Hit the showers and get out of here," Coach Hasson boomed. I was already ass naked, cupping my junk as I ducked into the showers.

"Bell's tonight?" Asher said from somewhere behind me and Jase grunted, "Yeah."

Jase didn't want to talk, he rarely did after running drills out on the field, but Asher talked enough for the three of us put together. When we'd cleaned the dirt off our skin and let the hot jets unknot the muscles in our bodies, we each grabbed our towels and padded back into the changing room. "What the fuck is wrong with you?" Jase barked at the few remaining guys who were all staring at us.

"I... hmm, shit..." It was Joel who stepped forward, his eyes avoiding his QB, opting for the floor instead.

"Spit it out, Mackey," I said, moving to my locker.

"Hailee, she hmm..."

Hailee?

What the fuck?

Then my eyes dropped to the bench in front of Jase's locker. The bench where his sports bag was. The one that should have been full of his clothes and wasn't.

"Oh shit..." I whistled between my teeth, unsure whether to be impressed or concerned for her life.

"She wouldn't fucking dare." Jase grabbed his bag and turned it upside down. "She took everything." He sounded calm. Deadly.

Shit. Hailee would pay for this, and there was something very wrong with me, because the idea made my dick twitch to life.

My history with Hailee Raine was complicated. When she and her mom first moved in with Jason and his dad, she'd been nothing more than his annoying step-sister. But I quickly learned Hailee Raine wasn't annoying at all. She was smart and quick-witted, and she didn't take Jason's shit.

From day one, she'd stood up to him; looked him right in the eye as he laid into her, laughing at her pigtails, glasses, and denim overalls smeared with paint. He'd called her Pippi Longstocking and said he didn't play with girls who looked like thrift store rejects. Hailee had kicked him in the shin and run off. But she hadn't told on him and she hadn't cried. That got my attention.

But six years was a long time. Now we were older, and Hailee was a different kind of annoying. All grown up, she'd filled out in all the right places since junior high. I'd noticed. Hell, we'd all noticed. It was why Jason had shut that shit down in ninth grade, the year she grew tits. It had been an unspoken rule before then, but that year Jason officially laid down the law.

Hailee Raine was off-limits to the team.

But that wasn't good enough for Jase. No, he issued a whole school lockdown. It was excessive. I knew it. Asher knew it. Everyone knew it. But since everyone also knew her step-brother's reputation of following through on his threats, no one dared ask her out. And for the last three years, Hailee had been a social pariah. She kept herself to herself, had a small circle of friends, and preferred to lose herself in the art studio than lose herself in school spirit. Although part of me couldn't help but wonder if she liked it that way, or if she'd just come to accept her fate.

I should have felt an ounce of guilt of over it—I didn't. Because the truth was, Jason wasn't the only one who had issues with his teammates, or anyone else for that matter, hooking up with Hailee.

"Found them." Grady, another senior, breezed into the locker room, holding a pile of clothes. "But you're not going to like what she did to your jersey." He unballed the white and cobalt-blue shirt and held it up, a strange mix of fear and amusement flashing in his eyes.

"Fuck," someone mumbled as we all took in the drawing of a pair of tits covering half his jersey. If it wasn't so weird it was actually a good drawing. Really good.

"I call a D-cup," someone else shouted. But Jason didn't respond. He simply snatched his jersey back off Grady, anger radiating from him, shoved it into his bag, and started getting dressed.

Jason liked to think he had Hailee under control. Liked to think he called the shots, that he ruled the roost. But over the past couple of years, she'd grown ballsy. Going up against us more. Against him. It was like she didn't give a fuck, and it had made for some entertaining memories.

There was just something about getting a reaction out of her that got my blood pumping. Although he'd never admit it, Jason and his step-sister were a match made in heaven.

Thank fuck my best friend had a shred of morality left. Because watching him jones after his sister would have been a step too far—even for me.

It wasn't that I wanted her.

I didn't.

I just didn't like the idea of anyone else having her either.

3

Hailee

ALL WEEK I waited for Jason to retaliate. But to my surprise, he never did. In fact, Tuesday morning when I'd left my bedroom to go downstairs, I had almost stumbled over a bag of my missing bras. It had taken a thorough investigation to deem them safe. There was no note. No hidden traps. Just my bras in all their super-supportive glory. Anyone else might have thought it was a white flag. But I wasn't anyone else. If anything, I knew the gesture was a decoy, intended to throw me off the scent of whatever he really had planned.

So all week I waited.

And waited.

My senses went on high alert whenever I spotted Jason and his friends in the halls at school. But they barely looked in my direction—just how I usually liked it. Except for Cameron. His eyes always lingered a little too long. As if he was plotting; planning my downfall. It was unnerving, but I didn't overthink it. Maybe he was feeling particularly douchebaggy this year? Whatever it was, I didn't care, because no matter what they dished out in my direction, I could handle it.

I'd been handling it for the last five and a half years.

Everyone thought Jason and I hated each other. But it wasn't about hating him, so much as hating everything he stood for. So he could throw a football? Big whoop. So could thousands of other eighteen-year-olds. Personally, I didn't understand the nation's infatuation. Playing sports didn't make someone a good person. It didn't make them trustworthy or kind. In my experience, football players were usually conceited assholes who cared more about their dicks and winning games than what was going on in the world around them. How *their* actions affected the world around them.

"Earth to Hailee," Flick glared at me and I blinked, stuffing down the memories.

"Yeah?"

She popped a chip in her mouth and frowned. "You're so weird."

"And you shouldn't talk with your mouth full."

"Don't look now," she lowered her voice. "But Jason just walked in."

So what did I do? I looked. Being told not to do something was like a red flag for me to react. Mom called me stubborn, but I preferred dogged. Jason didn't even glance over in our direction though.

Weird.

"Huh," I said, starting to feel a tad disappointed by his lack of retaliation.

"Don't tell me you actually *want* him to come after you?" Flick gawked at me, as I pushed a fry around my plate, coating it in a delicious ketchup and mayo combo.

"I'm not saying I want him to..." My words died on my tongue as I felt eyes on me. Lifting my face, my gaze collided with Cameron's.

"If I didn't know better, I'd say Cameron Chase has a crush. That's the fourth time this week I've caught him looking over here," she said, her lip twitching.

"Yeah," I snorted. "And pigs can fly."

"Would it be so strange? You've known him for years."

"You're serious?" It was my turn to gawk. "Did you forget that he helped my brother that time they stole my bike and clothes when I was swimming down by the creek and I had to walk three miles home in just my bathing suit and flip flops?" Granted we were only thirteen back then, but I'd had blisters for a week, and the sunburn had stung like hell. "Or the time in ninth grade when he and Asher snuck into the house when Jason was sick and decided to scare the shit out of me with those freaky clown masks? Or the time—"

"So they like to get a rise out of you... You know, some people call that foreplay." Her brows waggled suggestively.

"Oh my god, you *are* serious."

Flick shrugged. "I'm just saying, he's looking at you like you're oxygen and he's drowning."

No, he wasn't.

Was he?

I discreetly peeked over at the football team again. They always sat at the same tables; the ones next to the windows overlooking the athletic field. Cameron wasn't watching me now. He was talking to a petite blonde thing—a junior called Kayla, or maybe it was Kylie. I wasn't sure, because unlike most of the kids at Rixon High, I didn't make it my life's mission to know everyone. In fact, I could count my friends on one hand. But it was easier that way. When we'd started high school together, and people realized I was Jason's step-sister, they looked at me differently and I quickly became a stepping stone to Rixon High royalty.

Something I had no desire to be.

Ever.

I watched them together. Cameron smirking, her practically in his lap, all doe-eyed and coy, in a totally obvious kind of way.

"Is that jealousy I see plastered on your face?"

I leaned across the table and pressed my hand to Flick's forehead. "Are you sure you're feeling okay?" We'd never talked much about Jason and his friends, let alone *looked* at them. But I'd caught Felicity's eyes wandering in their direction more than once this week.

"Deny it all you want, but I know these things," laughter filled her voice, "and I'm telling you Cameron's into you."

Into making my life hell more like.

I rolled my eyes at her, but found my gaze wandering back over to him. The blonde was stroking his stubbled jaw now, her chest pushed up against his. God, I wasn't jealous. I was nauseous. The way girls threw themselves at them was disgusting. Raiders didn't date. They screwed around. Rotated through girls like an all you can eat buffet. And the girls at school were all too willing to be on the menu.

"Remember that quiz we had to do at the job fair last year?" Flick said, her eyes darting to the tables the football team occupied. "How many girls do you think answered jersey chaser for the 'where do you see yourself in five years time' question?"

I snickered. "Too many."

"It's so pathetic."

"Desperate," I added, feeling a strange dip in my stomach. Ignoring it, I pushed my plate away, slid on my glasses, and pulled out my sketch pad and pencils.

"What're you working on?" Flick leaned over to get a better look. "Wow, that's good, Hails, really good."

Pride swelled in my chest. I didn't draw for other people, but it never hurt hearing someone appreciated your art. The piece, a sketch of kids filing into school I'd titled 'first day rush', had taken me hours but it still wasn't quite finished. I liked to carry a project around with me for moments like this.

Moments where I needed to escape all the bullshit that came with being Jason Ford's step-sister.

"Hmm, Hails." Flick's voice ruined my concentration and I glared at her.

"What?"

"Is that any way to greet your... *friend*?

I glanced over my shoulder to find Asher Bennet standing behind me, a smug grin plastered on his face.

"What do you want?" Pencil poised between my fingers, spine rigid, I readied myself for whatever bullshit he was about to throw my way.

The tables surrounding us had grown quiet. Everyone knew Jason and I were step-siblings. Everyone also knew there was no love lost between us. He didn't usually come after me during school, preferring to keep our games out of the public eye, so whenever he or one of his friends approached me, it usually warranted everyone's attention.

"I just wanted to return this." He plucked something from behind his back, dropping it on the table in front of me.

My eyes widened and then narrowed at him with contempt. "Where the hell did you get this?" Heat flamed my cheeks as I covered the familiar black lacy bra with my hands, slowly dragging it toward me. It was a stupid question, one I already knew the answer to, but he'd caught me off-guard.

"You left it at my house." Asher stroked his jaw, raising his voice a few decibels to make sure everyone in the immediate vicinity heard him. "When we... you know..." His brows quirked up, a wicked smirk plastered on his face.

The table across from us all snickered, a low rumble of whispers starting to build around me. Son of a bitch. I balled my hands into fists, my nails biting into my palms. There was no way to spin this to my advantage and from the arrogant glint in his eye, he knew it.

I knew if I looked over at the football table, Jason would be watching his plan unfold just the way he'd hoped. I was foolish to let my guard down. But after three days of radio silence, a tiny part of me had hoped he'd finally called a truce. *Stupid girl.* There would never be a truce between us, and I'd stopped wondering a long time ago why he hated me so much.

But I refused to just roll over and take his shit.

I couldn't.

Keeping my glare on Asher, and not the football table, I stood up, and before I could stop myself, I slapped him. The crack of my palm against his cheek pierced the air and his eyes darkened. "What the—"

"You promised," I cried with Oscar-worthy gusto. "You promised you wouldn't tell anyone. I thought... I thought I meant something to you. I thought you *loved* me."

He jerked back. "L- loved you?" Asher laughed but it came out all strangled and wrong. "I never said—"

"Sure, you did." I inched closer to him, lowering my eyes and gazing at him with what I hoped were convincing puppy-dog eyes. "Right after we... *did it*, you said you loved me."

Out of the corner of my eye, I saw Jason moving toward us, anger burning in his blue eyes. Knowing I had his attention, I continued. "I know you're worried about what Jason will say, Ash, but it's okay." My hands slid up his chest and his expression fell. "We can be together. Jason won't... Oh, hi, Jason." I finally looked at him.

"What the fuck are you doing?" he seethed, derision rolling off him.

Stepping back, I moved closer to Jason, cutting us off from prying eyes since we had the attention of the entire cafeteria now. "You think you're so fucking slick," I said through gritted teeth, still smiling. "You'll have to try a damn sight harder than that to embarrass me."

The second I said the words, I saw his eyes light up. Crap. I usually didn't bite, but he got under my skin so much. Too late now though, I'd openly challenged him. And Jason *never* backed down from a challenge.

One of the few things we had in common.

"Jase." The sound of Cameron's gruff voice startled me. I hadn't even realized he had approached us. My eyes lifted to where he stood to the side of Asher. "Come on, she isn't even worth it," he said coolly, not even flinching as the words left his lips, his eyes refusing to meet mine.

But I did flinch.

Even now, after all these years, it was hard to forget Cameron wasn't a good guy. He was a jerk, just like my step-brother and Asher and the rest of the football team. But until this week, he'd never been so obvious about his dislike for me. Not that it really mattered because the feeling was entirely mutual.

Flick had it wrong.

So wrong.

Cameron didn't want me, he wanted to ruin me. And aside from being my step-brother's little bitch, I had no idea why.

"You should listen to him, Jase," I mocked. "Wouldn't want people to think you were—"

"Okay, Hails." Flick's arms came around my waist and she started yanking me away. "I think your work here is done."

The three of them stared after me, a mix of confusion, contempt, and challenge glittering in their eyes. Most girls would have been afraid. Most girls would have run off to the bathrooms and cried over the possibility of the most popular guys in school coming after them.

But I wasn't most girls.

"What the hell was that?" Flick hissed the second we spilled out of the cafeteria. She shoved my messenger bag at me.

"What? I wasn't going to stand by and let Asher do that."

"But calling Jase out like that?"

With a small shrug I took off toward the art studio. I had a free period next and Mr. Jalin was more than happy for me to use one of the rooms, as long as I cleaned up after myself. And I needed to paint away my frustrations.

Flick caught up to me. "Hey, I didn't mean—"

I ground to a halt and met her apologetic gaze. "I know. I just... ugh! He's so infuriating. Do you think I want to spend senior year going back and forth with him? Trust me, I don't. But I can't do nothing either."

I'd tried that before and it didn't work. In ninth grade I'd decided to ignore them. If I didn't react, they'd get bored, right?

Wrong.

The final straw had been when Jason paid Macaulay Denver to ask me out to the spring dance. He was so sweet and insistent, and we shared a common aversion to the football team. It had been impossible to say no to him, but I should have known it was all a ruse. I should have known my twisted step-brother had something to do with it. But I was fourteen and I wanted one night of teenage normalcy.

Macauley's mom had driven us to school and like a true gentleman, he'd opened the door for me and held my hand as we walked into the gymnasium. After finding us a table, Macauley had made sure I was comfortable before going to get us a drink. I'd watched the other kids dancing, laughing, and smiling, and for those few precious minutes, I'd felt like one of them. Until ten minutes later when I saw Macaulay making out with his *real* date, Sarah McKrinsky. Jason had taken great pleasure in telling me the truth, smirking down at me with Cameron and Asher flanking his side like evil lieutenants. I could have run out of there with tears in my eyes and my heart in tatters, but I didn't. Because Jason underestimated me. He failed to realize that every time he toyed with me, every time he tried to beat me down, it only made me stronger. And my walls were so impenetrable now, I wasn't sure there was anything more he could do to hurt me.

Much to my step-brother's annoyance, I'd stayed at the dance that night. Flick and her date were more than happy to let me play third wheel and we'd danced and laughed until the music died and the lights came up. Macaulay had even apologized; saying he felt bullied into going along with it. After all, you didn't tell Jason Ford no. Even then, at the tender age of fourteen, people treated him differently because of his talent on the field. Because of his father's legacy. Ninth-graders rarely had college scouts come out to see them, let alone ask for a verbal commitment to their school, but Jason did. I soon realized it was only going to get worse as he got older. Ignoring him wasn't going to work, so I had no choice but to step up and play his games.

It was hardly any surprise when I never got asked out again.

"I know, I know." Flick sighed. "I just worry about you. I know he's never taken it too far, but something feels different this year."

She wasn't wrong. I felt it too. The change. The shift in the air.

But what choice did I have?

This was my school, my *life*, and I'd be damned if Jason Ford stole that from me too.

4

Cameron

I left Asher and Jase in the gym with the excuse I had to meet with the guidance counsellor. I didn't, but they didn't need to know that. The halls were empty as I made my way to the art studio. Hailee had a free period which meant there was only one place she would be. So it was hardly a surprise when I found her in one of the smaller rooms. The door was ajar and I slipped inside, closing it behind me. It was a risk coming here, but no one would dare question me. And if anyone did run their mouths, I'd spin it to my advantage. Say I was doing Jase a favor, warning her to back off.

Hailee was straddling a chair, her back to me. Her dark blonde hair was pulled up in a messy bun, strands falling around her face as she swiped the paintbrush against the canvas in long angry strokes. Every now and again, she paused, inclining her head, revealing the delicate slope of her neck. The oversized shirt she wore—no doubt to protect her clothes underneath—combined with her black framed glasses, shouldn't have looked so appealing on her. But it did. It looked as sexy as fuck.

She chose that exact moment to pull out the ear buds I hadn't noticed she was wearing. Hailee's shoulders stiffened as if she sensed me, and she glanced over her shoulder. "Get out." Her voice was cold, her eyes not much warmer as they locked on mine.

Throwing up my hands in surrender, I said, "I come in peace."

"Do you take me for a complete fool?"

The verdict was out on that. The way she'd flipped Jason and Asher's little prank earlier was reckless. Amusing as shit, but reckless all the same.

"I'm here to run damage control."

"Damage control?" Her brow shot up, and Hailee swung her leg off the chair to stand up and face me. "We're not friends," she said lifting her chin in defiance, and my dick twitched.

Jesus, this girl made me crazy.

"No, we're not." But there had been a time when I'd wanted that—to be her friend.

Fuck, I shouldn't have come here. Scrubbing a hand over my face, I released a frustrated breath.

"What do you want, Cameron?" Hailee folded her arms over her chest, cocking her hip to one side. "I'm busy."

"You need to back down, Sunshine," I said, and her honey-brown eyes flashed with contempt. Damn this girl. This stubborn reckless girl. I hadn't realized but I'd started moving toward her as if she was reeling me in with some invisible thread.

"Cameron, what are you..." She swallowed, staring up at me as I stopped right in front of her. The air shifted around us, thick and heavy. I'd always kept my distance from Hailee. Looked but never touched. But standing here with her *right there*, I wanted to touch... fuck did I want to touch her.

Surprising us both, I reached out, plucking a strand of hair between my fingers. "Back. Down." I said quietly despite the warning woven into my words. "Jase needs to focus on the team, on the season; he doesn't need to be distracted with your games."

Her gaze widened, her soft-pink lips parted as she sucked in a sharp breath and swatted my hand away. "*My* games?" She almost choked on the words. "Fuck you, Cameron. You know this is all his fault. He's always hated me. He pushes and pushes. But I won't break. I'll *never* break." Hailee trembled, the vibrations rippling off her.

"Are you sure about that?" I cocked a brow at her, stepping further into her space, forcing her backward. Her legs must have hit the chair because she stumbled. My hand flew out to her waist, steadying her, and tiny bolts of electricity zipped through me as our eyes collided. Hailee stared at me, her gaze wide and clouded with confusion. Shit. She'd felt it too. I'd felt it Monday as well, the morning when I'd teased her about her t-shirt.

This was bad... really fucking bad.

Yet, I made no move to pull away. *Pull away dickhead.*

"Cameron. What the hell are you—"

I lowered my head, bringing us face to face. Her eyes simmered with anger, but I didn't miss the way her breath caught again. "Walk away, Sunshine. Jase will get bored eventually if you just back the fuck down."

"Been there, done that, and it didn't fucking work," she seethed. "Two words... Macauley Denver, remember that?"

Remember it?

I'd been plagued with the memories for weeks.

Ignoring her, I said, "One of you needs to back down before shit really hits the fan, and we both know he won't walk away."

Jase played with Hailee, but it was all harmless shit. Sure, she might have got her feelings hurt occasionally or suffered the odd embarrassment at the hands of the kids at school, but it could have been worse... so much worse.

This time was different though. Last season had been tough on Jason. Tensions between the Raiders and the Rixon East Eagles were higher than ever, and he was gunning for blood. I knew it was likely Hailee would be caught in the crossfire. Jason used her as his own personal punching bag. But after calling him out earlier in the cafeteria… Hailee might as well have been the red flag and Jase the bull. I didn't doubt he was already planning his retribution. And, this time, it wouldn't be some childish prank.

She inhaled a harsh breath and my eyes automatically went to her mouth. I closed the distance between us until my lips were hovering right over hers. "Last warning, Sunshine," I whispered, so close I could almost taste her. "Back down or don't say I didn't warn you."

Her palms shot out, slamming against my chest and I staggered back. "Fuck you, Cameron. Fuck all of you."

"Hailee, come on—"

I hadn't meant to use her name, it just tumbled off my lips. But she cut me off. "Get out. Get out before I scream, and I will. I'll do it. You might be a Raider, but I don't care." Her eyes were wild, drilling into mine with such hatred my stomach knotted. But it was a good thing. She needed to hate me.

With a smirk, I started backing away. "Don't come crying to me when he ruins you."

Her face blanched and I knew she remembered every prank, every time Jase came after her. Before she could ream me out some more, I slipped out of the room and got the hell out of the art studio.

Telling myself I hadn't almost just kissed her.

"So, WHAT DID MISS HAMPSTEAD SAY?" Asher asked as we met up outside class.

"She just wanted to run by my college applications again."

Jase scoffed. "Like she doesn't know exactly where you're headed."

"Nothing's a given," I said quietly as we made our way to the locker room.

"You'll be at Penn with me." He spoke the words with no hesitation. None. As if it was already a done deal.

I gave him a hard look. "*I'm* not the golden boy of Rixon." The corner of my mouth lifted. "There's no guarantee the scouts will—"

"They'll want you," he said, cutting me off. "You already know they're interested."

"I need to have other options though." Besides, I wasn't even sure if the call did come, that Penn was what I wanted. It was an Ivy League school and Ivy League meant expensive. So even though it was one of the top football programs in the country, when I had interest from Pittsburg and Michigan State that would most likely come hand-in-hand with athletic scholarships, there was a lot to think about.

"What's up with you?" Jase shoulder-checked me as he shouldered the door. "You've been in a pissy mood all morning."

"He needs to get laid," Asher chimed in, slinging his bag onto the bench. "What's it been, man, like a month?"

"Fuck off." I yanked off my tee and balled it up, throwing it at him.

"Party at my house tonight?"

"You know it. But don't invite Khloe or the cheer squad," Jase said. "It's only the first week of the semester and I'm about done with her shit already."

"Maybe we should invite Hailee?" Asher grinned. "Mix it up a bit."

Jase's eyes widened, his nostrils flaring. "Seriously, you're going to talk to me about her. *Now?* Do you want someone to end up in medical?"

Asher clapped him on the back. "Call it motivation. Coach said you needed to bring your A game this season."

"I always bring my A game, fucker."

"Well you can bring your A+ game then."

"Did I hear someone say party?" Joel stuck his head around the locker cages.

"Yeah, at my place tonight. Spread the word. But no cheerleaders. Invite the gymnastics team though, those girls are as flexible as fuck." Asher grinned. "Hey, Cam, maybe you can hook up with Miley?"

"Maybe I will." I smirked. Miley wasn't a stage five clinger like most of the girls at Rixon.

"You three going to sit around all day bitchin' like little girls?" Coach appeared in the door. "Or are we going to play some ball?"

We hurried to slip on our shoulder pads and cleats and filed out of the door onto the football field.

"Bring it in," Coach boomed, and we moved in to form two semi-circles around him, the front row taking a knee. "Okay, quiet down, quiet down." He waited for the rumble of our chatter to subside. "It's been a good week. You've come into the semester with the dedication and motivation I expect. Jason." He addressed my best friend, and our captain. "You're looking good out there, Son. Are you ready to take your team all the way this season?"

"Yes, Sir."

"I'm sorry." Coach Hasson twisted his face, cupping his ear. "I didn't hear you."

"I said, YES SIR," Jase yelled, his voice carrying across the field.

"That's more like it, Son. Last year was tough." He grimaced. "We knew Rixon East would come at us with everything they had, and they did. It should have been us going to that championship game. But this year, State is ours. Now gather in." We circled Coach, shoulder to shoulder, until he slipped into the formation, holding his fist in the air. Thirty-five fists followed, then Asher's, then mine. Finally, Jase threw his fist up and said, "Raiders on three. One... two..."

Our battle cry filled the air, the ripple of energy palpable. There was nothing more electric, more fulfilling, than standing side-by-side with your teammates, your family, ready for a new season. We all felt it: the anticipation, the hint of things to come. We'd been unlucky last year, losing out at a shot at the State Championship to Rixon East. The only silver lining was those motherfuckers took a crushing defeat against Fieldson Hills.

This year though, this year it was ours. Jase was consumed with the idea of winning, of being the best, of getting his Championship ring before we graduated. And nothing and no one would stand in his way. Jason Ford would knock down anyone who dared try and stop him, and I couldn't help but wonder if that extended to me. His best friend. His brother; maybe not in blood, but in all the ways that counted.

We all knew football meant sacrifice. It meant hard mornings in the gym and long days out on the field. It meant putting everything else second to the game: family, girls, classes, even though Principal Finnigan would have something to say about that. If you wanted to be the best, you had to give your all. Anything less was not an option. You had to live, eat, and breathe it until you bled your team colors. But it would all be worth it in the end. When the call came, it would all be worth it.

Wouldn't it?

5

Hailee

"I CAN'T BELIEVE he said that." Flick shook her head with incredulity as I told her all about Cameron's little stunt earlier, as we ate ice-cream over at Ice T's, a cute little place downtown.

"Believe it. I mean who the hell does he think he is?" Cameron hadn't uttered a word to me in years, except for the odd insult or veiled threat.

She licked her Oreo and strawberry cone, frowning. "And here I really thought he wanted you."

"Trust me, Cameron Chase does not want me," I snorted. "He just wants me to stop messing with his beloved quarterback."

"What are you going to do?"

"Do?"

"Yeah." Her eyes darted to mine. "I mean, he threatened you."

"It's nothing new, Flick." I'd been dealing with their shit for years. "If Jason backs down, so will I, but we both know that will never happen."

"So I guess I know the answer to my next question." Guilt flashed in her eyes causing me to incline my head as I studied her.

"Something you want to tell me?" My brow rose as I licked the spoon clean.

"Well, I was thinking, since it's senior year and all, and since we'll never get these experiences again..." Flick inhaled a deep breath. "That... maybe... weshouldgotothepeprallynextweekend." The words came out in a blast of strawberry scented breath.

"Hold up a minute. You want to go to that thing? We never go." We hated those things. Not to mention the fact it was an entire night dedicated to the football team in all their asshole-glory.

"I know, I know." She hung her head in shame. "It's just I made this stupid list."

"List?" That got my attention. "What list?"

Flick slid her purse onto the table and plucked out a small folded sheet of paper, hesitating. "It's stupid..." Her fingers clutched it like it was the Holy Grail. But now I was intrigued.

"Give it to me." I snatched it out of her fingers and unfolded it, smoothing the paper out on the table. "Number one, take up a new hobby." My eyes lifted to hers. "So that's why you signed up for book club?"

"I like reading." Her shoulders lifted in a small shrug as she stirred the straw around her glass. "Now I get to do it with sixteen other people."

"Okay number two, cut class. But we—"

"*Without* having a valid excuse." Flick gave me a pointed look. "Sneaking off to buy chocolate and tampons because you got your period does not count."

I stuck my tongue out at her. "Moving on. Number three, attend a pep rally. Oh, I know, we could paint our nails Raider blue and make banners too," I smirked, half-expecting her to laugh along with me. But she didn't.

Snatching the list back, Flick scowled at me. "You don't have to be such a bitch about it." Her expression faltered, and guilt coiled around my heart.

"I'm sorry..." I gave her a half-smile. "That was a shitty thing to say."

"Yeah, it was. I might not enjoy school spirit as much as everyone else, but it doesn't mean I don't want to experience everything just once, Hails. This is senior year. Our last year before we go off to college and..."

"You're scared?" I saw it now, the cloudiness in her eyes, how strange she'd been acting all week.

"I'm not scared," she let out a heavy sigh. "I'm just... look." Flick folded her arms on the table and leaned forward. "We can't all be like you, Hails. You're so hardened. Nothing anyone says or does affects you. Most kids our age hide behind a mask, pretending to be strong and untouchable, but not you. You don't have to pretend because it's just how you are."

"I'm not... hardened."

Was I?

And if I was it was only because my circumstances had made me that way.

"Do you know how many guys from school asked me out last year?" Flick asked, and I frowned, wondering what the hell that had to do with anything. "None, Hails. Not a single one."

"So? That's their loss, Flick. You'd be a catch—"

She shook her head, sadness washing over her. "You don't get it." Her walls slammed up and I hated it. We didn't fight, ever. So I didn't understand what was happening right now. "It doesn't matter... forget I said anything."

"No, wait." I laid my hand on hers. "Tell me. I'm your best friend, I want to know." I thought I *did* know everything about her, but obviously I was wrong.

Screwing her eyes tight, Flick sucked in a shaky breath. When she opened them again, fixing her soft green irises on me, my stomach sank, and I knew I wasn't going to like whatever she was about to say.

"It's you," she said flatly.

"Me?" I choked out, feeling like she'd ripped the rug out from under me, my stomach plummeting into my toes.

"Yes... no." She grimaced. "That came out wrong."

Me?

I was the reason guys didn't ask her out? That made no sense because they didn't ask me either. And it had never mattered before. We hung out with guys all the time at The Alley.

"I don't know what you... oh." The truth was written all over her face, I just hadn't wanted to see it.

"Yeah, oh." Flick gave me a weak smile. "You're off-limits, Hails, you know you are. No one will look at you because they're scared of—"

"Jason."

She nodded. "And I'm your best friend. Getting close to me would be like getting close to you and that would be too much of a risk."

"You're not a fucking risk, Flick," I said feeling my irritation levels rise. "Do you really want to go out with some douche who lets my step-brother dictate who he can and can't date?"

"No, I don't. But that isn't the point..." She left the words hanging.

"So what *is* the point?"

"I want to date, goddamn it, Hails. I want to go to Homecoming and Winter Formal. I want to go to Prom."

"Y- you do?" I sank back in my chair, the weight of her confession winding me.

"I love you; you know I do. But being your best friend isn't easy sometimes, Hailee, and you're so... oblivious to that."

"I'm not..." I pressed my lips together, swallowing the argument lodged in my throat. Because Flick was right. Until now, I had no idea she felt that way.

"I don't want to be the next Khloe Stemson. I don't want to join the cheer squad and throw myself at the Raiders feet, that's not what this is. I just don't want to graduate and have all these regrets." She wafted the list in the air with a heavy sigh. "I'm sorry if I hurt your feelings."

"I'm sorry I'm such a hardened bitch who ruins your life."

"Hails..."

"Joke." I held up my hands. "I'm joking." For the most part anyway. "I need to pee; I'll be right back. Can I get you anything else? My treat?"

"Hmm, I shouldn't." Her gaze flicked to the counter. "But I'd accept one of those rocky road brownies as a peace offering."

With a weak smile and a heavy heart, I stood up. "Consider it done." Making my way inside the store, I headed toward the back where the restrooms were.

Flick's admission had caught me completely off-guard. There was no denying Jason had made things difficult since I moved to Rixon, but it wasn't like he'd ruined my life. I still went to class, enjoyed art, and Flick and I participated in non-football-related school events all the time. Granted, we didn't have a huge group of friends and we didn't get invited to any parties, but we were fine. Content in doing our own thing.

Or, at least, I'd thought we were.

After washing my hands, I went to the counter to get Flick's brownie and a strawberry shake for myself. I didn't want her to resent me. We were best friends. Ever since I'd walked into seventh grade math and been seated next to the girl with eyes the color of sage, it had been the two of us against the rest of the world. But she was right, this was senior year. Our final year together. Flick had plans to go off to UPenn next year, and I was hoping to go out of state to Michigan. They had a great art program at their Stamps School of Art and Design. Come this time next year, there would be miles between us, so I guess the least I could do was support her with completing her stupid list.

Not totally on board with the idea, but willing to give it a shot for my very best friend, I paid the server and grabbed my items before heading back outside. But when my eyes landed on our table, I froze. I'd left Flick alone for all of ten minutes, but she wasn't alone now. Jason, Asher, and Cameron were sitting with her, and they were... laughing.

All of them.

Gingerly, I stepped outside and stood at the end of the table. "Did I miss something?"

Flick's face paled at the sound of my voice and I narrowed my eyes at her, silently asking what the hell was going on. "Hmm," she cleared her throat. "Jase and the guys were just going to the store to get supplies for the party."

Jase and the guys? She made it sound like they were old friends.

"And I care why?"

Flick sucked in a sharp breath but didn't get chance to answer because my step-brother rose from the table, his hard eyes fixed on me. "Asher thought you guys might want to come. I told him it was stupid idea."

"Let me get this straight, you're inviting us to a party?" It had set up written all over it.

Asher shrugged, shoving his hands into his pockets. "It's no big deal."

My eyes skirted to Cameron who was silent. I wanted to know what he thought about this after he'd warned me explicitly to back down. Was this a test? Some messed up way of seeing if I'd bite?

He was going to be sorely disappointed. Or depending on which way you looked at it, maybe he'd be impressed.

"Gee, thanks for the invitation but I'm busy washing my hair." I dropped Flick's plate in front of her and sat down. "Now unless you want something else you should—"

"What about you, Felicity?" Jase drawled, a wicked glint in his eyes. "You want to come party with us?"

My gaze widened and she lowered her head, heat flaming her cheeks.

"Shit, man, I think she wants to come." Asher's eyes lit up as if the idea of making Flick defect to their side was just too tempting. "Come on, Felicity, we'll look after you."

My head whipped up to where Jase was standing, and I glowered at him. "Mess with me, play your silly little pranks, fine, but leave her out of this, okay? She doesn't deserve your—"

"Hails," Flick said quietly. "It's fine, I know they're only joking."

"Naw, don't be like that, baby." Asher grinned at her. "You're right, *Hails* isn't welcome, but we'd make an exception for you. Right, Jase?"

His eyes lingered on my best friend, dark and searching, and too fucking long. He reminded me of the Big Bad Wolf ready to pounce on Red Riding Hood. The flush to Flick's cheeks deepened under Jason's intense regard. And before I knew what I was doing, I leaped up and slammed my palms into his chest. "Back off," I snapped, shoving hard.

"Jesus, woman, are you fucking mental? We were just having a little fun."

"Well, don't. She's never done anything to you."

Our eyes locked on one another, simmering with anger and hate.

"Not that I don't enjoy watching the two of you tear into each other..." Cameron's voice startled me, and I blinked, breaking my stalemate with Jason. His lip curved in a smug smile as if he knew he'd won this round.

Bastard.

"Yeah, yeah," Jason said, rubbing his jaw. "Well this has been entertaining, but we have more interesting places to be, little sister."

Little sister?

He was barely two months older than me.

"Yeah, like Jenna Jarvis' pussy," Asher snickered, and I shot him a disgusted look. "What?" He pouted.

"You're a pig."

"Naw, baby, I'm a Raider and we know how to ride real damn—"

"Let's get out of here already, I'm fucking bored." Cameron started walking away. Asher blew Flick a kiss before taking off after his friend, but Jason hovered. His eyes still trained right on me.

"What?" I barked.

Without another word, he shook his head and went after them.

"And you want to embrace *that*?" I said incredulously, dropping back down on the bench.

"I didn't... I'm not... God, you're right," Flick said, her cheeks still pink. But as I watched her watching the three of them stalk off toward Asher's car, laughing and joking, I realized she did want that. She wanted to go to their stupid party and get drunk and make out with some random guy. Maybe even make out with one of them. I suppressed a shudder.

I'd been so consumed with the rivalry between me and Jason, the endless war, and hating on the football team, that I'd failed to see what was right in front of me.

Flick humored me.

All this time I thought we were the same. I thought we shared a mutual hatred of all things school spirit and Rixon Raiders.

But she didn't, not really.

She pretended.

And she did it for me.

6

Cameron

"IS it me or did Felicity Giles get hot this year? Those fucking ugly overalls don't usually do it for me, but on her they look—"

"First Hailee, now Felicity?" Jase jeered. "Next thing, you'll be joining band and wearing one of those fucking awful sweaters." His brows quirked up as he shot Asher a pointed look through the rear-view mirror.

"I'm not saying I'd bang that, but you can't deny they both have that geeky hot girl thing working for them."

His words made my chest tighten and I rubbed the heel of my palm against my leg. Hailee wasn't geeky, she was... Hailee. Unapologetically herself. Always had been.

"Can we please not talk about her anymore?" Jase groaned. "I just want to get fucked up, find some bendy gymnast to fuck, and forget all about Hailee fucking Raine and her mother." His lips pursed, the blood draining from his knuckles as he gripped the steering wheel.

Just then Asher's cell pinged. "Oh shit," he said, and I glanced back. "Thatcher just tweeted throwing some serious shade our way."

"Let me see that." Jase's tone was cold as he reached his hand back waiting for Asher to hand it over. "Motherfucker," he breathed, tossing me the phone.

@ThatcherQB1: *Rixon East are ready to rumble with RHS this year. Raiders gonna run scared after the Eagles are finished with them #Eaglesforthewin #Raiderscansuckit*

"HE'S GUNNING FOR BLOOD," Asher said.

"He's all talk." Jase brushed him off, but I saw the tic in his jaw. There was no love lost between Lewis Thatcher and my best friend. They'd come through Pee Wee together, their rivalry only growing over time. Things had finally come to a head last year, when Thatcher's sister Aimee got involved. And the whole thing had blown up.

"We're stronger on paper and on the field," he added, arrogance rolling off him.

"No doubt," it was barely a grunt from the backseat. But then Asher shoved his face between the two front seats. "They're our third game, right?"

I nodded.

"So, let's get our hands a little dirty before then. Show Thatcher we're not taking any prisoners this year."

"I thought we were done with that shit?" I said. "Finnigan is just looking for an excuse to bench Jase."

"Finnigan can kiss my ass." Jase sneered.

Asher's house came into view and Jase parked up, effectively ending our conversation. We climbed out, grabbed the supplies from the trunk, and went around back where some of the other guys were already hanging out. Asher's parents were cool, and since they were out of town for business a lot, we usually hung out here. His house was bigger than most of our places, thanks to his dad's successful tech company. It backed onto a small lake where they had jet skis and a small motorboat, as if the huge pool and fire pit wasn't already enough.

It was pretty awesome.

Jase went to join the guys, leaving me and Asher to take the beer and snacks inside. I dumped the bags on the counter levelling him with a hard look. "Why the fuck do you keep bringing up Hailee?"

"That shit's funny. I've never seen Jase so bent out of shape over a girl."

"It's his sister, or have you forgotten that?"

"Still... it's not like they're blood-related."

"Something is very fucking wrong with you." I folded my arms across my chest, letting him deal with the bags. "Don't be stirring up trouble, Ash, we don't need it. Not this year."

"Yeah, yeah." He ducked into the refrigerator to stow the beers. When he was done, he leaned against the counter, his eyes searching mine. "I still can't believe it's senior year. Have you thought about what you might do?"

Dragging a hand down my face, I shook my head. "It's not that simple."

"Yeah, I know. But if you know Penn isn't going to be—"

"What's taking so long?" Jase appeared in the door, his eyes hard and assessing.

"Just grabbing some beer, man." Asher grabbed a six-pack and chucked a bag of chips at me. "Come on." He brushed past Jase and went outside.

"You okay?" Jase tipped his head at me, and I nodded.

"Yeah, I'm good."

His eyes lingered on me a second longer, then he spun around and followed Asher. I sagged back against the counter, releasing the breath I'd been holding. Jase didn't get it. He didn't get why anything would take precedence over football. Over college. I guess that's what made him different—what gave him an edge other players didn't have. He was detached enough from life to make the sacrifices required, and then some. He didn't worry about family because his team, football, was his family. I guess he'd learned that from his dad. But my dad hadn't been a rising football star, and although he supported me, supported the team, he also had other things going on that required his attention.

Sometimes, it felt like I was standing at a crossroads: one foot planted firmly in my dreams of football and college and the promise of going all the way to the NFL; the other remaining rooted in real life where dreams didn't always come true and life wasn't always fair. And balancing the two... well, it was hard fucking work.

"Yo, Cam, grab an extra bag of chips." Asher's voice cut through my thoughts and I stuffed down all my shit and locked it away tight. Because right now I was a Raider, and football and all that came with it, needed to be my priority.

"I'm just saying," Mackey stood tall, swaying slightly in the middle of our circle of chairs. "Alabama are looking tight this year, and Clemson are looking stronger than ever, but my money is on the Buckeyes."

A sea of crumpled Solo cups rained down on him as he held up his hands to shield his face. "Come on, Jase, man, help a guy out. Ohio State wanted you, right? What do you think?"

My eyes fell to Jase who was sitting in a chair, legs kicked out in front of him, his eyes slightly glazed from one too many beers. "There's no denying Ohio are going to be bringing everything they've got this year, but it's not this season I'm interested in, it's next season. And rumor has it, Penn have recruited one of the best QB's in the country." He smirked. "It's a motherfucking gamechanger."

Quiet laughter rippled around the fire pit. "Not that I'm knocking the Nittany Lions, I'm not," Grady said. "But you do know they haven't won a national championship since nineteen-eighty-six, right?"

Jase shrugged, arrogance rolling off him. "I heard Deontay Syracuse is going to commit to Penn. He's the best DT in the country right now. Together, we'll be unstoppable."

Someone let out a low whistle.

"What about Chase? They want you too, right?"

It was my turn to shrug, taking a big swallow of beer. Jase's eyes slid to mine but he didn't speak. "I'm still deciding."

The shrill of Asher's ring tone pierced the thick silence that had descended over us, and he clambered to his feet. "The entertainment has arrived." With a shit-eating grin he disappeared while Grady, Mackey, and a few of the other guys began scrutinizing Penn's two-thousand-nineteen line up.

When Asher reappeared, his arm was slung around a cute brunette I recognized from the gym team. "Girls, welcome," he declared. "Make yourself at home. Drinks are in the kitchen." He swung the girl around and pointed to the house. "Pool's right over there, feel free to get in. But if you do, you should probably know about the rule."

"Rule?" one of them asked.

"Yeah, it's this whole thing my dad has about keeping the water clean." He fought a smirk. "He prefers it if we all swim naked. Less chemicals."

"Yeah, but more bodily fluids," one of the guys howled, and laughter rumbled around us as the girls rolled their eyes, giggling and whispering about Asher's smooth-talking ways.

But it worked. A couple of them broke away from their friends and started peeling off their clothes. Granted they didn't get naked, but their tiny bikinis left very little to the imagination.

"Fuck yeah," Mackey said, jumping up and yanking off his jersey. "Wait for me." He took a running jump and bombed into the water, sending a shower of spray in the girls' direction. They threw their heads back, laughing, grabbed each other's hands and took off after him.

Things quickly escalated from the team hanging out and discussing the upcoming college football season to an all-out party. Asher cranked up the sound system before joining the girls in the pool, and Jenna Jarvis made a beeline for Jason, sliding onto his lap and running her fingers through his hair. He dipped his head, dragging his tongue along her jaw, and she opened up willingly, sucking it into her mouth. No sweet talk, no coercion, or promises of things he would never follow through on. But girls like Jenna were a dime a dozen. They knew what Jason was about and they were still willing to walk into the lion's den. Just for the chance to say they had their shot at taming him.

I was still watching them out the corner of my eye when Miley Connor stepped into my field of vision. "Cameron Chase, fancy finding you here." She grinned but not in that coy please-pick-me way but with more of a guy-to-guy way.

"What's up, Miley?"

"Not you, apparently." Her gaze dropped to my crotch, and I gave her a throaty laugh.

The other thing about Miley... she had no filter. Taking the chair beside me, Miley sipped her drink. She looked good, the cut-off shorts and tank top molding to her lean body, toned from hours of practice. Miley was like the rest of us, an athlete. She knew all about sacrifice, about being in peak physical condition. And unlike so many of her teammates, she didn't have time to chase football players. Not with her sights firmly set on the Olympics.

It's why I liked her.

With Miley I felt no expectation, no pressure to promise things I couldn't give her. We hooked up, used each other to escape, just for a little while. And when we were done, we went our separate ways until the next time.

"Why so glum, Chase? It's senior year," she said looking out over the party.

"Do you ever get tired of it?" I asked her quietly.

"I get tired of not being able to eat what I want when I want, if that's what you mean?" Miley let out a long groan. "What I wouldn't give to be able to go to Pepe's Pizza and eat a whole pepperoni and onion to myself and then make myself sick on cookie dough ice-cream. But it's the sacrifice we make." She glanced at me, smiling.

"A little birdie told me you're going to commit early to Alabama?"

"That birdie would be right."

"Nice." I envied her being so sure, so certain of her future.

"It's a big move but it's the best program in the country, and I want to be the best." She gave me a warm smile. "What about you? A little birdie, also known as our entire class, are saying Penn want you as well as Jason?"

"They're interested but I haven't committed yet."

"Ivy League," she whistled through her teeth. "Impressive."

"I'm not just a pretty face and one of the best wide receivers in the State, you know?" I grinned at her.

"No, Cameron Chase, no you're not. You're also very, very good with your tongue." Her eyes darkened with lust. "Want to get out of here?"

"I thought you'd never ask." I downed the rest of my beer and stood up, waiting for Miley to do the same. Asher caught my eye across the pool. He knew the deal with me and Miley, but he was too busy all up in one of her friends to give me shit about it.

"We're out," I said to Jase as we passed him.

"Here?" he asked, and I knew he meant were we going upstairs or somewhere else.

I looked to Miley who shrugged. "I'm easy."

"I bet you are," Jase snickered, and I threw him a harsh look.

"Watch this one, Jenna," Miley said with a hint of bitterness. "I've heard he bites."

Jenna lifted her face from Jason's neck, her lip curved with arrogance. "Oh, I know he does. But I bite harder."

Well, okay then.

"Come on, Chase," Miley laughed softly, and I jammed my hands in my pockets, following her toward Asher's house. "Fancy place," she said.

"Yeah, Ash's parents are loaded."

"You don't say."

We slipped inside and Miley paused, letting me lead the way. I stopped to grab a couple bottles of water and then led her upstairs to the guest room the Bennets let me use whenever I stopped over. I wouldn't exactly call it my room, but no one else stayed in here. They'd even given me a key last year.

"What is this?" Miley asked when I stopped outside the familiar door and dug the key out of my wallet "Your red room of pain?"

"Something like that," I smirked at her. "Why, scared?"

"Nah, Chase. You put on a good show, but I see underneath all that macho Raider bullshit."

Her words caught me off-guard, but I schooled my expression. "You know what this is, right?"

"Yeah, yeah," she replied giving me a little shake of her head. "We fuck, nothing more, nothing less. I'm not asking you for anything."

With a curt nod, I pushed open the door and pulled her inside. Sometimes, in the quiet moments after sex with Miley, I wondered what it would be like to open up to her; to tell her all my deepest fears, my darkest secrets. We weren't that to one another though, and I didn't want that, not with her anyway.

But life wasn't fair, and we couldn't always have what we wanted.

I knew that better than most people.

7

Hailee

"THIS IS A BAD IDEA." Flick snatched the bottle of vodka mixer from me and took a big swallow of it. "This is a very bad idea." She smeared the back of her hand across her mouth before hiccupping.

"Come on, we need to be quick." I grabbed her hand, pulling her through the trees bordering the Bennets' property.

"I can't believe I let you talk me into this," she groaned quietly as the woods grew denser, the shadows swallowing us whole.

"Consider it something to add to your list."

"Hails."

"Oh, come on, Flick. I already I said I'd go with you to the stupid pep rally, and I'll consider Homecoming—"

"You will?" The hope in her voice made me feel like the shittiest friend ever but I buried down the emotion, focusing on the task at hand.

When Jason, Cameron, and Asher had walked away from us at Ice T's, I knew I couldn't just leave it. Even if Cameron had warned me to back down. It was one thing to mess with me but to mess with Flick? That was completely unacceptable, especially after I'd learned she actually wanted to go to their stupid party. So, while she devoured her apology-brownie, I hatched a plan.

"Okay," I said pausing at the edge of the trees right where they met Asher's driveway. "Give me the drink." I needed some more Dutch courage for what I was about to do. It was stupid and reckless, and it could land me in hot water if anyone caught me, but it would be so worth it.

I chugged the remainder of the vodka mixer, my stomach churning as the bitter taste flooded my senses. When I was done, I tossed the bottle into the undergrowth and held out my hand. "Now give me the other stuff."

Flick hiccupped again before handing me the cannister and sticker. "Are you absolutely sure about this?"

"Do you even need to ask?"

"I guess not. But, Hails, you don't need to do this, not for me."

"Hush now, I need to concentrate." I read the instructions again, my glassy eyes making everything a little blurred. When I was sure I had it, I gave Flick my attention. "Wait here, okay? I won't be long." Slipping my hood over my head, I pulled the cord to conceal as much of my face as possible and slowly inched from the trees.

The front of the house was steeped in darkness; all noise and music coming from around the back. I'd never been in Asher's house before, but everyone knew his parents were rich. I had overheard kids at school talk about his infamous parties down by the lake his property backed onto. My eyes darted left and right, making sure no one was around, before I cut across the driveway to the row of cars. Asher's Jeep, Cameron's truck, and finally my target: Jason's restored 1969 Dodge Charger.

Moving around the body of the car, I crouched in front of the hood. My fingers trembled, my heart pounding against my ribcage, as I worked the sticker off the backing and positioned it front and center on the sleek black paintwork. Rubbing out any air pockets, I smoothed the Rixon East Eagles logo onto the hood, and then set to work on the spray paint.

"Hails," Flick's hushed voice carried on the breeze as I leaned over the hood to reach the windshield, spraying with as much accuracy as I could manage given the lack of light and my current lack of sobriety. "Hurry up."

"Coming, I'm almost done." Stepping back to survey my handiwork, I smiled to myself. Jason was going to kill me. If there was one thing he loved almost as much as football, it was this car. And when he realized... shit. It suddenly occurred to me I might not be the first suspect to pop into Jason's mind.

The Raiders had a messy history with Rixon East High. A rivalry dating back decades. A rivalry that had only burned brighter since Jason became QB One for the Raiders. Crap. What if he thought someone from their team had done it? I could be the match lighting a long-simmering fuse. It was too late to worry now though. I had no way of removing the sticker or spray paint.

Scooping up all the evidence, I shoved it in my pockets, and checked the driveway again before ducking back into the shadows. But the sound of voices startled me, and I dashed back to Asher's Jeep, crouching down behind it.

"You sure you're good getting home?"

It was Cameron. *Thank God.* At least it wasn't Jason; maybe I could still get out of this without being caught. The cars were parked in front of the double garage adjoining the house so if no one came around here, then I would be fine.

"Yeah," a female voice said. "I'm a big girl, I can take care of myself. It's cute you care though."

He gave a strained laugh and my stomach knotted. Cameron and a girl. It shouldn't have surprised me. The words Raider and manwhore practically went hand-in-hand.

"Thanks," he said. "For... you know."

"It's always a pleasure, Chase. I'd coming running any day of the week for that trick you do with your..." The soft purr of a car engine drowned out her words. Thank God, because I really didn't want to hear all about Cameron's amazing skills in the bedroom.

Shuffling to the other corner of the Jeep, I leaned up slightly to try to get a look at whoever Cameron was saying goodnight to. But all I caught was the flash of long dark hair before she climbed inside the Uber car.

Now was my chance, I had to get out of here. Crouching down again, I slipped out from behind the Jeep and ran. But right before I hit the tree line, the cannister fell out of my pocket, rolling to the floor with a loud *clunk*. I froze, my body paralyzed as I held my breath, waiting. Maybe Cameron had already gone inside, maybe he was—

"What the fuck?"

Shit.

Shit!

My pulse pounded against my skull as I tried to figure out my options. I could make a run for the trees and hope he didn't give chase, or I could turn around and fess up. Either way, it wasn't looking good for me. I'd hoped to be safely tucked up in bed when Jason discovered my latest handiwork.

Deciding to take my chances, I took one step, ready to dive for the trees, but footsteps crunched on the gravel behind me. "Who's there? Thatcher, if that's you, you'd better—"

I turned slowly, loosening the cord of my hood to reveal my face. Cameron's mask of fury faltered for a second, his eyes widening. But they quickly narrowed dangerously as he stalked closer. "Sunshine? What the actual fuck?"

"Hmm, hey." I gave him a wry smile.

He grabbed my arm and I wondered what the hell he was doing until he pulled me further into the shadows. "What the hell Cam—"

His head flicked up to the house where there was a CCTV camera. Crap. Why hadn't I thought of that? *Probably because you're drunk on vodka mixer and high on adrenaline, idiot.*

"Now," his voice was cold. "Want to explain to me what the fuck you think you're doing?"

"Hmm, about that... Well, I thought Jason's car needed a little facelift?" It came out more of question than the sarcastic wisecrack I'd been shooting for.

Cameron blew out an exasperated breath and I'm sure I heard him whisper, "You're not making this easy for me." But I figured my ears were playing drunken tricks on me. "You couldn't just walk away, could you?" His eyes pinned me to the spot.

But screw that.

And screw him.

"Then maybe you should rein your boy in." I jabbed my finger at him. "I can take him messing with me. But not Flick. She's not a part of this."

He leaned in, curling his fingers around mine. "And you don't think when he finds out you did this, he'll come after you with everything he's got? Think about it, Sunshine."

"Stop calling me that." I couldn't think straight when he said it.

Cameron's mouth curved, only a fraction, but enough for me to know he was enjoying this. *Asshole.* He was just like my step-brother. Worse even, because there had been a time when I truly believed he was different. But I was young and foolish and I'd learned my lesson where Cameron Chase was concerned.

"What are you going to do?" He frowned at that, so I added, "Are you going to tell him?"

"Let me worry about Jason, you just worry about yourself."

"What the hell does that mean?"

More voices pierced the air and Cameron glanced to the gate beside the garage. "Shit," he mumbled. "You need to get out of here."

"But what about—"

"Hailee, just go. Now."

"Hails?" Flick burst through the trees, her eyes glassy and wide, panic etched into her soft features. Cameron cussed under his breath. "Are you both drunk?" he sounded pissed.

"I... we..." My eyes moved to the gate, the clunk of metal catching my attention.

"Get her out of here, now. And don't come back." Cameron wasn't talking to me now, he was glaring at Felicity as if she was somehow to blame for all this.

"Don't look at her like that," I started but Flick already had her hand on my arm, trying to pull me away.

"Yo, Chase? You out here?" My step-brother's voice was close now. "I thought I heard a car."

"Go, *now*," Cameron's voice was a deadly whisper.

Vodka obviously gave Flick super-strength because she yanked me into the trees like I weighed nothing, Cameron's face no longer fully visible through the leaves. "What the hell was that?" she hissed.

But I couldn't answer because I didn't have one.

"Motherfucker!" The boom of Jason's voice, the anger dripping from every syllable, drowned out all my thoughts.

"Shit." I jumped into action. "We need to get out of here, now." My hand found Flick's and started pulling as I moved quickly through the woods. We'd walked to Asher's house from Flick's. She only lived a couple of blocks over, but it was far enough for Jason to find us if we didn't hurry the hell up.

Once we were clear of the Bennets' property, we ran. Neither of us were very athletic but we didn't need an excuse tonight. Our feet pounded the ground, trees and branches rushing past us, shadows dancing across my vision. When we spilled out of the woods onto the street, I'd never been happier to see Flick's house up in the distance.

"Come on," I said breathlessly, linking my arm through hers, and glancing over my shoulder one last time. "We should probably get inside."

Forty minutes later, we were both showered and lying on Flick's bed in our pajamas. "I can't believe Cameron caught you," she said, taking a bite of Twizzler.

"I wonder what he told Jason."

"I guess you'll know soon enough."

"What's that supposed to mean?" My brows crinkled.

"Well, if he does tell Jason, you can expect some awful retaliation, and if he doesn't, then I guess you're safe... for now."

"You make it sound like an episode of Game of Thrones."

"More like the Battle of the Sexes," she joked, and I nudged her shoulder with mine.

"It was weird though, right? Cameron could have cussed me out right there, but he didn't. He told us to go." Flick smirked, and I added, "What?"

"Nope. Nothing..."

"Come on, tell me."

"I know you think he doesn't want you, Hails, but you have to admit, it seemed a little bit like he was protecting you."

"*Protecting* me?" I sounded incredulous. "Two minutes earlier he was saying goodnight to his little fuck piece."

"Little fuck piece?" Flick exploded with laughter, rolling onto her back, but I wasn't laughing. I didn't know what I was anymore. Senior year was turning out to be more confusing than I anticipated.

I rolled over too, lying shoulder to shoulder with her. We both stared up at the ceiling, letting the events of the night settle over us. "Did you have fun?"

"Fun?" she balked. "Getting chased off Asher Bennet's property by Cameron after you tagged Jason's car, isn't my idea of fun, Hails. Why?" Suspicion dripped from her question. "Did *you* have fun?"

"I think I'm wired wrong," I admitted. Because while I'd been terrified coming face to face with Cameron, I couldn't deny a part of me liked it. The danger, the heart-pounding thrill as I stickered Jason's car with his rival's logo.

"You're not wired wrong," Flick sounded sad. "You're just so used to being on the defensive, to playing these stupid games with Jason, that it's altered your perception of what's fun and what isn't."

"You mean I'm hardened?" I flinched, remembering the word she'd called me earlier at Ice T's. It already felt like a lifetime ago.

"Yes... and no. I do think you're hardened, Hails, but you've had to be, I get that. But this thing with you and Jason, the constant back and forth; you don't have to prove anything to him."

Prove anything?

She thought I was trying to prove myself to him?

"That's not what I'm doing," I said, but as the words came out, I realized maybe she had a point. Jason had been so quick to write me off when our parents first got together. He never even gave me a chance. And maybe part of me engaging in this battle of wills with him was about more than knocking him off the pedestal the school, the town, put him on. Maybe deep down, I wanted him to realize I was a good person. A person worth knowing.

A *sister* worth having.

Ugh. I hated feeling like this. Weak and at his mercy.

I hated feeling like Jason's opinion of me mattered at all.

Rolling onto my side, I turned away from Flick. After a couple of seconds of silence, her voice drifted over me. "I'm sorry, I didn't mean to upset you."

"It's fine," I choked out, swallowing the tears threatening to fall.

I wouldn't cry.

Not over this.

And definitely not over my asshole of a step-brother and his friends.

"I just don't want to see you get hurt," she said, rolling behind me. Flick slipped her arm around my waist and tucked herself against my back. "I know you, Hails, and I know you'd never let things go too far, but Jason? I'm not so sure about him. He has to be the best, come out on top, whatever the cost. You should know that by now."

I did.

He was cold. Focused. Determined to succeed no matter what.

And for as much as I talked a good talk, even walked it sometimes too, I wasn't like him. I was hardened, yes, but I still had feelings. I still hurt. Cut me open and I was pretty sure I'd still bleed red, unlike Jason who would bleed blue and white. Or maybe even black to match the color of his soul.

My best friend was right. If I wasn't careful, this game between me and Jason was going to chew me up until nothing was left. It's what Cameron had been warning me about too. Jason wouldn't stop. He'd keep pushing, keep coming at me, until I surrendered.

But even knowing he might hurt me, that in the end, Jason might successfully smash through my walls, I still didn't know if I could do it.

I didn't know if I could walk away.

8

Cameron

"AFTER THATCHER TALKING shit on Twitter and Snapchat all week, my money's on him." Asher took a long pull on his beer, slouching down in one of the La-Z-boy chairs in his games room.

"Well he's got a fucking death wish, if it was." Jason's whole demeanor radiated anger. After he saw his car—and Hailee's handiwork—I thought he was going to detonate. Asher acted quickly and shut down the party, sending everyone home, while we tried to clean up his car and calm him the fuck down. We'd gotten the sticker off without any damage, but the paint was going to need removing professionally.

"We can't jump to any conclusions," I said. "If we go after Thatcher and we're wrong that could cost us—"

"Yeah, but come on, man," Asher folded his hands behind his head. "Who else is dumb enough to do something like... Hailee." His eyes lit up. "It could have been her."

"Nah, man," I said trying to act cool. "She's up for a prank or two but criminal damage?"

Jason was quiet. Too fucking quiet. I watched him out of the corner of my eye, trying to figure out what was going on in that head of his.

"You checked the CCTV?" he asked Asher who nodded.

"Like I said before, my old man switched off the system before the summer when it started glitching. He still hasn't gotten around to fixing it."

Thank fuck.

Jase grunted, rubbing his jaw. "Nah, Hailee wouldn't do it. She's ballsy but she's doesn't have balls big enough to pull something like this. It had to be Thatcher."

I didn't know what to do. On the one hand, I could fess up and deliver Hailee right at his feet... or, I could withhold the truth and give him more ammunition to go after Thatcher.

Either way, it was a shit show waiting to happen.

But could I rat Hailee out knowing Jason would come after her with everything he had?

"Still," I said making my decision. "Without evidence, you need to tread carefully. Finnigan is just itching for an excuse to come down hard on you. If he so much as gets a whiff of trouble with East he's going to pounce."

Jase sat back, considering my words. While Asher liked to stir trouble, I'd always been Jase's voice of reason.

"Fuck, I want to destroy that piece of shit."

"So, do it on the field, where it'll hurt most." Thatcher was much like Jason; hard-headed, arrogant, and devoted one-hundred-and-ten percent to the game. Losing to the Raiders would be almost as good as any retaliation Jase and Asher could dream up for him.

"Or we go across river and show that fucker what the Raiders are really about," Asher said around a shit-eating grin.

I cut him with a hard look, but Jase surprised me when he said, "Nah, Chase is right. Although I'm ninety-five percent sure it was him or one of his guys, we can't hit back. Not yet. Not with Finnigan breathing down our necks."

Asher grumbled under his breath but didn't argue. Jase's word was final, it always was.

"Doesn't mean I still don't need to get Hailee back though."

"Now we're talking." Asher rubbed his hands together, mischief dancing in his eyes. "Can we play with Felicity too?"

Jase's expression hardened; only for a split-second, but I saw it.

Interesting.

"Nah, Hailee is right, this is between me and her." Except he was all too happy to get us to do his dirty work now and again.

Asher shrugged. "Yeah, whatever, man."

"I'm going to get another beer," I said. "You guys want?"

They both nodded and I left them to it. I was right to lie to Jason. If he knew Hailee was the one behind what happened to his car... well, I didn't want to think about what he would do. But I realized now he wasn't ever going to give up this game of cat and mouse with her. And if he misdirected his anger at Thatcher toward her, things could still get ugly.

Unless Hailee was put in her place once and for all.

MONDAY ROLLED AROUND and everyone was talking about the upcoming pep rally. It was always a big deal with the whole school showing up to support the Raiders and welcome this year's Varsity team. Khloe had been blowing up Jase's cell phone all day wanting to know when they could get together to plan our *grand entrance*. Eventually, she'd pinned him down during his free period, but I'd left him to face her alone, saying I needed to show up for class. He'd pointed out that I was already late, but I'd just grinned and got the hell out of there.

I hadn't expected to walk straight into Hailee as I rounded the empty hall. "I need to talk to you." She grabbed my arm and yanked me into the janitor's closet.

"Hello to you too." I glared down at her, confused about how I felt about her manhandling me. On the one hand, my dick liked it. If the hard bulge in my jeans was anything to go by, it liked it a whole lot. But my head knew it was a dangerous game she was playing.

"Why didn't you tell Jason it was me?" Her eyes narrowed with suspicion, but I didn't blame her. How could I when she had every right to be wary of me?

"So, you heard the rumors then?" A slow smirk tugged at my lips. "About how Rixon East snuck across the river and tagged our captain's car? Tsk, tsk."

"Cameron..."

"*Sunshine...*" My smirk grew.

"God, you're infuriating." Hailee backed up, putting some space between us but it was the janitor's closet so there really wasn't much.

My brow quirked up. "Me? *I'm* infuriating? You might want to take a long hard look in the mirror, Suns—"

"*Stop* calling me that," she snapped, before releasing an exasperated breath. "Why did you do it? Why did you protect me?"

"You think that was me *protecting* you?" My gaze hardened as I folded my arms over my chest. "Sorry to burst your little bubble, but that wasn't me protecting you. That was me protecting my best friend from himself. From doing something really fucked up."

"He's a grown man," she scoffed. "I'm pretty sure he's quite capable of bearing the consequences of his actions." It was Hailee's turn to raise a brow.

"You don't understand."

How could she?

"Ha, football." The word was wrapped in bitterness. "It all comes back to football, doesn't it?" Hailee shook her head with incredulity.

"Jason has his whole career ahead of him. He doesn't need to be distracted by you and your inability to know when to quit."

"I..." Her expression slipped and a bolt of guilt went through me, but it was quickly followed by something else. The thing living inside me that had gotten used to watching Hailee battle with Jason. That enjoyed her smart mouth and reckless actions.

That craved them.

Shit, I was so messed up when it came to her.

"Admit it, Sunshine. You're just like him. You can't stand the thought of losing to him." I lowered my face to hers. "I think you like these games. Like all the attention we give you. The attention *I* give you."

Her eyes flared with anger as she sucked in a harsh breath. It was only a small action but enough to pull my gaze to her lips. Those soft-pink kissable lips.

Fuck it.

She already hated me, she might as well hate me some more.

I reached out for a strand of her silky hair, the same as I had when I'd paid her a visit in the art studio. "Cameron?" she asked, her voice uncertain and quiet and so unlike her. "Why are you looking at me like that?"

"Like what, Hailee?"

She swallowed, her tongue darting out to swipe across her bottom lip.

And I was done.

The thin rope of my control snapped, my mouth crashing down on hers as I threaded my hands into her hair and pressed us against the rack. Hailee's fingers gripped my jersey, pulling me closer... or was she trying to push me away? I didn't know, didn't care, because the taste of her lips on mine, the way my tongue slid against hers, it consumed me until I was drowning in nothing but Hailee fucking Raine.

My hand skated down her waist, sliding around to her ass to pull her closer, fitting our bodies together like two pieces of a puzzle. I was rock hard, my dick pressed up against her stomach, and fuck, if it didn't feel good. If *she* didn't feel good. But I was just getting into the kiss, rolling my hips into hers to get a little more friction, when she slammed her hands into my chest, shoving hard.

I stumbled back as she shrieked, "What the hell, Cameron?" Her cheeks were flushed, her lips swollen. "What the hell was that?" I don't know if she realized it, but her fingers ran across her lips, touching, as if she was unsure it had been real. But then her confusion melted away, replaced with anger.

Red hot, fiery anger.

And it was all directed on me.

"That was... you can't do that." The words came out harsh, but she was tongue-tied and I couldn't help but feel smug I'd affected her so much. Because fuck only knew, she affected me.

"I can't kiss you?" I teased. "I think I just did."

"Well, don't do it again." Her cheeks burned, the rise and fall of her chest quick. Oh, she wanted me to do it again all right, she just didn't want to admit it.

Stepping into Hailee's space until her back hit the storage rack, I stared down at her. She was still breathless, confusion clouding her eyes. "You want me," I said.

"I do not," she countered. "This... us... I hate you," she seethed, but I wasn't done playing with her. Sliding my hand along the curve of her neck, I leaned down, brushing my lips over the shell of her ear. "You can hate me all you want, Sunshine, but it doesn't change the fact you're probably wet for me right now."

Her soft gasp filled the small space and I felt her shiver. "Fuck you," she spat, trying to move around me, but I pinned her in place, sliding my leg between hers and pressing gently. I wanted to touch her, to test my theory.

But I knew I shouldn't.

Knew if I did, I might want to do it again, and that would be a dangerous thing indeed.

"Cameron, if you don't get off me in the next three seconds, I will—" A strangled moan left her lips as if she was fighting her own body when I ground my knee further into her and she practically rode herself against my leg.

"That feel good, Sunshine?" I did it again and her head dropped back, another soft moan slipping from her lips. But when my fingers dropped to the waistband of her jeans, and one of my fingertips stroked the bare skin above, she froze.

I felt the shift in the air, the temperature cooling right along with her icy glare.

"Get. Your. Fucking. Hands. Off. Me." The venom in her words had me backing away slowly. She looked furious, anger rolling off her in dark waves. But Hailee could deny it all she wanted; I felt the chemistry between us. The push and pull.

And I knew she did too.

Her eyes burned into mine, her body trembling. I'd never seen Hailee so worked up and shit, if I didn't want to believe it was my touch, my kiss, that did it. A beat passed as we stood there, locked in a battle of wills. Eventually though, her eyes flicked to the door and I stepped away, giving her free passage before I did something really fucking stupid.

Hailee rushed over to it, grabbing the handle, but at the last second she glanced back. "You think you can do whatever you like just because you're a Raider and it's fucking pathetic, but you don't scare me, Cameron. None of you do."

Defiance burned in her eyes and part of me was impressed. Even now, in a dark closet with me, she still tried to maintain the upper hand.

"Is that why you're running?"

"I'm not..." Her lips pressed together as she refused to go another round with me, and I smirked.

"I think we both know you're running," I said. "But you should be careful, Sunshine."

"Yeah." She raised her chin. "And why's that?"

"Because you can run but we both know you can't hide."

Hailee's brows knitted as if I was a puzzle she wanted to figure out, but then with a little shake of her head she left, my laughter following her all the way.

9

Hailee

CAMERON HAD KISSED ME.

Four days passed and I still couldn't quite wrap my head around it. We'd gone from arguing, slinging insults back and forth, to him pressing me up against the racking in the janitor's closet and kissing me. Only, kissing didn't do justice to the way his lips had felt against mine. If kisses had names, Cameron's would be called dangerous. It was like he'd taken all the hate between us, all the push and pull, and unleashed it on me. It hadn't been sweet or tender, or a recognition of long-buried feelings. It was a hate-kiss, fueled by the ongoing tension between us. It certainly wasn't because of emotions neither of us wanted to feel. Emotions I *refused* to acknowledge.

No. I wasn't accepting that as a possibility.

He was my step-brother's best friend.

A Raider.

Not to mention, he was one of my tormentors.

Cameron Chase was everything I hated.

And yet, I hadn't been able to forget the feel of his lips moving against mine, the way he'd held me, touched me. So I did the only thing I could—I spent the week pretending he didn't exist.

Of course, I didn't tell Flick; it would only fuel her theory that Cameron actually felt something for me. Even post-kiss I still wasn't convinced he did. His loyalty to my brother, the fact he was a Raider, the fact he'd spent just as many years taunting me as Jason, told me everything I needed to know about a guy like Cameron Chase.

But tonight, there was no escaping him.

"Remind me why we're here again?" I groaned, trailing after Flick as she moved deeper into the sea of blue and white.

"Because," she called over her shoulder, a cheesy grin plastered on her face. "It's senior year and we're embracing it, and you agreed to help your *best friend* fulfil her silly little list, remember?"

"How could I forget?" I stuck my tongue out at her. "Just so long as you're aware how painful this is for me. Did I tell you, I really *really* hate football?" My reply carried a little too loud causing a few people around us to throw daggers at me.

"Hails," Flick said, coming up beside me and shoving her arm through mine. "We're here to have fun. I know you hate football," she lowered her voice. "I know it's really hurting you to be here, but this is the last time we'll ever get the chance to do this. In four years time, you don't want to look back and regret not coming to one of these things."

I couldn't imagine a scenario where that ever happened.

My eyes scanned the football field, taking in the excited gaggles of girls, the ear-splitting noise, the marching band playing their little hearts out to a distracted audience. The air was electric, charged with the energy of eight-hundred kids all gathered to pay homage to their team. But the only thing it stirred inside me was a mild stomach ache and a bad case of eye rolls.

"Don't look so glum." Flick snickered, thrusting a handful of glow sticks at me.

"Am I supposed to know what to do with these?"

She shook her head, amusement glittering in her eyes, and held up her wrists. "Snap them and wear them."

"But why?"

"You'll see," was all she said as she grabbed my hand and pulled me deeper into the crowd, and it hit me how at ease she was with all of this.

The section of the bleachers we'd been ushered to sit in was crammed. Homemade signs littered the crowd, and kids spilled out onto the edge of the field. The cheer squad was gathered near the raised stage where Principal Finnigan and Coach Hasson were standing. It was football fanaticism at its finest, everyone waiting to get a glimpse at this year's Varsity team; the team they hoped would bring them home the State Championship.

Flick managed to find us two seats halfway up the bleachers next to a group of junior girls sporting the all too familiar Raiders logo on their cheeks. They were proudly waving their homemade signs for 'I heart Jason' and 'Call me Cameron'. They offered us spirit-worthy smiles but the nicest greeting I could muster was an eye roll and pursed lips. Even though they knew, like every other girl at Rixon, the most attention they could expect from my step-brother was a drunken fuck and tap on the ass on the way out, it didn't matter. I guess you got a free pass for being a cocky, conceited asshole when you were a five-star recruit, holding numerous season records, chasing the all-time State passing yards record. I only knew because Kent kept a board in the kitchen totaling all Jason's stats. Every morning as I enjoyed my coffee and Pop-Tart, I got a little reminder that Jason—*football*—was part of my life whether I liked it or not.

Only for another few months.

"I'm surprised you didn't make something." I nudged Flick, motioning to the girls. "Since you know... you're embracing this and all."

"Behave," she replied around a sardonic smile. "Oh look, it's about to start." Flick gave a little clap and I grumbled beneath my breath.

The marching band moved into formation, but it was impossible to hear them over the roar of the crowd. The force of it slammed into me, sending my heart freefalling, electrifying the hairs along my arms and the back of my neck. "Holy shit," I said to no one in particular. Glancing at Flick, I saw she was grinning, her eyes set firmly on the band as they performed the school's song. The team mascot, a giant blue Viking head, waddled onto the field facing off against a red and white Eagle. The crowd booed, laughter carrying across the bleachers like a wave.

"Is this for real?" I asked Flick out of the side of my mouth, aware of everyone around us being completely engrossed, watching a foam Viking try to take down a foam Eagle. Thankfully, the cringeworthy display didn't last too long, and they sauntered off the field, the Viking victorious, of course.

I was just about to ask Flick what we needed the glow sticks for, when the floodlights cut out, plunging the whole place into darkness.

"What the—" Adrenaline coursed through me, my heart catapulting into my throat, as neon lights stood out against the inky backdrop, and the opening beats of *Get Ready for This* blasted out through the PA system. I realized now all the signs and banners were painted in neon paint, and the cheerleaders were dressed in white shirts, blue neon Rs splashed against their chests, glow sticks around their wrists and ankles. Even I couldn't deny the black light set up was effective.

When their display ended, the crowd erupted again, sending tremors reverberating through the place, and I slipped my arm through Flick's. "This is crazy," I said, nestling into her side.

"It's something all right," she breathed out, and for a second my stomach sank. Surely, I wasn't going to lose my best friend—the one person who had always understood me—to *football*?

My thoughts quickly evaporated when the Imagine Dragons' *Whatever It Takes* boomed across the field. Not a single person remained seated. The eight-hundred strong crowd were on their feet, cheering and clapping, hooting and hollering. It was frenzied. Wild. It was high school lunacy at its best. And even I—the most anti-football person to have ever lived in Rixon—couldn't deny the atmosphere was electric. Infectious. Although I wanted to block it all out, to hate it as much as I'd always hated it; it seeped into me, coursing through my veins like wildfire. And no matter how dangerous you knew it was, how much safer it was to run away from the flames, you couldn't help but stop and watch them burn.

But the spell was broken when my eyes landed on my step-brother leading his team onto the field, the number 1 on his jersey lit up with neon paint; Cameron, number 14, on his right; and Asher, number 42, on his left. The three of them stood slightly ahead of the rest of the team. They reminded me of a general and his lieutenants leading their army to war;

heads held high, war paint streaked across their faces, helmets hanging at their sides like deadly weapons. Their names pierced the air as girls screamed and guys chanted. Even Flick looked ready to join in the chorus until I pinched her arm, levelling her with a hard look.

"What?" She shrugged. "When in Rome..." Her brows waggled before she turned back to the field and yelled, "We love you QB One, have babies with me."

"Oh my god." I clapped my hand over her mouth, drowning out her laughter. "You're demented."

"Takes one to know one," she mumbled, peeling my fingers away from her mouth. "Check out Cameron, he's looking mighty—"

"*Do not* finish that sentence."

It was too late. My eyes drank him in. The way his shoulder pads narrowed into his hips, how the tight-fitting pants clung to his muscular legs... and *other places*.

"You've got a little drool." Flick pressed her thumb to the corner of my mouth. "Right there."

"Fuck off," I grumbled, swatting her hand away. "Is this thing almost done?"

She pouted. "You're no fun."

"No, *this* is no fun." Now the initial buzz had worn off, I was ready to leave.

"Let's just stay for Coach Hasson's speech and then we'll go, okay?"

"Fine," I huffed, knowing she had me right where she wanted me. "But you owe me."

Even though, deep down, I knew it was the other way around.

An hour later, we still hadn't left. Flick was having fun and I guess my heart wasn't completely made of stone because seeing her so happy, kind of made me happy.

"I'm going to pee," I said to her as we wandered through the crowd. After Coach Hasson had worked everyone into yet another frenzy, he introduced his Varsity team for the season ahead. I knew each and every name, every face. We all did. The only difference was, I didn't care.

"I'll wait over by the 'cream the Eagle' stand," Flick replied around a mouthful of cotton candy. "This is good." She sucked her sticky fingers clean, grinning.

After the pep rally, everyone had moved to the parking lot where the social committee had set up stalls to raise money for the team. They'd kept the blackout theme but had strung up little neon lights between the stalls. It was annoyingly effective, just like everything else about tonight.

"I think you have to use the restrooms in the stadium."

"Great." Because I really wanted to go back in there.

I took off toward the imposing structure. Unlike most high schools in the area, Rixon High boosted a five-thousand capacity purpose-built stadium that, come game day next Friday, would be standing room only. The further away from the parking lot I got, the darker it became but I could just about make out the signage for the restrooms. Slipping inside, I hoped to find some other kids, but was greeted with nothing but deafening silence. The automated-lights flickered to life, calming my racing pulse, but I still hurried, eager to get out of here and back to Flick.

When I was done, I washed my hands and went back into the hall, waiting for the lights to flicker to life. But they didn't. So I inched forward, waving my hands in the air hoping to trigger the sensors. "Shit," I mumbled when nothing happened.

Wrapping my hands around my waist, I started toward the exit when a hand hooked around my mouth, yanking me into the shadows, drowning out the scream that ripped from my throat. A wave of fear washed over me as I was shoved into the wall, my eyes wild, straining against the darkness, searching frantically for something, someone... *anything*. But when a figure stepped in front of me, I pressed back against the cool cement, desperate to melt into the shadows and become invisible once more.

"Jason?" I snapped, the tremor in my voice betraying me. "Is that you?" Silence. "This is low, even for you." When the figure still didn't reply my voice cracked, "J- Jason?"

Even in the darkness, dressed in a black hoodie and sweatpants, a black mask hiding their face, I knew it was a guy. He was too tall, too broad and muscular... too deadly, to be a girl.

"Jason quit the *Friday the Thirteenth* act," I said trying to school the panic in my voice. "You got me, I concede." I held up my hands in surrender, but the figure watched on.

A little voice at the back of my mind whispered, *What if it's not Jason? What if it's a serial killer and you're about to be gutted like a fish?* But I stuffed down the thoughts. It was a knee-jerk reaction to the situation, to the fear clawing up my throat. It was Jason.

It had to be.

"Screw this," I murmured, steeling myself to run. But as I went to take off, another two figures rushed out of the shadows, grabbing my arms and pinning me against the wall.

"Jason," I hissed as my brain tried to process what was happening. "This isn't funny anymore. Tell your fucking idiot friends to back down before I scream."

Their hands tightened and I thrashed against them, but they were too strong, and I was probably going to have bruises tomorrow. "Cameron, Asher, you've done a lot of messed up things to me in the past, but this is—"

The figure—Jason—ate up the distance between us in long sure strides, stopping mere millimeters from my body. "Jason?" I breathed, no longer convinced it was him and that I wasn't about to be gutted like a fish.

Fear gripped me, as he dug his hand in his pocket. I sucked in a sharp breath as he began to lift his arm, waiting for the glint of metal. But it never came. Instead my vision went dark as something was shoved over my head and this time I did scream. The silence had been eerie enough. But this was worse.

This was fucking terrifying.

"Calm the fuck down," someone said, but the blood pounding between my ears made it difficult to distinguish if it had been Jason or Asher or Cameron. Or someone else entirely. My heart crashed violently against my chest, making it difficult to breathe as every possible scenario of what was about to happen flooded my mind.

"Please," I cried. "Just stop. Just—"

A hand fixed over my mouth again, and I gasped, fighting for breath, the smell of polyester overpowering my senses. But it all stopped when I felt something move against my stomach, painting torturous patterns. *Oh God.* My fight response withered and died, rendering me paralyzed, as I waited for the flash of pain. But it never came as a blunt object moved over my t-shirt. Confused, and drowning in a tsunami of fear and paranoia, I let my body go completely lax as my captors began to pull me away from the wall, guiding me to who only knew where. Seconds ticked by, my legs stumbling to keep with up them. And then the world came back in an overwhelming blur of color and noise as the hood was ripped off my head.

"W- what?" I blinked rapidly, sucking in greedy lungful's of air, as I staggered toward the sounds.

But as my vision began to settle, I realized something was wrong.

Very wrong.

I was on the fringe of the parking lot, looking out over the pep rally. And everyone was staring back at me.

Everyone.

The laughter started like a storm. The rumble of thunder far off in the distance, creeping closer with every crack of lighting. Until it was right on me; each rumble like a violent shiver up my spine, each crack like a jolt to my heart.

"Hails?" Flick pushed her way through the crowd, her eyes alight with panic. "What..." Her eyes dropped to my chest and she gasped, "Oh shit." The color drained from her face.

My fingers reached for the hem of the tee, stretching it out so I could just make out the words. There, painted in blue pen, was the words 'I ride Raiders for fun'.

Embarrassment burned through me, flaming my cheeks, as I met my best friend's sympathetic gaze. "I will fucking kill him," I ground out, not caring who could hear me.

She took a cautious step toward me. "Jason didn't do this—"

"Of course he did," I hissed, already searching the crowd for his smug face.

"No, he didn't, Hails." Something about the conviction in her voice gave me pause, and I slid my gaze to hers. "He's been here the whole time."

"But that's not..."

"It is, I promise."

Just then, I felt him. My eyes snapped up and sure enough Jason was there, in the middle of my gathered audience, his eyes hard on me. Flick was right. It couldn't have been him.

"And Asher?" I asked, my voice shaky.

"He was right there too. I watched them cream the Eagle three times in a row."

I didn't know what to feel when I finally said, "And Cameron?"

"He was there at the start, but I'm not sure... I didn't..." She sounded apologetic, and I didn't understand. She had nothing to feel bad about. It wasn't her fault.

"I see." My blood turned cold.

"Come on," she said, taking my hand. "Let's get out of here."

I let her lead me away from the whispers and stares and snickers. Jason and his douchebag friends had been mean to me for years. It was nothing new. Nothing I wasn't already used to. But this... this was different.

And I couldn't help but remember Cameron's words, '*don't come crying to me when he ruins you*'.

10

Cameron

"DO you need to tell me something?" Jase was blocking the door to Bell's, hands in his pockets, suspicion glittering in his eyes. We'd headed straight here from the pep rally, but I'd driven myself instead of riding with him and Asher.

"All you need to know is, I handled it."

"Handled it?" His brow rose. "I didn't know it needed handling."

Blowing out an exasperated breath, I ran a hand over my head and down the back of my neck. "Look, you can't afford to mess up this year. Hailee, she's a problem you don't need."

"So, you thought you'd fix it for me?" He straightened off the wall, folding his arms over his chest.

"I just don't want to see you mess up the season because of her."

He narrowed his gaze, searching my face for something. Something I didn't have the answer to. I held my breath, waiting. Relieved as fuck when a rare smile lifted the corner of his mouth. "Shit, man, I can't believe you did that. She looked ready to cry... and I don't think I've *ever* seen her cry."

My chest tightened remembering how Hailee had frozen up when I'd grabbed her. How her soft curves had tensed beneath my fingers. It had been the same when I'd kissed her, except then she'd quickly softened under my touch. Her body melting against mine even though she'd tried to fight it.

All week, after our janitor's closet kiss, I'd watched her. She had tried to avoid me; kept her head down whenever we passed in the hall at school, and I'd noticed she didn't sit in the cafeteria to eat her lunch. But there were moments when she didn't know I was watching her watch me. Mild curiosity was painted on her expression and something that looked a lot like lust shining in her eyes. Hailee could deny it all she wanted but kissing me had awoken something inside her. I'd felt it.

We both had.

But no matter how good she'd felt pressed against me, how good it had felt having my lips on hers, it was a problem neither of us needed.

So, I'd done what I should have done all along—I pushed her away the only way I knew how.

"Yeah, well, hopefully it'll keep her off your back for a while. But you need to stop that shit too. We have enough to worry about with Finnigan breathing down our necks, and then there's this shit with Thatcher—"

"Chill, man, it's all in hand." He clapped me on the back before yanking the door open. "Come on, drinks are on me."

I followed him inside where we were met with a low rumble of cheers. Bell's was our place; a bar run by an ex-Raider who decked the place out to be a living memorial to the team. Newspaper cuttings and photographs littered the wall, and there was a huge trophy case housing some of Jerry—the owner's—more treasured pieces of Raiders memorabilia: signed game balls, helmets, game ticket stubs. He even had his old jersey signed by Jerome Maddox, a Raider who went on to win two Super Bowls with the Pittsburg Steelers.

"Fellas," Jerry greeted us as we each took a stool at the bar. "What can I get you?"

"Two Bud Lights please, J." Jase got out his wallet, but Jerry shook his head. "First one's on the house. If you boys didn't keep using my place, business wouldn't be half as good as it is."

"Bell's will always be Raiders territory." Jase gave him a nod while Jerry got our beers.

"How're the team looking?" He handed us each a bottle without hesitation, another perk of being a Raider. "Think we'll go all the way to State?"

"You know it," Jase said.

"Gotta bring home the bling before you go off to college." He wiggled his ring finger, the light hitting his Championship ring. "I heard East are already talking a lot of smack." The corner of Jerry's mouth tugged up. Nobody had their ear to the ground as much as Jerry.

"East can bring it. They got lucky last year. This year, they won't."

"Damn right, Son. Damn right. I remember my senior year, nineteen-eighty-one, that season was brutal." His eyes glazed over with memories of the past. "Nobody thought we'd make the play-offs. Our last game was the Eagles at their place. It was a dog fight. By the fourth quarter we were trailing twenty-six-points to zero. We'd got guys bleeding, more injuries than we could count, and a team who was barely standing. I'll be honest with you boys, I thought it was over. We all did."

"What happened?" I humored the old man. I'd heard the story before; everyone who came through Bell's door had at one time or another.

"Coach Royston gathered us around and said to us... he said, 'strength grows in the moments when you can't go on, but you keep going anyway'. We came into that fourth quarter defeated, but we rose victorious and went on to win State. Bring it home this season, Son." He addressed Jason. "The whole damn town is counting on you."

Out of the corner of my eye, I watched my best friend. His eyes were narrowed, dark, his whole demeanor deadly. Winning State was the dream for most high school football teams, but it wasn't just a dream for Jason, it was a rite of passage. It was in his blood. And he wanted it more than anything else. He didn't only want it, he *needed* it. Sometimes I wondered if he needed it more than the air he breathed.

"You guys take it easy now." Jerry bid us a good night and went to serve some other customers, and we moved over to where the rest of the team had congregated.

"Why is it?" Grady piped up. "You two fuckers never have to pay for your beer, and the rest of us do?"

Jase raised an eyebrow as he slid into one of the booths.

"Because he's QB One, jackass," someone called.

"And Chase? What's he got that I don't?" Grady was smirking at me and I flipped him off.

"Try three offers on the table from Division One schools including Penn," Mackey grinned at me as if he was doing me a favor.

Asher stiffened beside me and then slammed his hand down on the table. "I don't know about anyone else, but I don't want to talk about free beer. I want to talk about kicking some Marshall ass."

A chorus of 'hells yeah' broke out in our corner of the bar. Jumping up onto the leather bench, he thrust his beer into the air. "What do y'all say? Do you think we can kick Marshall's ass?"

The whole place erupted and I rolled my eyes at Jase who just stared out at nothing as if Asher wasn't standing on the bench whipping Jerry's patrons into a frenzy. "I can't hear you." He cupped his ear, playing to his rapt audience. "I said, do y'all think we're going to kick some Musketeer ass on Friday?"

Kaiden jumped up, Mackey too. Until most of the younger players were up on their feet cheering and bouncing up and down. But I didn't move. Neither did Jase or a handful of the other senior players. We'd been there, done that. I didn't begrudge them lapping it all up—the attention, the thrill of wearing a blue and white jersey—but I knew there was a whole world waiting out there for me. A world outside of Rixon and the Raiders. And while their time would come; for me, for Jase, and Asher, it was already here.

It was supposed to be the defining moment of our high school football career and yet, already, I didn't know if my heart was in it.

And some days, I didn't know how to deal with that.

MONDAY SOON CAME AROUND and with it the anticipation for the first game of the season. "Mornin'," I said around a yawn as I padded into the kitchen, making a beeline for the refrigerator.

"Hey, sweetie," my mom gave me a warm smile as she helped my little brother, Xander, eat his cereal, but I saw the dark rings around her eyes.

"Ameron." He clapped vigorously, half-chewed cereal spraying from his mouth.

"Hi, buddy." I chugged a carton of milk while ruffling his hair.

"Ameron ootball day?" Xander grinned up at me as if I was the best fucking thing to ever live, and my chest squeezed. The little shit was cute and so oblivious, I envied him.

I envied a three-year-old.

How fucking pathetic.

"Yeah, buddy." I leaned back against the counter. "I have practice today. We've got our first game Friday."

"Ame day!" His eyes lit up. "Mama, we o to ame day with Ameron?"

"We'll see, baby." She gave him a tight smile, her eyes flicking to mine and then dipping. But not before I saw the flash of regret there. "We'll see."

"Maybe Asher's mom could bring him?" I suggested since it wouldn't be the first time Mrs. Bennet brought him along. "If you're, you know—"

"Yeah," it came out quiet as she cleaned up my brother. "We'll see."

"Good morning, family." Dad breezed into the room. "And how are we all this morning?" He pulled Mom in for a hug, dropping a kiss on her head, and they shared an intimate smile before he went to the coffee maker.

"First game of the season Friday then?" he directed at me. "How are you feeling?"

"Good," I said barely paying him any attention as I watched Mom scoop up Xander and disappear out of the kitchen. "I'm ready."

"It's a big year, Son." Dad sipped his coffee. "I wish things could be easi—"

"It's fine, Dad." I cut him off. I didn't want to do this, not this morning. "I haven't decided anything yet, there's still time."

He nodded, understanding simmering in his eyes. "I'll try my hardest to be there but—"

"I know." The words almost choked me.

"Marshall Prep could be a tough first game. They have a strong defense with that Belson kid, right?"

"Yeah, but I think we can do it. Our offense is looking tight and Coach has us practicing plays until we're blue in the face."

"Good, that's good. Xander will be at Katie's after school Monday, Wednesday, and Friday, we have appointments."

"Shit, Dad, I already told you I can take care of him. I can speak to Coach and maybe figure—"

"Cameron, it's senior year." He sighed, barely able to meet my eyes. "This year is important, Son. And Xander likes being with Katie. I know you're capable of helping, but this is important to us. Your future is important to us."

"How is she, Dad?" I forced the words out over the lump in my throat. "Really?"

He dragged a hand down his face letting out an exasperated breath. "Your mom is going to be fine, Son. Just fine. This new doctor is on the ball; they're adjusting her meds and running some tests. I have a good feeling about things."

"Good, that's good." Because God only knew we needed a break.

"I just need you to focus on school and football, Cameron." He approached me. "Promise me you'll do that?" Dad squeezed my shoulder and I managed a small nod.

"I promise." It came out strangled. Because what else could I do?

But as Dad said goodbye and went to find Mom and Xan, I couldn't shake the feeling there was something he wasn't telling me.

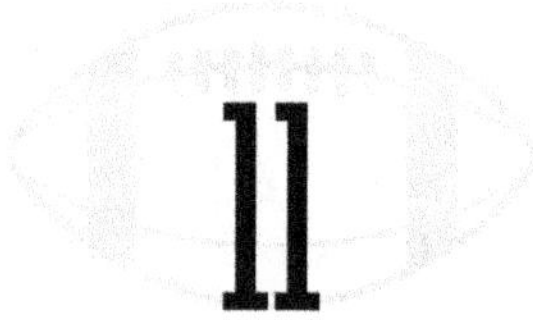

11

Hailee

"MORNING, SWEETHEART." Mom was busy making breakfast when I finally traipsed downstairs. "Don't forget we have to go pick out the wedding photos on Wednesday."

I silently groaned. "Great." Why I'd been roped into doing it when it should have been something a husband did with his new wife, was beyond me. But Kent was busy, suggesting I go in his place.

"Hailee Raine, can you at least try to pretend to be interested. This is important to me."

"I know, Mom, I just..." Pressing my lips together, I swallowed the words I wanted to say and forced a smile. "Wednesday sounds great. Can I bring Flick?"

"I already told Mr. Fetton to expect the three of us." She knew me so well. "So how was your weekend?" I detected a trace of suspicion in her tone.

"My weekend was fine." It came out a little sharper than I intended.

I'd spent most of Saturday in my bedroom. Flick had come over and we'd watched cheesy horror movies and binged on junk food; then yesterday, I'd worked on a couple of art projects.

Mom inclined her head, studying me. "Are you sure? You seem—"

"I'm fine." I smiled again.

"Because if something happened—"

"Nothing happened, Mom." It was possible she'd heard about the pep rally; rumors flew around our town quicker than lightning, but no way was I going to bring it up. I wanted to forget all about it.

"Okay." She conceded, something catching her eye over my shoulder. "Good morning, Jason."

I went rigid but didn't glance back to greet my step-brother. I hadn't seen him all weekend, and after Friday night, I really didn't want to. It might not have been his hands that grabbed me in the stadium and humiliated me, but I knew he put Cameron up to it. And like a good little lap dog, he'd followed his master's orders.

My muscles tensed as I braced myself for his smug remark about it. But it never came. Instead, he offered Mom a curt, "Morning," not sparing me a second glance.

Weird.

"Your dad already left," Mom kept her voice breezy.

"Got it." Jason grabbed an energy bar and one of his protein drinks and left. He didn't shoot me a scathing look or mouth any insults behind my mom's back.

It was certainly a first, and it had me more on edge than ever.

Mom sagged against the counter, releasing a heavy sigh. "He doesn't make it easy, does he?" Sadness washed over her features and I hated him a little bit more for making her feel bad.

"He's... Jason." I sipped my juice.

"I know, I know. He's under a lot of pressure with the team and college. But I thought... I hoped maybe with the wedding and it being senior year and all, he would—"

"Mom." Placing my glass on the counter, I went to her, taking her hands in mine. "Don't let him get to you."

"He's just different when Kent is around."

Yeah, because Kent was a buffer, absorbing some of his son's hostility toward me and Mom. And he always had an excuse for Jason's unwillingness to attend family meals or trips. 'He needs to focus on football', Kent would say, 'He's under a lot of pressure'. But Mom wasn't an idiot. Jason hated her almost as much as he hated me.

There had been a time when I'd wondered if Jason hated me *because* of her. I'd thought perhaps he was just an angry twelve-year-old, pissed his dad was trying to replace his mom. But we weren't kids anymore and Jason never did warm to Mom. And he'd only grown colder with me. Besides, from what I'd heard, Mr. and Mrs. Ford's relationship broke down long before Mom and I ever came on the scene. Mom had been a struggling single parent and Kent had been picking up the pieces of his life when they met, and while I hadn't been excited about the prospect of getting a new family, after what Dad did to us—to Mom—I only wanted her to be happy.

Even if she'd chosen an ex-college football player who coached junior high football, with a son who breathed football like it was air. But at least Kent didn't play anymore. That would have been too much to bear.

We hugged it out, and Mom pasted on her best smile. "Maybe he just needs some time to get used to it?"

"Maybe." I doubted it, he'd had years to get used to them being together before the wedding, but I didn't want to burst her bubble. "I have to go, Flick's waiting."

"Have a good day, baby." She kissed my head, and I grabbed my bag, before slipping into the hall, my stomach knotting tighter with every step.

ONCE SHE FOUND A PARKING SPOT, Flick cut the engine and turned to me. "Okay," she inhaled deeply. "You can do this."

"Do what?"

"Go in there with your head held high, of course."

"Right," I replied, confused. "Was there another option?"

"Well, I was prepared to add another thing to my list."

"You were?"

"Yeah." Mischief sparkled in her eyes. "I don't want to end up in the pen, but I'd do it, for you."

"In *the pen*?" I smothered the laughter building in my chest.

"Ride or die, baby." Flick waggled her brows. "I'm serious though, if you want to get payback, I'm in. So in. What Cameron did was—"

"I don't want payback," I said, my voice trailing off.

My best friend jerked back, eyes wide with surprise. "I'm sorry, I think I heard you wrong because it sounded a lot like you said, you *don't* want payback."

Shrugging, I said, "I don't. I'm done."

"Did something else happen?" She frowned. "Something you didn't—"

"You were right. It's gone too far and if I don't walk away, I'll be the one who ends up hurt. I can't play their games anymore. I'm done."

Something had changed when Cameron kissed me, not that I'd ever admit it to anyone. For a split-second, I'd actually thought he wanted me. His kiss was too intense. His touch too desperate. And I'd almost fallen for it; hook, line, and sinker.

But now, I realized it was all part of the game.

A game that, until the moment his lips fixed against mine, I'd always been more than willing to play. I'd even considered myself a worthy opponent. The girl who refused to let the Raiders trample all over her. But something was different this semester.

Cameron had gone after the one thing I'd always protected.

My emotions.

He'd made me feel something. Things I didn't want to feel. The rules had changed, and deep down, I knew if I kept playing the game, my reputation and sanity wouldn't be the only thing on the line.

"Wow, Hailee Raine, could it be that you've finally matured?"

"Piss off." I swatted her arm. "I just have more important things to focus on."

"You mean like helping me with my list?" She looked so smug, and I muttered indignantly under my breath. "You owe me, remember?" Flick added, giving me her best puppy-dog eyes.

As we climbed out of her Beetle, and made our way into school, I couldn't help but think I'd traded one form of torture for another.

"It's like you're invisible," Flick whispered on Thursday as we sat in our usual place in the cafeteria.

"Good," I mumbled around a mouthful of taco.

"Yeah, but I mean, it's weird, right?" Her eyes flicked over my shoulder and I knew she was watching the football table. "After last Friday I kind of expected you to get some backlash."

"Paul Rankle asked me if I do three-ways, and Finley Palmer asked me if I wanted to ride his dick in gym. I think that's backlash enough." There had been other things throughout the week: notes in English, and a couple of 'offers' at lunch, and every time I walked into class the room fell into hushed silence. But on the whole, no one said anything about Friday. I knew it didn't mean people weren't talking about it behind closed doors; they just didn't want to risk pissing off their beloved football captain.

"I guess," she said. "And I saw some stuff in the girls' bathroom—"

"You did?" My eyes widened. "Of course, you did." I let out an exasperated breath. Everyone knew girls were a cut above when it came to tearing into one of their own. Guys might have been the ones breaking hearts around here, but girls were the ones ruining reputations.

"It was probably Khloe and her bitch squad. You know she doesn't like the idea anyone else is 'riding Raiders for fun'." She air quoted the last words and I chuckled.

"Khloe is welcome to them." I discreetly glanced over my shoulder. Jenna Jarvis was draped over Jason like a bad rash while the rest of the gym team sat in amongst the team. My gaze ran straight over Cameron and the brunette cuddled up to him, and back to my friend. "Although it looks like the cheer squad is out and the gym team is in."

"Well, those girls are extra bendy." Flick mocked, and my face screwed up.

"There's a visual I don't need while I'm eating lunch."

"So, about the game tomorrow—"

"Not this again, Flick. I already told you, I'm not going." Attending a pep rally was one thing, but a football game? After last Friday, I couldn't think of anything worse.

"But you have to come." She pouted, giving me her best puppy dog eyes. "Or else I'll have to go alone, and you wouldn't want that, would you? Your best friend all sad and alone in a five-thousand strong crowd?" Her lashes fluttered.

"I hate you."

"No, you don't, you love me, and because you love me, you'll come to the opening game with me." It wasn't a question, so I didn't answer. But I did glare at her. Hard.

Flick's soft laughter filled our little corner of the cafeteria. "It's going to be so much fun," she said.

"Yeah, maybe they'll lose." I smirked, the idea filling me with a sick sense of satisfaction.

"Hails, you can't say that. It's like bad luck or something."

"Fine, fine." I pumped the air with my fist. "Go Raiders."

"Better," she nodded with approval. "Much better. We'll make a Raiders fan of you yet."

We cleaned up our table and headed out of the cafeteria but when we rounded the corner, Cameron was at his locker. His head snapped up, his eyes fixed right on me. But as quick as they locked on my face, they slid away. As if I was no one.

As if he hadn't kissed me the other night and then humiliated me in front of most of the school.

And the worst thing?

I didn't know which hurt more.

Friday night, I found myself returning to the one place I never wanted to step foot in again. But my best friend was relentless, and in the end, I figured it was easier to get it over with now than spend all semester trying to dodge her advances. I'd half-expected her to greet me with a Raiders jersey and matching ball cap, but she'd said we could build up to that.

Like tonight would *ever* happen again.

"It's exciting, don't you think?" She shouted over the noise of the crowd as we filed into the bleachers along with the rest of Rixon. The whole town had closed down for game night and those who weren't lucky enough to get tickets would be camped around their televisions ready to watch the Raiders' opening game against Marshall Prep's Musketeers.

"Exciting, yeah," I grumbled as we found our seats. The field was already a hive of activity; the marching band performing while the cheer squad worked the crowd into a frenzy.

Like the night of the pep rally, the air was electric. But tonight was different. More, somehow. The crowd was hungry for it, the energy of five-thousand people crackling around the Dawson Stadium. But nothing could have prepared me for the surge I felt when the team tore through the huge blue and white banner.

"My heart is beating so hard," Flick admitted, her eyes glittering with exhilaration, her skin flushed. She was one of them now. Her heart syncing to the thrum of the crowd, the beat of the band's drum. A good friend would have been excited for her; pleased she was having all these new life experiences she could tick off her list. But I guess I'd lost my good-friend title when I hadn't realized she wanted these experiences in the first place.

Imagine Dragons boomed across the field, barely drowning out the raucous singing as everyone chanted the lyrics at their beloved Raiders. My eyes immediately found number 1 and 42... finally landing on Cameron, the number 14 on his jersey standing out like a neon sign my eyes couldn't avoid if I tried.

"Don't hate me," Flick pulled my attention, pressing into my side. "But I think I kinda love this."

"I know," I whispered, my stomach dipping. Because I did. She was radiant. As if being here, in the crowd, was her calling.

"Just promise me you won't become one of them," I replied, trying to school my disappointment.

"Them?" she asked, barely able to tear her gaze off the field.

"Yeah, a Khloe Stemson or a Jenna Jarvis. Promise me you won't cross that line."

Flick's brows crinkled as if I was talking another language. But before she could reply, the team captains were called in for the coin toss. When Jason and his teammates stalked back to the rest of their team, she shrieked. "Yes! They won the toss."

"They did?" I asked, having no clue about what was happening down on the field.

"Yeah, see." She pointed to Jason and Cameron and a few others who were now jogging onto the field. "It looks like they're going to kick off to the other team."

"And I'm supposed to know what that means?"

She shook her head gently. "Just watch, you'll pick it up."

"If you say so."

"I do, now pay attention." Flick nudged her head to the field, and I groaned.

It was going to be a long night.

12

Cameron

MY MUSCLES PINGED WITH EXERTION, sweat rolling down my back and beading across my forehead as we huddled in the locker room, waiting for Coach. He strolled in with his assistant coaches, looking as cool as a cucumber.

"That's how it's done, ladies," he said yanking off his ball cap and running a hand through his graying hair. "Offense, keep working hard, running those rush plays we've been practicing, and we'll have Marshall eating out of the palm of our hand. Defense, keep them pinned down. Bennet, nice blocking, son. Their QB is completing three out of four of his passes but keep on him and he'll get tired." Asher grinned at me across the room and I rolled my eyes. "Watch out for their running back though, he has a tendency to go wide and slip our guys."

"I've got it, Coach." Asher held up his helmet. "No one is getting past me."

"Real glad to hear it, Son. Now gather round." He beckoned us in. "I know there's a lot of pressure right now. People were disappointed when we didn't make it past the first-round last year. Hell, I was disappointed, but this is a new season." Low rumbles broke out around me as the guys remembered how it had felt to get eliminated thanks to Rixon East.

"Okay, okay," Coach Hasson yelled over the noise, waiting for silence. "Let me tell you something about winning State. It isn't about luck or which school has the best players or the most money, it's about teamwork and heart. It's about grasping every opportunity and turning it into something to be proud of. Don't play for yourself, play for the other ten men on the field. The men watching you from the sidelines.

"This might only be the opening game, but right here, right now, you do what you do best; go out there and play like champions, do you hear me?"

"Yes, Sir."

"I said, do you hear me?"

"YES, SIR." Our voices melded together, echoing off the walls.

"That's what I like to hear. Asher, Son, take it away."

He moved into the middle of the huddle, eyes narrowed, shoulders squared. "Who are we?"

"Raiders," we all yelled in well-rehearsed synchronicity.

"I said who are we?"

"RAIDERS."

"And what are we?"

"Family," our voices echoed around the room, reverberating through my chest.

"And what are we gonna do?"

"Win."

"I said what are we gonna do?"

"WIN!"

"Damn right we are," Coach yelled over the noise. "Now let's go out there and play some ball." He thrust his clipboard in the air, and we rushed out of the locker room, fists pumping, spirits high. Adrenaline coursed through me as I bounced on the balls of my feet, stretching my neck from side to side. Game night was always a high; addictive and all-consuming. For those forty-eight minutes there was no room to think about anything else but the win.

The roar of the crowd as we re-entered the field was deafening, the glare of the Friday night lights blinding. We were gods now, and this was our arena.

"Soak it up, bro," Jase clapped me on the back. "This year is ours. You ready?" His eyes were dark, almost black. I'd never seen anyone get in the zone like he did.

Nodding, I pulled on my helmet, biting down hard on the mouth guard, and striding out to our end zone. Marshall were already on the field at the thirty-five-yard line, ready to kick off. Our players moved into position, waiting for the whistle. It sounded and their kicker punted the ball. My eyes fixed on it, tracking its projection as it sailed through the air, long and deep. "It's yours, Fourteen," someone yelled.

It kept flying, cutting through the air like a bullet. I dropped back, moving under the ball's trajectory, lining myself up for the catch. I didn't need to think, the actions were imprinted, instinctual like muscle memory. Knees loose, hands cradled, the ball landed with a *thud* and I tucked it into my body, locking my fingers around the leather.

"RUN!" Another voice yelled, echoed by Coach and his men on the sidelines, our four-thousand strong crowd in the bleachers. But I needed no encouragement, my eyes already scanning the field, anticipating the route home. Marshall's blockers were already moving downfield, a wave of black and yellow coming right at me, but I saw an opening and took off, pumping my legs as fast as they would take me. Adrenaline fired up my synapses, shooting around my body like tiny bolts of lightning, propelling me forward.

I passed midfield into the forty, the stampede of Marshall players right on my tail but I kept pushing. Kept moving. Catching a blur of yellow and black in my periphery, I tucked myself in, bracing myself for the hit, but it never came, one of our guys slamming into their blocker, taking him out of the play. Thirty yards... twenty... ten; they couldn't catch me now as I flew toward the endzone, nothing between me and the touchdown but fresh air. Slamming the ball onto the ground, I found myself jostled between my teammates as the crowd erupted.

"Ninety-five yards, baby," Grady shrieked. "That's how it done." He fist-bumped me as we moved upfield for our kicker to try for the conversion. The ball sailed cleanly through the uprights giving us the extra point, taking our lead to thirty-eight to six. Marshall needed a miracle now to claw back a win.

As we ran back to the sideline, Jase collared me, pressing his helmet against mine. "That is why Penn wants you, that right there." He gave me a rare grin. "One game down, another nine to go and then we're going all the way."

The conviction in his voice was deadly, and I knew Jason believed every word coming out of his mouth.

We would win State.

I would go to Penn with him.

And we'd have long and successful college football careers... *together*.

In his mind, there was no other option.

"Hey, you okay?" He grabbed my shoulder, eyes hard on my face.

"Yeah, I'm good." The lie rolled off my tongue. "Come on, we have a game to win."

WE WON forty-six to twelve in the end. Our offense was fast, our defense impenetrable. And in Coach's words, 'we outplayed them like a dream'. But the win was bittersweet.

After we'd left the field and gone back to the locker room, I'd picked up a voicemail from Dad saying they wouldn't be able to attend the game. He'd left it ten minutes after kick-off. So while my teammates were all pumped about seeing their friends and family who were waiting outside to congratulate us, all I wanted was some air.

It wasn't that I didn't appreciate people coming out to support us, I did, but it was a painful reminder I didn't have the people I wanted most waiting for me in the gathered crowd.

"Good game, Cam," Khloe sauntered over to me as I waited for the rest of the guys.

"Thanks," I grunted, kicking at the dirt with my sneaker.

She moved closer and her tits brushed my arm. "Are you heading to Bell's?"

"I'm not sure what the guys want to do yet." Or if I even wanted to celebrate.

My eyes scanned the parking lot to where Asher and some of the other guys were signing autographs and taking photos with fans, while Jase and his dad talked to Coach.

"Well, maybe we could—" Her voice trailed off as I spotted Hailee across the lot, walking with Felicity to her ugly fucking car.

What was she doing here?

She hated football, almost as much as she hated Jason. And after the pep rally, I never thought she'd step foot in the place again. That was kind of the point. Yet, here she was. Taunting me. Making me wish things were different.

"So, what do you think?" Khloe's hand laid on my arm, and I glared down at her, frowning.

"What?"

"I said maybe we can hang out sometime, just the two of us?" Code for: she wanted to fuck me.

"Listen, Khloe, I'm not..." Hailee's eyes found me, narrowing with contempt, hate radiating from her, even from all the way across the parking lot. Or maybe it wasn't hate at all, maybe it was jealousy.

Slinging my arm around Khloe's arm, I gauged Hailee's face for a reaction. Her lips parted as her breath hitched. *Bingo.* Dipping my head to Khloe's ear, I whispered, "I think you'd have better luck with Mackey. That kid is going places and I know he thinks you're hot."

Unlike me, who didn't do sloppy seconds, most of the guys shared girls around.

"Yeah?" She smiled up at me, but I still had my eyes fixed on Hailee.

She watched for another second before shaking her head a little and climbing in her friend's car. I'd wanted to get a rise out of her, to engage her after a week of us ignoring one another. It was supposed to make me feel better, to give me that tingle of excitement I felt whenever we interacted. But this time, all I felt was the bitter sting of dejection and a boatload of regret.

"Hey, man," Asher came over. "Was that Hailee I just saw climbing in Felicity's butt-ugly car?"

"Hailee? She was here? At a football game?" Khloe glanced over her shoulder with a sneer. "Wow, she's got bigger balls than I—"

"I think I see Mackey over there," I said, cutting her off.

"Yeah?" Hope sparkled in her eyes.

"Yeah, see." I pointed over to where he stood with the rest of the guys. "You should go say hi."

"O-okay. See ya." She walked away with a bounce in her step and Asher said, "What the hell was that about?"

Shrugging, I kicked the dirt again, "I told her Mackey was into her."

"He's into anything with a pussy."

"Lucky for her then."

"You okay, man? Your parents never made it?"

Giving him a little shake of my head, I mumbled, "No."

"Shit, bro, I'm sorry. Listen, you want to come back to the house and hang out? Mom's making lasagna." Despite his parents being out of town a lot, whenever they were back, Mrs. Bennet insisted on having quality family time.

"Nah, I should probably get home and make sure everything is okay."

"You're sure?"

"Yeah but tell your mom and dad I said hi."

Asher clapped me on the back before making his way over to his Jeep.

"Yo, Chase," it was Jase's voice. "Are you coming to Bell's?" He started walking over, a few guys lingering behind, waiting for their QB to give the order.

"I need to get home."

"Come on, bro, we always celebrate a win together." He was right, we did. But I wasn't feeling it tonight.

"I'm needed back at the house." It wasn't a complete lie.

"I know your mom has got stuff going on, but it's senior year." He sounded irritated. "They know you need to prioritize the team. You don't have to feel gui—"

"Tomorrow I'm there, okay?" I offered him a small nod, hoping he'd drop it.

He studied me for a couple seconds longer and then shrugged. "Yeah, whatever, man. I'll call you tomorrow." Jase was pissed but he didn't get it.

Maybe he never would.

And until recently, it had never been a problem.

13

Hailee

SINCE I'D ATTENDED the football game with her last night, Flick agreed to humor me at The Alley. It was our usual hangout, mostly because the football team rarely came around here. They preferred to go to Bell's, a bar downtown. The owner there was a huge football fan, letting the team come and go as they pleased. Needless to say, I avoided it at all costs. Even if they did have the best chili fries in town.

But The Alley was cool. It had roller skating; bowling; a small arcade; a diner; and, on a weekend, Tate, the owner, let local bands perform. He wasn't like Jerry, the owner of Bell's, who let the team drink and get up to no good, but it was still a good time.

The second reason I loved The Alley so much... It sat right on the Rixon/Rixon East divide with amazing views of the Susquehanna River. It was like my very own Switzerland. A football free zone, untouched by the rivalry between the Raiders and the Eagles. Anyone was welcome to hang out here, but Tate would kick your ass to the curb quicker than you could say 'go Raiders' if he got wind of any trouble.

Did I mention Tate was my kind of people?

"So, did you hate it as much as you expected?" Flick asked me as we got our milkshakes, and bacon and cheese fries and found a table.

"It was... okay, I guess. But I won't be rushing to get my tickets for next week's game."

"Spoilsport." She poked out her tongue at me. "The guys looked hot though, right? In those tight pants and shoulder pads." She practically panted.

"Doesn't really do it for me." I shrugged as I stirred strawberry sauce patterns in my shake.

"I'm sorry," Flick choked out. "But are you blind?"

"I just don't find football players hot." Except maybe one but he was an asshole that I wanted nothing to do with. Ever. Again.

Flick scrutinized me, her narrowed eyes searching my face. "What?" I asked, uncomfortable with her probing gaze.

"You're hiding something."

"Am not." *Great comeback, idiot.*

"Hails..."

"Flick..." I met her steely gaze with my own.

"It's him, isn't it? Cameron? Has he gotten under your skin?"

"What? No."

"You're being cagey. I know something happened. You might as well tell me now or I'll only—"

"Fine," I hissed. "Fine. Just keep it down, okay?" My eyes surveyed the immediate vicinity for any kids from school. Shuffling closer to the table, I leaned forward on my arms. "He kissed me."

"*Kissed* you?" Her eyes almost bugged out of her head. "And you didn't tell me? When did this happen? Was there tongue? Was he any good?" She groaned. "Of course he was good; it's Cameron Chase for Christ's sake."

"Flick." I gave her a pointed look. "Breathe."

"I... wow." A dreamy expression washed over her. "He kissed you." Her expression changed to a smug one. "I knew it. I knew he wanted you."

"Have you forgotten what he did to me?"

"Foreplay, Sista. I'm telling you, it's all foreplay."

"You have a very strange view of the world."

"I'm just saying, being a grade A asshole comes hand in hand with being a Raider. Those guys are... well, they're a law unto themselves. It's just how it is. You know Coach has all these rules about them dating and girls being a distraction."

"So that gives them license to sleep with half the girls at school and never call them again?" My brow rose. I wasn't buying into it, no way.

"That's not what I'm saying, but the whole town puts them on this pedestal. It's no wonder they're the way they are when you think about it."

"Is there something *you* need to tell *me*?" I flipped the tables on her.

"What? No!" She blushed and alarm bells rang out in my head. "I'm just saying..."

"Sounds a lot like you're defending them if you ask me."

"Oh, stop." Flick shot me a bemused look. "Everyone knows the guys on the team are manwhores. They don't date, they don't fall, and they certainly don't kiss girls for the sake of kissing them." It was her turn to raise a brow.

"They kiss girls for the sake of it *all* the time."

"Where did Cameron kiss you?"

"W- what?" I gawked at her, feeling myself grow hot.

"Answer the question, Hails."

"Where do you think he kissed me? On the mouth, dumbass." Although I couldn't deny the idea of him kissing me in other places had me pressing my knees together. *Get a grip Hailee Raine. You hate him, remember? Hate. Him.*

"No, I mean where did he kiss you? At a party? In the hall at school? At home? In your bedroom? *Dumbass.*"

"I... hmm... in the janitor's closet at school."

"Oh, this just keeps getting better." Flick smirked, amusement dancing in her eyes. "And how, pray tell, did you end up in the janitor's closet with him?"

"It doesn't matter."

"Doesn't matter? Are you freaking kidding me? I think it matters; I think it matters a whole lot. You like him, don't you?"

Like him?

I didn't like Cameron Chase.

I hated him with every fiber of my being.

"I'm not talking about this anymore," I said, stuffing a handful of fries into my mouth.

"Fine, but I know there's more to it. And just remember, Hails, the truth will come out, it always does."

An hour later, Flick had finally given up on the idea of there being more between me and Cameron. My silent treatment every time she brought him up probably had something to do with it.

"Hotties at two o'clock." She side-eyed the cute guys who had just walked in as we played air hockey. "The blond is cute," my best friend was still staring in their direction.

"Good that I like tall, dark, and handsome then." I flashed her a playful wink, sinking the puck in her open goal. The guys must have noticed us watching because one of them nudged the other, and they both glanced in our direction.

"What about Cameron?"

"Cameron who?" I cocked my head, but her smile faltered as if she saw straight through my ruse.

"Fine, play it that way. Maybe we should invite them over?"

"I don't... Shit, too late." I mumbled, dropping my eyes and whispering, "They're coming over here."

Flick did a little excited squeal.

"We're supposed to be having girls' night," I protested, but she simply rolled her eyes at me.

"What better way to make you forget all about he who shall not be named, than cute guys?"

"I don't know." I glanced over at them again. They had doubled back to the counter, probably when they noticed my frown, but they kept looking over here as they ordered drinks. I'd been joking when they first walked in, hoping to throw her off Cameron's scent. But now I wasn't so sure I wanted them to come over here.

"It's on my list," she blurted out. "Number ten, hook up with a random guy."

I sprayed a mouthful of soda into the air. "Easy there, who said anything about hooking up?"

I definitely wasn't looking for *that*.

"Says you." Flick sighed, lowering her voice. "You already lost your v-card. Now it's my turn, Hails. I don't want to be the only girl at college who hasn't done it yet."

"Flick, come on. It wasn't like the one time I did it was anything to shout home about." It had been awkward and over so quick I wasn't sure it had even happened, and I'd never seen the guy again. Not exactly a first time to remember.

"I'm not saying I want to sleep with him." Her gaze moved to the two guys again. "But I wouldn't say no to second base."

"I don't know—" But it was too late. The guys were already heading toward us, the blond making eyes at my best friend as the dark-haired one smiled at me. "Hey, I'm Toby."

"Hi," Flick said eagerly. "I'm Felicity, this is my friend Hailee. And you are?" She directed at the other guy.

"Jude," he said smoothly.

"Well, Jude, want to buy me a drink?"

Toby and I watched as Flick grabbed his hand and gave him no choice but to follow her back to the counter. "Is she always so..." His voice trailed off.

"No," I said fighting a smile. "She really isn't." And I wasn't sure what to make of this new version of my best friend.

"I guess it'll make me look like a complete jackass if I don't ask you if you want a drink?"

"No judgment here." I held up my hands. Then something occurred to me. "Hey, do you live around here? I don't recognize you from school."

"Ah, that would be because I go to Rixon East."

"I figured."

"I take it you're a Raider?"

"Is that what you're calling us these days?" The corner of my mouth lifted. "Actually, I hate football."

"For real? And they haven't cast you out yet?"

I laughed at that. Toby was funny and he had a nice smile. "Please don't tell me you play?"

"Do I look like I play?" He didn't. He was tall and lean, built more like a basketball player or swimmer than a football player. "Nah, it's not really my thing either. I'm more of a creative type..."

"No way, me too."

"Yeah?"

"Yeah, I'm hoping to go to Michigan next year to the Stamps School of Art and Design."

"Nice." Toby grinned and I found myself returning the gesture. "So, I know this might seem a bit out there, but we're actually heading to a party. Do you want to come?"

"Is this party in Rixon East?" I asked because no way I was going to a party my brother and his jock friends might be at.

"Yeah, it's across the river. That a problem?"

"It's not a problem for me," I replied around a smile, just as Flick and Jude returned.

"What's up?" Jude asked his friend.

"I invited Hailee to come party with us. You in?" He looked at Flick and her eyes lit up, locking on Jude. "I'm in."

"Cool," her new friend said. "You want to get out of here then?"

"Sounds good." I brushed my hands down my jeans and we followed the guys out of the building. They walked ahead slightly so Flick took the opportunity to loop her arm through mine.

"An East party; are you sure? If Jason finds—"

"Let him find out. He's not my keeper, Flick. What happened to 'oh, he's so cute'?" I gave her a pointed look as we trailed after Jude and Toby.

"Oh I'm in." She grinned. "I'm just making sure *you* know what *you're* doing."

"Everything okay?" Jude called over to where me and Flick had stopped. I grabbed her hand, started toward his car, and said, "Everything's fine."

Despite Rixon and Rixon East being divided by the Susquehanna River, it was only a fifteen-minute ride to the party. Jude pulled up outside a country house. Cars and trucks lined the street, the faint vibration of music filtering out of windows.

"Holy shit," Flick whistled between her teeth. "This place is—"

"Impressive, huh?" Toby got out and came around to open my door. I climbed out, suddenly feeling underdressed in my jeans, Vans t-shirt, and worn chucks. Rixon East was renowned for being more affluent that Rixon. Our neighborhood wasn't poor by any stretch of the imagination, but Rixon East boasted more estates nestled in the beautiful, leafy surrounds, and exclusive rentals along the river.

The house before us was no exception.

"You know someone who lives here?" I gawked, and Toby chuckled. "Yeah, he's my cousin. Come on."

"Cousin?" Flick mouthed as we followed the guys inside. I shrugged. It was too late now to worry about who Toby's cousin was.

Until we stepped inside, only to be met with a sea of red and white.

"Hmm, Toby, who did you say your cousin was again?" Flick asked, panic flashing in her eyes as she gave me a sideways glance.

"Lewis Thatcher, only the best damn QB in the state," Jude chimed in.

I almost choked on the air in my lungs. Toby's cousin was Lewis Thatcher, QB One for the Rixon East Eagles, and Jason's arch-nemesis.

Shit.

Flick's gaze widened over his shoulder, but I shook my head discreetly. No one knew who I was. We could enjoy the party, blend in, and stay under the radar.

At least that was the plan.

14

Cameron

"HERE YOU GO, BOYS." Sara, one of the servers at Bell's passed around our plates of food. Win or lose, it was our post-game ritual to all descend on Bell's on Saturday night, and when Jase had called me up this morning, I didn't hesitate to say yes.

When I'd gotten home last night, Mom and Xander were both asleep. Dad had two beers on ice, waiting to toast our first win of the season. We'd stayed up late, watching old game tapes, talking about Pee Wee and JV. But we didn't talk about the elephant in the room.

And this morning, when I finally dragged myself out of bed, my muscles sore and bones bruised, Mom seemed in good spirits. She'd even made us all breakfast. It was nice. Normal.

It was just like old times.

"You need anything else, you just give me a shout, okay?"

"I could use a good hard—" Mackey started but Sara cut him off. "You come back and see me when you're twenty-one, hot stuff." She winked, giving him a little smile before sauntering off, putting extra sass in her step.

Mackey sank back against his chair and groaned. "What I wouldn't pay to ride that."

"Sara's hot but she doesn't fuck football players," Asher said, squirting ketchup all over his meal. "Not even QB One, isn't that right, Jase?"

"She's got too much of a smart mouth for me. I like my women to talk less and suck more."

"Yeah," Mackey added. "But imagine what she can do with those pouty lips." A goofy expression came over him and Grady leaned over, hitting him upside the head. "Get your mind out of the gutter. We have a game to focus on."

"Dude, we just kicked Marshall's ass last night. I think we're allowed a little downtime."

"Fucking sophomores," someone grumbled.

"I heard that."

"Chill," Jase said to Mackey as he cut his Bell's Special Burger in half. The thing was just too damn big to try to eat whole. "We get it, you're amped, but Kaiden is right, the only thing you need to be focusing on is the next game, and the one after that, right up until week ten. Got it?"

"Got it," Mackey grumbled. "Doesn't mean I can't look though, right?" His eyes slid back to where Sara was serving another table.

Jase and I shared an amused look. We knew how it was: the raging hormones, the buzz of being gods amongst men. In a town like Rixon, making Varsity was a badge of honor that opened doors: to colleges, to girls, to a free pass for screwing up every now and again. But it also came with expectation and pressure. Expectation to be the best; to work hard and give your all. Joel Mackey might not have understood it now, but after a season under Coach Hasson and his team, he would. Those guys broke you down until you were nothing but blood and bone and then pieced you back together until you were hardened, inside and out. Until no team—no matter how big or strong or aggressive—was a threat. Rixon High's football program built warriors. Molded young men full of heart and grit and determination. As Coach Hasson liked to remind us every chance he got, 'great men aren't born, they're made'.

And Rixon High only made the best.

But there was no denying that sometimes it was a heavy burden to shoulder. And blowing off a little steam now and again was the only way to push through.

"So, Jase," Grady piped up. "What's the plan for Rivals Week?"

"That's for me to know and you to find out." The wicked glint in my best friend's eyes had my attention.

"Oh, come on. It's only two weeks away; you can tell us."

"My lips are sealed."

"But it'll involve a little trip across the river, am I right?"

"We should hit their place, tag some Vikings on their field house," Kaiden said.

"Or hack their social media accounts and troll the shit out of them." Mackey grinned, clearly impressed with his own idea.

"Speaking of which, Thatcher is talking smack on Twitter again." Kaiden held up his cell phone. "Check this crap out." He handed Jase his cell and the two of us scanned the screen.

@ThatcherQB1: What's black and blue and broken all over? The Raiders after we get a hold of them #comingforyou #rivalsweek

Jase tensed beside me. "He's a fucking idiot."

"If he keeps this up," Kaiden said, taking back his cell. "Their Coach will have to step in. Snapchat is one thing, but Twitter is a whole other beast."

"Don't sweat it. Come two weeks time, the only tweet he'll be sending is: hashtag it hurts."

The guys all howled with laughter, but I couldn't help but wonder what Jason had up his sleeve.

And if I even wanted to know.

AN HOUR LATER, we'd moved over to the pool table. "Chase, you're up." Grady motioned for me to take my shot just as my cell phone vibrated.

"Hang on," I said, retrieving it from my pocket. "It's my dad. I'll be right back." Going into the hall leading to the restrooms, I hit answer. "Dad?"

"Hey, Son." He sounded weary, his voice flat and empty. Worlds away from the guy I'd left at home earlier.

My senses went on high alert. "Is everything—"

"It's your mom, she..." My stomach plummeted as his voice cracked. He cleared his throat, forcing out the words, "I hate to call you when you're out with the guys, but we could really use you here. Xander is—"

"I'll be right there, Dad." Dread flooded me. Dad rarely called. If he did, it was usually because Katie couldn't watch Xan. So the fact he'd called on a Saturday night when I was with the team... I knew it was bad.

Asher found me staring at my cell phone. "Everything okay?"

"I'm not sure." I shoved it in my pocket, scrubbing a hand down my face. "He needs me back at the house."

"Your mom?"

"Yeah, I think so." My mind was shooting off in a hundred different directions trying to figure out what could have possibly happened.

"Shit, man, I'm sorry. Is there anything you—"

"No, it's all good. I'm sure it's fine. Xander probably got upset again." Asher knew more than most about my mom and her mood swings. It's why I stayed over at his place sometimes when things got too intense at home.

Four years ago, when Mom found she was pregnant with Xander, things were tough for a while. She and Dad weren't ready to be parents again. I was fourteen and my life already revolved around football, and they were my biggest supporters, never missing a single game. After my brother was born, Mom struggled. Doctors said she had postpartum depression. Dad took some time off to help around with the house and with my baby brother. With some medication and therapy, things improved and by the time Xander turned one, it looked like Mom was returning to her normal self.

But she never did, not really.

And we'd been watching her battle her own mind ever since.

"Tell Jase—"

"Tell Jase what?" He appeared in the hall, his brows bunched, arms folded over his chest.

"My dad needs me back at the house."

"Again?" He didn't even bother schooling his disapproval.

"Yeah, it's my mom…"

"I thought she was doing better?" I winced at the harshness in his voice. But I couldn't totally blame him for his lack of compassion. It wasn't like I went around broadcasting my family's issues, and Mom and Dad kept themselves to themselves these days. It was a sensitive subject; one Mom didn't want everyone to know about.

"She's doing okay, but something must have happened. I need to go." I went to move around him, but his hand shot out, pressing against my chest.

"You sure everything's okay?" His eyes searched mine and I wanted to believe he cared, that he wasn't just worried this was going to be a distraction for me. For the team.

"Yeah, man. I'll see you tomorrow." We liked to hit the gym Sundays, over at Asher's house. "Just do me a favor, yeah?"

"Anything," he said.

"Don't do anything stupid while I'm gone."

The corner of Jase's mouth lifted while Asher snickered. "Would we ever?"

I shot them both a hard look, hoping they would heed my warning, before slipping down the hall and out the back entrance, not wanting to face a barrage of questions from the guys.

I wanted to believe Dad when he said Mom was getting better, that this new doctor was positive he could help, but we'd been here too many times over the last three years. Every time her mood stabilized, and she started feeling like herself again, another wave of migraines, lethargy, and anxiety would strike. And every time it happened, the severity of her mood swings worsened. Sometimes it only lasted a few days, other times it went on for weeks. It's why, in the end, Dad hired Katie to watch Xander. He needed to go back to work, and I had school and football. I offered to help out more, to drop practice and prioritize my family, but he wouldn't hear of it. Neither of them would. Football was my ticket to college, my future. It didn't stop the guilt though. I carried it with me like a permanent weight in my chest.

Deep down, I think it's why things felt different this year. I was a senior now, playing in my final season. If everything went to plan, I would be leaving for college next summer; leaving Dad to raise Xander and look after Mom. I knew they didn't want me to put my life on hold, but I wasn't a kid anymore. And I couldn't help but wonder if now was the time I needed to step up and take more responsibility at home.

My house was only a few blocks over from Bell's and before I knew it, I was pulling into the driveway. It was late, almost nine-thirty. Xander should have been asleep by now dreaming of puppy-heroes and talking race cars, but something had obviously happened. With a heavy heart, dread knotting my stomach at the thought of what I'd find inside, I climbed out and made my way up to the house.

"Hey," I called out, closing the door behind me. "It's me."

"We're in here," Dad's voice filtered down the hall and I followed it into the living room. He sat in the armchair with Xander curled up in his lap. My little brother's eyes peeked open and he smiled. "Ameron is ome."

"Hey, buddy, come here." I crouched down, opening my arms. He leaped off Dad's lap and waddled over to me, his little legs moving as fast as they could. Scooping him up, I studied his face. He'd been crying, his eyes puffy and sore. My gaze flicked over his shoulder and Dad grimaced, running a hand down his face.

"What's up, little dude?"

"Mama ade me ry."

"I'm sure she didn't mean it." I ruffled his hair as he buried his face into my shoulder. "How about I tuck you in bed and finish that story we started the other night?"

Xan nodded, refusing to loosen his grip on my neck. "Come on then, buddy. Bedtime story it is." I carried the little man up to his room, wrestling him out of my arms and into his bed.

"You want a story?"

His lips pressed together as he dropped his sleepy eyes. Fuck, seeing him like that twisted something inside me. "Hey, Xan," I kneeled at the side of his bed, pulling the covers up around his little body. "Mom loves you. You know that, right?"

He peeked out at me from under his mop of brown hair. "I ow."

"Sometimes she's just not very good at showing it, buddy." I stroked his hair, moving it off his face so I could see his eyes. "But she loves you so much and I'm pretty sure you're her favorite little man, always will be."

"Eah?" His eyes lit up. "She ove me."

"That's right, she does. She'll make it up to you, okay?" She always did, whether it was ice cream at Ice T's or taking him to the park. On her good days, Mom found ways to erase all the not-so-good days from my little brother's mind.

"Kay, Ameron." He yawned, closing his eyes and snuggling into his pillow.

"Okay, buddy. Get some sleep." I dropped a kiss on his head. "I'll see you in the morning."

Xander was asleep in seconds. I tucked him in and creeped out of his room, pulling the door closed. I checked in on Mom, but she was sleeping too, her expression serene as if her dreams were the only place she found solace these days. The thought strangled my heart.

Before falling pregnant with Xander, Mom had been so full of life, my biggest supporter. It was hard to resent the little guy because I loved him something fierce. But sometimes, when she missed another game or forgot to ask how practice was, I couldn't help but wish for things to be how they used to be. Before she got sick.

Downstairs, I found Dad in the kitchen, nursing a glass of whiskey. "How bad was it?" I asked.

"I'm not going to lie, Son, I'm worried." His eyes shuttered as he inhaled deeply. "I've never seen her like that before, she was…." The pain in his voice broke me and I went to him, pulling him into my arms.

"It's going to be okay, Dad." I squeezed him tight, but as I said the words, I didn't know if I believed them. We'd been clinging onto the hope Mom was going to be okay for so long, I don't think either of us had really ever stopped to consider the alternative.

What if she wasn't?

15

Hailee

TWO HOURS into the party and we'd managed to blend. Toby and Jude kept our cups filled and the conversation flowing. It was refreshing being incognito; hanging out with people who didn't know me or my tenuous link to the Raiders. And when Toby had inched closer to me, his arm brushing mine, I didn't retreat. He was nice. He wasn't like his cousin and his jock friends who were busy playing beer pong outside while half-naked girls splashed around in the Olympic-sized pool desperately vying for their attention.

"This is fun, right?" Flick made a beeline for me when the guys disappeared.

"Yeah." I smiled, taking another drink from my cup. It was only punch, the bitter aftertaste of liquor barely noticeable.

"Toby is cute." She grinned. "Shame he's the cousin of the Eagles QB."

"Hush," I hissed, scanning the kitchen for any signs of him. "They can't know who I am, not yet."

"And if they find out?" She gave me a disapproving glance.

"They won't."

Flick looked ready to argue when explosions rang out around us. People started screaming and all hell broke loose. Grabbing my arm, she pulled me down behind the counter as blood pounded between my ears.

"What the hell is that?" Flick trembled as the loud pops continued to rain down on the house. "Gunshots?" She shrieked.

"No way," I said, breathlessly, my heart lodged in my throat. It was Rixon East, people didn't get shot here. But it sure as hell sounded like a gun fight.

"Motherfuckers," someone roared, and a group of guys in red and white jerseys rushed through the kitchen and out of the back door. The air smelled like bonfire, a smoky haze hanging in the air as I peeked over the top of the counter.

Flick gripped my arm. "Hails, what the—"

"Do you really think they would be out there if it was gun fire?"

"It's firecrackers," someone said, and my head whipped around to a guy who was moving closer to the windows. "My brother uses them all the time."

More people came into the kitchen, curiosity getting the better of them. I shrugged Flick off and went to the back door.

"Hailee, what the—" I pushed it open and stepped outside. The noise had stopped now but there was a group of guys fighting on the Thatchers' sprawling lawn.

"Oh, shit," someone yelled. "Fight."

People streamed out of the house eager to see whatever was going down. But when my eyes landed on Jason and Asher in amongst the brawl, I gasped. "Jason, what the hell?"

My step-brother's eyes snapped to mine just as one of the Rixon East guys landed a punch right on his jaw. His head snapped back, blood spraying into the air. "Jason!" My voice rang out across the yard as I pushed my way through the growing crowd.

"Wait," Toby said from somewhere behind me. "You know him?"

"Something like that," I murmured, watching as Jason fought off two guys while Asher got a handle on the third. "He's my step-brother." My voice was quiet as I forced out the words.

"Oh, shit," he said scrubbing his jaw. "I had no idea."

Why would he?

Jason lived in the limelight, not me. And he was a Ford, where I was a Raine. Unless you knew us, you would never put one and one together and come up with two.

The guys were circling one another now, the crowd amped up and bloodthirsty. One of the guys advanced on Jason but I yelled, "Stop."

Without thinking, I rushed into the circle and stood in front of him, using myself as a shield. "Move, Raider bitch," the guy spat, a nasty bruise forming around his eye. "Before I—"

"Back off, Thatcher, that's my sister. Do you really want to start something you know we'll finish?"

The guy—Lewis Thatcher—glared at me, his eyes sparking with interest as he rubbed his jaw. He was a mean looking guy: tall, built, with sharp eyes, and short spiked hair. But I was stuck on the part where Jason had called me his sister.

He'd never called me his sister before, not unless it came hand in hand with an insult.

"You've got five minutes to get the fuck out of here." Lewis Thatcher's shoulders relaxed as he stepped back, his friends doing the same.

"Flick?" I beckoned for her to come to me as she stood on the edge of the crudely formed circle, tears collecting at the corners of her eyes. "Let's go," I said, wrapping an arm around her.

Jason wiped his mouth. He looked wild, his eyes simmering with anger, blood smeared over his lip, hair disheveled. Asher didn't look much better. The two of them tipped their heads at Lewis Thatcher and his friends before slowly backing up. "Hailee, you and Felicity go wait down by Asher's Jeep."

"But—"

"*Now*, Hailee."

I flinched at the severity in his tone and Flick started pulling me away. "Come on, Hails," she said shakily. "We should go."

I glanced back to see Jason and Asher still facing off with the Rixon East guys. Surprised by the sheer relief I felt when they began to follow us.

We reached Asher's Jeep, parked on the street under the cover of shadows. "Get in," he said. "It's unlocked."

Flick wasted no time jumping inside, but I hesitated, my frantic gaze assessing Jason. "Get in the damn Jeep, Hailee," he growled when his eyes slid to mine. There was a deep cut in his lip and a dark shadow around his cheek, but it wasn't his injuries that had my attention. It was his eyes. They were completely black.

Feral.

"But—"

"Get. In. The. Fucking. Jeep." He gripped the door, waiting for me to slide inside. With a heavy sigh, I climbed in beside Flick, Jason slamming the door shut behind me. She threw me a concerned look but didn't say anything. The tension as Asher and Jason got in was so thick I could hardly breathe.

"Well, I didn't expect that," Asher said as he fired up the engine and pulled onto the road, his eyes sliding to my step-brother. "This could be a problem—"

"Don't," Jason cut him off, but I didn't miss the silent look they shared. I wanted to ask what he meant, why it could be a problem, but something told me I wouldn't like the answer. Defeated, I sank back against the leather seats, staring out of the window.

The ride back across the river didn't take long, but it felt like hours. No one spoke. Flick was quiet, her eyes closed, her leg shaking agitatedly. Every now and again, Asher's eyes met mine in the rear-view mirror, but I couldn't decipher the expression on his face. And Jason... well he was present physically, but he'd completely checked out. Lost to the anger radiating out of him like a force-field.

He was furious.

And something told me, it had everything to do with me.

THE NEXT MORNING, I lay in bed, not ready to face the aftermath of the night before. When Asher had pulled up outside our house, Jason had ordered me to go inside while the two of them stayed in the Jeep to talk. I only knew because I'd watched them from my window. Something was wrong, but whatever it was, they didn't feel it necessary to tell me. *Assholes*.

My cell phone bleeped, and I leaned over to grab it off the nightstand. I had two messages from Toby.

Toby: Did you get home okay? I was worried.

I smiled at that, opening the most recent message.

Toby: Good morning, just wanted to make sure Ford didn't kill you on the ride home.

Rolling onto my back, my fingers flew across the screen.

Me: I'm okay thanks. That was pretty crazy. Are things always like that at East parties?

Toby: Nah. Things only get crazy if your brother shows up.

So it wasn't the first time something like that had happened. Interesting. I stored that snippet of information for another time.

Me: STEP-brother. And trust me, I wish he wasn't.

Toby: I wondered why you didn't mention it...

Me: I didn't know it was important?

It wasn't exactly an opening line that worked well for me, 'Hey, I'm Hailee Raine, and by the way, my step-brother is Jason Ford'.

Toby: It's not. But next time, we should probably avoid an Eagles party...

My heart did an unexpected little somersault at the words 'next time'.

Me: Next time? How very presumptuous of you.

I was grinning now.

Toby: Is that a yes?

Me: I'll think about it

As I hit send my cell began to ring. "Hey," I said to Flick, my voice still thick with sleep.

"Hey. So... last night was interesting."

"Ugh. Don't." I groaned, throwing my arm over my face. "I can't believe they showed up there."

"I can't believe I thought we were in the middle of a shootout. My heart didn't stop pounding all night."

"Yeah, it was crazy. But guess who just texted me?"

"He did? That's funny because Jude texted me too." Her voice lifted.

"Oh." Suddenly I didn't feel so special. "Do you think they planned it that way?"

"Does it matter?" Flick scoffed. "They're hot and nice and they want us. Even *after* finding out who your brother is."

"Step-brother," I corrected her.

"Like that matters. Jason marched you out of that party like he was your dad."

"Please don't remind me." I'd get him back for that.

One day.

Pushing back the covers, I climbed out of bed, listening to Flick as she told me the ins and outs of her texts back and forth with Jude. Apparently, they had shared a secret kiss at the party and if I didn't know better, it sounded like my best friend had a serious crush.

Inside my bathroom, I listened for any signs of life from Jason's room. When there was none, I slipped out into the hall and downstairs. I loved Sunday mornings. Kent and Mom always left the house early to go play couples golf with our neighbors; and if Jason was home, he rarely surfaced before ten and then he usually headed straight over to Asher's house. But when I hit the bottom step and heard the low rumble of voices coming from the kitchen, I paused. Cupping my hand around my phone, I whispered, "Flick, I need to go."

"Go? But I was just about to tell you—"

"I think Jason and the guys are here. I'll call you later."

"Oh, okay."

We said goodbye and hung up, and I tiptoed down the hall. Jason was talking to Asher, but I couldn't hear anyone else. I hovered, straining to listen.

"He could use her against you," Asher said, and I heard Jason sneer.

"Like anything he could do to her would bother me."

"Dude, you might hate her, but she's still family. If your dad or her mom found out..." Asher's voice trailed off, and my spine went rigid as it dawned on me; they were talking about last night.

About me.

Without thinking, I stormed into the kitchen, my eyes immediately landing on Jason and Asher... and Cameron, sitting at the breakfast counter. Jason groaned, scrubbing a hand down his face, while Cameron grew tense. Ignoring him to focus on my step-brother, I said, "Why would they use me against you?"

"Hailee..." It was a warning, his voice low and cold. But screw that. They played enough with my life without dragging me into their rivalry with Rixon East.

"Fuck you," I spat, frustration and fury licking the inside of my stomach. "I didn't ask you to turn up at that party last night and ruin everything." Out of the corner of my eye, I noticed Cameron's expression harden, his fingers curl around the edge of the counter.

And then I realized I was only wearing my thin tank top and boy-short pajamas.

Great.

Just great.

"You shouldn't have been there in the first place. Fuck, Hailee, it's East territory. Those fuckers—"

"You think I care about that? About what team they play for? Me being there had nothing to do with you."

"Come on, *Hails*, you expect us to believe—" Asher swallowed his words when I levelled him with a hard look.

I threw up my hands, bitter laughter spilling out of me. "You're deluded, all of you." My eyes went wide. "If you must know, me and Flick went to that party because you made damn sure we don't get invited to any parties here. We didn't even know it was an Eagles thing until Toby said—"

"Toby, who the fuck is Toby?" Cameron finally spoke, and my gaze slid to his.

"You're actually going to sit there and act like you care?" I all but spat the words at him. In true asshole fashion he remained stone masked, my words rolling off his impenetrable expression.

Silence stretched out before us, the air growing dense. With an exasperated sigh, I looked to Jason again. "Why do you care so much that Lewis Thatcher knows who I am? It's never mattered before."

"Because they could come at me through you."

I scoffed at that. He was talking stupid. I was nothing to him, no one. So the idea someone would hurt me to get at Jason was the most stupid thing I'd ever heard.

"If that's the case," I said, "Then I'm surprised you didn't hand me over willingly." I locked eyes with him, daring him to prove me wrong.

Jason's jaw clenched as he curled and uncurled his fist against the counter, over and over, as if he was working the muscles in his hand as well as the problem in his head.

"Trust me, little sister," he seethed. "You don't want to end up in the middle of this."

"Are you fucking kidding me? I didn't ask to end up in the middle of *anything*." My voice was shrill, but I was so done with his shit. "You don't own me, Jason. Everyone else might treat you like the prodigal son of football, but I. Don't. Care." My blood boiled with contempt.

Jason stood up. "Fuck this shit," he said, storming out of the room.

"That went well." Asher gave me a wry smile, and I rolled my eyes. But he wasn't done. "You know, he's right. You think we make your life hell, but if you get in the middle of things with Thatcher and Jase, things could get very messy."

"What did he do that Thatcher would want to use me to get back at him?"

Asher went to reply, but Cameron said, "Ash, don't," shaking his head.

My eyes snapped over to his. "Really, you're going to keep me in the dark?"

"It's for your own sake."

"Oh please, like anything you do is for *my* sake."

"Aaaand, I'm out." Asher got up and started to leave. "Don't do anything I wouldn't, bro. Although looking as good as she does,"—his eyes raked over me, eliciting a shiver up my spine, and not the good kind—"I wouldn't blame you if you did."

"Pig."

"Bitch." He disappeared into the hall leaving me alone with Cameron.

The very last place I wanted to be.

16

Cameron

"HE'S A DISGUSTING PIG," Hailee said as the door closed behind Asher's retreating form.

"He's only messing with you."

"He called me a bitch." She gave me a pointed look, daring me to disagree.

"Yeah, but he didn't mean it." Asher was... complicated. He acted the spoiled football god better than most of us, but I knew him better than that. And the Asher Rixon High got wasn't the version I knew existed underneath his mask.

"Whatever." Hailee folded her arms over her chest, drawing attention to her soft curves.

Of course she'd had to storm into the kitchen wearing nothing but thin pajamas, her silky hair hanging over her shoulders like a huge fucking arrow saying 'look at my tits'.

I forced myself to look away, silently commanding my dick to stand down. "You okay?" I said, breaking the deafening silence. Hailee's eyes narrowed as they slid back to me, her expression murderous.

"I can't believe this," she muttered. "I went to that party to escape all your crap and now I'm in the middle of some stupid football rivalry thanks to my asshole of a brother. So, you tell me, Cameron, how the hell am I supposed to feel?"

"If it's any consolation, I told them not to do anything reckless."

"Oh wow, you did? Look how well that worked out." She sneered. "God, I really want to paint the crap out of something right now."

Silence enveloped us, the atmosphere toxic. Hailee had every right to be pissed. Hell, I was pissed too. I'd told them not to do anything stupid, warned them to stay out of Rixon East. But I should have known they wouldn't listen. Jason did whatever he wanted, when he wanted, consequences be damned. But he'd never had to worry about anyone but himself and the team before. East knowing about Hailee changed things. And whether he'd admit it or not, it made Jase vulnerable.

"I need to go." She started moving for the door, but I straightened off the counter.

"We should—"

"What, Cameron?" Hailee's eyes were saucers as she cut me with a look that made me feel five inches tall. "What should we do? Pretend like we can actually stand each other? Go another round of verbal chess? Or maybe you want to shove a bag over my head and ruin another perfectly good shirt?"

I heard her words, felt the venom behind them, but I was too distracted by her lips to really let them settle in my bones. Too focused on the way her mouth curved with every syllable.

"Oh my god," she shrieked. "You're doing it again. You're totally looking at my—"

I closed the distance between us, crowding her against the wall, snagging a wisp of her hair between my fingers. It was a bold move given the hate stare she was giving me, and the fact her step-brother was right outside, but it was a damn sight better than fisting her hair and smashing my mouth to hers, which is what I really wanted to do.

"Do you ever stop talking?" I asked.

"Do you ever consider getting professional help?" She looked away from me, her arms folded across her chest, as she fought a smirk.

"Oh, Sunshine, the only thing driving me crazy is you."

"This isn't a game, Cameron. This, us, it's not attraction you feel; it's hate. I. Hate. You."

Leaning in, I ran my nose along her jaw, sure I felt her body shiver, her breath catch. "Keep telling yourself that, Sunshine."

Her hands pressed against my chest as she glared up at me, but she wasn't fooling me. Hailee was pissed, yes, but she was also turned on. Her pupils were dilated, her skin warm and flushed. And I wanted nothing more than to find out all the other ways I could make her blush.

But she ground out, "I'm not doing this again with you. I won't be that girl." Giving a little shove, Hailee ducked underneath my arm and slipped away from me. "Stay away from me, Cameron."

But as she walked away from me, I knew I was screwed.

Because the rules had changed, and I knew I couldn't stay away from her.

Even if I wanted to.

After giving myself five minutes to calm down, I found Jase outside, throwing a ball. He looked like shit: a deep purple bruise around one eye and an angry cut on his lip. Anger radiated from him like a warning sign that said, 'stay the fuck away', but I wasn't anyone. And we needed to talk about this.

"I should've listened to you," he ground out, hiking the ball and sending it flying through the tire.

Folding my arms, I shrugged. "I told you it was a bad idea, but you couldn't have known she was going to be there."

"She shouldn't have been there, stupid fucking—"

"You know she wasn't there to stir trouble for you."

"Wasn't she?" He levelled me with a hard look. "How can I know for sure this wasn't all part of her plan to get back at me for your little stunt at the pep rally?" His brow rose. That was Jason though, so wary of everyone's ulterior motives. I guess it came with the territory; the higher you climbed, the less you could trust the people around you. Because everyone wanted a piece of a legend in the making.

"Because, man, Hailee might get off on your games almost as much as you do, but she's *not* you. Besides, she hates the limelight. Can you really imagine her going to an East party and announcing herself as Jason Ford's step-sister?"

He mulled my words over, his eyes hard on the ground. "She's made things real fucking difficult for me. My dad knows we butt heads, but if he found out I... fuck." His fist clenched at his side. "I don't know what I'm supposed to do here."

"East know she's family now, so you might as well start treating her like it. Rivals Week is the week after next. If they're going to try anything you can bet your ass it'll be then."

Jase jammed his fingers in his hair, tugging the ends in frustration. "She'll never go for that. And honestly, I'm not sure I can do it. I don't like her." He glanced up at me. "I'll *never* like her."

"You don't have to like her." The words stuck in my throat. "But she's in the middle of this now, whether you like it or not."

His grim expression told me he knew I was right. "She won't make things easy," he sounded defeated.

"She doesn't need to. One semester; we only need to get through one semester and then the season is done."

"One semester," he echoed as if he was trying it out for size. "I swear to God, man, if she screws anything up for me—"

"She won't." If Hailee knew what was good for her, she'd keep her head down and her mouth shut, and this thing with Thatcher would all blow over. And if it didn't... well, I didn't want to think about that right now.

"Fuck." Jase let the ball fly and it hit the outer rim of the tire. Jason didn't miss.

He *never* missed.

Looking my best friend in the eye, I said, "You need to keep your head about this, okay?"

"Yeah," he mumbled. "I just..."

"I know."

Football, this life, was all he knew. The air he breathed.

And for someone like Jason, losing even an ounce of control was not an option.

Monday morning in the weight room was a bitch. Coach didn't want us to get cocky after our crushing win over Marshall Prep, and had us work extra hard which meant practice was going to be a double bitch. He'd also given Jason and Asher an earful about their appearance, but he didn't ask questions —he didn't want to know. As long as they were fit enough to play and stayed out of Principal Finnigan's way, that was all that mattered.

The buzz in the locker room was infectious, everyone still riding the high of Friday night.

"So, I heard Levinson are looking good this season." Layton, one of the new players from JV said. "My cousin goes there, and he said—"

"Levinson can eat my ass," Asher howled. "Last season, weren't they like six losses to four?"

"Things change, man. I'm telling you, they got this new coach, and he's really worked them hard over the summer."

Asher shrugged. "I'll believe it when I see it."

"Don't get cocky, Ash," Jase chimed in. "We treat every game like we're playing the motherfucking championship game, you hear me?"

"Yeah, yeah, don't sweat it, man. We know the deal."

"Oh shit," someone chimed. "Yo, QB, you'd better come see this." It was Grady.

My spine prickled as Jase stalked across the room to him, peering over the guy's shoulder, his eyes hard on the screen. "Motherfucker," he rasped, his fist clenching against his thigh.

"Problem?" I asked.

"Time to get to work, ladies," Coach boomed. "And that better not be a cell phone I can see, Grady. Get it out of my sight, Son, and get out on the field stat. If you're not out there in ten, you can spend the next two hours running suicides. You feel me?"

"Y- yeah, Coach, I feel you." Grady mumbled as Jase stalked back to his locker. He looked furious, eyes thin, nostrils flared.

"What's up?" I asked, but he shook his head.

"Not now," Jase said. "We have a practice to get through."

That piqued my interest. Whatever he'd seen on Grady's cell had him all worked up which meant whatever it was, it wasn't good. And my gut told me there were only two things who could get to my best friend like that.

Lewis Thatcher.

And his step-sister.

17

Hailee

"WE NEED TO TALK." Flick was waiting for me outside English Lit, her expression grim.

"Okay..." My brows knitted.

"Not here." She glanced up and down the hall. "Come on." Her hand found mine, and we weaved our way through the stream of kids coming and going from class.

"Flick, hold up, what's—"

"Raider traitor." A shoulder slammed into mine, knocking me backward.

"Excuse me?" I spun around, glaring at the girl's retreating form.

"Okay, we need to go, right now." Flick grabbed my hand again and started yanking.

"Felicity Giles, will you just tell me what the hell is—"

"Thinks she's too good for us, for the Raiders." The words washed over me, my gaze landing on a group of girls over by the girls' bathroom door. They all burst into a fit of snickering when they noticed me watching them.

"What did you say?" I bristled, narrowing my eyes on their ringleader, but Flick didn't let up as she kept pulling me toward the main doors.

"You're a disgrace," someone else sneered until I realized everyone was looking at me.

Every. Single. Person.

By the time we reached the main doors, I'd been called every insult possible—whore, slut, skank—and a few more I'd never even heard before. We spilled outside and I sucked in a ragged breath, my chest tight as I glanced back at the doors. "What the hell is happening right now?"

Flick chewed her thumb, her eyes refusing to meet mine. "Flick," I urged. "What is going on?"

"Okay, don't panic..." Her gaze finally lifted. "But Thatcher posted something on Snapchat and people have been sharing it."

"He did?" I didn't even have Snapchat.

She nodded. "It's bad, Hails, really bad."

"I see." My voice was flat, my stomach churning. "Worse than the pep rally?"

Her lips pressed into a thin line.

"Show me," I said.

"Hails, I'm not sure—"

"Show me." Holding out my hand, I waited for her to give me her cell phone. She swiped the screen a couple times before handing it to me. A gasp slipped from my lips when my eyes landed on a photo of me. Except it wasn't me at all. It was my face photoshopped—pretty convincingly—onto a girl's body, and she was wearing an Eagles jersey, sucking provocatively on a popsicle.

"Ford's sister sucks Eagles dick good." My voice trailed off. "Where did that photo even come from?" Leaning closer, I got a better look. "Oh my god, is that one of my photos from the yearbook last year?" I remembered it now. I'd been in the art studio and Denny Marcus, the yearbook photographer, snapped me mid-laugh. "How the hell did they even get a hold of that?" I said, as if that was really the issue here.

"It doesn't matter. Now everyone thinks you—"

I glared at her. "Not helping, Flick."

"Sorry, I just... shit, Hails, what are you going to do?"

"Nothing. I'm going to do nothing." If I didn't stoke the fire, the flames would die out.

"When Jason finds out—"

"He'll what? Drive across river and defend my honor? Please." It came out bitter. "He won't care about this crap. We should get back in there." I flicked my head to the doors.

"Seriously? I thought we'd at least skip the rest of classes."

"It's one photo. I'm not going to hide because of one photo." Even if I did look like an advert for a cheap porn movie.

"Okay, if you say so." Flick trailed behind me as we re-entered the building. "What class do you have now?" she asked.

"Math."

"Asher's in that class with you, right?"

I frowned unsure where she was going with this. "When he can be bothered to show up, yeah. Why?"

She gave me a sympathetic look, and said, "Because something tells me this will only get worse before it gets any better."

Flick wasn't wrong. In math I received four hate-notes, had numerous paper balls thrown at me, and some of Khloe Stemson's friends spent the entire class kicking the back of my chair.

As I expected, Asher didn't show, but I'd spotted the team through the window, running drills on the athletic field.

"How was it?" Flick grabbed my arm as soon as I filed out of the room, keeping me close to her as we fought the crush.

"Is math ever fun?" I gave her my best smile, and she returned it with a pointed look.

"Okay," I conceded. "It was bad. By game night I fully expect to be forced to wear the foam Eagle costume and be thrown onto the field to receive a public beating from Vinnie the Viking."

Flick smothered a chuckle. "I'm sorry. I know it's not funny, but that conjures up all kinds of crazy visuals."

"Gee, thanks." I pressed my lips together, rolling my eyes, as we made our way down the hall. If I concentrated really hard, I could almost block out the insults.

Almost.

"Do you know what really pisses me off?" I said as we reached our locker bank. "When Cameron humiliated me, no one stood up for me. But now they all think I've been cavorting with the enemy and everyone is on a personal mission to defend *them*. It's pathetic."

"It's football," my best friend shot back.

I traded some books and closed my locker. It was history next, the only class I shared with Cameron... if he showed.

"Okay," I announced as we stopped outside my next class. "Wish me luck."

Flick rested her hands on my shoulder. "You got this. And if anyone gives you shit, just remind them that you ride Raiders *and* suck Eagles dick. Hell, girl, that's jersey chaser goals right there." She winked before spinning me around and shoving me into the room.

All eyes fell on me as I walked to the back of class. I liked to think I had excellent patience when it came to my fickle classmates, but after an hour of being kicked in the back last period, a seat on the last row seemed like the safest bet.

"Eagles whore," someone whisper-hissed as I passed them. But I didn't bite. I didn't hang my head or lower my eyes.

I wouldn't give them the satisfaction.

But my silence only fueled them, and the hushed insults began to ripple around the room like a rising wave, until the teacher, Mr. Henson finally intervened.

"Sorry I'm late, Sir." Cameron burst into the room and I dropped my head onto the table with a muted groan. I could survive fifty-five minutes of hearing I was a traitorous slut, but I couldn't handle hearing it in front of him.

His eyes found mine across the room, growing dark as he began to stalk toward me.

"Mr. Chase." Mr. Henson sounded pissed. "I'd like you take your usual—"

"Change of plan, Sir." He didn't even look at Mr. Henson. "I'll be needing a seat at the back. Jones," Cameron addressed the guy beside me. "Move."

The low rumble of chatter followed him as he reached the desk beside me. The guy already sitting there almost tripped over himself to move.

"Now, if everyone's in their seats," Mr. Henson cut Cameron with a harsh look, "We can get started."

Ten minutes into the lesson, Cameron rapped his pen against the edge of my desk. "What?" I mouthed, our hushed voices drowned out by the discussion happening between the teacher and a couple of kids up front.

"You okay?"

"What do you think?" I whisper-hissed, returning my gaze to the front of the room.

I ignored Cameron for the rest of class. When the bell finally went and everyone started packing up their things, a paper projectile landed on my desk. I casually opened it, keeping my hand over the page to avoid any wandering—namely Cameron's—eyes. Someone snickered as I balled up the vile note and stormed out of there.

I'd barely made it out of the door when I heard, "Who the fuck wrote this?" The harshness of Cameron's voice reverberated through me, making me flinch, but I didn't glance back.

I couldn't.

"Hailee, wait," he called, but I started pushing through the crowds as fast as I could.

I thought I could handle it. I thought it didn't matter what people said about me; the lies they told. But apparently even I had a line. And that line was a detailed account of what someone thought a traitorous whore like me deserved.

Traitorous whore.

Anyone who knew me, *really* knew me, knew I didn't date, let alone hook up with random guys.

Tears burned the backs of my eyes as I burst through the main doors into the fresh air. But I wouldn't cry. Not over a bunch of kids who had been all too happy to ignore me for my entire high school existence. Besides, it was anger, not pain, I felt.

"Hailee, would you just wait up—"

"Go away, Cameron." I waved him off over my shoulder as I made a beeline for the parking lot, ignoring the fact he'd called me by my name and not that stupid nickname he usually loved so much.

"Hey." His hand curved around my shoulder.

"What do you want from me?" I spun around, shrugging him off, narrowing my eyes right on him.

"I..." His response died as he stepped back, putting some distance between us. He swept a hand over his short hair.

"Just leave me alone, okay?"

But Cameron didn't move. He didn't do anything. He just stood there, watching me, his expression dark; his gaze so intense I felt stripped naked. I went to walk away, but he moved quickly, his hand snagging my wrist. "It's been like that all morning?"

"What do you care?"

Something flashed in his eyes, but he didn't offer me an answer, and I let out a heavy sigh. "You know," I said. "All I wanted was to get through senior year. I knew nothing would change with Jason, knew he'd still be obsessed with playing his stupid games. But I was fine with that. It was between us. I could still stay in the shadows..."

"I'll fix it," he said cryptically.

"Fix it?" My voice was incredulous. "You do know it's your fault I'm in this situation, right?"

"If you hadn't gone to that part—"

"You have got to be fucking kidding me? What is wrong with you? I'm seventeen, Cameron. I'm supposed to be going to parties, meeting boys, and getting drunk. But wait, I can't do that because you and my asshole brother made damn sure of it."

A couple of kids walked by us, their eyes wide with curiosity. Cameron grabbed my arm and pulled me toward his truck until we were secreted away between his vehicle and the one beside it. "I know we give you a hard time but it's better this way."

"Better?" I sucked in a harsh breath. "For who? You? Jason?" Anger vibrated in my chest as I glared at him.

"I..." he breathed out. "Look,"—Cameron pressed his hands either side of my head, caging me in. "I only did what I did at the pep rally because Jason was ready to destroy you."

"So you were saving me? Please." Bitter laughter rose up my throat. "You did what you did because you're just like him. He dishes out the orders and you come running like a good little—"

"Watch it, Sunshine." His words were low. Gravelly. As if this was all some game to him. But it wasn't a game, it was my life. And it was falling apart all because of them and their stupid rivalry with Rixon East.

"Or what?" My back pressed further into the side of his truck, pinned in place by his intense gaze.

"You really want to know the answer to that question?" Cameron's brow rose, a silent dare.

This felt different. I was angry, yes, but I couldn't deny there was something else simmering beneath my skin. Something unfamiliar. A deep yearning I tried to fight, tried desperately to ignore, every time I found myself in close proximity to Cameron Chase.

"What's the matter, Sunshine?" He leaned in, dipping his face to mine. "Cat got your tongue?"

"Why?" The word spilled from my lips. "Why are you doing this to me?"

"What is it you think I'm doing?"

I swallowed as his eyes flicked to my mouth, the way they had before in the janitor's closet and again in my kitchen the other morning. "Toying with me like this," it came out a whisper.

"What if I told you this isn't a game?"

Not a game?

What the hell did that mean?

"I- I don't understand."

Cameron moved closer, his legs brushing mine. My hands flew up, landing on his chest, desperate to keep him there. But the second I touched him, his eyes shuttered, a carnal growl rumbling in his chest. He swallowed it, shaking his head a little. When he met my gaze again, his irises had turned dark. His eyes hooded.

"Cameron?"

"Just give me a minute..." A beat passed, and another, energy crackling between us like an electrical storm.

I needed to go. I needed to push him away and move. But I was rooted to the spot, lost in his gray-blue eyes and all the things he wasn't saying. My heart galloped in my chest, my mind swimming with confusing thoughts. Cameron wasn't the good guy here, I knew that. Yet, I couldn't break whatever spell he had cast over me.

And I wasn't sure I wanted to.

What the hell is wrong with me?

"Cameron," I finally said breaking the tension. "I should go."

"You can't go," he said, his voice barely audible.

"Cameron, I'm not doing this." Whatever this was. "I'm not—"

One of his hands slid along my collarbone, gliding up my neck, his thumb stroking the skin there. I fought a moan. "You can hate me, Hailee. I deserve it, I know that. But don't insult me by pretending you don't feel this." He dropped his head to mine, inhaling deeply. "Tell me you feel it."

I could feel *something* all right, digging into my thigh.

Swallowing hard, I tried to process what was happening. Why my heart was a runaway train, crashing against my ribcage as if it was trying to escape. Why my skin tingled and I felt hot all over.

"You feel it," he whispered again, his warm minty breath dancing over my face. "I know you do." If I lifted my chin a fraction our lips would touch. We'd be kissing. But I didn't want that.

Did I?

"I..." I wanted to tell him I didn't feel it, that I had no idea what he was talking about, but there was obviously something very wrong with me because, I felt it. I did. But I couldn't tell him that.

I wouldn't.

Instead, "I hate you," spilled from my lips.

Before I could take back the words, Cameron's other hand cupped my neck and he fixed his mouth against mine, his tongue gently parting my lips and slipping inside. He kissed me slow and deep, right there in the school parking lot against the side of his truck.

And all I could think was Cameron Chase is kissing me...

Cameron Chase is kissing me...

Kissing me.

Heat flooded my stomach, making my thighs clench together, as he plastered me against his truck, kissing me deeper, harder. Our tongues dueled, fighting for dominance. But he won, and I softened under his touch. The way he nipped my lip, tracing his mouth over my jaw, my neck, sucking and nibbling.

"Cameron." It was supposed to be a warning, a signal for him to slow down. A reminder of where we were and what we were doing.

A reminder for myself to get a grip.

But pleasure escaped my throat, and I moaned softly.

"Fuck, you taste good," he murmured, his lips and hands exploring my skin, my body, as if he couldn't get enough of me. Which made no sense because we hated each other.

I hated him.

I hate him.

"Wait." I broke away and he groaned, dropping his face to the crook of my shoulder. "What the hell are we doing?" My voice trembled as I tried to regain control of myself, my stupid fickle emotions.

"Cameron," I said jabbing my fingers into his ribs when he didn't move. "Get the hell off me."

He stepped back, his lips curled in an annoyingly sexy smirk. "You're not making this easy, Sunshine."

"I swear to God, if you call me that again, I'll—"

"You'll what? Kiss me?" His smirk morphed into a smug grin.

"I'm leaving now," I said roughly. "Please don't follow me." *Because I might beg you for things I shouldn't want.* I slipped out from between him and his truck and started walking away but his hand snagged my wrist. "Cameron." His name left my lips a gentle sigh.

"Just tell me one thing," he said.

"What?" I gave a frustrated sigh. But it wasn't only Cameron I was frustrated with.

"Does hating me feel as good for you as it does for me?"

"Goodbye, Cameron." My eyes dropped to where his fingers were curled around my wrist and he released me.

"Whatever you say, Sunshine." He had to have the last words. "But just remember, Hailee." My name on his lips made my stomach do a little flip. "You can run but you can't hide."

18

Cameron

HAILEE HURRIED BACK INTO SCHOOL, but I didn't go after her. I needed some air. The girl got under my skin until I couldn't think straight.

When I'd followed her out here, I hadn't planned on kissing her again. I only wanted to talk, to find out what the hell was happening. But then I'd pulled her around the side of my truck and the temptation was just too damn much. Watching her fight herself over whether to admit she felt this thing growing between us, was the final straw.

Fuck.

She was messing with my head. Making me want things I couldn't have. But there were bigger things happening right now, like the fact someone had sent her a note in history loaded with dirty disgusting things that made me want to punch something—or someone.

When practice had ended and Jase had showed me the photo Thatcher had added to his Snapchat story, I'd almost lost it. What I hadn't expected though, was how the rest of the kids at school would react. The second I'd found her sitting at the back of class, I knew something was up. Hailee didn't hide; she usually sat up front, eager to answer questions and participate. But she was quiet, hiding behind her glasses, her eyes void of the usual spark I saw there. And the second I'd watched her read the note, saw her expression harden, the blood drain from her face, I knew it was only the tip of the iceberg.

Stuffing everything down, I went back into school heading straight for the cafeteria, surprised when I saw Hailee sitting with Felicity at their usual table.

"That shit Thatcher posted is everywhere," Asher said, coming up beside me, his eyes flicking over to the girls. "What did she say in history?"

"Not a lot, but someone sent her a note and it was bad."

"I heard a group of guys in the hall talking about her like she was—"

"Don't," I ground out.

He glanced at me. "What's up with you? You seem tense? Maybe you need to call up Miley and get her to help you work out those—"

"Seriously, bro, I said don't."

"Jeez, someone's on their period. Or is it this shit with Jase and Hailee? It'll blow over, you know?" He clapped me on the back. "Thatcher has bigger fish to fry."

I wasn't so sure about that.

Even though the photo of Hailee was obviously manipulated, kids saw what they wanted to see, and thanks to Thatcher, Hailee had become public enemy number one. It didn't matter I'd done something similar at the pep rally because that hadn't pitted her against us. For as fucked up as it was, to most girls at school, getting called out for riding Raider dick would have been a badge of honor. But sleeping with the enemy, even if it was only a rumor, was a crime our fans would not forgive.

"Come on, I could eat a small horse." Asher shoulder-checked me, moving ahead of me to the line. Except he didn't wait, he slipped right to the front, giving the diner lady a huge grin. They made small talk about the upcoming game Friday, while I grabbed a sub and added it to his tray. He worked his charm until she gave him a knowing wink, letting us slip past her without paying.

We wound our way through the tables toward Jase who was already sitting at our table, Jenna Jarvis practically dry fucking his leg. "What's up?" he said coolly.

"We've got a problem," I replied under my breath, motioning over to Hailee.

"She'll be fine." Jase swallowed his words as we watched a guy approach their table. Flick glowered at him as he dropped down on the bench beside Hailee.

"Maybe we should—" I started but Jase cut me off with a shake off his head. "She can handle herself," he said.

I didn't doubt that, but she was in this situation because of him. Because of us. And that didn't sit right with me.

The guy was saying something, a smug smirk plastered on his face, as he leaned in close to her. Too fucking close. He hooked his arm around Hailee's waist, and I braced myself to intervene, but she smacked him right across the face. The guy howled with laughter, backing away, but I saw the shock in his expression.

We all did.

Asher whistled through his teeth. "Shit, that girl's got balls of steel."

"She's going to need them," Jase grumbled as if he knew—and accepted—it was only going to get worse.

Well, screw that.

"It's so sad," Jenna said, twirling her hair around her fingers. "She could have been one of us, but instead she chose to fuck Thatcher just to get one over on—"

Jase shoved her off his lap and she landed on the bench beside him with a thud. "Ow, Jase, what the hell was that for?"

"I'm bored." His voice was cold. "Run along now."

"You bastard." Jenna kept her voice composed, but her cheeks flamed with embarrassment as she beckoned for her friends to follow her, and they sauntered away, trying to retain some dignity. Some of the guys howled with laughter but soon shut up when Jase sent them a hard glare down the table.

My eyes found Hailee across the room again. She had her head down, pushing a salad around her plate. "We should go over there."

"Did you get hit a little too hard in practice?" Jase snorted.

"I'm just saying, if we don't do something to end this, it's going to get a whole lot worse before it gets better. And if it gets that bad, and the wrong teacher overhears something, it could land on Finnigan's desk. And that is trouble we don't need."

My best friend regarded me for a second, scrubbing his face. "Fucking girls," Jase mumbled, shoving off the bench. He stood up and glanced back at the two of us, "Come on then, I'm not doing this shit alone."

"Oh, hells yeah, I'm in. Maybe I can tap up Felic—"

"She's off-limits," Jase barked.

"She is?" Asher jerked back as if he'd been slapped. "But why? I thought everyone except Hailee was fair game?"

"Because I said so, jackass."

Asher threw up his hands in surrender, his lips twitching.

When we reached their table, Hailee and her friend gawked up at us. "Yes?" she said flatly. "Can we help you?"

"No, but I think we can help you." Jase dropped down beside Felicity. Her eyes widened, glancing between him and Hailee and back again.

"What is happening right now?"

"You need us," he said as if it was that simple.

"Hmm, no," Hailee quipped. "No, we don't."

"That's not what he thinks." Jase flicked his head over where the guy who she'd slapped watched us. The little fucker looked ready to piss himself, his eyes darting to the ground when I narrowed my gaze right on him.

"Pfft," Hailee grumbled. "I handled him just fine."

"That you did, *Hails*," Asher added, sliding in next to her. I sat on her other side, watching her out of the corner of my eye.

"Don't call me that," she said, a defensive edge to her voice. "We're not friends."

"Looks like we are from where I'm sitting." He grinned.

"If I recall." Hailee glared at him. "None of this would be happening if you hadn't gate-crashed their party and started brawling with Thatch—"

"Brawling?" Asher quipped as Jase sat back, watching her with a dark expression. "Naw, baby, that wasn't a brawl, that was just the warm up."

Hailee sneered, her eyes quickly moving to her step-brother. "This has been fun and all, but you can go now." She wiggled her fingers in a wave.

"Yeah, I'm thinking this was a bad idea. I'm out." Jase got up and walked off while Asher threw me a 'what should we do now?' look. But before I could say anything, Hailee levelled me with a cold look, and said, "I don't know what *this* is, but I don't need you to pretend to be friends with me. I managed just fine without you all this time; I think I'll survive this."

"Fine," I said, realizing maybe Jase was right. Maybe coming over here was a huge fucking mistake. "Have it your way, Sunshine. Ash, let's go."

"But..." His eyes flicked to Felicity, but when I shook my head, he let out a long breath. "Fine, I'm coming. Don't do anything I wouldn't, ladies. See you around."

Everyone watched as we stalked away from Hailee and her friend, but they could look. If she was too stubborn to admit she needed us, then we'd just have to go around her.

"She's a handful," Asher muttered as he shouldered the door. "But her friend is quiet. I like that. Means she's probably a real freak between—"

"Do you think with anything other than your dick?"

"Football and pussy." He shrugged, a lazy grin splitting his face. "What else is there?"

I wanted to tell him that, one day, he'd meet a girl who made everything else pale into insignificance. A girl who would get under his skin and gnaw away at his soul. But he wasn't ready to hear the words... and I wasn't ready to admit I knew what the hell I was talking about. So instead, I slung my arm around his shoulder and said, "Come on, Casanova, we should probably show up for a class or two."

Our little stunt at lunch calmed the vicious rumors spreading through the halls, but it still didn't stop some guys, and girls, thinking they could talk about Hailee like she was the town slut.

"You need to do something," I urged Jase as we walked from last period to the locker room.

"Tried that, and she threw it back in my face."

"So, give the word for the team to quash the rumors."

He glared at me. "Why are you so worked up over this? It was just a photo."

"And you're okay with everyone thinking Hailee gives it up to the Eagles? To Thatcher?" My brow rose, challenging him. It wasn't like I could tell him the truth; that every time I heard someone call her a slut or whore, I wanted to break their face. He wouldn't want to hear that.

"You need to put an end to it, now. Before Finnigan hears something that gives him cause to look closer at this grudge between us and East."

Jase rolled his shoulders back, his hardened gaze locking on mine. But he didn't reply, he simply strolled into the locker room. Trailing after him, I went straight to my bench and began peeling out of my clothes.

"Yeah, well I wouldn't mind her sucking on my dick."

My eyes snapped over to two juniors huddled over a cell phone. "What's that?" I asked, pulling on my pants.

The one holding the phone paled. "Hmm, nothing, it's nothing." He dropped the cell in his bag and pressed his lips together.

"No, seriously, what was it?" Irritation rippled up my spine. "Because I know it's not what I think it is," I ground out, slowly approaching them. "I know you're not fucking stupid enough to be talking about your QB's stepsister like that."

Silence descended over the room, but I only had eyes for the junior who looked ready to piss himself. "Come on, Chase," he stuttered around a weak smile, as if we were old friends. "It's not like that… I wasn't…"

"So, tell me how it is?" I reached him, plucking the cell phone from his open bag. He was as white as a ghost now as I thrust the cell at him and barked, "Unlock it."

With shaky fingers, he swiped the screen and tapped out the pin. "I'm-I'm sorry, man, we were just goofing around."

I saw the flash of Hailee's face on the screen but kept my eyes locked on his face. I couldn't see that shit, not again. Not if I wanted to avoid making a huge fucking mistake. Grabbing him by his collar, I yanked hard putting us face to face. "This isn't just a team, it's a family. You disrespect one of us, your disrespect all of us. You want to talk shit about your QB's sister?" My breaths came hard as I narrowed my eyes on him.

"I… I'm sorry." His face was pale.

"Chase, ease up." Jase's demand barely penetrated my anger, but I felt him move behind me. "Chase." His hand landed on my shoulder and I flinched, shoving at the junior until he stumbled backward.

"You talking shit about Hailee?" Jase asked him.

"It wasn't—"

"Chase is right. This is a team. My. Fucking. Team." His voice was ice cold. "You feel me?"

The kid nodded, mumbling some incoherent apology.

"That goes for the rest of you." Jase swung around, running his eyes over each of his teammates. "Anyone else want to run their mouth off about Hailee?" He was met with silence. "Didn't think so. Hailee is off-limits. Always has been. If anyone needs reminding of that, I have no problem arranging it. This shit with the photo, it ends now."

My best friend's eyes slid to mine. His lips were pursed, annoyance pouring off him, but he gave me a little nod of understanding, and I returned it. Jase might not have wanted to intervene, but I'd given him no choice.

I only hoped I wouldn't live to regret it.

19

Hailee

AFTER JASON, Asher, and Cameron attempted to sit with us at lunch on Monday, things died down and, by the time Friday rolled around, the photo of me was old news. Instead, everyone was talking about the Raiders first game away from home against the Levinson Lions.

"Hi, Hailee," some girl I barely recognized said as Flick and I walked to lunch.

"Hmm, hi," I replied, my brows drawn tight, before glaring at my friend. "Okay, what the hell is happening now?"

She gave me a smug look, and I asked, "What?"

"I think you're Rixon's new hottest toy and everyone wants to play with you."

"Don't be ridiculous." So a couple of people had tried to talk to me, and I'd even been asked if I was going to watch the game tonight. I wasn't, obviously. But my total lack of school spirit no longer seemed to qualify me as a social leper. And for as much as I didn't want to admit it, Flick was right. People *were* interested in me all of a sudden.

With a chuckle, she looped her arm through mine as we entered the cafeteria. "You know, they came to sit with you for a reason."

"Yeah, but..." I hesitated. I knew what she was hinting at, but it didn't make any sense. "Let me get this straight. First, I'm treated like an outcast because Jason issued some kind of blanket Hailee-is-off-limits rule. Then I become the school slut for a fake photo circulated by Lewis Thatcher. And now, I'm what? Hot property because Jason and the guys sat with us at lunch; for all of five minutes, I might add."

"Jason and the guys?" Flick grinned, her eyes mocking me.

"Oh, piss off," I grumbled. "You know what I mean." It had been a simple slip of the tongue. Nothing more.

"I'm not saying it makes any sense, I'm just saying, I think he did something."

"Did something?" I scoffed. "He's barely said two words to me since Monday." There had been the odd grunt here or there when we passed one another at home, and he had actually sat down and eaten a meal with us last night, much to everyone's surprise. But I was under no illusion Jason and I were any closer to becoming friends. That ship had sailed long ago.

Not that I wanted that anyway.

I didn't.

Flick shrugged as we joined the lunch line. "But he might have said something behind the scenes. Told people they need to be a little nicer to you, perhaps?" Her brow shot up suggestively.

"You have met my step-brother, right? Being nice is not in his emotional capacity."

"He's a douchebag, I'm not denying that." Her lips pursed as if the words left a sour taste in her mouth. "But think about it. He's never let anyone else near you. The second Thatcher sent that photo though, he stepped up."

Stepped up? Is *that* what we were calling it?

"And I'm what?" I whisper-hissed, aware of all the prying eyes and ears within our immediate vicinity. "Just supposed to forgive the last six years and become Team Jason?"

Like that was ever going to happen. I loaded my tray with some lunch items and followed Flick to the service counter.

"I guess it does sound kind of lame when you put it that way."

"You think?" I shot back unable to keep the disbelief out of my voice.

"And how are my two favorite ladies?" Asher Bennet appeared out of nowhere and slung his arms around us, guiding us to our usual table. I ducked out of his embrace leaving him and Flick to walk together, shooting her a hard look in the process. She shrugged like it was no big deal.

Traitor.

"So." He sat down next to Flick as if he joined us for lunch every day. "I was wondering—"

"Steady there, you might get a headache." I smirked, stabbing a piece of pasta with my fork totally not pretending it was Asher's face.

"Ouch. So prickly, Raine. So prickly. Anyway, as I was saying." He gave my best friend his attention and she lapped it up, hanging on his every word. My stomach sank. "How would you girls like to come to a party tomorrow night?"

"No," I said at the same time as Flick said, "Yes."

Laughter rumbled in Asher's chest. "I can see we're going to have to keep an eye on this one," he said the words to Flick but directed them at me.

"You can go now," I huffed. It was bad enough he was sitting at our table. But flirting with Flick? That was enough to make me puke and I hadn't even taken a single bite of my lunch yet.

"You should come. There's no hidden agenda, I swear," were his parting words as he stood up, his eyes lingering a little too long on my friend. When he retreated back to his table, Flick squealed with delight. "A party," she shrieked, lowering her voice when I gave her an irritated glare. "A party at Asher Bennet's house. I can't believe this."

"You don't actually want to go?"

"Hails, come on." She groaned, rolling her eyes theatrically. "This has never happened to us before. And it's on my list."

"I think your list is fast becoming a way to talk me into selling my soul to the dark side."

"Oh, don't be so dramatic. It's just a party. And who knows, maybe you'll actually have some fun." She leaned in closer. "Besides, Cameron will be there." Her eyes danced with insinuation.

"Don't even..." I warned. I didn't want to think about Cameron, not here, not now.

Not ever.

But my eyes had a mind of their own, skimming over to where he and the rest of the team sat. His head lifted, his gray-blue eyes fixing right on me, but I darted away quickly, feeling my cheeks heat.

Oblivious, Flick said, "What?" She gave me innocent puppy dog eyes.

"It doesn't matter."

Inclining her head, she studied me. "It's okay to like him, you know?"

"I don't..." I inhaled sharply. I didn't like him. I didn't. "Whatever. Can we talk about something else?"

A slow smile tugged at her mouth. "Does that mean you'll come?"

"Do I have a choice?"

"No," her smile turned into a full grin. "No, you don't."

I WAS either a total doormat or the best friend a girl could have. The jury was still out on which as I downed the remainder of my drink, crushing the cup and throwing it in one of the trash cans Asher had strategically placed around his yard, which was as big, if not bigger, than everyone said it was. The place was freaking huge.

"I think I'm drunk," I declared.

"Shall we get another?" Flick didn't sound too sober herself as we meandered through the crowds of people all gathered to celebrate the team's win against the Levinson Lion's last night. According to everyone who was anyone it had been an easy game for the Raiders, taking them one step closer to the play-offs.

I hadn't even put up a fight when Flick turned up on my doorstep earlier with a bag full of clothes and a smile not even the most stone-hearted of people could have refused. But so far, it wasn't turning out to be all that bad. We'd managed to avoid my step-brother and his friends, or maybe they were avoiding us. Either way, we drank and danced and even joined in a game of beer pong or two.

It was strange at first, having people cheer my name.

My name.

Hailee. Hailee. Hailee.

But I couldn't deny, even in my slightly intoxicated state, it was thrilling. I was thrilled by people shouting my name. Oh God, I was turning into Jason. The idea made me shudder.

"What did you say?" Flick's head whipped around to mine.

"I didn't say anything."

"Yeah, you did. You said, you're turning into Jason."

"Did not." I poked my tongue at her, and she frowned.

"I need to pee. Crap, I need to pee so bad." Flick shoved me into a lawn chair, dancing on the spot like she had ants in her pants. "Stay right here, okay? I'll be back."

I waved her off as the world spun. Hoisting my legs over the arm of the chair, I dangled my head off the other one until I could see nothing but twinkling stars against a vast inky backdrop. It was so peaceful and calm, worlds away from the party I could vaguely hear going on around me.

"Comfortable?" a voice said from the shadows, and a face so breathtaking I sucked in a harsh breath, filled my vision. All intense eyes, straight-nose, and strong-jawed; even upside-down Cameron was beautiful.

I smiled up at him, giving a little sigh that pre-empted a hiccup. "Oops." I clapped a hand over my mouth smothering my dreamy smile. He chuckled, dropping into another chair close by. "I wondered where you'd disappeared to."

"You did?" I twisted my body to see him better but didn't sit up. I liked the feeling of being upside down. Weightless.

"Yeah, I was hoping I might get a dance with you."

"A dance, yeah, right."

He didn't laugh. *Why isn't he laughing?*

"You're not serious?" I almost choked on the words.

His shoulders lifted. "Sure I am." He sounded nonchalant. "I like dancing."

"Are you drunk?"

"Not as drunk as you."

I poked my tongue out at him and his eyes flashed like lightning in a storm. "So, it's Homecoming soon."

Homecoming.

Just the very word made me nauseous.

"I'd rather stick hot pokers in my eyes."

"So, you're not going?" he asked.

"No, I'm not going to Homecoming." *Was I?*

"Sure, you are, Sunshine. It's a senior rite of passage, you've got to be there."

"Flick wants to go." I folded my hands together, dropping them in my lap.

"Flick talks a lot of sense."

Peeking over at him, I asked, "Are you going to Homecoming?"

His expression darkened. "Kind of comes with the territory."

"Ahh, Homecoming Court, gotcha."

His face wrinkled with displeasure. "It's not really my scene, but Coach likes us to give back and everyone—"

"Hey." I threw up my hands. "Say no more Mr. Homecoming King."

"No, that'll be your brother."

"Step-brother," I groaned, and Cameron laughed. The soft sound drifting over me, wrapping me up like a warm blanket. "You have a nice laugh," I said, my eyes fluttering closed.

"And you're drunker than I realized. How are you getting home tonight?"

"I think I'm going to sleep riiiight here." I stretched my arms above my head, nestling further into the chair but then my world tilted as strong hands yanked me up.

"Oh no you don't," Cameron said. "You can stay here. Asher won't mind."

"Flick… I need to tell Flick." The words came out jumbled as he kept his arm around me and guided me back toward the house.

People called his name, called mine too, as he wound us through the sea of bodies still drinking and laughing. But it was strange. I didn't feel like they were laughing at me. Not this time. But then, maybe all the vodka in my bloodstream was giving me a false sense of confidence. Maybe I'd already fallen asleep and this was all a dream.

Either way, wrapped in Cameron's arms, it wasn't the worst place to be.

Even if I did hate him.

"Almost there," he said as we hit the top stair.

"Asher has a nice house," I mumbled as he paused at a door. I watched through glassy eyes as Cameron dug out a key from his wallet and unlocked the door. "That isn't creepy at all."

"You think I let just anyone stay in my room?" His eyes darkened, pinning me to the spot, stealing the snarky reply right off the tip of my tongue.

His room?

He had a room at the Bennet's house? But why?

Before I could ask the question, the air *whooshed* from my lungs as Cameron scooped me up like a baby and carried me into the room. "What the—"

"Relax, Sunshine, you're almost dead on your feet."

I was?

Now that he mentioned it, I did feel pretty tired and drunk.

Definitely drunk.

My fingers curled into Cameron's polo shirt and I breathed him in. "Hmm." My stomach coiled tight. He smelled good, too good. Like soap with a hint of something bitter, maybe whisky or tequila. So good that when he began to lie me down on the bed, I didn't let go of him and Cameron tumbled down on top of me. We landed with a soft *thud*, our bodies tangled, our faces almost touching.

"Shit, Hailee, I'm sorry..." He pressed his hands into the mattress either side of my head to take some of his weight off me. "I didn't mean—"

"It's okay." Reaching for him, I traced his jaw. He was so gorgeous it should have been illegal. The air shifted around us as I leaned up, brushing my lips over his, once... twice... until my mouth was slanted over his and I was kissing him.

I was kissing Cameron Chase.

And it felt good.

So damn good.

Heat exploded in my stomach, rushing out to my nerve endings, making my skin tingle and my body hum. I could kiss him forever. His lips were so soft and warm, and he tasted like everything I craved and never knew I wanted.

"Hailee—" his voice was raw.

"No," I whispered, peppering tiny kisses over his lips, sucking and nibbling. "No thinking." It didn't matter that we hated each other. Nothing mattered in this moment, except his mouth on mine.

Looping my arm around his neck, I pulled Cameron closer, nudging my nose against his. "Fuck," he breathed, adjusting himself over me so that we were two pieces of a puzzle slotted together. One of his hands slid to my thigh, and I hooked my leg around his hip, rubbing myself against him. Desperate to ease the ache growing deep inside me.

Cameron's eyes shuttered, his Adam's apple bobbing against his throat. But then he dipped his head, pressing a kiss to the hollow of my neck, sucking the sensitive skin between his teeth. I cried out, running my hands down his chest to the hem of his t-shirt. I needed to feel him. To touch him. I wanted to paint my fingers over every inch of his smooth skin.

He rocked into me, making us both groan. "Cameron, more..." I gasped. "I need more—" Something was building inside me, a firestorm sweeping through my belly and rushing to my core. My mouth sought his again, kissing him fervently.

But I quickly realized Cameron wasn't kissing me back. He was as still as a statue, the harshness of his breaths the only sound filling the silence. I pressed my mouth to his again just to be sure he wasn't kissing me back.

"Cameron." I eased back to look at him. "What's wrong?"

"We can't." His voice sounded funny, but he wanted this. I knew he did. It was right there in his eyes as they watched me. His hardness pressed into me, teasing me. Tempting me with all the things I wanted and shouldn't.

I leaned back in kissing him once more, needing him to kiss me back.

"Hailee." He broke away, staring down at me, his expression cold now. "Stop—"

Stop.

I blinked up at him, certain I'd misheard him. Because he couldn't possibly want to stop, not when it felt so good.

"We have to stop," he repeated the words, sending my stomach into a freefall.

That wasn't right. He was supposed to want more. To crave me the way I craved him.

Yet he'd said the word and now it hung between us like a glacier, cold and unforgiving.

I jerked away, flattening myself against the mattress, turning my head to the side to avoid his apologetic gaze. He let out a heavy sigh. "You should get some sleep. I'll find Flick and let her know you're up here."

Eyes screwed shut, tears burning my throat, I waited for him to leave.

I'd kissed Cameron. I'd practically offered myself up to him and he hadn't wanted me back. Rejection burned through me like acid until I felt nauseous.

About to tell him to go, to leave me alone, I felt the bed dip and he leaned over me, pressing a kiss to my head. "Goodnight, Hailee," he whispered, and then he was gone.

I grabbed a pillow and buried my face into it, letting myself drown in my mortification until I finally drifted off to sleep.

Sometime later, on the periphery of my dreams, I felt the bed dip beside me. "Cameron?" I mumbled barely awake.

"No, it's me."

"Flick?" My eyes searched the darkness, ignoring the giant pit in my stomach.

"Go back to sleep, Hails; it's late."

"Are you okay?" She sounded kind of funny.

"I'm fine," she sniffled, sliding underneath the covers. "Go to sleep."

"Night, Flick."

"Night, Hails."

But as the tug of sleep pulled me under, I was almost certain I heard my best friend crying.

20

Cameron

AFTER A RESTLESS NIGHT sleeping on Asher's couch, I finally dragged myself up and went into the kitchen, where I found him cleaning up the mess.

"Did something happen between you and Felicity?" I came right out with it.

"Happen?" He glanced over his shoulder at me. "Like what?"

"Did you sleep with her?"

"No, I didn't sleep with her. Why, did she say something?" He continued bagging up all the empty cups and bottles. Sometimes I wondered which he loved more; the party or the morning after, because I'd never seen a guy clean the way Ash did.

"No, but I saw her, and she looked upset." She hadn't wanted to talk about it, and I knew Asher had developed a weird interest in her. But from the deep frown etched across his face, maybe I'd jumped the gun.

"And you naturally think I had something to do with that?" His eyes widened with disbelief. "Cheers for the vote of confidence."

I helped myself to a glass of water and leaned back against the counter. "I just thought... forget it."

"Those girls have you all twisted up in knots. I saw you carrying Hailee up to your room, and I wasn't the only one." He gave me a pointed look. "I hope you know what you're doing?"

"She was drunk, and they had no way of getting home. What was I supposed to do? Leave her to sleep outside?"

"Before all this shit with Thatcher, that's exactly what you would have done. Hell, you probably would've have done a lot worse too." Rubbing a hand over my head and down the back of my neck, I released a heavy sigh. But Asher wasn't done. "You like her, don't you?"

"I—"

"Advil." Jase stalked into the room and I swallowed my words. "I need Advil."

"Yeah sure, man. You know where they are." Asher shot me a look that told me this conversation wasn't over.

"Who'd you end up with last night?" he asked Jase, who knocked back two pills and chugged a glass of water before sinking into one of the stools.

"Kayla, or Kylie, or fuck if I can remember."

"No way, I thought she had her eye on Cam?" Asher smirked at me and I flipped him off behind our friend's back.

Jase shrugged, none the wiser. "She wasn't complaining when I had my dick in her mouth."

"So, hmm," I cleared my throat. "You should probably know, Hailee and Felicity are asleep upstairs."

"What the fuck?" He stiffened, his mood turning blacker than a thundercloud. "I said invite them to the party, not invite them for a fucking sleepover."

"Hailee was drunk, right, Cam?"

"Yeah. I put her in my room."

Jase's eyes narrowed to deadly slits. "Your room?"

"Chill, it's not like that." I schooled my expression. "But I didn't know what else to do with her."

"And Felicity's up there too?"

I nodded, sure I'd caught a hitch in his voice when he said her name. "Did you say something to her?"

"Who?" He frowned.

"Felicity."

Jase reared back, his eyes wide. "What the fuck would I say to her?"

"I don't know, she seemed upset about something. I thought maybe Asher had—"

"Again, thanks for that," Asher added as he moved around the kitchen wiping the counters, whistling some tune far too upbeat for this time in the morning.

"No, I didn't say anything to her. I was too busy bending Kayla over your mom and dad's bed." He grinned at Asher, and the blood drained from his face.

"Tell me you didn't? Not again, man. You promised—"

"Relax." He chuckled darkly. "I used one of the guest rooms."

"She still up there?"

"What do you think?"

"Hit 'em and quit 'em, baby." Asher thrust his hips up slapping the air. When I rolled my eyes, he added, "You should try it sometime, Cam, or else Miley might get the wrong impression, thinking you're looking for something more than the little arrangement you've got going on. Speaking of the lovely Miley, I didn't see her last night?"

"Fuck off," I mouthed.

Just then, the sound of female voices floated into the room.

"Someone get rid of her, please," Jase grumbled but it was too late. Hailee and Felicity appeared in the doorway.

"Hmm, hey." She wouldn't meet my eyes and I knew she remembered. Fuck. I'd been hoping she was too drunk to remember.

"Ladies, come in, take a seat, breakfast will be served in..." Asher rubbed his jaw. "I don't suppose either of you want to make breakfast?"

Hailee climbed onto one of the stools, burying her face in her arm.

"Felicity?" Asher grinned at her.

"Ugh," she grumbled, her weary gaze flicking over to Jase. He sat rigid, doing nothing to hide his displeasure at the girls interrupting our morning routine.

"Fine." Felicity rubbed her hands together. "What have you got?"

"I think there are eggs, bacon, stuff to make pancakes." He beckoned her over to the refrigerator and the two of them set to work. It was weird. We'd never done this before. We always went out to eat, and I couldn't remember a time we'd ever included girls in our morning-after ritual.

"I'll be outside. I need some air," Jase disappeared out of the back door leaving the four of us. I reached over the counter, prodding Hailee's arm.

"Are you alive?" I whispered, and she peeked up at me. "Barely."

"Coffee?"

Giving a little shake of her head, she mouthed, "Water."

"Water it is." I grabbed her a bottle of water, careful not to get in the way of Felicity and Asher as they laid out all the ingredients; her barking orders at him, enjoying it far too much if the sparkle in her eye was anything to go by.

"Here." Sliding the bottle toward Hailee, I also threw her a box of Advil.

"Thanks." Hailee uncapped the bottle and popped two pills, washing them down in one. "I think I need to remember my limits."

"It's okay to let loose every now and again."

"If I recall, you were sober." Her eyes held an unspoken meaning and I felt sucker-punched.

Brushing her off, I said, "I had a couple of beers. Coach doesn't like us—"

"Stop, please stop." She held up her hand, burying her face again. "It hurts." Her words were mumbled.

"You sure you know what you're doing?" I asked Asher. He had a flour handprint on his face and another on his t-shirt.

"You're supposed to whisk the batter, not wear it," Felicity said looking over from the pan. The smoky scent of bacon wafted over to me and my stomach grumbled.

"I'll be back. Try not to kill each other." I shot Asher an amused grin and he flipped me off over Felicity's shoulder as she tried to show him how to whisk correctly.

Outside, Jase was sitting in one of the patio chairs. "She's annoying as fuck."

"Who, Hailee?"

"No, Felicity," he grunted.

"I don't know, she's not that bad."

Jase levelled me with a hard look. "Why are they even here?"

"Because you told Asher to invite them to the party..."

"Whatever. I just don't want her thinking this means something."

"Why would Felicity think—"

"Hailee, jackass. Keep up."

"You're in a delightful mood this morning."

"I'm just sick of this shit with Thatcher. Him finding out about Hailee was the worst thing that could have happened. Now I have to pretend to actually give a shit about her."

"If it makes you feel any better, I don't think she's going to get the wrong idea any time soon."

Hailee wasn't like most girls. She didn't see signs that weren't there. If anything, the years of back and forth with Jason had hardened her. Now she was wary of others; always questioning people's motives. In fact, they were far more alike than either of them realized. Except where Jason's cool exterior had rubbed off on her, she'd failed to make so much as a dent in his tough shell.

"Rivals Week." His voice was flat. "I usually live for this shit, but something's different this year."

He didn't need to tell me. I'd felt it ever since we walked into school on the first day of the semester. Maybe it was our impending final season as Raiders, the expectation of bringing home State. Or maybe it was the distance growing between us as our lives started to take different paths. I wanted college. I wanted a college career playing football. But I didn't want it the way Jase did. And over the summer, as the days until senior year had crept closer, the pit in my stomach had grown and grown until I felt pulled in two.

Part of me was still Cameron Chase, number fourteen, star wide receiver for the Rixon Raiders, waiting for the nod from a Division One team. But the other part didn't know who he was anymore. He was scared of the unknown; of what his family's future looked like if he left. And the two parts of me no longer married up.

"At least they're coming to our backyard. We don't have to worry about them pulling any stunts at their place on game night."

A couple of years back, in our sophomore year and Jason's first year as first string QB, we'd drawn the Eagles at their place. It was a dog fight; both teams battling it out for the win. Tensions were high and tempers frayed. Jase had got into it with two of their defensive ends after they kept playing dirty—repeatedly holding him and trying to grab his face mask—and an all-out brawl had happened on the field.

Jase clenched his fist against his thigh, his leg tapping against the patio. "I want to destroy him. I want to—"

"Breakfast is served." Asher's voice pierced the air and Jase shoved out of his chair, stalking inside.

He was losing it. But Rivals Week was always a big week on our calendar. Coach Hasson had already warned us to stay out of East this coming week, a warning we all knew had filtered down from Principal Finnigan. That didn't mean Thatcher and his guys wouldn't come at us though, and now he knew about Hailee, there was every likelihood she would be at the top of his shit list.

I went back inside, the scene of Asher and Jase eating breakfast with Hailee and Felicity, without trying to kill each other, was one of the weirdest things I'd ever witnessed.

"Dude, you need to try the bacon. The girl knows how to cook." Asher grabbed another piece off the plate and shoved it into his mouth, grinning over at Felicity.

"Must you be such a pig?" She scolded him and he actually blushed. Asher Bennet's cheeks turned beet red.

What the fuck was happening right now?

"This looks great, Felicity, thanks," I said, dropping onto the stool beside Hailee. She tensed, not looking at me as she pushed scrambled egg around her plate.

"Not hungry?" I asked, fighting a smirk.

"Piss off," she grumbled, resuming her plate art.

"So," Felicity piped up, completely oblivious to the various degrees of tensions lingering over us. "Rivals Week? How're you feeling about the big game Friday?"

Jase stared at her like she'd grown a second head while Asher chuckled. "You're becoming quite the fan, aren't you, Fee?"

"Fee?" She almost choked over the word.

"What?" He shrugged. "I figured you need a nickname now we're all friends."

Fee didn't look convinced. "Why is it," she said, her eyes sliding to Jase again. What was it with her and my best friend? "I never know whether to believe a thing that comes out of your mouth?"

"Because you shouldn't trust a Raider," Hailee spoke up.

"Now, now, Hails," Asher said smugly. "I didn't lie about the party, did I?"

"This has been fun and all," Sarcasm dripped from Jase's voice. "But are the two of you planning to get the fuck out of here anytime soon?"

Silence fell over the Bennet's breakfast counter. Felicity lowered her eyes, chewing her lip anxiously. But Hailee didn't look surprised. In fact, she looked oddly relieved as she met his icy stare with her own. "It would be my pleasure." She rose from her stool quickly, the metal legs scraping across the tiles, and snapped at Felicity. "Coming?"

"I... uh, yeah. Bye." Hailee's friend gave us a small wave and they both fled from the kitchen.

"You're a dick," Asher ground out, shoving his plate away from him.

"And you only just realized this?" Jase shot back, continuing to eat his breakfast like he hadn't just dismissed his step-sister and her friend away from the table like naughty children.

21

Hailee

I MARCHED out of Asher's house with Flick trailing after me. God, my step-brother was an asshole. He couldn't just be civil for ten fucking minutes while we ate breakfast. The breakfast my best friend had made for him no less.

Bastard.

"Hails, will you just slow down a second?"

"I need to get away from here, Flick." Anger propelled me forward until I was stomping down the Bennet's driveway, arms swinging by my sides, breaths coming in sharp bursts. "This, coming here, it was a bad idea."

"He's a jerk, you're right. But Asher is—"

I whirled around, glaring at her. "Please don't tell me you're developing a crush on *Asher Bennet*, the same Asher I know for a fact has slept with the entire girls track team." Probably all at once knowing him.

"No, I don't like him. Jeez, can you just breathe for a second?" She smoothed her hair back, composing herself. "I just think he's funny and he likes us."

"He likes us now, Flick. *Now*. After Thatcher discovered who I am. Don't you get how messed up that is? If we'd have never gone to that party with Toby and Jude do you really think we'd be here now?"

"Well... no." Her shoulders sank in defeat, hurt glittering in her eyes as they darted to the ground.

I felt like a mean bitch, but she was too quick to see the good in Asher. Too blinded by the promise of parties at his house and being sweet-talked by him in the cafeteria. Flick hadn't been the brunt of their jokes and mean pranks for the last five and a half years, but she had been right there beside me to witness it. So the fact she was ready to overlook that, made it all seem trivial somehow. As if none of it really mattered because they were Raiders. And if they extended you an invitation into their inner circle, you took it, regardless of whatever bullshit had come before.

"Look, I'm sorry, okay." I tried to school my irritation. "I know you want to fit in. I know you have your list and you want to make senior year one to remember. But it can still be fun without them." My eyes flitted over her shoulder and back to the house.

"What about Cameron?"

"What about him?" My chest ached remembering how he'd rejected me last night and then acted as if nothing had happened this morning.

"You like him," she added. "I know you do."

"It doesn't matter," I said quietly, feeling my chest constrict. "He's Jason's best friend, Flick, a Raider. Our worlds aren't supposed to co-exist." The quicker I got that through my stupid head, the better. Cameron was loyal to Jason, which made him my enemy. So despite any attraction between us he was a bad idea. *Really* bad. Because Cameron Chase wouldn't only hurt me. Given half a chance he would completely ruin me.

And I couldn't let that happen.

I wouldn't.

"But—"

"Come on." I cut her off, done talking about him. "We can walk back to your house."

She nodded, following me down the long winding driveway. "Hey, were you crying last night?" I asked, the vague memory suddenly flooding my mind.

"What? When?"

"When you came to bed? I thought I heard you crying."

"No." It rolled off her lips a little too quickly, and I glanced at her out of the corner of my eye. "If Asher hurt you Flick—"

"Hails, I don't know what you think you heard, but you're wrong. I'm fine. Everything's fine. As for Asher, like I said, I don't like him like that." I'd known Flick since we were twelve. I knew her tells. The little things she did when she wasn't being completely honest.

And right now, I knew she was lying.

But if Asher wasn't the one who had upset her… who was?

THURSDAY MORNING, things finally felt like they were returning to normal. I'd almost survived Rivals Week. There had been no more social media posts about me from Thatcher—he'd been too busy posting smack talk for tomorrow's big game—and Jason, Asher, and Cameron left us alone for the most part. I knew Flick was feeling dejected by Asher's recent change of heart where their blossoming friendship was concerned. But refusing to be thrown off course, she was focused on two things: her list and what to wear to Homecoming next weekend. The same Homecoming that despite recent events, she still insisted we attend.

"Looking forward to the game Friday?" Kent asked me as I entered the kitchen. Barely awake, I grabbed a mug of coffee and then slouched down on one of the stools.

"Game, what game?"

"I know you don't live under a rock, Hailee. It's Rivals Week. Not even you can ignore that."

"Oh, I'm not going."

"Of course you are. It's a big deal for Jason and the team, and we have tickets for the family section."

"Who'd you have to bribe to get extra?" Players were given two tickets each for their families and spares were like gold dust.

"Coach Hasson," he confessed, yanking on his tie as if the thing was too damn tight.

"Is Mom going?"

"She is. She wouldn't miss it for the world."

Of course not. I swallowed the words.

"I know things haven't always been easy between you and Jason, but I'm really hoping that now we're married, things will—"

"Good morning." Mom breezed into the kitchen looking far too bright and alert for seven thirty in the morning.

"Good morning, wife." Kent grabbed her as she passed him and kissed her with more gusto than I needed to witness. Ever.

"Do you mind?" I snorted.

Mom's dreamy gaze slid to mine. "Morning, baby." Her cheeks were flushed, and she sounded a little breathless. *Gross.* "How are you?"

"I was okay until you came in and started sucking face with Kent."

"Did he tell you the good news?" She beamed, untangling herself from his arms and making a beeline for the coffee maker.

"You're going to let me go to New York for my eighteenth birthday?"

"Nice try, but no, sweetheart. We have tickets for tomorrow's game."

"Oh, that." I gritted my teeth.

"Hailee, this is important to—"

"Jason. Yeah, yeah, I already heard a very compelling argument from Kent. If I agree to go, will you at least think about letting me go to New York?" One of my favorite artists had an exhibition coming up at The Met that I really wanted to see.

My mom and Kent shared a glance and he gave her a little nod. "Fine," she said. "If you come to the game Friday *and* the dinner Coach Hasson is throwing afterward, then yes, we'll think about it."

Dinner at Coach Hasson's? With the whole team and their families. I'd need reinforcements. "Is there a spare ticket for Flick?"

"I'm perfectly aware the two of you come as a package deal, Hailee." Kent gave me a warm smile. "Tell her we'll pick her up before the game."

"Fine, then you have yourself a deal."

A football game, and dinner at Coach Hasson's house, in exchange for a trip to New York for my birthday.

It was a small price to pay.

Later that day, I had a free period, so I headed to the studio. I'd only been there all of fifteen minutes when Mr. Jalin's voice echoed through the room. "Ah, Hailee."

Dropping the brush onto the easel, I spun my chair to face him, pushing my glasses up onto my head. "Hi, Sir."

"Nice." His thick-browed gaze swept over my canvas. "That's looking really nice, Hailee. I particularly like what you've done with the broad strokes." He moved closer, tracing the thick brush marks with his fingers, careful not to get too close. "You'll be using this for your final submission piece?"

"I think so."

"Good choice." He offered me a reassuring smile. "I think you'll do just fine."

"Thank you, Sir."

"Now for the real reason I'm here." Clasping his hands behind his back, Mr. Jalin regarded me with a reserved expression. "You're a very talented artist, Hailee. One of the best I've ever seen come through the doors of Rixon High. Coach Hasson and I were talking, and he wondered if this year, for the Seniors Night presentation, we tried something a little different."

"I- I'm sorry, I don't understand?" The mention of the football team had me a little tongue-tied.

"Every year, Coach Hasson likes to present his seniors with a memento. Usually it's a photograph to mark their time with the Raiders. But this year, we thought it might be nice to include a painting."

"You want me to... *paint* the team." I swallowed, my mouth suddenly dry.

"Well, yes, unless there's a problem?"

"No, no, Sir, I just..." I wiped my clammy hands down my apron, a hundred reasons why this was a bad idea flooding my mind. But despite my inner voice screaming at me not to do it, all I could think was Mr. Jalin, Rixon's Director of Arts; *and* Coach Hasson had asked me to do this.

Me.

"Seniors Night is a little over two months away," he went on while I was still trying to process what this meant should I agree. "It'll mean a lot of hours and you'll need to spend some time with the senior players, get out and watch them practice, but I think you can pull it off."

"Is there a particular style Coach Hasson has in mind?" My thoughts began shooting over in a million directions. Would he want something more traditional like a realism portrait or maybe something more fluid like an impressionist portrait? "Or do I have free rein?"

"It's all down to you, within reason of course." His expression turned serious. "This is not something to take lightly, Hailee. This project could really help you make a name for yourself locally."

He didn't need to tell me. For a small-town girl living in Rixon, it was the equivalent of being asked to do an exhibition at the Penn Museum or the Philly Museum of Art.

"I'll do it," I said with conviction. I'd just have to worry about the finer details later when I figured out the direction, I wanted to take it. "Thank you, Sir, for thinking of me."

"Just remember, we need this to be a success, Hailee. I've been battling the school board for years to funnel more money into our Arts Department. This could be the start of a mutually beneficial relationship between us and the Athletics Department."

"I understand." *No pressure then.*

"Coach Hasson would like to brief you further, so if you could arrange to meet with him as soon as possible." Mr. Jalin gave me a small nod before leaving me alone. It was almost as if the stars were aligning. Mom and Kent were insisting I attend the dinner at Coach Hasson's house tomorrow night and now I had a valid reason to be there.

But as I stared at my painting, getting lost in the swirls of blue and gray, nervous energy vibrated through me. Being around Coach Hasson meant being around the team. And being around the team meant being around Cameron; something I wanted to avoid at all costs. But this was too good an opportunity to refuse, and it would look great on my resume if I got accepted into Stamps. I'd entered the odd local show, and had some pieces displayed around the school before, but this could be a huge break for me.

There was just one fatal flaw with the plan—getting Jason to play nice long enough for me to complete the project.

22

Cameron

THE ROAR of the crowd was deafening. It had been for the entire game, which turned out to be brutal, just as everyone expected. The Eagles scored a touchdown, we scored one back; they sacked our QB, we took Thatcher down twice as hard. We were exhausted; mentally and physically broken, and despite outplaying them, the Eagles were leading by five. But we were fourth and goal, with eleven seconds left on the clock, which meant we had time for one final play.

And we needed it to count.

"Time," Coach yelled across the field and we moved in for his instructions. "Okay," he said. "They've got us pinned down, I know that. You know that. But this game should have been ours coming into the second half. Jase, what are you thinking, Son?"

We all looked to our QB and captain, hardly surprised Coach was letting him take control. He trusted Jase explicitly. We all did.

"We should run the Red 59 Counter Arrow," he said calmly, despite the fire in his eyes. He didn't just want this win, he needed it.

"Fourteen?" Coach locked eyes with me. "You ready for this?"

"I've got it." I nodded.

"That's what I wanted to hear. Now get out there and take care of business. Raiders on one."

Our battle cry rippled across the field, fueling us. Giving us the strength we needed for one final play.

"You ready?" Jase jogged over to me.

"Let's end them." Understanding passed between us as he offered me a rare smile.

"Go get 'em, bro."

We all moved into position behind the line of scrimmage, waiting for Jase's call. He reeled off the play before signaling, "Hut." Grady, our center, snapped the ball to him and he faked left. I took off, pushing past the safety. My best friend dropped back, hiked up his arm and let the ball fly, straight toward the end zone and my destination. I pumped my legs hard, running faster than I'd ever run in my life. We had to win, I had to get my hands on that ball.

It wasn't just about football, it was about Hailee. About wiping the smug grin off Thatcher's face when we beat them. But it was moving fast, too fast. Shit. In a risky move, I pushed off the ground and lunged forward, stretching my fingers until I felt my muscles rip, pain pinging through my shoulder. But it paid off as I felt the familiar smooth leather graze my fingers.

"Touchdown," the announcer yelled as my body collided with the hard ground. The crowd went wild as I lay there, staring up at the lights. My muscles hurt and my lungs burned, and I was pretty sure I'd pulled something, but it didn't matter. We'd done it.

I'd done it.

Jase and Ash were first to reach me, pulling me to my feet and then the rest of the guys were on us, jostling us around like we'd won the Championship game. But Jase wasn't celebrating with us, he was staring across the field, his eyes set right on Thatcher.

"Come on, man." I pushed through the crowd and slung my arm around his shoulder. "Not here, not now." I kept my voice low.

"One day," he ground out, his voice eerily calm. "One day."

Two hours later, still riding the high of our win against Rixon East, we were crammed into Coach Hasson's place for the annual Rivals Week dinner. It was a ranch style house overlooking the river with enough space to host the team and their families.

"Hmm, bro, why are Hailee and Fee here?" Asher nudged my arm and tipped his head to where the girls had just walked in, both looking like deer caught in headlights.

"Beats me." I took a long pull on my soda, feeling the deep ache in my shoulder.

Later, after dinner, Coach would turn a blind eye when we all raided his cooler for beers. But for now, while the team's families were present and sober, he expected decorum.

"They came with my dad and Denise," Jase grunted, joining us. My eyes went to the beer in his hand.

"Really?" I asked, my brow quirked up.

"What?" He shrugged. "I needed one."

Rolling my eyes, I fought a smirk. Jason didn't follow the rules, he made them. And I knew no one would give him shit about it.

"I knew they were at the game," Asher added still staring over at them. "But I had no idea they were coming here. I think she's stalking me."

I sprayed soda into the air, chuckling at the ridiculous statement. "You're not serious?"

"As a heart attack," he deadpanned, folding his arms across his chest as his eyes narrowed on Hailee and her friend. But they never so much as glanced in our direction.

It had been the same all week. After the disastrous morning at Asher's house, after the party, Hailee had avoided me like the plague. And I gave her space, because what else could I do? She'd kissed me... tried to do a whole lot more than that, and I'd rejected her. I didn't regret stopping play that night; she was drunk, and Jase was right along the hall buried balls deep inside one of the gymnasts. But I regretted how things went down between us.

I just didn't know how to fix things—or whether I should even try.

"Here he is," Mr. Ford's voice rang out above the noise. "The man of the moment. Congratulations, Son." He made a beeline for me, clapping me on the back. "That was a hall of fame moment right there."

"Thank you, Sir," I said, my eyes flicking to Jase. "Couldn't have done it without my QB."

"Right, of course. Good game, Son." Mr. Ford held out his hand to Jase who shook it with mild hesitation.

"Thanks, Dad." His words were clipped, and we all felt the tension between father and son.

"Jason," Hailee's mom burst through our small huddle. "That was... I'm so proud of you, sweetheart." She tried to pull him in for a hug, but he inched back. Denise faltered, covering his brush off with a wide smile. "We're all real proud of you, all of you. And to think you could bring home the big one this year."

We all smothered our laughter at her false enthusiasm, even Jase fought a bemused smirk.

"Okay, darling." Mr. Ford wrapped his wife into a side hug. "Let's leave the guys to have their fun. I want to talk to Henry."

Henry, or Coach Hasson as we knew him, was outside at his huge grill, a cloud of smoke billowing into the air.

"This is your year, Son, we're all counting on you," were Mr. Ford's parting words as they left us to *our fun*.

Thirty minutes later, we had all gathered outside on Coach's orders. He and his wife served us burgers and hot dogs, steak and ribs. It was good, but I missed my parents. They hadn't been at the game to see us beat the Eagles and they weren't here now to celebrate with us.

And I hated it.

This was the biggest season of my life, and they weren't here to see it, to share it with me. It fucking sucked but I had no choice but to plaster on a smile and celebrate with my teammates.

After everyone had eaten, Coach Hasson stood up, demanding silence.

"Speech," one of the guy's yelled and a ripple of laughter filled the air.

"Calm down, calm down," Coach said. "There are a couple of things I want to say, so bear with me. First off, I want to thank my wife, Sandra." He gazed warmly at the woman beside him. "Without her, I wouldn't be half the man I am. And I'm grateful she lets me welcome you all into my home year after year."

Everyone cheered at that, raising their glasses and bottles in the air to toast Mrs. Hasson. "Now to my boys." His eyes roved over every one of us. "You fought hard tonight. You didn't lie down when things got tough, you dug in your heels and kept on pushing. I'm real damn proud of you. Not only for showing those fellas across the river how we play ball, but for keeping your heads and not letting them provoke you into lowering yourself to their standards." His gaze landed on me, Asher, and Jason, conveying some unspoken message. "Rivals Week is done. We won. We draw the line here, you hear me?"

We each gave him an imperceptible nod, irritation rolling off Jase in waves. He respected Coach, listened to his orders on and off the field, but we all knew this thing between him and Thatcher was personal. So even though we'd won tonight, had handed Thatcher his ass on the field, we knew it wasn't over.

Not by a long shot.

Coach ran a hand down his face, swallowing hard. "I'll be doing all this again in a few weeks at Seniors Night, so I won't harp on too much longer. But know this, coaching the Raiders is a privilege, one I don't take lightly. And this year, is our year. I feel it in my bones, this year we're bringing it home."

The Hasson's yard erupted, my teammates making most of the noise as we whooped and cheered. He waited for everyone to hush before continuing, "And finally, I have an announcement to make. Where is Miss Raine?" He searched the crowd and my eyes spotted Hailee, her cheeks flaming with embarrassment as she held up a hand. "Miss Raine has kindly agreed to work with the team on an exciting art project this season. I'd like you all to show her the respect I know you're capable of."

A murmur of grumbles answered him, as Asher and I shared a confused look. "What the fuck?" he mouthed as I tried to process what Coach was saying.

Hailee was going to be working with the team? On an art project?

What the hell did that mean?

But more concerningly, why the fuck had she agreed to it in the first place?

I DIDN'T SEE Hailee for the rest of the night. That was until I went inside to get another drink and almost walked straight into her. "Shit." My hands flew out, steadying her. "I'm sorry."

"It's fine." She shrugged me off, smoothing her hair out of her face and tucking it behind an ear. "I was just..." Hailee pointed over my shoulder to the back door and started to move around me.

"Wait," I rushed out, grabbing her arm. Her eyes dropped to where my fingers curled around her wrist, and then slowly lifted to mine, her brow arched in annoyance.

"Sorry, I just... can we talk?"

"You want to talk, *here*?" She sounded incredulous and I couldn't blame her. Not after last weekend. But I needed to clear the air between us because all week it had felt like a heavy weight was pressing on my chest.

An idea sparked in my mind and my lip curved up. "Have you ever seen Coach's trophy room?"

"You know I haven't." Her mouth mirrored mine.

"Well, then, you're in for a treat." I waited, letting her make the decision. It was a risk given her family was here, but everyone was outside, enjoying the warm evening and good company.

"It's for research purposes only," Hailee said quietly, dropping her gaze.

"Research?"

"For the Seniors Night thing."

"Oh, yeah, that." I ran a hand down my face. I'd almost forgotten Coach's announcement that Hailee would be painting the seniors, but only because once I'd realized it might mean spending some one-on-one time with her, I couldn't think about anything other than me and her. Alone. Together.

"Cameron?"

I blinked down at her, shaking the thoughts from my mind. "Hmm, yeah, come on," I said before I did the sensible thing and walked away. "It's just down here."

23

Hailee

I FOLLOWED Cameron down the hall and into a big room, my eyes widening at the rows and rows of trophy cabinets and shelves. "Wow." I didn't know where to look first. "I had no idea."

"Yeah." He walked up to one of the glass cabinets. "Coach was a big deal back in his day."

"You don't say." I ran my eyes over the collection of silverware. "What's that one?" I asked pointing to a small bronze figurine.

Cameron gave a smooth chuckle. "That is the Heisman."

"Oh, I think I've heard of it."

His eyes widened with amusement. "It's kind of a big deal."

"Something to do with college football, right?"

He repeated my words, mumbling them under his breath. "How is it you've lived with Jason and his dad for six years and still don't know any of this stuff?"

"I have excellent avoidance skills." He gave me a pointed look and I felt myself blush. "I didn't mean..."

"So, you *haven't* been avoiding me all week?"

The air in the room turned dense as Cameron's gray-blue eyes stared at me intently.

Clearing my throat, I managed to choke out, "I think it was pretty clear after last Saturday—" He took a step forward and I swallowed, backing up, careful not to touch the trophy cabinets. "Cameron," I sighed.

"Yes, Sunshine?" The corner of his mouth tipped.

"You promised this was just for research purposes."

"Is that what we're calling it?" Humor danced in his eyes as he kept advancing on me, and despite knowing I needed to escape, I found myself lost in his stormy gaze.

My back finally hit the wall, the reverberation rattling my bones. I pressed my palms against it to stop myself from reaching out for him. But Cameron leaned in, touching his head to mine, completely overwhelming me. "I can't stop thinking about you," he admitted, so quietly it was more like a rush of warm air than actual words. "Last Saturday was me doing the right thing, Hailee. You were drunk and I—"

"You just want what you can't have." My eyes burned with defiance, willing myself to stay strong.

"I wish it was that simple." He let out a deep breath.

"What are we doing, Cameron?" *What are* you *doing Hailee?* I silently added as I breathed him in.

All week, I'd told myself avoiding him was for the best, that I needed to stay away from Cameron and his mind games. It was easy when I saw him with the team, the constant rotation of girls vying for his attention. Cameron Chase, wide receiver, number fourteen, belonged to Rixon. He was theirs to have, theirs to worship, theirs to love. But there were moments with him, when it was just the two of us, when it felt like he was mine. Like he was offering me a piece of himself.

And all I had to do was reach out and take it.

But I didn't want the scraps. I wasn't just another jersey chaser looking for whatever she could get. I wanted all of him or nothing. Something, I knew, he would never be able to give me.

"Tell me what you're thinking," he said, pulling me further under his spell.

It was just that though. A spell. And when it was broken, I'd be Hailee Raine, Jason's step-sister again and he'd be Cameron Chase, my brother's best friend.

Which is why, no matter how much I wanted him—and I did, I could finally admit it—I forced out the words, "I'm thinking this, us, it can never work."

Defiance glittered in his eyes as he lowered his mouth to mine. "Don't you know by now, Sunshine? I'm a Raider and Raiders never quit."

My stomach sank as Cameron kissed me. Not because the feel of his lips moving against mine didn't feel good, it did. It felt like my entire body was on fire, every stroke of his tongue making the flames lick higher and higher until I was burning with need. But because he'd proved me right. He was a Raider, he would always *be* a Raider. And one day, he and my step-brother would ride off into the sunset together, leaving me and the rest of Rixon with no choice but to stand by and watch.

And then where would that leave me?

"Cameron—" I breathed against his lips as they devoured me. Fixed over mine again and again, stealing the air from my lungs, and all rational thought from my mind.

"Just give me this, Hailee." He paused, his mouth hovering over mine, his eyes pinning me to the spot. "I need this, *please*." There was something so vulnerable about the way he said the words it made my heart ache. I leaned back, finally bringing my hands to his face, allowing myself to touch him.

Giving myself—him—this moment.

My fingers slid against his stubbled jaw, tracing the sharp angles of his face. I dropped my other hand to his bicep, painting the tattoo peeking out beneath his sleeve. "You like that, don't you?" he asked, and I nodded.

"It's beautiful." I'd never really found tattoos appealing before but staring at the cherry blossom and hummingbird inked on Cameron's arm, it made me want to draw on his skin. To brand him with my own mark.

"*You're* beautiful." His fingers gently gripped my chin, forcing my face back to his. Cameron didn't hesitate this time, tracing the seam of my lips with his tongue. His hands glided down my body, anchoring at my waist and pulling me flush against him. A small gasp spilled out of me when I felt the outline of his hardness against my stomach. I don't think I'd ever get used to the fact that Cameron wanted me. It made me drunk with desire. Turned me on in a way I'd never experienced before.

But most of all, it made all the memories of his complicities in Jason's games fade into nothing.

"I want to feel you," he murmured between kisses. "Let me touch you, Hailee." The raw desperation in his voice made my heart flutter wildly in my chest. And when one of his hands found the sliver of skin between my sweater and waistband of my jeans, I almost died, right there in front of his eyes.

"Cam—" My voice was shaky, my breaths coming in short sharp bursts.

"Tell me what you need, Hailee..."

My fingers twisted into his jersey as I yanked him closer, kissing him harder. Cameron's hand worked lower, expertly unbuttoning my jeans. He dipped his hand inside, grazing my damp panties.

"Jesus," he groaned, easing away from the kiss to look at me. He didn't say anything, just watched me, as he rubbed my clit over the thin material. My knees buckled, my stomach clenching with need, as I swallowed a moan. "I need to feel you, Hailee..."

I nodded, letting my head drop back against the wall. Cameron hooked my panties to the side and slid his fingers through my wetness, eliciting a string of tiny gasps from my lips. His eyes were wild, as they watched me. Dark and hooded, simmering with pure lust.

"Hailee," He swallowed hard. "I—"

"Yo, Chase, are you—" Asher burst into the room, his eyes going wide when they landed on me and Cameron tangled together like lovers in the dark. I panicked trying to push Cameron away, but he pressed me further against the wall, shielding me, his fingers still inside me.

"Hmm, Coach is looking for you, but I can see you're busy."

"Ash," Cameron growled.

He threw up his hands. "I didn't see a thing." There was a lilt in his voice. Humor. And I wanted the ground to open up and swallow me whole. "But you might want to... hurry." Asher tipped his head to the hall.

"Yeah, give me a minute." Cameron sounded cold now, and the fire died inside me. I tried to wriggle free again, but he was too strong, refusing to let me up.

"Hails," Asher smirked. "Looking good." He turned and left, pulling the door closed behind him.

"Oh my god," I cried squeezing my eyes shut.

"Asher won't say anything." Cameron finally withdrew his fingers and backed away. My eyes fluttered open and settled on him, but he looked right through me.

My stomach sank as I fumbled with my jean button. "I should go," I choked out, willing him to say something.

"Hailee, I'm sorry. It's just—"

It wasn't the words I wanted to hear, so I cut him off. "Yeah, me too," I whispered.

And then without looking back, I ran out of there.

"Where the hell have you been?" Flick hurried over to me, sliding her arm through mine. "You've been gone like thirty minutes."

Is that all it was? It felt like I'd been with Cameron for longer. Time had ceased to exist in Coach Hasson's trophy room. But I'd come crashing back down to Earth with a resounding thud when Asher stumbled in on us.

He'd seen us.

God, what a mess.

I believed Cameron when he said Asher wouldn't say anything, but it didn't make the fact he knew any easier.

"Are you okay? You look... I don't know, flushed."

Which, of course, only made me flush harder.

"I'm fine, I just ran into Cameron."

"Oooh." Her eyes danced with excitement. "And..."

"And what?" I frowned.

"And what did the two of you talk about?"

"Nothing important." I shrugged, guilt washing over me.

She gave me a strange look. "You're hiding something, Hailee Raine." Flick leaned in closer, lowering her voice. "Did you drag him off to the bathroom and kiss him again?"

Something like that. "Seriously?" I schooled my expression. "We're at Coach Hasson's home surrounded by the whole team, not to mention their families." Although now I came to think about it, I hadn't seen Cameron with his parents. I'd heard Jason say they never came around to his games anymore, since his mom had his little brother a few years ago.

"Yeah, I guess that could be awkward if Jason or your mom walked in." She smothered a snicker. "But you're going to have to get used to being around each other if you're doing the Seniors Night project, right?"

Right.

I silently groaned, wondering if I'd made a terrible mistake agreeing to this project.

"I know that look." Flick guided us back outside to the huge yard.

"What look?" I humored her.

"You're falling for him."

"Don't be ridiculous." A strangled laugh escaped my lips, but I wasn't laughing on the inside. Because she couldn't be right.

I couldn't actually be falling for Cameron Chase.

Could I?

24

Cameron

"YOU HAVE A VISITOR," Asher whispered as we jogged onto the field. My eyes followed his finger only to find Hailee sitting alone in the bleachers.

"She must be making a start on her art project."

"Art project, right," he drawled. "Is that what we're calling it? Because if the project includes getting up close and personal with her like I saw the two of you in Coach's trophy room on Friday night, then sign me—"

"Seriously, you need to stop talking," I ground out, searching the field for Jase. Asher noticed and smothered a laugh.

"Don't sweat it, he's working with Coach on some new plays."

I levelled him with a hard look, but it only fueled his curiosity. "So, what's the deal? Since when does looking out for her involve having your fingers buried deep in—"

"Ash, I swear to God if you—"

"Jeez." His hands flew up. "Joke, I'm joking. But I'm starting to think this thing with her isn't a game. You like her."

"I don't..."

He gave me a pointed look. "Oh fuck, you do, you totally like her. Jase is going to—"

"Never find out about this, you hear me? It was a mistake."

"Yeah, yeah, whatever you say, man." Asher clapped me on the back. "Just be careful. That chick is crazy. And this thing with her, Jase, and Thatcher is only going to get worse before it gets better."

Which is exactly what I was worried about.

We'd all expected Thatcher to make a move during Rivals Week but there had been nothing but crickets. It didn't mean he wouldn't hit back though, it just meant he was biding his time. Waiting to strike.

"Chase, Bennet, get your asses over here, ladies, we've got drills to run," one of the assistant coaches yelled. With a final glance at the bleachers and Hailee, I stuffed down all the thoughts running through my head and focused on the task at hand. Kicking some defense ass.

After a grueling practice, I hung back while the rest of the guys stalked into the locker room. Coach was busy talking to Hailee. She had a sketch pad in her hands and a smile plastered on her face as she showed him whatever it was she'd been working on.

"Chase, come over here, Son," his voice boomed across the field and I tore my helmet off and jogged over to them. "What's up, Coach?" My eyes grazed Hailee's face as I swept a hand through my damp hair, but she kept her gaze firmly on the pad in her hand.

"Can you show Miss Raine to the storage room? She wants to dig through some of the old picture albums for..." He glanced at her and she smiled.

"Inspiration."

"Inspiration, right." Coach pressed his lips together. "Can I trust you to show her?"

"Of course, Sir."

"And if you need anything else, just ask." He gave her a stern nod and left us alone.

"Hey." I gave her a smile. "How are you?"

"I'm okay, thanks." Her eyes darted around mine.

"Listen, I wanted to talk to you, after the other n—"

"Let's *not* do this," Hailee said, clutching the sketch pad to her chest like a shield. As if she needed armor against me. The thought punched me square in the chest. "I need to concentrate on this project if I want to get it done in time and I can't afford any... distractions."

"Is that what I am?" The corner of my mouth tipped. Being a distraction to her sounded like something I could get on board with.

"Cameron, I'm serious." She gave me a narrowed look, but I was sure I caught a sparkle in her eyes.

"No distractions." I held up my hands. "I promise. Come on, I'll show you where the storage room is, but I should probably warn you, it smells like years old cleats in there." Her nose wrinkled, and I chuckled. "Did you think painting the team would be all glamorous and shit?"

"I don't know what I thought." She was still clutching that shield of hers. "To be honest, I'm feeling a little out of my league here."

"Let me see what you have."

"Hmm, I don't know." Her fingers gripped the pad tighter. "It's only a rough sketch at the moment. I wanted to catch you in action." A sexy blush spread up her neck and into her cheeks and I didn't miss the way she almost choked over the word 'action'. "I'm thinking of doing a less traditional composition, something that captures the essence of the sport rather than just the player."

"Sounds... complicated." I had no fucking clue about art and compositions or any of that stuff.

"It isn't, not really. But I need enough raw material to work with."

"So, can I..." I held out my hand, hoping she would indulge me. Hailee peeked up at me with wary eyes, her fingers gently tapping the sketch pad. Awkward silence stretched out before us.

"It's okay," I started after what felt like an eternity. "You don't have to—" With a soft sigh, Hailee finally handed the pad over to me and I flipped it open.

"Holy shit, Hailee, this is amazing." She'd captured Grady, one of the other senior players, mid-drill, throwing his body against the blocking sled. It was only rough, but the lines and shadowing caught the impact in a way I would never have thought possible. "You're really talented." I started to flip to another page, but she grabbed the pad.

"Okay, that's enough."

"Hang on, I want to see more." I wrestled it off her, holding it just out of reach, and turned another page. My mouth fell open, the air sucked clean from my lungs.

"Like I said," her voice was small, uncertain, "It's just a rough sketch at the moment. Something to work with once I'm in the studio."

My eyes drank in every detail. The curve of my arm as I prepared to throw the ball, my wide stance and narrowed gaze as I sought out my teammate across the field. The intricate shading around the fourteen on my jersey, giving the illusion of the material moving with the air.

"Cameron?" Her voice was quiet, but it reverberated all the way down to my soul.

"Y- yeah, sorry." I closed the sketch pad and handed back to her.

"The final thing will be much better." Hailee tucked her hair behind her ear.

I knew I should probably say something, but I was speechless. "Come on," I managed to choke out, and we walked the rest of the way in thick silence.

It wasn't that I wanted her to think I didn't like the sketch, I did. I liked it a whole lot, but it had done something to me. *She* had done something to me.

And I didn't know how to undo it—if I even wanted to.

"Okay, this is it," I said, shouldering the door to the storage room. Hailee's eyes fell on the dusty boxes.

"There's a lot of stuff here."

"Yup. Coach is kind of a hoarder. Good luck with that." I offered her a smile, but she didn't return it.

Shit, I was being a dick. "So, Homecoming is this week." I tried to change tack. "Do you have a date?"

"A date?" The words got stuck in her throat.

"Yeah, you know, a guy asks you out, you dress up all pretty and he brings you flowers, and you pose for awkward photos." *Stop. Talking. Asshole.*

"Isn't that Prom?"

"Same thing." I shrugged suddenly feeling like a complete idiot. "So do you? Have one, I mean?" Why was I pushing this? I didn't want to hear about Hailee and her date.

"I do actually."

She did?

Fuck.

"Flick." Hailee frowned, watching me with a strange expression. "I'm going with Flick."

"Oh right." Relief flooded me, easing the tightness in my chest. "That's... nice." *Nice?*

"Are you okay, you're acting a little strange?"

"Me? I'm fine." I shrugged, backing up, but I hit the corner of a stack of boxes. "Shit." My hands shot out and I managed to steady them. When I looked back at Hailee, she was fighting a smile.

"So, I should, uh, go. I should go." What the fuck was wrong with me?

It was the damn sketch. It had voodoo powers or something because I felt all off-balance.

"Okay." She watched, her expression a lot more playful than it was five minutes ago.

"See you around?" My voice went up at the end making it sound like a question and I wanted nothing more than to bang my head against the wall. But before Hailee concluded I was completely certifiable, I gave her a little salute and got the hell out of there.

25

Hailee

"ARE YOU SURE ABOUT THIS?" I took a deep breath, running my hands down the pale-silver, fit and flare dress Flick had insisted I wear. It was the first one I'd tried on and she had leaped off the bed, shrieking with delight, declaring it 'the one'. But even now, in my kitten heels and subtle makeup, I wasn't sure.

"I think I'm going to throw up," I said, clutching my stomach as we approached the gym.

"Hails." Flick whirled around, the layers of her own dress fanning out like a cascading waterfall. "You've got this. It isn't ninth grade. You're not going to walk in there and be the laughing stock of the school. It's senior year. We're seniors and we deserve this. Okay?" She gave me a warm smile.

"Okay," I replied despite my mind screaming, '*no, no, no*'.

"Although it would've been a helluva lot more fun if we had dates," she added, and I elbowed her in the ribs. "I'm your date."

"I know, and honestly, I wouldn't want it any other way, Sista." She grinned at me. "Now what do you say, we go in there with our heads held high and have some fun?"

"Are you sure you don't want to ditch and hang out with Jude and Toby instead?" I knew he'd been texting her. Toby had sent me a few texts here and there too, only I got the impression he was a little wary now he knew who my step-brother was. But it was probably for the best. Toby was nice, and we'd hit it off, but he didn't set off a legion of butterflies in my stomach. He wasn't the guy consuming my every thought.

My body thrummed with nervous energy at the idea of seeing Cameron. All week we'd danced around one another; watching each other across the cafeteria, sitting close but not touching in history, and there had been another moment, Wednesday after practice, when I'd caught him looking at my mouth. Whatever this thing between us was, it was building. Growing into something *more* with every passing day. I knew it was dangerous getting tangled up with him; he was Jason's best friend. And I wasn't naïve enough to think he would ever be okay with me and Cameron. But I couldn't seem to stop myself either. I craved him. Craved the way he made me feel. The thrill of getting caught.

It was official, I was completely head over heels in lust with Cameron Chase. And he was in there, no doubt looking more drool-worthy than ever. He'd joked more than once about me saving him a dance. Granted, we probably wouldn't be able to have said dance because of my asshole brother, but just knowing he wanted to dance with me was enough.

Wasn't it?

Flick grabbed my hand and started pulling me toward the door. With every step the beat of the music inside mirrored my own heartbeat. *Boom. Boom. Ba-boom.* "You're nervous." She observed.

"No, I'm not. I'm just pissed you had me wear this dress."

"The dress looks hot, just like your hair and makeup. Now stop worrying. It's a dance. It's supposed to be fun."

Fun, right.

I could totally do fun.

But as we stepped inside, I was fourteen all over again, watching my date kiss another girl. Except Cameron wasn't kissing the girl he was talking to. But they did look pretty close; her hand on his arm as she smiled up at whatever he was saying. Flick noticed and yanked me in the other direction, an amused smile playing on her lips.

We found the bar—really, it was just a long table and Mr. Henderson dressed up in a tux making some funky looking drinks—and ordered two mocktails, and then went to sit at an empty table on the fringe of the dance floor. Khloe Stemson and the rest of the bitch squad were draped over their dates like cheap throws, but there wasn't a football player in sight between them.

"I guess they're still on the outs with Jason and the team." Flick mused, sipping her liquor-less mojito.

"And the gym team are still in." I flicked my head over to where Jason had Jenna Jarvis pressed up against the wall, attacking her neck with his mouth.

"She's a skank," Flick said coolly.

"Now who sounds jealous?"

"I mean just look at her. She knows he won't commit, and yet she still throws herself at him at every opportunity."

"Maybe it's just sex."

"Yeah right. Girls don't have *just* sex. They tell themselves that to make themselves feel better. But sex for girls comes with feelings. It's simple biology."

"Hmm." I held up a finger. "I had sex without feelings."

"That's different." She screwed up her face. "You're wired different."

"Hey." I swatted her arm. "I could have easily caught feelings for Austin, but after the sex, I realized it wasn't something I was in any hurry to do again." I flashed her a playful grin and her sullen expression slipped.

"Was it really that bad?"

"It wasn't good, that's for sure."

"So, why'd you do it?"

"I don't know." I shrugged. "I guess I just wanted to get it over with. And Austin had seemed nice at the time. It was so long ago, I'm probably revirginized."

Flick laughed at that. "We're a disaster. You're throwing Cameron death stares because he's talking to a girl, and I'm sitting here talking about sex when I have barely made it to third base with a guy." She groaned, dropping her head on the table.

"Come on, it's not all bad. Maybe you and Jude will..."

"Ladies, you came." Asher Bennet loomed down over me, a wicked glint in his eye. "And you both look smokin'."

"Smokin', really?" I scrunched my nose up. It was a miracle anyone fell for his charm, or lack thereof. Although not even I could deny he looked good in his charcoal dress slacks and crisp white shirt with the sleeves rolled up, his dark blond hair mussed up in his typical laid-back Asher Bennet way. "That's the best you can do?"

"As prickly as ever I see, Raine."

Flick peeked out from the table, gaping up at him. A slow grin spread over his face. "Me and you, Giles, let's go."

"Go? Go where?"

"To fuck in my Jeep, where do you think?"

"Oh my god," she breathed out, and I thought for a second she might faint.

"Dance floor, Felicity." Asher flicked his head to the crowd of kids dancing. "Let's dance."

"D- dance?" She mouthed at me and I gave her wide eyes.

"Go, it's what you wanted right? To dance and have fun." And I had no immediate plans to make a fool of myself in front of our entire class.

Cheeks a deep shade of red, Flick let Asher pull her up and they walked hand-in-hand to the dance floor. Last year, she wouldn't have looked twice at him or Cameron or my step-brother. But this year, she was different.

Maybe we both were.

I watched on as Asher danced circles—literal circles—around her, but she was laughing, her eyes sparkling with happiness. It didn't take long before he had the entire dance floor eating out of the palm of his hand and right at the heart of their attention was my best friend, in her crowning moment.

My gaze wandered over to where I'd seen Cameron before. He was alone now, watching Asher and Flick, a strange expression on his face. Feeling brave, I got up and made my way over to him but as I almost reached him, a girl tackle hugged him and he held her affectionately, smiling down at her.

The same smile he'd given me more than once. My stomach sank as I ducked into the shadows by the wall, pressing myself flat until the darkness swallowed me whole. What did I think? That I'd come here tonight, and Cameron would actually want to dance with me? To spend time with me? *Stupid, stupid girl.*

Swallowing my pride, I marched back to my table only to realize Flick was no longer dancing with Asher. I scanned the room when my purse vibrated.

Toby: what's up?

Me: At Homecoming and it kind of sucks

Toby: You should come party with us… it's not a football thing, I promise

Another party with Toby? Did I really want that? My fingers hovered over the reply button and then I was typing.

Me: Okay

I hit send before I could chicken out. I didn't really want to go, but the last thing I wanted to do was stay here and watch Cameron and some girl dance and make out.

Just then, I caught a glimpse of Flick. I rushed over to her, narrowing my gaze when I saw her grim expression. "What happened?" I asked.

"N- Nothing." She swiped at her makeup, smudging the streaks of mascara across her face.

"Flick, I know you've been crying."

"Not here, okay?" She said, her eyes darting around me as if she was looking for something. Or someone. "Can we just go?"

"Toby texted me, inviting us to a part—"

"That sounds perfect." She grabbed my hand and started pulling me toward the door.

"Good," I chuckled. "Because I kind of already said yes."

I had another message off Toby saying he was in our neighborhood and would be about ten minutes.

"Are you sure you're okay?" I asked Flick again as she wrapped her arms around herself, refusing to meet my eyes. "Did Asher do something—"

"I'm fine, Hails. I promise."

"I swear to God, if he hurt you, I'll kill him." His interest in my best friend was growing. The only problem was, I couldn't figure out if it was all a big joke or if he actually liked her. Either way, Asher Bennet would eat her alive, something I had no intention of ever letting happen.

"It's not Asher."

"It's not?"

"No."

"But it is a guy?" Because my gut told me it was a guy. Something was going on with my best friend, I just didn't know what.

Her eyes slowly slid to mine, and she pressed her lips together giving a little nod. "But I don't want to talk about it."

The fact she didn't feel like she could talk to me stung. But I hadn't exactly been upfront about Cameron either. So I offered her a warm smile, and said, "Okay, but when you're ready, I'll be here."

"Thank you." Flick sniffled. "Ugh, Homecoming sucks."

"I could have told you that."

"I just thought..." A heavy sigh escaped her lips. "I don't know, maybe this whole list is stupid."

Moving closer to her, I squeezed her hand. "It isn't stupid. It's brave. And I'm proud of you, Felicity Giles."

"Yeah?" Her eyes lit up.

"Yeah. You could have stood by and let me trample all over your senior year and you didn't." The glare of headlights blinded us both and I threw up my arm to get a better look at the approaching car.

"It's Toby, come on." Flick grabbed my hand and tugged me toward it.

"Eager much?" I murmured and she threw me a scathing look over her shoulder.

"Homecoming might have sucked, but the night is still young, and I don't plan on letting this dress go to waste."

"You do look pretty hot," I agreed.

"Damn right I do. Jude isn't going to know what hit him." Gone was the sad girl I'd found minutes earlier.

"Flick," I said. "You don't have to—"

"No, not listening. I need this, Hails." I wasn't exactly sure what she was referring to but the glint in her eye told me not to argue.

Toby rolled his window down, his gaze sweeping down my body, eyes darkening with lust. "Hey." He gave me a lazy smile.

"Hi."

"Hey, Toby." Flick's eyes looked past him into the car.

"Looking good, Felicity," Jude's voice drifted over to us and a wide smile stretched over her face.

"Ready to go?" Toby asked and she nodded eagerly, climbing into the back. I hesitated, my eyes glancing over to the gym.

"Hailee?"

"Yeah. I'm coming." I ducked inside and pushed all thoughts of Homecoming and Cameron Chase out of my head.

"WHY SO GLUM, SISTA?" Flick sipped her drink, swaying her body to the sultry beat. We'd been underdressed at the last party Toby brought us to, but tonight we stood out for different reasons.

So much for escaping.

"I'm just not feeling it," I said, scanning the room. Kids were crammed into every inch of the house. It was nowhere near as big as Lewis Thatcher's house, but I also hadn't spotted any East football players, so it had that going for it.

"Toby seems keen." Flick motioned over to the guys as they got us all another round of drinks.

"I guess."

My best friend's eyes narrowed and she grabbed my arm pulling me into her. "You're moping."

"I am not. I'm just..." *Totally not thinking about how good Cameron looked.*

"You should've just gone and talked to him." Flick let out an exasperated breath but I didn't reply. "Fine. Be a spoilsport. But please don't ruin my fun. I need this, Hails. In fact," she said conspiratorially. "I'm thinking I might do it."

"Do it?" I stared at her blankly.

"Sex, Hails. I might have sex."

My hand shot out, smothering her mouth. "Jesus, Flick, keep your voice down."

"What?" She grinned. "It's okay to say the words."

"Are you drunk?" We'd only had two drinks.

"No, I'm not drunk. I'm merely embracing this opportunity. Jude is hot and he's sending me all the right signals."

"So this doesn't have anything to do with whatever happened earlier?" My brow rose.

"It was nothing."

Oh, it was something all right, she just didn't want to admit whatever it was.

My eyes found Jude and Toby over her shoulder. They were heading back to us. "Just don't make any rash decisions. Jude seems like a nice guy, but your first time should be with someone you like... *really* like."

"Like you—"

"Is one of those for me?" I said, alerting Flick to the fact the guys were back. She shot me an appreciative smile, before turning to Jude and taking her new drink from him. "Want to dance?" she asked.

He shrugged but Flick wasn't deterred. Grabbing his hand, she led them into the next room where the dancing was.

"I like her," Toby said. "She's got real... character."

"Is that your polite way of saying she's pushy?" I laughed and he smiled.

"She goes after what she wants, nothing wrong with that." His eyes grew hooded as they lingered on me, and I lowered my gaze, needing to break the connection.

Toby was nice. A good guy. He was constantly checking if I was okay, getting me drinks, and making me laugh. And he didn't seem as put off that my step-brother was Jason Ford as I'd first thought. But despite everything he had going for him, Toby didn't set my world on fire.

He didn't make my heart beat wildly in my chest or stir desire in my belly.

He was sweet. Kind and attentive. He was everything I wanted to like.

Everything I *should* have liked.

There was just one small problem.

He wasn't Cameron Chase.

26

Cameron

"ARE you going to wear that thing all night?" I asked Jase, eyeing the cheap plastic crown on his head with amusement.

"I've already had three offers to suck my dick and Lisa Tenby let me finger fuck her in the girls bathroom so yeah, I'm wearing it all night. What's up your ass anyway?"

"Nothing, I'm fine." My eyes searched the sea of bodies, hoping to catch a glimpse of Hailee. But I couldn't see her.

I hadn't seen her for hours since I saw her and Flick arrive.

Jase glared at me, his hard gaze burning into my face as he sipped his drink. "You sure you're okay?"

"Yeah." I nodded, looking out over the crowd again. I didn't like school dances, never had, but when you were a Raider and played for Coach Hasson, they weren't optional. We were expected to show up, smile, and give the people what they wanted. Most of the guys lapped it up—the chance to be kings for the night. But not me.

"Miley's looking hot," Jase said and my eyes slid to his. "What's going on there?"

"It's just casual." I lifted my shoulders in a slight shrug.

"No shit. But come on, man, do you like her? I've seen the way she looks at you."

"We're just friends, Jase." Nothing more. Nothing less. But he didn't look convinced.

"Yeah, well, keep it that way. The last thing we need is any distractions. And she has trouble written all over her. I'm going to take a leak." He made his way across the room, parting the sea of bodies like he was the prodigal son.

And maybe he was.

For a town like Rixon, Jason was a ticket to having their name splashed in the national papers. People couldn't wait for the day, five years from now, when they could say they knew the new star of the NFL.

I spotted Asher over by the doors on his cell phone. Worry lines were etched into his face, and I straightened, my spine tingling. But before I could go over there and find out if he was okay, his eyes found me across the room and he grimaced.

We met halfway, just as he was ending the call. "Everything okay?" I asked him as he stood staring down at his cell phone.

"I, hmm, that was Fee."

"Fee? As in Felicity?"

"Y- yeah." He swallowed, running a hand through his hair. "She, uh, she asked me to get you to call her *immediately*."

"Me, but why would she want—Hailee." The air *whooshed* from my lungs. "You have her number?"

Of course he did, they had just been on the cell phone. But everything was a little hazy, my heart thundering in my chest.

"I put my number in her phone the time she cooked breakfast. You'd better call her, she sounded panicked. When I asked what was wrong she said there wasn't time to explain..." he added and my eyes locked on his.

"Text me her number and tell Jase I had to leave."

"Shit," he breathed. "What should I—"

"Tell him it's my mom or something." It didn't matter. I just needed to get to Hailee. If Felicity had called Asher....

"Cam?" Asher's voice pulled me from my thoughts.

"Yeah?"

"I said, are you sure you know what you're doing? Maybe this isn't a good idea—"

"Just text me her number."

"Shit, yeah. Okay." He started messing with his cell phone and I waited for the incoming message, and then I got the hell out of there.

Once I was clear of the dance, I pulled out my cell phone and called Felicity.

"Cameron?" she rushed out. "Is that you?"

"What happened?"

"I... she... crap, this is bad, Cameron. I don't know what to—"

"Slow down. Where are you?" I was almost at my truck.

"At a party, across the river."

Fuck.

"Okay." I schooled my anger. "Can you text me the address? It'll take me about fifteen minutes." If I broke the speed limit.

"Y- yeah. And thank you. I didn't know who else to call."

"Don't thank me yet," I said before hanging up. Reaching my truck, I almost yanked the door off its hinges.

An East party.

They'd left Homecoming and gone to an East party. Asher was right; I had no fucking idea what I was doing. Because it was the last place I should go. Especially without back up. But Hailee was there, and from the despair in Felicity's voice, whatever had gone down wasn't good.

Dammit.

As I reversed out of the parking bay and stepped on the gas, restless energy zipped through me. Hailee needed me. Okay, so the reality was Felicity needed me, but I wasn't about to split hairs over the fact she'd called me to help.

I couldn't deny a small part of me was pissed though. I'd spent most the night searching for Hailee, hoping to catch another glimpse of her, and all along she had been at an East party with that douche Toby no doubt. My hands tightened around the wheel. I'd always known Hailee was trouble. But if Jason found out about this, shit would hit the fan. I couldn't leave her there, though, I wouldn't. Because Hailee Raine was under my skin.

And even worse, I liked her being there.

"What the fuck happened?" I was out of my truck and on Felicity in a second, pulling Hailee's limp body out of her friend's arms and into my own.

"I... she... I don't know. God." Her voice quivered. "This is such a mess." Felicity wept as I slid my hands under Hailee's thighs and scooped her up, cradling her against me. She moaned, her head rolling to the side.

"F- Flick?" It was a garbled murmur.

"Ssh, I got you," I said, my voice thick. Glancing over at the house, it was obvious the party was still raging on inside.

"Cameron, we need to go. She needs—"

"Yeah." My eyes snapped back to Felicity. "Okay."

Coming around to open the back door of my truck, Felicity helped me get Hailee inside, and we laid her out across the seats. I went around the driver's side and climbed in, my hands gripping the steering wheel as I watched her through the rear-view mirror. She looked like a rag doll, her hair hanging loose around her face, makeup smeared around her eyes. The rise and fall of her chest labored.

Felicity slid in next to me and let out a deep breath. "I'm sorry," she said. "I didn't know who else to call."

"Tell me what happened." I still hadn't turned the key in the ignition, restless energy coursing through my veins.

"Drive, and I'll tell you." Felicity levelled me with a look that told me she knew exactly what I was thinking. "Cameron..." she added after a beat. "We need to go before someone sees you here."

"Fine," I ground out. "Fine."

Gunning the engine, I backed out of the driveway and pulled onto the street. "Okay, talk," I said as the house shrunk in the rear-view mirror.

"Toby texted her when we were at Homecoming, inviting us to another party. I got the impression Hailee was pissed at you, so we left."

Pissed... at me?

It wasn't a first, but I hadn't even spoken to her at Homecoming.

"Did he...?" The words lodged in my throat, anger rising in my chest.

"What? God, no. Toby is a good guy, Cameron. I swear. But something *did* happen. We were drinking the same thing and I was fine, but Hailee started acting really strange. I wanted us to come home, but she said she wanted to stay and have fun. Next thing I know, she disappears. We looked everywhere for her."

"We?"

"Yeah me, Jude, and Toby."

Toby.

I was already sick of hearing that fucker's name.

"What happened?"

"We couldn't find her anywhere but then someone said they'd seen her go into the pool house, the pool house everyone said was off-limits...." her voice trailed off.

"And..."

"And we found her like this, almost passed out on the couch. She was completely out of it. Toby and Jude went to get her some water and to find out what happened, so I called you and managed to drag her out of there."

"Why didn't you just wait for them to come back?"

"I guess I panicked. I mean, look at her. That isn't Hails, she doesn't get trashed like that. What if someone...?"

I glanced over at Felicity and her gaze darted away. "What if someone what, Felicity?" It came out raw.

She inhaled a harsh breath. "What if someone gave her something?"

My eyes went back to the rear-view mirror. She was right, Hailee wasn't drunk, she was completely wasted. "You think she was roofied?"

"Or something, yeah."

"Fuck." My back straightened, anger rippling up my spine. I wanted to turn the truck around, go back to the party, and beat the shit out of someone until I found out exactly what happened tonight. But I knew that wouldn't help the situation. And right now, it wouldn't help Hailee.

"Should we take her to the hospital?"

"I think she'll be okay," I said, checking on her again. "She just needs to sleep it off."

"She's supposed to be staying at my house, but if my mom and dad see her like this, they'll—"

"It's cool, she can stay with me." The words spilled out before I could stop them. I kept my eyes on the road but felt Hailee's friend watching me.

"You like her, don't you?"

I don't know why, but the fact it wasn't a question irritated me.

"I'm not doing this," I said, coolly.

"Okay." Felicity smothered a smile. "I won't say another word."

"Good." It was barely a grunt, but I didn't want to talk about this, not here. Not with her.

The ride across the river was quick enough and before I knew it, I was pulling up outside Felicity's house. "Are you sure you'll look after her?" she asked quietly. I huffed annoyed, and she swallowed, adding, "She's my best friend and you haven't exactly always been nice to her. I had to ask."

"I'll make sure she's okay." Hopefully everyone would be asleep so I could avoid any awkward conversations tonight.

"She acts tough but all this, your silly little games... she's not as tough as you think, Cameron."

I didn't trust myself to reply, so I gave Felicity a sharp nod and waited for her to climb out.

Ten minutes later, I pulled up at my house. Hailee still slept soundly on the back seat, murmuring softly every now and again. Climbing out of my truck, I went around to the back door. Her body was heavy with sleep, and whatever else was in her system, as I picked her up and went inside, taking her straight up to my room.

"F- Flick, what happened?" She began to stir as I lay her down on my bed.

"Ssh." I pushed the stray hairs from her face. "I'll get you some water."

"C- Cameron?" Hailee's eyes flickered open and she stared up at me, confusion clouding her expression. "What is—oh God." She clapped her hand over her mouth and retched.

"Shit, okay, up you come." Helping her off the bed, I half-carried her to the small bathroom adjoining my room. Hailee crumpled to the floor clutching the bowl, just in time for her stomach contents to make a reappearance. I crouched down, gathering her hair away from her face. She seemed so small and fragile like this; nothing like the strong, stubborn, reckless girl I knew her to be.

Someone had done this to her.

The thought sucker-punched me in the stomach.

Fumbling to flush the toilet, Hailee finally managed it before sinking back into my body with a pained groan. "Feel better?" I asked.

"I don't know what I'm feeling right now." Her voice was groggy, her words sluggish.

"Come on, let's get you cleaned up." I found her a spare toothbrush and towel before helping her stand. "I'll give you a few minutes. I can probably dig you out an old t-shirt if you want?" Her dress was wrinkled and stained but all I saw was how beautiful she'd looked at Homecoming.

"I, uh ... yeah, that would be good, thanks." She wouldn't look at me, and it stung. More than it should have.

Nodding over the lump in my throat, I left her alone and went to find an old football jersey she could wear. It was a dick move, one she'd no doubt give me shit about when she felt better, but I couldn't deny the idea of seeing her in my team colors was too tempting not to do it.

Knocking on the bathroom door, I pushed it ajar and slipped my hand inside. "Here you go."

Hailee snatched the jersey off me and closed the door in my face. I dropped down in the chair in the corner of my room, rubbing my temples. This was not how I saw the night going. I thought I'd go to Homecoming, hang out with the guys, watch Hailee from across the room and imagine dancing with her, claiming her as my own, right there in front of our entire class. But then Miley had cornered me and the next thing I knew I was being swept up in the Homecoming Court announcements.

I was just relieved Flick had called Asher. If she hadn't, it might have been Toby looking after Hailee right now, and not me. The idea made my chest tighten. Especially when I couldn't be certain it wasn't him who had slipped her something at the party.

Shit, she shouldn't have been there, in East territory. Thatcher had made it clear he was coming after her. This had his name written all over it. I was just relieved Flick had found her before ... Fuck. I couldn't even go there. The idea of someone touching Hailee, hurting her, was almost too much to bear. Inhaling a ragged breath, I tipped my head back and closed my eyes. It felt like an eternity until the sound of the bathroom door creaking made me open them. She stood there in nothing but my old football jersey and her panties... and I realized my plan had backfired. Because she looked completely at home in my jersey, not to mention as sexy as fuck.

"I, uh..." Her cheeks flushed a deep pink as she tugged on the hem of my jersey. "So I may have puked a little on my dress and I tried to wash it off and now it's all wet, and I couldn't—"

"It's fine." I stood up, closing the distance between us, telling myself to look anywhere but at her long, smooth legs. "How are you feeling?"

"Like I got hit by a truck. But I'll live." Her gaze dipped to the floor as she tucked her hair behind her ear. "I wish I knew what happened."

"We think you might have been slipped something."

"We?" Her eyes lifted to mine, and my chest tightened, doing all kinds of weird shit.

"Yeah, me and Felicity."

"She called you, huh?" An uncertain smile played on her lips. "Which is really odd because I had no idea the two of you were on a cell phone number exchange basis." Hailee let out a strangled laugh.

"She called Asher."

"Asher? Flick has *Asher's* number? How did I not know that?" She frowned. "So she called Asher, and what exactly?"

It was my turn to look at the floor. I played football against some of the biggest defensive ends in the game. Getting tackled to the ground by guys twice my size was all par for the course. Yet, Hailee, a girl half my size, completely disarmed me.

"She called Ash and asked him to have me call her."

"But why would she do that? And more to the point, why did you call her back?"

My eyes narrowed slightly. "Hailee, come on..."

"Why, Cameron?" Her eyes pinned me to the spot.

"Because you don't deserve any of this," I admitted. "And I was worried."

"But—"

"Come on." I cut her off. "It's late, you should probably get some rest." My head motioned to the bed, and her brow quirked up. I added, "I'll take the floor."

"Cameron." My name on her lips sounded good. Too fucking good. "I'm not going to make you sleep on the floor." Color crept up her neck and into her cheeks. Hailee ducked around me and got on the bed, slipping under the covers. Part of me had expected her to put up a fight; to insist I take her home.

But she hadn't.

And like the sucker I was, I wanted to believe it meant something.

Yanking off my t-shirt, I started unbuttoning my jeans while Hailee tried her best not to peek. But I felt her eyes on me more than once. I crawled on the bed beside her, careful not to get too close. Fumbling for the light switch, I plunged the room into darkness.

"Well, this isn't awkward at all," Hailee whispered. And even though it was dark, and I could barely see her, I was aware of everything. The soft sound of every breath she took, the warm current flowing between us. The way my skin tingled, and my pulse raced at her close proximity, despite the fact I hadn't even touched her.

Turning onto my side, I traced the profile of her face. "Get some sleep." I choked out the words to stop myself from doing something stupid. Like telling her it didn't feel awkward to me at all.

That it felt pretty damn near perfect.

"Night, Cameron."

"Night, Sunshine."

A beat of silence passed and then her sleepy voice cut through the quiet. "Cameron?"

"Yeah?"

"Thank you."

As I felt the pull of sleep, my mind was a jumble of thoughts. Of me and Hailee. Of all the reasons why this was a really bad fucking idea. But one thought stood out above all the others. It was the first time I'd ever fallen to sleep with a girl in my bed.

And I liked it.

I liked it a whole lot.

27

Hailee

"AMERON, AMERON'S HOME." The voice startled me, and I peeked open an eye, trying to get my bearings. *Where the hell am I?* I wracked my brain for an explanation when a dark-haired, chubby-faced boy filled my vision.

"You're not Ameron," he said, a cute little frown crinkling his face.

Ameron?

I groaned, pushing the hair from my face. What the hell—

Everything slammed into me at once. Homecoming. The party with Toby. Cameron holding my hair while I puked up everything but my soul in his toilet. The toilet in the bathroom next to his room.

His room.

Oh god, I was in Cameron's bedroom.

In.

His.

Bed.

I glanced over and sure enough, there lay Cameron, on his front, arm tucked under his head, snoring softly.

"Who you?" the boy asked as he clambered onto the bed, settling between me and Cameron.

"I'm Hailee."

"Ailee? I'm Ander."

"Nice to meet you." I gave him my best smile despite the panic rising in my chest "Hmm, Cameron?" I hissed. "Cameron, wake up. We have company."

"Xan?" Cameron said, his voice thick with sleep. "Shit, Xander?" He bolted upright, rubbing his eyes. They flew to mine, wide with alarm, and I chuckled, ducking my head.

"You ot a irlfriend, Ameron?"

"What, I... uh, no, buddy. This is my... friend—"

"Ailee." He nodded. "She pretty."

"Okay, buddy, time for you to go." Cameron scooped up the kid and climbed out of bed not bothering to pull on any clothes. "I'll be right back," he mouthed over his shoulder and I nodded, feeling my cheeks flush.

When they disappeared out of the room, I sank back into the pillows, groaning with mortification. I was in Cameron's bed.

Cameron's bed.

And we'd just been caught by the cutest toddler I'd ever laid eyes on.

Just when I thought my life couldn't get any crazier.

Two minutes later, Cameron stepped back into the room, taking the air with him. "Sorry about that." He ran a hand over his head, his eyes darting around me.

"Your brother is adorable," I said, pulling the sheets up around my body, aware I was dressed in only his football jersey and my panties, and he was wearing nothing but his tight black boxer briefs. *Keep your eyes on his face, Hailee. On. His. Face.*

"Yeah, although he's like a whirlwind."

"He's a cute kid."

"Don't be fooled." He laughed and we shared a rare smile. "How are you feeling?" Cameron sat on the end of the bed, his eyes burning into me.

"I'll be okay, I guess. I still can't believe someone did that to me." My head hurt and my muscles were like lead, not to mention the fact my stomach felt like something had died in there. But I had more important things to worry about right now, like the fact Cameron was right there, and he was almost naked; the hard planes of his body just begging to be touched.

God, I wanted to touch him.

What the hell was wrong with me?

"Yeah, well, people will do all kinds of crazy things in the name of football."

"Does that include you?" My brow rose, as I lowered my face, looking up at him through my lashes.

"I've done some stuff I'm not proud of, yeah." Cameron swallowed as if the words were hard to say.

"Well you came through last night, so thank you."

"It was nothing."

But it wasn't nothing, it was something.

The events of last night were hazy. But I remembered with perfect clarity Cameron had come running after Flick's SOS call.

He scooted closer, angling his body to me. I felt a little light-headed suddenly. "What can you remember about the party?" he asked gently.

"I..." A heavy sigh escaped my lips. "Not much to be honest. We left Homecoming and Toby came to pick us up. He said it wasn't a football thing, so I thought..." My voice trailed off, my gaze dropping.

"Why'd you leave Homecoming?"

My eyes snapped to his, but I didn't answer. What would I say? That I'd left because I saw him with a girl? Shrugging, I picked at his sheets. "I only went to keep Flick happy and she seemed upset about something, so we left."

"Funny." His brow lifted slightly. "Because she said you left because you were pissed with me."

My cheeks flamed. "*She* needs to learn to keep her mouth shut." I was going to kill her.

"I looked for you, thought I might cash in on that dance." His lip curved. "But you were already gone."

"Yeah, well, you seemed pretty busy to me, so I figured it was no big deal." Wrapping my arms around my waist, I lowered my gaze again.

"Hailee," his voice soothed something inside me. "What's... Miley..." He let out an exasperated breath. "You saw me talking to Miley."

"I didn't see you talking to anyone, Cameron, just drop it." I didn't want to feel like this, all over him talking to another girl. It was irrational. Illogical. It was completely pathetic. But I couldn't deny jealousy burned through me when he said her name.

"Miley's just a friend, you don't need to worry about her."

"It doesn't matter." I couldn't meet his eyes.

"Why are you being like this?" he asked.

I finally glanced up at him. "Like what?"

"A bitch."

"Way to remind me that you're not the good guy here." I threw back the cover and leaped out of his bed. "I should go."

"Whoa, slow down, Hailee. We should talk."

"We have nothing to talk about," I called out as I dove into his bathroom, hoping my dress was dry enough to wear otherwise it'd be awkward explaining to Mom and Kent why I was in just my panties and one of Cameron's old football jerseys.

"Thank God," I breathed as I found my dress mostly clean and dry. Throwing my dress over the towel rail, I splashed some water on my face and tried to tame my hair by running my fingers through it. It wasn't perfect, but it would do. Then I stole a blob of toothpaste to freshen up my breath. But when I looked up in the mirror, I was met with stormy gray eyes.

"Get out," I snapped at Cameron as he blocked the door, staring at me with a dark expression.

"Make me."

"Cameron, come on. You did a decent thing last night, but let's not turn it into something it's not."

"And what would that be, Sunshine?"

"Do you know what the trouble with you is?" I spun around and glowered at him. I was tired, thirsty, not entirely sure I was done puking, and so fed up of the constant games.

The back and forth.

The push and pull.

All these unwelcome feelings I felt every time he looked at me.

"Oh, I'd love to hear all about what you think is wrong with me." He leaned against the doorjamb blocking off my exit. Not that I was ready to leave; I still needed to get dressed.

"You're entitled," I said. "You're used to people giving in to your every demand. You want to skip class, that's fine because you're a Raider. You want to fuck girls and then kick them to the curb and not get any shit for it, cool, you're a Raider. You spend years making my life hell and then the one time you do something nice, I'm just expected to what? Drop my panties and let you—" I swallowed the words as Cameron's expression turned hungry, his lip curved in an infuriating smirk.

"Does the idea of me fucking other girls upset you, Sunshine?" He stepped forward, forcing me back into the bathroom.

"Cameron, come on, this is—" But he kept coming until my butt hit the marble counter. My hands flew out behind me, steadying myself, and he chuckled.

"Do you know what I think?" he said. "I think you're a judgmental bitch. You don't know anything about me or my life. You only see the game. You couldn't possibly pull your head out of your ass long enough to see what's really going on here."

My lips parted on a gasp. "I'm not..."

"But want to know what I really think?" Cameron dipped his head, crowding me further against the counter until the rough edge bit into my skin. "You don't hate me, you hate yourself. I'm everything you loathe, but you want me anyway."

"I..."

His mouth hovered over my lips, so close I could feel his warm breath. My body began to tremble, my stomach knotted so tightly I felt a little lightheaded.

"Why do you keep doing this?" I whispered, barely able to speak. Cameron was too much. His gaze unyielding, his body plastered against mine. His hands... God, his hands began to caress my sides, making it hard to think straight, let alone breathe.

"I just want you to admit it." He nudged my nose with his. "Admit you want me and then I'll leave you alone."

"You will?" I gulped, my mind swimming with all things Cameron Chase.

He nodded slowly, his eyes still locked on mine. I'd never noticed before—or maybe I'd just refused to see it—but they were a dark shade of blue with flecks of silver-gray streaked through them. They reminded me of lightning across a stormy sky. Fitting really, considering how dangerous Cameron was turning out to be for my carefully constructed life.

"I'm waiting, Sunshine," he said when I didn't reply.

"Fine. If it means you'll leave me alone... I want you," I said with as little emotion as possible. "It makes no sense, goes against everything I stand for, and to be honest, makes me real disappointed in myself, but it's the truth. Happy now?"

"Sunshine?" A slow smile tugged at the corner of his mouth.

"Y- yeah?"

"Shut up."

And then he kissed me. Cameron Chase picked me up like I weighed nothing, dropped me on the counter, and kissed me.

"Cameron, wait." My fingers gripped his shoulders, holding him back as I managed to break away. "What are we doing?"

He gave a throaty groan. "Let's call it working out our differences." One of his hands slid over my hipbone and underneath his jersey drawing a soft moan from my lips. "Don't over-think it, Hailee."

Don't over-think it.

Right.

I could do that.

I could totally—

Cameron dived at me again, attacking my mouth. He threaded his hand into my hair, drawing me closer, sweeping his tongue past my lips and into my mouth. And damn him, I went willingly. I'd spent so long fighting, of being on the defensive. I couldn't deny that, just for once, it felt good to give over. To switch to the offense for a change.

To stop thinking and just feel.

My legs wound around his hips and Cameron dragged my body to the edge of the counter, grinding into me. He was still half-naked and I couldn't resist reaching for his chest, tracing his abs with my fingers. His body was perfection, the hours of physical training and conditioning evident in the hard planes of his chest, the corded muscles of his neck and shoulders and thick biceps.

"Fuck, that feels good," he rasped against my mouth as I continued painting patterns on his skin. The knowledge I affected him the way he affected me, was powerful. Heady.

And I wanted more.

I looped my other arm around his neck, anchoring us together, kissing him deeper. I'd kissed other guys before. Guys from The Alley and the odd party we'd gatecrashed. But I'd never kissed anyone like this. It was fire and ice. Two opposites coming together with dangerous consequences.

Cameron rolled into me again, his hard length hitting the right spot. "Oh God," I moaned, a wave of need crashing over me. He was right. I wanted him.

I wanted Cameron Chase.

There was something very wrong with me to want the one thing I hated. But maybe Flick had been right. Maybe it had all been leading to this point.

"Not God, Sunshine,"—he nipped my ear—"Just Fourteen."

Gripping his chin, I stared into Cameron's stormy eyes. "You did not just refer to yourself as your team number?"

"I'm just a conceited jock, remember?" His brow arched, daring me to argue. But I wasn't looking to go another round of verbal chess with him, so I smashed my lips to his, demanding more. *Needing* more.

Cameron's fingers glided up my thighs to the edge of my panties and I froze. Kissing was one thing but letting him touch me... that was something else entirely.

"I need to feel you," he said huskily. "And I know you want it. You're practically riding my leg."

My head rolled back against the mirror as I levelled him with a hard look. He chuckled again, gently sliding off my panties until they were a puddle on the floor. The marble felt cool against my thighs, but when Cameron stepped between my legs again, his boxer briefs tented, I forgot all about the sting. "Are you wet for me, Hailee?"

"Why don't you find out?" I said, surprising us both. Cameron's brow shot up as he leaned in to capture my lips again, pushing his tongue against mine with a hungry growl. His fingers slid through my wetness, teasing me.

Cameron broke the kiss, touching his head to mine, his eyes simmering with heat as he slowly worked a finger inside me. I wanted to move, to escape from his intense gaze. But he had me trapped. Ensnared. And when he curled his finger upward and rubbed, I was done. Cameron Chase owned me now, and I'd willingly handed myself over.

"Fuck, you're so tight," he choked out, adding a second finger, stretching me.

My eyes fluttered closed as he started working me, long slow strokes, rolling the pad of his thumb over my clit.

"Eyes open," he demanded. "I want to see you when I make you come."

I swallowed the snarky reply on the tip of my tongue, moaning instead, as my body began to shudder. "I..." My voice was lost as intense waves of pleasure began to roll over me. "More," I breathed.

Cameron's other hand glided up my stomach, brushing the side of my breast. I arched into him, pushing my chest out, needing more.

Needing everything.

"So eager," he whispered against my lips.

"I'm going to... Oh God." His finger rolled over my nipple sending a bolt of heat shooting through me. I could hardly breathe but it didn't matter. Cameron had swept me up in his firestorm and I didn't mind the burn.

In fact, I *wanted* to burn.

I wanted to throw myself right into the flames.

"I can feel you, Sunshine." His voice lingered at the edge of my desire-induced delirium. "You're close."

I nodded, soft moan after soft moan spilling from my lips. Cameron did something with his fingers, something deeper, more intense, and my world exploded into tiny white stars. And there, on Cameron's counter, drowning in pleasure, trying to catch my breath, I realized he wasn't only dangerous on the field.

Cameron Chase was dangerous for my heart.

28

Cameron

HAILEE'S BODY melted against me, her breathing rapid and her skin flushed. Fuck, she looked good on my bathroom counter in nothing but my jersey. I'd never let a girl wear my number before, but I had a strange desire to make sure she never took it off. *Shit, Chase, get a grip.*

"I... Cameron," she breathed, fighting a smile. "I can't feel my legs."

Untangling myself from her body, I backed up, giving her some space. She was all over me and I wanted nothing more than to bring my fingers to my lips and suck them clean, but Hailee was panicking. I saw it written all over her face.

"You okay?" I asked, not caring I had a raging hard on that was impossible to hide in my tight boxers.

"I... that was..."

I braced myself for her smart-assed reply, but instead she caught me completely off-guard.

"Amazing," she sighed dreamily.

"Yeah?" Sounding far too pleased with myself, I cringed.

But it was her.

Hailee made some of the other shit disappear. The constant pressure. The worry over Mom. About picking a college. And although I enjoyed nothing more than the push and pull between us, I also just enjoyed her.

The quiet moments.

Being around Hailee was like a breath of fresh air, and I already craved another hit.

"I'll let you get cleaned up." My lip curved in a smirk. I couldn't help it. Knowing I'd made her come apart did things to me. Serious things.

Things I hadn't anticipated.

"Okay." She gave me a small smile and I left the bathroom.

If we didn't materialize soon, Xander would come looking. He had questions about my *friend*. Heaps of questions and I knew I couldn't trust him to keep quiet in front of Mom and Dad, so when I'd delivered him to the kitchen, I'd given them a brief explanation as to why I had Jason's step-sister in my bedroom on a Saturday morning.

Of course, they probably didn't expect me to have my fingers deep inside her and my tongue down her throat.

When Hailee reappeared, she was dressed, if you called wearing my jersey over the top of her dress, dressed. "I, hmm, is this okay?" Her eyes lowered the floor. "I didn't want to leave the house in just my dress."

"It's cool, you can borrow it, I have plenty more." Hailee sucked in a harsh breath and I backtracked. "I didn't mean... that came out wrong."

"It's okay." She moved to sit on my bed. "So..."

"Listen Hailee, I—"

Xander's screams pierced the air and my body tensed. "Shit." My heart lurched into my throat. "I need to go. Stay here, I'll be right back."

"O-okay."

I left my room and ran downstairs, taking two steps at a time. "Mama, Mama." Xander screamed and as I rounded the kitchen my world imploded. Mom was on the floor, pancake batter splattered up the cupboards, streaked across the tiles, and her blouse.

"Dad," I yelled, rushing to her side. "Mom, Mom, can you hear me?" I gently shook her shoulders. She was out cold, but I saw the gentle rise and fall of her chest. She was breathing.

Thank fuck, she was breathing.

Rolling her onto her side, I glanced back at Xander. "Hey, Buddy, where'd Dad go?"

"The tore o get srup."

"He left to get syrup?"

Xander nodded, his eyes wide and brimming with tears. "Mama kay?"

"Mom's going to be fine, buddy. Just fine." But as I said the words my stomach plummeted. Mom wasn't fine.

Not even a little bit.

"Oh God." At the sound of Hailee's voice, I sucked in sharply. "Is she okay?"

"Ailee," Xander shrieked.

"Hi, buddy." She went to him, stroking his hair.

"I know this is probably a lot to ask." I met her concerned gaze. "But can you get him out of his chair and take him into the other room?"

"Of course. Should we call 911?" Her eyes motioned to Mom's lifeless body.

"I don't—"

"Cameron?" Dad entered the back door. "What happened?" He dropped the bag of groceries on the counter, stuff spilling everywhere, and rushed over to me.

"I don't know, I heard Xander screaming and found her like this."

Dad ushered me out of the way and checked Mom over. "Karen, darling, can you hear me?" His fingers gently traced her face and she began to stir, and relief like I'd never known before slammed into me.

"C- Clarke? What happened?" Mom tried to sit up but crumpled back to the floor. Dad slipped his arm under her neck cradling her head in his lap. "You passed out, sweetheart."

"I- I did?" Tears collected in the corner of Mom's eyes and I was vaguely aware of Hailee's gaze burning into the back of my head. "Is Xander—"

"Xander's fine, Mom," I reassured her, sliding my eyes to Hailee. She gave me a small nod, my brother clinging onto her like a spider monkey.

"Why don't you and Hailee take him into the den while I call Doctor Kravis?"

"Are you sure—"

"Cameron, now, Son." Dad glanced down at Mom and I realized he wanted to protect Mom's privacy and dignity.

"Sure, if you need me, just shout." I went over to Hailee and Xander. "Come on, let's show Hailee your toys."

The second we stepped into the den, Xander wriggled out of Hailee's arms and plopped to the floor. "Ome on, Ailee. You ike Aze?"

"Aze?" she mouthed at me.

"Blaze and the monster machines."

"I, uh, I don't know that one."

I smiled, watching as Xander grabbed her hand and pulled her further into the room. And it occurred to me I wasn't the only one smitten with Hailee Raine. She listened patiently as Xan got her up to speed on all things Blaze. When he was absorbed in the game, Hailee crept away, coming over to me. "Is your Mom going to be okay?" she asked.

Moving to the couch, I waited for her to join me. "Honestly," I confessed. "I don't know."

"What's wrong with her?"

"She has postpartum depression and anxiety."

Hailee's brow crinkled and I knew what she was thinking. "But I'm not sure that's all there is to it," I admitted. "Dad said she's getting some tests."

"What tests?"

"I'm not sure." I buried my face in my hands, rubbing my eyes with the heel of my palms, letting out a shaky breath. I'd seen Mom lose it more times than I could count; I'd seen her in puddles of tears, sobbing about something as trivial as burning the dinner. I'd watched her unable to get out of bed for days on end, complaining she was too exhausted. But I'd never seen her unresponsive like that before.

"Hey." Hailee's fingers brushed my arm, coaxing me to meet her steady gaze. "If you need to talk, I'm here."

I stared at her, lost for words. She'd offered to be there for me, just like that. No judgement. No questions or ulterior motive.

It was more than I deserved and yet, I wanted to take it. I wanted to pour my heart out to this girl.

"Cameron?" Dad's head appeared around the door. "Can I borrow you for a second?" His eyes went to the girl beside me. "I'm sorry, how rude of me. I'm Cameron's dad, Clarke. You're Jason's sister, Hailee, right?"

"Yes, Sir, it's nice to meet you."

"I wish it was under better circumstances. My son said you got into a little bind last night and he helped you out?"

"He did," her voice was quiet.

"Well I'm glad you're okay. Cameron?" His gaze flitted back to mine, and I got up, following him into the hall.

"Is she okay?"

"Doctor Kravis wants us to go straight to Rixon General. Katie is coming by to pick up Xander—"

"Dad, I can watch—"

"You should get Hailee home and then go over to the Bennets', okay?" He gripped my shoulder, squeezing gently. "I'll call you as soon as we know anything."

"Okay." I ran a hand down my face. "I'll get Xander's bag packed."

He nodded. "She's going to be okay, Son." Dad gave a little sigh and walked off down the hall. I went back into the den to find Hailee on the floor playing racing cars with Xander. I watched them from the doorjamb, a tightness in my chest. She was smiling, letting my little brother run his red car over her legs.

As if she felt me watching, Hailee's eyes lifted to mine and she smiled. "Hi," she mouthed.

"Hey." I stalked toward them. "Guess what, buddy? Katie's coming to pick you up."

"Atie, I ove her." He gave a little clap and began clearing up the pile of cars. Hailee helped and in no time, there was no evidence of their game.

I scooped Xander up and threw him over my shoulder, toddler-laughter filling the room, easing some of the pain I'd felt at seeing Mom like that. "Are you okay to wait for Katie to come and collect him and then I'll drive you home?"

"Okay." Her expression slipped, but I didn't have time or energy to try to decipher it.

The drive to Hailee's house was quiet. I was lost in my thoughts; worrying about Mom, feeling guilty over Xander being with Katie instead of his family. Instead of me. And something had changed with Hailee. It wasn't so much what she said but everything she wasn't saying.

Hell, who was I kidding? She probably already regretted letting me kiss her, touching her the way I had. She'd softened at my house. Let her guard down. But now we were in my truck, going to her house, and it was like last night, this morning, had all been a dream. A beautiful nightmare where you wake up and realize the amazing memories aren't memories at all, but an alternate reality your mind created to taunt you.

My fingers tightened around the steering wheel as my emotions crashed over me like a tsunami.

"Cameron?" Hailee's voice grounded me, and I glanced over at her.

"Yeah?"

The blare of my cell phone cut through the tension and I glanced down at the console to see Jase's name flashing across the screen.

"Shit," I mumbled under my breath. Hailee must have noticed his name too because she angled her body toward the window, watching Rixon roll by.

Everything was going to shit, and I couldn't seem to find a way to smooth it over. I'd wanted us to talk. To figure out what this morning meant to her. To us. But there was no time now.

Hailee's house came into view and I breathed a sigh of relief when I realized Jason's car wasn't in the driveway. "He must be at Asher's already," I said.

"I guess."

I pulled up alongside Mr. Ford's truck and looked at Hailee. She was no longer looking out of the window, but she wasn't looking at me either.

"Hailee—"

"Cameron—"

We both chuckled, her eyes twinkling at me. "You go," she said.

Where did I begin? There was so much I wanted to say. But I couldn't seem to sort through my jumbled thoughts, so I said the first thing that came to mind. "You know we can't tell Jason about this."

Hurt flashed in her eyes. "Right, of course." Hailee grabbed the door handle and went to climb out.

"Wait, shit... that came out wrong. I didn't mean it like it sounded."

"It's fine." She wouldn't meet my eyes. "I know it didn't mean anything. It was just us working out our differences, right?" Her gaze finally slid to mine. She was pissed. And she had every right to be. But I couldn't think straight.

"Hailee, that's not—"

"I hope your mom is okay, I really do. Bye, Cameron," she said before shouldering the door and escaping from my truck. Frustration swelled in my chest. She was running. She could pretend it was my fault, but my fuck up was only an excuse—the out she was looking for to run from me. Again.

"This isn't over, Hailee," I said, locking my eyes on hers as she glanced back at me, daring her to deny it. Her lips parted as if she was going to say something. *Say something*, I silently begged.

But at the last second, she shook her head a little and walked away from me.

29

Hailee

AFTER CAMERON GAVE me a ride home, I spent the day holed up in my bedroom, working on the art project for Seniors Night. I'd managed to find enough photographs of the senior players in action from the storage room, to use. There were nine of them in total. Which meant nine individual paintings. Mr. Jalin was right; it was going to mean some serious hours in the studio, but I welcomed it.

After this morning at Cameron's house, I needed a distraction. Something to occupy my mind so I didn't spend every waking minute replaying the way he'd kissed me, the way my body had come to life at his touch. My skin began to tingle, my stomach clenching as I let the memories wash over me. Frustrated at myself, I shook away the intrusive thoughts and focused on the task at hand.

Drawing had always been a way for me to relax, to switch off from life and lose myself in nothing but the *swoosh* of a brush against a fresh canvas, or the *scratch* of a finely sharpened pencil against a crisp page in my sketch pad. I couldn't remember a time when I hadn't loved to draw. As a child, I was always doodling and coloring in and getting mom to carve shapes into potatoes so I could make crazy paintings. But when we'd moved in with Jason and his dad, it became much more to me than just a hobby. It was a way to express myself; to work out my frustrations.

And it was mine.

I didn't need a team behind me cheering me on, or an audience chanting my name. In some ways, art was as far away from sport as you could get, and the irony wasn't lost on me.

But I didn't only love it, I was good at it.

As I stared down at the sketch of Cameron, I couldn't help but smile. I'd captured his strength and physique to perfection. Without realizing, my fingers began to ghost over his face, covered by his helmet. Waking up in his bed this morning had been a shock, but it hadn't been as awkward as I'd expected.

As it should have been.

In fact, there had been moments when it didn't feel weird at all.

"Hailee, can you come down here please?" Mom's voice cut through my thoughts and I let out a heavy sigh.

"I'm busy," I yelled, adding more shading around Cameron's helmet

"It's important."

Relenting, I closed the sketch pad and went downstairs. "Yes?" I dragged myself into the kitchen.

"Attitude, young lady." Mom gave me a playful smile.

"Sorry, I was working." I pulled out a stool and plopped down on it. "The art thing Mr. Jalin and Coach Hasson asked me to do."

"Oh yes," Kent said. "How is that going?"

"Okay, I guess. It's not exactly my thing."

"It's football, Hailee, it isn't the devil's work."

"Kent," Mom said quietly.

He shook out his newspaper, offering me an apologetic smile.

"You wanted something?" I tried to change the subject, not wanting to get into all the reasons I loathed football.

"Me and Kent have been talking, and since you came to the game with us and Coach Hasson's dinner afterward,"—she grabbed a white envelope off the table—"Kent pulled a few strings and well, happy early birthday, baby."

I plucked the envelope from her, excitement dancing in my stomach as I tore into it and pulled out the contents. "You got me the tickets," I shrieked.

"We did."

"Thank you," I beamed, leaping down off the stool and throwing my arms around her. "Thank you so much."

"You're welcome." Mom hugged me back, laughing softly. "But—"

"No buts, Mom." Untangling myself from her, I pouted. "I'm eighteen."

"You're still seventeen for another two-and-a-half weeks, Hailee. And New York is a three-and-a-half-hour journey which is..." her voice trailed off as she glanced over at Kent.

"What your mom is trying to say is that we'd feel much better about you going all the way to New York... if Jason goes with you."

My stomach dropped. "No."

"Hailee, be reasonable," Mom chided. "We got four tickets for the exhibition. We thought you could take Flick, and Jason could ask Asher or Cameron."

"You honestly think they'll want to hang out at an arts exhibition with me for my birthday?"

This day couldn't get any worse. First, Cameron ruined what had been one of the best moments of my life, and now my mom and step-dad wanted me to play happy families with Jason—on my eighteenth birthday no less.

"I'd rather not go," I said, folding my arms over my chest.

"Go where?" Jason breezed into the room and I silently groaned.

"We got Hailee tickets for an exhibition she wants to see at The Met Museum in New York," Mom said, and he did a double-take.

"You're letting her go to New York? *Alone?*"

I bristled, my teeth grinding together.

"Well, no. Felicity would be going with her, and we hoped..." Mom looked to Kent again and he finally put his newspaper down. "We'd like you and one of the guys to accompany them."

"When is it?"

I don't know who was more surprised: me, Mom, or Kent. "What?" Jason added as we all stared at him. "I can't miss a game, but if it's a bye week, it should be okay."

"It's October nineteenth," Mom said.

"It's a bye."

"That settles it then," she said. "Isn't that great news, Hailee?"

"Great," I grumbled, shooting daggers at Jason. His eyes narrowed, but I found no malice there.

What the hell was happening right now?

"I think Asher's dad has a place we can stay, I'll ask him."

"You want to stay over?" I blurted out. This just got better and better.

"Well, yeah, unless you planned on sleeping in the car?"

Kent rose from the table, going to Jason's side. "That's a great idea, Son. I'm sure we'd both feel better knowing you were staying somewhere Neil vouched for." His eyes flicked to my mom's and she nodded around a smile.

"Just the one night, though."

One night in New York... with my step-brother and his friends.

Kill me now.

"And no partying," she added, her expression tight. Jason nodded, agreeing to her terms, but I saw the glint in his eyes.

"We should probably get going if we want to catch happy hour at The Royal," Kent said, checking his watch.

"The two of you will be okay?" Mom glanced between us dubiously. "There's money on the counter to order in and I left some snacks out."

"I think we've got it, Denise." Jason's lip twitched earning him a stiff glare from his father. He ushered Mom from the kitchen, leaving the two of us alone.

"Why?" I wasted no time asking.

"Why what?" Jason went to the refrigerator and got a beer for himself.

"Why did you agree to come to New York?"

"Do I need a reason?" He unscrewed the bottle, leaned back on the counter, and took a long pull on it.

"The Met is—"

"You think I actually plan on going to some stupid art exhibition?"

"But Mom said—"

"Let your mom and my dad think whatever they need to think to breathe easier. We can ride together and when we get there, we can do our own thing."

Of course, that was his plan.

Asshole.

"And here I thought you might actually have a decent bone in your body."

He stepped forward, his lip curved in an arrogant smirk. "Just because I've had to tolerate you over this shit with Thatcher doesn't mean we're friends. That's never going to happen, Hailee."

"Fuck you, Jason," I ground out, feeling my jaw tense.

His eyes sparked with something, but I didn't stick around to find out what because I was over his shit.

So over it.

When Sunday morning rolled around, my mood wasn't much better. Thanks to Mom and Kent, I was stuck with tickets to an exhibition I desperately wanted to see. But now they came hand-in-hand with Jason. God, he'd looked so smug last night when he revealed his grand plan. He had basically hijacked my birthday so he and his friends could go live it up in New York for the night because while Mom had gotten four tickets, I was under no illusion there wouldn't be five of us making the journey.

I was toweling off my hair, when a notification pinged on my cell phone. I ignored it since it was probably Flick. But when it pinged again... and again, I finally reached over the desk and grabbed it. Unlocking the screen, I frowned when I saw the number of texts I had from my best friend. Opening the most recent, I felt the blood drain from my face.

Flick: Call me. Now!

My stomach sank, but before I could reply, Flick's name flashed up on the screen, her ringtone cutting through the silence. "What the hell?" I murmured as I hit receive.

"Hails?" she sounded a little breathless.

"Yeah?"

"I'm outside."

"Outside?" I went to the window and sure enough, pulled up alongside the sidewalk was her yellow Beetle. "Why are you outside my house?" My voice trembled as my subconscious slowly began to wake up, alarm bells sounding in the back of my mind.

"Just grab your stuff and come on. Oh," she added. "And promise me you won't look at Snapchat."

"I don't have Snapchat, you know that."

"Good, that's good," she said, sounding distracted, as I shoved my feet into some ballet flats.

"I'll be right down." My heart crashed violently in my chest.

"Okay." Flick breathed a sigh of relief. "And Hails?"

"Yeah."

"I love you and I'm sorry. I'm so fucking sorry." The line went dead, and I stared down at my cell phone, my fingers shaking. Before I knew what I was doing, I'd opened up the App Store and found the Snapchat icon. *Promise me you won't look,* she'd said. Letting out a frustrated groan, I shoved my cell phone in my pocket and grabbed my purse.

Whatever it was, it couldn't be any worse than Thatcher's last photoshop prank.

Could it?

But as I left the house and saw Flick's grim expression, I knew I was wrong.

I just didn't anticipate how wrong.

30

Cameron

XANDER CRAWLED OVER MY LEGS, running his little car up and down, making all the noises to go with it. "Hang on, buddy," I said, feeling my pocket vibrate. I managed to retrieve my cell phone without interrupting his game.

Asher: You need to see this.

It was a nondescript weblink. I hit open and my world fell away.

"Ameron?" My brother's voice startled me.

"Hmm, sorry, buddy, I need to..." I swallowed over the huge fucking lump in my throat, moving him off my legs so I could stand. "I'll be back, okay?"

"Kay, o," he said. He'd learned a new word thanks to Asher, but since Xan couldn't say his b's or r's very well yet, 'bro' became 'o'.

I walked to the far end of the den and called Asher. "What the fuck am I looking at?" I hissed down the receiver as quietly as I could manage.

"I'm not entirely sure. Thatcher posted the link on his Snapchat story. It looked shady, so I checked it out."

"It's... *her*," I almost choked on the words. "It's Hailee."

"Fuck," Asher said. "I mean yeah, I thought... but, fuck."

"Has Jase seen this yet?"

"I don't know; he's on his way over here."

"Keep him there. I mean it, Ash, don't let him leave."

"Come on, man, you know he's going lose his shit when he sees this, if he hasn't already."

My notifications started blowing up, the persistent bleeping making it difficult to concentrate.

"Shit, it's everywhere," Asher let out a long breath. "My notifications are going off like crazy."

"Mine too," I said quietly, glancing over at Xander who was still playing with his toys. "I have to go."

"What are you going to do?"

"I don't know, but Hailee..."

"Shit, she's going to freak when she sees this, if she hasn't already."

Which is exactly why I needed to get to her. "I'll call you later. Just make sure Jase stays put at yours, okay?"

"Yeah, yeah, I got it."

"Hey, buddy." I went to Xander and scooped him up. "Let's go find Mom and Dad, shall we?" She'd spent the day at the hospital yesterday for monitoring, but they'd released her in the end, and this morning she'd seemed brighter.

"I'm Aze the Monster Achine." He looped his car through the air as I carried him down the hall to the kitchen, where Mom and Dad were seated at the breakfast counter looking over some papers.

"Everything okay?" I asked.

"Everything's fine." Mom gave me a warm smile that didn't quite reach her eyes as she pushed the papers to my dad and held out her arms for Xander. "And how is my favorite little man?"

"Mama, I'm Aze," he shrieked with delight.

"Sure you are, baby." She ruffled his hair, pressing her face closer to him.

"I need to go out, are you going to be okay—"

"We're fine, Son." Dad had collected the papers into one pile now. "You do whatever you need to do. We're going to take this little monster out for ice cream and then to the park, but we'd like to sit down later to talk to you about some things, okay?"

My stomach dipped. "What things?" I looked between them, trying to read between the lines. But when Mom dropped her gaze, shielding herself behind my brother, I knew. And the pit in my stomach split wide open.

"I can stay," I said. "If it's important, I can—"

"Go," Dad rose and came to me, squeezing my shoulder. "It can wait until later. Tell the guys I said congrats on the win Friday night."

"I, hmm... yeah, okay." My eyes flicked over to Mom and Xander again, and she gave me a weak smile. Something was wrong, something they needed to sit down and tell me about. I felt winded. I'd been waiting weeks to know and now the day they decided I was ready to know the truth, I needed to get to Hailee.

Fuck.

"It'll be okay," Dad added when I didn't move. "Everything will be okay, Son."

But I didn't believe him anymore.

Fifteen minutes later, I pulled up outside Felicity's house and cut the engine. I had been about to text her to find out where Hailee was, when she'd beaten me to it. Grabbing my cell phone, I quickly sent a text to Asher letting him know I was with Hailee. His reply came straight back.

Ash: Jase is here but he's ready to kill something. I might need reinforcements

A crazy idea popped into my head, but something told me she'd do it. Felicity would do anything for her best friend.

Me: I'm sending Felicity

Ash: Have you lost your fucking mind? He can't stand her!

Me: Just let her in when she gets there

Ash: I hope you know what you're doing...

I wasn't sure I knew anything anymore. So, ignoring his text, I inhaled a deep breath and climbed out of my truck, making my way up to Felicity's house. The door swung open and Felicity glowered at me. "She's upstairs." Her voice was flat as she stepped aside to let me past. "She won't talk to me about it. And I know it's not my fault, but I can't help thinking if I'd done more at the party then..." Sobs muffled her words as she buried her face in her hands.

"Hey," I said, feeling as awkward as fuck. "It's not your fault."

Felicity peered up at me. "You're right. This is all your fault." Her lips flattened into a grim line. "Well, Jason's fault. But that makes you guilty by association."

"Felicity, come on—"

"No, you come on, Cameron. Someone drugged her, stripped her naked, and *filmed* her..." She swallowed, a fresh wave of tears tracking down her face. "It's gone too far. I told her to stop. I told her to quit this thing with Jason. I told her..."

But it wouldn't have mattered. Thatcher wanted payback. He wanted to humiliate and hurt Jason the way he'd done to him.

And Hailee was the perfect target.

"I need you to do something for me," I said.

"Me?" Her voice shook, her green eyes wide with disbelief.

"I know it's a lot to ask, but I need you to go over to Asher's house and help him talk Jase down from doing something stupid."

The blood drained from her face. "You want me to *what*?" She clutched her throat.

"I know he can be... difficult." Felicity scoffed at that. "But the last thing we need right now is Jase going across the river and doing something that'll only make everything ten times worse." Not to mention jeopardize his whole future.

"Cameron, I don't know—"

"Please. There isn't anyone else to ask." And there was something about her. The way she'd taken control that morning in Asher's kitchen, making us all breakfast as if we actually deserved her kindness.

"Fine. *Fine*. But you owe me. And you'd better find a way to fix this because my best friend is up there, and she's broken. Broken, Cameron. And I hate it. I hate seeing her like that."

I dragged a hand down my face, blood pounding between my ears. Felicity was right, of course she was right. Jason, Asher, even me, we'd all had a hand in dragging Hailee into this shit.

Felicity was busy pulling on her shoes when she said, "My room is the last one on the left. I'll text you when we've contained Jason. And don't worry about my parents, they're out of town for the night."

I smiled at that. "Thanks."

"And there's a box of brownies on the counter in the kitchen." She pointed down the hall. "They're her favorites."

"Brownies, got it."

"And last thing, don't hurt her. I know you two have this weird thing going on where you both pretend not to care. But she cares. Hailee cares about you Cameron; she's just too damn stubborn to admit it. And I think you care too. So I'm warning you, as her best friend, if you hurt her, I'll find a way to destroy you. I'm talking full on Carrie-style revenge."

I choked over the breath in my lungs. "Jesus," I mumbled.

"I'm serious, Cameron." Her eyes narrowed dangerously.

Oh, I didn't doubt it. Asher was right, it was the quiet ones you had to watch.

Felicity gave me a curt nod and slipped out of the door, and I released the breath I'd been holding. Everything was such a fucking mess and the worst of it was, it wasn't over yet. When school rolled around tomorrow, everyone would have seen the video of Hailee. And she would have to walk the halls at school knowing they'd seen it.

My fist curled as I swallowed the roar building in my throat. I couldn't let my emotions get the better of me, not while Hailee was upstairs. So I stuffed it all down and went in search of the box of brownies and then I went to find her.

Brownies in hand, heart in my throat, I rapped my knuckle against the door only to be met with silence. "Hailee, it's me. Cameron." *Way to go, asshole.*

Silence.

"Hailee?" I peeked around the ajar door. "Can I come—"

"No," she snapped, barely meeting my eyes.

"Too bad, Sunshine, you're stuck with me." I slipped inside, closing the door behind me, aware the action seemed to suck all the air from the room.

Hailee was sitting in the middle of Felicity's bed, her back pressed against the headboard, knees bent, hugging a pink, fluffy cushion. Silent tears tracked down her cheeks. She looked so fragile and sad, a complete contrast to the girl I was used to dealing with. And the sight of her gutted me, squeezed my heart so tight I thought I might pass out.

"I'm so fucking sorry." I moved closer, my eyes flitting between the end of the bed and the desk chair. Opting for the safest choice, I dropped the box of brownies on the desk and took the chair.

"You... you saw the video?" She blanched, a fresh wave of tears flooding her eyes. "Did... did Jason see it?"

I pressed my lips together wondering what the fuck I was supposed to do here.

"Oh God," she groaned.

"Hey, it'll be okay. We'll make sure—"

"The whole school has probably seen it by now. You can't make people *unsee* it, Cameron."

No, I couldn't. But I could threaten any fucker who tried to bring it up, to ever mention that shit in the halls at school.

"I keep trying to remember what happened," Hailee said, her voice quiet. "Keep trying to see their faces, hear their laughter... but there's nothing. That's what I hate the most. That they did that to me, and I didn't even know. I mean what if they..." She retched and the sound was so full of pain, it ripped open my chest. "What if they tried to do... *more*."

"More?"

Her eyes slid to mine, widening with meaning. "No," I said, unwilling to believe it. "Thatcher is fucked up, but he wouldn't... Why, do you think someone hurt you?" The words lodged in my throat.

I'd assumed the video was the end of it, but what if it wasn't? What if someone had actually physically hurt her?

Bile rushed up my throat as I breathed in through my nose, trying not to lose my cool.

"No, I... I don't think so. I didn't feel anything... you know?" She gave a little shrug as if it was no big deal.

But it was a big fucking deal.

"Fuck," I ground out, clutching the back of my neck. "And I... we..." I'd touched her yesterday morning. Me. After someone might have... I leaped up, pacing back and forth.

"Cameron," Hailee said, but I couldn't think straight. I couldn't get the image out of my head of her lying there, out of it, while someone stripped the dress from her body, laughing, whispering taunts about how much she wanted it, how easy she was.

Bile rushed up my throat. No one had been recognizable on the video, the angle of the camera zeroed in on Hailee. Her body.

Hailee's hand curled around my arm and I froze, my heart jackhammering in my chest. "It's okay. I'm okay. I would know if anything had happened, and it didn't."

But it could have. If Flick hadn't have found her when she did, it could have.

Slowly, I turned to her. Hailee's eyes were red and puffy, and her smile didn't reach them. "None of this is okay," I said quietly. "When I think about them doing that to you... of them possibly hurting you, I..." Swallowing, I wrapped an arm around her waist, anchoring us together, and dropped my head to hers, breathing her in.

"It was just a cruel prank, Cameron." Both of Hailee's hands gripped my arms now, but I couldn't figure out if she was holding me closer or trying to keep me at a safe distance. "Jason will—"

"Ssh." I pressed my thumb to her lips. "Jase is the last person I want to talk about right now." This shit with Thatcher, between him and Hailee, it had to end.

It should have ended long before now.

Her eyes flashed with surprise as she sucked in a shaky breath. "Why are you here, Cameron? Why did you come?"

It was the question I'd asked myself more than once on the ride over here. But the second I'd opened that link, I couldn't think of anything but getting to her.

"Because I care about you, Hailee," I confessed. "I care about you so fucking much."

Her expression faltered and then she was burying her face in my chest, sobbing into my t-shirt. My hands slid into her hair, coaxing her face back to mine. "I will fix this, I promise."

I didn't know how yet but I would. It had gone too far. Hailee didn't deserve this. She'd never deserved any of it.

And I'd been too much of a fucking coward to stop any of it.

Tears collected in the corners of her eyes and I slid a hand down her face, brushing the drops of moisture away with the pad of my thumb. "Don't cry, Sunshine," I said. *I can't bear it.*

Hailee's mouth curved. "I really hate it when you call me that."

"And I really love the way you blush when I do."

"What are we doing, Cameron?" Her eyes pinned me to the spot, searching for answers. Answers I wanted to give her but wasn't sure she was ready to hear.

"What we should have done a long fucking time ago," I choked out, my grip on her tightening.

And then I kissed her.

31

Hailee

"CAMERON, WAIT." My hands slid to his chest, pushing gently. He jerked back, his eyes simmering with lust and something I didn't want to acknowledge. "We can't—"

"We can," he said without hesitation. "Tell me you don't want this, Hailee. Look me in the eye and tell me you don't want me."

I want you.

I want you so much it terrifies me.

But the words were lodged in my throat and all I could do was stare back at him.

"Hailee, I'm done pretending," Cameron breathed out, lowering his head to mine. "I want you. I've wanted you since the first day I laid eyes on you."

"We were just kids." I rolled my eyes. There was no way he could possibly mean that.

Could he?

Cameron's hands slid up my arms, resting on my shoulders. "I want you, Hailee Raine. *You.*" His eyes burned into me, igniting a fire in my stomach.

"But we... we hate each other." It was a useless argument. One I knew no longer applied where me and Cameron were concerned. The tug of his mouth into a smirk told me as much.

"Nah, Sunshine, it's not hate, it's—"

I smashed my lips to his. I didn't want to hear what he thought this thing between us was, not yet. I just wanted to feel. To forget. I wanted him to help me escape the shitshow my life had become, just for a little while.

Cameron groaned with approval as I pushed my tongue into his mouth, pressing my body against his. But it wasn't enough. I needed more.

I needed *all* of him.

My arms looped around his neck and pulled until we fell onto Felicity's bed landing with a *whoosh* of breath and a tangle of limbs.

"Shit... Flick," I rasped. "We shouldn't—"

"She's not here." Cameron stared down at me, his weight crushing me in the most perfect way. "I sent her to keep an eye on Jase."

"You did?" My brow rose, unsure how I felt about that.

"If you want to stop..." He started pulling away, but my fingers dug into his shoulders.

"I don't want to stop," I breathed out, my heart crashing violently in my chest.

"Thank fuck." Relief settled over him and Cameron dipped his head to kiss my jaw, moving lower to suck the hollow of my neck. A soft moan worked its way up my throat, spilling out as a needy sigh. He rocked back onto his haunches. "Up."

I sat forward, letting him work my t-shirt over my head, shivering as his fingers brushed my bare skin. Cameron yanked his own t-shirt over his head and my eyes drank in the inches upon inches of tanned muscles. Our eyes connected, as he crawled back over me, pressing me into the mattress. "I want to touch you, Hailee." His gaze held a silent question, and I nodded, my mouth dry, my mind clouded with desire.

Anticipation vibrated through me as he leaned forward, pressing a kiss to the curve of my chest. Cameron's hands slid underneath my back, fumbling with the clasp of my bra, and the material fell away from my body as he tugged it off, cool air dancing over my sensitive skin. His eyes darkened with lust, his Adam's apple pressing against his throat as his fingers traced over my pebbled skin. "Perfect," he whispered, before capturing one of the pink buds in his mouth.

I arched off the bed, smothering a moan. "You like that, Sunshine?" Cameron looked up at me through dark lashes. Pressing my lips together, I fought a smile, but he saw right through me, dipping his head once more to give my other breast the same attention. The feel of his hot mouth, the graze of his stubbled jaw against my skin, had my heart fluttering wildly, my stomach coiling so tight I gasped his name.

Cameron sucked and nibbled a path from my breasts up my collarbone to the slope of my neck. "What do you want, Hailee?" he whispered against the shell of my ear sending shivers rolling up my spine.

"You," I finally admitted. "I want you, Cameron."

His entire body seemed to relax as he smiled down at me. It wasn't arrogant or smug this time, it was genuine. Warm. And it softened something inside me.

"What?" he asked, still braced above me.

"Is this real?" I chewed my lip, nervous energy pinging through me.

"It's real." Cameron kissed me, deep and unhurried, his tongue swirling with mine as he rolled his hips against me. There was no denying he wanted me, I only hoped he wanted more than just this moment.

But I was too far gone to worry about the consequences now. I needed him. I needed him in a way that confused me and excited me and made my head swim with possibilities. He kept kissing me, silently reassuring me this was real. That I wasn't going to open my eyes and discover it was all a dream.

My hands ran down his chest, finding their way to the waistband of his jeans and I worked the button free, slipping my hands inside, grasping him.

"Fuck, Hailee," he choked out as I began to stroke him. He was so hard and heavy in my hand, his body responding to my touch. "That feels..." Cameron swallowed, kissing me again.

But then his hand snagged mine, pinning it beside my head. "Your turn." He smirked, pressing a quick kiss to my lips before leaving my body cold. Pushing his jeans and boxers off his hips, Cameron kicked them off before stripping me out of my leggings and panties.

"I could get used to this." His hungry gaze swept down my body as he palmed himself. But I only had eyes for him. His sculpted body and broad shoulders, his tapered waist that highlighted the delicious V most girls only dreamed about.

He climbed back onto the bed, kneeling between my legs. Running his hands up my calves, sending tiny bolts of electricity zipping through me. Lowering himself back over me, he gripped himself, nudging his erection against my clit. "Cam," I gasped. "C- condom."

"Wait," he said, his voice thick. "Just let me..." He rubbed himself against me again, sliding through my wetness, sending delicious waves rippling through me. "You feel so good, Hailee."

"More," I panted, twisting my fingers in the sheets. "I need..." My head rolled back, and I was vaguely aware of the tearing of foil, of Cameron's hands between us. And then he was there, pushing inside me, stealing the air from my lungs.

"Fuuuuck," he rasped, dropping his face to the crook of my shoulder. Warm lips kissed me, sucking and tasting, as I clung onto his shoulders. His arms hooked around my legs, dragging me closer, as he began to thrust into me. Slow at first, hitting a spot deep inside me that made my tummy clench and my breath catch in my throat.

"Oh God," I cried as Cameron picked up his pace, driving into me with deep measured strokes. I met him at every thrust, rolling my hips to meet his until nothing but the sound of skin on skin and our moans filled the room.

"Fuck, Hailee, I can't..." he mumbled against my mouth, our kisses growing messy; all teeth and tongue and hot desperation as we both raced toward the edge.

It started like a gentle wave rolling to shore and then crashed over me like a powerful tsunami knocking me over, leaving me boneless and breathless as I clenched around him.

"Shit," Cameron groaned, burying his face in my neck, sucking the skin there in a way I knew would leave a bruise, as he jerked inside me.

"That was..." his voice was muffled as we both rode the lingering waves of pleasure.

But no words seemed to do justice to what I felt. Being with Cameron had been amazing. It had felt right. Like a cleansing of the past. But most of all, it had changed everything.

And I wasn't sure I could ever go back.

"Are you okay?" Cameron asked me as we lay side by side sometime later, the sounds of our ragged breaths finally returning to normal.

"I will be," I said, pulling the sheet up my body. "Flick is going to kill me though."

He rolled onto his side, his eyes on me. "Nah, she won't. We can buy her new sheets."

I smothered a laugh. "I can't believe we did that."

"Believe it, Sunshine." Cameron leaned over, pressing a kiss to the end of my nose. "And that's only the beginning."

Beginning?

Surely, he didn't mean...

"Don't look so worried."

"But what about Jason?" I peeked up at him.

"What about him?" Cameron sounded cool, but I noticed the slight tic in his jaw when I mentioned my step-brother's name.

"For all we know, he was the one who put Thatcher up to this—"

"He's a douche, Hailee, I know that. But he's still your step-brother, he would never do that. Besides, him and Thatcher working together, I don't buy it..." Cameron trailed off and I frowned.

"Cameron, what is it?" His eyes had clouded with something.

"Do you regret it?" He brushed my jaw, leaning in to steal a kiss.

"Regret what?"

"This... us." Vulnerability flashed in his stormy gaze, making my chest constrict.

"No, I don't." I didn't regret a single thing that had happened between us this year because it all led to this point. Lying here in his arms, feeling safe and cherished. "Why?" I asked. "Do you regret it?"

A small smile tugged at the corner of his mouth. "The only thing I regret is not doing it sooner."

I swatted his chest, but Cameron caught my wrist, pulling me onto my side.

"I guess Flick was right all along."

"And what exactly did *Fee* say?" His brow rose playfully.

"She seemed to think that all this, the pranks and stuff, was some kind of weird foreplay."

"I guess you could say it was."

"Cameron, come on..."

He shrugged, running his nose along my jaw. I sucked in harshly, my eyes fluttering, hundreds of butterflies taking flight in my stomach. "I never hated you, Hailee. I hated that I couldn't have you. But Jas—"

"Don't," I urged. "Don't ruin this." Any mention of my step-brother was only bound to burst the temporary bubble of bliss we'd created for ourselves.

"You know, we'll have to talk about this, us, eventually," he said.

"I know. I just... I want it to be ours for a little while longer."

Cameron nodded, leaning in to capture my lips again. Our tongues swirled together in long, lazy licks. "Can I tell you something?" he asked finally pulling back.

"Anything." Easing away to put some space between us, I looked him in the eye. "You can tell me anything."

"I'm scared, Hailee. I'm so fucking scared there's something wrong with my mom."

Oh god, his mom. I hadn't even thought to ask how she was because I'd been dealing with my own crisis. "Is she—"

"She's okay. They released her yesterday after a few hours of monitoring, but I found them earlier looking over all these papers and they were both acting cagey. Dad said they want to talk to me tonight, that everything was going to be okay, but I have this feeling..." His voice broke, and my heart broke right along with him. Wrapping my arms around him, I pulled Cameron into me. "This year is supposed to be my year, Hailee. I'm supposed to be excited about college, about the future. And all I can think is what if something is wrong, really wrong..."

"It's okay," I said softly. "I'm sure it's all going to be okay."

"And the worst of it is,"—Cameron pulled back to look at me, his expression beaten—"I can't tell anyone. I mean, Ash knows some stuff, but Jase doesn't get it. He doesn't understand because football is everything to him. The end goal. But I have to think about Xander, my family. My dad wants me to focus on football, on winning State, but what kind of person does that make me?"

"Cameron, you're eighteen. It's senior year, I'm sure if things were... well, I'm sure your dad would tell you if he needed more help."

He gave me a small smile, but it didn't reach his eyes. "I don't know anything anymore," he sighed. "Football, the team... Jase; it always seemed so important but now Mom might be sick, really sick, and you're caught in the crossfire in this thing with Thatcher and I just don't know—"

"Ssh." I pressed my lips to the corner of his mouth. "I'm here, I'm right here." *I'll be here as long as you need me.*

Cameron held onto me like I was a life raft and he was drowning, and I realized there was so much more to the infuriating, cocky guy I knew him to be. He was shouldering the weight of the world; the pressures and expectations of the team against his family's situation. And now, for reasons I still didn't quite understand, he'd taken on my worries too.

I'd spent almost six years hating him. For being Jason's sidekick. For standing by, even helping, my step-brother make my life hell. I hated their stupid football team, that hadn't changed. I hated what they stood for, what they represented. The way people worshipped the ground they walked on and excused their shitty behavior because they wore a blue and white jersey. I hated the whole damn institution.

But I also couldn't deny that although I hated Rixon Raiders with every fiber of my being, I was pretty sure I was falling for one.

32

Cameron

I LEFT Hailee asleep in Felicity's bed. She was exhausted. After we'd talked and kissed and touched some more, she started to crash. So I'd told her to get some rest and that I would check in with her later. I needed some air. Not from Hailee, she'd been perfect. Everything I needed and hadn't even realized. But she'd said something when we were together, something I couldn't shake.

Heading over to Ash's house, I was hardly surprised to pass Felicity on her way out, Asher hot on her heels. "Do I even want to know?" I asked him as we both watched her storm from the house, fists clenched by her sides, anger rolling off her in waves.

"Just Jase being his regular asshole self." He shrugged. "I'll go make sure she's okay."

I gave him a nod and he took off after her. At least now we had the house to ourselves. I found Jase in the kitchen, nursing a funky looking protein drink.

"Did you do it?" I looked him in the eye, praying to God Hailee was wrong.

"What the fuck did you say?" Jase's eyes narrowed dangerously as he rose to his full height.

"Tell me you didn't do it? Look me in the eye and tell me you didn't set this whole thing up to ruin her?"

I hadn't even considered it until Hailee planted the seed. But as I'd lay there, watching her, it had taken root, growing into something ugly. Something I couldn't stop.

It was a stretch though. Jason hated Thatcher, so the idea of them colluding to hurt Hailee was out of the question. Especially given the history between them. But I couldn't help but wonder if he'd had a hand in everything going down the way it had.

"You think I had something to do with..." He dragged a hand down his face, letting out a heavy sigh. "No, I didn't fucking do it. But part of me wishes I had. Is that what you want to hear?"

"But Aimee—"

"Aimee has nothing to do with this."

"You fucked Thatcher's sister and sent him a video of the two of you." It was low, even for my best friend, and it had raised the stakes in their war. But he'd had his reasons. For as messed up as it was, Jase never acted without motivation or provocation and Aimee hurt him in a way few ever had.

"Yeah, well she was a conniving bitch who got what she deserved."

"There's something very wrong with you; you know that, right?" I hadn't known what he planned to do to Aimee, but even if I had, there would have been no stopping him. He'd let her in, only for her to throw it back in his face. And in his twisted logic, Jason had only been killing two birds with one stone.

"Go fuck yourself, Chase. You don't know what it's like walking in my shoes."

"Boo fucking hoo. You have this whole goddamn town at your feet. But it doesn't mean you can walk all over people, Jase. There are consequences to your actions. Just because you didn't pull the trigger on this doesn't mean it doesn't have your prints all over it. If you hadn't started this thing with Thatcher, Hailee would never have got caught in the crossfire."

"You think I give a shit?" He folded his arms across his chest, raising a brow. "You have no idea what it's like living with her. Pretending everything is fine when it's not fucking fine. My mom left because of her."

"Hailee?" I frowned, confused. "Your mom didn't leave because of Hailee. She left because your dad couldn't let go of his past." He was married to the game, the future he'd lost out on, the future Jase had within his grasp.

Anger ignited in his eyes, the muscle in his jaw pulsating. "I'm talking about Denise, dickhead. They were working things out until *she* came along." He all but spat the word.

"Jase, come on, it was over." Things had been rocky between his mom and dad long before Denise came onto the scene. "This thing with Hailee, it isn't fair. She isn't her mom. You can't keep punishing—"

"You think I'm punishing her?" He barked, a wicked glint in his eyes. "I'm not punishing Hailee; I just don't fucking like her. She thinks the sun shines out of her mom's ass. She has no idea what a homewrecking bitch she really is. Do you know she chased him? She spent months sniffing around my dad when he and mom were trying to work things out. I'd catch her calling him, even caught them almost fucking once, and I heard Mom call him out on it."

"Shit, man, I didn't know..."

"No, you didn't." His expression was guarded.

"You never said anything?" But then it was no surprise. Jase was a closed book to everyone around him. Me included.

"What was I supposed to say? My dad, a local hero, a man everyone worshipped, was a cheating son of a bitch who cared more about getting his dick wet with some whore than fixing his marriage?"

"Does he know you know?"

"What do you think?" he snarled.

Mr. Ford didn't know. If he did, there was no way Jase would have still been living under his roof because shit would have hit the fan long before now.

"You could have left with your mom, moved to Pittsburg and transferred schools?"

"And risked my whole future?"

Even now, with the truth laid out before him, it still all came down to football. I couldn't blame him for resenting Hailee's mom. Hating her, even. But Hailee wasn't her mom. She wasn't the responsible party here. She was just another innocent kid caught up in the mess her parent created.

And she had no idea about the truth of the situation.

"I get it," I admitted. "I'd hate her too. But Hailee is—"

"Hailee is a sanctimonious bitch who thinks she's better than me. She always has. Did you know her old man was a big hot shot football player at college?" I shook my head, anger rippling up my spine at the way he talked about her. But I wasn't about to start something I wasn't sure I could finish.

Jase went on, "Yeah, played running back for Rutgers. He knocked up Denise when they were in junior year and left her carrying the baby while he pursued football and pussy."

"I had no idea." But it explained some of Hailee's attitude towards football, towards us. The team.

She'd grown up with no father because he chose the game, the life, over her and her mom.

"If you hate her so much, why haven't you told her the truth?"

Jase's eyes darkened, but I saw the hesitation there. When he didn't answer, I added, "Know what I think? I think you're lashing out at her because you can't go after Denise. Deep down, you know your dad will pick Denise because he loves her, and people do crazy shit in the name of love. And that scares you."

I'd known Mr. Ford since I was just a kid and I'd never seen him act with Mrs. Ford, the way he did with Denise. He didn't just love her, he adored her. And for the first time ever, Jason wasn't first string in his father's life.

"You don't know what the fuck you're talking about."

"Don't I?" I knew I was right. Jason was still just a twelve-year-old kid who had found out his dad had fallen in love with another woman.

"No," Hailee's voice cut through the room and my stomach sank. Shit, she wasn't supposed to be here. She was supposed to be at Felicity's house, where I'd left her sleeping.

"What the fuck are you doing here?" Jase growled.

"I came to find Flick; she wasn't answering her phone."

He grumbled something under his breath, irritation radiating from him, but Hailee added, "You're joking, right? What you said about my ... my mom, it's just cruel joke?"

The pain in her voice cut through me like bullets. I wanted to turn around and say something to comfort her, to fix this, but I was rooted to the spot, unable to move, the weight of her stare burning into my back.

"It's the truth, little sister," Jase said mockingly, and I wanted to drive my fist into his face just to shut him up. "Your mom isn't the upstanding woman you think she is."

"No..." she whispered, her voice broken. "I don't believe you, you're lying. You're just trying to hurt me."

"Not so smug now, are you?" Jase laughed bitterly. "You hate me, hate everything I stand for because your dad was a piece of shit who didn't stand up and take responsibility for his mistakes, but it didn't stop your mom making a play for my dad. She practically begged him to fuck her. Was ready to spread her legs like a—"

"You need to back off." I stepped in front of Jason, shielding Hailee from him.

His lips curled in a vicious smirk as realization dawned in his dark gaze. "I knew it. I knew you were fucking hard for her. All these years, you went along with my shit, played the game, but it wasn't for my benefit, was it? It was for hers. You were protecting her. You chose *her* over *me*."

"I chose you, remember?" I gave him a pointed look, my fists curled at my sides as I forced myself to remain calm, to not get drawn into his malicious game.

"Nah, man." Jase shook his head. "You didn't choose me. You chose her. Are you fucking her?"

Hailee's harsh intake of breath made me flinch. But I didn't turn around to look at her still, I couldn't.

"I asked you a question." He scratched his jaw, waiting for an answer.

"No," I lied, hating myself. I looked my best friend dead in the eye and lied. But I knew if I confessed, this would end badly. Far worse than it was already heading.

"But you want to, don't you?"

"Jase, man, come on. Don't do this."

"Do what? Ask my best friend if all this time he's been planning on stabbing me in the back and all over some self-righteous bitch?" His eyes flicked over my shoulder to Hailee and my spine went rigid.

"It isn't like that and you know it." My teeth ground together behind my lips as I tried to get a handle on the anger boiling in my veins. But for as much as I wanted to protect her, to defend Hailee's honor against Jason and his cruel tongue, I needed his eyes off her and on me more.

"Nah, I don't know anything anymore." He inclined his head, rubbing his jaw harshly. "I trusted you. I trusted you with my life. It was you and me, bro. We were going to be unstoppable. Nothing was going to ever come between us, remember?" Jase ate up the distance between us until we were toe-to-toe, staring at me as if he no longer recognized me. Slamming his shoulder into mine, he said, "I hope she's worth it," and then he stormed out of the room.

I released the breath I'd been holding, turning slowly to face Hailee. She was pale, her face a mask of sadness as silent tears streaked down her cheeks. "Hailee, I—"

"Don't, okay." Her voice trembled as she backed up. "Just don't."

"I'm sorry. I'm so fucking sorry."

Silence enveloped us. Thick and suffocating. But I didn't know how to fix this. She wasn't supposed to be here, she wasn't supposed to hear any of this.

After a few seconds, Hailee finally broke the tension. "Is it true? Was he telling the truth?"

"I- I think so." I swallowed, my throat dry. Jason was a lot of things, but he wasn't a liar. If he did something, he owned that shit every time.

"But my mom wouldn't... she wouldn't do that." Hailee folded trembling hands around her waist, as if she was holding herself together. "Not after my dad..."

"Even adults make mistakes, Hailee."

"And Jason, what did he mean about you choosing me?"

Shit.

Shit!

"I, hmm..." I cleared my throat, trying to dislodge the giant fucking lump stuck there. "Maybe we should talk about this another time..."

"No, I think we should talk about it now." She glared at me and I wanted the ground to open up and swallow me whole. Nothing about this conversation would end well, not after Jase's revelation. But she was staring at me with those honey-brown eyes of hers, coaxing all my truths out of me, and I knew I had to confess.

"Sixth grade, when you first moved in with Jase and his dad..."

"I remember. I thought you wanted to be friends with me." Sadness washed over her.

"I did." My chest tightened. "I liked you. You were a breath of fresh air, always standing up to Jason and refusing to take his shit. I admired you."

"What changed?" she said coolly, the bite in her voice turning my blood to ice.

"Jason started to get jealous. He never said anything, but I realized the more I talked to you,"—and I'd talked to her a lot—"the more he taunted you. Right before summer, I called him out on it, and he told me I had to choose. Him or you."

Hurt flashed over her face. "And you chose him."

"I know it doesn't make any sense, Hailee, but I didn't choose him, I chose you. I saw the way Jason looked at you. He hated you. It was messed up, and I didn't really understand it, but I knew how cruel he could be. I knew he'd never leave you alone if I admitted the truth."

"The truth?"

"I liked you. Even back then, when I was too young to understand girls or any of that stuff. I knew you were different. You were the first girl I'd ever wanted to be around, to get to know."

"You made my life miserable that summer."

"I know." Guilt knotted my stomach as the memories washed over me.

We'd spent an entire summer taunting her, playing pranks, stealing her stuff, and making her life a misery. It was like Jason was testing me; making me prove my loyalty. And I'd gone along with it because I hoped if I played his games, he'd eventually back off and leave her alone. But he didn't. And by the time I realized he wasn't going to; it was too late. A line had been drawn between us. Hailee one side; Jason, me, and Asher the other. As the years went on, I told myself it was for the best, that admitting how I felt about her would only add fuel to the fire. So I stayed away. I played Jase's games and somewhere along the way, I even grew to enjoy them. Because provoking her, pushing her to retaliate, was my chance to get a rise out of her, to give me attention.

It was the only way I got to keep a piece of Hailee Raine in my life.

"Am I really supposed to believe, that all this time, you went along with his stupid games because you... *liked* me?" The doubt in Hailee's eyes was enough to slay me, but I looked her dead in the eye as I nodded.

"It makes no sense—"

"You're damn right it doesn't," she spat. "We're not kids, Cameron. This isn't junior high anymore. This is my life. And it's all been some big game to you. I've been a big game—"

"What?" Panic clawed up my throat. "It hasn't... that's not..."

"I need to go." She turned on her heel and made a beeline for the door, but I rushed over to her, snagging her wrist. "Wait," I choked out. "We need to talk about this—"

There was too much left unsaid. Too much I needed to try to explain. But when Hailee met my wild gaze again, I saw the defeat in her eyes.

"You know," she said softly, her flat tone cracking my chest wide open. "I always knew I was right about you. I can't trust you." She shrugged me off and fled the room, taking a piece of my broken, bloodied heart with her.

Earlier had been one of the best moments of my life. It hadn't felt like a betrayal or a game. It had felt real.

Right.

It had felt like a long fucking time coming.

But now, in the harsh light of day, everything had gone to shit. And I couldn't help but think, I only had myself to blame.

33

Hailee

"HAILEE, SWEETHEART, IS EVERYTHING OKAY?" Mom's voice drifted through the crack in the door, but I ignored her, the same as I had the previous three times she'd come to check on me.

After overhearing Jason and Cameron's argument, I'd fled Asher's house and holed up in my bedroom. Everything I thought I knew was a lie. Mom and Kent hadn't met after he and Jason's mom separated, at all. Mom was the *other* woman. And all this time, Jason knew.

He knew and he'd never breathed a word of it.

It wasn't any wonder he hated my mom, or me, for that fact. I'd always been so judgmental about him and the Raiders. Scarred by my own experiences of growing up without a father because of football. Gary Broker had been a rising star in the NCAA. He didn't have time to raise a baby, to play happy families with the girl he accidentally knocked up. He had better things to be doing with his time—the endless cycle of girls and parties and attention—and all I had was a couple of grainy photos of him and not a single good memory. Even after I was born, he still wanted nothing to do with me. There had been a handful of awkward meetings when I was a kid, but those didn't last past my seventh birthday when he finally grew up and settled down with his other family—the one he actually gave a shit about.

Mom had spent years drilling it into me; telling me that guys like him couldn't be trusted. Athletes. Jocks. Guys who were more focused on their careers than girls. But it was all a lie. Because we'd moved to Rixon and she'd managed to sniff out Kent Ford. Local football hero and legend in the making, if it hadn't been for his career-ending accident.

God, I was so naive.

All this time, I'd hated on Jason when Mom hadn't only betrayed him, she'd betrayed me too.

"Hailee," her voice pulled me from my thoughts. "I'm coming in, baby." She appeared around the door, giving me a concerned smile. "You've been up here hours; you missed dinner."

"I don't feel like eating right now."

"Did something happen... with Jason?" Her lips pursed as if it was a forgone conclusion. "He's acting more grouchy than usual."

Of course she'd assume it was him. Because for years she'd stood on the sidelines as we duked it out, and never once had she tried to fix the mess.

The mess *she'd* created.

"Were you ever going to tell me?" The words spilled out.

"Tell you?" she said, perching on the edge of my bed. "What on earth are you talking about?"

"How did you meet Kent, Mom?"

Her expression faltered but she quickly recovered. "You know this story, baby. We moved to Rixon and Kent was good enough to help me out with a flat tire and the rest as they say is history."

"I know."

"Know?" She inclined her head. "Hailee, I'm not sure—"

"Jason told me." She inhaled sharply, the noise puncturing the air, and my heart. But she didn't say anything. Didn't try to tell me I was wrong, that she had no idea what I was referring to. "You knew, he knew?"

I'd heard Jason tell Cameron he didn't think his dad knew so I'd assumed she was just as clueless.

"I suspected he knew something, yes." Mom lowered her eyes, but I saw the regret there, the shame coloring her cheeks.

"So, it is true? You had an affair?"

"Baby." She reached for me, but I snatched my hand back. "Matters of the heart are never that straightforward." Mom gave a little sigh.

"Matters of the heart?" I laughed bitterly. "You broke up their marriage, Mom. You ruined Jason's—"

"It's not that simple." Panic rose in her voice now. "Kent and Maryanne were having issues, he was lonely—"

"So, you thought you'd what? Offer a shoulder to cry on? A warm bed at night. Somewhere for him to escape his shitty marriage?"

"Hailee Raine," she scolded, her expression hardening. "I know you're upset, but I am still your mother."

Which was kind of the point. Adults were supposed to set examples, to be the ones scolding their kids for making mistakes. Not the other way around.

"You lied," I said. "All these years, you lied. I spent years in awe of your strength, Mom. You raised me alone, never asked dad for anything. I admired you for not taking the easy route, for not settling for just any old guy." And there had been quite a few along the way. "And I had to find out from Jason it was all a lie."

"Hailee, please, let me explain..." Tears rolled down her cheeks, but I wouldn't comfort her.

I couldn't.

"You raised me in your image, Mom. You made me believe in self-worth, in never settling for anything less than I deserve. But you also hardened me. All those stories warning me about guys like Dad, it messed with my head. And then you moved me to a town where football is more important than anything, and shacked up with a local football legend, no less. And I never complained. Not once. Because I was happy for you. Because it was your time to enjoy life, to be happy. And now I find out it's all a lie. That you went after Kent knowing he had a wife and a family.

"Get out," I said coolly.

"Hailee, now just wait a minute—"

"I said get out. I can't even look at you right now."

"Hailee Raine." She blanched.

"Get out," I yelled. "GET OUT. GET OUT. GET OUT." The words tore from my throat like an ugly explosion. Mom sobbed into her hands, fleeing from my room. I hadn't meant to lose my cool, but I couldn't look at her. I couldn't sit here and listen to her empty excuses.

She'd lied.

Day after day, she'd looked me in the eye and kept this dirty unforgiveable secret from me. I'd spent almost six years living with Jason, tolerating his bullshit, for her. Because she was happy. Because she deserved a man who treated her the way she deserved to be treated.

Grabbing the nearest pillow, I stuffed it against my face, screaming with frustration. I'd grown up without a father, but I'd never felt like I missed out. Mom was my mom and dad all rolled into one. She'd held me when I hurt, cried with me at sad movies, helped me with science projects, and homework. Where my dad had been absent for every milestone, Mom had been there. One-hundred and ten percent. They were the complete opposite of one another.

But in the end, it turned out they had one thing in common.

They'd both betrayed me in the worst possible way.

Sometime later, I woke up to the sound of raised voices. Disoriented, I sat up, rubbing my dry, sore eyes. I'd cried so hard I wasn't sure there were any tears left.

"You were fucking her long before Mom left," Jason roared, the anger in his voice evident even from my bedroom.

"Jason, you need to rein it in, now," Kent sounded calm, composed, as I crept out into the dimly lit hall. "You had no right telling her."

"How many times do I have to tell you? I didn't tell her. She overheard a conversation between—"

"You think I care how she found out, Son? This wasn't the right way..."

"You think there's a right way to find out your mom is a homewrecking who—" The sound of skin cracking pierced the air and I flinched, tiptoeing down the stairs.

"Touch me again..." My step-brother's voice was low. Deadly. And for a split second, I feared for Kent's wellbeing. But for as much as an asshole as Jason was, I didn't truly believe he would hurt his dad.

"Jason, I didn't... I'm sorry. I just don't appreciate you talking about Denise in such a way. This is a mess, Son. If only you had come to me sooner—"

"You would have what? Ended it? Tried to fix things with Mom?"

"That's not—"

"Didn't think so," Jason ground out. "Mom left. She left because of you. Because of *her*. And you wonder why I can't fucking stand her."

"Enough," Kent snapped. "Denise is my wife, Jason. Nothing you could have said or done was ever going to change that. I love her. And I'm sorry things happened the way they did, I truly am, but life isn't always easy, Son. It's messy and hard and sometimes it hurts."

I was rooted to the spot, my fingers curled around the bannister. I'd never heard Jason and his dad argue before. They weren't always warm with one another, but I figured that was down to Jason. He was detached, devoid of emotion. But now I realized there was far more to my step-brother than met the eye, and for as much as I didn't want to feel sympathy for him, I couldn't help it.

I'd known the truth for a few hours—he'd lived with it for years.

So why had he never told me? It couldn't have been to protect me, that made no sense. He'd expressed his contempt for me on more than one occasion. But a tiny part of me couldn't help but wonder if he wanted to spare me the pain that came with knowing.

A door slammed, jolting me from my thoughts, and I ran back upstairs, locking myself in my room. I might have felt sympathy for Jason, but Flick was right, I was hardened. Because although I knew he was in pain, although I knew he probably needed someone as much as I did right now, I couldn't be that person for him.

I couldn't forgive him.

By the time Monday morning rolled around, I was exhausted. I'd barely slept last night. My conversation with Mom, and the one I'd overheard between Jason and Kent, replayed over and over, until my dreams became a skewed reality; lies and truths becoming a tangled web of uncertainty. Jason hadn't returned home and I assumed he'd stayed over at Asher's, or his latest hook up's. I'd overheard Kent reassuring Mom things would blow over, as if the truth was just something we could all brush under the rug and ignore. But whatever they needed to tell themselves for an easy life.

"Good morn—you look like crap." Flick's brows knitted together. "What happened?"

"It's a long story."

"I've got precisely,"—she checked the clock on the dash—"eleven minutes, hit me."

So I told her what happened, from the moment Cameron showed up at her house yesterday, right up to when I'd heard Jason and Kent arguing last night.

"Okay, let me get this straight," she said, pulling into the school parking lot. "You had hot delicious sex with Cameron; found out your mom and Kent had an affair behind Mrs. Ford's back, effectively ending their marriage, *and* Jason knew all this time?"

"Don't forget the bit about Cameron being a jerk to me all these years because my step-brother made him choose between us." My lips flattened into a tight line.

"I don't even know where to start. Let's start with the sex." Her eyes twinkled with possibilities. "Yes, let's definitely start there, although you owe me so much for the fact you had sex in my bed. I mean, really? I had to sleep in there." Her nose wrinkled.

"Flick, focus." I groaned, burying my face into my hands, partly from embarrassment and partly from frustration that we were even talking about this. "Did you hear anything I just said? Cameron basically treated me like crap all these years because—"

"He was protecting you, obviously," she said the words without hesitation, her eyes rolling the way they did whenever she thought I was being dumb, as I peeked over at her.

"Protecting me, right."

"Come on, Hails." She leaned over, tugging my hands away from my face. "You can't deny it has a certain romantic poetry."

"Romantic poetry," I muttered under my breath, shouldering the door and climbing out of her car. "Well romantic or not, I'm not sure how I feel about it all."

"So, you're not going to have a Romeo and Juliet style reunion in the cafeteria?" Her brows waggled and I pursed my lips.

"You do know they both ended up dead?" My brow shot up and she smothered a laugh. "That won't be happening, Flick. Besides, you seem to have forgotten one very minor detail, I have to survive that first." I pointed at the gathered crowd, all staring in my direction.

"Shit," she whistled between her teeth. "Maybe we should cut class today. I'm not sure—"

"Nope." I hitched my bag up my shoulder and started forward, ignoring the chorus of insults.

Slut.

Whore.

Eagles skank.

I bit the inside of my cheek, forcing down the tears building. "I will not let Lewis Thatcher, or anyone else for that matter, run me out of school," I said with wavering conviction.

So they had all seen the video of me passed out and naked? Shame on them for watching it in the first place. I had bigger things to worry about now. Like my homewrecking mother and my conflicting thoughts for a stepbrother I'd spent the best part of six years hating.

Not to mention the guy who consumed my every waking thought but gave me whiplash at every turn.

Flick plastered herself to my side, slipping her arm through mine. "You're either very brave, Hails," she whispered, her hard gaze sending warning signs to a few girls nearby who were blatantly pointing and snickering. "Or very stupid."

"Yeah," I breathed out, feeling my classmates judgy stares brush up against me as we filed into school. "I'll let you know which when I figure it out."

What I really wanted was to turn and run, to get far far away from them. But I would not cower. Not today. Not over the video or my classmates. I was better than that.

Better than them.

And it'd take more than this to break me.

34

Cameron

"GET IT TOGETHER, LADIES," Coach boomed across the field as I fumbled the ball for the third time that morning. "Fourteen," he yelled. "Do we have a problem, Son?"

"No, Sir," I replied, cussing under my breath.

"And what about you, QB? Something you want to tell me?"

"No, Sir," Jase echoed my words, glaring at me across the field.

I hadn't seen him since he stormed off yesterday. But it was fine by me; I had bigger things to deal with.

"Okay, run it again." Coach Hasson sounded pissed, and I didn't blame him. We were unfocused, the tension between me and Jase rippling around the field like a storm on the horizon.

"How about you try to catch it this time?" Someone chuckled but I let it roll off my shoulders, moving into position for the play.

"Hut," Jase's voice echoed around us as Grady snapped him the ball, and I took off, looping behind him and down the right-hand side of the field. He let the ball fly and I tracked its projection, but something caught my eye.

Hailee.

She was sat in the bleachers, glasses framing her face, sketch pad balanced on her knees.

"Mother of God," Coach yelled, as my fingers grazed the leather and the ball rolled out of my reach. "Bring it in offense. Now."

I let out a heavy sigh as I jogged over to the sideline, but Jase stepped in front of me. "What the fuck is wrong with you today?" he said through gritted teeth and I shot him a hard glare. "You really want to go there?" I snapped.

"Maybe we should. Maybe if we aired all this crap between us, you'd actually manage to catch a fucking pass or two." He was toe-to-toe with me now, our shoulders squared, eyes locked on one another.

The entire field was quiet, tension crackling in the air as everyone waited to see what would happen.

"Walk away, Chase," he said coolly.

"You walk the fuck away."

"If the two of you don't get over here in the next two seconds," Coach boomed. "I'm going to knock your goddamn heads together."

Jase expelled a heavy sigh and shook his head as if he couldn't believe what had just gone down between us and then he did something I never expected.

He walked away.

Forcing myself to take a breath and calm down, I trailed after him, joining the huddle.

"Did I wake up in some alternate universe where my wide receiver can't catch the damn ball and my quarterback is growling at his teammates instead of talking to them with the goddamn respect they deserve?" His eyes drilled into me and Jase as we stood shoulder to shoulder, despite the vast fucking ocean between us.

"Sorry, Coach," Jase grumbled. "It's been a rough couple of days." His eyes slid to mine.

"I'm sorry, what did you say?" Coach Hasson cupped his ear. "Because it sounded like you grew a pussy overnight, Ford. It's week five. We're at the halfway mark, ladies. You think we can afford to drop the ball now, no pun intended, Chase? The play-offs are almost within our reach, but we need to keep our heads. Do you hear me?"

"Yes, Sir," a few of us mumbled.

"I'm sorry, I didn't hear you."

"Yes, Sir." Our voices melded into one.

"Good, now get out there and play like the team I know you can. Chase, Son, a word."

Jase's eyes followed me as I stayed behind while everyone else moved into position. "Do I need to be worried?" Coach didn't beat around the bush. "You're fumbling the ball, messing up plays, and I know you were late to conditioning this morning. Something you want to tell me, Son?" His eyes softened as he waited for answers.

Answers I didn't have.

Because while everything was falling to shit around me, I couldn't tell him.

I couldn't say the words even if I wanted to.

"I'm fine, Coach," I choked out, feeling the weight of the lie heavy on my chest. "I'll be fine."

His eyes narrowed with suspicion. "Let's go then. We've got a game to win Friday." Coach clapped me on the back, and I jerked forward, my eyes skirting over to where Hailee sat all alone. I wanted to go over there. To apologize for yesterday and explain everything, but what was the point? She'd barely looked at me all morning, her walls higher than ever.

I'd finally gotten my moment with her, only to have it ripped away from me in the blink of an eye.

And it sucked.

"Chase, let's go," Coach snapped, and I shook my head, ridding myself of the thoughts. I wanted Hailee. I wanted her so fucking much. But I wanted a lot of things. College. A football scholarship. A bright future.

But sometimes dreams didn't come true.

Sometimes they went up in flames and there was nothing you could do but try to avoid the burn.

"Okay, I gotta ask, what the fuck is going on with you and Jase?" Ash slammed his hand against the locker next to mine, blocking my exit.

"Not in the mood," I said, cutting him with a hard look.

"Tough shit because I tried asking him and he almost bit my head off. So now I'm asking you. And don't give me any of that, 'everything is fine' bullshit. I was at practice. I saw you fumble the ball like a pro. Let's not forget the fact the two of you looked ready to throw down."

"I said I don't want to talk about it." I spotted Hailee out of the corner of my eye and leaned back against the locker bank, following her with my eyes. She didn't look at me; she didn't have to. I felt her 'stay the fuck away from me' vibes from where I was standing.

"What's happening there?" Ash's voice cut through my trance. "Because I'm sensing some serious dark juju from her."

"Beats me." I shrugged, ducking around him and following Hailee down the hall.

"So, the two of you are—"

"Nothing." I winced, my chest squeezing. We weren't nothing. We were something.

Only I wasn't sure we were anymore.

"Jeez, getting answers from you is like prying Mackey off of Khloe's tits."

"So quit asking."

"Come on, man, this is me. I know something went down between you and Jase and I'd bet my inheritance it has something to do with her." He jabbed his finger at Hailee's retreating form.

"It's not my story to tell." I picked up the pace.

"What the hell does that mean?" he called after me, but I was too focused on the girl ahead of me. She veered to the left away from the flow of kids heading for the cafeteria and headed toward the arts department.

"Hailee," I shouted as she was about to disappear through the doors.

"Go away, Cameron." She didn't even glance back at me. She might as well have ripped out my heart and stomped all over it.

"I just want to talk, please." *I need to talk.*

"I'm busy. I have to work on the project."

Screw the damn project, I wanted to say. *I need you.*

"Please," my voice cracked, betraying me but it got her attention. Slowly Hailee turned to face me, her brows knitted together. "What, Cameron?"

"I..." the words lodged in my throat. "I'm sorry."

"That's what you wanted to tell me?" She scoffed. "I don't have time for this. I've had a really shitty morning."

"What's wrong—"

"Really, Cameron? Or did you just forget the video that Thatcher splashed all over social media?" Hurt burned in her eyes.

Fuck.

"I didn't... I mean, of course I hadn't..." But I had. I'd been so preoccupied I'd forgotten all about it. There had been weight conditioning, then practice, and my head was all over the place after the weekend. *Way to go jackass.* But now she mentioned it, I noticed the stares, the low rumble of whispers from a group of kids passing.

"What the fuck are you looking at?" I snapped, feeling my muscles lock.

"Cameron, don't." Hailee's warning barely penetrated the red mist descending over me.

"Surprised he wants Thatcher's slut—"

I was on the guy in a second. The air *whooshed* from his lungs as his back hit the wall, the sound reverberating around us. "What the fuck did you say?" My fingers tightened around his throat, the blood draining from his face.

"I... I..." The kid spluttered.

"Cameron, this isn't helping." Hailee moved into my periphery.

"You think you can talk about her like that?"

"Just stop." The sheer desperation in Hailee's voice made me loosen my grip and the guy slid down the wall, coughing and spluttering.

"Get the fuck out of here," I rasped, my eyes fixed on Hailee and not him.

He scurried away and I exhaled a long breath. "It's been like that all morning?"

Hailee stared at me as if she didn't recognize me and my chest squeezed.

"What was that?" She seethed. "I don't need you to protect me, Cameron. I was doing just fine without—"

"Hailee, please." I closed the distance between us, crowding her against the wall, and caged her in with my hands either side of her head. "I'm sorry, okay? I just—" Fuck. I was screwing everything up. But I couldn't think straight.

"I need to go." Hailee let out an exasperated breath, her shoulders sagging with defeat. I wanted to say something to fix it, to fix us, but she wasn't the only one broken anymore. And when I tried to speak, nothing but a heavy sigh escaped my lips.

"I'll see you around, Cameron." She gave me a weak smile and slipped out from between me and the wall, disappearing through the swinging doors, and all I could do was watch.

As THE WEEK WENT ON, things only got worse. Jase and I could barely be in the same room together without the tension reaching boiling point. Asher didn't know whose side to take or why he was even taking sides in the first place. And I wanted to kill someone every time I heard them mention the video of Hailee. Thankfully, shutting that shit down was the one thing we could agree on, and between us we'd quashed any mention of the video in the halls at school.

"Good morning." Dad breezed into the kitchen.

"Hey." I stirred the spoon through my cereal with little enthusiasm.

"Big game tomorrow?"

"I guess."

"Cameron, Son, everything is going to be ok—"

"I can't do this." I shoved the bowl away and stood up. "I can't pretend everything is fine; everything is not fucking fine."

"Son, look at me." Dad came to me, placing his hands on my shoulders. "We are going to get through this, Son, all of us. But what I need from you right now, what me and your mom both need, is for you to carry on like normal. Go to school, focus on football, and make us proud."

"But how can you..." The words died on the tip of my tongue. "I don't know how I'm supposed to do that, Dad, not when she's—"

"Ssh, Son, ssh." He pulled me into a hug, holding me tight. "We'll get through this, I promise. I just need you to be strong. Can you do that for me?"

Too choked to reply, I gave him an imperceptible nod. Dad's hand squeezed the back of my neck, lingering, as if he needed this moment as much as I did. When he pulled away to look at me, I saw the fear in his eyes. It mirrored my own. "Business as usual though, for now, okay?"

I swallowed, the dry air rough against my throat. Dad brought his head to mine and inhaled painfully. He didn't say anything this time; he didn't have to. Nothing was okay and everything was on the line. And part of me was pissed they'd kept this from me. But they were the adults, the decision makers. They got to choose how and when to break the news to their kids. Of course, Xander was too young to understand. All he knew was his mommy got sick sometimes, she shouted and cried and then held him tight and apologized over and over. And it was messed up but part of me envied him. On some level, his innocence would protect him from things to come.

My stomach plummeted. "I need to go," I rushed out, stepping out of Dad's embrace.

"Cameron—"

"I'm fine, Dad. I just need some air." And I needed for him to not be looking at me like that. Like the worst had already happened. "I have practice after school, so I'll be late."

"Xander will be at Katie's. Me and your mom will be—"

"Yep, got it." I grabbed my bag and keys and waved him off. It was a dick move. But I didn't know how to deal with this, how to handle the anger and fear festering inside of me. I didn't know how he expected me to go to school and play football like everything was the same.

When really nothing was ever going to be the same again.

We were all gathered around Coach Hasson for his pre-game pep talk. The last twenty-four hours had been a daze, my mind occupied with only two things: Mom; and this crap with Jase, Thatcher, and Hailee. She hadn't looked twice at me all week and I felt lost. It was crazy, how the one girl I'd spent the best part of six years keeping at arm's length had become the one girl I wanted by my side more than anything. I'd contemplated trying to talk to her again, to explain, but deep down, I didn't know what I would say. And if she rejected me again, I wasn't sure I could handle that.

"Fourteen, your head screwed on right, Son?"

"Sure, Coach." My helmet hung in my hand as I nodded.

"St. Odell have some big players. Keep your eyes open and your head down, you hear me?"

A round of grunts filled the locker room. "This is the one, ladies. We win this and there's no stopping us. We're the ones to catch, the ones to beat." His steely eyes ran over each one of us. "Gather in, Raiders on one."

The locker room electrified as we prepared to run out onto the field. I focused on the huge blue and white 'R' painted beside the door; our lucky charm, a reminder of who we were and where we were going.

"Hey," Jase came up beside me after the circle broke up. "You good?" It was the first time he'd tried to talk to me outside of practice in three days.

"If you're worried I won't get the job done," I ground out. "I will."

"Chase." He snagged my wrist and I glanced back at him. "Come on, that's not..." A heavy sigh escaped his lips. "This shit between us, it doesn't feel right."

"Yeah, well, a lot isn't right anymore." I shrugged him off and joined my teammates as we poured onto the field under the bright Friday night lights, silently praying I could make it through the next hour.

35

Hailee

"I CAN'T BELIEVE I let you talk me into this," I whisper-hissed at Flick as we sat wedged in between a sea of blue and white.

"Call it research." She flashed me a droll smile.

"More like a slow and painful death."

"Really, Hails? You're telling me not even a tiny part of you wants to be here to cheer him on?" Her brow rose, her expression dubious.

"Cheer who on?"

She gave me a knowing smirk. "If you think for one second that I believe this thing between you and,"—my best friend leaned in closer making sure no one around us could hear, not that anyone could over the simmering noise —"*Fourteen* is over, then you're more foolish than I... oh, here they come."

Imagine Dragons blasted over the PA system, whipping the crowd into a frenzy. Only it didn't spark the adrenaline in my veins the way it had before. Not when I'd spent the last week trying to avoid my peers, which was hard when you spent almost seven hours of the day with them. As if that wasn't enough, the atmosphere at home was toxic. And Cameron had barely looked at me all week. So sitting in amongst four-thousand Raider fans, cheering the team onto victory, wasn't exactly my idea of escaping all the shit going on in my life.

But Flick was nothing if not persistent, and if I pretended really hard and tried to avoid searching out Cameron across the field, I could kind of convince myself I was here for research purposes only.

Well, almost.

Going into the fourth quarter, the game was tied. It had been hard to watch. Something was wrong in the Raiders camp, everyone felt it. My step-brother was pissed, yelling at his teammates every time they fumbled the ball or didn't make the play, and Coach Hasson looked ready to blow a gasket on more than one occasion.

"This should have been a walk in the park for them," Flick grumbled beside me. She'd really found her stride as the team's latest fan, the blue and white ball cap sitting proudly on her head. "Come on," she yelled as our defense took down one of the St. Odell Saints offense; the crowd responding with a ferocious roar.

The players switched, my eyes tracking number fourteen as he jogged onto the field, moving into position. Jason yelled the play, and there seemed to be a collective intake of breath around the stadium as he hiked the ball to Cameron who took off down left field, right under its trajectory. The crowd was enraptured, a crackle of anticipation in the air, as he hooked his hand up ready to receive the ball. It was a good pass, an even better catch, and the crowd went wild, the noise deafening.

"Go, go," Flick yelled, her fingernails digging into my arm so hard I felt sure they might draw blood.

But I didn't cheer, I couldn't. My eyes were too focused on Cameron, the way he cut through the air, his strong legs eating up the yard markers. Thirty... twenty... ten.

"Oh God," my best friend breathed as the world slowed down. A Saints lineman appeared out of nowhere, set on a collision course with Cameron.

"Flick," my voice quivered as I watched, along with the rest of the crowd, as the huge defensive player ploughed into Cameron, knocking him into the air. His body sailed backward and he landed hard. The whole place winced, the four-thousand strong hiss of breath making my hair stand on end, nervous energy churning in my stomach.

It wasn't my first game. I'd seen other players take a hit. Watched as bodies were strewn across the field like rag dolls, but I'd never *felt* the impact before.

"Flick." My voice no longer sounded like my own as I clutched onto my friend while watching players swarm Cameron's lifeless body.

"He's fine," Flick said, her voice catching. "He'll be fine. Players take hits like that all the time."

But he didn't look fine.

He didn't get up and shake it off the way players usually did. He just lay there, unmoving.

Deathly still.

Dread washed over me, sending my heart into meltdown as it crashed violently against my chest. Game officials were on the field now, attending to Cameron, who still hadn't moved. *Why isn't he moving?* Jason ripped off his helmet and began to pace beside his best friend, dragging a hand through his damp hair, back and forth, over and over, while Asher looked on with the rest of their teammates.

"Get up," I breathed.

Why isn't he getting up?

After what felt like an eternity, Cameron slowly sat up and the entire stadium took that first breath with him. "Thank God," I gasped, barely able to get the words out over the lump in my throat.

Two officials helped Cameron to his feet, and Jason and Asher flanked his side as they ushered him to the team's area on the sideline. A slow round of applause built around the bleachers until everyone was on their feet clapping for their beloved number fourteen.

Play quickly resumed, as if my world hadn't almost ended, and the Saints took their offensive position. But I was too busy watching Cameron. He'd taken his helmet off now, his head hung low as one of the assistant coaches and the medical staff checked him over.

"Something's wrong," I said reaching for Flick when he leaped up throwing his helmet down and began to walk away. Jason went after him, the two of them locked in a battle of wills as Cameron glared at him and then mouthed something I couldn't decipher, my distance making it too difficult to read his lips.

"Is he...?" Flick swallowed her words as we both watched Cameron stalk off the field without so much as a backward glance.

"He left," I said, stating the obvious, feeling my stomach sink into oblivion. "He just left."

"Maybe you should go after him," Flick suggested.

"What?" I blinked at her. I couldn't think straight. Something didn't feel right. He'd been hurt, yes, but he'd seemed okay walking off the field, so what the hell had happened in those few minutes between him sitting down and storming off?

And then it hit me.

His mom.

Oh God, what if something had happened with his mom?

He'd been off his game all night; fumbling passes and misreading plays. Even a rookie spectator like me could see Cameron's head wasn't in it.

"There's only a few minutes left on the clock." Flick nudged me. "If you sneak out now, you'll miss the crush. He's probably in the locker room."

"Flick, I can't just..." She gave me a pointed look and I shook my head a little, hardly able to believe the next words out of my mouth.

"You'll be okay?" I asked.

A wry smile tugged at her lips. "Please, I was born for this." She tipped the bill of her cap. "Besides, I want to see them stick it to the Saints."

"Okay." I inhaled deeply. Was I really about to try and break into the Raiders' locker room?

Yes, yes, I was.

Because if Cameron was hurting, I wanted to be there for him. I wanted to comfort him the way he'd comforted me.

With a small nod, I apologized to the people on our row as I squeezed my way to the end. By the time I reached the bottom of the bleachers I was breathless and a little disoriented, but I quickly found my bearings and slipped into the stadium, making my way around the other side to where the locker rooms were. The crowd erupted overhead, the vibrations echoing throughout the place, making my pulse spike. From the ferocity of the roar, I knew the Raiders had scored, even before the PA system made the announcement.

When I finally reached the blue doors, I paused. I couldn't just burst in there. What if Cameron was showering? Or receiving medical attention?

What if he didn't want to see me?

Suddenly feeling way out of my depth, I leaned against the wall right opposite the doors. The game would be over in a couple of minutes which meant it wouldn't be long before the rest of the team would be in there.

"Excuse me, miss." A security guard approached me. "You can't be down here."

"I... hmm, I'm Hailee Raine." Recognition flashed in his eyes, but he let me finish. "Jason Ford's step-sister. I need to see him." It was the first thing that came into my mind.

"Well, of course." He smiled warmly at the mention of Jason. "Your brother played a great game tonight. Go Raiders." His eyes lit up as he fist-pumped the air. Realizing his momentary slip, he cleared his throat, his professional mask sliding back in place. "You can't go back there, but I'd be happy to let him know you're waiting out here."

Shit, that wasn't what I wanted.

"Thank you."

He nodded politely before slipping through the off-limits doors. I sank down on the cold floor, drawing my knees up. I should have snuck inside before the team came back. But it was too late now. I'd have to wait.

And I'd just have to hope that when he appeared, Cameron would talk to me.

SITTING THERE on the hard floor, I learned something new about football players—they liked to take their damn time in the showers. Thirty-five minutes after the stadium emptied, the players finally began to trickle out, hardly paying me any attention, too focused on whatever party they were heading to, no doubt. But when Asher and Jason appeared, I jumped to my feet and stepped forward.

"Hails, what a surprise." Ash gave me an easy smile, but I didn't miss the tightness around his eyes.

"I, hmm..." This wasn't awkward at all. "I came to see if—"

"He's gone." Jase's voice was cold, his eyes hard as they studied me. But surprisingly, for once, I didn't feel like his contempt was aimed at me.

"Gone?" I choked out.

But I'd been waiting here above forty minutes. Unless... crap. Cameron must have come back here, grabbed his things, and left the stadium immediately. In which case, I'd just missed him.

My stomach sank.

"So I'll let you guys talk." Asher gave me a nod before throwing his bag over his shoulder and addressing Jason. "Call me later if you want to hang." He took off down the long hall, and Jason let out a heavy sigh, moving to lean against the wall beside the door right opposite me.

"I never thought I'd be here." He broke the silence.

"You and me both." One of my shoulders lifted in a small shrug as I kicked my foot against the floor.

"I've never seen him like that, not in all the years I've known him. It's like he wasn't even on the field..."

"I think something is wrong."

"Wrong?"

"Yeah." I gulped wondering how much I should tell him. "With his mom."

"She has depression or some shit. I think having Xander screwed her up."

"Jason," I scolded, wishing I knew what had happened to him to make him so mean. "It's more than that. Maybe if you weren't so..." I let the words die on my tongue. I wasn't here to argue with him. I just wanted to be there for Cameron.

"Go on, say it. You think I'm too invested in football to see what's really going on here."

"Aren't you?" I clipped out.

"I... fuck." Jason's expression hardened but then softened when he let out an exasperated breath. "Something is really happening with his mom?"

I nodded. "I think so. He told me some things."

"What things?" That got his attention.

I pressed my lips together in defiance. It wasn't for me to reveal Cameron's secrets.

"He never said anything to me," Jason added when I didn't offer an explanation.

"Are you sure? Maybe he was trying to tell you all along and you just weren't listening?" My voice rose, the tension between us rising with it.

He dragged a hand through his unruly brown hair, his eyes darkening. "You should go after him."

"Excuse me?"

"Don't think this means I'm cool with the two of you. I'm not. But if what you say is true, Chase needs someone right now, and I'm probably the last person he wants to see."

"Jason," I sighed. "You're his best friend."

"A pretty shit one at that," he grumbled.

I was stunned speechless. Never once, had I heard Jason own up to his shortcomings. He was always so arrogant and cold. Infallible. Yet, he looked completely lost tonight; the fire in his eyes extinguished to nothing more than a dying flame.

"He'll come around," I said without doubt. Because the bond between the three of them exceeded right and wrong, good and bad. They were brothers. Bound together by invisible threads I would never truly understand.

"Just tell him I'm sorry," he said, and something passed between us. A mutual understanding I never thought we'd have. "Can you do that for me?"

Too choked to reply, I nodded.

"And Hailee?" He wasn't done. "What Thatcher did; it went too far, and for that, I am sorry."

I gaped at him unsure I was hearing correctly. This would forever go down as one of the most surreal moments of my life.

But I'd take it.

If it finally meant not being on the opposite side of the line from Jason, I'd take it.

FLICK AGREED to drop me off at Cameron's house. The ride over was quiet. I was too lost in my thoughts to really answer any of her questions. And there were many. I was thinking about the strange conversation with Jason. Distracted by the apprehension churning through my stomach.

Eventually though, she'd shut up and accepted silence as the soundtrack for the short journey.

"Are you sure about this?" Flick finally said as we pulled up outside his house.

"No, but I have a really bad feeling." Players didn't just storm off the field without good reason, not Raiders. And especially not star wide receivers.

"Should I wait..."

"No," I said. "I've got this." Besides, if the worst-case scenario became reality, and Cameron slammed the door in my face, I wouldn't want anyone to witness it.

"Okay, then, go get 'em, tiger." Flick reached over and squeezed my hand, offering me a reassuring smile. I climbed out and walked up to the Chases' door. The house was blanketed in darkness, no sign of life. Cameron's truck was parked in the driveway, but his dad's car was missing. I didn't know whether that was a good sign or not.

Taking a deep breath, I glanced back at Flick who gave me a thumbs up before pulling off and disappearing into the inky night.

"You can do this," I whispered to myself. But as I went to knock, I realized the door was ajar. "Cameron?" Ducking inside, I was greeted with silence.

"Cameron?" Blood pounded between my ears. It was quiet, the place steeped in darkness. But the door had been open. "Hello?" I called out again only to be greeted with sound of my own heart beating wildly against my chest.

Slipping my hand into my pocket, I clutched my cell phone, just in case, as I moved further into the house. "Cameron?" It was a whisper-hiss this time. But the place seemed deserted. And then I heard it. A gentle murmur. Racing down the hallway, I burst into the kitchen and skidded to a halt. "Cameron?"

He was crumpled on the floor against one of the counters, his face buried in his hands. Slowly he lifted his eyes to me and what I saw there in his gray-blue eyes broke my heart. Cameron Chase, wide receiver for the Raiders, was in pieces. His eyes were red and swollen, void of their usual sparkle, and his fists were bloody and bruised.

"Cameron." I dropped to my knees and scooted closer to him, taking his hands in mine, inspecting his injuries. "What did you do?"

"It doesn't matter," his voice cracked as he dropped his head back against the cabinet.

"These need cleaning, do you have a first aid kit?"

His eyes shuttered as he drew in a ragged breath that I felt all the way down to my soul. I wanted to comfort him, to wrap my arms around him and ask him what was wrong, but something held me back.

"Cameron, a first aid kit?" I said, distracting him, and myself.

"I, uh, yeah, there's one in the cabinet over there." He flicked his head, his eyes locking on mine. The intensity in his gaze almost too much to bear.

I found the first aid kit and hurried back to him, kneeling between his outstretched legs. "This might sting." He hissed as I wiped the blood from his knuckles, the skin angry and shredded. "I hope the other guy came out worse."

"I'm pretty sure the wall won," he said flatly, and my stomach dipped.

"Okay, next one." Silence descended over us as I continued to clean his wounds. Cameron didn't speak; he didn't need to—his pain swirled around us like an angry storm. When I was done, I set aside the first aid kit and gently brushed his jaw with my fingers. "Want to talk about it?" I asked quietly, letting my words settle between us.

"Talk?" he scoffed. "I'm not sure there's anything to say anymore, Hailee."

My chest constricted. "Try me," I said with an air of defiance. Because right now, Cameron needed someone. And I wanted to be that person for him.

I wanted to take away his pain and make it my own.

36

Cameron

"WHAT ARE YOU DOING HERE, HAILEE?" It was a shitty thing to say when she'd come after me, cleaned my busted knuckles and asked for nothing in return. But now she was asking, and I wasn't sure I had answers.

Everything was falling apart around me. All week, I'd barely managed to stay afloat, to keep my head above water. And then tonight, on the field, something had snapped.

I'd snapped.

"I..." She wrung her hands together, her eyes darting everywhere but at me. She was nervous, it oozed from her, hitting me like a brick wall. "I was worried about you." It came out softly as she finally settled her eyes on me. "You got hit and I didn't know if... and then I saw you storm out of there and I realized I never asked you how your mom was, and I thought—"

"She has a brain tumor." My chest tightened, the truth squeezing my heart like a vise. I sucked in, trying to get more air into my lungs. I hadn't meant to spew the words but seeing Hailee rush into the kitchen, the concern shining in her eyes, it broke something in me. Or maybe it fixed something.

I didn't know anything anymore.

"A brain tumor?" She paled. "Cameron, I'm so sorry." Throwing her arms around me, Hailee pulled me into her embrace, and I went. I went so fucking easily I knew if anyone could see me they would think 'what a pussy'. But I didn't care. Ever since sitting opposite Mom and Dad five nights ago, as they tried to explain to me what was happening, I'd been walking around in a daze. Unable to process the truth, my new reality.

Mom wasn't depressed, she had a tumor. For four years, we'd watch her lose herself to the mood swings, the highs and lows, and crippling lethargy. But it wasn't her mind at all. It was some invader, a four-inch tumor compressing her frontal lobe.

Hailee's hands rubbed my back as I clung to her, fighting the tears that had been stuck in my throat since Saturday. "Cameron," her voice was quiet. "Look at me." She gently pushed me away, holding me at arm's length. "I'm here. Tell me what you need. Tell me what I can do."

The relief was immediate, crashing over me like an unstoppable tidal wave. All week I'd wanted to talk to Hailee, to confide in her. To just *be* with her. It had been like wading through quicksand every day being pulled further and further under, threatening to be drowned in my anger and grief and confusion.

I shouldn't have been at school and I definitely shouldn't have been on that football field tonight. But Mom and Dad had made me promise I would carry on as normal.

Normal.

That was a fucking joke if I ever heard one.

They wanted me to be strong, to carry the burden and not crumple. But I wasn't strong; I was breaking at the seams. Slowly coming undone. And wrapped in the arms of the girl who had owned my heart for longer than I cared to admit, I finally let myself fall apart.

"Be with me, Hailee," I choked out the words from a throat that was raw from all the tears I'd cried. "Just be with me."

"I can do that." She gave me an uncertain smile, but it was enough.

In that moment, it was everything.

With no more words, I stood up, pulling Hailee with me and led her up to my room. Mom and Dad were on a rare night out. Doctor Kravis had arranged her surgery for next week, so Dad was insistent they spend some time together. Just in case.

Just in case.

Fuck.

"Cameron?" Hailee asked, as I froze up.

"Sorry, I'm—"

"Hey, it's okay." She squeezed my hand before moving ahead of me, pulling me gently toward my room. When we reached the door, Hailee didn't hesitate to go inside. The air was thick around us, the events of the last couple of weeks weighing heavily on us both.

"Cameron," she said releasing my hand and turning to me. "I—"

"Come here." I snagged her hand, tugging her into me until I was staring down into her honey-brown eyes which glittered with nothing but compassion and understanding. "You have no idea what you being here means to me."

"I went to the locker room," she admitted. "Right after you left the field. I went to find you. But you'd already left."

"I needed space. When that blocker tackled me, it was like everything slammed into me. Mom. This thing with you and Thatcher. Xander. It sounds dumb but my life flashed before my eyes and I..." I swallowed. It sounded crazy. But Hailee didn't look freaked out.

Not even a little bit.

"It's not dumb," she said. "You were hurt and given the circumstances... it's understandable, Cameron. You're under a lot of pressure and—"

"But that's just it." I ran a brisk hand over my head. "I'm under pressure because of football, because of the team. Even with everything that's going on, my mom and dad were so insistent I keep playing, that I go on like nothing has changed when, really, everything has changed. My mom needs surgery, she could..." Pain overwhelmed me and my eyes shuttered. Hailee's fingers twisted into my polo shirt as she leaned closer.

"Die," I forced out the word. "She could die, Hailee." My head dropped to hers, the weight of the truth almost breaking me.

"I'm sorry. I'm so, so sorry," she repeated over and over, her face brushing mine as she gently kissed the corner of my mouth. She couldn't fix this, no one could. We had to hand that responsibility over to the doctors at Rixon General and hope to God—*pray*—they could remove the tumor and give us back Mom in one piece.

I didn't realize I was crying again until Hailee kissed my cheeks. Fuck, I didn't cry. I was Cameron Chase, one of the best wide receivers in the state. I went up against some of the biggest, toughest defensive players in the country. But Hailee understood; on some level she got it. And I hadn't realized how badly I needed someone until this moment.

"Ssh," she whispered, her voice a gentle caress. "I'm here, Cameron. I'm right here." Hailee traced my lips with her fingers, chasing them with her mouth until we were kissing. Small uncertain kisses. My hands slid into her hair so I could tilt her face, deepening the kiss, sliding my tongue against hers, needing to be closer.

Needing more.

She kissed me fiercely, demanding the same back, pulling me closer, fitting our bodies together until we were a tangle of kisses and limbs, sighs and touches. I still felt hollow, the agony of what was to come heavy in the pit of my stomach, but Hailee filled some of the void. Each stroke of her tongue a patch on the hole in my heart; each touch of her lips a band aid for my grief.

"Is this okay?" she murmured against my lips, her hands dipping under my t-shirt and running over my warm skin. I nodded, too worked up to talk. I needed this.

I needed her.

More than I would have ever thought possible.

Hailee painted lazy patterns over my skin, taking her time to trace my abs. It was like the first time touching her again; my head clouded with too many emotions, too many thoughts. My body wanted her, my dick straining painfully against my jeans, but she deserved me to be one hundred percent in the moment. "Hailee, wait..." I couldn't believe I was saying the words.

She eased back, staring up at me, and her expression softened. "It's okay."

Taking my hand in hers, she tugged me over to the bed and shoved me down gently. I landed with a *thud*, falling back on my elbows. Hailee stripped slowly out of her clothes. Her sweater went first, revealing an expanse of creamy skin, followed by her jeans.

"Fuck, you're beautiful," I whispered, tracing my eyes over every inch of her. She dropped to her knees and reached for the button of my jeans, before tugging them down my legs, nudging me to lift my feet so she could remove them completely.

My eyes drank her in, the soft curve of her lips, the flush to her skin, as she realized I was commando.

"Do you have a condom?" she asked, and I nodded to the nightstand, my throat dry and my skin hot. Hailee got up and went over to the drawer, retrieving a foil packet, while I yanked off my t-shirt. Then she unhooked her bra and let it drop to the floor, before slipping her fingers into her panties and pushing them over her hips.

"Come here," I said, unable to disguise the sheer lust in my voice. She came willingly, climbing over my legs so she was straddling me. With one hand pressed into the small of her back, I buried the other one deep in her hair, angling her face to mine as I captured her lips. Hot, wet, desperate kisses. Hailee moaned my name and my dick twitched. I wanted to worship her, to spend my time acquainting myself with every dip and curve of her amazing body. But I couldn't wait. Not tonight. Not now.

"I need you," I whispered against her lips.

"So take me," she replied, gazing at me with lust and love.

Love?

The emotion slammed into me, taking my breath away.

Did Hailee really love me?

Shit, it wasn't possible.

Was it?

More importantly, did I love her?

Who the fuck was I kidding, I didn't love her.

So why the hell was my throat dry and my heart beating so hard I thought it might burst from my chest?

Hailee leaned back slightly, tearing the wrapper and rolling the condom over me. My head dropped back on a groan. Fuck, her touch was like kryptonite. But it was nothing compared to the way she felt sinking down on me.

"Cam," she breathed out, her body a quivering mess.

"I know, baby, I know." I curled my hand around the back of her neck gathering her hair in my fist, holding her still, needing to savor the moment. The feel of her tight around me, her skin against mine, her curves molded around my hard lines. But Hailee was impatient, rocking against me, the intensity of the position making us both groan.

"I need to move," she cried, her eyes glazed, skin flushed.

My hand dug into the swell of her hip as she began ride me, working me over and over, pushing away all the darkness until there was nothing but us. The sounds of our bodies moving against one another, our harsh breaths and quiet moans.

Feeling the familiar tingle at the base of my spine, I began to thrust upward, meeting Hailee every time she rolled her hips. "Harder Cam, harder..." she rasped, her nails raking down my chest, the sting taking me closer to the edge. Reminding me that I was alive. That I was here in this moment and that I had to fight.

For my mom.

My future.

My family.

Hailee's cries built, her pace quickening as she began to lose control. Pulling her hair gently to make her back bow, I dipped my head, sucking the hollow of her neck, nipping at the skin there, pushing her closer to the edge.

"Cam—" My name fell from her lips as she clenched around me, pulling me further into her body, squeezing me so tight I saw stars. I wanted to stay there. To live in this bubble and never leave. But her walls clenched me again, and I fell right over the edge with her, holding her close as my muscles locked up and I came hard.

I knew I'd have to leave eventually, but right there, in that moment, I never wanted to let go.

37

Hailee

"GOOD MORNING." The deep timbre of Cameron's voice sent shivers rippling up my spine.

"Morning." I peeked an eye open, fighting a smile as I stretched my body, my legs brushing his making my tummy clench.

"I was almost scared to wake up, in case last night was a dream." His eyes lit up with emotion.

Emotion I didn't want to get too lost in. Not yet. Not when there was still so much going on around us.

"Come here." Cameron dragged my body closer to his, igniting a fire in my belly. "I could get used to this," he said.

Burying my face in the crook of his shoulder, I let myself enjoy the moment. I was in Cameron's bed... again. And it didn't feel awkward or strange or like I was making a dreadful mistake, one I'd regret later.

It felt right.

"Thank you." His voice coaxed me out of his chest, and I gazed up at him. "For coming after me last night, thank you." Cameron touched his head to mine, inhaling a shaky breath.

"I wouldn't be anywhere else." Looping my arm around his shoulder, I breathed him in, the lingering scent of sex flooding my senses. "Should we expect a visit from Xander any minute?" I asked.

"He had a sleepover at Katie's, but I should probably warn you my mom and dad are home." My eyes widened and he smiled against my cheek. "Is that going to be a problem?"

"I don't know; you tell me."

"I want them to meet you," he blurted out, gently pulling away to see my reaction.

"I already met your—"

"I mean officially, Hailee. I want to introduce you to them as my girl."

His girl?

"Don't look so worried. This is a good thing." Cameron stole a kiss from me while I was still reeling from his words.

His girl.

He'd called me his girl.

"But Jason—"

"Will have to get over it. Life's too short, Sunshine. I realize that now. You never know what's around the corner and I'm not about to waste another second worrying about what Jase might or might not say because I'm in love with his step-sister."

"In love..." I choked out. "You *love* me?" My heart was going to burst out of my chest. He looked so calm, so normal, and I was having an internal conniption.

Cameron's lip curved, breaking into a wide smile as he chuckled. "You hadn't figured it out by now? I am completely,"—he kissed me—"and utterly." Kiss. "Ass over elbow in love with you, Hailee Raine."

"Oh."

Oh.

His brow quirked up. "I don't think I've ever seen you at a loss for words. I don't know whether to be flattered or mildly concerned." Amusement danced in his eyes.

"I- I think I need a minute."

"Should I..." He thumbed to the door and began to untangle himself from the sheets, but I wrapped myself around him, dragging him back to the bed. "Wait."

"Wait?" he smirked. "Is there something *you* want to tell *me*?"

"Cameron," I chided. "You can't just spring something like this on me and expect me to be okay with it."

"Well, I was kind of hoping you might feel the same..." He left the words hanging between us as he dipped his head, capturing my lips again. Rolling me onto my back, Cameron pressed the lines of our bodies together, erasing any space—and doubts—from between us.

"I—"

A knock at his door startled us both and Cameron froze above me. "Yeah?"

"It's just me, Son. Mom wants to know if you're hungry?"

Heat blazed in his eyes as he hardened between my legs. "I, uh, yeah sure, Dad." His voice cracked with lust. "But tell her to make an extra plate."

My cheeks burned as I silently shook my head with disbelief.

"I see ..." His dad cleared his throat. "Well, we'll... hmm, we'll see you both soon."

"Sure thing, Dad."

"Cameron," I hissed the second his dad's footsteps grew quiet. "What the hell?"

"Time to meet my parents." He winked, dropping a kiss on my head before clambering off me and the bed, not bothering to even try and hide his erection.

I wanted to be mad at him, to argue that this was moving too fast, that he was completely crazy. But as I watched him pull on his jeans and a clean tee, I couldn't find it in me to protest. Because he loved me.

Cameron Chase loved me.

Ten minutes later, I was having second thoughts.

"I'm not sure this is—"

"Hailee, stop." Cameron pulled me into his arms. "They're going to love you." He gazed down at me with such intensity I felt my throat constrict.

"Yeah, but—"

"No buts. I need you, okay?" His expression softened. "Please, do this, for me."

Arching my brow, I let out an exasperated breath. "You're not playing fair." I wanted to be there for him, I did. But it wasn't fair to use his situation against me.

Damn him.

"I told you once before, I'm a Raider. And Raiders never quit. Even if we have to play a little dirty sometimes." Something flashed across his face, but it was gone before I could decipher what it was. "Ready?" he added, and I gave a little shrug. "I guess."

Cameron led me into his kitchen, his hand firmly around mine. "Mornin'," he said without a care in the world. "Hailee's going to stay for breakfast. I hope that's okay?"

A woman with short dark hair and Cameron's gray-blue eyes beamed at us. "Of course, it's okay, sweetheart. Hailee, I'm Karen, Cameron's mom, it's lovely to meet you." She came over and hugged me. "And under better circumstances this time. I'm sorry you had to see that, sweetie," she whispered, and I swallowed over the lump in my throat.

"It's nice to meet you too," I said as Cameron wrapped his arm around me, guiding me over to one of the stools.

"Hailee," Mr. Chase said around a wary smile. "It's nice to see you again."

"Hello." I gave him a small wave as I sat down while Cameron helped his mom get some extra plates from the cabinet.

"How was the game last night?"

Cameron stiffened but quickly recovered. "Actually, I wanted to talk to you about that." He came and sat down beside me, taking my hand in his, as if he needed the contact. "While Mom is going through her… treatment," the word got stuck in his throat. "I think I should quit the team."

Mrs. Chase gasped, the sound almost painful, while Mr. Chase's brows pulled tight as he shifted uncomfortably on the stool. "Son, there is no need to—"

"Just hear me out, Dad, please." Cameron ran a brisk hand down his face.

"This week has been hell for me; my game was off. I'm angry, confused... it isn't what I need right now or what the team needs. I want to be here for you guys, for Xander. I *need* to be here." With the last word his chest heaved as if a weight had been lifted.

"But, Son, the scouts—"

"Don't matter, Dad. This is more important. Mom is more important."

I felt like an outsider. This was a conversation Cameron should have had in private with his parents, but then he was squeezing my hand back, his eyes settling on my stunned face. He gave me a smile so vulnerable yet reassuring at the same time, I realized that, despite my reservations, he needed me here. In some bizarre turn of events, I'd given Cameron the strength he needed to vocalize his thoughts to his parents.

"Oh, sweetheart, come here." Mrs. Chase's arms looped around her son's neck as she hugged him from behind, sniffling into his shoulder. "I'm sorry. I'm so, so sorry."

I swallowed back my own tears. This was a family; three people just trying to do their best with the shitty hand they had been dealt. Cameron's parents didn't push him to keep up football and school because of expectation or pressure, they did it for him. Because they knew what football and his future meant to him. But it was a burden too heavy for Cameron to carry. Last night was proof of that.

"You don't have anything to be sorry for, Mom. I've made my decision. I'll talk to Coach first thing Monday."

Mr. Chase was quiet, his eyes studying his son. "Don't make any rash decisions okay, Son? This is your future. We'll get through this, the same way we get through everything—together. If you need a break, fine. But it doesn't have to be the end of football. Not when you're so close to everything you've worked so hard for."

Father and son shared a long look, Cameron's fingers still firmly entwined with my own. Eventually, Mrs. Chase broke the stifling silence by placing plates of pancakes and bacon in front of us. "I hope you're hungry," she said, her expression warm as she watched me and her son.

"Mom. What's wrong?" Cameron asked, noticing her watching us.

"Nothing, sweetheart. I'm just glad you have Hailee." She swallowed, a mask of sadness falling over her as she settled her gaze on me. "I'm glad my son has you."

I nodded, too choked up to reply.

"I'm sorry." Mrs. Chase smiled. "I've made all this food and now everyone is sad."

"It's fine, Mom. Let's eat, I'm starving." He gave me a discreet wink and motioned for me to dig in.

And I did.

Because something told me no matter how scared this family was; right now, they needed to take comfort in the little things.

"Your parents seem nice," I said when we were back in the privacy of Cameron's bedroom.

"They're good people," he said, flopping down on the bed, pulling me with him. We landed with a soft *thud*, my body lying atop the length of his.

"They were cool about me being here this morning."

He shrugged. "I guess I didn't give them much warning, but I'm eighteen, Hailee. It's not like we're kids." Cameron brushed his nose against mine, kissing me softly. "I'm glad you were there with me. I've been trying to find the words all week, but every time I've tried to broach the subject with them, I just couldn't do it."

"You really want to quit the team?"

"Yes... no, I don't know." He pressed his head back against the pillows, eyes fixed on the ceiling as he let out a ragged breath. "It's just so much pressure, you know? If I can't pull it together, I'm a liability—"

"Yeah, but you don't need to quit. Coach will understand if you need some time out, they all will."

"Maybe." His eyes flicked back to mine. "Or maybe I've just realized there's more to life."

"You love football."

"I do." His eyes lit up. "But it isn't all I want. Not like Jas—" He stopped himself.

"It's okay, you can talk to me about this."

"It's always been his plan. We'd dominate Varsity together and then go to Penn, but everything's different now."

"Different?"

"Yeah," he smiled but it was full of sadness. My heart clenched for the guy I'd swore I wouldn't fall for and now I was in so deep I wasn't sure I'd ever find my way out.

And I was okay with that.

More than okay.

"There was a time when I wanted it, when I kept thinking, 'this is the month Mom will get better'. But she never did and with every episode my dreams moved further and further away until I was no longer sure they were mine anymore." Cameron paused, dragging his bottom lip into his teeth as if he was weighing up whether to say whatever was on his mind.

"What?" I pushed.

"And you happened."

"Me?"

"Yeah. That first day of semester, I saw you and it was like I was seeing you for the first time again."

"Cameron..." I ducked my head, my cheeks burning.

"Hey, don't hide from me, Hailee." His fingers slid under my jaw coaxing me back to him. "Don't ever hide."

"I just... this, us, it wasn't supposed to happen."

"But it did, and I meant what I said, the only thing I regret is that it didn't happen sooner." He tucked me into his chest, running his hand up and down my back, eliciting shivers up my spine.

"Cameron?"

"Yes, Sunshine?"

"Kiss me."

His hand glided up to my face, angling my head back so I could see his gray-blues glittering at me. He smiled warmly, setting off a legion of butterflies in my tummy, and said, "That I can do."

38

Cameron

I TUGGED at the collar of my shirt. It was a dark gray color, rolled up at the sleeves; worlds away from my usual football jersey or polo shirt. But I wanted tonight to be perfect which is why I'd called Flick asking her for some advice.

Taking a deep breath, I knocked on Hailee's door, praying to God she opened it and not her mom, or even worse Mr. Ford. It swung open and my heart skipped a beat. Hailee stood there in a denim skirt, a white t-shirt that scooped low on her chest, and wedged sneakers. Her dirty blonde hair was piled high on her head, her glasses keeping the loose strands off her face. It was simple, understated, but I'd never seen anything more beautiful.

"Hey," I finally said finding my voice. "I got you these." Thrusting the box of brownies at her, I rubbed the back of my neck.

"Have you been speaking to Flick again?" Her brow quirked up.

"Maybe." I smiled. "She mentioned you liked them when I came by... but we didn't get around to eating them."

Hailee's cheeks flushed a deep shade of red, her eyes darkening. I leaned in, unable to resist the pull, and kissed her cheek. "I missed you." I grazed my lips against her ear, and her fingers curled into my shirt, dragging me closer.

"It's only been a few hours." She turned her head slightly, her lips hovering over mine. Electricity crackled between us, the hairs on my arms standing to attention, along with other places. I was so gone for this girl, I might as well have handed over my heart and my balls in a neat little package and told her to give them back when she was done with them.

Stealing a quick kiss, I pulled away putting some distance between us. "We should probably get going, I made a reservation."

"You did?" Her mouth curved and I couldn't resist dipping my head to claim her lips again.

"You look beautiful, Sunshine."

"Cam..." Hailee sighed against my mouth, the soft noise a direct line to my dick. "Are you sure you don't just want to stay in?" Her arms looped around my neck.

I wanted nothing more than to take her up to her room and sink deep inside her, to lose myself in her, but I also wanted us to go out, to enjoy a night together before next week.

"We need this." I smiled against her. "Besides, I don't plan on letting you out of my sight tonight."

Hailee pulled back, frowning. "I can't stay out all night."

"Is your mom or Kent going have a problem with it?"

"Well, no, I don't think so, but—"

"Go and grab a bag, Sunshine, and I'll meet you in my truck."

"So bossy," she grumbled before turning on her heel and marching back up the stairs. But I didn't go to my truck. I waited. Unable to tear myself away from her even for a second.

When she came down the stairs a few minutes later, I pushed off the doorjamb and went to her. "Ready?"

She nodded. "Are you going to tell me where we're going?"

Hooking my arm around her waist, I kissed her head and said, "It's a surprise."

TEN MINUTES LATER, I pulled the truck into a parking spot and cut the engine.

"The Alley," Hailee said. "We're going to The Alley?"

"Yeah, is that okay?"

"Yeah, I mean, I love it here, but are you sure you want to be here?"

"What's wrong with here?"

"Nothing, it's nothing..." She pressed her lips together.

"Did I do the wrong thing? It's just Felicity said—"

"Felicity told you to bring me here?" Hailee stared at me with disbelief.

"Well, yeah. I wanted tonight to be perfect. She said you loved those brownies and that I should avoid wearing my football jersey and that you loved The Alley... so, here we are."

Her expression softened as she shuffled across the seat and leaned over to me. Cupping my face in her hands, Hailee kissed me. "It's perfect. I just didn't want you to feel uncomfortable."

That had my attention. "Why would I feel uncomfortable?" It was just bowling and a dinner. Nothing special.

"Because this is Switzerland."

"Switzerland?" Now I was the one gawking at her.

"Yeah." She chuckled. "In there you won't be Cameron Chase, wide receiver for the Raiders; you'll just be Cameron, my date."

"And that's a bad thing?" Because it sounded damn near perfect to me.

"Well, no, I just thought... it doesn't matter, it's silly."

"Hailee, stop. Nothing you could say or do is silly. Now tell me what's going on in that head of yours?"

"It's just you're used to hanging out at Bell's, or parties at Asher's house. This,"—her eyes flicked over to The Alley—"isn't exactly what you're used to." Hailee lowered her gaze and my chest tightened. She genuinely thought I gave two shits about where we were? We could have been in the school cafeteria surrounded by our nosy classmates and it wouldn't have mattered.

I stole another kiss from her before flashing her a smile. "Come on, or we'll be late."

"Late, but—" Her voice drowned out as I climbed out of the truck waiting for her.

"Ready?" I held out my hand as she came around to me, still frowning.

"What are you planning, Cameron Chase?"

"Why don't you come find out?"

Tate, the owner, met us inside. "Cameron, Hailee, glad you could make it. Your table is all set."

I glanced down at the girl beside me, grinning when I saw her dumbfounded expression. "Hmm, Tate," she said quietly. "What is happening right now? And how do the two of you know each other?" Hailee looked from him up at me and back again.

"My lips are sealed, Hailee, sorry." He gave me a knowing smile, leading us to the diner part of the building. I'd asked for a specific booth overlooking the river. The Alley might have been Hailee's Switzerland, but it didn't take long before people noticed us, whispering and pointing as we followed Tate, my hand on the small of Hailee's back.

"Everyone's staring," she whispered, her posture tense. I leaned forward, brushing the shell of her ear, and replied, "Let them look."

I had no problem with everyone knowing she was mine. In fact, if I didn't think she'd kick me in the balls, I would have kissed the crap out of her, giving them the show they were hoping for.

"I hope this is okay?" Tate said as we stopped at the last booth removing the handwritten 'reserved' sign. It was as private as it was going to get, but Flick had shot down my first suggestion of asking Tate for exclusive use of the place. 'Do you know Hailee at all?', she'd asked me with an air of amusement before proceeding to tell me I just needed to be myself—not Raider Cameron, but the guy underneath the bravado—and nothing else.

"It's great, thank you." I held out my hand and he shook it before leaving us to it.

Hailee stuttered, her eyes moving from the booth to me. "What is happening right now?"

"We're about to eat dinner and then I'm going to kick your very cute ass at bowling." I took her hand and gently nudged her into the booth, sliding in opposite her. "So, what's good here?" I picked up the menu.

"I can't believe you had Tate reserve us a table."

"It could have been worse. I could have booked out the whole place just for the two of us."

I'd expected to see her nose wrinkle at the obscene over-the-top idea, but it didn't. Instead, her pupils dilated, that sexy-as-fuck blush spreading up her neck. "Would you have wanted that?" I asked.

"Maybe." She chewed her bottom lip, desire simmering in her eyes.

My brow rose. "Yeah? Here?" I scanned the place quickly, imagining all the places I could lay her out and—

"Hailee?" A dark-haired guy approached the booth, his eyes darting between us.

"Hey, Toby." Her expression fell.

Toby.

My spine went rigid as I sat up straighter.

"Sorry, I didn't want to interrupt, I can see you're... busy." He swallowed thickly. "I just wanted to apologize for what happened. You didn't text me back and I..."

"You need to leave, now." I ground out, my fingers curled around the Formica table.

"Cameron," Hailee said gently. "It's okay. Toby, this is Cameron, my—"

"Her boyfriend." I locked eyes on him, sending him a silent message. Hailee's foot kicked me under the table and I jerked in my seat.

"Behave," she mouthed. "I'm sorry I didn't text you back, Toby, but it didn't feel right, not after..."

"Yeah, I get it." He ran a hand through his hair. "I just felt bad about what happened, and I wanted you to know I had no idea Thatcher was going to pull that shit. He might be my cousin but that was not cool."

"Are you done?" I said coolly.

Credit to him, the guy looked me right in the eye as he said, "Yeah, I'm done." His gaze slid back to Hailee. "And I'm sorry again. I guess I'll see you around."

She gave him a little nod and he left, and I breathed a huge fucking sigh of relief.

"You didn't have to be so rude." Hailee scolded, trying, and failing to keep the amusement out of her voice.

"Rude? That was me being polite, Sunshine."

"Cameron, come on..." She gave me a pointed look, but I wasn't about to waiver. Not on this.

"Hailee." I leaned forward, lowering my voice. "He took you to a party where you were drugged and..." The words lodged in my throat. "I'm *never* going to be okay with that." He was lucky I hadn't introduced my fist to his face.

"I know, I just... You did some pretty shitty things to me too, Cameron."

Her words cut like a knife and my eyes shuttered as I inhaled a deep breath. "You're never going let me forget, are you?" My stomach sank as I met her eyes once more, scared of what I might find there.

"I'm sure there are ways you can make it up to me." Lust dripped from her words and my eyes snapped to hers.

"Yeah?" I practically panted, and her smirk grew.

And just like that all thoughts of Toby and Thatcher evaporated.

An hour later, stuffed full of Alley burgers and milkshakes, we'd attracted quite the audience. But I only had eyes for the girl opposite me. With every question I asked, every graze of my fingers against hers, Hailee relaxed. We'd talked about everything: her mom, her dad, how she got into art, her plans for after graduation.

"So, Stamps is an art and design school?"

"Yeah," she said helping herself to a big spoonful of the sundae we'd decided to share. "It's part of the University of Michigan."

"You don't say." My heart picked up speed; a plan—albeit a crazy one—unfolding in my mind.

"What will you do if you decide not to play college football?" Hailee turned the spotlight on me.

"Honestly, I don't know. I've always liked numbers, so maybe business or finance or something."

"And you can do that just about anywhere," she said. "So you can stay local if your family needs you. Crap, I'm sorry. I didn't mean—"

"Hailee." I covered her hand with mine. "It's okay. I'm okay." Was I terrified about what next week would bring? Yes. But I had to trust the doctors knew what they were doing. And with Hailee by my side, everything seemed that much easier to process.

"Have you figured out what you're going to tell Coach?" She changed the subject.

"Not yet. But I can't think about the team until after the surgery."

Giving me a reassuring nod, Hailee smiled. "She'll be okay, Cameron."

"I hope so." I suddenly didn't feel hungry anymore. Because the reality was, I wasn't thinking past the surgery. The 'what ifs' or maybes. Because Hailee was right, Mom would be okay.

She had to be.

After beating me at bowling, twice, I drove Hailee back to my house. The tension between us was almost at breaking point. All night, Hailee had teased me with little kisses and subtle touches. I was surprised how tactile she was with me, given the constant stares and whispers aimed in our direction. But we were both too drunk on each other to care.

When I pulled into the driveway and cut the engine, Hailee turned to me. "Thank you, for tonight. It was perfect."

"No." I leaned over, capturing a strand of hair between my fingers. "You're perfect."

Hailee lowered her eyes, blushing. But I gently gripped her chin, forcing her to look at me. "Whatever happens next week, it won't change how I feel about you. I want you to know that."

"Cameron, I—"

"Wait, just hear me out, okay?" I needed to get this off my chest. "I might get angry and confused and I'll probably screw this up, but just know that I love you and I'm so fucking relieved I have you by my side going into this."

Hailee climbed across the console and onto my lap, slipping her legs over mine and looping her arms around my neck. "I'm not going anywhere. You should know by now, I don't break easily." She leaned in to kiss me, teasing me with her tongue.

"I never wanted to break you," I confessed. "I only wanted you to see me."

Pressing her head to mine, Hailee's eyes glowed with fierce possessiveness. "I see you, Cameron.

"I. See. You."

39

Hailee

"MAYBE THIS WASN'T such a good idea," I said as we sat in Cameron's truck in the school parking lot. He'd insisted on giving me a ride to school.

Twisting his body to me, he let out a long sigh. Kids had already started to notice us, and I knew it wouldn't be long before the entire school had heard, if they hadn't already after our date at The Alley last night.

"Hailee, look at me." My eyes slowly slid to his. "I love you. Nothing anyone does or says will change that."

Butterflies fluttered wildly in my stomach. I didn't think I'd ever get used to hearing him say those words. Even if I hadn't said them back yet.

A loud knock startled us, and Asher pressed his face up against Cameron's window. "Are you guys going to sit in there all morning?"

Cameron groaned. "I'm sorry." He mouthed at me, and I chuckled softly.

"Me and Fee are waiting."

That had me craning my head around Cameron to find Flick standing to Asher's side, looking like a deer caught in headlights. Shouldering the door, I climbed out of the truck and went around to meet my best friend.

"Hi," she said giving me a small smile. "This is... what is this exactly?"

I went to reply, but Cameron climbed out and wrapped his arms around me, pulling me back against his chest. "Me and Hailee are together now."

Flick grinned while Asher's eyes almost bugged out of his head. "Together, *together*? Or like fuck buddies together, because I thought—" His lips flattened at whatever Cameron was mouthing to him.

I glanced back at Cameron and he dipped his head, capturing my lips in a soft kiss. "I apologize now for anything that might come out of his mouth."

"I heard that," Asher grumbled.

"You were supposed to."

"Not that I'm not happy for you," he went on. "I am, but does Jase know about this?"

Cameron's arm tightened around me as he said, "It doesn't matter."

Asher looked past me to his best friend. "There is so much I want to say but, oh... speak of the devil."

We all turned in the direction he was looking to find Jason walking toward school with some of the guys from the team. As if he felt us watching, his eyes found us across the lawn, locking on me and Cameron. Everything slowed down: the stream of kids walking into the building, the incessant chatter and laughter, the oxygen filtering around my body. I'd known things would be awkward, but I hadn't expected it to feel like a new line was being drawn between us. I could practically feel the shift in the air, the invisible wall being erected between us. Me, Flick, Cameron, and Asher one side; and Jason on the other.

I shuddered at the realization.

"Hey," Cameron's voice anchored me back to him. "It'll be okay; he'll come around." He kissed my cheek.

Flick glanced at me nervously and I offered her a weak smile. But it was Asher who broke the stifling tension. "Well," he said. "I guess it's you and me, Fee, baby." He slung his arm around my best friend, who shot me a 'help' expression. A smile tugged at my mouth. It was a shame she had friend-zoned him for her mystery guy because despite Asher's manwhore tendencies, they made a seriously cute couple. But I had enough to worry about without getting involved in my best friend's love life.

"Are you ready?" I asked Cameron quietly, but of course Asher overhead.

"Ready? Ready for what?"

Cameron's expression fell as he said, "I have to talk to Coach."

WE SURVIVED the day at school. After the rumor mill almost exploded with news of me and Cameron, things settled down. But I was going to have to get used to my newfound popularity now I was with a Raider.

With a Raider. There was something I never thought I'd say.

"What are you smiling at?" Cameron asked me as he met me outside class.

"Oh nothing." I smirked, letting him take the pile of books from me. "But having a boyfriend has its uses."

We stopped by my locker and I traded the books I needed for homework with the ones in Cameron's arms. When I was done, I found myself crowded against the locker bank, stormy gray-blue eyes fixed right on me. The hall was emptying, but a few kids watched us with mild curiosity and amusement.

"We have an audience." My hands slid up his chest as I flicked my head to the group of junior girls openly gawking in our direction.

"We should probably give them something to talk about then." Cameron closed the distance between us, fixing his mouth over mine, his tongue slipping between my lips. "God, I love you," he breathed, pulling me closer.

"I love you too," I said a little louder than I intended earning us a round of hoots and hollers from a few of Cameron's teammates who passed us. "I'm in love with you."

It was the truth, I was completely and utterly in love with Cameron Chase.

"Yeah?" He pulled back. "You're not just saying it because you want my body or to say you bagged a Raider?"

I reached out, tweaking his nipple before drifting my hand down his solid chest, mentally counting off the ridges of his abs. "Well, this is definitely an added bonus..."

His smooth laughter washed over me, giving me a warm squishy feeling inside. "Fuck, we waited too long for this. You know that, right? It should have been me and you all along."

"I..." I didn't know what to say to that. But I didn't have to say anything because Cameron slanted his mouth over mine again. I was so lost in the kiss, in the rightness of his lips moving against mine, I almost didn't hear someone clear their throat.

But Cameron heard it and he pulled away, expelling a long breath.

"So, the rumors are true then," a girl with long dark hair said. "Cameron Chase is finally off the market."

"Miley, this is my girlfriend Hailee. Hailee this is Miley."

Miley.

I knew this girl. It was the same one from Homecoming, and I was pretty sure she was the girl from the night of Asher's party when I tagged Jason's car. "Hi." I lifted my hand in a small wave.

"Hey." Her cool gaze swept over me, but it didn't seem scathing like some of the girls in our class. "A little heads up would have been nice." She was staring at Cameron now, hurt lingering in her eyes.

"Give me a second," he said to me before guiding Miley down the hall just out of earshot. My stomach knotted as I watched them talk. They stood close, him staring down at her, her gazing up at him. She was gorgeous, lean and toned, an athlete for sure. And for as much as I didn't want to feel jealous, it burned through me like acid.

After a minute or two, Miley nodded and turned on her heel and walked off down the hall. Cameron approached me slowly, his eyes drinking me in. Trying to tell me things I couldn't quite decipher.

"So that's Miley," I said. "She's pretty. Were the two of you, like, a thing?"

"Hailee, don't do this." He let out a heavy sigh. "Miley is not important to me."

"But she was someone to you?"

Cameron crowded me against the locker again, cupping my jaw, angling my face to his. "Listen to me when I say this. It's *you,* I want. *You,* I need. Miley was someone to fill the void for a little while. But that's all. Me and you, *this,* it's real." He lowered his head to mine. "I need you, Hailee. I need you so much it fucking terrifies me." Vulnerability glittered in his eyes like stars across the night sky.

Lifting my hand against his cheek, I breathed him in, and said, "You have me." *Every single piece.* "Now take me home and show me just how much you need me."

CAMERON DIDN'T COME to school again after that. He wanted to be there for his mom's appointments and to help with Xander. So I was surprised when he asked me to go to the game with him Friday night.

"Are you okay?" I squeezed his hand as we watched the Raiders run out onto the field below. We were in the family section, using his two tickets reserved for his parents, and Asher had been kind enough to let Flick have one of his tickets since his parents were out of town.

"I'm okay." Cameron nodded before leaning down to capture my lips in a slow kiss.

"Hmm, guys, right here. I'm right here."

"Sorry." I peeked around Cameron and pouted at my best friend.

"You're so cute I can't even stay mad at you, ugh," she groaned, readjusting her Raiders ball cap. "I need a man."

"What about Ash—"

I clapped my hand over Cameron's mouth. "Don't put ideas into her head."

"He's nice and all," Flick said completely ignoring me and Cameron. "But he's not my type."

"There's another type beside cocky arrogant jock?"

"Sunshine," Cameron warned.

"What?" I played dumb. "It's true. You jocks are all the sa—"

He dipped his head silencing me with his lips and tongue. I melted against him and a couple of people behind us snickered.

"Cam," I breathed. "We have to... stop."

"You're no fun." It was his turn to pout.

"How's your mom, Cameron?" We both turned to Flick and her expression grew serious.

"She's doing as well as can be expected, thanks. The good news is her doctor seemed confident they got it all."

"That's great."

It was great. Karen had survived the surgery and her prognosis was looking good. She wasn't out of the woods yet, and she still had a long road ahead of her if the doctors decided she needed radiotherapy; but it was as positive as it could be given the circumstances.

Wrapping my arm around Cameron's waist, I snuggled into his side. Despite his mom's surgery going well, he'd still wanted to remain off the roster for tonight's game. Coach and his teammates begged him to be on the sidelines, but in the end, he decided to watch from the bleachers. I think, deep down, he was still waiting for the call to say something had gone wrong.

"She's okay," I whispered, squeezing him tighter. Cameron glanced down at me and smiled.

"I know." He kissed me again, and Flick grumbled.

"I think I liked you both better when you hated each other."

"You're practically glowing." Flick linked her arm through mine as we followed Cameron around the back of the stadium to meet the team and congratulate them on a well-deserved win.

"I'm happy," I admitted. "He makes me happy."

"Well, duh." She chuckled. "You managed to score yourself a Raider. I guess some things do come true."

I gaped at her unable to school my indignance, but she only laughed harder. "You should see your face. Just be thankful I didn't get you a shirt for your birthday with 'hashtag I ride a Raider' printed on it." Flick winked.

"You're just jealous."

Her eyes clouded for a second, the air around us cooling considerably, but then Flick was smirking as if nothing had just happened. "Of course, I'm jealous. I mean, I have eyes. Look at him."

So, I did.

Cameron was fist-bumping and guy-hugging his teammates. His friends. We hovered while he did his thing, letting Kaiden and Asher give him a play-by-play account of every touchdown as if we hadn't been front and center watching the whole game. But I realized it was probably just their way of including him in their victory.

"How are things at home?" Flick pulled my attention away from Cameron.

"It's weird. Mom and Kent are acting as if nothing happened, and Jason barely acknowledges either of them, so not much has changed there. I'm at that weird place where I want to be mad with her, but I'm not sure I have the energy to keep it up for much longer."

"Look," my best friend said. "She made a mistake. Yes, it was a pretty fucking epic one, but you can't help who you fall in love with. You of all people should know that."

"I..." Flick was right. She always was. But it didn't quell the sting of Mom's betrayal. I think I was more hurt by the fact she'd lied all this time than the fact she'd had an affair.

People had affairs all the time. I didn't condone it, but she and Kent were adults. They knew what they were doing. Jason and I knowing wouldn't have changed anything.

But something told me, he was in no rush to forgive his dad.

"And you and Jason, what's going on there?"

"Yeah, sister." He appeared out of nowhere. "What is going on there?"

Flick rolled her eyes at him, but he barely looked twice at her.

"Don't be a dick, Jason."

His hands went up. "I come in peace." His eyes flicked over to where Cameron was. "How is he?"

"Why don't you ask him yourself?" There was no malice in my words. Cameron was right; life was too short. After sitting with him in the hospital waiting room while his mom underwent a life-saving craniotomy, I realized this grudge between me and Jason, the stuff with Thatcher, it didn't matter. This was high school. Kids were mean and got off on bringing each other down. But the real world, where things were hard and painful and uncertain, was waiting for them. High school didn't define me. I knew my worth, and this moment, right here, defined me.

Jason ran a brisk hand through his damp hair as I stepped closer to him and lay my hand on his arm. "You should go talk to him; he misses you."

It didn't matter what Jason did or didn't think about me, our lives were entwined now. Whether he liked it or not. I loved his best friend, his brother in all the ways that counted, so we had to find a way to co-exist.

"I..." he hesitated.

"Go," I said quietly. "He needs you; he needs to know you're okay with all of this."

Cameron might have said he was ready to quit the team, but I knew he wasn't. Not really. But this thing between him and Jason was swaying him toward making the wrong decision. And regardless of what I thought about football, I didn't want him to give up his dreams.

As if he felt us watching him, Cameron's head snapped over to us. His eyes darkened when he saw Jason at my side. I dropped my hand to my stepbrother's back and nudged him forward. "Go, you'll regret it if you don't. Trust me."

40

Cameron

I WATCHED Hailee and Jason as he decided whether or not to come over here. She wanted him to, it was right there in her honey-brown eyes. But I didn't make a move; this had to be on him.

Hailee was in my corner now. She might have only been in my life officially for a few days, but she had been there every step of the way. At the hospital while we waited for Mom to come out of surgery, waiting outside the locker room while I told Coach I needed some time away from the team. She'd been there, no questions asked. She just got it. Understood what I needed. And she was there.

It meant the fucking world to me.

But Jason was wired different. In his eyes, empathy and compassion were weaknesses. Traits that meant letting people get close—something he rarely did. So when he started stalking toward me, I braced myself for whatever shit was about to come out of his mouth.

"Hey," he said.

"What's up?" I tipped my head. Since I could remember, the two of us had been inseparable, but now it felt like there was an entire football field between us.

"It didn't feel right out there tonight." Jase looked over at me, his hair falling over his eyes slightly.

"You got the win; that's all that matters, right?" I hadn't meant for it to sound like a dig, but he flinched.

"Come on, bro, it's not... Look, I screwed up, I get it." His expression didn't match the Jason I knew—the guy who was one step closer to State. "But you didn't tell me, you didn't—"

"You didn't want to hear it." My eyes shuttered. "You're not like the rest of us, Jase. You're so focused on football, on the future..."

"But this is different. I would've..." He let out a heavy sigh "How is she?"

"She's doing okay but they won't know if she needs radiotherapy yet." Doctor Kravis was remaining optimistic that he'd gotten all the tumor cells, but since it was a grade two meningioma there was still a chance it could come back.

"Fuck," Jase hissed out. "I'm so fucking sorry, man."

"She's alive and they got it, that's what we're focusing on right now."

The wait for her to get out of surgery was something I never wanted to experience again. Those six hours had been excruciating. If hadn't been for Xander's incessant questions and having Hailee right there beside me, I think I would have lost it.

Jase rubbed the back of his neck. He wanted to say something, I could see it in his eyes. "What?" I asked.

"Nah, it doesn't matter."

"Go on, say it."

"Do you think you'll come back to the team... now she's okay?"

I shook my head incredulously. Even now, he couldn't see past football.

"Fuck, that came out wrong." He scrubbed a hand down his face. "I mean, I get why you couldn't play tonight; to be honest, I'm surprised you came at all."

I hadn't wanted to, but Dad insisted. Even Mom had given her blessing.

"What I mean is, I need you. You and me, Chase. We need to see this thing through together."

"I don't know if—"

"I know." He held up his hands. "And I get it, I do. But we worked too hard for this, *you* worked too hard for it."

"Listen, Jase, I'm not sure Penn is—"

"Fuck Penn. You've got to do what's best for your family, I get it. It was always my dream anyway. But this year, it's ours. I can do it without you, but honestly,"—Jase locked eyes on me—"I don't want to."

"Worried you're nothing without your star wide receiver?" I smirked.

"Damn right I am. Kaiden is good but he's no Fourteen." He gave me a rare smile. "So what do you say, Chase? Are you in?"

"I can't promise anything but if Mom is okay and the doctors are happy with her progress then yeah, I'm in." Coach had already said I could cut back on practice if I needed to.

Relief settled in my best friend's eyes, his shoulders sagging, and for the first time in my life, I saw Jason Ford lower his walls. He really meant every word he'd just said.

And that meant something to me.

Despite all the highs and lows and events of the last few weeks, the fact he'd finally managed to look past himself and football, meant something.

"So, you and Hailee, huh?" He flicked his head over to where the girls stood pretending not to watch us.

"Yeah, is it going to be a problem? Because I'll lay it out there now; if you make me choose, it'll be her, every damn time." He was my best friend, but I was done being his puppet. I needed Hailee. I couldn't really explain it, but I needed her. And now I finally had her, I had no plans on doing anything to jeopardize that.

"Guess I'd better get used to it then." Jase shrugged but I saw the tightness around his eyes. "You know, we still need to get Thatcher back for what he did to her."

"Jase, I'm not sure—"

"He's going down, one way or another, he's—"

"Who's going down?" Hailee finally came over, guilt flashing in her eyes. "Sorry," she whispered. "I couldn't wait any longer."

"It's fine." I hooked an arm around her, pulling her into my side.

"So, what were you talking about?"

"Ask lover boy." The corner of Jase's mouth tipped and I flipped him off.

"Ask lover boy what?" Ash appeared, his arm slung casually around Felicity who looked less than impressed at being dragged into our small gathering.

"I think they're plotting something," Hailee said, throwing me a dubious look.

"No plotting," I said. "I promise." But Jase's eyes sparked with something dangerous, and I knew he wouldn't let this thing with Thatcher go.

"The guys want to know if we're headed to Bell's?" Ash asked, his arm still around Felicity.

"I'm not sure—" I started but Hailee pressed her hand to my stomach. "It's okay, if you want to go, we can go." She nodded reassuringly.

"Fee, baby, you in?"

"Do you promise to stop calling me that?" Felicity rolled her eyes at Ash.

"I promise to get drunk and try to feel you up." He winked and I caught Jase stiffen. I was missing something. Something that involved my two best friends and Felicity. But before I could try to figure out what the fuck was going on, Jase said, "Let's go then."

We followed him, as if the five of us, together, was just business as usual.

"Let me guess, this is on your list?"

"List, what list?" I asked Hailee, overhearing her and Felicity's conversation, as we reached the door to Bell's.

"Hmm, I didn't realize you were there." Hailee glanced back at me, her eyes wide as if she'd been caught with her hand in the cookie jar.

"Where did you think I was?"

"Already inside with Asher and Jason."

"I'll always be wherever you are." I leaned down, kissing her. In truth, I'd called Dad to check in on Mom, but he assured me she was fine, and Xander was with Katie. After the hardest week of our lives, he wanted—no, demanded—I try to enjoy a night with my girlfriend and friends.

"Oh God, I need a drink. Something strong. It's true the owner doesn't card the team here, right?"

I chuckled, still kissing Hailee. She broke away, looking at her friend. "You want to drink? *Here?*"

Felicity shrugged. "Desperate times, Hails, desperate times." She slipped inside leaving me and Hailee alone.

"She's acting strange." Hailee released a frustrated breath, and I hesitated, wondering whether or not to reveal my theory. "Cameron?"

Busted.

"So I, uh, I think something might be going on with Felicity and the guys."

"The guys?" Hailee blanched. "What do you mean *the guys?*"

"Asher and Jase."

"You think... no..." Strangled laughter spilled out of her. "Flick wouldn't go anywhere near Jason, and this thing with her and Asher is a joke. It's just a joke. I mean, it's Asher, he's..."

"Okay." I dipped my head to hers. "Just breathe. I'm probably wrong. It's probably nothing." I was pretty sure it wasn't nothing, but I could tell Hailee wasn't ready to hear it.

"Of course, you're wrong. She wouldn't... nope, I just can't." Hailee shook her head, a look of alarm plastered over her face before entering Bell's. I followed, regretting saying anything. But I knew Jase and I knew Ash and I'd sensed something going on for a while. And if I was right, it had disaster written all over it.

The second I stepped inside the bar, a wall of cheers and applause greeted me. Jase and Ash stood front and center, the rest of the team gathered behind them all chanting my name. I might not have been on the field tonight, helping them secure the win taking them one step closer to State, but this was their way of including me. Of showing me that no matter what happened from here on out I was still part of the team.

Still family.

"Good to see you, man." Grady came up to me, pulling me into a guy hug. "We heard about your mom. If there's anything I can do."

"Thanks, man, I appreciate it," I choked out the words over the lump in my throat. Kaiden was next, and then Mackey and some of the other sophomores. Each of them offered their words of support, each of them reminding me why I'd loved football so much, for as long as I could remember.

Because it was more than just a game.

It was more than the high of the win or the pain of the loss. It was brotherhood, and family, and knowing you had each other's backs no matter what.

"Hey." Hailee appeared at my side when the guys finally let me have some space. "Are you okay?"

"Actually yeah, I am." I kissed her, not caring who could see us, earning us another round of applause. Her fingers twisted into my jersey and when she pulled away, the cutest blush was smattered along her cheeks. "Oh God, that was so embarrassing," she murmured.

"You're a Raider now," I said fighting a smirk as I tucked her into my side, guiding us over to Jase, Ash, and Felicity.

"I guess I can thank the two of you for the warm welcome?" I asked the guys.

"We just want you to know the team are behind you one hundred and ten percent. Whatever you decide, we've got your back," Ash said.

"Always," Jase added and I don't know who was more shocked. Asher, me, or Hailee.

"Yeah, yeah," he grumbled. "Don't get too used to it. I'm still the cold-hearted bastard you all love to hate." His hard gaze skirted over to Felicity who pretended not to notice.

But I noticed.

I only hoped Hailee didn't because I didn't want tonight to end in drama. I wanted to enjoy the moment—my friends, my team, and my girlfriend co-existing in one of my favorite places.

After weeks of uncertainty, of feeling pulled in different directions, I finally felt like I could breathe. And I knew it was largely down to Hailee. She made all the other shit disappear. She kept me sane in the quiet moments, the moments where my thoughts turned dark and went to places I didn't want to be.

And although it was early days, I knew I didn't want to be anywhere she wasn't.

Without thinking, I jumped up on the nearest empty booth and waited for the place to go silent. Hailee stared up at me as if I'd lost my mind. And maybe I had, but if life had taught me anything over the last couple of weeks, it was that you never knew what was around the corner.

"I just want to say a few words."

My teammates all made a ruckus, stamping on the floor and banging on tables.

"Show the guy some respect," Jerry yelled from his position behind the bar, and I gave him an appreciative nod.

When everyone hushed, I continued, "At the beginning of this week, I'll be honest, I didn't know if I'd ever put on my jersey again. Football is important to me, but it's not everything. Family is what matters." My eyes found my best friends. "Friendship, having each other's backs, being there when things hit rock bottom, that's what makes being a Raider special. Is the thrill of the win, addictive? Hell yeah, it is. But it's knowing that if you lose, if your dreams go up in flames in front of your eyes, that you'll still have a team, a family, there to shoulder the burden with you.

"By now, you all probably know my family had some bad news recently. And it made me question everything I thought I knew. But regardless of what the next few weeks bring, one thing's for certain, I'll always be a Raider. And I couldn't think of a better team to win State with."

"Does that mean you're sticking around?" Grady yelled and I fought a smile.

"Well, you'll be needing your star wide receiver, won't you?"

"Hells yeah." He grinned and the place erupted.

Jase and Ash were on me the second I leaped down off the bench. Jase grabbed the back of my neck and pressed his head to mine, his eyes saying everything I knew he never would. And then Ash joined us, his arms looped around both our necks, pulling us close. "Thank fuck, I don't have to lose any more sleep over whose side I'm on."

A moment of understanding passed between the three of us. We were on the precipice of something, we could all feel it. All we had was this moment before everything changed.

"Do you think you'll commit when the scouts come out next week?" Ash asked and my eyes found Hailee standing with Felicity by the bar.

"Yeah, I'm going to commit."

Football was a part of me, a part of who I was. And I owed it to myself, to my family to see where it took me.

"Well don't keep us hanging. Where's it going to be?"

"Michigan," I said without hesitation. "I'm going to commit to Michigan."

It was a rash decision, one I knew I'd need to talk to my parents about, not to mention Hailee. But life was precious, and I didn't want to spend a minute wasting it. If things went south with Mom, I'd cross that bridge when it came. We still had nine months before college. A lot could change between now and then.

But here, in this moment, I wanted the dream.

I wanted football.

And the girl.

EPILOGUE

Hailee

"OH MY GOD, it's so big."

"I know something that's big," Asher turned around and flashed Flick a wicked grin.

"Asher, really." She rolled her eyes at him before settling her gaze once more on the New York skyline as we crossed the bridge. Jason grunted, his eyes thinning as he focused on the road, but I brushed it off because Cameron was wrong.

He had to be wrong.

Flick didn't like my step-brother—there was *nothing* to like.

"Are you excited?" Cameron's lips brushed the shell of my ear, sending a trail of heat zipping through me. I clenched my legs together and his smooth chuckle washed over me.

"Yeah, I've always wanted to see a Reba exhibition. I can't believe Kent managed to score us tickets."

"*You*, tickets," Jason said. "I told you already, I'm not going to some lame art show. Besides, Ash's cousins are going to give us the tour, right?"

"What?" I asked, looking from him to Cameron and back again. "You didn't say anything about Asher's cousins." This trip had officially been hijacked by my step-brother.

Fuck my life.

We might have found a temporary truce since everything with Cameron's mom happened, but I was under no illusion it would last. Too much had happened between us. But for a rare weekend, our differences weren't front and center. Cameron needed this weekend, we all did. And nothing was going to ruin it.

Not a damn thing.

THIRTY MINUTES LATER, after battling the city traffic, we were finally in the hotel.

"Holy shit, Hails, I can't believe it. Would you check out this view? I can see the Empire State Building." Flick's voice held a tinge of wonder as she beckoned me to the floor-to-ceiling window in our accommodation for the night.

The penthouse suite overlooking Fifth Avenue was ridiculous. But Flick had insisted I room with Cameron, so I couldn't complain too much. Jason and Asher were sharing the other double room—with two king beds—and Flick had happily taken the twin.

"New York," she sighed dreamily. "I still can't believe it. And,"—my best friend leaned in, whispering—"I heard Asher tell Jason his cousins are taking us to a club. A club, Hails. I'm so freaking excited."

My brows pinched as I tried to share her enthusiasm. "A club? I'm not sure—"

"Oh no you don't, Hailee Raine. This is a once in a lifetime opportunity. Do you know how many kids from school would kill to be here right now? We are embracing this."

"Let me guess," I said. "It's on your—"

"Ssh. Don't let the guys hear. It's bad enough Cameron overheard us before. I don't want them thinking I'm..." Her voice trailed off as something caught her eye over my shoulder. I glanced back to find Jason and Asher watching us.

"Are you two going to stand there all fucking day or can we get out of here?"

"Can you at least try to be civil?" I asked Jason, but he merely grunted and went to the refrigerator.

"So, how are my two favorite ladies?" Asher approached us but I ducked before he could collar me. His arm went around Flick though. It was becoming quite the habit.

"This is so cool," Flick beamed up at him. "I can't believe your dad is letting us stay here."

"Believe it, baby." He grinned back. "But you ain't seen nothing yet. My cousins know all the local hotspots."

"Asher, I'm not sure—"

"*Hails.*" He levelled me a serious look. "One night. We have one night. Turn that frown upside down and get on the love train."

"Love train, seriously?"

"It's okay for you, you've got Chase to attend to... your needs." His brows waggled. "The rest of us need to go hunting."

"Asher." Flick elbowed him in the ribs. "That's gross."

"Naw, baby. It's simple biology. Unless you're—"

"Is he bothering you?" Cameron came up behind me, looping his arm around me and pulling me back against his chest.

"Who, me?" Asher feigned surprise.

"What time is the exhibition?" Cameron brushed his lips over my ear.

"Not until two."

"So, we have some time to explore?"

"Yes, yes we do." Flick ducked out of Asher's hold and grabbed his arm. "We should go. I want to see everything."

"Of course you do," Asher grumbled, trailing after her like a lap dog.

"This should be interesting," I said as we followed them.

Me and Flick with my boyfriend, step-brother, and their best friend.

What could possibly go wrong?

"So, did you like it?" I asked Flick as we exited The Met. We'd cut the guys loose despite Cameron insisting he wanted to come. It was his trip too, and I didn't want to monopolize all of his time. Besides, I knew if Cameron came, Asher would want to come, and there was no way I wanted him making a scene in one of the most prestigious museums in the country.

"I..." She hesitated. "You like it and that's what's important. And at least I can say I visited The Met now."

"It was just so... inspiring. Her work is really something."

"And I'd love to hear all about it sometime but,"—she pointed at the guys standing at the bottom of the steps—"Who the hell is that?"

Jason was talking to a girl, a very well dressed, very beautiful girl.

"I guess it's Asher's cousin."

"He didn't say she looked like a super model." Flick grabbed my arm, pulling me toward them.

"I'm sure she's nice, despite being related to Asher."

"Hails, he's not *that* bad."

"But he's not boyfriend material either, right?"

She rolled her lips together.

"Flick?" I asked her again.

"I told you already, not interested. But it doesn't hurt to have a little fun."

"Hmm, I'm not sure Asher is the kind of guy you—"

"Fee get over here. I want to introduce you to Vaughn and Riley."

"Come on, Hails. He wants to introduce us to his cousins." She flashed me a playful grin, bouncing down the last few steps and sidling up to Asher as if they were the best of friends.

And it occurred to me, maybe that's where this strange thing they had going on was headed.

"Fee, Hails, this is my cousin Riley and his sister Vaughn."

"Hey," the guy said, his eyes running over Flick and then me. Cameron moved closer, whispering how much he'd missed me in my ear. Riley smirked. "She yours?"

"Actually, he's mine," I said, clasping Cameron's hand in mine.

"Noted." Riley's smirk morphed into an easy smile. "And you?" He flicked his head to Flick who blushed deeply.

"Me? I'm, uh, I'm very much... single," she croaked out.

"But you'll be keeping your dirty paws off her." Asher threw his arm around Riley and pulled him away.

"If I didn't know better," Vaughn said as she took off after them. "I'd say my cousin has a crush."

"Hey, man, you okay?" Cameron asked Jason who was rooted to the spot, watching Vaughn's retreating form.

"What? Yeah, I'm good." He glared at Flick. "You know she's joking, right? Ash doesn't want you. He just likes playing with you."

"I..." She snapped her mouth shut, embarrassment burning her cheeks.

"Jason don't be such a dick," I scolded.

"Yeah, man, come on. We only have one night," Cameron added. "Let's try to all get along."

"Whatever," he grumbled before stalking off after Asher and his cousins.

"Are you okay?" I asked Flick.

"Please, I'm fine." She smiled but it was forced. "Come on, we should keep up with them." Flick brushed past us and hurried after them.

"That was... weird."

"Don't worry about Jase," Cameron said, "He's just pissed his best friend is shacking up with his sister."

"You make it sound so romantic." I leaned up, pressing a kiss to his lips.

"Later," Cameron breathed. "Later, I'm going to kiss every single inch of you."

"Is that a promise?" My fingers twisted into his sweater, and he smiled.

"It is."

"I look forward to it." I stole another kiss. "Come on, before we lose them."

"Wait." He snagged my wrist. "What Asher said earlier, about the thing."

"The thing?" I vaguely recalled Asher asking Cameron if he'd told me about *the thing,* but I'd been too busy taking in the view of the city.

"Yeah." Cameron's throat bobbed. "I decided where I'm committing to."

My heart fluttered. "You did?"

"I did."

"It's okay," I said over the lump in my throat. We hadn't talked about it much, our relationship was new and I didn't want to make any assumptions. "Wherever you go, we'll make it work."

"Good, because I chose Michigan."

"Michigan... as in..."

A slow smile broke over his face as he nodded. "Is that okay?"

"You're going to go to school in Michigan?"

"If you want—"

"I want." I threw my arms around him. "I really want."

"Thank fuck because I kind of already made a verbal commitment."

I swatted his chest, hardly able to believe it. I'd known Cameron was looking at colleges again since his mom's surgery went well. But deep down, I'd expected him to follow Jason to Penn, and although I hated the idea, I would have never stood in his way.

"Jason—" I started but he cut me off.

"Is important to me, but this was my decision to make, not his."

And although he was almost six years too late, he'd finally chosen me.

Cameron

"What's up with you?" I asked Jase as we looked out over the club. Hailee and Flick were dancing below in the middle of the crowded dance floor. She'd wanted me to go with them, but I wanted her to enjoy some time with her best friend, and I wanted to talk to mine.

"You've had a stick up your ass all night. Is it her?"

"Her?" He eyed me coolly, taking a long pull on his beer. I had thought we might have a problem getting into the club, but it turned out Asher's cousins knew everyone and we'd all walked right in. It was pretty cool, even if I would have rather been back at the penthouse with Hailee. Alone and naked and buried so deep inside her I didn't know where she began and I ended.

"You know who I'm talking about." My gaze slid back to the girls as they laughed and danced, oblivious to all the guys staring at them with hunger in their eyes.

"You're okay with that?" Jase flipped the tables on me. "With her down there while they watch? If she was mine—"

"Are *you* okay with it?" I countered, and he knew full well I didn't mean his step-sister.

"What the fuck are you getting at?"

"You watch her, you know." I fought a smirk. "When you think no one is looking, you watch her."

He let out a strangled laugh. "I don't know what the fuck you're talking about. The only girl I've got my sights set on tonight is Vaughn."

"Really, man? She's Asher's cousin."

"Didn't stop you, did it?" He blew out a long breath and turned to lean against the balcony rail, giving the dance floor—and the girls—his back.

"I'm not doing this with you."

"Doing what? I'm not doing anything." His hard gaze flicked over me to Asher and his cousins. He looked hungry. Vicious. He looked like the Jase I knew before shit hit the fan.

I slammed my hand into his stomach as he stepped forward. "Don't do this. You don't need to prove anything. All you're going to do is hurt her—"

"Hurt who?"

With a disapproving shake of my head, I let him go. Jase lived for his games but one day they would come around and bite him on the ass. And for as much as I didn't want Felicity to get tangled up with him, maybe she was the girl to finally put him in his place.

"What's his deal?" Asher joined me, running his eyes over the crowd below.

"Who, Jase? Just his usual bullshit."

"He likes her, you know," he said as if it was nothing. "He won't ever admit it, but he does. She gets under his skin."

I side-eyed him but he was too busy watching the dance floor... the girls.

Felicity.

He was watching Felicity.

"And what about you?" I asked, uncertain whether this was water I wanted to tread. "Does she get under your skin?"

He shrugged, playing it cool. But I saw the tightness around his jaw. He liked her. Fuck. "Doesn't matter," he said. "She's not into me."

"And she's into Jase?"

"I'm not sure. She says she isn't, but I catch her watching him sometimes with this look in her eye, and I'm pretty sure something happened with them the other week at my house."

"What look?"

Asher expelled a shaky breath as he gripped the rail. "The look you used to give Hailee. The same look that says you want something even though you know it's a really fucking bad idea."

"It worked out for us, didn't it?"

He laughed at that, but it was full of bitterness. "You're the exception to the rule. Besides, you're not a cruel bastard like Jase. He'd tear Fee apart with his teeth and then feast on her bones just because he could." His jaw clenched. "And yet, my money says before the semester's out she lets him fuck her."

"Maybe she just needs to know there are other options on the table." I gave him a hard look.

"Maybe." Something flashed over his face, but he quickly schooled it. "Are we going down there before some stuck-up city suit steals your girl right out from under your nose?"

My eyes zeroed in on Hailee again. Asher was right, two guys were moving in on them. "Let's go," I said, draining my beer and slamming it on the ledge.

We made our way downstairs, weaving through the sea of bodies. I instantly locked eyes with the fucker watching Hailee. His eyes widened and then narrowed when I stepped up behind her, sliding my arm around her waist.

"Hey," she mouthed over her shoulder at me.

"I missed you." I kissed the tip of her nose before tangling our hands together and resting them on her stomach. The guy sneered before stalking off. I glanced over at Asher who threw me an amused smirk as he pulled Flick into his arms. She went willingly, a sloppy smile plastered on her face.

"How drunk is Felicity?" I asked Hailee as she rolled her hips against me, sending a trail of electricity zipping through me.

"Asher will look after her," she yelled over the music.

That was precisely what I was worried about.

"I'm not sure—" Hailee spun in my arms, slamming her mouth to mine. My hands slid down her back, finding the curve of her ass. She looked like sin in the skin-tight black sweater dress and kitten heels that made her legs appear longer.

Our tongues swirled together, slow lazy licks, mirroring the way our bodies moved. I didn't make a habit of dancing, but for Hailee I'd walk over hot coals. There was something magnetic about her. And I was completely powerless against her charms.

"Take me home, Cameron," she moaned against my lips. "I need you."

Fuck.

I wanted to throw her over my shoulder and get the hell out of here, but the night was still young and there was Felicity and my friends to consider. Although she and Asher looked more than at home wrapped in each other's arms.

"Later," I said, stealing another kiss. "Felicity wanted to make the most of the night."

Hailee's eyes darkened as she gazed up at me. "I love you." She fought a smile. "I love you so much."

I pulled her close, emotion punching my stomach. Hailee wrapped her arms around my waist and held on tight as we swayed, dancing to our own beat.

Only weeks ago, my future had been uncertain, a black cloud hanging over me, blotting out all the light. But now I had everything I ever wanted. I had the team, and State was within our grasp. Mom was doing as well as could be expected given the circumstances. And I had a girl who loved me unconditionally.

I was a lucky son of a bitch. But if the last few weeks had taught me anything, it was not to take anything for granted.

And I intended on making the most of my life—starting with the girl in my arms.

Hailee

"Where are you going?" Cameron murmured, his hand reaching for me as I tried to untangle myself from the sheets.

"Water," I said. "I need water." The air was different in New York. Thick and humid, it clung to your skin and made your lungs tight.

"Get me a bottle."

"Okay." I trailed my fingers over his jaw, heat flooding me as I remembered how intense it had been between us when we got back to the penthouse.

Pulling on Cameron's shirt, I quickly buttoned it up just in case anyone was still awake, although given the state of Jason, Flick, Asher, and his cousins last night, I doubted anyone would be.

Padding quietly into the hall, I hurried to the kitchen and got two bottles of water out of the refrigerator, pausing when I heard a noise. My heart leaped into my throat and I silently chastised myself. It was probably just someone snoring. But as I tiptoed back into the hall, I heard it again. A gentle creak. A muffled moan. My eyes strained against the darkness to find the source of the noise, only to be met with closed door after closed door. Until my eyes landed on the bedroom Flick had taken. The door was slightly ajar. She'd drunk a lot last night. Maybe she was sick? I hurried to her door, pausing outside. A muted sob pierced the air and I stepped into the room. "Flick, are you—"

A naked ass greeted me.

Jason's naked ass as he thrust into my friend.

"Oh my god," I breathed just as Flick's eyes snapped to mine over his shoulder.

"Hails," she cried, eyes wide with surprise and hazy with lust. Her body closed in on itself as Jason cussed under his breath, before rolling off my best friend.

My best friend.

... and my step-brother.

Together.

I turned on my heel and got the hell out of there. Cameron had been right. Something *was* going on.

Something between the two of them.

One of the people I loved most in the world.

And one of the people I hated most.

Life had just got a whole lot more complicated.

THE GAME YOU PLAY

To Nina
Thank you for believing in this story

PROLOGUE

"STUPID GIRL," I muttered to myself as I flushed the toilet and left the stall to wash my hands. The music pulsed through the walls, mimicking the thud of my heart against my ribcage.

He's doing it to get under your skin. Ignore him and he'll stop.

Easier said than done.

Jason 'asshole' Ford was the bane of my existence. Arrogant. Conceited. A total manwhore.

And the guy my heart had apparently decided it wanted.

Stupid, *stupid* heart.

Pressing my hands against the cool marble counter, I stared at myself in the wall-length mirror. I looked good. My hair was curled to perfection, hanging in long loose waves down my back; my makeup was smoky and seductive; and the black dress clung to my curves like a second skin.

I didn't only look good.

I looked downright hot.

"Get it together, Giles," I commanded to the girl staring back at me in the mirror. "He only has power over you if you let him."

And right now, the asshole was out there all over another girl.

A girl who wasn't me.

The knot in my stomach tightened as I inhaled a deep breath. "You've got this," I whispered.

Just then, a group of giggling girls spilled into the restroom, pausing to glance me over. I offered them a tight smile and hurried out of there. The New York club Asher's cousins had brought us to was something else. Nothing like the bars we had back home in our small town of Rixon. It was moody and dark, the furnishings sleek and sexy. Frequented by young, rich New Yorkers all looking to let loose and have fun.

I slipped into the hall connecting the cloakroom and restroom to the rest of the club, determined to enjoy the night. So what if Jason was practically dry fucking Asher's cousin? My body—and stupid foolish heart—might have wanted him, but my head knew better.

My head knew Jason Ford was a *really* bad idea.

What I needed was to find a nice guy who wanted to buy me a drink and dance the night away with me. And who knew, maybe I'd get to tick another thing off my list. After all, we were in New York. New freaking York. It was a small miracle my parents had ever agreed to let me take the trip for my best friend's birthday. Of course they only knew about the art exhibition we planned to visit and the sightseeing we wanted to do. But what they didn't know, wouldn't hurt them.

The thought made me smile, putting an extra bounce in my step, as I rounded the corner… and smacked straight into a hard, muscular chest. "I know you want me, Giles, but throwing yourself at me is kind of desperate."

"Fuck you, Jason." I glowered at him, stepping back to put a safe distance between us. Of course he took that as a challenge, the glint in his eye obvious as he inched closer.

"Jason," I warned, but he kept coming until my back hit the wall, knocking the air from my lungs.

"I know what you're doing," he whispered against my ear, his warm breath dancing over my skin. I gulped, my eyes fluttering closed. His voice was low, husky even, and if I didn't know him the way I did, it would have been easy to mistake his tone for seduction.

But I did know him.

And this was all a game to him.

"I'm not doing anything, Jason," I sighed, ignoring the little voice in my head whispering 'liar'.

He erased the sliver of space between us, plastering his body against mine in the dimly lit hall. "It won't work," he added, his tongue swiping my damp skin before nipping my earlobe. My knees buckled as a full-body shiver rolled through me.

"Jason." It was supposed to be another warning, but my voice betrayed me, his name falling from my lips on a breathy sigh.

One of his hands glided up my body. I fought the urge to lean into his touch, to seek more. He didn't care that he squeezed my breast a little too hard or that his fingers wrapped around my throat a little too tight. Because a guy like Jason Ford did what he wanted, took what he wanted, when he wanted it.

But I did care.

I cared that his rough touch lit up my body in a way it never had before. I cared that I wanted to let him do unspeakable things to me.

I cared that I cared.

Tears pricked the corners of my eyes, but I blinked them away, my gaze hard when he finally lifted his head to mine.

"Keep this up and you're going to get hurt," he said coolly. But the air around us was anything but cool.

It was blistering, crackling with tension, burning with anticipation.

"You're playing with fire, Felicity." God, even the way he said my name did things to me. "And do you know what happens when you play with fire?"

His liquor-scented breath caressed my face; his lips hovering dangerously close to mine. "You end up getting burned."

I should have told him to get the hell away from me. Or slapped his panty-melting face and walked away. Or even kneed him in the balls and run. But I did none of those things. Instead, I said, "Maybe I want to get burned."

Because I was Felicity Giles, a girl with a list and a serious case of the crazies.

Jason's brow lifted, his dark eyes studying me. Although looking into my soul better described the way I felt whenever his dark, intense gaze aimed in my direction.

Why couldn't I have wanted someone else, *anyone* else?

Seconds passed as we stared at one another. The music reverberated around us. Laughter and chatter lingering on the periphery of our dark corner of the hall.

"Jason?" I asked, finally breaking the silence, unable to bear it for a second longer.

"Fuck it," he breathed and then his lips were on mine, hard and demanding. Jason didn't just kiss me, he devoured me. His hands clawed at my dress, scraping the material up my legs until his fingers found the soft flesh of my thighs.

"Oh God," I moaned against his unyielding lips. My hands wound into his unruly brown hair as our tongues tangled together. It was messy and dirty and quite possibly the best kiss I'd ever have.

But nothing good lasted forever, and this was Jason. He wasn't a white knight swooping in to win the damsel's heart. He was the evil Prince out to wreck and ruin and leave a trail of broken hearts in his wake.

"Fuck." He tore himself away from me, his body literally jerking back.

Disappointment swelled in my chest as I watched his expression morph into sheer anger. "That was a mistake." His lip curled in disgust.

"Okay." I managed to choke out, smoothing down my wrinkled dress.

"I need to go; Vaughn is waiting for me."

My heart sank.

I could handle his taunts. I could even handle being called a mistake. But hearing him say he was going back to another girl after kissing me like that... it made me want to puke.

"You should probably hurry," I bit out. "Wouldn't want to keep her waiting."

"Shit, Felicity, I—" Something flashed in his eyes but I cut him off.

"Go Jason, just go." I stared at the patterns in the plush carpet.

His heavy gaze lingered on me for another second and then, like always, he was gone.

I WOKE STARTLED, my eyes straining against the darkness. Crap, my head hurt after one too many drinks. But I'd needed all the liquid courage I could get after spending the night watching Jason and Vaughn. His hand on her waist, her lips on his neck. The sexual energy rolling off them, infecting everyone in close proximity.

My stomach lurched and I pushed up on one elbow, waiting for the waves of nausea to pass. Just then, a creak out in the hall cut through the silence.

"Hailee?" I whispered.

Nothing.

Lying back down, I stared up at the ceiling, my eyes chasing shadows, when I heard the sound again. Ready to go out there and see who was up, I grabbed the covers. But my door swung open and Jason stepped inside.

"What are you—"

"Ssh," he hissed, stalking further into the room.

"You can't be in here," I said, curling my hands into the sheet, keeping them pulled up around my body. His eyes pierced the darkness. Watching me.

Stalking my every move.

Not that I dared breathe with him so close.

"Where's Vaughn? Shouldn't you—"

"Do you ever stop talking?"

"You're in my room in the middle of the night. You don't get to say what I can and can't do."

His lip curved deviously. "Wanna bet?" He edged closer, taking the air with him.

"Jason, this isn't funny..."

"You naked under there, Giles?"

Oh God.

Heat pooled in my stomach when it should have been fear. Because Jason didn't play nice, he played dirty.

Deadly.

Dangerously.

"You're drunk," I said, finding my voice again. "You should go."

"You sure about that?" He was at the foot of the bed now, looking over me like a dark prince.

"I..."

He needed to leave.

I needed to tell him to leave right now.

Jason liked this game too much. A game I should never have gotten tangled up in.

It had all started with a list.

My list.

My foolish little list.

It was supposed to help me rock senior year. To encourage me to do all those things I'd always dreamed of but never been brave enough to do. To shed my wallflower existence.

What I didn't count on was *him.*

I thought I was strong enough to play his game; to engage in war with an expert strategist.

I thought I could protect my heart and have some fun.

I should have known better.

I should have retreated instead of surrendering. But I handed over my heart without even realizing.

And now he owned me.

All of me.

Even if he said he didn't want me.

But now he was standing there, looking at me with hunger in his eyes. A hunger that matched my own.

He did want me.

Jason Ford wanted *me.*

And I knew, the rules had just changed.

1

Felicity

"ARE you going to ignore me forever?" I asked my best friend as we stopped at our lockers. She gave me some serious stink eye as she traded out textbooks.

"Hails, come on. It was a mistake. I made a mistake."

Slamming her locker shut, her eyes fixed on mine clouded with disappointment. "You slept with him," she hissed, lowering her voice. "You had *sex* with Jason. Have you lost your goddamn mind?"

"It was one time." *Barely one time when you really thought about it.* "And I was drunk; it was a mistake." One I wouldn't be repeating in a hurry. Not that the aforementioned asshole would want a second round. *Get a grip, Felicity.*

"And you think that's okay? You were drunk. Not to mention a virgin," her voice lowered dangerously, indignation flaming her cheeks. "And you let him—"

"It's done now." I gave her a tight smile, ignoring the knot in my stomach. "It will never happen again. But at least I can check another thing off my list." Strained laughter spilled from my lips, but Hails wasn't laughing.

She wasn't even smiling.

"This isn't funny, Flick." She let out an exasperated sigh. "I can't... I don't even know what to say right now."

"So don't." I shrugged. "Let's pretend it never even happened, okay. Jason who?"

But Hailee wasn't looking at me anymore. She was staring over my shoulder, her eyes narrowed with contempt. I didn't need to turn around to know who it was. I felt him. Felt his lips on my skin, his hands on my body.

A shiver rolled up my spine, quickly morphing into lightning bolts shooting around my body as I turned and met Jason Ford's arrogant smirk.

"Fee, baby, I missed you."

Silently groaning to myself, I forced a smile at Asher, Jason's best friend.

"It's only been a day, Asher. You might need to go see Miss Hampstead about your neediness. It's getting worse." My smile grew, but when I peeked over at Jason and saw his indifference my spine stiffened.

Asher glanced between the two of us, frowning. "What's—"

"So big game Friday?" Hailee cut him off, already tucked into her boyfriend Cameron's side.

Jason Ford, Cameron Chase, and Asher Bennet. The three of them were Rixon Raider royalty and they were hoping to take our football team all the way to State this year.

It was a big deal for our small town. An even bigger deal for Jason and his plan to go off and dominate college football at UPenn next year, hopefully earning him a place in the NFL draft.

"Really, Hails?" Asher mocked. "You're a fan now?"

She glared at him, earning her a low rumble of chuckles from him and Cameron. Jason watched on; his expression devoid of emotion. If anything, he looked... bored. My stomach dipped as I looked away.

Jason was complicated. Cold. Callous. And a complete asshole. Even if he was wrapped up in a frustratingly yummy package. Dark unruly hair, even darker eyes. The kind you got lost in, pulled so far under there was no hope of ever crawling back out. Broad shoulders and muscular arms and cut abs that were entirely lickable. I knew first-hand because I'd—

Don't *go there!*

Jason lived and breathed football. His commitment was borderline obsessive. But then, I guess if you wanted to be the best you had to give your all. Soul included.

"It's kind of hard not to be a fan when your boyfriend is the star wide receiver for the team." Hailee grinned up at Cameron. My best friend had done a real one-eighty since senior year began a couple months back. She had always hated the game. Hated her step-brother Jason even more. He, along with Asher and Cameron, had made her life hell ever since she moved to Rixon. But something changed this year. Cameron started looking at her with lust in his eyes and although she tried to ignore his charms, it didn't take long for him to break down her walls.

Our twosome soon became a threesome; a fivesome if you counted Asher and Jason. Although from the scowl Jason wore whenever he was around us, it was no secret he was tolerating his best friend's and step-sister's new relationship at best.

"Yeah, well, we need to be getting to practice so..." Jason's insinuation hung in the air.

"What's the rush?" Asher said, "We still have—" His mouth snapped shut when his best friend levelled him with an icy stare. "Ladies, it's been a pleasure." He trailed after Jason who failed to say goodbye, but then, he hadn't said hello either.

Cameron lingered, crowding Hailee against the locker and kissing her. I glanced away, giving them some privacy. I'd grown used to their PDA's over the last couple of weeks, but it didn't make them any easier to stomach.

After a minute or so, I peeked over at them. Faces pressed close together,

Cameron whispered something to Hailee that made her giggle. Jealousy clawed its way up my throat, but I stuffed it down. After everything they'd put her through over the last few years, she deserved this. The fairy tale romance. The happily-ever-after.

Cameron and Hailee were couple goals and I was so happy for them.

Not at all green.

Nope.

Not even a little bit.

My day didn't get much better. Hailee was barely talking to me, and all everyone else was talking about was the Raiders upcoming game against Millington. Which meant all day his name followed me, a whisper on the wind, taunting me.

But it was fine.

I was fine.

I'd wanted to lose my v-card and I had. Okay, so I hadn't anticipated giving it up to one of the most arrogant and conceited jerks I knew, but what was senior year if not a chance to try new things ... and then quickly regret *ever* going there.

Images flooded my mind as I pushed the sandwich around my plate. His hurried and needy and oh so hot kisses. His big strong hands splayed around my hip, my throat, possessive and dominant. The sting of him filling me... the almost tears.

"Flick?" Hailee narrowed her eyes at me. "Where'd you go just now?"

"Huh, I..."

"Forget it." She went back to her fries, and guilt coiled around my heart. I hated that things were awkward between us. But she had walked in on me and Jason doing it, so I knew I had to give her time to come around. My best moment it was not.

"You know, you can go and sit with him." I flicked my head over to where Cameron sat with the rest of the football team.

"I know. But we're not attached at the hip. Besides, he needs this." She glanced over at him. "After everything with his mom, he needs the team."

"How is she?"

"Dealing the best she can. But she's a fighter, and she really wants Cameron to focus on school and the team."

I nodded. "So if he's over there to bond with the team, why is it he hasn't taken his eyes off you?" My brow arched, and Hailee fought a smile.

"He wanted me to sit with them."

Swinging my leg over the bench, I stood up. "Come on, let's go," I said, prepared to take one for our team of two.

Hailee frowned. "What are you doing?"

"We're going over there. He might need the team, but he needs you too. And to be quite honest, I can't eat my lunch with him making moon eyes at you."

"Flick," she groaned, peeking over at the team. "I'm not sure..."

"Fine. I'll go by myself." I shrugged, grabbing my tray and moving around the table.

"Oh my god," Hailee breathed out. "You're serious, you're really going to sit over—"

But her words rolled off me as I made my way over to their table. A few of the guys glanced up when I reached them.

"Fee, baby." Asher's eyes lit up when he noticed me. "And to what do we owe this pleasure?"

"Room for one more?"

"Oh, sweetheart," one of the sophomore players, Joel Mackey, smirked. "You can sit right here." He glanced down at his crotch and I rolled my eyes.

"Back the fuck up, Mackey." Asher nudged the guy next to him and dropped his eyes to the space at his side.

Just as I went around to sit by him, Hailee approached the table. "I wondered how long it was going to take for you to give in," I heard Cameron say to her, quietly. He swung his leg over the end of the bench and pulled her down, slipping his arms around her waist. "Hi."

"Hi."

I sat down, trying to look at anything but Cam brushing his lips over hers. God, they were so in love. So happy. So freaking perfect. Something inside me twisted.

"You okay over there?" Asher whispered.

"Who me?" I flashed him a warm smile. Asher was... well he was like a stray who followed you around; cute and annoying. But he'd never been anything but nice to me.

"You don't need to do that," he lowered his voice so that it was drowned out by the conversation going on around us. "Not with me," he added.

"Do what?" I played dumb, ignoring the pit in my stomach.

His eyes flicked to where Jase sat. He was busy talking to one of the guys when a manicured hand slid over his shoulder. He glanced up, a sly smirk gracing his ridiculously perfect face, as Jenna Jarvis, star gymnast and head bitch of Rixon High, stared down at him with a salacious smile of her own. Without hesitation, Jase shoved his chair back slightly letting her drop onto his lap. She wrapped her arms around his neck and I almost gagged.

Suddenly, I felt Asher's arm go around the back of me. My eyes slid to his in question but in true Asher style he simply grinned.

My cell phone vibrated, and I dug it out.

Hails: Are you okay?

. . .

Me: Of course. Why wouldn't I be?

I didn't meet her heavy gaze despite feeling it burn into the side of my face.

Hails: He's just using her...

My eyes flicked to Jase and Jenna of their own volition.

Me: Doesn't matter. I knew what I was doing.

You didn't tame a guy like Jason Ford. You enjoyed whatever he was willing to give you and filed it away under 'fun while it lasted'. Jenna knew this, all the girls at school knew this, and yet, it didn't stop them trying to conquer him. To make him fall at their feet. And there had been many who had tried... and failed. But I didn't bunch myself with them because I was under no illusions when it came to Jason Ford, QB One, and Rixon's golden boy of football.

Hails: You deserve so much more xo

The xo made me smile. She might have been pissed at me for sleeping with her step-brother, but Hailee wouldn't stay mad for long. We were ride or die, and it would take a damn sight more than some guy to ever come between us.

Me: I love you too xo

I hit send and finally looked over at her, both of us grinning. But then something caught Hailee's eye and her face paled. I didn't need to turn around. I already knew what I'd find. But I did it anyway. To prove to myself —and maybe her—that I was in control of this situation. That Jason was just a semi-drunk lapse in judgment.

The second my eyes landed on them—Jenna plastered against him, their lips moving, tongues licking—I knew it was all a lie though. One I kept telling myself over and over, because if you kept repeating something, it had to be true, right?

My hands shook as I pushed my tray out of the way and stood up.

"Fee?" Asher's voice barely perforated the white noise in my head. Jason wasn't only kissing Jenna, he was devouring her, and I was pretty sure in about ten seconds they would be fucking in the cafeteria. Sexual energy rolled off them, hitting me like a wrecking ball.

"I- I have to go," I rushed out, trying to keep my voice even. "I forgot. I have an appointment with Miss Hampstead."

He frowned up at me; eyes narrowing, clouded with suspicion.

"I'll see you later, okay?" I forced a smile that I knew probably looked wrong.

"I'll come with you," Hailee said across the table.

"No, it's cool." I made myself meet her sympathetic gaze. "I'll see you in fourth period."

But the second I went to move I realized my mistake. To get out of the cafeteria, I'd have to walk directly by Jason and Jenna.

Crap.

Taking a deep breath, I grabbed my tray and kept my head held high. I was so proud of myself for keeping it together. Only a few more steps and I'd be clear of them and their live sex show. Until something brushed the back of my leg, and I froze. My breath caught as I willed myself to calm down. It was nothing. A gust of wind from an open window maybe, or dust particles in the air. Before I could stop myself, I looked down. Dark eyes stared back at me.

Jason.

It was Jason.

He stared at me, *through* me, as I stood there paralyzed. Jenna was still kissing him, trailing her treacherous mouth all over his skin. Skin that less than forty-eight hours ago, I'd tasted. Skin I had been kissing.

A violent shiver rolled up my spine, my stomach churning.

Move, Felicity. Just keep walking.

Jason's brow rose as he continued to stare at me, barely kissing Jenna back, but not stopping her either.

His intense gaze was cruel.

But then, I shouldn't have expected anything else.

Steeling myself, I narrowed my eyes at him, lingering for a second, and then put one foot in front of the other and kept walking. Telling myself he hadn't just ripped out my heart and stomped all over it.

2

Jason

"We need to talk," Cameron pressed his hand against my chest blocking my exit from the locker room.

"Not interested," I said coolly.

"We *are* doing this." His brow arched as he shoved me. It was only a mild push but enough for me to know he meant business.

"Fine," I shot back. "Say whatever you have to say, man, and let me get the fuck to class."

"You go to class now?" He smirked.

"Fuck you."

"Why'd you do it?" Cam let out a weary sigh, his eyes asking me a million things I didn't have the answer to.

Shrugging, I said, "Because I was drunk and she was there."

"Don't give me that bullshit. You like her."

"Like her?" I barked out. "I can't fucking stand her." Felicity Giles was exactly the kind of girl I spent my days trying to avoid. Needy. Desperate. Weird as hell.

"You really are a dick sometimes, you know that?"

"Never claimed to be anything else." I shrugged dismissively.

"I just don't get it. Vaughn was all over you. You could have taken her back to the hotel..." He let the words hang between us. We'd gone to New York for Hailee's birthday last weekend. Asher's cousin Vaughn had showed us around with her brother. She was hot. Slim with curves in all the right places, and Cam was right, she was up for it. Whispered it in my ear more than once during the night. But I hadn't gone there. Instead, I'd drank more than I should have, gone back to the hotel and found myself outside Felicity's room in the middle of the night.

"Look, it was just sex. Drunken sex. I was horny, and she was there." She might not have been my type, all geeky with no filter, but there was no denying Felicity was gorgeous. Long dark hair, narrow waist, and legs that seemed to go on for miles, even if she did stand a good few inches shorter than me. And her eyes, fuck. Two pools of sea-green that had worked some hypnotic voodoo shit on me.

Obviously.

"Just sex," my best friend repeated flatly.

"Yeah, just sex. She knows the score. It was a good time. Now it's over. So can we all just fucking move on?" I couldn't get distracted by some girl-drama, not when I had the play-offs in sight. My focus needed to be one-hundred-and-ten percent on the team. On winning State.

"So it wasn't a game?"

"Game? What the fuck are you talking about?" Irritation rippled through me.

"You didn't know?"

"Seriously, Chase, spit it out already."

Cameron was staring at me like I'd lost my fucking mind. And maybe I had. If I'd had known it would cause this much trouble, I never would have looked twice at Felicity. But then, my step-sister wasn't supposed to walk in on us.

He didn't reply, still gawking at me, so I added, "Look, I know she's Hailee's best friend, but she knows the deal. I didn't promise anything, and she didn't—"

"Will you just shut up a second," he ground out and it was my turn to gawk.

A beat passed. Another. The air charged around us.

And then he delivered the last words I ever expected to hear.

"She was a virgin."

"A virgin?" I choked out. "Is that supposed to be a joke?"

Felicity wasn't a virgin. Sure, she'd been tight, but I just figured she wasn't as experienced as Jenna or the other gymnasts and cheerleaders who rode dick like it was an Olympic sport. But she hadn't said a word when I'd gone faster. Harder. I always liked to be in control and that spilled over to sex. I never made a girl do anything she didn't want to, but I wasn't gentle either. I liked to fuck. And then I liked to get the fuck out of there. I'd tried the whole relationship thing once before and it had blown up in my face, and I wasn't *ever* looking to go there again.

I didn't do sleepovers and except for a handful of girls, I didn't do repeat performances. Sex was an outlet. Nothing more, nothing less. And like football, I excelled at it.

So how the fuck hadn't I realized Felicity was a virgin?

"You really didn't know?" Cam asked.

"Do you think I would have fucked her if I did?" He winced at my harsh tone. "She was practically begging for it."

I think. It was all a little hazy. But she'd wanted it as much as me.

"Nice, real nice." He deadpanned.

"Are we done? Because you're starting to piss me the hell off."

"Yeah, we're done." He let out an exasperated breath. "Just stay away from her, Jase. She's Hailee's best friend and things are already strained enough." He didn't say the rest; he didn't have to.

Things between us *were* strained. But then what had he expected when I found out about him and Hailee?

Growing up, she had been the bane of my fucking life. I'd hated her. Hated everything about her. But a lot had changed since senior year started. I guess that was a trending theme with it being the final year of high school.

Me and Hailee weren't exactly friends now, but for the sake of Cameron, we'd called a shaky truce.

"Is that all?" Anger laced my words. I was so fucking over all this bullshit.

"I know it's hard seeing me with her—"

"Save me the 'I'm sorry I chose your step-sister' speech."

"Jase, come on..." His hand curled around my arm. "It doesn't change anything. You're still my best friend. I've got your back. Always."

But it did change things.

It changed everything.

It had always been the two of us against the world. Now it wasn't.

And I didn't know what the fuck to do with that.

I PUSHED off the wall the second Felicity appeared. Mondays she stayed behind after school for book club.

Fucking book club. It sounded like something my grandma would have enjoyed if she were alive.

"Jason?" Her mouth fell open when she spotted me, those big sea-green eyes widening to saucers. "What are you—"

"Let's go, Giles," I said, trying to keep it as impersonal as possible. My dick had other ideas though, traitorous motherfucker, stirring to life the second my hand clasped around her tiny wrist. Remembering how it had felt to pin them above her head while I slid inside her, making her cry out my name.

"Go? Go where?" She huffed indignantly. "I'm not going anywhere with you."

"You think you have a choice?" I dragged her around the side of the building toward the gym. It was quiet, just like I knew it would be.

"Jason," she hissed, trying to yank free of my grip. But I kept walking, refusing to do this out in the open where anyone could walk by and see us.

Shouldering the door to the gym, I pulled her down the hall toward the locker room. The second we were inside, and the door closed, I was on her. Crowding her against the wall, I placed my hands either side of her head and glared at her. "A virgin? You didn't think to fucking mention that before we—"

Her scowl deepened, a low growl rumbling in her throat. It would have been impressive if she wasn't so tiny and vulnerable compared to me as I loomed over her. "It wasn't like you asked," she seethed.

"Because I didn't think—"

"Oh that's right." Her brow rose. "You're used to fucking skanks."

Jesus, this girl.

"Watch it, Giles."

"Or what, Ford?" she threw back without hesitation.

"Why didn't you tell me?" My voice softened, surprising me. It surprised Felicity too, if the hitch of her breath was anything to go by.

"It's not a big deal." She gave a lackluster shrug. "I wanted to get it over with, and you were available."

"Available?" I balked. She couldn't actually be serious. "You make it sound so—"

"What are you doing, Jason?"

What was I doing?

"Nothing, I just... shit, Felicity, you should have told me."

Sardonic laughter spilled from her lips. "What, so you could make it romantic? Buy me flowers and tell me how pretty I looked before dirtying me up. Please. This isn't a fairy tale and you're certainly no prince. It was just sex, Jason." Something flashed in her eyes, but she quickly schooled her expression.

It was too late though. I'd seen that look before. Right before I glided inside her.

Fuck.

Fuck. Fuck. Fuck.

Memories washed over me. Her damp skin, the little moans she made as I moved above her. Inside her. The way she'd clung to me, meeting me thrust for thrust.

"You're sure you were a—"

"Are you kidding me right now?" Her eyes widened.

"But you didn't..." The words got stuck in my throat.

"What, bleed? I did, you were just too wasted to notice." Shame colored her cheeks as she lowered her gaze.

I had been drunk, but I hadn't been that drunk. *Had I?* It had been dark and messy. A tangle of heated kisses and desperate touches. And then Hailee had burst into the room killing the moment and I'd pretty much hightailed it out of there, not bothering to check if she was okay.

"Can I go now?" she added, barely looking at me.

"I... what..." I choked out unsure why I felt like shit all of a sudden. So she was a virgin. It wasn't like I initiated it. She was as hot for me as I was for her.

Was I really hot for her?

I'd told Cameron it was just sex, convenient. But I couldn't deny I didn't like hearing her describe what had really gone down.

A girl's first time was supposed to be... more or something, wasn't it?

Hearts and flowers and mood lighting and all that shit. I didn't know because I didn't make a habit of fucking virgins.

"Why?" The word flew out of my mouth before I could stop it.

"Why?" Felicity frowned. "Why, what?"

"Why me?"

"Oh don't flatter yourself, Jason." She tapped my chest, smiling wryly. "I have a list and you were a means to an end."

A means to an... what the actual fuck?

"Now if you're done, I have places to be." She ducked under my arm and came up on the other side, but my hand shot out, grabbing her arm.

"What game are you playing, Giles?"

"Game?" Surprise flashed in her eyes, her earlier confidence slipping away. "You think this is a game?"

"You're telling me it isn't?"

The air electrified around us, crackling with sexual tension. My dick felt it. Hell, my entire body felt it. And it wanted more.

More Felicity.

More of her smart mouth and witty retorts. Her slender hips and pouty lips.

I needed to get a fucking grip. Because I had enough to worry about without adding a girl to the mix. Especially my step-sister's best friend.

"Go to hell, Jason." She stormed off, her anger almost palpable as she disappeared into the hall.

Long after she'd gone, I was still standing there. Processing our interaction. My body's strange response to her. She was pissed, that much was obvious—her attitude a front for her true feelings. Her closing line had been telling enough. She wanted me to stay the fuck away.

So why did all I hear was *game on*?

"Jason, can you come in here please?"

With a groan, I stalked down the hall and into the kitchen where I found my dad at the kitchen table, pouring over a stack of papers. "Yeah?"

"We'd like for you to join us for dinner today."

"I'm good, but thanks." No way did I want to sit around playing happy families with my old man, his new wife, and Hailee.

"Son," Dad let out a heavy sigh. "We need to move past this."

"I'm over it. I just don't want to pretend I actually give a shit."

"Jason," he snapped, eyes sliding to Denise. "I know you're hurting, but this is not the way."

Me and my old man were most definitely not father and son goals. To the rest of Rixon, Dad liked to exude togetherness. A team. The local football hero and the son set to follow in his path. But I knew the truth. I knew what Kent Ford was really about. There was a time when I'd worshipped the ground he'd walked on. But that was *before*. When he and my mom were in love. When our family was enough.

"I'll be in my room," I said, swiping a banana from the fruit bowl and retreating into the hall. Almost colliding with Hailee as she flew off the stairs.

"Sorry," she said. "I didn't see you."

"Yeah, okay," I grumbled. It wasn't like you could really miss me. Six one. Broad. Wearing my blue and white football jersey. "In a hurry?"

Hailee's brows pinched. "You want to talk?"

"Forget it." I waved her off.

"Jeez, I'm sorry. I just didn't expect... what you were saying?" Her expression softened, and I found myself humoring her.

"I said are you in a hurry?"

"Felicity's picking me up. We're going to The Alley."

Of course they were. I didn't get the appeal. It was a dive place on the Rixon/Rixon East border. Too many East kids came around there for my liking.

"You think it's a good idea to go there alone?"

"I won't be alone. I'll be with Flick. But it's nice to know you care." A hint of amusement played on Hailee's lips.

Before I could correct her, Felicity's horn blared outside. I knew because I'd been listening to the annoying-as-fuck sound for almost two years since she passed driver's ed.

"Right then, I'll guess I'll see ya." Hailee moved toward the door, but I called after her. "Yeah?" She glanced back.

"I didn't know."

"Know?" Her brows knitted.

I dragged a hand down my face wondering why the fuck I'd said anything to begin with. But it was out there now, hanging between us. "Yeah, about Felicity being a... you know," I explained.

My step-sister inclined her head, studying me for a second and then said, "Okay."

Okay?

What the fuck was that supposed to mean?

"I'm glad we cleared that up."

A hint of a smile lifted the corner of her mouth but then her expression turned serious. "I know we have to tolerate each other for Cameron's sake, but stay away from Felicity, Jason."

"I—" The words got stuck, but it was too late anyway. Hailee had already slipped outside and disappeared, leaving me standing there, wondering what the fuck just happened.

3

Felicity

"YOU'RE DISTRACTED," Hailee said over her sundae. "It's him, isn't it? Jason." There was a coolness to her voice that squeezed my heart.

"It's not..." I let out a heavy sigh, meeting her gaze. "I thought I'd feel good or relieved or something but now I just feel..."

I didn't know what I felt.

The list was supposed to help me push my boundaries, to step out the confines of my perfectly average life and take more risks. It wasn't like I'd planned to seduce Jason. To play his stupid game of cat and mouse. He was just there. Like a slow building wave that before I realized what had happened, crashed over me and swept me off my feet.

"Oh, Flick." Hailee reached over the table and grabbed my hand. "I could kill him for doing—"

"It wasn't his fault. I need you to know that. I—"

"You like him, don't you?"

"I can't really explain it but something's different this year." I'd never looked twice at Jason and his friends before. Neither had Hailee though, and look how that turned out. Now she was madly in love with Cameron and they were planning to go off to college together and have cute football playing babies.

"Did you think if you slept with him, he'd suddenly change? Because—"

"What? No. *No!*" I shook my head. "I know Jason isn't boyfriend material. Trust me, I know. But there's something... he makes me feel..."

Just then, the door opened and a swarm of people entered, all wearing red and white jerseys.

"Crap," Hailee grumbled as we watched the Rixon East football players stroll up to the diner counter.

"Don't they know this is Switzerland?" I whispered.

Tate, the owner of The Alley, refused to let the rivalry between Rixon High and the high school across the river, Rixon East, affect his business. Anyone was welcome here so long as they played nice. That meant no football jerseys, colors, or smack talk. It's why both football teams usually avoided the place like the plague.

"Apparently the rules just changed." Hailee retreated into herself, and I couldn't blame her. Lewis Thatcher, captain and QB for the Rixon East Eagles, had come after her once he discovered she was Jason's step-sister. It had been a shitshow, but since Rival's Week was done, we figured—*hoped*—the stupid pranks were over.

"Oh shit." I'd clearly spoken too soon as Lewis Thatcher entered The Alley, a smirk on his face as everyone sat up a little straighter. Like Jason, he was worshipped by his classmates and townspeople. But he wasn't in Rixon East now and technically, this was Rixon territory.

So what the hell was he doing here?

"Maybe we should go," I said to Hailee who was still gawking at them. "Hails?" I kicked her leg gently under the table and her head whipped around to me.

"Sorry, what?"

"I said maybe we should go."

"And let him win? No way." Defiance sparked in her eyes. "I doubt they even recognize—"

"Ladies," a deep voice said, and we both glanced up to find Thatcher and another guy staring down at us. "Hailee and, I'm sorry, I don't think I got your name?"

"You didn't," I sassed. "Because I didn't give it to you."

The whole diner had fallen quiet, everyone straining to hear our conversation. Hailee flashed me a look that said, 'don't make it worse', but no way was I just going to sit here while he taunted her.

"You go can now." I dismissed them with my hand and focused on Hailee again. Silently praying they left. But they didn't.

"I like this one," Thatcher's friend said. "I wonder what else her mouth can do—"

"You need to leave," Hailee ground out, her hands curled around the edge of the table, turning her knuckles white.

"Funny," Thatcher leaned down into her space, his lip twisted with amusement, "Because it sounds like a warning, and yet, I don't see anyone here coming to your rescue. Do you, Gallen?"

"Don't see no one, Cap." Thatcher's dog folded his arms over his chest, glaring at me.

My eyes surveyed the diner, searching for someone—anyone—who might help us. But the handful of kids I recognized from school all dropped their gazes the second I looked at them.

Cowards.

The rest of the kids watched with a mix of interest and sympathy, and I figured they were East kids. Used to Thatcher's games.

"What do you want?" Hailee sounded disinterested, but I caught the inflection in her voice.

"Want?" Thatcher grinned. "I want lots of things, baby." He plucked a strand of her hair and brought it to his nose, inhaling deeply.

Screw this. I dipped my hand into my purse and managed to dig out my cell phone without Lewis or his dog noticing. Quickly locating Cameron's number, I fired off a text and then slid it back into my purse.

"Rumor has it you're fucking Chase now?"

Hailee pressed her lips together refusing to answer.

"Get off her, you disgusting pig," I yelled, but panic filled Hailee's eyes as she shook her head subtly.

"Want me to shut her up, Cap?" The dog said. "Because I'd love nothing more than to watch her choke on my—"

"I'd like to see you try." The words spilled out before I could stop them. Hunger glittered in the dog's predatory gaze as his hooded eyes drifted down my body.

"Pig," I muttered, angling myself away from him.

"I want you to give your boyfriend a message for me—"

"Why don't you give it him yourself?"

Relief slammed into me at the sight of Cameron and Asher standing in the door. Thatcher immediately straightened, but he didn't leave Hailee's side.

"Are you okay?" I mouthed at her, and she nodded, unshed tears pooling in the corner of her eyes.

"Fee, baby, why don't you come on over here?" Asher crooked his finger at me, and I rose, ignoring the low growl coming from Thatcher's friend. When I reached him, Asher hooked me into his side and whispered, "You did the right thing."

Although with the anger rolling off Cameron, I wasn't sure. I didn't want to incite a fight, but I didn't want Lewis to upset Hailee any more than he already had.

"She yours, Bennet?" the dog asked Asher with a snarl. "Because if she's not, I wouldn't mind taking her for a ride; see if what they say about Raider chicks is true." His laughter filled the air and a few of his teammates snorted.

My stomach washed with disgust but Asher's fingers dug into me, grounding me. "What are we going to do here, Cam?" he said. "There's only two of us and eight of them."

"I'll handle it." Cameron inched forward, the air around him charged and dangerous.

"Hailee, come here." He gave her a reassuring nod, and slowly Hailee rose from the chair. But Thatcher's hand clamped down on her shoulder.

"Not so fast, baby, we're just getting—"

"Get your hands off her."

"Or what, Chase? You're a lover not a fighter and I don't see Ford anywhere, do you?"

Anticipation crackled in the air, the whole diner watching on with fascination. A few cameras were aimed in the direction of the stand-off between Cameron and Lewis Thatcher and I knew it wouldn't be long before it was all over social media.

"You don't want to do this, man." Cameron implored, holding his hands up. "It's a public place, people are filming."

Hesitation flashed over Thatcher's face, enough for Cameron to grab Hailee's hand and yank her toward him. "Go." He flicked his head toward us, and she hurried to Asher's side.

"Maybe we should call Jason," she said.

"That is the last thing we want to do right now. Your boy can handle it."

"What's going on here?" Tate appeared looking flustered. Planting his hands on his hips, he glowered at Thatcher. "You know the rules, Son. I won't have you coming in here disrespecting—"

"Easy, old man." He held up his hands, backing away slowly "We were just getting a bite and then leaving."

Leaving my ass.

If Tate hadn't showed up right when he had, we all knew things could have ended very differently. But Lewis Thatcher tipped his head toward the door and like good little minions, his teammates filed out of the diner, Tate following them out for good measure.

"Tell Ford we'll see him soon." Thatcher blew Cameron a kiss. "Nice seeing you again, Hailee."

Asher released me and threw himself into Cameron's path. "Don't do anything stupid, bro." He pressed his hand against Cameron's chest.

"I'm cool," he said, wrapping his arm around Hailee. "Let's go sit down."

"You mean let's wait until it's safe to leave?" I said unable to keep the sarcasm out of my voice. "What the hell was that?"

Asher and Cameron led us over to one of the booths at the back so we had a little more privacy. Hailee scooted in next to Cameron and Asher pulled me in next to him.

"He's gunning for blood." Asher scrubbed his face.

"Well, he ain't going to be gunning for blood in my place again." Tate appeared, his brows bunched together. "Cameron, good to see you, Son."

"Hey, Tate. I'm sorry about—"

"Now now, there's no need to apologize; but I won't have your little rivalry spilling into my business, you hear me?"

Cameron nodded, his jaw set.

"We had no idea they would show up here," Hailee added, the color finally returning to her cheeks.

"Yeah, well, the little shits planned it. A couple of them caused a distraction out back, or I would have been here sooner. You're more than welcome around here anytime, you know that. But not if—"

"We got it," Cameron said. "It won't happen again."

But it was promise we all knew he couldn't keep. Lewis Thatcher did what he wanted. No one could stop him from coming around here, except the police. And like the Raiders, the Rixon East Eagles were virtually untouchable.

Tate didn't look convinced, but he skulked away, mumbling something about 'football madness'. Few people in Rixon were anti-football. In fact, in my whole life I'd only ever known three people who weren't obsessed with the game: Hailee, Tate, and my mom. It was just a part of life here.

"Fuck," Asher breathed out.

"I second that," I said, dropping my head back against the booth.

"You okay?" Cameron asked Hailee, tucking her closer into his side. I envied them. Their closeness, their love. The way he looked at her like she was everything he needed, and he'd do whatever it took to keep her. I wanted that.

God, did I want it.

So why the hell did you have sex with Jason?

I ignored my inner critic, focusing on my best friend. "Maybe we should tell someone?"

"Tell who? Miss Hampstead? My mom? The principal?" She shook her head. "I can handle Lewis Thatcher."

"You shouldn't have to fucking handle him." Cameron slammed his hand down on the table, making me and Hailee flinch. "Jason should never have..."

"What did he do that was so bad?" I asked.

Jason and Lewis Thatcher's rivalry had grown with them from PeeWee through junior football camp. We'd all heard the stories of two of the best quarterbacks ever to come out of our district. The pranks and fights. But something had changed last year. The rivalry turned bitter. But no one knew the details, not even Hailee who lived with him.

"Nothing you need to worry your pretty little head over." Asher grinned.

"You think I'm pretty? How sweet." I shot back, my words dripping sarcasm. His expression fell and for a second I could have sworn he looked hurt, but then his smirk was plastered back in place as if it had never happened.

"You know Jase is going to want payba—"

"Not here," Cameron said quietly, and something passed between them. Something they didn't want me and Hailee knowing.

Dumb boys. I rolled my eyes.

"I don't want you or Jason going after Thatcher." Hailee grabbed his jaw, forcing him to look at her.

"We're not, I promise."

"Don't lie to me, Cameron. I expect it off Jason, but not you."

"What do you expect me to do? What he did to you—"

"Is done. Nothing you or Jason do is going to fix that. Let it go. I have."

Cameron dipped his head, capturing her lips in a slow, bruising kiss.

Asher cleared his throat, shifting uncomfortably. "Seriously, here?" he drawled, shooting me a bemused look.

"Sorry." Hailee's eyes slid to ours as she tried to break free from the kiss. But Cameron was stronger, planting big wet sloppy kisses all over her face.

"Aaaaand that's me, gone. Come on, Fee, baby, you can kick my ass at air hockey."

With a groan, I followed him out of the booth. Asher was the joker of the bunch: always smiling, always cracking a joke. With sandy blond hair, sparkling blue eyes, and a roguish smile, he was the epitome of the All-American boy next door. And somehow, I'd earned a spot in his life. Cameron constantly teased me about getting with Asher and sometimes, I did wonder what it would be like if I went there. I mean, he seemed interested, always teasing and flirting with me. But sadly, he wasn't the guy who turned my head and made my heart beat that little bit faster. Deep down, Asher was good. His heart was pure.

Which sucked for me... because apparently I preferred bad boys with dark hearts.

4

Jason

"WHAT THE FUCK HAPPENED?" I demanded the second Cam and Asher arrived at our regular spot in Bell's, a local bar run by an ex-Raider and one of our biggest fans. My eyes flicked to Hailee who was quiet and a little pale at his side. I barely even acknowledged Felicity. I couldn't risk her pulling that hypnotic voodoo crap on me, not here.

"Well?" I arched my brow, growing impatient.

"It was Thatcher. He showed up at The Alley."

"He was bothering you?" Meeting my step-sister's gaze, my eyes bore into hers, and she gave me a small nod.

"Fuck." I raked a hand through my hair, trying to rein in the anger I felt coursing through my veins. Thatcher was supposed to be my problem. Mine and the team's. He was never supposed to go after Hailee. But that shit was on me and I'd deal with it.

One way or another, Thatcher would get what was coming to him. Even if I had to bide my time until the season was done.

My fist curled against my thigh, anger radiating deep inside me. Fucking Lewis Thatcher.

"I'll get the drinks in," Asher said cutting the thick silence. Everyone seemed to inhale a breath as they were collectively waiting for me to get my shit together. I met Cameron's heavy stare. Concern shone in his eyes as he silently warned me not to do anything reckless.

But this was me we were talking about.

And when it came to Lewis Thatcher, the temptation to go across the river and cause a little chaos was usually too hard to resist.

"I'm good," I said, my eyes flicking past him to Hailee and then Felicity. Her eyes snapped to mine, narrowing slightly.

"I'll go help Ash." I walked away, barely able to stand the knot in my stomach. "Hey." Leaning on the bar next to Asher, I gave him a tight smile.

"Hey, you okay, man?"

I grunted some inaudible reply.

"This shit with Thatcher is getting hairy," Ash went on, "You should have seen him with his hands on Hailee. I thought Cam was going—"

"He touched her?" My jaw clenched.

"He was just trying to get a rise out of Cam. I managed to get Fee out of there before one of his guys..." he trailed off, watching me intently.

I knew what he was doing and I didn't like it.

"Anyway," he said when I didn't take the bait. "Cameron held it together. I'm not sure we'll be able to show our faces around there anytime soon though. Tate, the owner, wasn't too impressed."

"You know I haven't stepped foot in that place for almost two years, right?"

Asher shrugged. "I'd forgotten how cool it was."

"Cool, really?" I fought a smirk. "You're fucking weird sometimes."

"Fuck you, man." He shouldered me. "You have a plan, right? To get Thatcher back for pulling that shit with Hailee? I know she told Cameron not to do anything, but he can't just get away with it."

"And he won't," I ground out.

"Well you know I've got your back." He slung his arm over my shoulder just as Jerry brought our beers over.

"You two ain't cooking up no trouble, are you?" One of his bushy brows rose.

"Nothing you need to worry about J." I winked and the old man laughed.

"Seen that look one too many times. Just remember you got a load riding on the next couple of games. Don't go screwing up what could be a perfect season." His eyes slid to mine.

As if I'd ever let that happen. We were going all the way this year. Anything less was simply not an option. We'd lost out to Rixon East last year and it had fucking stung. But this year, State was ours. We were five for five. Another two wins and our ticket to the play-offs was in the bag.

We gathered up our drinks—beers for me and the guys, and sodas for the girls—and headed back to our table. Mackey and a couple of the other guys had joined us, and he'd wasted no time in turning his charm on Felicity.

"So, Flick. Is it okay if I call you Flick?" he asked around a suggestive smirk.

I slid into the booth, taking a long pull on my beer.

"You can call her Felicity, jackass," Asher piped up, smacking him upside the head.

"But I thought..." Mackey looked to her for help, but a slow smile spread over her face, and I braced myself for whatever shit was about to come out of her mouth.

"Asher is right," she purred, placing a hand on his arm. "It's only really a nickname my close friends use. Felicity is fine."

"Close friends?" The rookie's eyes lit up. "Baby, just say the word and I can make that happen."

The girls smothered their laughter while Asher hit him upside the head again. "Fuck, man, what was that for?"

"You need to work on your game, bro."

"Khloe didn't seem to mind last night when she was sucking my—"

A chorus of 'dude' and 'Mackey' rang out around us.

"Oh, it's like that now. Just because Hailee and Fli... *Felicity*," he shot her an apologetic look, "are here, we have to tone it down."

"That's right, dipshit," Asher replied. "Because we respect women."

"Dude, didn't you hear Jase telling everyone about the chick he banged over the weekend?"

Fuck.

My head snapped up. "Shut the fuck up, Mackey. It was just locker room talk."

"Locker room talk my ass. You said—"

"No fucking buts." I slammed my hand against the table, the crack reverberating through me. I chanced a look at Felicity, hoping she hadn't heard him. But from the way the blood had drained from her face, I knew she had.

Stupid fucking rookie.

"Excuse me," she nudged Asher, "I need to use the bathroom."

"I think I'll come with." Hailee followed her out and the two of them hurried off, but not before my step-sister glowered at me.

"What the fuck was that about?" Asher frowned at me.

"Maybe she got her period."

We all gawked at Mackey. "Or maybe," Asher drawled, "They need to pee."

"Nah, chicks go to the bathroom in packs when they get their period; it's called menstrual synchronicity or something."

"I'm pretty sure that has everything to do with chicks getting their periods together, not chicks peeing together."

"All sounds the same to me." He shrugged and someone balled up a napkin and threw it at him.

"Did something happen with you two?" Asher lowered his voice enough that no one else heard him.

"Who?" I played dumb.

"Jase, come on. She looked ready to puke all over the table."

"I have no idea what you're talking about."

"Of course you don't." He grimaced, turning away from me and joining in the rest of the conversation.

I don't know what they were all getting so hung up over. So me and Felicity had sex. It wasn't my fault she was a virgin and didn't tell me. Or that Hailee had walked in on us. If anything, it was a good thing... we'd fucked whatever this weird hate-lust vibe we had going on right out of us. *Except, you didn't finish **and** you stole her fucking virginity.*

Stifling a groan, I mumbled, "Be right back." Slipping out of the booth, I ignored the questioning stares. I don't know when I'd started caring about things so goddamn much, but I needed to clear the air. I couldn't afford any distractions this semester, and if my friends were going to keep bringing Felicity up, then she was just that. A distraction.

One I needed to nip in the bud sooner rather than later.

Determined, I headed toward the back of the bar where the hall leading to the restrooms was. Hailee and Felicity were just coming out of the women's bathroom when I entered. My step-sister immediately spotted me, her eyes on high alert.

"Hey," I said, raking a hand through my hair. "Can I get a minute?" My eyes found Felicity over Hailee's shoulder.

"I don't think that's a good—"

"Hailee," Felicity laid a hand on her shoulder. "It's fine. Go, we'll be right there."

My step-sister shouldered past me, pausing only to meet my eyes. She didn't speak. She didn't need to; her message glittering right there.

Don't touch.

Don't hurt her.

I'm warning you.

Jamming my hands in my pocket, I moved toward Felicity. "Come on." I slipped around her and down the hall. I knew this place well enough to know every nook and cranny. Shouldering the last door, I pushed it open and waited for Felicity to go inside. Her brow rose in question and I said, "Just to talk, I promise."

She gave me a tight nod.

The second I stepped into the storeroom and closed the door, the air seemed to disappear. Felicity watched me, her eyes clouded with hesitation.

"What the fuck was that back there?"

She jerked away as if I'd physically slapped her. "Don't act dumb, Flick. I saw the way you acted when Mackey was running his mouth."

"Yeah, well, I didn't plan on becoming *locker room talk*," she shot back.

"Is that what you think? That I was talking about you?" I stepped closer. "That was a mistake. *You* were a mistake. One I don't plan on making again."

Felicity's breath hitched, pain flashing in her eyes. "Fuck you," she seethed.

"Baby," I reached out, pulling a strand of hair. "We already did that."

"I hate you." Her voice trembled.

Good. She needed to hate me. I didn't need her getting the wrong idea about us.

About me.

For as much as I hated to admit it, Hailee was right. I needed to stay away from Felicity. She was too naïve, too fucking pure. Until New York, until *me*, she'd been a virgin for fuck's sake.

I stepped forward again, putting us almost chest to chest. I hadn't planned on getting this close, but there was no denying she pulled me in.

Almost made me want to finish what we started in New York. My eyes dropped to her lips; soft pouty lips I knew the taste of. Her tongue darted out as she watched me watching her.

"Jason, what are—"

"Shut the fuck up," I ground out. Her chest was heaving, matching the way she kept sucking in tiny harsh breaths. She reminded me of a doe. Innocent and vulnerable. Waiting to be picked off by the big bad wolf.

Before I knew it, I'd slid my hand to her neck, stroking my thumb along her damp skin. She was sweating. I made her sweat. It was heady, knowing the way I affected her. Knowing that if I dipped my fingers into her panties I'd probably find her wet for me. Even though she hated me, even though she didn't want this, her body did. Something we apparently had in common.

Her body shuddered, heat radiating off her.

Perhaps Felicity Giles wasn't such a good girl after all.

The idea made my dick twitch, straining against my jeans.

"You need to leave." Her body shook now, her eyes saying a million things she would never tell me.

"And why exactly would that be?" I leaned in, my lips ghosting over her jaw up to the corner of her mouth. She inhaled sharply.

"Jason, please, don't do this..."

"You want me."

"No." It came out a shaky breath.

"Don't lie to me, babe. I can feel the heat from your body, the way you're trembling at my touch. And I bet if I do this," I let my other hand drift down her stomach, down and down, until I grazed the apex of her thighs.

A soft moan slipped from Felicity's lips and I chuckled. "Bingo."

"Why?" she choked out, swallowing hard.

"Why?" I eased back to look at her. Pupils blown, skin flushed, her arousal swirled around us. "Because I can." My mouth hovered over hers, waiting. Anticipating what she might do.

Her eyes fluttered closed, her breathing ragged. I was barely touching her, and yet, she was so responsive. So easy to work up. Felicity Giles was nothing but surprise after surprise.

"Why me?" I asked against her lips.

"W- what?"

"Why did you pick me? I don't believe that bullshit about being a means to an end. Not when you could have your pick of guys who would have treated you—"

She snorted at that. "No one at school would dare ask me out."

What the actual fuck?

I blinked, hardly able to believe what I was hearing. Sure, Felicity wasn't classically hot; usually found walking the school hall looking more of a hot mess than a girl I wanted to fuck. But when you looked past the overalls and floral print shirts and hippy style she wore most days, she was beautiful.

"You really don't know?" she whispered.

My expression must have said it all, because Felicity let out a heavy sigh. "You," she said. "It's you. You told everyone Hailee was off-limits in ninth grade, and I'm her best friend. If anyone tries to get close to me, they're going to get close to—"

"Hailee."

"Hailee." Her lips pursed as she gave me a small nod. "Apparently, I'm not worth the risk."

She didn't date... because of me.

I guess I'd never really given it much thought before. She was Hailee's best friend; someone I was used to seeing around. Someone I barely tolerated. But now she was... *fuck!* I didn't want to feel guilty. But the unfamiliar emotion snaked through me.

A beat passed. And another.

"Jason, I should—"

"Wait, just wait a minute." I needed to think, and it was impossible with her standing there, so close, yet, so far away. My body hyperaware of hers.

"Are you okay?" Her voice was so small, so fucking quiet. I hated it, but I didn't know why.

"Okay, this has been... weird, but I'm going." She began peeling my fingers off her neck. I hadn't even realized I was still holding her like that because I couldn't think straight.

Felicity had almost made it to the door when I finally found my voice again. "Stop." I said, spinning around to meet her confused gaze.

"Jason, I—"

I was on her in a second, pressing her against the door, fixing my mouth over hers. Felicity slammed her hands against my jersey, pushing me away, but I was too strong and eventually she gave up, twisting her hand into the material and yanking me closer.

Demanding more.

Flattening my body against hers, I punched my hips forward. "Oh God," she moaned, her fingers scraping the back of my neck as we devoured each other. Tongues tangling and teeth clashing.

"Whoa." I jerked back, blinking rapidly, trying to clear my mind.

What the fuck was I doing?

"That was—"

"A mistake," Felicity said with a tinge of sadness.

"Yeah, I mean, I wasn't..." I backed up, putting some much-needed space between us.

"I get it." She closed down, wrapping her arms around her waist, barely meeting my eye.

"Felicity, I—"

"Let's *not* do this. I had zero expectations when we..." Her expression cooled like the air around us. "You don't owe me anything and I sure as hell don't owe you anything, so let's just pretend it never happened, okay? I'll go back to being your step-sister's best friend, the person you didn't realize existed."

Pretend it never happened.

"Fine. Sounds good to me," I said with an easy shrug.

"Great."

"Fine." The word echoed in my head. I was fine with that. I'd only come to talk to her to clear the air and avoid any more drama with the guys. Pretending it never happened was the perfect fucking solution.

After all she was right, she'd never been on my radar until recently; no one to me.

Better that's what she went back to. Wasn't it?

5

Felicity

"HAPPY GAME DAY." I flashed Hailee a wide smile, but she frowned.

"You're... happy."

"Is that a crime?"

"No, of course not, I just thought..."

"That I'd spend the week moping after Jason?" Laughter spilled out of me, but it was strained. "Like I already told you yesterday and the day before that, it was a mistake. A blip. Jason, who?"

Hailee's eyes scrutinized me. Sharp and assessing and filled with doubt.

"If it makes you feel better," I went on, filling the awkward silence, "I added another item to my list."

"You did?" Her brows went up as the school came into view.

"I did. Number eleven: Do not, under any circumstances, fraternize with the football team."

"Asher's on the football team." I felt her heavy gaze on me.

"Asher is a friend."

"Is that what we're calling it. He likes you, you know?"

"He doesn't like me. He likes the idea of me."

"We could double date." She sounded happy at the prospect; too happy.

"Hails," I glanced at her, "Don't get any ideas about me and Asher, okay?"

"Who, me?" She smiled deviously. "I have no idea what you're talking about."

"Hails, I mean it, Asher is..."

"Cute. Athletic. And totally into you."

"He isn't..." The protest died on my tongue. There were times when I did notice Asher looking at me with lust in his baby blues. But he was a guy and I was a girl. It was simple biology. Asher Bennet was a player through and through. The rumors I'd heard about his sexcapades were impressive to say the least. And he very much had a type. Much like the entire team.

And I was *not* it.

"I need to stop by the studio first thing. Coach Hasson and Mr. Jalin want to see how things are 'progressing'." She air quoted the words.

"Ah, yes, the Seniors Night portraits. And how are those coming along?" Hailee was secretive about her art, so the fact Coach Hasson had asked her to paint the annual senior football players commemorative portraits was no small thing.

In fact, it was pretty epic.

"Can I come with?"

"Hmm, I don't know, Flick. It's supposed to be a big surprise at the Seniors Night dinner."

"Please." I flashed her my best puppy-dog eyes. "The dinner is still three weeks away and I really want to see them."

"They still need a lot of work."

"Hails, they're going to be great. Mr. Jalin and Coach Hasson wouldn't have asked you if they didn't believe you could do it."

She gave me a weak smile, one that told me she wasn't as convinced as I was. "Fine. But you have to forget I ever showed you. Because Cameron has been hounding me to see his portrait and I told him no."

"Ahh, you love me more than you love him."

"Flick, come on. I love you both. Equally." Her lip quirked up.

Pulling into an empty parking spot, I cut the engine and twisted around to look at my best friend. "I'm sorry," I said, my voice nothing but genuine. "I'm sorry I almost screwed things up with you because of Jason. And I'm really sorry you had to see... well, *that*."

A violent shudder ripped through me at the memory of Hailee walking in on me and Jason. The confusion and hurt in her eyes.

The disappointment.

Her expression softened as she reached for my hand, squeezing it gently. "I'm sorry I freaked out. It's just we've hated him for so long and you're my best friend and I don't ever want to see you get hurt."

"You don't need to worry about me, Hails." My chest tightened. "I'm a big girl. Not even the likes of Jason can hurt me." But the second I said the words I knew it was a lie.

Because Jason had already hurt me. And I knew, given half the chance, he would completely destroy me.

But that wasn't going to happen, because whatever was between us, the weird hate-lust attraction we had going, was over.

So over.

Jason, who?

"Holy shit, Hails. That is..." I had no words to describe the work of art my eyes were currently soaking in. It was Cameron; a painting of him poised and ready to catch the ball. Even through his helmet you could see his fierce determination, the way his eyes were homed in on their target. Nothing but him and the ball, off-page, hurtling toward him.

"I've never seen anything like it." I reached out to touch it, but she swatted my hand away. "Crap, sorry," I said, leaning closer to get a better look. "It's so realistic. Like I'm watching him move for the ball. Even his shirt seems to be moving."

"That's what I wanted to capture; the urgency of the game, the adrenaline and power."

I glanced up at her, fighting a smirk. "Steady there, you're starting to sound like a true fan."

She blushed. "I guess he's rubbing off on me."

"Admit it, you love it." Pre-Cameron, I'd had to drag Hailee to her first game and she'd spent the whole time complaining. But now, my girl was on the way to becoming the Raiders number one fan. And I couldn't blame her. If I got to watch Cameron play, knowing he was mine, I'd be converted too.

"So can I see another?" I asked, eyeing the other canvasses, the paintings they contained all hidden with sheets.

"You really think it's good enough?"

"Babe, it's amazing. You're so talented. I wish I had your kind of natural ability... at anything."

"Flick, come on, you're good at stuff."

I snorted. "Hardly. Name one thing I'm good at?" Hailee tapped her lips, pondering it for too long. "See," I added, "Nothing."

"You like reading."

"So does half the population." I rolled my eyes.

"And you've been really good at stepping out of your comfort zone lately."

"I don't think they have a society for that at college, Hails."

"You like lists."

True. I did. Lists kept me organized; reminded me of things I needed to do. Lists for the grocery store. Lists of the celebrities I crushed on. Not to mention my senior year bucket list.

Lists made me happy.

"You're right. I am an excellent maker of the lists. It's an undervalued talent for sure."

"Oh come on." She nudged my shoulder. "You know what I mean. Just because you're not really good at one thing doesn't mean you're not good at lots of little things."

"Yeah, you're right." My smile was forced, the knot in my stomach tightening.

It wasn't that I was jealous of Hailee, I wasn't. She was gifted and I was excited for the Seniors Night unveiling. For her. But it only heightened my self-awareness of how lacking I was. It was senior year. The year of college applications and chasing future dreams. A future my parents had all planned out for me since the womb. They wanted me to follow family tradition; attend UPenn, get my business degree and work some white-collar job in the city.

Before senior year, I would have happily gone along with their plans. Because it was better than the alternative—*no* plan. But I was restless. A little voice whispering in my ear that if I went to UPenn and studied business and graduated ready to enter the big old world of white-collar employment, I'd regret it. It had been quiet before, easy to ignore, but now it was growing louder, a constant noise making itself heard.

That's how my senior year bucket list had first spawned. If I was going to pursue my parents' dream for me; instead of riding the bumpy road of uncertainty, I wanted to go out with a bang. Make senior year the best it could be.

1. *Take up a new hobby*
2. *Cut class*
3. *Attend a pep rally*
4. *Skinny dip down at the lake*
5. *Fall asleep under the stars*
6. *Go to a party at Asher Bennet's house*
7. *Drink (actual liquor) at Bell's*
8. *Go to Winter Formal... with a date (not a girlfriend)*
9. *Hook up with a random guy*
10. *Fall in crazy messy love*

I mentally recalled each item, checking the ones off I'd already completed. I'd joined book club, attended a pep rally, and partied at Asher's house. Thanks to Asher, I'd also got mildly drunk at Bell's. Number nine was a given, but I was considering giving myself a do over where that was concerned, because Jason was neither a random guy nor could our moment of madness be described as a 'hook up'.

"Hey," Hailee's voice perforated my thoughts. "Are you okay?"

"Huh, what?" I blinked at my best friend.

"You zoned out for a minute there."

"I'm fine."

"I didn't mean to hurt your feelings—"

"You didn't." My lips pressed into a thin smile. "Now what's a girl got to do to see the rest of them?" I inclined my head over to the other concealed portraits.

"Flick," Hailee groaned.

"Hails, come on... this is me." I turned on the puppy dog eyes and pout again, knowing she wouldn't be able to resist. But nothing could have prepared me for the next portrait, as Hailee pulled off the cover.

"Holy crap." The words fell off my lips in a *whoosh* of breath. It was Jason, staring right at me, his dark intense eyes fixed on my face, arm hiked ready to release the ball. I moved closer, awed by the detail. The muscles in his arm bulging, strong and powerful.

"I think it's my favorite so far," Hailee said. "Which is weird considering I still can't stand him. But he embodies the game. I think it's his eyes, the sheer determination in them. Like he *is* the game. I never really understood his obsession, but watching him train, seeing him out there on the field, I get it. He doesn't just like football, he—"

"Needs it." I couldn't take my eyes off him. I'd seen Jason play a few times now and it was always a sight to behold. But that was from the bleachers. This was intimate. As if I was right there on the field with him, watching him command the play, his team. A shiver ran up my spine and I sucked in a shaky breath.

"It's great, Hails. Really good." I tried to school my expression, but Hailee narrowed her eyes. Trying to deflect, I asked, "Who do you have left?"

"Jones, Merrick, and Killian. I'm almost done with the rest."

"I can't wait to see them all together. Coach Hasson is going to be blown away." My eyes flicked back to Jason's portrait, but I forced myself to look at Hailee. I needed to push him to the recesses of my mind; a memory I would only allow myself to recall when I was alone with a gallon of ice-cream in reach.

"I just hope the guys like them," she said quietly.

"They will," I reassured her. They couldn't not. But as she covered Jason back up, I saw the way her eyes lingered on her step-brother. The wariness in her gaze. Things had always been strained between them and although Hailee would never admit it, I knew she wanted things to be easier. For Jason to respect her. Especially now that she was with Cameron.

"He'll love it, Hails."

"I don't know—"

"Yes you do." My lips curved in a small smile. "It's okay to want his approval. He's your brother."

"*Step*-brother."

"Does it really matter? It's senior year. Soon we'll all be going off in separate directions. But you and Jason will always find your way back to one another, because like it or not, you're family. So yeah, it's okay to want him to like it, and it's okay if you want to try to smooth things over with him."

"You're a good friend, Felicity Giles." Hailee wrapped her arms around me, hugging me tight. "And I promise to do everything in my power to make your senior year as awesome as it can possibly be."

"Ride or die," I said.

Hailee pulled away, grinning at me. "Ride or die."

6

Jason

"YO, QB, CHECK IT OUT." Grady flipped me his cell phone. I caught it, my eyes narrowing on the tweet.

@ThatcherQB1: *Raiders better watch out, the Tigers are on the prowl #Tigersgohunting #Raiderscansuckit*

"Doesn't Thatcher's cousin play for the Tigers?" he asked me as I handed back his cell.

Shrugging, I grunted. "Fuck if I care. He's just bitter we put their asses in the ground Rival's Week." We'd played them a couple weeks back. It had been a dog fight, both teams refusing to roll over. But, in the end, we got the win, and Thatcher had gone back to Rixon East with his tail between his legs.

"Should we be worried?" Cam leaned in, whispering in my ear.

"Do I look worried?" Thatcher was clutching at straws. He couldn't touch me on the field, and he knew it.

"Hey." Cam's hand pressed against my chest as I went to move. "You sure you're good?"

"Millington are going down and I'm going to enjoy every fucking second." I grinned, but Cameron didn't share my enthusiasm. In fact, he looked miserable as hell.

"He can't touch me out there." My expression grew serious. "You don't need to look so—"

"Grady," Coach boomed, startling us. "That better not be a cell phone I can see on game night. Lock it away, Son. Now."

"Sorry, Coach," Grady grumbled, flipping me off when I smirked at him.

"Gather in, ladies," Coach Hasson's voice echoed around the locker room. We all moved in, dropping into formation around him. I kneeled, helmet tucked onto my knee, adrenaline pumping through my veins.

"Game six," he said. "Win tonight and we're only one more game away from securing our place in the play-offs. We're the team to chase, the team to beat. But that doesn't mean we can get cocky, you hear me?"

"Yes, Sir," rang out, vibrating through me.

"Millington have a strong defense and a quick offense. Don't underestimate them. I want eyes open, give Chase a clear path, and for the love of God, keep your eye on your QB."

Our defense grunted another, "Yes, Sir."

"Chase," Coach said to the guy standing at my side. "You good?"

"Yes, Coach."

"Glad to hear it, Son. Anything changes and you let me know, okay?"

Cam nodded, his eyes sliding to mine. So much passed between us my chest constricted. He'd missed our last game due to his mom being in the hospital, but he was back now and he was hungry for it. I saw it in his eyes, knew I was reflecting the same back at him. We were so close. So fucking close I could almost taste it. Last year, we'd lost out to a shot at the championship but this year it was ours. Do or die, I was getting my championship ring before I graduated.

"Anything you want to add QB?" Coach asked me, his eyes conveying every conversation we'd had during practice this week.

Keep your cool.

We're almost there.

Lead them to victory, Son.

Letting my eyes run over every one of my teammates faces, I said, "We do what we do every week, go out there and play like we want it. Like we deserve it. We're Raiders. And what are we going to do?"

"WIN," the roar of my teammates, my brothers, slammed into me, fueling the fire already raging in my chest.

"That's what I like to hear. Asher, Son, care to do the honors?"

"Sure thing, Coach." Asher jumped to his feet, bouncing around like fucking Tigger on steroids. "Who are we?" he cried.

"Raiders," our voices carried over the rumble of the crowd outside.

"I said who are we?"

"RAIDERS."

"And what are we?"

"Family."

"And what are we gonna do?" Asher grinned at me, cocky motherfucker.

"Win."

"I said what are we gonna do?"

"WIN!"

"Damn right we are," Coach punched the air with his clipboard and yelled, "Now get out there and show me what you're made of."

As we spilled from the locker room into the stadium tunnel, we sounded like a stampede, an army rushing into war. Flames licked my insides; hunger for the win coursing through my veins. I pulled on my helmet as we jogged onto the field, crashing through the cheerleader's banner like a powerful wave. The crowd was on their feet, cheering and yelling our names. The sheer force of their collective voices slamming into me. *Whatever it takes* by Imagine Dragons rose above the noise, igniting the whole place into a frenzy. This is what I lived for. On this sacred place, under the bright Friday night lights, I was the best. Worshipped like a god and revered like a star. I was an above average student, knew my way around an algebra textbook, knew my Shakespeare from my Miller, but out here... out here I was home.

I took a second, inhaling deeply, relishing the smell of freshly cut grass, letting my eyes run over the four-thousand-strong crowd. Four years, I'd played football here. Four years, I'd celebrated wins and defeats, although not many. Four years of blood, sweat, and tears. I was ready, *so ready*, for the next step in my football career. The NCAA. One step closer to the ultimate dream: The NFL. But I knew there was something about this time, senior year at high school. I'd grown from a boy into a man on this field and I would never forget my time playing under Coach Hasson, with guys I considered my brothers.

"Yo, QB, you good?" Asher yelled, and my head whipped over to him. I gave him a nod, jogging over to the rest of the guys. Anticipation rippled around us, the air crackling with excitement. It was addictive; better than any synthetic high.

"Hey, Jase." Grady flicked his head over to where Millington were huddled. "Looks like you've got a new fan club."

One of their players was glaring over at me. I stood taller, tipping my chin slightly, sending him a silent 'fuck you'. He narrowed his eyes, pointing his finger at me before dragging it across his throat.

"Yo, Coach?" I asked one of our assistant coaches. "Number twenty-three. What position is he playing?"

"Linebacker," he said warily. "Should I be concerned?"

"Nah, Coach. Just wondered."

He gave me a pointed look. "No bullshit out there, okay?"

"Did I hear someone say bullshit?" Coach Hasson called us in. "Listen up. Millington came here to win. If they don't, they can kiss a shot at the play-offs goodbye. So that means they'll be gunning for blood. Your blood. You hear me?" We nodded. "They're desperate and desperate men will do anything to get the win. Keep your cool and don't get dragged into their games. That goes for you too, QB."

"Yes, Sir." My eyes flicked over to Millington. Like us, they were now huddled around their coach, who was no doubt telling them to use every trick in the book to get the win they so desperately needed to keep their play-off dream alive.

The referee interrupted Coach's pep talk to inform us we needed to call the toss. I jogged out into the middle of the field with Cam and Asher flanking my side where we met the Millington players head on.

"Since they're the visiting team, the toss goes to Millington. What'll it be, Captain?"

"Heads," their captain said, as we all crowded in to watch the referee toss the coin into the air.

Tails. Eat shit. I grinned at him and then at number twenty-three who had come out to support his captain.

"It's your call, Raiders."

"We'll kick-off." I wasn't giving these fuckers even an ounce of breathing room.

"Sounds good. I expect a clean game. Captains, keep your players in check, and let's play us some football."

Asher and Cameron began to jog back to our team, but I couldn't resist glancing over my shoulder. Number twenty-three was jogging backward, his eyes fixed right on me, and even through his helmet, I didn't miss the words he mouthed.

Thatcher sends his love.

"Run, run," the whole crowd seemed to echo my words as Cameron took off with the ball, ducking and dodging the sea of orange and black players racing toward him.

"Motherfucker," I roared as he got tackled by a huge defensive end, his body slamming against the ground with a resounding *thud*. Right outside the end zone as well.

"They're all over us," Grady jogged over to me as we walked off field.

He wasn't wrong but I didn't want to admit it. Millington had brought their A-game and if we didn't turn it around soon our 21-18 lead was going to disappear down the drain.

I clapped him on his shoulder before cutting a path toward Merrick, one of our best defensive players. "Make them pay," I said, pulling his helmet to mine. "I refuse to lose to this bunch of pussies. You feel me?"

"I feel you, QB." His eyes sparked with hunger.

"Go get 'em."

Watching as our defense lined up at the scrimmage, Coach Hasson came up to me. "What the hell is happening out there? They got you spooked or something?"

I couldn't tell him that Thatcher's cousin, number twenty-three, was making it virtually impossible for me. He'd talked shit most of the game, pushing me, taunting me, trying to get me to take the bait. I hadn't... *yet*, because I knew Coach would rip me a new one. But I wasn't sure how much more of it I could take.

"Defense will take care of it," I grunted, watching as the Millington's QB called the play. He was cocky; a real showman, preferring to keep the ball and run than use his players and pass.

Sure enough, he faked the pass, rolled around to the left and took off downfield... right into the awaiting arms of our cornerback. Their bodies fell hard, the referee rushing over to the huddle already forming around them. But it was our player with the ball.

"Thank fuck." Clapping my hands, I yanked on my helmet, ready to get back out there.

"This is the one," Coach yelled, and my eyes flicked to the clock. There was time for one more play; two if we were lucky. We had to score; anything less and we risked giving Millington the chance to flip the game.

Giving Coach a nod, I jogged over to my teammates. "This is it. The play that ends these motherfuckers. Fourteen," my eyes found Cam across the huddle. "You get to sit this one out. We're going to run Blue Right Fourteen Reverse."

"But, Jase..." someone started, but I held up my hand.

"We go with the play, got it?"

"Got it."

It was a risk—not using Cameron—but you didn't make miracles happen by playing it safe, and we needed to hit Millington where they least expected it.

"Raiders on three." I shoved my fist into the center of the huddle, waiting for the other ten fists to follow. "One, two, three."

Our battle cry rang out around us, the crowd's roar igniting a firestorm inside me. They believed in us, in *me*, cheering us on until the bitter end. And we were about to give them the victory they deserved.

That *we* deserved.

Millington stepped up to the scrimmage, eyes hard, jaws set. They were the predators now, and we were the prey. But first they'd have to catch us.

"Blue Fourteen, Blue Fourteen, hut." The ball snapped to me and I caught it with nothing more than muscle memory. Dropping back, I extended my arm ready to hand-off the ball to my running back. He barreled past me and took off, as I darted right, ball cradled in my arm, head down. The fake play had given me the time I needed to gain yards, but it didn't take long for the Tigers' defense to realize I had the ball. They barreled toward me like a runaway train. I pushed harder, my muscles pinging with exertion, the air *whooshing* around my helmet as I kept running.

"Go, GO! The entire stadium seemed to yell, propelling me forward. Giving me the strength I needed to make one final push.

Someone reached for me and I leaped to the side, the *thud* of their body hitting the ground behind me reverberating in my ears.

Fifteen yards... ten... five. I was so close. So fucking close I could already hear the echo of 'touchdown' ringing in my ears. But a Millington player appeared out of nowhere slamming straight into me, the ball fumbling out of my hands. "Fuck," I grunted, the ground beneath me breaking my fall.

"That one's for Thatcher." Twenty-three came down hard on me. His elbow—or was it a fist—clipping my ribs with purpose. Once. Twice... Pain splintered through my side.

"Get the fuck off me," I sneered, pushing him off. He rolled away, clambering to his feet. The second I was upright, I got up in his face, barely aware of the game still going on around us. "What the hell was that?"

Dead Man Walking had the balls to smirk.

"Oh, you think this is funny. You piece of shit." I lunged for him just as the announcer called, "Touuuuuuchdown."

"FORD, GET THE HELL OVER HERE NOW," Coach Hasson barked just as my hand twisted into twenty-three's jersey.

"Better run, bitch b—"

Yanking him forward, I smashed my helmet against his. "Tell Thatcher if he wants me, to come get me. He knows where to find me." Anger radiated through me and when a hand landed on my shoulder, my head whipped around so quickly I got whiplash.

"Let him go, man," Cam said coolly. "He isn't worth it."

"How's your girl, Chase?" Twenty-three wore a shit-eating smirk. "When you're done with her, let me know. I wouldn't mind taking her for a—"

Cameron barreled me out of the way and tackled him, the two of them crashing to the ground. Suddenly we were swarmed by a sea of orange and black, blue and white, players pushing and shoving while Cameron wailed on twenty-three. His helmet was off now, Cam's too.

"Raiders, get the hell over to the sideline, NOW!" Coach grabbed my shoulder. "Rein your players in, Captain." His voice was icy cold. Enough that it snapped me out of the red mist, and I started pushing my teammates away.

"Go, get over there." I flicked my head to the sideline where the remainder of our team was gathered.

"Let's go, Chase." Coach and one of Millington's coaches pulled Cam off Thatcher's cousin; Coach Hasson handling my best friend while their coach helped his player to his feet.

"Coach, it wasn't—" I started, but he levelled me with a glare that said, 'shut the hell up'.

"We'll deal with this once we're in the locker room. Get in there and wait for me, you hear me?" Disappointment dripped from his words, sitting heavy on my chest.

I slung an arm around Cam's shoulder, but he shrugged me off, storming away. "Motherfucker." I threw my helmet down and kicked it, sending it flying into the water table.

"Ford!" one of the coaches yelled, but I didn't stop. I didn't even look back as I followed the rest of our team into the tunnel. We'd gotten the victory. But it had ended in a shitshow.

All because of Lewis fucking Thatcher.

7

Felicity

COACH HASSON'S voice echoed through the doors. He wasn't just pissed about what had just happened, he was furious.

"Maybe we should go?" I winced, as his tirade continued, eyeing Hailee as she paced outside the team's locker room like a caged animal. We weren't supposed to be back here but being the star quarterback's step-sister and star wide receiver's girlfriend swayed the security guy's decision to let us wait.

"You can go if you want to," she said, one arm wrapped around her waist, the other bent so that she could chew her thumb, "but I'm not leaving until I know Cameron's okay."

"Okay." I went to her. "We'll stay."

"I still can't believe he did that." Silence settled over us, but it didn't last long when a couple of minutes later, the door swung open and the team started filing out.

Joel Mackey noticed us first. "You better get in there, Hailee." He grimaced. "Your boy is in a bad way."

The blood drained from her face as she looked to me. "Can you... I mean..."

"Hailee," Jason's voice cut the air like a knife.

She rushed over to him. "Is he okay? What did Coach say? Is he hurt?" The questions spewed out of her and Jason looked completely out of his depth.

Dragging a hand down his face, he took a deep breath. "Cam needs you," was all he said, flicking his head to the door. "You should go be with him."

Her glassy gaze settled on me and I smiled. "Go, I'll be fine."

"Fear not, Hails." Asher appeared, making a beeline for me. "We'll make sure she gets home okay."

"You're sure?"

"Go, he needs you."

She gave me an appreciative smile before turning it on Jason. "Thank you," she mouthed before disappearing inside.

"Will Coach—"

"She doesn't need to worry about Coach," Jason said as he shouldered past Asher and disappeared down the tunnel.

"Come on." Asher slung his bag over his shoulder and motioned his head in the direction of his teammate, sending water droplets spraying everywhere.

"Asher," I moaned, following after Jason. "Now I'm all wet."

"And I haven't even touched you yet."

I glanced over at him, eyes wide and cheeks flushed.

"Relax, Fee, baby, I'm joking."

"Oh, okay." Embarrassment flamed my cheeks as we hurried after Jason.

Outside, most of the crowd had already dispersed. A few of the guys hung around to take pictures and sign jerseys and balls and other game paraphernalia, but Jason didn't stop for the die-hard fans. He didn't even acknowledge them.

"Go on ahead," Asher said, "I'll be right there." He stopped to take a photo with a couple of kids who had their faces painted with the Raiders logo.

When I reached Jason the words, "Where's Asher's Jeep?" fell from my lips.

"I drove."

"Oh," I said, eyeing his car.

Jason kicked the gravel, sending a plume of dust into the air. Everything about him screamed 'stay away'. A murderous expression. Waves of anger rippling off him. The way his jaw clenched so tight it looked painful.

He was a nuclear bomb just waiting to detonate.

And suddenly, I didn't want to ride anywhere with them. Even if Hailee had driven us here and was now attending to Cameron's *needs*.

"Change of plan." Asher sauntered up to us, his lip in a grim line. "My parents are on their... aaaaand here they are." Headlights illuminated the three of us, and I glanced over to where his gaze was fixed.

"They want to take me to dinner."

"They do?" My expression must have given me away because Asher chuckled.

"Don't look so worried, Jase can take you home. Can't you, QB?"

The guy in question grunted something inaudible.

"I can walk," I rushed out, wanting nothing more than the ground to open up and swallow me whole. "It's not far."

"Fee, baby, just get in the damn car." The words were for me, but Asher was looking at Jason, a silent message passing between them.

"You should come to Bell's later," he finally turned his attention on me. "Drinks are on me."

"I don't know," I said quietly. "Maybe, if Hailee—"

"Think about it." He winked and gave Jase a two finger salute before heading toward his parents' car.

Silence lingered, swirling with Jason's anger.

"I'll walk, you don't—"

"Get in the car," he ground out.

"Excuse me?" Indignation burned through me as I lifted a brow at him.

"I said get in the fucking car." He stomped around to the driver's side and almost tore the door off its hinges before throwing himself inside and slamming it shut.

I needed to leave. To put as much distance as possible between me and the brooding angry guy in the car. But there was something about his anger, the way he'd held back throughout the entire game. I'd watched him, even when I'd tried not to. Twenty-three had been all over him. But Jason hadn't taken the bait. Even when they were both up in each other's faces, he had maintained control. But something had changed when Cameron tried to intervene. And the only thing that tied Jason and Cameron together, except football, was Hailee.

The window rolled down, startling me. "Last time, Giles," his voice hit me straight in the stomach, "Get in the goddamn car."

Jason didn't take me home. He didn't even take me to his house, not that I'd expected him to ever do that. I didn't. But I also didn't expect him to take the road out of town and pull over by the lake. The sandy lot was quiet, nothing but the gentle rustle of leaves and my heart beating violently in my chest.

"So..." I said, trying to lighten the mood. "Nice view." Risking a peek over at Jason, I was surprised to see the corner of his mouth lift.

"Want to talk about it?"

"No, I really don't."

"What did twenty-three say to Cameron?"

"You noticed that, huh?"

"I..." My lips pressed together, not wanting to admit I'd noticed everything.

Brushing over my slip, he added, "You don't want to know."

"Try me."

Twisting his body slightly, Jason pinned me to his leather seat with those dark intense eyes of his. "It wasn't supposed to happen like this." His voice was cold. "She wasn't supposed to—"

"You think this is Hailee's fault?" Incredulity filled my voice. "You spent the last six years treating her—"

"I know." Jason's fingers jammed in his hair, tugging in frustration. "You think I don't know that? Hailee was nothing to me, *nothing*, and now... now she's in the middle of this thing with Thatcher and I don't know what the fuck I'm supposed to do. I don't know how to..." He stopped himself, pain glittering in his eyes.

"Care?" I whispered. "You don't know how to care?"

"I'm not the good guy here, Felicity. I want to win State, graduate high school, and get the fuck out of this town and go to college. That's it. That's my lot. And Thatcher is fucking everything up." The sound of his fist colliding with the steering wheel reverberated through the car. There was barely any air before but now I could hardly breathe; Jason's anger tangible.

"I just need for it to stop. Just stop for a fucking second." Head tipped back, he screwed his eyes shut, sucking in ragged breath after ragged breath.

"I'm here, if you want to talk." The words shattered the silence.

"You wouldn't understand."

"Because I'm not popular? Because I don't know what it's like to be put on a pedestal by the entire town? You're right," I gave a little sigh, "I don't know what it's like. But that doesn't mean I don't understand what pressure feels like."

Jason's eyes slid to mine, filled with a rare glimmer of vulnerability I knew not many people, if any, got to see. "Sometimes it feels like I can't breathe without the whole town watching." Surprise flashed across his face, as if he couldn't believe he'd said the words.

I waited, hoping he'd give me more. Hoping he'd let me in. But his stone mask was already back in place.

Jason was tortured. Over Hailee. Over his dad and her mom having an affair. His mom leaving. Carrying the weight of the team. The rivalry with Rixon East. It all sat squarely on his shoulders. And although I didn't want to understand him, to try to figure out what went on inside of the head of Rixon's prodigal son of football, part of me got it. Because although it wasn't the same, although I didn't have the pressure of an entire town rooting for me and my future; I had my parents' pressure. And sometimes that alone was almost too much to bear.

"Sometimes, when it all gets too much, I make a list." The words were out before I could stop them.

"A *list*?" Jason snorted.

"Yeah, it helps me process things."

"And these lists," his voice was drenched in sarcasm, "What do you put on them?"

"Anything really. Sometimes I use them to help me organize my life: to do lists, grocery store lists, homework lists—"

"You have a list for homework." His brow went up and then he smirked. "Of course you do. What else?"

"Celebrities I'd like to date, books I want to read, that kind of thing."

"And your senior year bucket list?"

"How did you...? Asher," I groaned. "Asher told you." I felt my cheeks burn.

"Don't worry. He didn't tell me what's *on* the list."

Because he didn't know. He and Cameron had overheard me talking to Hailee about it once. But I refused to share the details, because, holy crap, that would be embarrassing.

About as embarrassing as Jason asking me about it.

"Good. That's good."

"Why do you look so worried, Giles?" He leaned closer slightly, taking the air with him. "I'm not on the list, am I?"

Oh no.

He was doing it again. Looking at me like he wanted something.

Something I knew I shouldn't give him.

"We should probably head back," I said trying to keep my voice even. "It's getting late and you're meeting Asher at—"

"Giles," he said, sliding his hand along my collarbone and up my neck. His thumb stroking my pulse point. "Stop talking."

"But I—" The pad of his thumb moved against my lips, dragging downward and making my bottom lip *pop*. My tummy clenched; his touch like fire, burning me inside out. I didn't want to feel like this, to respond like this, but I couldn't help it. Where Jason Ford was concerned, my body had a mind all of its own.

"Don't you ever just want it to stop?" he whispered so quietly I almost didn't hear him.

"S- stop?"

"Yeah, the constant noise and pressure and... *everything*."

More than you know, I wanted to say; but I couldn't speak because his lips were right by mine.

"Ja—"

He kissed me. Just a gentle brush of his mouth over the corner of mine. It might as well have been a hot desperate kiss for the way my body reacted.

My breathing was labored but nowhere near as ragged as Jason's.

"Last chance to tell me to stop, Giles," he rasped, his eyes boring into mine.

Stop, the word formed on my tongue, but melted into nothing before I could say it. Because no matter how much I knew this was a bad idea... no matter how much I'd regret it later... no one had ever made me feel the way Jason did. So alive. So desired.

"I don't want you to stop," I breathed. The carnal growl that vibrated in Jason's chest turned my blood to molten lava. He wanted this.

Wanted *me*.

And in that moment, I didn't care if he'd regret it, or never look at me again. Right here, right now, I needed him to touch me. I needed him to make me *feel*.

He didn't devour me the way he had before. This time his kiss was slow, deliberate. He took his time acquainting himself with the shape of my lips, licking and nibbling. I slid my hand up and over his shoulder, feeling his hard muscle ripple beneath my touch.

"Get over here, Giles." His hand found my thigh and he helped me climb over the center console and onto his lap, straddling him.

"Fuck," he grunted, pain etched on his face.

"You're hurt."

"It's nothing." Jason dragged me closer.

It was close. Too close. Intimate and intense, the low body of his vintage car not built for heavy make out sessions.

There was a split second, as I settled over him, that our eyes connected. Eyes hooded, burning with lust, Jason looked deadly; but there was something else, something underneath the dark mask he wore. It was gone in an instant, his mouth quickly finding mine again as he ground into me, showing me just how much I turned him on.

And dear God, if that didn't go straight to my head.

I understood it now. Why girls chased bad boys, hoping to be the one to tame their wild ways. For this, right here, the ounce of power my body had over him. The way my kisses made him grow harder, made him hungry for more.

I wasn't foolish enough to believe it meant anything—I knew it didn't. But how could I not feel all warm and gooey inside knowing that out of all the girls he could have been here with, he was with me.

He'd *chosen* me.

Don't run away with yourself, Flick. He didn't choose you. You were there. Convenient. Like a grab-and-go snack. I shut the intrusive thoughts out. There would be time to analyze and regret later.

"You have too many fucking clothes on," his voice was rough against my skin, as he worked my Raiders sweater up and over my head. The thin tank underneath molded to my curves and Jason's eyes homed straight in on the swell of my breasts. "Gorgeous," the word formed on his lips.

I slipped my hand between us, desperate to feel his skin, to explore his body, sculpted to perfection from hours and hours of physical conditioning. But he snagged my wrist, smirking at me. It was almost dark now, the canvas of stars twinkling down on us like distant spectators; only the silvery hue of the moon illuminating our profiles. If it was possible, it made him look even more devastating.

"Ja—"

"Ssh." He silenced me with a finger pressed against my lips again, while his other hand slid down my chest, trailing a path between the valley of my breasts, and down my stomach. I sucked in a harsh breath when he grazed the waistband of my leggings but it didn't deter Jason. He continued his exploration of my body, touching and kneading, smoothing his fingers over my skin. But when he dipped his hand inside my leggings, I could barely contain the moan building in my throat.

"So fucking wet," he said gruffly, not giving me chance to catch my breath or process what was happening, as he pressed a finger inside me.

"Oh God," I moaned, rocking against his hand, needing more.

Needing so much more.

My head dropped back, exposing my neck and collarbone to him. Answering my silent plea, Jason dipped his head kissing the hollow of my throat, sucking gently. Driving me wild.

"Jase," I panted, the intrusion of a second finger making me wince. But only for a second, as pleasure flowed through me like a gentle wave.

I was lost in the intense sensations. The warm current flowing between us, *through* us. The intimate position. The feel of his hot mouth around my breast as he worked his fingers inside me, circling his thumb over my clit.

"I'm so close," I whispered, barely able to recognize my own voice. My legs began to shake as Jason went deeper, harder. I'd never let anyone touch me like this before. Not the way Jason did. As if it wasn't about my pleasure at all, but his. As if my body was his to play however he wanted.

It occurred to me, in that moment, maybe it was.

I dropped my head to look at him. Sure enough, he was watching me with eyes so dark they looked black. A lazy smirk was plastered on his face as he increased the tempo.

"You like my fingers inside you?" he asked as if I could possibly respond with anything other than a small nod.

"Oh God, Jason..." I couldn't breathe, my orgasm slamming into me like a tsunami.

"Come for me, Felicity," he rasped, still watching me. "Come all over my fingers."

His dirty words sent me over the edge, as my body clamped down. I took a shuddering breath, trying to swallow down the urge to call his name over and over.

I collapsed into him, sliding my hands around his neck. But Jason pushed me back, his eyes narrowed and clouded as he slowly brought his fingers to his mouth and sucked them clean.

My tummy clenched.

Christ, he was beautiful. A dark and dangerous angel.

"What?" I asked as he continued watching me, but his cell vibrated, cutting through the thick silence that had descended over us. Jason leaned around me and grabbed it.

"Is there a problem?" I asked when I noticed he'd gone tense beneath me.

"We should go. Everyone's meeting at Bell's." His voice was cold, detached, and I knew whatever had just happened between us was over.

I tried to temper the dejection squeezing my heart as I clambered off him and sat back in the passenger seat. He handed me my sweater without a word, fired up the engine and backed out of the sandy lot.

It wasn't until ten minutes later, when I climbed out of his car trying to reconcile what had just happened, I realized he hadn't let me touch him. Before he got the text, before the temperature had cooled a gazillion degrees between us, Jason had gotten me half-naked and played my body the way he played the game: sure and confident and one hundred percent in control.

But he hadn't let me touch him back.

If we hadn't been interrupted would he have?

Something told me it was better not to ask... because I probably wouldn't like the answer.

8

Jason

BELL'S WAS CRAMMED, everyone showing up to celebrate with the team. We usually partied at Asher's, but since his parents were in town, we'd come to the bar instead.

"Hey," he said, waving me over. "Where's Fee?"

"Fuck if I know."

"You didn't offer to bring her?"

"No I didn't offer to bring her. What am I, her damn babysitter?"

Asher eyed me carefully. "What's up? You seem pissy?"

My brow arched. "Thatcher sending his cousin to do his dirty work not enough reason to be pissed?"

"Yeah, I just thought... it doesn't matter."

He wanted to ask about Felicity; it was right there in his eyes. But she was the last thing I wanted to talk about—especially with him.

I'd fucked up again earlier. I should never have driven her out to the lake and kissed her. *Or put your hands on her.*

She just made it all so damn easy. Nothing like Jenna or the other girls I was used to being around. Felicity was just content being there; talking and listening. And some of the shit that came out of her mouth... well, it was gold dust, and strangely, I found myself craving whatever weird assed sentence was going to come out of her pouty mouth next. But nothing was as intriguing as the way she let me handle her body. She handed me complete control, as if she trusted me with every fiber of her being. Which was ironic considering I was the last person on Earth she should trust.

Despite her serious lapse in judgement where I was concerned, Felicity was a smart girl who gave as good as she got. But when I put my hands on her skin, my mouth on hers, something changed. It was addictive.

She was addictive.

But she was also off-limits for so many fucking reasons I should probably make a list.

Yeah, she'd love that.

I fought a smile.

"What's got you grinning like the Cheshire Cat?" Asher nudged me, taking a long pull on his beer.

"Nothing, just thinking." His frowned deepened as if I was a puzzle he was trying to solve.

"How's the ribs?"

"I'll live." I shrugged, chugging down my beer. Thatcher's cousin had gotten in a couple of hard digs, and I had a nice bruise forming, but it wasn't enough to do any real damage.

Just then, the door swung open and Cameron and Hailee walked in, Felicity trailing in behind them, looking like a deer caught in the headlights.

Fuck.

I hadn't anticipated seeing her again tonight.

"There he is," Grady called. "Get over here, Rocky Balboa, drinks are on the house."

The whole place cheered causing Cam to duck his head.

Pussy.

He never did eat up the limelight like the rest of us, and now he was with Hailee, he was even more inclined to linger in the background. I'd always given him shit for it. Back when we were kids and people began to take notice, I couldn't understand why he rarely lapped up the attention. But now I wondered if Cam was onto something. If maybe he knew all along that if you stayed in the limelight for too long, it would eventually burn your soul until there was nothing left but ash.

Cameron was sporting a nice shiner underneath his left eye. I had to give him props, I didn't know he had it in him. Because what they said was true: girls really did make you crazy. And my best friend was two screws loose over my step-sister.

"Fee, baby, you came."

"I... Hailee insisted." She kept her eyes on Asher, refusing to look at me.

It shouldn't have bothered me so much, but it did.

"Well, let's get you ladies a drink." He leaped up and slung his arm round her shoulders. I followed him up.

"I'll be at the pool table."

Hailee caught my eye, but I simply tipped my chin and kept on walking.

"Hey, Jase, good game tonight." A petite blond sidled up to me, running her hands suggestively up my chest.

"Hey..."

"Marissa," she purred, her eyes full of intention. "I'm on the swim team.

"You must love getting wet then," one of the guys hollered. I glowered at him, dragging my eyes back to Marissa, expecting to see her mild disgust at his words. But in true jersey chaser fashion she batted her eyes, fingering the collar on my Henley.

"Oh, I love getting wet." The words teased off her tongue slowly. "I don't suppose you could help me out with that, could you?"

Marissa was hot. Tight body accentuated by the mini skirt and one size too small Raiders tank she wore. Bringing my thumb to my lip, I let my eyes drift down her curves. She was exactly my type. Slim. Athletic. And down for whatever. But something was missing. That something was currently giggling at Asher like he hung the fucking moon.

"Jason." Marissa's hand grazed my semi-interested dick, commanding my attention. "I said do you want to get out of here?"

"Maybe later. It's still early."

Rejection flashed in her eyes, but then her seductive smile slid back in place. "You know where to find me." She flicked her head toward a group of girls.

"Yeah." I grabbed my bottle of Bud and took a long pull.

"Jason Ford passing up fresh pussy?" Grady came up beside me. "Hell must have frozen over."

"I'm not sure she could handle me." I smirked.

"Oh shit, you're bad, Cap. So fucking bad. But if you're not gonna indulge, mind if I—"

"Be my guest, man."

He slapped me on the back as he passed, making a beeline for Marissa and her carbon-copy swim team friends. He was quickly joined by Mackey and a couple of other rookies. They were worse than dogs in heat. Thank fuck I didn't have to work for it. Being QB One meant something in Rixon; but being Jason Ford—son of local football hero Kent Ford—*and* QB One meant everything. Guys wanted to be me and girls wanted to screw me. Everyone wanted their fill. And until recently, I'd soaked it up. But when everyone wanted a piece of you, the chance to say they knew you... partied with you... fucked you... or even fought with you, there wasn't much left to go around. It was a catch twenty-two, a rock and really fucking hard place. Because I loved the game, loved it more than anything in the world. Cut me open and I was pretty sure I'd bleed football. But it came at a price. One everyone thought they would happily pay until it's *your* life. Until you don't know who you can trust or who wants to use you as a steppingstone to their five minutes of small-town fame.

It's why I'd hated Hailee so much when she'd first moved here. She was so judgmental, sweeping in with her holier-than-thou attitude, assuming she knew what I was like.

Who I was.

So I liked sex, but didn't want to date or get tied down to one girl? The last thing I wanted was to put down roots here. Rixon was merely a steppingstone to bigger and better things. And I had one plan: to achieve what my old man couldn't and get drafted to the NFL. An injury had ended his career in senior year of college. His dream might have gone up in smoke but his legacy lived on.

Me.

And I was going all the way.

No matter the cost.

"Something on your mind?" Cameron pulled up a stool next to the high table beside me.

"Nah, just watching Grady make an ass of himself."

"You know, you can come sit with us."

"I know."

"What I'm trying to figure out is if you won't come over because of Hailee or Felicity or both of them?"

"Look, Chase, I'm happy for you, I am. Does it freak me out you're boning my step-sister? Hell yes." I shuddered. "But I get it. You need her, she needs you, yada yada yada."

"You say it like it's a bad thing."

My eyes levelled him. "You gave up Penn for her." Cameron had always been coming to Penn with me. We were going to dominate the Quakers and kick some Ivy League ass. But then his mom got sick and he and Hailee... well, things changed. He changed.

Cam let out a heavy sigh, raking a hand through his hair. "I thought we were over this? I get football is important to you, but there's more to life—"

"Is this the part where you tell me that one day I'll meet *the one* and realize I want to settle down, get married, and pop out a couple of kids? Because if it is, you're wasting your breath."

"I know Aimee hurt—"

"You think this has fuck all to do with Aimee? She was nothing but a conniving piece of shit like her brother."

"Jase, come on, this is me. You don't need to put—"

"Aimee was a mistake." A huge fucking mistake that came back around to bite me in the ass. If I'd have known she was Thatcher's sister from the get go, I never would have looked at her, let alone touched her.

"It's okay to admit you felt something..." Cameron trailed off when I glared at him. Hard. He didn't get it. I didn't want to feel. I didn't want to care about anyone other than myself and my future. Caring made you vulnerable. It opened you up to a whole world of hurt I had no interest in feeling. Besides, when I cradled the leather ball in my hands, I had everything I needed.

"Okay, I won't say another word. But you should still come sit with us. I know it'd mean a lot to Hailee." Cam stalked back to their booth, and I let my eyes drift over to them. Hailee was gazing up at him with stars in her eyes and Asher was busy entertaining Felicity with nothing but a beer mat and his nose. It would have been easy to go sit with them, to pretend I was okay with how much everything was changing. But then, Asher leaned forward, brushing a wisp of hair from Felicity's face and my hand tightened around the bottle. He was touching her and she was loving every second.

Fuck that.

And fuck them.

"Jerry," I called as I approached the bar. "I'm gonna need something stronger."

"Come on, Jase, you know I can't—"

"I like you, J, but it's either serve me the damn liquor or I'll go get it elsewhere."

He let out a resigned sigh and shook his head. "You remind me of him, you know. Back in the day."

"Spare me the 'you're just like your old man' crap." I nursed my empty bottle, waiting for Jerry to pour my new drink.

"Even sound like him too," his chest rumbled with laughter. "I'm cutting you off after two."

"Three." I rose a brow.

"Fine, three and you're done." He pushed a glass of whiskey toward me. It wasn't exactly the drink of champions, but I'd acquired the taste when me and the guys used to raid my dad's liquor cabinet back when we were kids.

Just like my old man, the words made me shudder. He was everything I was trying not to be. The prime example of someone letting it all go to their head. It didn't matter that Dad had me and Mom at home. Some skirt only had to bat her eyes in his direction and he'd be foaming at the mouth. My mom, now there was an example of a strong woman. She'd stuck by Dad through it all: the depression, the melancholy, the endless string of faceless women. But everyone had a breaking point, and Dad had found hers. Mom finally walked away and I had to choose—a new life, new school, and new team, or Rixon. A decision I would never forgive him for.

A decision my mom had never forgiven me for.

"There you are." A familiar hand slid over my shoulder.

"Jenna," my voice was clipped but it didn't deter her from sliding into the stool beside me.

"Drinking all alone?"

"Just catching my breath. You know how it is after a game."

"I know how it can be." She walked her fingers over my arm. "You look tense."

Tense was the fucking understatement of the year.

"I can help with that."

My eyes slid to hers in question. Of course I knew where this was going, the only way it ever went between us. But my dick wasn't in it, not tonight.

Unperturbed, Jenna leaned in, brushing her lips against the shell of my ear. "Meet me in the storeroom in five."

"Oh yeah, you going to make it worth my while?"

She pulled back, running her tongue across her bottom lip, a slow seductive sweep. "I think we both know that when we're done, you're gonna be feeling a whole lot better." She stood up, making a show of flicking her long blonde hair off her shoulder and letting me get a front row seat to her impressive rack.

"Five minutes." She mouthed before sauntering away, heading straight for the back of the bar.

"That one has trouble written all over her."

"Maybe I like trouble, old man."

"I knew another guy who said exactly the same thing once." Jerry gave me a knowing look, whipped the towel off his shoulder and began wiping the counter.

I hadn't wanted Marissa. She was new. All shiny and eager. Probably hoping she could impress me enough to want to stick around. But Jenna knew the score. She knew it was nothing more than sex between us. A way to burn off some steam and relax.

And given how tense I was, I knew I'd be a fool to resist what she was offering. Decision made, I downed the rest of my whiskey and made my way to the back. But before I disappeared down the hall, I glanced back, searching for my friends. For Felicity. She was still laughing at Asher, her eyes alight and lips curved. She looked happy. My chest tightened, Jerry's words rattling around my head. He was wrong. I wasn't my father.

I would *never* let myself become my father.

But I was no saint either.

9

Felicity

"ARE you sure he won't come back here?" I asked Hailee for the millionth time since we left Bell's.

"He rarely comes home Friday night, either crashing at Asher's or..." she trailed off, giving me a sympathetic smile.

Jason had barely looked twice at me at Bell's, and every time he did, it was with a scowl painted on his face. As if that wasn't enough, I'd watched him follow Jenna Jarvis into the back and return a while later with a lazy smirk and fresh wrinkles in his Henley.

"It is what it is." My lips pursed.

She shook away her grim expression. "Anyway, we didn't come back here to mope over stupid boys; it's girls' night. Are we going with Scott Eastwood in The Longest Ride or shall we go old school with a bit of R Patz in Breaking Dawn?"

Smothering a giggle, I shot her an incredulous look. "I still can't believe, you, Hailee Raine, are a closet Twihard."

"What?" She shrugged with no sign of remorse. "He's hot."

"If you say so. I'm more of Tim Riggins kinda gal. You can keep your sparkly vampires; I'll take Friday Night Lights any day of the week."

"Maybe that's your problem," she quipped, setting up the film.

"Says the girl dating her very own football star." I rolled onto my stomach and grabbed another handful of popcorn.

"I'm dating Cameron, the person. Who just so happens to play football."

"Yeah, yeah, keep telling yourself that." I grabbed a pillow and threw it at her. Hailee caught it and settled down on her bed, hitting the light switch and plunging the room into darkness.

"This is nice," she said through a yawn. "You, me, just like old times."

"Uh-hmm." I wondered if she'd still be saying that if she knew what I'd been doing with her step-brother less than a few hours ago.

Dear God, what had I done? Letting him touch me like that. But it was like I became someone else around him; someone who thrived on his cruel words and cocky charm.

It was unlike me. But maybe that was the problem. Maybe I liked the fact

I felt different around Jason. Powerful and sexy. Instead of the wallflower I'd been for most of my life.

Hailee was immersed in the film, *oohing* and *ahhing* to all her favorite parts, until my eyes grew heavy and the moving images started to blur.

I woke with a start. "Hailee?" I whispered, but she was out cold, her muffled breaths steady and shallow. The glare from the television illuminated the room, guiding my path as I climbed to my feet, stretching out the kinks in my neck. The digital clock on her nightstand read one in the morning. We must have been sleeping awhile.

Deciding to pee before I tried to get comfy again, I ducked into Hailee's bathroom. Not bothering to turn on the light, I left the bedroom door ajar instead. Once I was done, I washed my hands, catching my reflection in the small wall mirror. I looked the same. Same green eyes, same brown hair, and beauty spot on my upper left cheek. But I felt different. Something inside me was changing.

I was changing.

And I didn't know how to make it stop, whether I even wanted to.

"You gonna stand there all day or are you done?" The low growl catapulted my heart into my throat.

"Jason, what the—" He closed the distance, brushing past me to pull the door separating Hailee's side of the bathroom and her bedroom closed. "Let me out." My eyes narrowed as I took in his disheveled appearance; the bitter scent of whisky lingering on his breath.

"Why the fuck are you here?" he ground out, rubbing his jaw. There was a slight slur to his words and I realized he was drunk.

Crap.

I could deal with sober Jason, but drunk Jason... drunk Jason was what had landed me in this situation in the first place.

"I'm with Hailee. She invited me. It's girls' night," I said as if it mattered. Of course it didn't freaking matter.

Edging backward, my hands searched desperately for the door handle.

"You're everywhere, like a recurring nightmare." His words hit me straight in the heart.

"You came in here first—"

"It's my fucking bathroom." Anger blazed in his eyes as he stalked toward me, so close if he reached for me, I'd be right there.

"It's Hailee's—"

"I don't give a fuck. You shouldn't be here." He dragged a hand through his hair, pulling at the ends in frustration.

"So let me go," I whisper-hissed, done with his bullshit. I didn't ask for this. I didn't ask for any of this. Okay, so maybe I had a hand in blurring the lines between us, but he'd made it perfectly clear where we stood, and it wasn't like I was begging him to give me a chance.

"Is that what you really want?" His hand came for me, splaying against the side of my neck, his thumb tracing up and down.

"Yes," I said shakily.

"You sure?" Jason leaned in, his breath hot on my skin, his lips dangerously near the soft spot right beneath my ear. "Because I'm not so sure. I think you like this, like what I do to you." He inhaled deeply, inhaled *me*, and my legs almost gave way.

"Jason, stop." I fisted my hands at my sides, knowing if I touched him it wouldn't end well.

"Stop?" There was a wicked glint in his eye as he lifted his face to me. "You think *you* get to say when *this* stops?"

"I'm not going to play this game with you, not anymore."

He was drunk, his words crueler than ever, his touch harsher.

"Game? You think this is a game? This isn't a game; it's bloodsport, baby. And you... you couldn't have made it any easier if you'd tried."

Tearing myself from his hold, I stepped back, my body hitting the wall. "Get out," I said, coldly. "Now."

He blinked, confusion clouding his glassy eyes. "Feli—"

"Get. Out. Before I do something we'll both regret."

His heavy gaze lingered on me for a second before he staggered out of the bathroom, and I slumped against the wall, releasing the breath caught in my throat. Wondering how the hell I was ever going to survive Jason Ford.

EVERYTHING WENT BACK to normal after that. Whatever had happened between me and Jason in his car, was filed under 'epic screw ups', and I spent the weekend trying my best to forget our middle-of-the-night moment in the Ford-Raine bathroom. Of course, I didn't breathe a word of it to Hailee.

It had hurt, a sharp pain splintering my chest, that he could go so quickly from kissing me, touching me, to being with Jenna. But it was just another reminder I needed to push all thoughts of Jason Ford out of my head.

At least, that was the plan.

"Felicity?"

"Huh?"

"Are you okay, sweetheart?" Mom frowned. "I was calling you and you were completely zoned out."

"Late night studying," I said around a fake yawn. "You know how it is."

"I know it's senior year, baby, but I don't want you making yourself ill. A good night's sleep—"

"Makes for a healthy mind. Got it, Mom."

"You know your grandma, God bless her soul, used to drill that into me every day."

"I know, Mom." *Just the way you drill it into me.*

"Senior year." She slid a plate of pancakes toward me before helping herself to another mug of coffee. Apparently, once you were an adult, a healthy mind ran on a good night's sleep and two coffees before eight. "It only seems like yesterday you were born."

Silently groaning, I ate my breakfast while Mom took a trip down memory lane. By the time I was done, she was a little teary-eyed. "We're so proud of you, Felicity, and to think you're following in our footsteps."

"Sure thing, Mom." I regurgitated the same response whenever she brought up college.

"Although," she went on, "I'm not sure how your father is going to cope. He barely slept when you were in New York."

"It was one night," I reminded her.

"I know, I know. But New York is just so..."

I filled the silence with adjectives. *Big. Amazing. Inspiring. Alive.* I should have known she would say, "Overwhelming."

"I don't know, I kind of liked it." And it had absolutely nothing to do with giving a certain brooding Raider my v-card.

"Really?" Her nose scrunched up. "I found it to be so gaudy. Anyway, your father and I agreed, no more road trips until after graduation, young lady. I'm not sure his heart could take it, and you know Doctor Garrick said he needs to watch his blood pressure."

"Mom, I don't think my one-night stopover set off Dad's blood pressure, I think his endless late nights at the office did." He was rarely ever home and if he was, he brought his work with him.

"He just wants to provide for us, baby, for you. A strong work ethic is so important these days."

"I know," I murmured the words, suddenly feeling guilty. Dad did work hard for his family.

"One day you'll understand." Her eyes held nothing but warmth, as if she was doing me a favor. Protecting me. Keeping me safe from the monsters of the world. But what she failed to realize was, she was stifling me.

I was stifled.

But I couldn't tell her that.

Not unless I wanted to break her heart.

So I pressed my lips together and smiled, hoping she couldn't see I was already tainted by a monster.

A monster who wore a blue and white jersey and ate girls like me for breakfast.

"Miss Giles," the gruff voice startled me. "Just the girl I hoped to find."

My brows pinched as I gawked at Principal Finnigan, trying to rack my brain for any recent indiscretions he might be here to reprimand me for.

When the silence went on for a second longer than normal, I finally found my voice and said, "I'm sorry, did you want me, Sir?"

"Indeed." He smiled faintly. "This is Mya Hernandez, a transfer student from Philadelphia. I was hoping you could buddy up with her and help her settle in."

"Me?" I blinked, certain I'd misheard. "You want *me* to buddy up with her?"

"Well, I don't know of any other students called Felicity Giles, do you?"

"No, Sir."

"Well, then," he said, "I'll leave you girls to get acquainted. Mya already has her class schedule. If you have any issues, please see Miss Hampstead."

He smoothed down his blazer and took off down the hall, leaving me and the new girl staring awkwardly at one another.

"Listen, it's cool," she said with a hint of a Latina accent. "I don't need you to babysit me. Just point me in the direction of," she scanned the paper in her hand, "AP History, and I'll tell Miss Hampstead you were more than helpful."

"Mya, right?" I asked, ignoring her brush off. "I'm Felicity. It's nice to meet you."

"Yeah, whatever." She hitched her bag up her shoulders and glanced around.

"I love your hair, is it—"

"Natural?" Mya rolled her eyes.

"Sorry, I didn't mean—"

"No, I'm sorry." Her hard expression softened. "That was rude of me. It's just hard, you know, transferring partway through the semester of senior year."

"You're from Philadelphia?"

"Badlands," her voice lowered significantly.

"Isn't that like..." The words lodged in my throat.

"The ghetto?" Her brow went up as she gave a strangled laugh.

"That's not..." My cheeks flamed. "I didn't..."

"Badlands is not The Hamptons, that's for sure, but it was still home, you know?"

"You've been?" I changed tack. "To the Hamptons, I mean? I always wanted to go, but my mom and dad prefer culture to the beach." Quiet culture: museums and galleries and historical buildings.

"I went once. Didn't think it was all that. That whole scene isn't really my thing." Mya snorted, pushing her unruly spiral curls from her face. She was beautiful: all caramel skin with dark features, and a slim but curvy frame. She reminded me of Amandla Stenberg.

I smiled to myself. Girls at Rixon fit into two categories: Plastic Barbie jersey chasers and the rest of us. One look at Mya and I knew she was like me and Hailee. Well, pre-Cameron and a certain star quarterback that would remain nameless.

"What?" Mya frowned at me as I studied her.

Slipping my arm through hers, I leaned in close. "Are you a football fan, Mya Hernandez?"

"I prefer basketball."

My smile grew.

"Why are you looking at me like that?" She frowned.

"Oh nothing, but I think you and I are going to be great friends," I declared, dragging her down the hall. "Welcome to Rixon High."

"So this is the cafeteria," I announced as Mya trailed behind me. She had insisted on doing her own thing at lunch, and I had insisted she come with me to meet Hailee. Apparently, my persistence outweighed hers.

"Aaand it looks just like my old cafeteria except without the drug dealing and fights."

My head whipped around and I knew my mouth was hanging open like a fish.

"Joke," Maya said. "I'm joking. Well about the drug dealing, mostly."

"It was that bad?" I asked as we joined the line.

"Fallowfield High was a jungle. I'm lucky I escaped."

"How did you?"

"Long story," was all she said before turning her attention to the lunch items. "Same shit food though."

"Oh, I don't know. The tacos are usually good and Friday is spaghetti day."

"Hmm, sounds delicious," she replied drolly.

"Just wait, you'll see."

"And who might this be?" Asher had impeccable timing. I'd hoped to get Mya situated before introducing her to anyone else. But from the way his gaze drifted down her body and back up, I knew Asher would need no introductions.

"Asher Bennet." He held out his hand. "You must be the new girl."

"This is Mya," I said when she pursed her lips in defiance, staring at his hand like he had an infectious disease.

I was growing to like this girl more by the second.

Asher quickly recovered, running his fingers through his messy blond hair. "You like football, Mya?"

"It's not usually my scene, no."

"We'll have to change that then because you just landed yourself in Rixon."

"Am I supposed to know what that means?"

"You'll see." He winked at her before turning his attention to me. "Looking good, Fee, baby." Then he strolled away as if it was nothing.

"Why is everyone staring at us?" Mya asked.

"Because you just caught the eye of a Raider." My stomach knotted at the words, which was weird because if Asher turned his attention to the new girl, at least it meant he wouldn't be looking at me anymore.

Didn't it?

"*So* not interested." Mya loaded her tray with lunch items.

"Boyfriend?" I raised a brow.

"*Ex*-boyfriend. And I'm not looking to replace him anytime soon."

"Ah, I see. Bad break up?" We moved along the line.

"The worst." Pain flashed in her eyes, but it was gone in an instant. Mya was hardened. Aloof. She reminded me a lot of Hailee pre-Cameron.

We paid for our lunch and weaved through the masses to our table. Hailee was already there. She looked up and smiled. "You must be Mya. Welcome to Rixon High. I see Flick already got her claws in you." My best friend fought a grin.

"She's persistent, I'll give her that."

"Hey," I protested. "I am sitting right here."

"We know," they both said in unison and I gawked at them.

"I'm beginning to think this was a bad idea. Now there are two of you."

"Strength in numbers, am I right?" Mya held out a fist toward Hailee who stared at her. When she awkwardly bumped it against Mya's knuckles, it was my turn to snicker.

"Very ghetto," I mouthed at her.

"Heard that," Mya flicked her gaze to me and I blushed.

"Sorry."

"Nah, it's all good. I like it. Beats everyone else looking at me like they don't know whether to run the other way or ask me if I know Snoop Dog."

"Mya, that's not..." Hailee started but the words died on her lips. "Rixon is small town; there isn't a lot of diversity around these parts."

"I can see that." Mya let her eyes wander around the cafeteria. While I hadn't blinked twice at her style—the holey boy jeans, shirt tied around her waist, khaki tank top, and military style boots—others were looking.

"So break it down for me."

"Football team." I motioned over to where Asher and the rest of the team sat. He gave us a two fingered salute and Mya snorted.

"Is he always so..."

"Annoying?" I asked. "Pretty much. We hated on the team until this year but since Hailee is dating—"

"Hold up," Mya jerked back. "You're dating him?"

"Whoa, no. I'm with Cameron. See the one with the dark short hair, cherry blossom tattoo?"

"Nice, very nice. But still a football player? Damn, girl."

"Tell me about it." Hailee smiled shyly. "It was never the plan but..."

"You can't help who you fall for." Mya finished as if she knew all about complicated relationships. "Got it."

"Football is a huge deal here," I went on. "The Raiders have a real shot at State so expect things to get a little crazy around here over the next few weeks."

Mya grimaced. "Is there anything to do for fun in Rixon that doesn't involve football?"

"There's Ice T's, the ice cream parlor; and The Alley."

"Let me guess, bowling?"

I nodded. "It has a diner and arcade too. It's probably one of the only places untouched by football around here." Well, it had been until recently, but I didn't tell Mya that. I didn't want to scare her off for good.

"So we've got ice cream and bowling. Anything else?" She smirked.

"Hmm, in the summer we go down to the lake and swim, that's pretty cool."

"You're really living your best life here, huh?"

"Like I said, small town." Hailee smiled, forking some pasta into her mouth.

Mya's gaze flicked back over to the football tables. "Guess I'd better readjust my expectations then." There was something in her eyes, a sadness edged with lust. Mya talked a good game about hating football, just like the rest of us who tried to remain unaffected. But the truth was, when you lived in a place like Rixon, football infiltrated your life even if you didn't want it to.

When her eyes landed on mine again and she said, "Should I even ask if you have a basketball team?" I realized maybe I'd misjudged her after all.

10

Jason

"DID YOU SEE THE NEW GIRL?" Grady asked me as I got ready for practice.

I shrugged, pulling on my shoulder pads.

"I saw Bennet introducing himself." Mackey winked over at him. "You thinking of slumming it?"

"Not cool, bro," Asher's jaw clenched. "Not cool."

"What? I'm just saying she looks *Straight Outta Compton.*" He rapped the words.

"Mackey, do us all a favor and shut the fuck up, yeah?"

"Sorry, Cap, I was only messing around."

"Fucking idiot," Asher grumbled, shouldering him and heading out of the locker room.

"I think Bennet's got a crush on the new girl," Grady said, and snorts of laughter rang out around the room.

"Maybe you should all quit gossiping and focus on the game we have coming up?" I shot each one of them a harsh look before going after Asher.

I didn't give a fuck about some new girl, but I'd seen her sitting with Hailee and Felicity at lunch. Of course my step-sister and her best friend would take in the stray.

Rolling my eyes, I made my way over to Asher and Cameron. "Hey, you okay?"

"Who, me?" His brows waggled. "I'm good." Trust Asher to brush it under the rug.

"Who is she anyway?" I asked.

"I heard she transferred from Philly. Mia or Mya or something," Cameron offered. "The principal asked Felicity to help her settle in."

"Sounds about right."

"Okay, ladies, bring it in," Coach Hasson yelled. Once we were listening, he said, "Game seven and it's going to be a tough one. Fenn Hill are the team to beat this season. Their offense have been unstoppable, not to mention, they have eleven division one picks. And we're playing at their place. I'm not going to sugarcoat it; you're going to need to bring everything you have to get the win. And we need that win."

Because this win was our ticket to the play-offs.

"We've got this, Coach," I said with confidence. The Falcons were good, but we were better.

"I'm glad you think so, Son, because after Friday's game, you need to prove yourselves. I'm not going to rehash what happened because we drew a line under it Friday." Yeah, after he'd chewed us out like we were kids caught with our hands in the cookie jar, before issuing Cameron a warning. "But you'd better hope to God you don't pull that shit again. I don't care if their players are talking smack about your dead grandmothers out there. Let. It. Go. Do I make myself clear?"

"Yes, Sir."

"Good." His eyes landed on me. "Warm them up, QB."

"Let's go," I roared, leaping to my feet. After Friday's game, I was itching to get back on the field; to prove to everyone—and myself—that we were the best.

But then I spotted two familiar faces in the bleachers. Jogging beside Cameron, I grumbled, "What are they doing here?"

"Hailee needs to work on her last couple of raw sketches for the Seniors Night thing."

Pressing my lips together, I swallowed the reply on my tongue. Hailee I could deal with, but Felicity?

"I didn't sign up for this shit."

"Don't be a dick," Cam levelled with me with a hard look. "You know how important this project is to Hailee. Besides, she's been out here almost every practice and you haven't..." Realization sparked in his eyes. "But you're not talking about Hailee are you?"

"I have no idea what you're talking about."

A slow smirk tugged at his mouth. "Sure you don't." Cameron clapped me on the back before joining the rest of the guys in formation for warm-ups. "I'm going to enjoy watching you fall", he called, and I stared blankly at him.

Because what the actual fuck?

Practice was brutal. Coach made us run drills until my muscles burned and my bones ached. He was concerned about the game against Fenn Hill. It was right there in the way he pushed us harder. Demanded more. Insisted we give everything we had to give and then some. By the time we made it back to the locker room, I was ready to fall into bed and sleep for a week. Not that it was ever an option.

"Yo, QB, Thatcher is running his mouth again."

My spine straightened as Grady came over, handing me his cell.

@ThatcherQB1: *Better run, better hide, the Falcons are on the hunt #Falconsforthewin #Raiderscansuckit*

"He's really not giving this thing up, is he?"

"He's all talk." I flipped Grady's cell back to him.

"And if he isn't all talk?" Cameron dropped down on the bench next to me.

"I can handle Thatcher."

"Like you handled him when he was at The Alley putting his hands on Hailee?"

"That's not fair and you know it."

"You're right." He let out a strained breath. "I'm sorry. I just can't stand the idea that he was anywhere near her."

"It won't happen again," I said, even though I knew it was a promise I couldn't keep.

"You don't really think he'll show Friday, do you? Maybe we should talk to Coa—"

"Have you lost your fucking mind? The last thing we need to do is take this to Coach. If Finnigan finds out about this, it won't end well for any of us. He's already watching my every move." Determined to 'clean up' the reputation of the football team, the new principal had made it his priority to make sure his football team behaved. Except, it wasn't his team, not really. A fact he hated. But Coach Hasson and the school board could only protect us so much.

The need to get Thatcher back burned through me. But I had to be smart about getting payback. Because the team had worked too damn hard to risk everything.

I'd worked too damn hard.

"Thatcher will get what's coming to him," I said quietly, feeling vengeance boil my blood.

"That's what worries me." Cameron gave me a pointed look before standing up and grabbing his bag. "I'll see you tomorrow," he said before walking away.

There was a day when we did everything together. But now he had Hailee and everything was different.

And fuck me, if it didn't suck.

I grabbed my shit and headed out. I didn't expect to run into Asher and Felicity in the parking lot, laughing and joking like old friends.

"We're thinking of heading to Bell's, you want to come?" Ash said with an easy smile, as if she was part of our group now. I frowned, my eyes sliding to hers in question. She lowered her face, heat creeping into her cheeks.

"What, are you two now like fuck buddies or something?" Felicity blanched while Asher's eyes shuttered as he let out a heavy sigh.

"Jase, come on, it isn't like that—"

"Whatever. It's none of my business. You do you, but I think I'll pass."

"Maybe I should go," her soft voice drifted over me like a warm current. I was being a dick, but she was everywhere I fucking turned.

"You don't need to go. I said we'll hang out and we will." Asher narrowed his eyes on me, daring me to argue. Then it hit me, that maybe this was all part of some game. His way of trying to get me to admit I liked her.

I didn't.

She just got under my skin. That was all.

But as I skulked away from them, I wasn't so sure anymore.

"LET'S GO, ladies, onto the buses." It was Friday evening and the entire team and cheer squad were crammed onto four buses that would take us to Fenn Hill. Our fans following in their cars behind us.

It was a sight to behold; half the town making the forty-minute ride to come out and support the Raiders. But everyone wanted to see us win; to move one step closer to State. And it helped; having a big presence in the crowd at away games. Their constant roar like fuel to the fire.

Our fire.

I watched from the window as Cameron said goodbye to Hailee. Felicity and the new girl lingered on the periphery, pretending not to watch. All week I'd avoided her; and all week my mood had deteriorated.

Fucking girls.

Let them in and chances were they would screw everything up, but keep them at arm's length... and chances were they would screw everything up. It was a no-win situation.

I'd rationalized that my strange fascination with the girl who made lists and attended book club and owned some downright fucking ugly shirts was nothing more than the fact she'd been a virgin and I hadn't rocked her world because Hailee walked in on us.

The plan had been to fuck her out of my system with Jenna, but I was starting to wonder if I just needed to fuck *her* again. I shook the stupid idea out of my head. Going there with Felicity again was a one-way street to a headache I didn't want or need.

With everyone finally on board, Coach Hasson stood at the front, staring out at us the way he did whenever we had a big game ahead of us—which was every game we ever played.

"Listen up, ladies," he boomed. "I want your best behavior tonight. We're playing away from home which means you're not only representing your team, you're representing the school, and the town. I expect nothing but professionalism, understood?"

A grumble of 'Yes, Sir' echoed around me as Coach's hard stare bore into me. He was still pissed about the game against Millington and he had every right to be. But he wasn't the one out there, on the field. Sometimes decisions were taken out of our hands; sometimes the decision was made so quickly you didn't have time to weigh up the consequences. You were all up in some fucker's face before you could stop yourself.

"Hey, you okay?" Cameron nudged my shoulder.

I gave him a tight nod. I was more than ready for the game. Eager to get out there and kick some Falcon ass. It was everything else that was sitting heavy on my chest. As if I needed any extra pressure, Grady leaned over the top of my seat and shoved his cell in front of me. "Did you see this?"

"Grady," Cam warned, but it was too late. My eyes ran over the tweet, jaw clenching at Thatcher's taunt.

@ThatcherQB1: *What's that I hear? The Raiders crying like little b%&$es #Falconstakenoprisoners #Raidersbetterhide*

"He's just trying to get in your head." Cameron said, snatching the cell out my hand and shoving it back at Grady, mumbling something to him about 'stopping that shit'.

"Yeah, well it's working," I said coolly.

"You can't let him in, man. He knows the Eagles are out of the play-offs and now he's trying to sabotage our shot."

I concentrated on my fist as it pressed against my thigh, uncurling and curling it. Squeezing until the blood drained from my hand. Thatcher was under my skin, like an annoying itch you couldn't quite get rid of no matter how hard you scratched.

Asher's face appeared between the gap in the two seats in front of us. "Maybe we should just go over the river and give him what he wants?" Mischief lit up his face. Asher might have been the joker of the bunch, but he was always down for a rumble.

"Seriously, you think that's going to solve anything?" Cameron let out a frustrated breath.

"Better than sitting around waiting for him to come at us." Asher turned back around.

"Don't listen to him," my best friend's tone was serious. "Thatcher will get bored eventually."

But for as much as I wanted to believe him, I couldn't. Thatcher would keep coming, keep pushing my buttons, until eventually I snapped.

Because we were more alike than I gave him credit for. I'd hurt his sister... and now he was determined to hurt me. I'd been arrogant enough to think I was untouchable. Believed Thatcher couldn't hurt me because the list of people I gave a shit about was next to none.

But I cared.

Deep down, I fucking cared. And I hated it.

Because caring made me vulnerable.

It made me weak.
Something I couldn't afford to be.

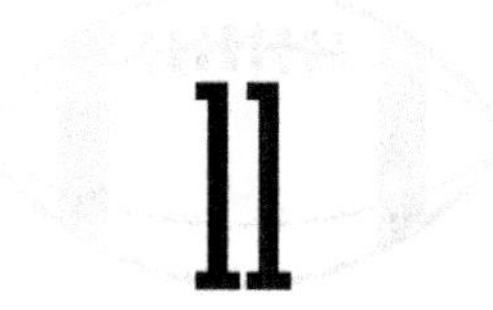

11

Felicity

"REMIND me why I agreed to come to this thing again?" Mya grumbled as I dragged her and Hailee to the concession stand for pre-game refreshments.

Fenn Hill had a much smaller stadium than our school, but it didn't stop the crowds swarming. Our blue and white painted faces and shirts and ball caps barely made a dent in the sea of yellow and green.

"It's fun," I yelled over the noise.

"Fun?" Mya arched a brow, glancing at Hailee who threw up her hands.

"Don't look at me. I'm only here for Cameron."

"I'm confused," our new girlfriend said. "I thought you hated the football team and the whole 'institution of the game'?" She air quoted Hailee's words from earlier this week.

"Oh, we do," I explained. "But we're also embracing it this year."

"Right." Mya frowned. "So which one do you want?"

"Want?" I spluttered, almost choking on her insinuation.

"Well, yeah. I mean it makes sense why she's here." Mya pointed at Hailee. "But what I can't figure out is why you're here if you're not crushing on one of—"

"There is no crushing," I rushed out, a little too quickly. "I so happen to enjoy the odd game of football. Even if the whole institution is whack."

"So you're in denial." Her brow went higher.

"I'm not..." The argument dried on the tip of my tongue. "I just want to support Cameron and the guys."

"*The guys?* You mean Asher and Jason—"

"Well, well, if it isn't Chase's girl and the sassy one." Thatcher's friend, the one he'd called Gallen appeared, his predatory gaze fixed right on me. "Looking good, baby."

"What the hell are you doing here?" I blurted out.

"I came to see the game, what else would I—"

"Is Thatcher here?" Hailee was as white as a sheet.

"You didn't think I was going to let Gallen here have all the fun, did you?" Thatcher rounded his friend and narrowed his eyes on Mya. "Who's the new girl?"

"No one to you," she retorted, folding her arms over her chest.

"I didn't know Ford had taken to slumming it with hood rats."

"You can't say that," I shrieked, stepping in front of Mya, shielding her from Thatcher's superior smirk. "You don't even know her."

"I have eyes, sweetheart."

People were watching now. Even the hot dog guy was gawking at us instead of doing his damn job.

"Just go," I lowered my voice, my eyes pleading. "You're making a scene."

Thatcher edged closer, taking the air with him, until my breath caught in my throat. "You've got balls; you know that, sweet thing? I was planning on playing with Chase's girl a little more, but perhaps I'll play with you instead." His hand snaked out and brushed the side of my neck, eliciting a violent shudder inside me.

"Get your fucking hands off her." Mya stepped up beside me, anger rolling off her. "Before I scream."

Thatcher's head whipped over to her and a twisted smirk graced his deadly expression. "Screaming only makes me hotter, baby."

Smacking his hand away, I stepped back, pulling Mya with me. Gallen smirked, making no disguise of the fact he was blatantly eye-fucking me.

Bile rushed up my throat. These guys were pigs. Worse than anything I'd ever witnessed from Jason and the team, and that was saying something. They didn't look like guys who wanted to have a little fun with us. They looked like guys who wanted to humiliate us.

To hurt us.

"Come on," Hailee said, her voice quiet. "We should go."

I pulled Mya away, trying to ignore the two sets of eyes biting into my skin. "Do I even want to know?" she asked as we abandoned hot dogs and melted into the sea of people.

"Oh, that was Lewis Thatcher, the quarterback and alpha-jerk of the Raiders rivals, The Rixon East Eagles."

"I'm sorry I asked." She half-laughed. "So when you said Rixon takes football very seriously, you really meant—"

"As serious as a heart attack." My lips curved in a tentative smile. "It can get kind of crazy. There is *no* love lost between Jason and Thatcher."

"And here I thought moving to some small town in the ass crack of nowhere was going to be boring."

"Hey," I protested. "Rixon isn't in the ass crack of nowhere."

"It isn't the city either. But I'm glad Principal Finnigan stuck us together." Her expression softened, something I suspected not many people got to see.

"Me too. Come on." Linking arms with her and Hailee, I pushed all thoughts of Thatcher out of my head.

We had a game to win.

"HOLY CRAP, THIS IS INVIGORATING." Mya grinned beside me as we watched our offence celebrate a touchdown. Their sixth of the game.

"What did I tell you? Hate the players, don't hate the game." Flashing her a wink, I chuckled, bouncing on the balls of my feet, waving my hands in the air like a crazy person.

Hailee was quieter, her eyes zeroed in on Cameron as he fist-bumped his teammates before jogging off field.

It was the fourth quarter and we hadn't seen Thatcher and his friend again. But we'd watched the Raiders kick the Falcons ass all over the field. Our fans, although four times smaller than the home fans, were louder, hungrier, and the buzz in the air was electric.

"Almost there," I squeaked, grabbing Hailee's hand and squeezing.

I knew how important it was for her to be here for Cameron after everything they had been through.

The final whistle went and our tiny section of the bleachers erupted. Even Mya was on her feet, hooting and hollering as the high of the win settled deep in our bones.

It was weird. Throughout high school I'd never been part of anything. I wasn't in band or on the cheer squad. I didn't get invited to parties or to join the debate team or compete for an athletics club. I had Hailee and our simple lives—hanging out at The Alley, gate-crashing the odd party, eating our body weight in ice cream at Ice T's—and it was enough.

Until I wanted more.

Until I wanted to soak up every experience I could in senior year and experience all the things I'd never gotten to because we'd been outcast by our peers all because of Jason and his stupid grudge against Hailee. But here, cheering on the team, I felt like I belonged.

As soon as the players disappeared off field, we all filed out of the bleachers and into the parking lot where the team buses were waiting. The second Jason appeared, leading the team out of the Falcons' building, a huge round of cheers greeted our heroes. The guys split off, searching for their friends and families among the gathered crowd. Cameron and Asher made a beeline for the three of us, while Jase chatted to Coach Hasson and his father. I pretended to listen to Asher as he recounted every play and pass, every tackle and sack. Really, I was watching Jason. His tight expression as his father gripped his shoulder as he talked animatedly with the coach.

"Fee, baby, what's got your..." Asher craned his neck around, the sparkle in his eye dimming. "Oh."

"Sorry," I gave him my best smile. "You were saying?"

"Well, I was about to invite the three of you to the party at my house tomorrow..." I hated the dejection in his voice but there was no use in trying to fix it. He'd seen me looking at Jason, and I knew he knew how I felt.

Even if I'd never told him.

"You like to party, Mya?" Asher slung his arm around her shoulder, and I swear a small growl formed low in her throat. "Message received." He edged away, shooting her a lazy grin. "But seriously, you should come tomorrow. My place is the only place to party. Hailee will be there, right, Hails?"

"I guess." She shrugged, glancing up at Cam who was too busy staring at her with such emotion I was pretty sure he hadn't heard a single word Asher had just said.

"I'll go if Felicity goes."

My head snapped over to Mya and she lifted a brow, some indecipherable expression on her face.

"What do you say, Fee, baby? Party at mine tomorrow?"

A few weeks back, my immediate answer would have been yes. It was on my list, a rite of passage for kids of Rixon High. But that was before sex with Jason; before the heated looks and stolen kisses. Before Asher's puppy-dog eyes followed me everywhere.

God, everything seemed so complicated now.

"Will there be dancing?"

"There is always dancing." His brows waggled suggestively.

"I'm not talking about *that* kind of dancing, Asher." I'd heard the stories.

"There can be any kind of dancing you want."

He was flirting. Nothing he hadn't done a hundred times before, but every time he did it, I felt more and more confused.

"Fine, we can go." My eyes slid to Mya who gave me a curt nod. She was hard to read. But I didn't miss the way her eyes lingered in Asher's direction.

She liked him.

He liked me. At least, I think he did.

And I liked Jason.

If this didn't have disaster written all over it, I don't know what did.

"Yo, QB," Asher beckoned Jase over. He strolled toward us, his eyes cool. "We heading to Bell's later?"

"Not tonight, my dad wants to... celebrate. But I'll be at yours tomorrow." His gaze found mine, narrowing. I could feel it running over my skin, burning. He looked wired. The adrenaline of the game, no doubt.

"You good, Jase? You look a little—"

Jason broke our connection to glare at Asher. "I'm good," he growled. "Coach wants us on the buses stat."

"Guess this is goodbye, ladies. Until tomorrow?"

Jason paused, glancing back at us. "You invited them?"

"Well, yeah, I didn't—"

"Whatever." He stomped off, and I let out a shaky breath.

"What crawled up his ass?" Asher asked Cam.

"I think it's just the pressure of everything."

Or the fact he was a moody asshole.

Coach Hasson and his assistants began rounding up the team to get on the buses, while a few fans lingered to wave them off. We hung back too because we were *those* girls now.

Strangely, I didn't mind.

"Do you think we should have told them?" I asked Hailee as she made moon eyes at Cam.

"And worry them for nothing? No." She folded her arms around her waist and I saw the flicker of doubt in her eyes. Hailee didn't like keeping secrets, least of all from Cameron. But we'd decided not to tell them about Thatcher being here to avoid any more trouble.

"Come on, we should go," Hailee started toward my car but paused when Thatcher appeared. He leaned casually against the hood, throwing a wolfish grin in our direction. I glanced back, hoping the team buses were still there, but they were already disappearing down the road.

Crap.

"Hmm, Hailee, what do we do?"

"Just play it cool," she said. "He won't do anything. He just wants to use us to get to the guys."

Which is exactly what I was worried about.

"He really doesn't know when to quit it, does he?" Mya asked as we inched closer.

"Ladies," he drawled just as his friend and another guy stepped out of the shadows.

There were still a few people in the parking lot, but they were all heading back to their cars, paying the three of us no attention.

"Should we shout for—"

"No," Hailee said, rolling her shoulders back. She was used to Jason's games; his cruel pranks. But this felt different. It *was* different. Hailee was no one to Thatcher, but she was someone to Jason and Cameron, and he knew it.

"What do you want, Lewis?" she said as we reached them.

"I want a lot of things." He let his eyes run down the length of her body.

"Yeah, well, so do I, but we can't always get what we want. You should probably leave."

"Or what?" He pushed off the hood. "I saw the buses leave. Your brother and boyfriend are on their way back to Rixon and you're here, all alone."

"She's not alone." Mya stepped forward.

"Yeah, she has us," I added, digging my hand in my pocket, my fingers grazing the corner of my cell.

"Ooh, I'm scared." The three of them burst into laughter. Until Gallen's eyes homed in on me... and my hand.

"What you got there, cutie?" He approached me and I backed away, my heart galloping in my chest.

"N- nothing," I cried, staggering back until my back hit the side of a truck. But Gallen didn't stop. He kept coming until he'd caged me in, his hands pressed flat either side of my head.

"You aren't trying to call for reinforcements, are you?"

"Fuck you," I seethed, my defenses working overtime.

His eyes flared, "Oh baby, I'd love nothing more than to fuck you." He trailed a finger down my neck and between the valley of my breasts. My chest heaved with a shaky breath as I turned my head away from him. But he grabbed my face roughly, pulling me back to him.

"Just one taste," he groaned, grinding his hips into me, as his tongue snaked out across my lips.

"What the hell is wrong with you?"

He grunted with pain, the unwelcome pressure of his body against mine disappearing as he stumbled away. "What the fuck?"

Mya advanced on him, her fist clenched.

"Fuck's sake," Thatcher grumbled. "If you want something done..." he trailed off, leaving Hailee to come up to me. "You," He jabbed his finger at Mya, "Keep your fists to yourself." He gave the other guy a nod and he grabbed Mya's hands pulling them behind her back.

"You can't do this," she thrashed against his body. But her fight only made the guy smirk.

"Now where were we?" Thatcher's eyes darkened. "What I'm trying to figure out is are you Bennet's girl or Ford's?"

"W- what? I'm not..."

Thatcher lowered his face to mine; so close I could feel his warm breath dancing over my skin. My stomach churned.

"Bennet wants you. I've seen it. The way he watches you, touches you. And Ford doesn't like it. I saw him tense just now."

He'd been watching us? Waiting for them to leave?

Oh God.

"I'm no one. I'm Hailee's friend, that's all."

"So you haven't given it up to Bennet or Ford? Maybe both of them?" His brow rose. "Maybe under this little miss innocent act you have going, you're nothing more than a dirty little slut."

I pressed my lips together, trying to swallow some of the fear and panic rushing through me. Not to mention the truth.

Thatcher narrowed his eyes, assessing me. "You're lying," he said. "You're someone all right and my money is on—"

"Shit, Cap," Gallen said, not so cocksure now. "Security. We need to go..."

"Yeah, okay." Thatcher stepped back, running a hand down his face, his eyes still fixed on me. "Until next time." He grinned.

Silence stretched out before us, the air turning icy cold. Then he said, "Oh, and tell Ford I'm coming for him."

12

Jason

"WHO THE FUCK are all these people?" I grumbled. I'd gotten to Asher's house an hour ago and grabbed a six-pack before taking my usual chair out back, but there were people everywhere.

"It's a party. We're celebrating, remember?"

Of course I fucking remembered. We were in the play-offs. But after a disastrous dinner post-game, with my father and Denise, I wasn't exactly in a people kind of mood.

"Did you invite the whole fucking school?"

Asher grinned. "Only the bright and beautiful. Who's beautiful?" he yelled and everyone went nuts, screaming and cheering. *Always the showman.* I rolled my eyes.

"Where's Chase?" I asked.

"Inside with Hailee, but I'd steer clear of them if I were you, seems like there might be trouble in paradise." Asher took a long pull on his beer.

I was already out of my chair though, stalking toward the house. The last thing we needed was our star wide receiver to lose his cool over some shit with my step-sister. The team needed Cam in the play-offs.

I needed him.

"Your funeral, man," he yelled.

Inside wasn't much better; bodies packed into every corner of the Bennet's huge house. They were rich—filthy rich compared to the rest of us—and they didn't mind Asher using the place for party central given they were out of town a lot. I couldn't figure which was worse: having parents who cared but were never around, or having a dad you didn't see eye-to-eye with who refused to stay out of your business. It seemed like parents were a pain in the ass whichever way you looked at it.

I searched the ground floor for Cam and Hailee before moving upstairs. Cam hadn't always had it easy growing up, and since the Bennet's had enough guest rooms to open a motel, they had given him his own room. He didn't use it much anymore, but I knew if they were anywhere, that's where they would be.

Raised voices made me pause when I reached his door.

"Tell him, Cameron."

"And then what? What do you think telling him will do except incite war?"

I crept closer, straining to hear, the hairs along the back of my neck standing to attention.

"So what do we do? Wait until Thatcher really hurts one of—"

I burst into the room, my eyes narrowed to slits. "Tell me what?"

"Jase, man, we didn't know—"

"Tell. Me. What?" I focused on Hailee since she was the only one who thought telling me whatever the fuck had happened was a good idea.

"Thatcher was at the game last night."

"What the hell did you just say?" I saw red, my fists clenched, liquid fury coursing through my veins.

"We saw him before the game and again after..." Hailee's eyes slid to Cameron who was deadly still.

"And why the fuck am I only just finding out about this?"

"Hailee only just told me. I swear, man."

"It's true," she added. "I didn't know what to do and Flick—"

"What does she have to do with all this?" Hearing her name set off my pulse, my heart jack-hammering in my chest.

"Thatcher's friend..." She hesitated, my mood darkening by the second. "He..."

"Hailee, spit it out or so help me—"

"Jase, man, you need to calm down," Cam offered, but I levelled him with a cold look.

"They really scared her, Jason. He had her pinned to the wall and he tried to—"

I couldn't hear anything over the roar of blood pounding between my ears.

"You okay, man, you look a little white?"

"H- he *touched* her?" The words almost choked me.

"Not like that, but he grabbed her and said some things. And his friend held Mya back after she punched him."

"She did what?" I rubbed my temples, this was getting worse by the second.

Hailee nodded. "She hit him and he left Flick alone but then Thatcher—"

My fist slammed into the wall beside me, the crack of bone against drywall reverberating through me. But I barely felt any pain, too consumed with the idea of Thatcher anywhere near Felicity.

"He knows she's someone, Jason." Hailee let the words hang between us, the insinuation like a slap in the face.

"Where is she now?" I asked, barely able to see straight.

"At home. She didn't want to come. I think it's affected her more than she wants to let on. She's been holed up at her house all day."

"And you? You're okay?"

If Hailee was surprised at my concern, she didn't show it. "I'm okay," she said, reaching for Cameron's hand. "I know this gives you reason to go after Thatcher, but it's what he wants. You're in the play-offs now. If you put one step wrong off the field, Principal Finnigan could pull you for the rest of the season."

Didn't I know it.

"You don't need to worry about me," I said, "I'll be fine. You two going to be okay if I go?" I lifted a brow at Cameron who gave me a tight nod.

"He isn't worth it," he reminded me. "Don't play into his hands."

"I don't plan on it." But Thatcher would get his, one way or another he would pay for all this.

But right now, I had bigger things to worry about.

Felicity's house was steeped in darkness when I pulled up outside. Cameron and Hailee had tried to warn me about coming here, but as soon as her name left my step-sister's lips, all rational thought went out of the window.

I had to know she was okay.

Maybe it was guilt over the fact she wouldn't be in this mess if it wasn't for me, or maybe it was because she meant more to me than I cared to admit. Whatever it was, I wasn't leaving until I saw her with my own two eyes.

So why had I been sitting here for the last ten minutes unable to get out of the damn car?

"Fuck it," I mumbled, shouldering the door and climbing out. I'd never called on a girl before; never stood on the doorstep and waited for them to appear. It wasn't my style. Wasn't something I ever imagined myself doing... yet, here I was.

But the second I hit the Giles' porch, I froze. It was late on a Saturday night. What if her parents were home? What if her old man answered the door and saw me standing here? He'd recognize me; everyone in town did. Then there would be questions, assumptions... Fuck.

There was no car in the driveway unless you counted Felicity's ugly sunflower yellow Beetle.

Retrieving my cell, I sent a quick text to Hailee.

Me: Are her parents home?

. . .

Haile: How the hell should I know? Is their car there?

Me: I don't think so.

Hailee: You should be good then. I hope you know what the hell you're doing.

I ignored that, not wanting to admit I didn't have the first clue what I was doing.

Knocking gently, I waited. And waited.

And waited some fucking more.

There was every chance she was asleep. But it wasn't good enough. I needed to see her, to hear her side of what happened.

I needed to know she was fucking okay.

Me: I need her number.

Hailee: No way.

Me: Please. I wouldn't ask if it wasn't important.

Hailee: If I do this, and I haven't decided I will yet, you have to promise me not to hurt her. Ever.

Shit. How could she expect me to agree to that?

Hailee: So.... what'll it be?

Me: I promise to only ever do what I think's best for her...

Hailee: Jason, that isn't the same thing.

. . .

Me: It's all I have right now. What's it going to be, little sis? Am I getting her number or am I breaking and entering your best friend's house?

Hailee: JASON!!! Don't you dare...

Me: I'm joking.

For the most part. Because I wasn't leaving without seeing Felicity. Another text came through with a cell phone number. I added it to my contacts and opened a new message chat.

Me: Open your door.

Felicity: Who is this?

Me: Come find out...

A couple of minutes passed, and I was beginning to think she'd barricaded herself inside while she waited for the authorities to arrive. But then the curtain twitched and a couple seconds later, the door creaked open. "Jason?" Felicity yelped. "What are you—"

"Don't I get an invitation inside?" I forced my eyes to stay on her face and not her bare legs.

"Why would I invite you inside?" She glared at me. "And what are you doing at my house anyway? It's late. I was asleep."

"Just open the damn door, Felicity," I breathed out. "Hailee told me what happened last night with Thatcher."

"So you came over here to do what exactly?" Her lips pursed, taunting me. Her eyes daring me to admit it.

"You're really going to make me say it?"

Silence stretched out before us while Felicity waited for me to make my choice.

"Fine, woman. I came because the second I heard he had his hands on you, I wanted to kill something." Preferably him.

Bitter laughter spilled out of her soft lips. "So you're jealous? That's it?"

Her brow shot up in challenge.

"Jealous of Thatcher?" I seethed. "I'm not fucking jealous."

"No? Because from where I'm standing, it looks like you are. Didn't you like hearing Thatcher and his friend had their hands on my body? They were so close to me, I could feel the warmth of their breath against my skin." My body began to tremble with rage as she kept talking. Kept describing what Thatcher and his guy had done to her.

"Felicity..."

"What, Jason?" she said, sharply. "Does it hurt to hear they wanted me? That they wanted to *hurt* me? Because I think he would have. I think he would have taken me right there—"

"Stop, okay," My chest heaved, and I rubbed my breastbone trying to ease the tightness. "Just stop."

"Why? Why should I?" Unshed tears collected in the corners of her eyes and I suddenly realized she wasn't baiting as much as unleashing her own anger at the situation.

"Let me in, Giles," I said, sliding my foot into the gap.

"No." A single tear escaped, rolling down Felicity's cheek. "You need to leave. Just go, Jason."

"Come on, babe. Let me in."

"You don't care about me," she whispered.

"I care," I admitted. "I wouldn't be standing here if I didn't."

Her eyes flew to mine, searching. Looking for answers I didn't have. It was a battle of wills and I didn't know who would break first.

"Fine," she eventually relented, "but you can't stay. My parents are—"

"Who said anything about staying?" I smirked as I stepped inside earning me one of her trademark eye rolls.

The door clicked shut behind us and I flinched, the sound like a gunshot to the chest.

What the fuck was I doing? She was okay, I could see that. Maybe a little shook up and angry, but she'd sassed at me the way she usually did. The fight sparking in her sea-green eyes.

"Nice place," I said, filling the awkward silence.

"It's not much different to your house." She smiled faintly, leading me down the hall I knew would open out to the kitchen.

"You didn't come to the party?"

"I didn't feel much like socializing." Her shoulders lifted in a small shrug as she went to turn away from me.

"Hey." I grabbed her arm and pulled gently, backing her up against the counter. Her breath hitched, her eyes alight with so much emotion I felt winded. How could one girl—one quirky, no-filter, pain-in-the-ass girl—affect me so much with a single look?

"You okay?"

"I..." Felicity slid her hands up my chest, her touch like wildfire, blazing a trail of heat. "I think so."

"Thatcher just wanted to scare you."

"Yeah, well, it worked."

My chest squeezed again. Too many people were being dragged into this thing between me and Thatcher. First Hailee, then Cam, and now Felicity. If I wasn't careful, soon there would be too many moving pieces for me to keep tabs on.

"What did you do that was so bad?" Her voice was quiet even in the silence.

Shit. She could have asked me any other question and I probably would have answered... but this was the one thing I never wanted her to know about me.

But instead of clamming up and distracting her with kisses and touches, I found myself saying, "There was this girl."

Felicity tensed, her eyes full of bewilderment. "A girl? Like Jenna?"

"No, not like Jenna." I grimaced. "Jenna is no one."

Felicity arched a brow at that.

"She's just someone to pass the time. A willing body." Jesus, it sounded so fucking awful out loud.

"Ew, gross," she mumbled, dropping her eyes.

"Hey," I slid my fingers underneath her jaw and tilted her face up, "you asked."

"I know, I just... ugh, I hate her."

"You sound a little jealous, Giles." The idea had me feeling a little smug.

"It's not exactly on my list to watch the guy I'm..." She stopped herself and I found myself wanting to pull the words out of her but I wouldn't. "It hurt seeing the two of you together is all."

"Together, me and Jenna weren't..."

Fuck.

Bell's.

"That wasn't what it looked like."

"You mean you didn't take her back to the storeroom and fuck her?" Her eyes darted away. "Could have fooled me."

My spine stiffened; the urge to argue with her strong. Felicity was only half-right; I hadn't fucked Jenna that night, but she had given me head.

Shame was a feeling I was unfamiliar with, but it didn't dull the impact.

"I didn't fuck her," I said, as if it mattered.

"Whatever, Jason." She looked at me again. "This, us, it's all a game. And like I said the other night in your bathroom, I'm not sure I want to play anymore."

The bathroom. Shit. That had been a mistake. I was drunk and angry and she was right there, my own personal punching bag.

Rather than acknowledge that clusterfuck, I inched closer, erasing the sliver of space between us. "You sure about that?"

Felicity's lips parted on a soft intake of breath. "What are you doing, Jason?" Her voice trembled.

"I thought it was obvious. I'm here because I couldn't stand the idea of Thatcher hurting you."

"Because you're jealous." It didn't come out sassy this time.

"I'm not..." Rubbing the back of my neck, I mulled over what to say next. When really all I wanted to do was kiss her. After all, didn't they say actions spoke louder than words?

"You're so fucking beautiful." My lips hovered dangerously close to hers. It would have been so easy to crash my mouth down on hers. But I wanted to savor her, to taste every inch of her skin.

I wanted to lose myself in her, and that disarmed me.

"Your eyes are so dark," she said. "It's like they're black."

"They say the eyes are the window to the soul. So what does that say about me?"

"I think it says you're deadly." Felicity leaned into me, our noses brushing, lips almost touching.

"Deadly, huh?"

We moved closer still.

"And dangerous..."

"Definitely dangerous," I echoed, tasting her. Once. Twice.

"Don't prove me wrong, Jason," her words slammed into me but I didn't have time to process them, because her mouth sealed over mine and I knew the game had just changed.

And I wasn't sure of the rules anymore.

13

Felicity

JASON WAS IN MY HOUSE.

It shouldn't have been the only thought consuming my mind as his lips trailed over my skin, nipping and sucking, but it was.

Jason was here.

Because he was worried.

About me.

I didn't know what to do with that.

I wanted to store it for future reference; to lock it away for the next time I needed to remind myself he wasn't just a conceited asshole. But I knew it was a dangerous thing—to let myself believe this meant anything more than right here, in this moment. Jason belonged to Rixon. He had the hearts of almost every single person in our small town. There wasn't room for mine too. Yet, I found myself falling down the rabbit hole anyway.

Somehow, we managed to make it upstairs to my room without breaking contact. Our clothes scattered in a haphazard trail from my door to my bed which looked better than ever with a half-naked Jason Ford sprawled over it.

"Come here." He crooked a finger at me, pushing up on his elbows to watch me. When I reached the bed, he shuffled to the edge, planting his feet on the floor. "You always sleep in a Raiders t-shirt?" He fingered the oversized blue and white shirt, pulling me until I stood between his legs.

"I'll take the fifth," I said around a coy smile.

"You will, huh?" His hands painted a torturous path up and down my legs, every time inching higher until his fingers were brushing the apex of my thighs. "I like you in Raider colors." His eyes glittered with lust, but I tried hard not to read between the lines.

Don't get sucked in.

Don't fall for his bedroom talk.

Don't let this become more than it is.

"But I think I prefer you like this." He pushed the shirt up my hips, all the way over my body until it was bunched around my shoulders. I pulled it off the rest of the way, baring myself to him.

"Perfect," his voice was strained and I loved it. Loved that I affected him so much because God only knew, he made me melt.

The old me, the me before senior year, wanted to ask a million questions.

What did this mean?

Did he want me or just hot anger-fueled sex?

Did he feel even an ounce of what I felt for him?

But the new me, the girl with a senior year bucket list, stuffed down all the doubt and willingly walked into the lion's den. Because deep down, maybe I did want my chance to tame the beast.

Jason smoothed one of his hands up my stomach causing me to shiver. "You like that?" He asked huskily, staring up at me with a lazy smirk. "What about this?" His fingers closed around one of my nipples, pinching, and a bolt of pleasure shot through me.

"Oh God." I tried to swallow the moan building, but his touch was like kryptonite.

His other hand joined the party, rolling and plucking until my knees began to buckle.

"Jason, stop, I can't..."

"Too much?"

I nodded, my body melting against him. Before I could catch my breath, he'd pulled me onto the bed and rolled me beneath him. "Do you have any idea how much it turns me on knowing no one has been here?" He slid his hand between us, cupping me. "Except me."

Jason pressed a finger against me, rubbing me through my damp panties. I wanted him to pull them to the side and touch me, *really* touch me, but he seemed content in taking his time. Teasing me. Driving me wild.

He rocked back, standing at the foot of the bed. His tight-fitting boxers left very little to the imagination and I almost came right there when he grasped himself, squeezing roughly.

"Jason..."

"What do you want, babe?"

Everything, I wanted to say. But instead, I squeaked, "You."

Eyes dark and hooded, he climbed back over me, kissing me deep and hard. Our tongues danced a fast-paced rhythm, tangling and swirling together until I wasn't sure where I ended and he began.

His hard length rocked against me, making me wetter, needier. My sexual experiences left little to be desired compared to this. Jason was barely even touching me and I felt him everywhere; my synapses firing off in all directions, heat swimming in my veins.

My hand glided down his hard abs, cut to perfection from hours and hours of physical conditioning. But when I grazed his dick, Jason snagged my wrist, pinning it to the mattress at the side of my head.

"Patience," he said against my lips before diving back into the kiss. His tongue stroked every inch of my mouth before he moved to my jaw, drifting down the slope of my neck and along my collarbone. I writhed against him, desperate for him to end the sweet torture. But something told me he was only just getting started.

The thought both exhilarated and terrified me.

On a normal day, Jason was a lot to handle. Too much. But like this—half-naked, his skin pressed up against my skin, his mouth latched onto my neck, his hands curled into the flesh on my hip—he was lethal.

Jason broke the kiss again but only to move down my body. He dipped his tongue into my navel, swirling it around. Something so insignificant wasn't supposed to feel so erotic, but it did. My toes curled, my body aching to be closer to him.

"These need to go," he whispered against the inside of my thigh, dragging my panties down my legs. I was naked now, fully exposed to the guy I knew would never give me everything I needed.

Everything I wanted.

But I couldn't find it in myself to care, not with his mouth hovering over my most intimate place. "Has anyone ever kissed you here?" he asked huskily.

"N- no," I panted.

He grinned wickedly before diving for me. His mouth and tongue hot and heavy as he licked and stroked. Jason pressed a finger inside me, then another. I moaned, his name falling from my lips like a prayer.

"You taste so fucking good." His other hand trailed back up my body, resting between my breasts, pinning me to the bed as he dived back in, eating me with an intensity that had me moaning and bucking off the mattress.

But Jason was a tease. Pulling away every time I almost fell off the edge. Taunting my warm skin with tiny kisses along my inner thighs, rewarding my cries with a deeper press of his fingers. My hands fisted his hair, desperately trying to move his head to where I needed him most, but he was strong.

And I was a breathless wrung out mess.

"Jason, please..."

Finally, he relented, attacking me with his mouth, his tongue licking and flicking my clit with fervor. My body began to tremble, the force of my orgasm tearing through me before I had time to prepare myself.

Jason climbed back up my body, licking his fingers clean before tracing them over my lips. "See how good you taste." I sucked one into my mouth, high on the lust burning in his eyes, the carnal growl rumbling in his chest as I tasted myself on his finger.

"I think I'm dead," I breathed out, barely able to form words.

"They don't call me God for nothing." He smirked before kissing me, long and deep and painfully slow.

"I want to feel you," I yawned, my hand drifting down his cut abs.

"Later," he insisted, rolling off me and tucking me into his body, my back to his solid chest.

"Are we spooning?" I asked, confused he wanted to cuddle rather than have sex.

"You're exhausted," was all he said as the weight of what had just happened settled over us. After a couple minutes of silence, I asked, "Jase, what are we doing?"

He stiffened behind me and I half-expected him to get up, yank on his clothes, and make a run for it. But he didn't. His lips pressed tiny kisses along my shoulder, stirring a fresh wave of desire in my tummy.

"That feels so good," I whispered, tilting my head to one side.

"*You* feel good."

Three little words that took root in my chest and exploded into hopes and dreams and things I knew better than to want with him.

Oh God. What had I done letting him into my house?

Into my heart?

I closed my eyes, trying to rein in the panic swimming in my veins. My mom had always told me to wait, to give myself to the right guy. The guy who would protect my heart, keep it safe, and treat it with respect.

And here I was, in bed, selling my soul to the devil. Because even though I wanted more, even though I wanted him to say this was the start of something, I knew better.

Jason Ford was a beautiful disaster waiting to happen.

And I was right in the eye of the storm.

My eyes fluttered open, and I stretched, my muscles still drenched in pleasure.

"Jason?" I smiled around his name. "Did I fall to—"

Crap.

I bolted upright, the stream of light like a bucket of icy water. It was morning, which meant—

"Felicity, baby, are you awake?" Mom's voice filtered through the door.

"Jason?" I whisper-hissed, my eyes darting around the room, hoping I might find him hidden in the closet.

He wasn't of course.

There was no sign of him. No puddle of his clothes on my floor and the slightly indented sheets beside me were already cold.

Jason had left, and it had been awhile.

"Flick, sweetheart, are you awake?" A knock sounded on the door, before it clicked open and Mom's head appeared.

"Hi, Mom." I gave her a weak smile, pulling the sheet up around my body. "How was date night?"

"Oh, you know your father, it was all very nice." Code for they went to their favorite restaurant, ate their favorite meals, and then moved on for dancing at their favorite bar.

"One of these days, you should surprise him." The words spilled out.

"Surprise him?" Her brows pinched. "I'm not sure your father would appreciate that. You know he doesn't cope well with change."

"It was just an idea." I ducked my head, feeling silly suddenly. I never commented on my parents' relationship. They were happy, content in their life together. So what if they liked routine?

"Are you okay?" Mom asked. "You look a little... I don't know... sad."

"I'm fine, Mom, just tired." I yawned for effect.

"Are you seeing Hailee today? We miss her."

I miss her too. I swallowed the words. We hung out all the time still, ate lunch together at school every day, and did all the things we did pre-Cameron, but she had someone now.

Someone who wasn't me.

"I'm not sure. I think she said something about hanging out with Cameron and Xander." Cameron's baby brother was the cutest and he'd taken a real shine to my best friend. But then, who wouldn't?

"You could go with them? Just because she has a boyfriend now, doesn't mean—"

"Mom," I sighed. "It isn't like that. I'm happy for her. She deserves this."

"Oh, sweetheart, I didn't mean... Of course you should be happy for her. I just meant, I remember what it's like to lose your best friend to a guy." She gave me a warm smile. "Your day will come, Felicity. High school can be a confusing time. But soon you'll be in college and I'm sure you'll meet a nice, intelligent young man who will sweep you off your feet."

"Like Dad swept you off your feet?"

Her eyes lit up. "Exactly. Guys in high school have a lot of growing up to do. Why date a boy when you can wait a few months and date a man; am I right?" She winked playfully.

"Oh God," I grumbled, throwing a pillow at her. "Get out of here. It's too early for this."

"Okay." Her soft laughter washed over me. "But if you hurry, I'm making bacon and eggs."

"Sure thing, Mom."

She left and I sank back down against the pillows, trying to ignore how much her words affected me.

Grabbing my cell off the nightstand, I closed my eyes and took a deep breath. Maybe this was the start of my fairy tale? Maybe this time I would get my prince?

But when I finally looked at the screen, there was nothing.

Maybe Jason didn't want to wake you? I knew better though. Jason had bailed when things got too intense. Yet again, he hadn't let me touch him. He hadn't wanted to have sex with me. He hadn't even bothered waking me to say goodbye. Because he was keeping me at arm's length. He'd given me so much last night, but he refused to give me the one thing that I really wanted.

His heart.

14

Jason

"SO WHAT HAPPENED?" The first words out of Cameron's mouth weren't a surprise. Of course he was going to want to know what happened with Felicity. But what was I supposed to tell him when I still didn't know what the fuck had happened?

"So you did go over there?" Asher added, shooting me a sly grin. "I knew the excuse about your old man was a lie."

"We talked," I deadpanned, loading more weights onto the chest press as Cam got into position.

"Talked." His brow went up. "You expect us to believe that?"

Shrugging, I played it cool. They didn't need to know Felicity and I had shared a moment. Whatever the fuck that meant. Or that I'd held her like she was the most fucking precious thing in the world. Then as soon as she had fallen to sleep, I'd hightailed out of there without so much as a goodbye because I'd panicked. Because for the first time since Aimee, things felt quiet. There was no expectation crushing my chest; no weight of the team, of winning State, there was just me and a girl and silence.

They didn't need to know that at all.

"Believe what you want; it's the truth. She told me exactly what happened with Thatcher and his goons and then I left."

"Right," Cameron said, leaning down on the bench. "And I'm not head over heels in love with your step-sister."

"Really?" It was my turn to raise a brow. "You're really going to throw that shit in my face?"

"It's in your face whether I throw it or not." He blew out an exasperated breath. "Hailee and I are endgame. The sooner you get on board with that, the easier things will be on all of us."

"Endgame. You think you and her are..." Fuck. I couldn't even say the word. I knew he loved her; knew she felt the same... but endgame?

From the look of complete seriousness on Cam's face though, I had underestimated just how deep his feelings ran.

"I'm following her to college, man. You think I'd be doing that unless I plan on putting a ring on it one day?"

"Fuck off," I said. "Now I know you're yanking my chain because there's no way in hell you're seriously suggesting one day you might—"

"Marry her?" A faint smile tugged at his mouth. "Serious as a heart attack."

Asher snorted and I levelled him with a hard look. "Are you hearing this?"

"Oh I'm hearing it and I can't say I'm surprised."

I groaned, spotting the bar for Cam. "But we're too young for all that shit. We've got our whole lives to settle down." It wasn't even on my radar yet.

Girls were a commodity, something to help me unwind after a tough game or a grueling training session. Besides, I didn't have time to worry about anyone else; not when I had to prove myself at Penn next year.

So why did you go over there, jackass? I ignored the little voice rattling round my head. I could be worried about Felicity getting caught in the crossfire without getting attached. It didn't mean anything, except my heart wasn't as black as everyone made it out to be. She was Hailee's best friend, and innocent in all this shit with Thatcher.

That's all it was.

"Hailee grounds me," my best friend said as if it was the simplest thing in the world. "When everything was falling to shit, and stuff with Mom was at its worst, she was there. No questions asked. Not because I wear a Raiders jersey or because she sees me as a meal ticket." He flopped back on the bench, heaving a deep breath. "I'm lucky to have her."

Yeah, until she grew bitter and began to resent his ass for the commitment and dedication required to make something of yourself in one of the country's top college football teams. High school football stars might have been treated like gods amongst men, but college was a whole other level of worship. Especially if you made waves, which I fully intended on doing. Penn hadn't asked me to commit early because they thought I'd be a valuable asset to their team—they thought I had potential to be *the* asset.

Even if I wanted someone by my side through it all—*and I didn't*—there wasn't enough to go around. I couldn't be committed one hundred percent to the game *and* committed to some girl. Being the best required sacrifice, one I was all too willing to make.

"It's not for me," I said with conviction.

"No one would put up with your brooding ass anyway." Asher grunted as he worked the free weights.

It was a joke.

He was joking.

Yet, it didn't stop the strange tug in my chest.

"Seniors Night next week. You ready, man?" he asked changing the subject.

"Figured I'd wing it." I shrugged, folding my arms over my chest.

"Coach will be pissed you haven't got some motivational speech prepared."

"Coach can suck it."

"Try saying that to his face." Asher smirked, his expression sobering with his next words. "You know it's funny, I've waited my entire life for this. State. College. But now it's almost here all I can think is I'm not ready to say goodbye."

"Nawww, you gonna miss us, Bennet?" I mocked.

"We can't all be untouchable like you, Jase. Yeah, I'll miss you guys. You're my best friends. Starting college, having to prove yourself all over again… I'm not going to lie, it freaks me the hell out."

His words sank into me. I'd never really given it much thought. Not when I'd had my eyes set on playing for the Penn Quakers for pretty much my entire life. It was in my blood; my legacy. My old man had the perfect career there until an injury ripped the dream out from under him. And when I came along, his dream became my dream. I'd been working toward taking Penn by storm for as long as I could remember. Now it was almost time. So while I loved my friends like brothers, I wasn't worried about going off to college next fall. Because I'd been counting down the days since my old man gave me my first football.

And it was almost time for my dreams to become a reality.

"So you and Felicity, huh?" Hailee breezed into the kitchen.

"Excuse me?" I played it cool, leaning back on the counter, draining the rest of my protein shake.

"She said you had a good *talk* Saturday night?" She gave me a suspicious look.

"We talked, yeah. I wouldn't say it was good."

"So nothing happened?"

"Why?" My brows furrowed, "did she say it did?"

"Nope."

"Well then, nothing happened."

"Jason, don't do that. Don't deflect. I told you not to—"

Pushing off the counter, I brushed past her. "You don't need to worry, *little sis*, me and Felicity are just friends."

"Friends?" She snorted. "You really expect me to believe that you and… you're up to something."

Letting out a frustrated breath, I spun around, meeting Hailee's narrowed gaze. "What the fuck do you want from me? I overlooked the fact you and Cameron—"

"Oh, for Christ's sake, we love each other, we're in love. Trust me, it would be a damn sight easier if I didn't love your best friend. But I do. And I won't apologize for that. If only you'd drop this macho don't-care-about-anyone bullshit maybe you'd understand. Or even let someone—"

"Careful, *Hails*, you're starting to sound like a romantic, and I know you know better than to think life is one big ole fairy tale and everyone gets their happily-ever-after."

"Agh," she threw up her hands, "You're so frustrating. I give up." Hailee stomped out of the room and I couldn't help but smirk. Getting under my step-sister's skin had once been one of my favorite pastimes, but now I saw it for what it was; juvenile sibling rivalry that had crossed a line.

I downed the rest of my shake and grabbed my keys.

"Jason," Denise's voice grated across my skin like nails on a chalkboard. "I was hoping to catch you before you left."

"I need to go, or I'll be—"

"This won't take a minute." She gave me a strained smile. "It's Hailee, she still won't talk to me."

"Not my problem."

"I know the two of you still don't see eye to eye, but I thought... well, I thought after everything, you might talk to her for me?"

"You want me to talk to Hailee about how you what? Ruined my family? Lied to her all this time? Stood by and did nothing while we terrorized each other? Tell me, Denise, what exactly should I talk to her about?"

Shame burned her cheeks as she spluttered, desperately trying to take control back of the conversation. I might have tolerated Hailee now because of Cameron and our shared hatred for our parent's deceit, but I didn't owe Denise anything. She represented everything I despised.

"Jason," she sniffled barely holding back the tears, "that's not fair. Me and your father never meant to hurt anyone."

"That's just it though, Denise, isn't it? No one is ever supposed to get hurt but they always do." The words hit me square in the chest.

It was the truth. People always found a way to hurt one another. Screw each other over in the name of love... greed... jealousy.

"I can see this was a bad idea; forget I said anything." She hurried out of the kitchen, her sobs punctuating the tension.

I probably should have felt even an ounce of guilt at making my stepmom cry, but the truth of it was, adults were supposed to set the standards. To teach their kids respect and integrity. My old man might have taught me how to throw a perfect pass, but he failed miserably when it came to teaching me how to be a stand-up guy. Even after losing his shot at going pro, after meeting Mom and settling down, he couldn't give up his football-star life. He and Mom spent years pretending, years of playing their roles as doting father and mother, husband and wife. When really it was all a sham. Mom stayed with him out of obligation, while he clung onto a dream that would never be his, finding solace at the bottom of a bottle or a stranger's bed. I never wanted to treat someone the way Dad treated Mom. Someone he was supposed to care about, to love. Which is why I planned on never settling down. I'd seen enough news articles on football players and the impact of the game on their personal lives and relationships to know that it wasn't worth the headache or heartache.

It wasn't worth it.

But football, the game, *that* was worth it.

It was all I needed.

By the time I arrived at school, first class was already in session. Not that it mattered I was late. Teachers regularly turned a blind eye to my tardiness or absence. Instead of sneaking into AP Math, I decided to hit the gym. After my run in with Hailee and then Denise, I needed to burn off some extra steam, and practice wasn't until after school.

But even after a good work out, I was still restless. It coursed through my veins, making it hard to focus. Usually, I'd text Jenna or one of the other gymnasts or cheerleaders to see if they wanted to help me relax, but the only person I wanted to text was the one person I shouldn't.

I'd snuck out of Felicity's room yesterday morning for a reason. To avoid any awkward conversations, where she got the wrong idea, and I had to dig my way out of the hole I'd gotten myself into in the first place. But my dick seemingly didn't appreciate not getting his because before I knew it, he had me pulling out my cell phone and texting her.

Me: Where ru?

Felicity: You are alive then? I thought maybe you'd been abducted by aliens...

Me: I didn't want to get you into trouble with your parents.

Felicity: That almost sounds sweet... if it were true.

Me: It could be true.

It wasn't, but I wasn't about to tell her that.

. . .

FELICITY: But we both know it isn't. What do you want, Jason? I'm in class...

I SMIRKED AT HER REPLY. Even via text conversation I could imagine her sassing me; hand on one hip, eyes wide and simmering with indignation. Her mouth all pouty and begging for attention.

Fuck.

This had shitstorm written all over it; yet, I couldn't seem to stop myself. I was so used to girls doing whatever I asked, jumping at a chance to be with me, that Felicity's banter was refreshing. So much so, I wanted more. Craved it like an addict craved their next hit. Because while I didn't need a distraction from football, maybe a distraction from all the other bullshit around me was exactly what I needed.

ME: Meet me after class.

FELICITY: I can't. I have this thing called class; you should look it up sometime.

ME: Skip. I bet it's on your list...

THE THREE LITTLE dots indicated she was replying, but time passed and still nothing. I'd been joking about the list thing but figured I'd hit the jackpot.

ME: I'm right aren't I? It's totally on your list.

FELICITY: I've cut class before.

ME: And I'm a virgin. Come on, skip class and check another thing off your list... I'll make it worth your while.

. . .

FELICITY: You really shouldn't make promises you have no intention of keeping!

ME: Maybe this is one promise I want to keep?

I WAS PRETTY sure I wasn't supposed to feel so smug about luring her in, but I couldn't deny it left me feeling all kinds of awesome.

When she didn't reply, I typed another text.

ME: We can finish what we started at your house?

FELICITY: When you came over and we TALKED?

ME: The only words I remember you saying are, 'Oh God' and 'More'. Come on, Giles. It's senior year. You're running out of time and you know you want to.

PLEASE WANT TO. I stared at my cell, willing her name to appear.

FELICITY: You're going to have to work A LOT harder than this.

SHIT. I hadn't expected it to get this far, not really. But now she was in, I didn't plan on backing out. One more taste. That's all I needed.

At least, that's what I kept telling myself as I sent:

ME: Challenge accepted.

15

Felicity

"HEY," Mya jogged up beside me. "What's got your attention?"

"Oh nothing." I shoved my cell in my pocket and flashed her a bright smile.

"Oh, really, the same nothing that had your attention at lunch and in government?" Her brow rose. "Come on, you can tell me. It's one of them, right? Asher or Jason."

"Ssh," I grabbed her hand, pulling her closer.

"Shit, my bad. So I'm right?" She lowered her voice conspiratorially. "It *is* one of them. You know I heard Jason left the party in a hurry Saturday." Her brows waggled.

Pressing my lips together, I kept walking, but Mya followed. "You can talk to me, you know?" she went on, "I know what it's like to want someone... *bad* for you."

My eyes darted to hers. "I don't..."

"Girl, it's written all over your face every time he enters the room."

Oh God.

The color drained from my cheeks. "Is it that obvious?"

"Seriously?" Mya's mouth lifted in a half-grin, not that anything about this was amusing. "You're fooling nobody but yourself."

"Crap. This wasn't supposed to happen. I wasn't supposed to..." I stuffed down the words.

"Fall for him?"

"I'm not... it isn't like that. I know it's doomed. He's Jason Ford for Christ's sake. But there is something there." Something that was proving pretty damn hard to ignore. Especially since he wasn't making it easy to forget him.

My cell vibrated again, and Mya nudged me, urging me to look at it.

Jason: Dancing naked under the rain?

"That is Jason, right? *The* Jason Ford? Because damn girl, what did you do to him?"

"It's silly really." I didn't return his text, giving Mya my full attention. "I created this list for senior year, kind of like a bucket list."

"Neat."

"You think?"

"Yeah, I mean, life is for living, right? If having a list keeps you accountable, then why not, I say." Mya slipped her arm through mine. "So what exactly is on this list, or is it a secret?"

"I don't go around publicizing it, if that's what you mean."

"It's something for you, I dig that. But Jason knows about the list?"

"Yeah, Asher let it slip."

"Asher?" Something flashed in her eyes. "What's his deal anyway?"

"What do you mean?" We reached the room where book club held their weekly meetings.

"Doesn't matter," she backtracked. "This your stop?"

"Yeah, I pushed myself to take up a new hobby this year."

Mya glanced at the temporary sign on the window and frowned. "And you chose book club? That doesn't sound very bucket list."

"Hey, it's a start."

"Yeah, but come on, you can do better than *book club*."

Her words sank into me, cracking open every insecurity I'd ever felt about myself. All my fears about becoming my parents.

Mya was right—book club was safe. It wasn't pushing any limits or breaking any chains. It was something my mom would have done when she was at school.

I shuddered.

"Oh dear God, I'm becoming my mother," I grumbled, suddenly wishing I'd have signed up to wizards and muggles or JROTC.

"You want to make memories, right?" I nodded, unsure where she was going with this. "Then you need to think big. You need to think so big that when you look back at high school in twenty years' time you can say you had zero regrets."

"Zero regrets, I like the sound of that." Even if it did terrify me.

"Ready to show me that list?"

Was I?

I doubted I'd ever be ready, but if I wanted senior year to be epic, maybe I needed Mya's help more than I cared to admit.

"I'M HOME," I called, dropping my keys on the sideboard and making my way into the kitchen.

"Hey, sweetheart, how was your day?"

I spent the day evading this hot guy's text messages, overhauled my bucket list with my new friend from the city, and seriously considered cutting class.

But not wanting to give my mom a heart attack, I went with, "It was the usual. You're home early?"

"Dentist appointment. I scheduled you for next month."

"Thanks, Mom."

She pushed a glass of juice toward me before going back to the pan of spaghetti. It was Tuesday which meant spaghetti. Tomorrow would be pot roast, and Thursday Mom liked to live on the edge with steak *and* chicken fajitas.

"Me and your father were talking yesterday and thought now is a good as time as any to start contacting businesses in the city who might be able to give you an internship next summer."

"It's only November, Mom. Isn't that a little premature?"

"Absolutely not. Making the right contacts now could be crucial for your future."

"I'll get right on that," I murmured, tapping out a tune on the counter. "Hey, Mom." I asked after a couple of minutes silence. "What's the most adventurous thing you did in high school?"

She glanced over her shoulder, brows pinched with confusion. "Adventurous thing?"

"Yeah, like sneak out after dark or make out behind the bleachers."

"Felicity Charlotte Giles, what on earth has gotten into you?" A slight pink streak appeared across her cheeks.

"It's for a school project," I lied. "For English."

"A project you say, well," she dried her hands on the towel shoved into the waistband of her pants, "Let's see, there was that one time me and your father played hooky to go down to the lake for a picnic. We'd been dating six months and he wanted to make it special. Then there was the time we made out at the back of Mr. Kavendish's classroom during Romeo and Juliet, that was particularly daring."

"Rad, Mom." I mocked, feeling my stomach sink.

"Sorry if my stories aren't cool enough for you, baby, but we were good kids. We didn't go looking for trouble and we were happy to live within the rules."

I knew the story well. My parents were high school sweethearts who went on to college, graduated, and found jobs in the city. Together. Then I'd come along, their unplanned surprise, and upset all their plans. They never made me feel anything less than loved and cherished, but sometimes I wondered if their overbearing interest in my future was their response to having a child they weren't prepared for.

"Do you ever regret only ever being with Dad?"

The lines around her eyes deepened. "The school really wants to know this stuff?"

Shrugging, I quickly fumbled for something to say. "They want us to compare senior year back in the day to senior year now, that kind of thing.

They didn't really give us set questions or anything. I just thought... well, you and Dad have been together forever. That can't have always been easy."

"Were we young? Of course we were. But when you know, you know, sweetheart. And I took one look at your father and knew he was the one."

"What do you think has been your recipe for success?" Because where a lot of marriages ended in heartache, my parents had weathered the storm.

"Hmm, let's see. Communication, never going to sleep on an argument, and routine."

"Routine?" I squeaked. "Jesus, Mom, you make it sound so romantic."

"Baby, your father is about as romantic as that wooden spoon." She flicked her head to the utensil rack. "But he's always been there for me, and that's what really matters. I'd rather have a lifetime of your father than a few months of fire and passion."

I found it a little sad that she didn't think you could have both. But who was I to judge? They were happy enough and one hundred percent committed to each other and our family.

"Favorite senior year memory?"

"That one's easy." She smiled wistfully. "Prom. It was magical. Just how the movies portray it. Your father bought me a beautiful corsage and drove us to the school gym in his rusty old Buick. We coordinated our outfits and danced the night away with our friends. It was perfect."

"I bet there was a rockin' after party?"

Mom laughed softly. "There was none of that back in my day." I didn't believe that for a second which could only mean one thing: my parents weren't invited, or more likely, they refused to go.

"Felicity, is everything okay?" Mom switched direction. "You seem distracted lately and I'm not going to lie, baby, it's worrying me."

"I'm fine, Mom." *Except I can't stop thinking about a guy. A guy I know will break my heart if I give him even half a chance.*

"Don't drop the ball now, okay?" Her expression softened. "A lot of people think once college applications are done, senior year is a chance to let your hair down. But it's a chance to start thinking about the future, about the kind of person you want to become."

"Got it, Mom, hair down, future." Her words left a bitter taste in my mouth.

"You've been such a good girl, Felicity. Now Hailee has a boyfriend, I worry you might lose focus. The football team are a bad influence. Athletes get so much handed to them for free but real life isn't like that."

"Cameron is a good guy."

"I'm sure he is, baby." She gave me a dubious smile. "But you want more out of life than to end up as some trophy girlfriend, don't you?"

"Whoa, slow down." My hands went up, my eyes wide. "We're talking about Hailee and Cameron, not me."

Mom came over and brushed my bangs from my face. "You're beautiful,

Felicity. Inside and out, and boys will notice that. I only hope that when they do, you choose wisely."

"Mom, I'm a teenager. We're supposed to screw up and get it wrong occasionally." I laughed but it came out all strangled.

"We're Giles', sweetie. You know what that means." The urge to roll my eyes was strong but I remained expressionless as she said, "Planned, prepared, and punctual. That's all you need in life."

"Sure thing, Mom. I'm going to head upstairs and do my homework. Get a head start."

Her face lit up. "That's my girl. I'll shout you when dinner is ready."

With a small nod, I left Mom with her plans and headed for the sanctuary of my bedroom. Inside, I kicked off my shoes, grabbed the folded scrap of paper from my bag, and dropped down on the bed. My list was a mess. Nothing planned or prepared about it. But I couldn't deny that despite my mom's unintentional warning, Mya's additions made my pulse race.

1. ~~*Take up a new hobby*~~ *Explore alternate career paths*
2. *Cut class*
3. *Attend a pep rally - DONE*
4. ~~*Skinny dip down at the lake*~~ *Get a tattoo*
5. *Fall asleep under the stars*
6. ~~*Go to a party at Asher Bennet's house*~~ *Crash a party in style*
7. *Drink (actual liquor) at Bell's – OVERDONE*
8. *Go to Winter Formal... with a date (not a girlfriend)*
9. ~~*Hook up with a random guy*~~ *First time do over*
10. *Fall in crazy messy love (with someone NOT JF)*
11. *Do not fraternize with the football team!!!*

Snatching my cell off the nightstand, I found her number.

Me: So my new list...

Mya: Don't tell me you've already changed your mind?

Me: No, no, it's just my mom, she's big on being planned and prepared...

Mya: Good thing your mom isn't the one with the list then ;)

Me: Ha-ha! Am I silly? Is this whole thing stupid?

Mya: You're scared?

Me: My parents have my whole life mapped out for me. What if I do the list and realize their life isn't the one I want?

Mya: I think that's okay. Wanting to make our parents happy is perfectly normal, but not at the expense of our own hopes and dreams.

I mulled over Mya's words, but another text came through before I could type a reply.

Mya: Did you figure out what you're going to do yet?

Me: No...

Mya: Okay, when you were little, what did you want to be?

Me: What does this have to do with my list?

My cell started blaring, Mya's name flashing across the screen. "Hello?" I said.

"It might seem dumb, but just hear me out, okay?"

"Fine," I grumbled. "I've always loved animals, but my parents never let me get a cat or dog. They were worried about allergies and safety and all that stuff. One summer, I found a stray dog. Scrawny undernourished little thing, but it had the cutest face and I wanted it to be mine so bad. I lured it into our garden shed, gave it some blankets and food."

"What happened?"

Sadness washed over me. "Mom found out and made me take it to the local pound. I cried for a week." A tiny part of me was still bitter about it all these years later.

"Dogs, really? I had you down as more of a girl scout."

"Nope. I always wanted to be veterinary doctor."

"So start there..."

"Start where exactly?" She was making no sense.

"You're not sure you want to follow in your parents' footsteps, right? So you need to figure out your own path."

"I guess." A heavy weight settled on my chest. "I'll see you tomorrow."

She chuckled softly. "Is that your way of telling me I overstepped?

"Not at all. You've given me a lot to think about. Thank you."

"Hey, what are friends for, right? I'll see you tomorrow."

We hung up and I stared up at the ceiling, replaying the conversation.

I'd always been the good girl. Agreeable and passive, all too willing to go along with my parents hopes and dreams for me because it was what was expected. But if senior year so far had shown me anything so far, it was that some things in life required you to take a risk. They required you to let go of all your insecurities and doubts and take a leap of faith. Maybe they would work out and maybe they wouldn't, but at least you would know you tried.

I wanted that.

I wanted to take risks and throw caution to the wind.

I wanted to go after what I wanted. Have fun discovering a new path, one I carved for myself.

I wanted to fall head over heels in love despite everyone warning me it would only end in heartache.

God, did I want that.

But could I really do that with Jason, knowing it would never mean the same to him as it would for me?

My cell bleeped, another incoming text. I opened it eagerly expecting some more advice from Mya, but Jason's name stared back at me.

Jason: What are you doing right now?

After typing and deleting at least three replies, I went with the truth.

Me: Lying on my bed about to start some homework.

Jason: You're killing me, Giles. Come meet me... or better yet, I could come to you. I remember your bed... it's comfy.

I fought a grin. To my complete surprise, Jason was turning out to be very persistent.

Me: No and no. I need to get this done and my mom is home.

Jason: Mom's love me.

My chest squeezed at his playful words. Damn him for doing this to me, offering me glimpses of the guy I knew was hiding beneath his cool, indifferent exterior. Glimpses of a guy I knew would never surface permanently.

Me: I'm not sure my mom would.

Jason: She's not a fan? I'm wounded.

Me: Like you don't have enough middle-aged women fawning over you.

Jason: But I don't want them…

My heart fluttered at his words. At everything he *wasn't* saying.

Me: Goodbye, Jason. I'll see you at school tomorrow.

Jason: You know I didn't get to where I am without a fuck load of persistence and focus… When I want something, I go after it.

I didn't text back. I didn't know what to say. But proving himself true, another text came through.

Jason: We both know you're going to end up under me again, Giles. Why not save us both the heartache and give in?

Me: And for a second there, you actually had me fooled. Goodbye, Jason.

He didn't reply but it didn't matter. The damage was already done. He'd gone and pushed the right button to piss me the hell off. But he'd also made a huge dent in my armor, and I knew if he kept it up, I wouldn't be able to resist for much longer.

Even more alarming, I really didn't want to.

16

Jason

SMIRKING TO MYSELF, I hit send on my latest text to Felicity.

Me: Skinny dipping in the lake?

Felicity: Are you serious? Do you know what kind of things lurk in there?

Me: I can think of a few...

I smiled, my eyes darting around the cafeteria to make sure nobody was paying me any attention.

Felicity: Behave!!!

Me: Come on, Giles, say yes. Let's cut class and live on the wild side...

Felicity: I have study hall.

Me: Study hall? It's senior year...

Felicity: We don't all have a free pass to do whatever the hell we want. Unlike some people...

Me: Think of your list!

Felicity: Goodbye, Jason.

Damn, she was really playing hard to get. I thought I almost had her the other day, but then right at the last minute, she'd pulled the rug out from under me. I wasn't used to working so hard for a girl. But Felicity wasn't just any girl. A fact I could finally admit to myself without breaking out in a cold sweat.

I risked peeking over at where she, Hailee, and Mya sat at their usual table. "Looking for me?" Jenna's hand slid over my eyes, her lips grazing my cheek. I peeled her fingers away and glanced up at her.

"What the fuck was that?"

She reeled back, indignation flaring in her eyes. "What, I can't say hello now?" Flicking her silky blonde hair over one shoulder, she sat down next to me.

"That wasn't hello; that was you marking your territory."

"Don't be such a drama queen. It was one little kiss; we've done much more than that in public before."

My spine snapped straight, the knot in my stomach tightening as I glanced over at Felicity. She was busy talking to Hailee, not paying me any attention. But if she looked over here...

Why does it matter? It's not like you're hers or anything.

"Jason?" Jenna's hand grasped my knee. "I said where did you get to Saturday at the party? I looked for you."

Forcing myself to look at her and not at Felicity, I said, "I had shit to take care of."

Her expression hardened. "Shit to take care of? That's all I'm getting?" She was drawing attention now; my teammates pretending not to listen as they ate their lunch and talked among themselves.

"Careful," I ground out. "You're starting to sound like a girlfriend and we both know I don't do girlfriends."

Her hands slid up my chest as she leaned in, giving me a perfect view of her rack. "You keep saying that, and yet, you keep coming around for seconds and thirds and fourths..." She licked her lips in what I assumed was an attempt at seduction. But all it did was make me bristle.

"I come around because you're good for it. Nothing more, nothing less." I pulled Jenna's hands free of my chest and shoved them back at her.

Someone snorted. Everyone watching to see what I would do next. Everyone including Felicity. Her gaze burned into me, forcing me to look at her. There was so much in her eyes, I didn't know which emotion to pluck out first.

But Jenna shrieked, "You're such a self-absorbed asshole, Jason. One of these days you'll come around and I'll tell you no." She sounded genuinely hurt as she fled from our table.

"There goes gym pussy for the foreseeable," someone groaned. But I didn't give a fuck. I only had eyes for the girl glaring at me like I'd just called her out in front of the entire cafeteria.

My cell vibrated and I pulled it out.

Felicity: What the hell was that?

Me: I have no idea what you're talking about...

My eyes lifted to hers again as I fought a grin.

Felicity: Jenna seemed upset.

Me: Don't know. Don't care.

Felicity: What do you care about, Jason?

You. I care what you think. But I couldn't type the words. Not here, not now.

Maybe not ever.

"Someone interesting?" Asher called across the table.

"Nah, just my old man."

"Right." He saw right through my ruse. "I'll catch you later."

I watched through narrowed eyes as he rose from his chair and made his way over to Felicity and the girls. Without asking for permission, he dropped into the seat beside her and slung his arm over her shoulder. Challenge danced in his eyes as he glared at me across the room.

Motherfucker.

I loved Asher like a brother, but he was pushing this thing with Felicity too far.

"What's up with that?" Grady nudged my ribs. "You think he's banging her?" He flicked his head over to where Asher was holding court with Felicity.

"How the fuck should I know?" I growled.

"Whoa, dude, no need to get pissy with me. I figured if anyone knew the deal with them two, it'd be you. Although I can't see it myself. She's so fucking weird. Has stage five clinger written all over her."

"Grady?"

"Yeah, Cap?"

"Shut the fuck up."

He ducked his head, forking a mouthful of salad into his mouth. The guy had no fucking filter.

Asher caught my eye again, a smirk tugging at his lips. Without another word, I jerked away from the table and stood up. "I'm out," I said.

"See you at practice?" Grady asked, and I nodded.

As I stalked out of the cafeteria, I sent Felicity another message.

Me: Do you want him?

Felicity: Excuse me?

Me: Don't play dumb, Giles. Do. You. Want. Him?

Felicity: Careful, Jason. You sound awfully jealous for someone who doesn't care…

My jaw clenched, anger radiating through me. She knew exactly which strings to pluck to get a reaction. But jealous?

I didn't get jealous.

I was Jason fucking Ford.

But as I moved down the hall, kids diving out of the way to make room for me, all I could picture was Felicity smiling up at Asher, his arm hung over her shoulder. And I wanted to kill something.

"Run it again," Coach yelled from the sideline. There wasn't a muscle in my body that didn't ache, but I welcomed the burn. The burn numbed everything else. Tamped down all the unfamiliar emotions that had taken root in my chest, snaking through me like slow acting poison.

"If I didn't know better," Asher taunted from the scrimmage line. "I'd say you had a bad case of blue balls."

"Fuck off, Bennet," I snapped, getting ready to call the play.

"I'm just saying, you don't seem yourself."

"Ash," Cam warned from his wide position.

"Chill, he knows I'm only yanking his chain." He flashed me a smug grin.

I called the play and barked, "Hut," as I received the ball and dropped back to make the pass to Cam.

"Nice," Coach boomed. "Keep playing like this and we won't have anything to worry about Friday. Everyone hit the showers, I'll see you tomorrow."

Yanking off my helmet, I tucked it under my arm and started toward the locker room.

"Hey," Ash jogged up beside me, "Serious talk. You okay? I was only—"

"What the fuck are you doing?"

"I'm not doing anything."

"Don't give me that bull." My eyes slid to his, narrowing. "You're pushing me. Why?"

"I'm not…" He pressed his lips together, mulling over his reply. "Fine. I don't get it, okay? You like her. I know you do. And for some bizarre reason, she likes you too."

"And?"

"You're too fucking stubborn to do anything about it."

"Maybe I don't want to do anything about it." The lie soured on my tongue. I wanted to do something about it all right, but I knew I shouldn't.

The rest of the guys gave us a wide berth as we slowed down.

"Come on, Jase, this is me. I know you better than that and I know no girl has ever got under your skin the way she has. Tell me I'm wrong?" His brow rose.

It was my turn to smother my reply.

"Didn't think so." He flashed me a knowing grin.

"You like her," I said.

"It doesn't matter." Asher shrugged in that easy laidback way of his, but I saw the tightness around his eyes.

He *did* like her.

Probably a whole lot more than he'd ever admit.

"So what's the plan? Try and talk me into giving her a shot and then you hang back in the wings waiting for me to screw it up and swoop in and fix her broken heart?"

It was a joke. An attempt to wipe the smug smile off his face. But it backfired because the second the words left my mouth, I realized it was probably true. I would screw it up and he would be there, waiting to wipe away her tears.

"Admit that you like her, and I'll back off," he said. "I know it kills you seeing me flirt with her."

"You've lost your fucking mind." I barged past him and kept walking. Asher didn't know the first thing about what I felt.

Dammit, I didn't even know.

"Jase, man, when are you going to stop and pull your head out of your ass?"

Stopping, I glanced back, eyes narrowed to slits.

"She won't wait forever." He just wouldn't stop pushing. "And yeah, maybe I will be around to help her forget all about you. Then what? You just gonna sit by and watch me move in on your girl?"

My girl?

It shouldn't have sounded so damn good.

"You'd choose her over me?" I deflected his slip of the tongue.

"What are we, five?" He ran a hand down his face. "All I'm saying is, you'd better figure out what you want because I'm sure there are plenty of other guys just waiting to take your place."

"Is that a threat, Bennet?" I stood taller, irritation rippling up my spine.

"You're a dick, you know that?"

"Never claimed to be anything else."

"Just don't destroy her, man. She's strong but she's not that strong." He moved around me, not sparing me a backward glance, while I was left standing there wondering when life got so complicated.

The answer as clear as day.
Felicity fucking Giles.

I WAS DONE WAITING.

The plan was simple—lure Felicity into meeting me and fuck her clean out of my head. Because Asher was right, she was under my skin. Burying herself deeper and deeper. She'd been the one to tell me she wouldn't play my games, yet it felt like she was running circles around me. And for as much as I wanted her, wanted to taste her lips again, to soak up the quiet that existed whenever she was around; deep down, I knew this thing between us could never work.

Me: Tonight. You, me, and every item on your list you haven't completed.

Felicity: I never had you down as a dog lover…

Me: WTF?

Felicity: Nothing, forget I said anything.

Me: You're so fucking strange.

Felicity: So you like to keep reminding me.

Shit. Not the best way to score brownie points. Considering my reply, I went with the truth, for once.

Me: What if I told you, I like your brand of strange?

Felicity: Hold the phone. Did Jason Ford just admit he likes something?

Me: Easy there, Giles. I said I like your strangeness… I'm not sure it's a reason to be flattered.

Felicity: You like me.

Yes.
Yes, I do.

But I couldn't tell her that. So instead, I went with something typical jock-asshole.

Me: I'd like you bouncing on my dick more.

Felicity: Okay.

My eyes almost bugged out of their sockets.

Me: Okay, you want to bounce on my dick? Because I've got to say, Giles, I'm a little surprised...

Felicity: Very funny! Okay, I'll meet you...

My pulse ratcheted.

Me: Yeah? After school? Or now?

Felicity: Cutting class is on my list.

I smirked triumphantly. I fucking knew it.

Me: Meet me after second period, round by the locker room.

Felicity: You've really given this some thought.

Me: I think about a lot of things.

Her. Naked. Underneath me.

Felicity: Goodbye, Jason. I'll see you soon.

17

Felicity

I'D LOST my freaking mind.

It was the only explanation as I hid out in the girls' bathroom until the hall had emptied. When a good five minutes after the start of third period had passed, I slipped out of the bathroom, ducked down the hall and straight out of one of the side entrances. My heart pounded in my chest as I crossed the lawn and went around the back of the building. But it was nothing compared to how it galloped away when I spotted Jase's Dodge Charger, the engine humming just like the gentle hum beneath my skin.

He looked completely at ease as I opened the door and slid inside. "I didn't know if you would come."

"Just drive," I clipped out, my eyes wide as they darted around looking for any sign that I'd been caught.

"Don't look so worried," he said smoothly. "No one will even know you're gone."

I threw him an 'are you for real' look and he chuckled darkly.

"It's easy for you to say," I said. "You're allowed to do whatever you want and no one bats an eye."

"Oh, I wouldn't be so sure of that."

His eyes swept over me, making me shudder and my tummy clench. But I tried to ignore his suggestive tone, the flare in his eyes.

Too late, you already gave him all the power agreeing to cut class.

"If you want to go back, I can—"

"Just drive," I repeated.

"As you wish." Jason smirked as he pulled off and headed out of the school gates. "You know, it might help if you breathe."

I shot him daggers and he chuckled again.

A few seconds of silence passed and then he said, "I was sorry, about Sunday morning."

"No you weren't," I replied, resigned more than angry. Jason was Jason. He hadn't promised me anything, and I hadn't asked for anything. So the fact I was in the car with him when I should have been sitting in third period

English wasn't lost on me. But I couldn't seem to make rational decisions when it came to Rixon's bad boy star quarterback.

Maybe I was more like Jenna Jarvis and the gymnastics team and cheerleaders than I realized. But they didn't have a list. They didn't want to live every second of senior year as though it was their last.

I did.

At least, that was my excuse for my behavior of late.

"You're not what I expected, Giles," he murmured, his words making me sit a little straighter.

"Am I supposed to know what that means?"

I was me. Nothing more, nothing less. Until recently, Jason had made no effort to hide the fact he found me annoying. But now he looked at me differently, talked to me in a way I never expected.

It was all very confusing.

Any normal girl might have believed it meant she was special or that she was capturing the heart of the guy she liked. I knew better. I knew you didn't capture a guy like Jason, you were granted an audience; allowed to breathe, to talk, to *be* in his presence.

And for some reason, right now in this moment, he had chosen me. Given *me* the royal nod. I smothered a nervous laugh.

"What?" he asked as my eyes drilled holes into the side of his head.

"Nothing."

"I can hear you thinking from all the way over here, spit it out." The corner of his mouth lifted.

"I'm just wondering what it's like to be you. Loved by an entire town, worshipped by most of your classmates. Guys want to be you, girls want to..." The word lodged in my throat.

"You can say it, Giles, I won't tell."

"Fine, girls want to fuck you even though they know that's all they will ever get from you."

That made him shift uncomfortably in his seat.

Good.

Asshole.

"Maybe I'm worth the ride," he threw back, and I snorted.

"No one is *that* good in bed."

"Is that a challenge?" He glanced over at me, daring me with his dark intense gaze.

"Shouldn't you be watching the road?"

"I don't know, the view from here is pretty incredible." He winked before turning his attention back to the road.

I silently screamed at my emotions to batten down the hatches because whether he knew it or not—planned it or not—Jason was knocking down my defenses one by one.

He's Jason Ford. Jason freaking Ford. He doesn't date.

He doesn't do commitment.

He doesn't fall in love.

Internal pep talk over, I smoothed down my skirt and said, "So where exactly are we going?"

"It's a surprise."

"I bet that's what you say to all the girls." I winced at how desperate the words sounded. But I had a serious case of foot-in-mouth syndrome on a good day, let alone when Jason was around to flummox me with his smooth lines and easy charm.

I waited for his reply, but it never came. Instead, he pressed his lips together as if to keep his reply from escaping.

Weird.

Silence followed. Thick and heavy; the kind that didn't feel uncomfortable but wasn't entirely comfortable either. I forced myself to look out of the window, to watch the town roll by, giving myself space to breathe and prepare for whatever Jason had up his sleeve.

Eventually, we began to slow, but only because Jason had turned off the main road onto an overgrown track that meandered through the trees.

"The lake?" I asked, a thrill shooting through me. He'd brought me here before, but we'd parked in the sandy lot at the entrance. Jason showed no signs of stopping this time.

"Don't worry," he said, "we're not going swimming. Not today, anyway."

The car jerked and bounced over the uneven terrain. I hadn't been out here in years, since me and Hailee had stopped swimming at the lake a few summers ago.

"What?" Jason's gravelly voice washed over me.

"We used to love it out here."

"So why'd you stop coming?"

"You're kidding me, right? The summer after you stole Hailee's clothes and bike and she had to walk home half-naked in the blistering heat... sound familiar?"

His lips pursed.

"You were a total jerk to her."

The car came to an abrupt stop near the water's edge. "Yeah, well things change."

"Do they?" I asked, desperate to know what he was thinking, to get inside his head and uncover his deepest darkest secrets.

When he didn't answer, I whispered, "What are we doing, Jason?"

"I thought it was pretty obvious." His lip curved smugly.

"Jason..."

"What do you want from me, Giles?"

"I want to know you. Not the Jason Ford everyone else gets to see, the *real* you."

"The real me, huh?" he scoffed. "I don't think anyone wants to know the real me. All they want is the football star, the jock, the guy who can propel them to social greatness. People want the illusion, not the real thing."

"I do." The words came out small.

"And what if you don't like what you find?" His expression softened, not much, but it was there. "What if underneath the number one jersey there's nothing but darkness?"

"I don't believe that. You care, Jason, I know you do. About Hailee, about your friends..." *About me.* The words lodged in my throat. "You're not just the conceited asshole you let everyone believe you are."

"Let's get one thing straight," he said, his eyes pinning me to the spot. "I am. I'm not the reformed bad boy and I'm not looking to be changed by..." He swallowed the words and I felt myself flush with indignation.

"You think I want to change you?"

"All girls do."

"Let's get one thing clear, Jason," I shot back, my voice low and sultry, "I'm not all girls."

Heat flashed in his eyes as he leaned closer, taking the air with him. "I'll break you. You know that, right? This, whatever this is, won't end well."

Run, the little voice in my head screamed, *run far away and never look back.*

But I didn't reach for the door handle. Instead, my hand reached for him, twisting into his jersey and yanking his mouth to mine.

"You're fucking crazy," he murmured, meeting my lips halfway, attacking me with his mouth, with frantic licks of his tongue. Jason kissed like it was the final play and the whole game was on the line.

His hands wasted no time running down my body, palming my breasts through my sweater. "Off, now," he commanded as if his words were gospel. Perhaps they were, given how quickly I helped him peel it over my head. His lips twisted in a wolfish grin as he appraised my body. "Ever been fucked on the hood of a car, babe?"

We were back to that.

Not Giles.

Babe.

I didn't know which I hated more.

"Jason," it was a breathless whisper, "you know I haven't."

"That's right you haven't because I'm the only guy to ever have this." His hand glided down my stomach, finding the waistband of my leggings.

"God, I hate you," the words flew out of my mouth before I could stop them.

His head lifted, confusion pinching his expression. "Funny, because from where I'm sitting, it looks a lot like you'd do anything to bounce on my—"

"Jason! Stop."

"Stop?" His brow shot up. Before I could process what was happening, Jason pulled me onto his body, forcing my legs apart to straddle his thighs.

"You want me to stop?" He rocked into me, his erection hitting my stomach.

"I... yes... no." I tried to smother the moan building.

"Which is it, Giles, because you're sending me mixed signals over here?" He continued rocking into me while his hands played lazily with my breasts.

"I can't think when you're..." Pleasure rippled through me. But it wasn't enough.

It wasn't nearly enough.

"What, babe? You need more?" Jason's hand slid up my throat spanning my neck so that he could push me backward gently. Then he sucked the skin there.

My hands twisted harder; pulling him in, pushing him away, I was no longer sure.

"Say it," his voice echoed around us. "Tell me you want me, want this."

"I..." *Don't do it, don't give him so much power over you.*

"Say the words, babe." His thumb pressed into my center, causing me to jerk above him.

"I want you," my voice trembled, mirroring my body. "I want... this." The words left me in a sharp exhale. Victory flashed in his eyes, the air around us shifting as an understanding settled between us.

I did hate him.

I hated that he made me feel so alive, so desired.

I hated the way he knew exactly how to kiss me, touch me, to get me to fall at his feet.

But most of all I hated how I didn't hate him, not even a little bit.

"Relax," he said as if he knew I was all up in my head. "If it makes you feel any better, I hate you too." His thumb brushed my neck slowly before he chased his touch with his lips. "I hate how I can't stop thinking about you." *Kiss.* "I hate that you say the most ridiculous things." *Kiss.* "But most of all I hate that Thatcher and his goon had their hands on you. I hate..." His lips touched my skin again as my heart crashed against my ribcage.

This wasn't the plan.

He wasn't supposed to say all of this, to feed the small part of me dreaming of a different time and place. A time and place where Felicity Giles could ever end up with a guy like Jason Ford.

I waited for his words, greedy for more. But they never came, replaced with hot kisses as he dragged his tongue up and down the hollow of my throat. Disappointment flooded my chest but deep down, I wasn't surprised. Jason would never admit the truth. That there was something between us. That this was more than just sex. And for as much as it hurt, maybe it was better this way.

His hands were all over me now, his mouth the same.

"Jason," I said, gently tugging his hair. "Slow down."

He lifted his face, brow arched. I took advantage of the moment, pushing my hands against his chest to move him back. Then I fumbled around to find the recline handle and pulled.

"What the fuck?" he grunted, and I stifled a giggle. Jason needed control. He needed to hold all the power. But this time, I wanted to be in the driving seat.

I wanted to drive *him* wild.

"What game are you playing, Giles?" he asked, his hands gripping my hips as I gently rocked above him. We both groaned, and another thrill shot through me. He was at *my* mercy now.

With my newfound confidence, I hooked my hands into the waistband of my leggings and pushed them down over my hips. It was no easy feat getting them off, but I managed. If Jason noticed my clumsy striptease, he didn't comment, his hooded gaze too busy eating up every inch of my bare skin.

"Fuck, you're beautiful," he whispered.

Yeah, fuck. His words were like a poisoned arrow through my heart.

As if he noticed my hesitation, challenge glinted in his eye. He was ready to pounce, to take back the power and flip this whole thing on me. But I wasn't backing down. I wasn't just a pawn in his game.

I was the goddamn queen.

And this queen wanted her king to kneel at her feet.

Sliding my hands around my ribs, I unhooked my bra and let it slide down my arms. Jason didn't speak, he didn't have to. His eyes betrayed every thought running through his head, and even though I knew it was only temporary, I had him right where I wanted him.

"Take it off," I demanded, my eyes fixed on his jersey.

"Okay, I'll play, babe." There was a hint of amusement in his voice as he leaned forward to yank his jersey off. He was so beautiful; a perfectly sculpted Adonis. Who in this moment, was mine. Not Jenna Jarvis' or the gymnast team's. Not Rixon High's or the team's or even the town's.

Mine.

But you can't keep him, Felicity. Don't forget that. ***Never*** *forget that.*

My hands trailed down his abs, counting every ridge until my fingers hovered precariously close to the waistband of his sweats. Without giving myself any time to hesitate, I gently pulled, waiting for Jason to lift his butt off the chair so I could wiggle them off his hips.

Holy crap. He was rock hard.

His smooth chuckle sliced through the tension crackling around us. My eyes lifted to his. "What?" I asked.

"I'm just wondering if you're brave enough—"

I palmed him roughly, his groans filling the car. "Shit, Felicity." My name on his lips was like music to my ears.

"Condom?"

"Glove compartment."

Of course he kept a stash of condoms in his glove compartment. I rolled my eyes and his brow rose, his gaze hooded, hazy with lust.

With great skill, I managed to lean over and retrieve one. Jason surprised me by capturing my wrists and pulling me down. He kissed me hard, bruising my lips and leaving me breathless. I could almost feel his mind working overtime, hear his thoughts.

But I was too far gone to care. I needed Jason more than I'd ever needed anything before.

It was terrifying.

Exhilarating.

And completely crazy.

He watched me, pupils dilated, as I freed his dick and tore open the wrapper, rolling it over him. His breath was ragged, his muscles rippling with every sharp intake of oxygen.

One hand rested on his shoulder, I rose over him, hooked my panties to one side, and slowly sank down on him.

"Fuuuuk," Jason ground out, his hand clamping down on my hip, trying to steady me. But I wasn't about to let him take the lead. Not now, not when I finally held some of the power.

Even if it was only temporary.

18

Jason

FELICITY LOOKED LIKE AN ANGEL. Eyes clouded with pleasure, lips parted in a soft moan.

A dirty sassy angel.

My angel.

She'd caught me completely off guard when she took control. I didn't think she had it in her, but I should have known better because where Felicity Giles was concerned nothing was as it seemed.

And I fucking loved it.

"Yeah, just like that," I hummed, driving my hips up as she rocked above me.

It didn't matter we were by the lake, in the middle of the day where anyone could see us. The second my lips touched her, I knew there was only one way this ended. From the way she was riding my dick, she did too.

My hands roamed over her body, desperate to touch and explore every inch of her skin. Her soft curves, the gentle slope of her hips, her perfect tits.

I couldn't get enough of her.

"Jason..." My name slipped from her lips, caught somewhere between a sigh and moan, the needy sound a direct line to my dick.

I wanted to take to control, to grab her waist and show her exactly how I liked it, how I needed it, but she'd worked her voodoo bullshit on me again because I couldn't do anything but sit back and enjoy it.

Enjoy her.

Every roll of her hips. The way she rose above me ever so slightly, holding the tip inside her and then sinking back down slow and deep. I'd never worried about a girl owning me before because there had never been a girl who had come close. Not even Aimee held that mantle. Felicity was different though. She was everything I never knew I needed.

It was a damn shame I couldn't keep her. And I couldn't. Because while she felt fucking fantastic riding me, this, right here, was where we had to end. Before she became the wrong kind of distraction.

The kind of distraction I'd vowed never to fall for.

My chest tightened as I tried to get my head back in the game. "What is it?" she asked, barely able to catch her breath. "What's wrong?"

"Nothing," I replied coolly. "Come here." My arm looped around her waist as I sat up putting us chest to chest.

"Jason, what are you—"

"Ssh." I whispered, rocking back and forth, the intimate position so much deeper and intense. I could feel every inch of her pressed against every inch of me and it was fucking breathtaking. In that moment, it was hard to deny how perfect she was. The way her body molded to mine, like two pieces of the same puzzle.

"You weren't supposed to..." her voice was broken with pleasure.

"Do you have any idea how crazy you drive me?" The words hung between us as I slowly regained control of her body.

Her.

Felicity buried her face in my shoulder as my hand threaded into her hair and our rhythm increased stealing the breath from my lungs. *I'm going to fuck you right out of my head.*

She froze, her body rigid above me.

Shit.

I hadn't meant to say the words aloud. But now they were out there; a vast ocean between us.

"Felicity, I—"

She grabbed my lips, forcing them together as she moved faster. Harder. Chasing the fall.

Her body began to tremble, her breath choppy and labored. The familiar tingle at the base of my spine told me I was close. Ready to fall right alongside her; she just needed one final push. Dipping my head, I closed my mouth around her nipple and bit down gently. Her cries echoed around us, pleasure crashing into me like a freight train. But like any good high, the inevitable comedown sucked ass.

Felicity clambered off me, grabbing her leggings and sweater and awkwardly dressed herself.

"That's something for your list," I said through strained laughter. I sounded like a fucking idiot. As if some lame assed joke about her list changed the fact I'd accidentally slipped out I wanted to fuck her out of my head.

"We should get back to school." Her voice was cold, sending the temperature inside the car down by a few degrees. "I don't want to miss fifth period."

"Uh, yeah." I tucked myself back into my sweatpants and pulled on my jersey. Things had gone from great to shit in two seconds flat all because of my big fucking mouth.

But this is what you wanted, right?

One more time with her. A chance to rectify how things had gone down in New York.

The ride back to school was painful. Felicity barely looked twice at me and every time I tried to fill the suffocating silence, the words died on the tip of my tongue.

It was a clusterfuck.

Exactly what I'd known would happen, but I'd gone and done it anyway. Felicity wasn't Jenna or any of the other chicks I usually went with. She was different.

I was different around her.

All too soon we rolled into the parking lot, school looming up ahead. "Felicity, I—"

"Save it, Jason. I knew what this was. I knew and I came anyway. But it's done now, right?" She didn't sound sad or pissed, just resigned. "You've fucked me out of your head so I guess we can just both move on."

"I..." *Say something. Say anything.* But nothing came out, my thoughts too incoherent to form words.

"Okay then..." Felicity grabbed the door handle and pushed. But not before turning back to me. "I guess it's true what all the girls say about you," she said, holding my conflicted gaze.

"Yeah, and what's that?" I managed to choke out.

"You're worth the ride." Her eyes didn't sparkle and her voice was devoid of any emotion. "See you around, Jason."

Then she was gone.

It fucking stung to see her walk away, but I knew it was better this way. Better she thought I was just a cold-hearted bastard who had used her in a game of push and pull. Cat and mouse. But the truth was, I wasn't so sure anymore. And although I'd never do it, for the first time in my life, I wanted to chase the girl.

Life wasn't a fairytale though. The only happy ending I needed was the one where I won State, went off to college, and made my dream of going pro a reality.

"Okay, ladies, gather in." Coach beckoned us over. "Two games to go before the play-offs." The guys began cheering but I barely managed a grumble.

"Okay, okay, you're excited, I get it. You've earned it. But we need to keep our heads. Tomorrow is Seniors Night, which means best behavior. There'll be the formal walk out at the game and then the presentations at the party afterward. Mrs. Hasson is cooking up something special for the occasion so I want to see you all in your best clothes. Grady," he looked at the guy across from me, "that means you too, Son. If I see you in so much as a pair of sweats or a jersey, I'll break out my old dinner jackets. Consider yourself warned."

A few of us snickered while Grady flipped me off behind his helmet.

"Any questions?"

"No, Sir."

"Good. Don't forget we have Miss Raine's unveiling too. I want you to remember to show her some respect. She's worked tirelessly on this project and I think I speak for the whole team when I say I'm excited to see what's she's created."

My eyes went to Cam who had a goofy grin painted on his face. He was so gone over my step-sister it left a sour taste on my tongue.

"It's just nearest and dearest Friday. Right, Coach?" I don't know why I asked the question, and I instantly wanted to take it back when all eyes landed on me. Asher was smirking but Cam looked worried. I hadn't told them about earlier with Felicity, but they knew something had happened because I'd been a dick during practice, taking my frustrations out on my teammates.

"Something you want to tell us, Jase?" Coach asked with a hint of amusement.

"Nah," I kept my voice even. "Just wanted to make sure we weren't inviting the entire class."

"Rest assured it'll be intimate, Son. The team, close family... girlfriends," he scoffed at that, "and the cheer squad."

A rumble of appreciation echoed around the field.

"*Best* behavior, remember?" Coach shot us a bemused look. "Okay, get out of here. Jase, a word please."

I hung around, waiting, while my teammates headed for the showers. "What's up, Coach?"

"All set for tomorrow?"

"Sure thing." I ran a hand over my damp hair and down the back of my neck.

"I just wanted you to be aware. Principal Finnigan has asked your father to give a speech at the presentation."

My spine stiffened. "I see."

"Now, I know the two of you haven't always seen eye to eye, but he's your father Jason, and the town consider him to be—"

"A local hero." As if I needed any more of a reminder.

"It's out of my hands but I wanted to give you a heads up."

"Thanks," I grumbled.

"Piece of advice, Son. It's important to know where you came from, but you don't have to let it define you. You've earned this, Jason, and when we're crowned State champs, you can rest easy knowing *you* made it happen. Not your father or his legacy. Football might be in your blood, but you have a rare gift that's all yours, Son. Own it."

"Thanks, Coach." I barely got the words out over the lump in my throat.

He gave me a small nod. "Now get in there with the rest of them."

As I walked off field, I couldn't help but wonder what it would be like to be normal. To walk out tomorrow with my family, a girlfriend maybe. People who loved me unconditionally, not because of who I was and where I was going, but for the person behind the jersey.

The person behind Rixon's golden boy of football.

I couldn't even remember the person I was before. Before Varsity football, and state records; before being scouted by some of the best colleges in the country. Most people spent their whole lives chasing their dreams, trying to turn fantasy into reality. Yet, here I was, barely eighteen, with the whole world at my feet. My dreams were right there for the taking. It should have been the best fucking time of my life and it had been until recently. Until I started to care. But I couldn't afford to care. I couldn't afford to open myself up to distractions. To make myself vulnerable. Not now. Not when I was so close.

Later that evening, I found myself in the last place I wanted to be: riding with Hailee in awkward as fuck silence. She didn't mention Felicity and I didn't ask. I figured her lack of third degree meant Felicity was keeping secrets from her best friend, which suited me just fine.

"Thanks for helping me do this," she finally said as we pulled up outside the side entrance to the Arts Department.

"Yeah, well, Coach gave me no choice." I dragged a hand down my face.

"I see." Her expression hardened. "I just thought... It doesn't matter, come on." Hailee climbed out of my car and I let out a heavy sigh, thumping the wheel. It wasn't supposed to sound so bitter, but it was too late now. Reluctantly, I shouldered the door and followed Hailee into the building.

"So there are nine portraits in total," she said without looking at me. "Each one has been wrapped for transportation and Coach and Mr. Jalin already took the display equipment over to his house.

"Got it." The Arts Studio wasn't a part of school I was familiar with, but Hailee seemed completely at ease as she guided us through the network of adjoining rooms. The air was thick with the smell of paint and cleaning fluid.

"It takes some getting used to."

Silence settled between us. But it felt suffocating.

"So art, huh? Cameron says you're pretty good."

"I hope so since it would be kind of embarrassing if Coach unveils the portraits and they resemble children's artwork." Her lips curved slightly, and I found myself smiling back.

"I guess it was a dumb question."

"Not dumb," she gave me a half-smile. "I know this is weird for you, Jason. Me being a part of your life. But it would make things a lot easier if we could at least try to get along?"

"It'd really piss our parents off." I smirked. But Hailee's smile was gone. "You want to forgive her?"

"I don't want to forgive her, no, but I don't know how much longer I can freeze her out. It's senior year. I leave for college next year." Sadness edged into her expression.

"So, what? They get a free pass just because we're flying the nest?"

"Jason," Hailee pinched the bridge of her nose. "Don't you find it exhausting all the time?" When I looked at her with a blank expression, she added, "Holding onto so much hate and bitterness?"

"I don't hate everything."

She gave me a pointed look and I felt my jaw clench. "You don't know what it's like to never know someone's motives, to not know who you can trust," I said. "People think it's so easy being the hotshot football player, but do you know how old I was when scouts first started approaching me?"

"Thirteen?"

"Eleven. I was in sixth grade. While most kids were playing king of the hill and capture the flag, I was running drills and working with my dad on conditioning programs." Because there was no other path for me. I was going to fulfill his dream whether I liked it or not.

"I had no idea—"

"It doesn't matter." I shrugged dismissively, kicking the floor with my sneaker. "By the time you arrived in Rixon, I'd caught the eye of four Division One teams. Four. People started taking notice. Suddenly my life wasn't my own; it was my old man's, my football coach's, even the town's. When all I wanted was to play football."

I always loved the game, that was never the issue. But I hadn't realized back then, that one day, it would mean shouldering the expectation of an entire town.

A flicker of sympathy passed over Hailee's face.

"Shit, you don't want to hear this, we should probably—"

"Thank you," she said, "For telling me."

Why had I told her?

It was a long time ago and I wasn't a kid anymore. Being in the spotlight came with the territory, and the light would only get brighter when I went to college. To survive you had to build walls. Maybe I'd built them higher than others, but it was only because I wanted it more than most.

"It explains a lot." A smirk tugged at her mouth.

"Oh yeah?"

"All that pressure, the expectation... it explains why you're a grade-A asshole." Hailee laughed softly, her eyes twinkling. But I didn't laugh. I didn't even smile. Because she was right.

I was an asshole because I could be. People treated me like the prodigal son of football and somewhere along the way, I started acting like it. But what most people didn't realize was, it was a defense mechanism. A way to protect myself.

"I'm joking, Jason." Hailee added when I didn't reply.

"No you're not."

"Then maybe, but now? Now, you're not so bad." She grabbed the door handle to studio two and slipped inside. "What the—" Her words trailed off and I stepped up behind her to see what had rendered her speechless.

Art supplies were strewn everywhere. Red and white paint was splashed up the walls, and across the canvasses lying haphazardly around the place.

"I can't believe someone did this." Hailee's voice trembled as she swiped tears from her eyes. "It's all ruined; the Seniors Night project is ruined."

I looked at my step-sister, the person whose life I'd made a misery in the past, and felt like the worst kind of shit. For so long, I'd used Hailee as a punching bag to deal with my anger at her mother and now she was being used in the same way by someone else.

All because of me.

For a moment it was like I was looking in on us, for the first time actually looking beyond the armor I put around myself, the 'hurt people before they hurt me' principles I lived by, and I didn't like what I saw.

I stepped closer to her and I put my hand on her arm, causing her to jump slightly, as her attention shifted from the ruined canvasses. "We got this, okay? What do you want me to do to help?"

Hailee took a deep breath. "Can you help me get them back on the stands?"

I nodded.

The silence was deafening as we worked together to clean up the studio. I spotted my face amongst the chaos. Cam's too. Some of the canvasses looked worse off than others. When we stood back to survey the wreckage, Hailee let out an exasperated breath. "Tell me this isn't what I think it is," her body shook with anger. "Tell me Thatcher didn't break in and ruin my hard work because of some stupid football rivalry. Tell me, Jason." Her eyes flew to mine, pinning me to the spot, making me feel five inches tall.

"I can't," I ground out, my fists curled tightly against my thighs as I took in the devastation. Art wasn't my thing, but I knew how hard Hailee had worked on the project. How many hours it had taken her to paint each portrait.

A beat passed.

Another.

Until I could hear nothing but the roar of blood between my ears, the *thud thud thud* of my heart against my ribcage. "I'm so fucking sorry," the words sliced through the air like a hot blade through ice, as my fist smashed into the wall.

"Shit, Jason," Hailee rushed over to me, trying to get a look at my hand. But I shook her off, cradling it against my chest.

"It's fine," I said. It wasn't, but I'd had worse. It was nothing a little ice and a few shots of whisky wouldn't solve.

"You weren't supposed to see it until tonight." She sniffled, ignoring my apology.

"I never realized you were so talented." Even covered in red and white paint splatters, I could make out the intricate detail of my helmet, the way my shirt seemed to ripple as I hiked the ball. It wasn't just good.

It was fucking incredible.

"You should have seen them before..." she trailed off, sadness radiating from her.

"Can you fix them?" The one of me was the most affected but at least four seemed to have escaped the paint splatters.

"I'm not sure. I'll need to talk to Mr. Jalin."

"Hailee—"

"I know what you're going to say, Jason, and I get it. If we bring Thatcher into this, Principal Finnigan will intervene. But I have to tell Jalin. I'll think of something to protect you, but everyone's going to know something happened when we unveil them tomorrow. Maybe if we get this place tidied up and I speak to him, we can control the story."

It wasn't ideal. But it wasn't like we had a list of options.

"When did you get so devious?" I asked around a half-smirk, brushing over the fact she was prepared to lie to protect me because I didn't know what the fuck to do with that.

"I learned from the best." She shot me a knowing look.

"You know, if I didn't hate you so much, I think I could probably grow to like you."

"The feeling is entirely mutual." Hailee mirrored my expression. "Come on, we have a lot of work to do if we want to get this place tidied up before class tomorrow."

I pulled out my cell phone.

"What are you doing?" Hailee sounded wary.

"Calling in reinforcements."

19

Felicity

"WANT TO TALK ABOUT IT?" Mya asked me.

"Nope. I want to get wasted, flirt with cute guys, and then eat my body weight in ice cream. Maybe not in that order." I took a long pull on the liquor Mya had sequestered off her grandmother. It almost blew my brains out the first sip I had, but at least it left me numb.

"I hate to break it to you," my partner in crime said, "but I'm not exactly sure this is the place to meet guys."

We were down by the river, huddled on a bench. It probably wasn't my brightest idea ever, but I couldn't sit at home, wallowing. Deflecting Mom's incessant questions. It wasn't like I could call Hailee; not when she was off with Jason preparing for the Seniors Night thing tomorrow. At least it was family and close friends of the team only. I wouldn't have to survive sitting there, watching him, remembering how he made me feel... how he trampled all over any hopes of there being something real between us.

Fuck you right out of my head.

He hadn't meant to say the words. I'd seen the surprise in his dark eyes, the flash of panic. Any other girl would have probably slapped him across the face and run a mile. But not me.

What the hell was wrong with me?

"You're in deep with him," Mya said, and my head whipped up to hers.

"Huh?" I slurred.

"I said, 'you're in deep with him'."

"I'm not... I wasn't supposed—"

"Girl, we both know it doesn't work like that. You don't get to decide who you fall in love with."

"I'm not in love with him."

"Maybe not now. But it's there, inside you. You want him."

"I do," I admitted, my eyes darting to the ground beneath me. "He's different with me."

"They always are," she sighed, her voice distant.

"Your ex?"

She gave a small nod. "Reeled me in before I could even see what was happening."

"He hurt you?"

"He didn't just hurt me," Mya gave me a sad smile, "he completely destroyed me. Jermaine was my best friend growing up. Our momma's were girlfriends, got pregnant together, raised us together. We were all tight."

"What happened?" I asked, surprised Mya was finally opening up to me.

"He fell into a bad crowd. At first it was just young boys thinking they be gangsters. But last year, things changed. He changed. He was the same old Jermaine when it was just the two of us, but he started running for a crew. I begged him to stop, but money talks and he thought he was invincible."

"Sounds like someone I know," I grumbled.

"Jermaine wasn't involved in some high school football rivalry, Felicity. He was running drugs and errands for the kind of people you don't say no to."

"Oh." My cheeks heated.

"I know this rivalry has you all on edge," her expression softened, "but it's not life or death."

"Did Jermaine—"

"Die? No, but he did get taught a lesson after he screwed up, and I..." Mya gulped, her whole demeanor turning dark. "I was collateral."

My eyes grew to saucers. "You mean you were... *hurt*?"

She nodded slowly. "My momma finally told J we were done and she shipped me off to the ass crack of nowhere to finish up senior year. I haven't heard from Jermaine since." My new friend shrugged as if it was nothing, but pain radiated from her.

"You'll be safer here," I said, as if that mattered.

"Safe but not whole. I spent my entire life with Jermaine at my side. Even though I know it's for the best, even though I know I couldn't stand by any longer and watch him ruin his life, it doesn't make it any easier. If I'm not there, who's going to protect him?" A single tear slipped from the corner of Mya's eye, but she quickly swallowed the rest down, and I couldn't help but wonder what she'd been through to have hardened so much.

"He'll be okay," I added.

She gave a little shrug. "It doesn't matter anymore."

But something told me it did. She was lying to herself. Just like I'd been lying to myself. About Jason. About my perfectly mapped out future courtesy of my parents.

"So what's the history between you and Jason?"

"That is a story for another day."

"I'm not going anywhere." Mya gave me a pointed look.

"Jason is ... well, he's complicated. He's always been this asshole, you know? Untouchable. Cold. Cruel. He made Hailee's life hell ever since she moved to Rixon. I never liked him, hated what he stood for, how he treated her."

"What changed?"

"Everything." I smiled sadly. "Everything changed. I started to see glimpses of behind his mask, and I was so sick of being the good girl. Of being the girl always overlooked. And he'd look at me with this intensity... But it was nothing more than a game."

A game I'd lost.

Silence descended over us while we both got lost thinking about the guys in our life we wanted but couldn't have. I grabbed the bottle of liquor and took another mouthful, wanting nothing more than to erase the pit in my stomach.

"You're vibrating," Mya said after a couple of minutes. "It's Hailee."

"Let it go to voicemail." I waved her off, tracing patterns into the fluffy white clouds drifting across the dusky sky. The vibrations finally stopped, only to start again seconds later.

"She's calling again."

"She probably just wants to tell me all about Cameron. He's always doing cute things for her."

"He seems nice."

"He's the best," I sighed dreamily.

"Makes you wonder why a guy like him is friends with a guy like Ja—"

"Nope." My head snapped over to Mya. "You promised. No talking about him."

"I know, but—"

"No buts, Mya, please."

"Okay." She held up her hands. "I'm sorry. I didn't mean to upset you."

"I'm not upset, I'm just..."

What was I? Hurt? That was a given. Embarrassed? Dreadfully so. But most of all, I was annoyed at myself. At how easily I'd given in to Jason's charms, when all along I knew it was a game. A game that, once upon a time, I had no intention of playing.

Gah. I was so stupid. Jason had played me hook, line, and sinker. Letting me believe I had the upper hand, that I was calling the shots, only to rip the ground out from beneath me.

"She's still calling," Mya's concern perforated my bubble. "Maybe you should take it?" She handed me my cell.

"Hey, Hails," I tried my best at sounding sober.

"Thank God," my best friend sounded fraught. "I've been trying to call you for the last five minutes."

"Sorry, I was just... downstairs getting a drink." It was almost true.

Mya shot me a bemused look. "What?" I mouthed, shrugging. She rolled her eyes and went back to whatever—or whoever—had her attention on her cell.

"The portraits..." It was only then I realized she sounded upset.

"What happened?" I bolted upright, dread creeping up my spine.

"Thatcher, he... he completely trashed the studio."

"He didn't?" I gasped, my eyes growing to saucers. Hailee had slaved for hours over the Seniors Night project. "How bad is it?"

"Pretty bad." She sniffled and I knew she was probably putting on a brave front. "The guys helped me tidy up most of the mess but at least two portraits are ruined."

"Oh God, Hails, I'm so sorry."

"Yeah, it sucks. Mr. Jalin thinks we can still pull something off in time for tomorrow, but I'm not so sure."

"How's Ja—" His name stuck in my throat.

"He's acting surprisingly cool. But I know he's already plotting revenge. He just has this look, you know?"

Her words sent chills through me.

"Yeah," I whispered.

"Anyway, we're all heading over to Bell's. I think they want to cheer me up."

"That's nice."

"So, you'll meet us there?"

"I..." Mya must have overheard Hailee because she was shaking her head mouthing, "No," at me.

"Sure. Why not. I'm with Mya so it'll be the two of us."

"Okay," Hailee said. "I need a drink. Something strong."

Liquor sloshed in my stomach at her words. I needed water. But she didn't need to know that.

"We'll see you soon." I hung up and downed the rest of the liquor.

"This is a bad idea." Mya glared at me.

"I know." I clambered to my feet, swaying slighting as the cool air wafted around me. "But didn't you suggest I should add crashing a party to my list?" My lip curved deviously.

"This is *not* what I had in mind. I won't say I told you so when things go to shit because it's not my style, but I will say this: I think you should call Hailee back and say you've changed your mind."

"Noted." I gave her a defiant nod.

Mya rolled her eyes. "Fine, come on. Let's go cause some trouble."

"Trouble?" My lips curved into a thin line. "Who said anything about trouble?"

But she was right. I was drunk. And Jason was an asshole.

This couldn't possibly end well.

"Hails," I called across the bar. It was crammed for a Thursday, but I figured someone had told everyone that Jason, Asher, and Cameron were here, and like bees to honey they couldn't resist.

Very sexy, very lickable, very bad-for-your-heart honey.

"Are you drunk?" Hailee's eyes narrowed, her forehead crinkling like old lady skin.

"Who, me? Never!" I flashed her a mischievous smirk.

"Do I even want to know?" She cut me out, going straight to Mya.

"She called me." The traitor held up her hands. "I'm merely the wingwoman."

"And the liquor thief," I mouthed.

"Liquor thief?" Hailee looked really worried now. "Did something happen?"

"Happen? What could have possibly happened?"

She grabbed my arm and pulled me close. "Flick, talk to me. This isn't like you."

Lots of things weren't like me nowadays.

I let out an exasperated breath. "I just need to cut loose. Blow off some steam. Have a little fun." I waggled my brows suggestively.

"Are you sure you're okay? Maybe we should—"

"Fee, baby," a voice came from behind Hailee. "Get your cute ass over here."

I went to move around her, but she cut me off. "Flick, talk to me."

"I'm sorry, Hails," pulling her into my arms, I hugged my best friend tight. "I'm so sorry."

"Sorry?" She eased back. "For what?"

"The portraits of course."

Mya shook her head discreetly, but I levelled her with a look that told her this was between me and my best friend.

"You're sure you're okay?" Hails asked.

"Just feeling the pressure of senior year is all. You know how the parentals can get."

"Your mom—"

"Is the last thing I want to talk about. Let's forget all about parents and jerk face football players and just enjoy ourselves."

"You do know it's a school night?"

I shrugged. "One night won't hurt."

"Flick—" But I was already gone; weaving my way through the tables to where Asher and Cameron sat.

"Something you want to tell us?" Asher asked me as I slid into the booth next to him, a goofy grin plastered on my face.

"We're here to take Hailee's mind off things, right?" I arched my brow. "I figured what better way than to let loose a little." My gaze landed on Asher's beer and it was his turn to arch a brow.

"Seriously?" he asked, but I was already snatching his bottle away and bringing it to my lips. "Well, okay then."

"Flick," Hailee and Mya finally caught up to us. "Is that really a good idea?"

"It's on my list remember," I said giving her my best puppy-dog eyes.

"No way, you don't get to pull that crap with me, not tonight."

"Ah, the elusive list." Asher's arm went around my shoulder and I leaned into him slightly. He wasn't Jason, but he smelled good and the weight of his arm around me was nice.

Too nice.

"When do we get to find out what's on the list?"

"Never." I grinned at him.

"Bet I could persuade you to tell me."

"Oh yeah, and how do you plan on doing that?" I was flirting... with Asher and it felt good. He'd moved closer but so had I.

"I'm pretty creative, I'm sure I can think of—"

Someone cleared their throat and when my head lifted over to where the sound had come from, I was met with an icy cold stare that didn't just give me chills, it froze the blood running through my veins.

"What took you so long?" Asher asked, edging away from me but not removing his arm.

"Jerry wanted to shoot the shit." Jason's eyes didn't leave mine for a second but then moved to where Asher's hand rested on my shoulder. If looks could kill, I was pretty sure we'd both be dead.

"Mya, right?" he asked sliding in beside her. "You know who I am?"

"Everyone does." She shrugged, sitting a little straighter. I mirrored her action, desperate to see what he said next. Jason leaned in, his mouth dangerously close to her ear, and whispered something. Her gaze widened and then narrowed.

"Thanks," Mya said coolly," But I couldn't be less interested if I tried." She shot me a reassuring look, but the damage was done. Jason had flirted with her... right in front of me. Acting like it was nothing.

Like *I* was nothing.

Just like you're doing with Asher.

"I'll be back," I said to no one in particular as I hurried from the booth. The room began to spin, but I kept going until I was in the hall leading to the restrooms.

"Felicity, wait up," Mya called.

"I'm fine." I waved her off, staggering toward the girls' bathroom.

"It's okay," she said, gently grabbing my arm. "He's just trying to make you jealous. I would never—"

"I know." I finally met her eyes.

"Look, from one broken girl to another; you can't let him win. You deserve more. You deserve everything he won't give you."

"I know," the repeated words came out a whisper.

"So act like it," Mya said. "Throwing yourself at his best friend is only lowering yourself to his level. You're better than that. You're better than him and if he's going to get another chance with you, make him earn it."

"Earn it… right?" I half-smiled. "And how do I do that again?"

"Make him think you don't need him."

"By *not* flirting with Asher?"

"His friends are definitely off-limits but I didn't say anything about other guys." Mya grinned mischievously. "So what do you say? Shall we get back out there, find us a couple of cute non-football players, and make your guy crazy jealous?"

My guy.

As if Jason would ever allow himself to belong to anyone.

"I guess."

"Not good enough," her expression darkened, "If I can survive leaving my home and the guy I've loved since I can remember, I'm sure you can survive a night of harmless flirting in the name of making Jason Ford realize what he's missing."

"Ssh." My eyes darted around the hall. The last thing I needed was the wrong person overhearing our conversation—or any person for that matter.

"Okay, that's it." A look of determination flashed across her face. "I was ready to drag you out of here screaming and kicking but I can see it's worse than I thought. So one night. You get one night."

"One night?" I had no idea what she was talking about.

"Less talking," Mya grabbed my hand, "And more drinking. We've got work to do."

20

Jason

"BRO, if you clench any harder, your jaw is going to break." Asher chuckled, taking a long pull of his beer.

"She drives me fucking insane," I ground out, watching on as Felicity and some douchebag from the soccer team laughed like they were old friends.

"She's a girl. It's what they do. So you and her—"

"Never going to happen."

Felicity disarmed me. Every moment I spent with her, I felt my walls chip away a little more. I couldn't afford to be defenseless, not in a world that would chew me up and spit me out quicker than you could say, 'Go Raiders'.

I glanced over at him and noticed his eyes fixed in another direction... where Mya was also talking to some guy.

"New girl, huh?"

"What?" His head whipped around.

"You and the new girl?"

"I heard you the first time. I just have no fucking clue what you're talking about."

"Of course you don't." I scrubbed my jaw. He was right. If I clenched any harder there was a good chance I'd need emergency dental work. But ever since she returned from the restroom, Felicity had been talking to anyone and anything with a dick that wasn't me.

"Well, aren't we a pair?" Asher just wouldn't shut the hell up. "You won't admit you want Fee and I can't admit I like the new girl."

"So you do like her? Knew it." I smirked.

"She's... different."

"You're not wrong there." I downed the rest of my beer.

"So you and Fee?"

"There is no me and *Fee.*" What kind of fucking nickname was that anyway?

"You know I only pushed you before because I wanted you to pull your head out of your ass, right?"

"I know," I grumbled. When Cam and Asher had suggested we all come to

Bell's to take Hailee's mind off the mess at the studio, I hadn't anticipated on it turning into a session with *Dr Phil.* All I wanted to do was drink and forget about Thatcher. Numb the burning desire to ram my fist straight into his face.

I would never forget the look on my step-sister's face when she saw the devastation he'd caused. Part of me didn't want to care, didn't want to feel responsible for it.

But I did care.

I was responsible.

And it was a hard truth to swallow.

Asher slung his arm over my shoulder as we watched the girls flirt shamelessly with the two douchecanoes. "I don't know about you, but I'm not going to just sit here and watch this shit." He gave me a pointed look, one that should have had me following him as he cut across the bar to them. But I didn't go.

I couldn't.

Because going would be admitting something I wasn't ready for.

So I sat there like a fucking statue watching the girl who had completely flipped my world on its head as she batted her eyes and twirled a strand of hair around her finger.

My hand curled around the table. *Walk away,* I silently willed the douche to excuse himself. Because while I couldn't go over there and stake my claim, I wasn't sure I was strong enough to stand by and watch someone else make a move on Felicity. Not when I could still taste her on my lips, remember how good she felt bouncing on my dick, how fucking easy it was to lose myself in her.

"Penny for your thoughts?" Hailee came up beside me.

"Just chillin'."

"I don't think I've ever seen her like this before," she said, guilt ripping through me. "Did something happen between the two of you?"

"Hailee—"

"I know, I know. But I know Felicity and this isn't her."

"I can't be who she needs."

"I want to agree. I want to tell you to walk away and save her the heartache. But something tells me you're both already in too deep for that." My step-sister looked at me as if she could see right through me.

I hated it.

"You have to make a choice, Jason," she went on. "Take a chance on her or let her go. Because this—whatever this is that you're doing right now—it's hurting her. And I won't stand by and let you hurt her, I just won't."

Pressing my lips together, I gave her the silent treatment. I wasn't having this conversation. Not here. Not now. And most definitely not with her. My step-sister. Hailee fucking Raine; the girl I'd hated for so long I didn't know how to deal with my newfound concern for her.

"Hey," she laid her hand on my arm when I didn't reply, "I'm not your enemy, Jason."

Slowly, I slid my hard gaze to hers. She was right. The lines had been redrawn and somehow, we were on the same side now, but it didn't mean I had to like it, or even accept it.

"Yeah, whatever." I shrugged her off, finding Felicity in the crowd again.

Maybe I couldn't go claim her, but I could sit here and watch. I could make sure that douchecanoe kept his hands firmly to himself.

"I hope you know what you're doing," Hailee let out a heavy sigh. "I'm going to find Cameron."

"You do that," I grunted. "I need another beer." Catching Jerry's eye, I tipped my empty bottle toward him. He gave me a terse nod, disappointment glittering in his eyes. He could judge all he wanted. Jerry didn't know what it was like to shoulder the expectation of an entire town... your classmates... teammates. He didn't know what it was like to want something so bad you had to give up everything else.

No one did.

"Are you going to handle that?" Asher asked me sometime later, "Or am I?"

Inhaling a deep breath, I watched Felicity sway on her feet as she attempted to make Hailee and Mya dance with her. It had been the same for the last hour; Felicity trying to coerce the girls into dancing, them telling her no.

"Shit, she's going to—"

Mya caught her fall.

"Someone should have taken her home an hour ago," I said.

"Hailee tried. Mya too. She's on a mission, man."

Hailee caught my eye across the bar, her expression full of challenge. *Are you going to step up?*

I rubbed my temples, exhaling a shaky breath, holding her steely gaze. It was a bad idea—the fucking worst. But I couldn't take another second of Felicity flashing her bedroom eyes at some random guy or dodging advances from some dickwad who didn't deserve to touch her.

"Here." I thrust my bottle of water at Asher. I'd stopped drinking a while ago, right around the time Felicity began to try—and fail—to turn Bell's into a club.

"Good man." He clapped me on the shoulder. "Just go easy on her, she's wasted."

"Yeah, yeah. See you tomorrow." Our eyes connected and I saw his concern. Asher might have had a crush on the new girl, but he cared about

Felicity, and I couldn't decide if I was relieved she had him in her corner, or insanely jealous.

Maybe both.

Hailee and Mya noticed me first. "Oh it's you," Felicity slurred, her body falling limp against me. "I'm not sure I like you anymore." Her hands pressed against my chest, my body vibrating with heat.

Jesus, even her touch was magic.

"House key?" I asked Hailee over her shoulder.

"Pocket I assume."

"If her parents wake up and discover me in their house, you'd better have a damn good cover story ready." I kept my voice low.

"We can take her," Mya said over my shoulder. But I ignored her, slipping my arm around Felicity's waist and tucking her into my side.

"I'll see you back at the house." I gave her a tight nod. Hailee returned it, amusement dancing in her eyes. But it was nothing compared to the curious stares aimed at us as I herded Felicity out of the bar. I was just relieved that Jenna and the gym team were nowhere to be seen because that was one shitshow I didn't need right now.

"Jason?" Felicity murmured.

"Yeah?"

"Whatever you're doing, stop. I hate you." She sucked in a shaky breath. "And I hate myself for ever thinking you could change."

"Yeah, yeah, Giles. You hate me, I get it. Now get your drunk ass in the car."

Fifteen minutes, and one emergency stop later, thanks to Felicity thinking she was going to puke all over my car, we were at her house. I dug the key out of her pocket, Felicity cradled in my arms, and unlocked the Giles' front door. She let out a soft moan when her head bumped the wall as I slipped inside.

"Ssh." My fingers traced her cheek. The last thing I needed was Mr. Giles to find me carrying his daughter upstairs but yet again, all rational thought had flown out of the window.

Thankfully I remembered the layout of her house so I didn't have to worry about walking in on her parents sleeping.

"Okay, let's get you into bed." I dropped her down onto the mattress and began the torturous task of undressing her.

"No," she murmured, trying to fumble with her clothes. "I can do it."

"You can barely talk, let alone get undressed." My fingers peeled hers away. "Let me do it."

"Why?" she murmured, her head rolling like a rag doll. "I'm no one. Nothing."

"You're not nothing." I brushed the hair from her face, fighting a smile, and ignoring the giant lump in my throat.

Couldn't she see she was someone to me? That she was slowly becoming too important, which is why I had to walk away? Before we were both in too deep and things became too messy.

Felicity relented, her body pliant as I peeled her shirt and jeans off before tucking her into bed. Her eyes were closed, her breathing deep and steady. She'd drunk a lot tonight. Too much. And I knew it was my fault for how things went down earlier.

"Fuck," I muttered, stepping away from her before I did something stupid. Something more stupid than sneaking into her house on a Thursday night while her parents slept down the hall.

But I couldn't seem to drag myself away either. Because in that moment, with her passed out on the bed, I could pretend. Pretend she was mine and I was hers. Even if it was only a dream. One I knew could never become reality.

Leaning against her desk, something caught my eye. Reaching for the stack of papers, the familiar crest stared up at me. "What the..." My eyes squinted as I snatched up the college application, a sinking feeling tugging at my stomach.

There was no way.

No way she was applying to Penn, *my* fucking school.

Yet, there it was, staring me in the face, like a giant screw you from the universe.

"J- Jason?" Her soft voice hit me dead in the chest. "Are you still here?"

I wanted to go to her, to reassure her everything was okay. That she was just disorientated from all the liquor in her bloodstream. But I was paralyzed by the papers in my hand. At what they implied.

Penn was Ivy League, one of the best colleges in the country. What were the chances that Felicity also had plans to go there?

Unless... no. She wouldn't pull that kind of crazy shit.

Would she?

Suddenly I couldn't breathe. My chest tightened around my lungs like I'd been sacked by a hulk of a linebacker. Quietly hurrying to the door, I glanced over at her one last time before ducking out of her room and retracing my steps out of the house.

Felicity was never supposed to be a distraction. She was never supposed to bury her way under my skin.

Only she had.

And for as much as I'd resisted, for as much as I knew it was a terrible idea, deep down, I had been coming around to the idea of exploring this thing between us. The inexplicable pull. But I wasn't looking for anything serious. Didn't have time for it. Not now. Not when I went off to Penn next fall. So the idea she would be there, on campus, showing up all over the place… I couldn't deal with that shit.

It was better this way.

Better she hated me.

Better she got all ideas of her and me out of her head.

Felicity deserved Prince Charming, not the misunderstood Knight with a chip on his shoulder and hate in his soul.

The vibrations of my cell pulled me from my thoughts and I dug it out my pocket. "Yeah?"

"Check your snapchat," Grady said. "We've got a problem."

"Do I even want to know?"

"I think you'll want to see this, Cap."

"Fine," my jaw clenched, "thanks for the heads up."

I waited until I was in my car to open up Grady's message and when I did, I knew only one person was responsible.

Thatcher.

21

Felicity

"I THINK I'M IN HELL."

"No," Hailee said, "that's just your hangover talking."

"Don't say that word. It's evil."

"What did your mom say?"

"Oh, I hid out in the bathroom until she left for work. But if I don't make it through the day, I'm ready to fake a stomach flu. So ready."

"That was some impressive display last night." She gave me a pointed look; one I felt all the way down to the pit of my stomach.

"Honestly, I don't know what to say." My cheeks flushed.

"You could start with the truth."

"I'm not sure you're ready to hear it." I peeked over at her while the rest of the student population filed down the hall, moving to their classes.

"Hey," she grabbed my hand, "It's okay. You don't need to protect me. I know you like him. I know he likes you—"

"He doesn't like me, Hails." My head shook side to side. "I'm just a game to him."

A game I could never win.

"So what was last night then?"

"What do you mean?"

"I mean, why did my pig-headed step-brother pretty much carry you out of Bell's—in front of everyone might I add—if you're just a game?"

"He did?"

I had hazy memories of being wrapped in his arms but I hadn't considered what it meant. That he'd done it in front of other people. Our classmates. Hailee was staring at me like she expected an answer, so I said, "Because he's trying to win student of the year? I don't know."

"God, you're dense sometimes. He likes you. It's written all over his face every time he looks at you."

"Hails, I don't know what you think you know, but Jason doesn't like me." At least, not in the way I wanted him to.

"Come to the Seniors Night thing tonight."

"I can't. It's family and friends of the team only."

"Well I'm a guest of honor *and* I'm family. You can be my plus one."

"I don't think it's a good idea."

"Look," Hailee pulled me closer to the locker bank. "Jason is as stubborn as he is good at football. But he's different with you. I can't explain it, but ever since New York, he's been different. Come tonight, be there for him. And maybe after, the two of you can talk."

"You really think it's a good idea? He made it seem like..." My voice trailed off before I revealed too much.

Everything was so confusing. He said one thing but was constantly doing another. And despite my head knowing it was better—easier—to walk away, my heart didn't want that.

"Don't you at least want to know where you stand?"

"I guess..."

"So come."

"Fine, I'll come." I was going to the game anyway and even if Jason didn't want me there, Hailee, Asher, and Cameron would make me feel welcome.

Butterflies tickled my insides. I didn't want to get my hopes up again, not where Jason was concerned. But I had hazy memories of last night. Of him undressing me and tucking me in. Of his fingers tracing my face as if I was the most precious thing in the world. He could be so gentle and tactile and warm with me. A stark contrast to the cold icy version everyone else got to see.

"Don't look so worried." Hailee squeezed my hand, offering me a reassuring smile.

But this was Jason she was talking about.

Which meant I didn't need to be worried.

I needed to be terrified.

I SHOULD HAVE KNOWN the night was doomed when the Raiders lost. The entire game had been like pulling teeth. We scored a touchdown. They got one back. We sacked their QB, they took down ours even harder. Jason was off his game, so much so we'd all witnessed Coach Hasson chew him out on the sideline more than once. It was a shitshow and everyone felt the tension on the field.

By the time we arrived at the Hassons', nervous energy coursed through my veins.

"Relax," Hailee said. "It's going to be fine."

"Did you watch the same game I did?" I asked incredulously. "We practically got our asses handed to us."

"It was one game and it isn't like they needed the win or anything."

"Hails, you have so much still to learn."

She chuckled, cutting the engine. "I know I talked you into coming tonight for Jason; but confession time, I partly did it for me."

"Hails, he's seen the portrait. He knows how good you are."

"I know but this is different." Her voice cracked. "It's like baring myself to everyone, and that terrifies me."

I twisted around to her. "You are so talented, babe. You have nothing to be worried about. Mr. Jalin managed to fix the damaged portraits and everyone is going to love them. *All* of them. This is your time to shine, Hails."

She gave me a slight nod, but I could see the fear in her eyes. Reaching over, I squeezed her hand. "You've got this."

"*We've* got this." Her smile grew.

"Ride or die."

"Ride or die." Hailee gave me a small nod, before we got out of the car and made our way around the side of the house. The team were already there, their expressions somber, the mood still tense.

"Ah, Miss Raine," Coach Hasson made his way over. "Just the person I wanted to see."

"Hi, Coach, tough game."

"Hmm." His lips pressed into a thin line. "We're not going to dwell on that tonight. We're here to celebrate our seniors and your talent. Mr. Jalin informed me of the *incident*." The way he said it suggested he knew there was more to it than what he'd been told.

"Unfortunate to have happened the day before the presentation," he added.

Hailee tensed but kept her expression neutral. "These things happen. I'm just relieved Mr. Jalin had the foresight to take photographs of them."

"Indeed. Now if I could borrow you for a quick moment to run through the plan."

"Hmm, sure." Hailee looked to me and I nodded.

"Go, I'll be fine." Glancing around the Hassons' yard, I spotted Asher and Cameron with their parents. The rest of the players were standing with their families.

But not Jason.

He was sat in a chair on the edge of the gathering, drinking a beer. Jenna Jarvis sat proudly on his lap, like the Queen Bitch she was. A potent mix of anger and jealousy skittered up my spine when her eyes lifted to mine and glittered with victory.

"Flick, what's... Oh." Hailee reappeared. "What the hell is he playing at? She isn't even supposed to be here, it's a closed event," she mumbled beneath her breath.

"It's fine," I steeled myself, ignoring the ache in my chest. "Let's go get our seats."

"You're sure?"

"I'm here now, aren't I?" And it wasn't like seeing Jenna all over Jason was new to me. I'd been there and done that enough times, I didn't just own the t-shirt, I had that crap trademarked.

I trailed after Hailee, keeping my eyes ahead. If Jason noticed me, he didn't let it be known. Asher on the other hand, beamed at me as we approached the long table. They had been arranged in a giant U shape with the lectern at the front surrounded by Hailee's portraits behind in a sweeping arc, and rows behind for the rest of the guests.

"Fee, baby, this is a surprise," Asher said quietly, his gaze moving past me, probably to Jason.

"Hailee invited me as her plus one."

"Screw that, you can be my plus one. Come on." He patted the seat beside him.

"Isn't someone sitting there?"

"You." He smiled and some of my nerves subsided.

"Hey, Felicity," Cameron added once I was seated. "How are you?"

"I'm good. Sorry for gate-crashing." I gave him a tight smile.

"Never. You're Hailee's best friend which makes you one of us. Besides I think Mrs. Hasson got carried away with all the food. The more the merrier."

"Thanks." Before I could stop myself, I'd lifted my gaze over to where Jason and Jenna sat. He looked indifferent, barely touching her, but she was wrapped around him, hands splayed on his chest, her body turned into him slightly, sending a clear signal to everyone—*to me*—that tonight, Jason belonged to her.

"He's pissed we lost," Cameron said.

"Nah, he's pissed his head wasn't in it and that's *why* we lost."

"Ash," Cam warned.

"He needs to figure his shit out before the play-offs or we can kiss State goodbye."

"What?" I asked, the three of them staring at me.

"You should talk to him." That was Asher.

"She's going to, right, Flick?" Hailee added. "After the presentation."

"I, uh, I guess." My eyes found him again only this time he was staring back. His eyes narrowed and dark. Anger rippled off him, palpable even from our position all the way across the yard.

"Ignore her." Asher leaned in.

"Easy for you to say." I tried to give him an easy smile, but I knew it probably looked strained.

"He doesn't want her. She's just convenient. Or a bad habit. Yeah, she's a bad habit." His lip kicked up.

"You know what they say about bad habits, right?" I said. "They're hard to break." My stomach sank.

"Don't give up on our guy yet. I don't know what happened today but something's eating at him." I gave him a pointed look and he added, "More than usual."

"You really want me to do this?" The words flew out of my mouth. "Me and Jason?"

Asher sucked in a harsh breath, his eyes shuttering. But when they opened again, he was looking at me with nothing but understanding. "Did I wish for a second that things could be different? That maybe I'd caught your eye first? Hell yeah, I do." He swallowed thickly. "But you can't help who you fall for and I always knew it was you and him."

"I'm not sure there's a me and him, Asher."

"That's because Jason doesn't know how to let people in. He doesn't know how to trust anyone. But you're changing him, Fee, baby. Which is why you can't give up on him yet. He might not realize it yet, but he needs you. And something tells me, you need him too."

"I..." The words died on my lips. "You're a good friend, Asher Bennet. He's lucky to have you."

"You've got me too." He grinned. "No matter what happens, I'll always be here for you."

"That means a lot. You're going to make some girl very happy one day."

"I'm not so sure about that." He chuckled, but it came out strangled. "Here we go."

I followed Asher's line of sight to where Coach Hasson was standing next to the lectern. Jason had finally moved to an empty seat at the table. Of course it had to be right opposite me. His hard gaze burned into the side of my face as I tried to concentrate on Coach Hasson.

"Okay, okay, settle down." He waited for silence to fall over the yard. "Tonight we celebrate our seniors. Their commitment and dedication, their leadership and talent. But it isn't only a celebration of the past, it's a celebration of the future. Of the young men you're becoming and the doors that await you. I have a whole other speech somewhere," he pretended to check his pockets, "But for now, I'm going to hand it over to a man who knows all about what it takes to be the best. Kent Ford."

Hailee stiffened beside me and I leaned in. "Did you know about this?"

"He never said a word," she whispered.

"Maybe that's why he was off his game." It would make sense. Everyone knew there was no love lost between Jason and his father, despite the united front Mr. Ford liked to present to everyone.

Jason's dad moved to the lectern, brushing down the lapels of his dinner jacket. He looked good, much like an older Jason. Same unruly brown hair, same dark intense eyes. But age had mellowed him, or maybe that was Hailee's mom. Either way, he looked happy. He looked like a man content with life. A man in love.

I found Hailee's mom in the outer row of seats. She beamed at her husband, radiating happiness. "Look at your mom," I said quietly.

"I'd rather not," Hailee groaned.

"Hey." I took her hand under the table. "She's happy. They're happy. I know she hurt you, but you can't help who you fall in love with." God, I sounded like Mya and Asher. I knew Hailee carried a lot of resentment toward her mom and the lies she'd told. But if I'd learned anything over the last few weeks, it was that sometimes your head and heart went to war and it wasn't always your head that came out the winner.

It was so easy to judge, but it wasn't until you were in that situation, trying to do the right thing, that you realized just how powerful the heart was. I mean, here I was, completely aware that Jason didn't want me, not the way I wanted him, but I was willing to put myself on the line one more time to try to reach him. To try to show him that sometimes you had to take a risk.

"Hey," Hailee nudged my shoulder, "Are you okay?"

"Yeah." I flashed her a weak smile. "I'm fine." The lie was so regular now, it rolled off my tongue with ease. Even if every time the two little words spilled from my lips, it killed another little piece of my heart.

22

Jason

I WANTED TO RUN. The urge to get up and walk away from my old man, from Coach, my teammates, and best friends, Hailee, even Felicity, coursed through me. Like deadly poison, it burned, eating away at my soul.

The last thing I wanted to do was sit here and listen to Kent Ford spout shit about hard work and sacrifice and family. Because he was a liar. Sure he'd loved the game, and he was a damn good player back in the day, one of the best, but he didn't know what it meant to make sacrifices. He was a have-your-cake-and-eat-it kind of guy, and like so many players before him, I suspected he loved what the game could do for him more than the game itself.

But still, I didn't move.

People thought I was cold, that I didn't care. Sometimes I wondered if I cared too damn much. I just didn't let people see it.

"Welcome to Seniors Night," his strong voice carried across the Hasson's yard, "The final home game of any season always holds a special place in my heart, but tonight was something else. Tonight, I watched my son continue the Ford legacy in Raider history. It's just a shame his game was off, but what player doesn't have his ups and downs." He gave the crowd an easy smile, even earned a laugh or two. But I wasn't laughing. I wasn't even smiling. Because I knew it wasn't a joke.

He and Coach were pissed we didn't get the win and they weren't the only ones, My old man was telling me in front of everyone I hadn't been good enough tonight and it fucking burned. So much so, part of me wished I'd have gotten up at his wedding and talked about his failure as a father and husband just to see how he fucking liked it.

The feeling of never quite being good enough, even though you thought you gave your all.

But the truth was my head wasn't in it tonight. Too consumed with Thatcher's latest threat. With Felicity's sea-green gaze every time she'd looked my way at school. I couldn't tell anyone about Thatcher though. Until I figured out what the fuck to do, I had to lie and pretend everything was fine.

Everything was not fucking fine.

It was falling to shit around me. The pieces of my carefully constructed world falling apart all because I couldn't keep my dick in my pants and out of the girl who made me fucking crazy.

"I know all about the sacrifice and dedication; the blood, sweat, and tears that go into winning a State Championship," Dad flashed his championship ring to his enthralled audience, "that's why I know you'll bring it home this season. Because you're fighters. Because you're the best. Because you're Raiders. And Raiders—"

"Never quit," rang out around me, reverberating through me, stoking a fire in my soul. Even though I was pissed, even though this was the last place on Earth I wanted to be right now, it didn't matter. Football was in my blood, part of my DNA, and when my teammates and our supporters cheered our name, it called to something inside me.

My eyes found Felicity across the yard. She was watching me, a faint smile gracing her lips. Why she was here I had no fucking idea, but deep down, I wanted to believe she came for me. Not that I could ever tell her that.

"Okay, okay, I'm going to wrap this up so we can get to the good stuff."

"Yeah, Mrs. H's chicken wings," someone yelled, earning him a round of hoots and hollers.

Dad grabbed his drink off the lectern and raised it high. "To the seniors of 2019. May your futures be filled with opportunity, success, and most of all… football."

The place erupted, everyone cheering for the man I hated so much I could barely look at him. It probably wasn't healthy, the amount of resentment and bitterness I carried around with me, but I didn't know how to let go.

I didn't know how to forgive him.

Parents were supposed to set the standard. They were supposed to help shape us into the adults we would one day become. Which meant I could look forward to becoming a cheating son of a bitch who cared more about looking good in front of his town, and getting his dick wet, than his family.

The man of the moment approached me. "Jason," he stuck out his hand. "I'm proud of you, Son. So damn proud."

I stared at his hand, wishing I could leave him hanging. But everyone was watching, waiting to see the special moment between father and son.

"Thanks," I choked out, grabbing his hand and shaking.

His eyes held so many apologies, but it was too little too late. I wasn't sure we'd ever find our way back to one another. Not after everything.

Coach chose that exact moment to intervene and I breathed a sigh of relief as Dad took his seat. "Thank you, Kent," he said, offering a nod of appreciation. "I know it means a lot to the team to have you here. You're a true inspiration to the guys and proof that dreams can come true.

"Now we move onto the presentation. Every year, I like to give each of my seniors a token gift to remember their time at Rixon High. To remind them where they came from. This year, we've done something a little different. In an effort to work across departments, I approached Mr. Jalin, our arts director, about an exciting opportunity for one of his students. Miss Raine, if you'd like to come up here."

I watched from across the way as Hailee stood up, cheeks flushed and eyes wide, and walked toward the coach.

"What Miss Raine has created for this year's presentation is nothing other than incredible. And I hope you'll join me in applauding her talent. Seniors of 2019, we present your senior year portraits." He and Hailee began uncovering each portrait. The crowd hushed into awed silence. Even I couldn't deny the impact of the nine paintings side by side.

"I think you'll agree they really are something special."

"Thank you," my step-sister said, barely able to look at her audience.

One by one, Coach called up the seniors, presenting them with their portrait. Hailee posed for photos, graciously accepting a chaste kiss on the cheek from each of them, all except Asher who picked her up and twirled her around, and Cam who pulled her into his arms and kissed the crap out of her, audience be damned.

"And last but by no means least, our quarterback and captain, Jason Ford."

The crowd's applause faded into white noise as I got up and moved toward Hailee. She was smiling at me with such uncertainty, I felt like a complete shit. But when I reached her and she wrapped her arms around me, it was my turn to choke. Hailee didn't speak, she didn't need to. That one gesture spoke volumes.

When she pulled away, her smile was no longer uncertain but full of understanding. It only twisted the knife deeper. I'd been such a dick to her: making her life hell ever since she arrived in Rixon. Yet, here she was forgiving me for everything as if it was the simplest thing in the world.

"I hope you like it," she said taking the framed photo down from the easel and presenting it to me.

I'd seen the portrait yesterday, but it had been ruined with red and white paint splashes.

"Well, Son," Coach said, filling the awkward silence. "What do you think?"

"I..." The words lodged in my throat along with the giant fucking lump that had been there for the last couple of minutes.

"I think you've stunned him into silence."

Hailee's brows furrowed. "Are you okay?" she whispered.

"It's good, really good," I managed to choke out. "Thanks."

"Okay, now we've got all the formalities out of the way," Coach declared, "let's eat."

Mrs. Hasson and some of the other player's moms began uncovering all the food laid out on a long table at the edge of the gazebo. Most of the guys wasted no time joining the line. But Cam and Asher came over to us. "You've been holding out on us, Hails," Ash said.

"You saw them yesterday."

"No, I saw the mess Thatcher made." I winced at the mention of his name. "You're super talented and I don't know about these two goons, but I'll be hanging mine above my bed."

"Thanks, I think," she chuckled.

"Where's Fee?" he asked.

"She's hmm," Hailee's eyes flicked to mine, "around."

Code for: she didn't know if she should come over here.

My chest tightened.

"Are you hungry?" Cam asked her.

"I could eat." Hailee blushed, and I groaned.

"Seriously, can you two at least pretend to be talking about food." Shouldering past him, I headed for the line, only to be intercepted by Felicity.

"Hi," she said, her smile not quite reaching her eyes.

"Hey."

She winced at my cool tone, but shook it off maintaining eye contact. "I just wanted to say congratulations."

"Thanks." I went to move around her, needing to get away, but she grabbed my arm. "I was hoping we could talk, later, maybe?"

"There's nothing to say."

Hurt flashed across her face. "Jason, please, I came tonight for—"

"Hey, Cap, you gotta try this," Grady yelled, and I took the opportunity to slip away. He shoved a sophomore out the way to make room for me and handed me a plate. "What was all that about?" He tipped his head to where Felicity was still standing, watching us.

"Nothing."

"So last night was..."

"Nothing." I shrugged.

"Doesn't look like nothing from where I'm standing. It looks like you got yourself a stage five clinger."

"She's Hailee's best friend," I deadpanned.

"Never shit where you eat, man." He slung his arm around my shoulder.

"It isn't like that."

"For you, maybe, but she's got that look." He glanced back again but I didn't look, not this time. "And we both know you don't need that shit right now."

"Do me a favor, Grady?"

"Yeah?"

"Shut the fuck up."

His expression fell. "Sorry, man, I'm just yanking your chain." We moved up the line, loading our plates with barbecue. "Did you decide how to deal with the Thatcher problem yet?"

Shaking my head, I glared at him. Hard.

"Shit, my bad. I'm just concerned he's going to lure you into doing something real fucking stupid."

"Why don't you worry about you and leave Thatcher to me, yeah?"

"Sure, Jase, I just—"

"Let. It. Go," I hissed.

"Whatever you say, man." He held up his hands. "This barbecue looks good."

"So let's eat."

And forget all about Felicity and Thatcher.

After everyone had stuffed their faces, we all settled down again. The clink of Coach's fork against his glass ushered everyone into silence. I pulled at the collar of my shirt. It felt like it was getting tighter by the second, squeezing the air from my lungs and making it difficult to breathe.

"You've got this," Cam mouthed at me.

"Now that you've all filled your bellies, I'm going to handover to Jason. Before I do though, I wanted to take this opportunity to say a few words about this young man."

Silently groaning, I buried my face in my hands.

"Jason Ford came to me an angry, hot-headed young man. He pushed every boundary I set, broke every record before him, and worked harder than any other player I've ever had the pleasure of working with. But with great talent comes great responsibility, and four years ago, if someone asked me if Jason had what it took to be QB One, I would have had to think about it.

"You see being quarterback requires leadership; it requires a player who understands the importance of teamwork, someone who calls the plays but might not always get the glory in the end zone. Jason had talent in spades. Still does. In fact, I'd go out on a limb and say I've never seen a senior player command the field the way Jason does." His eyes landed on me and he gave me a nod of encouragement. "But talent is only part of it. If you want to go all the way, you have to keep your eye on the prize. You have to forget all the other crap off field, the rivalries and drama, the girls and parties. You have to leave all that at the door and give one hundred and ten percent every time you step out on the field. Jason isn't perfect and he still has a way to go, but if anyone can go all the way, it's him. Which is why I want to present Jason Ford the Rixon High School 2019 MVP *and* Coach's Player of the Year Award. It has been my pleasure watching you grow into the player you are today, Son. Now you go out there and make Rixon proud."

His compliment swirled around me, weighing heavily on my shoulders as

I went to him, accepting his firm handshake and the two trophies. But Coach went one step further, pulling me into a hug. "I'm proud of you, Kid. Real damn proud. Just don't forget where you came from when you go off and dominate the NCAA."

"Thanks, Coach." I stepped up to the lectern, adjusting the mic. "Hey everyone, I'm Jason."

A few snickers rang out and Grady flipped me off.

Fucker.

"Coach asked me to say a few words, but public speaking isn't exactly my forte. I prefer kicking ass on the field."

The guys burst into hoots and hollers and Coach had to step in to quiet them down.

"Being QB One for the last four years has been a privilege. Football is my life. It's all I've ever wanted to do. All I can ever imagine doing. And I'm grateful to have had the opportunity to work with Coach and his team.

"But Coach is right; being a Raider is more than just football, it's family, and I love you guys like brothers. Well, most of you; the jury is still out on Mackey." I smirked at the sophomore watching me with hunger in his eyes. Hunger I remembered. He wanted to be me one day. To be standing here addressing his teammates, his brothers. But he was too distracted by the girls and parties and the god-like worship we received every time we walked the halls at school.

"Coach talked a lot about sacrifices." My eyes found Felicity. "But when you want something bad enough, when it's all you can see, there isn't any price too high to pay. Mark my words Raiders, one day, it'll be my name in the Hall of Fame. One day, you'll all get to say you knew an NFL legend."

It sounded arrogant; a pipe dream that might never come true. But I didn't work in what ifs and maybes, I worked in hard facts. And I was going all the way.

No matter the sacrifice.

"Here he is, the man of the hour." Dad grabbed my shoulder and pulled me into his side. "We're proud of you, Son, real damn proud."

I smiled tightly at the group of men gathered around my old man.

"Must be something, Kent, watching your kid follow in your footsteps."

"It's something all right." His hand tightened. "The question is though, does he have what it takes to go all the way?" It came out lighthearted but I didn't miss the lingering bitterness.

"Coach seems to think so, and I for one, am rooting for you, Jason." Grady's dad chimed in, tipping his beer in my direction. I gave him a small nod of appreciation.

"He just needs to learn to rein in his emotions. Take tonight for example..."

I tuned out, my teeth grinding behind my lips. I didn't want to hear about how I messed up or how I threw away the team's perfect season.

"Excuse me," I said, shucking out of his grip. "But tonight is supposed to be a celebration, so I'm going to do just that, celebrate." Stalking away, I didn't expect to hear him call my name.

"Jason." I turned slowly, narrowing my eyes on my old man. "I was just shooting the shit with the guys, you know how it is."

"Whatever," I grumbled.

"You're annoyed."

"I'm not annoyed, I'm just... It doesn't matter." I let out an exasperated breath.

"I think it does." His audience had dispersed, leaving the two of us and a boat load of shit I didn't want to deal with.

"You know," he stepped closer, hands jammed deep in his pockets, "I remember what it was like to be young. To have the world at your feet. To think you're invincible." Pain flashed in his eyes. "But we're all human, Jason. We all make mistakes."

"You are such a fucking hypocrite," I spat the words. "Standing up there tonight to talk about sacrifice and dedication and what it means to be a team."

"Watch your tone, Son," he said coolly, glancing around to make sure no one had overheard me. Because God forbid someone actually saw the real us, the father and son behind the fake smiles and state records. "I know you're still upset over me and Denise—"

"Upset? Is that what you think? That I'm upset about you and Denise?" Bitter laughter rumbled in my chest. "I'm not upset about you and Denise; you two deserve each other. You have no fucking idea what it's been like growing up in your shadow, a man respected and revered by an entire town. Knowing that without you, I probably wouldn't be where I am today, but at the same time, knowing I'm *who* I am because of you. Cold. Callous... Cruel."

"Jason, I—"

"Save it, Dad," I ground out. "You have everything you need now, right? You have Denise and a son you can live vicariously through. And me? I've got football. At least I know the game will never disappoint me."

23

Felicity

"HAVE YOU SEEN JASON?" were the first words out of Hailee's mouth as she hurried over to us.

"No, we've been here the whole time," Asher said.

"Crap, he and his dad got into it and Jason stormed off. He looked pretty pissed. I was going to go after him but someone stopped me to talk about the paintings."

"Fuck," Cam grumbled, pulling Hailee onto his lap. "This is the last thing we need."

"You should go after him," Asher said to me while I obsessed over how his best friend held my best friend. Intimately. Tenderly. As if she was the most precious thing in the whole world.

"I don't know," I said, dejection crawling up my throat like a cockroach, "he didn't seem pleased to see me earlier." In fact he'd acted like seeing me was the last thing he wanted. "Maybe I should just leave."

"Ride or die, remember?" Hailee said, her eyes pleading with me. "At least try to talk to him. He looked really upset."

My heart ached for Jason and I wanted to go after him, I did, but I wasn't sure my heart would survive another rejection.

"He needs you, Fee." Asher gave me a half-smile. "Besides, if you don't go after him, one of us has to and I'm sure he'd rather see a pretty face than Cam's ugly mug."

"Fine, I'll go." I stood up. "Any ideas where I should try to look?" Coach Hasson's place was like a maze.

"Try the boat shed or down by the river."

"Okay, wish me luck."

The three of them smiled. "Good luck," Hailee said. "And don't take no for an answer."

On shaky legs, I crossed the Hasson's yard, taking the path away from the main patio down to the river. It was dark out, nothing but the silvery hue of the moon lighting the way.

"Jason?" I whisper-hissed. "Are you down here?"

Met with nothing but silence, I kept walking, bypassing the boat shed.

There was no one down here. I dropped down onto a rickety bench, watching the river shimmer and dance in the distance.

All night Jason had avoided me. But despite his cold shoulder, Hailee was right. I needed closure. I needed to know once and for all where I stood. Whether I'd dreamed up the growing connection between us. Because I knew what I felt, and Jason liked me. He just didn't know how to handle it.

The seconds ticked by, the air like cold fingers ghosting over my face and neck. Shucking into my jacket, I stood up, ready to admit defeat and return to my friends when I heard a rustle. "Jason?" I called.

"You shouldn't be down here," he said from the shadows. I stepped closer, the sliver of moonlight bouncing off his hard profile, making him look even more intimidating than usual.

"I came to see if you're okay. Hailee said she saw you arguing with your dad."

"Hailee needs to learn to mind her own fucking business." His tone matched his eyes.

Cold.

Guarded.

Completely devoid of emotion, despite the anger rippling off him in dark waves.

A shiver skittered along my spine and I hugged myself tight. "Jason, come on, talk to me, please."

"And say what? I thought you got the memo yesterday."

"So that's it?" I stuffed down the sting of his harsh words. "You're just going to walk away and pretend this, *us*, is nothing."

"It *is* nothing," he ground out. "I don't know what else I can do to make you see that. You said it yourself, Giles; you were nothing more than a game. A game I won, and now I'm done with you."

Tears pricked the corners of my eyes, but I would not cry, not in front of him. He didn't deserve my tears.

Not a single one.

"Why are doing this? Why are you being so cruel? You care, Jason," I said, steeling myself, "I know you do. You're just scared. Scared of letting yourself feel something. Well, newsflash, I'm scared too. But I'm here. I'm willing to take a risk on you. On us." My chest heaved with the weight of the words but Jason looked unaffected.

Indifferent.

"There is no us." His sharp words made me flinch. "Why can't you just accept that?"

"Because I don't believe you. Last night—"

"You think last night meant something?" He sneered, the harshness of his stare like a hundred tiny daggers cutting into my skin. "I was doing Hailee a favor and saving everyone anymore embarrassment. You were a fucking mess."

The words crashed over me, making my heart lurch into my throat. Blood pounded between my ears.

A fucking mess.

He hadn't saved me because he cared... he'd saved me out of pity.

"God, I'm stupid." *So stupid.* "I let them all convince me you liked me, that you needed me. But you don't need anyone."

People with no hearts didn't have room to care about others let alone *need* them.

"Finally figured it out, huh?" He scratched his jaw absentmindedly.

"I hope you find what you're looking for, Jason," I said with nothing but quiet confidence. I might have been breaking inside, but he wouldn't see me crumble.

Jason didn't say anything as I turned and started walking away. But then his voice perforated the heavy silence. "Oh and Giles..."

"Yes?" I snapped over my shoulder, barely hanging on by a thread.

"You might want to think about applying to another school. Penn isn't big enough for the both of us and I don't know what crap you're trying to pull but I don't want you there."

My lips parted on a pained gasp. I wanted to argue, to tell him me applying for UPenn had nothing to do with him and everything to do with my parents, *my* future, but a figure burst from the shadows.

"Hey, baby," Jenna said, sidling up to Jason as if I wasn't standing right there with tears in my eyes. "Miss me? Oh, hey, Felicity, I didn't see you there."

She saw me all right.

She just got great satisfaction over watching the blood drain from my face.

"You might want to run along now, unless you want to see the show, if you know what I mean." She smirked before pressing her lips to Jason's, making sure I got a front row seat.

He wasn't invested in it; he wasn't touching her or kissing her back. He was watching me. His hard eyes silently daring me to call him out.

It took everything I had not to jump on her back and tear her away from the guy who had unknowingly stolen my heart.

No, that wasn't right. He hadn't stolen it. I'd handed it over willingly. Secretly hoping it was enough.

That *I* was enough.

When all along, I knew wasn't.

Jason Ford was the devil in sheep's clothing and I was nothing more than a game wrapped up in a pretty package.

Something to pass the time.

A game he'd already grown tired of.

"I never had you down as a voyeur," Jenna's voice snapped me from my morose reverie. "But if you want to watch, maybe you'll learn a thing or two." She snickered into Jason's shoulder.

Damn that hurt. I didn't want to believe he'd told her that I'd given up my v-card to him, but at this point, anything was possible. Because I didn't know Jason.

Maybe I never had.

"You're welcome to him." I barely managed to choke out the words.

Just for a brief moment I thought I saw a flash of regret in Jason's gaze, but then he captured Jenna's mouth and closed his eyes, losing himself in the kiss, showing me he hadn't changed at all. He was still the cold-hearted bastard he'd always claimed to be. Only it was too late. He'd reeled me and then spat me out, not caring that he'd smashed my heart into a thousand pieces.

Pieces I knew would never heal right.

Somehow, despite the gaping hole in my chest, I managed to turn and walk away from them with my head held high.

From Jason.

For what I promised myself would be the final time.

"This is nice," Mya said as we ate cookies and ice cream and watched cheesy movies. It had been Hailee's idea after the disastrous end to last night.

I hadn't even stopped to tell them I was leaving, I just needed to be far, far away from Jason and his poisonous words.

"I can't remember the last time I had a girls' night."

"Pre-Cameron we did this a lot. Although most of our sleepovers ended up with Hailee plotting revenge on Jason."

"Hey," Hailee said, "We still hang out. You make it sound like now I have Cameron, I'm not around."

"I'm joking, Hails. I'm happy for you, I am. After everything they put you through, you deserve all the happiness."

"Your brother sounds like a grade-A asshole." Mya's eyes crinkled.

"My *step*-brother is an asshole. But he's different lately." Her gaze flicked to mine.

"Yeah, well, different or not," I sighed, "he's still a cold-hearted bastard."

Mya and Hailee both looked at me with sympathy in their eyes. "Please don't do that; don't look at me like he ripped out my heart and trampled all over it. I wanted closure and I got it."

"Yeah, but I still can't believe he did that. And with Jenna, of all people."

"Really, Hails? Because this is Jason we're talking about. He's disappointed me at every turn, why should last night have been any different?"

"I just thought that this time he would..." She swallowed the words.

"I know," I said quietly, "me too."

Although I knew exactly who Jason Ford was, part of me had still foolishly hoped he had changed. That I'd changed him. I had managed to convince myself I was different to the Jenna Jarvis' of the world when all along I was exactly the same.

It was a bitter pill to swallow. But at least I'd seen his true colors once and for all. I could move on knowing I'd tried to smash through Jason's steel walls. Even if it did suck that I failed.

"If you ask me, you're better off without him. Jason Ford loves only two things: himself and football."

"You're not wrong there." Hailee leaned over to high five Mya.

"Anyway, enough boy talk. I thought this was supposed to be girls' night. What are your plans for after high school, Mya?"

"Ooh straight into the heavy stuff, I like it." She crossed her legs in front of her and pushed her spiral curls from her face. "I always wanted to do something to help people, you know. Like drugs counselling or a school guidance counsellor."

"Psych major?" I asked.

"Maybe, or education. I haven't really narrowed it down, but I'm applying to Montclair State and Michigan. I want to go out of state but not too far away."

"Me and Cameron are headed to Michigan."

"No way."

Hails nodded. "He was supposed to go to UPenn with Jason, but—"

"But he realized he couldn't bear to be apart from Hailee and applied to Michigan instead." The way my best friend blushed at my words was so darn cute.

"Wow, that's... serious."

Hailee shrugged. "I couldn't imagine going without him."

"I miss that," Mya sighed. "Having someone to make plans with. What about you, Flick? Given anymore thought to your plans?"

"I thought the plan was to study business." Hailee frowned at me.

"It was... I mean, it is."

"But..."

"But I might be having teeny tiny second thoughts."

"Oh shit, do your parents know?"

"What do you think?" My eyes rolled dramatically.

"I thought you were happy applying to UPenn and following in their footsteps?"

"I mean, yeah, I was. It's always been the plan. Instilled in me from day one. But now, now I'm not so sure it's what I want."

Jason's cruel words from last night filled my head. He thought I was applying to UPenn because it was where he was going, but it couldn't be further from the truth. I was applying because it was expected. Because my parents wanted me to follow in their footsteps and continue their legacy. The exciting world of white-collar employment. And until recently, I had been all too happy to make them happy.

"You never said anything," Hailee sounded dejected, her expression crestfallen.

"You know me, Hails," I gave her a tight smile, "I'm a people pleaser, not a rulebreaker." Until Jason. I left that strictly to Hailee and her vendetta against the guys.

"But this is your future. You can't do something just because your parents want you to."

"I know." It had just taken me a while, and a little push from Mya, to find the courage to pursue my own path.

"So what are you going to do?"

That was the million-dollar question. I could pursue business at UPenn and make my parents happy or I could go after what I wanted. Chase my dreams.

The only problem was; I still didn't know what they were.

"I'm going to work on my list."

"Your list?" Hailee groaned. "Hasn't that already caused enough trouble?"

"Actually, Mya helped me rethink a few things. I think it could be good for me to work toward completing it, and who knows, maybe I'll figure out exactly what I want to do with my life."

"Now that sounds like a plan I can get on board with." Mya grinned, her eyes sparkling with eagerness, as if I was a project she just couldn't wait to get her hands on.

"You know I've got your back, whatever you decide," Hailee added. "Just because I have Cameron now, doesn't mean I'm not one-hundred percent here for you."

"Thank you. But first things first..." I dug my cell out of my pocket and found Jason's number.

"Is that what I think it is?" Hailee craned her neck to get a better look.

"Yep. I need to draw a line under Jason and his games." My thumb hovered over the 'delete' button. Drawing in a deep breath, I closed my eyes, and pressed it.

"To new beginnings." Mya declared, raising her soda in the air.

"New beginnings," I echoed, clinking my glass against hers.

But the sound of Hailee clearing her throat cut through our soft laughter. "Now are you going to fess up about what *really* happened between the two of you?"

Well, damn.

"Seriously? You want to know? I figured you were mentally scarred from New York."

"I don't want to know the graphic details, but yeah, I want to know." She gave me a tentative smile. "After all, I need to know how badly I need to get him back for hurting you." Her mouth curved into a devious smirk and soon the three of us were falling around my bedroom floor in fits of laughter.

And the ache in my heart faded.

Just a little bit.

24

Jason

"ARE you going to drill daggers into my head all morning?" I finally dragged my eyes to Hailee's, and she clucked her tongue in disgust. "Whatever's on your mind, just spit it out so I can finish my breakfast in peace." I all but growled the words.

"I'm just wondering what made you this way. I know you have Daddy issues, but join the fucking club. Most of us have parent issues. Which makes me think there must be something else. A reason you're so... so cruel."

"I don't have to answer to you." My eyes narrowed.

"You're right, you don't. But I'm asking anyway." Hailee glared right back. "Why? Why did you do that to her?"

"Am I supposed to know what the fuck you're talking about?"

Her nostrils flared, a streak of pink coloring each cheek. My step-sister was pissed and instead of trying to cool the flames, I was stoking them. But she didn't have the first fucking clue about why I did the things I did.

No one did.

"Felicity came to Seniors Night for you," she hissed. "To be there for you. And you went and threw it back in her face. I know the two of you have been meeting. I know she slept with you... again. I know everything."

It wasn't her harsh tone that had me internally flinching, it was the fact Felicity had told her everything. Things I'd thought had been just between the two of us. Not that it mattered now.

None of it did.

"Yeah, well, it's over."

"Are you even listening to yourself? You were seeing her in secret... why?"

"I don't—"

"Because you care about her. Stop pretending you don't. You think we don't all see the way you look at her? Even Thatcher and his goons noticed. You watch her. You watch her when you think no one is looking, so don't stand there and tell me whatever was happening between the two of you was nothing." Hailee slammed her hands down on the table, making the breakfast bowls clatter.

"So I care?" I yelled back, my thin rope of control snapping. "It doesn't matter. None of it fucking matters. I can't afford any distractions next year."

"If you care about someone, they're not a distraction, Jason," her voice softened a fraction, "they're a support."

"It doesn't matter."

"Stop saying it doesn't matter. It fucking matters," she roared back, her chest heaving with the strain of her words. "Felicity deserves better. And you promised; you promised me you wouldn't hurt her..." Tears pooled in her eyes, twisting my gut.

"No, I didn't," I said coolly.

"Yes, you did."

"No, I didn't. I promised to only ever do what I think's best for her, and this... this is what's best."

Hailee shook her head, cussing under her breath. "That doesn't even make any sense. If you wanted to fuck Jenna, you could have at least waited until Felicity left. She was right there and you rubbed Jenna in her face. So tell me, Jason, how is that what's best for her?"

"She needed to know we were done." The words almost got stuck in my throat and I sucked in a harsh breath.

"Oh my god, listen to yourself. You make me sick." She slumped back in her chair defeated. "I really thought you were changing. I thought you'd finally shed that hard shell of yours. But it really was a game, wasn't it?"

I gave her a dismissive shrug.

"You think the whole world revolves around you. That just because you're some football god you can do whatever the hell you want. But this is high school, Jason. Soon you won't be at the top of the food chain anymore and I hope you get a taste of your own medicine."

"Are you done?" I growled.

"Done?" She smirked. "I'm only just getting started. You're so self-centered you can't even see what's going on around you. You didn't stop for a second to consider Felicity's feelings. It never even occurred to you that maybe she has her own shit going on. You automatically assumed she was applying to UPenn to follow *you* there. Jason Ford. Football star and epic asshole." bitter laughter spilled from Hailee's lips, "but you couldn't be more wrong."

"What the hell is that supposed to mean?"

"Maybe you should have pulled your head out of your ass for five seconds and asked her about her own life. But now you'll never get the chance."

"Yeah? Why's that?" I sounded composed but her words had completely disarmed me.

Hands pressed firmly against the table, Hailee stood slowly, the chair scraping against the tiles, the sound cutting me right to the bone. "Because, dear brother, you might have won *the game* but the only real loser here is you." She walked to the door, glancing back at the last second. "And Jason?"

"Yeah?" I croaked.

"If you know what's good for you, you'll stay away from Felicity. She doesn't need you back complicating her life anymore than it already is."

Her warning hung between us, and I knew whatever progress we'd made in patching up our relationship had just been torn wide open again.

And I only had myself to blame.

"Hey," Cam said as I entered the gym. We had morning practice, and I'd been bracing myself for his tirade. So his greeting was unexpected to say the least.

"You're still talking to me then? Because after the lecture Hailee gave me this morning, I wasn't sure if I should wear body armor."

"Come on, Jase," he let out a heavy sigh, "you had to know it wouldn't end well. You really hurt—"

"Yeah, yeah, save me the speech. I already heard it." We moved over to the chest press and started adding weights.

"So what happens now?"

"Nothing happens. It's done, we're done. Felicity knew what she was getting into."

"But—"

"There are no fucking buts," I ground out, irritation swimming in my veins. "It's done. Over. Did you know she applied to Penn?" My brow rose.

"Hailee mentioned it, but I didn't, no. You think she did it because she knew you were going there?"

"I don't know what the fuck to think, but she can't go there."

"Jase, you can't tell someone where they can or can't go to college, man. It's her future and Hailee said something about her parents being alumni."

"I don't care if her parents are best friends with the Dean, she can't go there." *I can't have her there, everywhere I turn.*

When I met Cam's eyes again, he was scrutinizing me. "What?" I barked.

"What's really going on with you?"

"Save the *Dr Phil* routine, I had enough of that from Asher."

"You called?" he appeared out of nowhere.

"Great, now I have to listen to the two of you bitch."

"Nope." Ash held up his hands as I got situated on the bench. "No bitchin' here. The way I see it, now you've cast Fee aside, she's fair gam—"

"Don't even fucking think about it." My chest rumbled.

"About what?" He played dumb.

"Ash, don't push him."

"Push him? How could I possibly be pushing him when he chewed her up and spit her out like she's nothing?" His smile was easy, but his tone was cool.

Yeah, Asher was pissed and I couldn't blame him.

"You want my sloppy seconds, Bennet?" I swallowed the guilt crawling up my throat, and doing what I did best, I dialed up my asshole meter. "She's all yours."

"You're a heartless fucker, you know that, Ford?" he said before storming off.

Cam shook his head, rubbing the back of his neck. "Was that really necessary?"

"He's wanted her since day one."

"And you'd be okay with him being with her? Because you know he'll probably go after her just to prove a point."

Shrugging, I pushed the press harder, grunting with exertion. "Like he said, she's fair game." The words snaked around my heart.

"I don't believe you," Cam said. "You're a cruel motherfucker but you care about her."

"Yeah, well I don't care enough."

I half-expected Cam to take a page out of Asher's book and storm off, but he didn't. Cameron was loyal to the bone. It's why it had taken him so long to go after what he really wanted: Hailee. Still, he wasn't impressed with my attitude and for the next ten minutes, we worked in painful silence. All while he studied me, trying to see past my icy exterior. But if anyone was an expert on keeping their emotions locked down, it was me. I'd had years of practice and I wasn't about to open up now.

I had more important things to think about.

By the time lunch rolled around, all I wanted was to eat my turkey sub in peace. But even that was too fucking much to ask.

"You know, if you want to go over there, I'm sure they wouldn't—"

My head snapped up to Grady and I levelled with him a hard look. "Jeez," he breathed out. "Someone has a giant stick up their ass. I'm just saying—"

"Well, don't."

As if they heard our argument, Asher and Felicity both looked over at us. Ash held my stare, a silent 'fuck you' glittering in his eyes. I let my eyes run right over him to her. The blood drained from Felicity's face as she tried to remain unaffected, but I saw the tell-tale signs. Wide eyes, the way her breath hitched, and I knew if I was close enough, if I ran my fingers up her neck, her skin would be warm.

Felicity wasn't the only one affected though. My heart was racing like I'd just done an hour of cardio. It beat so hard I felt it in my skull. Curling my hands into fists, I pressed them into my jeans, urging myself to calm the fuck down. She saw it though. She saw it and instead of letting it go, she decided to bait me. Sliding closer to Asher, Felicity leaned into him, laughing at something he said.

"Easy, bro," Grady said under his breath. "Before you break something." He got all up in my face, blocking my view of Asher and Felicity. "It's not worth it," his voice was low.

"Yeah, I'm cool." I sat back, forcing my hands to uncurl.

"Eyes on the prize, remember?" Grady moved back, squeezing my shoulder. "You need to get laid, work off some of that tension, Cap."

"Did someone say my name?" Jenna appeared, a seductive smile on her face. "Hey, baby." She made a show of wiggling onto my lap, draping her arm around my neck like she belonged there.

Like *I* belonged to *her*.

"S'up?"

"You, if I have anything to say about it." Dipping her hand between us, she grasped my junk.

Grady bellowed with laughter, high-fiving a couple of the players. "Yo, Jenna, where's the rest of you?"

"The girls will be here soon enough." She shot him a suggestive wink.

"Mr. Ford, Miss Jarvis," Principal Finnigan appeared out of nowhere, clearing his throat. "Please keep it clean. This a school cafeteria, not a strip club." His narrowed gaze fixed right on me, his disdain for everything I represented etched into every line of his face, and there were plenty. "All set for Friday?"

I gave him an imperceptible nod.

"Well, I look forward to it." He stalked off to his next unsuspecting victim.

"Dude needs to get laid," someone said, causing our table to break out in laughter.

"He really doesn't like you, does he?" Mackey asked.

I shrugged. He didn't like me, but it didn't matter. Soon the season would be over and then he couldn't touch me.

Grady threw me a look, but I shook it off. I wasn't about to do anything stupid, anything to jeopardize the team's shot at the Championship. But after that, Thatcher was mine. All I had to do was keep my cool and refuse to be drawn any further into his games.

Jenna swept her hair off her shoulder and dipped her mouth to my ear. "I want you, let's sneak off to the locker room."

It would have been so easy to say yes.

So easy to let her drop to her knees and help me forget all the bullshit.

"Jason, what do you say? Shall we get out of here?" She nipped my ear, but I was too busy watching Felicity.

Watching her watch me.

"Maybe later, yeah?" I gave Jenna an easy smile, sliding my eyes back to Felicity.

But she was gone.

25

Felicity

"OKAY, well thanks for getting back to me. Please keep me in mind if anything comes up." I hung up, rubbing a hand down my face.

"No luck?" Mya dropped down beside me.

"No. I called every veterinary clinic within a fifteen-mile radius."

"Well, that sucks. What about pounds?"

"There's only two locally. One does offer volunteer positions, but they have no vacancies and the other one is undergoing a restructure so they're not taking on new staff at the moment."

"You could widen the radius."

"I could but anything further and my parents will get suspicious."

Mya nudged my shoulder. "You could always just tell them."

"I could but I want to be sure first. If I tell them and it doesn't work out, I'll be causing a lot of heartache for nothing."

"You really think they'll be that upset? Veterinary school is a solid plan."

"But it isn't *their* plan and it's at least eight years in school."

"But do *you* want it?"

"I think so. I mean, I've taken all the right courses and I love animals. But I'll need to talk to Miss Hampstead about changing my application and I'll definitely need to find some hands-on experience."

"Ooh, you could do some dog walking for your neighbors or run a doggie day care service on the weekend."

"Oh yeah, my anti-pet parents would love that while they overreacted every day that I was going to get Tetanus, or the house invaded with fleas, or the neighbors complain about barking."

"Okay I get it, over-cautious parent alert. There must be a vacancy somewhere for you."

"Hey, what are you two doing out here?" Hailee's brows bunched. "I went to study hall but you weren't there."

"I wanted to get a head start on calling local veterinary clinics and Mya found me out here."

"Any luck?"

"Nothing yet. I may have to figure out a plan B."

"Have you tried the clinic in town?" she asked.

"No, it's too close to home. If Mom and Dad find—"

"You don't have to tell them why you're doing it yet, just that you want to try new things."

"I don't know... it would be ideal being so local." I wouldn't have to worry about travel time and maybe I could help after school.

"You should call them," Mya said, handing me her phone, the clinic's number already punched in.

"Now?"

"Can you think of a better time?"

Hailee sat down beside me, the two of them giving me expectant stares.

"Fine, but I bet they have nothing." I'd left it too late to try to find something.

I hit call and waited.

"Hello, Rixon Veterinary Clinic, Regina speaking. How can I help you?"

"Hmm, hi, Regina. I'm a senior at Rixon High School and I was wondering if you have any volunteering opportunities? I'm considering studying animal science at college and really wanted some hands-on experience."

Mya gave me a little thumbs up.

"I didn't catch your name?"

"Oh? I'm sorry, it's Felicity."

"Well, firstly thanks for thinking of us, Felicity. I'd love to be able to tell you we have something right now, but unfortunately—"

"You don't." My shoulders slumped. "I expected as much."

"I'm sure you can appreciate, we have a rigorous process in place for all of our volunteers and we only recently recruited."

"Of course, I completely understand."

"That said, I might be able to arrange you a visit to our sister-center across town."

"The pet rescue place?" I asked.

"Yes, A Brand New Tail. There's no permanent volunteer spots at the minute but I'm sure George, the manager, wouldn't mind showing you around."

"That would be great, thank you."

"Excellent. Drop me an email and I'll forward it to George. We can also add you to the waitlist should anything come up..."

"Thank you so much." We said goodbye and hung up.

"So..." Mya asked.

"They can let me look around, but they don't have anything permanent right now."

"Well, it's a step in the right direction." She gave me a reassuring smile. "And who knows. Maybe you can work your magic on George and get him to give you a shift or two?"

"Mya!" My cheeks burned. "I would never—"

"Relax, I'm joking. But it's good to see you smile, girl."

It felt good to smile. Until I spotted Cameron, Asher… and Jason heading in our direction. My breath caught in my throat. Even now, after everything, my heart still wanted him. The rest of me wanted nothing more than to watch him combust into flames, but my heart, well it wasn't quite there yet.

Before they reached us, Jason split away from his friends and took off toward the gym. I let out a little sigh of relief, ignoring the way my stomach sank, and pasted on the brightest smile I could for Cameron and Asher.

"Ladies," Asher said. "We missed you at lunch." His eyes settled on mine, asking me things I didn't want to answer.

"We had a… thing." Mya winked at me.

"A thing. I like things. You could have invited me."

"Asher," Hailee warned.

"It's okay, Hails. You don't all have to pretend this isn't awkward. But I'm fine. Truly."

"That's the spirit, Fee, baby. So what's happening?"

"Felicity is trying to figure out her future," Hailee said.

"Sounds interesting. Anything we can help with?"

"Not unless you know of a veterinary clinic taking on volunteers."

"Huh." Asher's brows pinched. "I never had you down as a cat lover."

"Hey, I like dogs too. Anything soft and cute really, I don't discriminate."

"You've tried the one downtown?"

I nodded. "They have nothing. I'll figure something out." I waved him off, hoping to deflect the attention from me to someone else. The last thing I needed was Asher on the case. He was worse than a dog with a bone.

"We should probably head to practice before Coach comes looking for us." Cameron reached for Hailee, pulling her to her feet. "I'll miss you."

"Miss you too," she said, kissing him.

"Miss you three," Asher added around a grin.

Cameron flipped him off behind Hailee's back.

"You'll be at the game Friday, right?" Asher turned his attention to me and Mya.

"Actually," I tucked my long bangs behind my ear, "I don't think so."

"What the fuck? You have to come. It's our final game before the play-offs."

"Hails will be there, right, Hails?"

"Yes, she will," Cam answered for her.

"See, you have to come."

"Hailee can hang out with Cam's parents." His mom and dad were making the trip to Brennington since she was finally feeling a little better.

"What about you, Mya? Can I count on you to be there, cheering us on?"

"Oh shoot, did you say Friday? I think I'm washing my hair."

"*I think I'm washing my hair*," he muttered beneath his breath, rolling his eyes. "If you don't come, you can't come party with us afterwards."

"Whatever will we do?" Mya clutched my hands, feigning disappointment.

"We could always hang out at The Alley?" I suggested. "Or maybe get drunk down by the river again, that was fun. Oh, I know, we could—"

"Okay, okay, you both made your point. But let's face it, whatever you do, wherever you hang out, it's not going to be half as much fun as being with me." Asher's amused gaze lingered on Mya until he winked and walked off, not bothering to wait for Cameron.

"You really shouldn't encourage him," he remarked.

"He can handle it," Mya scoffed, her eyes tracking Asher's retreating form. She could play down the chemistry between the two of them, but she wasn't fooling anyone.

Jealousy stirred in my chest, which was crazy. Because I didn't want Asher like that. But I couldn't deny his attention softened the blow of Jason's rejection somewhat. Not to mention the part of me that worried if Mya and Asher hooked up, I'd lose my two closest friends to Raiders.

"Hey, are you okay?" Mya nudged me again and I flashed her a weak smile.

"Me? I'm good."

"Everything's going to work out, Flick. I can feel it in my bones."

"Speaking of bones," Cam cleared his throat, "I'd better go before Coach breaks some of mine for being tardy. I'll see you tonight?" he asked Hailee.

"Of course. Bye."

He pulled her in for one last kiss and disappeared after Asher.

"What?" she said, noticing us both glaring at her.

"You two are so cute it's disgusting." Mya grinned.

"So disgusting," I added around a smirk despite the sinking feeling in my stomach.

I wanted that.

Wanted someone to look at me the way Cameron looked at her.

But I would never get it so long as I was stuck on Jason.

"Felicity, sweetheart, is that you?" Mom's voice filtered down the hall as I kicked off my shoes and dropped my keys on the sideboard.

"Hey, Mom." I entered the kitchen.

"How was book club?"

"Good, thanks. No Dad?"

"He needed to stay late at the office."

"Again? He's always working."

"Sure is. You know how it is, got to keep that roof over our heads. Well, you will soon enough." She chuckled.

"So I've been thinking," I said, sliding onto one of the stools. "Since its senior year and all, that I might like to do some volunteering."

"What a wonderful idea." Mom came over to the breakfast island to join me. "I'm sure me or your father can arrange some work experience with—"

"Actually, Mom, I was thinking I might do something else."

"Something else?" Her brows pinched. "I'm sorry, I'm not sure I understand."

"I just realized there's so much I've always wanted to do and time's running out, so I thought now might be a good time to experiment."

"Hmm, that sounds kind of distracting, sweetheart. You have book club; that's outside the box."

Dear God, if she though book club was outside the box, I had no hope getting her on side for my new plan.

"It's not exactly giving me major life experience though, Mom. I want to learn something new, try new things. Before I know it, college will be here, and I'll have a full schedule of classes. I don't want to leave high school with any regrets."

"No, you're right, you're absolutely right." Her bright smile gave me a smidgen of hope. "I bet if your father speaks to Killian at the bank he could help out or I could ask Mrs. Fenton if she has anything suitable."

My bubble burst almost as quickly as it began inflating.

"Mrs. Fenton from the care home?" Disbelief filled my voice.

"That's the one. I'm sure the residents would love to have a visit from you."

"That wasn't quite what I had in mind, Mom. I was thinking something more along the lines of working with... animals."

"Animals?" she barely contained her surprise. "But why on earth would you want to work with animals?"

"Well, I did always want a pet, remember? And imagine how much fun it must be working with all cute little puppies and kittens."

"Cute and dangerous, Felicity. And don't even get me started on the allergies."

"Mom, I don't have allergies."

"Because we raised you in a pet free environment."

"I'm not sure it works that way."

"It seems like an awful waste of your time when you could be getting real hands on experience in the workplace."

She didn't get it. She never had. Which is why I'd never veered from the plan. *Their* plan.

It was just easier that way. But now I'd considered a different plan, I couldn't just switch it off. If my brief time with Jason had taught me anything, it was to go after what you wanted.

"I think it'll be good for me," I said defiantly, feeling something stir in my chest.

"I'm not sure I agree, sweetheart. And I can only imagine what your father will say; but if it's something you really want to do," she gave a resigned sigh, "then I suppose it would be okay, as long as we've checked out they have up to date health and safety policies."

"Really?"

"You've worked hard for the last three years, Felicity. You deserve some downtime."

It wasn't exactly a gleaming endorsement, but I'd take it.

"Thanks, Mom, it means a lot to have your support." Whether or not she'd feel the same if she knew the truth was another matter.

"Sweetheart, all I want is for you to be happy," she reached over the counter, "you know that, right?"

I nodded over the lump in my throat. She wanted me to be happy... doing what had made her so happy. But I wanted more. I realized that now. I wanted to chase my own dreams even when they led me down the wrong path. I wanted to make mistakes and learn from them. I didn't want to settle for average anymore; not when I could have amazing.

There was still one fatal flaw in my new plan—I wasn't sure I would ever be brave enough to tell my parents.

26

Jason

"LET'S GO NUMBER ONE, you're slacking," one of the assistant coaches yelled across the field. I cussed under my breath, pumping my legs harder, pushing through the wall of pain closing in around me.

I was fucking tired.

Thanks to Thatcher and the shit with Felicity, I was barely sleeping. My muscles ached and my head pounded but it was practice and I had a job to do. Giving anything less than one-hundred and ten percent was not an option.

"That's it, QB, keep it up."

I felt eyes on me as I ran the drill again. Looking around, I found Asher glaring at me. The little shit was still pissed over our last conversation about Felicity and it sucked that I couldn't tell him the truth. But he'd get over it. He always did.

"Hey," Cam said, jogging over to me. "You okay?"

"I'm good. Ready to kick some Brennington ass Friday." It was our last game and we were playing at their place. Then we had a rest week before the first round of the play-offs.

"You and your dad figure things out?"

We'd barely spoken since Seniors Night but that was nothing new.

"Not really."

"I know you're angry at him for everything but maybe—"

"I appreciate the advice, I do." I grunted as my hands closed around the pass from Grady. "But I'd rather not do this. You're with Hailee now, save it for her."

"I can be here for both of you. Besides, Hailee and her mom are patching things up."

My brow arched. "Guess we're not so similar after all." Because I could barely look at my old man for his indiscretions, let alone try to smooth things over.

I guess it was different for me, though. I'd known for years who my father really was. Long before Denise and Hailee came on the scene. She was just the final straw where my mom was concerned.

So no, I wasn't in a hurry to forgive the man who had ruined our family. But I was in a hurry to get the hell out of this town. A clean break. That's what I wanted. To escape out from under the shadow of Kent Ford and forge my own legacy.

"Heard anything more from Thatcher? I was thinking perhaps we should have told Coach—"

"You think he doesn't know exactly what happened with the art project? He's not an idiot. But he can't afford Finnigan sticking his nose where it doesn't belong."

"Has he said anything to you?"

"No, but he's hinted at it."

"So what are you going to do? Thatcher won't—"

"If Thatcher knows what's good for him, he'll stay across the river until after the play-offs."

"You really think he'll do that, after everything?"

I didn't, but there was no use telling Cam that. Not when he wanted to run off and tattle to Coach.

"I don't know how many times I have to say it," I ground out, "I can handle Thatcher."

Cameron didn't look convinced, but I was done arguing over something that I couldn't change. Thatcher wouldn't stop coming until he got what he wanted.

Me.

So it was my plan to lie low and stay out of trouble at least until we were crowned State champs.

"Jase, get over here, Son." Coach beckoned me over with his usual crooked finger.

"He doesn't look too happy."

"I'm sure it's nothing," I grunted, ripping off my helmet and shouldering past Cam to head for where Coach and one of the assistant coaches were talking.

"What's up, Coach?"

The assistant coach excused himself and left us to it. Coach Hasson gripped my shoulder. "Walk with me."

We looped around the guys and walked to the other end of the field. The air was frigid, the first signs of winter evident in the dewy grass. "Talk to me about what happened with Miss Raine's art project."

"We told you, Coach. It was an accident. We were moving the—"

"I know what you told me, Jase, but I'm asking for the truth." He gave me a pointed look. "There are rumors circulating that the Eagles had something to do with it. Wouldn't happen to know anything about that would you?"

"Not me, Coach." I jammed my hands into the waistband of my pants and kept my expression neutral.

"Jase, level with me. If it comes out Thatcher and his band of idiots from across the river were responsible, I won't be able to protect you from Principal Finnigan and we both know he's just waiting for an excuse to pull you from the team."

"I don't know what to tell you, Coach." Rubbing the back of my neck, I gave him a half-smile.

"This rivalry will be the death of me." He shook his head with frustration. "I'm going to miss the hell out of you next year, but I can't say I'll miss you and this Thatcher kid going at it every time I turn my back."

"I'm so—"

"Listen to me and listen to me good, Jason. Four more games. That's all that's standing between you and the championship. It would be a damn shame if you ruined what has been a near perfect season because you didn't know when to quit it. Keep your head on straight, you hear me?"

"Yes, Sir."

"I mean it, Son. If I find out you're planning a retaliation on the Eagles, you won't have to worry about Finnigan because I'll be the one making you sit out. I've turned a blind eye for too long where the two of you are concerned. Stupid high school pranks are one thing, but when it starts affecting the people around you, that's when it's time to call it a day."

If he wanted to make me feel guiltier than I already did, he'd succeeded. It slithered through my gut, twisting and tightening.

"You're a good kid, Jason. I meant every word I said at Seniors Night, but sometimes you're blinded to the game and that makes you your own worst enemy. From someone who remembers what it's like to want it so bad you can't see anything else, it's a big old world out there, and there is room for more than just football. It doesn't feel like it now, when you're on the precipice of greatness, but trust me when I say, it's true." He gripped my shoulder again. "Now get out of here. I don't want to see you again until we're boarding the buses for Friday's game, okay?"

"But, Coach, that's still two days away."

"I'm giving you all some well-deserved downtime. I'm not worried about Friday and neither should you be. It's what comes after that matters. You've worked hard this season Jason, try being an eighteen-year-old kid for once; you never know, it might suit you." Coach winked at me, before straightening his ball cap and strolling off toward the gym.

Downtime?

It didn't figure into the equation. There was always something to be working toward, training for. Even when the season was over, I was in the gym working out, or working with the guys on drills. Perfecting the play, strengthening any weak links in the chain.

"Well?" Cam strolled over to me. "What's the verdict?"

"He wants us to take some downtime."

"Downtime? Sounds good to me." He grinned.

It was in that split second, I realized how much we'd changed. Maybe it was Hailee or his mom being sick or the looming future, but football was no longer the most important thing in Cam's life anymore.

Maybe it never had been.

I didn't ever think anything would come in between us, our plans, but it had. Yet, I couldn't blame him. I'd never seen him as happy as he was with my step-sister.

It had never been in my plan to meet someone, to let someone in. To distract me.

Then *she* came along.

Felicity Giles.

Fuck, had she taken me by surprise. A dark-haired angel with no filter and crazy fashion sense. She was everything I didn't want or need, and yet, she'd infiltrated my steel exterior before I even had time to realize what was happening.

"You're thinking about her, aren't you?" Cam's voice burst my daydream.

"Who, Hailee?" I quipped.

"You know exactly who I mean." He smirked.

"Doesn't matter."

"You keep saying that..."

"Because it's true. We're done." We had to be.

"If you say so."

I did.

Even if it was the biggest lie of all.

"And that's how it's done, ladies," Coach yanked off his ball cap and thrust it in the air. "A damn near perfect season." If we hadn't have blown our last game.

It was a bitter pill to swallow, but it didn't matter. We were in the play-offs. One step closer to the end goal.

"Get showered and get changed. I want to get out of here and back home stat."

A chorus of 'Yes, Coach' rang out around me, the buzz of the win still crackling in the air.

"Hey, Cap, check it out," Grady flashed me his cell.

@ThatcherQB1: *Raiders might have made the play-offs but Ford is going down #youredone #watchyourback*

"He's just pissed the Eagles are out and we're in," I said, feeling my stomach knot. "Let him talk shit, we all know who's the better team."

"I still think we should go across the river and show him who's boss." Ash slung his towel over his shoulder.

"You over your tantrum?" My tone was cool.

He shrugged as we hit the showers. "I figured if anyone's going to show to the party later, I need to make the peace."

"Oh, so it's like that, huh?"

Asher's mouth curved. "What can I say, gotta give the people what they want."

"Fucker," I muttered under my breath.

After a quick shower, we got dressed and gathered by the buses where Hailee and some other fans hung around to congratulate us. "Great game," she said to Cam and Asher, completely ignoring me. I edged away, hitching my bag over my shoulder. It was on the tip of my tongue to ask where Felicity was, but that would suggest I cared.

"Hey, Jase, we're going to ride back with Hailee. You want a ride?"

My eyes slid to hers in question, and she gave a dismissive shrug.

"I'll ride with—"

"Just get in the damn car, Jason," she sighed.

"You heard the woman, *Jason*, get in the damn car." Ash winked, and I flipped him off. He was so smug I wanted to tell him to fuck off. But I didn't. Instead, I gritted my teeth behind my lips and got in the car.

Wondering when I became such a pussy.

Two hours later, everyone who was anyone was crammed into Asher's house.

"Okay fuckers, quiet down." He jumped up on the breakfast counter and thrust his beer in the air. "Now I know Coach said it all last week at Seniors Night, but this is my house and I want to say a few words."

A couple of the guys cheered while Grady balled up a napkin and launched it at him. "Get on with it," he yelled.

"This won't take long," Ash grinned at him, waggling his brows, "just like Mackey in the sack." Another round of hoots and hollers broke out around me.

"Last year should have been ours; we should have been in that championship game, bringing home the crown. But this year... this year it's ours. I love you guys and I don't know what I'm going to do when the season's over. So raise your drink in the air and let me hear y'all. Who are we?"

"Raiders."

"And what are we going to do?"

"Win!"

"Damn right we are. Now let's celebrate like the winners we are and get fucked up." He chugged his drink down and thumped his chest like Tarzan. Cam laughed beside me, but I barely smiled. Because celebration or not, something was missing.

I followed Cam outside to our usual seats where Hailee joined us. "Everything okay?" Cam asked her as she slid onto his lap.

"Yeah, fine."

"They're not coming?"

She shook her head, her eyes finding mine. "I don't think so."

"Maybe it's for the best," Cam said quietly as I focused on my beer, scratching off the label with my thumbnail.

"Yeah." Hailee's eyes burned into the top of my head.

"Shots," Asher appeared with a tray of Jell-O shots.

"Nah, man," I grumbled, not in the mood.

"Aw come on, man, we made it. A near perfect season and State in our sights." He thrust a cup at me, waiting for Cameron and Hailee to take theirs.

"I can't believe this is almost the end." Ash's expression fell as he raised his cup in the air. "It's been the best four years of my life. To good friends, football, and the future, whatever it may hold." Something flashed over his face, but it was quickly gone as he downed his shot.

"Pittsburg won't know what hit them," Cam said, tossing his empty cup on the tray.

"Yeah," Ash shrugged, "but it won't be the same will it?"

A good friend would have reassured him, would have promised things wouldn't change.

But he was right.

Come graduation nothing would be the same anymore.

27

Felicity

"YOU MUST BE FELICITY. I'm George, welcome to A Brand New Tail."

"Hi," I smiled at the man. He was younger than I expected; with sandy blond hair and a bright smile. He couldn't be a day older than twenty-five.

"Thank you so much for this."

"No problem. Regina said you're thinking of applying to study animal science at college?"

"It's a possibility but I know it's super competitive and some hands-on experience would really help my application."

"Can I ask why now? Most of our volunteers from high school start with us in junior year."

"I've always loved animals and vet school is something I've always had in the back of my mind, but my parents... well, they have a different idea where my future is concerned."

"Ah," he smiled. "Say no more. My parents wanted a doctor and got a vet tech instead."

"How'd they take it?"

"It was a shock at first, but they came around to the idea. In the end, I think all our parents really want is for us to be happy. Shall we get started?"

"I'd love that."

For the first time since Mya talked me into this whole thing, I felt a seed of hope blossom in my chest. George got it. He'd been where I was now and come out the other side without too many bumps and scrapes if his senior position here was anything to go by.

"First things first. This is Serena, our front of house manager." He motioned to the pixie-haired woman manning the desk. "Serena, meet Felicity. I'm giving her the grand tour."

"Hey, doll," she smiled warmly. "High school junior?"

"Senior, actually," George corrected. "She's a bit of a late starter."

"No time like the present. Don't let him scare you off, Felicity, was it?" I nodded. "George is all bark and no bite. Excuse the dog pun, you get a lot of those around here." She gave me a wink and went back to whatever had her attention behind the desk.

"Don't mind her," George said, leading me through a door into a long hall. "So out there was what we call, 'the floor'. And everything beyond this door is what we refer to as 'the back'."

"Got it."

"I figured we'd start with the fun stuff and work backwards."

"Sounds good to me." The place had a very distinct smell. I couldn't quite put my finger on it, but it was there.

"We have a permanent staff of four. Me, Serena, Joseph, and Maggie, and a team of five volunteers who help us out on a week-to-week basis depending on how busy we are." George kept walking, leading me to the far end of the hall. "Serena handles front of house, all customer enquiries, and adoptions. Maggie and I deal with new arrivals; we run full check overs, update vaccination boosters, administer medication and treatment in any cases requiring it. And Joseph is our resident animal whisperer."

"Animal whisperer?"

"It's what we like to call him. It's his job to look after the animals day-to-day, but the guy has a rare gift with them, even the most severe cases we see. In my five years being here, I haven't seen a case he hasn't been able to crack."

"Wow, he sounds wonderful."

"He's really something. Unfortunately, he's taken a rare day off, so you won't meet him today."

Disappointment settled in my chest, but I tried to shake it off, remembering Hailee and Mya's words of encouragement. This was a positive step in the right direction.

"And here we are. This is what we like to call, 'the zoo'."

The second George opened the door, I realized why. Assaulted with overzealous barks and wary purrs, I stepped into the room. Even a few growls greeted me.

"Okay, okay, quiet down." George dragged his keys along the nearest cage. "I brought someone to meet you all, but you have to promise to behave."

"There are so many."

"We don't just take cases from Rixon. We cover the surrounding areas too, so things can get pretty crazy. We're almost at capacity right now. Twenty-five cats, eighteen dogs, and Earl."

"Earl?" I asked, my eyes wide as I observed the vast room. It was clearly divided into cats and dogs with an examination table and apparatus set up in the middle. The crates were big and spacious, each equipped with food and water bowls and scratching posts for the cats, a few toys for the dogs.

"Our rabbit. We technically only take cats or dogs, but he was found in the alley behind the building and Serena begged us to take him in.

"Someone just left him there?"

"You'd be surprised where people dump their unwanted pets."

My heart clenched as I found the long-eared rabbit in a special cage away from the other animals. He was so cute and defenseless; the idea someone could just toss him away made my heart ache.

"So when an animal first arrives, the first port of call is a full health check..." For the next ten minutes, George explained how they processed new animals and how they used a digital matching service to try and rehome as many animals as possible.

"The average stay with us is eleven weeks, which means we're doing a fairly good job of finding animals new compatible homes. We have a thorough screening process and insist potential adopters attend one of our information sessions before jumping headfirst into anything. And we're proud to hold an eighty-five percent rehoming success."

"Eighty-five percent? But what happens to the other fifteen percent?"

"Oh, they usually become lifers here or we transfer them to a more suited center." He moved over to a cage and crouched down. "Now this is Boomer. He's a black lab who's been with me since the beginning."

The dog stared up at me, leaning up to sniff the air around me. "Hi there, boy."

"You want to meet him? He's as friendly as they come."

"I'd love to." A little thrill shot through me as George unlocked the cage and pulled open the front gate.

"He's a little unsure of new faces so give him a minute."

"Hey, Bo—"

The huge dog leaped toward me, knocking me back onto my butt.

"I think you have a fan," George chuckled but I had my hands full of dog as Boomer nudged and licked my face, coaxing me to run my hands through his soft, glossy fur.

"And George said you were shy." I glanced over at him and he blushed a little. He was kind of cute, made ten times cuter by the fact he cared for all these animals.

But I wasn't here to crush on George, I was here to soak up everything I could about what it entailed to work in a place like A Brand New Tail.

"You like that, huh?" I scratched under Boomer's neck and he lifted his head from side to side so I could get better access.

"Okay, Boom, back in you go. Joseph isn't on shift today, but I'll make sure you get to stretch those legs later." He patted Boomer on the head before gently herding him back into his cage.

"They all get daily exercise?"

"They do. Twice a day. And then Joseph usually has them out in small groups in the yard. It's important for socialization and preparation for their new homes."

I nodded, eagerly soaking up every word. "I always wanted a dog or a cat, but my mom was concerned about allergies."

"I have three pets." George scooped a handful of doggy treats out of a jar and began working his way down the low row of cages. "A spaniel and two cats."

"Where did you study?"

"I did animal science at Penn's School of Veterinary Medicine. I graduated last year, got my licenses, and Regina offered me the position of center manager."

"Wow, that's amazing."

"I always imagined I'd work at a veterinary clinic, but once I started volunteering here, I couldn't imagine being anywhere else. There's something magical about bringing together a rescue pet and a new owner." Pride radiated from every word and I realized I wanted that. I wanted to make a difference to animals *and* people.

"You have that look," he observed.

"I do?"

"Yeah," he smiled, "The newbie sparkle. I remember it well. It looks good on you." His eyes widened at his slip of the tongue, and I smothered a giggle.

George was flirting with me. It was probably unintentional and harmless, but it felt nice all the same.

"And that was really inappropriate. I'm sorry. Sometimes I speak before I think. I can assure you, I'm usually much more professional."

"It's okay."

Awkward silence stretched out before us despite the little flutters in my chest.

"So, hmm, yeah this is the 'zoo'. We also have a surgical room, a recovery room, and a couple of isolation pens for the worst cases."

"It hurts my heart knowing people can be so cruel to something so cute."

"We see it all here. It's definitely not for the faint of heart, but it only makes it all the more rewarding when a dog who has only ever known neglect and abuse finds a loving home. You want to see the rest of the place?"

Nodding eagerly, I said, "I'd love to."

I ENDED up staying most of the afternoon. George was happy to talk shop and I was more than willing to listen. It couldn't have gone better… until he reminded me there were no volunteer openings, and the bottom fell out of my happy bubble.

"Of course, I understand," I said, wringing my hands in front of me.

"I think you'd really fit in here." A gentle blush creeped into his cheeks again and there was no mistaking he was flirting. "But my hands are tied. Hopefully you got a real feel for what it's like though?"

"I did, thank you."

"Well, it was nice to meet you, Felicity. If you have any questions or need any help with your application, just give me a shout." He fumbled in his pocket. "Here's my card."

"Thanks." I plucked it from him and held it close to my chest as if he'd just offered me the universe. "I should probably let you get back to it. Wouldn't want to keep them waiting." My head flicked over his shoulder.

"Yeah, I have big shoes to fill today since Joseph is on vacation."

"I'm sure you'll do a great job."

"I'll try."

Neither of us made any effort to move but it was starting to feel awkward, so I gave him a small wave and walked away. It had been such a bittersweet experience; confirming my unexplored desire to work with animals but tempered by a sting of regret. Frustration because I hadn't been braver to go after what I wanted last year or whenever my mom and dad brought up college.

And knowing it might have been too late.

28

Jason

I WAS on the way out when Hailee's voice stopped me in my tracks. "Maybe you should call George and see if he can..." The conversation became muffled but I caught the odd word.

Flick.

Ask.

Risk.

"George?" I doubled back and breezed into the kitchen.

"Good morning to you too," my step-sister grumbled as she poured herself a glass of juice.

"So who's George?" I leaned against the door jamb casually.

"No one."

"You make it too easy sometimes, you know that, right?"

"And you make it so easy to hate you." A smirk spread across her face. "Don't you have to be at school bright and early for practice?"

"They'll wait for me."

"So arrogant."

"So prickly," I shot back. "So, George?"

"Is no one."

I didn't like the way she was deflecting. Hailee only usually did that if she didn't want me to know something. And right now, there was only one person she didn't want me to know about.

Felicity.

"I'll find out, *little sis*," I warned. "One way or another, I'll find out who George is." Grabbing an apple from the bowl, I bit into it, sending her a pointed look.

"You don't care remember? So why would you possibly want to know who George is?" I glared harder and she chuckled. "Not so arrogant now, are you?" Her brow shot up.

Without another word I stalked out of the kitchen, the muscle in my jaw working overtime.

Fucking George.

It shouldn't have mattered who he was. He could have been the Giles' new pool boy or a family friend for all I knew. But it didn't stop my mind zipping off in a hundred different directions, all of them ending at the same point. George wasn't no one.

He was someone, and I fucking hated it.

By the time I'd arrived at Asher's house, George had taken on a life of his own. Snowballing into Felicity's life. Maybe they were dating. Maybe he was an ex looking to rekindle their relationship. Or maybe Felicity was pursuing him. That one especially stung.

"Good mornin'." Asher took one look at me when he climbed into my car and let out a low whistle. "What happened now?"

"Who's George?"

"George? Is this some kind of test? Am I supposed to know who George is?"

"Just answer the fucking question."

"Curious George? George Foreman? George Clooney?" Asher mocked, and I stared at him blankly. "No? Well, in that case I have no idea who George is." My hands tightened around the wheel as I took the turn for school. "I'm guessing from the way you're strangling the life out of your steering wheel that wasn't the answer you wanted?"

"It's nothing."

He snorted. "If you say so."

A beat passed. And another. Until I finally choked out, "I heard Hailee on the phone to Felicity."

"And what? You're worried George is swooping in to mend her broken heart? I'd call that a sweet dose of 'I fucking told you so'."

My chest rumbled with indignation as I swallowed my reply. It pained me to say it, but Asher was right.

"What, no comeback?" he added.

My eyes slid to his, silently pleading for him to drop it. But I'd picked the wrong friend to confide in for that.

"Didn't I tell you this would happen?" Ash ground out. "Felicity is a catch, bro. If you weren't so hung up on her, I wouldn't have hesitated to try my luck there. But there are a lot of other guys out there, Jase."

"I know. Fuck, you think I don't know that?" The words came out strained.

"So what happened?" Out the corner of my eye, I watched as he twisted around, running a hand through his messily styled hair. "Talk to me; let's try to fix this before it's too late."

"Coach is going to be pissed if we're late," I said, deflecting.

"Jase, man, come—"

"Just do me a favor and look out for her, yeah?" I lowered my voice, finding an empty parking spot. Cutting the engine, silence descended on us.

Asher wanted to say more, to argue I was making a huge mistake, but I'd already made my bed. This morning was just a blip. Surprise at hearing her and Hailee talk about another guy so soon. But it was bound to happen eventually. Felicity might have been quirky, but she had a caring personality and the kind of smile that lit up an entire room. Any guy would have been lucky to have her. *I* would have been lucky to have her. In another life, maybe.

I shouldered the door, not even bothering to wait for Ash, and headed for the locker room. I needed to hit something. I needed to hurt.

But most of all, I needed to forget.

Practice didn't help much. I skulked through two classes, barely listening to the teachers, before joining my teammates at lunch. They chatted around me, excited for a week's rest before the first play-off game next weekend.

"I come bearing good news." Asher dropped his tray down and sat beside me. "George is no one." He leaned in, keeping his voice low. "Well, he's someone, but he's no one for us to worry about."

"Us?" I said coolly, irritation shooting up my spine.

"Who knew you could be so possessive?" He pinned me with a sarcastic look. "Anyway, George is the manager at a pet rescue place Felicity is trying to get some volunteer experience at."

"What the hell does she want to do that for?"

"I heard Hailee telling Cameron she's thinking of a switching her degree to animal science or something. But she needs hands-on experience for her application."

So George wasn't some new guy she was dating. I should have felt relief coursing through me.

I didn't.

Because I couldn't help but wonder if her change of plans had anything to do with my knee-jerk reaction to finding out she had applied to Penn.

"Okay," I grunted.

"Okay?" Ash drawled. "I bring you the four-one-one and all you can say is, 'okay'?"

"Like I said before, it doesn't—"

"Matter, yeah, I got the memo. Guess you won't be interested to know George gave Flick his card and told her to call him if she needed *anything*. I don't know about you, but that sounds a lot like code for—" Asher groaned with pain as my elbow jammed into his ribs. I casually went back to my sub, pretending like he hadn't just blown my world wide open.

So George wasn't a new guy she was seeing. But by the sounds of it, he wanted to be.

I'd pushed her straight into his open arms.

And I didn't know what the fuck to do with that.

My mood only got worse as the day went on. So when my cell vibrated as I was walking to my car at the end of the day, and I opened the incoming Snapchat message, I almost saw red. The grainy image was accompanied by only two words.

Time's up.

Fuck.

Thatcher wasn't backing down, and I wasn't sure how much longer I could avoid him. Maybe it was better to end it now. Him and me. One on one.

Against my better judgment, I typed back.

Name your time and place.

His reply was instant.

No man's land… Friday after sundown.

It was a stretch of land down by the river not far from The Alley. We used to hang out there when we were kids, before the rivalry between The Raiders and The Eagles became more than just a few harmless high school pranks.

Done. Just you and me.

Oh you know it. I'm going to enjoy making you bleed.

Big words for a guy who's waited almost eight months to get revenge.

All good things come to those who wait.

. . .

I DIDN'T REPLY. There was no point. We could go around in circles all day about the fact he was choosing now to strike, but it wouldn't change anything. I just had to figure out a way to walk away from this thing in one piece. Because while he had everything to gain, I had everything to lose.

I WAS SITTING in the yard, drinking a beer, when Hailee found me. "Out here drinking all alone, it must be bad."

"Just needed some air."

"Want to talk about it?"

"No, I really don't. But thanks for the offer," I tacked on the end.

"Someone hold the phone, hell must have frozen over," she chuckled, dragging another chair over to mine. "You must be excited for the play-offs."

"I'm ready. It's like my whole life has been leading up to this point, you know?"

"I really don't." She gave me a hesitant smile. "But I've been around you long enough to know how important this is to you."

"So what? We're friends again?"

"I'm not sure we were ever friends, but I'm done holding onto so much hate and bitterness. I want to enjoy the rest of senior year."

"To non-friends?" I held up my beer and Hailee frowned. "Here," passing her an empty, I clinked the neck of my bottle against hers.

"Truce?" she added.

"I think I can agree to that."

"I know I gave you a hard time about Felicity and I'm not going to lie, I spent a couple of days planning on ways to make you pay, but I think I've realized it's for the best."

Her words coiled around my lungs making it difficult to breathe.

"Yeah?" I barely managed to choke out.

"Yeah. The two of you are from completely different worlds, and football will always be the most important thing to you. And that's okay. Felicity needs someone solid, someone who can put up with her brand of crazy."

"Someone like George?" The words were out before I could stop them.

"Oh God, please don't tell me you're jealous of George?"

"Should I be?"

Her expression fell. "I really don't know how to answer that."

"So she wants to be a veterinary doctor or something?"

"Yeah, it's all kind of new. She was supposed to be studying business like her parents both did. But she made this list and it pushed her to reassess things, to go after things she wouldn't have before."

"Like asshole football players who don't know what they want?"

"Exactly like that." Hailee burst into quiet laughter. "Maybe in another time and place you two would have figured things out."

"Maybe." I liked that idea; Felicity and me together in a few years' time. Me the hotshot NFL player and her the big-hearted animal doctor.

"How did you know Chase was the one?" I asked even though I felt fucking stupid the second the words left my mouth.

"It wasn't really a case of knowing. It was just a realization that life was better with him around than not, and when things went bad with his mom, I wanted to be there for him. I wanted to be his person."

I took a long pull on my beer mulling over her words. "I always thought I was his person." My lip curved in a half-smirk despite the knot in my gut.

"One day, you'll get it. Maybe not now but one day..."

"I almost had it once you know."

"Aimee?"

"Yeah." I stared off into the distance remembering a time that felt so long ago but wasn't that long at all.

"What happened?" Hailee asked. "I mean, I know a little, but I'd rather hear it from you."

Sliding my eyes to hers, I let out a weary sigh. "Aimee was... different. Special." At least I'd thought she was. But that was before I knew the truth. Before I ever met Felicity and realized what I felt for Aimee was nothing but puppy love.

"She hurt you?"

"She didn't just hurt me, she completely fucking destroyed me."

29

Felicity

I WOKE to the sound of my cell vibrating. Leaning over, I fumbled to find it, and lifted it to my ear. "Hello?"

"Felicity, it's George."

"George?" I rubbed the sleep from my eyes unsure I'd heard him correctly.

"George from New Tail. I hope I didn't wake you?"

"Is it that obvious?" A soft chuckle left my lips.

"Sorry, I figured with it being a school day you'd be up and at it."

"I'm not really a morning person."

"I remember it well." I heard his smile. "Anyway, I just wanted to call and let you know that a position came up, so if you're still interested—"

"Interested?" I bolted upright. "I would love to."

"Well, that's great. When can you come down and fill in the paperwork?"

"Today, I can come today," the words spilled out in a frenzy. "I have classes until three-thirty, but I'm free after that."

"I'll need to check what we have going on today, but I can't see it being a problem. I can email you later to confirm," he hesitated, "or shoot you a text?"

"Either is fine." Excitement danced in my tummy. "I'm just relieved and excited, definitely excited. You were so certain nothing was available, I'd kind of given up hope."

"Well, I'm glad to be calling with good news." George gave me a list of what to bring in with me later before we said goodbye and hung up.

I leaped out of bed with a spring in my step, and quickly shot a text to Hailee and Mya.

Me: George just called... there's a position for me.

Hailee: That's amazing, I'm so happy for you.

. . .

Mya: That's great. All that flirting must have paid off.

My stomach knotted. Is that why George had suddenly found me something? Because he liked me? I didn't want to owe him anything.

Dammit.

I typed another quick text to Hailee.

Me: You don't think George found me something because he thinks I'll owe him now, do you?

My cell rang and I hit answer. "Mya seems to think he's doing this because he likes me," I rushed out.

"Good morning to you too," Hailee laughed softly.

"Sorry, I was just so happy and now I'm panicking."

"Did he give you that vibe just now?"

"I don't know. He was friendly, but he seemed like a nice guy."

"He knows you're in high school, right?"

"Of course."

"So he's probably just doing a nice thing. You said he's fresh out of college himself, so he probably just appreciates how much this means to you. This is a good thing, Flick."

"You're right," I breathed a sigh of relief. "You're totally right. It's Mya's fault."

"She likes to mess with your head. But she means well."

"I know. Thanks. I should get ready for school. Do you want a ride?"

"Cameron's picking me up, but you can ride with us?"

"Is Jason... actually, don't answer that. I'll meet you there. I think I have to get Mya anyway."

"Okay, and Flick?"

"Yeah?"

"I think Mya's right. I think this could be a really good thing for you."

"Thanks, I'll see you at school." I hung up and let out a shaky breath, nervous energy radiating through me. Getting this break at A Brand New Tail was a good thing but it meant pulling the plug on my parents' dream for me.

Something I didn't relish doing.

"Hey," Hailee chased me down after class. The day had flown, my head too consumed with George's early morning call to concentrate. "Are you headed straight there?"

I nodded. "I didn't want to risk going home and running into Mom. This way I can hopefully calm my nerves before I get there."

"And what has you all worked up?" Asher peeked over Hailee's shoulder, grinning at me.

"The pet rescue place called Flick; they have an opening for her."

"Georgie boy pulled some strings, did he?"

"How do you know about George?" My brows bunched together.

"I, uh," he stuttered, guilt swimming in his eyes. "I overheard Hailee telling Cam all about it."

"Okay."

"I'm proud of you, Fee, baby." He hooked his arm around my neck and pulled me in. "Those furballs are going to love you."

"I hope so, I could really—" Asher yanked his arm free and jerked away from me.

"Hey, guys," Mya said, joining us.

"Mya," he said smoothly, the reason for his sudden change apparent. "Nice shirt."

"This old thing." She pulled at the frayed t-shirt and chuckled. "Thanks, I guess."

Hailee and I watched the two of them. Asher was smitten, his eyes tracking Mya's every move. But she seemed indifferent to his attention.

"So what are you girls up to later? I know Flick is heading to puppy heaven but what about you, Hailee? Mya?"

"Me and Cam promised Xander we would take him to Ice-T's."

"Just don't feed that little shit any of the candy. We made that mistake once."

"I think we've got it covered." Hailee smiled.

"Mya?"

"I'm living the dream tonight with Mr. Galveston's homework."

"History?" Asher winced. "Ouch."

"Do you even do homework?" She threw back.

"I do it... occasionally," he added. "But just because I play football doesn't mean I'm a dumb jock. You're looking at a GPA of 3.33 right here."

"Athletic and book smart. I am impressed."

"You should be."

"Okay," I interrupted. "Not that I'm not enjoying watching whatever this is," I wagged my finger between them, "but I need to go. I don't want to keep George waiting."

"Call me as soon as you get done," Mya said, "I want to hear all about dreamy George."

"Dreamy George?" Asher frowned. "Isn't he the manager of the place?"

"The very young, very cute manager," Mya nodded. "Flick's words, not mine."

"You have a crush, Fee, baby? I'm wounded."

"I do not have a crush." Heat spread along my neck and into my cheeks. "George is... nice. He's also going to be my boss so..."

"Kinky." Asher grinned, his eyes dancing with amusement.

"Gross," I hissed, waving him off. "Right, I'm out of here. I'll call you both later. Asher, it was a pleasure as always."

"The pleasure is all mine," he called as I left them to it. "Oh and Fee? Make sure George keeps his paws to himself. See what I did there... paws." He exploded with laughter as I rolled my eyes and headed out of the building.

Wondering what I was getting myself into.

TURNED OUT, I had nothing to worry about. When I'd arrived at the center, Serena had welcomed me, handing me a stack of paperwork to fill in. Then she traded me the papers for a volunteer handbook which she left me to study while she dealt with some clients. George eventually showed up to walk me through the volunteer schedule and list of duties. I'd missed the latest round of volunteer training, so for now I'd have to learn the ropes as I went, but I was just relieved to be there.

"I had no idea there was so much involved in pet adoption," I said, shadowing George as he scrubbed a new arrival: Benji, a cute one-year-old puppy, brought in by his parents who were getting a divorce and no longer wanted him. He was so frickin' cute, with big, round eyes and thick soft fur, the color of the sand.

"Our matching process is rigorous and time consuming, but it means better success rates. Something we're very proud of."

"I'm so excited to get started."

"And we're excited to have you. You'll get to meet the other volunteers over the weekend. I think Sandie, Hale, and Lisa are in Saturday, and then Tom and Beth are down for Sunday."

"There's five of them?" I asked, confused.

"Yes, didn't I already explain that?"

"You did, but I'd just assumed someone had left since the position came up." And I definitely remembered him telling me there were at capacity.

"Ah." George flushed bright red. "We shuffled things around and managed to find you some hours after all."

"Wow, that's... wow."

"It's actually great timing as Sandie recently announced she's pregnant, so she'll be looking to drop her hours as her pregnancy progresses."

"Oh, okay then, if you're sure." I couldn't shake Mya's insinuation George's motives weren't entirely innocent.

"There's nothing to worry about, I promise. I know how important hands-on experience can be for a college application, so if we can do our bit to help you..." He let his words hang.

"Thank you, that's very kind."

He beamed, the color in his cheeks returning to normal. "You want to takeover while I grab the rest of the supplies?"

"For real?" I started pushing my sleeves up.

"Of course, get in here. Benji is one of our friendlier arrivals."

"He's so cute. I can't wrap my head around the fact they no longer wanted him."

"He'll be rehomed in no time. He's one of the better cases, trust me. Okay, if you get in here," George held onto Benji but stepped back letting me slip around him, so I was closest to the tub and the puppy, "that's it. Now slide one hand to his collar." Our fingers brushed as he withdrew his hand and it was my turn to blush. George cleared his throat and jerked back.

"You can start rinsing him off and then dry him with that towel." He flicked his head over to the counter and a stack of towels.

"Rinse and dry, got it."

"Excellent, I'll be right back."

George left and I took my time washing Benji. He was a placid thing, letting me scrub and run my fingers through his soaked coat. "You like that, boy?" I cooed earning me an eager lick to the face. Laughter bubbled up, the smile on my face so wide it hurt. But there was something so right about being here, that I felt happiness wrap around me like a warm blanket.

"We good in here?" George's voice perforated my bubble.

"We're fi—" Benji chose that exact moment to shake off his fur, spraying droplets of water everywhere. "Oh my..."

George handed me a towel. "Here, get dried off while I pat him down."

"Does that happen a lot?"

"Yep, hazard of the job I'm afraid," he chuckled.

"It's funny," I said toweling myself off, "I've kind of drifted through high school, never being sure what I wanted to do. Happy to go along with my parents' plan for me. But being here, it's like I know this is what I want to do. Gosh, I bet that sounds so cliché."

"It doesn't. I felt the same, back in the day. I knew being a doctor was what my parents wanted for me. But I'd be at the hospital, visiting my gran when she was sick, or hanging out with my dad on his rare day off, and I never felt that connection. I knew it would be rewarding, to heal people, save lives. But it never felt like what I was destined to do."

"How am I going to tell them?" I whispered the words.

"If it makes you happy, eventually it'll make them happy."

He made it sound so easy.

"Look at it this way, you could spend the next four years of your life at college, surfing along studying a course that's okay, or you could spend the next four years of your life studying something that excites you. Something you feel passionate about. Who knows where the future will take you, but wouldn't you rather be on a path you choose? Sorry," George added. "Like I said before, sometimes things just spill out before I can stop them."

"I admire it actually. It's nice to meet someone who understands where I'm coming from."

"Surely there must be someone? A best friend? Boyfriend?"

"Best friend, yes. Boyfriend, no." My stomach dipped. "But I'm not sure Hailee really gets it. She's always known what she wanted to do."

George's expression had changed, his eyes fixed on mine, searching for something.

"George?" I asked, breaking the strange tension that had descended over us.

"What? Sorry." He shook his head. "It's been a long day. Where were we?"

Benji chose that moment to shake his fur again, soaking George. I grabbed some towels and hurried over to them. "Thanks," he said, "that'll teach me for not paying more attention."

The moment between us had passed, but I couldn't help but wonder what had him so distracted in the first place.

30

Jason

"YOU'RE SURE ABOUT THIS?" Grady asked for the twentieth time that week.

"This thing needs to end now."

"I'm not disagreeing, I just don't understand why you're not taking Bennet and Chase for back up. Well, Chase I kind of get. If Thatcher had come after my girl the way he went after Hailee, I wouldn't be able to—"

"Grady..."

"Shutting up," he groaned. "So we're really doing this?"

"*I'm* doing this. I just need you there in case things go south."

He let out a low whistle. "And you're sure we can't hold off doing this until after we win State?"

"It has to be now."

"If Coach—"

"Coach won't find out." Thatcher was many things, but he wasn't a snitch.

"I could call a couple of the other guys—"

"If you're having second thoughts, man, I'll go alone."

"Nah, I've got you. I just think this is a bad idea. A really bad idea."

I didn't disagree but Thatcher wanted his pound of flesh and he was determined to get it one way or another. At least this way, if I met him one on one, it would be a fair fight. Besides, it wasn't the first time we'd rumbled. I knew I could take him.

"Noted. I'll see you in ten."

"Yeah, yeah. See you there." I hung up and grabbed my keys off the sideboard. It was almost sundown. Cameron was out with Hailee, and Asher's parents were in town for a flying visit and had insisted on taking him for dinner. Dad and Denise were off doing whatever the fuck they did on Friday nights. The coast was clear.

Until I walked out of the house.

"Aimee?" I stared at the girl who had screwed me over once upon a time. "What the fuck are you doing here?"

"Hey, Jason," she gave me a tentative smile, "it's been a while."

"Not long enough." My teeth ground together. "Let me guess, your brother sent you."

"Actually he doesn't know I'm here. If he did..." She trailed off, her eyes darting to the ground. "Can we talk?"

"You can say whatever you came to say, yeah, and then you can get the fuck off my property."

"Jason..." she let out a heavy sigh, running a hand through her hair. When I didn't respond she added, "That's fair enough. I guess I earned that."

"You've got to be fucking kidding me," I mumbled beneath my breath.

Aimee lifted her eyes to mine again, sympathy and regret swimming in her brown irises. "I suppose it's too late to say I'm sorry?"

"Apologies mean nothing out of the mouths of liars."

"I never meant to hurt you... it just all went too far and—"

"Save it," I snapped, my chest heaving with frustration.

There had been a time when I'd wanted the girl standing before me. Wanted her so bad, I let down my walls. Opened up to her. There wasn't an inch of her skin I hadn't tasted. A dip or curve or blemish I hadn't trailed my lips over. I thought I'd known everything there was to know about the quiet girl from across the river... until I'd found out she was none other than Lewis Thatcher's little sister.

Anger rushed through my veins, igniting a firestorm in my chest. There had never been any love lost between me and Thatcher, but Aimee had changed everything. Turned our rivalry into a war that spilled off the field and into our lives, affecting everyone around us.

"You got your revenge, Jase, isn't that enough? What you did to me—"

"Don't fucking talk to me about what *I* did. You reeled me in for weeks, let me believe what we had was real. I felt things for you I had never felt before and it was all a lie."

I had been falling in love with her. I couldn't pinpoint the exact moment it happened. Even at the time I hadn't realized. It was *after*, when I learned who she really was, that I understood how deep my feelings ran for Aimee Thatcher—my enemy's sister.

"It wasn't," she cried, swiping at the tears falling from her eyes. "What we shared was real. It was real. It wasn't supposed to be, but I couldn't help it. I couldn't help falling for you."

Closing the distance between us, I stopped right in front of her. Looming over her, my eyes narrowed to deadly slits. "You played me, Aimee. You made me weak and defenseless and then, when I was completely at your mercy, you stabbed the knife in my back and watched me bleed out."

"Jason..." Aimee's voice trembled as she craned her neck to look at me. "I'm sorry, I'm so sorry."

"Yeah? Well, I'm only sorry I didn't completely destroy you." The words came out low and deadly, laced with the pain of our past.

When I'd found out who she was and what she'd planned with her brother, I'd concocted a plan of my own. I would never forget the look on Thatcher's face when he opened the video message of me fucking his sister. It had been all the revenge I'd needed, but it had been the catalyst for everything since.

"You were always mean, Jason, but I'll forever regret turning you into... *this*." A violent sob spilled from Aimee's lips as she stepped back, putting some much-needed distance between us.

"I only came to warn you," she added. "Lewis is out to destroy you. He wants to make sure you never see the play-offs. If you have any sense, you won't go."

I ran a hand over my head and down the back of my neck, the weight of her words pressing on my chest like a ton of bricks. "Is that all?"

"I mean it, Jason," she warned, "he's out for blood. *Your* blood."

Another time, another place, I would have replied with some cocky statement about him being all talk and no action. But the stakes had changed. I went after his sister and he'd come after mine, but I hadn't retaliated then. I'd been biding my time, waiting for the right time to go after him.

But my time was up.

I had to decide.

Fight.

Or flee.

Something Hailee once told me flashed in my mind, and I couldn't help but think, no matter what I decided, there would be only one loser at the end of this.

Me.

"You should go, Aimee." Shouldering around her, I headed straight for my car. The sooner we got this over with, the better.

"Jason, don't do this..." Her cries bounced off the window like rain against glass. Aimee made it sound like I had a choice but running was never a choice, and my mind was already made up.

Grabbing my cell phone, I shot Grady a quick text before firing up the engine and gunning out of the driveway. Aimee's defeated figure shrank in the rear-view mirror. I'd played in my fair share of dog fights. Football games where players broke the rules and cared more about hurting each other than scoring a touchdown.

As far as I was concerned, this wasn't any different.

Thatcher wanted my blood?

Fine.

But I'd make him work for it.

It was quiet down at No Man's Land when we arrived. Grady sat tense beside me, tapping his fingers against his thigh.

"Nervous?" I asked, surveying the stretch of land in front of us. It was right beside the bridge, sheltered by the huge cement pillars. Part of it ran underneath, only accessible when the river ran low. Which wasn't often. When we were kids, we'd hang out down there, daring each other to try to make it across. Kids doing the kind of shit kids do.

This wasn't like that though.

This was different.

"What's the plan?" Grady ignored my original question.

"Plan?" I side-eyed him. "I'm going to beat the shit out of him and send him crawling back across the river with my initials scratched into his fucking skin."

"Jesus, Cap." Grady let out a low whistle. "Are you sure we shouldn't call—"

"The less people involved, the better. If you want to walk, walk. I won't hold it against you." I wasn't scared; I was fucking furious. It burned through me, liquid fire in my veins.

"Fuck that. I'm staying. Just promise me if things get too messy, we'll leave."

"Yeah, whatever." The lie rolled off my tongue. No way was I leaving until Thatcher got the message loud and clear not to mess with me and mine.

"Shall we then?"

We climbed out, the bitter fall wind slamming into us. "Shit, it's cold."

"Grow a pair, Grady." I smirked as I flexed my arms either side of me and took off toward the riverside. Thatcher was waiting but he wasn't alone.

"Surprised you came," he drawled.

"I'm a man of my word."

"Interesting." He inclined his head, scratching his jaw. "You didn't come alone." Thatcher's hard gaze moved to Grady.

"Neither did you." My eyes went to the goon at his side.

"Didn't want to miss you get your ass handed to you, Ford," Gallen said, stepping up to his teammate.

Anger shot up my spine knowing that he'd put his hands on Felicity.

"Yeah, yeah, are we doing this or what?"

"Oh, we're doing it. But you really should have brought reinforcements." His lip twisted as a handful of other Eagles' players stepped out from the shadows.

"Whoa, this isn't what was agreed," Grady said, edging closer to me.

Thatcher shrugged, yanking his hoodie and shirt clean off in one. "Yeah, well, the game just changed."

My eyes ran over each of them; players I recognized. Players I'd gone head to head with on the field more times than I could count. Players who I knew would do anything for their captain and quarterback.

Even if he was a complete dickwad.

"The difference between me and you?" I said. "I refuse to take my players down with me."

"The righteous Jason Ford everyone," Thatcher swept his arm around him, "how fucking poetic."

Letting out a fake yawn, I glanced at Grady. "Bored yet? I know I am." Grabbing the hem of my hoodie and jersey, I pulled them off, throwing them down at my teammate's feet.

Thatcher glanced back at his audience, ready to showboat a little more, but I was done talking. Head down, shoulder cocked, I tackled him to the ground. We landed with a *thud*, his grunts filling the air while I rammed my fists into his side.

"Motherfucker!" He roared, bucking and thrashing against me. His fist came up hard, crunching into the soft flesh of my neck and I rolled away, momentarily winded.

"Cheap shot, Ford," he gritted out, clambering to his feet.

Before I could anticipate his next move, two of his teammates wrestled me to my feet, restraining my arms behind my back.

"Hey, hey," Grady rushed over to us, "that wasn't—" His head snapped back as Gallen's fist caught his cheek, and the two of them began going at it.

"Is this how you win?" I seethed, "by playing dirty."

"No," Thatcher grinned, "this is how I end your season." His fists slammed into my ribs. Over and over. Knocking the air clean out my lungs. Pain ricocheting through me. The hands restraining me loosened their grip and I dropped forward onto my knees, my hands breaking my fall.

"What's the matter, Ford, cat got your tongue?"

Thatcher edged back, giving me space to clamber to my feet. I could already feel the bruising around my ribs, the damaged tissue. But I was used to a little pain, I thrived on it.

Wiping my bloody lip with the back of my hand, I lifted my chin in defiance. "It'll take a lot more than that to put me down." I threw all my weight up and forward, our bodies crashing together, bone on bone, skin on skin. Pure hatred on pure hatred.

"You're a fucking lunatic," I spat the words at him as he slammed his head into my mine, missing my nose and grazing my jaw. It stung something fierce, but I forced down the pain, locking it away where I'd deal with it later.

I'd had worse. Thatcher could do his worst but there was only one of us walking away from this in one piece, and it wasn't him.

31

Felicity

"WE HAVE GOT to find somewhere new to hang out on a Friday night," Mya grumbled, her eyes running around The Alley.

"Hey, it's not that bad."

"Not that bad? Girl, I just watched two man-boys get excited over winning at air hockey. Not sexy."

"I don't know." My shoulders lifted in a small shrug. "I kinda like it." The Alley was familiar, like your favorite pair of sneakers. The ones you couldn't bear to throw out no matter how worn and stinky they were.

"One day, I'm going to take you to the city." Mya's eyes lit up with promise. "Oh yeah, we could hit a club or two and find us a nice pair of—"

"You guys have got to come see this." A guy rushed into the diner, breathless and red-faced. "Jason Ford and Lewis Thatcher are down by the river, beating the shit out of each other."

The room spun, my hands gripping the edge of the counter so tight the blood drained from my fingers.

"Flick, breathe," Mya's voice called to me. "Just breathe." Snapping out of my trance, I met her worried gaze. "It's probably nothing. You know how rumors fly around here."

It wasn't nothing.

I felt it in my bones.

Just then, my cell phone blared to life. "It's Hailee," I said, staring at the screen, willing her to tell me it wasn't true.

"Hails?" her name came out strangled.

"We're on our way there now but you're closer."

"I can't... I'm not..."

"Fee, baby," Asher came over the line. "How're you holding up?"

"I don't... It's true? He's down there *fighting* Thatcher?"

"We're not too sure what the fuck is happening right now which is why we need you to go down there. Now, Felicity."

I couldn't speak, the words lodged up against the giant lump in my throat.

"Asher? It's Mya. She's spaced out or something. Yeah, okay. We can do that. Should we call... No, okay. Got it." She thrust the cell phone back at me.

"We need to leave, now."

"But—"

"Pull yourself together, your man needs you."

"He's not—"

Mya slammed her hands down on the table, leaning over to shove her face in front of mine. "You need to get it together, okay?" I nodded. "Jason can hold his own, but Asher is worried... it doesn't matter. We need to go stat. You can either stay here and freak out, or you can come with me and hope to God you can talk some sense into him before it's too late."

"The play-offs," I shrieked, leaping to my feet. If Coach or Principal Finnigan found out about this, Jason could be forced to sit out of the play-offs.

Mya rolled her eyes dramatically. "Now she gets it. Come on, we're wasting time." She'd rolled up the sleeves on her jacket and pulled her spiral curls into a messy ponytail which made me wonder how often she did this kind of thing for Jermaine.

"Too many times," she said as if she heard my thoughts. "Now let's go. Jason needs you."

I COULD BARELY SEE for the sea of people—Rixon and Rixon East kids—all mingled together, desperate to get a glimpse of Thatcher and Jason, their quarterback Kings going at it.

"What the hell are we supposed to do now?" I asked Mya, clutching onto her hand like it was my lifeline.

"Flick, over here," Hailee's voice settled some of the unease swimming in my stomach.

"Thank God," I all but fell into her arms, taking comfort from her hug. "This is crazy. Hey, how'd you get here before me?"

"Asher drove like a crazy person." She gave him a scowl. "But we're here now, and the guys called the cavalry."

"The cav—" the words died on my tongue as the entire team filtered in behind Asher and Cameron.

"We need to disperse this crowd," Cam said, his brows pinched with concern. "Any suggestions?"

"Leave it to me," Asher said, grabbing a couple of the guys and whispering in their ears. Soon they had disappeared into the crowd.

"Come on," Cam grabbed Hailee's hand and motioned for us to follow. We had to push and shove our way through the wall of bodies, but when I finally saw Jason, I froze. The sight of him shirtless and bloody was sensory overload.

"Flick?" Mya yelled over the noise: the grunts and groans from the two fighters in the middle of the crudely formed ring, the bloodthirsty cheers from our classmates. "Hold it together," she scolded, yanking on my arm, jerking me into action. "He's okay, see? You need to really worry when—"

Thatcher got in a good hit, the crack of bone on bone reverberating through me so violently, my stomach lurched, bile rushing up my throat. I swallowed, dragging in a lungful of fresh air. "Someone has to do something."

"We are, if you'll just keep moving."

"Thank fuck," Grady rushed over to us, sporting a black eye of his own.

Cam shook his head at his teammate, disapproval written all over his expression. "Save the lecture, man, I'm fully aware of what a clusterfuck this is," Grady winced.

"I'll deal with you later," Cameron seethed. "Right now, we need to figure out how to end this."

"I've tried, twice. This is the thanks I got." He pointed to the ugly bruise forming around his eye.

"Okay, go find Asher and help with the crowd. We've got this."

We did?

Because my legs felt ready to give out on me as I clung to Mya.

"Okay," Asher reappeared, breathless and flushed. "I'm here, what's the plan?"

"I'm thinking you two should get in there before you lose your quarterback for the play-offs," Mya deadpanned.

"Man, I love a woman who tells it like it is." Ash grinned at her. "Yo, Thatcher," he sauntered toward them, "Having all the fun without me?"

"Fuck off, Bennet, this is between me and Ford." Thatcher wasn't unscathed, blood trickling from a cut in his lip, another under his eye. He also had a nasty bruise ripening around his ribs.

"Sorry, bro, but we kind of need our QB for the play-offs; you know, the ones you didn't make this year."

"What the hell is he doing?" Mya lurched forward but Cam cut her off with his arm.

"He's got this."

"The hell he does, look..." She flicked her head to where a couple of Eagles' players were closing in on him.

"Fuck, okay, you three stay here."

"Cam," Hailee said, "I'm not sure this is a good idea. Maybe we should call the police?"

"If it comes to that, we will, I promise. But for now, just stay here." He levelled her with a look I rarely saw from him.

"That boy has more restraint than me," Mya remarked.

"That's what I'm worried about." Hailee reached back for my hand and we stood there, the three of us, watching while the guys we cared about faced off with Thatcher and his bunch of goons.

"Whatever Asher did, it worked. Look, people are leaving."

We glanced back to find the crowd slowly dispersing, being herded away by the remaining Raiders.

"It's over, Thatcher," Cameron stepped between him and Jason.

"You think just because you showed up with your girl in tow that it's over? It's over when I say it's fucking over." He was incensed, anger rolling off him like a tidal wave. "In fact, since she's here," his eyes found Hailee, "why don't you come over here and experience what it feels like to be with a real ma—"

Cameron's fist drove straight into his face. Thatcher grunted in pain, staggering back, but he quickly righted himself, spitting blood onto the ground. "So you do have balls, Chase? I was beginning to think you didn't after you let me and the guys mess with your girl time and time again."

"Cameron, don't." Hailee tore her hand free, moving toward them, but before she got there, Grady appeared and scooped her up, bringing her back to us.

"Stay out of this, Hailee, trust me."

"Aw, you don't want to play? What about your girl, Ford, does she like to play? It sure looked like it from the—"

"Thatcher," Jason's tone was icy cold.

A chill ran up my spine watching them. There was so much anger and hatred between them, I knew I was missing some of the pieces of the puzzle.

"Lewis, stop," a girl's voice shattered the tension.

"Aimee, I thought I told you to stay the fuck out of this?"

Her dark hair whipped around her as she ran toward them, putting herself in front of Jason as if she was shielding him.

"Hailee," I asked, the knot in my stomach tightening, "who is that?"

"I think that's Aimee."

"Aimee?"

"Yeah, Thatcher's sister, Jason's ex."

Jason had an ex?

I had vague lust-haze filled memories of him mentioning a girl, but he hadn't gone into detail. She hadn't even been a blip on my radar, but now she was there; a real-life person. And she was standing in front of Jason like he was hers to protect.

"Oh, shit, Flick, I didn't..." Hailee's voice became white noise as I watched the unfamiliar girl face off with her brother. She hadn't frozen on the side lines or stood by and watched; she'd run straight into the fray.

To protect Jason.

But why would she do that? Unless...

"Hey, you don't know anything yet, so stop thinking whatever you're thinking right now." Mya nudged my arm, giving me her trademark death stare.

"I'm not leaving until you walk away, Lewis. This has gone too far. Jason only did what he did because he was hurt."

"You think I give a shit about that? He sent that video to—"

"Hurt me. *Me*, Lewis. If anyone should be standing here demanding revenge, it's me." Aimee's expression turned sad. "Look, I know you only want to protect me, to get back at him, but this is his future."

Thatcher's jaw clenched, his eyes burning with hatred for the guy I realized I knew nothing about. Not really. I thought he'd let me in, let me see a side of him no one else got to see, but Jason was a locked box.

Maybe he always would be.

Tears burned the backs of my eyes as I slowly began to edge away from my friends.

"Felicity, where the hell are you going?" Mya hissed, trying to reach for me, but I shrugged her off.

"I can't be here." I couldn't see Jason's past play out right in front of my eyes. It hurt too much to see their history.

To *feel* it.

"Don't run, not now. Not when he needs you."

"Jason doesn't need me, Mya." I smiled sadly, letting the tears fall freely now. "He never did."

Without a second glance, I walked away. Ignoring her calls, Hailee's too. Blocking out the sound of Aimee's voice as she tried to reason with Thatcher. The low rumble of whispers as the Raiders and Eagles stood guard.

But most of all, I ignored the sound of my heart breaking.

32

Jason

"THIS ISN'T OVER," Thatcher spat as he finally relented, letting Aimee slip her arm around his waist and lead him away. She glanced back, her eyes saying things I didn't want to hear.

Cam and Ash were on me in a second, helping me stay upright as they guided me over to our friends and teammates.

"Fuck, man, you're a mess," he released a shaky breath. "You need the ER?" I threw Grady a 'fuck you' expression, and his hands went up. "Is it too early to say, 'told you so'?"

"Grady?" I hacked up a mouthful of blood, leaning on Ash for support. My ribs burned like a motherfucker and I wasn't one-hundred percent sure Thatcher hadn't broken something.

If he had, I could kiss the play-offs goodbye.

That was assuming this didn't land on Principal Finnigan's desk first thing Monday morning.

Fuck.

I'd really fucked up. But I'd been caught between a rock and a hard place.

"Yeah, Cap?" Grady asked.

"Shut the fuck up."

"Come on, we should probably get out of here before the cops show up." Cam barely met my eyes, disappointment radiating off him.

But screw him.

He didn't know the whole story yet, no one did.

I'd tell them eventually, but first I needed a shit ton of Advil and a bottle of Jack.

I managed to crawl into the back of Asher's Jeep, Mya climbing in behind me while Cam and Hailee sat up front. There was no sign of Felicity, but I was almost certain I'd seen her there, standing with the girls.

Maybe I dreamed it up.

A mirage in the middle of one of the worst fucking beatings of my life.

A beautiful angel in the middle of my own personal hell.

"Guess the rumors are true," Mya said, studying me intently.

"Yeah, and what do they say?" It hurt to fucking breathe let alone talk, but there was something about the way she looked at me that had me intrigued.

"You're not just a pretty face." Her lip curved. "Before you pass out, tell me one thing. Was it worth it?" She kept her voice low, as if we were sharing some big secret.

"So worth it." I sank back against the leather, swallowing a groan and closing my eyes. "So fucking worth it."

Her hearty laughter was the last thing I heard.

"WHAT THE FUCK were you thinking, bro?" The veins in Asher's neck throbbed with frustration. "We're this close to State and you go and screw it all up and for what? To say you have bigger balls than Thatcher? It makes no sense, none."

"Ash, leave it," Cam said coolly, his eyes hard on me.

"Leave it? Are you fucking kidding me? He's out. When Coach gets wind of this, and he will, he'll have no choice but to pull your," he jabbed his finger at me, "ass from the team. All that hard work for nothing. I just don't get it. You told us all to leave it, so then why the fuck did you—"

"ASH!" Cam roared, and his eyes grew to saucers.

"What?"

"I said, leave it."

"Yeah, whatever, I'm out. I need a beer or something." He stormed from the room, the door slamming behind him.

"That went well," I smirked, the pain meds and whisky slowly working their way through my system.

"Jase, come on, cut him some slack. He's only worried. We all are."

"Yeah, yeah, save me the Mother Teresa routine. I knew what I was doing when I went down there."

"So why'd you do it?"

"Like you don't already know."

"For her?" His brow hit his hairline. "But why?"

Why?

That was the question I'd asked myself over and over since getting back to Ash's house.

"Because the thought of him hurting her any more than he already had kills me."

A slow smile cracked his face.

"What?" I asked.

"Took you long enough."

"Doesn't change anything," I groaned, pain burning through every part of me.

"I think it does. I think it changes everything."

"I'm not that guy, Cam. I'm not like you."

"You just got your ass handed to you... for a girl. I think you're more like me than you give yourself credit for."

I snorted. "I had him." There was no way Thatcher had the upper hand on me. Sure, I was bloody and bruised but so was he. My knuckles were busted wide open to prove it.

"So in the end you risked everything... for a girl."

"Not just any girl." My head dropped back, my eyes shuttering as the reality of everything sank in.

Asher was right. I'd blown everything I'd ever worked for. But it wasn't for nothing.

It was for her.

And I'd do it again. Over and over, if it meant protecting Felicity from the likes of Thatcher and his goons.

"He has some images of her... *us*." I groaned the words, guilt slamming into me. It was all my fucking fault. Thatcher might have been unhinged but I'd given him the ammunition he needed to come after Hailee and then Felicity. All this time, I'd thought by not caring, by not giving a crap about anyone around me, I was protecting myself. But they weren't the weak link.

I was.

"Images, what kind of... oh, shit."

"Yeah," I breathed out. I still had no idea how he got them, but I'd seen them with my own eyes; me and Felicity in my car down by the lake. "He threatened to send them viral unless I agreed to the fight."

"Did Aimee know? She was the one who messaged Asher."

"I have no idea why the fuck she was there. She turned up at my house to warn me it was a setup, that Thatcher intended on fucking me up enough to ruin my shot at playing in the play-offs."

"First Hailee, now you and Felicity. This isn't just some harmless prank, Jase; it's more serious than that."

"You think I don't know that?"

"We have to report him."

"I started it." I ground out. "None of this would ever have happened if it wasn't for that video I sent him of me and Aimee."

"True but that was between the three of you." Cam rubbed his temples. "You never passed that shit around. He's out of control and there's still nothing stopping him from sending those images to everyone. We have to report him."

"Give me some time to figure this out, yeah?"

"Jase..."

"Twenty-four hours, that's all I'm asking."

"Fine. But if you don't handle this the proper way, I will. Coach and

Principal Finnigan are going to blow a gasket when they find out about this, maybe the truth will soften the blow."

I didn't share his optimism, but it was hard to worry about the play-offs when I currently felt like I'd never lift a ball again.

"You look like shit. You sure I can't take you to the ER?"

"Nah, I'm good. Got everything I need." I flicked my head over to the bottle of Jack and box of pills.

"Okay, get some rest. If you need anything..."

"Thanks, and Cam?"

"Yeah?"

"Was she there? I mean, I think I saw there but it's all a bit hazy."

"She was there," he hesitated, "but she left."

"Right." His confirmation hurt more than any bruise caused by Thatcher's fist.

"She'll come around." He lingered by the door.

"You think?"

"I know so." A faint smile tugged at his mouth.

"How's that?"

"Because that's what you do when you love someone." Cameron slipped out of the room as if he hadn't just delivered a bomb.

He thought Felicity loved me?

After everything I'd done to her, the way I'd treated her.

It wasn't possible.

Was it?

Did I even want her to love me?

It was crazy.

Her and me.

I cared about her, sure. I wouldn't have done everything I had for her if I didn't.

But love?

I wasn't in love with her.

She was nothing like my usual type. Quirky and irritating. Unapologetically weird with her lists and lack of filter. But she was also kind and compassionate and she didn't take herself too seriously. And she had a banging body hiding underneath those god-awful overalls she wore.

My heart began to crash violently against my ribcage, my palms growing clammy. I was having some kind of reaction. A moment of complete 'oh fuck' clarity.

I was ass over elbow in love with Felicity Giles.

When I woke up the next morning, I was pretty sure I was in hell. So when a knock sounded on the door, I croaked, "Come in," hardly caring who it was. I just needed some damn pain meds.

The door swung open and Hailee's head peeked into the room. "Oh my god," she hurried over to me, unshed tears in her eyes.

"I hope you're not going to cry on me," I said gruffly, "because I don't do tears."

"What the hell were you thinking?" Perching gingerly on the edge of the bed, Hailee grabbed the box of pain meds and gave me two, handing me a glass of water to wash them down with.

A pained groan rumbled in my chest but I stuffed it down. "Thanks."

"Are you sure I can't persuade you to go the ER?"

"Not gonna happen. But I'll go see our physician Monday."

"Coach is going to lose his shit."

"It is what it is."

"Jason don't do that. Don't downplay the fact you just threw away the play-offs to try to defend my honor."

"Of course you think this about you, little miss 'look at me'." Even though it hurt like a bitch, I chuckled. The look on Hailee's face was just too damn priceless.

"You mean, you didn't do this to get Thatcher back for trashing the portraits?"

"Oh, I definitely got a couple of hits in for that." I managed a wink despite the bruising around my eye. "But no, it wasn't about you."

"So what the hell... Felicity." Her eyes widened. "This was all for Felicity."

"How'd you guess?"

"Because this isn't you. Well, it is, I mean you're not exactly known for your cool headedness. But you wouldn't risk everything, the play-offs, if it wasn't important." The understanding in her eyes was almost too much to bear. "What did he threaten to do?"

"He has some photos of us. Threatened to send them viral if I didn't agree to the meet. I couldn't do that to her, not after everything." Flopping back onto the pillows, I stared up at the ceiling.

"So all this? Pushing her away, shoving Jenna in her face, acting like you didn't care, it was all to distance yourself? To protect her?"

My eyes slid slowly to hers. "He knew she was someone to me. He knew she was my weakness, so yeah, I thought if I pushed her away, if I pretended I didn't care, he'd forget about her. I didn't know he had the images. He must have had one of his guys keeping tabs on me."

"Oh, Jason." Hailee did something she'd never done before; she grabbed my hand and squeezed gently. "You care. All this time you cared. You know you have to tell her, right?"

I gave her a pointed look.

"Jason, come on, she thinks you and Aimee—"

"Aimee is nothing to me."

"I know that, but Felicity saw the way she jumped in to protect you. Put yourself in her shoes. She didn't even know you had an ex."

"Fuck," I breathed out, pain splintering through me. Only this time, it wasn't just the physical kind.

Everything was so fucking messed up.

"You have to fix this. Otherwise, it was all for nothing."

That's where she was wrong though.

It wasn't all for nothing.

Because if I knew anything about relationships, about love, it was that you protected the people you cared about. You stood up for them and made sacrifices.

And I'd just made the ultimate one.

I'd sacrificed the one thing I wanted more than anything. But even now, even knowing I probably wasn't going to see a single play-off game, I didn't regret it.

I only regretted not choosing Felicity sooner.

33

Felicity

I WAS IN DREAM HEAVEN. Jason's greedy lips tracing featherlight kisses up the slope of my neck, the heat of his body radiating around me, his delicious scent assaulting my senses.

"Open your eyes, babe,"

"I don't want to," I murmured, feeling desire swirl low in my tummy.

"Felicity." His voice was so real. "Open your eyes."

"No, don't make me. I don't want this to be over." It was too nice here. Wrapped in his arms, safe and protected. Cherished. I snuggled my face into his shoulder, breathing him in.

"Jason," I sighed, his name sweet on my tongue.

"Yeah, babe?"

"Make love to me, please." I wanted him. More than I'd ever wanted anything. Certain, if he didn't touch me soon, I'd drown in the flames raging inside me.

A throaty groan filled my ears as his lips brushed the shell of my ear. "Open your eyes and ask me again."

Damn him. Even in my dreams he was insufferable.

"Fine, all good things have to come to an end eventually," I mumbled to myself because I knew the second I opened my eyes—

"Jason?" I grabbed the sheets, my body paralyzed as he loomed over me. "B- but what are you... *Jason?*"

"Hey." His swollen lip curved into a hesitant smile. "I'm sorry I scared you."

"Scared me?" I sucked in a harsh breath, my back plastered against the pillows. "You almost gave me a heart attack."

"Among other things." A faint smirk played on his face.

"Oh God," I mumbled, turning my face into the pillow. It hadn't been a dream at all. Jason was here, in my room.

He'd kissed me... and I'd begged him to make love to me.

The universe owed me some good karma in the future after all the shit it had put me through lately.

Sensing my impending meltdown, Jason backed up, giving me some space. My eyes adjusted to the darkness, revealing the extent of his injuries. I reached for him instinctively, ghosting my fingers over the dark bruises around his eyes. He leaned into me, exhaling a shaky breath.

"Why, Jason? Everything you've worked for..." my voice trailed off, the weight of what had happened on Friday night settling over us.

"For you," he whispered.

The words were like a gunshot to my heart.

Two little words I'd never in a million years expected to hear.

"Me?" I choked out, my eyes searching his for any signs this was a joke. That it was all a part of his cruel game.

"We should probably talk."

"Talk... you broke into my house in the middle of the night... to *talk*?"

"I was supposed to wait." He raked a hand through his unruly brown hair, letting it fall haphazardly around his face. "Had it all planned out and everything. But I was lying in bed, trying to ignore the pain, and I couldn't wait another second longer. I had to see you now."

"You did?"

I'd spent all weekend fretting over him, greedily absorbing any minute details Hailee would feed me.

Jason nodded, a small uncertain smile lifting the corner of his mouth. He winced at the involuntary action.

"It hurts?"

"Like you wouldn't believe. But not as much as it hurts knowing I might have screwed things up between us."

Us.

He thought there was an us still?

Maybe I was still dreaming, stuck in some beautiful nightmare.

"Is this real?" I asked quietly. He leaned in, cupping my face, brushing his thumb over my lips. Raw desire blazing in the depths of his eyes. "Does this feel real?"

"Honestly, I'm not sure." I could barely think straight with the way my heart was galloping in my chest, crashing against my ribs looking for a way out.

"What about this?" Jason moved closer, his lips touching mine.

"I'm still not sure, you should probably do it again. Just so I can be certain." I fought a smile and he chuckled, the sound like a salve to my battered heart.

Slowly, he threaded his fingers into my hair, tilting my face ever so slightly to align our mouths at the perfect angle. "Jason," I pleaded, desperate for him to kiss me, to show me this was real. But he hovered there, staring at me with such intensity I thought my heart might explode. His eyes were dark and hooded and filled with so much emotion, I couldn't breathe.

I couldn't do anything but wait.

"You are the single most important thing in my life, and I'm sorry. I'm so fucking sorry," he said with complete conviction.

Then he kissed me.

But it wasn't just a kiss at all.

It was Jason willingly handing over his heart. With every press of his lips, every stroke of his tongue, he silently told me everything I'd so desperately craved to hear from him as his mouth moved over mine. He might have been the one in control, setting the pace, but I was the one with the power. It simmered between us. An unspoken admonition. He was apologizing to me through actions, not words, but the ball was in my court regarding what happened next.

"Jason, wait," I said, physically forcing myself to break the kiss.

He dropped his forehead to mine, letting out a pained groan. "Hey," I said, sliding my hands gently against his cheeks, forcing him to look at me. "I'm here, I'm right here, but you're right, we should talk."

There was so much we needed to figure out. Things I needed to know before I let him off the hook.

"I can come back later," he started to pull away, "when it's—"

"Jase?"

"Yeah, Giles?"

"Shut the hell up and lie down with me." I shuffled over to make room for him and threw back the cover. His brow went up but his expression quickly softened.

"You're sure?"

"Get over here before I change my mind." My parents were sleeping right down the hall, and I didn't want to think about what my dad would do if he found me with a boy in my bed, let alone a Raider, but I wasn't about to give up the chance to have Jason here like this. In my bed, heart on his sleeve and ready to talk.

He kicked off his sneakers, his hoodie going next, before slipping in beside me. We lay on our sides, facing one another. "What did you mean, you did it for me?" I asked.

"Thatcher knew you were someone to me. He sent me some messages, threatening to come at me through you. So I distanced myself." His eyes shuttered. "Pushed you away."

"I see." I shuddered thinking about everything we'd been through the last few weeks, everything he'd put me through.

Jason pulled the covers up around us, refusing to let me escape from the conversation. "But it didn't matter because he knew the truth and he already had his ace card up his sleeve," he hesitated, guilt swimming in his eyes. "He had some images of us, down by the lake that day."

"No!" Panic flooded me, embarrassment flaming my cheeks, as my thoughts shot off in a hundred different directions.

"I'm so fucking sorry. I still can't figure out how he got them, but he threatened to make them viral unless I agreed to meet him."

"He has images... of me. Us?"

"I'm going to go to the authorities. It's gone too far. I realize that now. I will do everything in my power to make sure he doesn't release those photos."

Tears pooled in the corners of my eyes. I wasn't a slut. I didn't sleep around or date guy after guy after guy. But I'd done things with Jason... things I didn't want anyone to know about, let alone *see*. "Oh God, if my parents—"

"Hey, hey," he pulled me into his arms, tucking me against his solid body. "It won't come to that, I promise."

Hands pressed against his chest, I closed my eyes and inhaled a shuddering breath.

"I'll fix it, Felicity, you have my word." I didn't just hear the words, I felt them. Jason meant every single one. He'd done all this for me, to protect me. It was a lot to process.

Suddenly, a thought popped into my head. "What about Aimee?" I craned my head back to look at him.

"Aimee is no one."

"Jason..."

"She was someone, once upon a time. But that shit was over a long time ago."

"She's Thatcher's sister?" He nodded, his fingers tracing up and down my spine, making it difficult to concentrate. "You were together?"

"You really want to know this stuff?" he asked, and I gave him a weak smile, nodding. "I hadn't seen or spoken to Aimee in months until yesterday."

"Oh, that makes me feel better."

"Good, I don't want you to ever worry about other girls. There is no one but you."

"Jenna?" my brow rose accusingly.

He snorted. "A means to an end."

"Whatever happens next between us, promise me you'll never ever refer to me as a means to an end."

"You're not a means to an end, Giles. You're endgame."

If I wasn't already head over heels in love with Jason Ford, those three little words would have spun my world.

"Endgame? Sounds... serious?"

"Oh it is." He pecked the end of my nose. "Dead serious."

"I'm not entirely sure I understand exactly what it means, you might have to break it down for me." I fought a grin.

"It means you're mine."

"I'm yours, okay, I think I can get on board with that." Warmth spread through me. He said the words as if they were the simplest thing in the entire world. And I loved it.

I loved him.

I had for a while now. I'd just been too scared to admit it.

"Anything else?" I lowered my head, looking up at him through my lashes, acting coy.

"Yeah, I think it means come game day, there's only one number you'll be wearing." He captured my lips in a bruising kiss. "Mine."

THE NEXT TIME I woke was to my alarm and a very hard, very warm chest. I untangled myself from Jason's embrace and reached behind me, desperately trying to locate my cell to make the noise stop.

"What the—"

"Sorry," I whispered, "Alarm."

"Shit," he bolted upright and quickly sank back down, groaning in pain. "I didn't mean to fall asleep."

"I'm glad you did." Pushing my bed hair out of my face, I smiled at the sight of Jason sprawled out in my bed. At some point in the night, he'd taken off his jeans and jersey and climbed back in beside me, sliding his bare legs against mine.

It had been heaven.

"How long do we have before your parents surface?"

"Not long." I'd had the foresight to set my alarm thirty minutes earlier than usual so he could sneak out before they got up.

"Come here." He hooked his arm around my neck and pulled me down to him, his lips finding mine in a clumsy kiss.

"Ew, morning breath," I complained.

"You think I give a shit about that? Lips, now," he growled the words, fixing his mouth over mine, making a show of pushing his tongue deep into my mouth and tangling it with my own. My tummy clenched; a delicious ache spreading through me.

"How long did you say we have again?" Jason rolled onto his side, sliding my leg over his hip and rocking his erection into me.

"Not long enough." A soft moan spilled from my lips as he continued grinding against me. "Oh God, that feels..."

"Fuck, I need to stop. I need to—" A knock at my bedroom door had us both freezing.

"Morning, baby, are you awake?"

"Uh, yeah, Mom," I croaked, barely able to form words as Jason pressed into me again, a smug smirk gracing his bruised face.

"I'll make coffee. See you down there."

I waited a second to make sure she had left and then swatted Jason's chest. "You're so bad," I scolded, but his expression was twisted with pain. "Crap, I'm sorry. Where does it hurt?"

"Everywhere, but nowhere as bad as here." He grabbed my hand and closed it around his rock-hard dick.

"Jason!"

"You're telling me if I do this," he slipped his fingers inside my panties, "I'm not going to find you wet?"

"Oh God..." I pressed my lips together as he rubbed back and forth, sliding through my wetness. "We can't..." I moaned, lost in sensation.

"For once, I'm inclined to agree." His fingers disappeared and my eyes fluttered open, only to find him sucking them clean. "Later." Promise burned in his eyes as he leaned in, kissing me. Swirling his tongue around mine, letting me taste myself on his lips.

"How will you sneak out?" He could barely sit up, let alone execute a stealthy escape plan.

"Who said anything about sneaking out? Moms love me, remember?" My eyes widened to saucers and his face broke out in a wide grin. "Gotcha."

"Haha, now go, before my dad wakes up."

Jason climbed out of bed and grabbed his clothes.

"Your ribs," I blanched at the huge purple bruise painted along his side.

"It's nothing," he played it down, but I saw how carefully he pulled on his jersey and hoodie, pain behind his eyes with every movement. "I'll see you later, okay?"

It was on the tip of my tongue to ask what happened when we got to school, but Jason had already slipped into the hall. He glanced back, his eyes saying all the things we were yet to say.

Things I never thought we'd get to say.

And I knew in that second, this time it wasn't a game or some cruel prank.

It was real.

Jason Ford, Rixon's golden boy of football, was mine.

34

Jason

"ARE YOU SURE ABOUT THIS?" Cam asked me as we made our way into school. Everyone was looking; kids, teachers, even the few parents doing the morning drop off. I knew what they saw.

Jason Ford.

Star football player.

Cocky arrogant troublemaker.

People usually turned a blind eye. Usually excused my antics as 'boys being boys'. But not this time.

This time, people had gotten hurt.

I'd gotten hurt.

But they didn't know the truth. They didn't know I'd done what I'd done out of a need to protect Felicity. To stand up for the girl who consumed my every waking thought.

They didn't know at all.

As far as I was concerned, it could stay that way. I hadn't fought Thatcher for glory or in the name of the Raiders reputation, or even my own. I'd done it because when it came down to it, I was just a guy who loved a girl and refused to let some fucktard like Lewis Thatcher ruin her because of his beef with me.

I spotted her first. She was talking to Hailee and Mya near their locker bank, ignoring the rumble of whispers and gossip flying up and down the hallway.

"So did the two of you talk about what happens now?" Cam asked me as we slowly approached them.

"Nope." I couldn't tear my eyes away from her to answer him. Felicity was wearing boy jeans, slung low on her hips, a slither of skin on display where her shirt didn't quite meet the waistband. It was baggy around her midriff, tight over her chest, and hung off one shoulder. Her long brown locks were swept over one shoulder, her face void of makeup, her expression animated as she talked to her friends.

"So what's the pla—"

But I was already gone. Cutting through the stream of kids. Hailee noticed me first, her lips breaking into a wide grin. Mya was next, smugness dancing in her eyes, as if she knew this was a forgone conclusion. I gave zero fucks about their reactions though. The only girl I cared about still hadn't noticed me as I moved up behind her. Sliding my hands around her eyes, I leaned in and whispered, "Guess who?"

"Hmm, Asher?" She chuckled as I spun her in my arms and glared at her.

"Try again, Giles."

"Hi," she said around an uncertain smile.

"Hi."

Hailee and Mya backed up, giving the two of us space. The whole school seemed to have stopped around us, everyone watching their King fall for his Queen.

"Is it me or is everyone watching us?" Felicity cast a quick glance around.

"They're waiting to see if the rumor is true."

"Oh yeah?" Her smile grew. "And what rumor would that be?"

"That QB One is officially off the market." I inched closer to her.

"And is he?" She matched my step.

"I think it's pretty safe to say, he's taken."

"Damn, just when I'd finally plucked up the courage to tell him how I feel. Ah well, I guess I'll have to wait until whoever it is dumps his sorry ass."

"Did I ever tell you, you're so fucking weird?" I lowered my head to hers.

"Did I ever tell you, I have a serious thing for football players?"

"Players, plural? Because I know a couple of the guys who would love to hook—"

She swatted my chest. Before she could move her hands, I captured her wrists, keeping them pressed there.

"Something you want to tell me, Giles?"

"You first, Ford, I have a reputation to protect." She winked and I let out a hearty chuckle. This girl...

This fucking girl.

Leaning in, I brushed my lips over her ear and whispered, "I am so fucking gone for you."

Felicity eased back to look right in my eyes. "Is that your way of telling me you love me?"

Swallowing thickly, I nodded, aware this wasn't exactly how I planned to tell her.

"Good job, because I am completely and utterly gone for you too."

I didn't care we had an audience. I didn't care people had their cell phones out recording the moment QB One publicly handed over his balls to a girl.

I didn't care one bit as I pressed Felicity against the lockers and kissed the ever loving shit out of her. People would just have to get used to it because she was mine, and I was hers, and I intended on reminding her of that every second of every day.

"Ford, my office, now!"

All eyes went to me as I stood up and padded across the locker room. A couple of guys clapped me on the back, silently offering their support. But this was my burden to bear, and mine alone. Until I stepped inside his office to find I wasn't alone.

"Coach," I said coolly, waiting for the shit to hit the fan, sliding my eyes to the silent figure already seated in front of his desk.

"Sit," he barked, and I took the other empty chair. "I don't think I even need to ask my next question to know the answer. You're a mess, Son. A real damn mess."

I shifted uncomfortably on the plastic chair, trying to find a position that didn't make my lungs feel like they were on fire.

"As soon as we're done here, you head straight to medical. You hear me? If you've broken anything so help me God..."

I nodded, knowing this was one of those times Coach wouldn't appreciate a smart assed reply.

He tore off his ball cap and rubbed his head with sheer frustration. "Four more games, that's all I asked for. And you couldn't just listen. You know I'll have to go to Principal Finnigan with this, right? If he hasn't already found out since it seems to be the only thing on kids' lips this morning."

"Sorry, Sir." It sounded so lame in comparison to what was at stake, but it was all I had.

"So you're confirming his story?" he looked to Asher who rubbed the back of his neck.

"I, uh..."

"It's okay, bro. I already confessed I screwed up by goading Thatcher into that fight and you had to come save my sorry ass."

What the fuck?

I stared at Ash like he'd lost his goddamn mind. Or maybe I had. Because nothing he was saying was making any sense.

"Well, Jason, what do you have to say for yourself?"

"I, hmm, I..."

"It's okay," Ash whispered and my eyes slid back to his in question. He nodded, his eyes hammering home everything I didn't want to believe.

He was taking the fall.

For me.

My teeth ground together behind my lips as I tried to figure out what the fuck to do. If I let him take the fall, chances were his season was over. But if I told Coach the truth, my season was over, and maybe Asher's too for the fact he tried to save my ass.

Fuck.

"I haven't got all day, Son."

"It's okay, Jase, just tell him."

I couldn't do it. I couldn't be that guy. Not after everything.

"Sorry, Coach, but I have to tell you the—"

"The truth is, Coach," Ash cut me off, "Lewis Thatcher is a sick fuck who has spent the last three months coming after Jason through his friends and family. Jason didn't want to tell anyone to protect his step-sister and girlfriend."

"Girlfriend?" Coach frowned, rubbing his jaw.

"Felicity Giles, you may know her?"

"The name does ring a bell."

"Thatcher threatened to hurt Felicity over and over, but Jason refused to take the bait. His final threat was more persuasive," Asher threw me a sympathetic glance. "I knew if Jason found out about the threat he'd go after Thatcher, so I arranged the meet."

"And what exactly did you expect to achieve, Son?"

Ash shrugged in that easy way of his. "World peace?" I snorted. "Fuck if I know. But I couldn't just sit around and do nothing. Anyway, the whole thing was a set up. They jumped me and I had no choice but to call for back up."

"Which is when you intervened?" Coach cocked his brow at me.

"I... yes."

"To save your teammate's hide?"

"Yes, Sir."

"But we played straight into Thatcher's hand because he'd wanted Jase there all along."

"I see, and the rest of the team? How do they figure in all of this?"

"I took them as back up, but that was it." I ran a hand over my face.

"You have proof of Thatcher's threats?"

Asher nodded. "I have screenshots of everything."

"You do, since when?" I asked.

"Since I knew that one day we might need them."

"There's also a video and some photos, Sir. But they're hmm, quite graphic."

"You should have come to me with this. You should have come to me the second Thatcher upped the ante."

"Yes, Sir," we grumbled in unison.

"Will Miss Raine and Miss Giles attest your story?"

I nodded.

"Right, well, I have no choice but to take this to the Principal. Given your history with him, I wouldn't expect him to be on your side. You know what that means?"

Another, "Yes, Sir," filled the room.

Coach let out an exasperated breath. "I'll do my best, but it could be out of my hands. Now go on, get to class, both of you. And damn well stay there until I say otherwise."

We left his office in silence, but the second we were out of earshot, I grabbed Ash's arm. "What the fuck was that in there?"

"That was me saving your ass, so don't be a dick and mess things up. Stick to the plan."

"The plan? You do realize you just took the fall for something that could end your football season?"

"I know and I'd do it again if it means you get to play."

"But... why?" I was stunned.

"Because you're one of my best friends and I know how much State means to you. Besides, Finnigan is just looking for an excuse to come down on you and this could've opened up a whole can of worms you don't need." He went to walk off, but I tightened my grip on his arm.

"Asher, come on, think about this, it's crazy."

"Actually, it's pretty simple. I'm your friend and this is what friends do. You can thank me later." With that he yanked his arm free and strolled off as if he hadn't just saved my dream and let his go up in flames.

Later that day, I had another score to settle.

"Jason?" Jenna's eyes widened as I crowded her back into the girls' locker room. Girls gasped, some shrieking as they hugged clothes to their half-naked bodies.

"Everybody out, now," I roared, knowing full well that no one would complain. One by one, Jenna's friends and teammates scurried out of the locker room, leaving her at my mercy.

"J- Jason, you're scaring me."

"Good, you should be fucking scared." I closed the distance between us until I could smell the cloying stench of her perfume.

"What is it, what's wrong?" She tried to regain control of the situation. Batting her eyes, brushing her hair back to reveal an expanse of tan skin, the curve of her tits.

"Not going to work, Jenna," I seethed. "You see, I had an interesting chat with Aimee Thatcher earlier. Ring any bells?" Her face blanched, her eyes filled with fear. "I mean, you must know her right, since you've been visiting her house, drip feeding Thatcher things about me. About my. Fucking. Life."

"It isn't... it wasn't like that."

"So you didn't spread your legs and let him fuck you while whispering all my secrets in his ear?"

"It's all your fault," she shrieked, thrusting her hands into my chest and beating hard. "You dropped me like I was nothing. And for Felicity Giles, a fucking no one."

"Watch it, Jenna. You might think you're the Queen Bee around here, but I can soon strip you of that title." I could destroy her without even breaking a sweat. But I wasn't out for blood yet, I was out for answers.

"How'd you do it?"

All morning, I'd been pondering how Thatcher got the photos of me and Felicity. I'd assumed he had one of his guys following me, but it seemed a stretch. Even for Thatcher. It wasn't until Grady mentioned he'd seen Jenna talking to some Eagles players Friday as the fight dispersed that my mind began piecing together a more likely scenario. A quick call to Aimee confirmed my suspicions. Thatcher's guy was in fact, a girl. A girl who, against my better judgment, had an up close and personal relationship with me.

"Jason, I—"

"Answer the fucking question."

"I followed you, okay? I'd been watching you, noticed you always texting someone. It didn't take a rocket scientist to figure out who, the way you two sat staring at one another across the cafeteria." Jealousy dripped from her words. "I didn't plan to follow you, but I saw Felicity sneaking out and before I knew it, I'd gotten in my car. It was just a lucky break."

A low growl tumbled in my chest and the blood drained from her face again. "I didn't... that's not what I meant. I just meant it was a coincidence. Please, Jason, what are you going to do?"

I slammed my hand against the wall beside her and ground out, "Only what you deserve."

Then I walked away without a backward glance.

No matter our history, Jenna made her bed when she came after Felicity.

She could fucking rot in it.

35

Felicity

"HOW ARE we getting on in here?" George's head appeared around the door just as I got Benji back in his cage.

"We're good. I just finished grooming Benji and I was going to get started on Meagan and Frieda next." They were two of the cutest puppies I'd ever laid eyes on; mini Schnauzers I'd have struggled to tell apart if it wasn't for their contrasting collars.

"Actually, you have a visitor." Something flashed over his face.

"Visitor?" I washed my hands and dried them on paper towel. "Here?"

"He's waiting out front."

He?

I followed George out into the hall, my mind working overtime. As we reached the doors separating the front and back of the center, George paused. "I just want you to know you've already made an impression here. You're great with the animals, eager to learn, and Serena loves you, which is always a bonus." He gave me a tentative smile. "The position is yours for however long you want it."

"What are you—" George pushed opened the door and I gasped. "Jason? But what are you...?"

"Hey," he gave me a hesitant smile as he approached us. "Thanks, man," he held out his hand to George, "I really appreciate it."

"Umm, yeah, sure." My new boss ran a brisk hand over his head, guilt flaming his cheeks.

"Wait a minute." My gaze narrowed, sliding between the two of them. "Did he put you up to this?"

"He may have had a hand in it," George admitted sheepishly.

"Let me guess," I let out an incredulous sigh, "you're a Raiders fan?"

His cheeks turned beet red.

"I don't know what to say." I'd thought maybe George had found me a position because he liked me; it had never occurred to me he'd done it because Jason had asked him to.

"Can I borrow her?"

"She's all yours." There was an undertone to George's words that confirmed Mya's suspicion. He did like me. But he knew I belonged to someone else.

I gave him a half-smile. "Thank you. Should I still come by tomorrow?"

"Of course, Felicity. Like I said, the position is yours for as long as you want it."

With a small nod, I let Jason take my hand and lead me out of New Tail.

"You have some explaining to do," I said the second we were on the sidewalk.

"And I will." He pulled me in front of him, so we were face to face. "But first..." Jason slid his hands into my hair, tilting my face. His lips brushed over mine, slow and tender at first but it quickly became something else. Jason licked the seam of my mouth, pushing his tongue inside, finding mine. He tasted like mint, taking my breath away, as he explored every inch of my mouth. Branding me.

Possessing me.

Imprinting himself on my very soul.

When we finally broke away, we were both flushed and breathless.

"Hi," he said quietly.

"Hi." I fought a grin, still hardly able to believe this strong, scary football god was mine.

"What?" he asked.

"I just can't believe we're here, after everything."

"Believe it, babe." He dipped his head, nudging his nose against mine, stealing a chaste kiss. "Because you're mine now and there's no escaping me."

"Good job I have no plans to run then. Now," I slid my hands up his chest, "Fess up. What did you say to George to get him to give me a position?"

"It was nothing a few play-off tickets couldn't solve."

I balked. "Tickets. That's all I'm worth? Wait until I see him."

"Don't give him a hard time over it. I think he would have agreed without me throwing in the tickets to soften the deal."

"How did you even know... Asher," realization dawned on me. "Asher told you."

"He was only trying to help." Jason pulled me closer, his lips finding the soft skin beneath my ear. "I missed you."

"It's only been a few hours."

"Too fucking many."

"Is this the kind of boyfriend you're going to be? Needy?"

Jason lifted his head and frowned at me. "Needy? I'd handcuff you to me if I thought it wouldn't cause some serious trouble with your parents."

"Jason!"

"What?" He played dumb. "I can't help it if all I can think about is kissing you, getting inside you."

"Ssh, you can't say things like that to me here."

He leaned back in, brushing the shell of my ear with his lips. "Babe, I can say whatever the hell I want."

He was so bad.

So very bad and so very all mine.

It was going to take some getting used to.

"What did Principal Finnigan say?"

He took my hand and started leading me across the street to his car. "He's yet to make a decision. But it's not looking good for Asher."

"I still can't believe he did that."

"Really?" His brow shot up. "Because when I think about it, it's exactly the kind of crazy shit he would pull."

"He's a good friend."

Jason opened the passenger door for me and I slipped inside, waiting for him to get in. Once the door slammed shut behind him, the air in the car turned thick. "Do you wish it'd been him?"

"What?" I asked taken aback.

"Do you ever wish it was him you'd fallen for?"

"No." I didn't even need to think about it. "There was never a choice, Jason. You don't get to choose who you fall in love with."

"You love me, Giles?" His eyes slid to mine, dark and uncertain and so vulnerable it made my heart melt.

"I love you so much it terrifies me."

"Good." He leaned across and kissed me. "We can be terrified together."

TEN MINUTES LATER, Jason pulled up to his house, and cut the engine. "Nervous?" he asked, reaching over and tangling our hands together.

"Nervous? What could I possibly have to be nervous about? I've been in your house more times than I can count. Hailee's mom loves me." It came out smug despite the butterflies fluttering in my stomach.

"No one's home, babe." His smooth laughter filled the car.

"Oh," I stuttered, heat spreading through me. "Where are they all?"

"Hailee's with Cameron, and Denise and my dad are off doing whatever the fuck they like to do on an evening. The house is ours for at least the next four hours."

"Oh." This time I gulped.

"Hey," Jason's hands glided up my arm until he was brushing my neck. "You good?"

"Yeah." I blinked over at him. This was Jason. Nothing I hadn't already experienced—*and survived*—before.

"No pressure, okay?" His eyes searched mine. "We can go in there and watch TV and eat our body weight in chips. Or we can go in there and do homework. I just really, really want to go in there... with you."

"Okay."

"Yeah?"

I nodded, finding the courage to step out of his car. I don't know why I was so nervous suddenly. I'd let him claim me in front of half our class today at school. But this felt different.

This felt like coming out to each other, and after everything we'd been through, there was a little voice at the back of my mind whispering for me to be careful. To not jump in headfirst with him in case he had a sudden change of heart.

But it was too late.

I was already in deep waters hoping Jason would throw me a life raft.

Hoping *he* would be my life raft.

We entered the house in silence. It was the same four walls, the same collection of gaudy ornaments lining the shelves, and family photos Hailee's mom had scattered over the walls. Everything was exactly the same.

But I was different.

We were different.

"Is this weird for you?" Jason asked, no doubt sensing my hesitation.

"A little. I just... I never thought we'd get here and now we are and I'm so happy, I am. But—"

"You're worried I'll hurt you again." Shame washed over him. "Wait here." Jason dropped a kiss on my head before disappearing down the hall.

I stood there, arms wrapped around my waist, wondering what the hell could be so important he had to abandon me.

When he returned, he had that sheepish look again. "Jason," I said, "what did you do?"

He was holding a white plastic bag. "I was trying to think of a way to show you I want this. That I'm serious about *this*." He motioned between us. "So I got you something."

I peeked over, trying to see what was in the bag. But nothing could have prepared me for the Penn hoodie he pulled out.

"I wasn't sure of your size." He handed it to me. It felt soft and heavy in my hands.

"I don't understand..."

"Well, you're going to need one come next fall." Nervous energy radiated from him. "I have one too, but mine's black."

"You're telling me you got us matching hoodies?" My heart swelled.

"Well, yeah." He lowered his face, rubbing the back of his neck, looking up at me through thick dark lashes. "Isn't that what couples do?"

I had no words.

None.

I think Jason had stolen them all right around the time he completely stole my heart.

"I know I said I don't want you there, at Penn, but I was just lashing out. Of course I fucking want you there."

"Four years, that's a long time." I smirked. "What if things go south and we have to be around each other all the time?"

"Not possible." He hooked his arm around my neck and pulled me flush against his chest. "I already told you, we're endgame. So if you have doubts, I suggest you run now. Because I am locking you down for the next four-and-a-half years at least."

"Only four-and-a-half years?"

"When I enter the draft, I might need to cut you loose."

"Works for me, dating a pro football player isn't on my list."

His fingers dug into my sides, tickling and pinching. My laughter spilled freely, filling the space between us, the remaining cracks in my heart.

"I fucking love you." Jason's hand curved around my neck. "I never thought I needed anyone. But I need you, Felicity. I need you so much it hurts." He pressed his head to mine, breathing in sharply.

"So take me," I whispered.

"Yeah?" His eyes were wide and full of wonder.

And hunger.

So much hunger, my legs turned to jelly.

"I'm right here, what are you waiting—" The air *whooshed* from my lungs as Jason hoisted me over his shoulder and carried me up the stairs, ignoring my cries for mercy.

Inside his room, he slowly lowered me to the floor, letting every inch of him press up against every inch of me. We stood there, our eyes locked on one another's, neither of us saying a word. Simply soaking up the moment.

Eventually, I broke away, moving deeper into the room of the most complicated, most gorgeous guy I'd ever laid eyes on.

It was just as I expected. Dark and manly. Slate gray walls with splashes of black and chrome. The bed was drenched in black sheets with silver flecks. It reminded me of a storm. Alluring and mysterious from a distance, but deadly if you got too close.

Just like Jason.

"You're the first girl to ever see inside this room except Hailee," he said. I turned to meet his sincere gaze. He'd moved back to the door jamb, leaning against it casually, watching me.

"It's very... you."

Prowling toward me, Jason took an ounce of air from the room with every step, until he was on me, the air gone and my lungs burning with need. "You are so fucking beautiful. I don't deserve you."

I reached up and palmed his cheek, his scruff like sandpaper beneath my skin. "It isn't for you to decide what you deserve."

"The things I want to do to you would definitely make me undeserving."

My lips parted on a soft '*Oh*'.

"Last chance," he warned, his eyes darkening to the color of his sheets.

"I'm not running," I said defiantly.

"Good, because I'd chase you to the ends of the earth. You're mine, Felicity. Every single piece of you."

36

Jason

MY EYES TRACED over her face, taking in the flush of her cheeks; her slightly parted lips, soft and pink and utterly kissable.

"Where to start?" I pressed my palm against Felicity's breastbone, dragging it down her sweater until my fingers found the hem. Slowly, I tugged the material up her body, letting it bunch around her shoulders. "Fuck, I want to taste every inch of you."

"Jason," my name sounded like fucking heaven on her lips. I dropped to my knees, tracing my name on her stomach with my tongue. I wanted to mark her. Brand her in every way possible until we were bound so tight, she could never leave me. Because there was no going back now. I meant every word I'd said to her. She was endgame. I still wanted football, I still wanted Penn, and the NFL, and everything that came with it, but I didn't want any of it if Felicity wasn't right by my side for the ride.

Kissing a path to her bra, I slid my arms around her back and unhooked the clasp. My mouth greedily sucked one of her breasts, and then I gently bit her nipple. Her body jerked with pleasure, so I did it again... and again, until she was writhing in front of me, clawing at my shoulders.

"You're teasing me," she moaned, burying her fingers in my hair and yanking sharply.

My girl had claws and it was such a fucking turn on, I thought I might explode right there and then.

"I'm only just getting started." I climbed up her body, pulling her sweater and tank top off, letting her dusky pink bra slink off her arms and drop to the floor. My own hoodie and shirt went next. Hooking my arm around her waist, I pressed my hand against the small of her back until we were skin on skin, her delicate curves flush against my shredded muscles. Everything about us was different.

Hard and soft.

Rough and smooth.

Cruel and kind.

But we fit to perfection. Two parts of the same whole.

Her hair hung between us like a silky curtain, so I wound it around my fist, gathering it at her nape and pulled gently, forcing her to arch her back. Giving me perfect access to kiss and suck the hollow of her neck. I took my time, tasting and savoring her salty sweet skin.

"More," Felicity's cries filled the room, "I need more." Her nails grazed my shoulder blades.

"I got you, babe." Our lips met, hot and wet and needy; our tongues lapping and stroking and exploring. Her kisses were addictive and I knew no amount of hits would ever be enough.

Felicity became impatient, her hands tracing my abs, painting a torturous path down to the waistband of my jeans. She expertly popped the button and shoved her hand inside, grasping me. "Fuck," I choked out as she pumped me slowly. "This isn't what I had in mind," my voice cracked with raw lust.

"I can't wait. I need you," she breathed, "now."

I wanted to make her wait, to reacquaint myself with every inch of her body, and then all the parts I'd yet to explore, but truth be told, I couldn't wait either. My need for her was like a firestorm raging inside me, burning higher and higher with every touch, every taste.

We made quick work of each other's jeans and underwear, then I scooped her up and dropped her on the bed, not bothering to ask permission. Felicity giggled, the sound so fucking perfect I wanted to bottle that shit for a rainy day.

"Come here." She crooked her finger, scooting up the bed and letting her legs fall open. There wasn't so much as a hint of shyness or uncertainty in her eyes, her love for me blazing in her sea-green gaze.

Crawling over her, I slid between her legs, my rock-hard dick settling at her entrance. "Do I need to stop?" I arched my brow at her, hoping, praying she wouldn't make me.

"There's only ever been you," she said, "and I'm on birth control. But I know you've been with other—"

"No one."

"What?" She blinked up at me.

"There hasn't been another girl since New York."

Confusion swam in her lust-filled eyes. "But Jenna—"

"I never slept with her, I just let you think... Fuck." I dropped my head to her shoulder, regretting so much that happened between us. In trying to protect her, I'd hurt her, and it would always be there, in the background.

"Jason, look at me," her voice coaxed me out of hiding. "I don't care about what happened before, I only care what happens now and in the future." She hitched her legs higher, almost pulling me into her body. We both groaned at the intimate contact.

"So if I do this." I rocked my hips, pushing another inch inside her, "you're not going to hate me?"

Licking her lips, Felicity looked right at me, a seductive smirk spreading across her lips. "Didn't I tell you? There's nothing more I love than to hate you." Sliding her hands down to my ass, she pressed me further into her.

"Fuck," I groaned, bolts of pleasure shooting off in all directions inside me. "Do you have any idea how good you feel?"

"Show me," it came out breathy.

I rocked forward again, my hand sliding up one of her legs, anchoring us closer, making it so much deeper. My other hand found her neck, my fingers splaying around her possessively as I pulled out before sinking into her heat again.

My lips claimed Felicity's again, my tongue loving her mouth, the way my body loved her. "I love you," I whispered against her swollen lips, "I love you so fucking much."

"I love you too, Jason. I do."

My pace quickened, needing more. Needing everything she had to give. Our skin became damp, our kisses clumsy, all while Felicity met me thrust for thrust.

My partner.

My equal.

The girl who taught me there was more to life than the game.

Who taught me how to love.

The girl I planned on keeping for as long as she would have me.

THE NEXT MORNING rolled around too quickly. I'd dropped Felicity off at home last night and then gone home and drunk one too many whiskies. I was so fucking happy things between us were finally good, but there was still a lot hanging in the balance. So when Coach called me and Asher into his office after a grueling practice, I knew the wait was finally over.

"Come in, ladies," Coach motioned for us to take a seat. "Principal Finnigan has consulted with the school board, and in light of everything, they have decided to suspend you from the team, effective immediately."

Asher let out a heavy sigh, leaning forward on his elbows. "And Jase?"

"Principal Finnigan pushed for a suspension but the board felt that since you were coming to the aid of your teammate that a more lenient punishment was adequate." His mouth pulled into a grim line. "You're out for next week's game but if we make it through to the next round, you can play."

I sank back in the chair, running a hand down the back of my neck. I could play. If we made it to the second round of the play-offs, which I had every faith we would, I could play. But it came at a price.

Asher's season was over.

"Coach," I said ready to defend my teammate, my brother.

One of the best friend's a guy could ever have.

"It's fair," Ash interrupted me. "I won't contest. Besides, maybe they'll let me wear Vinnie the Viking. Go Raiders." It came out drolly despite the defeat in his eyes.

"Ash—"

"It's cool, bro." He shrugged. "I knew what I was doing when I went down there to meet Thatcher."

Coach Hasson watched us, watched me. He knew. Deep down, I didn't doubt he knew the truth, but he was letting it play out this way because sometimes good men had to make sacrifices, and without Asher's sacrifice, the Raiders would be going into the play-offs without their star player.

"I'm sorry it came to this, real damn sorry," he addressed Asher. "You're a good kid, Bennet, and I don't doubt you're going to have a successful career with the Pittsburg Panthers. Principal Finnigan might get the final say on whether or not you play, but it's my team and my field and I expect to see you sitting there on the bench supporting your teammates, you hear me?"

"I wouldn't be anywhere else, Coach."

"Good, now get out of here."

The door clicked shut behind Asher, sucking the air from the room.

"You know, I couldn't sleep last night. I lay there worrying I was about to lose not one but two of my best players going into the play-offs. It's a Coach's worst nightmare."

"Coach, I—"

"You listen up and listen good, Jason," he gritted out, disappointment rippling off him. "I don't know all that happened with Thatcher and quite frankly, I don't want to know. But you have got to learn to channel your anger, Son. You think I don't know kids like you and Thatcher? Hell, I used to be you. I thought I was untouchable, a god on and off the field. But my old man refused to let me forget who I was and where I came from. He kept my feet firmly on the ground.

"I know you and Kent have issues, I know it hasn't been easy growing up in his shadow, but for the love of God, do not throw away what could be the opportunity of a lifetime for the likes of the Thatcher's of the world. You're better than that. You take all the crap, all the anger and resentment, and channel it into football. Or if that fails, you find yourself a damn good woman to help keep you grounded."

I chuckled at that. I'd gotten to know Mrs. Hasson quite well over the years and it wasn't any secret she kept Coach in line.

"This Miss Giles. You think it could be serious?"

"I think so, Sir."

"Good, you hold onto her and don't let go, you hear me? When you have the world at your feet like you do, girls are a dime a dozen. They'll all want a piece of the action, the glory, but it's a rare thing to find a girl who will see beyond all that. A girl who will stick around long enough to realize there's more to you than football."

"Got it," I said, trying to disguise how deeply his words affected me.

"There's just one last thing before you leave. I thought you might like to know the school board are issuing a full investigation into Mr. Thatcher and Miss Jarvis. They won't get away with this, Jason. But I'm begging you. Let the authorities handle it from here on out."

"I think I can do that, Coach."

"Glad to hear it. Okay, get out of here. We have a game to prepare for. Just because you're out for the first game doesn't mean I don't expect one-hundred-and-ten percent at practice, okay?"

Nodding, I moved to the door, pausing. "Hey, Coach, you ever get into trouble back in the day?"

"Does a bear shit in the woods?" A rare smirk lifted the corner of his mouth. "Now go, before I change my mind."

The locker room had cleared out by the time I was done. Only Asher remained, sitting on the bench near his locker cage. "Hey," I said, dropping down beside him.

"Hey," he mumbled, kicking his sneakers against the floor.

"Why, Ash?" I'd already asked him the question but that was before the sentence had been handed down.

"Because this was always how it was supposed to be; you get the girl and the glory."

"Ash, come on..." I nudged his shoulder with mine.

"It's all good." Raking a hand through his hair, he finally lifted his eyes to me, but his smile was distant. "It's your dream, man, so make it count."

With a small nod, he got up and walked out of the locker room. Leaving me sitting there with nothing but my regrets.

They said heavy was the head that wore the crown. Well my crown was coiled in guilt and shame, and it weighed a fucking ton.

37

Felicity

MY EYES FLICKED to the wall clock for the tenth time in less than ten minutes.

"Felicity, sweetheart, is something wrong with your food?"

"No, Mom, it's great." I forced a smile, pushing the noodles around my plate. "I... umm... it's just, well, there's something I want to talk to you about. Two things actually." I'd hoped to sit down with her and Dad, but he got held up at the office again, and I figured it might be a blessing in disguise. If I broke the news to her first, then she could help break the news to my dad.

"I'm listening." She placed her silverware down and leaned in attentively. "Whatever it is, baby, I'm sure it doesn't warrant all this worry." Her eyes softened.

"So funny story, I—" The doorbell startled me, making me choke on the words yet to come.

"Are you expecting someone?"

I was... but he was fifteen minutes early.

Damn him.

"I'll get that, Mom." I was up and out of my chair before she could stop me, all but running down the hall. Yanking the front door open, I hissed, "You're early."

"Hailee said you might need some moral support." Jase's brow went up. "And I brought back up."

"Back up?"

He pulled his arm from behind his back, revealing a bouquet of hand tied roses. "They're beautiful." I went to take them from him, but Jason snatched them out of reach.

"Actually, they're for your mom. Hailee said they were her favorite."

"Are you sure you haven't done this before?" Stepping to the side, I let him enter. But Jason paused, turning to meet my dreamy gaze.

"Only for you. Only ever for you. You owe me, Giles." He grinned, leaning in to steal a kiss.

"Felicity, sweetheart," Mom's voice filtered down the hall, "is everything okay?"

"Fine, Mom. I'm coming."

"Already?" Jason whispered, tracing his mouth down my neck. "I haven't even touched you yet."

"Behave." My hands pressed into his chest. "This has to go well." Because if it didn't... well, it didn't bear thinking about. I went to go, but he grabbed my wrist, pulling me back to him.

"Hey, it's going to be okay, Felicity. Whatever happens, we'll deal with it, okay? Together."

Any apprehension I felt melted away. Jason might have been new to the whole relationship thing, but so far, he was doing a pretty amazing job.

"Ready?" I asked him, feeling myself fall into his dark intense eyes. Our mouths fused together again, like magnets unable to fight the attraction.

"Felicity?" Mom's voice was closer now.

Crap.

Lips still attached to Jason's, I slid my eyes to the hall to find her standing there, watching us with a mix of mild curiosity and panic. "Hmm, hey, Mom." I finally detached myself from my boyfriend's mouth. "Surprise."

"Surprise? I'm not sure I follow..." her eyes narrowed, moving from me to Jason and back again. "Is that who I think it is?"

"Hi, Mrs. Giles. I'm Jason. Jason Ford." He stepped forward, thrusting the bouquet of flowers at her. "It's a pleasure to meet you."

"These are for me?" She was giving him a serious case of the mom-stares.

"They are. A little birdy told me they were your favorite."

"They're very beautiful. Thank you, Jason." Mom graciously accepted the flowers despite the scowl on her face. "Now would you care to explain why you're in my house, kissing my daughter?"

"About that, Mom. I can explain. Jason is..." The words were right there, on the tip of my tongue, but I froze.

I totally and utterly froze.

Fingers sliding against mine, Jason's touch slowly thawed the panic coiled around my throat. "I'm Felicity's boyfriend."

"B- boyfriend. Oh my... Well, that is a shock. *Boyfriend*?" Her eyes went to mine and I managed a small nod. "I see, and how long has this been going on?"

"It's fairly new," Jason said with an easy confidence, and I was beginning to wonder if there was anything he couldn't do. "But rest assured, I care about your daughter very much."

"That's... good to know." Her hand slid to her neck as if she was having a hard time breathing. "Maybe we should all sit down." Mom spun around and disappeared down the hall, and I slumped against Jason.

"This is not how I wanted this to go," I let out a heavy sigh. "Did you see her face? She's mortified."

"Hey." Jason's fingers slid underneath my jaw, tilting my face to meet his steely eyes. "At least she knows now. She'll come around."

"How can you be so sure?"

"Because she loves you."

"Okay." Inhaling a deep breath, I said, "Let's go finish this." Because her world was about to spin one more time before the evening was over.

I only hoped we all survived.

We found Mom in the living room, sipping what looked like a glass of liquor. Dear God, I'd driven my mother to drink. *There's one for your list.*

"I'm so sorry, Mom. This wasn't how I wanted you to find out. I was trying to tell you over dinner, but the words just wouldn't come out."

"I won't deny it's a lot to process. I had no idea you were even dating; you never said anything." Hurt flashed in her eyes, making guilt snake around my heart.

"I'm not dating, I mean, I wasn't... Me and Jason just sort of happened." My eyes lifted to his. "I didn't plan for any of this."

"Well, if there's one thing I know, it's that you can't help who you fall for. I mean, take me and your father for example." She smiled wistfully. "I just thought you had more sense, sweetheart."

"Mom!" I scolded.

"Forgive me, Jason, I didn't mean to sound so insensitive. I'm sure you can understand I'm not bowled over at the idea of my daughter dating a football player, let alone Rixon's star quarterback."

He stiffened beside me, squeezing my hand a little tighter. "We're not dating, Mom," I said. "I love him. I'm in love with him."

If she'd been surprised in the hall watching me kiss Jason, it was nothing compared to the expression she wore now. "Felicity Charlotte Giles, in love, really?"

"Really."

"And you," she glared at Jason. "What are your intentions for my daughter?"

He cleared his throat and I wanted the ground to open up and swallow me whole. Jason might have signed on for my brand of crazy, but he was about to learn I had nothing on my mother.

"I'll be honest, it's not a question I imagined answering so soon." Strangled laughter rumbled in his chest. "But I love her, ma'am. She makes me want to be a better man. Makes me want things I wasn't sure I ever wanted. I understand you have concerns, I would too. But please know I would never do anything to hurt her."

Mom's expression barely softened. "You've certainly got a charm about you, don't you?"

Oh dear God, despite her stone mask, my mother was flirting with my boyfriend.

I was never going to live this down.

"I try," Jason quipped back, and I stamped on his foot. He smothered a grunt.

"Your father isn't going to like this, sweetheart."

"I was kind of hoping you might help soften the blow." I flashed her my best puppy-dog eyes. "But before you make any decisions, there's probably something else you should know."

"Oh God, you're not pregnant, are you?"

Jason started choking beside me while Mom stared at me expectantly. And I sat there, shrinking into the chair, wondering when life got so complicated. Knowing the answer was simple.

Jason freaking Ford.

After I broke the news to Mom that I planned on switching my business degree to animal science, and she'd had a semi-meltdown, I let Jason drag me away to give us both some space. I'd broken her heart but as he kept reassuring me, it would heal. Because that's what hearts did. Sure, maybe they never quite got pieced back together the same way, but they would carry on beating.

"How are you feeling?" he asked me as he drove to wherever it was he was taking me.

"Sad, but mostly relieved. I'm their only child, their baby. I didn't want to hurt them."

"She'll come around, I promise." His hand splayed over my knee, rubbing gently. I covered it with my own, grateful for his reassurance.

"And my dad?"

"Him too. It might not happen overnight, it might not even happen over a few months, but it will happen." I murmured some incoherent reply, too depressed to answer. "You deserve all your dreams, Felicity, and they will realize that one day."

"Where are we going anyway?" I changed the subject. I wasn't feeling in the mood, but Jason had insisted he had something to show me. I never could resist him, and I wasn't about to start now.

When we turned off the main road out of town and took the familiar dirt path down to the lake, I groaned. "Seriously? You brought me here, now? The last thing I want to do right now is bounce on your—"

"Giles?" He cut the engine.

"Yeah?"

"Shut the fuck up and get out of the car."

Well, okay then. Rolling my eyes, I shouldered the door and climbed out. The lake shimmered under a blanket of twinkling stars. "God, it's so beautiful out here."

Jason came up behind me, wrapping his arms around my waist. "A little birdy told me you almost completed your list."

"Almost."

There were only three things remaining: fall asleep under the stars, get a tattoo, and go to Winter Formal with a date. Although I still wasn't sure about getting a tattoo. It seemed so permanent.

"What if I told you, you can tick two of those things off tonight?"

"We're going to sleep out here?" Because I was pretty sure my boyfriend didn't have his tattoo license, and Winter Formal wasn't for another couple of weeks.

I craned my face around to his, unable to hide my grin. "Only if you want to," he said.

"But it's freezing."

"So technically, I thought we could sleep in the car, but the view is the same."

"It's perfect." I brushed my lips over his. "Thank you. But that's only one—"

Jason shoved something into my hand. I plucked open the note.

Roses are red, violets are blue
I'd really like to go to Winter Formal with you?

Stifling a giggle, I said, "Fess up. Asher wrote this, didn't he?"

"He may have helped a little."

Turning in Jason's arms, I leaned up, touching my forehead to his. "I'm glad the two of you are okay."

"You really think I want to talk about Ash right now?"

"What else did you have in mind?" I asked, coyly.

"First." he dipped his head, kissing my collarbone, sucking the sensitive skin between his teeth. A shiver rolled through me, my eyes fluttering closed. "I want your answer."

"Yes," I breathed, desire humming through me.

"Good." Jason spun me so that my ass hit the edge of his car. "Now I'm going to make love to you on the hood of my car and then we can cuddle talk about the final thing on your list before we fall to sleep under the stars, sound good?"

Looping my arms around his neck, I smiled. "It sounds perfect."

EPILOGUE

FOUR WEEKS later

Felicity

"My god, I can't watch," I buried my face into Hailee's arm as we watched from our preferential seats. Mya was with us, as well as Jason's dad and Hailee's mom, and Cameron's parents. Asher was on the outs with his parents since the suspension, so they hadn't made the trip.

A collective *'oooh'* roared through the crowd as the Bulldog's defensive end took down Cam for the third time.

"Is it always this tense?" Mya asked, to which me and Hailee both answered, "No."

"Sorry I asked." She held up her hands, grabbing another hand of popcorn.

"Seriously?" I gawked at her.

"What," she shrugged, "I'm hungry."

I couldn't eat. I was too nervous. My heart had been in my mouth for most of the game. I knew how much this meant to Jason. He'd played it down a lot around Asher; trying to smooth the cracks that had appeared between them ever since Asher took the fall about the Thatcher ordeal. But when it was just the two of us, when I was lying in his arms, nothing between us, I felt his fear. Fear of failure, of letting his team down, his coach, the entire town.

But most of all, of letting himself down.

He'd worked so hard for this, they all had, but no one wanted it more than Jason. It wasn't just some high school accolade; it was his legacy. His way of proving himself. So watching him and the rest of the team get their asses handed to them, was almost too much to bear.

"Run," Hailee yelled, "Run."

We both held our breath, waiting for the moment our offense reached the end zone, but a Bulldog defensive player came out of nowhere and slammed into Grady, knocking him clean off his feet.

"Dammit."

"At least he almost got there that time," Mya remarked.

I levelled her with an incredulous look. "Just because your guy isn't out there on the field doesn't mean you can't at least pretend to be interested."

"I'm interested." She sat a little straighter. "And what do you mean, *my guy*?"

"You know exactly what I mean." She and Asher had gotten closer since I got with Jason but they were both still pleading the fifth on whether it was more than friendship.

"We're just friends."

Case in point.

Rolling my eyes, I settled my gaze back on the field, searching out Jason. Pride radiated from every bone in my body. Not because he'd led his team to this point; the whole town knew he'd do it, but for the fact he was mine.

For how far we'd come.

Rixon's complicated, brooding, cruel, star quarterback was changing right before my eyes. He was warmer and more open, no longer afraid to tell me how he felt. Even less afraid to show me. He'd even made an effort to get to know my parents, although that was a work in progress. My dad was taking some warming up to the idea I had a boyfriend, let alone a boyfriend by the name of Jason Ford who I planned to go off to college with next year.

Of course, Jason still liked to talk dirty and make me blush at every opportunity, but I didn't mind. In fact, I'd grown to love it. He pushed my boundaries and I pushed his right back.

And I couldn't wait for the next summer when we left for UPenn to start the rest of our lives.

Together.

Jason

"Raiders, gather in," I yelled like a general commanding his army. My teammates huddled together, waiting for my words of encouragement. For the profound speech to carry them into the fourth quarter.

"Listen up," it came out breathless. I was running on empty; we all were. "No team ever wants to be in this position; going into the fourth trailing by eight points. But we can do this. I know we can. Forget all the other games, forget what happened last game." When we'd almost fumbled our comfortable win by giving the opposing team room to score a touchdown with two minutes on the clock. Luckily, we were able to get the conversion before the final whistle, but it had been the most stressful two minutes of my life.

"Four years and it all comes down to this. Whatever happens, I'm proud to call myself a Raider, and you should be too. Hands in, Raiders on three."

The huddle grew tighter as my teammates dropped their hands on mine. My eyes found Asher on the sideline and before I could think about it, I yelled, "Yo, forty-two, get your ass over here," giving zero fucks he wasn't supposed to move from the bench. He deserved this as much as the rest of the guys.

"Feeling the pressure, QB?" he smarted as he jogged over to me.

"You deserve to be here." I held his eyes, silently telling him everything I'd been too chicken shit to say.

Thank you.

I owe you.

You're the best friend a guy could ever have.

He gave me a curt nod and then said, "Are we doing this or what?"

"On your word, Ash."

"Raiders on three. One. Two. Three..." Our battle cry rang out around me for the last time, our six-thousand strong crowd echoing the word at us.

It was something to behold, standing there on Hershey Stadium's now tarnished field, the blinding Friday night lights blazing down on us. Making us seem larger than life. Worshipped and adored. The next time I did this, my jersey would be Penn Quaker red, white, and blue, and I'd be a rookie. But I was ready. Hungry for it.

College.

Football.

A fresh start with Felicity.

It couldn't come soon enough. But first, we had a game to win.

Felicity

"Are you sure this is a good idea?" I asked no one in particular as I stared up at the neon sign reading *Ink City*, nervous energy vibrating through me.

"He'll love it," Mya whispered in my ear as the guys jostled one another, the effects of our few celebration drinks showing. "Besides, it's the last item on your list, you can't back out now."

I nodded slowly, watching the guys. They were buzzed, we all were. Still riding the high of the win. The Raiders had done it, in the last minute of play. Cam getting the final touchdown.

"My parents will—"

"*Never* find out about it. Stick to the plan."

"The plan, right." I took a deep breath. Hailee caught my eye and frowned.

"What are you two up to?"

Ignoring her, I moved to the front of our group and grabbed the door handle. "Are you guys doing this or not?"

"Fuck, I love it when she takes charge," Jason smirked, and I rolled my eyes right back.

"Oh, I'm in," Asher bounced on the balls of his feet. "I'm so fucking in. State Champs 2019, here I come."

"I hate to break it to you, *Champ*," Mya clapped him on the shoulder, "But can you claim the title if you didn't actually play?"

"Way to burst a guy's bubble." He scowled but it quickly melted away. He was too damn wired. We all were. The after-game celebrations had been crazy, everyone rushing onto the field to celebrate with the team. Then there had been dinner at the hotel's restaurant with close family and friends. Afterwards, Coach finally let us off the hook. Officially, we weren't supposed to leave the hotel, but unofficially, Coach agreed to turn a blind eye as long as we all surfaced tomorrow morning for the buses home.

"Either way," Asher went on, "I'm getting it done. No girls at college are going to know I didn't play. They're only going to see 'State Champ' and flock to me like—"

"Flies to shit?" Mya deadpanned.

We all streamed into the store, instantly assaulted with the sound of tattoo guns and rock music. Jason walked up to the desk and did all the talking. "Three?" he called over to us and the guys nodded. But before he could confirm with the receptionist, I called, "Make that four."

"Holy shit, Fee," Asher whistled between his teeth. "For real?"

"Just something small," I said, my eyes sliding to Jason. "It's the last thing on my list."

"Hell yeah, you heard my girl, make that four."

His girl. I don't think I'd ever get used to hearing him call me that.

"Take a seat and Auden will be with you shortly."

Jason came over to me, dipping his head to my ear. "You sure about this?"

I gave him a little nod, not trusting myself to speak. We'd talked about what I might get if I went through with it. After all, it was the only remaining item on my list. But when he saw it, he was going to freak.

I'd already fallen in crazy messy love with him, so I might as well get the crazy messy tattoo to go with it.

Jason

"What's taking them so long." I growled, pacing back and forth outside the room where Felicity currently was, alone with Auden, with his hands on her body, touching her.

"Chill, man." Cam's hand clamped down on my shoulder. "He's only doing his job."

"Yeah, well, she should have let me in there with her."

"Maybe she was worried about passing out or getting sick."

I threw Ash a hard look. Like I gave a shit about that. My favorite version of Felicity was first thing in the morning, hair all mussed up and crazy, her eyes heavy-lidded with sleep, her skin damp from my touch.

I loved sleeping with her, but it usually didn't lead to much actual sleep.

It wasn't my fault she was so irresistible, and I was a hot-blooded guy who was powerless against her voodoo magic.

The vibration of the gun behind the door finally stopped. "Thank fuck," I grumbled, moving closer.

A few minutes later, it swung open and Felicity skipped out.

"About time."

"Sorry," she said meekly. "It hurt more than I expected."

"Can I see?" I asked expecting a tiny heart or some script-font life quote girls liked to get. She'd had a few ideas but had been tightlipped about a decision. So when she said, "Don't freak out," the floor went from under me.

"What did you do?"

Felicity glanced around the store, and moved in closer. She lifted her sweater up, yanking the neck of her tank down, and everything slowed down.

"Tell me that says what I think it says." My heart was pounding so hard I thought I might pass out.

"Oh, it says it all right." Asher was beside me, staring at the curve of Felicity's perfect breast like he'd never seen a girl's naked tits before.

There in tiny Varsity font, stamped right across where her heart lay, were four little words that shouldn't have pleased me so much.

Property of a Raider.

"Flick," Hailee gasped, her eyes growing to saucers, "Please tell me that's temporary."

"It's not." She dropped her sweater, meeting my gaze. "Now, no matter what happens, a part of my heart will always be yours."

"Holy fucking shit," Asher slapped his hands against his thigh. "If you don't put a ring on it, I will." He smirked at me and I glared back, sending him a silent message.

Over my dead body.

THE HARDER YOU FALL

To My Readers
Thank you for loving the Raiders as much as I do!

1

Mya

I WOKE STARTLED, grasping the barely familiar sheets in my fingers as I tried to regulate my breathing.

It was just a dream, I silently whispered.

Just a messed up, distorted version of things. It wasn't real.

"It's not real," my shaky words pierced the silence.

When I'd first moved to Rixon from Philadelphia, the nightmares had been every other night. My aunt wanted me to see a therapist, but I wasn't about to sit in front of some shrink and let them dissect my dreams. I knew what haunted me in my sleep. I didn't need to give it a name or reason or excuse.

Sometimes people experienced bad things and it left marks. Scars invisible from the outside but so real on the inside that you never forgot. You just learned how to deal. How to get up each day, paste on a smile, and survive.

Surviving in a place like Rixon might not have been a matter of life or death, but it still had its moments.

I finally pushed back the cover and climbed out of bed, trying to tame the dark, unruly spiral curls out of my face. My bedroom in my aunt's house was small but cozy. She'd never had children, but she had tried her best to make it homely for an eighteen-year-old girl who was more of a stranger than family. Lilac wasn't my color, but I appreciated the effort.

My favorite thing about my new space was the small adjoining bathroom. Aunt Ciara's room adjoined the master suite which meant we didn't have to share. A luxury I hadn't been afforded back in Philly.

After washing my face and brushing my teeth, I pulled on some clean clothes and made a second attempt at fixing my hair, eventually settling on dragging it into a ponytail. The girl in the mirror looked like me but she hadn't felt like me in a really long time. I guess that's what happened when you were forced from your home, your life, and shipped off to live in the ass crack of nowhere. If I hadn't been paired with Felicity Giles on my first day at my new school, Rixon High, I didn't doubt my existence here would be almost intolerable.

As it was though, I had become fast friends with Felicity and her best friend Hailee Raine. Those girls were something else; refusing to conform to the Rixon way of football and more football. I decided to overlook the minor detail that they were both dating football players now. And not just any football players; Rixon Raider royalty to be exact. The irony wasn't lost on me, or them for that matter. But you couldn't help who you fell for. I knew that better than anyone.

My cell phone vibrated and I grabbed it off the desk, reading Felicity's text.

Flick: Running late... I stopped over at the Ford's.

Rolling my eyes, I typed a quick reply.

Me: Say no more. I'll see you in a few.

That was what I loved about Felicity. Despite being in a relationship with one of the broodiest, meanest, and downright arrogant guys I'd ever met, she hadn't wavered in her friend-ability. Every morning, even if she was a little late sometimes, Felicity picked me up for school. And every morning, we talked about all the things girlfriends should talk about.

My cell vibrated again and I smiled, eager to see whatever zany reply Flick had cooked up. But when I ran my eyes over the screen, I froze.

J: I need you, Mya. Please...

I quickly deleted the message and shoved my cell in my jean pocket. Trying to ignore the way it burned a hole. If I texted him back, we'd go around and around in circles like we always did.

Jermaine might have needed me.

But it wasn't enough.

I wasn't enough.

I never would be.

So I did what I'd done every day since arriving here. I grabbed my school bag, headed downstairs and waited for my ride.

Because sometimes pretending was better than facing the truth.

"Mya, come in," Miss Hampstead, the school guidance counselor, smiled up at me from behind her desk. "How are you?"

"Okay, I guess."

"You guess?"

"It's Monday morning," I said. "Can things ever really be okay on a Monday morning?" My lips curved into a tight smile.

"Oh, I don't know." She laughed softly. "I quite like Mondays. The start of a new week, the endless possibilities, the chance to be better."

"Spoken like a true guidance counselor."

We both laughed at that.

"So I just wanted to check in and see how you're doing? Your teachers are all very pleased with your progress and your grades are looking great. Have you given college anymore thought?"

"Actually, I have." I unzipped my bag and dug around inside, pulling out the stack of papers. Handing them to her, I sat back and waited. Miss Hampstead took her time, running her eyes over my notes.

"Excellent. We can set aside some time before the holidays to get these submitted if you'd like?"

"Sounds good to me."

"I noticed you've picked two out of state schools and Temple University."

I nodded, feeling my throat close. "I want to keep my options open."

"Having options is good. Not that I suspect you'll have any problems, with your transcripts looking as strong as they do."

I tapped my knee rhythmically, forcing a smile. "Great, can I...?" I thumbed to the door.

"Actually, before you go, I just wanted to ask how things are... socially."

"Socially?" My brows pinched.

"Yes. I'm aware you've made quite good friends with Hailee Raine and Felicity Giles."

"That's correct."

"And they are currently dating Cameron Chase and Jason Ford."

"Miss Hampstead, if you have something to say, just say it."

She let out a small sigh, her expression softening. "I'm sure you're more than aware of the recent issues between Jason, and Lewis Thatcher over at Rixon East High."

"It's hard *not* to be aware." Football was to Rixon what oxygen was to the human race.

"I just want you to be careful, okay? You're new here and you're..." She swallowed hard.

"You can say it, I am fully aware that I'm the odd one out."

"Rixon is a good town with a lot of good people, Mya. But small towns like this can also be difficult places for... outsiders."

"You mean people of color?" My brow rose sardonically.

She sighed. "Rixon High likes to pride itself on being inclusive, Mya, but the reality is over ninety-six percent of our students are White American."

"I'm in the four percent club, got it."

"Mya, I know this isn't an easy conversation to have, but I just wanted you to know that I'm here, if you need anything to make your time with us easier, or if a problem arises."

"Sure thing, Miss Hampstead. I appreciate it." But what I really wanted was to get the hell out of her office.

"Okay, well, I think that's it for now. My door is always open."

With a small nod I left her, only to bump into another face of concern.

"Hey, everything okay?" Felicity was waiting for me.

"Yeah, just the usual. Newsflash, did you know ninety-six percent of the student body at Rixon High are white?"

"She said that?"

"Yep."

"Wow, that's... I don't really have any words."

"Welcome to my world," I grumbled as we made our way toward class.

"So, me and Hailee were talking at the weekend and we think we should do something epic for New Year." Felicity looped her arm through mine.

"How epic are we talking?" I gave her a sideways glance. "Because the last time you wanted to do *something epic* you got a very real, very permanent tattoo."

Her cheeks flushed. "Not that epic. But Rixon on New Year's Eve is hardly anything to shout home about. Usually, Asher has a big party and everyone gets so wasted they can't even remember what year it is the next morning."

"I thought you never went to his parties before this year?"

"We didn't. But people talk." She shrugged. "Anyway, I told you about the time we went to New York with the guys?"

"You mean the time you gave it up to Jason?"

"Ssh!" She hugged me closer. "That is not the point right now. Asher's cousins are super rich and know all the best clubs. And this time, you can come with us."

"Hmm, I'm not sure. That sounds kind of—"

"You have to come. Even if we don't go clubbing, we can stay in the swanky penthouse again and have our own private party. It's our last New Year's before college. We've got to make it one to remember."

"It sounds kind of expensive."

"Oh hush, we'll probably just throw in some cash for gas. Asher's dad will handle the penthouse and the guys will buy all our drinks. The only thing you'll really need is a killer outfit."

"It'd just be the six of us?"

She shrugged again. "I guess, unless Vaughn and Riley join us again. But I'm not sure how I feel about her coming around Jason."

I grabbed her hand, inspecting her nails. "Is that your claws I see coming out?"

"Uh, Mya, you didn't see her. She was like a freakin' model."

"Hmm, have you looked in a mirror lately? You're gorgeous, girl. Besides Jason loves you." Even I couldn't deny Rixon's star quarterback loved my friend something fierce. He'd softened a lot since they'd finally got their act together.

A bolt of pain shot through my heart but I ignored it.

"Yeah, you're right. You're totally right." She gave me a warm smile. "Oh look, class calls. See you at lunch?"

"Yep, if I survive two hours of biology."

"Good luck with that." She chuckled.

We parted ways and I headed into class. Felicity knew bits and pieces about my past, about Jermaine. But she didn't know all the gritty, painful details.

No one did.

And I never wanted them to.

———

Before I joined Felicity and Hailee in the cafeteria for lunch, I headed to my locker to trade some books. Once I was done, I finally caved and checked my cell phone, instantly regretting it. Four messages. Three from Jermaine, and one from my girlfriend, Shona.

J: Call me, I need you.

J: Why you gotta be this way, Mya? I miss you. I love you. I need you… I'm nothing without you, baby girl.

J: For real, it's going to be like that? Your mama won't even tell me where you're at.

Shona: It's bad, girl. Call me xo

My stomach sank, my insides torn apart as my head and heart warred over what to do. Part of me, the part who would always be a young naïve girl in love, wanted to call Shona and see what was going down. But the other part, the part who knew making that call only led down a road to more hurt and heartache, quickly deleted all four text messages.

When I'd first left Fallowfield Heights, our small neighborhood in the heart of Badlands, Mom had wanted me to get a new number, but I couldn't do it. I couldn't cut myself off completely. Maybe one day, I would.

But today was not that day.

Pushing down the worry, I made my way to the cafeteria, aware of the odd stare as I wound my way through the tables to get to Felicity and Hailee. I let them roll off my back though. You soon got used to being one of the four percent—one of the only Latina girls in a predominantly white school. Even if the licks of curiosity, of wariness and disapproval were like a thousand tiny blades over my skin.

Rixon High didn't only love a minority story though. It loved any kind of gossip it could get its hands on, and despite being the girlfriends of two of the most popular guys in school, my friends weren't immune to their peers' scrutiny. Sure, they didn't have to deal with insults or rumors based on the color of their skin or where they came from, but they had to deal with their fair share of bullshit. And like me, they handled it with grace and the attention it deserved.

"Hey," Felicity caught my eye. "We were just talking about you."

"All good I hope?"

A couple of girls watched me, eyeing me discreetly while they pretended to talk, as I sat down and pulled out my lunch.

"Mya, what's... Oh." Hailee's expression hardened. "Ignore them, I do."

"I'm pretty sure they don't whisper about you for the same reasons as they whisper about me." Irritation rippled through me as I stared right back, daring them to say something. When they didn't, I casually flipped them the bird.

Hailee snickered while Felicity whipped her head over in their direction. "You really think they're offended because you're Latina?"

"Oh, I know they are." I sat back in the chair, taking a bite of apple.

"It's just so... so narrow minded. We had an African-American president for Christ's sake."

"People are threatened by what they don't know. And I don't need to point out the obvious. Rixon is the epitome of hick town."

"We are not... Okay," Felicity backtracked. "Maybe we are, just a little bit."

"I almost wish you hadn't gotten with Jason just so I could make a play for him and really give the people of Rixon something to talk about."

"You could always make a play for another football player." Hailee smirked, not saying the words we all knew she was thinking.

"Me and Asher are friends. Just friends."

"But you could be more. You could be friends who—"

"Do *not* finish that sentence."

"What?" Her hands went up. "I'm just saying, I've been sensing some more-than-friends vibes from the two of you."

I frowned at that. Sure, me and Asher had hung out a couple of times with Felicity and Hailee and the guys, but that was inevitable. Our best friends were all in relationships with each other.

Our lives were entwined whether we wanted them to be or not.

"I didn't come here to meet someone. I came here to avoid guys. Period."

"Yeah, but come on, Mya, it's senior year." Felicity gave me her puppy dog eyes, the ones that had gotten us into trouble more than once since I'd arrived here.

"Exactly."

They both rolled their eyes, chuckling at my reasoning. But they didn't get it. They didn't know that while I'd escaped to Rixon, part of me was still back in Fallowfield Heights with Jermaine. They couldn't understand how it felt to know you'd left the one person you promised you'd always be there for, alone. They couldn't appreciate what it was like to be scared for someone's life. For your own life.

They couldn't know.

Because although I was sitting at their table, sharing and laughing and joking about our lives and friends and what we were going to do over the weekend, the fact of the matter was they belonged here.

And I didn't.

Regardless of how much I pretended.

2

Asher

"WHAT DO YOU THINK HE WANTS?" I asked my best friend, Jase, as we made our way to the locker room. Coach had sent a text out at the ass crack of dawn, insisting the team be there at eight thirty sharp. It was weird. Especially since the season was over and we were State Champs.

Only by association. "Thanks for the reminder," I grumbled to myself.

I hadn't played in the championship game, or any of the play-off games for that matter. Instead, I'd sat on the sidelines, cheering my team, my brothers, to victory, all so my best friend and captain, Jason Ford, could play.

"Fuck if I know," he said, shouldering the door. The second we stepped inside, the rest of the team cheered, chanting Jason's name like he was the motherfucking King.

I guess to them, he was.

He'd taken them all the way to State. In a place like Rixon that meant something.

It meant every-fucking-thing.

A couple of guys caught my eye, sending me a nod of appreciation. Some of them knew the truth—knew that the only reason Jason had got to play in the play-offs was because I'd taken the fall for him a few weeks back.

Rixon High had a long-standing rivalry with the next school over, Rixon East, and things had turned ugly between Jason and their captain, Lewis Thatcher. It had all come to a head a few weeks ago, when Lewis lured Jason into a fight. Coach and Principal Finnigan had caught wind of it and threatened to kick him off the team. But it never came to that.

I stepped in and turned the heat from Jase to me. People knew I was always down for a rumble and they knew I was stupid enough to do something like try to protect Jason. And even though, deep down, I was pretty sure Coach knew the truth, he let me take the fall. Because Jason was the best. Jason was the player the team needed to go all the way.

And me?

Well, I guess I was expendable.

It had sucked watching my team fight their way through the play-offs for victory. Cut me to the bone when Jase had called me out onto the field during the championship game, going against Coach's and Principal Finnigan's orders for me to remain on the bench at all times. But I took it like the man I was. Football meant everything to Jason. But it was never the end goal for me. And I couldn't see his dreams of going pro go up in smoke all because of some stupid fucking rivalry gone bad.

"Ladies, look alive," Coach Hasson boomed, strolling into the locker room looking far too alert for a Tuesday morning. "Now, I know you didn't expect to be here today. The season's done, it's almost the holidays, and God only knows you all deserve some downtime after the play-offs." Another chorus of cheers rumbled around the room. "Okay, okay, quiet down."

"Guys, come on," Jason yelled when they showed no signs of calming down.

Silence ushered over us and Coach gave Jase an appreciative nod. "I'll miss that, Son," he mused, stroking his jaw. Not saying the words we all knew he was thinking.

There would never be another Jason.

Someone to lead the team the way he had.

Jason was the stuff legends were made of and there wasn't a single person in the room who didn't believe he was going all the way to the NFL.

"I wish I could say this is good news, but honestly, after the last few months, I'm not sure you'll agree."

Jase stiffened beside me and Cameron shot me a frown.

"The news won't break officially until this afternoon, but I've been given permission to tell you first." Coach paused, stress lines crinkling his eyes. Whatever he was about to say wasn't good. Which meant it could only be about one thing.

Lewis Thatcher and the Rixon East Eagles.

"Formal charges are being brought against Lewis Thatcher. I also learned this morning that Washington pulled his scholarship."

"Fuck yeah," someone hollered as the guys began discussing Coach's announcement.

"Did you know?" I whispered to Jase who was still as statue beside me.

"No," he clipped out, his expression strained.

"Hey, man," that was Cameron. "This is a good thing."

"They'll probably want Hailee to testify."

"Shit, I didn't—"

"Bring it in," Coach yelled. "I'm not done yet."

There was more?

I wasn't sure Jason could take anymore, volatile energy rippling off him in dark waves. I couldn't blame him though. If Thatcher had come after my sister and put his hands on my girl, I would've wanted blood too.

"There has always been a bitter rivalry between Rixon and Rixon East. It's older than you or me. But Principal Finnigan, and Principal Castrol over at East, have decided it's time to lay the past to rest and make an example of what happened this semester. Rivalry on the field is one thing, but when it spills out into the community and starts affecting innocent people that is unacceptable." His hard gaze found the three of us. "Do I make myself clear?"

"Yes, Sir," everyone grumbled in unison.

Coach continued. "Both Principals have decided that, in a show of good faith, an exhibition game will be held in the new year to raise funds for a local charity that supports young peoples' mental health and wellbeing."

"You expect us to play them again?" someone balked but Coach didn't get a chance to answer because Jason stormed out of the locker room, letting the door slam behind him.

Coach let out a resigned sigh. "Can I trust the two of you to handle that?" he said to me and Cameron, and we nodded. "This isn't an opt in, opt out scenario. Principal Finnigan made it very clear he expects everyone to play, especially the senior players."

"Leave it to us, Coach," Cameron said, going after him. I lingered, confused about what he was saying.

"You too, Bennet. Principal Finnigan agreed you've served your punishment."

"I'm playing?" I didn't know how I felt about that.

"You're still a Raider, are you not?

"Yes, Sir."

"Then you're playing. Now go, make sure he doesn't do anything stupid." With a sharp nod Coach Hasson dismissed me, and I took off after my best friends.

IT DIDN'T TAKE LONG to find them. I only had to follow the sound of raised voices outside the gym.

"Are you fucking kidding me?" Jase ground out, his back to me. "You're taking his side?"

"I'm not taking anyone's side," Cameron shot back. "But you really want to piss Finnigan off when we're so close to being done with senior year? It's one game. And maybe they have a point, maybe after everything, this is a good thing. Set a good example for the younger players coming up through the ranks."

I jammed my hands in my pockets, watching the two of them go at it. Cameron had always been the voice of reason, the person who had talked Jason out of doing something really fucking stupid more times than I could count. Me? I usually acted as the devil on his shoulder, goading him into some stupid prank or fight over the river in Rixon East territory.

Today though, I remained quiet.

"If I ever have to look at one of their players again it will be too soon," Jase spat, dragging a hand through his hair.

"Come on, man, Thatcher is off the team. Without him, it'll be different."

"How can you be so... so fucking calm knowing what they did to Hailee?" He was seething now, his jaw clenched in anger.

Cam let out a heavy sigh, tipping his face into the crisp morning air, his breath like a faint plume of smoke drifting skyward. "It's over," he slid his eyes to Jason's. "Hailee is good. We're good. And I want to focus on our last few months as seniors. Thatcher is going to get his, I promise."

I hoped for everyone's sake, he did. Because from the murderous glint in Jason's eyes every time someone mentioned his archrival, I suspected our best friend wouldn't be able to let it go if the law didn't find Lewis Thatcher guilty.

"What?" Jase finally noticed me standing there. "You got nothing to say?"

"Cameron's right." I stepped forward. "Let's do it, one final play. Go out with a bang."

"We're State Champions. It doesn't get much fucking more *bang* than that."

Wincing, my eyes shuttered. Jason didn't mean it as an insult. But it sure felt like one, when they'd earned it and I hadn't.

"Jase," Cam warned, noticing my crestfallen expression.

"Shit, Ash, I didn't mean it like that." Jason cussed under his breath. "I just wanted to enjoy the holidays. I didn't want another game with the Eagles looming over us."

"One final play," Cam reiterated. "Ash is right. We do this, together. One last time. Then we walk away with no regrets."

"Fine," Jase grunted. "But if it all goes to shit, I'm blaming the two of you." He said the words to both of us, but his eyes were on me, something passing between us. I wanted to believe it was gratitude, but I wasn't sure. Jason wasn't exactly good with his feelings.

"I can take the heat if it all goes wrong, no problem. It's what I do best." It was a joke, but neither of them laughed.

Jason groaned and then looked at Cameron. "One condition."

"Name it," Cam replied.

"You break it to the girls."

Laughter spilled out of me and the two of them looked at me like I'd grown a second head. "All I'm going to say is, good luck with that. It was nice knowing you both." I clapped Jason on the back and left them to argue who was going to tell Hailee and her best friend Felicity, Jason's girl, about the exhibition game.

Telling myself I wasn't bitter.

Even if it was a huge fucking lie.

"Hernandez," I called out, spotting Mya Hernandez, my newest friend courtesy of Hailee and Felicity.

"Go away, Asher," she replied over her shoulder, but I broke into a jog, cutting her off before she could duck out of the building.

"Why the cold shoulder?"

"Not a cold shoulder, just a… shoulder." Mya grinned and shit if I didn't drown in her big brown eyes.

"Asher?" she snapped.

"Uh, yeah?"

"I'm guessing you didn't just chase me down to stare at me like I've got something on my face." Leaning in, she flushed a little. "I don't, do I?"

"No," I laughed. "You're good."

A little too good, if the way my body moved in closer was anything to go on. But then, it had been weeks since I'd gotten any.

"So… what do you want?"

"You wound me, Hernandez. I thought we were friends."

"No, you decided we were friends after you lost Felicity to Jason."

"I didn't lose…" She gave me a pointed look and I changed direction. "Fine, I thought Felicity and me were friend goals, sure. But what can I say? She doesn't know what she's missing."

My chest tightened. Not because I wanted Felicity. I didn't; she was my best friend's girl. But there had been a time, when Hailee and Flick first started hanging around with our group, that I'd thought maybe… nah, who the fuck was I trying to kid? She only ever had eyes for Jason.

I was just the funny friend. The guy who made the girls laugh.

"Goodbye, Asher." Mya tried to move around me, but I stepped into her path.

"Not so fast."

"Asher, come on." She swatted my chest. "I have shit to do."

"Yeah, like what shit?" I smirked.

"Homework and shit."

"Can I come?"

"You want to come and do homework with me? Hmm, how about hell to the no?"

"Come on, Mya, it wouldn't be the first time we've hung out."

"That was different." Her brows drew together. "That was with the group."

"So this could be our group."

"Two people hanging out is not a group, it's a pair. It's… weird."

"But I've never been to your aunt's house."

"Because we're not friends." Mya darted around me, hurrying out of the building, but I gave chase.

I needed her.

"Mya, wait up." She was already weaving between the cars in the parking lot. "How are you getting home?" I knew Felicity usually gave her a ride and she was with Jason.

"They're called legs," she yelled over her shoulder. "You should try using them someday." She had the balls to wink at me.

Shit, this girl. She was like no one else I'd ever met. Ever since Mya Hernandez had arrived at Rixon High a couple of months back, she'd slid right into our group. Flick had been tasked with taking the Philly transfer under her wing, but Mya didn't need a babysitter. She'd proved that more than once.

Mya Hernandez was a fighter. Not scared to wade into a fight to protect those she cared about. But it wasn't her strength that intrigued me. It was her scars. The ones she thought she kept hidden.

Cussing out the stubborn girl, a new plan hatched when thunder rumbled overhead. I ran to my Jeep and ducked inside just as the first fat drops of rain began to fall. Throwing it into reverse, I backed out of the lot and tailed Mya as she pulled up her hood and hurried down the sidewalk.

Slowing to a crawl, I wound down the passenger window. "Get in," I yelled.

"What?" She glared at me. "No. No!"

"A ride," I explained. "That's all I'm offering."

"Just a ride? Because if this is a ploy to get an invitation into my aunt's house, it won't work." Rain pelted down on Mya, dripping off the peak of her hood and onto her thick lashes.

"You need me, Hernandez, admit it." I leaned over and pushed open the door, waiting. "Get in."

To my surprise and relief, Mya climbed inside, shaking off her hood before pushing it down. Her tight spiral curls seemed wilder, framing her face.

"Thanks." She belted up and tucked her hands under her thighs.

"Scared you won't be able to keep your hands to yourself?" I teased, expecting some sassy retort. But Mya was quiet, too fucking quiet.

"Mya?" I asked.

"Just drive, Asher." She gave a resigned sigh, as if she'd broken her cardinal rule by accepting a ride home from me.

And I didn't know which cut worse.

That she was disappointed at herself for giving in to me. Or the fact she felt the need to resist me in the first place.

3

Mya

"WELL, THIS IS ME." Asher's Jeep slowed to a stop outside my Aunt Ciara's house. It was an old farmhouse style place on the edge of town. A world away from the likes of Asher's house with its huge yard, double garage, and lakeside setting. His was one of the biggest houses in town, a constant reminder that me and my new *friend*—and I used the term loosely—had completely different lives.

I was the girl from the hood, running from her past and trying to hold it together long enough to finish senior year. While Asher was... well, he was the All-American boy next door. Popular, athletic, and drop dead gorgeous—if you liked that kind of thing. Messy blond hair, pantie-melting blue eyes, and a smile so charming he had half the town falling at his feet.

He was also a giant pain in the ass.

Unlucky for me, his chosen ass of the moment was mine.

"Thanks for the ride." I began to shoulder the door, but he snagged my wrist. My eyes flew to where his fingers curled around my wrist; his sun-kissed skin still three shades lighter than my caramel skin.

Just another reminder of everything that was different about us.

"Invite me in, Hernandez. I bet your aunt would love to meet me." He had the audacity to wink. I smothered a groan.

"My aunt isn't exactly a fan." My brow rose, gaze darting to where he was still holding me. Asher released my wrist and ran a hand through his hair.

"Let me guess, she doesn't want a Raider sniffing around her niece?"

"Try, white boy," I murmured beneath my breath.

"What did you just say?" Asher said. "Because I know you didn't just say what I think you said."

"Nothing," I bit out. "I said nothing."

His eyes narrowed, searching my hardened expression for the truth. "Your aunt got a problem with the color of my skin, Hernandez?" He actually sounded offended. "She doesn't even know me."

"Welcome to my world."

"Nobody cares about that shit, Mya. In case you haven't noticed, it's the twenty-first century."

"And the fact you just said that tells me everything I need to know." Indignation skittered up my spine. "Thanks again for the ride. I'll see you at school tomorrow." I slipped out of the Jeep, my chest tight with frustration.

Of course Asher didn't get what it was like for me in a place like Rixon. Why would he? He was a guy. A privileged white guy, born and raised here.

He was also a Rixon Raider.

Something I'd quickly learned meant something around here.

I didn't look back as I hurried toward my aunt's porch. She wasn't home, rarely was thanks to her job at the Seven-Eleven in the next town over. But I didn't want to tell Asher that. He was worse than a dog with a bone and I knew if he realized I was home alone, he'd find a way inside, and then I'd never get rid of him.

Almost home free, I let out a small sigh of relief but then his voice made every muscle in my body lock up.

"What the fuck just happened?"

I swung around to find Asher standing there, his eyes full of apology and confusion. He looked so freakin' adorable, in an annoyingly cute puppy-dog kind of way.

"Go home, Asher." I remained guarded. Because if you gave Asher Bennet even half an inch, he wouldn't hesitate to take a mile.

"Mya, come on. What was all that?"

"You wouldn't understand," I whispered, hating the icy fingers of vulnerability wrapping around my throat.

"Try me." He stepped forward, taking the air with him. Which was ridiculous since we were standing outside, surrounded by nothing but the chilly Pennsylvanian air.

"Asher... please..." I didn't want to do this. Not here. Not now.

Least of all on my aunt's porch.

"Mya..." he countered, determination burning in his baby blues.

"Thirty minutes and then you're gone."

"If that's your attempt at an invitation inside, I gotta say, you really need to work on your manners, Hernandez."

Rolling my eyes, I dug out my key and opened the door, not waiting for Asher as I slipped inside. I'd lived here for almost three months, but my Aunt Ciara's house still didn't feel like home.

I wasn't sure it ever would.

"Nice place," Asher said, the door clicking softly behind him. Although it might as well have been a gunshot to the heart, the way it reverberated through me. Making me painfully aware that we were all alone. In my territory.

The only place I had in Rixon to call mine.

"Can I get you something to drink?"

"You got any snacks back there?" Asher craned his neck, his amused gaze going over my shoulder.

"Come on," I grumbled, "I'll see what I can find." If there was one thing I'd learned about Asher Bennet since my short time at Rixon High, it was that the boy could eat. Sometimes, I wasn't sure where he put it all. There wasn't an ounce of fat on him, nothing but solid muscle pulled taut over broad shoulders and narrow hips.

He followed me into the kitchen and took a seat at the counter. "Your aunt's not here, is she?"

"You caught that, huh?"

"Were you lying to me, Hernandez?"

"I was... maybe." I sighed, getting to work on making him a sandwich. "We only have turkey, cheese, and some questionable pickles."

"It'll do." He made himself comfortable. "So how long has your aunt lived in Rixon?"

"Since I was little. I never visited her before though." She always came to us. Mom never spoke much about why her only sister moved away from Philly, but as I grew up, I pieced together the story. My aunt Ciara had run. Escaped the neighborhood for a better life. She was older than Mom by almost a decade, and as soon as she graduated high school, she packed a bag and got the hell out of dodge.

"What you said before, about me being white, would that really be a problem for her?"

Sandwich made, I pushed the plate toward Asher and grimaced. "Yes... and no. My aunt met a man here. A white man. I don't know the whole story, but I heard my mama talking once and whatever went down between them, my aunt and the man, it wasn't good."

"Wow, okay." Asher took a huge bite of the sandwich, barely chewing it before he swallowed. "So I'm going to be judged based on one man's actions. How progressive of her."

"In case you haven't noticed, Rixon isn't exactly diverse."

He shrugged, taking another bite. "But we're not all the racists you paint us to be either."

"Do you realize how bigoted you sound right now?"

"I don't—"

"I left my home, my very diverse neighborhood, and moved to the ass crack of nowhere where football is religion and I'm one of only a handful of kids to walk the halls at school who don't fit the white profile."

Asher straightened, his expression hardening. If I didn't know better, I would have said he looked possessive. But that opened a whole other can of worms I wasn't ready for.

"Has someone said something to you?" he asked. "Because if they have—"

Leaning back against the counter, I let out an exasperated breath. "Asher, listen to what I'm saying. It isn't about what people are or aren't doing or saying..." It was, but that wasn't the point right now. "It's about how alienating it can feel for someone who wasn't born here, who isn't white, to try to assimilate while staying true to their roots."

Asher's brows crinkled as he quietly processed my words. I didn't want to have this conversation, especially not with him. But over the last few weeks, Asher had wormed his way into my life. Whether I'd wanted him to or not.

"I guess I didn't think..." He dragged a hand down his face.

"It's okay. It's tough being a Raider." I teased, wanting nothing more than to deflect the limelight away from me.

"You'd tell me though, right, if someone did say anything to you about... you know?"

"About the fact I'm a Latina girl from the hood?"

"You are so much more than that, Mya." His eyes burned with something I'd seen before. At first, it had been when he looked at Felicity. But then his sights had shifted from her to me, right around the time she and Jason became more than just two people who liked to drive each other crazy.

I still didn't know how I felt about it.

Dropping my gaze, I ran my finger over the worn wooden countertops. My aunt had opened her door to me without question; welcoming me into her home and heart. She didn't say the words, but I think she saw a lot of her younger self in me. A girl desperate to escape. Only I never wanted to escape. I just knew I couldn't stay there anymore without losing a part of myself.

So here I was in Rixon. Hiding. Pretending everything was okay. Trying to outrun a past that I knew would one day catch up with me.

"You are so fucking beautiful it hurts."

My eyes snapped to Asher's and he cussed under his breath. "Shit, Mya, I didn't... I mean, I did, but I didn't. Fuck."

"I think you should go," I said calmly, giving no hint at the band of horses galloping through my chest.

"It just came out. I didn't... Let's rewind. Pretend I never said it."

"Asher." I gave him a pointed look, fighting a smile. "You don't think I'm beautiful?"

"What? No... I do. Of course, I do, but I thought..." Asher cussed again. "You're fucking with me, aren't you?"

My lip curved in a faint smile. "I'll see you tomorrow, okay?"

He stood up, an apology dancing in his eyes. "Don't let this make things weird between us, Hernandez. I can appreciate a beautiful woman even if I know she belongs to someone else."

"I don't—"

"It's written all over your face. Besides, Hailee and Flick talk. A lot."

"They told you about—"

"They wouldn't do that, no. But sometimes I hear things... see things," he said cryptically. "Whoever he is, he doesn't deserve you."

"Yeah, and what makes you say that?" I lifted my chin ready to defend Jermaine. I guess some habits were harder to kick than others.

"Because he let you run. And if you were mine, I'd chase you to the ends of the Earth before I ever gave you up."

My.

Heart.

Stopped.

Beating.

"And on that note," Asher smirked, a trace of vulnerability in his expression. "I'll see myself out. Until tomorrow, Mya Hernandez."

I watched as Asher walked away trying to figure out what I felt most confused about: that Asher had called me beautiful, or that his parting words had sounded a lot like a promise.

An hour later, I was busy at the stove when the front door rattled. "Mya?" My aunt's voice drifted down the hall.

"In the kitchen," I called back, stirring the pan of tomato sauce.

"Ooh, something smells good."

"It's just spaghetti." Glancing back, I smiled. "How was your day?"

"My feet are ten degrees hotter than hell, but I'll live. Did you throw in some of those chilies I like?"

"Yep."

"Good girl. I taught you well."

Making her extra hot tomato sauce was one of the first things Aunt Ciara taught me when I'd arrived. Everything about my aunt from her five-three stature to her petite frame and sparkling eyes screamed sweet. But Ciara Hernandez liked her food hot. Eyes burning, mouth-watering, get-the-fire-hose hot.

"I saw Mrs. Clements. She said you had a visitor."

My spine stiffened at the disapproval in her voice. "A friend gave me a ride home, yeah."

"And did this friend also come inside the house?"

"Aunt C, I'm eighteen." I kept my cool, offering her a placating smile. "I didn't think it would be a problem."

"She also said she thought he was a football player." Her brow lifted, voice drenched in accusation.

"Asher plays for the team, yes."

"Mya, girl, don't be telling me you brought that Bennet boy into my house."

"He's just a friend."

"Yeah, and it was your friendship with Jermaine that landed you here. Do you really want to go—"

"That's not fair," I said, quietly feeling the weight of her words settle heavy on my chest.

She clucked her tongue. "Those Raiders are bad news. Walk around this town like they own the damn place. Get away with murder too. I'm not sure I like the idea of you taking up with one of them."

"I'm not taking up with anyone. There was a storm. He offered me a ride home and it seemed rude to just send him on his way, so I invited him in. It isn't a big deal."

Aunt Ciara's expression softened as she looked to the ceiling, no doubt silently asking the Lord for guidance. When she settled her big eyes back on me, she said, "I know how hard this is for you, Mya. I've been there, remember? I've walked the path you walk now, except I had no one to turn to or guide me right. You're here to finish senior year, to get your diploma, and get into a good school. To put your life in Fallowfield Heights behind you. You are such a bright young girl, and you have such a bright future ahead of you, but you have to stay on course."

"It was just a ride home, Auntie."

"A ride home with a white athlete who thinks he can take what he wants when he wants without consequence."

"Auntie, that's not—"

"I know how it sounds." She sighed. "But it's the truth, whether you want to hear it or not."

There was no use arguing with her. Aunt Ciara was a woman scorned, her heart still wounded by the young man who'd promised her the world and gave her nothing but a broken heart and countless black eyes.

"I don't pick my friends based on the color of their skin, Aunt C. That's not who I am."

"And I wouldn't want you to. You're better than that. But the lines blur so easily, Mya. And boys like that Asher Bennet and his football friends are used to the people falling at their feet."

I went back to stirring the tomato sauce. "We're just friends," I uttered again.

But every time I said the words, the lie coiled a little tighter around my heart. Because I wasn't sure me and Asher were just friends. Yet, I knew we could never be more.

So where the hell did that leave us?

4

Asher

"FEE, BABY, CAN WE TALK?" I jogged up beside Felicity, laughing when she gave me her deer-caught-in-headlights expression. "Chill, Jase is in the gym. He'll never have to know." With a wink, I slung my arm around her shoulder.

"Asher! You can't do that. If Jason sees... you know how jealous he gets." She batted my arm and it fell away, much like my bravado.

"So it's like that, huh?" I pouted dramatically. "Fine. I'll just have to go harass Hailee. At least she won't—"

"I didn't say we couldn't talk." Felicity smiled. "It's just Jason is really wound up about the exhibition game. I'm worried about him."

"Thatcher is off the team. There's nothing to worry about."

"I know that, and you know that, but Jason is..."

"Jason," I said, needing no further explanation. "I'll talk to him."

"Thanks. I tried to help him last night, but he didn't want to know."

"Are you sure you were doing it right?" I frowned, fighting a smirk. "Because it's not that difficult, Fee, baby. You just put the p—"

"Asher, stop!" she shrieked, swatting my chest, her soft laughter washing over me. It wasn't so long ago I'd work hard to hear that sound. But that was before I realized she was meant to be with my best friend. Now I loved her like a sister.

And I needed a sisterly favor.

"What do you want?" she asked, trading out some books in her locker.

"So this is going to sound weird but I don't have anyone else to ask."

"Okay." Her brows bunched together as she glanced over at me.

"It's about Mya."

"Oh no; no you don't." She slammed her locker closed. "I'm not getting in the middle of whatever weird thing you two have going on."

Weird thing?

"Did Mya say something to you about me?"

"I wouldn't tell you if she did. She's my friend. And you're..." Felicity hesitated.

"*Also* your friend?" My lip curved.

"Well, yes, but it's different. You're my boyfriend's best friend. And Mya is one of my best friends. I can't be in the middle of this. Whatever *this* is."

"I need to know what happened with her ex."

"Oh hell no, Asher Bennet," her voice rose again but Felicity quickly schooled her panic. "You can't ask me that." Her hand wrapped around my arm pulling me into the locker, carving out a sliver of privacy in the emptying hall. "What kind of question is that?"

"Well, I thought it was a perfectly reasonable question until you went all psycho on me." I grinned because making light of things was my default setting. Even if I wanted to kidnap Felicity and hold her hostage until she told me every little detail about Mya and her ex.

She reared back, studying me. "Did something happen between the two of you?"

"I have no idea what you're talking about."

"Asher..."

"Fine. I may have let it slip out I thought she was beautiful. Yep, I may have said that."

Fuck.

I felt like a giant pussy admitting it. But if anyone would understand it was Felicity Giles.

"I see."

My eyes narrowed. "What the hell does that mean?"

"I, hmm, nothing. It means nothing." Her lips thinned and I didn't like the cautious look in her eyes. "What did she say?"

"She kicked me out of her aunt's house quicker than you can say, 'Go Raider's'."

"That sounds like Mya."

"So," I flounced back against the locker bank. "I need to know what happened between them."

"Why?"

"Because I need to know what I'm up against here."

"You like her," she deadpanned. "You *really* like her."

"You sound surprised?" My brow quirked up.

"No, I mean Mya's hot and you're... well, you're you." Felicity's eyes went wide, darting around us as if she was worried Jase might appear at any second. "But I didn't think it was anything serious."

Ignoring that, I said, "I'm flattered you think I'm hot, Fee, but that ship has sailed." My smile fell, my heart falling right along with it.

Jesus, I was confused.

I liked Mya, there was no denying that.

But my heart couldn't forget the first girl it had felt something for.

Something real.

"Asher..." Sadness washed over her.

"Hey, it's all good, right?" I flashed her a reassuring grin, turning my easy charm back on. "We're friends and you're with Jason now. Everything worked out the way it was supposed to, but now I need you to help me."

"With Mya."

I nodded.

"I'm not sure she's looking for anything right now. Things with her ex ended badly and..." Guilt glittered in Flick's eyes. "I've already said too much."

Actually, she hadn't said enough.

"Listen, you can either help me or I can find out myself."

"Why is this so important to you?" Felicity stared up at me as if I'd lost my damn mind.

And it occurred to me, maybe I had.

But I saw something in Mya, felt it every time I was around her. I couldn't explain it, but I couldn't just ignore it either. Especially not since my two best friends had gone and gotten themselves loved up.

"Do you actually like her, or is this just some game, because I'm not—"

"Come on, Flick, you know me better than that. I like her, okay? There's something in her eyes..." I swallowed the words, realizing how fucking stupid I sounded. "She ever talk about me?"

"I..."

"Shit, don't answer that." I'd obviously misread the situation. *Way to go, jackass.*

"Want my advice?" Felicity asked.

"Always."

"Don't force it. If it's meant to be, things will find a way of working themselves out. And if it's not meant to be, you can still be friends. Besides, it's not like Mya will be here forever. She'll have to go home eventually and then there's college."

My chest tightened at that. I hadn't really given much thought to what happened down the line. Focusing only on what happened now.

Or what I wanted to happen.

"You can't escape destiny," I said with arrogant conviction, earning me a snicker from Flick.

"And you and Mya are destiny?"

"Written in the stars, baby. She's running from her past. I'm..." Shit. I swallowed the words but there was no avoiding Felicity's scrutinizing gaze.

"You're what?"

"Nothing. Thanks for the help. I'll catch you later?"

"Later?" Her face paled.

"Yeah, you guys are still coming over, right? I thought we were having a movie night?" And since I was the only one with the home movie theater, we usually crashed at mine.

"I..."

"You have other plans." My chest tightened.

"It's just with this exhibition game and Jason walking around like a bear with a sore head, I wanted to do something to cheer him up."

"Hey, you can be cheery at my house... aaaand you don't mean that kind of cheering up. You mean cheer-sex."

"Asher!" The skin along her neck flushed pink.

"Fine. Go cheer-sex your guy. I guess I'll make do with Hailee and Cameron."

"Hmm..." Guilt flashed in her eyes and I groaned.

"Let me guess. The cheer-sex stuff comes after a double date?"

"We just didn't think you'd want to—"

"I get it. Nobody likes playing third wheel." Or in this case, fifth. "Well, have fun." I didn't mean to sound as bitter as I did. But fuck, if it didn't sting being dropped by your best friends for couples' night.

"I'm sure it would be okay if you came with us."

"And cramp your style? Nah, I'm good." I forced a smile. "You guys go have fun. I'll be fine."

"You're sure? I made reservations at that new restaurant on the edge of town. Jason's dad recommended it."

"Does Jason know that?"

"It can be our secret."

"Sure." I had enough of those, what was one more?

"We'll all hang out tomorrow?"

"Yeah, of course." It came out strained. "Have fun tonight." I gave her a two-fingered salute and stalked down the hall, wondering when life got so fucking complicated.

On the face of it, everything had changed at the beginning of senior year, when Hailee and Cameron started eye-fucking each other across the cafeteria. But the truth was, things had felt off for me for a while. Before the girls turned our world upside down.

Senior year was supposed to be the best time of our lives. But sometimes it felt like a noose around my neck.

I shouldered the door and stepped out into the murky cold air, when I spotted a blur of spiral curls, ripped jeans, and military boots. "Oh, hell no," I murmured as I cut across the lot. "Mya, wait up," I yelled.

I hadn't seen her all day, and I was pretty sure it was because she was avoiding me.

"You need a ride?" I asked, slowing down to her pace.

"I'm good but thanks for the offer." She wrapped her arms around her waist, hugging her jacket tight to her body.

"Come on, it looks like another storm is about to hit and your aunt lives three miles out."

"I don't know..."

"I'll be on my best behavior. Scout's honor."

"You expect me to believe *you* were a boy scout."

"Okay, you got me, but I swear I have no ulterior motive this time."

Her dark eyes searched mine, eventually softening around the edges. "I wouldn't say no to a ride downtown."

"You're not heading home?"

Mya shrugged. "My aunt has her friends coming over and I don't much feel like listening to them gossip. And Flick and Hailee are..." she trailed off.

"It's cool, I just got the memo. Sucks to be us, huh?"

"Better than them trying to get us to triple date."

"Ouch!" Strangled laughter rumbled in my chest despite how much her words stung.

"Shit, Asher, I didn't mean—"

"Don't sweat it. I have tough skin, Hernandez. But since we've both been blown off by our so-called friends, we could, I don't know, hang out maybe?" I steeled myself for her rejection.

So color me surprised when the word, "Okay," slipped from her soft pink lips.

"Yeah?" my eyes widened.

"Yeah, so long as you don't make a bigger deal out of this than it is."

"And what is this?" I teased.

"Two *friends* getting milkshakes at The Alley?"

"You have yourself a deal, *friend*."

Mya rolled her eyes as if she knew exactly what was going through my head. But there was no way she knew.

Because if she did, I was pretty sure she'd be running for the hills.

"I USED TO LOVE THIS PLACE." I glanced around The Alley, taking in the familiar Formica tables, clink of the pinball machine, and smell of fried food.

"Why did you stop coming?"

"Once we made Varsity, it was just kind of off-limits. Everyone knew Tate, the owner, didn't stand any football rivalry bullshit so we just avoided it."

"Because you wanted to cause trouble?"

"Not really, but coming here meant shedding our jersey's and in case you haven't noticed, we're not about that."

She glanced down at me. I was sure her eyes lingered on my chest a little longer than necessary. "You're not wearing your jersey today."

"Things are different now the season is over." The words came out strained as I led Mya over to a booth.

"But there's the exhibition game."

"Yeah, but it's not like State. There was a lot riding on that. We had a lot to prove. This game is just a way for Principal Finnigan and Principal Castrol to look good in front of the press. Finnigan has been wanting to clean up our reputation since he transferred here and this gives him a platform to do that."

"I don't think I'll ever understand how one town can be so obsessed with football." Mya picked up a menu, and I found myself lost in the way she studied it, her big brown eyes sweeping over the laminated card, sparking with interest.

"Stop," she let out a small sigh.

"Stop what? I'm not doing—"

"I can feel you watching me." Her eyes flicked to mine. So dark and intense... and pissed.

"Right. Sorry."

"You promised, Asher." Mya lay the menu flat, pressing her hands against it. "Friends, remember?"

"Friends, got it... and why is that again?"

She blew out another exasperated breath. "Because I'm not looking for a relationship. And you're..." Mya shook her head. "We're just not compatible."

"You haven't even given me a chance. It makes sense. You're friends with Hailee and Felicity and we're all always hanging out anyway."

"Which is just another reason it makes no sense. Flick and Hailee are my only..." Mya pressed her lips together.

"Your only what?"

Leaning across the table a little, she whispered, "My only friends here. If we did try dating, which we are *not* doing, and it went wrong, I'd lose them."

"They wouldn't choose me over you."

"No but they'd choose their boyfriends." Something flickered in her eyes.

"You're so certain we wouldn't work out. Why is that?" I scrubbed my jaw, half-surprised, half-relieved she wasn't just shutting down this line of conversation.

"Look around you, Asher."

Frowning, I glanced around the diner. A few kids watched us, curiosity glittering in their eyes. But it wasn't anything outside the usual. Kids tended to know when a Raider was around. It's just how it was in Rixon; came with the responsibility of wearing a blue and white jersey.

"In case you haven't noticed, having an audience comes with the territory."

"Wow, arrogant much?"

Laughter rumbled in my chest. "Just telling it like it is. I could care less if we have an audience. I only see you, Mya."

Her lips parted on a small gasp.

"What, no sassy comeback?"

"I do not sass."

"Sure you don't." I smirked, loving our playful interaction. But it ended all too quickly, when Mya's smile slipped away.

"You don't think they're looking at us wondering what someone like you is doing here with someone like me?"

"I don't give a shit what they think, and you shouldn't either."

"It's easy for you to say," she threw back and I tugged my hair in frustration. Mya was a complicated girl. Walls so high and reinforced I wasn't ever sure I'd get through them. But then, sometimes, she'd give me a look that said, 'don't give up'.

"Come on, Hernandez, work with me here. I won't let them bother me, if you don't let them bother you. Or I could go over there and ask them what the fuck their problem is?" I went to get up, but Mya's hand snagged my wrist over the table.

"No," she rushed out. "Don't, please."

"So you'll ignore them?"

"Them who?" Her voice dripped sarcasm but I'd take it.

"That's my girl," I said, grinning like the damn Cheshire cat. Mya's eyes widened in surprise at my slip of the tongue.

If only she knew the truth. Knew that it wasn't a slip of the tongue at all. It was a test. A promise of things to come. Because one day, Mya Hernandez would be mine.

She just didn't know it yet.

5

Mya

EVERY TUESDAY WITHOUT FAIL, I spoke to Mom. Sometimes we'd speak for hours, other times it was shorter, and if she got upset, we usually ended the call and promised to talk again soon. But today, the first time in almost twelve weeks, she didn't pick up.

"Come on, Mama," I muttered, hitting call again. It rang out, the drone of the dial tone echoing through my mind. "Aunt C, have you heard from Mama today?"

She appeared in the door. "She texted me a couple of days ago. She isn't answering?" Aunt Ciara eyed the phone in my hand.

"No. It's Tuesday. We always talk on Tuesdays." Panic flooded me. "What if something happ—"

"Breathe, Mya. Breathe." My aunt hurried to my side. "I'm sure it's nothing."

Just then, my cell phone blared to life. "See, nothing to worry about."

"Mama?"

"Mya, mi pequeña. I'm sorry I missed your call. I was washing my hair and didn't hear my cell."

"That's okay." Relief sank into my bones. Aunt Ciara pressed a kiss to my head before leaving me alone. "How are you?"

"You know how it is, baby. Gotta keep working."

I stiffened. "I know, Mama."

"But enough about me, tell me all about you. How is school? Did you pick a college yet?"

"I'm still weighing up my options, but my guidance counselor is going to help me before school gets out for the holidays."

"That's good, baby, real good. Mi pequeña graduating high school and going off to college. I couldn't be prouder if I tried."

"I haven't been accepted yet, Mama."

She grunted. "They'd be foolish to turn you down, baby. Always were booksmart."

"So I was thinking," I hesitated, bracing myself for her response. "Maybe I could visit over the holidays. Just for a few days?"

"Mya, baby, you know that isn't a good idea."

"I haven't spoken to him. I've ignored all his texts, just like I promised. But I miss you. I miss you so much, Mama. And Shona and the girls."

"He's still calling you?"

"Texts mainly."

"I don't like it, Mya. I don't like it at all. Maybe I should talk to Keelan and—"

"No, Mama, you can't. You promised," I cried, fear edging into my voice.

"Ssh, baby. You're right, that wouldn't end well. But I wish you'd change your number. Be done with him once and for all."

"I am done. It's over." My chest cracked.

Silence followed.

A beat.

Another.

Until Mom let out a heavy sigh. "I didn't want to tell you, but you should know, Jermaine dropped out of school."

"*No!*"

School was his last hope. The one place he had people anchoring him to something more than a life of drugs, gangs, and an early grave.

Not the only thing. I shut down the little voice. I'd tried… and failed. Walking away from Jermaine was the hardest thing I'd ever done, but it wasn't only about him anymore. It was about me too. My life, my dreams.

My safety.

"He's running for Diaz officially."

That's what Shona must have called to tell me. Jermaine was in deep with Diaz and his crew now.

Guilt snaked through me. When I'd left, Jermaine was still in school. He still had a chance. But if he'd initiated into Diaz's crew, there would be no easy way out now. Tears pooled in my eyes as I remembered our last conversation, right before Mom shipped me off to Rixon.

"Fuck, Mya, baby, you weren't supposed to be there… you weren't supposed to get hurt." He tried to cradle my face, but I jerked back, shielding my bruised cheek with my hand.

"Don't touch me," I ground out shakily, pain radiating from various parts of my body.

"But I need you… I need you, Mya. I always need you."

"So stop," I cried. "Walk away before it's too late. Keelan said he'd give you a job."

"Glass collecting at the bar?" He scoffed. "I can't be collecting no glasses, Mya. I got a rep to protect."

"Do it for me, J; for us. I can't stand by and watch you do this to yourself no more. Look at yourself. Look at me. What happens next time it goes wrong? What happens when it's not someone's fist but a bat or… gun."

"Nah, baby. This isn't shit, just a little warning."

"A little warning?" I gasped, the air leaving my lungs on a painful breath. "They held me down while they beat you. And then they..."

"Mya, mi pequeña?" Mom's voice pulled me from my thoughts, and I swiped at my eyes, trying to compose myself.

"I'm still here." I forced the memories back into their box, locking it tightly. "Think about the holidays, okay, Mama? I could just come for a couple of days and stay at the house. Shona could visit. Or maybe you could come here?"

"You know I can't, baby." Sadness lingered in her voice.

"Aunt Ciara wouldn't mind. In fact, I'm sure she'd love to see—"

"Mya, enough. Keelan's calling me on the other line, I gotta go, baby. But be safe, okay? And we'll talk soon. I love you, Mya."

"Love you too, Mama." Swallowing down the dejection, I ended the call and clutched my cell phone to my chest.

Everything was a mess. All because I fell in love with the wrong boy. People said all you needed was love. But they were wrong.

So wrong.

Love wasn't always enough to save somebody. Two people could love one another with everything that they were and it might still not be enough to make their relationship work.

Jermaine Kingston had taken my heart and promised to keep it safe. But he'd failed me. And something told me if I gave Asher a chance, he'd also hurt me. Even if he didn't mean to.

My heart had been shattered once.

I wasn't sure it would survive another heartbreak.

"There you are," Felicity said on Friday morning as I headed into the building. "I was beginning to think you were avoiding me."

"I just needed some space."

"Anything I can help with because if Asher is—"

"It's not Asher," I said a little too quickly. "I guess I'm just missing home, what with it almost being the holidays."

"Are you going to see your mom?"

"I want to, but she doesn't want me to go back."

"Because of Jermaine?"

Nodding, I pulled off my hat and stuffed it in my backpack. "She's worried I'll fall back into old habits."

"But you wouldn't, right?"

"Me and Jermaine are over, but feelings don't just switch off, Flick. I can't say for sure how I'd act again if I saw him. I found out he dropped out of school."

"I'm sorry."

"It's not your fault. It just means he's in even deeper with the crew now. I guess I'd hoped me leaving would..." I trailed off, spotting Asher and the guys across the hall.

"We'll talk later." She gave my hand a little squeeze, smiling as Jason stalked toward her.

"Hey." He kissed her deeply, pressing her back against the lockers.

"Mya," Cameron said. "How's things?"

"Good thanks. You?"

"Can't complain."

"Asher," I said, noticing he'd made no effort to say hello.

"Hey." He barely looked at me.

Felicity and Jason finally broke away from one another and she shot me a 'what's all that about' look. I shrugged.

"Felicity said you didn't ride in with her again." Jason looked at me.

"She did, did she?"

My friend's gaze went wide, guilt swirling in her hazel eyes. "I... oops."

"It's no big deal."

"The weather is getting bad out there. You can't trust the school bus and I don't like the idea of you walking all that way alone."

"I... appreciate your concern." This was too fucking weird. "But I'm a big girl, I can handle myself."

"Oh, I don't doubt it." Jason chuckled. "But it's worrying my girl, so do me a solid and either ride with her or find another ride."

"Jason!" Felicity shrieked, mouthing a silent apology at me.

"Are we hanging at yours tonight?" Jason asked Asher.

"I guess," he grumbled.

"What the fuck is wrong with you?"

"Nothing." He pasted on an easy smile, but it didn't reach his eyes.

"Schools almost out for the holidays and you're acting like a little bitch."

"You know what? Fuck you, Jase. I'm out of here." Asher spun on his heel and stormed off down the hall.

"Nice, man, real nice." Cameron side-eyed Jason who frowned.

"Am I missing something? Because I asked a simple question."

"Jason," Felicity pressed a hand against his chest. "Go easy on him. It's been a rough few weeks and I think he was hurt we didn't invite him the other night."

"Hmm, you didn't invite me either," I spoke up.

"Well, yeah," Felicity said. "We didn't want you to think we were trying to push the two of you together."

"I get it and honestly I really don't care." I did, a little bit. But I wouldn't ever admit that to them. "But Asher cares. He's gone from losing his two best friends and the girl he wanted, so yeah, cut him some slack."

Jason growled while Felicity gasped. It was Cameron who spoke though. "You really think he's upset?"

"He's upset about something, and my money is on the fact he feels left out."

"But we haven't—"

"If you're going to try and tell yourself you haven't excluded him, you're lying to yourself. And I get it, I do. But look at it through his eyes."

The three of them stared at me like I'd grown a second head. "Okay, good talk. I'll see you at lunch?" I asked Felicity, who nodded, her mouth still hanging open.

I hadn't meant to defend Asher but something about the dejection etched into his expression had hit me right in the chest. He was lost all of a sudden, trying to find his new place in the world. Something I could empathize with.

But I didn't want to have common ground with the football player with a dangerous smile. Because common ground connected us. I was pretty sure he already felt it. But if he knew I also felt it, he'd use it against me.

And I wasn't sure I could resist his attack forever.

I didn't purposefully search him out, but when I entered the library where I'd been hiding out for the last couple of days, there he was.

"Fancy seeing you here," I whispered, dropping into the seat beside him.

"Needed some space and this seemed like a good bet."

I smothered a laugh.

"What's funny?" his eyes slid to mine in question.

"Where do you think I've been hiding the last two days?"

"Here?"

I nodded.

"No shit. Guess we're more alike than you give us credit for."

We sat there, in a secluded corner of the library, in comfortable silence. After a few minutes, I pulled out my jotter and began doodling.

"What are you doing?" Asher leaned over, his head almost touching mine as he watched me sketch.

"Nothing really. I just find it soothing."

"You're an artist?"

"God, no. Hailee is an artist. I just like to doodle."

"It's cool," he said. "Reminds me of street art. You know, the kind kids graffiti on abandoned buildings and road signs?"

My pulse ratcheted. "I guess."

"He taught you, didn't he?" he asked quietly.

My eyes lifted. "How do you do that? Know what I'm thinking without me even speaking?"

"I know you, Mya, even if you think I don't."

The air around us crackled, thick and heavy and alive.

"Asher, I..." I swallowed over the lump in my throat.

"What's his name?"

"Jermaine," I croaked.

"Is it over between you and him?"

I nodded.

"Do you still love him?"

"I... yes." A pained sigh rolled off my lips. "I think a part of me will always love him."

"But you're not in love with him?"

"N- no."

Asher inched closer; so close I could feel the warmth of his breath. "I can work with that."

His hand slid along my neck, teasing my curls. My head knew it was a bad idea; was silently screaming at me to stop him. But my heart, my battered bruised heart, craved the attention.

Craved his attention.

Asher's lips hovered over mine, my heart crashing in my chest like a heavy base. *Ba-boom. Ba-boom. Ba-boom.*

"I can't wait to taste you, Mya." His voice was thick with lust, his words laced with intention.

"Asher," my fingers curled into his hoodie. "Kiss—"

"Mr. Bennet," Mrs. Hegarty, the librarian boomed. "This is a library, not your own personal flirt shack."

He sank back in the chair, pinching the bridge of his nose as he expelled a long breath.

"Ms. Hernandez, I am most surprised," she said, as if she didn't notice it was me as she approached us.

"Sorry, Mrs. Hegarty. It won't happen again."

"Yeah, sorry, Mrs. H. It was my fault, not Mya's."

"Oh, I don't doubt it, Mr. Bennet. Now if you're not in here to study..." Her unamused gaze flitted to the doors behind us.

"We'll be out of your hair in a minute."

"Good." She spun on her heel and disappeared behind the stacks.

"Well, that was not how I saw that going," Asher said but I was too fixated on the librarian's words.

"What did she mean? Your own personal flirt shack?"

"That's what you're taking from this?" Asher gawked at me.

"You bring girls here a lot?"

"Are you kidding me right now? You followed me here."

"I didn't... it doesn't matter." I grabbed my bag. "I should go."

"Mya come on, we should talk about what just happened."

"Nothing happened." I stood up but Asher caught my hand.

"I'll let you run, for now." His thumb smoothed over the curve of my fingers and I suppressed a shiver. "But this thing between you and me, it's only a matter of time."

I walked away and didn't look back. Even though I felt his eyes burning into me every step of the way.

6

Asher

"WHY THE FUCK is your house full of people?" Jason hissed.

"Nice to see you too, man."

"I thought it was just going to be the six of us?"

My eyes went over to where Hailee and Cameron were greeting a very confused looking Felicity. "It was, but then Dad called and said they couldn't make it home, so... party central at your service."

"You okay?" He eyed me carefully. "You seem... wound up."

"Me? I'm fine. Nothing a little shot of Tequila won't fix. Am I right?" I hollered and the house exploded with cheers as people raised their cups and beers, fist pumping the air like they were at a *Black Hearts Still Beat* concert.

"You could have given us a heads up. I'd rather not entertain the masses tonight."

"You're still pissed about the exhibition game?"

"I just thought it was going to be low key. The three of us and the girls." His eyes flicked over to where Flick stood.

"Something going on with the two of you?" I asked. He seemed off, and if it wasn't the game, it only left a handful of things. Felicity was at the top of the list.

"Nah, we're good."

As if she heard him, Flick came over to us, tucking herself into Jason's side. "This is... wow. I was not expecting this tonight."

"School's out for the holidays. It's almost a new year. Graduation is right around the corner. What's not to celebrate?" I shrugged.

"Are you okay?" she narrowed her eyes at me.

"Jeez, what is up with everyone? Can't a guy be psyched for the holidays?"

"Asher," Felicity edged closer to me, laying a hand on my arm. "You can talk to us... if something's wrong."

Just then the front door opened and another swarm of people poured in. It was getting rowdy but I hadn't exactly considered the consequences after the strained conversation with my father. His parting words had been to keep things respectable if I had friends over. But all I'd heard was, 'throw the biggest fucking party you can'. Because this—rebelling against his orders—was the only way I maintained a tiny bit of control over my life. But no one knew that. Because I was Asher fucking Bennet.

Mr. Popular.

Skilled athlete.

Notorious flirt.

And persistent joker.

I was the life and soul of the party. Not the fun sponge, absorbing the good times away, and bringing the mood down.

"Duty calls," I said to my friends, unable to stand their looks of concern for a second longer.

Tonight was about celebrating.

It was about getting wasted and having fun.

But most of all, it was about sticking it to the man I called Dad and the future he had all laid out for me.

———

"Don't you think you've had enough?"

Cameron eyed the cup in my hand, and I raised it into the air; liquor—vodka, tequila, whisky, I'd lost count of what I was drinking—sloshing up the sides.

"Oopsie," I hiccupped before chugging down the rest of it. "Now, I've had enough." Wiping my mouth with the back of my hand, I strained my eyes to see better. Everything was spinning.

Whoa.

Why the fuck was everything spinning?

"Maybe it's time to—"

"Party!" I yelled, grabbing the nearest body to me and thrusting its arm in the air. A girl's laughter washed over me.

"Hey, Asher," she said.

"Hey... uh..."

"Lucy."

"Lucy, hey." I smiled, turning on the Asher Bennet charm. "How about me and you—"

"Okay, that's enough." A heavy arm landed on my shoulder, pulling me away from the pretty blonde and marching me down the hall.

"Hey, man, I was just about to—"

"Hit on your teammate's girl?"

"Shit, that was Felicity? I didn't—"

"Jesus, how much have you had to drink? It wasn't Felicity; it was Lucy, Peterman's girlfriend."

"Fuck," I slurred.

"Yeah, fuck." Cameron manhandled me into the bathroom at the back of the house. I stumbled onto the toilet and dropped my head into my hands.

"Everything's spinning."

"I'm not surprised. Ready to tell me what's really going on?"

"What do you mean?"

"The party. You drinking your way through your dad's liquor cabinet like you're on a one-way mission to getting your stomach pumped."

"We're celebrating."

"Celebrating, you really expect me to believe that? I know you, Asher, and something's up."

"You think you know..." I grumbled, swaying slightly. My hand shot out, steadying me. "You haven't got any idea what it's like sometimes."

"So talk to me, man. I'm right here."

"It's my..." I slumped off the toilet and yanked the lid up just in time to empty my stomach contents into the bowl.

"I'll get you some water." The door opened and closed as Cam left me to nurse a stomachache—and my pride—on the expensive floor tiles.

After flushing the toilet, I managed to pull a hand towel off the rail and turn on the faucet. I cleaned my face and laid down on the tiles as the room spun around me.

When the door opened again, I held out my hand, not bothering to open my eyes.

"Here."

Shit.

That wasn't Cameron.

"Thanks." I took the bottle from Mya and dragged myself into a seated position. The water tasted like shit going down, but it soothed my throat.

"When did you get here?" Mya hadn't arrived with Felicity and I hadn't seen her all night. Unless...

"I've been here long enough."

Fuck.

"Want to talk to about it?"

"Is that why Cameron sent you in here?" I peeked up at her. "To try to coax the truth out of me?"

"No, I offered."

"Why? I'm no one to you, right?"

"Asher, that's not fair." Mya perched on the edge of the bathtub.

My friends didn't live in houses like this. Houses with an excessive number of bathrooms and guest rooms and jet skis on the lake. But their jealousy was misplaced because what they didn't know was, money meant fuck all when it came at a price.

A price I'd never asked to pay but had to anyway.

"No? Well life isn't fucking fair." I closed my eyes, bringing a hand to my head, hoping the room would stop spinning.

"What am I going to do with you?" Mya sounded closer. She *was* closer. I felt her fingers on my forehead, softly brushing the hair from my face.

My eyes snapped open, my fingers curling around hers. "What are you doing?" I ground out, hating that I sounded like an ungrateful bastard. But her touch was like kryptonite. Hitting me right where it hurt most—my heart.

"Just because we can't be together doesn't mean I don't care about you. Now stop being a stubborn ass and let me help you."

Mya gently pulled me up until I was sitting. I still felt as sick as a dog but at least everything was stationary now. "Cameron and Jason must really hate me, huh?"

"Hate you?" Her brown eyes softened. "Those guys love you like a brother. You're lucky to have them."

"Right, that's me, Asher Lucky Bennet."

Shit, I'd heard that one too many times over the years.

You're lucky to have this life. This house, and everything that comes with it.

Don't be so sensitive, Asher, you're lucky to have parents who can provide for you.

You're lucky I'm allowing you to play football at all.

"Did something happen, Asher? Because you're not making any sense."

"I drank most of my old man's liquor cabinet. I don't even know what day it is right now."

Lies.

It was all lies. I knew exactly where I was, what day it was, and who was here with me. But I didn't want Mya to see behind my façade. Behind the guy everyone loved.

Because I knew she might not like what she found.

"Come on, I think the party's over." Mya stood up and held out her hand, waiting for me to give her mine.

The second our skin slid together, I felt it. The electricity. The connection. It simmered between us. Hooking my other arm around her waist, I pulled her flush against me and pressed my head to hers. "Tell me you don't feel that?"

"Asher..." Mya's eyes shuttered as she sucked in a harsh breath.

"Tell me."

"I... I feel it." She sounded so resigned. So sad. "But it doesn't change anything."

"Because I'm white? Because you think I give a shit about that?"

"Not just that, no. We come from different worlds, Asher. I have... nothing, and you have everything."

My eyes closed, swallowing down the bitterness. She didn't get it. No one did. Because, on the face of it, I had the nice house and rich parents, and the Raiders jersey on my back. I was supposed to be grateful. I couldn't possibly know hardship.

Easing back to look her in the eyes, I let out a heavy sigh. "I thought you of all people might look past all that stuff. I thought you might see me."

"You're talking in riddles, Asher, and your breath smells like something died." Mya's hands pressed against my chest, the corner of her mouth tipping in a small smile. But I knew she wasn't pushing me away because I had puke-breath, she was keeping me at a safe distance.

"I'm not," I whispered. "You just need to look harder."

"You think you can stand?" Mya asked me and I grinned.

"I'm not falling at your feet... yet."

"Even drunk you're insufferable. Wait here, okay? I'll be right back."

Satisfied I was propped up against the counter, Mya yanked the door open and ducked into the hall. Part of me wondered if she was doing a runner, getting as far away from me as possible. But the other part, the part clinging to the idea of there being an us one day, was hardly surprised when she reappeared.

She felt it.

Mya felt this thing growing between us.

I just had to get her to see it was worth taking a chance on.

"Jason and Cameron are going to close the party down. Come on..."

"You trying to get into my room, Hernandez?" I looked at her with a lazy smile. She rolled her eyes not giving me an answer.

I figured it was better than an outright rejection.

Hand wrapped around mine, Mya led us into the already emptying hall. Fortunately for me, we were able to slip up the second, less used set of stairs without anyone noticing.

"Which one is your room?"

"Mya I'm quite capable of getting to my own room."

She let go of my hand and gave me a pointed look. I took a small step and another but before I knew it, I staggered forward almost crashing into the wall.

Except Mya broke my fall.

"You were saying?" There was a teasing note in her voice, but her eyes held a glint of concern I didn't want to see there.

"I'm never going to live this down, am I?"

"Oh, I don't know about that, Mr. Football Hotshot. Come on." She held out her hand again and I took it, relishing the way her skin felt against mine. So warm. So soft and smooth.

So right it left me a little breathless.

"I'm not tucking you in," Mya threw over her shoulder. "So don't get any ideas."

Pouting, I let her pull me along the hall to my room. "You know," she said, "I don't think I've ever been in a house so big."

"What's home like? Your home in Philly?"

"It's not like this, that's for sure." Mya pushed open the door and found the light switch, but I said, "Don't. I just want to get into bed and forget this ever happened."

Mya guided me over to the bed and I flipped down onto it face first. Her amused laughter echoed in my skull. "I'll get you some water and Advil."

I don't know how many minutes passed before she returned, the liquor-haze making me heavy, pushing me toward the edge of oblivion.

"Asher?" Her voice pulled me back into consciousness and I rolled over, cracking an eye open.

"Thanks," I said, eyeing the bottle of water, box of pills, and gum.

"You should get some rest. I'll—"

"Stay, you should stay."

"Asher, I don't think that's a good idea."

"You're right, it's not. It's probably the worst idea I've ever had." I pushed up onto my elbows, kicking off my sneakers.

Mya hesitated, her eyes glittering with indecision. She wanted to go, that much was obvious. But something made her stay.

Padding over to the door, she closed it, before moving to the two-seater couch pushed up against the wall.

"You're not sleeping there," I said, suddenly feeling very awake.

"Who said anything about sleeping? I'll sit for a little while and make sure you're okay."

"I think the chances of me hurting myself in my sleep are pretty slim."

"You might choke on your own puke."

My stomach lurched and I grimaced. "That is..."

"Disgusting?" Mya smirked.

"Can we pretend you didn't see me half-passed out earlier, hugging the toilet bowl?"

"Too late," she replied.

"You're loving this, aren't you?" I groaned, tipping my head back and taking in a deep breath. "This was so not how I saw this going." The words came out small.

The bed dipped beside me and Mya's hand rested on my arm. "What happened tonight, Asher?"

Our eyes collided.

Time stopped.

It would have been so easy to tell her, to let her see inside the guy with the world at his feet.

"I... My dad called, it was a rough conversation."

Her brows furrowed. "You threw an impromptu party and then got ass over elbow drunk because of some argument with your dad?"

"Well, when you say it like that..." Strangled laughter spilled out of me, but it quickly died when I felt my stomach churn again. "Fuck." I clambered off the bed, making a beeline for the bathroom adjoining my room, leaving Mya, and all thoughts of my dad behind.

7

Mya

"HOW IS HE?" Felicity asked as I entered the kitchen. Jason and Cameron had cleared the house in less than thirty minutes and were now bagging up all the empties while Hailee and Felicity wiped the counters.

"He's finally asleep."

"I don't think I've ever seen him like that," she said.

"I'm going to help the guys." Hailee gave me a smile before leaving us alone.

"What do you know about Asher's parents?"

"His parents?" Flick frowned. "They're mega rich." She glanced around the huge kitchen as if a person's worth amounted to state-of-the-art appliances and sparkling marble counters.

"Yeah, but what do you *know* about them? Like, why are they never around?"

"His dad is in the tech business. Developed some security system for rich celebrity types. So he's away a lot schmoozing them and having meetings, I guess."

"So you don't really know?"

"I... I never really thought about it. It's just always how it's been. They're good people though. You know they gave Cameron a room here for when he needed to get away from his family, and Mrs. Bennet used to help his mom out with Xander."

Xander, Cameron's little brother, was the cutest kid I'd ever seen, but it didn't explain anything about Mr. and Mrs. Bennet.

"So they were around more when Asher was younger?"

"They went to his games when they could, but they've always travelled a lot."

"Both of them? Doesn't that seem a little weird to you?"

"Where's all this coming from, Mya? Jason and Cameron seem to respect Mr. and Mrs. Bennet. They're pretty cool parents. If you ask me, Asher's lucky to have them."

Lucky to have them.

Asher had mumbled something similar. But he was so wasted it was hard to decipher what was real and what was the liquor talking.

A couple of beats passed before Flick said, "You think something happened with his dad?"

"I'm not sure. He wasn't making a lot of sense. Hey, don't tell Jason any of this, okay? I'm not sure Asher will remember any of tonight and I don't want to seem like I'm poking my nose in where it doesn't belong."

"I would never..."

"I know."

"What will you do?"

"I'm not sure yet. Part of me wants to dig around and find out what's going on with him, but the other part..."

"Is scared?" Her brow arched.

"I'm not—"

"You like him, don't you?"

"Felicity, come on. You know I'm not looking for that."

"I know, but sometimes it comes whether you want it or not."

"I don't want to give him the wrong idea about us."

"Asher is a good guy, Mya. He would never hurt you." The unspoken words glittered in her eyes.

"It could never work," I said, mentally running over all the reasons me and Asher were a terrible idea.

"There was a time I would have said the same thing about me and Jason," Felicity pointed out.

"Yeah, but that's different."

"Is it? I know you think you come from different worlds but what's that saying, 'opposites attract'? Who knows? Maybe you're exactly what each other needs."

My eyes darted to the doorway. "I should probably get home, my aunt will be—"

"Want a piece of advice? Don't run. These Raider boys have a way of getting what they want, and whether you want it or not, I think Asher wants you."

I gawked at her, the air sucked clean from my lungs. He'd made no secret of the fact he felt something for me. Even made me admit I felt it too. But everything was so easy for him or, at least, I'd thought it was before tonight. But now I didn't know what to think. I'd heard no rumors around town about his father; nothing to make me question the kind of childhood he'd had.

From the outside, Asher Bennet had it all.

Money.

Looks.

A bright future ahead of him.

Everyone knew looks could be deceiving though, and I couldn't shake the feeling there was more to Asher than met the eye.

I knew I should walk away. Walk away and forget all about the football player with the easy smile and glint in his eye. But the fixer in me couldn't just forget.

Mom always said I was drawn to broken things. Right since I was a little girl and used to feed the neighborhood's stray cats. Then Jermaine came along with his crooked smile and nose for trouble and that was it, I'd never wanted to fix something as much as I'd wanted to fix him.

"Mya?" Flick's voice pulled me from my thoughts, and I blinked over at her.

"Yeah?"

"Are you okay?"

"Just tired. I should go."

"You could always stay here. It's late and I don't like the idea of you walking home alone."

"It's not that far." And I'd walked through much worse neighborhoods at night.

"Let me ask Jason—"

"Ask me what?" He appeared at the door, his brows drawn tight.

"Can you give Mya a ride home?"

"It's fine, I can walk."

"Come on, tough girl," he teased. "I only had one beer."

Riding with Jason, alone, was the last place I wanted to be, but Flick gave me a nod of encouragement before gazing up at him with stars in her eyes. "Thanks, babe," she said. "I'll finish cleaning up. Call you tomorrow." That was for me.

I gave her a tight smile before following Jason out of the house. His restored Dodge Charger glistened in the moonlight. "You going to stand there all night or get in?" he said.

"You didn't have to do this."

"You're one of Felicity's best friends which makes you my friend. Now get in the damn car."

Feeling my jaw clench, I yanked open the door and slid inside.

"There," Jason smirked, "that wasn't so difficult, was it?"

I shot him a pointed look but he only chuckled.

Silence settled over us as Jason backed out of the Bennet's large driveway and took the road out of town.

"I take it Felicity told you where I live?"

"There isn't much she doesn't tell me," he said dryly.

"I'll bear that in mind."

"How was Ash when you finally left him?"

"Passed out hugging a pillow."

"He say anything to you?"

"Just a lot of jumbled nonsense. What do you think happened?" I glanced at him sideways, wondering if Jason had his own theories, and whether or not he'd share them with me.

"He's been acting weird for a while. At first, I thought it was just about Felicity. He likes... liked her." Jason cleared his throat. "For a second I thought she was actually going to come between us."

I shifted uncomfortably in the leather seat, jealousy edging into my thoughts.

"But now I'm thinking it has nothing to do with her." His hard gaze burned into the side of my face. "He likes you, ya know?"

"So everyone keeps telling me."

"You're not feeling it?"

"I... it's complicated."

"Because of your ex?"

"Let me guess, Felicity told you—"

"Actually, she didn't. But I'm no fool, Mya. I know you're running from something."

It wasn't like I tried to hide who I was and where I came from, but it unnerved me that Jason saw through me so easily.

"Look, whatever's going on with Ash, something tells me he's not going to come to me or Cam with it. But maybe he'll open up to you."

"You want me to use his feelings for me against him?"

"That's not..." he let out a heavy sigh. "I'm worried about him. I've never seen him so out of control. It's Asher, he's like sunshine on a rainy fucking day or something. But tonight was different. He was..."

"Dark," I whispered.

"Yeah. I don't know what the fuck is going on with him but whatever it is, he needs someone there for him."

"He has people. He has you and Cameron and Felicity and the rest of the team."

Jason grumbled, "Does he know that though?"

"I just don't want him to get the wrong idea." My hands curled into fists, pressing against my thigh.

"I'm not asking you to marry the guy. Just be a shoulder to lean on, an ear to listen. Things haven't been the same between us since everything went down and I know he feels pushed out because Cam's with Hailee and I'm with Felicity."

When I didn't answer, Jason's words swirling around my head, he added, "He's a good guy, Mya."

That was the problem though. Asher was good. He deserved a girl who could be in the moment with him one hundred percent. I wasn't sure I could be that for him.

I wasn't sure I wanted to be.

"You don't think it would only make things worse for him?" I asked.

"What the fuck does that mean?"

"It doesn't matter," I huffed indignantly, annoyed at myself for even bringing it up. Maybe Flick was right, maybe I was making a bigger deal out of it than it needed to be.

We rode the rest of the way in silence. It was one thing I liked about Jason; he didn't feel the need to fill awkward silences. He also didn't push. He'd said his piece and now the ball was in my court.

Only I didn't know what the hell I was going to do about it.

"WELL DAMN, girl, if you don't look like a bird is nesting in there." Aunt Ciara eyed my wild curls with amusement.

I smoothed a hand over my bed hair and waved her off, making a beeline for the coffeemaker. I'd had a restless night, replaying things over in my head. The drunken conversation with Asher. The friendly advice from Felicity, and the strange ride home with Jason.

"Rough night?" my aunt asked.

"Something like that." I made myself a mug of coffee and sat down at the kitchen table.

"I was talking to Maeve yesterday and she told me the best news. Her grandson, Tyrese, is coming to stay for the holidays. Isn't that great?"

My brows pinched, blood pounding between my ears. "Tyrese?"

"He's a good boy. Studying business at UPenn, I think. Visits his gram whenever he can. I'm surprised he's still single."

"Aunt C," I groaned, not liking where this was headed.

"Now now, don't go getting all riled up. We know better than to meddle. But would it really hurt you to come visit them with me one day?"

Yes, yes it would. It was bad enough she had an opinion on everything but now she was trying to set me up with her friend's grandson. It couldn't get much worse.

"It won't hurt for you to have another friend here, Mya," she said when I didn't answer.

"I have friends."

"And I'm sure they're great. But Tyrese is..." She hesitated.

"Black?" I questioned, disappointment dripping from my voice.

"That's not what I was going to say. But now that you bring it up, yes, he is. He's a good solid Afro-American man who has been raised to respect women. After Jermaine, he could be just what you need."

"I'm sure he's a good man." I rose from the table slowly, letting the chair scrape across the tiles. "But I'm not interested." Dumping my mug on the drainer, I walked out of there, not bothering to stop at the sound of my aunt's voice.

She'd gone too far this time.

Thinking I needed her all up in my business. Jermaine wasn't just some guy I'd foolishly fallen in love with. He'd been my best friend since forever. We had history; our lives were entwined. He was a good guy but like so many before him, he had been tempted by the easy money running for Diaz's crew could give him. Opportunity didn't come knocking in our neighborhood.

Drugs, gangs, and crime did.

I slammed the bedroom door behind me and made my way over to the bed, only to be interrupted by the blare of my cell. Glancing at Shona's name, I ignored it, dropping onto my bed and clutching a pillow to my chest. Mom was right. Unless I made a clean break, I would never escape my ties to Fallowfield Heights. But it was my home. Not to mention the fact my mom would never leave there. How was I supposed to just forget them? To turn my back on my roots?

The answer was, I couldn't.

Not yet.

8

Asher

"YOU LOOK LIKE SHIT." Jason smirked at me as I padded into the kitchen, the smell of bacon turning my stomach.

"Fee, baby, not that I don't usually love seeing you in my kitchen—"

"You need to eat," she cut me off, grabbing the pan and shaking the contents onto a plate. Usually I would have been the first to dive in, but I could barely look at it without my stomach churning.

"I really don't," I grumbled. "I need water and Advil. Lots of Advil."

It wasn't unusual to see them in my kitchen on a weekend, especially after a party. But this was one morning I didn't want company. My head was pounding, my body felt like it had gone ten rounds with our defensive line, and I had murky memories from the night before... memories I'd rather forget.

"Which one of you put me to bed?" I asked Jason, and Cam who was awfully quiet. They glanced at each other and then me.

"You don't remember?" Cameron asked.

"I have a few black spots."

"We didn't put you to bed, man. Mya did."

"What the fuck did you just say? Mya wasn't even at the party." I knew, I'd looked for her enough. But that was before all the tequila... and Jack... and shots.

Too. Many. Fucking. Shots.

"She turned up," Flick added, pushing a plate of breakfast toward me. I just stared at it, trying to sort through the hangover haze clouding my mind.

"She was here?"

"Yup." Jason bit into a piece of crispy bacon.

"Well, shit." It was one thing for my friends to see me trashed, but Mya? That wasn't supposed to happen.

Fuck.

"Did she... say anything?"

"After watching you puke for an hour? The girl was traumatized."

"I didn't—" A hazy memory flooded my mind. Mya's hand against my skin. It was hard to tell if it was real or just a figment of my imagination. I guess drinking half your old man's liquor cabinet would do that to you.

"Ready to tell us what the hell happened?" Jason glared at me.

"It was nothing." I shrugged dismissively, pushing eggs around my plate.

"Ash, man, if something is going on—"

"Nothing is going on. I'm fine, promise. It's been a crazy few weeks, and I just felt like a blow-out." I could barely look at them, even if I felt their hard eyes burning into the top of my skull.

"Yeah, well don't make a habit of it. School might be out for the holidays, but we still need you fit and ready for the exhibition game."

"I thought you were still pissed about that?" My brow rose and Jason shrugged.

"Any chance to show Rixon East who's on top and I'm there. Besides, Felicity talked me around." His eyes flicked to hers and she blushed.

"I take it you figured out how to—"

"*Asher!*"

Chuckling, I went to the faucet to get another glass of water.

"So Mya didn't stay?" I finally asked the question I'd been wondering ever since hearing her name.

"Jason gave her a ride home after she made sure you were all tucked in." Amusement laced Cam's words, but I didn't give him shit for it.

"Okay," I grunted.

"This shit must be killing you; knowing she was here but not being able to remember what you said to her?"

"Jason," Flick shot me an apologetic look.

"I'll make it right with her," I said with conviction.

Whether or not she'd give me a chance though, was another matter entirely.

"You MUST BE Mya's aunt. Nice to meet you. I'm Asher, Asher Bennet." I held out the bunch of flowers, realizing I had severely underestimated Mya's warning when the petite woman glared up at me. "I know who you are. What do you want?"

"I... uh, is Mya home?" I scratched my jaw, feeling the weight of her stare press down on me.

"She's busy."

"Ma'am, I mean no disrespect, but I'd really like to—"

"Asher?" Mya appeared, eyes wide with an indecipherable emotion. "I wasn't expecting you."

"I know. I just wanted to drop by and give your aunt these and hopefully talk to you."

"Mya," her aunt warned.

"You should put the flowers in water, Auntie. I'll be right there, okay?"

I stood a little taller at Mya coming to my defense but as the two of them stared at one another, locked in some silent conversation, I knew there was far more to this than her aunt just not liking white guys.

Shit.

"Five minutes," her aunt said before snatching the flowers out of my hand and taking off down the hall.

"What are you doing here?" Mya hissed as she slipped out onto the porch, closing the door behind her.

"I wanted to see you."

"You could have called or texted."

"I wanted to see you, Mya. After last night—"

"You can remember everything?"

"About that. I didn't say or do anything inappropriate did I?"

"You were pretty out of it." She smiled, but it didn't reach her eyes.

"What?" I asked, sensing she was keeping something from me. But if she was about to tell me, it never came. Instead, she let out a weary sigh.

"You really shouldn't have come here."

"I just wanted to say thank you. The guys told me what you did." I reached out, plucking a spiral between my fingers. "I would have preferred you hadn't seen me like that but I'm glad it was you taking care of me."

"Asher, what happened yesterday?"

The ground moved from under me. "What do you mean?" I choked out. "Nothing happened."

But I saw it in her eyes.

Mya knew.

Maybe she didn't know everything, but she knew enough.

She knew I was lying.

Glancing back at the house, Mya's lips pulled into a flat line. "I can't talk right now. But I could... come over later?"

"Yeah?" My chest almost burst.

"Well, your home movie theater is pretty awesome."

"Oh it's like that, huh?"

"How else would it be?"

Was she flirting with me? Because it felt a hella lot like she was. I fought a grin.

"Pick you up at six?"

"I can make my own way there."

"Okay." I didn't want to push her, not yet. "Should I invite the others?" I asked.

"Won't they be busy? It's Saturday, the night of dates and dreams and all those other things regular couples do."

"So it'll just be the two of us?" I clarified because my mind was spinning in a hundred different directions.

"Asher?" she said, her silky voice grounding me.

"Yeah, Hernandez?" I couldn't keep the smile off my face.

"I'll see you later."

Slowly backing away, I kept my eyes on her. Mya was beautiful. The dark wash denim overalls molded to her curves. The black tee underneath highlighting the tone of her skin. Everything about Mya drew me in. She was fierce and unapologetic and completely herself.

And I wanted to know her.

All of her.

"Don't be late," I mouthed and she chuckled, waiting until I was on the sidewalk.

"Oh, and Asher?" she called out.

"Yeah?"

"Don't get any ideas about what this is."

"You mean a movie with a friend?" I smirked. "As if I could forget."

This time felt different though. She might have wanted to play it down as nothing more than friends hanging out but there was a sparkle in her eyes I hadn't seen before.

A sparkle I suddenly wanted to see all the damn time.

By the time Mya arrived, I no longer felt hungover. Which was a good thing considering how many snacks I'd prepared. Everything from nachos to popcorn, pretzels to candy. I may have gone a little overboard.

"Jason, Cameron, Hailee, and Flick did a good job with the clean-up." She pretended to run her finger along the sideboard, inspecting it for dust. "I hope you tipped them well. Although, I'm surprised you haven't got a housekeeper."

"We used to have one, when I was younger," I admitted. "But as soon as I turned fourteen, she left."

"I can't imagine what that's like, always having someone to do everything for you." Mya's eyes clouded.

"There's just you?"

"Me and my mama, yeah."

"What happened to your dad?"

"I thought I was coming over to watch a movie?" She deflected and I couldn't blame her. I didn't like to talk about my family either.

"We can work up to that." I led Mya toward the back of the house, pulling open the door to the basement level home movie theater.

"I got a bunch of stuff from the store earlier. I hope you're hungry?"

She shot me an uncertain smile. "You didn't need to do that, Asher."

"I know, but I wanted to. I feel like, after last night, I owe you." Raking a hand through my hair, I dropped down on one of the couches, chuckling when Mya took the one furthest away from me.

"Do I still smell?"

"You do remember." She gasped.

"Bits and pieces. It's very hazy though. What'll it take for you to put me out of my misery and tell me if I said anything inappropriate?"

Mya hesitated for a second, as if mulling over her answer, then cracked a small smile. "You were ever the gentleman."

"I highly doubt that." But I'd take it. I'd take anything she had to offer me.

Jesus, I was so pathetic, begging for scraps of attention from a girl who had made it clear on more than one occasion that she wasn't going to cross whatever invisible line she'd drawn between us.

But she's here. And she's flirting back.

"Listen, I'm sorry about earlier, with your aunt. I guess I didn't really believe you when you said she had a problem with white boys."

"She doesn't have a problem with white boys, Asher. She has a problem with *me* dating a white boy."

"Good job you're not dating one then." I fought a grin, watching her reaction. But Mya wasn't like most girls. You had to work for her blushes and little expressions of surprise.

It was one of the things I liked most about her.

"What movie did you have in mind?" She switched the subject.

"Take your pick." I flicked my head to where I'd sorted out a pile of DVDs. While she was deciding, I went and got the snacks, adding bowl after bowl to the small coffee table.

"Wow." Mya observed the spread. "That is a lot of food."

"You have seen me eat, right?"

She laughed at that, sitting back on the other couch.

Screw this.

I stood up and stalked toward her. Mya's eyes went big, tracking my movements until I hovered right in front of her. "Asher, what are you...?"

"Chips," I deadpanned. "I need chips." Shoving my hand into the bowl, I scooped up a handful, winked at her, and sat on the end of her couch. She narrowed her eyes at me, pressing her pouty lips into a thin line.

"Problem?" My brow rose.

"Just play the damn movie," she mumbled.

But the movie wasn't distraction enough. It didn't stop me from watching her out the corner of my eye, stealing discreet glances as she laughed and gasped and buried her hands into her face. There was something so fucking pure about seeing Mya this way. Completely uninhibited and free. It did all kinds of crazy things to me; made my heart race and my palms sweat. It also made me act like a dumbass because before I knew what I was doing, I'd shuffled closer to her and grabbed her hand in mine. I half-expected her to tear her hand away and chew me out. But Mya was full of surprises, letting our joined hands rest between us as if it was the simplest thing in the world.

Then the stars aligned.

Mya almost jumped out of her skin when the bad guy appeared out of the shadows, brandishing a knife and ready to kill. "Holy shit," she shrieked, her ass lifting at least two inches off the couch. Laughter rumbled deep in my chest as I slipped my arm around her shoulder and pulled her into my side. "It's okay," I teased, "I'll protect you."

"Asher..." Her hand went to my stomach, my muscles contracting beneath her touch, blazing a path of heat *down, down, down.* My eyes dropped to hers, hooded and hungry.

"Asher, what are you..."

"Just one taste," I pleaded, needing to kiss her so much it hurt.

"I—" she started, but my hand slid into her hair, tilting her face to mine. "We shouldn't..." It was a cracked whisper, her eyes telling me something different. Silently giving me permission.

The movie raged on around us, the explosions and cries from the surround sound system drowning out to nothing but white noise, as I gently brushed my lips over hers. Mya let out a little whimper, her fingers curling into my t-shirt. My pulse ratcheted, my body burning for the girl who tasted like strawberry kisses.

"Asher, this is a bad idea." Her words should have doused me in cold water, but they didn't. Because Mya didn't pull away. She didn't shove me back and run. Instead, she pressed her lips to mine again, pulling my body into hers. I went willingly, pressing Mya into the back of the couch, learning the shape of her mouth, the curves of her body.

I'd only been half serious when I told Flick I thought me and Mya were written in the stars, but kissing her, feeling her underneath me, I felt a cosmic shift. Maybe this—*us*—wasn't destiny but we were so fucking right for each other I wanted to scream it from the rooftops.

So when she breathed, "Stop, Asher. You have to stop," as if we were doing something wrong, I knew it was a mistake.

Because nothing was wrong about this.

Not one single thing.

I just had to make her see it.

9

Mya

ASHER KISSED ME.

He wasn't supposed to kiss me.

I wasn't supposed to *let* him kiss me.

But the way he looked at me, with so much yearning and hope; it cracked right through the last of my defenses. Leaving me unprotected and powerless against his charms.

I didn't feel vulnerable the second his lips touched mine though, I felt alive. Warmth coursed through me like wildfire. His weight pressed against me, overwhelming in the best kind of way.

A fighter at heart, I'd always had to fight for what I wanted. A girl growing up, in a man's world ravaged by drugs and crime. For so many years, I'd stood by Jermaine's side, defending him, refusing to let him fall deeper into the trap. I'd looked out for him right since we were kids, when I never had anyone looking out for me. But here in Asher's house, tangled in his arms, his lips hovering right over mine, I felt safe. I felt like he would never let anything hurt me.

It should have been a relief. Here, with him, I could finally breathe. But the strength of my developing feelings for him scared me. Because here, behind closed doors, it was just the two of us. There was no judgment or stereotypes, whispers or glares. No black, brown, or white. No rich and poor. There was only lust and desire and a connection I was no longer sure I could fight.

"Why do you like me?" I blurted out, killing the moment. But fear was a strong motivator.

Asher stared down at me, confusion crinkling his eyes. "I've never met anyone like you, Mya," he said. "You're strong and beautiful and loyal. You're not intimidated or in awe of the team, and you are so fucking beautiful it hurts."

"You already said that." My lip curved.

"I did?" His eyes danced with humor. "Your beauty deserves repetition."

"You're such a cheese ball."

"Too much?" He grinned. "I'm sure I can think up some other adjectives..."

"No." My fingers ran up his chest finding his jaw. "I think I got it."

Asher fixed his mouth over mine again, slipping his tongue between my lips. My little voice of reason silently screamed at me to stop, but with every stroke of his tongue, every press of his lips, it grew quieter and quieter until all the reasons why this was a bad idea melted away.

I let my hands glide over his shoulders, tangling my fingers into the hair at the nape of his neck. Asher broke the kiss, brushing his nose over mine, before tracing his lips over my jaw and down the slope of my neck. Sucking and nibbling and grazing his teeth against the sensitive skin, sending thousands of tiny shivers rippling through me.

"I want you, Mya," he rasped. "I need you."

The sheer desperation in his voice had me gripping his chin and lifting his face to mine. "What happened yesterday, Asher?"

Indecision flickered in his eyes. He wanted to tell me, but something held him back.

"What happened with your ex?" he countered.

Damn him.

We were back to this. Both of us needing more, neither of us willing to share. But one of us had to make a move, to give an inch.

Something told me it wasn't going to be him.

Taking a deep breath, I started. "Jermaine is... *was* my best friend." I pushed Asher off me gently, needing air. He sat back, raking a hand through his perfectly messed up hair.

"We grew up together, were in the same class at school. Our mamas always used to joke that we were two halves of the same whole." Asher let out a small breath and my eyes slid to his. "I won't lie to you, Asher. He was my everything."

"What changed?" His voice was tight.

"I don't need to tell you that where I come from, it isn't like Rixon. When you're a kid it's easier to ignore what happens on street corners, but once you hit high school it's reality. Drugs, gangs..." I hesitated, unsure of how much to tell him. Not because I was protecting Jermaine, that ship had long sailed, but because I was protecting myself.

If I told Asher, if I let him into that part of my life, there was no undoing it. I'd forever be the poor girl from the wrong side of the tracks.

"He fell in with some bad people. Things got out of control and he got hurt." *I got hurt*, the words teetered on the tip of my tongue.

Asher's brows bunched together as he studied me, seeing right through my defenses. "And..."

"And I knew I'd lost him. Next time it wasn't going to be a gang jumping him, roughing him up. It was going to be a car rolling by with a gun. My mama wanted me out of there and my aunt was all too willing to let me stay with her. Your turn," I said, wavering under the intensity of his stare.

Asher, like Felicity and Hailee and everyone else at Rixon High, knew one version of Mya. Sure they saw the military boots, the denim overalls, and plaid shirts, but she was still a tamed down version of herself. Because I knew the other version of Mya, the *real* version, and this place, these people, wouldn't mesh.

"My dad is an asshole," Asher deadpanned, his face devoid of emotion.

"Okaaaay. I don't really know what to say to that."

"Everyone thinks he's this awesome self-made man who provides for his family but he's a mean son of a bitch. A real devil in sheep's clothing."

"No one else knows this?"

He shrugged, not meeting my eyes. "Money talks, I guess. And don't get me wrong, on the face of it, he's generous. He donates to charity, helps out my friends' families. Supports the team. But everything comes with a price where Andrew Bennet is concerned."

"And you have to pay it." I whispered.

"Four years." Asher tugged at the ends of his hair. "He gave me four years of high school, but senior year is almost up."

"What happens after high school?" Dread slithered up my spine.

Asher ran a hand down his face, his expression contorted with pain. "I become his puppet."

I didn't know what that meant but I could feel the torment radiating from him.

"My father was never the athletic type. He didn't play football or run track or anything like that. His talent was computers and tech. Figuring out how things work and making them work better. I was never interested in that stuff and I was always a big disappointment to him. Football... that was my passion, and I was good at it. Not as good as Jason," he gave me a wry smile, "but I could have had a good college football career. So the deal was I got to play at Rixon if I walked away from football in college and focused on academics."

"Asher, that's not—"

"Fair?" he scoffed. "My old man doesn't care about that. All he cares about is his business and making sure I'm ready to take his place and finally become the son he's always wished he had."

"What about your mom? How does she feature in all this?"

His expression darkened and I knew I'd hit another chord. "She's the reason I got four years."

"What do you mean?"

"Before high school, Dad tried to make me quit football, said it wasn't becoming of a Bennet. He'd never hid the fact he resented he got me instead of a carbon copy of himself. When I was a kid, Mom sheltered me from a lot of that, but I didn't realize just how much she protected me until I got older."

His eyes settled on a spot on the floor, his fists curled tight and rubbing against his thigh.

I reached for him, uncurling his fingers and sliding them between mine. Asher looked at me and I smiled. "I'm right here," I whispered.

"Mom knew how important it was for me to play with Jason and Cam. So she sacrificed herself," he almost choked over the words.

"I don't... what do you mean?"

It was her husband, it didn't seem like that big of a deal for a wife to support her husband, unless... "Asher?" I said when he didn't answer. His eyes were closed, his chest rising and falling with his ragged breaths.

"When I say he's mean, Mya." Asher's eyes opened. He looked broken and it made my heart ache. "He isn't just mean with his words."

"Oh." The unspoken words hung between us.

"Did he ever... hurt you?"

"When I was younger, he'd get so mad at me. Mom always stepped in though. I thought she tempered his anger, but he'd take it out on her when I wasn't around. She was good at hiding it but there's only so much makeup can disguise. Thankfully, he was away a lot for work so it was just the two of us and Serena, the housekeeper. But then the summer before high school he started going on about how it was time for me to learn the business and show more interest in my future.

"We got into a big fight when he said I couldn't try out for the football team in high school, but Mom intervened, made me leave the house. When I finally returned, they sat me down and told me that they had come to an arrangement. Mom would start accompanying Dad on his business trips and I got four years of football with my friends. He'd always wanted her to be more involved, but she wanted to raise me."

There was so much I wanted to ask. So much that didn't make sense. But I could see the emotional toll it had taken on Asher to finally tell someone the truth.

To tell *me*.

So instead of pushing for more than he was ready to give me, I shuffled closer to him and wrapped my arms around his neck. "I'm sorry," I said quietly.

"That's the first time I've ever told anyone the truth." Asher eased back to look at me. "I'm glad it was you, Mya."

"I won't tell a soul."

"I know," he said. "I have to tell them eventually. They're already asking why I haven't formally committed to the Pittsburgh Panthers next fall. They don't know it's because my future is already sealed at Pittsburgh, and it doesn't involve football."

"They'd understand."

"Maybe. But I don't want it to come between us, not when we only have a few months left of senior year. Besides, you know what Jason is like. If he found out the truth..."

He wouldn't be able to bite his tongue. Because despite all his flaws Jason Ford protected those he cared about, and Asher was like family to him.

"There's more, isn't there?" I couldn't stop the words from tumbling out. But something about the whole thing didn't sit right with me.

"Yeah," Asher let out a weary sigh. "If I don't keep my end of the bargain and go to Pittsburgh like a good little lap dog, Dad will cut me off. No trust fund, no college, no future."

"There are other ways, Asher. Scholarships for one." I knew from Felicity that he'd been offered at least two athletic scholarships.

"It's not that simple." He ground out. "It won't only be me that suffers. I have to think about Mom. Me and Dad are all she has."

"I'm just saying—"

"Can we not do this right now?" His eyes were soft despite his callous tone. "It's been a rough couple of days and I'm exhausted."

"You're right. I'm sorry. I should go—" I went to stand but Asher caught my hand.

"I don't want you to leave."

"You don't?"

He shook his head. "Stay."

"Asher, I'm not sure..."

"Look, I know you don't want anything serious and I know you're still hung up on your ex, but I like you. I like you a lot. I can go slow, if that's what you need."

He looked so adorable staring up at me with his big blue eyes. "Give me a chance, Mya, please. That's all I'm asking."

There were so many reasons it was a bad idea.

So many.

But how could I deny him when he'd trusted me with something he'd never trusted anyone else with?

"I'll stay but I'm not making any promises. Our lives are both complicated and us being more than just friends will only complicate them further."

"I can live with that." He got up and hooked his arm around my waist, drawing me into his body. His eyes homed in on my lips and he started to lean in.

"Asher, friends don't kiss."

"Maybe we can be the exception to the rule," he said around an irresistible smile.

A dangerous smile.

A smile I knew would get us both into a lot of trouble.

10

Asher

MYA STARED UP AT ME, lust and indecision swirling in her eyes. She wanted me. She wanted *this*. But she was still fighting it.

"I promise I won't fall in love with you, if that's what you're worried about," the words were barely a whisper against the corner of her mouth. "I know we're heading in different directions. I know this is only temporary, but you make all the shit fade into the background."

"Asher," she breathed, pressing her forehead closer to mine.

"I won't hurt you, I promise." *But you might destroy me.* Because although I'd promised her I wouldn't fall in love with her, I could already feel myself doing exactly that. It was a small price to pay though, if it meant having her in my life.

Mya fisted my t-shirt, fighting whatever battle raged inside her. Maybe it was her lingering feelings for her ex, or maybe it was the fact he'd hurt her and she didn't want to trust another guy so soon. Whatever it was, I wanted to prove her wrong, to show her nothing else mattered except the way we made each other feel.

This time when I brushed my lips over hers, Mya didn't resist. She pulled me closer, anchoring us together, deepening the kiss. Our tongues tangled in soft lazy licks, setting my body on fire. My hands glided down her spine, finding her perfect ass, pressing her into my rock-hard dick.

"See what you do to me," I said against her swollen lips. "See how much I want you."

Mya whimpered, rubbing herself on me, letting me rock into her at the perfect angle. I wanted to strip her down and take her right here on the couch, but I knew she wasn't ready. She was only just getting her head around us being kissing friends.

"Come on," I said, pulling away, smirking at how flushed and breathless she was. Leading her back up to the first floor, we walked in comfortable silence upstairs to my bedroom. "At least I can walk in a straight line tonight," I joked.

"I should probably text my aunt," she said.

"What will you tell her?"

"That I'm staying with the girls."

I gave her a curt nod. I didn't expect her to tell her aunt the truth, but it still stung knowing I was her dirty little secret.

"It's just easier this way, Asher," Mya added, sensing my change in mood.

"It's all good," I said around an easy smile as we entered my room. "At least your aunt gives a shit what you're doing and who you're with."

My dad hadn't cared in a long time. As long as I wasn't tarnishing his reputation, he'd pretty much washed his hands of me. Most kids eagerly awaited the day their parents went out of town and left them home alone, but I'd been used to my own company since ninth grade.

"You want a t-shirt to sleep in?"

"I... uh..." Mya lowered her eyes, toying with the hem of her shirt. "I guess."

With a quiet chuckle, I went over to the dresser and pulled out a clean Raiders jersey.

"Oh, hell no, I'm not wearing that." Her nose scrunched up in disgust.

"Please." I stuck out my bottom lip. "For me?"

"Asher, come on... isn't there some kind of jersey ritual where you should only let your girl wear your number?"

"That's a thing?" I teased. "I never knew."

"I'd rather sleep naked than wear that thing."

"Really? Because that can be arranged."

Shaking her head, Mya fought a smile. "Fine, give it here."

"The bathroom's through there." I pointed to the door.

"Oh, I remember." She gave me a bemused look as she stalked past me, my jersey in a death grip. "I hope you cleaned up after last night," her voice drifted back to me and I smothered a laugh.

While Mya got changed, I stripped out of my clothes and dumped them on the chair. I didn't expect to turn around and see her standing in the doorway watching me through hooded eyes. "See something you like?" My brow quirked up as I patted my abs.

Heat blazed in her eyes as she let her gaze run down my body. "Nice... tattoo." She grinned.

I stepped toward her. "We both know you weren't looking at my tattoo, Hernandez." It was my turn to let my eyes trace over her body. "Fuck, you look good in my jersey." It clung to her curves, hinting at her killer body underneath.

"At least it covers my ass," she shot back, fingering the hem which landed almost at her knees.

"I should probably check." I spun a finger and mouthed, "twirl."

She rolled her eyes. "You wish."

Oh how I did.

"You're not sleeping like that, are you?"

"I always sleep like this," I said. "But if you think you can't resist touching me, I can put something on."

"I..." Mya swallowed. "I think I'm capable of resisting."

"Wanna bet?"

"I'm beginning to think this was a very bad idea." Mya got that caught in the headlights look again. Before she could bolt, I hooked a hand around her waist and pulled her closer.

"I'll behave, I promise." Ducking my head, I kissed the tip of her nose. "Thank you for agreeing to stay with me."

I wouldn't tell her, but it meant a lot she'd agreed to stay. Not only because I wanted her something fierce, but because it got lonely sleeping in an empty house day in, day out.

"Just don't get too used to it," she replied, eyes dancing with amusement. "It's one night."

"Better make the most of it then." Without giving her any warning, I bent down, slid my arm under Mya's knees and scooped her up.

"Asher, what the hell?" she shrieked, clinging onto me. I walked us over to the bed and dropped her down on the mattress, her laughter filling my room.

"I couldn't resist. You look good on my bed." Almost too good. Especially wearing my number. Her eyes fell to my black boxer briefs and I rose a brow at how her gaze lingered on the outline of my dick.

"You're making it really hard for me," I warned her, smirking at my double entendre.

"I have no idea what you're talking about." Innocence edged into her expression, but I knew better than to be fooled by her attempt at demure.

Mya was anything but innocent.

Kneeling on the bed, I crawled toward her, wrapping a hand around one of her ankles. Her skin was so soft and smooth. I wanted to acquaint myself with every inch of her body. My palm glided up her leg, brushing her inner thigh. Mya's eyes flared, her breath catching.

"Asher..."

"One day," I said huskily. "You'll be moaning my name."

"You're so full of it."

"Oh, you think?"

This is what I needed from Mya. The banter, the games, and teasing. She made it so easy and she gave as good as she got. And I fucking loved it.

My fingers traced the contour of her leg again, inching higher and higher, disappearing beneath the blue and white material.

"Asher." It was a warning this time. "I didn't agree to this."

"Kissing friends only, right? So what about if I kiss you right..." Dipping my head, I ran my tongue over her warm skin, "here."

I didn't kiss her panties, but I did let my mouth linger there enough that her hand shot out and grabbed my shoulder. "You're not playing fair."

"No?" I looked along the line of her body, meeting her eyes, blowing soft puffs of air against her. Mya stifled a moan, her legs tensing either side of my head.

I wanted nothing more than to hook the lacy material to the side and taste her, but I wouldn't, not without her explicit permission. Lifting myself up, I moved over her, bringing my eyes level with hers. "Hi," I said.

"Hi." Mya smiled, her eyes sparkling with desire.

"I'm not going to kiss you there, not yet, not until you beg me."

"Asher..." it came out a pained groan.

"Yeah, Hernandez?"

"I've been thinking about our situation."

"Situation, is that what we're calling it?"

"Yeah, and I think kissing is allowed. Maybe some clothed groping."

"So I can do this." I smoothed my hand up her stomach, over the jersey, and rested it against the swell of her tits. "And you're not going to knee me in the balls?"

"Your balls are safe." She laughed. "I meant what I said though. We need to take this slow. Friends... with kissing benefits."

"Don't forget the clothed groping."

"That too." Mya leaned up, kissing me slow and deep, her tongue exploring every inch of my mouth. My dick hardened, nudging up against her.

"Shit, that feels good," I rasped, pretty certain that if I created enough friction, I could get us both off. I broke the kiss, grinding my hips, watching her eyes flutter closed. "What about this? Is this okay?"

"Hmm-mm," she murmured, pulling her bottom lip between her teeth, stopping herself from saying whatever was on her mind.

"And this?" I dipped a hand between us, rubbing her through her damp panties.

"Asher, don't..."

"Don't what, Mya?"

"Don't stop," she panted the words, letting her head fall back as my fingers continued moving over her.

"Let me touch you. I *need* to touch you." I was so fucking hard for her. I wanted to feel how wet she was, slide my fingers into her and make her come.

"N- no." Her voice quivered, her body trembled. "Not yet."

What the hell did that mean?

Not yet as in right now?

Or not yet as in a week... a month... *never*?

I withdrew my hand, stroking the side of her neck as I kissed her senseless. It was messy, all teeth and tongue and sweet desperation. But I couldn't get enough of her.

Mya hitched her legs around my waist, letting me press deeper into her. If it wasn't for the thin material of my boxers and her panties, I'd be buried deep inside her. But as it was, I could almost imagine it.

"One day," I repeated the words over and over. Against her mouth, her damp skin, as I rocked harder and faster, driving us both toward the edge.

"It feels..." Mya took a shuddering breath.

"I know." It shouldn't have felt so good, but it did. And we still had a layer of clothes between us.

"Oh God," she cried, "More, I need more." Mya grabbed my hand and pushed it between us. I took the hint, rubbing her again but she whispered, "Touch me, Asher."

I jerked back, staring down at her with surprise. "Yeah?"

She nodded, capturing my lips again, kissing me like she was drowning and I was the last source of air.

Tentatively, I dipped one finger inside her panties. Mya let out a soft moan, her nails digging into my shoulder. I added another finger, letting them slide between her wetness and push inside her.

"Is this okay?"

Suppressing another moan, Mya nodded. My thumb found her clit, rubbing slow torturous circles. "God, that's..." The words stuck in her throat as her body began to shudder. "Asher..."

"I've got you, Mya." I pressed my fingers deeper, kissing her neck, sucking the soft skin between my teeth. My other hand slid up her stomach, underneath the jersey this time. I found the shell of her bra and yanked it down, teasing her nipple with my fingers.

"Ah, God," she cried. "I'm going to..." Mya buried her face into my shoulder as she shattered around my fingers. Slowing my pace, I drew out her orgasm, holding her while she rode the waves of pleasure.

"You okay?" I asked, slowly detangling her from my chest.

"I'm good." She smiled up at me, but I saw the hesitation there. Mya was already second guessing what had just gone down between us. But I didn't want her to regret it. I didn't want her to regret a single second with me.

"Come here." Hooking an arm around her waist, I pulled her into me, her back to my chest.

"What are you doing?"

"Spooning. Friends can spoon, can't they?" My hand rested against her stomach as I breathed her in.

"Yeah," she chuckled softly. "Friends can spoon."

"Night, Mya."

"Night, Asher."

Silence enveloped us and it wasn't long before Mya's breathing evened out. I was tired too, but I didn't want to sleep. Not yet. I wanted to soak up her being here, in my arms. She might have needed the friend label for now, but as I lay there, listening to her little snores, I made a silent promise to myself.

One day Mya would call me more than just 'friend'.

I WOKE TO AN EMPTY BED. Limbs heavy with the lingering trace of sleep, I pushed up onto one elbow. "Mya?"

Nothing.

Rolling over, I fumbled on the nightstand and grabbed my cell phone. My heart sank at the text message on the screen.

MYA: Sorry I bailed. Needed to get back... I'll see you soon though xo

ME: You ran.

MYA: I didn't, I promise. I just... I need time. You said you could give that to me.

I WANTED to tell her to stop fighting it, but I didn't want to push her away. It was bad enough she'd snuck out on me this morning.

ME: I won't let you run, Mya...

MYA: I'll see you soon, okay?

ME: Yeah, whatever.

I THREW my cell down on the bed and flopped back against the pillows. Last night had felt like a breakthrough. Mya had finally let down her walls enough for me to clamber over the side. But I should have known it was only temporary. She was too hung up on her ex, on all the reasons we couldn't work. I didn't want to be second string... not again.

I'd watched Flick fall hopelessly in love with my best friend. The first girl

I'd ever felt something real for, even though I'd known any hope of us was doomed from the start. Mya was different though. Sure, there were obstacles but nothing worth having came easy.

I was prepared to fight for her.

But I couldn't be the only one willing to go all in.

11

Mya

I RAN.

Again.

This time I wasn't running away from people who had the power to hurt me though. I was running from the one person who wanted to heal me.

Waking up wrapped in Asher's arms had been a harsh reality check. I couldn't keep running; it was time to move on. To put the past behind me and get closure on that part of my life. The only catch was I knew it meant I had to go home.

"I've been thinking," I said as Aunt Ciara plated up bacon and eggs. "I want to go home for Christmas."

She clucked her tongue. "Mya, you know that's not—"

"Hear me out, okay?" I grabbed the glass of juice and took a big swallow. "I'm done with Jermaine, with that life. But I need closure, Auntie. I need him to know it's over, once and for all."

"Your mama isn't going to like it."

"She'll understand. I need to go back and make things right." Because while Jermaine had been the reason I'd run, I didn't doubt he thought I'd betrayed him.

After all, I had just up and left. If our roles were reversed, I'd want answers too.

"I'd ask you to come but..."

"Ain't never going to step foot in that place again, and neither should you, girl. You're free of that life now." Her expression softened, eyes glazed with unshed tears. "I know you think you have to do this, Mya, but you don't owe that boy nothing."

She was wrong though. I might not have owed it to him, but I did owe it to myself to do this.

Jermaine had once been everything to me. Best friend. Protector. Lover. You didn't just get over the kind of history we shared. And if I was truly going to give Asher a chance, give *anyone* else a chance, I needed to put Jermaine in the past once and for all.

First stop: getting a new cell phone number. Second stop: visiting Mom and saying a proper goodbye to my friends.

"This isn't about him, Aunt C. It's about me. My life is here now. But if I'm going to truly move on, I need to do this."

"Your mama will probably already have plans with Keelan."

"I know. I was thinking I'd go as soon as possible. That way I can avoid their plans and be here with you on Christmas Day."

Mom and Keelan's relationship was complicated. He'd never lived with us, but he'd had my mom eating out of the palm of his hand for as long as I could remember. They met when she started working at his club, The Diamond. Everyone in our neighborhood knew Keelan King. He'd once ruled the streets until he'd finally moved into more legitimate businesses. He still ruled his club with an iron fist. No gang activity. No drugs. And no touching his dancers.

For a neighborhood in Badlands, Mom could have ended up with much worse.

But I still didn't like him. I didn't like the way he held so much power over her. Money talked though, and it was something we'd never had enough of. Mom liked to think she was his queen, but I saw it for what it was; a man taking advantage of the situation. You didn't walk away from someone like Keelan; he decided when he was done with you.

"I don't like it," Aunt Ciara said. "But I won't stop you. Just be careful. After what happened before..."

"I've got this, I promise." It was only a couple of days. I'd visit my mom, see my friends, and try to talk to Jermaine before I left. If I called Shona and let her know to keep it on the down-low, there was no reason everyone had to find out I was back unless I wanted them to.

"I'm proud of you, you know?"

"You are?" I asked.

"Damn straight, I am. People think walking away is the easy way out but it's the other way around. Staying is easy, it's walking away that's hard. I know you care deeply for that boy but sometimes love isn't enough."

She didn't need to tell me that.

It wasn't enough for Keelan to make a real commitment to Mom, and it hadn't been enough to make Jermaine make better life choices. It wasn't enough for Mr. Bennet to respect his son's hopes and dreams, and it wasn't enough to make me stand by and watch Jermaine throw away his life.

But coming here, to Rixon, I'd also seen glimpses of when it was enough. It was enough for my aunt to take me in, no questions asked. It was enough for Jason to put his future on the line for Felicity, and it was enough for Asher to try to protect his mom.

Sometimes love was enough.

I just hadn't had the fortune of experiencing it much yet.

At least if I put Jermaine behind me once and for all, I could carve my own path, decide who was worthy of *my* love.

"Mya?"

"Y- yes?" I blinked over at my aunt.

"Where'd you go just now?"

"Nowhere, Auntie." Forcing a smile, I stuffed a piece of bacon into my mouth, swallowing the lie. Because I had been somewhere.

I'd been wrapped in Asher Bennet's arms. Content. Happy.

Safe.

"I CAN'T BELIEVE you're leaving." Flick frowned, watching as I stuffed a clean pair of jeans into a backpack.

"I'm not leaving," I said. "I'm getting closure."

"Closure, right. And this closure wouldn't happen to have anything to do with a certain Raider who I know you spent the night with, would it?"

"He told Jason?" My eyes almost bugged out, my stomach knotted into a tight ball.

"No, he didn't tell Jason. Asher wouldn't do that to you. Your aunt asked me how the sleepover at my house went last night. I put two and two together."

"Crap, you didn't—"

"Drop you in it? Of course not. I told her we had a great time braiding each other's hair and baking cookies."

"Very funny." I balled up a t-shirt and threw it at her. Flick caught it, her shoulders shaking with laughter.

"So... what happened?"

"I don't want to talk about it."

"That bad, huh?"

Letting out an exasperated breath, I sat in the chair. "It wasn't bad... it was..."

"Ooh, something happened." She clapped her hands, excitement dancing in her eyes. "Tell me something happened."

"It's not a big deal."

Felicity's brows crinkled. "If it wasn't a big deal, you wouldn't be acting so shady. Spill..."

"We kissed and then he... uh, there was some groping. *Clothed* groping."

"Because that makes all the difference." She rolled her eyes. "Did you... you know?"

"Come? Maybe... possibly..." Heat crept into my cheeks.

My friend let out a squeal of delight. "This is so exciting. Wait," her frown reappeared, "why don't you seem as excited about this development as I am?"

"Because it's complicated."

"Because of your ex?"

"Among other things."

"You're still hung up about the race thing? Because I'm telling you, no one will bat an eye if the two of you hook up."

But they would.

Asher was a white privileged athlete, with good grades and a bright future ahead of him. A future I was almost certain the town wouldn't want tainted by their beloved Raider hooking up with the poor Latina girl from the hood.

"I'm not getting into this again." I sighed, resuming packing my bag. "I'm going home for a couple of days to see my mom and friends. Some space might do us good."

"Does Asher know about this?"

"I don't need his permission, Flick." My tone was defensive.

"I'm not suggesting you do. But you've got to see it from his point of view. It looks like you're running."

"He said the same thing." I pressed my lips together.

"At least explain it to him. Otherwise, he's likely to think you're running back to your ex."

"I would never—"

"I know that and you know that, but he doesn't know that."

"Fine," I conceded. "I'll text him."

"Good. Then hurry up and do whatever you need to do so you can get back here and we can celebrate."

"We're celebrating?"

"Hells yeah," she shrieked. "This is huge. And perfect. We can all hang out now without anyone feeling left out and New York will be even better once you and Asher—"

"Whoa, slow down there. I'm not sure where this thing with Asher is going to go, Flick."

"Oh hush, you want him. He wants you. What's to figure out?"

If only life were that easy.

"Please don't say anything to anyone, not yet." My expression turned serious. "I'm not ready for anyone to know yet. That means Jason too."

"Can I at least tell Hailee? She'll be so happy for you."

"Felicity," I groaned.

"Fine." She held up her hands. "My lips are sealed. You deserve to be happy, Mya, with someone who will treat you right."

Her words hit me right between the chest, but I brushed them off. "I need to finish packing. Are you going to help or keep up the *Dr. Phil* routine?" My brow rose.

"Hey, I only care about you."

Stopped dead in my tracks by her admission, I gave her a sad smile. "I know, I'm sorry. I guess I'm more nervous about going home than I thought I would be."

"So, don't go."

"I have to," I said defiantly. "It's just something I have to do."

IT WAS over an hour's ride to the city. I'd stuffed in my earbuds and hit play on one of my favorite playlists. It didn't distract me enough though and before I knew it, I'd opened my chat history with Asher, re-reading our most recent messages.

Just like Felicity had warned me, he hadn't taken the news I was returning home for a couple of days well.

ASHER: What the fuck, Mya? I thought you were done with him?

ME: I am. That's why I have to do this. I'm not trying to hurt you and I'm not going back there to fix things with him. But I need closure. Surely you can understand that?

ASHER: I don't know what to think right now. I woke up after one of the best nights of my life to find you gone and now I find out you're leaving town. It feels a lot like you're running to me.

THAT ONE HURT.

Because although I hadn't told him yet, last night had also meant something to me. More than I ever thought it would. Which is why I had to do this.

A clean break.

My thumb scrolled the messages down to my last reply, the one that had gone unanswered.

ME: You said you'd wait for me... I'm asking you to keep your word.

. . .

The only difference between mine and Jermaine's relationship, and the one in the song? I'd never loved the way he'd lied. I'd just loved him. Let my love for him blind me to the truth.

Jermaine was never going to choose me over his reputation. It was the one battle I couldn't win, no matter how hard I fought.

My cell phone bleeped and my heart kicked up a notch, hoping to see Asher's name flash across the screen, sinking when it wasn't.

Shona: Where u at?

Me: Just outside Kessington. C U soon xo

Shona: We got some catchin up to do, girl. Party at mine 2nite?

Me: Shona, come on… you know I can't b parading around like that

Shona: It's my house. We'll keep it low key. Besides, Jesse is home. He'll look out for us. Plsssss. I've missed you, girl…

Me: I've missed u 2 xo

I silenced my incoming notifications and watched as the semi-familiar streets became streets so familiar I could pick out every other store. I hadn't given much thought to what it would feel like to return but now I was here, I realized how strange it felt.

How it didn't feel like home anymore, not even a little bit.

12

Asher

"SON," my father's deep voice echoed over the line.

"Dad," I clipped out, spinning the football with one hand.

"We'll be back in town in a couple of days. Your mother wants to decorate and have dinner, just like old times." There was a hint of sarcasm in his words.

"Old times, right."

"Asher, could you be a little more interested please? This is important to her."

"Of course, Dad. Whatever Mom needs."

"We'll be in town for the remainder of the holidays. I don't have to be back in the city until January fourth."

"That long?"

That was a little over two weeks away. I hadn't survived two weeks with my parents in what felt like forever.

"Your mom had hoped we could all spend New Year's together."

"Actually, about that. The guys want to go to New York. Vaughn and Riley invited us. I thought we could—"

"Very well, I'll arrange the penthouse. Just the five of you?"

"Six, I think."

"Six?"

"Felicity's friend Mya is coming with us."

"Ah yes, the new transfer. Is she someone you have your eye on?" He cut straight to the point in true Andrew Bennet fashion.

"Can we not do this, Dad, please?"

He scoffed. "It's a perfectly reasonable question, Asher. You're eighteen, a young man, and you have yet to bring home a girl for us to meet."

Because you're never home and I would never willingly introduce my girlfriend to you. "That's because I haven't found anyone I want to bring home yet."

"So you and Miss..." he hesitated.

"Hernandez."

"Hernandez? Are her family immigrants?"

"Excuse me?" I choked out.

"It's a South American name is it not?"

"Oh my god," I breathed. "You're serious."

"It's a perfectly reasonable qu—"

"Actually, Dad, it's not. It's presumptuous and irrelevant."

"It's hardly irrelevant if you have plans to date the girl," his tone was scathing.

My blood boiled beneath my skin. All this time I'd been reassuring Mya that her skin color wasn't an issue, failing to realize that it might be a problem for my own father and his ideas of my future.

"And if I do want to date her?"

Silence filled the line, making my body tense. Finally, my old man released a heavy breath. "I'm a man of my word, Son," he said. "You still have until the end of senior year. But just remember, Asher, the mistakes you make now will follow you into adulthood."

I wanted to ask what the fuck that was supposed to mean but I didn't want to enrage him. Not when he and Mom seemed to be going through a calm period. The fact she wanted to decorate for the holidays was a telltale sign things were okay between them.

"You don't need to worry, Dad," I said in an attempt to placate him, and get him off the phone. It was bad enough they were coming home soon without spending my last couple days of freedom arguing with him.

"Very well, we'll see you soon. Invite the guys to join us for dinner if you'd like."

"Yeah, maybe." Although after confessing everything to Mya, I wasn't sure how much longer I could keep lying to them.

"Yo, Ash, you down there?" Jase's voice rang out through the house and I dropped the free weights, grabbing a towel to dry off. I'd barely made it off the bench when he and Cam appeared in the door.

"How long have you been down here? We've been calling."

"A while." I caught the bottle of water Cam threw me, uncapped it and took a long pull. "Thanks."

"You look like shit," Jase remarked, arms folded across his chest, eyes narrowed with scrutiny.

"I'm okay." After the conversation with Dad and finding out Mya had gone back home for a couple of days, I'd hit the gym. Pushing my body to its physical limit. The adrenaline didn't erase the memories, but it helped temper the frustration swimming in my veins.

When my friends didn't reply, watching me as if I was a freak show, I added, "It takes a lot of hard work to look this good, you know." My lip curved convincingly.

"So this hasn't got anything to do with the fact Mya just up and left to go back to Philly?"

"Nope." I said, dropping back onto the bench and staring up at the ceiling.

"Did something happen between the two of you?" Cam asked.

"Yeah," that was Jason. "Because I tried to get it out of Felicity, but she wouldn't give it up. Not even after I did that thing she loves with my ton—"

"Whoa, too much information," I protested, throwing an arm over my eyes.

When I'd been working out, the pain and resistance had demanded my full attention, but now I was done my muscles slowly began to contract and relax, letting in the torrent of thoughts I'd rather keep out.

"So you and Mya?"

"There is no me and Mya," I grumbled.

She'd run.

For all I knew she was headed straight back into her ex's arms.

My fist clenched against my thigh.

Fuck.

"But something did happen?"

I glanced over at them. "I thought so, but I got it wrong."

"She'll come around," Jason said it as if it was a given, but I wasn't so sure. Mya had spent the night in my bed, in my arms, and then literally ran home from me. It didn't get much suckier than that.

"We have places to be anyway."

"Yeah?" My brow rose.

"Yeah." He smirked. "If you'd have bothered to check your phone, you'd know. Get ready and meet us out front in five."

They turned and walked away but I called after them, "Where are we going?"

"To initiate the next generation."

That got my attention. We'd dominated the team for so long, there hadn't been any need to initiate the players coming up through the ranks. Sure, we gave the younger players shit but everyone knew the deal. You either made the cut or didn't, and if you did, you were as good as family. But this year was different; this year we were handing the reins to them. Aside from the exhibition game next month, our time as Raiders was officially over.

I should have known Jason wouldn't walk away without putting the rookies through their paces.

And bad mood or not, this was one show I didn't want to miss.

An hour later, Cam, me, and the rest of the senior players stood behind Jason with the junior and freshman players huddled in front of us. The line had been drawn but we all had two things in common: we were Raiders, and we were freezing our balls off.

"Listen up and listen good. Just because our time at Rixon is almost done doesn't mean I'm going to walk away without knowing we're leaving the team in good hands."

A couple of guys grumbled at Jase's stern words. I rose a brow at Mackey, one of the youngest players on the team. He pressed his lips together and dropped his eyes to the ground. *Little fucker.*

"It's time to prove yourselves. To show me and the rest of the senior players that you've got what it takes to lead the team into next season and defend the championship. We have the game with the Eagles coming up and although some of you might think it's just a friendly scrimmage, it isn't. It's a chance to put this bullshit rivalry behind us. It's time to show them and everyone else who we really are." He glanced at me. "Ash, if you'll do the honors."

I stepped forward, bouncing on my toes, clutching my helmet by my side. "Who are we?"

"Raiders." It was a guttural roar that almost put me on my ass. A grin tugged at my lips. Jason didn't need to worry about leaving the younger players in charge of the team. They were fighters. Hungry for it. They were more than ready to fill our shoes.

Throwing my head back, beating my fist on my chest, I yelled, "I said who are we?"

"RAIDERS."

"And what are we?"

"Family."

"Damn right we are," I added, going off script. Hooking my arm around Jase and Cam's necks, I crushed them into me. "And what are we gonna do?"

"Win." The words reverberated through me, igniting the familiar fire in my chest.

"I said what are we gonna do?"

"WIN!"

Fuck, I was going to miss this. Miss them. I didn't allow myself to go there often. To a place where I no longer had my guys—my brothers—at my side. Football, playing with Cam and Jason for the last four seasons, had been everything to me. A gift. One I both appreciated and resented.

"Hey, you okay?" Cam whispered as the rest of the guys got ready to prove themselves to Jason.

"Yeah, it's just everything's changing." The two of us watched our best friend bark orders at his successors, while Grady and Merrick, a couple of the other seniors, helped him whip them in shape ready for the first drill.

"Change isn't always a bad thing."

"Isn't it?" I threw him an uncertain glance.

"The Panthers isn't the only team interested in you. If you're having doubts, you can always go somewhere else." Cam meant well but he didn't know all the facts. He didn't know that despite the Pittsburgh Panthers wanting me, I'd already turned down their offer.

Now was not the time to tell him.

Clapping him on the back, I forced an Asher Bennet kilowatt smile. "Come on, we have some rookies to terrorize."

For as bittersweet as it was, running drills with my team again was exactly what I needed. The initial burn of frigid air filling my lungs, the ping of my muscles as I sprinted up and down the field, the thrill of rushing our offense players to the ground. Football might not have been my destiny, but it would forever be a part of me. One day in the future, when I was stuck in some boring computer class, or shadowing my old man in a meeting with some stuck-up celebrity type, I'd remember this time.

When football was religion and people worshipped the ground we walked on.

"Yo, Cap," I called out to Jason. "I'm thinking we need to put the offense through their paces, they're looking a bit sloppy."

"I like your style, Bennet," Grady said, jogging up beside me. "What you thinking?"

"Bull in the ring."

He howled with laughter while a couple of the younger players paled. Bull in the ring was an age-old drill that was mostly considered too aggressive for practice these days.

"Ste, you're up first."

"Me?" He blanched. "Why am I up first?"

"Because you've got some big shoes to fill next year, *QB1*," I teased. Ste was a good kid; showed real leadership potential, but he was no Jason Ford.

I doubted Rixon High would see another Jason Ford for a very long time.

"Shit," Ste cussed beneath his breath.

"Yo, Cap, you ever shit yourself before a little game of bull in the ring?"

Jason sauntered over to me, arms folded across his number one jersey, and cut his glare to Ste. "You want to take this team all the way, Kinnicky?"

"Y- yeah, you know I do, man."

"So man up and get in the fucking ring," Jason growled the words, shooting me and the rest of the seniors an amused smirk.

"Get it, Kinnicky," Mackey yelled. "You've got this." The rest of the freshman and junior players started cheering their future quarterback on while we moved into position, ready to rush the shit out of him. Nine seniors versus one junior. It was typically the defense players who formed the ring, but this wasn't about physical strength as much as it was about mental strength. And Ste Kinnicky, future quarterback and leader of the Rixon Raiders was about to show us all just how big his balls were.

"You ready, Kinnicky?" Jason asked and the junior pulled down his face guard and nodded sharply.

"Okay, on my count. One... two... play."

"You THINK they've got what it takes?" I asked my best friends, tipping the neck of my beer toward the table of younger Raiders. We'd finally called time on the drills when a storm rolled in and fat drops of rain had started to fall. In true captain spirit, Jase told everyone to head to Bell's, adding that the drinks were on him.

"Kinnicky has the skill but I don't know if he has the heart." He stroked his jaw. "Mackey, though, now that kid is hungry for it."

"He's hungry for something all right," Cam chuckled. "Check him out, trying his luck with Sara again."

The regular waitress at Bell's, Sara, was used to our banter: the cat calls and sexual innuendo. But Mackey was like a dog with a bone and no matter how many times she knocked him back, he got right back up and tried again.

"Hey, Jase, did you ever get in her panties? You can tell us." Grady piped up, earning him a slap upside the head from Cam. "What?" he groaned. "It's just a question."

"I'm with Felicity now, fucker. Show some respect."

"Jeez, it's not like she's here right now. I'm just shooting the shit."

"Yeah, well don't." Jase grunted, leaning back in the booth.

"You've changed, man. And if that's what it means to be pussy-whipped, count me out."

"Nawww, Grady, you sound jealous," I taunted.

"Jealous? Fuck that. The two of you are no fun now. I mean, don't get me wrong, I like Hailee and Felicity, I like them a lot; but shit, guys, there's too much pussy in the ocean to be shacked up before we all go off to college."

"You'll see," Jase said smoothly. "One day, when you're least expecting it, some chick will come along and knock you on your ass."

"Nah, it's not my style. I prefer to hit it and quit it. Am I right or am I right, Bennet?"

"Yeah, is he right, Bennet?" Jason rose an amused brow.

Smug fucker.

"What's that look for?" Grady caught on to the silent conversation happening between me and my best friend.

"Nothing. It *is* nothing, right, Ash?"

"Wait a minute." Grady sat up straighter. "You hitting that sweet Latina ass?"

"Grady," I warned, levelling him with a hard look.

"What? It's all cool with me. She has a Rihanna look about her. You know from the *Talk That Talk* single cover."

We all gawked at him and his eyes widened. "What? She's hot and that song is dope."

"Who are you right now?" Laughter rumbled in my chest, but it came out strangled. I didn't like hearing Grady talk about Mya. Even if it was his attempt at a compliment.

"So are you?"

"Am I what?" I asked.

"Banging Mya."

"Grady?"

"Yeah?" He grinned.

"Shut the fuck up."

Before I make you.

13

Mya

"I THOUGHT you said it was going to be low key?" I yelled over the music to Shona, but she was too busy eye-fucking one of her brother's friends to notice.

"Yo, Mya, get over here and show me how you work it." Some guy I recognized from school crooked his finger at me, a lazy smirk plastered on his face.

"In your dreams, Diego. Don't you know Mya is still J's girl?"

I bristled. Shona's head whipped round finally giving me her attention. "Oh, hell no, Kris, you did not just say what I think you said."

"Shona," I hissed, grabbing her hand. "Leave it, it doesn't matter."

"It matters," she gave the guy some serious stink eye. He threw up his hands, mumbling an apology. "That's right, homeboy, you'd better apologize to my girl."

"You need me to kick his ass to the curb?" Jesse, Shona's brother, appeared with his friend Leroy in tow.

"S'all good." She barely looked at Jesse, giving Leroy the once over. "But you can get me and my girl a drink."

"Shona, don't be hitting on my friends." He frowned, glancing at me with an expression that said 'help a guy out'. I shrugged. We both knew there was no stopping Shona when she had her sights set on something, or someone.

"What can I get you, Mya?" Leroy asked.

"Just a soda pl—"

"She'll have a proper drink, like me."

"Shona, I don't think that's a good idea." I glanced around her house. Every inch of space was crammed with bodies and I couldn't help but notice there wasn't a single white person anywhere.

It wasn't something I'd ever noticed before.

But that was before. When I'd lived for my best friend's parties, When Fallowfield Heights still felt like home. When I didn't feel the need to permanently watch over my shoulder for any signs of trouble.

"Hey," Jesse's hand landed on my shoulder, "You're good here. Jermaine knows better than to come around causing trouble."

"I know." I gave him a tight smile. "I'm a'ight."

"Good. So how is it livin' out in the country? Shona says you're at some fancy ass football school."

"It isn't exactly fancy, but they sure do love football."

"They treating you right? Or do I gotta roll up on your new classmates and give them a little warning, Jesse Byrd style?"

Fighting a smile, I replied, "It's mostly been okay."

"Mostly?" His brow rose.

"I'm a four percenter."

"Huh?" Confusion crinkled Jesse's eyes but Leroy returned with our drinks, saving me an explanation. Taking a sip, I was relieved to find barely any trace of liquor. The last thing I needed was to end up drunk.

Just in case.

The opening beats to the latest Drake song blasted through the speakers causing Shona to shake her booty. "Dance with me." She grabbed Leroy's hand and all but dragged him into the middle of the room.

"Damn, she never listens." Jesse shook his head in mild disgust.

"Has she ever?" I chuckled watching her grind up on Jesse's friend. He'd looked bewildered at first, but it didn't take long before his actions mirrored hers, his hands running up and down her body as they moved and popped to the sultry beat.

"She tell you about Jermaine getting kicked out of school?"

I nodded, pressing my lips together to stop myself from going there.

"He's in deep with Diaz. Be careful, Mya."

"I'm a big girl, Jesse." My eyes slid to his. "I can take care of myself."

"Oh, I don't doubt it." His eyes danced with amusement. "But you're like family to me, always will be, and I'd hate to see you get hurt again."

My breath caught in my throat. We'd never talked about what happened, but Jesse had been there when Shona found me. He'd driven us to the ER. Had almost lost it that night, wanting to go find Jermaine and beat the crap out of him for putting me in harm's way. Between me and Shona, we'd managed to convince him not to do anything reckless. Jesse Byrd might have been six feet two of pure muscle and brawn, but he was no match for Diaz and his crew.

"I'll be okay, promise."

He didn't look convinced, but he knew me well enough to drop it. We watched Shona and Leroy practically dry fuck until Jesse finally snapped. Grunting under his breath, he stormed toward them, ripping his baby sister away from his friend. She flounced over to me and grabbed her drink, hardly fazed.

"He needs to lighten the hell up."

"You two were getting pretty hot out there."

"We were dancing."

"So I didn't see him rubbing up on you?"

Shona smothered a giggle, and I rolled my eyes. "You need to find yourself a decent guy instead of acting thirsty every time a guy looks in your direction."

She fake gasped. "I do not act thirsty."

"You know it's true. But you're worth more, Shona."

"Listen to you, acting all boujee now you livin' in that hick town."

"You do realize that's a complete contradiction, right? You can't be boujee and hick?"

"Whatever." She stuck her nose in the air, flicking her braids off her shoulder. "All I'm saying is you don't be calling me no more, too busy with your new friends."

"You know it's not like that." Guilt snaked through me. "I just..."

"Yeah, I know." Shona shoulder checked me. "I'm messing with you."

"I got a new cell phone number. So now we can talk all the time. You'll just have to save me as 'boujee bitch' or something." I grinned.

"You really think I'd be letting Jermaine look at my cell? I've barely spoken to him since you left."

Silence filled the space between as we both looked out at the sea of bodies. There was a thin layer of smoke, the bitter twang of weed permeating the air.

"Shona," I said, finally breaking the tension between us. "You get why I left, right?"

"Sure, I get it. Part of me was so fucking relieved when your mom told you to pack your bags. But the other part, the selfish part, can't forgive you for leaving me behind. I know that makes me a bitch, but I can't help it."

"I know." I threw my arms around her and hugged her tight. "I'm sorry I left too."

"You just make the most of it and remember you got out, Mya. You escaped this place." She eased back, flashing me her megawatt smile. "Now, tell me about those white boys you been hanging out with." Her smile turned suggestive.

"They're just... guys."

"You like one of them."

"No I don't." *Liar.*

"Oh you do, it's written all over your face. Lemme guess, he's a Justin Timberlake. You always did have a crush on JT back in the day."

"He's not—" A commotion over by the door caught my attention.

"Mya, yo, Mya, you up in here?" Jermaine's voice filtered through the house and my spine stiffened.

"Fuck," Shona hissed. "Don't worry, babe, I'll get Jesse and Leroy to deal with him."

"And cause World War Three?" I glared at her. "I knew he'd find me. I just thought it'd be on my terms." Placing my drink down, I began moving past her.

"Wait, you're sure about this?" she asked me.

"Better than the alternative." Silent understanding passed between us. If I didn't go to him, Jermaine and his guys would cause problems for Shona and her brother. Something I couldn't let happen.

"He puts a single finger wrong and you call me, 'kay?" Jesse gave me a reassuring nod.

Nervous energy vibrated through me as I cut through the sea of bodies and made my way to the front of Shona's house. Jermaine stood in the door, his eyes hard and cold. It had been three months since I'd seen him. Three months for him to beef up, cover more of his dark skin in tattoos. Three months to let his love for me turn to hatred.

"Mya, baby, looking good," he said smoothly, letting his gaze run down my body. I shuddered, his attention no longer familiar and safe.

"J," I said coolly. "It's been a while."

"Yo, Shawn, you guys get out of here. Me and my girl gotta talk." I internally flinched.

His girl.

He still thought of me as his girl. But I hadn't been his girl since the day I left Fallowfield Heights.

His guys moved around him, ready to disperse into the party but I said, "They leave. I'll talk to you if they leave."

Jermaine's brow rose. "It's like that, huh?"

"It's like that," I deadpanned, folding my arms over my chest and glaring at him.

"A'ight. I'll meet you later," he said to them, and they all filed out of the house.

"I see you got yourself some lap dogs." I didn't want to think about what he'd done to earn their respect.

"Come on, My, why you gotta be this way? I thought we could talk." He swaggered toward me. "Talk, kiss... make up. You owe me, girl." His hand reached for me, but I swatted it away.

"I owe you nothing more than an explanation."

"So it's like that, huh?" Jermaine rubbed his jaw.

"Let's go outside, I need some air." I couldn't breathe with him looking at me like that.

Shouldering past him, I slipped into the cool night. Shona lived in one of the nicer parts of the neighborhood, so we were afforded some privacy. I moved around to the side of the house, where I knew there was a bench, and sat down. Jermaine followed but he didn't sit. Instead, he towered over me. He seemed taller. Older in the face somehow. No signs of the young man I'd left behind.

"How's your mama?" I asked, breaking the silence. "Bet she was real disappointed you dropped out of school."

He clucked his tongue, shrugging. "I did what I had to."

"Bullshit. School was the *only* thing working for you."

"So what? I could look forward to a life of working at the Seven Eleven or collecting glasses for Keelan at the bar. Fuck. That."

"At least it'd be safe. At least it'd be an honest job."

"Shit, Mya, three months in wherever the fuck you been and you already talking shit. They brainwashed you out there? Filling your head with dreams of a better life?" He snorted. "I got news for you, baby girl. This is all we got. Life ain't never gonna be no different."

My heart ached at his words. For the boy I once knew. Jermaine was blinded by the promise of money and status. He couldn't see there was another way, like too many men in our neighborhood.

"It didn't have to be like this," I whispered, tipping my head back against the cladding.

Jermaine took my hand in his, sliding our fingers together the way he had so many times. But where it once brought me peace, it felt wrong now.

"It was always you, Mya. You were my anchor in this fucked up place we call home. As long as I had you nothing else mattered."

Tears pricked the corner of my eyes. "We both know that's not true. I was never enough. If I was, you would have stopped."

"You left me, you fucking left me," he repeated, again and again, his voice cracking with pain. I wanted to console him, to give him comfort the way I had so many times before. But I didn't.

I couldn't.

"I left because I knew if I stayed, I'd never get out. And I want more, J. I want to go to school and get a degree. I want a house and a family and a job. I want more than... than this."

"You always were too good for this place." He stared off into the darkness.

"I'm sorry I ran, I am. But I had no other choice. I watched you get beaten within an inch of your life and then I was assaulted. They assaulted me with your blood on their hands. Do you have any idea what that was like? I thought they were going to..." The words lodged in my throat as the hazy memories flooded my mind.

The pain.

The crunch of bone on bone.

Their laughter.

So much laughter.

Blood. Everywhere.

"It's the life, Mya."

"Oh God," I yanked my hand away and jumped up. "Listen to yourself. Even now, even sitting here listening to me tell you why I left, it's still not enough. You should go."

"Baby, don't do this." He stood up, trying to pull me into his arms, but I resisted, stepping back out of his hold. "You make it sound like it's all on me, but you knew who I was. You knew where my life was going and you loved me anyway. And what, now you think you just get to run away and pretend like we're nothing to each other? Fuck that. You're mine, Mya. You'll always be mine. You can't run forever." His eyes turned hard. "One day, you'll come running back. Ain't no outrunning the hood, baby. You know that."

It was a silly thing we'd grown up saying. I'd beg Jermaine not to hang out with Diaz's crew and he'd tell me it was destiny. But it was never destiny. It was a choice, and he'd already made the wrong one.

"Goodbye, Jermaine," I said, slowly backing away.

"You're making a mistake, Mya," he ground out, his eyes swirling with so much anger and sadness it physically hurt to walk away from him. But I had to do this. I had to put him in the past. Because love wasn't enough. Not for us.

"This isn't the end," he called after me, as I spun on my heel and took off around the back of Shona's house. I didn't look back. I didn't let myself cry or scream or fall apart.

Not until I reached the back door and fell into Jesse's waiting arms.

14

Asher

"SO I HEAR Coach Hasson has you all locked into an exhibition game next month?" My old man talked a good talk, but I heard the disapproval in his voice. It wasn't what he said, it was how he said it.

My friends were none the wiser as they ate my mom's lasagna and drank Dad's twenty-one-year-old single malt as if everything was fine.

"Yeah, it kinda came out of left field," Jason said. "But if it means I get to play one last time with the team and raise money for a good cause then count me in."

"I'd better dig my checkbook out then." Dad smiled, but it only reminded me of a sly fox.

Everyone laughed, the mix of Mom's strained laughter to Dad's hearty over-the-top chuckle almost too much to bear.

This wasn't the first time I'd played happy families with my parents and best friends. Dad liked to showboat. He liked to present a united and strong front, and usually I played along without too much difficulty. But this was different. This felt like the last supper before walking the green mile to a death sentence of security systems and business meetings, brightly colored ties and business suits.

"That would be very kind of you, Mr. Bennet."

"Please, Jason, we've talked about this before. Call me Andrew."

My best friend nodded, and I'm sure I caught him slightly starry-eyed as he watched my father command the table. Jason and his old man, Kent Ford, weren't exactly close. There was a lot of resentment and bitterness there, but it still felt ironic that he respected my dad so much. *If only he knew*.

Forcing the thoughts down, I forked some more lasagna into my mouth. Mom cast me appreciative glances every now and then. This was all for her. Dinner. The fake conversation. Dad might have been a cold, cruel son of a bitch, but in his own twisted way he loved her. And if there was one thing Andrew Bennet never did, it was sever a business agreement.

Marriage.

Fatherhood.

Business.

It was all the same to him. A series of transactions where people exchanged money and services, promises and sacrifices to move forward and better themselves.

Dad got reassurance his son would follow in his footsteps. Mom got some semblance of family.

And I got four years of football with my friends.

"Asher, Son, are you listening?"

Speak of the devil. My father glared at me.

"I, uh, sorry."

"I was just telling the guys how excited we are about having you keep up the Bennet tradition of going to Pittsburgh in the fall."

Blood pounded between my ears. He could talk about anything, and yet he chose the one thing I didn't want to talk about.

"Andrew let's not bore them with stories of how proud we are. There's still so much food and I made dessert too."

"It's okay, Mrs. Bennet," Cam said. "We can always spare a few minutes to talk college, right, Jase?"

"Sure thing. I can't wait for the summer to come around."

"Your father tells me Miss Giles will be following you to Penn?"

"She's not following him, Dad," I jumped in. "She was always going there."

"Really?" He looked genuinely surprised. "I never realized she was so intelligent. It's time you found yourself a nice—"

"Andrew, please. Let's not embarrass Asher in front of his friends."

"I'm just saying, Julia, that a good woman can be the making of a man. I mean, look at us." He patted Mom's hand, his eyes sparkling with a fierce possessiveness that could easily be mistaken for adoration.

I knew better.

I knew Mom was a pawn in his games, just the way I was.

"Actually Mr... I mean, Andrew, Asher does have his eye on a girl."

My head snapped over to Jason and I dragged my finger across my neck. He smirked while Cam spluttered over a mouthful of whisky.

"Ah yes, the Hernandez girl." Dad's smile grew tight. "Well, I guess it's better to have your fun now before you settle down and focus on the future."

My friends frowned at that. Jase cleared his throat, no doubt ready to come to my defense, but Cam discreetly nudged him, giving a little shake of his head.

Fuck. This was turning into a shit show. I hadn't wanted to invite them over, but I knew it made Mom happy when she had guests to entertain. And my friends seemed like a safe choice.

Now I was seriously wondering if there was something wrong with me.

This wasn't safe. Having them here wasn't reassuring.

It was painful. Cutting me up inside as if I'd swallowed tiny shards of glass.

I dropped my silverware on my plate, the clatter piercing the tense silence. Running a hand through my hair, I gave Jase a pleading look. I'd never asked him to bail me out of one of Mom and Dad's dinners before. But tonight was different.

Tonight I needed my friends.

Jase cleared his throat. "That was great, Mrs. Bennet. I can't wait to see what's for dessert. Then we need to make tracks. We're meeting the rest of the team at Bell's for our annual pre-Christmas thing."

"You are?" Dad's expression darkened. "You never mentioned it, Son."

"Guess it slipped my mind," I grumbled.

"Well, that's just lovely," Mom added. "Team spirit is just so important these days. I'll get these cleared away and serve dessert so you boys can be on your way. Asher, a little help?"

"Sure thing, Mom." I stood up and began loading plates into my hands. I knew Jason and Cam didn't understand the strange atmosphere at dinner, but it was better that way.

For now, it was better they didn't know the whole story.

At least, that's what I kept telling myself.

"WANT to tell us what the fuck that was all about?" Jase kept his eye on the road as we drove away from my house. It wasn't until the shadow of the building disappeared in the rear-view mirror that I finally felt the weight ease off my chest.

"Just my old man being his usual hard ass self."

He side-eyed me, his hands tightening around the wheel. "Something's going on with you. You don't want to tell us yet, that's cool. But drop the charade. We've all been there. Me with my old man. Cam with his mum. It's okay to let people in, Ash. You don't have to carry whatever it is that's got you so worked up alone."

"Fee's good for you, man." I ignored his grand speech and deflected the spotlight from me to him. "And despite everything that happened, I'm happy for you. You two deserve each other."

"So that's how it's going to be?" he asked.

"For now, yeah. But I'll let you know when I'm ready to talk."

"We'll be here, you know that." Cam leaned forward from the back seat and squeezed my shoulder.

The familiar streets of our small town rolled by. I couldn't imagine moving to Pittsburgh, living in a strange place with strange people. But I guess my future was tainted by the fact it wasn't truly *my* future.

"Hey," I said after a little while. "This isn't the way to Bell's."

"You caught that, huh?" He smirked, signaling left and pulling onto the street where Felicity lived.

"Guys, if this is your attempt to cheer me up, I'm really not in the mood to play fifth wheel." I'd done enough of that lately.

He chuckled, not saying another word as he pulled onto Flick's driveway and cut the engine. "Trust me," he said cryptically. "I think you'll like this surprise."

Surprise?

What the actual fuck?

We got out and I reluctantly followed Jason and Cam up to the Giles' house. The last thing I wanted to do was hang out and watch them with their girlfriends. They usually tried to keep PDA's to a minimum around me.

Tried and failed.

And I got it, I did. They were in love. So deeply gone for their girls that they couldn't keep their hands off them. But that shit was nauseating on a good day, let alone on a day where everything seemed like such a fucking mess.

Jason didn't knock. He just walked right in like he owned the place. It didn't surprise me. He already had Mr. and Mrs. Giles wrapped around his finger, despite their initial concerns about their daughter dating Rixon's golden boy of football.

We followed the girly laughter into the living room and my eyes almost bugged out of my head. "Mya?" I choked out. "What are you...?"

She stood up, pushing her wild curls out of her face. "Hey."

I noticed Fee and Hailee grinning at us out of the corner of my eye.

"Can we talk?"

"I... uh... sure," I said.

Jase clapped me on the back, moving around me as I stood rooted in place, staring at Mya.

"Come on," she said, taking my hand and leading me away from our friends.

I was so surprised, so fucking confused, I trailed behind her like a lost puppy.

Mya kept going until we reached the back door. "It's cold," she said. "But I thought we'd have more privacy outside?" She glanced back at me and waited.

"Sure."

Releasing a small breath, Mya nodded, before slipping outside. She wasn't wrong. The frigid air wrapped around us like icy fingers. Or maybe it was just trepidation at whatever it was she wanted to talk about.

"Fuck," I breathed, jamming my hands deep in my jacket pockets.

Mya chose the swing seat. It was big enough for two, but I was still so stunned at seeing her, I opted to stand.

"So," she started, "I have something for you."

"You do?"

"Yeah." A tentative smile tugged at her mouth as she reached into her pocket and pulled out a tiny scrap of paper. "Here."

I took it from her, my brows pinched in confusion as I read the number written on it. "I'm not—"

"It's my cell phone number. My *new* cell phone number."

"I don't understand." I scratched my cheek.

"I'm done, Asher. I went back there and saw Jermaine thinking I needed closure, but I realized something. That part of my life was over the second I packed my bag and left. So I'm done."

"You're done?" I sounded like a parrot but I couldn't process what she was saying.

"I still want to take things slow, but what I'm saying is, if you still want me, I'm yours."

Yours.

She'd said, 'I'm yours'.

The words spun around my head until they finally settled into four little letters.

Mine.

Mine.

Mine.

Mya was saying she was mine... if I still wanted her.

I dropped to my knees in front of her and let the scrap of paper flutter out of my hands as I cupped her face. "You're done with him?"

"So done." She grinned, her eyes full of promise.

"You really want to be mine, Hernandez? Because I'm going to be needy. So fucking needy." I admitted. "Waking up and finding you gone, it hurt. More than I ever thought it would." Leaning in, I rested my head against hers. "But finding out you'd gone back home, imagining you with him, that almost damn near killed me."

"I'm sorry. I just... I got scared, Asher. The way I feel about you scares me."

"Yeah?" Pulling away, I looked into Mya's eyes, needing to see the truth there. "How do you feel about me?"

"Like I could lose myself."

"I'll never let that happen," I said. "Know why?"

"Why?"

"Because I'll always find you, Mya." Burying my fingers in her hair, I leaned in and tasted her lips. Once. Twice. Three times. Just to be sure this was real.

That *she* was real.

Mya looped her arms around my neck, drawing me closer. I rose up on my knees, leaning into her, pressing her back into the Giles' swing seat. She said she wanted to go slow, but I couldn't resist hitching her leg around my hip and grinding against her.

"Asher." One hand curled into my jacket. "We should probably..."

Don't say it.

Don't fucking say it.

"Slow down."

A groan of frustration worked its way up my throat, but I smiled at her as I slowly eased up. "You're going to drive me insane, Hernandez."

Mya smiled. And it was so pure, so fucking honest, I felt myself fall even deeper into her.

"I'm sorry."

"Never be sorry with me. Ever. You like something we're doing, tell me. You don't like something we're doing, tell me. You need me to slow down, tell me. You need me to speed up..." my brow rose suggestively. "Definitely tell me."

She batted my chest, gawking at me as if I'd lost my damn mind.

"It's one of the things I love most about you, Mya. You're not afraid to speak up. I don't ever want to silence you. No matter how blue my balls become."

"Oh God, stop." She was laughing now. "You have a hand. Use it."

I crowded her again, kissing a path from her lips to the shell of her ear. "Oh, I do," I whispered. "And I always think of you."

"Asher..." My name on her lips was like music to my ears.

"Come on, you, let's go hang with the others."

"For real?" The surprise on Mya's face was so fucking adorable. As if part of her actually expected me to throw her over my shoulder and stalk off to my cave to have my way with her.

I mean, thinking it wasn't the same thing as doing it. Right?

I dropped a kiss on her head before pulling her up and hooking my arm around her shoulder. "Me and you, Mya. On our terms, okay?"

"Okay." She swallowed nervously.

I chuckled, leading her back inside to join our friends, feeling like the motherfucking King of the world.

15

Mya

THE SECOND we stepped into Felicity's living room, silence fell over the four of them. Jason smirked, grumbling something that sounded like, 'about fucking time'. Flick elbowed him in the ribs, making him grunt in pain. Asher chuckled, taking me by the hand and pulling me over to the empty loveseat. He sat down first, tugging me down beside him and wrapping his arm around me as if it was the most natural thing in the world.

"So," Flick said, her eyes darting from me to Asher and back again, "does this mean you two are together now?" She fought a grin.

"We're..." I looked at Asher, unsure I wanted to define or put a label on us when everything still felt so new.

"Taking it slow," he answered for me. "But just so we're clear, I don't intend on looking at another girl, let alone touching one." He wasn't looking at me, but I felt the words all the way down to my soul. It was his not so discreet way of letting me know he was all in, and I couldn't deny it did soften something inside me.

"That is so cute." Flick was grinning now.

"Fucking nauseating if you ask me." Jason groaned.

"Do I look like I care?" Asher pulled me closer, dropping a kiss on my head. "I finally got the girl. I think it gives me a free pass for tonight at least. Besides, I have to watch you clean Fee's teeth on a regular basis." He flipped Jason off.

"Just be thankful you don't have to watch me clean her pus—"

"JASON!" Felicity shrieked, clapping her hand over his mouth. "That is disgusting."

"Nah, babe, it's fucking delicious," he mumbled against her palm.

"Seriously though, man, we're happy for you." Cam gave us a small nod, shifting Hailee who was curled in his lap, her head resting on his chest. "At least now we can go out without you moaning like a little bitch," he teased.

"Fuck you. I just so happen to be an awesome fifth wheel."

"Hey." I pinched his rib. "What are you trying to say?"

Asher's eyes slid to mine, shining with lust and other things I wasn't ready to acknowledge. "You know I want you, Hernandez. It's you who's got us moving at a snail's pace."

"Ash..." My cheeks burned as I felt everyone watching us, no doubt wondering what he was talking about.

"Say it again," he breathed, eyes wide with awe.

"Say what?" My brows knitted.

"Ash. You called me Ash."

"I did?" I hadn't even noticed.

"Yeah, you did. You know what that means, Hernandez?"

"No, but I have a feeling you're going to tell me."

He leaned in, brushing his nose over mine, completely forgetting we had an audience. "It means you must really, *really* like me."

"You're okay I guess." I smothered the laughter building.

"Say it, Mya. Admit you like me."

"You really need to hear me say it?" He'd pulled me into his bubble and I couldn't deny him even if I'd wanted to.

He gave me a small nod, his eyes pleading with me.

"I like you." It was a whisper, meant only for his ears. But in true Asher Bennet fashion, he threw his head back and roared, "She likes me. Mya Hernandez likes me."

Laughter exploded all around us, our friends infected with his excitement.

"You're crazy," I said, fisting his jacket, coaxing him to come back to me.

"Yeah, you're right, I am. I'm crazy for you." He attacked my mouth with his, kissing me clumsily. Greedily. Pushing his tongue into my mouth and tangling it with my own.

This didn't feel like going slow. It felt like falling recklessly and hopelessly into each other, giving no thought to how hard we might crash.

"Asher," his name was a breathless whisper as I tried to hold onto my last shred of defenses against him.

But it was futile.

Asher was my weakness.

"What's got you so happy?" Aunt Ciara eyed me across the table the next morning.

"Nothing," I said, averting my eyes.

"Don't be thinking I'm some fool. You've got that young and in love look. Please tell me you didn't fall for that athlete's charm?"

"Asher, Auntie, his name is Asher."

"I don't need to be knowing his name. He's bad news and I thought you were smarter than this, my girl."

"Auntie, please." Guilt coiled around my heart. I didn't want to disappoint her. Not when she was one of the last people left in my life who cared.

My visit home had been a disaster in more ways than one. My mom had barely been around, tied up at The Diamond with *work*. She'd invited me to hang out there with her, but I couldn't bring myself to be in that place. To see her draped over Keelan, waiting on his every need, or even worse up on stage dancing for him and his friends.

A painful shudder worked through me.

When I'd given her my new cell phone number, she'd hugged me tight and told me it was the right thing. That she was real relieved I was finally letting go of Jermaine and my life in Fallowfield Heights.

A life that included her.

"Now you're frowning like your whole world just ended. What is going on with you, Mya?"

"Mama just let me walk away." I hadn't said much about my trip and Aunt Ciara hadn't asked. She knew how fickle her sister could be. It was one of the reasons she'd barely visited us when I was younger.

"Because she knows you'll have a better life, better opportunities out of that place."

"Yeah, but she's my mother. I thought she'd at least seem sad."

"Mya, she loves you something fierce, but she's also different to you and me. Sofia needs to feel needed. She needs the validation a man's love gives her. After your daddy left..." Aunt Ciara hesitated.

My father was never around. He left before I was even born. It had taken a while to accept I was never going to know him, but I had made peace with it a long time ago.

"He broke something inside her," she went on. "Something that Keelan fixed. He might not be who you or I would choose for her, but he's always provided. He kept a roof over your head and food on the table."

"I know," I whispered.

But it came at a price. And that price was her love. He'd demanded it to its fullest. And somewhere along the line, I had to compete for her attention.

Until somewhere along the line, I stopped.

"Now tell me about this Bennet boy."

"Really?" My face lit up and part of me hated how much I'd already let Asher get under my skin. "You want to know?"

She clucked her tongue. "If it puts a smile on your face, I suppose I can listen for five minutes. But don't get the wrong idea, Mya. I still think this is a bad idea. This town is more backward than you think. It won't easily accept one of its football stars going out with one of us."

"There is no them and us, Auntie."

Her brows pinched and I knew she saw right through me. Because while I so wanted to believe my own words, part of me knew she was right. But it was too late now. Asher wouldn't let me run anymore.

And I didn't want to.

I wanted to do what I did best for something I wanted; for the people I cared about.

Fight.

"ARE you going to get Asher a gift?"

Eight little words I never expected to hear. But I should have known Felicity would already be planning our wedding. She hadn't stopped grinning ever since me and Asher entered her living room together, two days ago. Now it was the day before Christmas Eve and she was asking me about gifts.

"No, I'm not getting him anything. We're not—"

"Oh my god," she groaned. "If you say you're not together one more time, I will explode. Have you seen the two of you? You can barely keep your hands off one another." A smirk tugged at the corner of her mouth.

"We're not *that* bad."

"Try telling that to someone who'll listen. You've got it bad, girl. Almost as bad as Asher."

"I just... crap, it wasn't supposed to happen this fast."

She was right.

Me and Asher had been inseparable for the last forty-eight hours. It was only when Flick insisted I help her with some last-minute shopping, and Asher's mom needed his help with preparations for the Christmas Eve party they were hosting, that we'd actually left each other's sides.

"You should get him something."

"Don't you think it's a little soon for gifts? We're not even official."

Flick gave me a pointed a look as she inspected some wallets in the men's section. "Do you plan on hooking up with other guys?"

"You know I don't." I rolled my eyes.

I hadn't planned on hooking up with any guys when I'd moved in with my aunt. But here I was, Asher Bennet's unofficial girl.

"Asher made it pretty clear he only has eyes for you." Felicity cut through my reverie. "So label or no label, you're together. I don't know what the big deal is. This is a good thing, Mya. That boy is crazy about you." She traded one wallet for another. "You're coming tomorrow, right? To the party at the Bennets'?"

"I don't know." Asher had said he wanted me there but after everything he'd told me about his dad, I wasn't sure it was a good idea.

"You have to come. We're all going. It would mean a lot to Asher if you were there."

My heart clenched. I wanted to be there for him, I did. But I didn't want to make things any worse for him.

"You're worried his parents won't approve?" Flick lowered her voice.

"If people can't accept me because of where I come from or the color of my skin that's on them," I replied, the half-truth souring on my tongue. "I just don't want..." Pressing my lips together, I swallowed Asher's secret. The one I'd promised *not* to repeat.

"You're acting strange." Felicity frowned at me.

"It's all right for you," I deflected. "Jason's family all love you."

"And Mr. and Mrs. Bennet will love you too. You just have to give them a chance to see how good you are for their son."

I pretended to look at some nearby sweaters, letting my fingers run over the soft material.

"We all know something is going on with Asher," Flick came up behind me. "I know Jason talked to you about being there for him."

"That's not what this is," I rushed out, glancing back at her.

"Mya, I would never think that. All I'm trying to say is, if you ever need to talk, about anything, I'm here."

"Thanks, I appreciate it."

She smiled, mischief sparkling in her eyes. "Now about his gift. I have an idea."

I followed Felicity as she weaved through the racks like a girl on a mission. But we never reached our destination because she stopped in her tracks, anger rolling off her.

My eyes immediately found them; a group of girls from school, talking in hushed whispers, judgmental gazes narrowed in our direction.

"We should probably go," Flick said, her words clipped, but one of their voices drifted over to me.

"Don't know what he sees in her. I mean he could do *so* much better than her."

The words reverberated inside me, and something snapped. Before I knew what I was doing, I marched over to them. "Do you have a problem?" My brow went up and I folded my arms over my chest. But I was met with a wall of icy resistance.

"So you can say it behind my back," I scoffed, "but you won't say it to my face?"

"Mya." Felicity grabbed my hand. "Come on, they're not worth it."

"You're right, they're not." My fists clenched at my sides as I glared at the girl who had spoken loud enough for me to hear. Back in Fallowfield Heights, if someone dissed you like that, you called them out on it, and eight out of ten times it usually ended up getting physical. But this wasn't my old neighborhood and the last thing I wanted to do was live up to the stereotype they had of me.

It almost killed me to walk away, even if Felicity was right. They weren't worth it. Vicious gossip was nothing new. I'd been on the receiving end of whispers and disapproving looks since I arrived in Rixon and became a member of the four percent club.

"Ignore her," Felicity said as she ushered me out of the store. "Kellie Ginly is just a jealous bitch."

"She's on the gymnastic team, right?"

Flick nodded. I'd heard the stories. Knew all about Asher's preference for flexible gymnasts who all looked like carbon copies of one another. Blonde. Big boobs. Tanned legs that went on for miles.

Past preference, I reminded myself.

"Asher hasn't touched any of them in months," she reassured me.

"It doesn't matter."

"Sure it does. You don't always have to act so tough around me, you know. You're one of my best friends, Mya."

"I just hate it, you know? I left Fallowfield Heights because I knew Jermaine was only going to drag me down with him. But being here, the constant stares and whispers; it's like a permanent reminder of the very thing I'm trying to escape."

"You can't let them win. The people who matter, who know you, don't care about any of that. *Asher* doesn't care about any of that. Besides, where's the girl who told me to stand up for my man?"

"Oh she's in here somewhere," I said.

"Well, time to dig deep and find her because the Ginleys are good friends with Mr. Bennet which means Kellie will most probably be there tomorrow night. And if you don't claim Asher, she'll have no problem stepping into the role for you."

My chest tightened as I imagined her trying to make a move on Asher.

"Now I'm certain I should avoid the party."

"What?" Felicity gawked at me. "Why the hell would you say that? Didn't you hear anything I just said?"

"Oh I heard you all right," I ground out unable to think about anything but how hard I'd beat her ass if she so much as looked at Asher tomorrow night.

Because official or not, he was mine.

Just like I was his.

16

Asher

THE HOUSE LOOKED like *Buddy the Elf* had paid an overnight visit, if Buddy used high end ornaments and garlands to adorn every shelf and flat surface.

"What do you think?" Mom asked, putting the final touches on the main tree. There were at least another three scattered around the house, but this one... this was the showstopper.

"It looks great, Mom." I grimaced.

"Gosh, just think, this is the last Christmas you'll be here." Her voice cracked and I felt like an absolute shit. Me and Dad were all Mom had, and she was right, I was leaving next fall.

"Don't get upset. I'll still visit. We'll still celebrate the holidays together."

"You're a good boy, Asher." She stepped back to admire her handiwork, wrapping her arm around me. "Thank you for doing this."

"Mom, come on..."

"No, Son. I know this isn't easy on you and I know you don't understand why I tolerate your father. But he's all I have."

"Hey," I gave her an easy smile despite the knot in my stomach, "let's not do this now. It's your big night. Your guests will be arriving soon."

"How did I get so lucky with you, my sweet boy?" She rested her head on my shoulder as we both stood there staring at a Christmas tree so perfectly dressed it was impossible to see the imperfections.

Much like our family.

To the outside world we had it all. Money. The big house with the ostentatious yard. A successful career that saw my parents rub shoulders with celebrities and folks so rich it made us look dirt poor. But it was all a front. The shiny perfect life hiding a dark truth.

"Is your friend still joining us?"

Earlier, I'd caved and told Mom all about Mya after she caught me repeatedly checking my cell phone. I'd hesitated at first, but after the disastrous dinner the other day, I needed to have her in my corner.

"I hope so."

"If she's even half as special as you say then I'm sure she'll be here."

My eyes flicked to the front door. Guests would be arriving any second and within the next hour, our house would become the who's who of Rixon.

The doorbell rang and Mom clutched her heart, startled. "Goodness, it's showtime."

Showtime.

The word echoed through my skull almost as familiar as my own name. She'd said both to me enough growing up.

Time to put on a show.

It's showtime, my sweet boy.

Let's take our places.

The script was our lives, our house the stage, and we always performed to our best. But lately, the cracks had begun to show. Mom was more emotional, and I felt myself fall further and further into the black cavernous pit inside me.

"Clark, Karen, so good to see you both." Mom pulled Cam's mom into her arms. "Gosh, you look radiant."

"I feel good, thank you, Julia."

"And Xander," Mom craned her head around Karen's shoulder. "Is he here?"

"Actually, we got a sitter. Thought I'd enjoy a rare evening without a toddler stuck to my side like glue. He's fast asleep waiting for Santa."

Mom cast me a wistful glance. "I remember it like it was yesterday. Well, I'm glad you're both here. Andrew is around here somewhere. Come through, let's get you both something to drink."

My friends trailed in behind them, carrying an assortment of gifts and bags.

"What the hell is all that stuff?"

"Ask Felicity," Jason grumbled. "She insisted on bringing gifts for everyone."

"It's polite."

"It's overkill, babe." Jason pecked the end of her nose. "Where's the bar? I need a drink."

"Mya?" I asked Flick.

"She'll be here."

But she hadn't rode with them. My gut twisted. Cameron must have noticed my frown because he squeezed my shoulder as he passed me. "She'll come. Give it time."

"Jase's dad isn't coming?"

Hailee blanched. "He and my mom got into it. They said they'll be here, but it was bad. I haven't seen them argue like that in a long while."

"Rough." I guess we weren't the only family hiding secrets. "Looks like we all need a stiff drink then. Follow me."

THE CLINK of silverware against glass ushered the room into silence. It was standing room only at my mom's annual Christmas Eve party, the sea of familiar faces all watching my father as he took center-stage to give what I could only assume would be another stellar performance.

I spotted Coach Hasson and his wife, Sandra. Then Jason's dad, Kent and Hailee's mom, Denise. They'd finally made it although I'd noticed they hadn't spoken a single word to one another since arriving. Apparently, the Bennets were better actors than the Ford-Raines.

But one face was missing.

While my friends stood hand in hand with their girlfriends, I stood alone.

I'd checked my cell at least fifty times, wondering where Mya could have possibly gotten to, not wanting to believe that she'd actually stood me up on what was proving to be one of the shittiest nights of my life.

"Welcome, friends, to our annual Christmas Eve celebration," Dad started. "I think I say this every year but the chance to spend quality time with those we love is something I don't take for granted. So thank you for choosing to spend your evening with us. We hope you enjoy the good food, good drinks, and questionable conversation. Merry Christmas, everyone."

"Merry Christmas." The crowd's cheer rattled in my chest and I felt like raising my glass in the air and declaring my own version of Merry Fucking Christmas. Because nothing about watching my friends and their families hang onto every word of my father's speech felt merry.

"That seemed a little on the short side," Jason whispered out of the side of his mouth. "I was expecting an ode to Asher; apple of my eye, fruit of my loins type of speech."

"Fuck you." I mouthed, cracking a small smile. Dad wasn't wrong, the drinks were good, the lingering warmth of his whisky running through my veins giving me a slight buzz.

"Son," a heavy hand landed on my shoulder. "Can I borrow you for a second?"

"Sure thing, Dad." *It's not like I have a choice.*

"I'll return him to you in one piece," he said to my friends.

It was a joke.

A fucking joke.

And yet, it felt like a gunshot to the chest.

"What's up, Dad?" I cleared my throat, aware of the slight slur to my words.

"You know the Ginlys, don't you?" He guided me over to a tall man with thinning gray hair. "Malcolm, you remember my son, Asher."

The man extended his hand. "How could I forget? Congratulations on a great season, son."

"Thanks." I gritted out. Of course he fucking remembered me. I'd been in his daughter's class since grade school. Not to mention the fact, I knew he was an avid Raiders fan.

So what the hell was my father playing at?

"Malcolm was telling me earlier that Kellie has just accepted a full athletic scholarship to Pittsburgh. Isn't that great?"

"Yeah," the blood drained from my face, as realization dawned on me. This was a set up. My father's attempt at keeping my eye on his future and off distractions.

Distractions like Mya.

My heart withered in my chest. He was never going to accept me dating her. No matter how bright or intelligent or beautiful she was.

Mya didn't fit into the plan.

His plan.

So this was my father's lame-assed attempt at redirecting things.

"Ah, talk of the devil. Hey, sweetie." Malcolm placed his arm around Kellie's shoulder and pulled her into the conversation. She batted her eyes right at me, smiling coyly. "Hey, Asher."

"Kellie." I gave her a dismissive nod.

"Did you hear?" She tucked a lock of blonde hair behind her ear. "We're going to be Panthers together, isn't that great?"

"It's—"

"Asher?"

My pulse spiked at the sound of Mya's voice but it was nothing compared to the way my heart went into overdrive as I turned around and laid my eyes on her. No, that didn't do justice to the way I drank her in. Fuck... she looked...I swallowed hard trying to gather my thoughts. But all I could see was the black silk gliding over her body like a waterfall, ending just above her knee, cinching at her waist and flowing over her hips. Her wild curls were tamed off her face with a big Diamanté hair clip and her shoes... holy crap, her shoes were six inches of pure sex.

"You came." The corner of my mouth lifted as I raked a hand through my hair.

"I did." Mya grinned back. "These heels are killing me though and I could really do with a drink."

"Then let's get you a drink." I stepped toward her when my father's cough yanked me back.

"Aren't you going to introduce us, Son?"

"Of course." I gave Mya a tight smile, hoping she could see the apology in my eyes for whatever shit was about to come out of his mouth. Stepping to the side of her, I gave my father my full attention, silently begging him not to be an ass.

"You must be Mia," he said warmly. "Asher's friend from school."

"It's My—" Mya's hand slid against mine, and she squeezed gently.

"It's Mya," she said politely. "You have a lovely home, Sir."

"Thank you. I'm sure it must be a lot for you to take in."

She went rigid beside me and I wanted to lunge at my father and ask him what the fuck his problem was. But if I wanted Mya to stick around, I knew that was the wrong move.

"Well, if you'll excuse us. Mr. Ginly, Kellie," I said with as much gusto as I could muster. "Enjoy the rest of the party."

Dad gave me a curt nod, his eyes filled with an unspoken warning. But nothing could dampen my mood now Mya was here.

She made me soar.

And the quicker I got her away from his toxicity the better.

Grabbing her hand, I guided her through the house to the kitchen, hardly surprised when I found my friends crowded around the huge breakfast island playing beer pong.

"Mya, you made it." Flick was the first to spot us. She came over and took my girl's free hand. "You look amazing. No wonder you're late. Come on, I'll get you a drink."

I let her go, wandering over to the guys.

"Told you, you had nothing to worry about," Jase said smugly. "She cleans up good."

"I don't know," I mused. "She looks... different." Sure, Mya had a sexy and seductive thing working for her tonight, but I couldn't help but wonder if her extreme makeover was all for show.

"Are you fucking blind? She looks hot as sin."

That was just it though. To me Mya always looked hot. It was her unapologetic, individual style that caught my eye in the first place. The way she carried herself, the way she wore her own skin. But tonight she looked like every other woman in the room, dressed to the max, wearing far too much makeup, and even faker smiles.

"For real? You're sulking because she dressed up?"

"It's not that. It's just I can't help but think she did all this to fit in."

"She seems happy." Cam flicked his head toward the girls who were drinking and talking. Mya seemed at ease, her smile warm and eyes alight with interest.

"Well this has been enlightening and all," I declared. "But I need some time with my girl."

Jase gave me a sly grin. My friend's quiet laughter followed me as I approached the girls. Felicity saw me first, her eyes dancing with approval as I slid my arms around Mya and pulled her against my chest. "Hi," I whispered against the shell of her ear, desperate to kiss her there.

Her breath caught as she turned slightly to see me. "Hi, yourself." There was something in her eyes, a fierce possessiveness I'd never seen before.

"You okay?"

"I'm good. You?" she replied coolly.

Yeah, something was definitely off with her.

"Come on." I grabbed her hand and led her out of the furthest kitchen door, the one leading to the second set of stairs. It was quieter back here; the area usually off limits for guests.

"Asher, where are you—"

"You'll see." I pushed open the bathroom door and pulled her inside. Mya watched me intently as I stalked toward her. Her hands went behind her on the counter. Fuck, she looked good. There was no denying that. I wanted to unwrap her like a present and explore every inch of her body.

"You look... shit, Mya, I don't even have words."

Beautiful.

Alluring.

Mine.

I traced a hand down the slope of her neck. "You didn't need to do all this though."

"You don't like it?" Hurt flashed in her eyes, and I dropped my forehead to her shoulder.

"You're killing me here, Hernandez, in the sweetest possible way. But it feels like..."

Mya eased back, sliding her finger underneath my jaw and lifting my face to hers. "Like I tried too hard?"

Silence passed between us.

"Did you?" I asked.

Her fingers curled into my shirt, anchoring us together. "This is all for you. I promise. It's stage one of your present."

"Stage one?" That had my attention. "I like the sound of that."

"You should." She smirked, toying with my lapels. Our bodies were flush; the rise and fall of our chests synchronized. "What did your father want just now?"

I stiffened, sensing the coolness in her words again. "Forget about him, Mya." My lips brushed over hers. "It's just you and me. No one else matters."

"He wants you to be with someone like her, right? Someone like Kellie?"

Fuck.

This was so not where I wanted this conversation to go. But I knew better than to lie to her.

"I think it was a lame attempt at setting us up together, yeah."

"She's going Pittsburgh next fall?" Possessiveness dripped from her words and I liked it.

I liked it a whole lot.

Mya was jealous. It was usually such an ugly emotion. I knew, I'd felt it enough in the past. But knowing Mya cared enough to be jealous... well, it turned me the fuck on.

"You sound a little jealous there." I brushed her neck again, unable to resist dipping my head and swiping my tongue across her collarbone, sucking the skin gently between my teeth. Mya moaned softly, her grip on me tightening.

"Kellie might want me but it's not her skin I'll be tasting tonight." I kissed and sucked her neck some more, letting my hands glide up and down her silk covered body. "It's not her curves I'll be touching. It's not her I want inside of... God, do you have any idea how much I want inside of you?" Rocking against Mya, I made sure she could feel just exactly how much I wanted her.

"Ash..." she breathed.

"There'll always be other girls waiting in the wings," I said, my lips barely touching the corner of hers, "but none of them are you. And you, Mya Hernandez, are all I want."

"I want to give you your Christmas present now," Mya said, a little breathy. "But we should probably get back to the party before someone notices we're gone." She straightened her dress, smoothing out the material over her hips. "Shall we then?" Her eyes flicked to the door but all I could do was stand there and watch her.

She was mesmerizing.

Strong.

Beautiful.

Mine.

"You really got me a present?" I'd gotten her a little something but I hadn't expected anything in return. So color me surprised when the corner of her mouth kicked up in a seductive smile.

"Yeah, I got you a present. Me." Her tongue darted out, wetting her lips, as she let her gaze fall down my body and slide back up. When her eyes met mine again, she smiled. "Merry Christmas, Ash."

17

Mya

"MYA, it's so lovely to meet you," Asher's mom beamed at me. "You look stunning, sweetheart."

"Thank you, Mrs. Bennet." I blushed under her regard. "So do you."

"I was so excited when Asher told me he had invited a girl. He's never brought a girl home before."

Asher's fingers clutched my hip, and I wasn't sure if he was reassuring me or cringing at his mom's confession.

"I love the tree. It's so pretty."

Mrs. Bennet's eyes widened with delight. "You do? We spent all afternoon putting together the finishing touches. I've always loved the holidays." Her expression turned sad. "Well, you two love birds have fun, and I hope we get chance to talk more soon."

As Mrs. Bennet excused herself, I couldn't help but smile. She'd been nothing but nice to me. But it wasn't meeting his mom I was worried about. It was Mr. Bennet.

He'd spent most of the evening watching us. I don't think Asher noticed, too buzzed and high on us. *Me.* He'd barely let me out of his sight, completely oblivious to the way people watched us laughing with our friends. But I saw them. I felt their stares of disapproval brush up against my skin like tiny shards of glass. Even dressed to the nines in a dress I couldn't afford, I still wasn't good enough. Of course, in a town like Rixon, people talked. Everyone knew I was the transfer from Philly. They knew a girl like me didn't really belong in a town like this. Yet, with Asher's constant attention, and our friends' presence, it was easy to pretend I did. To pretend that they were only staring because they envied me, envied the way Asher touched the small of my back or kept kissing my shoulder. He was so attentive and sweet. I was determined not to let the narrow-minded views of his parents' friends ruin the night. Besides, I still had to give Asher his present. If I could only figure out how to get him alone later.

We wandered back over to our friends. The girls were busy making cocktail concoctions, so I took a seat at the counter.

"The boathouse."

"Excuse me?" I said to Jason who was watching me, a knowing glint in his eye.

"You're trying to figure out how to get five minutes alone with him."

"I'm not... okay, I totally am. They have a boathouse?"

Of course they had a boathouse. There wasn't anything this house didn't have.

"They don't really use it anymore," he said. "But it's warm and out of sight and you won't be disturbed down there."

My brows knitted. "Okay, this is weird."

He shrugged. "There's nothing we don't know about each other, Mya, it's just how it is." Jason flicked his head over to Asher and Cam as they goofed around. "He's falling you know."

"I know," I whispered, curling my hands around the stool.

If I'd learned anything about Asher in my short time at Rixon, it was that he wore his heart on his sleeve. Sure, it was usually wrapped up in layers of jokes and humor, but if you looked hard enough, you'd find it right there. Vulnerable and defenseless.

I knew what he felt for me was more than just some crush. Because I felt it too.

"Just do me a solid and make sure you're there to catch him, yeah?"

Covering my mouth, I smothered a soft laugh.

"What?" Jason asked.

"Nothing." Everyone seemed so certain it would be me who hurt him.

I didn't know what to think about that.

"I'm glad he found you, Mya."

"What are you two talking about?" Asher appeared at my side. He spun the stool and took my hand, pulling me up, letting his hand drift down over the curve of my ass.

"Oh, you know... life, the universe, all that other boring shit," Jason grunted, giving me one final pointed look. "I'll catch the two of you later."

The guys exchanged a nod before Asher anchored his hands at my waist. "Having fun?"

"Surprisingly, yes."

"You'd tell me, right? If anyone said anything to you."

"Stop." I kissed him. "Worrying. I'm fine, everything's fine. In fact, I was hoping we could go somewhere..."

"Somewhere?" Confusion crinkled his eyes, but they quickly widened. "Oh, you mean..." He swallowed hard. "Fuck, Mya." Asher pulled me closer, brushing the stray curls from my face and letting his lips linger near my ear. "You're serious?"

"I know I said I want to go slow, but this isn't about taking it slow or moving too fast, it's about what I feel. What *we* feel." I eased back to look at him. "I want you, Asher."

Awe glittered in his eyes as he dipped his head and kissed me softly. "I can't believe I'm saying this," he groaned. "But we need to wait. At least until the adults have drained the bar."

"Oh, okay." Dejection cinched my chest, and I dropped my eyes to the floor.

"Hey, hey." Asher tilted my face back to his. "I want you. I want you so fucking much it hurts. But the things I want to do to you, *with* you, require time. I don't want to screw this up."

"Has anyone ever told you, you're a sweet talker, Asher Bennet?"

"It may have been said before." He kissed me again, hard and long, making a total scene of it. I heard a couple of gasps of astonishment but refused to give them credence. I wasn't here for them, I was here for Asher.

For us.

"So, Mya Hernandez," Asher lifted his head, grinning at me. "Do you think you can wait a little longer for me?"

I gave him a salacious smile. "If you promise to make it worth my while."

"Fuck, I deserve a medal for this." His gaze raked over me for the hundredth time tonight. I loved the way he looked at me. His heated gaze made me stand taller.

Leaning up, I nipped his earlobe. "Maybe we should spike their drinks, speed things up?"

Asher laughed at that, letting his gaze drift past me to the party going on behind us. He went rigid and I knew he'd spotted them, our small audience. "Or maybe I should just fuck you right here against the counter and give them something to really lose their shit over."

I pulled out of his arms, wrapping my arms around my waist, staring at the floor. Asher let out a heavy sigh, sliding his fingers underneath my chin and angling my face back to his. "Crap, Mya, I didn't mean... I see them, you know. I've seen them all fucking night."

"Ignore them." I pressed a hand to his cheek. "I am." He remained still, his hard eyes still staring past me. "Ash, look at me. No one else matters but us."

Even if I didn't fully believe my own words, I'd believe them tonight for him.

"Thirty minutes. I'll give them another thirty minutes and then I'm going to take you down to the boathouse and bury myself so deep inside you that all I can see is you, Mya."

"Thirty minutes," I repeated, my body on fire at his words.

It wasn't long to wait but it already felt like forever.

WE WAITED ALMOST AN HOUR. Teasing each other with barely there touches and fleeting glances while the party went on around us. Jason and

Cameron teased us, fake gagging and rolling their eyes every time we fell into our own little bubble.

"Your dad is toasted," Asher said to Jase as we lingered in the kitchen. It had been our safe haven for most of the night; the adults preferring to stick to the huge reception room, letting the catering staff wait on them with trays of canapés and flutes of expensive champagne.

"My mom isn't much better," Hailee mused, looking a little glassy-eyed herself. "But at least they made up."

"That is one thing I never need to witness again. I still can't believe I walked in on them almost... fuck, nope, not going there." Jason shuddered, downing the rest of his beer. "Right," he slammed it down. "I don't know about anyone else, but we're calling it a night."

"We are, are we?" Felicity arched a brow.

He roped an arm around her neck and pulled her close. "Do you want to get fucked before I pass out, or not?"

"*Jason!*"

"Dude, there are some things I never need to hear," Cam protested.

Laughter rumbled in Jason's chest. "Like you aren't going to be boning my sister in about twenty minutes time."

"Dude!" We all shrieked this time.

"I think that's our cue," Asher whispered against my ear, sending a delicious shiver up my spine.

"Merry Christmas, Mya." Flick launched herself at me, hugging me so tight I could hardly breathe.

"Merry Christmas," I chuckled at her enthusiasm.

"I'm so happy you found each other," she whispered, "be careful with his heart."

"Babe, let's go," Jason said, pulling her away. "Merry Christmas, Mya, Asher. We'll see you guys in a couple of days."

"Have a good one, man." Ash fist bumped him, and then Cam, before burying his face in my hair.

"Ash?" I whispered. "What are you doing?"

"Smelling you. You smell so fucking good, I could eat you."

"What are you waiting for then?"

He pulled back, his eyes hooded, nostrils flared. "You sure about this?"

"Do you want to unwrap your present or not?"

Asher tipped his head back and groaned, the sound reverberating deep in his chest. I chuckled softly, enjoying teasing him. The air crackled around us, charged with anticipation.

My hairs stood on end as he took my hand and led me to the door. "What if someone sees?"

"At this point, I honestly couldn't give a fuck."

The house was emptying now, the music mellowing. "It's almost midnight," I said, noting the time on the wall clock as we left the house and stepped into the cool December air.

Asher was quiet as we walked across his vast yard toward the lake. I'd only been out here a handful of times, but the Bennets' yard never failed to take my breath away. It was the stuff of movies. A huge pool, sun loungers dotted around the edge, a huge canopied area for the summer. Beyond that, a neatly mowed lawn that ran all the way down to the small lake where they had their own jetty and, just as Jason had said, a boathouse.

"It looks... abandoned," I said, noting the dark building hidden beyond some trees.

"It doesn't get much use these days but when I was a kid I was always out here. My grandpa, my mom's dad, loved to tinker on the boat. I'd spend hours watching him from the mezzanine."

We reached the door and Asher paused, curving his hand around my neck and drawing me close. His lips found mine in an urgent kiss. "Thank you," he breathed. "For being here tonight."

"I'm glad I came. Your dad might be a complete ass, but your mom is sweet."

He winced.

"Hey," I said. "Just because she makes some decisions you don't understand or agree with, doesn't mean she doesn't love you."

"For as much as I want to confess all my deepest darkest secrets to you, I want to do this much more." Asher kissed me again, pushing his tongue deep into my mouth, his body caging me against the door. I felt him hard at my stomach.

"Merry Christmas, Mya," he whispered.

"Merry Christmas." I pulled back to look at him. The moonlight reflected off his profile, making him seem ethereal. An angel caught somewhere between the light and the darkness.

Asher grinned, before pulling me inside and pushing me against the cladded wall. "I had this all planned out," he said. "There are candles and a blanket upstairs, but I'm not sure I can wait. I need you, Mya. I need you so fucking much it hurts."

I ran my finger across his brow, studying his face. Asher Bennet was gorgeous. From his piercing blue eyes to his playful smile and mussed up blond hair. On the face of it, he was perfect. But it wasn't his perfect eyes or perfect smile or perfect teeth that drew me in, it was his imperfections. His maddening persistence. The darkness that sometimes shrouded his expression. The way he cared too much.

On paper we were complete opposites but when you stripped away our exteriors, you were left with two people betrayed by the people they were supposed to be able to trust. Two people who were completely wrong for one another.

But as I was quickly learning, sometimes wrong felt perfectly right.

18

Asher

I INCHED BACK FROM MYA, slowly unbuttoning my shirt. Her eyes tracked my movements, heavy-lidded with lust. We'd danced around one another all night. It had been the sweetest kind of torture, having her right there in plain sight but being unable to touch her the way I wanted.

The way I needed.

"See something you like, Hernandez?" I asked smugly, as I shuck out of my navy dress shirt. The material dropped to the floor as I began snapping my belt and unbuttoning my slacks. Mya swallowed, her hand gliding up the side of her neck. She was so fucking sexy.

"Come here." I crooked my finger at her and Mya came willingly, falling into my arms. Her hands slid up my bare chest, her touch like kryptonite; making my heart race and my knees weak.

"Jesus," I breathed, sucking in a harsh breath as she gently rolled one of my nipples between her fingers.

"You have too many clothes on." My hand drifted up her spine, locating the delicate zipper hidden beneath the seam of her dress. It slid down with ease, and Mya let the silky material fall down her arms, revealing a lacy black bra.

"See something by you like, Hotshot?" Mya smirked, pushing the dress over her hips and down her body until she was standing before me in nothing but her underwear.

"I think I just died and went to heaven." I didn't know where to look first. The swell of her perfect tits, the curve of her waist and flare of her hips. Her perfect ass.

"Kiss me," she whispered, staring up at me with anticipation.

"Kiss you?" I said, hooking an arm around her waist and erasing the space between us. Until we were skin on skin, racing heart against racing heart.

"I'm going to kiss every single inch of you, Mya. And when I'm done, I'm going to start all over again."

She shivered at my words, inhaling a shaky breath as I swept my fingers across her collarbone.

"Tell me what you want." I whispered against the corner of her mouth.

"You, Ash… I just want you." Mya wriggled closer, grazing my rock-hard dick. We both groaned. I dropped my hands to my jeans ready to kick them off, but Mya beat me to it. Her greedy hands dipping inside, stroking me through my boxer briefs.

"Fuck," I hissed.

I don't know how it happened, but Mya took control. Backing me up against the far wall, she ran one of her hands up and down my abs, dipping her head to nip and suck my neck while her hand worked me through the thin material.

"Mya, wait…" But before I could stop her, she dropped to her knees, yanked down my jeans and boxers and sucked me into her mouth. "Holy fuck." Sensation exploded up my spine as she ran her tongue up and down my length, pumping me with her hand. Slow torturous strokes that damn near blew my mind.

God, I never wanted her to stop but this wasn't supposed to be about me. It was supposed to be about her. About me showing her how I felt.

"Mya, babe, stop." I wound my hand into her curls and tugged gently. She looked up at me, eyes glazed with desire.

"Is something wrong?"

"Yeah, something's wrong." I pulled her to her feet, spinning us so her back was pressed against the wall. "This is about you, not me." My hand glided down her flat stomach, dipping inside her lacy panties. "I want to watch you come." Without warning I pushed a finger inside her.

Mya gasped, her eyes fluttering closed as her body arched into my touch.

"Eyes open, Mya."

She pinned me with a heated stare as I worked her with my fingers. No more words passed between us, just the sounds of her quiet moans and my labored breaths. It was intense. We both felt it. The shift between us. The tether binding us together.

"Asher," it was a shuddering breath but she might as well have reached into my chest and ripped out my heart.

It was hers now.

Whether she wanted it or not.

I didn't give Mya chance to catch her breath. Sliding my hands under her legs, I scooped her up and carried her over to the old boat. It was covered in a dust sheet that crinkled and crunched as I laid her out before me.

"Shit," I rasped, "Condom."

"No," she shook her head, biting her bottom lip. "I'm on birth control and I'm clean. I need to feel you, *all* of you."

Thank fuck for small mercies.

Pushing my boxer briefs off, I stroked myself a couple of times before leaning over her and covering her body with mine. Mya hitched her legs around my hips, steadying herself with a hand on my shoulder, as I teased her with the tip of my dick, letting it glide through her wetness.

"More," she begged, her voice thick with need.

Slowly, inch by inch, I pressed into her. "Christ, Mya, you feel..." The words lodged in my throat as I went deeper, grinding against her in a way that had us both moaning in pleasure.

Pressing my hands flat against the sheet, I stared down at her. I watched as her eyes rolled back every time I ground into her; watched the way her tits jiggled behind their lacy confines. "You are so fucking perfect," I rasped, thrusting harder, needing more. Needing to bury myself as deep as I could possibly get inside her.

But it wasn't enough. I needed to consume her. To imprint myself on her the way she'd already imprinted herself on me.

I needed to mark her.

To make her mine in every sense of the word.

Running a hand up her stomach, I toyed with the lacy shell of her bra before yanking it down. I licked her hungrily, before drawing her nipple into my mouth, sucking gently.

"Oh god... Ash..."

I released the dusky bud with a *pop*, moving to the curve of her breast. This time I sucked harder until blood rushed to the surface, bruising her skin.

"Did you just bite me?" Mya asked breathlessly, beads of sweat forming on her smooth silky skin as I continued to rock into her.

"Are you complaining?" My brow arched, the familiar tingle at the bottom of my spine building.

"God, Asher," she moaned my name. "Why does this feel so right?"

"Because it is right." I lowered my head to hers, every inch of me pressed up against every inch of her. "You can't tell me you don't feel this." Pulling one of Mya's hands off my shoulder, I slid my fingers through hers, pinning it at the side of her head. I rocked slower... harder... deeper, pushing us both toward the edge.

"Fall with me, Mya. Fall with me."

Her walls clenched around me, making us both cry out, as she came. Another thrust and I followed, jerking inside her.

"That was..." she tried to catch her breath.

"Epic... Earth shattering... The best you ever had," I said around an arrogant smile.

Mya chuckled, brushing the damp hair out of my face. "I was going to say intense."

"Not quite what I was going for, but we can practice." I pecked her lips. "Lots and lots of practice." My dick stirred to life again, but I ignored him, focusing on the girl beneath me.

My girl.

"I wish you could stay the night."

"Asher..."

"I know, I know. But this, us, it means something to me, Mya." *It means everything.* My thumb brushed over her lips as the unspoken words played on repeat in my head.

"It means something to me too." Her eyes burned with possessiveness.

"So we're really going to do this?"

She already knew I was in, but I needed to hear her say the words too.

"Yeah, we're doing this."

"You know I'm never going to let you go, right?"

"Asher..." Mya gazed up at me, letting out a resigned sigh. "It's senior year. College is right around the corner..."

"So? We have time, babe." I kissed her softly, letting my lips linger on hers. Mya didn't say anything else on the matter and I didn't want to taint what had been one of the best moments of my life.

Untangling myself from her, I held out my hand. Mya stared at it, confusion clouding her eyes. "The night isn't over yet," I said.

She slid her palm against mine and I led her further into the boathouse to where the stairs led to the mezzanine. "Watch your step."

"You could have at least let me put on some clothes."

"Wait here." I left Mya at the top step and located the box of matches I had left out here earlier. Once I'd lit the candles, I beckoned her over to the makeshift bed.

"You did all this?"

"If you're impressed by a few blankets and candles, I really need to up my game. Come lie with me?"

"Asher, if we fall asleep..."

"We won't, I promise. I'm just not ready to say goodbye yet."

I pulled the blanket over us and wrapped an arm around Mya's waist, snuggling as close as possible. It was perfect; our legs tangled, our slick bodies meshed together like two pieces of a puzzle.

"You know," Mya broke the silence, her voice barely a whisper. "When I first got to Rixon and learned how football obsessed the town was, I was dreading it. I'd left my home, my mom, my friends and..." she trailed off.

"It's okay, you can say his name." As much as I hated it, Jermaine was a part of her past. A part of what made her who she was in this moment. I didn't ever want to imagine them together. Him loving her, *hurting* her. But I couldn't pretend he didn't exist either.

It helped knowing I was the one here with her now. Lying beside her, my kisses on her lips, my touch all over her skin.

"I felt like an outsider. Part of me still does. But right from first moment I met you, you made me feel a part of something."

My chest tightened at her words, emotion clogging my throat. I was falling ass over elbow in love with her, but I didn't want to say the three little words I knew would be too much for her to hear yet. So I swallowed them down, storing them away for another day.

"Will your parents wonder where you've gotten to?" Mya asked, changing the subject.

"Dad will be slumped over a glass of whisky by now, wondering where he went wrong in life to end up with me for his son, and Mom will be crying over the family albums."

She turned in my arms to face me, her hands pressed against my chest as she gazed up at me. "I hate that you've carried this for so long.

"It is what it is."

"You deserve more though, Asher. You deserve a father who loves you and sees you for what you are. Not for what he wants you to be."

"Yeah, well, we can't always get what we want."

"Sometimes we do." She smiled, pressing a kiss to my lips. "Sometimes we get given exactly what we need when we didn't even know it."

"Are you saying you need me, Hernandez?"

"Maybe, just a little."

I tucked her against me, determined to make the most of every second we had together. But reality was a cruel bitch and all too soon, Mya was telling me to wake up.

"I really should go," she said.

I hadn't meant to fall asleep. But everything was so quiet with her. So peaceful.

Around Mya I could breathe. I could forget about all the other bullshit and imagine a future where I got to choose my own path.

Reluctantly, I got up, helping Mya to her feet. Dropping a kiss on the end of her nose I told her to wait while I went back downstairs and gathered up our clothes, yanking on my slacks before helping Mya back into her dress. When we were both dressed, I pulled her into my arms. "Best. Christmas. Ever."

"I should probably go..."

"Wait, I have something for you." I'd almost forgotten the small velvet pouch in my pocket. I dug it out and dropped it into her hand. "Merry Christmas, Mya."

Eyeing me carefully, her brows pulled tight, she pulled open the pouch, tipping the contents into the palm of her hand.

"It's a bracelet," I added, nervous energy radiating through me.

"It's beautiful." Delicate leather strands weaved together loosely to create a braid that held in place an oval silver charm. "What does it say?" Mya lifted it to her face to get a better look at the tiny engraving.

"Forty-two." We said in unison, our eyes colliding.

"It's your number."

"You didn't like the idea of wearing my jersey, so I thought maybe this was a good compromise." When she didn't say anything, my chest grew tight. I ran a hand down my face and added, "It was supposed to be an inside joke."

"It's..."

Fuck. It was too soon.

"Listen, forget it." I went to snatch it back, but Mya closed her fingers around it.

"Asher, it's perfect. It's just... well, I feel bad now. I didn't get you anything."

Slipping my arms around her, I pulled her closer. "You gave me everything tonight." I pecked the end of her nose. "Can I do the honors?" My eyes dropped to the bracelet and she nodded.

It fit her wrist to perfection. I held her hand, smoothing my thumb over the curve of her hand. "You know what this means, right?"

"That I owe you a present?"

"No." I smiled. "It means you're wearing my number, which means you're mine now."

"I guess I'd better not lose it then." Mya brushed my jaw before kissing me softly. I wanted to deepen it, to push my tongue into her mouth and explore every deep dark place inside her.

I wanted to stay here forever.

Because once we walked out of here, our perfect bubble would burst and reality would come crashing down around us.

19

Mya

"I KNEW IT." Flick screeched down the line. "So how was it? I want details, all the glorious details. Was he hung? I always imagined he was—"

I cleared my throat. "Are you done discussing the size of my..." I hesitated.

"I think the word you're looking for is boyfriend." She smothered a laugh.

"My boyfriend... wow, that's going to take some getting used to."

"Yeah, yeah, but back to the size of his—"

"*Felicity!*"

"What?" I could imagine her pouting. "It's girl talk. I tell you all about Jason's skills in the bedroom."

"I never ask though. You just dump that shit on me without warning."

She chuckled at that. "It's not like I can tell Hailee. She freaks out because he's family. Anyway, I don't want to talk about Jason right now. I want to talk about you and Asher. Was it magical? Did he make you see stars?"

"Who are you right now?" My face scrunched up.

"A girl in need of details, that's who. I still can't believe you did it in their old boathouse."

"It's not like we had options. Besides, there was something thrilling about it." Knowing we could get caught at any moment.

"And he gave you a gift. So romantic." She sighed dreamily and I knew I'd lost her to wedding bells and white dresses.

"Earth to Felicity, it's still early days." My eyes dropped to the bracelet wrapped around my wrist. "He still has to tell his parents and I still need to tell my aunt."

"You really think she'll be upset?"

"Upset, no. Disappointed, hell yes. She's warned me off white boys several times since I got here."

"But Asher isn't just any white boy, he's..."

"Different," I said quietly, feeling my heart clench.

"Have you broken the news about our trip to New York yet?" she asked, and I pressed my lips together, the silence deafening. "Mya, you have to tell her. We leave in two days."

"I know, I'm working up to it." Aunt Ciara and I were in a good place. We'd enjoyed Christmas Day together and I'd even gone to church with her and her friends. I didn't want to rock the boat, not when things were so good; but Felicity was right, I had to tell her.

About New York...

About Asher.

"Just do it. Quick and to the point, like ripping off a Band-Aid."

"Easy for you to say," I grumbled.

"You think it was easy announcing to my dad that I was dating Jason Ford? Hell no. But we have to make our own decisions, Mya. Even if they turn out to be mistakes."

"Thanks for the vote of confidence." My stomach twisted.

"I don't mean I think Asher is a mistake. If anything, I think you're finally thinking straight. I meant your aunt has to let you make your own way."

"I hope you're right." Because I could only imagine how much grief she was going to give me when I broke the news to her.

"Anyway, did you still want to come over later? The guys are having guys night at Bell's so I thought me, you, and Hailee could have girls night at my house."

"Will you stop asking about the size of my boyfriend's dick?"

We both exploded with laughter. It felt good, easing the heavy weight that had settled on my chest as we talked about my aunt.

"Just give me a ballpark figure and we can move on."

"I'm hanging up now."

"Nine inches," she snorted down the line. "It's got to be at least nine—"

"Goodbye, Felicity."

"Nine-and-a-half?"

Her voice faded away as I hung up, still chuckling at her outburst. Pre-Jason, Felicity had been sexually repressed. Or at least, that's the impression I'd gotten. But now she was all too willing to share. Still, I loved her in a way I hadn't anticipated. She would never replace my childhood friends from Fallowfield Heights, but Felicity had done a pretty good job at filling the hole left when I moved to Rixon.

Against all my better judgment, and my misguided expectations, I was making a life for myself here. I had friends, real tell-it-as-it-is friends. I was making good progress in my classes. And I had Asher.

The boyfriend I never knew I wanted.

I was falling hard and fast for him. It wasn't supposed to happen. I wasn't supposed to let it happen, but I was tired of fighting my feelings. Of always being the tough girl.

I was tired of letting other people dictate my life.

So what if me and Asher came from different sides of the tracks?

Attraction didn't discriminate based on color or background or life experience. It wasn't black or white but various shades of gray; prisms of color. My world had been dark when I'd moved to Rixon; dreary and desolate. All the pain and anger I felt bleeding into a black stain on my soul. But Asher, my girlfriends, even some of my teachers at school, were splashes of vibrancy, refusing to let me live in the shadows.

And if I admitted it to myself, I kind of liked living in the light again.

"Mya, it's so lovely to see you again. Come in."

"Thanks, Mrs. Bennet."

"Julia, please call me Julia. Asher," she called out over her shoulder, "your friend is here."

Asher rushed into the kitchen, sliding to stop in front of me. "Girlfriend, Mom." He grinned at me. "Mya is my girlfriend."

The word did all kinds of things to my stomach.

Closing the distance between us, he kissed me softly, not caring his mom was right there, pretending not to watch. I let out a contented sigh and gazed up at him. "Hi."

"Hi," Asher replied. "I'm glad you came."

I'd almost told him no when he had invited me over but before I could make my excuses, Asher had dropped it out that his father was on a last-minute business trip. He said his mom was excited to meet me again, in less chaotic circumstances, and I didn't have the heart to trample over his enthusiasm.

"I hope you're hungry, Mya. I took the liberty of making us all some lunch."

"Oh, you didn't have to do that, Mrs.... Julia."

Asher moved to my side, taking my hand as we followed his mom further into their huge house. "Thirty minutes," he whispered against my ear. "She gets you for thirty minutes and then you're all mine."

Desire licked up my spine but it was nothing compared to how my heart went haywire when he kissed the sensitive skin beneath my ear. "Ash..." I breathed, shooting him a look that said, 'behave'.

He slowed our pace a little, waiting for his mom to disappear into the kitchen. Then he pressed me against the wall, pinning my hands at either side of my head. "You want me to behave when all I can think about is being inside you again?" Asher's eyes turned as dark as night. "You drive me crazy, Mya." He leaned in, flicking his tongue against my damp skin, dragging it up toward my jaw, setting off a flight of butterflies in my stomach.

"Ash, we should—"

His mouth crashed down on mine, hard and demanding. I melted against him, my lips parting with surprise, letting his tongue invade my mouth. Asher rolled his hips into me, swallowing my soft moans.

"Asher, Mya?"

"Shit," he rasped as I gently pushed him away, trying to catch my breath.

"Thirty minutes," I said, willing my heart to calm down.

"Thirty minutes," he repeated, heaving a deep sigh, his eyes still burning into mine. Silently promising me so many things. Things I'd thought I didn't want but craved so intensely I felt a little lightheaded.

We could manage thirty minutes without tearing each other's clothes off, couldn't we?

But as Asher took my hand again, his fingers brushing mine, I knew he wasn't the only one who was going to suffer over lunch.

I already missed his intense touch.

"There you two lovebirds are." Mrs. Bennet gave us a wistful smile as we entered the kitchen. "Sit, sit. This food won't eat itself."

"It looks amazing, thank you so much," I said, letting Asher pull out my chair and help me get seated. Something I'm not sure had ever happened in my entire life.

Once we had our plates loaded, Mrs. Bennet started with the questions. "So, Mya, what colleges are you applying to?"

My eyes flicked to Asher and back again. "I've applied to Temple University and two out of state schools. Michigan and Cleveland." I knew Asher was supposed to be going to Pittsburgh. I also knew Cleveland was only about a two-hour drive from there.

I also knew it was far too soon to be thinking about any of this.

"Cleveland, how lovely," she said, smiling knowingly, as if she knew exactly what I was thinking. "Pittsburgh is only about a two-hour ride from Cleveland, if I'm correct." Mrs. Bennet gave her son a meaningful glance, but Asher didn't share her enthusiasm.

My heart sank.

"Mom," he ground out, rubbing a hand over his face. "Can we not do this?"

"What? I'm just making polite conversation."

"I haven't made any decisions," I rushed out, no longer hungry. Asher's eyes burned into the side of my head, but I couldn't look at him.

"Of course," Mrs. Bennet added, sensing the sudden tension settling over us. "It's a big decision and you have plenty of time. Unlike Asher who's been destined for Pittsburgh his whole life."

Steeling myself, I finally met his eyes. His face was pale, drained of blood and humor. His eyes so full of pain my heart ached for him. "Yep," defeat clung to his voice, "Pittsburgh here I come. Go Panthers."

Mrs. Bennet sniffled, clearing her throat. "Excuse me, I need to use the bathroom." She hurried away from the table, leaving me and Asher sitting there, staring at each other, neither of us able to find the words to fill the silence.

"You really applied to Cleveland?" he finally asked, surprising me.

"It's one of my choices, yeah."

"You never said anything."

"You never asked." We hadn't gotten that far yet; sharing our hopes and dreams for the future. But I guess that's what happened when you were so caught up in defending your present to everyone around you; you didn't think much past tomorrow or the next day or the one after that.

Silence filled the space between us again. I didn't really understand what was happening, but everything felt wrong. Reality forcing its way into the cracks of our new relationship, pushing us further apart.

"I'm sorry," Asher's voice punctuated the air. "I didn't mean... shit, Mya, I don't know what I'm doing here. I thought we could have lunch with my mom and everything would be okay. But he's always there, standing over my shoulder, pushing me toward the future he wants for me."

"It's okay." I reached across the table and held out my hand. Asher slid his palm against mine, exhaling a shaky breath, his eyes shuttering.

"I should let you go." He might as well have reached inside me and grabbed my heart. "I shouldn't drag you into this shit with my dad. It's only going to get worse." Asher's eyes flicked to the door his mom had disappeared through.

"I'm right here," I said. "I'm not going anywhere."

"Mya, I said I *should* let you go, not that I will. I'm too selfish to give this thing up. I need you."

I need you.

Three little words I'd heard before. Three little words that, in the end, weren't enough. This time was different though. I had to believe this time was different. That those three little words were enough.

That *I* was enough.

That how we felt about each other would be enough.

Asher's room looked different in daylight. It was as big as I remembered, but now I could take a proper look at his space, while he made himself comfortable on the bed.

"I'm over here and you're all the way over there." Asher stuck his lip out, pouting dramatically.

"I want to know you."

"You can learn everything you need to know about me over here." His brow waggled suggestively as he patted the space beside him. I ignored him, running my fingers over a shelf full of football trophies and awards.

"Football really is at the heart of Rixon, isn't it?" Picking up a small bronze statue, I brought it closer to inspect the engraving plate.

"MVP for my Pee-Wee team. I was twelve." His warm breath danced over my skin, making me shiver.

"I thought you were staying over there?" My gaze went to the bed.

"Why would I be over there, when you're over here?" Asher kissed the sliver of bare skin along my shoulder. "Football is my past; I think I've finally accepted that." He took the statue from me. "I'm going to play one last time with my team and then I'm going to focus on other things. Like you." Leaning around me, he placed the trophy back in its rightful place before turning me in his arms.

"But you love football," I said. "Maybe there's a compromise? Maybe you can have both. Football and—"

His brows knitted as he scrubbed his jaw. "For someone who didn't like football a few weeks back, you sure sound disappointed that your boyfriend might never play again."

"I can't deny there was something appealing about those tight white pants." My hands ran down his arms, loving how his muscles contracted under my touch.

"I'll keep a pair just for you." He winked, but I saw the lingering sadness in his eyes.

"Is your mom likely to come upstairs?"

"Nah, I think we're safe."

"Good." I brushed the hair away from his face, inching closer.

"Oh yeah?" Asher's eyes lit up. "Is that your attempt at seducing me, Hernandez?"

"Is it working?"

He leaned in, until our noses were touching. "You don't need to seduce me, Mya. I'm already yours."

His words sank into me, softening my hard, jagged edges.

"You really mean that, don't you?" I asked, not really wanting to be *that* girl. The girl unsure about everything, who constantly needed reassurance from her boyfriend. But after Jermaine; after all the broken promises and lies, it was hard to trust so easily.

"I mean it, babe. Every single word. But maybe I should show you." Asher dipped his head, pressing his lips to my neck. "Maybe you need a reminder."

20

Asher

"ARE you going to sit there all night wearing a shit-eating grin?" Jason grunted as he slid into the booth with our beers.

We were at our table in Bell's. It was quieter than usual; people still visiting family and friends for the holidays. After two days of strained meals and awkward conversation, it'd been a huge fucking relief when my father announced he needed to leave for urgent business. The smug bastard had simply smirked when he'd asked me if I'd liked my presents. As if they hadn't been a giant slap in the face; every other gift a Panther branded item of clothing or college accessory. Like I needed any more of a reminder that, come next August, I would be going to my father's alma mater to become his puppet.

Unsurprisingly, there hadn't been a Panther's football jersey in sight.

So what had I done? I'd immediately invited Mya for lunch, thinking it would be nice for her and Mom to spend some time together without Dad's shadow looming over them. Big-fucking-mistake. Mom had gone and brought up college and the conversation had quickly gone to shit. I'd half-expected Mya to make her excuses and get the hell out of there.

But she hadn't.

My girl had sat there with my mom, who had hardly been able to look at me, while we pretended everything was fine. It was such a relief when we finally went up to my room. Mya had let me lose myself in her without question. I needed her and she was there. I could still feel her now, wrapped around my dick, her breathy moans in my ear. The way she cried my name over and over, as if I was her salvation.

Because fuck only knew, I was beginning to think she was mine.

"Jase, ease off." Cam came to my defense. "We were the same."

"Were?" I snorted. "He's worse than a dog in heat." My eyes went to Jase.

"Fuck off," he mumbled. "We're not talking about me and Felicity, we're talking about you and Mya. Although I don't think I need to ask how it feels now you finally got the girl."

"What's that I hear, fuckers?" Grady joined us, sliding in beside Jase. I smothered a groan. I hadn't expected him to be here. "You and Mya going steady?" he asked.

"We're... going. She met my parents Christmas Eve and came over for lunch with my mom earlier."

"Holy fuck, that's... good for you, bro. What did they think?" I reared back, eyes hard on him. "Whoa, I wasn't throwing shade," he blurted out. "I just meant did they like her?"

Awkward silence fell over our booth as I replayed my father's blatant disapproval, not to mention his arrogance when he'd met Mya.

"My mom loved her," I finally said, the words like sandpaper in my throat. "My old man, not so much. He tried to set me up with Kellie. Turns out she's also going to Pittsburgh next year."

"Shit, man, that's rough. How'd Mya take that news? You know how persistent Kellie can be."

"I'm not worried about Kellie." She wasn't even on my radar.

"You should be. She and those gymnasts can be fucking mental. Look at Jenna." Grady's eyes slid to Jase who had gone eerily quiet.

"Let's *not* talk about Jenna." She'd caused enough shit between him and Felicity without rehashing it all.

"So what's the deal? Why the long face? Wouldn't she put out?"

"Grady, man, I swear if you don't shut the fuck up..."

"Jeez, Bennet, lighten up. I'm going to shoot some pool with Merrick and the guys. Catch you later."

Jase and Cam gave him a sharp nod, but I stared out at nothing, clutching the neck of the bottle in my hand like a vise.

When Jase settled his attention back on me, his brow rose. "Talk."

"Later," I said non-committally. "We need to figure out plans for New York. Riley and Vaughn have this whole bar crawl thing planned but it sounds like a lot of hard work."

"Can't we start at the penthouse and end up at a club?" Cam asked.

"That's what I was thinking. We can get some drinks, snacks, and the penthouse has a wicked sound system. I could ask Riley and Vaughn if they want to bring some friends?"

Jase ran a hand down his face. "Set it up, but don't let Riley and Vaughn turn it into something huge. I don't want to spend the night with a bunch of rich kids from the city."

"I'll tell them to keep it tight." I pulled out my cell to text Vaughn, since she was more likely to respond than Riley.

"A whole night of freedom," Jase grumbled. "I can't fucking wait. We're running out of places to fuck."

"Seriously, man?" Cam shook his head. "Do you have to do that?"

"What? Like you and Hailee aren't—"

"Dude!" I levelled Jase with a hard look. "There's a line. Don't cross it."

"Bunch of pussies." He smirked, taking a long pull on his beer.

"Don't even try to act like Fee hasn't gotten you right where she wants you. You're whipped, bro, admit it."

His expression darkened but then melted away, morphing into a proud smile. "I can own that shit. I, Jason fucking Ford, am so fucking whipped by my girl and I love it."

"Say it a little louder for the people in the back," Grady yelled, and Jason flipped him off, earning him a round of snickers and cheers.

"When's the wedding?" someone called, and the blood drained from his face.

"Oh, now he shuts up." Cam snorted. "You should see your face."

"Fuck off, Chase. We all know you'll be the first one down the aisle with Hailee."

He shrugged. "One day."

"What about you, Ash, man; you think Mya's wife material?"

My throat went dry, my fingers tightening around the bottleneck.

"Yo, Cap," Grady shouted across the bar, saving me from Jason's question. "You feel like getting your ass kicked at pool?"

"Like that'll ever happen." Jase stood up, arrogance pouring from him. "Rack 'em up, Grady, and prepare to eat shit." He sauntered off leaving me with Cameron.

Eyes narrowed right on me, he said, "I'm here."

"I know." I lifted my face to his.

"Whenever you're ready."

I nodded, feeling the teeth of the truth nipping at my heels.

Time was running out.

But I still wasn't ready.

"Do you think this is a good idea?" Cam whispered as we trudged around the Giles' back yard, wading through the bushes lining their house. "Couldn't we just have knocked?"

"It's been too long since we pranked Hailee," Jase slurred. "She needs a little reminder who's the better sibling."

"*Step*-sibling," I corrected.

"Step, smep. She needs bringing down a peg or two since she got with Chase."

"I'm standing right here," Cam protested.

"Yeah, yeah, man. You owe me too. My *step*-sister. Really, man, you had to go there?"

"How many drinks did you have tonight?" I asked him.

"I'm fine."

"You're drunk, and when Felicity sees what you've done to her mom's plants, she's going to have your balls."

"Just because Hailee has your balls in her purse, doesn't mean the rest of us let our women run the show."

Cam dropped into one of the garden chairs. "I'm just going to sit here and watch you show *your woman* who's boss."

"I'm with him," I slowly backed up, leaving Jase to try to scale the wall by himself.

"Bunch of pussies," he murmured, trying to get a foothold in the wooden lattice. "We've got to take back our balls, I'm telling you. These girls think they can just swoop in and turn our lives upside down and have us running around after them, I'm a Raider for fuck's sake. And Raiders never..." he trailed off when he noticed us glaring at him. "What?"

I nudged my head over his shoulder to where the girls were standing looking less than amused.

"Jason Gary Ford, what the hell do you think you're doing in my mom's hydrangeas?"

"Babe, I can explain..." Jase dragged a hand through his hair, inching closer to them. "We thought it would be funny."

"He," Cam coughed, "he thought it would be funny."

"Traitorous motherfucker."

"Please tell me you weren't going to try to scale the wall?" Flick broke rank and stepped up to him, pressing her hands to his chest forcefully.

Jase shot her a lazy smile. "I wanted to see you."

"You could have called or knocked. God, you stink. Just how much did you let him drink?" Her eyes went to me.

"Don't look at me. I'm not his keeper."

"Or me," Cam added. "Blame Grady."

"Grady? Grady who isn't here right now trampling through my mom's plants and trying to climb the lattice."

"Don't be pissed, babe." Jason hooked his arm around Felicity's waist, dragging her closer. "I missed you." He buried his face into her neck and she shrieked.

"Get off me, you're drunk."

"Maybe you should just invite us in?" I suggested, "before he really makes a scene."

Mya shook her head at me, the faintest of smiles tugging at her lips. Without a word, I rose from the chair and did my best to walk in a straight line to her. "Hi."

"Hi," she said, her smile growing. "Just how drunk are you?"

"Not as drunk as him." I thumbed to where Jason was slowly breaking Flick's resolve, the two of them kiss-fighting. "But a little more drunk than Cam."

"Sounds about right," Hailee said as she brushed past me to go get her guy.

"Miss me?"

"Miss you?" Mya chuckled, smoothing her hands over my shoulders. "It's only been a few hours since I last saw you."

"Admit it, you missed me."

"Ash..." She lowered her eyes, touching her head to mine.

"It's okay, Mya," Jase called over. "We're all slaves to love here."

"Oh God, stop," Flick smothered a laugh. "You're here now. I guess you might as well come inside."

"Shall we?" I said to Mya. She took one of my hands and turned to go back inside. But I paused, letting my eyes sweep down her body. "Nice pajamas."

"Behave," she scolded. "Or I'll call you a cab."

Jase snickered but my girl shot him a hard look. "You too, Ford. It might be your girlfriend's house, but you interrupted girls night and I'm not afraid to send you packing."

"Warning received, loud and clear."

"You really showed her, Jase," I teased.

"Fuck off," he mouthed as we all headed inside. It was late and both me and Cam had tried to talk Jason out of coming here to sabotage the girls' night. But I wasn't about to let him go off alone. Besides, the chance to spend more time with Mya was just too good to refuse.

The girls ushered us into the living room, practically shoving us onto the couch. "Now," Felicity started, "What to do with the three of you."

"You can do whatever you'd like, babe," Jason smirked, letting his hand run down to his crotch.

"Dude, we're right here," I reminded him.

"Maybe you should fuck off then."

"What about a game of truth or dare?" Hailee suggested. "Jason goes first since he's the mastermind behind all of this."

"Truth or dare is for pussies," he grunted, his hungry eyes fixed on Flick like a predator stalking its prey.

"We'll make it worth your while." Mya stepped between Hailee and Felicity, throwing her arm around their shoulders. I sat up a little straighter, frowning.

"Oh yeah, Hernandez," Jason said. "And how exactly do you plan on doing that?"

"I dare you to kiss Asher—"

"What the fuck?" We both shrieked. "No way!"

"Kiss Asher," my girl stood her ground, "and I'll kiss Felicity."

Holy shit.

My jaw almost hit the floor as Flick nodded. "Ooh, good one. What do you think?"

"Babe, I'm not some pre-pubescent guy who gets off watching two girls..." His words trailed off as Felicity dragged a finger down Mya's neck, toying with the neckline of her pajama tank.

"You were saying?" She had Jase's full attention now. He narrowed his eyes, nostrils flared.

"For real, you want to do this?" His hard gaze found me around Cameron. "You want to see me kiss Asher?"

"Dude," I interjected. "You're not actually considering this?" Seeing Mya kiss Felicity would be as hot as fuck, but no way did I want to kiss my best friend—*a guy*—for it.

No way.

"I'm game, if you are."

It felt like we were spectators to some private challenge between Jase and Felicity. Challenge glittered in their eyes, the air thick with tension.

"You'll really make it worth our while?"

She nodded and I tried to catch Mya's attention, but she was too busy watching Jason and Felicity.

"Fine. Ash, man, get over here."

"I'm not kissing you, Jase. No fucking way."

"Don't be such a pussy. I've seen your dick more times than I can count. What's a little kiss between friends?"

"You've lost your goddamn mind," I ground out as Jason stood up, coming around the couch toward me. "Keep your drunk ass away from me."

"You know he'll win," Cam said. "Might as well get it over with."

"Thanks for the help, man. Big fucking thanks." I jabbed a finger at Jase, warning him to stay back, but the huge drunken idiot launched on top of me, pinning me to the couch.

Laughter exploded all around us as I tried to wrestle him off, but the motherfucker was just too strong. He caged my body, using one of his hands to grip my face. "Just one little kiss, pucker up."

"Jason, get the hell—" His mouth pressed down on mine, hard and wet and as weird. as. fuck. I went still, clamping my lips together to avoid an accidental slip of the tongue. Shoving with all my might, I slammed my body forward, sending Jase falling back onto his ass.

"Don't *ever* do that again." I smeared his kiss off my lips with the back of my hand. He clambered to his feet, a shit-eating smirk plastered over his face.

"Aww, don't be so sensitive. You've got pretty nice lips... for a guy."

Cam snorted beside me and I levelled him with a look that said, 'you're next'.

"That was... wow, I did not expect that to happen." Flick looked a little flushed. Her eyes dancing with a mix of surprise and curiosity. "Okay, I guess it's our turn. Mya..."

"Felicity." She smirked at her friend, gently cupping her face. The two of them inched closer, and I found myself sitting straighter again. They were almost nose to nose, lips to lips, when they both turned their head at the last second and grinned. "Gotcha."

"I can't believe you actually thought we'd do it," Felicity added around a smug grin.

"You tricked us?" Jase growled.

"And you fell for it hook, line, and sinker. Want your balls back now?"

"You're in so much trouble, babe." He advanced toward her, but she edged backward.

"It was a joke, Jase. Don't be so—"

"You'd better run."

"Oh shit." Flick spun on her heel and took off out of the door, laughter drifting back to us as Jason took off after her.

"I guess we won't see them again tonight," Mya said, her eyes sliding to mine. "Am I in trouble too?"

Heat trickled down my spine. "Do you want to be in trouble?"

She came over and climbed on my lap, tucking her body tight to mine. "Would you be disappointed if I said I want to hang out with Cam and Hailee and just enjoy being a normal couple?"

"Actually," I pecked the end of her nose. "That sounds pretty damn perfect to me."

21

Mya

"MYA, I'M HOME," my aunt's voice rang out, startling me.

I let out a heavy sigh. This was one conversation I knew I couldn't escape. What was it that Felicity had said 'rip it off like a Band-Aid'? Only I was pretty sure this Band-Aid was going to leave a deeper cut.

I found Aunt Ciara in the kitchen, unpacking a small bag of groceries. "A little help." Her eyes widened with meaning, and I chuckled, setting to work alongside her.

After a couple of silent minutes, she huffed out, "For the love of Jesus, Mya, spit it out."

"How do you do that?" I asked.

"You think I don't see the way you're holding it all in?" Her brow rose.

"Felicity and Hailee invited me to New York with them for New Year's."

"New York, huh? Sounds fancy. Fancy and expensive. You know we don't got spare money lying around for—"

"Actually, it's all taken care of."

She stopped what she was doing, fixing her suspicious gaze on me. "Let me guess, those Raider boys are picking up the tab."

"Asher's family has a penthouse we can stay in. It won't cost a penny. I'll just need some gas money and an outfit, but Felicity has already said I can borrow something."

"Asher's family," she repeated, her tight expression telling me everything I needed to know.

"It's not a big deal, Auntie," I said, grabbing the last of the groceries and putting them away.

"The fact you're saying it's not a big deal, tells me it is a big deal. I thought you were going to be cautious where the Bennet boy was concerned?"

"Asher, his name is Asher, Aunt C. Besides, would it really hurt for you to be happy for me. I have friends, Auntie, good friends. And Asher is, well, he's a good person."

He was good and kind and he liked me.

He didn't see Mya, the girl from the hood; he saw Mya, the girl who had left her home, her life, for something better.

"And what do his parents think about you heading off to New York with their son for New Year?"

"I... I don't know." The truth teetered on the tip on my tongue. "But Asher doesn't care what they think. He's serious about this thing between us. I am too."

"Mya, Mya, Mya," she made a drawn-out groaning sound, "I thought you were more sensible than this."

"We care about each other," I said, my voice cracked with frustration. "Isn't that enough?"

"For now, maybe. But what about after graduation? What then? You'll go off to different schools and he'll what, wait for you?" she asked incredulously. "I've heard rumors about that family, about his father's connections. You think he's going to sit by and watch as his only son dates you?" Her tone was almost scathing, as if I was the villain here. Not Mr. Bennet and his bigoted ideals.

The need to defend Asher, to defend our fledgling relationship burned inside me. "Asher is—"

"Going to break your heart. I'm sorry, Mya, I know you don't want to hear it but he's going to go off to college; meet some rich, white girl his parents approve of; and leave you high and dry."

"You're wrong." Anger slithered through me, making my body tremble and tears sting my eyes. "I know you only want to protect me, Auntie. But I know Asher and you're wrong about him."

Maybe this thing between us was doomed to fail. Maybe it was destined to be nothing more than a short whirlwind of stolen kisses and secret touches. But in my heart of hearts, I knew Asher would never purposefully hurt me. He didn't have it in him.

"I love you," I said quietly, my heart aching for the crack forming in our relationship. "But I've made my choice. I choose Asher."

Aunt Ciara's expression hardened, her lips thinning with disapproval. She didn't say anything, she didn't have to. I felt her disappointment. It permeated the air, making it dense and oppressive. But then my cell phone blared to life, drowning out our tension. I ignored it, trying to think of how to smooth over the crack forming between us.

"You should probably answer that." She bit out when it blared again.

"Fine, I'll be up in my room." I marched out of the kitchen, desperate to hear Asher's voice, only to be disappointed when I saw Shona's name flashing on the screen.

"Hey, this unexpected."

"A girl can't call her girlfriend no more?"

"Shona, it isn't even like that." Closing the door behind me, I dropped down on the edge of the bed. "How's it going?"

"How do you think it's going? Jermaine about damn near lost his shit when he found out you'd left... again."

"I told him—"

"Don't matter what you told him. He isn't going to let this thing go."

"He has to. I'm done. I've moved on. I..." Asher's infectious smile flashed in my mind. "I'm seeing someone."

"The white boy JT lookalike?"

"And he plays football," I teased, trying to lighten the tense mood.

"Damn, girl, it's like I don't even know who you are anymore." Silence lingered over the line.

"He's a good guy, Shona."

"Whatever you say. I just don't want to see you get hurt again," she let out a heavy sigh. "Listen, I was calling to tell you Jermaine came around asking about you. I didn't tell him nothing, but I don't think he's going to forget you anytime soon."

"He has to," I repeated unsure who I was trying to convince more.

Her.

Or myself.

"My life is here now, Shona. He doesn't know I'm in Rixon. He can't ever know."

"Chill, girl. I ain't going to say nothing. But I can't guarantee Jesse won't get involved if he keeps coming around here."

"I'm sorry."

"Nah, you're not. But I get it. You had to get out. Stay safe, girl."

"You too," I whispered. Shona hung up and I clutched the phone to my chest. Jermaine wasn't going away. Even though I'd changed my number and told him we were done, he was still there. Haunting me like a ghost.

I didn't expect Aunt Ciara and Shona to understand my relationship with Asher, but it sucked that I had to constantly defend it to the people closest to me. Aunt Ciara had her reasons, but Asher wasn't her ex. He wasn't going to make false promises only to break my heart and leave me bloody and bruised and alone. And Shona... well, she didn't get it. Where we came from you didn't date white boys.

Even though their disapproval didn't surprise me, a small part of me had hoped they would see things from my perspective. That they would at least try to understand what it was like to be an eighteen-year-old falling headfirst for a guy who made her laugh and feel safe and cherished. A guy who wouldn't bring pain and danger and heartache to my doorstep. But the louder their warnings got, the quieter my conviction became, the two halves of me at war.

Asher wouldn't hurt me. I didn't doubt that.

But trying to live in Asher's world with him, that might just destroy me.

"Not that one," I said, cringing at the thought of myself in the floral print dress Felicity was holding up against her body.

"You're right, it's too… happy."

"Happy? Are you saying I'm *not* happy?"

She glanced over at me, fighting a smirk, as I lounged on her bed, surrounded by clothes. "Do you think you're happy?"

"I'm happy with Asher. He makes me happy."

"You are so cute right now. He'd love it."

"Don't you dare tell him I was sitting here making googly eyes. I have a rep to protect. A thunderstorm rep, apparently."

"I didn't say you were thunder but you're definitely not sunshine either."

I poked my tongue out at her and picked the silky dress—the one I'd worn to the Bennets' party—off the pile. "I could wear this again."

"No, he's already seen you in that. Besides, that was parental approved. This is New York. You need something… *more*."

"More, right." I rolled my eyes, letting the soft material flutter through my fingertips, remembering how Asher's eyes had widened when he saw me in it. The way his breath had hitched. The hunger in his expression.

"Show me what you brought over again." Flick beckoned at me.

Digging out the bag of worn jeans, denim skirts, shorts, and tank tops, I pulled a face. "This is definitely not going to cut it."

"It's okay, we still have time. I must have something in here." She began sifting through her wardrobe again.

My eyes flicked to the dress Flick planned to wear. It was a deep shade of green, cut low in the front and even lower in the back. Her mom had bought it specially for her, wanting her daughter to look the part for our big trip to New York.

I couldn't deny jealousy had simmered in my veins when she'd told me. I wasn't jealous of her, or even the dress, but I couldn't ever remember a time my mom had taken me shopping. And for as strong as I tried to be, I couldn't pretend my friend's sparkly new dress wasn't a reminder of everything I'd lost.

Everything I never had.

"Okay, I think I've got it. Show me those jean shorts again. The dark wash ones."

"These old things?" I'd breathed life into an old pair of jeans by cutting off the legs, but they hardly screamed New York club vibe.

"I think they might work with this." She spun around, presenting me with a sequined black halter that was too short to be a dress but long enough my midriff wouldn't be on display. "The back is cut low, so you won't be able to wear a bra." Flick flipped the hanger so I could get a look.

"Not a problem." I climbed off the bed. "Can I try it on?"

"Uh, yes! I need to see it. Try it with the heeled boots."

"Are you sure you don't mind me borrowing all this stuff?"

She gave me a pointed look. "As if you even need to ask."

"Thank you." Snatching up the shorts and boots, I disappeared into her small bathroom and stripped out of my clothes and shimmied into the outfit. The girl staring back at me was taller, thanks to the killer heels, but she was also older somehow. Wiser.

Felicity was right. I didn't look like a picture of happiness, my resting bitch face making my expression too serious. But I saw the subtle change in my eyes. The little sparkle. And I knew the root of it. The girl beyond the door, determined to make me look the part for our big night out. The boy I'd be walking hand in hand into the club with. Rixon was changing me and it wasn't all bad. In fact, some of it was good.

Very good.

"The suspense is killing me," Flick called through the door. "Are you done?"

Taking a deep breath, I toyed with the material in the front, so it hung just right. "Okay," I stepped back into the bedroom. "What do you think?"

Her eyes went wide and she clapped, letting out a little shriek of approval. "Hell yes. Asher is going to die when he sees you."

"Well hopefully he won't die. I kind of like having him around."

"This trip is going to be the best." Felicity beamed. "Just promise me you'll stick up for me if Vaughn makes a play for Jason."

"I got your back." I shot her a playful wink. "Is Asher close to his cousins?"

"Not really. I mean, they seemed friendly enough when we went before, but they don't keep in regular contact or anything. Why do you ask?"

"No reason." The lie soured on my tongue. But I couldn't tell her how the little voice in my head was whispering all kinds of things to me.

"They'll love you, Mya," she said trying to reassure me. "You have nothing to worry about."

"Yeah." I forced a smile, telling myself it didn't matter what they thought.

Even if I knew, deep down, it did.

22

Asher

OUR TRIP to New York was finally underway. The smaller Rixon grew in the distance, the more I could breathe. My arm tightened around Mya, and she gazed up at me.

"I can't wait to see the skyline." Her smile was easy, her words light, but I felt the lingering tension between us.

I'd been a dick the other day at lunch with my mom. But when she'd brought up college, I had immediately gone to a dark place. I knew Mya thought it had something to do with her applying to Cleveland, but she was so far off the mark. That was the only good thing to come out of that conversation. Cleveland wasn't Pittsburgh but it was close e-fucking-nough. Two hours was nothing. We could have stopovers, spend the weekends together, see each other every other day if we wanted.

But that was the dream.

The reality was much different.

The reality was that my father wouldn't want me going off to Pittsburgh still dating Mya. He'd want me single; available to date a long list of suitable girls.

Girls like Kellie Ginly.

Pittsburgh was a long way from Rixon though, long enough that we could keep it a secret from him, if it came down to it. Because I couldn't lose her.

"Where'd you go?" Mya brushed her nose across my jaw, commanding my attention.

"Just thinking."

She cupped my face, turning me into her. "No thinking. Not today." Mya kept her voice low, her words only meant for me. "We're going to go to New York, to celebrate the new year, and have an amazing time with our friends. The rest can wait, okay?"

Nodding, I pressed my head to Mya's, letting my lips brush over hers. Her fingers tightened into my hoodie as she leaned closer, letting me deepen the kiss.

This.

This was what I needed.

Her kisses.

Her touch.

Just her.

Someone cleared their throat, Jason I think. But I didn't care, and I didn't stop. I kept kissing Mya, letting my tongue glide and tangle with hers. Igniting a firestorm inside me, flames searing me inside out.

I would gladly burn for this girl.

"I hope to fuck they aren't going to do this for the whole ride." There was no mistaking it was Jase this time. Mya chuckled against my mouth, the sound wrapping around my heart like a vise.

"We should stop," she breathed.

"No," I slid my hand into her hair, anchoring her face to mine, "we should keep going."

"Ash..."

"Mya..." She didn't resist when I captured her lips again, kissing her harder. Deeper. Kissing with her with everything I had.

"Babe, if they carry on," Flick said, "we might have to stop."

I finally broke the kiss, sliding my eyes up front to where Felicity sat beside Jason in the front of the minivan we'd hired. She leaned closer, whispering something to him. "Fuck," he muttered, his eyes hard on the road.

"Everything okay up there?"

His eyes met mine in the mirror, and he grumbled, "I don't know whether to high five you or throw you out of the van."

"Me? What the hell did I do?" I smothered a grin, settling back against the seat with Mya tucked into my side.

Rixon was miles behind us now. Exactly where I wanted to leave it. Because my girl was right; this was our weekend.

And not a single thing was going to ruin it.

"Holy crap," Mya gasped as we stepped out of the elevator and into the foyer of the penthouse. It was all glass and chrome and high-end decor. Completely over the top, and probably unworthy of its thousand-dollar-a-night price tag, but Dad's brother, Uncle Mich, was all too willing to accommodate me and my friends. They were constantly trying to one up each other. *Let the kids borrow the penthouse. Let the kids vacation in the Hamptons*. Riley and Vaughn worked it to their advantage more than me though. Probably because their father cared even less than mine.

Well, mine cared... just about the wrong things.

"It's something else, right?" Flick breezed past us as if she owned the place, Jason trailing after her.

"I can't... wow." Mya's eyes were big, awe glittering in her dark irises. "Your uncle owns this?"

"Yeah. My dad uses it for business sometimes." I moved up behind her, wrapping my arms around her waist. "It's just an apartment." My breath brushed the shell of her ear.

"It's really not. It's... too much. I knew you were rich, Asher, but this is... wow."

I chuckled but it came out strained because I knew what she was thinking. "You belong here, with me," I said.

I didn't want her to doubt us. Not in Rixon, not here, not anywhere. But I tried to put myself in her shoes, to imagine what it must be like to be the girl plucked out of a bad neighborhood and thrust into my life.

Mya's hand slid atop of my arms, hugging me back. "How many bedrooms are there?"

"Enough." My voice was husky as I imagined her laid out before me in nothing but a smile and lust in her eyes. "But if we don't hurry, Flick and Hailee will claim the best ones."

She turned in my arms. "They can have them. I've got all I need right here." Mya leaned up, running her tongue along the seam of my mouth. I opened willingly, desperate to taste her again. We'd practically made out the entire journey and it still wasn't enough.

I still needed more.

"Well, fuck me, it's true." My cousin Riley's voice was like a bucket of cold water. Letting out a heavy sigh, I pressed my head to Mya's, giving myself a second.

"You must be Mya," he said, coming closer.

"Hi, it's nice to meet you."

"I'm Riley and this moody bitch is my sister, Vaughn." He flicked his head to the sullen girl standing at his side.

"Hey," she said coolly, giving Mya the once over before raising a brow at me. "Cousin."

"Vaughn, it's good to see you," I said, letting her slide her slender arms around my shoulder in an awkward hug.

"We brought supplies, they're in the car," Riley said. "Where are the guys? Thought the three of you could come give me a hand and let the girls all catch up."

Vaughn glanced at me again, before she settled her focus back on Mya. I moved closer to my girl, wrapping my arm tighter around her waist, not liking the way my cousin was looking at her.

"Actually," I said, feeling all kinds of protective. "Why don't you two get the supplies and I'll send the guys down in a second?"

"Yeah, whatever." Riley gave me an easy smile, but I saw the tightness around his eyes. "Come on, sister of mine." He marched out of the penthouse, Vaughn following behind.

"So they're your cousins," Mya said, her eyes still trained on the door. "I can see the family resemblance between you and Riley, and Vaughn seems... nice."

I bristled at the tightness in her voice. "Don't worry about Vaughn."

"Oh, I'm not worried," Mya stood a little straighter, shooting me a bemused look. "She isn't the first white girl who's looked at me like I'm dirt on her shoe, and she won't be the last." She shucked out of my hold and took off deeper into the suite.

Cussing under my breath, I ran a hand down my face. This trip was supposed to be a chance to enjoy ourselves, to be a normal couple away from people's judgment.

But it was already turning into a fucking disaster.

"You good?" Cam asked me as we leaned against the balcony, watching the girls dance on the floor below. The club Riley and Vaughn had brought us to was crammed, bodies packed in like sardines. But upstairs in the VIP section it was more laid back, which was why we were up here while the girls were down there.

"Yeah, I'm good."

"Mya seems to be enjoying herself."

I let out a heavy sigh. "It's like when it's just us, or we're with you guys, things are great."

"But?"

"But not everyone's happy about us. You know what Rixon is like, what the kids at school are like. Hell, even some of the guys on the team give me shit about liking Mya."

"They don't mean anything by it."

"Don't they? You think I don't see how people look at us?"

"They're just curious, man. It's nothing personal."

"It feels fucking personal." I scrubbed my jaw, glancing back at the girls. "You saw how surprised Riley and Vaughn were, and they live here."

Wasn't New York like the city of diversity or something?

"Did they say something to you?"

"Riley? Nah, he was just surprised. I know he doesn't give a rat's ass who I'm with. But Vaughn made it obvious she didn't approve." My jaw clenched. Vaughn had since apologized for her initial reaction to Mya, but the damage was already done, and the two of them had steered clear of one another during the pre-club drinks back at the penthouse.

"I just thought we could come here and leave all the bullshit back in Rixon. But it's never going away is it? There will always be people who look at us together and disapprove."

"Fuck them all. They don't matter," Cam said. "People will always cast judgment. But you're better than that. Rise above it and just do you." He clapped me on the shoulder. "I see the way you look at Mya, you're in deep with her."

"Gone," I said quietly. "I'm totally gone for her."

It was fucking terrifying how strongly I felt about her. How desperately I wanted to make this thing between us work.

Despite all the obstacles stacked against us.

"Then that's all that matters. The rest is all white noise."

But it wasn't. It was incessant chatter, a constant hum in the background that, no matter how much I tried, I couldn't ignore.

"She told Hailee and Flick she's applied to Cleveland," Cam went on. "You know, it's only a couple hours from Pittsburgh."

"I know." I curved my hands around the railing.

"So, how do you feel about that?"

"Relieved." So fucking relieved. "But my old man isn't going to be impressed."

"What's it got to do with your dad?"

"I..." The words were right there. *Tell him. Just rip off the Band-Aid and tell him.*

Before I could get them out, Cam's expression darkened. His eyes narrowed past me. "Fuck," he hissed.

"What is—" I turned just in time to see some douche put his hands on Mya.

I took off, shouldering past a few people, ignoring Cam's yells as I hurried down the stairs and onto the dance floor. I'd lost Mya and the girls in the crowd, but I could just make out the tall fucker who had put his hands on my girl.

Anger swam in my veins as I pushed and jostled bodies out of the way, bursting through the crowd. "Touch my girl again and you'll..." The words dried on my tongue as I took in the scene before me. Mya was all up in the guy's face as he clutched his junk, eyes watering, face contorted in agony.

"You fucking bitch," he seethed.

I wedged myself between them, murder in my expression. "What the fuck did you just say?"

"You'd better put a leash on your bitch or—"

Before I knew what was happening, Mya shot around me and drove her fist straight toward the guy's face.

"Whoa there, Rocky." Jase appeared out of nowhere and caught her around the waist hauling her backward before she could do any real damage.

"You'd better keep an eye on that one," the guy mumbled, already backing up. "A girl like that will get you into all kinds of trouble."

"Get the fuck out of here." Jase clapped me on the back, a shit-eating grin plastered on his face. I'm glad someone found the situation funny, because I sure as shit didn't. But I breathed easier when I found Mya safely tucked between Flick and Hailee who, I noticed, each had a hand wrapped around her arm.

With the help of his friends, the guy limped away, taking his wounded pride with him.

"You okay?" Jase asked Mya and the girls as I stood there, trying to rein in the anger still vibrating through me. I wanted to go after the guy, I wanted to—

"He touched my ass." Mya was in front of me now, her hand touching my arm. She gave me a weak smile. "I might have overreacted a little. I'm sorry, I didn't mean to cause a scene."

Shit. She thought I was embarrassed?

Closing the distance between us, I hooked an arm around her waist and pulled her against my chest. "*Never* apologize for defending yourself."

"He was hardly attacking me, Asher," she said, rolling her eyes.

"No, but he put his hands on you without your permission. If you hadn't have kneed him in the balls, I would have." I would have done a whole lot worse than that.

"You mean you burst through the crowd, ready to defend my honor?"

"Mya, I'm pretty sure I'd walk over hot coals for you." I gazed down at her, trying to show her just how much she meant to me. But sometimes actions weren't enough. Sometimes you had to take the simplest approach and tell someone how you really felt.

Pulling her out of earshot of our friends, I brushed a stray curl from her face and leaned down, inhaling a shaky breath. "I know it's only officially been a few days and I know it's complicated and we don't know what the future holds, but I'm pretty sure I'm falling in love with you, Mya Hernandez."

Her lips parted on a soft gasp only I heard. "You weren't supposed to fall in love with me, Asher," she breathed. My heart crashed violently against my ribcage waiting for her to put me out of my misery. "But I'm glad you did."

"Yeah, and why is that?" I was fishing but I needed to hear her say the words too.

I needed her to feel the same.

"Because," she sucked in a sharp breath, "I..." Mya swallowed the words I so desperately wanted to hear. But she wasn't fooling anyone. I saw the truth glittering right there in her eyes.

She felt it, I knew she did.

"It's okay," the words came out strained. "You don't have to say it back yet."

"Ash..." Mya's eyes fluttered closed just as Khalid's *Better* blasted through the sound system. I turned Mya in my arms, tucking her body close to mine and began dancing. She might not have been ready to say the words, but she was here with me. For now, it was enough.

We moved together; Mya rolling and popping her hips, grinding on me in a way that had my dick straining against my jeans. I ran my hands up the curve of her waist, appreciating how good she looked in the halter top and shorts, how her dark caramel skin glistened under the club mood lighting. Mya tipped her head back against my shoulder, taking one of my hands in hers and pressing it to her stomach as we rocked in synchrony. The lyrics serenaded us like our own private song.

I was uncertain about a lot of things. My future. How the fuck I was supposed to sacrifice everything I loved just to keep my father happy and my mother safe. But this, standing here with Mya, knowing she was going to be in my bed at the end of the night, I was sure about.

In that moment, nothing felt better.

Until she dipped her hand around her back and let it slide down the front of my jeans. "You're playing a dangerous game, babe," I whispered against the shell of her ear as I rocked into her hand, groaning into the crook of her neck.

"Maybe I like danger." She pushed our joined hands beneath the swathe of sequined fabric covering her midriff and the waistband of her shorts.

A quick glance around told me no one was paying us any attention. We were just another couple out enjoying the night. Lingering between one year and the next. Mya slid her hand over mine, moving my fingers higher and higher until they grazed the curve of her breast.

Her very smooth, very *naked* breast.

Fuck.

I'd assumed she was wearing one of those cleverly disguised strapless bra things.

"Are you trying to kill me?" I groaned again, earning me a soft chuckle.

"It's almost midnight," she said, tilting her face so that her lips almost touched mine. "I want you inside me when the clock strikes twelve."

Fuck.

Fucking fuck.

I almost exploded right there and then. My eyes darted wildly around the room, desperately searching for somewhere—*anywhere*—I could make her wish, and all her dreams, come true. Because while I wanted nothing more than to sink deep inside of Mya, I drew the line at fucking her in public.

My eyes found Jase over the crowd and he smirked, as if that fucker could read my mind. I flipped him off. He pulled out his cell and typed something, my own cell vibrating to life seconds later. Discreetly, I dug it out of my pocket.

Jase: The car is out back. You can thank me later.

. . .

Me: Do I even want to know how you know that?

Jase: I like to be prepared.

I laughed at that. Smug bastard. Before I could type a reply, the screen lit up again.

Jase: I know I give you shit but I'm happy for you, man. Now go before I rethink my offer... happy new year!

Me: Thanks, I owe you.

Mya brushed my cheek with her nose as I pocketed my cell phone. "Please tell me that was our fairy sexmother?"

Fairy sexmother?

What the actual fuck?

"Who are you right now?" I stared at her with a potent mix of awe and lust.

"I'm just a girl who needs her boyfriend."

"Come on." Tangling our fingers together, I led Mya away from the dance floor. We didn't stop for our friends, or for the DJ as he announced the five-minute warning to the official countdown, and we sure as shit didn't stop for security as they yelled at us not to go through the emergency exit.

We spilled out into the night, the sleek black limo that had brought us to the club right where Jase had said it would be.

"Seriously?" Mya said, her brow arched. "I thought we'd go to the bathroom or something."

My lips curved mischievously. "Consider it a gift from your *fairy sexmother*. Now," I yanked the door open for her, "get inside before I fuck you on the hood of it."

23

Mya

ASHER FOLLOWED me into the plush limo, closing the door behind him and locking it. His eyes burned with hunger, his hot gaze setting my already warm skin on fire.

"Two minutes," he rasped as I sat down on one of the leather benches running down either side of the vehicle.

"W- what?"

"Two minutes until the clock chimes twelve."

"Oh." The word left my lips on a small gasp, remembering how I'd told him how I wanted to welcome in the new year.

I hadn't meant to say the words but dancing with him had been so sexy, his hands painting a trail of heat over my skin. Teasing me. Torturing me to the point of needing him so much I couldn't think of anything else.

I would never forget the way he burst through the crowd, like a knight-in-Henley-armor, with murder and possessiveness shining in his eyes.

"I want to go slow, take my time..." Asher crawled over me, pressing me into the soft leather bench, running his hand up my chest and palming my neck gently. "But I don't think I can."

"So don't." I dragged my teeth over the lobe of his ear, biting hard. A groan rumbled in his chest as his hand slid up my thighs, finding the waistband of my jeans.

"These need to come off, now," he said against the corner of my mouth.

Asher rocked back onto his haunches, and I lifted my ass off the bench, letting him pull the shorts off. His eyes went to my lacy black panties, and another groan worked its way up his throat.

"Your turn," I panted, trying to reach for him. Asher chuckled, staying just out of arm's reach as he unbuttoned his jeans and freed his dick, pushing his boxer briefs and jeans down his hips in one swift motion.

"What are you waiting for?" I needed him.

Needed him to ease the deep ache inside of me.

He smirked, stroking himself up and down, his eyes pinning me to the spot. We were half-clothed, inside a limo, in some back alley in New York, but it didn't matter.

Prowling forward on his knees, Asher grabbed my ankles and wrapped them around his waist, pulling me around him so he could nestle between my legs. His hard length nudged up against me, sending sparks shooting through my body. I tried to reach between us to guide him right to where I needed him, but Asher snagged my hand, shaking his head with a dirty smirk.

"Ten," he said, bumping up against me again, letting the tip of his dick hit my tight bundle of nerves. "Nine." Asher leaned down, capturing my lips in a slow kiss. "Eight." Rocking his hips, he ground against me but didn't give me what I needed most.

"Seven," I said, realization dawning on me as I kissed him, almost frenzied, dipping my hands underneath his Henley and raking my nails down his chest, eliciting a low growl from his chest.

"Six." It was a garbled noise in his throat as he continued dragging himself through my wetness, teasing me.

"Five." I covered his hand with mine, feeling him hard and heavy and wet between us.

"Four," we both panted, our breaths mingled with raw lust. "Three..." It was a breathy moan as he pressed closer still but not close enough. "Two..." Asher kissed me again, stealing my breath.

"One." He thrust inside of me in one smooth glide, my head bumping against leather, my fingers curling around his bicep. "Mya, fuck," he barked, pulling out and pressing back into me.

Harder.

Deeper.

I hooked my ankles together, careful not to dig the heels of my boots into his back.

"It's like you were made for me." Asher kissed the corner of my mouth, dragging his tongue over my lips and plunging deep inside as he continued rocking into me, circling his hips in that perfect way that had me arching off the bench.

"Oh God... Ash... it's..." I never wanted him to stop. The way his body moved over mine, strong and sure and so damn right. It was the most intense sex I'd ever had.

"Say it," he whispered against my lips. "Tell me you're mine, Mya. Tell me you won't let anything come between us."

"I'm yours." The words were caught somewhere between a promise and a breathy moan as I felt the waves of pleasure begin to build inside me.

"You and me, babe." He flattened his body to mine, pressing deeper. So deep I could feel him everywhere. "It's you and me."

Asher hooked my leg higher, his movements slowing as he traced letters of love across my skin. "Ash... what are you...?" I gazed up at him, flushed and breathless and aching.

"I lied," he whispered. "I need you to say it, Mya. I need to hear the words." He stole my breath as he slowly inched out of me.

"I..." Sparks of pleasure shot through me as he moved in lazy shallow strokes that had my stomach coiling tight and my legs quivering.

"More," I cried, gripping his shoulders, arching my body into him, desperate for more.

"Tell me you feel it," Asher kissed my lips, before dragging his tongue up the slope of my neck. Over and over, licking and nipping. Teasing and tasting.

"I feel it." My head was clouded with sensation, dizzy with need.

"Mya..." My name sounded like a prayer on his lips as he filled me again in one smooth stroke. "God, you feel so fucking good."

"Harder, I need you to go harder." Beads of sweat trailed down the valley of my breasts; Asher's skin slick against mine, his weight too much and not enough all at the same time.

The limo rocked beneath us. The boom of fireworks exploding overhead. Until soon I saw explosions of my own. My body shuddered, Asher's name falling from my lips over and over.

"Fuck, Mya," he let out a guttural groan, lifting his head to meet my sated gaze. "I love you. You know that, right?"

Pressing my lips together, swallowing the emotion clogging my throat, I nodded. Asher dropped his head to mine, letting us ride the lingering waves of pleasure. "You are everything I need." His lips found mine. "You, Mya. Happy New Year."

It was a new year.

New possibilities and fresh beginnings.

A chance to carve out a better future for myself.

But there wasn't only me to think about now.

There was Asher.

The guy who was slowly teaching me love knew no bounds.

"I love you." The words spilled from my lips in a single breath.

"You love me, Hernandez?" Asher asked around a grin, before brushing his lips over mine. Once. Twice. Three times. As if he needed reassurance this was real—that *I* was real.

"I love you, Asher," I repeated the words, teasing the words off my tongue. "I'm in love with you. I should have said it earlier, but I guess I was scared."

"You don't ever have to be scared with me, Mya." Asher pressed his head to mine again, taking a deep breath.

"I know." A full body shiver worked its way through me as the weight of our declaration settled over us. "Just promise me one thing, okay?"

"Anything."

"Promise me, you won't break my heart."

"Never."

Our lives were entwined now, the bonds between us weaving tighter and tighter with every moment we spent together. Until I didn't know where I ended and he began.

It both terrified and exhilarated me. The way we'd fallen so hard and fast, swept up in the allure of each other.

But I was no fool.

Even now, lying there beneath him, his taste on my lips, his love in my heart, I knew that after the fall usually came the crash.

I only hoped my heart would survive.

"What time is it?" Ash dragged my body back toward him.

"Just after nine."

"Fuck, my head..."

"Yeah?" I snorted. "I told you to lay off the shots." After we'd finally left the limo we had returned to the club and celebrated the new year with our friends. A little too hard if the throb in my skull was anything to go by.

Leaning over, I grabbed a bottle of water off the nightstand and uncapped it. "Here." I took a big gulp before passing it to Asher. He peeked an eye open, grinning up at me. "Hi," he said.

"Hi."

"Last night was kind of crazy, huh?" His heated gaze went right through me and a delicious tingle worked up my spine.

"It was—"

"Wakey wakey, lovebirds," someone hammered on the door. "Breakfast is here."

Asher's stomach rumbled as if on cue.

"You're hungry?" I asked incredulously.

"Yeah, but not for food." He tried pulling me down on top of him, but I resisted, planting my hands firmly on his chest.

"We should join them. I don't want your cousins to think I'm rude."

"Fuck my cousins. Did they even come back here with us?"

"You don't remember?"

"I'm not going to lie; everything is a little hazy. Not the limo though. I remember that." His eyes flared again, and I knew he was thinking about what we did in there.

"Vaughn dragged some guy back with her. Riley was flying solo though."

"Huh." He scrubbed a hand over his face. "Guess I drank more than I thought."

"At least you didn't puke this time." The corner of my mouth tipped as I teased him.

"I didn't say anything last night, did I?"

My heart stopped. Blood pounding between my ears.

"What do you remember?" It came out strained.

"I remember some fucker putting his hands on you... the limo... shots. But I definitely have a few black spots."

Disappointment and dread sat in the pit of my stomach.

He didn't remember.

Asher didn't remember our confession to one another.

"Mya, what is it?" He leaned up, brushing my face.

"N- nothing. I should get cleaned up." I began climbing off the bed but before I got a foot on the floor, my body had been yanked back and Asher was looming down over me.

"I love you," he said, apology shining in his eyes.

"You remember?" Confusion swirled in my chest, making it hard to breathe.

"Of course I remember. I was joking. It was supposed to be a joke to see if you'd own up to it."

"A test." My brow went up. "You mean it was a test?" I batted his chest. Hard.

"No..." The blood drained from his face. "Shit. I screwed up, babe. Forgive me?" His eyes went soft, his bottom lip sticking out.

"Don't do that to me, Asher. Don't make a game out of how we feel about each other." My hands glided up his collarbone, looping around his neck. "I might be strong, but it doesn't mean you can't break me."

"I'm sorry." He covered my face in closed-mouthed kisses. "I'm a dumbass who doesn't think. I remember everything about last night. Well, the important bits." Asher leaned down, running his nose along my cheek, his mouth lingering at my ear. "I remember how it felt being inside you in the limo."

His teeth grazed my lobe and I felt him grow hard at my stomach. "Ash..." I licked my lips. "Maybe we have time to—"

"Rise and shine, lovers. If you're not out here in five, I'm coming in," Jason yelled. "Consider yourselves warned."

"Ugh." Asher rolled off me and flopped down on the bed. I giggled into his arm.

"We should get dressed."

"He's such a fucking cockblock."

"We have time," I said, stroking my finger up the cut lines of his torso.

"Time, you think we have time?" His eyes simmered with possessiveness. "I don't want time, Mya. I want forever."

I gulped hard. The weight of his words pressing down on me.

On us.

But yet again, I was saved by another knock at the door. "Guys." It was Hailee this time. "I'm not sure I can keep Jason out any longer.

"Coming," I called. "We'll be right there."

Before Asher could grab me again, I slipped off the bed and grabbed some clothes before disappearing into the adjoining bathroom. The door clicked shut, the sound ricocheting through me. It was one thing to declare our feelings for each other... but to want forever... that was something else entirely.

Part of me wanted to believe Asher was joking; making some flippant spur of the moment comment. But the other part knew better.

Asher Bennet didn't let people in. He guarded his heart—his truths—with wit and humor. Even his best friends in the whole world didn't know about his dad.

But I did.

Asher had trusted me with his deepest darkest secrets. So when he looked me in the eye and told me he wanted forever, I believed him.

Even if it was crazy.

"Fee, baby, this looks really good, but I'm not sure I can stomach it." Asher groaned, pushing away the plate of food and dropping his head on the counter.

"It's not like I cooked it." She chuckled. "All I did was serve it."

"Still, it looks great," I said, digging into my plate of bacon and pancakes. A glass of water and a couple of Advil had worked wonders on my hangover.

"Ash, man, I know you're hurting right now, but please stop calling my girl 'Fee, baby'."

"Don't be such a caveman," Flick rolled her eyes at him.

"Yeah, Jase," Asher mumbled from his arm. "Don't be such a caveman."

"Okay, then, let's see how the fuck you like it." Jason set his sights on me and I frowned across the counter at him. "Hey, Mya, baby," he said huskily, "how are your pancakes?"

"Hmm, good, thanks." I slid my eyes to Asher who had gone tense.

Jason smirked. "You've got a little syrup right there." He stood up and leaned over the counter, his arm coming toward me. "Here, let me get—"

"Don't even think about it." Asher wrapped his hand around Jason's wrist, his eyes narrowed to deadly slits.

"Now you know how it feels."

"Not the same thing at all, and you know it."

"Yeah." Jason grinned. "It was just too tempting to fuck with you. Now eat something, it'll make you feel better."

"He this bossy with you?" Asher glanced at Felicity who blushed a deep shade of red.

"Oh, you have no idea."

"You love it," Jason said around a mouthful of bacon.

"Maybe." My friend was beet red now. "Just a little."

"I can't believe it's January first," Hailee said. "Graduation will be here before we know it."

"Bring it on if you ask me. I can't wait to get the fuck out of Rixon."

"Jason!" Felicity scolded.

They started bickering but Asher had my full attention. He was still curled in on himself, face hidden in the crook of his arm. I rested my hand on his thigh, squeezing gently. It was a show of support; a way to let him know I was here for him.

I didn't expect him to straighten, clear his throat, and say, "So I have something to say and I need you to let me get it out, okay?" His eyes flicked to mine and I silently asked him if he was sure.

"It's time," he breathed.

Anticipation rippled around us, the air thick and heavy.

"Whatever it is, we've got your back," Cam broke the awkward silence while Asher tried to find the words.

"Yeah, we're here, man," Jase added. "One hundred percent."

"I know and I appreciate it. More than you know." Asher pushed off his stool and stood up, raking a hand through his tousled bed hair. "Fuck, I don't even know how to say this."

"Ash..." I started but his eyes cut to mine, the pain behind them making the words dry on my tongue.

"Asher, it's okay," Felicity said quietly, coming around to me. "We're all here."

"Ah, fuck it," he expelled a long breath and then fixed his eyes on his two best friends and then he said the words I knew it would kill him to say.

"I won't being playing college football next season."

24

Asher

THE TWO GUYS who knew me better than anyone stared at me as if they no longer knew who I was.

"You're joking," Jase laughed but it was a strangled kind of sound that made me internally flinch. "It's a joke."

"It's not a joke, Jase," I said grimly. "I won't be playing football for the Panthers."

He sat straighter, running a brisk hand down his face. "You've lost your goddamn mind."

"Jason." Felicity shot him a harsh look before settling her eyes on me. "But you love football," she said.

"Yeah, well, football isn't going to secure my future. And we can't all be like you, man, with a shot at going pro."

Jason winced at the bitterness in my tone. I wanted to tell him it had nothing to do with him and everything to do with my piece of shit father, but I couldn't find the words.

I was still surprised I'd even told them the truth about college.

"So if you're not going to play football, what the fuck are you going to do?"

"You know Pittsburgh is my old man's alma mater. I'm going to study business and when I graduate..." the words lodged in my throat. "I'm going to help Dad expand his tech business."

"If that's what you want, man." Cam smiled but it didn't quite reach his eyes. "Then good for you."

"I still don't get it," Jase narrowed his gaze, scrutinizing me as if he saw right through my bullshit. "You can study and play football. Why would you—"

"Gotta grow up one day, right? Figured I might as well get a head start. Besides, it won't be the same without you guys."

"Ash, man, come on, this doesn't make any sense." I'd expected this, expected Jase to be the one who wouldn't let it go. "You're a Raider," he said. "The dream was always college football."

"Yeah, well, dreams change," I said, exhaling a shaky breath as I locked eyes on him. Jase didn't get it. How could he? Football had always been everything to him, the dream *and* the end goal. And despite his rocky relationship with his dad, at least Mr. Ford understood what it was like to want something so badly it consumed your every waking minute.

Right from when he first held a football, Jason was a star in his father's eyes. I was nothing but a bitter disappointment to mine.

And now I'd disappointed my best friend. The guy who had been my captain and quarterback for as long as I could remember.

We were locked in an impasse. Jason wanted to say more; it was right there in his eyes. The need to unearth my reasons, to know why it had to be like this. And I was silently pleading with him to let it go.

In the end, it wasn't me who walked away like I'd expected. It was Jason.

"Fuck," I hissed, clenching a fist against my thigh. Mya got up and came to me, wrapping her arms around my waist.

"He'll come around."

"Excuse me," Felicity jumped to her feet. "While I go beat some sense into my boyfriend."

"We should probably make a start on getting the bags," Hailee said to Cameron who was staring at me with an apologetic expression.

"He'll cool off. This is your decision, not his."

"Thanks." I gave him a sharp nod, unwilling to offer him any further explanation.

"I shouldn't have said anything," I said the second me and Mya were alone.

She craned her neck to look at me. "Maybe the whole truth would have been better."

"I tried but I'm not ready. If you think this changes things, them knowing the whole story will really screw things up."

"They're your friends, Ash, they'll understand."

Looping my arms around her, I held Mya tight to my chest. "I'm not ready."

I didn't know if I ever would be. I'd lived with this lie for so long it had become an extension of me. A ten-foot wall erected out of lousy jokes and false smiles. Telling them would be like baring myself to the world, the *real* me. Not the version people knew and loved. But the other version.

The dark tainted version that had anger simmering in his veins and pain festering in his heart.

"Okay," Mya whispered. "We'll figure it out."

"As long as I have you, it'll be okay." My lips fixed over hers, finding solace in her softness, the little noises she made as my tongue stroked hers. Being with Mya was going to be complicated. But my whole fucking life was complicated.

At least with her by my side, I didn't have to face the shitstorm alone.

AFTER GIVING EVERYONE A RIDE HOME, I returned the minivan to the rental place and picked up my Jeep. Mya had offered to ride with me, but I needed space. Time to clear my head, ready to deal with Dad's bullshit when I got home.

Pushing open the door, I steeled myself when his voice drifted down the hall. "Asher, Son, we're in the kitchen."

Waiting to pounce, no doubt.

I ditched my bags by the staircase and made my way toward the back of the house.

"Happy New Year, sweetheart," Mom greeted me first, her smile too wide, her eyes red and swollen.

She'd been crying.

Which meant he'd upset her.

Anger boiled in my blood. "Happy New Year, Mom. Dad." I gave him a sharp nod while I hugged Mom.

"Did you have fun?" she asked, her voice significantly lower than usual.

"New York was great, thanks." I forced a smile. "Did you have a nice evening?"

Dad and Mom spent every year at The Danforth, the only five-star hotel and restaurant in a twenty-five-mile radius. They always hosted an extravagant and exclusive dinner. It was the perfect place for Dad to rub shoulders with the other businessmen and wealthy people living in the local area.

"It was..." She hesitated, telling me all I needed to know, "lovely."

Dad grunted. "The Ginly's were there. Good people. Malcolm and I were hoping that since you and Kellie will be attending Pittsburgh in the fall together, that maybe you could—"

"The rest of the year is mine," I ground out. "Isn't that what you said?"

"I did. But then I didn't expect you to be gallivanting around town with the Hernandez girl."

"Mya. Her name is Mya."

"I know very well what her name is, Son. What I can't quite understand though is if you're dating her to make a point or because you genuinely care about the girl?"

"Care about her?" I spat. "I don't fucking care about her. I love her. I'm in love with her." My chest heaved with the weight of the words.

"Love?" He chuckled darkly, the sound making my muscles tense. "You're eighteen, Son. Love is for fools."

Mom let out a pained gasp behind me, and then fled from the kitchen.

"Nice, Dad. Real nice."

"Your mother knows how I feel about her."

I wasn't sure being a possessive jealous asshole translated into love, but what the hell did I know?

"Mya isn't going anywhere," I said resolutely. "So you need to get to used to that. I've kept my end of the bargain. I'm still going to Pittsburgh; I'm still going to focus on my degree and leave football behind."

"Son." My father rubbed his brow. "Mya is... not suited for our world. I'm sure she's a lovely girl, but—"

"Save your condescending racist bullshit for someone who cares. There are still five months until graduation. Five months where I get to say how I live my life."

He bristled, irritation flashing in his eyes. "Watch your tone, Asher. You might still have five months, but if you think for a second I'll just stand by and watch you screw up your life for a girl who probably only sees you as her meal ticket, you've got another think coming."

He was deluded.

Completely and utterly deluded.

Mya didn't love me because of my family's wealth. She loved me in spite of that.

But he saw all relationships as business transactions. What one person could do for another. In fact, I was pretty sure there was a dollar sign right where his heart was supposed to be.

"I'm done," I said, moving toward the door.

"You're making a terrible mistake, Son. Mark my words, one way or another, that girl will ruin you."

With a final shake of my head, I walked away from him. From the one man I should have been able to look up to and go to for advice. But Andrew Bennet was no more of a father to me than Cam's dad or Jason's dad had been. It wasn't any wonder, I craved the affection he'd never afforded me. And now I'd had a taste of it, I wasn't sure I could ever give it up.

My father's warnings be damned.

"Are you sure you're okay?" Mya asked me for the third time since I'd picked her up. As if my mood wasn't bad enough after my conversation with Dad, her aunt had scowled at me from the window, her disapproval burning into me.

"I'm good," I said tightly, stuffing another fry in my mouth. I'd brought her to Bell's for some food and then the guys were going to join us with Hailee and Felicity.

"Ash... if something happened when you got home—"

"I said I'm good," I snapped, then let out a heavy sigh, dragging a hand down my face. "Sorry, that was uncalled for. My dad ambushed me; it wasn't pretty."

"Let me guess," her expression fell, "he's not happy about us?"

"I don't give a flying fuck if he's happy or not. I'm happy, *you* make me happy." I reached across the booth for her and Mya laid her hand in mine. "Five months," I said gruffly, her touch already soothing the tension coiled tightly in my chest. "We just have to survive another five months and then we can escape to college and not have everyone breathing down our necks."

"Asher, I still haven't decided which college I'm—"

"Asher, my man." Grady and Merrick approached us when all I really wanted was to tell them to fuck off so I could beg Mya to say she'd choose Cleveland.

I *needed* her to choose a school close to me.

"Didn't expect to see you here." His eyes flicked to Mya in question.

"We're meeting the guys," I said. "They'll be here soon."

"Jerry will need to hang a sign soon." Grady snorted.

"Come again?"

"First Cam, then Jase, and now you. Shit, man, these girls must have golden fucking pussies or—"

I was up and out of the booth in a second, my hands fisted in Grady's sweater. "What the fuck is your problem?"

"Whoa, Bennet, relax," Merrick came to our teammate's defense. "He's just goofing around."

"Yeah, well I'm fucking sick of it."

Grady shoved me off him and the two of us squared up to one another, eyes narrowed, jaws set.

"Asher..." Mya had gotten up too. I felt her move to my side. "He's not worth it."

"You think just because Bennet's showing you some attention, you're special?" Laughter rumbled in Grady's chest as he tried to save face. We had an audience now, everyone including Jerry watching.

Mya inched forward, her lips pressed into a thin line as she went toe to toe with the Raiders defensive end. "Jealous, Grady?"

"Jealous?" he stuttered over the words. "Why the hell would I be jealous?"

Mya arched her brow, a smug smile tugging at her lips. "Because you'll never come close to getting a piece of ass as hot as this." She blew him a kiss before sauntering off toward the restrooms like nothing had happened.

The three of us watched, mouths hanging open.

"Holy shit, Bennet. That was..."

"Hot as fuck." Merrick finished for him.

"Don't get any ideas," I said, feeling my chest tighten again. "She's mine."

"Yeah, but how yours are we talking?"

"Grady."

"Yeah, man?"

It wasn't a question, but I answered him anyway. "Shut the hell up."

The friction between us had dissipated, replaced with a different tension. I saw the hunger in his eyes, but I wasn't sure it was Mya he wanted, not really. My girl had struck a chord with him. He was jealous and instead of being happy for us, he lashed out.

Since I knew all about that, I decided to cut the guy some slack.

"Jesus, Bennet, she's a firecracker, that one," Merrick added.

"Yeah, but is she a firecracker in the sa—"

I levelled Grady with a hard look and he swallowed the words. "No more talking shit around Mya, got it?"

"Yeah, I got it," he grumbled, rubbing his jaw.

Mya returned a couple of minutes later, slipping her arm around me. "Miss me?"

"Always."

She smirked over at Grady and Merrick who had taken up residence at the booth over from ours. "Think he got the message?"

"Oh, he got the message all right. But now he wants his very own Mya-doll."

"He does?"

I nodded, fighting a smile. "I think you have a new fan club."

"Grady?" Mya shuddered, her expression one of disbelief. "But he's so... *Grady*."

I chuckled at that. "Sorry for acting like a caveman earlier. Lately my default setting is to attack."

"I know exactly how you feel," she whispered. "When do your parents leave?"

"Tomorrow, thank fuck."

"And they'll be gone for how long?" Her fingers toyed with my collar and I struggled to think straight, my thoughts shooting off in a hundred different directions, all which ended with her. Naked. Underneath me.

"I'm not sure. Could be four days, could be a week. Why?"

Mya's eyes darkened, her teeth biting into her bottom lip. "No reason."

"You want to play house with me, babe?"

"I wouldn't say no to it." She gave me a coy smile, and just like that all thoughts of my dad and Grady and her aunt disappeared.

25

Mya

THE REST of the holidays were uneventful. Asher's parents ended up being away for almost a week and by the time they got back, which was supposed to be this evening, school was looming.

"I don't want to go back to reality," I said to Asher, as we lay curled up on his bed.

I'd spent almost every waking minute at his house; sometimes just the two of us, sometimes with our friends. Aunt Ciara and I were barely talking; her disapproval at how easily I'd given Asher my heart too much for her to accept.

But I was happy.

Asher made me happy.

I knew the road ahead was littered with bumps and obstacles but being with him felt too good to worry.

He peppered my face with big wet kisses. "I don't think I can let you go."

"You have to," I giggled, pressing my hands against his chest, pretending to resist.

Asher rolled us so I was beneath him. Brushing his nose featherlight across my jaw, my cheek, he kissed the corner of my mouth. "I wish they didn't have to come home and ruin this."

"No you don't," I sighed, looping my arms around his neck. "You love your mom."

"You're right, I do. But sometimes, fuck, Mya, sometimes I wish she'd stand up to him. Money isn't everything. We'd make it work somehow. I hate the idea that she's beholden to a life of misery with him."

Brushing the golden strands of hair from his eyes, I gave him a small smile. "He's her husband and despite all his faults, she loves him. Staying isn't always the easy way out, Ash."

I knew that firsthand.

"Yeah, it's just... the price feels too high, ya know?"

"I know. But she has to follow her heart and make her own mistakes. Otherwise she'll just end up resenting you."

I hated that, in their own way, Asher's parents had both let him down.

He deserved so much more. He deserved to have all his dreams come true. But it was my past and his present that had led us here, to this exact moment, and I couldn't regret or feel sorry for that.

Our experiences shaped us. Molded us into the people we were today. Pain, heartache, happiness, and hope, all contributed to who we became. So while I wished things had been different for both of us, I also knew we were the people we were now because of everything we'd been through.

I buried my face into Asher's chest, relishing how good it felt to be in his arms.

"I know there are a million reasons why I probably shouldn't say this," he whispered into my hair. "But pick Cleveland, Mya. Pick me."

"Ash..." My hands tightened around him.

"I don't need an answer yet," he said. "I just wanted you to know, I don't care about how long it has or hasn't been, or what the next five months might bring. I know what I want and I want you, Mya. Always."

I didn't answer him.

I couldn't, the lump in my throat too big.

But if I'd have been brave enough to give him an answer, I was pretty sure it would have been yes.

MONDAY MORNING ROLLED AROUND TOO QUICKLY. Asher insisted on giving me a ride, pulling the boyfriend card. It was a nice normal couple thing to do. But the second we climbed out of the Jeep, I remembered that nothing about our relationship was normal; at least not in the eyes of most of our classmates.

"Ignore them," he said, grabbing my hand in a show of a solidarity. Asher pulled it to his mouth and kissed my knuckles. A couple of girls sneered in my direction. I sneered right back.

"Hey, there you are." Felicity made her way over to us. "I see you have quite the audience." She glanced over at another huddle of girls who were pretending not to watch us. "You know they're just jealous that Asher is officially off the market."

"Maybe I should just pee on him now, get the message across."

"I'm down for most things," Asher grinned at me, "but I draw the line at that."

"Where are the guys?" he asked Flick.

"Jason said something about hitting the gym."

"He's taking the exhibition game seriously, huh?"

"I guess."

"You can go," I said. "I can walk to class with Felicity."

His eyes slid to where the girls were still huddled, and still staring.

"Go," Flick urged him. "We've got this."

"See you at lunch?"

I nodded, leaning in to kiss him. Felicity squealed under her breath, but it barely registered when his lips touched mine.

"Try to ignore them," he whispered.

"Them who?" I grimaced.

"That's my girl."

"Go, before I beg you to stay."

Asher took off toward the gym, leaving me and Felicity to head into school together. She looped her arm through mine. "You two are so f'in cute, I can barely stand it."

"They're still staring, right?" I said through gritted teeth.

She glanced back and let out an irritated sigh. "Yep."

"Guess I'd better get used to it now the cat's out of the bag."

"They'll get over it. Come lunch there'll be some new drama or scandal for them to salivate over."

"I hope you're right because we've only been here ten minutes and I already want to punch something."

We'd barely made it into the building when a saccharine sweet voice said, "Hey, Mya."

"Hmm, hey, Kellie, right?" My mean girl radar went on high alert.

"Yeah, we met briefly at the Bennets' party."

"Yeah, I remember," I said, coolly.

"Well, anyway, I just wanted to say hey. We should totally hang out some time. You too, Fee."

"Felicity," she corrected. "My name is Felicity."

"Oh, my bad." Kellie laughed, the sound like nails grating on a chalkboard. "I just heard Asher call you Fee this one time and figured—"

"It's a nickname my *friends* use."

Ouch, burn. I stifled a snicker.

Kellie's eyes widened with surprise, but she recovered quickly, pasting on a false smile. "I should go but don't forget what I said about hanging out."

"Like that is ever going to happen," Felicity mumbled under her breath.

When Kellie was gone, I turned to her, my brows pinched. "What the hell was that?"

"I think that was a perfect example of keeping your friends close and your enemies closer."

"Just what I need," I groaned, "more enemies."

"You don't need to worry about Kellie, she's no one."

But even I knew it was always the *no ones* you had to worry about.

"You're vibrating." Asher dropped his gaze to my pocket, but I nudged his face with mine, coaxing him back to me.

It was lunch and we were sitting with the guys and the rest of the team. It was weird, sitting here as his girlfriend rather than his best friends' girlfriends' friend. But no one gave us shit about it. In fact, no one cracked a single joke.

The fact wasn't lost on me.

"Did you orchestrate this?" I asked him, ignoring the vibrations in my pocket.

"I have no idea what you're talking about."

My eyes narrowed, as I glanced around the table. A couple of the guys smiled, but no one made a single remark. Not even Grady, who always had something to say.

"So you're telling me this is just business as usual?"

The corner of Asher's mouth tipped. "I said *I* didn't do anything..." he let the words hang, but it was when his eyes slid to Jason that realization dawned on me.

"You did this?" I asked the brooding quarterback.

"I may have said something."

I didn't know whether to be flattered or offended. My natural instinct was to tell Jason I didn't need his help, that I could fight my own battles. But as I was slowly learning about my friends, you didn't have to fight things alone.

"Thank you," I said, offering him an appreciative nod.

He shrugged as if it was nothing.

It wasn't.

Asher slipped his arm around my waist and pulled me into his side. "You're one of us now," he whispered against my ear.

I couldn't help but smile. But it quickly fell when I felt someone watching me. My eyes searched the cafeteria, landing on Kellie Ginly at the gymnasts' table. Her mouth curved when she realized I'd noticed her.

"What's wrong?" Asher asked, commanding my attention. I hadn't even felt myself tense.

"Nothing," I lied, sliding my eyes back to Kellie. She wasn't watching now, busy talking to her friends.

Asher played with the bracelet ringing my wrist. "I know you're technically already wearing my number," he said. "But the exhibition game is my last game and well, I'd really like it if—"

"Yes," I breathed, leaning back to kiss him.

He chuckled. "You don't even know the question yet."

"You're going to ask me to wear your jersey to the game."

"Actually, I was going to ask you if you'd wear one of those Vinnie the Viking hats."

"Liar."

His arms looped around me tighter. "So you'll do it? You'll wear my jersey?"

I nodded, feeling my heart flutter in my chest.

"Everyone will know you're mine." I felt him smile against my hair.

"Isn't that the point?" I glanced back at him, our eyes locking on each other's. Asher's gaze burned with pride.

"I hadn't expected you to say yes."

"I'm not ashamed of you, Asher. I'm not ashamed of us. And I'm done hiding."

The way gossip flew around the halls at Rixon meant everyone probably already knew about us, and if they didn't, they would come game day.

"My mom and dad will be there..." He let the words hang.

"Good," I said. "They should be."

"I think I like this side of you." He dropped a kiss on the end of my nose.

"Isn't jealousy and possessiveness supposed to be a turn off?" My brow rose.

"Maybe but it's having the opposite effect on me." His eyes darkened, and I leaned in, brushing my lips over his.

"You want to skip fifth period?" I asked.

"Fuck, yes I—"

"Okay, you two," Jason's voice cut through air. "Break it up before we all see something we can't ever unsee."

Asher flipped Jason off, laughter rumbling in his chest. "Tonight," he whispered back at me.

I gave him a small nod, my stomach coiled tight at his promise.

I was already counting the hours.

By the time the final bell went, I was more than ready to get the hell out of school. Being Asher Bennet's girlfriend would have elevated anyone to celebrity status in the halls of Rixon High but being his girlfriend *and* the Latina transfer from Fallowfield Heights... well that shit made me infamous.

I spent the entire afternoon overhearing my name in hushed conversations. Some were simple curiosity at the outsider who had managed to land herself one of the most eligible guys in school. But others were so farfetched, my eyes ached from all the rolling. And some were just too close to the truth that I'd sat and listened, my heart almost beating out of my chest.

Apparently, everyone had a story about me now, and if they didn't, they knew someone who did.

But I forced myself to let their words roll off my back. Asher loved me.

Me.

He knew about Jermaine and my life in Fallowfield Heights, and he loved me anyway.

At least, that's what I told myself as I filed out of class to meet him.

But when I turned the corner and found him talking to none other than

Kellie Ginly, I froze on the spot, my resolve crumbling around me. She spotted me over his shoulder, her saccharine sweet smile growing into something twisted and ugly and too big for her heart-shaped face. She laughed at something Asher said, making a show of tucking a strand of poker straight blonde hair behind her ear.

And then she touched him.

She laid one of her perfectly manicured hands on his shoulder and leaned in, like they were two old friends sharing a private joke.

The hall was already emptying around us, but Asher had no idea I was standing there, watching them. How perfect they looked together. His All-American good looks and her beauty pageant complexion.

But she knew.

Her eyes flicked to mine more than once, a wicked glint there.

A warning.

She might as well have pissed up his leg and claimed her territory.

But he's not hers, he's yours, a little voice reminded me.

Refusing to be the girl who was intimidated by someone like her, I steeled myself and marched up to them. "Hey," I said, my voice weaker than I wanted it to be.

"Oh, Mya, hey." Kellie flicked her hair off her shoulder and smiled. "I was just filling Asher in on our class notes since he missed it."

"That's... nice of you." I forced out the words.

Asher's gaze burned into the side of my face, but I couldn't look at him. Not until I'd reined in the anger and jealousy coursing through my veins. Surprising me though, he slipped his arm around my waist and kissed my cheek.

"I missed you," he said as if Kellie wasn't standing right there.

"Awww, you guys are the cutest. I was so surprised when my dad told me you were dating someone. I told him, 'Asher doesn't date, Daddy', but then I saw you guys at the party and well, I was wrong. You're a very lucky girl, Mya."

I barely managed to choke out a garbled, "Yeah."

"Thanks for the notes, Kellie. See you around," Asher dismissed her, his eyes only for me.

"Oh yeah, sure. See you." She trotted off.

"She's wrong you know?" he said before I could even formulate words.

"Wrong?"

"You're not the lucky one. I am." Asher pressed me against the locker, hands either side of my head.

"You two look good together," I said, the words spilling from my lips in a blast of jealousy.

"I'm not going to let you do this, Mya."

I pressed my lips together in defiance, hating the way he saw right through me.

"It's you I want, *you* I love." He leaned in, his lips brushing the shell of my ear. "You I'll be buried deep inside of later. Kellie Ginly is no one to me. No. One. How could I even see her when all I see is you?"

He pulled back to look at me, his expression softening. "Better?"

"A little," I said, feeling some of the anger ebb away. "But you should probably keep going. Just to be sure."

I was joking but challenge flared in Asher's eyes.

A challenge I'd gladly let him win.

26

Asher

"LOOK ALIVE, LADIES," Coach Hasson boomed as he entered the locker room. "It's a full house out there and the Eagles are looking for blood." A wave of grumbles rose around me. "I want a clean game, got it?"

"Yes, Sir." Our collective response echoed off the walls.

"This marks the start of a clean slate. We go out there and win the way we know how, through hard work, teamwork, and giving it our all. Jase, Son, do you want to say a few words?"

My best friend stalked into the center of the room, helmet hanging by his side, hunger glittering in his eyes. "Being a Raider, leading this team, has been a privilege and something I will never forget. But Coach is right. This game is a chance to put all the bullshit with Rixon East behind us. A chance to show them once and for all who the better team is on and off the field. Kinnicky, I'm looking to you tonight to step up to the plate and prove you've got what it takes to lead after I'm gone."

My gaze snapped to Cam who looked as confused as I did.

"Coach, I'll lead the team into the game," he said, "but I think Kinnicky should take my place in the third quarter."

"Are you sure that's—"

"It's the right call." Jase nodded at Kinnicky across the huddle. The junior looked ready to piss his pants, but he managed to stand tall and return his quarterback's nod.

"Well, all right then." Coach looked to me. "Asher, how about it, Son? One final time."

My chest tightened, Coach's words like a vise around my throat.

This was it.

The last time I'd ever put on my jersey and play with my teammates. My best friends and brothers, for all intents and purposes.

"Asher..."

Everyone was staring at me, waiting for me to leap into action and get them pumped up. But there was something so bittersweet about it, I could barely find the words.

Until Jase caught my eye and said, "Together, we'll do it together."

With a tight smile, I moved into the center with him. He slung his arm around my shoulder and shouted, "Who are we?"

"Raiders," the team replied.

"I said who are we?" My voice rang out, strong and clear, spurred on by my best friend's reassurance.

"RAIDERS." The team echoed back at us, their collective roar sending a surge of energy coursing through me.

"And what are we?"

"Family." Jase squeezed my shoulder, his eyes sliding to mine, saying a hundred things I knew I'd never hear. This time, on the field as a team, and off the team as brothers, it was everything.

"And what are we gonna do?" I grinned at him, falling into my role with such ease, despite the deep ache in my heart.

"Win."

"I said what are we gonna do?"

"WIN!"

Adrenaline pumped through me, the kind of high that could only come from being surrounded by your teammates; the guys who had seen you at your best, your worst, even your butt nakedness. Four years of my life had been dedicated to them. To the team. Four years that had flown by too quickly.

And now, it was at an end and I would never have this again.

"One more time," Jase said quietly, squeezing my shoulder, and I knew his words were for me and me alone. He might not have understood my decision to give up college football, but right now, it didn't matter. All that mattered was going out there and playing the best game we could possibly play.

Kicking some Eagle ass in the process.

Adrenaline pumped through me as I pushed my legs harder, eating up the distance between me and my target. Head down, shoulders squared, I drove straight into the offensive player's side, tackling him to the ground. He landed with a loud thud, fumbling the ball.

"Nice, Bennet," someone yelled as the rest of our players closed in.

We were winning comfortably in the fourth quarter, the Eagles disorganized and sloppy with no Lewis Thatcher to lead them. It didn't stop us from going hard. The hunger for the win tethered us, pushing us harder, faster.

I'd been prepared not to play with my team again, but now I was out here, the roar of the crowd fueled me. And knowing Mya was out there watching me only made me stand taller.

God, I was going to miss this. I'd been lying to myself; thinking I could go off to college and focus on school instead of football. But being out here, wearing a blue and white jersey, it meant something.

Something I couldn't just forget.

"Nice tackle, Son," Coach said, offering me a stiff nod, as I jogged off field to let the offense do their thing.

"This one's for you," Jase clapped me on the back as he jogged out to the huddle, ready to give the play.

"How does it feel being back out there?" Coach asked me, keeping his eyes ahead.

"It feels good, Sir."

"The Panthers will be lucky to have you next season, Son." The words hung between us, and I half-expected him to call me out on why I hadn't yet committed to the team.

He didn't though. Jason threw a perfect ball to Cameron who took off down field, every single Raiders fan making the run with him.

"Go, go," Coach yelled, thrusting his clipboard in the air, as if it was the final play in the Championship game.

"Touchdoooooown!" the announcer yelled over the PA system, sending the stadium into a frenzy.

Jase caught my eye across the field, understanding passing between us. Football would always be a huge part of us, of our friendship. I didn't doubt that. But he was only just beginning his journey. While mine... mine ended here.

And I had to be okay with that.

"You did it," Felicity and Hailee rushed over to us. Jason caught his girl, pulling her in for a kiss.

"We never doubted you for a second." Hailee smiled, nestling into Cam's side.

"Where's Mya?" I searched the crowd for her jersey but couldn't find her among the friends and family who had flooded the field to help celebrate our win.

"She got a call," Flick said, coming up for air. "I'm sure it's nothing."

"Son," my dad's voice cut the air like a knife and my spine snapped straight.

"Mr. Bennet," Jase said coolly. "Nice to see you."

The air turned tense as my friends watched our interaction. They still didn't know the whole story, but I figured they had begun to slowly piece things together.

"I wanted to be here to show my support for the team. I've donated a sizeable check to the charity."

"That's great, Sir," Cam said, ever the peacekeeper.

"Where's Mom?" I asked him.

"She's talking to Cameron's parents. You know how he gets whenever Xander is around."

She loved that kid almost as much as she loved me.

"I should probably go and say hello." Cameron gave me a nod. "I'll catch you later at Bell's?"

But just as he turned to head over to the bleachers, something caught my eye. "Is that—"

"Oh God," Felicity breathed as she took off toward Mya and the tall black guy she was talking to.

"What the fuck?" Jason grumbled.

"I think that's Mya's ex."

"Shit."

I was already moving but Dad's voice gave me pause. "I really don't think now is the time for this, Son. Miss Hernandez and her friend obviously have some things to talk about."

They were beyond the perimeter of the stadium, huddled by the fence. It was too far to read Mya's expression, but my gut told me it wasn't a friendly visit. And if my dad thought for one second I was about to leave Mya—the girl who owned my fucking heart and soul—alone with her ex, he was sorely mistaken.

"We should go and make sure she's okay, Mr. Bennet," Jase said, clapping me on the back. "Come on."

We broke out into a steady jog. "I take it this is a surprise?" Jase side-eyed me as we slowed our approach.

"He isn't supposed to know she's in Rixon." A whirlwind of emotions churned inside me. I didn't know what to think, what to feel. I had so many questions, but nothing outweighed my need to get to Mya and make sure she was okay.

Felicity had already reached them, taking Mya's side as she continued to talk to Jermaine. Although now we were closer, I could see that they weren't talking at all—she was begging him to leave.

"Babe, everything okay?" Jason was as cool as a cucumber as he strode up to Flick.

"Yeah, we're okay. Mya was just introducing me to her friend Jermaine." Her eyes flicked to mine. But I was too busy watching my girlfriend watch her ex.

"I'm Jason," he extended his hand to Jermaine. But the dude just stared at it. "And this is Asher."

His eyes slid to mine, sharp and assessing, even if his posture was still relaxed and easy. "Asher." He rolled my name around on his tongue. "You the guy tryin' to make a move on my girl?"

"J," Mya said. "I'm not your girl anymore."

Her eyes finally met mine, swirling with too many things.

"Don't be like that, baby girl. You know me and you got history. We're always gonna have history."

"Exactly. History. We have *history,* Jermaine, as in, it's in the past." She let out a strained sigh. "You should go."

"We drove all the way out here to see you and you gonna dismiss me, just like that?"

"Jermaine, please." Mya's voice cracked.

"Maybe you should leave," Jason said. I was still rooted to the spot, my thoughts running at a mile a minute trying to figure out why he was here.

How he was here.

"Really, you're going to pick these white boys over me? I came for you, baby girl. Came to make things right between us."

"You shouldn't have," Mya almost choked over the words, and I could see she was hanging on by a thread. "I'll call you later, okay?" The words spilled from her lips in a hurried jumble. "Let me finish up here and then I'll call you."

"A'ight. We can stick around a while."

What the fuck was happening?

Was she having second thoughts after seeing him again?

Jason glared at me, his heavy stare nudging me do something. To say something. But I was paralyzed by the situation. By the idea that Mya had anything to do with Jermaine being here, in Rixon.

"Come on," Felicity urged Mya to start walking. "We should get back to everyone."

But I couldn't move. Mya caught my eye, silently begging me to go with them.

"Go on ahead," I said tightly. "I'll be right there."

A sly smirk tugged at Jermaine's mouth, as if knew exactly what I was thinking. Jason gave me an understanding nod, herding the girls away despite Mya's protests. When they were out of earshot, I edged closer, locking eyes with him. He was taller than me by about an inch but where I was broad, the guy was lean.

"You the one my girl's fucking around with?" He got straight to the point.

"She isn't your girl and that's none of your fucking business."

"You think a chump like you is going to keep her?" He arched a thick, dark brow. "Mya doesn't belong in your world. She belongs with me."

"That must be why she's here with me and not back in Philly with you then."

We'd moved closer now, standing almost nose to nose. My own anger and possessiveness reflected back at me in his eyes.

"I was her first," he drawled, and I was almost certain the guy was high. "Her first kiss, her first fuck, her first everything. You think she's just going to forget that? Forget what we had? Why do you think she came home? Because she needed a little of what only I can give her."

Don't let him provoke you. I forced myself to take a step back, fists clenched tightly at my sides. "Mya ended things with you. If you care about her at all, you need to let her go."

"Let her go?" He sneered, clucking his tongue. "I'll never let her go, she's in my blood. I need her."

"Asher," her voice reverberated inside me and I closed my eyes, inhaling a ragged breath. "Let's go, *please*."

Our eyes met and I couldn't do anything but go to her.

"Well, would you look at that," Jermaine mocked. "You running around after her like a little bitch boy."

My body locked up as I glanced back, but Mya slid her hand in my mine and pulled me away. "Don't," she said. "He's not worth it."

He wasn't.

But Mya was.

As we walked away, I couldn't help but think that I'd made a mistake going too easy on the guy.

27

Mya

THE MOOD WAS tense as we rode to Bell's. Asher's parents had insisted on taking us out for dinner.

All of us.

Jason and Felicity were riding together, and Cam and Hailee were riding with his parents. Which left me to ride with the Bennets. After witnessing me arguing with Jermaine, I was surprised my invitation hadn't been revoked.

Asher was quiet, too quiet; but his dad... well, his dad was deadly silent.

Thankfully, we pulled into the parking lot within minutes, and Mr. Bennet cut the engine. "We'll see the two of you inside," he said, motioning for his wife to join him. They disappeared inside leaving me with Asher.

"Tell me there's a reasonable explanation for him being here?"

"What the hell is that supposed to mean?" I ground out, not liking the accusation in his voice.

"You told me he didn't know where you were. You looked me in the eye and told me—"

"I didn't tell him." My blood ran cold. "He convinced my friend, Shona, to tell him. She tried to call me, but it was too late."

Asher ran a hand down his face, cussing under his breath.

"Ash..." I laid a hand on his arm, hating the distance between us. "Seeing him surprised me as much as it did you."

"So that's your ex?" A sad smile tipped the corner of his lips. "I thought he'd be... taller."

I managed a small laugh. "When I talk to him later, I'll tell him he can't be here. That it's over. I'll make him—"

The color drained from his face and I knew I'd messed up. "You're not seriously going to meet him?"

Guilt slithered around my heart. "I have to. If I don't..." I didn't like to think about what Jermaine would do. No, the only logical plan was to meet and talk to him and hope I could make him see sense.

"I'll come with you," Asher said, defiance burning in his eyes.

"I don't think that's a good idea."

Yanking his arm away, Asher folded into himself. "Do you still want him?" His eyes slid to mine, the vulnerability in his expression like a hammer to the chest, cracking my ribs wide open and leaving my heart bloody on the floor.

"No. *No,* Asher. I love you. I'm in love with *you*. But Jermaine is... complicated. I have to talk to him." I shuffled across the seat and cupped his face, gently pressing my forehead to his. "I am so sorry he's here. But he's a part of my past, a part of who I am. I thought you accepted that."

His hand drifted to my cheek. "I do. I just... shit, Mya. Seeing the two of you like that. I wanted to kill him with my bare hands."

My eyes fluttered shut as I drew in a harsh breath. I didn't want Asher anywhere near Jermaine. It had been hard enough watching the two of them square up to one another while Jason and Felicity all but dragged me away.

"We should go inside," he said, breaking the heavy silence. "Everyone is waiting."

I leaned in to kiss him, but Asher turned his head, my lips grazing his jaw. His rejection burned through me like acid. But I couldn't blame him. Knowing about my past with Jermaine was one thing, having it shoved in his face was another.

We climbed out of his dad's car and walked into Bell's together, despite the growing distance between us. Felicity and Hailee came straight up to me while Asher disappeared into the sea of people gathered to celebrate the Raider's win.

"Are you okay?" Flick asked, her eyes gleaming with concern.

"I can't believe he's here." I swallowed hard. "He's not supposed to be here."

The second I'd turned on my cell and saw all the missed calls from Shona I knew something was wrong. But it was the single text of Jesse that confirmed it. Jermaine and his guys had followed Shona home to an empty house and threatened to trash the place if she didn't tell him where I was. I knew my best friend and I knew how feisty she was, and deep down, I knew she wouldn't have given up my whereabouts unless she felt she had no other choice.

"Where is he now?" Hailee asked.

"I told him I'd meet him later to talk."

"What the hell, Mya?" Flick's eyes almost bugged out of her head. "You know that is a bad idea. Asher will—"

"What else would you have me do?" I gritted out, trying to hide the nervous energy coursing through me.

Her eyes flitted past me and I didn't need to turn around to know who was watching me. "Okay," she let out a weary sigh, "let's just try to get through dinner and then we can figure out what to do."

With a small nod, I followed them to the long table Jerry had arranged for us. Mr. Bennet sat at the head of it, with Asher to his left and his wife to his right. His cold gaze met mine as he said, "Jason, son, why don't you move up one and let the girls sit together?"

He didn't need to say the words for me to know I was being cut out. I glanced at Asher, half-expecting him to come to my defense, but he didn't, not this time.

My blood ran cold.

What had started as one of the best days of my life, standing in the bleachers wearing my boyfriend's number as I cheered him and his team on, was turning into my worst nightmare.

As I took my seat between Felicity and Hailee, I'd never felt more of an outsider. Felicity grabbed my hand under the table and squeezed. "Just breathe," she whispered.

Cameron's mom sat opposite me, a picture of happiness as she played with Xander who sat between her and Mr. Chase.

"What's your name?" he asked me.

"Hi, I'm Mya."

"It's nice to meet you, Mya," Cameron's mom smiled. "I'm Cameron and this little monster's mom. You're Asher's girlfriend, right?"

I nodded, too choked up to reply.

"Asher ot a irlfriend." Xander picked up his sippy cup and thrust it in the air, sending juice flying everywhere. "Asher kissy his irlfriend."

Cameron, Hailee, and his parents smothered their laughter while the other end of the table remained quiet. It was like being stuck between sunshine and a thunderstorm.

"Xander, remember what we talked about, buddy?" Cameron gave his little brother his best serious stare.

"Me gots to behave if I want to be a big boy."

"That's right, buddy."

"Cam?" A little grin tugged at his mouth.

"Yeah, Xan?"

"Do you kissy Ailee still?"

Quiet laughter came from the dreary end of the table and I peeked around Felicity and Jason at Asher. A half-smile barely hid his amusement. But when his eyes met mine, it melted away replaced with regret.

God, I hated this.

I hated that Jermaine, and his dad, and my aunt, had the power to come between us so easily.

I hated that no matter how much we tried to be strong, there would always be something—*or someone*—trying to come between us.

Asher looked away first, giving the server his full attention. Cameron's mom offered me a knowing smile, but it did little to ease the tightness in my chest, because not only did I have to survive this dinner.

I also had to survive seeing Jermaine again.

For the next hour, I ate and smiled and pretended that on the inside it wasn't killing me to sit there and act as if everything was okay.

In some ways, it was a relief I wasn't seated closer to Asher and his parents. Xander provided constant amusement, entertaining us with his random toddler outbursts, and Mr. and Mrs. Chase were both warm and friendly, treating me with the respect Mr. Bennet hadn't afforded me. But I'd kept an ear on the conversation between Asher's and Jason's parents. Surprisingly, Mr. Ford didn't bring up football, and I wondered if Jason had warned him to not mention it.

"A toast," Mr. Bennet's deep voice commanded our attention. He stood up, glass raised. "To good friends and future adventures."

Everyone lifted their drinks, a collective chorus of, "good friends and future adventures," echoing around us.

He was a good actor, giving no hint at the real man hiding beneath an expensive suit and fat checkbook.

"You're all welcome to join us back at the house for a nightcap."

"Oh, we couldn't possibly," Cameron's mom said. "We have to get this little monster home to bed."

"Of course," Mrs. Bennet gave her friend a weak smile.

"Kent, Denise?"

"Not tonight, Andrew. Early start in the morning. But thank you for dinner. You didn't have to pick up the tab."

"Don't be silly, Kent. What's a little dinner between friends?" They shook hands and Jason's dad helped Mrs. Raine-Ford into her coat.

I stood too. "I'm going to go," I said to Hailee and Felicity. The sooner I met with Jermaine, the sooner I could try to put today behind me.

"Thank you for a lovely dinner." I forced myself to look at Mr. Bennet. His jaw clenched as he gave me a brief nod.

"Goodnight, Mya." Mrs. Bennet rose, beckoning me around the table. I went to her and she wrapped her slim arms around me. "I'm sorry," she whispered. "But please, don't give up on my boy. He needs you, more than you know."

Pulling away, I gave her a tight smile. Asher stood up and for a second my heart soared. He was going to say something, to give me a sign we were still okay. But he wasn't looking at me, his eyes narrowing dangerously. I turned slowly, the air sucked clean from my lungs at the sight of Jermaine and two of his guys standing in the door of Bell's.

I felt the weight of the stares of my friends and their families as my past and present collided in a way I never anticipated.

"What the hell are you doing here?" I rushed over to Jermaine, glowering at him.

"Got bored of waiting, baby girl." He ran his thumb over his bottom lip, smirking.

"You need to leave, now."

"What? We not welcome or somethin'?"

"Jermaine, please." I let out an exasperated breath, noticing how out of place he looked, standing there in his baggy jeans and hoodie, his hair braided back in slick cornrows.

"Mya," it wasn't the voice I wanted to hear. In fact, Mr. Bennet was the last person I wanted anywhere near Jermaine and his friends. "You should ask your friends to leave. We don't want any trouble."

"And who the fuck are you, old man?" One of Jermaine's guys stepped forward.

"Easy, Shawn." Jermaine's hand shot out. "I only want to talk."

"You should have waited," I said quietly.

"Well, I'm here now. Let's roll, unless you want to introduce me to your friends."

This wasn't the boy I knew. Jermaine was all grown up, commanding the room with an arrogance that scared me. I knew what it meant to run with someone like Diaz. It's why I let my eyes run down to the waistband of his jeans, searching for the outline of a knife. Or even worse, a gun.

When my gaze settled back on his face, his smirk melted away, and for a second I saw a glimmer of the boy I'd once loved. "Seriously, Mya, you think I'd come here packing?"

Mr. Bennet cleared his throat, hovering precariously close to us.

"Let's go outside and talk," I said, desperate to get them as far away from my friends and their families as possible.

"I'll come with you," Felicity appeared out of nowhere, flanking my side in solidarity. It warmed my heart knowing she was willing to take a stand for me, but I refused to drag her into this.

"Wait for me, okay?" I met her concerned eyes. "I'll be right back."

I didn't look for Asher.

I couldn't.

But as I followed Jermaine out of Bell's, I was sure I heard his father say, "She doesn't belong here, Son, let her go."

"What the fuck, Jermaine?" I slammed my fists against his chest the second we were outside. "What the hell do you think you're doing?"

"Easy, Mya, girl." He laughed. He actually laughed at me like he wasn't here to ruin everything. "I needed to see you."

"See me? You needed to see me?" I yelled, aware that I was losing it. My tight grasp on control was slipping through my fingers. "This is my life, Jermaine. *My life*, and you shouldn't be here."

"We'll give the two of you some space," one of his friends said, shooting me an amused look.

"Fuck you," I growled, feeling the thin rope of my control snap. I knew people like him. Gangbangers who thought they didn't have to live by the rules of society.

It was a hard to believe Jermaine was one of them now, that he'd chosen them over me.

"Be careful, baby girl." Jermaine inched closer, looming over me in a way that had once made me feel safe and protected.

"Tell your boys to back off. You want to talk, I'll talk. But not with them leering at me."

He gave them a brief look. One look that had them walking away without protest.

"Who are you?" I whispered.

"I grew up, Mya. Found my place in the world." He tried to touch my cheek, but I turned away. "It's time for you to come home. I can keep you safe now."

"Because you're in Diaz's crew? Diaz can't keep you safe," I snorted. "He'll only get you killed." I forced out the words over the giant lump in my throat.

Even now, despite everything that had happened between us, I didn't want to see the boy I grew up with get hurt.

We were at an impasse again, the same impasse we'd been at too many times before. Jermaine didn't believe he deserved a better life and nothing I could say or do would change that. He was bound to Diaz's crew now. Blood in, no out.

"We're done," I said, remembering all the pain and heartache he'd caused. "Nothing you say or do will change that." Stepping back, I hugged myself tight, creating a wall between us.

Jermaine went to close the distance, but I thrust out a hand. "Come any closer and I'll scream, and someone will call the police." I was surprised Mr. Bennet hadn't already.

"You wouldn't," he drawled, the surprise in his eyes contradicting his words.

"Try me."

"Shit, Mya, you've changed."

"Yeah," I lifted my chin in defiance. "well, so have you." Turning to leave, I spotted my friends in the window of Bell's watching through the blinds. I didn't expect to see them standing there. I didn't expect Jermaine to grab my wrist forcefully and yank me back.

And I didn't expect my boyfriend's friend to fly out of the bar and tackle Jermaine to the ground.

But if I'd learned anything about Asher and his friends in my short time in Rixon, it was to expect the unexpected.

28

Asher

I HAULED ass after Jason but he was too quick. He'd knocked Jermaine out of the way before I could reach them. The two of them started going at it, fists flying and bone crunching. Cameron appeared just as the other two guys pounced. There wasn't time to think. I'd had enough scuffles on and off the field to know that if a fist was flying at your face, you either ducked and tried to make a run for it, or you hit back. I threw my knuckles straight into one guy's face and his head snapped back, pain splintering through my wrist.

"Motherfucka," he grunted, trying to grab me. I dodged his reach and tried to get to Jason who was still whaling on Jermaine, the two of them trading insults as well as fists. Felicity had her arms wrapped around Mya who looked desperate to step into the fray and I shot her a pleading look to stay put.

"The police are on their way," someone yelled, but it wasn't the three of us who needed to worry. We were Rixon through and through and I knew the attending officers would take one look at us and know who we were.

"You need to walk away, Son," Dad commanded, but I ignored him, jogging over to Jason. Blood dripped from a deep cut in his lip, but he didn't look worried. Once upon a time, he'd lived for this shit.

"You should go before the five-o arrive," I ground out. Jermaine flashed me a wolfish grin.

"Me and you, preppy, let's go." He bounced on the balls of his feet, taunting me with his eyes and crooked finger. "Come on, you know you want to."

"Jermaine," Mya cried as Hailee and Felicity tried to pull her away. "Just go."

"You should listen to him, man." Jason hacked a mouthful of blood and spat it out at his feet. "This is our territory. Raider territory."

But Jermaine's eyes were set on me, jealousy etched into his expression. "Bet it kills you knowing I had her first. Once you taste black you never go—"

Several people yelled as my fist drove straight into his nose. Jermaine staggered back, blood splattered over his face and hoodie.

"You're dead, motherfucka." He pointed two fingers at me and pulled the trigger. Mya rushed to my side, yanking me backward by the arm just as sirens sounded at the end of the street.

"J, let's roll," one of his guy's said.

"Yeah, a'ight." He scratched his jaw, indecision flickering in his eyes. He didn't want to leave Mya, to walk away; but to everyone's relief he did. The three of them piled into a beat-up Chevy and peeled out of the parking lot.

"What the hell were you thinking, Jason?" Felicity shrieked, throwing herself into his arms. He tipped his head at me, understanding passing between us.

He had my back.

Which meant he had Mya's back.

"Are you okay?" Mya asked, gently cradling my hand in hers. My knuckles were split open, blood seeping through my fingers. "You need this looked at."

The adults swarmed us, the moms fussing over us like we were little kids needing some TLC, while the dads quietly watched on, waiting for their opportunity to strike.

My father would never let me hear the end of this. He'd told me as much inside, when Mya left to talk to Jermaine. It's why Jason had gotten to them first; something I wouldn't forgive myself for in a hurry.

"Ash... please, say something."

But I couldn't bring myself to look at her. I was angry and confused and my hand hurt like a bitch.

"Oh, Asher, what a mess." Mom offered me a sad smile. "We should probably get you home and take care of this."

Mya slowly released my hand, her fingers lingering as if it pained her to let me go. "I should probably go," she said so quietly it cut right through me.

"That's probably a good idea," Mom replied, sounding more like my dad than she ever had before.

"I never meant for this to happen, Mrs. Bennet." The vulnerability in Mya's voice coaxed me to look at her. She looked so broken... so defeated. I wanted to wrap my arms around her and tell her everything would be okay. But before I could get out the words, Mom ushered me away.

"Now do you believe me?" my father said as we approached him.

"Not right now, Andrew," Mom brushed past him, leading me to the car. I noticed Jason's dad talking to the police officers, no doubt smoothing things out with them.

Mom climbed into the car, but Jason jogged up to me, shoving his hand against the door. "What are you doing?" he asked, his brows knitted in confusion.

"Leave it, Jase."

"No fucking way, man. I didn't just take a beating from that punk so you could walk away from Mya with your fucking tail in between your legs."

"It's complicated." My teeth ground together.

"Looks pretty simple to me. She's shaken up and you're running."

"I'm not..." I let out a weary sigh. "Jase, please, drop it." My eyes went to my dad and then found Mya across the parking lot. Her breath hitched, unshed tears glistening in her eyes.

"Asher, Son, it's time to go." Dad's tone was final, the coolness in his voice making me wince.

"There's something you're not telling me, isn't there?" Jase asked.

"I'll talk to you later, okay?" I yanked open the door and slid into the car, slamming it behind me, the sound reverberating deep inside my chest.

My father climbed in a second later, the temperature turning subzero.

"How is your hand, sweetheart?"

"I'm fine, Mom." I clutched my bloodied hand to my chest, staring out of the window as Bell's grew smaller behind us.

"Those boys were—"

"Gangbangers, Julia. Those young men were gangbangers and thanks to Asher's *friend* they have tarnished the team's victory and our son's reputation."

"Lay off it, Dad," I grunted, the adrenaline finally subsiding, giving way to the pain radiating deep inside my metacarpals.

"I'll lay off you, Son, when you do the right thing and end it with the Hernandez girl. She is nothing but trouble. You saw her. She knows one of them; intimately might I add."

"Asher," Mom glanced back, "Is it true? Did she... have a relationship with one of those... those men?"

Mom was visibly shaken by the night's events, but I didn't like how easily persuaded she was by Dad.

"Jermaine is Mya's ex. It ended badly," I admitted, hating that I was proving my father right. "But it's over and she's here to escape that life. He wasn't supposed to know she was in Rixon."

"See, Julia. She's dragged her gangbanger friends into our lives and now none of us are safe."

"For real, Dad? Don't be so melodramatic. It was a fight. It was hardly a gang war."

"No." He caught my eye in the rear-view mirror. "But what happens now? Do you think he's just going to go on his way?"

I didn't want to think about it. I wanted to go back to earlier, before I ever laid eyes on him. When I was thinking of how badly I wanted Mya. When I was foolishly making idle plans for our future once graduation was out of the way.

But for as much as I wanted to ignore his words, the reality was, my dad was right. Despite how fucking hard it was to admit it. Jermaine had been nothing more than a faceless name; an imaginary guy that couldn't touch our relationship. A guy I hadn't had to compete with.

But now he was real.

Now, I knew he had a wicked glint in his eye, an arrogant swagger, and a mean left hook.

And worst of all, I knew he wasn't going anywhere fast. Not unless Mya knew some magical way of sending her ex on his merry fucking way.

Fuck.

I clenched my fist involuntarily; completely forgetting that my knuckles were split open. But pain was good. Pain numbed all the other thoughts festering inside my mind.

Soon enough, Dad turned off the road into our driveway. Without a word, I climbed out and made for the house. I didn't want to listen to any more of his bullshit, and I certainly didn't want to see the look of disappointment in Mom's eyes.

"Asher, wait," she called. "I should really look at your—"

"I've got it, Mom." Digging my key out, I unlocked the door and hurried inside. I needed space. I needed to be alone. But the screech of tires had me glancing back.

Headlights illuminated the driveway and my mother shrieked. Bolting out of the house, I came slamming to a stop when my eyes landed on Jermaine. "Where is she?" he yelled, his eyes wild.

"You need to walk away, son." Dad moved casually toward him, shielding Mom.

"She's not here," I added, inching closer to Jermaine who was acting like a caged animal.

"She didn't leave with you?" He faltered, only for a second, and Dad dug out his cell phone, dialing nine-one-one. But before it connected, Jermaine pulled out a gun and aimed it straight at him. "You don't wanna do that, old man," he said.

Everything slowed down.

The thud of my pulse against my skull.

The beat of my heart in my chest.

Dad dropped his cell and lifted his hands.

Slowly.

Slowly.

Slowly.

"You don't want to do this." He sounded so calm, so composed. Like he'd been held at gunpoint a hundred times before.

"A- Andrew." Mom's cry pierced the silence and Jermaine swung his aim around. I dove in front of her, throwing up my hands too.

"Mya told me about you, you know?" I said, hoping to keep his thoughts on me and off the trigger. "She said you were best friends. Grew up together and everything."

"She talked about me?"

"Yeah, man. You were her first everything, remember?"

"So why the fuck is she runnin' from me?"

"I can't answer that. But why don't we call her?" I went to lower my hand, but he jabbed the gun toward me. "Whoa, easy." My heart was in my throat. "I'm just going to call Mya and tell her you're looking for her."

I didn't want this psycho anywhere near her, but I didn't know what else to do.

He had a gun.

A loaded fucking gun aimed right at me. Maybe if I could call her or text her, I could warn her. I could get her to alert the authorities.

Think, Asher, think! I inched forward, careful to keep my mom behind me. "Asher, Son—"

"Ssh, Dad, I got this."

"Jermaine, you don't want to do this. Imagine what Mya will do when she finds out—"

"Don't be talkin' like you know her. You don't know her, I know her." He turned the gun into himself, tapping it against his chest.

"Why don't you let my parents go on inside and we can talk? Man to man."

Mom whimpered, and I heard my dad quietly trying to comfort her. I needed them out of here, somewhere safe. Somewhere where he couldn't touch them.

Shit. I was in over my head.

"Call her," he demanded. "Tell her to come here."

As slowly as possible, I dug my cell out my jeans pocket and dialed Mya, all while keeping one eye on Jermaine.

"Asher," she breathed. "Thank God. I thought—"

"I need you to come to my house."

"Asher, what is it? What's wrong?"

"Jermaine is here," I kept my voice as even as possible. "He wants to talk to you."

"H- he's there?" Hushed voices came over the line. I could pick out Jason and Felicity in the background.

"Hurry," I added, before hanging up. "It'll take her at least ten minutes."

"I got time. I got all the fucking time in the world."

Mya made it in less than seven minutes, but it had felt like a year. The second she stepped out of Jason's Dodge Charger, Jermaine seemed to relax. "You came."

"What's going on, J?" Her tone was soft, but I didn't miss the sheer horror in her eyes as she noticed the gun in his hand. "What did you do?"

"Nothin'. I didn't do nothin' yet. I just needed you to listen."

"And you thought following my boyfriend home and threatening him and his parents with a gun was the way to get my attention?"

"I wasn't thinkin'. Shit, Mya, everything's so fucked up."

"I can see that," she seethed and I tried to catch her eye to silently ask her what the hell she was doing. But then it dawned on me; she wasn't trying to aggravate him, she was trying to draw his attention off us to her.

"Asher, Son, we should go inside and call the police," Dad whispered.

"You two go." I kept my eye on Mya. "I'm not leaving her."

"Asher," Dad hissed. "Now is not the time for heroics."

"I'm staying."

He and Mom moved toward the house just as Jermaine advanced on Mya. I didn't have time to think as I lunged for him. He was so focused on her, he didn't see me until it was too late. My body slammed into his and we toppled to the ground.

"NO!" someone yelled as a gunshot went off. The gun clattered to the floor and Mya kicked it clear of Jermaine.

"You're okay," I rasped, a little winded from the fall.

Sirens sounded in the distance, and Mya helped me clamber to my feet. "What were you thinking?" she scolded me before falling into my arms. I held her tight as I searched for my parents to check they were all right. But something was wrong.

Dad held Mom in his arms, his face ashen, his crisp white dress shirt stained red. "Dad?" I croaked, shoving Mya away and rushing over to his side. "What happened?"

I'd seen my father wear many expressions. Anger. Indifference. Arrogance. But I'd never seen him look scared until that moment.

"The bullet…" was all he managed to say.

Two little words.

Words that should never have passed his lips.

Two little words I knew would change everything.

29

Mya

"WHAT DID YOU DO?" I lunged for Jermaine as he staggered to his feet. "What the fuck did you do?" My fists rained down on his chest, his face. My nails scratched, tearing flesh and drawing blood, as I shrieked at him over and over until my lungs burned and tears stung my eyes.

Eventually, strong arms wrapped around my waist, hauling me off him. "Easy, Mya." It was Jason. "Easy."

"I... fuck." Jermaine's eyes were wide and skittish as the drone of sirens drew closer. "I didn't mean to... fuck!" He rubbed the heel of his palms against his forehead.

"Yo, J, we need to roll," one of his guys yelled, but it was too late. The flash of blue and red illuminated the inky sky. The Chevy gunned to life, speeding away as Jermaine's friends abandoned him.

"You're dead, you're fucking dead." Asher rushed at my ex, tackling him to the ground, the two of them a blur of limbs.

"Asher, *no!*" The words tore from my throat as I watched the guy I love rain fire and fury down on the guy I'd once loved. Jermaine didn't fight back. He just lay there, letting Asher beat him to a bloody pulp until the blood on his hands swirled with Jermaine's blood.

"Do something," I cried, barely aware that Jason was holding me up.

A couple of officers arrived, dragging Asher off Jermaine. He fought against them, thrashing and yelling, tears streaming down his face. It wasn't until the EMTs arrived and started working on Mrs. Bennet, that he finally calmed down.

"I need to go to him," I whispered, pain coiled so tightly around my heart I could barely breathe.

"I don't think that's a good idea. Let me go talk to him." Jason handed me off to Felicity who I hadn't even realized was there.

"Ssh," she hugged me, "it's going to be okay."

But nothing was okay.

Mrs. Bennet was bleeding out on the ground while her son sat motionless, his eyes completely devoid of emotion, his hands and face and clothes caked in blood. His mom's. Jermaine's.

His own.

"This is my fault," I sobbed into my friend's shoulder, clutching her arm like it was the only thing anchoring me to Earth.

"Don't say that, you couldn't have known he would do this."

But she was wrong.

I should have known Jermaine wouldn't just let me walk away.

I'd been too blinded by love though. Gotten too comfortable being in Rixon, with Asher and my new friends. I'd foolishly let myself believe things could be different, that I deserved more from life.

The EMTs got Mrs. Bennet secured onto the stretcher, and I tore from Flick's hold, hurrying over to them. "I'm sorry." I reached for her. "I'm so, so sorry."

"I hope you're happy," Mr. Bennet said coldly. "None of this would have happened if it wasn't for you."

"I didn't... I wasn't..." The lame excuses dried on my tongue, a garbled sound escaping my throat, as every whisper and rumor about me came true.

"Mom." The pain in Asher's voice made my legs buckle, the sheer force of his agony hitting me like a tsunami. Felicity caught me as father and son walked beside Mrs. Bennet's lifeless body.

"We need to move out," one of the EMTs said, motioning for everyone to give them room.

Jason came over to us and I grabbed his hand. "What did he say?"

The small shake of his head told me everything I needed to know, and a fresh wave of tears rushed to the surface.

"Asher," I yelled, my voice cutting the air like a knife. He slowed down, moving aside to let the medics load his mom inside the ambulance. His eyes found mine, but it wasn't my Asher staring back at me.

"Oh God," I choked out, hardly able to breathe through the tears.

"She'll be okay," Felicity said, unable to disguise the quiver in her voice. "They'll save her."

"I should go with him, he needs me." I tried to break free, but Jason hooked his arm around my waist, tucking me into his body.

"Let him be," he whispered. "Right now, he needs to be with his family."

"Miss Hernandez?" A deep voice said, and I peeked out the comfort of Jason's big body to find an officer staring at me with sympathy. "I'm going to need you to come with me."

"Go with you?" Flick stepped in front of me, shielding me. "Go where?"

"We'd like Miss Hernandez to come down to the station and answer a few questions."

"She can give you her statement here. She's in no state to go anywhere right now."

"It's okay," I said, untangling myself from my friends.

"Mya, you don't have to do this. Not right this second."

My gaze flicked to where the ambulance was backing out of the Bennets' driveway, a strange numbness seeping through me.

"Miss Hernandez, this way please." The officer took my arm, leading me toward the cop car.

"Jason," I heard Flick hiss, "do something."

"Hang tight, Mya, we'll figure all this out," Jason called after me.

But it was too late.

The damage was done.

Mrs. Bennet was leaving the scene in an ambulance and I was leaving in a police cruiser.

And my past... my past had finally caught up with me.

"Thank God you're okay." Felicity ignored the officer at the desk and slung her arms around me.

"Hey," I croaked. "Thanks for waiting."

"Are you kidding me? They led you away like you're somehow responsible for all this. It's not right."

I hugged her again, feeling a rush of emotion. "How is he?" My voice was cracked, my throat raw from all the tears. From reliving what had happened at the Bennets'.

"Mrs. Bennet is still in surgery; they don't know anything yet."

My eyes shuttered as I sucked in a harsh breath. "But how is *he*?"

Flick pressed her lips together, shaking her head a little. "He's... broken. Jase and Cam are with him right now."

"Will you take me there?"

"Mya, listen..." she hesitated. "I'm not sure that's a good idea. Mr. Bennet is—"

"I need to see him, Felicity, please."

"Okay. Let me make a quick call. I'll meet you outside." She hurried away before I could argue. I knew she was calling Jason to see how things were at the hospital, and I also knew I didn't care. I had to see Asher.

It had been the longest, haziest ninety minutes of my life. The officers had arrested Jermaine and wanted my statement. But I hadn't anticipated how hard it would be to recall everything.

After I was debriefed and given the card for the presiding officer in the case, I went in search of Felicity. She was on the phone, pacing in front of her car. "She has a right to be there," I heard her say. "No, Jason, I... okay, okay. I have to go." She noticed me standing there. "Love you too, bye."

"Any news?" I wrapped my arms around myself, a chill working its way up my spine.

"Not yet. Listen, why don't I take you home? It's been a traumatic night for everyone and I'm sure your aunt will—"

"I know you're only looking out for me, but I have to see him, Felicity. Put yourself in my shoes."

"Okay," she said weakly. "I'll give you a ride."

"Thank you."

"You should probably know the story already broke on local news channels," she said, as we climbed into her sunshine yellow Beetle. The car had always made me smile, but not tonight.

"I can only imagine what they're saying." I pressed my head against the window as the town I'd come to call home rolled by.

"Pay no attention."

"Easy for you to say. It wasn't your gangbanger ex who shot the wife of one of the town's most respected businessmen." Bile clawed its way up my throat and I retched.

"Shit! Here." Flick handed me a bottle of water from the center console.

"Thanks." My head rolled back against the headrest as I took a big swallow, letting the cold liquid douse the flames in my throat.

"What will happen to him? Jermaine, I mean?"

"They're going to push for aggravated assault with a deadly weapon. If she... d- dies..." The words lodged in my throat, silent tears rolling down my cheeks.

Felicity reached across and grabbed my hand. "Don't think like that. She'll be okay. She has to be okay."

THE CLOYING SCENT of disinfectant assaulted my senses the second I stepped foot inside the hospital. I hated these places. Sure, they were a place of help and healing, but most of my experiences were wrapped up in tragedy and trauma. Not to mention the last time I was in a hospital bed was because my boyfriend's enemies had left me beaten and bloody on the ground. I could still remember lying there, trying to ignore the pain radiating through my body. I could still hear their taunts, see the bloodlust in their eyes as they made me watch as they beat Jermaine, before turning on me. I could still remember praying for a way out of a life I was sure would get him killed. If not both of us.

It seemed like some bad kind of karma that I was here now, awaiting news of whether my boyfriend's mom was going to survive.

"Jason said they're on the third floor, come on." Felicity took my hand, and I was so grateful to have her beside me.

People watched as we approached the elevator, their curious stares brushing up against me. I knew news had already broken about the shooting, but the hospital was in the next town over. People couldn't know I was the girl from the incident. But they only had to take one look at my brown skin and my disheveled appearance to draw their own conclusions.

It seemed so petty now, to worry about their narrow-minded views when Mrs. Bennet was lying on an operating table as the surgeons tried to save her life.

The elevator doors pinged open, pulling me from my inner turmoil and Flick ushered me inside. "How are you holding up?" she asked me.

"I feel like I'm in a bad dream," I said quietly. "Like any moment I'll wake up and realize none of this is real."

But it was real, and it wasn't going away.

"At least they got Jermaine. You don't have to worry about him anymore."

Strangely, that didn't make me feel any better.

We stepped off the elevator a few seconds later, and I immediately saw him.

"Asher..." I breathed, his name a pained sigh on my lips. He was standing against the wall, his head tipped back, eyes closed. Someone had tried to clean the blood off his hands and face, streaking red all up his neck and arms.

Jason spotted us first, his eyes darkening when they landed on me. "Hey," he said slowly approaching us. "I thought I told you—"

"Jason," Flick warned. "She has every right to be here."

"I just want to see him," I sniffled. "To see how he is."

"His mom's bleeding out in the OR. How do you think he is?"

Guilt slithered through my chest as I gaped at him. This wasn't the guy who had held me earlier, offering me comfort and reassurance. This was the formidable Jason Ford I'd heard so much about. The guy who protected his own and guarded his heart. The guy who wasn't afraid to draw lines in sand between him and his enemies.

I'd stood on the same side as him until now.

"I..." Tears clogged my throat.

"Jason, that isn't fair."

"Fair?" He snapped at Flick. "None of this is fucking fair, babe. I just had to hold my best friend while he puked his heart and soul up because he thinks his mom is going to die. Do you know what that feels like?"

They started arguing, their hushed voices and harsh words born out of fear and frustration. I inched down the hall, desperate for Asher to look at me. Needing him to acknowledge I was here. But when his eyes finally found mine, there was nothing but pain.

He pushed off the wall and began to move toward me. I wanted to run to him, to throw myself into his arms and beg him never to let go. But I didn't move a muscle.

"Hi," I said at the same time as he said, "Mya."

I gave a small half-hearted laugh, relief seeping into every fiber of my being that he was standing here with me. "I came straight away," the words rushed out. "Is there any news?"

Asher swallowed, raking a hand through his blood tinged hair. "Not yet."

"I'm so sorry," I whispered, stepping forward to hug him.

I just needed to touch him, to know he was okay.

"Mya." Asher stepped back, my hands grasping thin air. "You shouldn't have come."

"W- what?" My arms went around my waist; but I wasn't shielding myself this time, I was holding myself together.

"You can't be here right now."

"But I came... for you. I want to be here for you, Ash... I'm here for you." I was rambling now, but everything was slipping through my fingers.

"You should go."

Go?

He wanted me to go?

It made no sense.

He needed me.

We needed each other.

"Mya, why don't we go downstairs to the cafe and get a drink?" Felicity gently grasped my arm.

"Asher?" I whispered when his broken gaze dropped to the floor.

"You've done enough, Mya," he said flatly, still refusing to look at me. "You should go."

"Come on, let's go see if there's any update." Jason draped his arm around Asher's shoulder and began leading him back to the waiting area.

"Asher, wait..." I cried.

"Mya, don't do this, not here," my friend said softly. "Come on." She wrapped her arm around me and led me back into the elevator.

"W- what just happened?" I asked the second the doors pinged shut, my heart breaking inside my chest.

"He's confused, Mya. Give him time."

"Time," I repeated, numbly.

I could give him time.

I'd give him all the time in the world if I thought it would fix anything.

But I'd seen the emptiness in his eyes. No amount of time was going to fix this.

Nothing was.

I'd given my heart to the boy with the charming smile. But Asher was no longer smiling.

And my heart was no longer whole.

30

Asher

"SHE'S STABLE."

Two little words that felt like everything and nothing all at once. The surgeons had worked on Mom for over three hours, removing a single bullet from her neck. It had lodged in her throat causing severe blood loss. After she went into cardiac arrest on the operating table, they decided to induce a coma to try to minimize the damage to her brain. It wasn't great news, but she was alive, and that's all that mattered.

"Would you like to come and see her?" The nurse with kind eyes glanced between me and Dad. He nodded. "Follow me."

My friends whispered words of encouragement as I followed the nurse and my dad down the hall. Every muscle in my body ached, my chest heavy. And my eyes, my fucking eyes were dry and sore from all the tears. But as the nurse stopped outside a private room, the blinds drawn, I inhaled a deep breath, steeling myself for whatever we would find on the other side of the door.

"Before we go inside," she said, "you should probably prepare yourselves. Mrs. Bennet underwent lifesaving surgery. There's going to be a lot of wires and tubes, but they are all there to help her, okay?"

"I'd like to see my wife now." I winced at how cold Dad sounded but if it affected the nurse, she didn't show it.

I guessed she was used to seeing people at their very worst in a place like this.

She pushed open the door and led us inside. "She's looks more peaceful than I expected," the words came out choked as I moved to stand beside her. "Hey, Mom, I'm right here." I went to take her hand, hesitating when I noticed the central line disappearing into her skin.

"It's okay, Asher, you can hold her hand."

Gently grasping her hand in mine, I let my eyes run over her features, swallowing the huge sob building in my throat.

"I'll give you some time. If you need anything just press the buzzer."

"Thank you," I said, aware of how still Dad was.

The nurse left us in silence. Nothing but the gentle hum and steady bleep of the machines helping to keep Mom stable.

"This is on you, Son," Dad's voice didn't waver. He didn't yell or breakdown and cry. He was completely and utterly devoid of anything.

Yet, I knew it was an act. Another performance where he refused to let me see his true feelings.

"Dad, I—"

"You brought that girl and her thug boyfriend into our lives. I told you... I told you she would ruin you."

Guilt wrenched through me, squeezing my heart like a vise. "This wasn't supposed to happen."

"But it did." Disappointment drenched his words. "Your mom may never recover from this, and for what? Because you wanted to prove a point and date the Hernandez girl."

That wasn't it at all. But words failed me. It was hard to argue with him when Mom was lying there hooked up to machines because of Jermaine. A guy who never would have entered our lives if it wasn't for Mya.

Pain splintered through me. I didn't think it was possible to feel more hurt than I had when I saw Dad cradling Mom's body, blood covering her, fear shining in her eyes. But I was slowly realizing there wasn't a limit on how much agony a person could feel. I hadn't only almost lost Mom tonight, I'd lost Mya too. The one person who made everything seem brighter was now the one person who would forever be a reminder of this moment. Of standing here and watching my mom lifeless and pale in a hospital bed.

I pushed all thoughts of Mya out of my head. Right now, I needed to concentrate on my family.

"I need to make a call," Dad said suddenly, pacing across the room. "I trust you'll stay with her?"

"Of course."

"I'll be back." His tone was cold, sending chills up my spine.

I dropped into the chair beside Mom and let my head fall back, closing my eyes. The last four hours felt like a bad dream. People in Rixon didn't get shot. But it wasn't a dream, and Mom had been shot by my girlfriend's ex. It was hard to believe that only a couple of days ago I was planning our future and now I couldn't think past the next hour or the one after that.

My cell phone vibrated, and I pulled it out of my pocket, wincing at the blood still streaked over my hands.

Mom's blood.

Mya: Felicity said your mom is stable. That's good, Ash... really good. I'm thinking of you both. You know where I am if you need me xo

. . .

I STARED at the screen for a couple of seconds, before powering it off and placing it on the small nightstand. My head wasn't in the right place to deal with Mya, not yet. Things were different now, I knew that. She had to know too. But I didn't want to say something I might regret later down the line.

Running a hand over my face, I dropped my weary gaze to Mom again. It was inconceivable how someone who looked so peaceful could be walking the thin line between life and death.

"You have to pull through," I whispered, the words ripping out my heart. "I need you, Mom. I need you."

She was the one redeeming thing about our family, the glue that bound our fragile state together. Without her, we would be nothing.

Tears rolled down my face as I let my worst fears take hold.

She had to pull through.

Because if she didn't, the hole she would leave behind would be irreparable.

FOUR DAYS.

I sat by my mom's side for four days, waiting, hoping, *praying* the doctors would give us the news we wanted to hear.

But four days passed and nothing changed.

Her condition was stable, but the doctors didn't want to prematurely wake her for fear of sustained damage to her brain from the severe blood loss.

"Hey, man," Cam slipped into the room, bringing me a fresh coffee. I'd lived on the stuff since I figured everyone would frown if I sat here drowning my sorrows at the bottom of a bottle of whisky.

"Thanks." I sipped at the cup, barely tasting it.

"How is she?"

"The same." I rubbed my face. "It's weird, you know. I've been used to not having her around much. But this is fucking torture. Knowing she's right there but might never..." I swallowed down the swell of tears.

"She'll come through this, Ash."

"Yeah, maybe." I could feel the darkness edging into my thoughts. I wanted to be positive; to listen when the doctors said it was the best-case scenario right now. But it was so fucking hard when she was just lying there, unmoving. Motionless.

Lifeless.

"The team all send their thoughts. They all want to come show their support, but Coach told them to hold off until you're ready."

"I'm not," I rushed out. "I appreciate it, I do, but I'm not ready for them to be here. You and Jase are different, but not the rest of the team, not yet."

"I get it. But just know she's in everyone's thoughts. You both are."

"Thanks, man."

"How's your dad handling it?"

"You'd have to ask him," I grumbled.

"That bad, huh?"

"We haven't exactly talked much. He blames me."

"Come on, Ash, that's... It wasn't your fault."

"No?" My brow rose. "If I hadn't gotten with Mya, Jermaine would never have—"

"You can't think like that, and you can't change the past." He gave me a pointed look but I couldn't bear his sympathy. The pity in his eyes. "Have you spoken to her?" he asked.

"She texted me a few times but honestly, she is the least of my worries right now."

"Asher," he let out a heavy sigh. "That isn't fair and you know it."

"Fair?" I scoffed, making a strangled sound in my throat. "None of this is fucking fair. My mom was innocent, Cam. She shouldn't be the one lying there."

"*No one* should be lying there," he said calmly. "And I'm so sorry it happened, I am. But you love her, man. What happened doesn't change that."

"Doesn't it?"

"Mya loves you and she's holed up at her aunt's, hiding..." he hesitated, letting his words trail off.

"Hiding?"

"It's nothing, forget it." Cam rubbed his face, but I saw the flash of guilt in his eyes. "You need to focus on your mom. We can handle the rest."

"Handle what?" I levelled him with a hard look. "What aren't you telling me?"

"Seriously, man, I shouldn't have said anything. It's nothing."

"Cameron..."

He blew out an exasperated breath. "It's just you know how people can be around here. They close rank, and your mom and dad are like Rixon celebrities."

"Cam, what the fuck happened?" A growl rumbled in my chest.

"Felicity and Hailee took Mya for ice cream at Ice-T's. There was an incident."

"With Mya?" My chest tightened and I rubbed my breastbone.

"A couple of girls gave her shit. It got ugly. Tim didn't want any trouble, so he asked Mya to leave."

"Fuck." My hand flew out connecting with the side of the bed, pain radiating through my knuckles. Luckily it wasn't my already busted up hand.

"Felicity and Hailee gave him a piece of their mind, but she's been at her aunt's ever since."

"Maybe it's for the best," I mumbled, cradling my hand. "Maybe she should just go back to Fallowfield Heights."

"For real? You want her to leave?"

"How I am ever going to fix this, Cam? Tell me what the fuck I'm supposed to do here?" My voice was shrill, desperation laced in every word. "Because the way I see it, my mom pulls through and wants nothing to do with the girl who brought this to our doorstep, or she doesn't pull through and..." I couldn't even say the words, the lump in my throat too big.

Swallowing, I took a couple of deep breaths.

"It's not easy, I know—"

"It's fucking impossible." Frustration welled up inside me. "If I try to fix things with Mya, it's like I'm choosing her over my mom. And if I just end things with her, I'm just like everyone else who has ever let her down. But it's my mom, Cam. The one person in my life that has sacrificed so much for me."

A frown crossed his expression. "What do you mean?"

"It doesn't matter," Sadness clung to my words. "I hate that Mya is going through this, but I can't be who she needs right now. Not until my mom wakes up."

And maybe not even then, the words teetered on the tip of my tongue.

Cam stood up, offering me a sad smile. "You know, I love you like a brother, Ash, I do, and I hate that this is happening. But I know what it's like to almost lose someone you love, to feel like they're slipping through your fingers, and I know what it feels like to want, *need*, someone to blame. But this is not Mya's fault. She came to Rixon to escape her psycho-ex. Put yourself in her shoes for a second—"

"Cameron, I don't—"

"No, bro, you need to hear this. Something is happening with you, something big. You think we don't see it, but we do. And I'm going to go out on a limb and say it's something to do with your old man. He's made it pretty clear he doesn't approve of Mya. But don't let this," his eyes flicked to my mom, "give him the ammunition he needs to make you end things with her. You found your person, Asher. Don't let her go just because things got hard all of a sudden. You need her just like she needs you. And if you don't try to make things right with her, one day down the line, when your mom is better and this all seems like a bad dream, you will regret it."

"Cam?"

"Yeah?"

"You can go now," I said.

He hesitated, disappointment edging into his expression. Part of me wanted him to push, to make me listen to his lecture. He was only telling me the truth after all.

But there was one giant problem with that.

The truth hurt.

And I was maxed out on my daily dose of pain.

31

Mya

"THAT'S IT," my aunt stormed into my room, "you're getting out of that bed even if I have to drag you." She hurtled toward me like a bull, and I bolted upright, holding out my hands.

"Okay, okay, I'm getting up."

"Praise the Lord." She backed off. "I have been going damn near out of my mind worrying about you."

"I'm sorry, Auntie," I whispered. "I just—" Tears gushed from my eyes and I grabbed a pillow, burying my face into it.

I hated this.

The permanent pit in my stomach, the endless tears and overwhelming heartache.

Almost a week had passed.

Seven days without Asher by my side, reassuring me we could get through this. Seven days of not knowing whether he would ever speak to me again let alone forgive me.

Seven miserable days without the guy I'd come to love more than anything.

If it wasn't for Felicity and Hailee, I might have driven myself insane with worry. As it was, they'd kept me updated about his mom's condition. Which hadn't changed since she came out of surgery.

At first, I'd tried to keep myself busy. To go on with life as normal. I managed four days. Four days until Kellie Ginly and her gymnastic friends cornered me at Ice-Ts and ripped into me as if I was the one who had pulled the trigger. School had been hard enough that day, facing the onslaught of whispers and stares. But it was nothing compared to having Kellie all up in my face, telling me that I ruined Asher's life.

I couldn't remember a time I'd ever let someone speak to me the way she'd belittled me. But I'd just stood there, taking her abuse and insults, letting them seep into my pores, sinking deep inside my bones. Because I *did* feel partly responsible. Part of me, no matter how misguided or irrational, felt like I deserved her wrath. She was Asher's people long before I ever arrived in Rixon.

And me?

I was just the Latina girl from the hood who had ruined his life.

"I know, child, I know." My aunt plopped down on my bed, wrapping her slender arms around me. "Love is a cruel, wicked thing. But this is not your fault, Mya, you hear me?" Slipping her fingers underneath her jaw, she tilted my face up. "Tell me you know that."

"I... I know."

"You need to believe it too. What happened with Mrs. Bennet was nothing but a tragic accident. Me and the ladies at church have been praying for her."

"Y- you have?"

She clucked her tongue. "Don't sound so surprised. Just because this town has never welcomed me with open arms doesn't mean I'd ever wish harm to anyone. We are all God's children, Mya. A fact some of the good people of Rixon seem to forget. Has he called yet?"

"I... no." I shook my head, shame and embarrassment burning through me.

"If he's worth your love, he will. And if he doesn't, then you know he's not."

"He blames me."

"No, he doesn't. But sometimes, blaming someone is easier than accepting the truth."

"I just feel like this is karma. That I'm paying my dues for leaving Fallowfield Heights and abandoning Jermaine."

"Mya, Mya, Mya, for a bright, intelligent girl, you really are quite the fool sometimes. This isn't karma. This is life. And life can be hard and messy and painful. You got out of Fallowfield Heights because you knew if you stayed, you'd end up hurt again, or worse. Ain't no life for a girl like you there. Your mama knew that. Keelan knew that. And deep down, Jermaine knew that. Don't ever feel guilty because you got out. Because you made the hard decision and walked away."

"Why couldn't he just let me go?" I cried, clinging onto her. "Why did he have to come back?"

"Because while you were strong enough to let him go, he was weak. Jermaine will pay for his sins, Mya. One way or another he'll pay."

Even now, it still didn't make me feel any better. There had been too much hurt and pain.

"Your guidance counselor called," Aunt Ciara said. "She'd like to see you tomorrow if you're up to it?"

Drying my eyes with my sleeves, I nodded. "I should go back to school anyway."

"That's my girl. Don't ever forget who you are and where you came from, Mya. Being born and raised in Fallowfield Heights is a part of who you are but it doesn't define you."

"Thank you, for everything."

"For my favorite niece, anytime." Her laughter made me smile. We'd had a rocky time recently, but when all was said and done, we were family, and no matter what happened, I knew she would be there for me.

"Hey," I said as I walked up to Felicity, Hailee, and the guys.

"Mya, thank God." Felicity enveloped me in a hug. "I've been so worried."

"I'm okay." I wasn't, but I would be.

I had to be.

"Hey, Mya." Hailee hugged me next, concern radiating from her.

"How is he, really?" I asked, my eyes finding the two people who would know better than anyone. But I was greeted with silence.

Eventually Jason cleared his throat. "I've got to go, catch you later." He kissed Flick before heading off into the building.

"Did I do something wrong?" I clutched the strap of my backpack.

"It's not you." Felicity gave me a warm smile, but I knew she was lying. Jason blamed me. Just like everyone else in town.

"I have a meeting with Miss Hampstead, I'll see you later." Hurrying away from them, I kept my eyes down, trying to block out the low hum of whispers following me.

I heard she's in a gang.

The bullet was meant for Asher instead.

She should just go back to where she came from before anyone else ends up hurt.

But my once thick skin was worn now and no matter how much I tried to ignore them, their voices only rang louder.

"Mya, come in."

Miss Hampstead liked to provide service with a smile, and today, despite the circumstances, was no different. I guess that was a prerequisite of being the school guidance counselor; you smiled regardless.

"How are you?"

"I'm holding up, if that's what you mean."

"And Asher, is he—"

"Asher is focusing on his mom right now."

She flinched. "Of course. Well, I really just wanted to make sure you were okay. I know how quickly rumors circulate the halls at school let alone the town."

"It's nothing I can't handle."

Four months ago, I would have believed that. But that was before Asher had smashed through my walls and buried his way deep inside my heart.

"Do you want to talk about it?" Her expression softened as she relaxed in her chair.

"What is there to say?"

"Oh, I don't know. Lots of things I should imagine. How did seeing Jermaine again make you feel? How do you feel now he's been arrested with the probability of spending a long time behind bars? I should imagine it's put a huge strain on your relationship with Asher. Maybe we should start there?"

"You want to know how I feel?" Miss Hampstead nodded and I sighed. "I'm tired." My lips thinned, a vortex of emotion swirling inside me.

"I'm tired of people thinking they know about me, about my life. I'm tired of being judged on the color of my skin and not what's beneath it. I'm tired of people asking me how I am, knowing that they probably won't like my answer. But most of all, I'm scared. I'm so scared that Juli... Mrs. Bennet won't pull through and that I'll lose Asher for good and that I'll never be able to walk down the street again without people looking at me like I'm the one who pulled the trigger. So yeah, that's how I'm feeling."

Silence enveloped us as my words, my pain, hung heavy in the space between us.

"That's... a lot to carry around with you."

I drummed my fingers against my thigh, desperate to escape her small office, even if part of me wanted to stay here forever.

"Maybe some time off—"

"You think I should hide?" I scoffed, indignation skittering up my spine. "*That's* your solution?"

"Mya, calm down."

I. Lost. It.

"Don't tell me to calm down. My ex-boyfriend came here and threatened my boyfriend and his family with a gun. A *gun*, Miss Hampstead. Mrs. Bennet was shot and everything is falling apart around me and I don't know how the hell I'm supposed to deal with that." My chest heaved as I purged all the frustration and anger and fear and heartache.

Asher didn't need to tell me what, deep down, I already knew.

Regardless of what happened to his mom, we were over.

There would always be a part of him that would blame me, just like there would always be a part of myself that blamed me. We couldn't move on from that. Even if we did work through it and find our way back to one another, it would always be there. Festering in the background like a wound that refused to heal. Spreading bigger over time. Its poison slowly bleeding into everything around it.

"Here." She pushed the tissue box toward me. "Feel better?"

"A little, I guess." I gave her a half-hearted shrug, surprised at how much lighter my chest felt.

"You need to talk, Mya. If not to me, then a friend or your aunt. You've been through a lot, and it isn't over yet."

"I know."

The police would want me to testify against Jermaine. I was a crucial witness. But testifying against him could make me a target again. Especially if the police used his gang affiliations to build their case.

"My door is always open, whatever you decide. And try to remember that when people judge you, Mya, it says more about their character than yours."

"Is that your way of saying we're done?" I managed a tentative smile, and Miss Hampstead chuckled.

"I have a feeling we've dug deep enough today. I know this is hard and things feel like they'll never fix themselves right now, but you will get through this."

"Thanks." Grabbing my bag, I stood up and steeled myself for class. Because something told me if I wanted to survive the next few weeks at school, I was going to need all the strength I could get.

"HEY, MYA," Cameron jogged up beside me as I was heading out of school. It had been a relief when the final bell rang and I could escape the constant whispers and stares.

"Hey." This wasn't awkward, at all.

"Can we talk?" he asked.

"I was going to walk home but I wouldn't say no to a ride." It was cold out and thanks to a diet of saltine crackers and milk, my energy levels were low.

"Come on." Cameron smiled, leading the way to his car. "Ladies first." The passenger door swung open and he motioned for me to get in.

"I can see why Hailee loves you."

"I try." He chuckled, moving around to the driver's side. "How are you holding up?" Cameron asked as he drove out of the parking lot.

"I'm not going to lie; it's been a tough few days."

"You know, I talked to him, tried to make him see this is not your fault."

"You didn't need to do that." My voice quivered but I forced down the tears. I'd cried enough.

"Yeah, I did. Asher needs you, Mya. More than he knows right now. Something's different with him this semester. He's... distant and closed off and I sense this building tension between him and his dad. At first, I thought it was just about you. But then he told us he wasn't going to commit to the Panthers and something didn't fit. Jason's right, football was always the dream. Maybe me and Ash don't stand a chance of going pro like Jase but it's still in our blood."

"Why are you telling me all this, Cameron?"

"Because I know he's pushing you away and I know you're probably going to let him. And I get it, I do. But what the two of you have, it deserves to be fought for."

"I can't be the only one fighting though." My head dropped back against the seat, a harsh breath leaving my lips. "You know everyone told me he'd hurt me. My aunt, my friends back home, even Miss Hampstead warned me about getting involved with a Raider."

"You're talking like you've already given up." His heavy gaze burned into the side of my face but I didn't look at him.

I couldn't.

"He won't even reply to my texts, what would you have me do?"

"Actions speak louder than words, Mya. He's in a bad place, and I'm worried if someone doesn't pull him out soon, we'll lose him."

His words were like a knife to the heart. I'd walked away once from a boy I loved to save myself, but could I do it again?

Asher wasn't Jermaine. He would never readily hurt me, but the universe was cruel and unforgiving, and here we were, facing the ultimate test.

A test I wasn't sure I'd survive.

But if it meant saving Asher...

"I'll think about it," I said, before I could take back the words.

"That's all I ask." Cameron gave me a gentle nod. "That's all any of us can ask."

32

Asher

"ANOTHER, J," I slammed down the empty glass and flicked it toward him.

"You're done, Son. I already let you have more than I shoulda."

"Come on, Jerry. You know what happened. You know my mom is... fuck." I jammed my fingers in my hair, pulling the ends in frustration, the bite of pain a welcomed reprieve from the constant numbness in my chest.

"I'm real sorry, kid, but you won't be getting anymore liquor from me. You should go home, Son, get a cold shower and—"

"You know what, J, go fuck yourself." I pushed back the stool and stood up, swaying as the motion hit me.

"Whoa there." Jase grabbed my arm steadying me. "Everything okay here?" He eyed me and then glanced over at Jerry.

"Make sure he gets home, okay?"

"Will do." Sliding his arm around my waist, Jason started dragging me toward the door, but I paused at the last second, looking over my shoulder. The whole room was spinning, but I could see Jerry. Two Jerry's in fact. "I'm sorry," I yelled, "about before."

He waved me off as if it was nothing. But it wasn't.

It was something.

It was the darkness gnawing at my soul. The growing pit in my stomach with every day that passed and Mom didn't wake up.

"Come on, man, I got you." Jason helped me out of the bar and into his car. I landed with a thud, my head rolling against the leather seat.

"You didn't call," he said when he climbed in. He and Cameron had been around as much as they could, but they had lives too. School and girlfriends and their own families to worry about. Besides, I knew I was shitty company, slipping further and further into the black hole trying so desperately to swallow me up.

"I just needed some space, ya know?"

"I'm taking you home."

"No, no." My voice cracked. "Anywhere but there, please. I can't stand it there."

He let out a heavy sigh, raking a hand down his face. "We could go to mine, but Denise has some friends over while Dad is out of town."

"Just take me anywhere. I don't care." I let my head rest on the window and closed my eyes. Alcohol had seemed like a good idea when I'd turned up at Bell's almost two hours ago. But as the buzz slowly wore off, everything seemed to multiply. It was too much for one brain to handle and I wanted to tear my skin off just so I could breathe.

"I'm losing it," I murmured, squeezing my eyes so tight the skin around my face pinched.

"You're not losing it. You're under an immense amount of stress."

"I keep dreaming she's gone. I wake up and go into her room only to find the bed freshly made and all the cards gone."

"She's not gone, Asher. And you're not going to lose her. Your mom will pull through this, I truly believe that."

We drove in silence after that. I knew Jason probably had heaps of other things he wanted to say but I wasn't exactly in a receptive mood.

When we pulled up to Felicity's house, I finally broke the silence. "What the fuck is this?"

"This is my girlfriend's house," he deadpanned.

"I can see that, but what the fuck are we doing here?"

"You didn't want to go home, and we couldn't go hang out with Denise and her friends, so I brought you to option C."

"I can't go in there." I shook my head.

"Chill. Her parents are out and she's home alone studying."

"You're sure about that?" I couldn't ask him the words on the tip of my tongue. But he knew.

Of course he fucking knew.

"She's not here, you have nothing to worry about."

My eyes slid to the house again. Part of me hated that I felt relieved Mya wasn't here, but I couldn't deal with her. Not yet.

"Is there liquor?" I asked, already feeling the numbing effects of the liquor wearing off.

"Her dad might have a beer or two in the refrigerator, but I think you've had enough."

"I'll have had enough when I pass out and forget the shitshow that is my life."

He rolled his eyes, shouldering the car door and climbing out. I didn't really want to see Felicity. But it was better than sitting at home, listening to the chime of the clock, the whir of refrigerator. Listening to every-fucking-thing that wasn't the phone ringing with news of Mom.

Cussing under my breath, I got out of the Dodge Charger and followed Jase up the Giles' driveway. He knocked and seconds later, the door swung open.

"You look like shit," she said to me, the pity in her eyes too much to bear.

"Hello to you too," I replied, suddenly a lot less drunk than I was two minutes ago.

"Well, don't stand out here all night. The neighbors will talk." She beckoned me inside. Jason stood back, leaning against the wall. No doubt watching with amusement as Flick treated me like a naughty schoolboy.

The second I stepped inside, she pulled me into her arms, hugging me. "You're okay," she whispered. "You're going to be okay." I let myself take her offer of comfort. It was stupid but I needed a woman's touch.

I needed my mom.

Bile rushed up my throat, but I swallowed it down. "Thank you," I managed to croak out, finally untangling myself from Felicity's arms.

"I would have come to the hospital again, but Jason said..."

"Yeah, sorry about that. I just... it's hard."

"I know." She gave me a sad smile. "But if you ever need me, all you have to do is call."

"I think Jase might have something to say about that." The corner of my mouth tipped. It was the first joke I'd cracked in days.

"Nah, man." Jase shut the door and came around to stand beside Flick. "We're here for you, whatever you need."

"Does your dad have any whisky?" I asked Felicity. "I could really use whisky right about now."

"Asher, that isn't going to help." She frowned. "But I have some homemade cookies."

My stomach rumbled. "The ones with the chocolate chips?"

"Come on, let's see what I can find."

Jase came over and slung his arm around my shoulder. "Everything is going to be okay, Ash," he said as if he truly believed the words.

I only wished I could believe them too.

"WHERE HAVE YOU BEEN?" I growled at my father as he entered Mom's room. It felt more familiar than our house lately, but then I had spent every waking minute here. Until the nurses began insisting I left to shower and eat and do all the things I needed to do to take care of myself. But I didn't care about myself.

I cared about the woman sleeping in the bed. Except, she wasn't sleeping, not really.

Dad fussed with his tie and I knew exactly where he'd been. "Work," I snapped. "You've been working."

"Watch your tone, Son," he said. "Business doesn't just stop because..." His eyes flicked to Mom, the blood draining from his face. "How is she?"

Surprised at his reluctance to argue with me, I replied, "The same. The doctors said they're thinking of waking her soon but it's still too early to know what sustained damage there is."

"You spoke with the doctors?" It was his turn to look surprised.

"Well they couldn't speak with you since you weren't here."

"Asher, please." He walked around the bed and leaned down to press a kiss to Mom's head. It was funny, watching him treat her as something fragile and precious. Dropping into the chair opposite me, he clutched Mom's hand in his. "It's this place... I can't..."

"I know." But whereas Dad chose to run, I chose to stay.

I would always stay.

It's what made us so different.

"How do you do it? Sit here, day in, day out, watching her as if she might wake up at any second, knowing she won't?"

"She gave up everything for me," I bit out. "It's the least I can do for her."

"Son, I want you to know—"

The door creaked open and both our heads snapped up to see who was entering.

"Mya," her name fell from my lips in a whoosh of air.

"You." Dad shot out of his chair. "You have no right to be here," he yelled.

Mya's eyes went wide, darting between us. "I- I should go. This was a mistake."

"You're damn right it was; you've caused enough pain already," my father seethed at her, spittle flying from his mouth. But he didn't approach her. Thank fuck, he didn't approach her. I couldn't bear the thought of him laying one hand on her.

Inhaling a shaky breath, I moved around the bed, putting myself between him and Mya. "Give me a minute, Dad," I said, keeping my eyes locked on her. She slipped out of the room, and I followed, ignoring Dad's grumbles of disapproval.

Mya didn't wait. She kept walking, hurrying down the hall.

"Wait." I grasped her arm, pulling her around. "What are you doing here?"

"I came..." Her voice wavered, unshed tears glistening in her eyes. "For you, Asher. You won't return my calls or texts. I haven't seen you in days. I just needed to know you were okay."

"You can't be here," I said, still stunned she was even here after the way I'd dismissed her before. I'd ignored her for the best part of two weeks. Yet, she was here. Standing in front of me, silently begging me to let her in.

Fuck.

I fisted my thigh.

She smothered a sob, turning from me to walk away, but I grabbed her arm again, pulling her to the side. "I didn't mean..." Shit, what did I mean?

"I just had to know the truth." Mya's expression was crestfallen.

"The truth? I don't understand."

"I just needed to look you in the eye and see it." Silent tears ran down her cheeks now, gutting me in a way I hadn't been prepared for. "You used to look at me with such adoration. But now you look at me like you can't stand to be around me... like you blame me. And I get it, I do. There is nothing more I wish than to take your mom's place. But I can't change what happened. I can't do anything. So instead of sitting at my aunt's, driving myself crazy with worry over you, I had to come and see for myself."

"Mya, that's not fair—"

"None of this is fair." She gave a small shrug. "I'm going to testify, Asher. I want you to know I'm going to do everything I can to make sure you and your family get justice for what happened. But I'm not going to cling onto the hope that things between us will ever heal. I can't."

I dragged a hand down my face, trying to process everything she was saying. "You're breaking up with me?" Disbelief coated my words.

"You can't break up with someone you already lost, and I lost you the second that gun went off." Pain flashed in her eyes and I wanted to do something—*anything*—to take it away. But it was like my head and heart were at war. My heart knew how special she was, how much we needed her. But my head; my stupid, foolhardy head, looked at Mya and saw Jermaine. Jermaine holding a gun up at my parents, at me. Saw my mom bleeding out, cradled in my dad's arms.

It was like no matter how much I tried, I couldn't separate the two.

"I was going to do it, you know? I was going to accept a place at Cleveland. I want you to know that, Asher. I want you to know I was going to choose you." Mya pushed damp curls from her eyes and sucked in a harsh breath. "I really hope your mom makes a full recovery. Goodbye, Asher."

I should have gone after her. I should have told her that we could figure things out, that I just needed time to get my head around everything that had happened.

But I didn't.

I took the coward's way out.

I stood there as Mya walked away from me for the last time, my heart breaking all over again.

33

Mya

"OH MY GOD, did you hear? Asher's mom finally woke up." Kellie Ginly locked eyes on me as I tried to give her and her friends a wide berth, her mouth curving deviously. "He called to tell me last night."

I faltered for a second. He'd called her? But I quickly pushed aside the hurt. It wasn't the important titbit of information I'd overheard. Mrs. Bennet was awake and that was all that mattered.

"That's amazing, I bet he's so relieved." Her friends quickly burst into questions.

How is he?

What is the long-term damage?

Is he coming back to school soon?

I hitched my backpack up my shoulder and carried on down the hall. Three weeks had passed since that day in the hospital when Asher let me walk away. I hadn't gone with the intention of ending things between us, but the second Mr. Bennet saw me standing there, I knew I had to let Asher go. I'd already caused enough pain and heartache for his family without making things worse.

The closure had been a good thing. News spread quickly that I was no longer Asher's girl and within a few days people's interest in me simmered. There were still the whispers and stares, but it was nothing I wasn't used to. I filled my days with class and my new part-time job stacking shelves at the Seven-Eleven where my aunt worked. Felicity and Hailee remained loyal in their friendship, but it wasn't the same now me and Asher were no longer together.

To the outside world, I had moved on. But I didn't anticipate getting over him anytime soon. Asher Bennet had imprinted himself on my soul in a way that I wasn't sure I'd ever recover from. To deal, I kept my head down and my focus on college. I'd decided to accept an offer from Temple University to study social work. If growing up in Fallowfield Heights had taught me anything, it was that more help was needed in communities where young men and women felt they had no choice but to turn to gangs, drugs, and a life of crime. It felt like coming full circle somehow, and I was counting down the days until graduation.

"There you are." Felicity found me by my locker. "I've been texting you."

"I think my cell is on silent."

She rolled her eyes. It was a common occurrence these days. "Asher called Jason earlier, his mom is—"

"Awake, I know."

Flick's brow pinched. "You do? Did he—"

"I overheard Kellie Ginly telling her friends."

"Kellie... but how would she know?"

I shrugged, trading out some books. "Apparently Asher called her last night."

"But that doesn't make any sense. He doesn't—"

The reverberation of my locker slamming shut cut her off. "I don't want to talk about him."

"But—"

"Felicity, you promised."

"I know, I know, it's just, she's awake. This is a good thing." She looked so hopeful. I didn't have the heart to tell her that some things couldn't be fixed. That just because Mrs. Bennet was awake didn't mean me and Asher were going to find our way back together.

"You're right, it is great news. I'm happy for them." Shoving the books into my backpack, I shouldered it and took off down the hall.

"That's it?" Flick hurried after me. "That's all you have to say?"

"What else is there to say?"

"I don't know. I guess I just thought..."

"Life isn't a fairytale, Felicity. Not all stories get a happy ending."

"But..."

I let out an exasperated breath and levelled her with a hard look. "You're my best friend and I couldn't have gotten through these last few weeks without you, but you need to let this go. I've accepted it's over between me and Asher. You should too."

I'd just walked through the door after a long shift at the store, when my cell phone blared to life.

"Hey, Shona," I said, kicking off my shoes and letting the cool tiles soothe my burning soles.

"Hey, girl. How's it goin'?"

"It's... going. How are you? How are things back home?" After Jermaine had forced her to give up my location, Shona had felt responsible for everything that had gone down. But I didn't blame her. I'd asked her to keep it a secret; I'd burdened her with that.

Me.

"Diaz is actin' like it's all business as usual, but since Jermaine's arrest, things feel... different."

"Keep safe, yeah?" I said.

"I will. Jesse and Leroy watch me like a hawk."

"Leroy, huh? You got your way then?" I smirked.

"He gave in eventually." She chuckled. "Jesse gave him a black eye for it though."

"I'm glad you have him to look out for you."

"Any developments with JT?"

"It's done." The words punched my chest. "But I found out his mom finally woke up."

"That's good news, right?"

"Yeah." I couldn't keep the pain out of my voice.

"Hey, it's almost spring break. We should totally hit the city. Girls' trip. It's only weeks until graduation and then college will be calling your name and I'll never see you."

"Shona..."

"Yeah, yeah, I know. We can't all be brains like you. But I'm proud of you, Mya. I'm so fucking proud you got out and made a life for yourself, even if you do live in some hick town in the ass crack of nowhere." Her laughter soothed the ache in my chest. "I know things suck right now but soon this will all be behind you."

"I know." But the idea of leaving Rixon, of leaving my aunt, and the place I'd come to call home, didn't fill me with joy. *Because Asher is here*, a little voice whispered. But come the summer he wouldn't be here. He'd be in Pittsburgh, moving on with his life.

Moving on from me.

"Listen, Shon, I need to go start dinner. But I'll call you soon."

"You'd better," she warned. "Laters."

Pocketing my cell, I got up to go into the kitchen, but a knock at the door made me pause. Traipsing back into the hall, I checked the peephole before opening the door. "This is a surprise," I said to Felicity who stood on my aunt's porch.

"We're going out."

"We are?" My brows knitted together.

"Yep. I miss hanging out with you. I know things are awkward, but you're still one of my best friends, so get ready and let's go."

"Flick, I'm not sure..." We hadn't been out since the Ice-Ts incident.

"Ten minutes. You have ten minutes and then we have to get Hailee."

"Where are we going?"

"Worry less about that and more about what you're going to wear." She frowned at my work uniform. "Is that tuna fish I smell?"

I sniffed myself and realized she was right, I stank. It must have been when I'd cleaned up a spillage in aisle three. "I'll need to take a quick shower," I said.

"The clock's ticking." Mischief twinkled in her eyes.

"This is just like old times," I said, half-mockingly. When I'd first arrived in Rixon and she'd taken me under her wing, we'd gotten into all kinds of trouble together. It felt comforting to know that after everything, she was still here.

"Eight-and-a-half minutes," she grumbled. "Let's go, Hernandez."

But as she started marching me up the stairs, I was sucker punched by her words.

Hernandez.

No one ever called me that.

No one except Asher.

Bell's was crammed. I couldn't believe I'd let Felicity talk me into coming here. But I couldn't deny there was a part of me that wanted to see Asher. To witness his easy smile once more, and to know he was okay.

That's all I'd ever wanted.

"Breathe," Flick whispered to me as we moved deeper into the bar. The whole team was here with their friends and girlfriends. I spotted Kellie and the gymnasts straightaway, and the cheerleaders holding court the other side of the room. It looked like the entire senior class had come out to celebrate the Bennets' good news, and my heart swelled for Asher.

"Look, Cam saved us a seat." Hailee pointed to a booth away from the football team.

"I hope you're going to marry him one day," I said, hardly surprised that he would do such a nice thing for me.

Felicity offered to go and get our drinks while we weaved through the huddles of people to reach Cameron.

He stood up, letting Hailee slide in. I took the other side.

"Thanks for this," I said, drumming my fingers against the table.

"It's the least I could do. I'm glad you came." His eyes slid from me to Hailee. "I'm going to go hang out with the guys, but I'll come check on you later, okay?"

She nodded, leaning in to kiss him. My heart ached watching them. But if two people deserved happiness it was the two of them.

"This is silly," I said when he'd gone. "You don't have to sit over here with me. I'll go and you can—"

"If you think we're going to abandon you, you really don't know us at all," Hailee replied around a small smile. Flick appeared seconds later, sliding a tray of drinks onto the table. "We're celebrating. My treat." She handed me a bright pink cocktail.

"What is it?" I sniffed the contents.

"Happiness and sunshine in a glass. Drink up."

"Isn't Jerry going to get into trouble for serving everyone?"

"Asher's mom is awake; it's a private celebration." She winked at me, slurping at her own drink.

"Have you seen—"

The words died on my tongue as Asher filled my line of sight. He was joking with a couple of his teammates, his hair pushed back in that messy style of his, his smile easy and eyes bright.

I swallowed, feeling tears pool behind my eyes. "He looks happy," I whispered. Just then, Kellie Ginly sauntered over to him and hugged him, making a show of kissing him on the cheek.

"It doesn't mean anything," Felicity said under her breath, a hint of disapproval there.

"It doesn't matter. He's a free agent."

"Mya, you don't mean that."

"So, do you have any plans for spring break?" I changed the subject, forcing myself to look away from Asher and Kellie. He wasn't mine anymore. He could hug and kiss whoever he wanted. It was something I was just going to have to get used to.

"I think Cameron and Jason want to take Asher away for a few days; maybe to his Dad's place in the Hamptons."

It was like I couldn't escape him.

But slowly, I was becoming okay. I glanced back and found Asher watching me. Our eyes locked, so much passing between us. My pulse spiked. His mouth curved into a smile and he gave me a little nod before turning away.

I smiled to myself. Things between us would never be the same, but maybe, just maybe, we could find peace after everything.

"Come dance with us," Felicity pouted, her eyes glassy with the effects of all the sugary sweet cocktails she'd consumed since we arrived at Asher's house.

I hadn't wanted to come when they'd announced the party was moving to the Bennets'. It didn't feel right. But the need to be in close proximity to Asher, to see him happy, was too much of a temptation, plus, she wouldn't take no for an answer and no one else seemed to care whether I was there or not. People were too happy and relieved to have their loveable funny party host back. And Asher played up to the role flawlessly. But I couldn't help but wonder how much was real or whether he felt forced to oblige them. It wasn't my place to ask him though, and despite caving to Felicity and Hailee's insistence I come with them to the party, I kept my distance.

"I owe you an apology," Jason came up beside me as I watched the girls twirl and dance without a care in the world.

"I'm listening," I said, running my thumb around the rim of my cup. It had been tempting to get drunk and join the celebrations, but I didn't want to lose control, not surrounded by Asher and his adoring fans.

Especially not with Kellie Ginly throwing me icy stares like we were mortal enemies.

"Asher is like family and you're—"

"Not?" My brow rose.

"I'm sorry, okay. I shouldn't have treated you like you had a hand in all of this. Because for the record, I know you didn't. What happened, that's all on your piece of shit ex. Me and you, we're good."

"As far as apologies go that sucked." I smirked. "But I'll take it."

He barked a laugh, shaking his head with disbelief. "I'm glad you're here, Mya. We all are." Jason gave me a look I didn't quite understand before he stalked over to Felicity, hooking his arm around her waist. The two of them started dancing as if they were the only two in the room, and I had to turn away, their love too much to bear.

"I'm surprised to see you here," another voice said, this time one I never wanted to hear again.

"It's a party."

"Yeah, at your ex's house. I mean how pathetic do you have to be?" Kellie Ginly glowered at me, flicking her hair off her shoulder. She looked cute in a skintight knitted dress that scooped low in the front and landed just below her knee. It was demure but sexy and even I couldn't deny she looked killer.

She looked like a girl out to impress.

My stomach knotted.

"What do you want from me, Kellie? In case you didn't get the 4-1-1, me and Asher are over. I'm only here to celebrate, just like everyone else." I moved around her to leave, before I said or did something I would regret. But she caught my wrist, demanding my attention. "You should do Asher a favor and just leave. He doesn't need you anymore, not now that he has me."

My eyes widened, just for a second, before I schooled my expression. But she saw it and she was about to go for the jugular. "Oh, you didn't know? I've been helping him through this difficult time. Even spent some time with him and his dad. Andrew is such a lovely man. Good taste too." She smiled but it looked more like a snarl. "He's so relieved Asher decided to get rid of the trash."

"What the fuck did you just call me?" I stepped into her space, all rational thought flying out of my head.

"You heard me, Latina. Trash."

Clenching my fists at my side, it took everything in me to walk away when all I wanted to do was hit her right in her pretty, perfect face.

"That's right," she called after me. "Run back to whatever ghetto you came from."

I hurried through the Bennets' house, desperate to get away from Kellie and her poisonous words. I needed air. I needed to—

"Mya?" I collided with a wall of solid muscle, and Asher's hands steadied me. "What happened?" His jaw clenched.

"I'm fine, I just need... air, I need air. I have to go but I'm so happy your mom is awake. It's great news." The words spilled from my lips as I tried to gently shuck him off my arms. I couldn't stand him touching me, holding me with concern in his eyes.

We weren't those people to each other anymore.

Spinning on my heel, I took off again, pushing and jostling bodies out of the way.

"Mya, wait," Asher called, making me move faster. I couldn't do this with him. Not here, not now.

I never should have come here. I knew that now. There would always be people like Kellie Ginly waiting to strike, to act like their white privilege made them better than me. More worthy.

More suited to be by Asher's side, living in his world.

34

Asher

"MYA, WAIT A SECOND, PLEASE," I said, snagging her wrist. My touch stopped her dead, her gaze going straight to where our skin met. Heat flowed between us and I wanted nothing more than to pull her into my arms and hold her. To feel her body pressed against mine.

But I'd lost that right, and it hurt something fierce.

She turned slowly, letting her eyes drift to mine. "Please, let me go," it came out a strained whisper, as if saying the words caused her physical pain.

Immediately releasing her, I stepped back, raking a hand through my hair. "I'm sorry. I didn't... You came."

"You know how persistent Felicity can be." She gave me a weak smile. "I'm so happy for you, Asher, and your mom."

"Thanks." The air cooled between us, the fleeting moment when I'd grabbed her wrist long gone. "She has a long road to recovery, but the doctors are pleased with her progress so far."

I couldn't even begin to describe the sense of relief that had hit me when Mom's eyes finally flickered open; how good it had felt to feel her fingers squeeze mine. She'd been disorientated and groggy and was barely able to string a syllable together, but she was awake.

It was like all my prayers had been answered.

All but one.

Dad was the biggest surprise of all though. He'd burst into tears, collapsing at the side of the bed when he had entered the room and seen her. In all my eighteen years on the planet, I don't think I'd ever seen him cry or show an ounce of emotion toward us. His sudden change of heart didn't erase the past, but it gave me a smidgen of hope, that maybe, just maybe, they could figure their shit out. That almost losing Mom would make him realize that he needed to atone for the sins of his past. Even if we never found solid ground again, I would breathe easier knowing Mom was happy and healthy and cared for.

"I'm so happy for you." Mya smiled again, a real honest-to-God smile. One that wasn't tainted by all the pain and heartache between us. It meant a lot.

It meant every-fucking-thing that she was here.

That even after the way I'd treated her, how my father had treated her, and Kellie and Vaughn, and the kids at school; she still cared enough to come and celebrate our good news.

But her smile quickly faded as something caught her eye behind me. I glanced back, narrowing my gaze as Kellie hovered nearby, watching us like a hawk. "What is she—"

"I should go," Mya rushed out. "Send my love to your mom." She spun around and took off down the hall toward the front door.

Kellie's eyes burned holes into the back of my head as I tried to piece together what the fuck had just happened. Mya was running, but I wasn't sure she was running from me. And if she wasn't running from me...

Marching up to Kellie, I said, "Did something happen with you and Mya?"

"I'm surprised she was here in the first place." Kellie twirled a strand of hair around her finger, a flash of contempt crossing her expression. "I mean, doesn't she realize how sad it makes her look? Not to mention desperate."

"Excuse me?" My jaw clenched, my teeth grinding together.

"Well, it's obvious she's only here because she still wants you. Like that is *ever* going to happen." Her shrill laughter filled the air, making me flinch.

"I'm going to ask you one more time, Kellie. What. Did. You. Say. To. Her?"

"Asher, I..." Panic flared in her eyes, but she quickly recovered, smiling at me like I hung the moon. "I was just making sure she knew she wasn't welcome around here anymore. Your dad would—"

"My dad... what the fuck does my dad have to do with this?" He was at the hospital with Mom. He'd barely left her side since she'd woken up yesterday.

"He came over for dinner the other week, remember? We got to talking and he said he was glad you finally came to your senses about her."

"That's all he said?" I gave her a pointed look.

"Well, yeah, I mean, he was upset, and you know how men get when they've had a drink or two." Her laughter was strained now.

"Kellie..." My patience was wearing thin, my good mood quickly turning dark.

"Fine." She huffed as if I was the one inconveniencing her. "He told my father he was glad you'd finally taken out the trash, okay?"

Anger rippled up my spine, my hands curling into tight fists. "And let me guess, you thought you'd pass the message on?"

"I didn't... I was just trying to help. You can't honestly want anything to do with her after what she did."

"Mya didn't do anything. Fuck." My eyes frantically searched the hall, but Mya was long gone.

Trash.

He'd called her trash, and Kellie had reiterated the words like a mindless puppet.

Deep down it didn't surprise me, but it didn't make it any easier to hear.

"You should leave," I seethed.

"L- leave?" She blanched. "I don't understand. I thought—"

"You thought what? That now me and Mya are no longer together, I'd get with you?" A dark chuckle spilled from my lips. "I wouldn't touch you if you were the last girl on the planet."

Tears glossed her eyes. "But we're—"

"What? The same? Well suited? Destined to be?" I mocked dryly. "You don't know anything about me!"

People were watching now. Jason and Cameron slowly inching their way over to us, concern pinching their expressions.

"Asher, calm down." Kellie tried to save face. "You're making a scene." She fluffed her hair as if it held the power to fix the mess she'd created.

It didn't.

"Get the fuck out of my house and don't ever come back." My best friends came to my side, Hailee and Flick watching on from over by the door.

"You heard him," Jase said coolly. No one ignored his word. In Rixon High, Jason Ford's word was final. Kellie sniffled back a tear and spun on her heel before running out of the house.

"And don't let the door hit you on the way out," I yelled, my chest heaving.

"What was all that about?" he asked.

"How much did you hear?"

"Enough to know she pissed you the hell off."

"She was fucking with Mya." Shame burned through me. I'd done this. I'd given people the impression I blamed her.

I'd stoked the flames.

"Fuck. I think I really screwed up, you guys."

"No shit." Cam folded his arms across his chest, pinning me with a hard look.

"We all screw up," Jase added. "We're guys, it's what we do. But the question is how do you plan on fixing it?"

"I don't know," I admitted.

But I'd figure it out.

I had to.

Because losing Mya for good was not an option.

It never was.

I'd just been too blinded by pain and grief to see it.

"Can't you drive any faster?" I tapped my hand against my knee, my eyes searching the dark empty streets for Mya.

She wasn't answering her cell. Fuck knows, I'd called it enough. I knew Mya would most likely ignore me, so I used Felicity's phone. But still, she didn't pick up.

"There." I saw the shadowy silhouette of Mya's profile up ahead. "Stop the car."

"Asher, just give me a—"

"Stop the damn car," I rushed out, my hand already clutching the handle ready to push. The car slammed to a halt and I leaped out. "Mya, wait up," I called.

"Go away, Asher." She stepped up her pace but there was no way she could outrun me.

I broke into a jog, darting across the street and falling into step beside her. "Don't you know it's not safe to walk home alone?"

"The only danger I see out here is you." Her eyes simmered with emotion as she looked up at me.

"Let me walk you the rest of the way home, please?"

"It's a free country, you can do whatever you want," she shot back, but there wasn't the usual amount of fight in her words.

I knew I'd done that. I'd dimmed her spark.

And I hated myself for it.

I glanced back, but Felicity had already pulled a U-turn and disappeared. I owed her big time; not only for bringing me here but trusting me enough to be alone with Mya.

"I kicked Kellie out of my house," I said.

"You did?" Her eyes were fixed ahead, but I couldn't take my eyes off her.

"I know what she said to you, what my dad said about you. And it makes me sick to my stomach thinking that you might think I agree with them, about any of it."

"Asher," she sighed, coming to a stop. "Don't do this, *please*."

"Do what? What am I doing, Mya?" We'd turned into one another, like magnets.

I'd watched my two best friends fall ass over elbow in love, hard and fast. And I'd wanted it too... shit, I'd wanted it so badly. To have that one person who got you. Who loved you unconditionally. But I hadn't known how powerful it could be when you found them. How something inside you shifted, making room for the ties that bound you together.

"You're acting as if everything is okay between us."

"I'm not... fuck, Mya. I'm so fucking sorry."

"Asher..." she breathed my name. "Don't make this any harder than it needs to be. I'm so happy your mom's awake but this, us, it's over."

Over.

The word splintered through me like a knife to the stomach.

We weren't over.

We couldn't be.

"I deserve that, I do. I deserve for you to walk away and never look back. But you can't look me in the eye and tell me you don't still feel it." I inched closer, bringing my hand to her cheek. Mya turned into me, pressing her skin against mine, her shoulders dropping slightly as if my touch unwound something deep inside her.

"You feel it," I whispered, my mouth hovering near the corner of hers. I hadn't planned to chase after her and kiss her. There was too much I needed to say first. But now I was standing here, with her so close, it was impossible not to be swept up in the pull.

"Asher, please..." Mya's voice cracked, her eyes fluttering closed as I kissed the corner of her mouth.

"I'm sorry. I'm sorry for pushing you away. I'm sorry for treating you like you were to blame. But most of all, I'm sorry for ever letting you think I didn't want you anymore." My hand curled around the back of her neck, drawing her closer, touching my head to hers. "I will always want you, Mya. You own my heart and I don't ever want it back."

I eased back to look at her. Tears streaked down Mya's cheeks, her eyes glittering with so much emotion it knocked the air clean from my lungs. "I want to believe you," she whispered. "I want to believe we can get through this. But your dad—"

"Is *not* important." I captured her lips again, kissing her softly and with caution. The last thing I wanted was to scare her away, but I needed this. I needed to taste her, to take comfort in her.

"I thought she was going to die." My confession pierced the silent night. "I saw her lying there and I thought she was going to leave me. It doesn't excuse anything I did or said to you, but I was scared. I was so fucking scared, Mya." My hands cupped her face. "It felt like I had to choose. You or her. It's fucked up, I know, but you deserve the truth."

"You blamed me."

"I didn't, not really. But I can't deny it was hard to separate my thoughts about you with my thoughts about Jermaine. So many times I wanted to call you or text you or just hear your voice, but the more time passed, the more the darkness consumed me."

Mya's hand had slid to my sweater, curling into the fabric. "And if she hadn't woken up?"

God, I didn't want to think about that. But I knew why Mya was asking the question and she deserved an answer.

"If Mom hadn't woken up, I would've needed you more than ever. Even if I couldn't see it at the time."

"I think your friends know you better than you know yourself."

"Is that so?" I was hardly surprised Cameron had said something to her since he'd chewed me out too.

"You're lucky to have them. Have you told them the truth yet?"

"No, but I will. Everything's different now. But I didn't come here to talk about them, Mya. I came here for you." Indecision flickered in her eyes and I rushed out, "What you said before, about accepting a place at Cleveland—"

"I changed my mind," she said a little too quickly. "I'm going to Temple University. They have a great social work program and I want to help communities that need it most."

"I see." My heart didn't just sink, it withered and died in my chest. She'd really moved on. I couldn't blame her, but fuck, it hurt.

"It's something I need to do. For me, Asher. I spent most of my life looking out for Jermaine, and then I came here and met you. Even when I said I wouldn't let myself fall in love again, you went and stole my heart anyway. I can't be the girl who's always fighting for someone to love her. Jermaine. My mom. You. I'm tired of fighting. For once I want someone to fight for me. To *choose* me. But until then, I'm okay with fighting for myself, for going after what *I* want."

Mya palmed my cheek, brushing the tip of her nose across mine. The intimate action sent a shiver shooting up my spine. But it was bittersweet. Even when she fixed her mouth over mine, kissing me hard, letting her tongue slip between my lips and stroke my tongue, I knew it wasn't the ending I'd hoped for.

It was Mya's way of saying goodbye.

But screw that.

She couldn't walk away, not again. Not when I'd bared my soul to her and laid all my cards out on the table.

"I won't let you walk away," I murmured against her, deepening the kiss. "I won't lose you again, Mya." Emotion clogged my throat and I finally broke away, inhaling a ragged breath. "I can't lose you."

Mya lowered her face, looking up at me through thick lashes. "Then fight for me, Asher," she said before turning and walking away.

35

Mya

"HE'S WATCHING YOU AGAIN," Felicity whispered, hardly being discreet about the fact she was watching Asher watch me.

He was finally back at school, although I'd heard he wasn't doing all his classes. Things were relatively normal again in the halls of Rixon High. I'd barely heard my name whispered in class and if I entered a room, people looked away rather than staring like I was about to pull a gun on them and fulfil the stereotype.

It was almost as if someone had told them to back off, but I didn't want to make assumptions.

"Quit it." I nudged Felicity in the ribs, and she sprayed a mouthful of soda everywhere.

"What?" She played dumb. "I wasn't doing anything."

"You're staring at him."

"But he looks so... so—"

"Desperate?"

"I was going to say lost."

"Flick..." It wasn't like I couldn't feel Asher watching. His gaze was like a laser, smoldering into the top of my head as I pretended to eat my lunch.

"You should talk to him."

"I'm good, thanks." Surprisingly, it was the truth. I missed Asher something fierce. I missed being part of the group. But I couldn't deny that since I'd walked away from him, I also felt empowered.

While I accepted his apology, I hadn't just rolled over and given in to him. I'd stood tall and put myself first for once. In some ways, I had Asher to thank for giving me the push I needed to embrace my future at Temple University. Going out of state for college would have only been me running further away, and deep down, I didn't want that. I needed to own all the parts of me: the girl from the hood; the girl trying to find herself in a town that didn't accept her; and the girl I knew I could become. I was all those parts and if someone was going to love me, they had to accept all of me.

"You're really going to do this, huh?" Felicity pulled me from my thoughts. "You're really going to make him suffer?"

"I'm not making him suffer, Flick. But I'm not going to just roll over either. He hurt me, *really* hurt me. Part of me gets it, after what happened to his mom. But I've had a lifetime of pain to deal with. Next time I trust someone with my heart, it'll be because they earned it."

"But look at him... I mean, he's so... sad."

Before I could stop myself, I'd looked over at Asher's table. He was surrounded by his teammates, the conversation and laughter going on all around him, but his eyes were fixed right on me.

I inhaled a shaky breath. Of course, it wasn't the first time I'd stolen glances of him around school. I always knew when he was nearby. Just because we were no longer together didn't mean the connection between us was severed. If anything, it burned brighter; snapping taut whenever our paths crossed. But it was easier to resist the pull now. Easier to ignore.

At least, that's what I kept telling myself.

In that one simple look, Asher was able to tell me everything I didn't want to hear.

He was sorry.

He loved me.

He wanted me back.

But words weren't enough, not this time.

I was the one to break our connection, to lower my eyes and focus on the food in front of me. Felicity grumbled beneath her breath, clearly frustrated at my behavior. But this was one thing she couldn't fix.

The only person who could was sitting across the cafeteria.

And even then, I wasn't sure there was anything left he could do to make me change my mind.

"This was a great idea," I said to Felicity as I helped her herd the last couple of puppies into the tub. "I feel better already."

"It's impossible not to love these little guys, even if they get overexcited at bath time." She scrubbed a spaniel's ear, sending the tiny ball of fluff into an excited frenzy. "Quick," she shrieked, "grab a towel."

Laughing, I leaned over and helped myself to a freshly folded towel. It was my second time helping Felicity out at A Brand New Tail, the local pet shelter where she volunteered a couple nights a week, but I hadn't been here since pre-Asher.

I'd forgotten how good for the soul the little furballs could be.

"So are we hitting The Alley after we get done?" I asked drying Maximus off while she handled his brother Caesar.

"Actually," she peeked over at me, "we're... hangingatmyhousewiththeguys."

"Felicity, seriously?"

"I'm sorry, but when I told Jason we were hanging out with Hailee, he got all needy and jealous and wanted to come with us, and I thought it would be less awkward if we all hung out at mine."

Levelling her with a hard look, I let out a heavy sigh. "That makes zero sense. You know that, right?"

"I thought you'd be cool with it, since you're playing hard to get and all."

"I'm not playing hard..." I stopped myself. "Fine, it's fine." It was just six friends getting together, I could handle it.

"Asher offered not to come," she added, casting me a furtive glance.

"He did?"

I didn't know how to feel about that.

"Yeah, said he didn't want to make you feel uncomfortable, but like I told him, you're cool with everything." Her lip curved, a familiar glint in her eye. "You *are* cool with everything, right?"

"Who me?" I smiled sweetly.

"I don't know how you do it."

"Do what?" We finished up drying the puppies before placing them back in their crates.

"Pretend you're over him."

"I'm not. Over him, I mean."

"Well, duh, took you long enough to admit it." She grinned.

"Oh hush." I rolled a towel and whipped her arm with it. "You know what I mean. Just because I'm not falling at his feet, doesn't mean I don't care about him."

I still cared.

I cared too damn much and that was half the problem.

"So why put yourselves through this? I don't get it."

With a half-hearted shrug, I let my eyes wander anywhere but to her. "Because I'm tired of always being cast aside when things get rough. I wasn't enough for Jermaine and Asher made me feel that all over again."

"Oh, Mya, you know it wasn't like that. He loves you, but he's a guy and we all know how emotionally stunted they can be."

"It's not good enough," I said around a sad smile. "I chose him, Flick. I put him first. He asked me to pick Cleveland, and I was going to do it. But I'm done being that girl."

Felicity stared at me, but I saw no judgment in her eyes this time. "Okay," she said quietly. "If that's what you need to do, then okay, I'm right behind you."

"Thank you."

"Hey, that's what best friends are for. Now let's get cleaned up so we can go make your boy suffer."

I rolled my eyes, smothering a chuckle. It wasn't quite what I meant, but I'd take it.

Because it was better than her trying to play Cupid.

"You'd better get in here if you want pizza," Jason yelled the second we stepped into Felicity's house.

"He has a key now?" My brow quirked up.

"I... uh, sometimes he waits for me to get done at the shelter."

"And what do you parents think about that?"

"Usually my mom tries to feed him."

"And when they're not here?"

She flushed. "What they don't know won't hurt them."

"Scandalous."

Our laughter ushered the Giles' living room into silence as we entered.

"About fucking time." Jason grumbled around a mouthful of pizza. "Get over here." He patted his lap, pulling Flick onto his the second he could reach her.

"Hey, Mya, how did you enjoy puppy season at the shelter?" Hailee asked, pushing a half-empty pizza box toward me.

"It was... just what I needed." My eyes found Asher across the room. He offered me a small nod in greeting but didn't say anything.

"What are we watching?" I forced myself to look away, even if I could still feel his intense gaze on my face.

"Yeah, Cam, why don't you tell them what we're watching," Jason teased, throwing a handful of popcorn at him.

"There is nothing wrong with *The Kissing Booth*."

"Did you suddenly grow a pussy overnight?"

"*Jase!*" everyone yelled.

"Oh, lighten up. If Cam wants all of us to get in touch with our feminine sides, I'm down. Just don't blame me when I raid the place for ice cream and want to braid your hair."

"You're so weird." Felicity rolled her eyes.

"Is that so, Giles?" He cocked his brow. "Takes one to know one." Jason attacked her with his mouth, planting wet, sloppy kisses all over her face.

"Get off me, you big jerk." She tried to bat him off, but it was futile. His arms were wrapped tight around her waist, anchoring them together.

Hailee and Cameron shared a knowing smile, in that way only two people in tune could. And me and Asher, well, we sat there pretending everything was fine.

"Guys, seriously?" He finally groaned.

"Sorry," Jason replied. "We'll do better." He moved Flick off his lap and tucked her into his side, before grumbling. "Are we watching the movie or what?"

I sat there like a statue while I was pretty certain Felicity and Jason spent more time watching each other than the movie; they were barely able keep their hands off one another. Hailee and Cam weren't much better, and by the time the credits rolled, I jumped up, desperate to escape the overpowering sexual tension.

I escaped to Felicity's bathroom. It had been the longest two hours of my life, my body hyper aware of Asher sitting across the room in Mr. Giles' favorite armchair. After washing my hands, I dried them on a fluffy hand towel. I liked Felicity's house. It wasn't small but it wasn't huge either. I felt at ease here. Comfortable. Unlike Asher's house where I'd always felt out of place. Like Cinderella swept up into a fairytale.

Except Cinders had gotten her Prince in the end.

Clutching the rim of the basin, I took a couple of deep breaths and looked at myself in the mirror. I could do this. I could totally do it. All I had to do was go back out there and pretend like everything was fine.

"Asher," I gasped as I opened the door to find him standing there.

"You took your time."

"I..."

"I'm joking, Mya." His lip curved into a tentative smile.

"Oh, right. Well, I guess I'll just get out of your way." I went to move around him, but he filled the space, making no effort to move. Our chests brushed as I tried to wiggle through the tight gap. His smell, the cologne I loved so much, punched me right in the stomach.

But then, Asher was backing me into the bathroom, giving me no escape.

"Asher, what are you—"

"I've tried, Mya. I've tried so fucking hard to give you space, to figure out how to fix this." He motioned between us. "So you need to help me out here. You need to tell me what I have to do to fix it."

I edged back as he advanced with slow, sure strides. The air crackled around us, the bonds between us twisting and tightening. "Tell me what to do." Asher loomed over me, the edge of the counter pressing into my back.

"Asher..." My hands slammed against his chest as I desperately tried to resist his charms. His smell. The way he looked at me with so much love and yearning. "It's not that simple."

"It is that simple," he countered. "I love you. I fucking love you, Mya." Asher's chest heaved with the weight of his words as he leaned in to touch his head to mine. "I need you, babe. I need you more than I need air. It's like I can't breathe when you're not around."

A tremor tore through my reinforced walls, shaking their foundations. He sounded so desperate. I wanted nothing more than to take away all his pain. Even now, *I* wanted to fix *him*.

"Asher, it's not—"

"Ssh, don't say it. If you don't say it then there's still hope." His eyes shuttered as he inhaled a shaky breath, trying to rein in his emotions.

Oh God. What was I doing?

The boy I loved more than anything was standing in front of me breaking and I was forcing myself not to put him back together. But if I gave in, if *I* fixed this, I knew it would only be temporary. Because there was still his father to contend with. The trial. His mom, and Jermaine. Not to mention come the fall we would both be at colleges across state.

"Asher, look at me." He opened his eyes and I fell headfirst into a pool of sparkling blue. "I love you, I do. But sometimes love isn't enough."

"It is." His hands cradled my face, brushing his lips over mine. "It is enough, Mya, and I'm going to prove it to you. I just need you to wait for me. Promise me, you'll wait for me while I figure out how to fix this."

I let out an exasperated breath. "Asher, I'm not—"

"Promise me." There was so much pleading in his eyes, so much emotion, I couldn't deny him.

But I couldn't say the words he wanted to hear either.

So I pressed my lips together and gave him an imperceptible nod, all while my heart was screaming, *don't let me down.*

36

Asher

I DIDN'T GO to school Monday. I wasn't ready to see Mya again. Not until I figured out how the hell to fix everything. So I spent the day at the hospital, sitting with Mom. She was in and out of it for most of the morning, but I kept reminding myself the doctors said it was to be expected.

"A- Ash," she stuttered, her voice a low croak as she crooked a shaky finger toward me.

"Hey, Mom," I moved to the side of the bed, taking her hand in mine. "It's good to see you awake, but try not to talk, okay?"

She gave me a weak smile. Her skin was pale and her eyes sunken into their sockets. She'd definitely seen better days, but she was here. She was lucid and she knew me.

For now, it was enough.

"Son," Dad entered the room behind me, but his eyes immediately went to Mom. "Julia, you're awake." Hope filled his voice.

The man was transformed. From brooding, cold businessman to warm, concerned husband. The way he came around the other side of the bed and affectionately gazed at Mom, brushing fuzzy hair from her face. "I just spoke with your doctor. He'll be by shortly. Can I get you anything?"

She gave a little shake of her head, squeezing my hand. "I- I have... all... need." Her speech was slowly returning, which the doctors had told us was a good sign, but it was going to take time. Lots and lots of time. With rehabilitation and therapy, they expected significant improvement, but given the nature of her injury and damage to her brain from the cardiac arrest, they couldn't say whether she would make a full recovery.

"My-ya... o- okay?"

I froze, my eyes wide as I tried to figure out if I'd heard right.

"Darling, I don't think now is the time to—"

"Ssh." Her eyes slid from his to mine, tears collecting in the corner. "I sorry, A- Ash. S-so sorry."

"Ssh, Mom, it's okay." I leaned over to press a kiss to her head, guilt snaking through me as I fought my own tears. It was the first time she'd been lucid enough to try and engage in a conversation and of course, *this* was what she wanted to talk about.

"You don't need to apologize for anything," I said, giving her a warm smile.

"N- not your fault," she rasped, each word taking her at least twice the regular amount of time to get out. "N- not her fault."

The room felt like it was closing in around me. I stood up and said, "I'm going to get some air, okay? I'll be right back."

"A- Ash... didn't m- mean upset..."

"I'm okay, Mom. I'll be okay." I gently pressed my head to hers, relief slamming into me.

She was here, and she was okay.

That's what I needed to cling to.

I slipped out of the room and sat in one of the chairs lining the corridor. Tipping my head back, I closed my eyes and inhaled a deep, steady breath. It had been almost a week since she'd woken up. A week of trying to accept my new reality. Of me and Mya tiptoeing around each other. Of trying to wrack my brain for a way to fix everything.

Mya was right. I needed to fight for her. I needed to show her that I chose her, regardless of the consequences. But it was fucking hard when I was so preoccupied with Mom. Even when I'd gone into school, my mind had been elsewhere.

Then we'd all been at Felicity's and I'd caved. Cornering Mya in the bathroom had been a jerk move, but I just needed to talk to her, to touch her, to feel something—*anything*—from her. A small sign we could find our way back to each other.

"Can I sit?" Dad's deep voice pulled me from my thoughts, but he didn't wait for my reply as he dropped down beside me. "She's asleep. One minute I was talking, the next..."

"The doctors said that's to be expected in the early days."

"I know... I know... it's just... Jesus, it's hard," he breathed. "I've never been more terrified than I was holding your mother, covered in blood—"

"Don't, Dad, please don't." I remembered every second of that night. The blood was imprinted on my soul.

Would be for a very long time.

"I swear my whole life flashed before my eyes," he went on, and I realized it was the first time he'd wanted to talk, *really* talk, about what had happened.

I guess I just didn't expect he'd want to talk to me about it.

"All the mistakes, the way I've treated you both."

"If this is the part where you apologize and we become a shiny happy family, you're about ten years too late," I said with a resigned sigh. I couldn't even find it in me to be angry anymore. I was too exhausted. Like I'd finally woken up from a month-long bad dream.

In some ways, I guess I had.

"You think I don't know that? The damage is done; between us at least," he trailed off, silence stretching out before us. "I can't change the past, Son. But I can change the future. I can try to change who I am."

I gave him a sideways glance, raising a brow. "Actions speak louder than words."

"I know they do." He let out a shaky breath, as if he was purging his need to control everything. Transforming right in front of my eyes. "I'm going to make this right, Asher. Your mother has always been there, right by my side; the dutiful, loving wife. When I think of how I've treated her... treated you both..."

"Dad," I warned, grinding my teeth together.

I didn't want to do this. Not now.

Not ever.

Did I want him to be there for Mom and make things right? One-hundred percent. But I didn't want to listen to his bullshit excuses about why he'd been such a cold-hearted bastard most of my life.

"I'm sorry. I just..." He exhaled. "They say it takes losing everything to realize what you had, and, well, almost losing your mother, it was like something shifted inside me, Asher. Something fundamental."

Didn't I know it?

I'd lost Mya, let her slip through my fingers.

And now when I needed to fight for her, I wasn't sure how to do it.

Actions speak louder than words. The thought hit me like a wrecking ball and I blurted out, "Will you be okay sitting with Mom for a while? There's something I have to go take care of."

His eyes narrowed a fraction, but not in their usual cold, assessing way. "Do I even need to ask where you're going?"

"You can ask, but you won't like the answer." Standing up, I loomed over him. "You said almost losing Mom shifted something inside you. Well, it changed me too, Dad. And do you know what? Life is too short. It's too fucking short to worry about what people think or what they might say if you go against the grain.

"I love Mya. I love her so much. And I pushed her away. I pushed her away because I thought it was what I *should* do; what you and everyone else thought I should do. But screw that. Mya is a good person. So much better than you or me. She's strong and brave and beautiful on the inside and out, and I'm so lucky to have called her mine." *And such a fucking idiot for ever pushing her away.*

Dad stared up at me, his lips pressed into a thin, disapproving line. This was usually the part where he went off at me about responsibility and reputation and all the other bullshit rules he'd lived *his* life by. But I realized now, this wasn't his life.

It was mine.

"What?" I said, disarmed at his silence. "Don't you have anything to say?"

"Oh, I have plenty to say." His expression softened in a way that rendered me speechless. "But something tells me you're not going to listen anymore, so I think I'll save my breath."

My mouth tipped at one corner. "I think that's the most real thing you've said to me in years."

He chuckled at that.

It was weird.

The whole fucking thing was weird.

We'd been at odds for so long, I'd forgotten what it felt like to be on the same side. Even if we were still sitting at either end, a vast space between us. It didn't matter though. He needed to focus on Mom. If he was going to prove he'd changed, that losing Mom had made him realize what was important in life, then he needed to let me walk away and make my own decisions. He needed to let me walk my own path.

A path I hoped led me straight back to Mya.

"You sure about this?" Jason asked as I folded the last note and added it to the pile.

"Never been surer." I looked at my two best friends and grinned. "But if this doesn't work, you'll probably have to lock me up in a cupboard until graduation because I can't promise I won't do something stupid."

"Don't talk like that." A dark look crossed Cameron's expression.

"I'm joking," I laughed. "It was a joke." Well, for the most part. Although I was pretty certain I would go off the deep end if Mya didn't take me back.

I needed her in a way I couldn't explain.

A way I didn't even want to try to understand.

"I gotta say, man," Jase said, "I didn't know if you had it in you."

"Fuck off," I grunted. "We can't all be like you."

"What do you think he'll say?" Cam asked me, wariness in his eyes.

"Honestly, it doesn't matter; not anymore. He hasn't been my father in a real long time." I hesitated.

"Tell me I'm not going to have to kick Mr. Bennet's ass all over town, because you know I'll do it, even if it'll land me in a whole world of trouble with Penn."

"There are some things I need to tell you, yeah." I dragged a hand down my face. "But I want you both to know that the only reason I didn't tell you is because I was ashamed. Well, that and my father is a piece of shit and as good as blackmailed me."

"What the fuck, man?" Jase's eyes bugged, the vein in his neck throbbing violently.

"If I tell you—"

"*When,* when you fucking tell us. I'm not kidding, Ash, if something happened—"

"Jase." Cam laid a hand on his shoulder. "Let him talk."

"Thanks." I gave my calmer friend an appreciative nod. "If I tell you everything, I want something from you in return."

"Anything, you know that," Cam said without hesitation.

"It ends with us," I said. "As much as it pains me to say this, Mom is going to need him and he's changed, I really believe he has. I don't want what I'm about to tell you to go further than the three of us, okay?"

"But Mya knows?" Jase rubbed his jaw.

"She does."

"Good," he said, his shoulders dropping. "I'm glad you have her, man."

I didn't have her yet, but if my plan worked out, I would soon enough.

First though, I needed to lay all my secrets to rest.

I needed to tell my friends the truth.

37

Mya

I DIDN'T SEE Asher all week. By the time Friday rolled round, I was beginning to think he'd given up on us.

On me.

Then I found it. A folded white note that fluttered out of my locker when I'd gone to collect some books I needed.

Mya

I thought long and hard about how to fix things between us... in the end I realized actions speak louder than words.

I love you more than words can say
And I know you love me too
So take a risk on me today
And let me show you the story of me and you

I GLANCED ROUND, half-expecting Asher to leap out from somewhere and say, 'gotcha'. But no one appeared. In fact, no one paid me any attention as I re-read the note, absorbing every detail. It made zero sense. Until my cell vibrated.

ASHER: Your driver awaits outside.

HE WAS SERIOUS, he really wanted me to cut class.

. . .

Me: You've lost your damn mind.

Asher: I'm crazy. Crazy for you. Now hurry or you'll miss your ride.

He'd lost his goddamn mind. But I couldn't deny a thrill shot through me at his boldness. My cell vibrated again, and I smiled when I read his words.

Asher: Time's ticking, Hernandez.

Hernandez. God, it felt like forever since he'd called me that. Since things had been easy between us.

Before I started second guessing myself. I shoved my books back into my locker, slammed it shut, and hurried down the hall. My eyes immediately found Jason's sleek Dodge Charger across the parking lot. He stood propped against it with a smirk plastered on his ridiculously handsome face.

"Your chariot awaits," he said with a hint of amusement as I reached him.

"Do I get to know where we're going first?"

"Not a chance." His smirk grew. "If you want this you have to trust me."

"Just like that?" My brow rose, my gaze hardening despite the butterflies stroking my stomach.

"You either want him to make things right or you don't."

"I'm scared," I admitted, unable to meet his eyes.

"That's not a bad thing, Mya," Jason replied, the softness in his voice making me look at him again. "If you weren't scared it would mean you don't care. And we both know that's not true."

"Okay," My lip curved a fraction. "Let's do this."

"Thank fuck, I thought I was going to have to kidnap you."

Rolling my eyes, I climbed into his car, clutching the note like it was my lifeline.

"Ready?" Jason said.

I nodded, too nervous to speak.

"Relax," my chauffeur said. "You have absolutely nothing to worry about."

But we both knew he was lying because this was it.

This was the moment me and Asher moved forward together or walked away for good.

"Okay, this was not what I was expecting."

Jason's car rolled to a stop outside my aunt's house. "Are you sure he told you to bring me here?"

"I'm only the driver." He flicked his head to the door. "But there might be someone waiting inside for you."

Hope swelled in my chest as I hopped out of the car and hurried up to the house. But when the door swung open to reveal Aunt Ciara standing there, my heart sank.

"Don't look so disappointed." She chuckled, ushering me inside. "Your boy left you something." Aunt Ciara pulled another white note out of her pocket and handed it to me. "I love you, Mya, and all I want is for you to be happy. Lord only knows you deserve it. And I can admit when I was wrong about someone. I'll see you later, okay?"

With a wink, she disappeared down the hall and left me standing there in disbelief. My hands trembled as I opened the note and read Asher's handwriting.

Here marks the spot I first called you beautiful... and it's true, Mya. So fucking true. You're beautiful inside and out and I'm so thankful I let it slip out that day. Because if I hadn't, maybe we wouldn't be here now.

But this is only the beginning...

Now you must go back to the start
To find out when you stole my heart
The clue is home to Milton and Shakespeare, Steinbeck too
Hurry though, Mya, because I'm waiting for you

Swiping a rogue tear from my eye, I folded the note back and stuffed it in my pocket. "I'll see you later," I called out to my aunt before slipping back outside, relieved to find Jason still waiting.

"So?" he asked when I climbed into the car. "What did it say?"

"He didn't tell you?"

"It was a need to know basis," he grumbled. "Apparently, I didn't need to know everything."

Stifling a snicker, I handed him the note. "What the fuck does it mean?"

"It means we're going back to school."

Because I knew exactly where the next clue was.

"The library?" Jason gawked at me. "What the hell does the library have to do with anything? Wait a minute..." His eyes lit up. "Did the two of you get freaky in the stacks?"

"*Jason!*" I groaned. "You can stay out here for that."

"Oh, hell no. I have chauffeur rights. Let's go."

"Fine but stay quiet." The last thing we needed was to upset Mrs. Hegarty.

The library was almost empty, and I had no problems locating the chairs me and Asher had sat at all those weeks ago. "Crap," I whispered when I realized a couple of guys were studying there.

"What?" Jason asked.

"That's where the clue will be."

He puffed his chest dramatically. "Have you learned nothing from being with Asher? Come on." Stalking up to the guys, Jason glared down at them.

"Hmm, can we help you?" One said quietly, glancing nervously to his friend.

"Yeah, I need you to mov—"

"Jason," I interjected, offering the guys an apologetic smile. "Sorry about my friend, he has no manners. I'm looking for something. You didn't happen to see a white note lying around, did you?"

"This white note?" The other one grinned, plucking the note from his piles of books. "A *friend* asked us to look after it."

"He did, huh? Well tell your *friend*, thanks." I snatched the note from him and headed for the door.

"You're no fun," Jason protested.

"I'm plenty fun. Now back up so I can read it."

I wanted to kiss you so badly that day... I almost strangled Mrs. Hegarty when she interrupted us! Do you remember? The words were right there on your tongue. You wanted me to kiss you because you felt it, Mya. You felt the connection between us.

And when you forgive me and we make up, I'm thinking we should probably revisit the library and make up for that day.

But that can wait because it's time for your next clue...

I drank too much because life got hard
But you were there like a shining star
You held my hand and comforted me

And soon you became all I could see

"Got it," Jason said, snapping his fingers. "It's his house, right? The night he got wasted."

"Dude, back the hell up." I looked over my shoulder, frowning at him.

"I'm right though, aren't I?"

"You're annoying."

"But you need me, so come on, Hernandez, let's get this show on the road."

My stomach was churning by the time Jason pulled into Asher's driveway. I'd only been here once since the incident; the night of the party when all people had been thinking about was celebrating Asher's good news. But now, in the harsh light of day, it seemed wrong to be here.

"Hey, you okay?" Jason asked, his eyes burning into the side of my face.

"I'm not sure I can do this." The memories of that night strangled my voice.

"Mya, look at me." His commanding tone coaxed me to glance over at him. "You need to do this. If not for Asher, then for yourself. What went down here was not your fault, okay?"

"Okay." I nodded unsure whether I believed him.

We climbed out together and I was relieved to have someone by my side, even if it was Jason. "Do you think he's here?" I asked as we slowly advanced on the house.

"I'm not—"

"There you are." Felicity burst from the front door. "I've been waiting all morning."

"Hmm, hello," I said, my brows pinched.

"Oh, don't give me that look. Like you didn't know I'd have a hand in making this happen."

"The thought hadn't really crossed my mind." I'd been so swept up in it all, I hadn't stopped to think about what it took to pull off something like this.

"It's amazing, right? He put so much thought into everything." She clapped her hands, excitement dancing in her eyes. "And the notes. I almost died."

"Hold up," Jason growled. "*You've* seen the notes?"

"Well, yeah. Why, haven't you?"

"No, I haven't seen the fucking notes. Unbelievable." He skulked past us, into the house.

Felicity laughed at her boyfriend's tantrum. "He'll get over it. How are you holding up?"

"I'm... okay, I guess. This is all..." I swallowed. "It's a lot to take in. I still can't believe he did all this."

"You haven't seen anything yet." She winked. "Come on. I think he left a thing or two for you." I took Flick's hand and let her pull me inside. "You want some space?"

"Yeah, actually, I think I do. Is that okay?"

"We'll be in the kitchen. Find us when you're done."

Inhaling a deep breath, I made my way to the back of the house, where the downstairs bathroom was located. Inside, I found a white note propped up against one of Mrs. Bennet's marble soap dispensers.

I didn't know if you'd get to this point. I know it's a lot to ask of you to be here, so thank you. Thank you for trusting me.

I can't remember much about that night. I'd drunk so much. But everything I can remember is you. Your voice. Your gentle touch and soft skin against mine. How good it felt. You were like a bright light in the darkness. My own North Star in dark skies. And even though everything's a little hazy, I remember being hit with this overwhelming need to make you mine, in every single way possible.

I wanted to keep up with the little rhymes, but I'm not going to lie... I never was very good at poetry. Besides, I think you know this next one.

Your next clue is where we shared our first proper kiss...

I DASHED out of the bathroom, running down the stairs to the basement. Part of me wanted to find Asher there waiting for me. But I knew our story wasn't finished. Deep down, I knew there was more to come. So when I spotted the next note laid on a cushion on the couch where we'd first made out, I snatched it up and greedily drank up the words.

Do you remember?

Do you remember how good it had felt to have my body pressed against yours? The way we kissed like we were both running out of air?

Do you remember telling me to stop?

I would never ever take advantage of you or push you to do something you didn't want to do, but in that moment, you really tested my resolve. I wanted to drown in you, Mya. To never come up for air.

You do that to me.

Only ever you.

...do you remember what happened next?

Tears streaking down my face, I took off back upstairs, taking the stairs to the second floor. The second I stepped into Asher's bedroom I was assaulted with memories of him. Us. Nights tangled in his sheets. Mornings wrapped in his arms.

I dried my eyes with the backs of my hands, searching for the next note; hardly surprised when I found it in the middle of his bed alongside a tiny velvet pouch.

Now this is where we go off course a little... but if it leads you back to me quicker, then I can live with it.

Open the pouch, Mya.

Have you opened it yet? They should all make sense but in case they don't, here's a little reminder.

The heart represents the first time you said, 'I'm yours'. We were at Flick's house (and while she desperately wanted to be included in our little trip down memory lane, I needed to speed things along. I'm a patient guy... but where you're concerned, I'm not THAT patient).

The boat represents the first time you gave yourself to me. Best. Night. Of. My. Life. Hands down. I predict the only days that'll ever top that are the day you become my wife and the day you give birth to our child. Because, babe, I want it all with you. Every-fucking-single-thing.

The Empire State Building represents our night... and what an amazing night it was... in New York. We might have said the words for the first time that night, but I'd felt them long before that. In fact, I'm pretty sure I fell in love with you that night you tucked my drunk ass in bed.

Am I winning you over yet?

You're probably getting a little hungry and thirsty by now... you should probably head out to get a drink

---

THE TEARS WOULDN'T STOP. No matter how hard I tried to swallow them down, they kept falling.

"Mya?" Felicity came into the room, wrapping me in her arms. "Oh, sweetheart, you weren't supposed to get upset."

"I just... God, I've been such a bitch."

"No, *no!*" She held me at arm's length. "You needed to know he loved you the way you love him and that's okay. You've both been through so much. But it's okay to need someone, Mya. It's okay to give them another chance."

I dried my eyes, clutching the bracelet charms in my hand.

"Can I see them?" Flick asked, and I uncurled my fingers. "Shall we add them to your bracelet?"

"I'd like that." I nodded and let her do it. When she was done, I admired them. "It's beautiful."

"He did good. But don't you have somewhere else to be? What does your clue say?"

"Bell's," I said with conviction. "He wants me to head to Bell's." It was the only place that made sense.

"Well, then, what are we waiting for?"

FELICITY DROVE me to Bell's. I think Jason was happy to stay behind given that I couldn't stop crying. Asher hadn't only played with my emotions, he'd completely wrecked them.

"Hey, Jerry," she said as we entered the bar. "I think you might have something for my girl."

"Hey girls, why don't you hop on up to the bar and I'll be right with you." He disappeared out back while we got comfortable on the stools.

Felicity reached over and took my hand in hers, squeezing. "It's going to be okay, Mya."

I was starting to get that.

It wasn't just about Asher's grand gesture, it was about the way Jason and Cameron stepped up to look out for me, and the way Felicity and Hailee were always there no questions asked. Maybe I would always be the odd girl out in Rixon, but they only ever made me feel like I belonged. I'd built a family for myself here, a life, and that was something I would always be grateful for.

"Here we go," Jerry reappeared, carrying a black drawstring bag. He dumped it on the bar and handed me a note. "I'll leave you two girls to it." He gave me a knowing wink before busying himself at the other end of the bar.

"Is everyone in on this?" I asked incredulously.

"Only the important people," Felicity replied. "Well, don't just stare at it, open it." She motioned to the note in my hand.

I know football isn't your sport. I know it pained you to wear my jersey at the exhibition game, to stand in the bleachers supporting me. But you did it anyway. You constantly pushed yourself out of your boundaries... for me.

You chose me.

You fought for me.

I thought I was fighting too. I thought because I almost beat the shit out of Merrick, or because I barely spoke to Vaughn in New York, or because I went against my dad's orders by being with you, that I was fighting too.

But I realize now it wasn't enough.

I wasn't enough.

And I'm so fucking sorry, Mya.

So let me show you I'm ready.

Meet me at the place where young men who think they have it all figured out become Gods and Kings.

Because this King is ready to claim his Queen.

I SUCKED IN A SHAKY BREATH, his words reverberating through me, leaving me breathless.

"Now that one, I did not see. Holy shit, I think I picked the wrong Raider."

"Felicity!" I nudged her shoulder as we both read it again. "The place where men become Gods and Kings... what does he—"

"The football field, where else?" she said as if there was no question.

And she was right.

Of course she was right.

"Are you ready?"

"I think so," I choked out over the huge fucking lump in my throat.

"Well before we go, you should probably look the part." Her eyes dropped to the bag on the counter. "You've come all this way; you might as well go the whole nine yards."

38

Asher

"SHE'LL BE HERE," Cameron said as we stood centerfield waiting for any sign of Mya and Felicity.

"And if she doesn't show?"

"She'll show," he said with absolute conviction.

"How can you be so sure?" I asked him, bouncing on the balls of my feet.

My heart had been in my throat all fucking day. It had all seemed like the perfect plan when I was putting it all together, but now as I stood on the football field, surrounded by my teammates, I wasn't so sure.

If she didn't come... fuck, I didn't want to fall to my knees and cry like a pussy in front of them all, but I was pretty certain that's exactly what would happen.

Cam was on his phone when he glanced up. "Showtime."

"They're here." My pulse spiked.

"They're here." He gave me a reassuring nod. He'd been great about this whole thing. Jason too. It hadn't been easy aligning all the pieces, but we'd called in some favors here and there, and I may have dropped my father's name once or twice; but this was it, make or break.

"Okay," I said jogging into position. "See you on the other side." It was impossible to see her, my vision blocked by the wall of bodies all facing the bleachers where I knew Hailee and Felicity had led Mya to wait. I could imagine her standing there in my jersey, wondering what the fuck was going on.

At least, I hoped she was.

"Who are we?" Jason roared.

"Raiders," my teammates voices echoed through the air.

"I said who are we?"

"RAIDERS."

"And what are we?"

"Family."

"And what are we gonna do?" Jason glanced back at me, giving me a sharp nod.

"Get the girl," they yelled in unison.

"I said what are we gonna do?"

"Get the girl!"

Adrenaline pumped through me as the guys began to close rank, jogging into two lines—offense and defense—until they were stacked in front of me in a long vertical ladder leading straight to Mya.

Grady glanced back, shooting me a shit-eating grin. "You got this, bro," he mouthed, and I nodded.

I'd done some questionable things over the last four years. Partied too hard. Fucked too many girls. And partied some more. I'd lied to my friends and played a role in a game I never wanted any part of. I'd grown bitter and resentful and I'd dealt with it the only way I knew how—by plastering on a fake smile and making some lame ass wisecrack and raising a glass to the perfect life everyone thought I had.

But this, standing here waiting for my cue, was the first time I felt at peace. There wasn't a single doubt that this was the right decision.

Now all I had to do was convince Mya.

The opening beat to *Whatever It Takes* by Imagine Dragons boomed over the PA system and slowly, pair by pair, the two lines separated until I could finally see her.

Mya.

My Mya wearing my number, staring at me as if I'd lost my ever-loving mind.

Maybe I had.

Maybe this was an over-the-top cheese fest of epic proportions. But she deserved it. Mya deserved to know unequivocally that I loved her and that I chose her. And what better way to show her than in the presence of my teammates. My brothers.

My Raiders family.

I jogged toward her, high-fiving my teammates on the way down. When I'd first asked them to help me out, they'd all given me a ton of shit and Grady had asked to see my newly grown vagina. But Jason, being Jason, had soon insisted they fall in line. We were a team. And if one of us needed help, we stepped up. End of.

Slowing my pace, I came to a stop just in front of Mya.

"Hi," she said softly.

"Hi, yourself."

"I... I don't even know what to—" Her eyes widened to saucers as they finally took me in. "Asher..." she croaked.

"Yes, babe?" The corner of my mouth tipped as realization slowly seeped into her expression.

"Why are you wearing that?"

"What this?" I pinched the cherry and white jersey and pulled it away from my chest. "Figured I should get used to it."

"B- but why?"

I took a step closer. "Because come fall, I'm going to be playing for the Temple Owls."

"You are?" The surprised expression on her face was adorable.

I nodded, fighting a grin. "It isn't official yet, but it will be soon enough. What do you think?" Turning on the spot, I paused long enough for her to get a good look at the name printed on the back.

"Hernandez," she whispered.

"That's right, babe." I faced her again, closing the distance between us. "You're wearing my name and I'm wearing yours. Do you know what that means?"

Her lips parted but the words got stuck.

"It means," I leaned in, hovering my lips over hers, "I'm yours and you're mine."

"I think I like the sound of that," her voice quivered, but the smile on her face said it all.

"Yeah?"

"Yeah," she breathed. "There's just one tiny problem."

I reared back, my brows bunched together. "I won't be at Temple in the fall."

"You won't?"

What the actual fuck?

Mya shook her head. "I won't be there... because I accepted the place at Cleveland."

"You what? I'm not following."

Guilt sparkled in her eyes. "After that night at Felicity's, I knew there was no way I could walk away from you. I just needed time to figure things out. So I accepted the place at Cleveland. I was waiting for the right time to tell you."

Cupping the back of her neck, I drew her close to me. "Well, you're going to need to un-accept it. I want Temple, Mya. I want Temple with you."

"You're sure?"

"More than anything. Where you go, I go, Hernandez." Her body relaxed against me at my words.

"But what about your dad?"

I eased back to look at her. "Who do you think pulled some strings with the administration at Temple?"

"He did?"

"He owed me, and now," I kissed the end of her nose, "now we're even."

"I don't know about this." Mya drummed her hand against her thigh as I pulled into a parking bay at the hospital and cut the engine.

"Hey," I said, leaning over to take her hands in mine. "Stop overthinking it."

"I'm not... it's just..."

"You're scared?"

She nodded, her bottom lip trembling. Without hesitation, I closed the distance between us and captured her mouth in a deep kiss. My other hand buried into her hair, loving how soft her spiral curls felt against my skin. "I love you, Mya. Nothing will ever change that."

"She really wants to see me?"

Emotion clogged my throat. After I'd sat and told my mom the plan I had to win back Mya, she'd looked at me with such pride, I may have shed a tear or two. Then she'd slowly uttered that she wanted to see my girlfriend as soon as possible.

"She does," I choked out, brushing my thumb over Mya's neck. "But if you're not ready—"

"I'm ready." Conviction burned in her eyes.

"That's my girl."

We climbed out of my Jeep and made our way inside. A couple of people stared, glancing at our joined hands, disapproval shining in their eyes, but it only made me hold her tighter.

I was done caring what people thought.

"I hate these places, so much," Mya murmured as we stepped into the elevator.

I moved behind her, wrapping my arms around her waist and dropping my chin to her shoulder. "Yeah, I'll be glad when she's finally home." But I knew it could be a while. Mom was showing progress, but the doctors were concerned about the extent of the damage caused to her brain.

"I don't think I'll ever forgive myself," Mya whispered.

"Hey, don't do that. We promised, remember? Jermaine did this, not you. If I hadn't gone for him—"

"He would have shot you or me."

Silence enveloped us as we waited for the doors to ping open.

"When we walk out of here, we do it together, okay? And we leave the past where it belongs."

Mya turned in my arms, gazing up at me with so much love it knocked the air from my lungs. "Together." She leaned up to kiss me, but all too soon the doors pinged open and the noise of the busy hospital floor cut through our intimate moment.

We walked hand-in-hand to Mom's room. Dad had made a substantial donation to the hospital to give her the best room available. It had a couch and a foldaway bed that Dad slept on most nights. He'd even gone as far as to notify all his clients he was taking an extended leave of absence to care for Mom.

It was more than I ever expected but no less than she deserved.

It shouldn't have taken almost losing Mom for him to step up to the plate, but I was just relieved he'd come through when she needed him most.

She stirred the second we entered the room. "Hey, Mom," I said, letting go of Mya to move next to the bed. "I brought someone to see you."

Mom's eyes tracked Mya as she approached us. My heart jack-hammered in my chest, my palms growing slick. I knew Mom didn't want me to bring Mya here for any other reason than she wanted my girlfriend to know she didn't blame her. But there was still a seed of doubt. A tiny part of me that expected the rug to be pulled from under me at any second. Mom didn't blame Mya. Dad has conceded and helped me with Temple University, albeit begrudgingly.

It all felt too good to be true.

But when Mom lifted a shaky hand toward Mya and my girl fell at the side of her bed, clasping her hand with tears rolling down her cheeks, I knew we were going to be okay.

The past had hurt us all, but it hadn't destroyed us.

I watched as the two most important women in the world to me shared an intimate moment. Mom had pulled Mya close, barely saying a word, but she didn't need to. Her eyes said everything she couldn't yet say.

"A- Ash..."

I went to Mya, covering their joined hands with my own. "I love you both, so much. And I know we'll get through this, okay? Because we're going to need you healthy and happy one day, Mom."

Her eyes widened and I chuckled. "Don't worry we're not making you a grandma... yet." I winked at her, but Mya's elbow caught me in the ribs.

"I am so sorry Mrs.... Julia. You know how he gets when he's excited about something. But you don't need to worry. We plan on going to college before any of that happens."

"We'll see," I grumbled, wrapping myself around her and kissing her neck. I knew people would think we were too young, too irresponsible to know what we wanted in life. But I'd been looking out for myself, craving love and attention, for as long as I could remember.

And now I'd found it?

I didn't plan on ever letting it go.

"Now THERE's a sight for sore eyes," I said gruffly at the sight of Mya standing there in nothing but my Raiders jersey and her black lace panties.

After spending the afternoon with my mom, I'd persuaded her to come home with me. We'd ordered in and gone down to the home theater room to watch a movie. It was nice. Normal.

It was a slice of heaven in the living hell we'd been through the last few weeks.

Now we were upstairs, ready to sleep. But I hadn't expected her to come out of the bathroom wearing my jersey.

"I thought you'd like it." She toyed with the hem of the material, flashing me her smooth caramel thighs.

I pushed up on one elbow, letting my eyes rake over her. She was so beautiful, and every inch of her was mine.

Would be for a very long time if I had anything to say about it.

"I thought we were going to sleep?" I said, tracking her movements as she approached the bed.

"We are." Mya smiled coyly, longing glittering in her eyes.

I swung my leg over the bed and curved my hand around her waist, drawing her closer, letting her settle between my legs. "Thank you for today. I know it wasn't easy."

She gazed down at me. "I'm glad I went. I think, in a way, I needed to see her. I needed to know she didn't blame me."

"No one blames you, Mya. Not even my old man." Her brow rose at that. "He'll come around." And if he didn't, it didn't matter. He'd cut me loose from my Bennet empire obligations and stepped up to take care of Mom.

If I never spoke to him again, we were even, and I could live with that.

"It doesn't matter," she said. "I don't need his approval."

"That's my girl." I curled a hand into the hem of the jersey and pushed it up her body so I could kiss her navel.

"Ash..." she breathed, letting her fingers play with my hair.

"I don't think I want to sleep anymore." It was late and we had school tomorrow but all I could think about now was being buried deep inside her.

"We really should—"

"Ssh." I kissed her stomach again, swirling my tongue around her belly button. "I can be quick."

"Not too quick I hope." She pulled my hair, demanding my eyes.

I smirked at her sass. "Don't ever change, Mya. Not for me. Not for anyone." My hands slid down her back to palm her ass, guiding her down into me. Mya kneeled either side of me, lowering herself down slowly. I imagined her naked, taking my rock-hard dick inside her.

"Fuck," I rasped as she wiggled against me, sending sparks of pleasure shooting up my spine. "Not enough," I whispered, my lips finding the hollow of her neck as I gathered her wild curls in one hand and pressed her closer. I wanted to taste every inch of her, devour her. I wanted to brand her with kisses and imprint myself on her soul.

I wanted to bind us in every way possible.

But something told me Mya would rip me a new one if I got down on one knee and spontaneously proposed. So for now, I settled for kissing her. For letting my hands wander beneath my jersey, tracing letters of love on her skin.

"What do you want, Mya?" I kissed the corner of her mouth. "Tell me what you want."

"You," she said softly. "I just want you."

"You have me, all of me."

"Show me." Her eyes flared with lust.

"Show you?" I arched a brow. "It would be my pleasure." Guiding her down onto the bed, I settled over Mya and brushed my nose over hers, pecking her lips. Letting my tongue slide into her mouth, pouring every ounce of love I felt into her. We'd made it. We'd overcome the odds.

Our past and present had collided in a way neither of us saw coming, but the future?

The future was ours.

EPILOGUE

Mya

THREE MONTHS LATER...

"MYA HERNANDEZ," Principal Finnigan called my name and I moved across the stage, the chorus of cheers and whistles making my cheeks heat. My eyes found Asher across the stage where he stood with the rest of our graduating class, his eyes alight with happiness.

"I love you," he mouthed, and I grinned. God, I loved him. I loved his over the top boyfriend antics and the way he wasn't afraid to tell me he loved me every second of every day.

I loved him so much I was already dreaming of crazy things like moving into our first apartment and getting married and having cute blue-eyed, blond-haired, dark skinned babies.

I was *that* girl now.

Completely smitten. Completely gone.

Completely his.

And I wouldn't have changed it for the world.

After everything that had happened with Jermaine, Julia, and Asher's dad, and even Kellie Ginly, I knew we could weather whatever storm hit us next. Because I wasn't naïve; I knew there would be other people out there who didn't approve of our relationship.

They could all go fuck themselves for all I cared.

Asher Bennet was mine, and I was his.

And nothing was ever going to change that.

"FUCK, YOU LOOKED HOT OUT THERE." Asher hooked his arm around my waist and attacked my mouth, planting big wet sloppy kisses all over my face.

"Ash..." I chuckled, pressing my hands against his chest. "Stop, we're in—"

"Don't care, babe." His warm breath tickled my ear. "I don't fucking ca—"

Someone cleared their throat and we both turned slowly to find Mr. Bennet standing there glaring at us. "Dad," Asher mumbled. "Your timing is impeccable as always."

"Asher," he regarded his son. "Mya."

Mr. Bennet no longer looked at me like I was dirt on his shoe, but he hadn't exactly welcomed me into the family with open arms either. He was amicable. Polite and civil, but he made no efforts to get to know me.

Strangely, I was okay with that.

He needed to focus on his wife and helping her heal. Even if he had a problem with me still—and part of me knew he probably did—Julia called the shots now. And she loved me in a way I never saw coming.

In a way I wasn't sure I deserved.

"Is Mom—"

"A- Ash."

Asher broke away from me and went to his mom, falling into her open arms. We weren't sure she would make it to graduation, but Julia was defying her doctors at every turn. Proving to everyone she was strong.

"Mya." Her eyes met mine over his shoulder, a faint smile tugging at her lips. "I- I'm p- proud of you." She stumbled over the words a little, but her speech was improving every week.

"I'm so happy you made it Mrs... Julia."

She beamed, gently pushing Asher to arm's length. "W- wouldn't m... m-miss it for the world."

"I love you, Mom." Asher's voice cracked. "I love you so damn much." He reached back, searching for my hand. I slid my fingers into his and his shoulders immediately dropped, relief oozing from him.

"My two favorite girls," he said, glancing between us, so much emotion in his blue gaze my breath caught.

"There you are." Felicity breezed up to us, looking radiant in her gown. "Hi Mrs. Bennet, it's so good to see you."

Julia smiled, happiness glittering in her eyes.

"Where's Jase?" Asher asked.

"Talking to Coach Hasson. He's no longer a Raider but he still can't let go."

"You should know by now, Fee, baby, once a Raider, always—"

"A Raider," the two of us answered, sharing a smile.

"Damn straight."

"Well, if you don't mind, I need to borrow Mya for a little while."

My eyes slid to Asher's and he grinned. "Fine by me."

"I'll see you later," I said.

Asher's parents were letting him host a graduation party, one last time before we headed to the Hamptons for summer vacation and then all went our separate ways for college. Since the guys had summer practice we were leaving early. It was hard to believe we would all be in different colleges. Lucky for me though, Jason and Felicity would only be across the river at UPenn so we'd still see each other.

"Come on." Felicity grabbed my hand, flashing me a knowing smirk. "I promise to return her in one piece."

My brows furrowed, trying to decipher the intent in her expression, but before I could figure out what the hell was going on, she was pulling me away from Asher and his parents, towards her bright yellow car.

"No way." I shook my head, gawking at the scraps of lace and silk. "No fucking way."

"Come on, he'll love it. Tell her, Hails." She flicked her gaze to Hailee who threw up her hands.

"Don't drag me into this. Besides, I'm with Mya on this one. It's..."

"Obscene," I said.

"It's sexy," Flick countered. "Jason loves it when I—"

I clapped a hand over her mouth. "We don't need to hear about how much Jason loves *anything*. I'm not wearing that." Asher loved me regardless of what I wore, and it wasn't like we needed any help in the bedroom. He was insatiable, and I was all too happy to oblige him.

Felicity pouted. "I still think you should get it."

"It's a party. A party Asher is throwing." I gave her a pointed look. "I'll be lucky to drag him away from the guys for ten seconds let alone long enough to seduce him with... *that*." My nose scrunched up as I looked at the lingerie again. I wasn't opposed to wearing pretty things, but it was too much.

"You're no fun."

"But you love me." I nudged Felicity's arm and smiled at her.

"Yeah, I do. Come on, let's look in the other section."

We wandered around the store, stopping to look at a rack of bras. "Does anyone else wish we were doing something low key to celebrate?" I asked, fingering a simple black bra with a small heart detail in the front.

"You're not feeling the party?" Hailee asked.

"It's cool, I just... our time together is limited. I thought it might be nice to hang out, just the six of us."

"If you tell Asher that, he'd cancel in a heartbeat," she replied.

"I know but I don't want to ruin his fun." Asher deserved a party. After a tough few months, he was finally in a good place. His mom was in and out of physical therapy, but she was home and doing okay. His dad had turned over a new leaf, being the husband he should have always been. And we'd recently had news Jermaine had pleaded guilty to aggravated assault with a deadly weapon which meant there would be no trial and the prosecution were confident he would receive the maximum sentence.

It wasn't easy hearing my oldest childhood friend would spend a long time behind bars, but it was no less than he deserved and I'd made my peace with the fact I hadn't been able to save him. Love wasn't always enough, and that was okay. To make a relationship work it required compromise and trust, communication and respect. Both people had to accept responsibility for their actions and hold their hands up and apologize when they got it wrong. They had to fight for each other and stand up for what they believed. But most of all, they had to realize you couldn't change someone who didn't want to change themselves.

"Know what I think?" Felicity pulled me from my thoughts.

"What?" I asked.

"I think tonight is going to be epic."

"Oh yeah," I chuckled, "and why's that?"

"Because, my friend," she looped her arm through mine, "we survived high school. And if we can survive high school, we can survive anything."

"Where is everyone?" I asked as we approached Asher's house. It was steeped in darkness, no sign of life as we reached the door.

"You'll see," Felicity replied cryptically, a knowing glint in her eye.

"What did you do?" Hailee whisper-hissed.

"Me? Oh, this isn't me, this is all—"

"Ladies." The familiar cadence of Asher's voice hit me and my stomach clenched. "Welcome to the party."

"Party?" I gawked at him. "You do know the definition of party is people? Noise and laughter. Music." My eyes went to the house again as I strained to hear something—*anything*—which hinted at the chaos inside.

Felicity shot me an amused look. "Don't say I didn't tell you so." She disappeared inside, Hailee trailing after her.

"What was all that about?" Asher's eyes danced with intrigue as he closed the distance between us, hooking his arm around my waist and bringing me flush against his body.

"Nothing," I smiled coyly. "What's going on, Ash?" My brow rose as my hands smoothed up his hard chest.

"Don't you trust me, Hernandez?"

"Always," I said without hesitation. "But you're up to something."

"Maybe." He kissed the end of my nose, one of his hands brushing my face. "Come on. I think this is a surprise you'll like."

Taking my hand, Asher led me into the house. I'd never felt comfortable here but over the last three months it had become my second home. With his parents spending so much time at the hospital, we'd stayed here a lot. And even when his mom was finally released, I still came over. She loved spending time with us.

A sultry beat drifted down the dimly lit hall, sending shivers up my spine. That, and the sight of Asher in dark jeans and a fitted Henley. He always looked good, but tonight he looked good enough to eat. I smiled to myself, still in awe of how a girl like me had caught the eye of someone like him. But Asher had taught me that what people saw didn't define us. It was what was on the inside that counted. And our souls were the same.

"Asher, what is—" The words died on my tongue as we entered the living room. Jason was serving the girls cocktails from the temporary bar set up in the corner of the room while Cam messed with the docking station, selecting a song he knew we loved.

"Surprise." Asher pulled me in front of him, pressing up against me and wrapping his arms around my waist.

"But the party..."

"Is right here. There is no one else I'd rather celebrate with tonight than you and my best friends, Mya. Congratulations, babe," he whispered against the shell of my ear. "Tonight, we celebrate."

Asher

"How the fuck did we get so lucky?" I asked my two best friends in the whole world.

"It's a question I ask myself every second of every day. She's everything I never knew I wanted." Jase took a long pull on his beer, not taking his eyes off Felicity for even a second. The girls were dancing together, laughing and smiling, twirling around without a care in the world.

"This was a good call," Cam added, shifting forward as he tracked Hailee's movements. "I'm not sure I could have survived another party."

"Hey, my parties are fucking epic."

"Yeah, but this is a thousand times better," he grumbled.

"You're not wrong," Jase agreed as the three of us sat there watching our girls. The girls who had come out of nowhere and knocked us so far on our asses I wasn't sure we'd ever get up again.

"If I die tonight," I proclaimed, the buzz of liquor simmering in my veins. "I'd die happy."

"No one is dying." Cam elbowed my ribs. "Don't be saying that shit."

"Sorry, man, I wasn't thinking." The pain in his voice sobered me. We'd all been through a lot senior year. Some happy, some not so happy, and some downright ugly. But we'd made it and now we had our whole lives ahead of us.

"It's cool," he said. "I just... well, I guess with college approaching, it's..."

"We get it." Jase glanced over at him. "But whatever comes our way, we handle it together. No amount of distance changes that. You're still my best friends. My brothers. We're Raiders and no matter what color jersey you wear, we'll always be Raiders."

"College," I breathed. "I'm so fucking relieved Mya will be there with me."

"Tell me about it. I thought I had it all figured out," Jase said. "I thought I didn't need anything except football. But that girl right there," he tipped the neck of his bottle toward Flick, "I need her more than air, and it fucking terrifies me."

"Never thought I'd see the day." Cam smirked at him.

"Fuck off."

"Nah, man, it looks good on you. *She* looks good on you."

"You should see her when she's riding my—"

"And there's the Jase we all know and love." Laughter rumbled in my chest. "You think we gave them enough time?"

"Yeah." He slammed his bottle down on the coffee table. "I think they're done."

"Thank fuck for that," I mumbled, need pulsing through me.

We each stood up and approached the girls. But I didn't pay any attention to what my friends were doing. I only had eyes for Mya, for the way the black knee-length dress molded to her curves like a second skin.

"Ash?" she gazed up at me as I pulled her into my arms.

"Needed you, babe," I whispered against her ear before flicking my tongue over her salty sweet skin. Mya curled her hands into my Henley, letting me sway us to the music. "Are you enjoying the party?"

"Yes." She grinned at me, her eyes glassy with one too many cocktails. Mya didn't let her guard down a lot, but tonight, with our friends, she had. It made my heart swell watching my girl let her hair down and enjoy herself. It's all I wanted; to see her happy.

After everything, she deserved it.

I turned her in my arms, pulling her body flush to mine, letting her roll her ass against me. My hands found the swell of her hips and my lips found her shoulder. I was hardly surprised to see Jase already had Felicity pinned against the wall, kissing her like he thought she might disappear any second.

"Asher..." Mya turned into me. "I need—"

"Come on." Taking her hand, I pulled her out of the room and into the hall. But I couldn't wait. I needed to taste her, to feel her skin on mine. Crowding her against the wall, I leaned in, kissing her hard. Our tongues slid together, dancing to their own rhythm.

"Feel what you do to me," I whispered against her lips. "Feel how much I want you." Grabbing her hand, I pressed it against the growing bulge in my jeans.

"The feeling is entirely mutual," she breathed, pupils blown with lust.

"Oh yeah, is that right?" My smile turned wicked as I dipped my hand underneath her dress, pushing the material up her thighs. Letting my fingers tease her soft skin. I moved higher and higher until I found her panties.

"Ash..." It was a needy moan.

"So wet," I said, kissing the corner of Mya's mouth as I rubbed her over the lacy material.

"Remember what you said to me once?" Her words surprised me and I eased back to look at her. "You said you'd chase me to the ends of the Earth before you ever gave me up."

"I remember." The words got stuck over the lump in my throat. It seemed like so long ago when we'd been dancing around one another.

"Prove it," she said, and before I could register her words, Mya ducked out from between me and the wall and took off up the stairs.

"I'm coming for you," I called after her, the soft sound of her laughter like music to my ears.

"I'm counting on it," she said as I gave chase, the two of us running down the hall toward my bedroom. Either Mya was quick or I was more buzzed than I'd first thought, because she made it into my room before I could grab her.

The second I burst through the door, I ground to a halt, my mouth hanging open at the sight of her standing there in nothing but black lace panties and a matching bra. "I think I must have died and gone to heaven."

"I'm real, Asher," she smirked, toying with the strap of her bra.

"You sure, Hernandez? Because fuck... you look like an angel standing there." I dragged a hand through my hair, trying to rein in my emotions.

"Touch me and find out." Challenge shone in her eyes as she began to back up, stopping only when the bed hit the backs of her legs.

"Challenge accepted." Peeling the t-shirt from my body, I quickly unbuttoned my jeans and pushed them off my hips. Mya's hungry gaze pulled me toward her, until I was close enough to feel the heat from her body. "You are the most beautiful thing I've ever seen." I ghosted a finger down her neck and between the valley of her tits.

"Tonight was perfect," she said.

"*You* are perfect."

"We did it, we survived high school."

I moved closer, burying a hand deep into her thick curls. "We did," I whispered, brushing my lips against hers. "And now we get to live, Mya. We get to chase our dreams, together."

My hand dropped to the curve of her ass, pressing her against my dick. But it wasn't enough. In one swift motion, I picked Mya up, forcing her legs around my waist. Her shrieks of surprise filled the room but quickly turned to giggles when I turned around and dropped down on the bed with her straddling me. Her hand slid to my jaw, anchoring me in place as she kissed me. Teased me with her tongue and teeth. My fingers found the clasp of Mya's bra, pulling it off her body while she worked a hand between us, freeing my dick from the confines of my boxer briefs. Our kisses grew frantic. Dirty wet kisses as we explored one another's body. I would never get enough of this, of her.

Mya grasped me in her hand and sank down on me, making my world shatter with sensation. "Together," she repeated, smothering a moan as her eyes fluttered closed.

"Together," I ground out, letting my fingers dig into the flesh of her hips. "Always."

Mya began moving, riding me in a way only she could. I couldn't speak, couldn't do anything but watch and feel; surrender myself completely to the girl who owned me.

Heart.

Body.

And soul.

I couldn't fall any harder than I had for Mya Hernandez.

And I'd show her every day how much I loved her.

Forever.

THE ENDGAME IS YOU

PROLOGUE

Cameron

"THIS IS THE LIFE," Asher said as he laid back on the lounger, folding his arms behind his head.

He wasn't wrong.

His family's place in the Hamptons was something else. We'd been out here before, him, Jason, and me, but this time was different. Better. This time we had our girls with us, and it was our final summer together before we went off to college. Hailee and I were heading to Michigan next week to get settled before classes started. Then Jason and Felicity would be moving to UPenn in a couple of weeks, with Asher and Mya across the river at Temple University.

It was the end of an era. No more Raiders, no more high school, but a new adventure.

I flicked my eyes to Jason who was sat in a chair, elbows propped on his thighs, chin resting on his fists. "They'll be okay, you know." I chuckled, sliding my gaze to where the girls were currently dipping their toes at the water's edge.

"It's not them I'm worried about," he grunted. "It's them." Jason tipped his head to where a group of guys were checking out our girlfriends, clearly unaware that we were sitting in wait.

"You need to lighten up." I gave him a pointed look. "Soon we'll be at college and you know there's going to be plenty more where that came from."

"Ugh, don't remind me." Jason Ford, prodigal son of football and Rixon's golden boy pouted.

"For real, you're worried about college dick?" Asher asked. "Felicity has your tattoo on her skin. She's not going anywhere."

Jase reared back. "Of course she's not fucking going anywhere. But it's college. Coach Hasson ran a tight ship, but it'll be a whole other level at college. I can't expect her to sit around and wait for me."

"Well, no, she'll probably do that thing called make friends. I've heard all the kids are doing it." Laughter rumbled in Asher's chest.

"Fuck you." Jase kicked his lounger and Asher almost went flying.

"You're really going to have to learn to rein in Mr. Possessive Asshat, you know?" I said.

"Just put a ring on it, then every fucker will know she's taken."

"Don't be stupid, he's not going to—" My brows pinched. "Jase, man, please tell me you're not actually considering it. We're eighteen."

"Like you wouldn't put a ring on Hailee's finger in a heartbeat."

He had a point.

But we had time. I wanted us to both enjoy each other first. Fuck knows we'd earned it.

Jase shot up out of his seat. "He's dead."

"Whoa." I leaped up after him, blocking his way forward. "They're talking." Glancing back, I watched the group of guys laugh with the girls. It seemed harmless enough... until one of them made a beeline for Hailee.

"Let's go," I growled, possessiveness streaking through me.

"I guess I'd better come make sure the two of you don't do something stu—Oh, hell no." Asher whipped off his sunglasses and gawked in their direction, watching as one of the guys offered to put lotion on Mya's shoulders.

"I'll take the two on the left." He barged past us. "You two take the others."

Hailee

"Come on, don't be like that. Just because you got guys waiting for you doesn't mean we can't hang out."

"Is this asshole for real?" Mya arched a brow.

"Bitch please, you should—"

"Oh, hell no, you did not just call her a bitch." Flick stepped up to the douchebag and glared at him. "My boyfriend would kick your ass all over this beach."

"I'd like to see him try." The guy laughed, glancing at his friends who chuckled.

"That can be arranged," Jason, Cam, and Asher closed in around them.

"Oh, hey, babe." Flick grinned. "This is Tom. He was just telling us how he thinks we should ditch you guys and hang out with them instead."

Mya shot me a knowing look. Flick was a bit of a loose cannon where Jason was concerned. It was crazy, but she loved his possessive alpha side. She said it got her all hot for him, so I was hardly surprised she was enjoying this.

"Flick," I warned, because while she might have enjoyed seeing her guy get pissed, it usually didn't end well for everyone else.

Cameron moved around us, pulling me into his side. "Hi." He smiled down at me as if we were the only two people on the overcrowded beach.

"Hi." My fingers splayed over his hard abs, loving how warm his skin felt. "We should probably intervene," I whispered, "before he does something stupid."

Jason was all up in the guy's face, eyes narrowed dangerously. "I suggest you take a walk, now."

The air crackled around them and I silently willed the guy to walk off. This was supposed to be a relaxing weekend before we all went our separate ways. I didn't want to have to call Kent to bail his son out of county jail for assault.

Thankfully, the douche must have recognized the emergence of Jason's dark side because his hands went up. "Shit, yeah, man, my bad." They started backing up.

"Yeah, you'd better run," Flick yelled.

"Seriously," I said. "Do you have to provoke him?"

She shrugged, launching herself into Jason's arms. "It's all the testosterone. It gets me hot."

"Gets you wet more like." Jase nipped her bottom lip before capturing her lips with his.

"I love you guys, but that was too much information," Mya grumbled.

"Jealous, babe?" Asher prowled toward her. "Because I'm pretty sure I can help you out with that."

"Asher, don't you dare." She backed further into the water's edge.

"You should know not to dare me by now. I never lose." He winked before diving at her. One minute Mya was standing there, the next she was over Asher's shoulder, shrieking like a banshee as he ran straight toward the ocean.

"He's so gonna get it," I said around a smile, watching as Asher dropped her into the water.

"He's gonna get something all right." Jason barked out a laugh.

"Why is everything about sex to guys?"

"And girl." Flick snickered, holding up a finger.

I rolled my eyes, unable to smother the laughter building in my chest as Jase dipped my best friend and smothered her with wet, sloppy kisses.

Despite all his alpha ways, they were so freaking cute. Even if she had completely lost her mind and let someone tattoo 'Property of a Raider' on her skin. But that was Felicity Giles, a girl who loved with her whole heart and lived every second like it was her last. I was excited for them to go off to UPenn and chase their dreams. Even if Cameron and I would be a nine-hour ride away in Michigan.

"You okay?" Cam looped his arm around my neck and gazed down at me.

"Yeah, I'm good."

I had great friends.

The most perfect boyfriend.

And our whole lives ahead of us.

Cameron

"We're lucky bastards, you know that, right?" Asher tipped his beer toward where the girls were laughing and talking, sipping the sugary sweet cocktails Felicity had insisted on making.

After a day at the beach, we'd headed back to the house. The place had a grill too mammoth not to put to good use. A cloud of smoke currently drifted into the sky as Jase flipped burgers and steaks.

"Yeah, I know." Hailee caught my eye and smiled; and fuck, if it wasn't like a bolt of lightning to my heart.

I loved that girl. I loved her more than I had ever loved another person, and the thought of starting my life with her should have been the happiest moment of my life. Except I had a gnawing guilt over leaving Rixon, of leaving my mom and dad and my kid brother, Xander. Mom was better, she was, but it didn't stop the trickle of fear I felt every time I imagined being a nine-hour ride away and getting a call that she was sick again, or that Xander was having bad nightmares still.

I wanted to be there for them, always. But Hailee wanted Art School, especially STAMPS at the University of Michigan, and she deserved it.

She deserved it so fucking much.

"You all set to be a Wolverine?" Asher asked.

"I guess."

"Don't sound too excited about it."

"It just won't be the same, ya know?" I took a long pull on my beer.

"Yeah, being a Raider was something special, a once in a lifetime experience. But college will be good, you'll see."

I wished I could be as laidback as Asher. Even after everything he and Mya had been through with her ex, and with his mom getting shot, he still managed to paste on a trademark Bennet smile.

I envied him. His ability to dust himself off and embrace everything life had to offer.

I wanted it; I did. But fear held me back. Fear about the future... about everything changing.

Rixon was my home.

But Hailee was my heart and I knew I'd follow her anywhere.

"Yo," Jase yelled over his shoulder. "Steaks are almost done."

"And that's our cue to get the salad," Felicity mumbled.

"And the sauce. Don't forget the hot sauce." Asher smirked. "Oh and bring some pickles and some of those—"

"Babe," Mya clipped out. "You have legs."

"Yeah, but I'm supervising Jase."

I snorted at that.

"It's a good thing I love you." She rolled her eyes playfully before taking off after the girls.

"I love her so fucking much," he said, as if it was the simplest thing in the world.

But I got it.

We all did.

We were young. Three guys chasing their dreams of football, fame, and fortune. But we'd already found our forever girls.

And that was worth everything.

Every fucking thing.

Hailee

"I am stuffed." Felicity sat back rubbing her swollen stomach.

"You'll be stuffed later," Jason smirked.

"Is that a promise?" Desire glittered in her eyes.

"Guys, really?" I groaned, and Cameron squeezed my hand, fighting a smile.

"What?" She shrugged. "We're all friends."

"Damn right, we are."

Jason reached for his beer and thrust it in the air. "No matter what the next four years bring, you'll always be my best friends."

"Aww, love you too." I poked out my tongue at him and everyone laughed.

"You're not so bad, Raine."

"Likewise, Ford."

It was hard to believe there had been a time when Jason and I couldn't stand one another. He still drove me crazy sometimes, but I loved him like a brother. He was fiercely protective of those he cared about, and that now included me.

"But seriously, guys, we might not be Raiders anymore, but we will always be friends. Distance won't change that."

"Easy for you to say," Cam said, glancing between Jase and Asher, "you'll be a stone's throw away from each other."

He chuckled, but I heard the strain there. Cameron was coming to Michigan for me, for *my* dream, and I couldn't help the tiny pang of guilt I felt. He reassured me all the time it was the right move, but I didn't ever want him to regret it.

Or resent me.

My shoulders sank.

"Hey." He squeezed my hand and I lifted my eyes to his. "I'm joking... it was a joke."

"I know."

"You think he'd really go anywhere you're not?" My stepbrother asked me.

"Jase," Flick warned.

"It's okay," I said, forcing a weak smile. "Nine hours is nothing. We can still see each other at the weekend and at holidays."

"Damn right we can." Asher tipped his beer at us. "Nothing, not college, distance or time, is going to ruin this."

His words settled over the six of us, turning the air thick with anticipation.

College was a big step. Things would change. *We* would change.

But was Asher right?

Were the bonds between us strong enough to survive?

PART I

Sophomore Year

1

Jason

"OKAY, GATHER ROUND," Coach Faulkner called us in, and we fell into position around him. Shoulder to shoulder, teammate to teammate. The anticipation of a new season was thick in the air. Last season, as a freshman, I'd been so close to tasting victory, but in the end it had been Cornell who took the title.

It had been a bitter pill to swallow. I wanted to be the best, to win, to prove myself.

But this year... this year it was ours. We were thirsty for it: training harder, pushing harder. I might have only been with the Quakers for a year, but I felt at home here. We had strong leadership, a strong defense, and one of the best offenses in the whole damn country.

It was our year to bring that trophy home.

So the grim line on Coach's face had a pit carving through my stomach. Something was about to happen. Something that affected the team.

Fuck.

"I've got some news, ladies, and you're not going to like it." He yanked off his Quaker ball cap and rubbed a hand over his jaw. "Manella is out."

A collective grumble filled the air.

Lincoln Manella was our running back, our fucking captain. It was his senior year; he was supposed to be entering the draft next spring. He couldn't be out.

"Just got word from his old man. He tore his ACL and needs surgery."

"Fuck," I breathed, flicking my eyes to my friend Gio. His lips pulled into a thin line.

This was bad.

Very fucking bad.

"So, what's the plan, Coach?" Jared Galloway, our starting fullback and one of the senior players, asked.

"We need a new captain."

All eyes slid to me.

"Whoa." I held up my hands and stepped back, bumping into the player behind me. "It should be an upperclassman."

There were guys on the team who had more seniority than me, more experience. Just because I'd arrived last year a true freshman, taking the QB position from the senior player before me, didn't mean I'd wanted or been qualified enough to be the captain.

"It should be you, son." Coach tipped his chin in firm reassurance. He believed in me, he trusted me… and it floored me.

I'd led my high school team, carried that responsibility with pride and tenacity. But this was different.

This was college.

"I agree," Jared said. "You more than proved yourself last year, Jase. You might only be a sophomore, but this is the right call."

"Anyone got a problem with this?" Coach scanned the fifty young men surrounding him and not a single one of them stepped forward to disagree.

"Decision made. Congratulations, son." A small smirk graced Coach's rugged face. "You just became our fearless leader."

The team broke out into a chorus of hoots and hollers as everyone congratulated me on the promotion. But I stood there blindsided, completely in shock, with only one thing on my mind.

I did not see that coming.

Felicity

Hot wet lips trailed up my neck, kissing and biting, teasing. A soft moan spilled from my mouth, lulling me from my nap, as I tilted my head, welcoming the delicious sensations.

"I missed you," Jason whispered against my throat.

"It's only been a few hours."

Even if it felt like more.

"It's too many." He let out an exhausted sigh, tucking my body into the hard curves of his.

"What time is it?"

"Six thirty."

"Crap." My eyes flickered open. "I was only supposed to have a twenty-minute power nap."

"Long day?" he asked, nuzzling my neck again. I loved it, the feel of Jase's five o'clock shadow rough against my soft skin, his arms wrapped possessively around my body as if he might never let me go.

And I didn't want him to.

This guy owned my heart and soul and I didn't ever want it back.

"Yeah," I admitted. It was only two weeks into the semester and classes were already kicking my ass. I shuddered to think how intense things would get in junior year once clinical practice started.

"You've got this, babe." Jason nibbled my earlobe sending volts of electricity shooting through me. "You just need to believe in yourself."

"I actually signed up for some extra tutoring."

"You did?" I felt him tense behind me.

"I almost failed last year, Jason." My brows furrowed, disappointment sitting heavy in my chest.

"But you didn't," he reminded me.

"No, but this year is only going to get harder."

I thought my love of animals, dedication to animal welfare, and determination to succeed was enough. Turns out, it wasn't.

"Hey." Jason shuffled us so that I was on my back and he was leaning over me. "You've got this." He slid his fingers into my unruly curls and kissed me, his tongue curling around mine, stirring my body to life.

"I have some news too," he breathed the words against my lips.

"Tell me." I cupped his face, pushing his away gently so I could look into his eyes.

"Linc had an accident. He's out for the season."

"Oh God, Jason, that's awful." Lincoln had really taken Jase under his wing last year, so I knew how hard this would hit him.

"That's not all..." He hesitated, a flash of fear streaking across his eyes. "Coach wants me to be captain. He thinks I'm ready."

"Jason..." I smiled so wide my cheeks hurt. "That's amazing. I'm so freakin' proud of you." I slung my arms around his neck and crushed him to me, peppering his face in sloppy kisses. "My boyfriend, QB One *and* captain of the Penn Quakers."

But he didn't revel in my excitement. He was still and quiet.

Too quiet.

"Jase?" I held him at arm's length. "What is it?"

"What if I'm not ready? What if I screw it up? Fuck, you should have seen the way they were all looking at me. As if I had the answers, the power to make things happen."

"Babe, listen to me and listen good. You, Jason Ford, are one of the best quarterbacks in the country right now. You came into a well-established team and proved yourself in your freshman year. You ranked *third* for the most passing yards in a single season." Pride flooded me. "Third, babe. That's huge. Not to mention the fact you blew the Quakers passing yards record out of the water."

Jason was already in the Penn Quaker Hall of Fame; he'd already made Quaker history. But with that kind of accolade came the pressure to always do more, to constantly be better.

"You've got this, Jason," I said with complete conviction, ignoring the niggle of doubt that this was going to take my boyfriend away from me even more than football already had.

Didn't captains have to spend more time with the coach, watching game footage and devising plays? And then there would be the rest of the team.

The captain was a leader, a father figure, the guy everyone went to when they needed an ear to listen or a shoulder to lean on.

But if anyone deserved it, it was Jason.

So how could I even contemplate feeling anything besides pride for him?

The answer was, I couldn't.

I knew what football meant to him. Jason had given everything to the game he loved. Hours of conditioning and practice. He was one hundred and ten percent committed to his team, to forging a successful football career for himself. And I was the lucky girl who got to stand at his side and watch him flourish. So I stuffed down my reservations, plastered on my best smile, and said, "I'm so proud of you."

"And I'm so fucking lucky to have you in my corner." Jason captured my lips in a slow, deep kiss. The kind of kiss that we sank into, exploring each other's mouth with easy familiarity. But like every time we touched, it soon turned into more. Heat simmered between us, rising into an inferno neither one of us could control.

Jase slid his hands to the hem of my t-shirt and began working it up my body. His lips brushed a path up my stomach, his tongue dipping into the valley of my breasts as he pushed the material over my head.

"God, Jason," I moaned, jamming my fingers into his thick, dark hair. He continued painting my skin with his lips, tracing letters of love and promises of forever over my chest and collarbone.

"I need you."

He pulled away, leaving me cold, to yank off his jersey. My eyes traced over his body, his chest, shredded with muscle, all hard lines and deep grooves.

"Sometimes I forget how gorgeous you are," I whispered, reaching out to touch him.

He'd always been physically fit, a sculpted work of art thanks to all the conditioning and hours spent in the gym. But since playing college ball, his body had matured and refined in a way that left me breathless every time I saw him naked.

"You look like you want to devour me." He smirked, holding my heated gaze with his own.

"I do," I confessed.

Jason dived for me and we became a clash of limbs, fighting to undress the other, desperate to touch and feel and taste. I was hardly surprised he got me naked first, pinning me to the bed and dipping his head to flick his tongue over my nipple. I cried out, arching into his mouth. His smooth chuckle reverberated around my sensitive skin, sending shivers skittering up my spine.

Nothing would ever compare to this, to the feel of him touching me... owning me. I loved it, almost as much as I loved him.

"I want to take my time," he rasped as he punched his hips forward rocking into me, "but I'm not sure I can."

"So don't," I practically pleaded. We could play afterwards. Right now, I needed to feel him inside me, above me, riding me hard and fast until neither of us knew where I ended and he began.

Jason ripped my panties off; ripped them clean off my body before sinking inside me without warning. We both groaned, his hands tangling with mine either side of my head. "I love you, Felicity, so fucking much."

"Then show me..." My voice cracked as he pulled out and rocked forward again, sheathing himself deep inside me.

Jason loved like he played football. With complete determination, skill, and confidence. He knew exactly how to play my body, the way he played on the field, and he knew exactly how to make me come every damn time.

"Fuck, babe, nothing... *nothing* will ever feel as good as this." He thrust into me again, over and over, splintering my body apart in the best kind of way. Jason kissed like a man starved, dragging the oxygen from my lungs and taking it for himself. One of his hands slipped down my thigh, hitching my leg higher, letting him drive deeper.

"Jason... God..." I breathed, trying to ground myself, but it was too much.

It always was.

"Let go, babe." He kissed me slower, mimicking the shallow rock of his hips as he drew pleasure from my body.

My legs began to tremble, sweat beading on my skin and slipping down my body. I pressed my lips together, trapping the moan building into my throat. I was so close.

"I can feel you, Felicity, feel you squeezing my dick." He whispered the dirty words against my ear as I unraveled. "Come for me, babe. Come all around my..."

I shattered around him, crying out his name, over and over.

Jason flattened himself against me, slamming into me with renewed vigor as I rode the lingering waves of pleasure.

His body locked up tight, his jaw tense with concentration as he jerked inside me.

We lay there, silent and sated and I'd never felt happier. We'd had an amazing freshman year together, and now we had three years of living as a couple, in a cute little off-campus apartment a few minutes' walk away from Penn.

But no matter how happy I was, how madly in love with Jason I was, there was always a little voice of doubt in the back of my mind.

Jason was already Quaker royalty. In one season he had won the hearts of his teammates, coaches, and fans. And now he was captain. He would soon be thrust into the public eye more than ever.

No matter how hard I wanted to believe in the fairytale, the truth was he would always be in the spotlight, and I would always be the girl at his side in the shadows.

But it was something I was just going to have to learn to live with, because giving this up—giving *him* up—wasn't an option for me.

Ever.

2

Felicity

VETERINARY MEDICINE WAS both my dream and nightmare. I loved animals. I loved them with every fiber of my being. There was something about being surrounded by crates of four-legged friends that brought me peace, and it had been at A Brand New Tail in Rixon that my dream to become a vet had been born. However, the truth was, I was barely staying afloat. The course was naturally science-based but I'd underestimated just how hard it would be to stay on top of multiple classes. This semester alone, I was studying general pathology, parasitology, and microbiology.

If I wanted to stay on track, I needed help.

Which is why I'd signed up for the tutor program.

Butterflies zipped around my stomach as I headed for the Hill Pavilion. I was meeting Darcy for coffee nearby and to discuss a schedule. All tutors were fourth year or post-grad students, and I was hoping she could help me keep my head above water this year.

But when I reached the coffee shop, I saw no sign of her. I checked my watch. I was almost five minutes late. Glancing around the place again, I decided to wait by the noticeboard. It was chock full of advertisements for roommates, social clubs, and local bars hosting live music nights.

Someone tapped my shoulder and I spun around. "Can I help you?" I frowned at the guy.

"Felicity Giles by any chance?"

"Um, yeah."

"I'm Darcy, your tutor." The guy smiled and my eyes widened.

"*You're* Darcy? But I thought..." I stopped myself. How rude and presumptuous I'd been.

His smile grew timid. "You thought I was a girl?"

"Sorry." My cheeks pinked.

Darcy shrugged. "I'm used to it. Unfortunately for me, my mom had a strange affinity for Jane Austen in her younger years." He held out his hand. "It's nice to meet you."

"That's... I really don't know what to say." My awkward laugh echoed around the high ceilings.

"Shall we?" He motioned to one of the tables. "I already got myself a coffee. What would you like?"

"Oh no, you don't have to do that. I'll just—"

"Felicity, relax. I can afford to buy coffee for a pretty girl." His eyes twinkled.

"I have a boyfriend," I blurted out. God, this was beyond awkward. I bet he thought I'd lost my mind.

"Good thing I'm only here to tutor you then. What's your poison of choice?"

"Latte, please," I conceded. "Cream and sugar."

He gave me a reassuring nod before heading for the line while I got comfortable at the table. My phone pinged and I dug it out of my bag.

QB#1: Hope tutoring goes well.

Me: Just arrived. Shouldn't you be practicing, Captain?

I smiled.

QB#1: You can tell Darcy from me that she'd better take care of my girl.

The knot in my stomach tightened. Jason thought Darcy was a girl, just like I had when I pulled one of her—*his*—tickets off the advert pinned to one of the course noticeboards.

Crap.

He wasn't going to like this. It wasn't about *not* trusting me. Jason had a problem trusting anyone with a dick around me. But it worked both ways. If I knew Jase was getting tutoring from a girl, that he was spending a lot of time with someone who wasn't me, I'd be jealous too.

It was just the way we loved each other. Deeply. Obsessively. Completely.

Darcy chose that exact moment to return, placing my latte down in front of me. "I didn't know if you'd eaten or not, so I grabbed two blueberry muffins."

"I already had breakfast, but thank you."

"Hey, more for me, right?" His smile was easy, his eyes warm. Darcy didn't give off creeper vibes. He was nice, friendly, even if a little forward.

"So, Penn Vet, how's that going for you?"

"I want to say it's a breeze, but then I wouldn't be sitting here."

"Yeah, freshman year can be a shock to the system, but it gets easier, I promise."

"Why do I feel like you're sugarcoating the truth?" Our laughter swirled around us. "Thanks, for the latte." I brought the glass to my lips, reveling in the bittersweet smell of cream and coffee beans.

"Anytime. So why don't you tell me what you struggled with last year and we can look at your classes for this semester and figure out a plan of action."

"Sounds good." Some of the tension left me. Darcy was my tutor. This was strictly a business relationship. Jason couldn't get pissed about that. Besides, he knew I was his.

I felt a lick of determination skitter up my spine. I needed this if I was going to be able to survive sophomore year. I needed help.

And Darcy Bannerman came highly recommended.

After almost two hours, and a rigorous plan, Darcy and I packed away our things and left the coffee shop. "So I'll see you Wednesday?" he said, waiting for me to move ahead of him.

"Sounds good," I said, ducking around him and stumbling straight into—

"Jason?"

"Hey," he shot me a smile that made my knees weak. "How was tutoring?" His arms went around me, as he dipped his head to kiss me.

"It was good. I... uh... this is Darcy, my tutor." I wriggled free of his grasp to step aside and introduce them.

The second Jason's eyes landed on Darcy his expression darkened. "*You're* the tutor?"

"Darcy Bannerman." He held out his hand. "You must be the boyfriend."

Jason narrowed his gaze, staring at Darcy's hand as if it was contagious.

"Jase." I hissed, elbowing him in the ribs.

"Jason. Jason Ford."

"As in starting quarterback Jason Ford?" Darcy's brow went up.

"Felicity didn't tell you?"

I rolled my eyes at that.

"No, it never came up."

"Okay," I rushed out. "This has been fun and all, but if you'll excuse us, Darcy, I need to talk to my boyfriend about the etiquette of conversation." He chuckled as I pulled Jason away. "What the hell was that?" I hissed once we were out of earshot, marching down the street.

"You failed to mention your new tutor was a guy." Jason fell into step beside me.

"That's because I didn't know."

"Yeah, I suppose Darcy is a pretty girly name."

"Jason." I glowered at him. "Is this going to be a problem?"

"Will you get a new tutor if I say yes?" His brow arched in challenge. I wanted to believe he was joking.

I knew he wasn't.

"If I'm going to pass this year, I need all the help I can get, and Darcy comes highly recommended."

"I bet he does," Jason grumbled, his eyes going over his shoulder, but Darcy was long gone.

Usually, I loved this side of him. Possessive and dominant. But now he was just being stupid.

"Jason, look at me." I stopped, gripping his jaw, forcing his eyes to mine. "There is nothing to worry about."

"And if our roles were reversed. If it was me spending time alone with a tutor who just so happened to be a hot girl?"

"You think Darcy's hot?" I hadn't really noticed.

"Don't push me, Giles."

Giles.

A shiver ran up my spine. He only called me that when I'd really pissed him off.

"I'd hate it, okay? But I would trust you. Because that's what you do when you love someone. You trust them."

His hard expression melted away, giving way to something that looked a lot like regret. "Shit, Felicity, I trust you, I do." He pulled me into his arms, brushing his nose over mine.

"I know you do." My hands curled into his Quakers hoodie. "But I need this Jase. I need to get a handle on classes before I sink too deep."

"And he's really the best?" He studied me.

I nodded.

"Okay," he breathed. "But if he so much as looks at you the wrong way, I will—"

"Ssh, my Neanderthal." I kissed him softly, but Jason took control, sliding his hands into my hair and slipping his tongue past my lips.

"Get a room, Ford," someone yelled, and we both turned to find a group of football players.

"Are you guys working out today?" I asked.

"Yeah. With Linc out—"

"I get it."

"Tonight. Me, you, and our favorite takeout?"

My smile fell. "I'm volunteering at the shelter."

He mumbled his displeasure under his breath.

"I won't be late. Why don't you hang out with the guys at The Gridiron and I'll meet you afterward?" The sports bar was on my route home from Paws, the animal shelter I helped at sometimes.

"Yeah?"

I nodded, and Jason leaned in capturing my lips again. "I know I'm a lot," he whispered, "but it's only because I'm so fucking crazy about you."

Love wrapped around me like a warm blanket as I fisted his hoodie tighter. "The feeling is entirely mutual."

"Yo, Ford," Gio yelled. I liked him. He was American-Italian and hailed from Verona County in Rhode Island. He had an adorable habit of cussing in Italian. It wasn't any wonder they called it the language of love; his accent was so freakin' dreamy.

"Yeah, yeah, Abato," Jase shouted back. "That's my cue." He stole another kiss. "I'll see you later."

Pressing my lips into a small smile, I nodded. "Go show them who's boss, Captain." I smirked. Jason chuckled, giving me a flirty wink before taking off toward his friends and teammates.

I watched them jostle him, fist bumping and laughing. He looked so happy, so free. He'd slipped into college life with ease. Even with his intense athletic schedule, he was doing well in his classes and keeping up with the workload. Nothing fazed him.

Unlike me, who had almost failed my freshman year.

I shook off the feelings of inferiority. This year would be better. This year I would give my studies everything, and now I had Darcy in my corner, everything would work out.

Except as I headed for my first class, I couldn't stop the seed of doubt taking root in my stomach.

Jason

"What's up, man?" Gio asked as he spotted me on the weight bar. "You seem... tense."

"Felicity got a tutor."

"And that's a problem wh—" Realization dawned on his face. "The tutor is a guy?"

My jaw clenched as I pictured that fucker's face. I didn't know him from Adam, but I already didn't like him. He'd be spending time with Felicity. My woman, the other half of my fucking soul. Possessive asshole or not, I was not okay with some guy spending quality time alone with *my* girl.

"It's just tutoring." He snorted. "You don't have anything to worry about."

"Don't I?" My brow rose.

Felicity was gorgeous. All seductive curves and wild spirit. I saw guys around campus watching her, wishing they could have a taste. They soon backed the fuck off when they saw me, but still.

"Seriously, bro, Fee wouldn't look twice at another guy. She doesn't get all crazy possessive when we hang out with the cheer squad."

Oh, she did. I just didn't advertise the fact. Freshman year, Felicity had almost attacked a girl for trying to get my number at a party. Instead, I'd dragged her to the nearest bedroom and fucked the anger right out of her.

Our love was like wildfire. It burned constantly. Throw water on it and it simmered to a gentle flicker, but add a strong wind and it became an inferno. Ferocious and unpredictable.

"This is why I don't have a girlfriend," Griffin joined us. "Too much drama for my liking."

"Dude, you don't have a girl because you're a walking, talking STI." Gio exploded with laughter but it became muted when Griffin punched him in the arm.

"I had chlamydia once. One fucking time. She told me she was—"

"Rule number one, Griff," I said. "Always wrap it."

"Yeah," he dragged a hand through his hair, "And what's rule number two?"

"Get a steady girl and then you won't have to worry about wrapping it."

Gio and I shared a knowing smile. He wasn't in a serious relationship like me and Felicity, but he had steady pussy.

"Nah, I need to sow my wild oats before I settle down." Griffin grabbed some free weights and started pumping.

"You just haven't met the right girl," I said. I didn't make a habit of sharing my personal life, but Gio and Griffin were my closest friends on the team. Both juniors, they'd taken me under their wing last year. It wasn't the same as having Cameron and Asher—guys who had known me most of my life—in my corner, but I trusted them. And sometimes, when I needed to, I confided in them.

"You guys want to get a drink at The Gridiron later?" I asked them.

"Fee giving you a free pass?" Gio smirked and I flipped him off.

"She's working a shift at the shelter. She'll meet us after. I'm going to invite Asher and Mya too."

He'd been nagging me to get together, but it had been a crazy couple of weeks.

"I'll ask Jordan if she wants to come."

"Pussy whipped." Griffin coughed under his breath.

"We're friends."

"Friends with benefits," I corrected.

"Yeah, I guess."

"Count me out," Griffin said. "But enjoy couples' night." He squeezed Gio's shoulders before heading for the chest press.

"I hope his dick falls off."

I chuckled. "He just hasn't met—"

"The right girl, yeah." Gio looked conflicted but I didn't ask. If he wanted to talk about Jordan, he'd bring it up. "How are you feeling about being captain?" He changed the subject.

"It's an honor." It was. I'd come to Penn wanting to go all the way, and this was just another step in the right direction.

"But..." he prompted.

"Linc left some big shoes to fill."

"Nah, you've got this. If it wasn't going to be this year, it would have happened when he graduated. This spot was yours the minute you stepped foot into the locker room."

"Thanks, man, I appreciate it."

"No need to thank me, Jase. You're one of the best; the kind of leader this team needs to go all the way. I have faith in you, man, even if you don't."

"I guess we'd better get to work then." I smirked, brushing off his compliment no matter how much it meant to me.

"Yeah." He chuckled. "We'd better."

3

Felicity

"FEE, BABY, GET OVER HERE."

"Asher?" I smiled, surprised to see him standing at the bar next to Jason and… "Mya!"

A high-pitched squeal broke from my lips as I bypassed Asher to go straight to his girlfriend. "It's so good to see you."

"Girl, it's been three weeks."

"Three weeks too many." I hugged Mya tighter, uncaring that she preferred to keep PDAs to a minimum. "Tell me everything. How are classes? The new place? I want to know it all."

"Are you okay?" She eyed me with suspicion.

"What? I can't be happy to see one of my best friends?" I smiled, but it felt weak.

"Don't worry about me or anything," Asher grumbled, making Jason, Gio, and Jordan laugh.

"So needy." I locked my arms around his neck and hugged him. "It's good to see you, Ash."

"Not as good as it is to see you." He held me tight until familiar fingers pried me away.

"Okay, put my girl down, Bennet, before I have to snap your fingers and ruin your football career before it even gets started."

Asher released me and Jase pulled me between his legs. "I missed you."

"I want to say I missed you too, but the shelter had two new rescues, Pug puppies… they were so cute."

"Great, I've been axed for goddamn dogs."

"Aww, you still own my heart." I kissed the corner of his mouth. "But these were some really, *really* cute puppies."

"Well if you'd rather stroke those than…" he whispered the words only meant for me as he trailed a finger down my neck. A shiver rolled through me and I swallowed a whimper.

"Didn't think so." Jason kissed the end of my nose. "Hey, Hugh, get my girl a drink," he called over to the bartender.

"Sure thing. Your regular, Fee?"

I nodded. "So, what have you guys been talking about in my absence?"

"Oh, you know, trying to deflate this one's head since he got promoted to captain." Asher pinched Jase's cheek, and he batted him away. "How does it feel to wear the crown?"

"Asher," Mya sighed.

"He knows I'm proud. I'm like the proud brother he never had. But that shit's got to weigh a ton."

"I was born ready," Jason said, but I saw the tightness in his eyes. He was having doubts about his ability to lead.

We all knew he had nothing to worry about though because he *was* born ready.

"That's the spirit, bro." Asher clapped him on the shoulder. "Now Fee is here, we should toast."

"We don't need to—"

"To Jason," he thrust his beer in the air, "may your leadership be firm and your game strong. Congratulations, man."

Jason

I tried to heed Asher and Gio's words. Every day we practiced, every day we studied game tapes and devised new plays, I tried to hold onto the fact that I'd waited for this day my entire life. But with the opening game finally here, I couldn't deny I had a constant gnawing in my stomach.

It didn't help that Felicity was spending more and more time with tutor boy. She was finding one of her classes, parasitology or something, particularly difficult. But it wasn't like I was around much to help, or even could if I was.

The team had become my life the last couple of weeks. Everything building to this moment.

"Okay, ladies, look alive." Coach Faulkner moved through the locker room, fierce determination etched in the lines of his face. "Tonight, we're going to go out there and show everyone why it should have been us bringing that trophy home last season, you hear me?"

"Yes, Coach." Our battle cry echoed off the walls, reverberating all the way down to my soul. Hunger pulsed inside me as adrenaline trickled through my veins. No synthetic high could ever replicate this; the moment you stepped out on that field. The second we became gods among men: worshipped and adored, immortalized in the chants of the crowd, every sigh and gasp and cheer. It was our oxygen, our life-force. And I would let it fuel me, push me harder and faster until we won.

"Number one," Coach fixed his eyes on me, "you ready?"

It was the million-dollar question.

I felt strong.

One hundred percent on form.

But I also felt humbled; honored to captain my team, to walk them into battle and lead them to victory.

Because losing was not an option.

"I feel ready, Coach."

"Glad to hear it, son. Dartmouth are looking strong, but they don't have our heart. They don't have our drive or our thirst." He jabbed his finger into the air. "They don't have what it takes to go all the way. Bring it in."

The sound of our cleats against the locker room floor was like the beat of a drum.

"Quakers on three. Jason, do the honors."

I punched my hand into the middle of the tightly knit circle as fifty other hands followed suit.

"One... two... three... Quakers."

We broke formation to file out on the field. I grabbed my helmet and jogged ahead, my heart racing, blood pounding between my ears. But it was nothing compared to the roar of the crowd as we jogged out onto Franklin Field.

"Soak it up, man," Griffin yelled around a shit-eating smirk.

And I did. I slowed to a walk, soaking it up. There had been something special about playing in my freshman year. But this, being here as captain, was the pinnacle of my football career to date. I needed to take a minute, to allow myself a second to process everything. My eyes scanned the VIP section and found Felicity. She was grinning from ear to ear, sitting beside Jordan who was here to support Gio on a 'purely platonic' basis. I called bullshit, but whatever. I could just make out Felicity mouthing the words, "I love you."

In that moment, with my girl in the bleachers, the thirteen-thousand strong crowd all shouting my name, I felt like a god. Worshipped. Adored. Loved.

I felt unstoppable.

This was my calling, my domain... my kingdom.

And I was born to rule.

Felicity

"Oh my god," I breathed as I watched Jason fall back, search the field for his wide receiver, and send the ball flying toward him. He caught it, tucking it into his body and sprinting toward the end zone.

"Go, go," Jordan yelled, and the entire crowd seemed to yell with her.

"Touchdooooown," the announcer's voice filled the stadium, and everyone went wild.

"They've got this," Jordan said around a big smile.

"Yeah." I dropped down in my seat and searched for Jason. He was celebrating with his teammates, high-fiving and fist-bumping. He looked completely at home out there, as if he was born to play.

I didn't doubt he was. Some people possessed that natural talent, a destiny written in the stars. We were watching football greatness unfold right before our eyes, and I didn't think there was a person in the crowd who doubted that Jason Ford, a boy from a small town in Pennsylvania, would one day grace the NFL with his talent and charisma.

The cheer squad broke into a sideline celebration and I smothered a groan.

"Hey, turn that frown upside down." Jordan nudged my shoulder.

"They're just so obvious." I heard them talk about Jason, watched them lust over him despite the fact everyone knew he was off the market.

"Please tell me you're not worried about the likes of Shelly and Farrah?"

"She wants him." Shelly Halstead had wanted Jason since the first day he stepped foot on campus.

"Half the girls here want him."

My lips pressed into a thin line, but Jordan only laughed.

"He loves you; everyone can see that. You have nothing to worry about."

I liked Jordan. She was one of my few girlfriends here. It wasn't that I'd purposefully avoided making friends during freshman year, just it was hard when your boyfriend was the new football star. Girls either looked at me as the competition or they were brazened enough to try to use me as a steppingstone to get to Jason and his friends. I'd quickly given up trying to form genuine friendships. I had Jordan and Mya, and I spoke to Hailee all the time despite the nine-hour distance between us.

"It's just... a lot," I whispered the confession, hating myself for even saying the words.

Jason gave me no reason to worry. He was unwavering in his love for me. But as I watched the team celebrate; watched the cheer squad lick their lips and bat their eyelashes in his direction; listened to thousands of people chant his name; I couldn't help but think the very thing he loved would one day be the thing that drove a wedge between us.

Jason was going places.

And I barely had my head above water.

Jordan pulled me into a side hug. "You and Jason are endgame, Fee. I see the way he watches you, the way he tracks your every move. That guy is head over heels in love with you. All this: football, the crowds, the high; it would mean nothing if he didn't have you by his side."

As if he heard her words, as if he felt the doubt swirling around me like a storm cloud, Jason looked up, searching the bleachers for me. I couldn't see his eyes behind his helmet, but I felt them.

And I couldn't ever imagine *not* feeling them.

The party was wild. But there was something about winning the first game of the season that had everyone worked up. Jordan and I lingered on the periphery with a couple of the other girlfriends, sipping our sugary sweet mixed drinks, while Jason, Gio, Griffin, and a handful of their other friends took shots.

"Okay, okay, let me get up here." Griffin jumped up on the huge breakfast island and ushered the crowd into silence. "I think I can speak for everyone when I say we were all fucking bummed when Coach gave us the news about Linc. But I think I can also speak for everyone here when I say we never doubted Jason would be there to pick up the pieces." He fixed his eyes on Jase and raised his beer in the air. "I'm proud to call you my friend, man, but I'm even prouder to call you my captain. And I know... I just fucking know, you're going to take us all the way this season."

The room exploded with cheers and hollers, quickly turning into chants of, "Speech, speech."

Jason cleared his throat, looking more than a little displeased at Griffin's little stunt. "Those of you who know me, know I'm a private guy, so I'm going to keep this short. Linc is a good guy, one of the best. He took me under his wing last year and guided me right, and for that, I owe him. I'm fucking honored to lead the team in his stead. To Linc." He tipped his beer forward and nodded at his rapt audience.

"Linc." The name echoed through the room, a somber reminder of how fragile this life could be. How, one minute, you could be on the cusp of football greatness only to have it all ripped away in the blink of an eye. Or, in Linc's case, a simple wrong landing during a basketball game with his younger brothers.

Jason's eyes found mine across the kitchen, and he stalked toward me.

"We're going to dance," Jordan announced, shooting me a knowing glance.

I gave them a small wave, heat coursing through my veins as Jason drank me in. I was wearing skinny jeans and a fitted Quaker tank top, no different than half the girls here. But the way he looked at me... it was as if I was the only girl he could see.

The only girl he wanted to see.

"Hey." He crowded me against the counter.

"Hey." I smiled. I couldn't help it. Jason would always bring out the best and worst of me. "Nice speech."

"You know I fucking hate doing that."

"I know." I ran my fingers over his jaw. He didn't resemble a twenty-year-old sophomore. He was all man. Tall, broad, and muscular with a five o'clock shadow over his angular jaw, Jason had graduated Rixon a boy on the verge of adulthood and matured into a confident, self-assured guy who knew without doubt what he wanted from life.

"Congratulations, QB One." Fixing my mouth over his, I kissed him.

Jason groaned against my lips, tangling his tongue with mine and sliding his hands into my hair.

"Fuck, babe, no win will ever taste as good as this."

His words made my heart swell, even if I knew he was just caught up in the moment.

Because for as much as I wanted to believe I came before football... part of me wasn't so sure.

4

Felicity

I WOKE UP ALONE, again. It was the third morning in a row. Jason seemed to spend every spare second he had in the gym, or with his coaches, or cramming in extra study hours so he didn't fall behind in his classes.

The Quakers were on a winning streak and no one wanted to lose momentum.

Grabbing my cell off the nightstand, I smiled at the text message from Jason, but it didn't quite reach my eyes.

It never did these days.

QB#1: Sorry... I know I promised to be there this morning, but the guys texted wanting to get an hour at the gym before classes. Everyone is feeling tense about the game Friday.

Me: Go do your thing. I can't wait until tonight xo

Wednesday night was always date night. We didn't always go out, but we always cleared our schedules for each other. Sometimes we went across the river to hang out with Asher and Mya, sometimes we caught a movie downtown, or sometimes we stayed in and just enjoyed a slice of quiet in our crazy lives.

QB#1: Tonight? Shit, I told the guys we'd get together to watch the tapes from the game last week.

My stomach sank. He'd forgotten about date night.

. . .

Me: Oh, okay. Well, I could always use some extra hours studying. We can take a raincheck.

QB#1: I'll make it up to you, I promise.

Me: I know xo

I did. Jason would strive to lavish me with a romantic meal at our favorite restaurant or a seductive night in, worshipping every inch of my body until I'd forgotten all about his indiscretion.

Except, the further into football season we got, the less time we spent together, and the more my heart ached.

"Whoa, who died?" Darcy chuckled as he greeted me at the coffee shop.

"Huh?" I frowned.

"The glum face? Is everything okay?" He ushered me to a table.

"Yeah, I'm fine."

"You know, I'm a good listener as well as an excellent tutor."

"Modest too, apparently." I managed a weak smile.

"Let me guess, guy troubles."

"How did you—" I stopped myself. The last thing I wanted was to discuss Jason with my tutor.

"Nine times out of ten, it is." He shrugged as if it wasn't a big deal, but something told me it was. "Want to talk about it?"

"Not really, no." I pulled out my notebook.

"You know, I wouldn't have put you with Mr. Hotshot Football Player."

"What is that supposed to mean?" My defenses went up.

"I just meant... football players usually attract a certain type of girl."

"You don't know anything about me or Jason, Darcy." I really didn't appreciate his tone or the insinuation in his words.

"Sorry, this is coming out all wrong." He ran a hand through his hair. "All I mean is, I've been on campus long enough to witness my fair share of heartache." There was something in his tone... something personal.

"You don't like the football team very much, do you?"

"I guess you could say that." His expression hardened.

"They don't all fall into the typical jock stereotype, you know?"

"I'm sure there are exceptions to the norm."

There were. Jason, Asher, Cameron, even Gio, and Griffin—for all his goofy ways—were good guys. They played hard and they loved hard.

"But..."

"But I guess I don't understand how intelligent, independent, ambitious girls are so willing to be second string to a sport."

I didn't know what I'd expected... but it hadn't been for him to pick up on my insecurity.

"When you love someone, Darcy, you support their passions, their hopes and dreams." It came out harsher than I intended.

"I can see I hit a nerve. I didn't mean—"

"Jason and I love each other very much. He supports my dreams and I support his."

Why was I justifying myself to him? I didn't owe him or anyone else an explanation about why I was with Jason. You didn't choose love, it chose you, and Jason Ford had stolen my heart a long time ago.

"I'm sure he's a good guy." Darcy finally opened his notebook.

"He is."

I'd wanted to come to our tutor session and focus on something else besides the gnawing pit in my stomach. But now there was an awkward tension in the air as Darcy talked me through the life cycles of protozoan parasites.

We worked like that for an hour, in stilted conversation potted with thick silences.

I'd never been more relieved when he announced we were done. I hurried to pack up my things and abruptly stood.

"Felicity, wait," he said. "I owe you an apology. My prejudices about the football team, are just that, mine. I watched a couple of my good friends get hurt pretty badly by jocks... it left a sour taste in my mouth. I'm sorry."

"I appreciate your words. But I meant what I said, Darcy. You don't know anything about mine and Jason's relationship." And I intended on keeping it that way.

"You're right, I don't. As long as you're happy, right?" He gave me a goofy smile, but it was like a punch to the stomach.

Because I wasn't happy lately.

"Same time Thursday?"

I hesitated. I could request a different tutor and hope they had even half as much as knowledge and Darcy's ability to break down the science and explain it in a way that I understood.

But that felt like the coward's way out.

He was entitled to his opinions, even if they had hit a sore point.

I gave him a small nod and said, "I'll see you then."

Jason

"You think we're ready?" Griffin asked me as we filed out of the room adjoining the locker room. We'd been watching game tapes from Dartmouth's game against Yale last week. They were the team to beat. The team we needed to beat to stay at the top of the league.

"We're ready," I said with complete confidence. Since our opening game, we'd gone from strength to strength. Being quarterback always gave you a natural leadership role in a team, but now that I was captain, something had clicked. We all felt it. But it was more than that. I had something to prove. To myself, Coach, the team, the fans... Linc.

I needed to take them all the way.

Anything else was *not* an option.

"We're heading over to the house if you want to come for a beer?" Gio said.

He and Griffin lived with a few of the other guys in a big house just off campus.

"Not tonight." I wanted to make it home in time to see Felicity.

Between classes, the team, and her work at the shelter, we'd barely seen each other. I wanted nothing more than to take my sweet time exploring her body before I sank deep inside her.

"Hot date?" Griffin smirked and I flipped him off.

"Actually, I missed date night." Guilt snaked through me. But I could make it up to her. I couldn't, however, make it up to the game Friday night if we weren't ready.

"Oh shit, you're gonna be in the doghouse, man."

"Nah, Felicity understands." But as I said the words, my stomach knotted. I was asking a lot of her. We both knew the level of dedication and discipline playing college ball would require, but even I'd underestimated just how intensive it would be. Playing for the team didn't only mean practice and games. It meant bonding with the guys, being a brotherhood... a family. You couldn't just shirk your way out of that. Especially not when you were the captain.

"I'll catch you later," I said to the guys as we filed out of the building. It was already dark.

I jogged to my car and climbed inside. Then I checked my cell. There was a text from Cameron, but nothing from Felicity.

With a heavy sigh, I fired up the engine, backed out of the parking lot and took off toward our building to make it up to the girl I loved more than I ever thought possible.

Our apartment in Powelton Village was less than a ten-minute ride. The closer I got to our building, the more I couldn't help but feel like I'd messed up. Wednesday was always date night. It was something we'd started back in freshman year, to make sure we put aside some time each week for the two of us to just be Jason and Felicity.

I pulled into my allotted parking spot and cut the engine. It was almost nine thirty. Late, but not too late to salvage the night.

Grabbing my cell, I found Cameron's number and hit dial.

"What did you do?" he asked.

"How do you know I did anything?"

"Because it's nine thirty on a Wednesday night..." He let the words hang.

"I think I messed up tonight." I dragged a hand over my face.

"It can't be that bad."

"It's date night and it slipped my mind."

"That doesn't sound so scandalous." He chuckled.

"I'd arranged to watch game tapes with the guys, so when I realized, I—"

"You chose the guys over Felicity."

Fuck. The fact he answered for me only cemented my guilt.

"When you say it like that it does sound like a dick move."

"Fee knows the deal. She knows what it means to be on the team."

"Yeah, I guess..."

Silence fell over the line until Cam said, "Things are okay between the two of you, right?"

"Yeah, I think so. I mean, we're not spending much time together lately. She's at the shelter or with tutor boy. And I'm either trying to study or with the team... Why? Has she said something to Hailee?"

"What? No! Even if she had I'm not sure she'd tell me."

I scoffed at that. "Bullshit. My sister would tell you everything."

"Did you just refer to Hailee as your *sister*?"

"No," I grumbled at my slip of the tongue.

"You did. I heard it as plain as day. You said—"

"Okay, Chase, don't get too excited. It doesn't mean anything."

"Oh, but it does." I heard his smile. "Wait until I tell her you've progressed to sis—"

"I'm hanging up now."

"I'm sorry." His laughter subsided. "Your secret stays with me, I swear."

"Hmm. I should never have called you." That's what I got for seeking out some advice.

"Yeah, you should. You needed someone to tell you to pull your head out of your ass, go find your girl and grovel."

"You're right." That's exactly what I intended on doing.

"Are the girls still planning to take Mya away for her birthday?"

"I think so," I said. "Asher suggested we could go stay with him."

"I'm easy. It'll be good to see you."

"Yeah, you too. Thanks for the chat."

Cameron's laughter filled the line again. I was fucking ecstatic that he found this funny. "Anytime. Now go grovel."

We hung up and I climbed out of my car, grabbing my bag from the trunk. Our apartment was on the top floor with views of the Schuylkill River.

When I got inside, it was quiet. "Babe?" I called.

Throwing my keys onto the sideboard, I moved deeper into the apartment. The lonely plate on the draining board made my chest tighten. She'd eaten alone.

It shouldn't have mattered as much as it did.

Felicity

I heard Jason before I felt him. Measured footsteps in the hall, the creak of the bedroom door, the rustle of him stripping out of his clothes. Part of me ached to glance over my shoulder and greet him. But the part that had stewed all night on Darcy's words kept me rooted in place, eyes closed and heart heavy.

The covers moved behind me and a rush of cool air hit my back, and then Jason's hard, warm body brushed mine. "Babe, you awake?" He slipped his arm around my waist and tucked me into the lines of his chest. Usually this was my happy place, but tonight, the distance between us felt bigger than ever.

What was happening?

We'd survived freshman year. That was supposed to be a couples big test, wasn't it? Survive freshman year—the lure of new experiences and endless parties—and you could survive anything.

Jason's lips ghosted over my neck, trailing a path to my ear. "I'm sorry," he whispered, and those two words damn near broke my heart. They were so full of regret and sincerity, but they didn't promise the one thing I really needed to hear.

That it wouldn't happen again.

5

Jason

WE WERE LEADING the Ivy League four to none, with three games left to play. The pressure was on after what could only be described as a flawless season. Probably my best football season to date. My passing yards total was already a season best and I was currently tied second with a kid out of Cornell on the Division I FCS season passing yards leaderboard.

I was heading for the single most perfect season of my life... and yet, my personal life was a fucking mess.

Letting out a frustrated breath, I pushed open the door to the hotel bar and found Asher and Cameron sitting in wait.

"Hey, it's good to see you." Cam got up first, pulling me into a guy hug. Seeing my friends was like coming home. I loved my team at Penn: the guys, the coaches, the fans; but it wasn't Rixon.

"Sorry I'm late."

"Don't sweat it, we know the drill." They did. They'd seen me captain the Rixon Raiders, witnessed how deep I became when handed such a responsibility. I didn't just carry my own thirst for the win, I carried every single player's.

"Everyone is on edge. This could be a perfect season—Penn's first in almost a decade. It means a lot to the team, to Coach."

"And it should," Asher said, taking a long pull on his beer. "Just don't let it go to your head."

"Fat chance of that." Cam shot me a smirk, and I flipped him off.

"Between classes and the team there isn't time to let it go to my head, trust me." The bartender pushed a beer toward me, and I nearly drained the thing in one.

Fuck, I needed this. A night shooting the shit with my friends; friends who didn't want to talk plays or game tapes or team stats.

The girls had gone to a fancy spa in Michigan to celebrate Mya's birthday in style, while we'd decided to join Asher at his place. Thanks to his sizeable trust fund, their apartment building was like a five-star hotel, complete with a fully equipped gym, bar and restaurant, and roof top terrace.

"So, I was looking at your stats," he piped up. "You know Heisman could come knocking this year."

I snorted. "There hasn't been a Heisman Trophy winner come out of the Ivy League since the fifties."

"It could happen. You're dominating ESPN chatter."

Yeah, when hell froze over.

"I'll just be happy to see us maintain our perfect record and win the league."

We fell into easy conversation. Time and distance didn't sever our bond. If anything, our friendship was stronger than ever.

"So my mom is having a Thanksgiving thing," Asher announced. "She's keeping it low key. She wants to invite Kent and Denise; your mom, dad, and Xander," he said to Cameron.

"Yeah, sounds good. What about Mya's aunt?"

He let out a weary sigh. "It's a work in progress. She and Mya got into it the other week, don't ask me what about. Probably me or the fact that Mya is getting too involved in her studies."

"Isn't that supposed to happen?" I asked.

"Yeah, but she's volunteering at a community project and she comes home with all these stories about the kids..."

"She wants to save them all," Cameron said, and Asher nodded.

"And she can't, ya know? I'm just worried she'll get too attached."

"Nah, she's strong," I said, "and she wants to help. There's nothing wrong with that."

Mya had grown up in a rough neighborhood. She'd witnessed firsthand what deprivation, crime, and drugs could do to a person. So the fact she wanted to be a social worker and try to make a positive impact was commendable.

"Says the guy who's been spending more time with his team than his girl." Asher's brow quirked up.

"She's always with tutor boy." I bristled. Darcy's name was becoming a regular mention in our conversation. I fucking hated it, but it wasn't like I could complain, not when Asher was right. I was spending more time with the team than Felicity. But it was only for another few weeks. Once the season was over, things would settle. We could be us again.

"Dude, you're not seriously jealous about a guy who enjoys talking about animal science all day?"

"You're forgetting that Felicity also likes talking about that stuff."

"He's her tutor. You're her... person."

Cameron chuckled. "He's right, you know. You and Felicity are going the distance. All couples have highs and lows."

"Well being in a low fucking sucks."

"You're still... doing it, right?"

I gawked at Asher. "What are we, five?"

"I'm just trying to help." He shrugged.

"Yeah, well maybe we should change the subject." Dissecting my relationship with Felicity was making me cranky.

"If you make it as one of the Heisman finalists, we can take a trip to New York for the weekend to celebrate."

"Seriously, Ash, the chances of me getting shortlisted are almost non-existent." I rubbed my jaw.

"Still, I'll ask my old man if we can reserve the penthouse for the weekend. That way, even if you don't shortlist, we can still go, but it can be a commiseration instead of a celebration." A shit-eating grin tugged at his mouth.

"There's something very wrong with you," I grumbled.

"But you love me."

Yeah, I did. He might have been like sunshine on a fucking rainy day, but Asher was my best friend. Cameron too. Almost fifteen months had passed since we left Rixon for college, but they were still my guys.

Always would be.

He pulled out his cell phone and I frowned. "What are you doing?"

"Texting my dad."

Cameron smothered a chuckle and I rolled my eyes. "Of course you are."

Felicity

A weekend with Hailee and Mya had been just what I'd needed. We'd spent an entire day and night being pampered and primped, finishing off the day with cocktails in the tropical al fresco style bar. This morning we'd enjoyed a champagne breakfast and then gone our separate ways. Mya and I had flown back to Philadelphia together.

"Oh my god," she murmured as we came through arrivals to find Asher holding a huge 'welcome home' sign. "He did not."

"Oh, he did." Laughter spilled from my lips. I scanned the arrival lounge for Jason, my heart sinking when I didn't spot him.

"My two favorites." Asher approached us.

Mya grabbed his face and squished her nose against his. "It's a good thing I love you."

"What, you didn't like my sign? It took all morning to paint."

"You have completely lost your mind."

"Fee, baby," he kissed Mya before stepping around her, "get over here."

"Hey, Ash." I gave him a hug. "Have you seen Jason?"

"Actually, he asked me if I minded giving you a ride."

"He did?"

I dug out my cell phone checking my messages again.

Nothing.

"He got caught up and didn't want to keep you waiting. Come on, the

Jeep is out front." He grabbed Mya's overnight bag and started toward the door. But I hesitated.

"Hey," Mya said. "I'm sure he wanted to be here."

"Yeah."

I'd confided a little to Mya and Hailee about how strained things had become between Jason and I lately, but I hadn't wanted to put a dampener on our time together. Besides, they had both found their feet at college. Hailee and Cameron had a group of friends they regularly hung out with, and Mya was friends with a ton of her fellow social work classmates. It seemed like it was only me who, a year later, still hadn't slotted into college life.

We piled into Asher's Jeep and I sat quietly in the back while Mya caught him up on our time at the spa. My cell burned a hole in my pocket. I wanted to text Jason and ask why he hadn't been able to pick me up, but I didn't. Because I was pretty sure I already knew the answer.

It was only a fifteen-minute ride to Powelton Village. Asher rolled to a stop outside my building and twisted around to face me.

"Thanks," I said.

"Anytime. Don't be too hard on him, yeah?"

My brows pinched. Wasn't he supposed to side with me? After all, Jason had abandoned me at the airport in favor of hanging out with the team.

"I'll see you both soon."

"Don't be a stranger," Mya said around a warm smile.

I climbed out, dragging my small suitcase behind me. Usually, I'd be excited to see Jason after time apart, but the permanent knot in my stomach only twisted tighter.

Asher honked his horn and I waved, watching as the Jeep disappeared into the steady stream of traffic. There was no sign of Jason's Dodge Charger in the parking lot, and my heart sank a little more.

I rode the elevator up to the top floor, silently planning a hot bath and comfort food. But when I stepped inside the apartment, the gnawing pit in my stomach was replaced with butterflies. A vase of red roses greeted me, a card propped up against the glass. I plucked it up and opened it.

Felicity,

Be ready by 7.

Wear something sexy.

J

I COULDN'T HAVE FOUGHT the smile pulling at my lips if I'd tried. It didn't fix everything, and I knew we still needed to talk, but it was exactly the sign I needed.

NINETY MINUTES LATER, the knock at the door made my heart flutter in my chest. I opened it gently, hardly able to believe my eyes. Jason looked devastating. The slim-fit dark jeans hugged his muscular thighs, and the black dress shirt molded to his broad shoulders and thick arms. He'd left the collar open and rolled the sleeves to his elbows. His hair hung over his eyes a little, in the way I loved so much.

Sweet baby Jesus, he stole my breath.

"Hey." A faint smirk played on his lips as he let his eyes glide slowly down my body and back up again. I'd opted to wear a tight sweater dress that finished just below my knee. It skimmed my curves and scooped low on my chest. Demure yet sexy. Although from the heat in Jason's gaze, I felt stripped naked.

"Fuck," he breathed, leaning in to brush his lips over my cheek. "You look stunning."

"You don't look so bad yourself."

"I'm sorry I wasn't at the airport. I wanted to surprise you and I knew Asher could give you a ride home."

Home.

I loved hearing him refer to our apartment as home. It was so intimate, so permanent. It made it easy to forget the last few weeks and how strained things had been between us.

Jason tucked a curl behind my ear, letting his thumb brush my cheek and hover over my bottom lip. "I really, *really* want to fuck you right now."

"Jason." My breath caught, desire pooling in my stomach.

"But I made reservations, so that will have to wait." He ran a hand down his face, torment glittering in his eyes as if he wasn't sure.

"We could always stay home?" I batted my eyelashes.

"As tempting as that sounds, I have some making up to do. Dinner *then* sex." He fixed his mouth over mine. It was hard and bruising and a promise of things to come. A shiver ran down my spine as I melted into him. "I know things have been hard, but I love you, Felicity. So fucking much."

Jason

It took everything I had not to drag Felicity into the bedroom, strip the ridiculous sexy dress from her body and make love to her. Need pulsed through me as we kissed. My fingers slid into her silky strands, loving how soft it felt against my skin. She smelled amazing, like a vanilla and strawberry sundae. I wanted to taste her, trail my tongue up and down her body until she was a writhing mess beneath me.

Fuck, I wanted her.

It made me realize how much we needed this. We'd still been having sex. I was a hot-blooded guy and Felicity had a body built for sin. But I couldn't remember the last time we played. Spent hours exploring each other's bodies, finding new ways to make each other come undone. We were both busy, both exhausted by the time bedtime rolled around.

"What?" Felicity whispered, uncertainty shining in her eyes as I studied her.

"Just thinking how much I've missed you."

"I've missed you too." She curled her freshly painted nails into my shirt.

"Well, tonight is ours," I said with confidence, threading our hands together.

"I can't wait." She smiled up at me, and my heart beat harder.

That single look... it was everything. And I knew that no matter how hard or demanding college got, we'd be okay. Because this girl—this beautiful, intelligent, driven woman—was mine.

6

Jason

THE ROOFTOP WAS a fancy restaurant with incredible views of the city. The floor-to-ceiling windows made it feel like you were dining under the stars, even if it was too cold to sit out on the terrace.

"That was amazing," Felicity let out a contented sigh as she placed down her silverware.

"I thought we could have dessert to go."

Her cheeks pinked as my mind filled with images of her laid out beneath me. "Jason, stop." It came out a little breathless.

"What?" I smirked. "I'm not doing anything."

"You know exactly what you're doing." Her brow went up.

"Excuse me," a voice said, and I shot the balding guy approaching our table an irritated look. "I hate to disturb you, but are you Jason Ford?"

"He is," Felicity answered for me.

"My son is a huge fan. He'd never let me hear the end of it if I told him I saw you and didn't ask for an autograph."

Fuck. He wanted to do this now? When I was thinking about pulling Felicity into the nearest bathroom and eating her for dessert?

"I wouldn't usually ask, but my son, well, he's sick. It's been a tough year and I just know this would make his day."

Double fuck.

"Here." Felicity leaned over and handed me a clean napkin while the guy thrust a pen into my hand.

"What's your kid's name?" I asked.

"Daniel. He's eleven, followed your whole career."

I uncapped the pen and scribbled a message before handing both of them to him. "Would you like to get a photo?"

"That would be... thank you," he stuttered, digging out his cell.

Felicity came around to us and took the phone. "Say Quakers."

I bit down on my cheek to stop chuckling.

"I took a couple." She handed him the phone.

"Thank you so much. My son will be so excited."

"You tell him to stay strong."

"I will, and thanks again." He sniffled, and I could see the flash of pain in his eyes.

Shit, was his son really sick?

Something twisted inside me.

"Wait," I exhaled. "Maybe I could try to organize tickets for you to bring him down to a game."

"You could?" The guy went slack jawed.

"Yeah." Grabbing another napkin, I asked for the pen back and wrote down our PR's number. "Call this number tomorrow and they'll get you set up."

"That is... thank you. Thank you so much."

"Anytime."

"Enjoy the rest of your evening."

The guy walked away, looking back one last time. He waved the napkin and mouthed 'Thank you' again.

"Jason, that was—"

"Don't," I breathed. I didn't want tonight to be about football, but this was my life, and it would only get more intense as I progressed through college, moving ever closer to my NFL dream.

"Excuse me," I signaled to the server, "can we get the check please?"

Despite our private table in the corner of the room, other people had started to glance in our direction. If we didn't get out of here soon, there was every chance we'd never make it.

"I'm sorry." I ran a hand down my face. "I thought we'd have more privacy."

"This is your life, Jason, I understand." There was a flicker of sadness in her voice that damn near gutted me.

"But I don't just want it to be my life, babe. I want it to be *our* life. Look, I know things have been intense the last few weeks... but the team—"

"Are important, I get it. This is your dream. I knew what I was signing on for."

Except she didn't. No one truly could until they'd lived it.

"I guess I just feel like everyone has it all figured out. You're doing amazing, and I'm so proud of you, Jason, I am. You manage the team, your classes. Hailee and Cameron are loving Michigan and have made a whole life for themselves. Asher and Mya are... well, they're Asher and Mya, nothing fazes them."

I didn't like hearing Felicity talk like that, as if everyone had found their place except her. Especially not when her place was right by my side.

"We should go..." She grabbed her purse.

"Talk to me, please. I don't want football to come between us, not tonight."

"It isn't just football, Jason, it's... everything."

Well, shit.

I'd known things were bad. But perhaps I'd underestimated how much.

"Look, let's go back to the apartment and talk. I hate that you're feeling like this."

"Okay." Felicity gave me a small nod.

I dug out my wallet and pulled out some bills, adding them to the check. "Come on." I reached for her hand. "Let's go home.

Felicity

The night had been perfect. The restaurant was romantic with its sultry mood lighting and incredible views. The food was to die for. And being with Jason away from all the pressure of classes and the team was heavenly.

Until the stranger had approached asking for an autograph, and just like that the illusion came crumbling down around us, giving me a snapshot of what life with Jason would always be like. The more successful he became, the more recognized he became. The more recognized he became, the more the spotlight would shine down on him. And the more the spotlight shone, the more I wilted into the shadows.

"It's chilly," I said, as he held open the door for me and we spilled out into the inky night. Thanksgiving was in less than three weeks, and with it, the end of the football season.

Until next year.

"What are you—"

"Ford? What the hell, man," Griffin ambled over to us, a small group of people trailing behind. "Fancy running into you guys."

"Hey, Jason. We were just talking about you."

My spine bristled at Shelly Halstead's dulcet tone. She didn't even look twice at me, fixing her overly made up eyes right on Jason.

"All good, I hope?" He gave a strained laugh, clutching my hand tighter.

"Oh, you know it." She smirked, licking her lips seductively.

"We're meeting Gio and a few of the guys at The Gridiron. You and Fee should come, hang out."

"Actually, we're just on our way home," I said, giving Griffin a weak smile.

"Come on, one drink." He pouted.

"You should totally come, Jason." Shelly twirled a strand of hair around her finger. She couldn't have been any more obvious if she'd tried.

But what did I expect?

Jason was the star... and I was invisible by all accounts.

"You should go," I said before I could stop myself.

He gave me a confused look.

"Go, hang out with your friends. I'll see you back at the apartment."

"What are—"

I took a step backward right as Griffin and Shelly grabbed Jason and started steering him in the opposite direction. "We'll return him to you in one piece," Griffin called, but I was already hurrying away from them.

Tears burned the backs of my eyes as I folded my arms around myself and tried to fight the wave of emotion crashing over me.

"Felicity, wait..."

His voice gave me pause but it only made me angrier. It was irrational, I knew that. But I also knew Shelly had completely dismissed me just now, as if I was no one. Insignificant. Just a bug to be stepped on.

"Felicity, will you just wait a second?" He snagged my arm and I finally stopped, inhaling a ragged breath. "What are you doing?"

I pressed my lips together, willing myself not to cry. But tears clung precariously to my lashes.

"Felicity, babe, look at me." Jason began to turn me in his arms. "What the fuck is going on?"

"She just acted like I wasn't even there." I could barely look at him. This wasn't me. I wasn't insecure about a jersey chaser.

And yet...

"Shelly, you're worried about *Shelly*? She's no one to me, you know that."

"I know." My bottom lip quivered.

"Have I ever given you a reason to doubt me?"

I shook my head, unable to find the words to even begin to explain what was going on in my head, when I didn't even truly understand it myself.

"You know I wouldn't have gone with them just now, right?"

My eyes dropped, hating that such a lovely night was ruined.

"Look at me." Jason slid his fingers under my jaw and tilted my face. "I need to hear you say the words, Felicity."

"I know," I whispered.

"Good." His lips thinned. "Now can we please go home and salvage what was supposed to be a romantic night?"

"Okay," I said the words, but I didn't feel them. I was still stuck on that sidewalk, watching Shelly blatantly lust after my boyfriend as if I was nothing.

Wondering why it mattered so much.

Jason

Felicity was quiet the whole way home. Fucking Griffin and Shelly. It was as if the universe just wanted to fuck with me a little more, planting them right outside the restaurant. One minute we were all standing there, and the next, Felicity was telling me to go with them, as if I'd ever just abandon her like that.

Fuck. It stung.

By the time we made it up to our apartment, the air was thick and suffocating around us. I wanted to apologize, to spend the night showing her how much I loved her. How much I fucking needed her. But now… now I didn't know what to say, let alone know how we even got to this point.

The second she opened the door, Felicity took off into the apartment.

I snagged her wrist. "Wait, we need to talk."

"I'm tired, Jason. I think I'm just going to—"

"Fuck. That," I ground out, feeling the edges of my control fray.

She spun around to face me, her eyes holding so much defeat, I felt sucker punched. "I don't want to do this right now."

"Do what? You're talking like we're over or something."

Her eyes flickered to the ground. It was only a split second, but it was enough for my heart to plummet into my fucking toes.

She wanted to end it?

No.

No way.

It was just an argument. A silly argument after a few weeks of strain. It was nothing we couldn't fix. But then she said seven little words that made me stumble back.

"I'm not sure I can do this anymore."

"What?" I blinked at her. "What the fuck did you just say?"

We stared at each other for the longest second. Tears glossed Felicity's eyes, streaking down her cheeks.

"Hold up, this is all because Shelly was there?"

"She acted like I was no one, Jason. Do you have any idea how horrible that makes me feel? Knowing that she thinks she can have you? As if I'm nothing."

"Babe." I stepped forward, needing to touch her. Needing to stop any more ridiculous words coming out of her mouth. "You know what she's like." A lot of the cheerleaders were the same, all desperate to bag a player. And unfortunately for me, I was at the top of the food chain. But I'd never even looked, let alone touched.

Not when I had all I could want right here.

"I thought I was strong enough..." she murmured, dropping her gaze again. "I thought we would come here, and I'd be at your side..."

"You are at my side." I grabbed her shoulders. "You're the only one I need at my side. I know I've been prioritizing the team, but it's just for a few more weeks and then the season is over, and things will calm down." My eyes bored into hers, pleading with her to believe me. "Shit, babe, where is all this coming from?"

"I'm barely keeping my head above water, Jason. And you… you make it look so easy. You have friends, the team, an endless stream of girls vying for your attention. That guy tonight, at the restaurant, he's going to be the first of many. And I'm proud of you… God, I'm so proud of you. This is all you've ever wanted..."

My jaw clenched. The more she spoke, the more resigned she sounded. I gently laid my hand along the side of her neck. "I need you to hear what I'm about to say. You think I'm not blind with jealousy over the idea of you spending all your spare time with tutor boy? That it doesn't drive me crazy knowing you've found someone to connect with about the thing *you* love? I. Fucking. Hate. It." My fingers brushed her throat, feeling her pulse flutter beneath my fingers.

"I hate that you've found it hard to make friends and I hate how much I've let you down. But do you know what I hate the most? I hate that you're standing there, doubting that I want you." My hand dropped to the neckline of her sweater dress, gently tugging it down to reveal my brand on her skin. My thumb traced the small lettering. "What does it say?" I asked her.

"J- Jason."

"Tell me what it says."

"P- property of a Raider."

"Damn right it does. You're mine, Giles." My hand slid back to her neck, holding her gently as I stared right into her eyes. "None of this means anything if you're not by my side."

Her lip quivered as she bit back a fresh wave of tears.

"I love you, woman. I love you too fucking much to ever let you walk away from me."

"It's only going to get harder," she breathed. "Classes, your football career. What if I'm not strong—"

"Ssh." I slid my thumb over her lips, leaning down to touch my head to hers. "You're one of the strongest people I know, babe. Your heart, your compassion, the way you love so fiercely. I'm a lucky bastard to call you mine. I know things are hard right now, and I hate that I've made you doubt me, doubt us... but I need you, Felicity. I will always need you."

A whimper escaped her lips, but I swallowed it, sealing my mouth over hers, and kissing her with everything I felt. The good, the bad... the downright unthinkable. Losing Felicity was not an option.

Not today.

Not tomorrow.

Not ever.

I just needed to figure out a way to show her that.

7

Felicity

I COULD TASTE the salty wetness of my tears as Jason pushed his tongue into my mouth and kissed me. Only, he didn't just kiss me, he branded me. Marked me with his teeth and claimed me with his touch.

There were still things we needed to talk about, insecurities I needed to address, but for now, I allowed myself to get lost in the way he dominated my every thought.

"You look so fucking sexy in this dress." His hands slipped down the back of my thighs and he hoisted me against him, forcing my legs around his waist. I could already feel him hard at my stomach. Thick and ready. Desire pulsed through me like a heartbeat.

"Jason," I gasped, as he stalked me across the room and pushed me up against the wall.

Everything became desperate. We clawed at each other's clothes, skin, and muscle. My fingers raked across Jason's shoulders and back as he trailed hot wet kisses down my jaw and throat, lingering on my pulse point, flicking his tongue over my burning skin.

My hair cascaded around me as I dropped my head against the wall, greedy for more. Jason walked his fingers down my stomach, finding the hem of my dress and pushing it up my body, before sliding his hand between us.

"Oh God," I cried as he rubbed me over my lace panties, creating an intoxicating friction.

"Fuck, babe, you're so wet." Hooking the material aside, he pushed two fingers inside me. A garbled moan broke from my lips as he added his thumb, dragging it over my clit. "This is mine," he uttered against the corner of my mouth. "Always." He curled his fingers, rubbing harder. "Forever." He nipped my bottom lip, soothing the sting with his tongue. "Mine."

A wave of intense pleasure crashed over me as I cried his name over and over. My hand went to his belt buckle, pulling it free and working his jeans off his hips just enough that his dick sprung free.

I needed him.

I needed him more than I had ever needed him before.

My hunger was frenzied, coursing inside me like wildfire. Jason's eyes locked on mine as he slowly rocked forward, filling me to the hilt. "Fuck," he breathed.

"Move," I begged, my voice thick with lust. "I need you to—" The air *whooshed* from my lungs as he pulled out and slammed back inside of me.

He wasn't gentle or tender, slow or sweet. Jason wasn't making love to me now, he was imprinting himself on my soul, trying to carve his name on my bones.

"Mine," he growled against my ear before running his tongue down my neck, licking and sucking.

"Jason, I can't... it's—"

"Ssh." He pressed his head against mine, pinning me to the wall with his intense gaze. "I know what you need, Felicity. I will always know." He punched his hips forward making us both cry out in ecstasy.

My hands wound around his neck, holding on for dear life. I would ache tomorrow, the wall rough against my back, my thighs pressed wide to accommodate Jason's big body.

But right there, in that moment, I didn't care. Because we were just two people so desperately and irrevocably in love that we were drowning in each other.

And I didn't ever want to come up for air.

Jason

I told Coach I was going to be late to morning conditioning. After last night, I didn't want to just up and leave this morning. I meant everything I'd said, but I wasn't dipshit enough not to know that it wasn't about what *I said*, it was about how *Felicity felt*.

I watched her sleep for a while. The soft rise and fall of her chest, the slight scrunch to her nose as she dreamed—of me hopefully—and the way her perfect fucking tits jiggled with every breath.

Felicity was all I ever wanted. Every part of me was tied to every part of her, so the fact she doubted this, doubted us, it fucking killed me.

I'd tried to show her last night, but I knew sex wasn't the answer.

But fuck, if it hadn't blown my mind all the same. It felt like forever since I'd taken her so urgently. I hadn't wanted to stop, high on the feel of her thighs pulling me closer, her perfect body pinned against the wall, on display for me. Her tattoo taunting me while I rocked into her over and over.

I reached out, tracing the curve of her hip where the sheet had fallen down her body.

"Jason," she murmured.

"It's me. Go back to sleep."

"You're still here?"

"I told Coach I'd be late." I shuffled down the bed, pressing my body against the soft curves of hers.

"You did?" She finally cracked an eye open.

"Yeah. After last night..."

"Ssh." Her finger pressed against my lips, the way mine had hers last night. "I don't want to talk; I just want to enjoy this."

Pushing the hair from Felicity's face, I brushed my nose over hers. "I love you. You know that, right?"

"I know." Her hand splayed over my chest, right where my heart lay. "I love you too."

My shoulders sagged with relief. I hadn't realized how much I needed to hear those words until now. "We'll get through this, I promise." Because anything else was not an option.

Felicity nodded. "What time do you have to leave?"

"I still have an hour."

"Better make the most of it then." She reached down and grasped my morning wood, sending a bolt of pleasure up my spine.

"Actually," I couldn't believe I was doing this, "I was hoping to take you to breakfast." I kissed the end of her nose.

"Yeah?" Her uncertain smile made my heart crack wide open.

Damn, I had some making up to do. But I didn't want to rush headfirst into shallow apologies and hasty grand declarations of love.

I wanted to show her, without doubt, that she was it for me.

But first, I wanted to take my girl to breakfast and feed her.

"Good?" I asked, watching with rapt fascination, and a touch of jealousy, as Felicity devoured her blueberry muffin.

"So good." She grinned.

Mr. Java's was a coffee shop off campus. It was less crowded, and we'd been able to grab a table by the window.

"So did Mya mention the Thanksgiving thing Asher's mom is throwing?"

"Yeah."

"And?"

"I assumed we'd go." Felicity smiled. "She said I can invite my parents, or I'll see them before."

Things with Felicity's dad were still strained. He didn't look at me like I'd stolen and corrupted his only daughter anymore, but he still wasn't my biggest fan either.

"Then we'll all come back here on Friday to watch the game."

Fuck.

The final game.

The season close was fast approaching.

"Asher also mentioned the possibility of spending a weekend in New York after the season is over. It could be pretty romantic."

"That sounds nice." Felicity smiled but it didn't reach her eyes.

"Babe, me and you, we're—"

"Hey, I didn't expect to see you here." Tutor boy loomed down over us, setting my jaw on edge.

"Oh, hey, Darcy. You remember my boyfriend, Jason?"

"As if I could forget. You're big news around campus."

"We've had a good season so far." I sat back in my chair, dragging one leg over my knee. Darcy was a preppy type. Slacks and a sweater, hair slicked back, and a messenger bag looped over his shoulder. He was everything I wasn't, everything I didn't want to be. Yet, I couldn't help but wonder if Felicity ever wished she'd fallen for someone more like him.

What the fuck was I doing?

Felicity didn't want someone like Darcy Bannerman. She needed someone to temper her wild spirit, put up with her special brand of crazy.

She needed me.

"We all set for our session later?" He ignored my eyes drilling into his head and focused solely on my girl.

I had the sudden need to claim her, right there in the middle of the fucking coffee shop. I shifted uncomfortably, pissed that he was invoking such a carnal reaction from me.

Now you know how Felicity feels, asshole.

"Yeah, I'll see you later, okay?" Her polite dismissal made my heart soar.

"Uh, sure." Tutor boy hesitated. "I'll see you later. Jason, it was a pleasure."

I bet it was, asshole.

He left the coffee shop and Felicity let out a little sigh of relief. "You can stop glaring now." She chuckled.

"Do you ever wish—"

"Don't even say it. I don't want Darcy, he's my tutor."

"Yeah, but he gets all that stuff you love so much."

God, why was everything so fucking messed up? It was like we took one step forward and two steps back.

"Jason, I love you." Felicity shuffled forward on her chair. "I guess I just underestimated how hard all this would be."

"I know and I wish it could be different. But—"

"I get it, I do. I would never ever want you to give up your dream. You've worked too hard for it."

"I love you."

The words were fast becoming a stitch for the frayed seams of our relationship. But I didn't know how to fix it. I didn't know how to make Felicity believe I needed her.

Her green eyes fluttered closed and when she opened them again, all I saw was a girl desperately trying to cling onto her dream.

She gave me a sad smile and said, "I know."

Felicity

"Hello, do you mind if I sit here?" I said to the girl meticulously unpacking her supplies onto the small desk.

"Sure." She barely glanced at me.

After breakfast with Jason on Monday, I'd decided to brush myself off and revert back to my old habit of making a list. Back in high school, it had helped me feel in control of my life, so why not here?

But instead of writing a college bucket list, I'd decided to keep it simple. One task a day.

Today's task: make a new friend.

It sounded simple, and yet, it was something I'd struggled with. Even in my classes full of likeminded students, I'd failed to really connect with anyone. But I'd noticed Elodie and she was always alone, always sitting at the back of lectures. So I'd decided that maybe she was like me; maybe she also found it hard to connect.

"I'm Felicity," I said. "Felicity Giles."

"Oh. My. God," she breathed. "I thought it was you." Her whole face transformed. Gone was the shy, quiet student I'd seen around classes, replaced with a starry-eyed girl who stared at me like I was the second coming.

"I mean, I've heard your name around... but I didn't know... wow. You're like dating Jason Ford. That is... wow. I'm a huge fan."

My lips pressed into a thin line. I couldn't escape. No matter where I turned, who I talked to, I would always be *Jason Ford's girlfriend.*

"That's me." I gave her a weak smile. I didn't have the heart to ruin her morning since she seemed so excited to be talking to me.

"I'm a huge fan... huge. Followed the Quakers my whole life. My dad played for them... he's kind of Quaker royalty. That's why I keep myself to myself." She glanced around conspiratorially. "And oh my god, I'm doing it, aren't I? I'm totally being that weird obsessed fan that I try so hard to avoid."

"Yeah, you kind of are." Strangled laughter bubbled in my chest.

"I'm sorry, it's just... damn, girl." She clutched the edge of her desk and leaned closer. "You're dating *Jason Ford*, one of the best quarterbacks the NCAA has seen in at least a decade. That's got to be something."

Oh, it was something all right.

"Hey, would you like to get a coffee after class? In a totally non-creeper kind of way. I'm Elodie by the way. Elodie Faltham."

"I..."

This so wasn't how I'd seen the conversation going. I'd wanted to make a friend, to strike up conversation with someone who wouldn't automatically pigeonhole me as Jason Ford's girlfriend. But maybe she got it, maybe she understood more than most.

"I promise I'm not usually this weird," she added as if she could hear my inner turmoil. "I'm just passionate about the things I love, and it just so happens I really love football, almost as much as I love animals." Her smile grew.

That sealed the deal.

A girl who could love football *and* animals...

Despite her shaky introduction, Elodie Faltham sounded like my kind of girl.

8

Felicity

"HOLY FREAKING CRAP, THIS IS AMAZING," Elodie shrieked beside me as the team jogged out onto the field.

Jordan had needed to go home for the weekend, something to do with a family emergency. She kindly offered to donate her ticket to my *new friend.* I wasn't sure Elodie warranted friend status yet, but we had hung out a couple of times, and we always sat together in class now. After her initial excitement that I was dating Jason, she reined herself in, and kept our conversation to safer topics like my volunteer work at the shelter and her dream of one day working with big cats in African reservations.

"I mean, I've been to all their games, but I've never even come close to scoring seats this good. Thank you so much." She gave me a big grin and I couldn't help but be infected by her enthusiasm. She reminded me of... well, me back in high school, eager to soak up senior year and all that came with it.

"Oh my god, there he is." She pointed to Jason and I let out a small chuckle.

"Yep, that's him."

"Oh God, I'm doing it again, aren't I?" Her brows knitted. "I'm sorry, it's just—"

"It's okay. Enjoy it."

The atmosphere in Franklin Field was electric, everyone high on the team's perfect season so far. If they won tonight, it would leave them with two games to play and the league title in sight.

I knew how much it meant to the team, the fans, and the coaches. But most of all, I knew how much it meant to the guy wearing the red and blue number one jersey.

"If they win this game, the season could be theirs. Only Dartmouth has a shot at taking it from..." She launched into an analysis of the Ivy League, but her words barely registered as I watched Jason command his teammates. They respected him, followed his orders, and paid attention when he talked. It was something to behold.

We were in a better place since the weekend. There were still some things we needed to work through, but something had shifted.

"Felicity?" Elodie nudged me.

"Huh, sorry?"

"I said are you sure about me coming to the party later? I've never been to a football party before."

"It's just like any other college party really, except with more cheerleaders."

"Actually," her cheeks pinked, "I've never really been to a college party before."

"I've probably been to less than you can imagine," I admitted.

"What, no way? Your boyfriend is—"

"I think we've established who my boyfriend is." I gave her an amused smile. "But I haven't exactly spread my wings since coming to Penn."

"Well, we can be out of our comfort zone together." Elodie shot me a conspiratorial wink.

"Aren't you worried about people finding out about your dad?"

She shrugged. "Honestly, I think I've been using him as a reason not to push myself into new social situations."

"So tonight, we party?" A trickle of excitement zipped through me. I'd always gone to parties with Jason, stood and watched from the sidelines as he and his friends let loose and enjoyed themselves. Jordan had been around this semester, but last year it had mostly been me. So I couldn't deny it felt nice to finally have someone in my corner.

Even if she was infatuated with my boyfriend.

Jason

"Congratulations." Felicity rushed over to me as I found her in the lingering crowd.

I pulled her into my arms and kissed her. Adrenaline still pumped through my veins, a firestorm showing no signs of letting up. I either needed a strong drink or to be buried deep inside my girl. But there was a party... a party I'd promised the guys I would make an appearance at.

Fuck.

"I'm so proud of you."

We'd beat Yale 28-17. We were unstoppable, a relentless storm determined to blow right through every team we came up against. And next on the list was Cornell.

My eyes went over Felicity's shoulder when I realized we had company. "You must be Elodie," I said, pulling Felicity into my side. "I'm Jason."

The girl's eyes went wide, her mouth hanging open.

"El, we talked about this," Felicity said as if they were old friends. I'd heard all about Elodie Faltham, daughter of Quaker legend Marcus Faltham, star running back in the late eighties. She was Felicity's new friend.

Although I was beginning to think there was something wrong with her with the way she was gawking.

"H- hi, it's an honor." She held out her hand, and I stared at it, frowning. "Oh, right, sorry." She jammed it into her pocket. "I'm not usually this nervous. It's just I'm a huge fan."

"Guess it runs in the family, huh?"

"Yeah." She gulped. "My dad started me young."

"I know that feeling," I grumbled. "Are you ready to party with the team?"

"I..." She rolled her lips together, but I could see she was almost ready to burst with excitement.

"She's a little excited."

"The team is going to love having Quaker royalty in the house."

"Oh no, you can't tell them, please?" Her whole demeanor changed.

"Sure, yeah, okay." I glanced at Felicity and she gave me an imperceptible shake of her head.

Just what I needed. A party I didn't want to go to, a girlfriend who was questioning our relationship at every turn, and a fan who looked like she'd never partied in her life.

Tonight, was going to be a fucking disaster.

THE PARTY WAS ALREADY in full swing by the time we arrived. Felicity wanted to run by the apartment and change. She'd let Elodie borrow an outfit and the two of them looked dressed to kill. It didn't worry me where Felicity was concerned—everyone knew she was off limits. But Elodie was fresh meat and so far out of her comfort zone she may as well have worn a neon sign.

"Oh wow, that's a lot of people," she breathed, her eyes wide with wonder as she took in the house.

"Don't worry," Felicity squeezed her hand, "we'll get a couple of drinks inside you and you'll be fine."

"I'm sure Griffin or one of the guys will be more than happy to help—"

"*Jason.*"

"What?" I balked. If Felicity thought I was going to spend the night playing babysitter, she was sorely mistaken. I wanted to show my face, have a couple of beers, and then get the hell out of there.

"We can't just let the guys loose on her."

"Relax, I'm joking." Mostly. But Elodie was already gone, walking into the house as if she was entering a magical wonderland or some shit.

I hooked an arm around Felicity and dragged her into my side. She pressed a hand against my chest, gazing up at me. "Are you okay being here?"

"I am." She nodded. "Who knows, maybe I'll even have some fun?" Her eyes flicked to Elodie.

My brows knitted together. "Are you saying you don't have fun with me?"

"You know what I mean." She leaned up to kiss me, scraping her nails lightly over my jaw. Blood flowed straight to my dick and I groaned under my breath when she grabbed my hand and yanked me into the house.

"Yo, Ford, get over here."

Music pumped out of a speaker somewhere, bodies already grinding and rubbing on each other. Griffin and Gio made a beeline for me, pulling me into a guy hug. I tried to keep hold of Felicity's hand, but she let me go, mouthing, "I'm going to find Elodie," who had already disappeared into the sea of people.

"Behave," I yelled, because although we were in a house full of teammates, Felicity was still my girl.

And I really didn't want to spend the night fighting off the vultures.

Felicity

"I think I'm drunk," Elodie giggled, burying her face in Griffin's shoulder.

"How many did she have?" he asked me, and I shrugged.

"About four." As opposed to my eight, but even after double the amount of drinks, I still wasn't as drunk as my new friend.

"Four? Holy shit, she's—"

"Happy." Her head snapped up. "I'm sooo happy. Let's do more of those funky smelling shots." She started to reach for the rest beside her six-foot two leaning post, but Griffin wrapped her into a bear hug. "Oh no you don't, new girl."

"I'll have one," I piped up.

"I think you've had enough," Jason ground out.

"Oh, don't be such a spoilsport." I tapped his cheek. "We're having fun."

"Fun." Elodie punched the air, almost falling backward but Griffin steadied her. He seemed smitten, a glint in his eye.

"You need to watch Griff," I whispered to Jason, swaying gently. "He's looking at El the way you look at me."

"Oh yeah?" He dipped his head to mine, electricity crackling between us. "And how do I look at you?"

"Like you want to devour me."

Jason smirked, stealing a chaste kiss. "You're fun when you're drunk."

"Then I should probably drink more." I shot him a saucy wink before diving for the tray of shooters.

I don't know what came over me, but for the first time in a long time, I felt like my old self. Fun and free and not tied down by the weight of expectation and responsibility. It was ironic really, but it seemed that the quiet, shy girl from my class had unleashed something inside me.

I downed the murky looking drink and wiped my mouth with the back of my hand, enjoying the burn as it slid down my throat.

"Your girl is on form tonight, Ford." Griffin said, his arm still wrapped around Elodie.

"Fee is the best," she slurred. "I think I have a girl crush."

"Okay, drunk girl." I wrangled her off Griffin. "We are going to dance."

"Dance?" She shrieked. "But I don't dance."

"Well," I grinned, "you do now."

THE ROOM WAS SPINNING. Sweat coated my skin, little beads of moisture trailing down my back and chest as we moved to the beat. I'd lost track of time, dancing and laughing. No one bothered us, not with Jase and Griffin standing watch like two sentries put on the Earth with the sole purpose of protecting us.

"I think Griff likes you," I said to my new friend. She'd switched to water earlier, protesting when Griffin had insisted she drink it. But I knew she'd thank him tomorrow morning when she woke. Although I had a sneaky suspicion she wouldn't be waking up in her own bed.

"I don't feel so good," I reached out for her, a wave of nausea crashing over me.

"Shit, Felicity—"

Strong arms caught me. "I'm taking you home."

"But I'm still dancing." I stared up at my savior.

"Babe, you can barely stand." Jason pulled me into his side and said something to Elodie and Griffin. Over the music and the blood pounding between my ears, I could barely make out a single word.

Then we were moving. Cool air rushing over my skin and dousing the heat coursing through my veins. "Wait." I sagged against Jason's body. "I don't feel so good."

"I got you, babe," he said, sounding far too sober. Come to think of it, I hadn't seen him with a drink for hours.

"Why aren't you drunk?" The words came out a garbled mess as he propped me against the wall so I could catch my breath.

"I had two beers then switched to soda."

"But why? It's a celebration... everyone came to celebrate you." All night I'd watched people gravitate to Jason. He was the sun and they wanted to be in his orbit.

Or was it gravity?

Huh.

"I wanted you to enjoy yourself."

"But you could have relaxed too."

"I think you underestimate the level I will go to protect you." He kissed the end of my nose. "How are you feeling now?"

"Okay, I think. Your swoony words sobered me a little." A smile tugged at my lips.

"One-hundred percent truth, babe."

"God, I love you. I love you so much I wish this didn't ever have to end." A rush of love swelled inside me, like rising waters threatening to pull me under.

"Good thing it doesn't ever have to end then. Come on." He started to pull me along with him.

"It will though. One day you'll be super famous, and I'll be a college dropout. I'll still love you then, you know... even when you're a hotshot in the NFL and I have to get my glimpses of you on ESPN."

"You're drunk, babe."

"That may be so, but I'm also a realist... and this... us... it isn't endgame. It's—" My ankle rolled, and the world began to fall away.

"Shit, Felicity."

"I'm flyiiiiing." I chuckled, throwing my arms out to the side and bracing myself for impact.

But it never came.

"You caught me," I said, staring up at intense dark eyes I didn't think I would ever forget. Because those eyes were my world. Everything I ever wanted.

"I will always catch you, Giles."

God, how I wanted to believe him.

9

Jason

"THIS IS IT, ladies. Win tonight and the title is ours." Coach leveled us with a hard look.

Our win against Cornell last week meant we could be crowned league winners tonight, instead of our last game. And the best fucking part? Cam and Asher were in the crowd, thanks to their teams having bye weeks.

"I couldn't have asked for more from you this season," he went on. "Losing Lincoln was a blow, but, Jason, son, you rose to the challenge and got the job done."

Everyone cheered, the stamp of their cleats against the floor and the shrill of their hollers rattling inside my chest.

"It's so close we can almost taste it. Penn hasn't had a season like this in almost a decade. Go out there and do what you were born to do. Now everyone get in here."

We rose like an army answering a battle cry and wedged around Coach in a circle. "Quakers on three." He gave me the nod and my voice pierced the air.

"One... two... three... Quakers."

Gio clapped me on the back, his eyes dancing with anticipation. "Yo, Griff, is your girl gonna be out there?"

"Fuck off, she's not my girl."

"Not what I heard," I added around a smirk.

Since the party, Felicity and Elodie had hung out a lot. She'd even talked me into going on a couple of double dates with Griff and her new friend. He didn't want to put a label on it, but the two of them seemed close. I'd seen the protective glint in his eye that night. He barely let her out of his sight. Elodie was a strange one. At times, she was desperately quiet and introverted, and then other times she was vibrant and talked at a mile a minute. But Felicity liked her. And there wasn't much I wouldn't do for that girl.

As we grabbed our helmets and filed out of the locker room, my mind went to that night again. Felicity had been ass over elbow drunk, spewing all kinds of shit about us, about me. Things I didn't ever want to hear. But when she'd woken up the next morning, hungover and dehydrated, I hadn't had the heart to bring it up with her. So we'd danced around it. If she remembered, she never said anything, and I tried every day to reassure her that I loved her.

To reassure her that her fears were never going to manifest into reality.

Things were better... but they weren't perfect. She was still hanging around with tutor boy and I was still with the team more often than not.

Hopefully though, after tonight that would all change.

"You ready for this?" Gio shoulder-checked me as we spilled onto the field. It was a blessing to have our penultimate game at home. If we won tonight, the atmosphere in Franklin Field would be explosive, and the hunger for it burned in my veins.

"Born ready," I muttered, letting the crowd's cheers wash over me. Felicity was the girl for me. I felt it in my soul as sure as I knew the sky was blue and the grass beneath my feet was green. One day, I would put a ring on her finger and my kid in her stomach. She was my heart. But football? Football was my calling.

I just had to find a way to make the two symbiotic.

A big hand landed on my shoulder and I looked up to find Griff staring at me. "I finally get it," he mumbled.

"Yeah, and what's that?" I teased.

"I like her, man. I really fucking like her."

My lips curved. "Well hold that thought, because we have a game to win." I clapped him on the back and started jogging toward the rest of our team.

"How'd you do it?" he called.

I spun around, jogging backward. "Do what?"

"Focus on football *and* a girl?"

"You just gotta show her what she means to you."

The words were like a punch to the stomach. My step faltered as every memory Felicity and I shared slammed into me one after another.

Everything was so clear... I didn't know how I hadn't seen it before.

I knew what I had to do.

I knew how to fix us.

Felicity

Tears streamed down my face as I watched Jason and his teammates celebrate. The thirteen-thousand strong crowd was on their feet, clapping and cheering, celebrating right along with them.

I watched with nothing but pride and love as Coach Faulkner found Jason and pulled him into a hug before holding his shoulders and saying something to him. Jason nodded, his eyes wide with understanding.

"Your boy did good." Hailee nestled into my side, her own pride and excitement swirling around us. This moment didn't only mean a lot to me, it meant a lot to all of us. Cam, Asher, Hailee, even Mya. We knew what football meant to Jason, what *this moment* would mean for him.

I dabbed my eyes, trying to get a hold of my emotions. Being here to witness this, seeing the guy I loved more than anything make his dreams come true… well, it was easy to forget all the strain and distance between us over the last few weeks. My heart swelled for him. The boy from Rixon with a dream of making it. A boy who had stolen my heart and refused to let it go.

He wanted football *and* me.

If only it were that simple.

"Flick, you should go down there," Asher said, nudging me from behind.

"What? I can't just—"

"He's looking for you."

Sure enough, Jason was searching the crowd for me. We hadn't been able to sit in the VIP section since there was six of us, so I'd given Elodie my ticket and she and Jordan were down there, while I sat in the bleachers with my friends.

The second Jason's eyes found mine, everything melted away. On shaky legs, I hurried down the steps to the barrier. Jason jogged toward me, his smile radiant and eyes filled with sweet relief.

"You did it," I breathed, pressing my palms against his shoulders. His hair was damp and messy, his Quaker jersey streaked with mud and grass stains as his helmet hung at his side.

"I can't…" He swallowed roughly. "This is… I can't believe it."

"Believe it, Jason." One of my hands slid to his cheek. No matter what happened between us, wherever our road led, I would always want this for him. Even if it became the thing that ultimately destroyed us, Jason deserved this.

He deserved his dreams to come true.

"I am so proud of you." I leaned down to kiss him, and a chorus of cheers broke out behind us. My cheeks pinked and I tried to pull away, but Jason slid one of his hands around the back of my neck, anchoring me in place. "Babe, I couldn't have done it without you," he whispered against my lips. "I need you, Felicity Charlotte Giles. I will always need you."

I opened my mouth to reply, but the guys charged at him, yanking him backwards.

"Sorry, Fee," Griff yelled. "But we need to borrow our fearless leader."

Laughter escaped my lips as I watched them.

Part of me wanted to hate the very thing that might one day take Jason from me, but right there, in that moment, I could only feel joy.

Jason

We didn't stay and party with the team. Despite their protests, after a couple of drinks, a lot of high fives and congratulations, I wanted nothing more than to celebrate with my friends and my girl, so we left.

"Shit, man, that was really something." Asher clinked his beer against mine as we sat huddled in a quiet booth toward the back of the bar underneath Asher and Mya's building. I hadn't wanted to be accosted by adoring fans, not tonight.

"You know, after that performance, teams will be lining up for you?"

"Don't speak so soon, there's still another two years left." And after Linc, we all knew how quickly your dream could go up in flames. His surgery had gone well, but his rehab would take a while. *If* he played again, there was every chance he wouldn't be the same player.

Asher snorted. "We'll see. Come graduation, you'll be signed with the Eagles or the Steelers, I'll be ready to start up a new branch of my old man's business, and fuck knows what this one will be doing."

"Hey." Cam punched his arm. "I have plans."

"Care to share then? Because I don't think I've ever heard you talk about what happens after graduation. In fact, I wouldn't put it past you to have a ring on her finger and a kid on the way." Asher smirked.

"Who's got a kid on the way?" Mya and the girls approached, frowning at the three of us.

"Umm, no one." He hooked an arm around her waist and pulled her down beside him.

I got up to let Hailee squeeze in between me and Cam, before pulling Felicity down on my knee. Scooping her hair out of the way, I nuzzled her neck. She leaned back, wrapping her arm around my neck. "Tired?" she asked.

"I'm okay." I breathed her in before kissing her soft skin. A shiver ran through her body, igniting the fire in my veins.

"Don't mind us," Asher grumbled.

"Like you aren't a total horn dog after a game." Mya rolled her eyes and we all burst into laughter. It felt good.

It felt fucking amazing sitting there with my girl and my best friends in the whole world.

"So the Heisman—" Asher started, but I silenced him with a dark look.

"Heisman? What's he talking about?" Felicity glanced back at me.

"Ash seems to think Jason stands a good chance of being nominated," Cam answered her.

She twisted around to look at me. "Well, do you?"

I shrugged. "I doubt it. The Ivy League is usually overlooked."

"But there's a chance?" Hailee asked, and I met my stepsister's inquisitive gaze with a small nod.

"I guess."

"Holy shit, Jase, that's huge."

"The announcements aren't until early December, but seriously, you guys, don't get your hopes up. I'm not." I grabbed my beer and took a long pull. Felicity threaded our fingers together, her touch like a balm to my bruised and battered body. The game had been a dog fight. Brutal and relentless. But in the end, we had come out on top.

"Well, either way, my dad reserved the penthouse. It's ours for the entire weekend."

"We already booked our flights," Cam said.

"And I thought we could ride together?" Asher eyed me.

"Yeah, sure." I leaned back against the leather booth.

"You just won the Ivy League. You could try to seem a little more... I don't know, hyped."

"I'm hyped," I grunted. "It's just all on the inside."

The girls snickered. My arm snaked tighter around Felicity's waist and I let out a weary sigh. I was crashing, and I wanted nothing more than to go home, get naked, and fall to sleep wrapped in her arms.

Usually after a game, the adrenaline lingered. The high of the win or low of a defeat pulsing through my veins like a synthetic drug. But we'd done it. We'd won the title with a near perfect season. All the pressure had melted away, and I could finally relax.

I'd really done it.

"One more drink and then I think we'll head out," Felicity said, as if she had a direct line to my thoughts.

I fucking hoped she didn't.

Because there were things she didn't know yet.

Decisions I'd made that would affect us both.

"We can stay," I said. There was no pressure here. No guys chanting my name or fans wanting autographs. These guys knew me well enough to keep me grounded, to give me space.

And I fucking loved them for it.

10

Felicity

"SO, YOU AND GRIFF?" I waggled my brows at Elodie across the table.

"Are just friends." She pursed her lips, pretending to finish up the notes she was making.

"Friends who spend almost every night together?" My brow arched.

"Griff is..." She let out a long breath, tapping her pen against her lip. "He's complicated."

"Aren't they all? But the season is over now." The Quakers had ended with a perfect season, only making their title win all the sweeter.

"I'm happy to see where it goes, but I'm not under any illusion it's the real deal. Besides, Griff is a jock, his eyes will wander eventually." My stomach twisted and she paled. "Oh shit, Fee, I didn't mean..."

"I know." I did. She was firmly in the Jason/Felicity fan club.

"You guys are okay, right? Things seem... good."

"We're fine."

Elodie smiled. "And you have your weekend away to look forward to. New York in December will be so romantic." She let out a dreamy sigh.

"Yeah, it will be nice." I was looking forward to seeing Hailee and Mya and spending some quality time with them without the pressure of classes. "I can't believe the semester is almost over."

"And we survived."

"We did," I said around a smile. I didn't doubt that my sessions with Darcy had a lot to do with my improved grades, but I was still relieved. I only had a couple more papers to submit before I was officially done for the holidays.

"Is that the time?" Elodie frowned. "I need to go." She collected up her things and stuffed them in her bag.

"Hot date?" I snickered.

"Griffin is taking me to The Gridiron for burgers."

"Romantic."

"We can't all be you, jetting off to New York for a weekend of romance." She stuck out her tongue before moving for the door.

"Hey, Elodie," I said as she grabbed the handle.

"Yeah?"

"I'm really glad I talked to you that day in class."

"Yeah." She beamed. "Me too."

Elodie left and I got comfy on the sofa. Grabbing my cell phone, I noticed I had a new text from Jason.

QB#1: Need to talk… are you home?

Me: Yeah. Elodie just left. Is everything okay?

QB#1: I'll be home soon.

My brows pinched. If Jason wanted to make me worry, he'd done a pretty good job of it. By the time I heard his key rattle in the door, I had a giant pit in my stomach.

Sitting forward, I waited for him to enter the apartment. "Hey." I searched his face for any sign of what was wrong, but he wore a mask of indifference.

"Hey," he said weakly, dropping down on the couch. Before I could ask what was wrong, Jason pulled me into his arms, burying his face in my shoulder.

"Jason, what is it? What's wrong?" Dread snaked through me.

His body trembled beneath my fingers as I held onto him as tight as he held me. Nudging him away with my shoulder, he finally straightened to look at me. "Coach called me."

"He did?"

"I'm in, babe… I made the final four."

"The Heisman Trophy?" My eyes grew to saucers. "Oh my god, Jason, that's amazing."

"I think I'm in shock." Another shudder rolled through him.

"Hey." I cupped his face. "You deserve this; you deserve it so much. Oh my god, your dad is going to freak."

"I already called him. He got all choked up."

"Well, yeah he did." I smiled. No one wanted this more for Jason than Kent Ford. "I thought you were coming here to tell me something bad."

"What?" Jason's brows furrowed. "What would I be—" his expression fell. "Us. You thought I was coming to talk about us."

"Honestly, I don't know what I thought, but you were so certain you wouldn't make the final cut."

"Come here, woman." He anchored his hand at the nape of my neck and guided my face to his. "What do I have to do to show you that me and you... we're endgame?"

"Jason..." I averted my gaze to escape his intense stare.

"No, babe. You need to hear me when I say it's you." He forced me to look at him. "It's always going to be you."

"I love you, Jason," I said, because it was true. It would always be true.

No matter where the future took us, my heart would always belong to Jason Ford.

Jason

"Good evening and thank you for joining us. Without you, the fans, college football and the Heisman Trophy would not be what they are today. I'm honored to be here this evening, representing the Heisman Trophy Trust. Congratulations to this year's finalists for their incredible feats on the field this college football season. We have so enjoyed watching you and following you in this year's Heisman race..."

The Heisman Trophy Trustee's voice was drowned out by the blood roaring between my ears as I sat beside the other three finalists. My heart was beating like a bass drum in my chest, my palms were slick, and sweat beaded across my brow under the glare of the lights as the Trustee continued her speech.

"And now it's time to welcome a new member into our Heisman family. It is my pleasure to announce this year's winner..."

Time slowed down. I never expected to be here tonight. I never expected to be announced as a finalist... but now I was here, now it was a possibility, I wanted it.

I wanted it so fucking much.

"Jason Ford, University of Pennsylvania."

Cheers erupted behind me as I stood and shook hands with the other finalists, hardly able to believe my ears.

I'd won.

I'd fucking *won*.

"Congratulations, man," one of them said, but it all became white noise to the thrum of my heart in my chest.

This was... I had no fucking words.

Nothing.

It was a good thing Cameron and Asher had helped me write an acceptance speech just in case... because, fuck.

I moved toward the aisle behind me and my dad grabbed me, pulling me into a bear hug. "I'm so proud of you, son. So fucking proud."

"Thanks, Dad," I managed to choke out over the giant lump caught in my throat.

Denise was next, her overpowering perfume making me cough as she enveloped me into a hug. "Congratulations, Jason. I know what this means to you."

We'd had a tenuous relationship when she and Hailee first moved in with me and my old man. Right up until senior year, I'd wanted nothing to do with her or her daughter. But as I moved along the line to my stepsister, I could no longer imagine not having her in my life.

"I'm so proud of you." Hailee hugged me, and I let her. Because I was no longer that same boy who had tormented her, and she was no longer the girl who rubbed me the wrong way.

"Get over here, bro." Cameron and Asher pulled me into a big group hug. The three of us silent as we acknowledged this moment.

The two of them had been there for every high, every low. They had seen me at my best, my worst, and every shade in between. And their loyalty and friendship had never faltered, not once.

Before I broke away, Ash grabbed my neck and pulled me close, "Now you go up there and own it, you hear me?" He shot me a wink, stepping aside to let me kiss Mya's cheek.

"Go get her, tiger," she whispered.

Felicity was waiting on the end, tears brimming in her eyes as she watched me close the distance between us. She looked stunning in the jade-green dress that fell over her curves like a silk waterfall.

"You did it," she breathed as I hauled her against my body, not caring we were in a room full of people, live on national television.

"I couldn't have done it without you." I couldn't explain it to her, but Felicity grounded me in a way that no other could. Her wild spirit and empathy, her passion and insecurities, everything about her anchored me. I needed that.

I needed it more than I'd ever realized.

"Go," she nodded to the stage, "they're waiting."

Stealing a kiss that barely touched my bone-deep need for her, I looped back around to the other row of chairs to shake hands with my coaches.

"Never doubted you for a second, son," Coach Faulkner said, giving me a rare smile.

"Thanks, Coach."

"Now get up there and do Penn proud."

With a swift nod, I made my way to the stage. "Congratulations, Jason." Someone guided me to the podium where the trophy was situated. I curled my hands over the bronze sculpture and lifted it in the air to hair-raising applause.

My heart beat so hard I felt a little lightheaded, but I couldn't wimp out now. This meant everything... *everything* to me. Placing the trophy back on its stand, I pulled the scrap of paper out of my pocket and looked out over the crowd.

"This is... wow. I should warn you now, I perform much better on the field." Emotion welled up inside me and I inhaled a shuddering breath, but the gentle laughs from the crowd settled my nerves. "I want to thank my team first. At the beginning of the season we lost our captain, Lincoln Manella, and Coach Faulkner asked me to step up as captain."

"Hell yeah, he did," Asher yelled, and everyone chuckled again.

"The team didn't only accept my leadership, they respected it. My O line: Gio, Klein, Macca, Treyvon, Austin, Louis, Paulie. Those guys have been unbelievable this season and I couldn't have done it without them. All my teammates have supported me and made this possible. I want to thank my coaches for guiding me right and keeping me grounded. For imparting their knowledge and pushing me to work harder." I gave an appreciative nod in the direction of Coach Faulkner and his team.

"I want to thank the team at Heisman for everything this weekend. For allowing me and my family to be here. It's an honor to stand on the same stage with some of my childhood idols." I glanced at the line of previous winners standing tall, all here to celebrate this moment. "I want to thank my dad, for pushing me to go harder, faster... for showing me what it takes to be the best. To my stepmom and sister, for being here today despite our history. My friends, my brothers in all the ways that matter, for always having my back. I'm so grateful. To the other finalists here tonight, it has been an incredible experience sharing our journeys and being in the company of such talent."

Taking another deep breath, I steeled my spine. "Earlier in the season, someone suggested that I could be in the running for the Heisman Trophy, but I dismissed it. No way a kid out of a small town in Pennsylvania, playing for an Ivy League team, was going to end up here tonight. But here I am." Another round of applause washed over me and I soaked it up. "So to anyone sitting at home, thinking it will never be them, that they will never make it... play harder, work harder... *love* harder, and the rest will follow."

My hand slid into my dress slacks pocket, my body vibrating with restless energy. I felt like I'd been standing up there for an hour, not ten minutes. But there was still one person left to thank.

Rubbing a hand over my jaw, I forced down the wave of emotion threatening to bring me to my knees. "Before I say goodnight, there's someone else I need to thank tonight." My eyes found her down in the audience. "Two years ago, I believed the only way to get to the top was with rigid determination and narrowed focus. I won't sugarcoat it; I was a bit of an arrogant ass. But then Felicity barreled into my life and showed me it didn't have to be like that. Love doesn't make us weak, it makes us strong. Football will always be the dream, always. But what's a dream without a pretty girl by your side and a future laid out before you?"

I left the stand and walked along the far aisle to Felicity. Her eyes widened, filled with fresh tears. "J- Jason, what the hell are you doing?" She pressed a hand to her mouth as I dropped to one knee and presented her with the ring box I'd been carrying all evening.

"Felicity Charlotte Giles, you once permanently inked my stamp on your skin, but what I didn't tell you that day was, you're permanently tattooed on me too. You own me, babe. And I wasn't kidding when I said we're endgame."

Mya and Hailee let out little shrieks of approval as I flipped the lid.

"So, what do you say, Giles? Want to really make this a night to remember and say yes to marrying me?" The words coiled through me, filling me with so much emotion I had to blink the tears right out of my eyes.

"You're crazy." She slid off her chair, kneeling with me.

"Crazy about you." I grinned. "I know this season has been hard. I know the next two seasons will probably be equally as hard. But I thought that maybe if you're wearing my number as well as my ring, it would help you remember that I'm all in, babe. I'm so fucking in."

"Yes," she cried. "Yes, I'll marry you."

I'd won a ring once. A championship ring in my senior year of high school. It had meant everything to me at the time; but this, right here, sliding the princess cut diamond band onto Felicity's finger showed me it was nothing compared to this moment.

Because no matter where my football career took me; no matter if I entered the draft and landed a spot with an NFL team, it would be nothing without this girl by my side.

Football was the dream.

But Felicity?

She was my endgame.

PART II

Junior Year

11

Asher

"I CAN'T BELIEVE it's junior year already," Mya let out a small sigh as the six of us sat around the electric fire out on the terrace on the roof of our building. Summer was slowly retreating, giving way to the crisp mornings and cool evenings.

It had been a crazy year. Jason and Felicity had gotten engaged after he won the Heisman Trophy, seven months ago. Their relationship had only gotten stronger after he put that ridiculously big diamond on her finger. I couldn't speak for Cameron, but I felt the pressure. We were still young—we still had two years of college left—but I wanted that.

I wanted to bind Mya to me in all the ways that mattered.

She'd rip me a new one though if I even tried to get down on one knee. She wanted us to enjoy life, to make the most of college and classes and football. If anything, I was the Flick in our relationship; wondering when this smart, gorgeous, humble girl was going to slip through my fingers. But I wasn't about to confess that to her or my friends, so I pulled her closer and kissed her hair, reminding myself of how fucking lucky I was.

"You ready for another season?" I asked Jase.

"You know it."

It had been a summer of football camps, some time visiting my folks and Mya's aunt back in Rixon, and a week at the Hamptons.

"You think the Wolverines can go all the way this season?" I asked Cam.

He gave me a half-shrug. "Who knows?"

"What the fuck is that supposed to mean?"

"Ash," Hailee warned, and I frowned.

What the hell was happening right now?

"Xander got upset when we left," Cam blew out a long breath, running a hand down his face. "He said some things."

"Shit, man, I didn't realize." Xander was almost seven and he adored his older brother to the point where he struggled with Cam being away so much.

"It's just hard, ya know? I want to be there for him, but I'm not always going to be around."

"It's not your fault." Hailee rubbed his arm.

"Sorry for being a dick." I apologized.

"Nah, it's not you, it's me," he murmured.

Being an only child, I didn't get what it felt like to carry the responsibility of a sibling, especially a little kid who had already been through so much.

He still had nightmares about his mom being sick, even though everyone thought he was too young to remember. I'd only seen Xander a handful of times since we graduated, but the last time I'd seen the little guy, he'd seemed lost. Wearing a vacant look, he'd barely smiled unless his big brother was giving him his full attention.

I knew Cameron carried a lot of guilt over leaving. His heart torn between the girl he loved and the little brother he wanted to protect.

"But your mom is okay, right?"

"Yeah, she's fine. But she and my dad are both at a loss about what to do with him. He's so... different."

"He'll be okay," Hailee said. "As soon as we can, we'll bring him out to Michigan and show him the sights again."

Cameron leaned down and kissed her. "Thank you."

"Are you excited about classes, Mya?" Flick asked, changing the subject to safer shores.

"I can't freakin' wait. Although I wish it was senior year so I could jump into field practice."

"I'm not going to lie, I'm a little scared about clinical practice."

"Nah, babe." Jason hooked his arm around Felicity. "You've got this."

"And hey, at least *tutor boy* will be around to help you if things get too much." I smirked and Jase flipped me off.

"Really, you went there?" A low growl rumbled in his chest.

"Joke. I'm joking."

"Yeah, well it doesn't matter," Felicity said. "Darcy graduated. He's no longer at Penn."

"Thank fuck," Jason murmured, and she elbowed him in the ribs.

"Without Darcy I probably would have flunked my classes."

"You would have figured it out."

The two of them started bickering quietly while the rest of us watched the flames lick the inky sky. There was something about ending the summer with your girl and best friends and stepping into a new year. It was a tradition we'd started the summer before college. One I intended on keeping. We may have had less and less time for one another now we were all at college, but when we came together it was like no time had passed.

"What are you thinking?" Mya brushed the hair from my eyes.

"Just how perfect this is."

"Another year," she sighed.

"Another year closer to the rest of our lives together."

"Ash..."

"I know. No rush, right?" I touched my head to hers.

"We have time." Mya brushed her lips over mine and I was a goner.

There wasn't anything I wouldn't do for this girl. If she wanted time, I'd give it to her.

So long as she knew she was my forever.

"God, Asher, it's—"

"Fuck, babe, I know." I thrust up inside Mya again, curling my hand around her hip, encouraging her to ride me harder... Faster... *Deeper*.

"You feel incredible." Leaning up on my elbows, I took one of her perfect tits in my hand and flicked my tongue over the dusky bud. Mya cried out, throwing her head back as I sucked and laved, teasing her sensitive skin with my teeth.

I wanted to mark her, to brand her permanently as mine. I'd never been a possessive asshole, at least not like Jason... until Mya came along.

I couldn't explain my need to possess and consume her. I wanted her tied to me in every way possible.

Heart, mind, body, and soul.

I guess you could say I was a lot to handle. But Mya loved me. She loved our life together. And we openly talked about the future.

"Fuck." She ground her hips slower, rocking in tortuous circles, making my body tremble with pleasure. "Fuuuuck."

Mya smirked, aware of the power she held over me. I'd gladly handed over my balls to her when I'd chosen Temple—chosen *her*—over my place at Pittsburgh. But I wouldn't have changed it for the world.

When you'd grown up under the stifling expectations of my father, having something—*someone*—to call your own, to love and cherish and worship... well, it was a rare thing of beauty.

Need burned through me and I flipped Mya onto her back, slamming inside her, so deep she cried my name. Threading our fingers together, I pressed our hands beside her head as I pulled out and rocked back in, over and over, driving us to the point of sweet ecstasy.

"I'm close." She raked her fingers down my spine, moaning into my ear as I trailed hot wet kisses down her throat.

A familiar tingling started at the bottom of my spine just as Mya pulled me deeper into her body, locking her legs around my hips and shuddering around me.

I kissed her deeply as I fucked her into complete submission.

Nothing... *nothing* would ever feel as good as this.

Except maybe our wedding night.

Or the day I watched her birth our kids into the world.

Okay, so I was a little more than ahead of the game. But I was a Bennet. I had a game plan. One that included me and Mya and a happily-ever-after.

Mya

Sunlight framed Asher's face, making him look angelic. Although the way he'd loved my body last night was nothing short of sinful. A shiver ran through me just thinking about how he'd flipped me onto my back and fucked me as if it was the last time he would ever get to be inside me.

I let my fingers linger on his chest, tracing his cut abs, loving how warm his skin was. Sometimes it was hard to believe this was my life. I was halfway through my bachelor's in social work and living in an amazing building with my boyfriend. It was a far cry from life in Fallowfield Heights. But I'd earned it. I'd made sacrifices and worked my ass off to get here.

Asher, and all that came with being his girlfriend, was just the icing on the cake.

"You should probably move a little lower." His voice was thick with sleep.

"No can do, I'm meeting Faith for a run." I dipped my head and kissed him. It was supposed to be a chaste gentle peck, but when I tried to pull away, Asher buried his hand in my thick curls and captured my lips with his.

"Good morning," he breathed, finally letting me up for air.

"Morning." I smiled. I couldn't help it. I was one of those annoying girls now, sickeningly in love with her boyfriend. A football player no less.

"Are you going to the gym with the guys?"

"Yeah, I think Aiden wants us there."

I kissed him again. "Well, don't work too hard."

"What do you want to do later? I was thinking we could get dinner at Dukes or we could stay home and Netflix and Chill." His brows waggled.

"Or… we could go to The Hideout for open mic night."

"Yeah?" He frowned. "You enjoyed that?"

"What?" I batted his chest. "Faith is on the roster tonight and I want to support her."

"But what about supporting me and my very, *very*," he grabbed my hand and cupped it over his morning wood, "real problem?"

"You're insufferable," I chuckled.

"No, I'm just a guy in love with a girl." Asher nuzzled my neck, sucking and licking.

"I know what you're doing." I tried to push him away.

"I have no idea what you mean." He sucked harder, making blood rush to the surface, bruising me.

"Ash, you'll make me look like—"

"You're mine. I'll make you look like you're mine."

With a heavy eye roll, I untangled myself from him and climbed out of bed before he could grab me again.

"Tell Faith we'll be there," he called, just as I disappeared into the bathroom.

Every time. I smiled to myself.

Every damn time.

"So you're coming tonight, right?" Faith pressed her hands to her knees, breathing deeply.

"Wouldn't miss it for the world." I smiled.

Faith and I had been friends since our first day of freshman year. We'd met in orientation and never looked back. Like me, she wanted to make a difference: to work with those less fortunate, and help kids flourish, despite their often dire circumstances.

Felicity and Hailee aside, she was my best friend. So of course, I was going to be at the poetry slam night at The Hideout later.

"Asher's coming too."

"You know, it's cute that he wants to support you supporting me, but it wouldn't hurt him to relax the reins now and again."

My brows furrowed. "What's that supposed to mean?"

"I'm just saying, he's like your shadow. It's... a lot."

We stretched our calves before breaking into a gentle jog through Fairmount Park.

"We enjoy each other's company. Is that such a crime?"

"No." She chuckled, but it did little to ease the knot in my stomach. "I just think it would be nice to hang out occasionally without Asher tagging along."

"We hang out, Faith." We hung out all the time with the rest of the people from our class.

"Forget I said anything." She brushed me off, but her words lingered.

Before the summer, Faith had ended her relationship with her childhood sweetheart Max. She said they'd outgrown each other. I knew she'd embarked on a summer of self-discovery and sex with strangers, but I hadn't expected her to come back so judgmental of my relationship with Asher.

Awkward silence followed us as we jogged under the leafy canopy of the oak and ash trees.

"I know things have been hard since you and Max—"

"Honestly?" She shrugged. "I feel like a new woman. I'd been with Max since junior year in high school and I hadn't realized how suffocating our relationship was until I walked away."

"I'm glad you're in a better place, Faith, I am. But some of us are happy in our relationships."

"Asher is a total babe, and he's rich. Trust me, I get it."

She got it?

My stomach sank. Is that what she thought? That I was with Asher for his money?

"I love Asher," I said defiantly, annoyed at myself for even feeling the need to defend our relationship. "It has nothing to do with how wealthy his family is."

"I know you do." She shot me a weak smile. "But do you really think you'll go the distance?" Faith picked up her pace and left me trailing behind...

Wondering what the fuck had just happened.

12

Asher

"YOU DON'T HAVE to come tonight, you know?" Mya said, making me frown.

"What? Why wouldn't I want to come?"

"I know poetry isn't your thing and I think some of the guys from our class are going to be there. You'll probably be bored."

I glanced over at her. "Are you trying to get rid of me?"

"What? No! I'm just giving you an out." She shrugged as if it was nothing.

An out?

What the actual fuck?

"We always spend Sunday together," I said.

"I know and I love it, I do." Mya came toward me and I opened my legs, letting her slip between them. Linking her hands behind my neck, she gazed down at me. "I just didn't want you to think you have to come."

"Is everything okay?" My brows furrowed deeper. "You're acting weird."

"Everything's fine." Her lips pursed a little and I knew everything was not fucking fine.

"You want me to come, right?"

Shit. I sounded like a pussy. But we always spent Sunday's together during the semester. It was our way of making time for each other when the weeks got busy and our schedules got hectic.

"Of course." Mya brushed her lips over mine, but I intensified the kiss, sliding my tongue into her mouth and tangling it with hers.

"Keep kissing me like that and we'll never make it out of here."

"Now there's an idea," I chuckled.

"I can't believe it's junior year already." She exhaled a small sigh.

"Believe it, baby." I kissed her again.

"Okay, I'm going to finish getting ready and then we can head out." Mya's hand lingered on my shoulder and then she walked away, disappearing into the bathroom.

My cell phone vibrated, and I plucked it off the coffee table, scanning the text message.

. . .

Diego: A few of us are hanging out later, you should come.

Me: It's Sunday. Got plans with Mya.

My teammates knew the deal.

Diego: You are so fucking pussy whipped...

Me: Never claimed to be anything else.

I smirked, running a hand over my jaw. The guys liked to bust my balls about Mya, about how serious I was about her. But I didn't give a fuck. I loved her. And I'd almost lost her once... there was zero chance of me ever losing her again. I didn't care that it was college, that it was supposed to be the time for partying and sowing your wild oats. Football wasn't my life like it was for so many of my friends, like it was for Jason. I loved playing and I enjoyed the brotherhood and camaraderie, but it wasn't the end goal for me. I had zero intention of going pro.

Diego: Well, you know where we'll be if you change your mind.

Wasn't going to happen but I appreciated him getting off my back about it.

The Hideout was crammed but Faith had reserved a table upfront for Mya and a couple of their other friends. It was an eclectic crowd. Preppy types with something to prove. The stoners, all high on weed, free love, and peace. The drama students all desperately trying to get their big break. Then Mya and her friends; the ones out to change the world and make a difference. There wasn't a jock in sight, but I didn't care because although football was a big part of my life, it didn't define me. I had ambitions and plans just as much as the rest of the people here.

"You know, Asher," Rex, one of Mya's friends said, "it's nice you support her passions."

I frowned at that. "Is that not what two people in a relationship usually do?" Taking a long pull on my beer, I offered him a tight smile.

"Of course." His laughter came out strangled. "I just meant, what with you being on the football team and all."

"We're not all the conceited, selfish, shallow guys you paint us to be, ya know?" My lips thinned.

"I didn't... that's not..." He pulled at the collar on his sweater. "That came out wrong."

"Relax, Rexy boy. I'm secure enough to not give a crap about your stellar opinion of me."

"Asher, I didn't..." He released a heavy sigh, running a hand down his face. "You really love her, huh?"

I looked at the guy, *really* looked at him. He'd only really migrated into Mya's group last year, but I'd been around Rex enough times to know the dude had confidence issues.

"Have I ever given you or the gang reason to think I don't?" My brow arched.

The 'gang' was tight. They looked out for each other, hung out a lot, and shared the highs and lows of their emotionally demanding course. And until today, I'd never really questioned my position among them. But in less than a couple of hours, Mya had suggested that I didn't have to tag along, and now Rex was acting like I didn't belong.

Not how I saw the beginning of semester going.

As if she heard my thoughts, Mya glanced over at me and mouthed, "You good?"

I nodded, because I wasn't about to let Rex, or anyone else for that matter, know how I really felt.

Maybe I should have taken Diego up on his offer after all.

Faith took the stage and we all clapped. Aside from Hailee and Felicity, she was Mya's best friend. Freshman and sophomore year, we had hung out with her and her ex-boyfriend a lot. It had been nice, having another couple on campus to do things with. But Faith and Max had broken up before the end of sophomore year and that was that.

"Hey everyone. I'm Faith and this poem is called Freedom..."

Freedom is the power to breathe. To live and grow and feel.
Freedom is the power to speak. To think and consider and be.
Freedom is the power to love. To ask and give and hold.

You told me you loved me, but you hurt me the most. You took all that freedom and stripped it from my soul, leaving me weak and ruined.

You gave me your word, you promised me the world… and then stole it away in the blink of an eye.

Freedom is the power to change. To realize I'd become who you wanted me to be. Not who I needed to be.

Freedom is the right to say no. To protect my heart and body and soul and refuse to submit.

Freedom is the me saying I'm done… you don't get to hold all the cards anymore.

I'm free.

And you're no one.

The room was silent, the pain and passion in Faith's words rippling in the air, making it thick and heavy. She was Mya's friend, not mine, but it didn't take much to figure out she was talking about her ex. I shifted uncomfortably in my chair. I knew Max. I'd witnessed them as a couple: saw the way he'd loved her, the way he'd made her laugh. He'd wanted more and she hadn't. That's what Faith had told Mya, so the fact she was standing up there, publicly dissecting their relationship, and making him sound like a possessive asshole, left a sour taste in my mouth.

From the earsplitting applause she received, it was apparent no one else agreed with my assessment of her poem.

"Holy. Shit. Girl," Mya said, "that was awesome."

"I've been feeling inspired." Her twinkling gaze landed on mine and she narrowed her eyes. But as quickly as it was there, it was gone, as she lapped up the praise from her friends.

"Rex, help me get the drinks in?" Faith crooked her finger at him, and he went willingly.

Mya slid into his seat and looped her arms around my neck. "What did you think?"

"It was... a little harsh."

She reared back, confusion clouding her eyes. "What do you mean?"

"Come on, babe. She made Max out to be a complete asshole."

"It wasn't necessarily about Max."

"It was so about him. She dumped him, and yet she stood up there making it sound like he was some possessive narcissist, which we both know couldn't be further from the truth."

"Huh. I guess I didn't think about it like that."

"He wanted more, and Faith freaked."

"It's just slam poetry, Ash. You don't need to get so upset over it."

"I'm not upset," I sighed, running a hand over my head. "I just think it's a little unfair."

"You know what she's like." Mya brushed her nose over mine, stealing a kiss. "She's all for girl power and independence."

"And making her ex out to sound like a total asshole apparently," I grumbled.

"It's their business. Who are we to say how someone should or shouldn't feel? Max was a good guy, but he was kind of intense, always glued to her side. I guess she felt smothered."

"Is that what earlier was about?" I asked, the chips falling into place with a resounding *thud*.

"What?" Mya's gaze widened.

"When you said I didn't have to come tonight. Did Faith say something to you about me?"

"I..." Mya let out a small breath. "Not exactly," she admitted. "She's just in a weird place and wants to make the most of her newfound freedom."

"So she did say something to you?"

Un-fucking-believable.

"She didn't mean anything by it."

"Did you?" My body vibrated with a sense of impending doom. I couldn't really explain it, but I knew this wasn't going to end well. Yet, for some reason, I couldn't let it go.

"Asher, stop... this is silly."

"I don't think it is," I said.

First Mya, then Diego and Rex, and now Faith's stupid poem.

"Do you feel smothered by me?" Before I could stop them, the words spilled from my lips, and Mya's breath hitched.

"Where is all this coming from?"

"Answer the question, Mya," I ground out. The chatter and laughter went on around us, but it barely penetrated the roar of blood between my ears.

"You're being ridiculous." Her gaze went over my shoulder. "They're coming back. Please don't make this into something it isn't."

But the seed was planted, and I couldn't shake the feeling, I wasn't really welcome here tonight after all.

Standing, I shoved my hands in my pockets. "I'm going to hang out with Diego and the guys. I'll see you back at the apartment later."

"Leaving so soon?" Faith shot me a smug look.

"Yeah," I replied. "I guess it wasn't my scene after all."

And then I got the hell out of there.

Mya

"I should go after him." My chest constricted as I watched Asher walk away from us. He'd been so upset, so weird over Faith's poem.

But then, I'd screwed up earlier.

I'd seen the dejection in his eyes when I'd suggested he didn't have to come.

God, I should never have said anything. We always spent Sunday together. And I loved it. But Faith was in a weird place and Asher was a lot like Max. When he loved, he loved with his entire being. It had taken some getting used to, being the center of his universe, but I never felt smothered.

Overwhelmed sometimes, sure, but never smothered.

"Let him go." Faith shrugged, taking a long slurp of her drink. "You guys can kiss and make up later."

"She's right, you know," Bella, our other friend, said. "A little time and space never hurt... besides, makeup sex." She waggled her brows.

"Ugh, no thanks." Faith rolled her eyes. "Max was always so clingy after an argument."

"So, the poem," I asked, changing the subject. "Was that—"

"About Max? Yeah... he was just so stifling sometimes. It was like I couldn't breathe. He'd want to talk about our life after college, having a family and settling down..."

"He thought you were the one," Rex said, frowning.

"I guess. But it's college... we're supposed to find ourselves and spread our wings. Not... clip them."

"It's why I stick to my three-date rule." Bella nodded.

"But what if you met the right person?" I asked.

"Like you and Asher?" She gave me a warm smile. Unlike Faith who glowered.

"What?" I glared back.

"Asher is a nice guy, but do you really think he's the one?"

"Faith," Rex hissed under his breath.

"No, it's okay," I said, feeling a trickle of irritation up my spine. "Let her make her point."

"All I'm saying is, you met in high school, under... difficult circumstances. You went through something huge together. That kind of trauma can bind two people together. We see it all the time in class. That shared experience can become a dependency... a crutch. But unless you give yourself time and space to come to terms with that trauma, you can't really know who you are or what you want."

Faith had a point. We'd studied enough about attachment, shared trauma, and trauma bonding for me to know that people often did mistake shared trauma for compatibility. But what me and Asher had wasn't some product of our experiences.

When my ex, Jermaine, had found me in Rixon and shot Asher's mom, part of me had felt sure Asher would never be able to forgive me. At the time, I hadn't been sure *I* would ever forgive myself. But Asher loved me *in spite of* that. He'd done nothing but prove to me he was in.

All in.

When I didn't answer, Faith let out an exasperated breath. "Look, all I'm saying is, we're halfway into college. Do you really want to spend your entire college experience tied to another person who may or may not end up being the one? Because I sure as hell don't."

I pressed my lips together, considering her words. Asher had gone against his father's plans for him and followed me to Temple University.

He put me first every single time.

Above the team. Above his family and friends.

Faith was wrong. I didn't need to spend the next two years questioning anything. Because I knew. In my heart of hearts, I knew how Asher felt about me. And I knew how I felt about him.

"You're wrong," I said, standing.

"Seriously? You're going after him?" Faith gawked at me, while Bella gave me a discreet thumbs up.

"I get Max wasn't it for you, but Asher is it for me. You're one of my best friends and I'll always be here for you... but don't project your shit onto me, okay?"

Faith smothered a gasp and I offered her a weak smile. "I'll see you in class."

I didn't wait around to hear her reply. I had to go after my guy.

13

Asher

"YO, man. We weren't expecting you." Diego swaggered over to me. He had an Owls ball cap pulled on backwards and his jeans slung low on his hips.

"Do you ever wear a shirt?" I asked, meeting his fist bump with my own.

"And deny the ladies all this?" He swept a hand down his cut abs. "Nah, bro. So, what's up? I thought you and Mya had plans?"

"We did." I pressed my lips together, smothering a groan.

"Oh shit, trouble in paradise?"

"Honestly, I don't know what the fuck happened. One minute, everything was fine, the next..."

"You need a drink. Yo, Broderick," he hollered over his shoulder. "Get my guy, Asher, a beer."

Ten seconds later, Broderick appeared. "Hey, man."

"What's up?" I gave him a small nod.

"Not a lot. Just shooting some pool and deciding who to take for a ride tonight." He smirked, and the two of them high-fived, laughing and jostling each other.

"Ash and Mya had a fight," Diego said.

"Oh shit. You need me to hook you up? Jada is here and she brought plenty of friends."

"I'm good, thanks." Jada was a cheerleader and more than happy to service the football team.

"You need to relax, man," he said. "Have a drink. Get your dick suck—"

"Do not finish that sentence," a familiar voice said, and Diego let out a low whistle.

"Mya?" I turned to meet her narrowed gaze. "What are you—"

"Can we talk?" Her brow went up.

"We'll give the two of you some space." Diego dragged Broderick away.

"You left," she said.

"I didn't think I was welcome there." I rubbed my bottom lip, hating the distance between us.

If Cameron and Jason were here, I knew they would tell me to grow some balls. But I'd always worn my heart on my sleeve, I wasn't about to change now.

"Ash." She inched closer, so close I could smell her perfume. "What has gotten into you?"

I reached for her, but Mya batted my hand away, pressing her palms flat against my chest and pushing me into the wall.

"You knew what you were signing on for with me," I said. "I'm intense and needy and so fucking gone for you."

"Faith said some things..." Her eyes glittered with emotion. "But she doesn't get it. No one does. The way I feel about you. The way you make me feel..." Mya leaned in, letting her mouth hover over mine. "You're it for me, Asher Bennet."

"Yeah?" My throat felt dry, my heart beating hard beneath my ribcage.

She nodded. "I'm sorry I made you doubt how I feel about us."

My hand slipped around Mya's neck, holding her there and touching my head to hers. "I'm sorry I overreacted about Faith's poem. But the idea you might not feel the same—"

"I do." A grin spread across her gorgeous face. "And I'm right here."

I captured her lips, pushing my tongue into her mouth. She tasted so fucking good. I wanted to take my time exploring every inch of her.

"Erm, babe, unless you want an audience, maybe we should take this back to our place." Mya buried her face into the crook of my neck, and I wound my hands around her body.

"I love you."

"I love you too, Asher." She lifted her eyes to mine. "So much."

"This year is going to be amazing. I promise."

"I know." I saw nothing but complete conviction there, and it was such a fucking relief.

"And I promise to give you space, even if I do hate every second that I'm away from you." My lips curved but I meant every single word.

"Well, I promise to always come back to you. How does that sound?"

Ducking my head, I brushed my nose over hers. "It sounds pretty damn perfect."

Mya

"Jesus, babe," Asher rasped as I ran my tongue along his shaft. He'd already made love to me once and again in the shower. But there was something about tonight's events that made me crave him.

His hands slid into my curls, guiding my mouth deeper over him. "That feels so fucking good."

Despite his vice-like hold on me, Asher let me set the pace. After more than two-and-a- half years together, I knew exactly how to bring him to the edge. My hand jacked him slowly in rhythm with my tongue, as I licked and flicked, sucking him like a popsicle.

"Fuck, Mya..." he choked out as I took his dick deeper, relishing the clean taste of him.

Our eyes connected, and I held his stare as I ran my lips up and down, swirling my tongue over the tip. "I'm close..." His grip on my hair relaxed a little and I knew I had him right where I wanted him.

Asher's head rolled back, a string of cuss words leaving his lips on breathy moans. I sucked him harder... *deeper*... flattening my tongue against his shaft and bobbing my head up and down.

"Fuuuuck," Asher went to pull away, but I tightened my hold on him, not letting him go until I'd swallowed down every last drop.

Licking my lips, I sat up.

"Do you have any idea how fucking sexy you look like that?" He wound his hand around my wrist and tugged me forward. I went willingly, letting Asher pull me across his body. He leaned down, kissing me hard, not caring that he could taste himself on my tongue. Desire pulsed through me, but it was late, and we had class in the morning.

Asher must have had the same thought because instead of deepening the kiss, he rolled me over and spooned me from behind, wrapping his big body around mine. "We should fight more often," he teased.

"That wasn't a fight, babe. A fight requires raised voices, some smashed glasses, and a fist or two."

He chuckled. "My little fighter."

"What we had earlier was... a moment."

"A moment. I can live with that. Let's just not make a habit of it." He snuggled me tighter.

Sometimes, when we were like this, it was hard to believe this was my life. The girl from Fallowfield Heights living in a prestigious apartment building in the city with her rich football-playing boyfriend.

Asher was everything I never wanted... and everything I never knew I needed.

"Penny for your thoughts?" He ran his nose along my shoulder.

"Just thinking how I ended up here."

"You need me to remind you? Because I can. I can spend the entire night reminding you of exactly why we're perfect for each other."

A shiver rolled through me at the intention in his words.

"Do you think it will always be like this?"

"I think life will have its ups and downs," he said, "but we'll get through whatever storms blow our way."

Glancing back, I smiled. "You always sound so sure of everything."

"Because I am. I love you, Mya. I love our life together. And I'm excited about what the future brings."

"Even if I want to stay in the city?" I wanted to work in the kinds of neighborhoods where I'd grown up. I wanted to make a difference to kids like me. I was one of the lucky ones, I got out. But so many kids thought their destinies were already decided for them. I wanted to show them there was always another way.

"I already told you, if that's what you want, that's what we'll do."

Rolling over, I stared up at Asher. He was so handsome, his features older and wiser, a young man on the cusp of great things. Turned out, Asher was whip smart like his father. He'd never wanted his father's life, but since starting his business degree two years ago, Asher had come to love the very thing he'd once resented.

"But what about your dad's business?"

"We'll figure it out. He's been wanting to expand. This could be the perfect opportunity. We have time." He kissed the end of my nose.

But two years was nothing. Once we threw ourselves into classes and the football season, junior year would pass us by in the blink of an eye, and we'd be one step closer to making the big decisions.

"Hey, Mya," Bella beckoned me over. "How are you... after, you know..."

"I'm good, thanks."

She nodded. "Have you seen Faith yet?"

"No, but honestly, it's not a big deal. She's entitled to her opinions, so long as she doesn't keep trying to—"

Bella widened her eyes and I turned just in time to greet Faith. "Hey," she said around a sheepish smile. "Can we talk for a second?"

"I'll just..." Bella left us to it.

"I'm sorry about last night. I had no right to—"

"No, you didn't," I said flatly. "Mine and Asher's relationship is just that, Faith, ours. I won't justify my decisions to you, and I don't expect you to judge me for my actions, the way I won't judge you for yours."

"You're right, you're totally right." She ran a hand through her silky red hair. "I'm just trying to be more in control of my life and sometimes it spills out. It won't happen again, I promise."

"Good."

"Did you find Asher?"

"Yeah."

"He probably hates me now, huh?"

"He doesn't hate you, Faith. He just doesn't understand you sometimes. Max was a good guy. I know you two had your differences, but I think the poem threw Ash for a loop."

"I can see that. To be honest, I think the poem was less about Max and more about me and the pressure and expectations I put on myself."

"You'll get there, Faith. Don't be so hard on yourself."

I wanted to graduate and become a social worker, but not the same way Faith wanted it. She lived and breathed it, out to prove to everyone that she could make it. Her tenacity was inspiring, but I also wondered if it was impacting on her personal life. Asher hadn't been wrong, Max was a great guy. Solid and dependable with plans for the future. Most girls dreamed of meeting a guy like that. But not Faith, she'd run the second things got too serious.

"You're a good friend, Mya." She took my hand in hers. "Asher's lucky to have you." There was something in her eyes that looked a lot like regret, but I didn't ask.

Faith needed to work things out for herself.

"Come on," I said. "We should get to class."

Asher

"You made a quick exit last night," Diego said as we worked out next to each other.

"Yeah, we had shit to take care of."

"I bet you did." He shot me a knowing grin and I managed to flip him off.

"You know you're punching above your weight with Mya, right?"

"Fuck you, D." I chuckled. Of course I knew Mya was too good for me. But she was mine, and I didn't plan on giving her up for anything.

"I'm just busting your balls, she's a good girl. One of the best. She volunteering again at the center this semester?"

"Yeah, her field practice isn't until senior year, so she'll want to get all the hands-on experience she can."

"She's a better person than me. Some of those little punks would be cruising for a bruising with the way they talk to the staff there."

"It's what she wants to do," I said as if was that simple. And in a way, it was. But Diego was right, the New Hope Community Center worked with some of the most challenging kids living in and around Strawberry Mansion.

"Don't you ever worry about her being there?"

"What kind of question is that, D? Of course I fucking worry. She's my..." *Everything.*

Mya was my everything.

But she wanted to make a difference. She wanted to try to break the cycle of crime, drugs, and poverty so many of the kids in Philly found themselves in. It was important to her.

"It's not the nineteen-fifties," I said. "Women don't want to stay at home, raise the kids, and play Suzy Homemaker."

"Hey, my momma did just that and she's one of the best women I know." His eyes lit up with fondness.

Diego's mom was a great woman. I'd met her last year, when she'd showed up with Pastel de Elote for the team.

"Mya wants to make a difference," I said unsure who I was trying to convince more, myself or Diego.

"I hear ya, man. All I'm saying is, it's a crazy world out there. Don't think I'd ever rest knowing my girl was in the thick of it."

My brows furrowed. He made it sound like Mya was going off to war.

But in some ways, she was.

The world needed people like Mya. People willing to put themselves on the line and advocate for those without a voice.

I was proud of her—so fucking proud.

But part of me would always worry. Because that's what you did when you loved someone.

14

Asher

"LOOKING GOOD, BENNET," Coach yelled across the field as I ran drills with Diego and a hulk of a guy called Brian. "Run it again."

Our offensive line got into position, moving toward us like a well-oiled machine. I broke formation, tracking the wide receiver and making the lunge. Our bodies collided with a *thud* and we went down.

"Fuck, Bennet, you knocked the wind right out of my sails," Farrow said.

"Hell yeah, I did." I clambered up and offered him a hand up.

"Okay, hit the showers," Coach said, "you're done for the day."

I pulled off my helmet, dragging in a lungful of fresh air.

"You're looking good out there, bro," Diego said approaching me. We fist bumped but his eyes flickered over my shoulder. "You have company."

I turned to find Mya sitting in the bleachers. A smile tugged at the corner of my mouth. "I'll catch you in a bit."

He rolled his eyes, but I was already gone, heading in her direction.

"Hey," she said, coming down onto the field.

"This is a surprise." I kissed her cheek.

"I had a free period. I wanted to come and see you in action."

"Oh yeah? I thought football players didn't do it for you?" My voice was teasing.

"Oh, I don't know." Mya came closer, trailing a finger up my dirty jersey. "One football player caught my attention."

"Yeah?"

"Yeah, number six. He's looking—"

I grabbed her and started tickling her sides. "You want a piece of Farrow? I'll see if I can hook you up."

Her laughter wrapped around me like a warm blanket. "Okay, okay, you got me."

I eased up and leaned in to brush my nose over hers. "What are you really doing here?"

A knowing smile lifted the corner of her mouth. "Sally called. They need an extra hand tonight. They've got some new kids and want all hands on deck. I said I'd be there."

"Okay. Just be careful, okay?"

"Always." Mya kissed me.

"What time will you get done?"

My body stirred to life at her proximity. I was going to have a serious case of blue balls if she was going to be home late.

"I don't know. I wouldn't think any later than nine."

"Enough time for you to come home and show me just how much you like football players then?" I smirked as my hands dipped around to her ass.

"Behave."

"With you? Never. I should probably go before Coach chews me out. But text me later?"

She nodded, taking a step backward. "Love you."

"I love you more." *So fucking much.*

I headed for the gym unable to hide the shit-eating grin lifting the corners of my mouth.

Yesterday had been rocky there for a moment, but everything had righted itself in the end. We'd had some of the best sex of my life. A new season was looming, and the team was looking stronger than ever. And I had a full schedule of classes I couldn't wait to get stuck into.

Life was great.

But there was still a small part of me that thought Mya underestimated just how much I loved her. I knew she wanted to stay in the city after graduation, and I knew she assumed I'd want to return to Rixon and help my old man with the company.

But she was wrong.

I just had to figure out a way to show her just how serious I was about our future together.

Mya

"Hey, sorry I'm late." I ran a hand through my hair and gave Sally, the New Hope Community Center coordinator, a big smile. "Tell me where you want me, and I'll jump straight in."

"We had some new kids signposted to the program, three brothers. They recently got placed into foster care. "The elder two, Jay and Mario are a little uncertain, but I've paired them up with Pat and Hershel."

"And the youngest?"

"Hugo, he's only six. His file says he's been a selective mute for the last two years."

My heart clenched. I'd seen a lot during my time volunteering with New Hope. It ran a *Big Brothers, Big Sisters* style program for kids in the foster care system, but instead of one-to-one activities, it operated at a community level. They held weekly sessions, and monthly group events, as well as providing ongoing support to the foster families and their charges.

"Here." Sally thrust a file at me. "It makes for difficult reading. Hugo is ready and waiting when you are."

I sat down on the leather bench in her office and flicked open the file.

Hugo Garcia aged six. Two siblings, Jay, aged eleven, and Mario, aged fourteen. Father unknown, mother known to authorities since Mario was just three, after she started turning tricks to make ends meet. A history of narcotic use, neglect, and poor school attendance.

"Jesus," I breathed, trying to get a hold on my emotions. No matter how many case files I read, it never got any easier.

"Jay and Mario have friends, they were able to get out of the house, but Hugo..." Sally's voice trailed off.

"It says here he likes football."

She nodded. "Came in clutching a stuffed Eagles mascot."

"I can work with that." At least, I hoped I could.

"If anyone can reach him, Mya, it's you."

Her words touched something inside me. All I wanted was to make a positive difference on the lives of the kids I encountered, so to have my mentor say that was everything.

I left Sally and went to find Hugo, spotting him the second I stepped into the main hall. A small kid with a head full of brown, curly hair, he watched the other kids and volunteers play a game of hacky sack.

I grabbed a soft football out of the box and made my way over to him. "Mind if I sit here?"

His silence and lack of eye contact spoke volumes. Instead, Hugo gave me a half-shrug and shifted along the bench.

"I'm Mya. I was hoping we could hang out."

More silence. But I didn't let it faze me. You had to have thick skin to work with these kids. Kids who had seen and experienced things no kid ever should.

"Is that Swoop?" I motioned to the tatty stuffed eagle in Hugo's hands. He was clutching onto the thing so tight I was surprised it hadn't ripped clean in two.

But he didn't respond.

"I'm not a huge fan, but my boyfriend plays for a college team. He's pretty good."

Hugo glanced at me, his stare so dull and lifeless it twisted my insides.

What had this poor kid seen to make him choose not to communicate? To build walls so high he didn't know how to break through them? To choose isolation and solace over comfort and security?

"His name is Asher, he plays defense."

Hugo averted his gaze again, and the seed of hope that had flourished in my chest withered and died. But I'd keep pushing. Slowly and surely, I'd prove to this six-year-old with pain in his eyes that he could trust me.

Two WEEKS and three more sessions later, Hugo still refused to talk. He barely engaged in sessions, choosing to color or read a book in silence. His brothers had flourished, although Jay preferred the physical activities laid on by the center while Mario preferred the more creative ones.

"There you are." Asher looped his arms around me and pulled me against his chest as I added milk to my cereal.

"Sorry. I couldn't sleep."

He made me drop the spoon and turned me in his arms. "The kid?" His brows furrowed.

"He's just so... sad. It breaks my heart."

"Babe, we talked about this. You can't fix every kid who comes through the doors."

"I know." I bristled. "But you haven't seen him, Ash. He just sits there, completely closed off. I've spent almost ten hours with him, and he hasn't said a single word to me."

It was no time in the grand scheme of things, but it was the first time I'd worked with a selective mute before. It was hard not to let my own frustrations bleed over.

"You promised you wouldn't get too involved."

"I'm not," I snapped a little too harshly, and Asher arched a brow. "Sorry, I just—"

"You care, I get it. But some of these kids have experienced enough trauma to warrant a lifetime of therapy. You said he was getting professional support?"

I nodded. "Someone has been working with him at school. But so far, nothing."

"Know what I think?" He leaned down, touching his head to mine.

"What?"

"The little guy will talk when he's good and ready."

"I wish it were that simple." My shoulders sagged.

"Maybe he just needs a reason to talk."

"What do you mean?" It was my turn to frown.

"Maybe he needs some motivation, and I'm not talking getting a sticker or lollipop at the end of a session with the school shrink."

"Like a bribe?"

"Let's call it gentle persuasion."

"Actually," I said, an idea forming. "You might be onto something."

"Yeah?" Asher grinned. "And here was me thinking I was talking complete crap."

"There's this intervention a lot of schools use called the 'mystery motivator'. I might be able to adapt it."

"Sounds good. You said he likes football, right? Maybe we could arrange something once the season starts? Bring the kids out to a training session or even a game."

"You'd do that for them?"

"For you, babe. I'd do it for *you*." He kissed the end of my nose.

Ideas started firing off in my head. The only time Hugo even looked remotely interested in me was when I'd mentioned my boyfriend played college football. I'd tried to incorporate football into our activities and conversations as much as I could without coming on too strong. It was important to go at Hugo's pace, to gradually earn his trust.

"I'll talk to Sally and see what she thinks. Thank you." I threw my arms around his neck and kissed him. Asher grew hard against my stomach, and I eased back to look at him. "Seriously?" I smirked.

"What? My dick just so happens to be very, *very* attracted to you."

"Well, I hate to be a buzz kill..." I let my mouth linger on his, running my tongue over the seam of his lips. "But I have an early class." Slipping out from between Asher and the counter, I grabbed my bowl and sashayed away.

"You're killing me, Hernandez," he called after me.

"Love you too," I replied around a smile.

Because I did.

I loved Asher the way the stars loved the night.

Unconditionally.

Irrevocably.

Endlessly.

15

Asher

"BENNET, GET IN HERE, SON," Coach Johnson called as I passed his office.

"What's up, Coach?"

"Just checking in. Wanted to see how you're feeling about the upcoming season?"

"I feel good, sir. The team is looking strong. I think we might have a real shot going into the playoffs."

"I agree. That kind of attention will bring scouts. You're a junior now, son. It's time to make some decisions about your future."

"Already made them, sir."

"I thought you might say that." He rubbed his jaw. "But I'd hoped to convince you to reconsider. When scouts come knocking, I'd really like your name on their list."

"I don't know what to tell you, sir. Going pro isn't in my plans."

"Well, shucks, Bennet. Never thought I'd see the day a talented young man such as yourself would give up a shot at the big leagues for a woman."

"She's not just any woman, sir." A smirk played on my lips.

"No, son, I guess she's not." There was no malice in his expression; just mild disappointment, and a shit ton of respect.

"I'm sorry it wasn't the answer you'd hoped for, Coach."

"Me too, son. Me too. Now get out of here."

I gave him a nod and walked out of there. I knew the guys wouldn't understand, but it wasn't their life.

Back in senior year, at high school, I'd watched my mom almost die from a bullet meant for me. I'd watched the fear in my old man's eyes as he held the one woman who had always stood by his side, despite his flaws—and he had many. I'd made a promise to myself that day if Mya ever gave me a second chance—which she had—I would never do anything to jeopardize that.

Mya wanted a career, she wanted to make a difference. Her plans didn't include being with an NFL football player. And I didn't want anything that didn't include her. I wanted roots, a life together. I didn't want to be thrust into a world of football and fame.

Exiting the gym, I pulled out my cell and scrolled to my dad's number.

"Asher, this is a surprise," he said.

"Hey, Dad. I was hoping we could talk."

"Is everything okay, Son? You sound—"

"Everything's great. There's just some stuff I need your help with."

"Okay." He took a breath. "You want to talk about it now or should I drive up there?"

"Yeah?" I smiled.

There had been a time when Andrew Bennet was too focused on work to drop everything and come running. But he wasn't that guy anymore. I hadn't forgotten the way he'd treated Mya in the early stages of our relationship, or the cold-hearted bastard he'd been growing up, but I had found it within myself to forgive him. He loved Mya. She'd opened his eyes to so much more than a life of hard work and sparkling reputation. Between her and Mom, he was no longer the monster I had grown up with. I'd earned a second chance with Mya, so it seemed only fair, I gave him one.

"Of course, Asher. How about I come this evening? We can go to that quaint little place you took me and your mother last time we visited."

"The Hideout? Actually, I have somewhere else in mind."

"Whatever you want. Will Mya be joining us?"

"She has a shift at the center, but she might be able to join us after, if you're still around."

"I can always make time for Mya." I smiled at that. "I'll see you both later."

We hung up and I checked my wristwatch.

Only five hours until I could start putting Operation Future into action.

Mya

"It's good to see you again, Hugo," I said, sitting down beside him. He was busy coloring in another picture of Swoop, the Eagles mascot. Sally had printed a bunch off for him. It was his favorite activity; one of the only activities he engaged with.

"That looks great," I added when he didn't acknowledge me. "I thought we could try something different today. I'm hoping you'll like it." I placed the blank cards and envelopes down in front of me. I'd spoken to Sally about my idea and she and Hugo's social worker were all for it.

He finally lifted his dull brown eyes to mine. "Hi, there," I said, giving him a soft smile. "Would you like me to tell you about the activity I thought we could do?"

He gave me an imperceptible shrug, but I took it as permission.

Hope unfurled in my stomach. I didn't want to get overexcited, but this was huge. I gently pushed a card and pen toward him. "So, I know how you love football. Your brothers have been telling me all about it." I winked and his little brows furrowed. "They said you want to be like Fletcher Cox when you're older?"

He stared back at me with a blank expression, but I kept going. "I want you to think about football for a minute. I want you to think about the way it makes you feel and why you love it so much, and then, when you're ready, I want you to write one wish down on the card. It can be anything to do with football, okay?"

Seconds ticked by as Hugo stared at the blank card. I didn't push. I didn't speak. I just sat there quietly, waiting. For this to work, he had to engage with the process... he had to own it.

After a few minutes, I was worried he wasn't going to bite. But then, slowly, Hugo picked up the pen and began drawing. His grip was shaky, the lines messy and unintelligible. But we could figure out the details later. I just needed an idea to work with.

"Finished?" I asked once he'd stopped drawing. He gave me his sad eyes again and nodded. It was a small action, but it was something.

"You did great, Hugo. Do you mind if I take a look?"

He slid the card across to me. Thankfully, I could just make out the football field and huge bird-like man in the center.

My lips curved as I realized what he was telling me. "You'd like to go to the Lincoln Financial Field and meet Swoop, huh?"

Emotion welled inside me. It was something so innocent and pure, it made my heart ache.

"Well, I can't promise anything," because that was the number one rule of working with kids—no promises—"but I'm going to see what I can do, okay?"

A flicker of interest passed over his face.

"But you have to do something for me too."

His expression fell.

"I'm going to put your wish in this envelope and we're going to keep it over there on that bookcase." I pointed at shelves across the room. "See." Taking the pen, I stuffed the card inside the envelope and wrote 'Hugo' across the front. "It's going to stay right there... and when you're ready to try to make it come true, all you have to do is ask me."

His eyes widened a little, fear glittering there.

"I know it's scary," I spoke gently. "I know you haven't spoken to anyone in a really long time, but you don't have to be afraid anymore, okay? The Hansons are a good family. They want you and your brothers to feel safe.

"It doesn't have to be today or the next time we meet, but I'd really like it, if, one day, you use your voice to ask me for the envelope."

Hugo studied me, his murky brown eyes fixed on mine. I wanted to know what he was thinking, what he saw when he looked at me. But I knew it wasn't that simple. In this field, patience was your best friend. Progress was often made in baby steps, and just when you thought you were moving forward, something would happen to set you back again.

"Do you think you can give it a try? I'll put the envelope over there for safe keeping, and when you're ready to ask me for it, I'll be right here waiting."

Hugo shifted on his chair and I hated that it was because I was pushing him into a state of discomfort. But I'd read up a lot on selective mutism and it often came hand in hand with social anxiety disorder. Overcoming it wasn't going to be easy, but he was still young. With the right interventions and support, there was no reason why Hugo couldn't slowly regain his speech and confidence.

But then he looked at me again, and although he didn't nod, I saw his answer.

Hugo would try.

And I would wait.

Asher

"I'm sorry I missed your dad," Mya said as we lay in bed.

"It's okay. Rough night?" She'd gotten home a little after ten.

"I offered to stay and help Sally clean up."

"Of course you did." I smiled, stroking her warm skin. "How did it go with the kid?"

"I'm not sure yet. But I'm hoping it'll reach him." She snuggled closer. "So what brought your dad to Philly?"

"I wanted to talk to him, and he offered to drive up."

Mya rolled onto her stomach, gazing up at me. "What did you need to talk to him about?" Her nose scrunched up.

"Things."

"Things." Her brow arched with suspicion, and I chuckled.

"I wanted to feel him out about opening a second branch of his business here."

Her eyes went wide. "You did?"

"I was serious about what I said, Mya. You want to put down roots here, and if I'm going to work for the family business, that doesn't just happen overnight. We'd need to find premises, employ a team, source clients."

"Wow, you've really given this a lot of thought."

I reached for one of her spiral curls and twirled it around my finger. "Coach asked me today about going pro. Said I have a shot—"

"Ash," she frowned, "I don't want you to give up that dream for me."

"It isn't just about you. It's about me too. And honestly, I don't want it. I love football, but it's not my life. You are." Her breath caught, but I wasn't done. "I know we're young, and I know you probably think I'm crazy for even talking about starting a family, but I want that. I want a life with you."

"Actually..." Mya pressed her lips together and looked up at me through her thick lashes. "I've been doing some thinking myself..." She hesitated. "How do you feel about fostering?"

"As in fostering kids?"

"No, puppies." She rolled her eyes. "Of course, kids. I was talking to Sally tonight and she was telling me all about the family who have taken in Hugo and his brothers, and what they're doing... it's incredible. I always thought the way I could help and make a difference was to be out there in the community, working at grass roots level. But maybe this is something else to consider."

"I'm not going to lie, babe, I don't know the first thing about fostering. Don't you have to be settled? Have a good job, a house, that kind of thing?"

"There is eligibility criteria, yes. But it isn't as rigid as you think. You have to be over twenty-one and have a stable living arrangement, but the rest is pretty flexible."

"Fostering, huh?" I didn't know how to feel about opening up my home to a kid who wasn't mine. I'd always imagined we'd start a family with a baby, *our* baby.

"It's not something we have to decide or even talk about yet. I just think it's something I might want to do one day."

"You have a big heart, Mya Hernandez." I brushed my thumb over her cheek, letting it linger on the pillow of her lip.

"I just want to help. You came into my life when I needed someone. I'd like to think I can pay that forward one day."

Well, shit. When she put it like that... but fostering? That was huge, and we were so young.

"I don't want this to be another issue between us," she said as if she could hear my thoughts. "I was just saying it's something I'd like to think about, one day."

"I know."

But I also knew Mya, and once she got something in her mind... Yeah, this wasn't going away anytime soon.

I could give Mya a lot of things: money, love, a happy life... but could I give her this?

There was only one thing for it. I needed a beer and some guy time with my best friend.

16

Asher

"HEY, THANKS FOR COMING." I got up to greet Jason. We guy-hugged before taking a seat at the bar.

"Anytime. What's up?"

"I... fuck, I don't even know where to start."

"Is everything okay? With Mya? Your mom?" Concern filled his eyes.

"Yeah, they're fine."

He frowned. "So, spit it out."

"Mya wants to foster kids."

Jase reared back. "She wants to *what*?"

"Yeah, I know." I scrubbed my jaw.

"Like now or after college?"

"After college. You have to be at least twenty-one to get a license." Although her birthday was in a few weeks, I was pretty sure no one was going to entrust a kid's wellbeing to a college student.

"I thought she wanted to do the social work thing?"

"She does... at least, I think she still does. It kind of took me by surprise."

"Yeah, I bet." He flagged the bartender and ordered a drink. "So how do you feel about it?"

"Honestly? I don't know. I mean, I want kids. I can't wait to get her knocked up." Jase shook his head at that, and I frowned. "What?"

"We're barely twenty-one."

"I know, but I've always wanted a family."

"I'll say it again... we're *twenty-one*."

I flipped him off. "You're telling me you don't want the big house and lots of kids?"

"One day, when we're much, *much* older. I want to enjoy Felicity first. Make a life together, ya know? Besides, if I draft—"

"Which we both know you will," I smirked.

"Life will be crazy."

"Yeah, I get it." I ran my thumb over the neck of the bottle. "I told Coach I'm not looking to go pro."

He let out a long breath. "I always knew you were unsure, but I didn't think you'd made the final decision."

"It's just not what I want. I love football. I love being on the team. But I want more after college."

"Like babies?"

"Fuck off." I chuckled.

"It's a damn shame, Ash. You could have gone all the way."

"Maybe, maybe not. But I don't yearn for it the way you do. I thought maybe breaking free from my old man's expectations, I'd find my passion for it again. But honestly, it never came. I'm happy where I am. And once we graduate, I want to expand the business here. I spoke to my dad and he's going to put out some feelers."

"Well, if that's what you want then good luck to you." He lifted his beer and topped it toward me.

"It is."

"But back to the fostering thing." Jase's expression sobered. "Is it a deal breaker?"

"What? *No!*" Panic snaked through me. "I'd do anything to make Mya happy."

"Yeah, but come on, Ash. Taking on the responsibility of a kid who isn't your blood?"

"I'm not saying it would be easy, but I have money, resources... shouldn't I use them for a good cause?"

"You're a better man than me. I'm not sure I could do it."

"I'm still not convinced I can." But for Mya, I'd try. "Speaking of kids, have you spoken to Cam?"

"Yeah, he's really worried about Xander. Apparently, he's getting into some trouble at school."

"Shit." I'd known things were bad, but we hadn't talked in a few days.

"I think he'd move back to Rixon in a heartbeat if it wasn't for Hailee." Jason let out a weary sigh. "I'm worried about them."

"They'll figure it out. Xander is one of the most loved kids I know."

"Yeah." He said. But he didn't look convinced.

And maybe he was right. Maybe sometimes love wasn't enough.

"It's good to see you," I said.

I had friends at Temple. Diego, Aiden, Farrow, and the rest of the team. But none had ever come close to filling the hole left behind by Jason and Cameron.

What we had was rare.

Special.

It was a fucking blessing.

And I thanked the universe every day for giving me two of the best friends a guy could ask for.

"Mya, it's so lovely to see you." Mom pulled my girl into her arms and my heart swelled watching the two of them.

They'd formed a special bond after the shooting, and it was a giant relief that the two most important women in my life got on.

"Son." Dad extended his hand and I accepted it. "It's good to see you both."

It had only been a few days since he drove out to see me, but it was the weekend before the team's first game, so we wanted to do dinner before life became too hectic to see them.

"Something smells delicious." Mom beamed.

"I slaved for hours over this, you'd better enjoy it," I teased, shooting Mya a knowing wink.

"Let me guess, sweetheart," Mom said to Mya. "You did all the heavy lifting." She chuckled.

"Ash likes to think he prepared everything, but sitting on the stool, giving me instructions on how to chop the onion—"

"Hey, I helped."

"Give up now, Son," Dad suggested, managing a rare smile.

"Fine, fine. Steal all my thunder."

"Oh, hush." Mom came over and ruffled my hair, her eyes clouded with melancholy.

She'd found it hard after everything to let me go, but she understood, perhaps better than anyone, my desire to follow Mya to Temple.

"Why don't you get your parents a drink?" Mya said, "and I'll finish up in here."

"Sure thing." I moved around Mom and went to her, pressing a kiss to her forehead. "Holler for me if you need any help."

"I think I have it handled," Mya mumbled, going back to stirring the contents of the pan.

"Come on, why don't we wait in the living room?" I got them a drink each and we made our way through the apartment. I took a seat in a chair, leaving the couch for Mom and Dad.

"How are classes?" Mom asked.

"Good."

"And the team?"

"We're looking strong. It should be a good season."

"That's great, Andy. Isn't that great?" She frowned, as my father toyed with something on the sideboard.

"Andrew?"

"What is this?" He turned slowly and my stomach sank.

Shit.

He was holding the fostering information leaflet Mya had brought home for me to look at.

"Asher, what is this?" he repeated.

"Relax, Dad," I replied. "It's just a leaflet."

"About fostering."

"I'm sure it's nothing, Andy. Probably something to do with Mya's course. Come sit down," Mom patted the couch.

He dropped the leaflet on the side and joined us. "Tell me you're not seriously considering fostering, Son?"

"And if we were?" I sat straighter, feeling a lick of irritation up my spine.

"Be reasonable, Asher. You're just kids. You have your whole lives ahead of you to think about kids. I thought you wanted to focus on the business, on growing—"

"I do," I snapped, hating that no matter how hard he tried to be better, to do better, underneath it all, Andrew Bennet was still the same rigid, narrow-minded man he'd always been.

"Did you know that lots of young professionals foster?"

"Sweetheart, this is... well, it's a lot." Mom looked flustered. "I thought Mya wanted to graduate and do her social work training?"

"She does, but her heart is with working with kids. This is the best of both worlds."

"Now, hang on a minute, Son. It sounds like you've already made the decision. You're in junior year. There's still two years left of—"

"Hmm, is everything okay?" Mya appeared in the doorway.

"Actually," I said, standing. "I was just telling my parents about the fostering thing."

"You were?" Her eyes darted to them and back to me, confusion glittering in her gaze.

"Yeah, my dad noticed the leaflet and had some questions." I gave him a tight smile.

"I see. Well, it's really only a pipe dream at the moment," she said.

"Asher made it sound like it's already decided," Dad clipped out and I heard my mom shush him.

"He did, did he?" Mya narrowed her eyes, slowly approaching me. "What are you doing?" she mouthed.

Roping my arm around her waist, I pulled her close. "I've been thinking... and I think we should do it. As soon as you turn twenty-one, we should see about getting our license and—"

"Whoa, slow down." Strangled laughter spilled from her lips. "We still have to graduate."

"I know. But I've been thinking about Xander and Hugo and all the work you do at New Hope. If we can give some kid a safe place and security and a chance at a better future, we should do it."

Deep down, I think I'd known the second Mya brought it up that it was the right move, but we were young, and it was a big decision.

I wanted it though.

I wanted it with Mya.

Her lip curved. "Yeah?"

"Yeah." I nodded. "I can start the business and you can stay at home with the kids and play Suzy Homemaker." It was my turn to smile.

Mya batted my chest. "You did not just say that."

"Oh, I did." Parents forgotten, I dipped my head, and brushed my lips over hers. "We'll need a house, something with more space and a yard; oh, and a dog. I've always wanted a dog."

"You're crazy."

"Certifiable." I grinned, but the rough bark of my father's cough, ruined the moment.

"Son, we should probably talk about this."

"Actually, Dad," I said, tucking Mya into my side. "I don't think there's anything else to talk about. We're doing this. You can either get on board with it, or not. But it won't change anything."

Not a damn thing.

Because I wasn't lying when I said I'd give Mya everything she wanted. As I stood there, with my girl by my side, and my parents watching on as if I'd lost my damn mind, a sense of peace washed over me.

And suddenly, nothing about it seemed crazy anymore.

It felt good.

It felt *right.*

It felt like things were exactly the way they were supposed to be.

Mya

"I can't believe you told your parents we're going to foster." I lifted my head off Asher's shoulder and smiled up at him.

"It just came out. He started berating me and something inside me snapped."

"He's just worried, they both are."

"And I get it, but I'm not a kid anymore. We're old enough to make our own decisions."

"And you definitely want this?" I stared at him with wide eyes.

"I want you to be happy, Mya. I want to make a home with you, start a family."

God, the conviction in his voice was everything. Overwhelming in the best kind of way.

Asher meant every word and it just filled me with so much emotion, I bit down gently on my lip. "You know, *if* we look into doing this, it probably means putting a baby on hold for a few years."

Why did the thought of making babies with Asher make my heart flutter?

Because he's your forever guy, your happily-ever-after.

"And that's okay. I'm in no rush for anything. I just want to know it's in the cards."

"It is. It definitely is." I relaxed back into the crook of his arm. "I think I want two kids. A boy and a girl."

"A boy and a girl and a house full of foster kids."

"I don't know about a house full." One would be enough. But ever since I'd had the idea, I couldn't get it out of my head.

"You know, there's something we probably need to discuss first." Asher slid off the couch and onto his knees in front of me. He pulled my hand into his and pressed his lips together.

"Oh my god," I breathed. "Tell me you're not about to do what I think you're about to do?" My heart crashed violently against my ribcage.

"I think I am." His voice trembled. "I didn't plan it like this... Fuck, I don't even have a ring. But I love you, Mya. I love you so fucking much, and sitting here, talking about babies and the future... well, it's got me feeling all kinds of crazy."

"Asher, you don't need to do this... not now... not like this."

"Yeah, babe, I kind of do. Because ring or no ring, I love you and I want to spend the rest of my life loving you. You want a house full of foster kids, but I just want you, Mya. Say yes... say yes and make me the happiest guy on the planet."

"Yes," I cried, launching myself into his arms. We landed in a tangle of limbs and laughter.

"Yes?" Asher stared up at me, and I grinned.

"Yes, I'll marry you, you crazy idiot."

"Oh fuck, did I really just do that?" The blood drained from his face. "I can't believe I did that. I don't even have a ring for fuck's sake."

"Asher, look at me." I gripped his jaw. "I don't need a ring. I don't need a romantic gesture or a huge public display of affection. I only need this." My other hand went to his breastbone, right where his heart lay.

"Yeah?" His voice was small.

"Yeah."

"Good." His expression morphed into pure joy. "Because I'm not taking it back ever. You're mine now, Mya Hernandez, and I'm never letting you go."

17

Asher

"HOLD ON, I'm just connecting Cam now."

"Ash? What is it?" Cameron's face appeared on the screen.

"Can you see us?" I asked, and he nodded. "Jason and Fee too?"

Another nod.

"Okay." I took a deep breath, hugging Mya to my side. "We have something to tell you..."

"Oh my god, you didn't?" Felicity shrieked, clutching Jase's shoulder.

"We did," Mya said, shooting me an infectious smile. "We're engaged."

"Congratulations," Hailee and Cameron said.

"Nice one," Jase grinned, and Fee blurted out, "Let's see it then."

"Well, I... so, funny story..."

"Asher Bennet," she groaned. "Please tell me you didn't propose without a ring."

"It just sort of happened."

"Oh shit," Jase breathed. "You didn't get a ring."

"Hang on a second, it isn't like that," I argued, and Mya buried her face into my neck, smothering her laughter.

"Ash, I was counting on you for the grand romantic gesture," Felicity let out an exasperated breath.

"I think it's sweet," Hailee added. "Spur of the moment. I like that."

"Back up, Giles," Jase was no longer looking at us. Instead, his eyes were fixed on his fiancée. "What the fuck is that supposed to mean? I made a big gesture. Or have you forgotten when I got down on one knee on *national television*?"

"Don't be silly, babe, I haven't forgotten, and it was very sweet, but I had high hopes for Asher and Mya."

"Guys," I interrupted. "It's not like I don't plan on getting a ring. We're going shopping in the week to look—"

"No, no, no." Fee looked mortified. "You can't let Mya pick her own ring, it's bad luck."

"Well, I'm glad we decided to call our *friends* and share our happy news with them."

"Ignore them," Hailee said. "I think it's great news. I'm so happy for you both."

"Thank you." Mya leaned her head on my shoulder.

"Have you talked about wedding plans yet?"

"Seriously?" I balked. "I didn't even get a ring..."

Mya dug her fingers into my ribs, and I yelped. "No, we haven't," she said. "Sometime after graduation. We're in no rush."

"You're the last man standing now, Cam," I smirked. "You know that, right? It's time you upped your game."

"Ash..." Hailee warned.

"Relax, he knows I'm joking."

"Trust me, when I do finally pop the question, I'll make sure to have an actual ring."

"Burn," Jason hissed, unable to hide his amusement.

"Okay, this has been nice and all, but I want some alone time with my fiancée."

"Not until you put a ring on—"

I hit end call and dropped my cell on the counter, pulling Mya around to me.

"Ash, that was rude."

"Nah, they get it." Cameron and Jason were as infatuated with their girlfriends as I was with Mya. They understood what it was like to want to bury yourself so deep inside her, you didn't know where you ended, and she began.

"I need you, Mya." Heat coursed through my veins.

"Well, I'm right here." She licked her lips.

I prowled toward her and ran my hand along the curve of her neck. "Mine," I breathed.

Mya's breath caught, her eyes fluttering closed. "Is this real life?" she whispered.

"Does this feel like real life?" I asked her, leaning in to swipe my tongue over her salty sweet skin.

She reached for me, curling her hands into my Temple U hoodie. Without warning, I slipped my hands to the backs of Mya's thighs and hoisted her against me. Her legs wound around my hips and she shrieked with surprise. Spinning us around, I dropped her on the counter and pushed myself between her thighs. "I love you, Mya. Today, tomorrow, and all the days after."

"Show me..."

Oh, I would.

I intended on showing her all night long.

Mya

"Hey, Mya," Sally looked up from her desk. "The boys are running late."

"Everything okay?" I frowned.

"I think Hugo had a bad day at school. Mariah said some kids have been giving him a hard time."

"They're six."

"I know, right? Kids can be so cruel. But hopefully seeing you will cheer him up."

"Oh, I don't know about that."

"Hey, none of that. You're making a difference, Mya. You just have to trust the process. Be there. Show up. These kids need to learn to trust adults again."

"You're right." I nodded.

"And who knows, maybe today will the day he decides to use his words."

But it wasn't.

As soon as Hugo and his brothers arrived at the center, it was apparent that whatever had gone down had made him even less willing to engage.

But I wouldn't quit. I would be patient. I would wait. And eventually —*hopefully*—I would help.

Another week passed, and I was no closer to getting Hugo to open up to me.

I knew not to take it personally; it wasn't about me. It was about the little boy with eyes the color of honey, clinging onto the stuffed Eagle as if it was his life raft.

While he sank further into himself, his brothers flourished in their new foster home and sessions with Pat and Hershel. Jay liked football, basketball, dodgeball; any sport that involved a ball really. Although Mario enjoyed sport, he was also super creative. He and Hershel had started painting a mural on one of the walls inside the main hall. For a fourteen-year-old, the kid oozed talent. When it was finished, I was hoping to invite Hailee down for the unveiling. I knew she'd have something to say to Mario about it.

"Hey, buddy," I said, sliding onto the bench beside Hugo. "How was your week so far?"

Silence stretched before us as he half-heartedly colored in another printout of Swoop.

"So, remember my boyfriend, Asher? The football player? Well, it's his first game tomorrow."

A flicker of interest flashed across Hugo's face, but he didn't meet my gaze. "The Owls play at the Lincoln Financial Field too, but I bet you already knew that."

More silence. I ran a hand down my face, racking my brain for something, *anything*, that might get Hugo engaging with me. Sally caught my eye across the room and gave me a reassuring smile. A smile that said I was doing the right thing, no matter how useless I felt.

But Hugo didn't engage. He didn't smile or gaze up at me, eager for my tidbits about Asher and the team. He just sat there, coloring in and clutching his stuffed toy as if I wasn't even there.

By the time the session was over, I was emotionally weary. Asher was picking me up and we were going to watch a movie, so once I'd helped clean up, I grabbed my purse out of the locker in the staff room and headed out.

"Bye, guys," I said to Pat and Hershel. They gave me a quick wave and I made a beeline for the door.

Asher met me halfway. "Hey, how was it?"

I shook my head, noticing Sally waiting with the Garcia kids.

"Is that your boyfriend?" Jay called over.

"Jay," Sally warned.

"It's okay," I said, approaching them. "This is Asher, my boyfriend." My lips curved, as I discreetly watched Hugo. He peered up at Asher and then my fiancé did the most incredible thing. He crouched low and held up a fist.

"Hey, you must be Hugo. Mya has told me all about you. She said you want to be just like Fletcher Cox when you're older?"

Jay and Mario could barely contain their excitement, but not Hugo. He simply stared up at Asher, his eyes wide and lips parted.

"Is that Swoop?" Asher asked, completely unfazed at Hugo's lack of reply. "Can I see him?" He slowly extended his hand but didn't get too close.

"Asher," I whispered, not wanting him to scare Hugo. But then slowly, Hugo pushed Swoop forward and placed him in Asher's open palm.

"He looks like he could do with a bath."

Hugo smiled. It was only small, full of trepidation and uncertainty.

But it was a smile.

I looked up at Sally and I knew the emotion in her eyes mirrored the emotion in mine.

"Did Mya tell you it's our first game of the season tomorrow?"

Hugo nodded.

This was freaking huge. I'd spent weeks trying to get the little boy with pain in his eyes to engage with me, and Asher had managed to do it in under a minute.

"I'm going to ask our running back to score a touchdown just for you." Asher handed Swoop back and held up his fist again. "What do you say?"

Hugo made a small fist and bumped it to Asher's. "Awesome. Mya can let you know next time how we got on, okay?" He stood up. "What about you two, you like football?"

Jay pulled up to his full height and puffed out his chest. "Hell yeah." Sally cleared her throat and he murmured, "I mean, sure do."

"What's your name, kid?"

"Jay, and this is my brother Mario."

"Well, it was nice to meet you all. Perhaps I can drop by with a few guys from the team one day and we can hang out?" I nudged him, and he added, "If Sally says it's okay." He shot my mentor a blinding smile.

"I'm sure we can figure something out," she said returning it with her own.

"You three be good, okay? And I'll see you soon." Asher took my hand and guided me away, the sounds of Jay and Mario's excited chatter following us.

"I can't believe you just did that. You were so good with him."

"Nah." Asher gave me a coy look. "I didn't do anything, not really."

"You did. Hugo hasn't responded to anyone at the center like that, or his foster parents. It was... wow."

I couldn't even be envious that Asher had made the breakthrough with Hugo I so desperately wanted, because seeing the guy I loved interact so easily with the lost little boy had been nothing short of heart melting.

"I think I just fell in love with you all over again."

We reached Asher's Jeep and he pulled me into his arms. "He's a cute kid. I can see why he's got you all tied up in knots."

"I just want to reach him, ya know?"

"I know." He leaned in, kissing me softly. "I meant what I said. Me and the guys will drop by one session and play some ball with them. I don't know why we've never thought of it before. Maybe we could get a regular thing going. Coach would love that, having the team giving back to the community."

"That would be... the kids would love that." The other volunteers too no doubt. "You're really okay with this, aren't you?"

"With what?" His brows bunched together.

"The fostering thing... the work I do."

"Mya, I don't know how to make this any clearer to you, but I will always, *always* support your dreams. I fell for your spirit, your passion and drive... your big heart. I'm crazy in love with you, Mya Hernandez, and one day I'm going to put a huge ring on your finger and claim you as mine in front of all our friends, family, and our houseful of foster kids."

"I'd like that."

"Good, because it's happening, Mya. We just gotta finish school first." Asher gazed at me with such reverence it took my breath away.

There had been a time when I had questioned what I'd done to deserve Asher, but I realized now it wasn't about being deserving. Our souls were the same. We loved hard and we fought hard for those we cared about. *That's* what brought us together, and that's what would set the foundation of our life together.

And I couldn't wait.

18

Mya

"THAT'S QUITE the man you have," Sally said when I arrived at New Hope on the Monday after Asher's first game.

"Yeah, he's really something."

"Gosh, I remember that feeling," she sighed. "To be so in love it radiates from your pores." She grinned.

"Crap." I blushed. "I've become *that* girl, haven't I?"

"Yeah, hon, I think you have. But it seems Asher worked his magic because I spoke to Mariah earlier and they had a really good weekend with Hugo."

"He spoke to them?"

"No." Her expression fell a little. "But he was using non-verbal cues and even joined in some of their activities."

"That's amazing."

"I have a good feeling about this, Mya."

I left Sally to her paperwork and made my way into the main hall. I instantly saw the difference in Hugo. He was no longer huddled at one of the tables, clutching his stuffed eagle. Instead, he was on the fringe of the game. He wasn't exactly participating, but he wasn't *not* participating either.

Smiling to myself, I made my way over to him and crouched down. "Hey, buddy. You want to join in?"

He shrugged.

"Maybe there's something else you'd like to do?" He slid his small hand into mine and my heart swelled. Hugo led me over to his usual table and helped himself to a sheet of paper and a crayon, scribbling something. He thrust the paper at me, and I read it aloud.

"Did they win? The Owls?" I smiled, and he nodded. "They sure did, buddy. The running back scored two touchdowns just for you."

His whole face lit up.

"In fact, I have a photo. Asher asked me to show it to you." I dug it out of my pocket and passed it to him. We'd gone to the mall and had it printed out so Hugo could keep it. It was a shot of Asher and the Owls' running back, Aiden, celebrating. They were pointing right at the camera, right at Hugo.

His smile grew.

"You can keep that. See, Asher and some of team signed the back for you." His little fingers clutched the photograph as if it was the most precious thing he'd ever received.

"Remember your envelope is waiting. Whenever you're ready," I said.

I didn't push. It had to be on Hugo's terms, if ever. But he'd made such a huge step and it was all thanks to my fiancé.

God, I would never tire of saying that.

At least, until he was my husband.

I swallowed down the rush of emotion. Something brushed my hand and I looked down to find Hugo tugging my fingers.

"What's up, buddy?" He beckoned me down to him, so I crouched down to meet his eye level.

Tentatively, he leaned in, cupping his hands around his mouth. "O- open envelope please," he said.

"Yeah?" My heart almost burst.

He nodded, looking skittish. I didn't want to scare him off, so I steeled myself and kept an even tone. "That's really great to hear, Hugo. Shall we go get it down?"

"Yes, please." His voice was barely a whisper, but his words were perfect.

I stood and held out my hand. Hugo took it, and everyone in the center stopped to watch as we crossed the room and I plucked the envelope off the shelf, handing it to him.

"Go ahead, open it," I said. "And then we can see if we can make your wish come true."

Asher

"Stop," Diego grunted. "You're like a fucking yo-yo."

"I'm just nervous."

"Dude, it's a bunch of kids. What could possibly go wrong?"

Diego had clearly never met some of the kids Mya worked with. They wouldn't hesitate to tell us if what we had planned was totally lame and uncool. But hopefully they would all enjoy it.

Especially Hugo.

Mya had come home that day—the day he finally chose to use his words—a teary-eyed emotional mess. I'd held her while she cried her happy tears and then she'd given me a blow-by-blow account of what had happened.

The little guy had done amazing, so it was only right he got to see his wish come true. Coach had been able to pull a few strings, and together, he and Sally had arranged the event at the football field today.

"They're here." I spotted Mya and Sally and a handful of the other volunteers walking out of the tunnel with Hugo, his brothers, and some of the other kids in New Hope's program for kids in the foster care system.

They were wide-eyed, their expressions full of wonder as they took in the vastness of the Lincoln Financial Field stadium.

"Come on," I said to the guys. "Let's go introduce ourselves. And remember, keep cussing to a minimum."

"Yeah, yeah, Bennet, keep your hair on. I think we can behave for an hour." Aiden chuckled.

"Hey." Mya reached us. We were here on official team business, but it didn't stop me leaning in to press a chaste kiss to her cheek. "They're so excited," she whispered.

"How are you all doing?" I asked the huddle of kids. Jay and Mario were grinning ear to ear, but most of the other kids looked like Hugo, completely awestruck.

"You ready to play some ball with us?"

A chorus of 'yeahs' filled the air. "Well, before we get started with some warm-up activities, I have a little surprise for you. Bring him out, Coach," I yelled.

"You did it," Mya breathed, reaching my hand, as we watched Swoop the eagle traipse out onto the field.

Hugo clapped his hands with glee, and I crouched down to his level. "What do you think, buddy?"

He looked at me with tears shining in his eyes, and whispered, "Best. Day. Ever."

Mya

"Hey guys, over here." Faith beckoned us over to where she and Rex were sitting. "We didn't think you were going to make it."

"We almost didn't," Asher murmured, and I elbowed him in the ribs.

"Play nice," I mouthed.

When Faith had called to ask if Asher and I would meet her for drinks, I'd almost told her no. Things between us were okay, but I'd had no intentions of putting her and Asher in a room together anytime soon. But he'd overheard the call and said everyone deserved a second chance. So here we were, meeting Faith and... Rex, for drinks.

Odd, she hadn't mentioned him in her original invitation.

"I hear congratulations are in order," Rex said to Asher.

"Yeah, thanks."

"Listen, I hope there are no hard feelings about before. You guys are perfect for each other, and I was being a judgmental bastard."

"No hard feelings." Asher squeezed my hand under the table, his touch lingering on my finger.

We still hadn't picked out a ring, but honestly, I didn't need one. I had everything I could ever want. We were engaged, I turned twenty-one soon, and things at the center were going great since Asher got the team involved.

The session that day had gone so well, both Coach Johnson and Sally had wanted to make it a regular thing. She was currently looking at setting up the infrastructure to make it a permanent feature of the center's program.

It had been such a great day, watching the kids interact and bond with the team. Hugo had followed Asher around like a lost puppy and the two of them had become fast friends. So much so, that Asher had signed up for the program's in-house training sessions so he could be an official volunteer.

Life was good.

Perfect, even.

We'd celebrated our engagement over the weekend back in Rixon. Asher's mom had invited my aunt for dinner and the five of us enjoyed good food and easy conversation, the tension of our past staying right where it belonged. Even Asher's dad had managed to congratulate us, hugging me tight and telling me that the wedding was taken care of; all we had to do was let him know what we wanted.

But I didn't want a big fanfare. All I needed was something small with the people I cared about most in the world.

"I like this place," I said, glancing around the coffee shop Faith had picked. "It has character."

"Right? We come here a lot."

"You do?" I frowned, glancing between her and Rex. Guilt shone in Faith's eyes.

"Actually, that's why I asked you to come. There's something I have to tell you... and I don't want it to be weird, all right? But you're one of my best friends and I know I was a total bitch at the beginning of the semester—"

"Faith take a breath. What is going on?"

"Oh, Boo Boo, just spit it out already. She isn't going to care."

Boo Boo? What the hell?

Asher almost choked on his coffee.

"Me and Rex, well, we're—"

"Together. We're together, okay?" He huffed dramatically. "Good. Now we can all move on with life."

"I'm sorry, can we just back up a second, to the part where you just said the two of you are..."

"*Together*?" Rex smirked.

"I did not see that coming." Asher let out a low whistle and I nudged him again.

"I know, I know." Faith buried her face in her hands. "I'm a complete hypocrite."

"How long has this been going on?" I asked.

"Officially, a couple of weeks."

"And unofficially?"

"We were fucking most of the summer."

"*Rex*!" Faith hissed.

"So the summer of sexual inhibition and self-discovery was—"

"I lied. And I feel like a horrible person. But things with Rex were confusing and I didn't want to jump headfirst from one relationship into another. God, you must think I'm such a bitch."

"Faith, stop." I sighed. "Are you happy?"

"Yeah, I mean... it's new and unexpected. But Rex is so different to Max."

"Well, duh." He grinned, sliding his arm around her shoulder.

"I'm sorry, but I don't see it, at all," Asher said.

"That makes two of us," Faith offered him an uncertain smile. "But the heart wants what the hearts want, am I right? Listen, I really am sorry about everything I said to Mya."

"She's forgiven you," he said, "so I guess that makes us cool."

"As long as you're happy," I added, "what me or anyone else thinks shouldn't matter."

"You're right, it shouldn't. But I don't always find it easy to shake people's expectations."

"You'll get there, Boo Boo." Rex nuzzled her neck, and I sat there watching, completely bewildered. They were so... different. Faith was all about appearances and what other people thought, and Rex was... Rex. He didn't really conform to gender stereotypes or label himself as straight or gay.

It was weird... but even weirder was the fact that as I watched them whisper to one another, wrapped up in their own little bubble, it didn't seem weird at all.

"Well, I don't know about anyone else," Asher said. "But I'm really glad we cleared the air."

My friends chuckled, and I smiled, a strange sensation washing over me.

I'd been Faith once upon a time. A girl lost and unsure of her place in the world, wanting to break free from the stereotypes forced on her. Then I'd found Asher and he'd taught me love had no limits. It was hard and messy and chaotic, but worth the fight and the tears and the heartache.

Love was what made us human.

But how someone else loved us made us feel more than human.

And Asher...

He loved me enough to make me feel like the luckiest girl in the world.

PART III

Senior Year

19

Cameron

"CHASE, A WORD?" Coach beckoned me toward his office, and I weaved my way through the locker room. The air was warm, the smell of sweaty cleats and wet grass lingering.

Practice had been grueling, and I knew Coach Byford probably wanted to know where my head was at.

"Hey, Coach."

"Take a seat, son." He motioned to the seat opposite his desk and I sat. "Do I need to be worried?" Fingers steepled, he sat back, studying me.

"It's my brother, sir. He's..." Fuck. I didn't know what the hell was going on with Xander. He'd only been in second grade a few weeks and my parents had already been called in four times.

Four.

"He's finding it tough."

Coach whipped off his ball cap and let out a long breath. "That's rough, Cameron. I feel for the little fella, I do. But this is your senior year, son, and the team have a real shot at going all the way. I need to know my best wide receiver has his head on straight."

"I know, Coach. I'm sorry."

"You're a good brother, Cam, and you're a good guy. But the team needs you, here, on the field."

I nodded, unable to reply over the lump in my throat.

"Scouts are going to be making the rounds soon enough, and you've got it, son. But you need to leave all the other crap at the door, okay? When you come into my locker room, you come with a clear head and—"

"And hunger for the win."

"Damn straight. Now get out of here."

I got up and made for the door, but Coach's voice stopped me at the last second. "And Chase?"

"Yes, sir?"

"You ever need to talk, my door is always open."

"Thanks, Coach." I gave him a small nod before slipping back into the locker room. My quarterback, a guy called Dominic Sanchez, was waiting.

"Everything good?"

"He's worried." My lips pursed.

"Does he need to be worried?"

"I'll be okay."

He clapped me on the back. "Do you know what I think you need?"

"No, but I'm sure you're going to enlighten me."

Dom guided me over to our corner of the benches. "You need to go find that woman of yours and let her help relieve all the tension you got going on, if you know what I'm saying."

"Amen to that, brother." Dylan, our running back, held his hand out and the two of them fist bumped.

"Beats hanging around with you bunch of losers." I shot back around a smirk. But it was all front.

It had been for a while.

I loved my team. I loved my classes and living in Michigan with Hailee.

But I didn't love being four-hundred miles from home, from my kid brother and his struggles.

Everyone—Mom, Dad, Jase and Asher, even Hailee—kept telling me it was only eight more months. Eight more months until we could move back to Rixon and be closer to my family. But I couldn't shake the pit in my stomach, the feeling that this was only the beginning, that Xander knew something the rest of us didn't.

And that terrified the shit out of me.

"Hailee?" I threw my keys on the sideboard and moved deeper into our loft apartment overlooking the Huron River.

The chilled beats of Röyksopp drifted down the hall and I knew exactly where to find her. Grabbing a beer from the refrigerator, I kicked off my sneakers and headed for the mezzanine. Sure enough, Hailee was standing over a canvas with her back to me, paintbrush in hand.

I leaned against the wall for a second, drinking in the sight of her. While I'd found it hard being away from Rixon—from my family—Hailee had flourished at Michigan. She loved every second of her arts degree and her talent had grown substantially. So much so that last spring we'd decided to get a bigger place, somewhere to accommodate her growing collection of paintings and sculptures.

Our new place was perfect. It was an industrial warehouse that had been converted into huge open plan apartments. Ours was lucky enough to have a mezzanine that was perfect for Hailee's studio, without her feeling locked away in a different part of the apartment.

Her body swayed gently to the music as she brushed long sweeping arcs over the splodges of color already decorating the canvas. Almost four years later, and I still didn't really understand most of her art. But I loved watching her. Her work attire didn't hurt the eyes either.

She currently stood in an oversized white shirt that grazed her thighs. Hailee had pulled her hair into a loose bun at the nape of her neck, and from the way the shirt was hanging off one shoulder, I knew she'd probably left some buttons open.

Taking a long pull on my beer, I placed it on the sideboard and quietly moved closer. She was too lost in her art to notice me. Or, at least, I was thought she was, until she said, "How long were you watching me?"

"Busted." I smiled, brushing the stray hairs off her neck and leaning in to press a kiss there.

A shudder rolled through her, and Hailee glanced back at me. "What is it? What's wrong?"

Her words wrapped around me like a warm blanket. She knew. Hailee always knew when something was wrong, but I tried my best to make sure she didn't know just how much I was struggling. I didn't want to be a burden, not on her. Not when she'd worked so hard to get here. Studying at STAMPS art and design school had always been her dream, and I'd be damned if I did anything to ruin that.

Besides, it was only eight more months.

"Practice was tough."

Her brows furrowed. "Let me finish up here and we can—"

"Is it an important piece?" I flicked my gaze to the canvas.

"Just something for me."

Thank fuck.

I pulled the brush from her fingers and threw it down on the tray.

"Cameron, what are you—"

My fingers slid to her neck, my thumbs smoothing over her soft skin. Hailee's breath caught. "That bad, huh?" Her eyes darkened.

"It was pretty bad." I'd fumbled the ball, barely caught Dom's passes, and defense had taken me down seven out of ten plays.

It was a fucking shit show.

"I'm sorry." She fisted my hoodie, anchoring us together. "What do you need?"

"You," I breathed against her lips. "I only need you."

Hailee

I felt Cameron's torment as he kissed me. I knew he was worried about Xander; it had gotten worse every year that we were away from Rixon. He constantly reassured me he was okay, that he wanted to graduate from Michigan before we decided what to do *after*, but it was taking its toll.

His tongue slipped past my lips, curling around mine. Cameron kissed the way he played ball, sure and steady and in complete control. And it wasn't long before our hands were searching for skin, desperate to touch and explore.

"This needs to go," he said between kisses, fingering the buttons of my work shirt.

"Here, let me." I broke away, helping him undo the buttons, baring myself to him.

More often than not, I painted in just a shirt. I liked the freedom and it saved on laundry.

Cam dipped his head, kissing the curve of my breasts as he backed me against the wall.

"We could take this downstairs," I suggested. It was a mess up here.

"No," he breathed. "I need you, Hailee." His fingers went to his sweats, pushing them down his hips right along with his boxers. His hoodie and t-shirt went next until he was standing in front of me stark naked.

God, he was beautiful. Strong and stacked, his torso was a solid slab of muscle, each ab perfectly chiseled and defined.

I reached for him, trailing my hand over the cherry blossom snaking up his arm. Next, I traced the tattoo he'd gotten of the artwork I'd painted on him with my own hand in senior year. It was our initials—HR and CC—looped together with a delicate heart over his pec.

"What?" he asked, his voice a hushed whisper.

"I love you, Cameron." *So much it scares me.*

He crowded me against the wall and picked me up, pressing my back against the bare brick. "Not as much as I love you." He grasped himself and lined himself up with my center, pressing into me.

"Oh God," I moaned as I sank down on him.

Cameron stilled, touching his head to mine and taking a shuddering breath.

"It's okay." I laid a hand on his cheek. "I'm here, Cameron, I'm right here."

Burying his face in my neck, he pulled out slowly before thrusting back inside. It was deep like this, intense and overwhelming in the best kind of way.

"Harder," I said, letting my head fall back. "Take what you need."

Cam squeezed my hip, hard enough to leave a bruise as he rocked into me over and over. "Fuck, Sunshine," he groaned. "You feel like heaven."

He attacked my mouth like a man starved, all tongue and teeth and teasing strokes.

"Cameron..." His name was a breathy plea on my lips as I drowned in sensation.

"Feel me, Hailee." *Thrust.* "Feel what you do to me." *Thrust.* "Nothing... *nothing* will ever feel as good as this."

He went harder... faster... *deeper*, driving me into the wall until I knew

I'd have friction burns. But it didn't matter. Cameron needed this and I wanted to be the one to give it to him.

Only ever me.

"I love you," he panted against my damp skin. "I love you so fucking much." Cameron kissed my throat, licking and sucking, branding me with his lips and searing me with his touch.

"Harder," I cried, clinging onto Cam's broad shoulders for dear life as he pushed me toward the precipice of sheer bliss.

"Fuck, Hailee." He slammed inside me, once, twice... until I shattered around him, crying his name over and over.

Cameron stilled, riding his own waves of pleasure. He gathered me into his arms and just held me.

"It's okay," I whispered against the corner of his mouth. "It's going to be okay."

But as I said the words, I knew it was a lie.

Because this was one thing I didn't know how to fix.

Cameron

"Come here," I patted the bed and Hailee climbed in beside me. After we'd cleaned up, she had reheated some leftovers and we'd eaten together before calling it a night.

I was weary from practice and Hailee was tired from the way I'd used her body against the wall.

"How are you feeling?" she asked me.

"I'm just worried about him."

"I know. But you can't fix everything, Cam."

I couldn't, I knew that. But if I was there, if Xan had me there to talk to, to distract him...

Fuck.

Guilt chewed me up inside. He was my kid brother. My little shadow. He was lost and no one knew how to help him.

"They're coming to the game Friday?"

"Yeah, Dad booked them into the hotel on Denton Avenue."

"I'm sure seeing you will cheer him up."

"Yeah." He usually perked up whenever I went home or he visited us, but as he'd gotten older, he'd started to pull away. Although I knew it was irrational, I couldn't deny it felt like he was punishing me.

"Can I ask you something?" Hailee sat up, and I nodded. "Do you ever regret coming to Michigan with me?"

"What? *No*! Hailee, that's not—"

"I'm not trying to make you feel guilty, I'm not." She gave me an uncertain smile. "I'm just trying to understand how I can help. It's senior year. I don't want you to spend our last year here together resenting me."

"Hailee, stop." I cupped her face, stroking her cheek. "I don't ever want you to feel that way."

"So, you're happy here?"

"I..." I couldn't do it. I couldn't lie to her, not when she'd been there every step of the way.

"I can't help but wonder if he'd be this way if I'd have stayed." The words were like a sheet of ice between us and I instantly regretted them.

"You never said anything." Her voice cracked. "All this time and you never—"

"I didn't want you to think I didn't want to be here. I do, so much. But he's my brother, and he isn't getting better, he's getting worse."

"So, what do we do?" Her eyes filled with tears and I hated that I was the one to put them there. But this conversation was long overdue.

Over the last couple of years, Xander had become the elephant in the room. But I constantly reassured her this was what I wanted. Because it had been.

When my mom got sick, Hailee had stood by me through the hardest few weeks of my life. I wanted to come to Michigan for her, to put her first. But now I was stuck between a rock and a hard place. Xander was family, my blood, and everything in me was screaming at me that he needed me... but Hailee, she was my heart, my home.

How the fuck was I supposed to choose between them?

The answer was, I couldn't.

20

Cameron

"CAMERON." Xander shot at me like a bull out of a gate and I opened my arms catching him.

"Hey, Xan, it's good to see you." He clung to me like a spider monkey, so I slid my arms under his butt and carried him into our building.

"How's school?"

"Ugh. Don't ask. I hate that place."

"No way? Don't you have Mr. Gellar? I remember that guy, he was always a hoot."

"Well, he's a real asshat now."

"Hey, watch it," I scolded him, and he grumbled, "Sorry, Cam."

Hailee and my parents trailed in behind us, and I lowered my brother to the floor to greet them properly.

"Son, it's good to see you." Dad stepped forward and pulled me into his arms. I could see the worry lines around his eyes, but they were no longer because of mom. Instead they were caused by the seven-year-old currently drilling holes into the side of my head.

"Hey, Dad."

"Cameron," Mom nudged her way between us, looking up at me with weary eyes. "Has it really only been a few weeks?"

"Yeah." I chuckled, but it was strained.

"And Hailee," Mom went to my girl. "You get more beautiful every time I see you."

"Thanks, Karen."

"Excited for the game tonight?" Dad asked.

"Yeah, but I'll not be excited about spending the day with this little squirt tomorrow." I tackle hugged Xander, and his laughter was like music to my ears.

"Oh, Clarke, look."

Xander instantly stiffened at Mom's words. "Relax," I said. "She's just happy—"

"Yeah, whatever." He shirked me off and went and sat on the couch. We all watched him, silence descending over the four of us.

"Why don't I make some coffee?" Hailee suggested, giving me a reassuring smile.

"Thanks," I said, sliding my eyes back to Xander. He'd pulled out his handheld computer game, his thumbs working overtime as he pressed the buttons.

"How is he, really?" I asked my parents and their expressions fell.

"We don't know what to do anymore, Cameron. He's completely shut us out."

"I'll talk to him." I ran a hand through my hair, releasing a heavy sigh. But as I watched my brother, one of the most important people in my life, I feared talking wasn't enough anymore.

Hailee

"Are you excited to watch Cameron?" I asked Xander as we sat in our seats. It was the opening game of the season, and a big rivalry game against Ohio State, so the atmosphere in the Michigan Stadium was electric.

Karen and Clarke sat on the other side of Xander, giving the two of us some space. I'd noticed how strained things were between them and their son, and my heart ached for them all.

He shrugged, and I nudged his shoulder. "It's okay to be excited, you know. But if you're not, that's okay too."

"I just really miss him," he admitted.

"He misses you too. So much. He talks about you all the time."

"He does?" He stared up at me with big blue eyes, just like his brother's.

"Yeah. Cameron loves you so much, Xander."

"But he left." His lip quivered, but he steeled his expression.

For a seven-year-old, Xander Chase had excellent resolve. It's why his mom and dad struggled so much to get him to open up to them.

"You know Cameron leaving had nothing to do with you, don't you?"

He shrugged again, just as the team jogged out onto the field. The noise was deafening and Xander seemed to shrink into his chair. He leaned into me as if he needed the protection, but he didn't get too close.

My heart swelled with pride at seeing Cameron in his maize and blue jersey.

When they had found out his mom was sick, he'd been prepared to give up his dream of football. But, in the end, he hadn't had to. His parents were so proud of him and everything he'd achieved so far at Michigan. But senior year was his year.

At least, I hoped it was.

"They're looking good," Clarke yelled over the chorus of cheers and chatter. "Strong."

"It's their year." I grinned at him.

"I really hope so."

Xander peeked up at me and I frowned. "What?"

"Are you and my brother going to get married one day?"

"I..." I stuttered over the words. "Maybe. I mean, I hope so."

Karen and Clarke smothered their laughter.

"Why?"

Please don't say you don't want us to. My heart galloped in my chest as he stared up at me before beckoning me closer. I dipped my head and waited.

"Maybe if you do, and you come back to Rixon, I can come live with you."

Oh God.

My heart.

It broke for the boy looking at me with nothing but hope and sadness in his eyes.

It broke for his parents, trying so hard to be unaffected by their son's growing detachment.

But most of all it broke because I couldn't give him the answer he thought he wanted to hear.

"Hailee?" he said.

"Uh, it's not something I can really answer, buddy."

Disappointment flashed in his eyes.

"We still have to get through college and then figure out what we want to do."

"You'll be coming home though, right?"

Crap.

This was not going well.

I was digging a deeper and deeper hole. I glanced over at Karen, but she and Clarke were deep in conversation.

"Wherever we decide to settle down, you will always be welcome, Xander." I chose my words carefully. "If we get a place big enough, you can even have your own room. We can decorate and—"

The announcer's voice came over the speaker and relief flooded me.

I gave Xander a reassuring smile, but he barely returned it, and I hoped the game would be enough to take his mind off things.

Cameron

"Okay, listen up and listen good, ladies," Coach said, his eyes glancing to the scoreboard. We were tied with a little over a minute on the clock. "We've got a shot at one final play, and we need to make it a good one. Because anything less is not an option, you hear me?"

"Yes, sir."

"Good. Now get out there and show them why that championship is coming home this season."

"Dom, take it away, son."

"Hands in," he yelled, and we all piled our hands in the center.

It had been a brutal game, our teams matched in speed, strength, and grit. But with Hailee and my family in the audience, I'd found my flow, scoring touchdowns on five out of seven passes. The only problem was Ohio had also scored.

"Wolverines on three."

"One… two… three… Wolverines." We broke from the huddle and Dom jogged beside me. "You ready?"

I gave him a stiff nod.

He curled his hand around my neck and pulled me into him, our helmets crashing together. "We've earned this, Chase. It's senior year and that championship is ours, you hear me?"

Adrenaline pulsed through me, the roar of the crowd like liquid ecstasy coursing through my veins.

When I was out here, on the field with my team, playing to the cheers of over one-hundred thousand fans, it was easy to forget about all the other shit. Xander. Hailee. My future. Decisions I wasn't sure I was ready to make.

Out here, it all went away until there was nothing but me, the ball, and a line of defensive players all looking to stop me from reaching my destination.

I knew it wouldn't last though. When the final whistle sounded, and the noise stopped, it would all come rushing back.

But for now, I was invincible.

"Let's give them a show," I called to Dom and he grinned.

"What are you thinking?"

"Remember when we were goofing around with Dylan the other day?

"Yeah?"

I nodded.

"It's a big risk."

"We can pull it off."

"Let's do it then." He jogged off toward Dylan to give him the instructions as the rest of us moved into position.

The crowd quieted as we waited for the clock to resume. If we wanted to score, we needed to move fast and execute the play to the letter.

"Blue twenty-two," Dom yelled. "Blue twenty-two." A couple of players dropped back, and the offensive line began shuffling, trying to read the play.

I stayed light on my feet waiting for the snap to Dom. He caught it and hiked the ball to Dylan who began charging for the line of scrimmage, only to slow at the line and pass back to Dominic. The offense scrambled and I flew. Pumping my legs hard, I moved into the open space, extending my hand to give him the signal. The ball cut through the air and I leaped, curling my hand around the leather. The confused Ohio players immediately switched direction to close in around me. But I was too fast, cool air whipping through my helmet as I push harder… *faster*… nothing but the end zone and victory in sight.

Fingers grazed my shoulder as a defense player reached me, but I shirked him off, dodging right and straight into the end zone.

"Touchdooooown," the announcer's voice rang out through the stadium, the collective hoots and hollers of the tens of thousands of fans deafening.

My team jogged over, all wanting to celebrate our first win of the season against one of our biggest rivals.

"That's how you get shit done," Dom said, smashing his helmet to mine. "Fuck, I could kiss you."

"Please don't," I chuckled, trying desperately to hold onto the high. But no sooner had it arrived than it started to dissipate.

Xander was out there somewhere with my parents. They would look to me for answers, answers I didn't have.

"Get over here," Coach yelled, and we all jogged toward him. "What the hell was that, Sanchez?"

"That was getting the job done, sir."

"That flea flicker your idea, son?"

"The credit is all Chase's, sir."

Coach set his eyes in my direction. "Risky move."

"Knew we could do it, sir," I said, feeling the weight of the shoulder pads start to crush my lungs.

I needed to get off this field, and fast.

"Lucky for you, it worked."

I went to move around him, but Coach caught my arm, and I glanced back. "You played well out there tonight, son. Keep it up and you'll have nothing to worry about when the scouts come around."

His words only made my chest tighter. "Thanks, Coach," I mumbled, before tearing off my helmet and jogging toward the tunnel. I needed a shower and then I needed to find the one person who could make it all go away.

Not even an hour later, I filed out of the stadium to find Hailee, Xander, and my parents waiting for me.

"Congratulations." My girl rushed into my arms and wrapped herself around me. "You were amazing."

"I don't feel so amazing. Their defense are like giants."

She stepped back, narrowing her eyes. "Are you okay?"

"Nothing a little TLC from my favorite girl won't cure." I leaned in to kiss her, forgetting we had an audience.

Until my brother made a retching noise.

"Get over here, squirt," I said, crooking my finger. Xander came willingly, wedging himself between Hailee and me.

"We need to talk," she mouthed, flicking her eyes to him.

Dread snaked through me.

Something had happened.

"Are you okay?" I mouthed back, and she nodded, but there was a sadness in her expression that had alarm bells ringing.

But in true Hailee fashion, she pasted on a smile and said, "Right, who wants ice cream?"

"Can I have sprinkles?" Xander slipped out of my arms and stared up at us.

"Of course you can, buddy. You can have whatever you want."

"I want three flavors."

"You got it, Xan."

We moved over to where Mom and Dad were hovering. "Congratulations, Son."

"Thanks, Dad."

"You pulled out a nice play at the end."

"Coach almost blew a gasket."

"I bet. But it paid off."

"Come here, sweetheart." Mom pulled me into a hug. "I'm so proud of you."

She told me every time we were together. It was as if after her illness she wanted to treasure every moment, imprint every memory. She was healthy now, but I guess something like that changed you.

I knew it had changed me to some extent.

"The team not celebrating?" Dad asked as we headed for their SUV.

"Yeah, there'll be a party or something."

"You can always go after we—"

"Don't do that," I said. "I want to be here, with you guys." My arm slipped tighter around Xander.

"You're a good man, Cameron." Dad squeezed my shoulder.

"Thanks." Emotion clogged my throat, but it was nothing compared to the way my heart squeezed at how tight Xander clung to me as we made our way across the parking lot.

21

Hailee

"IS HE ASLEEP?" I asked.

"Yeah, finally."

"Come here." Crossing the room to Cameron, I pulled him into my arms. "It's going to be okay."

"Is it?" His voice cracked. "Because I'm not sure anymore."

Xander had wanted to stay with us at the apartment, so we'd agreed he could. Karen and Clarke had watched on with a mix of dejection and relief as we left their car and made our way into the building. They were staying at a hotel two blocks over, but would join us for breakfast in the morning.

"Tell me what he said to you at the game." Cameron stared down at me with so much pain, I wanted to take it from him.

"He asked if we were getting married..." I took a deep breath, knowing how greatly my next words would affect him., "and then he asked if he could move in with us."

"Fuck, he said that?"

I nodded, giving him some space to digest things.

Cameron ran a hand over his head and cupped the back of his neck. "What am I supposed to do here?"

"You just keep doing what you're doing. Xander knows you love him, Cameron. He knows your mom and dad love him. He's just a little messed up right now, but he'll grow out of it."

"Will he?" Cam dropped down onto the edge of the bed, burying his face in his hands. I sat beside him, offering my comfort if he needed it.

"You know, tonight, at the game, I wanted it. I wanted to go pro. I don't know what happened. One minute, I was worrying about Xander and my parents and you, and the next, I was so wrapped up in the game..."

"Hey, don't feel bad." I cupped his face, forcing him to look at me. "You should never feel bad for wanting to follow your dreams, Cam. Ever."

"I still can't believe he said he wants to live with us."

"It's like he's waiting for you to go home."

"I know."

"Do you want that?" I asked, unsure I wanted the answer. "To go back to Rixon?"

"I just want to help him."

"Even if it costs you your dream?"

He let out a weary sigh. "You're looking at me like it's not only my dream I'm sacrificing."

My stomach knotted. "So, you are considering giving everything up?" The words spilled out before I could stop them. "I'm sorry, that's not fair."

It was his brother. His kid brother who had almost lost his mom. I couldn't resent that.

I wouldn't.

Not when I'd pulled him away from them.

"I wish I could wave a magic wand and make all this better for you and Xander."

"I know you do, and I love you for it." Cameron reached for me, fisting the oversized Wolverines t-shirt and pulling me into his arms.

"We get through senior year and then I go home, at least until this stuff with Xander gets better. He needs me, Hailee. I can't just turn my back on him. I can't..." His eyes shuttered, torment etched into the lines of his handsome face. "But if you don't want to follow me, I'll understand. I know you have a better shot at following your dreams here or in Philly."

"Stop." I leaned in touching my head to his. "Where you go, I go."

"Yeah?" Relief washed over him.

"Cameron, as if you need to ask."

"It won't be forever, I promise," he breathed the words as if they were hard to say. "Just until he's in a better place."

"It's okay. He needs you."

"And I need *you*. I will always need you, Hailee. I hope you know that." He stared at me with such intensity, I sucked in a sharp breath.

"I do."

Cameron

"Can't I stay another night?"

"We need to get home, sweetheart," Mom reached for Xander, but he dodged her advance. The flash of hurt in her eyes gutted me.

"Xander, please, don't make a scene. Cameron and Hailee need to—"

"Hey," I said, finally making myself known. "Are you all set?"

"Yes," my parents said at the same time as Xander grumbled, "No."

"I think Hailee wanted some help, if you two want to—"

"Sure thing." Dad squeezed my shoulder, guiding Mom away.

"Hey, squirt. What's going on?" I sat down beside my brother.

"I don't want to go back to Rixon."

"No? But what about school? Your friends?"

"I know Mom and Dad call you and tell you everything, Cam." He flicked his knowing eyes to mine.

"They're worried. We all are."

"It's not like I try to make people hate me." He shrugged.

"Nobody hates you, Xan." God. He was seven. It was too young to harbor such negativity but here we were.

"Well, they don't like me. Harry Jones and his friends all say I'm weird."

"You are not weird." A sense of protectiveness flooded me, and I wanted nothing more than to call Jase and Asher and ride down to Rixon and hunt down Harry Jones and teach the little punk a lesson or two.

"It's okay, Cam. I know I'm not like most other kids."

Fuck.

His words were so innocent, but there was so much conviction behind them that he might as well have punched his little fist into my chest and ripped out my heart.

"You've gotta tell me how I can fix this, Xander."

He looked at me with big, sad eyes and said, "When are you coming home?"

"As soon as senior year is done, I'll be back. It's not long really, not when you take out the holidays and spring break."

"And then I can come stay with you and Hailee?"

Jesus. This was really happening. My kid brother was choosing me over our parents.

"You can come and stay, yeah. Hailee told me the two of you talked about it?"

"She didn't really give me an answer."

"You'll always be welcome to stay over, Xan, you know that. But Mom and Dad would be really upset if you didn't want to live with them anymore."

"But I want to live with you." He twisted his hands in his lap.

I wanted to ask him why, to make him tell me why he felt this way, but I knew he didn't have the answers. If he did, we wouldn't be sitting here right now.

"Xan, look at me." I slid my fingers under his chin and tilted his face to mine. "Do you have any idea how much we all love you?" His lip quivered. "Mom and Dad would do anything to make you happy, but you need to talk to them, buddy. They can't help if they don't know what's wrong."

Silent tears began rolling down his cheeks and he wrapped his arms around me, burying his face into my chest. "I don't want anyone to leave me, not again," he murmured against my sweater.

"Seven months, Xan," I said, rubbing his back. "Seven months and I'll be home." But as I said the words, I already knew I'd be looking at my schedule to see where I could make more trips back to Rixon. I couldn't ignore this, not anymore. Something was going on with Xander, something huge, and he needed me.

"HEY, you don't call, you never write," Asher chuckled. "I'm beginning to think you don't love me anymore."

"I texted you just the other day."

"Text smext. I need to hear your voice."

"I'm hanging up—"

"Relax, I'm just busting your balls. What's up?"

"I need to cancel guys weekend."

"What?" he gasped. "No way!"

We'd arranged a weekend away since we all had the same bye week. It never happened, so we'd planned on making the most of it.

"I'm going home, I need to—"

"Xander?"

"Yeah. He needs me."

"So, we'll all go," he said, as if it was the simplest answer.

"But we have the tickets." We were going to catch an Eagles game. Jase's dad had some old friends in high places and they'd managed to get us VIP passes.

"Xander is more important. We can take him to a Rixon Raiders game and boost his cool-o-meter. The girls will be lining up for a chance with the Xan-man."

"Ash, he's seven." I pinched the bridge of my nose.

"Nothing wrong with starting early."

"I can't believe they gave you your foster license." He and Mya had been approved over the summer. They didn't plan to become active foster parents until after graduation, but they had wanted to be prepared.

"What? The kids love me." He chuckled. "But seriously, me and Jase can come with you. Xander will love it. We'll be like the four amigos causing chaos. Just like old times."

"I appreciate it, Ash, I do, but..."

"You need some bro time?"

"Yeah, I think we do. He's got this crazy idea into his head that he wants to live with me and Hailee when we move back to Rixon."

"Hold up." I heard the surprise in his voice. "You made the decision?"

"Yeah, I think so. He's getting worse. My mom and dad don't know what to do with him anymore. Things will be easier if I'm around."

"I get it, I do, and I hope you don't think I'm talking out of line here, but do you think that's the right move?"

"What do you mean?" My brows bunched together.

"Xander is already incredibly attached to you. If you go back, it might only compound that. He needs to deal with whatever it is going on in his head. The counselor should be able to help."

Xander had recently started sessions with a new therapist. But he was resistant, unable to articulate why he felt the way he felt.

"How are your mom and dad holding up?"

"It's taking its toll. Mom isn't sleeping and my dad just throws himself into work and then feels guilty."

"That's rough. I'm sorry, Cam. If there's anything we can do..."

"Thank you. I'm hoping if I'm around more, he'll settle down at school. I made him a calendar of every weekend I'll be home."

It had been Hailee's idea. We'd printed it out and it doubled as a countdown until graduation. Mom had helped Xander pin it on his wall beside his bed, and every morning, he crossed off another day.

I couldn't get back to Rixon every weekend, not with games, but I'd managed to work it so I could go home at least once a month. Then there were longer holidays like Thanksgiving and Christmas.

It was a lot to juggle but I needed to make it work.

"So if you're planning on returning to Rixon after graduation," his voice sobered, "what does that mean for the draft?"

"I haven't gotten that far yet."

Xander needed me *now*. He needed to know I planned on being around more. Everything else had to take a backseat for now.

"I get it. I'm here, whatever you or your family needs."

We chatted for a little bit longer. I asked about Mya and we talked about Hailee's latest installation at an independent gallery in the city. By the time we hung up, I felt lighter.

Talking to my best friends had that effect on me. We'd been through so much together. It felt good knowing that they always had my back, no matter what.

Over three years apart, but we were stronger than ever.

Brothers bound by choice not blood.

Family.

And I wouldn't change them for the world.

22

Hailee

SENIOR YEAR WASN'T QUITE what I expected. I thought Cameron and I would enjoy our last year of college, that I would flourish with my art and he would carve out a name for himself among NFL scouts.

The reality was quite a bit different.

After that first game, when his parents and Xander had visited, Cameron began splitting his time between Michigan and Rixon as much as he could.

Sometimes I went with him, but most of the time, I didn't. I had classes, friends, various installations across the city.

I had a life... *here.*

But more and more, his life became back in Rixon.

I watched him pack his weekend bag with a tightness across my chest. It was the third time this month.

"I thought you were going to try to stick to the schedule," I said.

"I was." He leaned down and kissed my hair. "But Xander has been doing better. I don't want to ruin all his progress."

"But what about classes Monday?"

"I spoke to Professor Joffrey. As long as I get a copy of the notes and submit my essay on time, he's happy to excuse me."

"And practice?" The team were on a winning streak, and Coach Byford was determined for them to go all the way to playoffs.

"I'll be back. I told Xan it's a fly-by visit. If I leave tonight—"

"Tonight?"

"Yeah, I thought I told you that was the plan?" Cam stuffed another t-shirt in his bag.

"We just got home, it's late." Not to mention the fact he'd just played a football game. "You can leave in the morning. You'll be there tomorrow night and then you can have all day Sunday together."

"I promised him I'd take him to the park."

"You can't go to the park Sunday?"

"Hailee..." Cam paused what he was doing and lifted his eyes to mine. "I need to do this."

"I know. I just don't like the idea of you driving through the night after a game."

"I'll be careful, I promise. I'll stop halfway and get some rest."

My lips pursed. I didn't like the sound of that any better.

"What?" he asked.

"I just worry you're pushing yourself too hard. I know you want to help Xander, but you can't be everything to everyone, Cam. Something has to give eventually."

And the way we were headed, I was starting to wonder if it was me.

If I was the thing to give.

Between practice, classes, and going back and forth to Rixon, Cameron was barely here anymore. Yet, I couldn't say anything, because if I did, it made me a terrible person.

So I stuffed down my reservations, put on a smile, and played my role as supportive, understanding girlfriend.

And it was slowly breaking my heart.

"It isn't forever. The holidays will be here soon enough, and then once it's the new year, and he knows there are only a few months before graduation, I think it'll be easier."

Cameron was in too deep to see that he was feeding Xander's attachment issues. I knew Asher had tried to talk to him about it; Mya had told me the last time we spoke. But again, I didn't feel able to say anything because Xander was his brother. His baby brother. And after what they went through almost losing their mom… I couldn't criticize his choices.

Even if I didn't fully understand them.

"I think I'm done." He zipped the bag and stood, running a hand through his damp hair. "I'll see you Monday, okay?"

I nodded, a rush of emotion clawing up my throat.

"Please be safe, and call me when you stop, no matter the time."

"I'll text. You need to get some sleep."

Like that would come easy knowing Cameron was on the road in the middle of the night, running on nothing but adrenaline and energy drinks.

"I will." He slid his hand along my jaw and tipped my head back, grazing his lips over mine. "I love you, Hailee."

"I love you too."

I went to deepen the kiss, but Cameron had already pulled away, slinging his bag over his shoulder and making for the door.

While I stood there watching as he took another piece of my heart with him.

I WOKE to the sound of my cell phone blaring. A smile tugged at my lips at the prospect of speaking to Cameron, but when I saw Felicity's name, disappointment snaked through me.

"Hey," I said, around a yawn.

"Did I wake you?"

"I must have fallen asleep."

"Late night?"

"I barely slept. Cameron drove back to Rixon through the night and I couldn't settle."

"I thought he was going this morning?"

"Me too," I said, my chest tightening.

"He's going home a lot, huh?"

"Yeah, I guess..." I trailed off, unsure of what she wanted me to say.

Everyone knew Cameron was going back and forth. It wasn't some big secret. But it did make me wonder what our friends were saying about it.

"Has Jason said anything?"

"Like what?" Felicity asked.

"I don't know... ignore me."

"Hailee, did something happen?"

"No... yes..." I released a weary sigh. "I don't know."

"Okay," she said, "start from the beginning."

So I did. I told her how Cameron and I made the calendar for Xander, how it was supposed to help him count off the days until he saw his brother. I told her how the visits were becoming more and more regular, and the time we spent together was becoming less and less. I even told her how we'd barely been intimate lately.

"What, like no sex, *at all*?"

"We've fooled around a little, but no, no sex."

"God, Hails, how are you functioning right now? I can't go more than a couple of days."

"It's not by choice, trust me."

Cameron was always too tired or too wound up to get into it, so I'd stopped trying.

"I feel like we're drifting apart, and I don't know what to do about it. And I hate myself for even thinking it because it's Xander. Of course Cameron should be there for him."

"Well, yeah. But you're important too, babe. He shouldn't be neglecting your relationship either."

"How do I say anything without coming across as a selfish, horrible person though?"

"I'm thinking it's less about saying anything and more about finding the spark again."

"The spark?" I said with skepticism.

"Yeah, you know, put on something sexy and wait for him to come home and then seduce him."

I smothered a groan. "Sometimes I really wish you wouldn't suggest things you clearly do with my step-brother."

"It's just sex, babe. Everyone does it."

Some more than others apparently.

"Do you think I'm crazy?" Because I was starting to feel that way.

"What? *No*! No way. You're totally justified to feel upset."

"I'm not upset, Fee, I'm just..." Oh, who I was trying to kid? I *was* upset and that only made me feel guiltier which in turn upset me more.

I was a mess.

All because my boyfriend was trying to do right by his family.

"It's okay. You're entitled to your feelings, just don't let them fester. Cameron loves you Hailee, so much. Besides, if he ever hurt you, Jase would—"

"Don't you dare tell him any of this." Panic welled inside of me.

"I won't."

"I mean it, Felicity. It's bad enough I have to listen to your freaky sex talk knowing you're boning my brother, without you discussing my sex life with him."

"But he could talk to Cam and—"

"Felicity, I'm serious. I will revoke your best friend status if you breathe even so much as a word of this to Jason."

"Relax, I'm joking."

"You'd better be." Because I was not ready to get relationship advice from Jason, no matter how close we were these days. "I'm sure things will be okay. It's just a weird time."

"Atta girl. And don't forget what I said about seducing him. You can thank me later," she added, and I rolled my eyes.

"Yep. Got it," I said, wanting to end this line of conversation.

"Let me know how it goes."

"Hm-hmm, talk to you soon. Bye."

"Hailee, wait—"

I hung up, letting out an exasperated breath. A second later, my cell pinged.

Flick: Rude much? It's a good thing I love you. Call me soon xo

I chuckled. I couldn't help it. Since Jason had proposed almost two years ago, Felicity had morphed into this confident, sexy, no-holds-barred kind of woman. I didn't blame her. She was engaged to one of the NCAA's players of the decade. Jason had already earned himself numerous records, and a spot in the Hall of Fame. And ESPN were already naming him as a sure thing for next year's draft. It wasn't just Jason though, it was her. After a rocky start, Flick had found her feet with her studies. She had everything going for her. The guy, the career... the huge diamond ring on her finger.

I'd been nothing but happy for them when Jason proposed. Same with Asher and Mya. But another year had gone by, and Cameron still hadn't popped the question. I wasn't in a rush, I wasn't. But lately, I couldn't help but wonder if he was just waiting for the right time... or if he was stalling.

"Ugh, stop," I hissed at myself.

I was letting my mind play tricks on me. Just because Cameron wanted to be there for Xander, it wasn't any reflection on our relationship.

So why couldn't I seem to separate the two?

And why, every time he left, did it feel like the space between us grew?

Cameron

"Hailee, I'm home." I threw my keys down and kicked off my sneakers. I was bone-tired and weary. It had been a long ride back to Michigan, only made ten times worse given how badly Xander had reacted when it was time for me to leave. It had taken almost two hours to calm him, and then I'd wanted to stick around and make sure he was okay, which meant I'd missed practice.

It was late, past ten.

The lingering smell of lasagna wafted down the hall. But it wasn't until I entered the kitchen and saw the barely touched meal, I knew I'd fucked up twice today.

Our small table was set for two, complete with candles and wine glasses, and a glass of freshly cut flowers. Trudging to the refrigerator, I was hardly surprised to find a bottle of wine chilling and a container of our favorite dessert from the restaurant across the street. Hailee had gone to a lot of trouble, yet, she'd never said a word.

Because she wanted to surprise you, asshole.

I let out a frustrated groan. I hadn't texted. After sending the initial text to say I was leaving, I'd been so caught up with Xander and then my own thoughts, I'd completely forgotten to text her.

Pulling my lifeless cell phone out of my pocket, I plugged it into a power outlet and waited for it to come to life.

I had text after text from Hailee.

HAILEE: It's me. You said you'd be home by now but you're not here and your cell is ringing out. Let me know you're okay.

. . .

Hailee: Since you're still not answering, I called your mom. She said you left Rixon at one. What the hell, Cameron? You texted me at eight this morning and said you were leaving. What is going on?

Hailee: I consider myself a pretty understanding person... but what the actual fuck, Cameron? It's almost nine-thirty and I'm going to bed. Not that I imagine I'll get any sleep because my boyfriend is unreachable, and no one has spoken to him all day.

Guilt trickled down my spine. It seemed so fucking inexcusable now, but at the time, after leaving Xander, all I'd wanted was some time with my thoughts. One hour had turned into two and two into four. I'd made one quick stop for gas and to use the restroom and then got back on the road.

I hadn't stopped to think about Hailee.

I hadn't stopped to think about anything besides my kid brother back home, breaking his heart because I was leaving him again.

It was *all* I could think about.

And, in this moment, I realized how screwed up that was. I'd taken a lot for granted these last few weeks. Hailee. The team. My classes.

Hailee.

Fuck.

I glanced at the table again. She'd planned an entire romantic evening and I hadn't even fucking called her to tell her the change of plans.

With a heavy heart, I moved through the apartment to our bedroom. It was quiet, but nothing could have prepared me for the sight of Hailee asleep on the top of the bed, clutching a pillow, her new lingerie accentuating her womanly curves.

She hadn't just planned a romantic meal; she'd planned a night of seduction. Probably in hopes of rekindling our usually healthy sex life. But with everything lately, I was normally too exhausted.

In fact, I couldn't remember the last time we were intimate. I wracked my brain. There had been the night a few weeks back, against the wall. Surely it hadn't been that long?

Crap.

I'd royally fucked up.

"Way to go, Chase" I grumbled to myself. She'd fallen asleep crying, that much was obvious, and it cracked my heart wide open.

"I'm sorry." I moved nearer, brushing the hairs from her eyes. Hailee stirred but didn't wake, so I wiggled the covers free from underneath her body and pulled them up over her.

"I'll make this up to you, I promise," I whispered.

Because I would.

One way or another, I would find a way to show Hailee how much I loved her.

23

Cameron

WHEN I WOKE UP, Hailee was gone. The bedsheets were cold and the hole she left was vast.

I ran a hand down my face before leaning over and grabbing my cell phone off the nightstand.

Me: I'm sorry.

I waited.

And waited.

But nothing came.

I didn't blame her. Roles reversed, I'd be pissed too.

My fingers flew over the screen.

Me: I'll make it up to you, I promise.

My cell pinged, but it wasn't the name I wanted to see.

Jase: What the fuck did you do to my sister?

Jesus. She'd told him? Okay, I knew the likelihood was that Hailee had told Felicity and she'd told Jase, but still, I didn't like thinking they all knew what a selfish asshole I'd been.

It had been a lapse in judgment. I'd taken for granted that Hailee would be waiting, that she'd understand where I was coming from.

A whole day, asshole. I ignored the little voice of reason and climbed out of bed. I needed a shower and some food since I'd gone to bed on an empty stomach.

Hitting call, I waited for Jase to answer.

"I fucked up."

"Yeah, you did," he ground out. "What the hell were you thinking? She was going out of her damn mind."

"I didn't... shit, Jase. Things were hard with Xan when I went to leave. He was a mess, I was a mess. I just needed space, ya know?"

"I get it. He's going through some stuff and you're carrying that responsibility, but Hailee is your—"

Everything.

She was my everything.

"Yeah, I know," I forced the words out over the lump in my throat.

"Talk to me, Cam. Where's your head at?"

"He needs me, that's all I know. When I'm there, he's better, and Mom and Dad can breathe again."

"Shit, it's that bad?"

"Yeah. His therapist is talking about attachment disorder. But his symptoms are atypical. Kids with AD don't usually form secure attachments to any of their caregivers, but he's become overly attached to me." I inhaled a shaky breath.

Xander was seven. Every year that passed since my mom's illness, he'd withdrawn more and more. It was as if he wanted to escape my parents when they offered him nothing but love and comfort.

I hated it.

I hated that I didn't understand why he felt that way, even though I knew it wasn't something he chose to feel.

The whole situation made me feel powerless, but being there for him, for my parents, was something I *could* do. It was something I could control.

"He'll get through this, Cam," Jase said. "You all will."

"It's just something I have to do."

"I get it. So does Hailee. Just don't shut her out, okay? You need her."

"I know." Pain laced my words. "I'll fix it."

"Good, because I really don't want to have to drive up to Michigan and kick your ass." I heard the smirk in his words.

"You think you could take me?"

"I know I could."

"You wish, asshole." Laughter rumbled in my chest and it felt good.

I couldn't remember the last time I laughed.

"How's stuff with the team?" he asked.

"Coach is going to tear me a new one for missing practice."

"He'll understand."

"You haven't met Coach Byford." I hesitated, hardly able to believe the words teetering on the tip of my tongue.

"What?" Jason asked.

"Nothing." I couldn't say it. Not to him.

"Shit, Cam," he breathed. "Tell me you're not seriously considering quitting the team? In your *senior year*?"

"I don't want to." I didn't. "But it means I could go home at the weekend and travel back for classes."

"And what is my sister supposed to do while you're driving back and forth?"

"Jase, come on..."

"I'm not trying to be a dick, I'm not. But we literally just spent five minutes going over the fact you need to let Hailee in, not push her away."

"It's not like that. I just..."

Jase let out an exasperated breath. "You need to figure out your priorities here, Cam. Graduation is in less than seven months. Less than six if you take out the holidays and spring break. It isn't that long. If you walk from the team, you'll regret it."

"But if I don't, and Xander gets worse..." How could I live with that?

"I wish I had the answer," he sighed.

"Yeah, me too."

"Just talk to Hailee. Any decisions you do or don't make need to be done with her. It's only fair."

"I will, I promise." If she wanted to talk to me anytime soon that was.

"I gotta shoot, Felicity is—"

"Yeah, yeah. Go tend to your girl." I smiled. Jase was different but he wore it well.

"I'm here, Cam. Always."

We said goodbye and I hung up. Opening my message history with Hailee, I started typing.

Me: We need to talk.

Hailee

I stared at Cameron's message, the permanent knot in my stomach tightening.

He wanted to talk.

My mind automatically assumed he wanted to talk about us... and I hated it.

I hated that I was that girl now, insecure and uncertain of her relationship, of her man. But last night, after the gnawing worry, followed by frustration and then a deep sense of disappointment, I'd fallen to sleep clutching my tear-stained pillow.

The vibration of my cell jerked me from my reverie.

. . .

CAMERON: Hailee, please.

HAILEE: Okay.

CAMERON: I have practice straight after classes but after? At the apartment?

HAILEE: I'll be there.

POCKETING MY PHONE, I made my way toward the Art and Architecture building for my morning classes. I didn't know how things had gotten to this point, but I didn't know how to fix them either.

"Hailee," Devyn waved as she approached me. "I'm glad I caught up to you."

I frowned.

"Dominic said Cameron missed practice. Something about an emergency at home? I hope everything's okay?"

Devyn was a sweetheart. She was Dominic's twin sister and the two of them were best friends. So much so, they shared an apartment off-campus. She also happened to be a huge football fan, so Cameron and I hung out with them a lot during the season.

"It's Xander, he's going through some stuff."

"That must be rough, the age gap." She hooked her arm through mine as we headed into the building. "Cameron is a good brother."

"He is." I really didn't want to talk about this.

"You know, I heard my brother and a couple of the guys talking... Crap, this is going to sound so wrong..."

"Just spit it out, Dev," I said, smothering my irritation.

"They're worried." She gave me a sympathetic smile. "He never hangs out with them anymore; he's distracted at practice... they're saying his heart's not in it anymore. There's even talk of Coach giving the second string more time on the field."

Her words reverberated through me, but Devyn wasn't done. "Has he said anything to you? Doesn't he want to play any—"

"What? *No*! Cameron loves the team. He'd never walk out on them. He's just finding it hard to balance everything."

"That's what I told Dominic. Cam knows there's too much on the line this season. Especially since the championship should have been theirs last year." She let out a little huff.

"Listen, Dev, it was good to see you," I rushed out, "but I need to use the bathroom before class. Catch you later?"

"Huh, sure." Her lips curved. "I'm sorry if I overstepped—"

"You didn't. I just really need to pee." Offering her a small wave, I hurried down the hall toward the nearest bathroom. Inside, I ducked into the first stall and closed the door, inhaling a ragged breath.

The guys thought Cameron wanted to quit.

I knew things had been tough, but I didn't realize it was affecting his performance so much.

Because he didn't tell you.

My heart sank.

When Cameron's mom had gotten sick, he'd turned to me. I had been his person. His safe place. But he wasn't turning to me now.

Whether he realized it or not, Cam was shutting me out.

And I was letting him.

Cameron

Blood roared between my ears as I sat and waited for Hailee to get home. We hadn't spoken again all day, despite me reaching for my cell at least five times.

There was so much I wanted to say to her, to explain, but every time I tried to start typing, I couldn't find the words.

I hoped talking face to face would go better.

The door opened and I heard the soft thud of her sneakers against the floor. "I'm in here," I called, and seconds later, Hailee appeared.

"Hey." She gave me a tentative smile.

I wanted to go to her, to pull her into my arms and beg for forgiveness, but there were things we needed to discuss. Things I needed to say without the distraction of her close proximity.

"Sit, please."

She did, folding her hands into her lap.

"I owe you an apology. I fucked up, and I'm sorry. I'm so fucking sorry."

"I just don't understand..." she said. "I know things are hard right now, but you didn't even think to call me. Do you have any idea what that feels like?"

"I... I'm sorry."

"Wait." She held up her hand, silencing me. "I'm going to ask you something and I want the truth, Cam. I think I deserve it."

"Okay..." My brows furrowed, not liking the finality in her tone.

"Do you want to quit the team?"

I reared back, my eyes growing to saucers. "How did you—"

I was going to kill Jason.

"So it's true?" Disappointment washed over her, the distance between us vaster than ever.

"No... I mean, I thought about it, but—"

"You thought it about it and you never said a word. What is happening to us, Cameron? Because when the semester started and you began pulling away, I told myself it was just the pressure of balancing everything. Then you started going back and forth to Rixon more and more, and I got it, because it's Xander. He's your blood, your family. But what I didn't anticipate was that every time you left, it would drive the wedge growing between us deeper.

"I think I've been understanding. I've tried to be there for you, for Xander, even your parents. I don't grumble or complain, or trash talk you to our friends. Because I get it. I get you want to do the right thing. You wouldn't be the guy I fell in love with if you didn't. But something is happening to us and I'm starting to wonder if it has anything to do with everything else going on, or if it's just us. If maybe you're starting to feel like..." Hailee's bottom lip quivered but she swallowed her emotion. "*I'm* the burden."

Without speaking, I got up and crossed the room to her. Dropping to my knees, I looped my hand around the back of her neck and pulled her to me until our heads were pressed together. "You are not a burden."

"So, what is it? Why do I feel like I'm losing you?"

Her words snaked through me, lashing my insides. "Because I'm an asshole," I breathed. "I take your love for granted. I take *you* for granted, and I shouldn't."

"I just don't understand how we got here?" Hailee was holding back her tears. I heard them in her voice.

"I love you. I love you so damn much, and I know things haven't been right for a while and I—"

The blare of my cell cut through the air, and Hailee's gaze darted over my shoulder.

"I'll leave it," I said.

But it didn't stop ringing.

"Maybe you should get it; it could be your mom."

My eyes shuttered, my heart torn in two. I wanted to put Hailee first, to prove to her she was the most important thing in my life...

"Cam, it's okay." She took my hands and gently moved out of my hold. "Go, they need you."

And I need you. But the words wouldn't come out.

I got up and ran a hand over my face. Hailee had curled up on the chair, her expression crestfallen. "I'm sorry," I mouthed as I snatched up my cell phone and hit answer. "Dad?" I said, panic flooding me as I wondered what Xander could have possibly done this time.

"Cameron, Son..."

"Dad, what is it?"

"It's your mom... She's in the hospital."

The world fell away as I tried to process his words.

"What do you mean, she's in the hospital?"

"She... she collapsed. They think she had a seizure."

"Where's Xander?"

"He's with Asher's mom. He was there when it happened. I found them—"

"Dad?" My voice cracked.

"We need you, Son. We need you to come home."

24

Hailee

WE GOT a flight to Philadelphia and rented a car to drive to Rixon. It was the quickest option.

Cameron had barely spoken a word on the ninety-minute flight from Detroit. He'd clutched my hand the entire way there though, as if I was his lifeline.

The second I pulled up outside the Rixon General, Cameron grabbed the door handle. "I need to—"

"Go," I said. "I'll find somewhere to park."

He gave me a small nod and climbed out, jogging across the street and disappearing inside.

My heart ached for them. First Xander, now this. I didn't want to assume the worst, but I knew that if anything happened to Karen, the Chase men wouldn't survive it.

I found a parking spot and cut the engine. I wanted to go to him, to see how Karen was. But I needed a minute.

I didn't get it though. My cell phone started ringing.

"Jason?"

"How is he?"

"I- I don't know. His dad called and everything was a blur after that. We just got to the hospital."

"Is he there? Can I speak to him? He isn't answering his cell."

"N- no. I'm in the car still."

"Hailee, what is it? What's wrong?"

The tears I'd fought so hard to contain exploded, streaming down my cheeks like unstoppable rivers, the noise of my heavy sobs audible.

"Shit, Hailee, don't cry. He'll be okay. They'll all be okay."

"They won't. If she doesn't make it... I'll lose him, Jase. I know I will." Every fear and insecurity I'd felt over the last few weeks battered me like an unforgiving storm.

If his mom was sick again, he would quit the team—maybe even quit college—and move back to Rixon. Because that's the kind of guy Cameron was. He made sacrifices for the people he loved. And they would need him.

His family would need him.

"You're his family too," Jase said, and I didn't even realize I'd said the words aloud.

"You know what I mean. He'll be here and I'll be there."

"But you'll get through this. You will. Listen, did the two of you get a chance to talk?"

"We were talking when his dad called. Why?"

"Cameron loves you, Hailee. He needs you. I know it might not always seem like that, but we're guys, we get shit wrong sometimes. Don't give up on him, okay?"

Silence filled the line. I wanted to heed his words, to be a pillar of strength for Cameron and his family, but the truth was, I was scared... scared of what the future would bring for us.

"It was you, you know?" Jason's voice grounded me.

"What was?"

"It was you and Cam that made me realize there's more to life than football."

I snorted. "You hated me back then."

"I didn't hate you, Hailee. I just..."

"Yeah, I know."

We had a lot of history—a lot of bad history—but we weren't those people anymore. Jason was one of the most important people in my life.

He was family.

"Cameron loves you and even if he tries to push you away or cut you loose, it'll only be because he thinks he's doing right by you. If his mom is sick again, and I really fucking hope she isn't," he let out a weary sigh, "you're going to need to be his strength, Sis. Even when he doesn't think he wants you to be."

More tears flowed down my cheeks and I bit back a huge sob.

"You hear me?" Jase said. "You might not be a Ford, Hailee, but you are my sister in all the ways that matter. And we don't quit, okay? We fight."

"Yeah, okay."

"Good, now go be with our guy. And tell him I'm here. Whatever he needs, all he has to do is call."

"Thank you, Jason."

"Anytime. Now brush yourself off and be the badass Hailee Raine I know you can be."

Cameron

"Dad."

His head snapped up and he was out of his chair in a second, rushing toward me and pulling me into his arms. "You're here, thank God, you're here."

"How is she? What are they saying?"

"They're still running tests."

"Do they think it's the same as before?"

He paled. "It's the most likely scenario, Son."

Fuck.

"But they said she was okay. She got the all clear." Mom had the surgery and they'd gotten the tumor.

"We always knew this was a possibility, Cameron."

Yeah, but how unlucky did someone have to be to have it come back? I couldn't get my head around that. Hadn't we dealt with enough already?

"Xander—"

"He's okay." Dad squeezed my shoulder. "I checked in with Julia earlier."

But I knew the truth. Xander wasn't okay.

"It's like he knew," I said.

"Whatever do you mean?"

"It's like he knew she was going to get sick again and that's why he kept pushing her away."

"Cameron, he didn't know. He couldn't have."

Of course, I knew that. But it didn't stop me wondering if he sensed something.

"Hailee," Dad's gaze moved over my shoulder.

"Hi, Clarke. I'm so sorry." She didn't think twice about hugging him.

"I'm glad you're here." Dad held her at arm's length, offering her a warm smile.

"I wouldn't be anywhere else."

My chest squeezed, remembering the conversation we'd been having as my dad called. The conversation we still needed to have.

The conversation that would have to take a backseat.

"Shall I get us some coffee?" Hailee suggested. It was late, but I wasn't leaving until I got to see Mom.

"That's a great idea," Dad said, digging out his wallet. "Here, let me—"

"Don't worry, I've got it." She offered him a smile.

"Thank you," I said, and Hailee took off down the hall.

"I'm so glad she came with you, Son. You're lucky to have her."

He was right, I was.

Hailee hadn't given coming with me a second thought. She'd gotten on her phone the second I told her I needed to get to Rixon ASAP.

But I couldn't stop thinking about what she'd said earlier.

I couldn't stop wondering if she was right.

It was almost eleven when they finally let us in to see Mom. The doctor confirmed that she'd had a seizure due to a new glioma.

My mom had *another* brain tumor.

I didn't know what the fuck to do with that.

"I'll give the three of you some space," Hailee said as we reached Mom's room.

"Thank you." Dad slipped inside, but I stayed back.

"I'm not sure I can do this again," I confessed, my heart numb from the news.

"Sure, you can." Hailee enveloped me in her slim arms. "You're so strong, Cam. And I'm here, I'm right here. Whatever you need."

I wanted to tell her to take me away from here. To hold me tight and never let go. But my dad needed me, my mom too. And Xander.

Fuck... Xander.

"This will destroy Xander." I swallowed hard, dropping my gaze to the floor.

"Look at me," Hailee said, sliding her hand to my cheek. "You can do this, Cameron. They need you."

Touching my head to hers, I tried to draw comfort from her. The girl who had stood up beside me through this once already.

"I can't lose her, Hailee. I just can't."

"Ssh," she whispered. "We don't know the prognosis yet. Go be with her and your dad. We'll worry about the rest later." Hailee's lips hovered over mine, touching but not kissing. I felt her uncertainty, and I knew I'd been the one to put it there.

But I couldn't do this, not right now. Not when I didn't know if my mom was going to make it or not.

"I won't be long," I said, pulling away.

"Okay, I'll be right out here." Hailee stepped back, wrapping her arms around her chest, barely able to meet my gaze.

I should have apologized, explained that my head was all over the place. But I didn't.

I couldn't.

Because this wasn't like before.

This time, I couldn't afford to fall apart. Not when my family were already holding on by a thread. This time, I had to step up to the plate and be the brother Xander needed, the son my parents needed.

This time, I had to put them first.

Hailee

"Hi, sweetheart." My mom came to me in a dream, only when I opened my eyes, she was standing right there.

"Mom?" I pushed up, my muscles sore from sleeping on the row of plastic hospital chairs. "What time is it?"

"A little after one."

It had been two hours since Cameron and his dad had disappeared into Karen's room.

"I must have fallen asleep."

She nodded. "Cameron called and asked me to come and get you."

"He did?" I frowned, glancing down the hall where I knew he was with his parents.

"They're going to stay with Karen. He didn't want you to be out here all by yourself."

"Oh, okay." My stomach dipped.

"Come on, sweetheart. Let's go home."

But as I got up and let her lead me away, all I could think was I was leaving my home behind in that room.

"It's so good to see you, Hailee. I just wish it was under better circumstances." Mom made small talk as we walked to her car. It was dark out, a blanket of stars kissing the inky sky. Such a beautiful scene for such a tragic night.

"Did Cameron say anything else?"

"Just that he didn't want you to be alone and that you needed to get some rest too."

I toyed with my cell phone, desperate to text him. But I knew he needed some time with his mom and dad to come to terms with everything.

"It's such a shame. Karen is a good woman."

"She is."

We climbed into the car and I let my head fall against the glass, fighting the wave of tears building inside me.

"Hailee?" Mom asked. "Are you okay?"

"I'm fine," I murmured.

And then I puked all over myself.

I WAS SICK.

By the time Mom had gotten me home, I could barely stand. At first, I'd thought it was just an emotional response to everything that had happened, but I spent most of the night with my head down the toilet bowl.

"How are you feeling?" Mom slipped into my room with a glass of ice-cold water and some crackers.

"Like I got hit by a truck." I tried to sit up but my stomach roiled.

"Have you heard from Cameron?"

"Nothing." I stared at my cell, willing it to vibrate.

"I'm sure he'll call. It's a lot for them to process." She placed the glass down and pressed her hand against my forehead. "You don't feel feverish. It could be something you ate, or a stomach flu."

"I'll be okay." I brushed her off.

"Cameron will probably have to stay away if he's going to be visiting his mom in the hospital. At least until it passes."

Great.

Just what I didn't need.

"I'm really tired, Mom." I'd barely slept a wink.

"Sure, baby. I'll let you get some rest. If you need anything..."

"I know, and thanks, for everything."

"Hailee, you're my daughter. I will always be here for you. I hope you know that." She gave me a warm smile, before leaving me alone.

The door had barely closed before the first tear fell.

25

Hailee

AFTER TWENTY-FOUR HOURS, I finally felt human again. But my heart was still bruised. Cameron had texted a couple of times to say he was spending the day with Xander, and that he would stop by later today.

That was five hours ago.

Mom insisted, I rest. She also insisted I drink regular fluids and nibble crackers to replenish myself. I think secretly she just loved having someone in the house to fuss over.

"Can I get you anything else?" she called, and I shook my head with silent laughter.

"I'm good, Mom, thanks."

"Okay, baby. Holler if you need me."

Our relationship hadn't always been easy, but she was trying. And after Karen's devastating news, I knew I probably needed to try harder.

I wanted to call Cameron, to see how his mom was doing, and to ask if they knew anything more. But I didn't want to crowd him.

So, I opted for calling my best friend instead.

"Hailee, thank God," Felicity said on the third ring. "I've been so worried. How are you? And Cam? And Karen. Oh God, Karen..."

"Breathe, Flick," I chuckled softly, not that anything about this situation was funny.

"Seriously, how are you?"

"I feel a bit better now, but it wasn't pretty."

"I can't believe you got so sick. Do you think it was something you ate?"

"I don't know. But I feel okay now."

"Well, that's good. And Cam? He must be beside himself."

"I don't really know. He's with Xander."

"You mean you haven't seen him today?" She sounded surprised.

"Well, no. My mom thought he should stay away until I knew it was only a twenty-four-hour thing."

"Makes sense, I guess. But you've spoken to him, right?"

"I..."

"Hailee?"

"He needs to be with his family right now," I said, unable to keep the sadness out of my voice.

"But you're his family."

I'd thought so too, once upon a time. But I wasn't so sure about anything anymore.

"Has Jason spoken to him?"

"Yeah, they talked earlier."

I sucked in a harsh breath.

"Shit, Hails, I didn't mean to—"

"It's okay. I'm glad he has Jason to talk to."

If he wasn't going to turn to me, he needed to turn to someone.

"I just don't understand it. You've always been so good together."

Her words made the knot in my stomach tighten. "He doesn't want to choose," I said quietly.

"But there doesn't have to be a choice, does there?"

There did though. Or at least, I knew Cameron enough to know that's what he thought. He was an all or nothing guy. I'd seen how much it had affected him not being able to be there for Xander. He'd persisted for me. He'd continued our life in Michigan... *for me.*

But I realized now, his heart wasn't in it.

"He needs to be here with his family."

"You really think he'll quit the team? Leave college?"

I didn't want to believe it when we'd first talked about it, but Karen's diagnosis changed everything. And I knew...in my heart of hearts, I knew I'd already lost him.

Silent tears clung to my lashes.

"I'm so sorry," Felicity said as if she'd worked it out too.

"It's okay," I choked out. "He needs to be here for them."

Even though I knew the words to be true, it didn't make them hurt any less.

"Hailee," Mom yelled. "Cameron is here. I'm going to meet Kent for dinner. We'll be back later."

"Listen, I've got to go."

"Do you want me to come there? I can drive down—"

"No," I said, drying my eyes. "I'll be okay."

"Well, call me later."

"I will. Bye." I hung up and took a deep breath.

"Hailee?" Cameron's voice made my heart soar, but it quickly crashed back down to Earth.

"Come in."

The second he stepped into the room, I saw my greatest fear etched into every single line of his face.

He looked at me with sad eyes and said, "I think we need to talk."

Cameron

"It's okay," Hailee said, completely catching me off guard. I'd come here prepared for a battle. After spending the day with Xander trying to figure out how to tell the girl I loved more than anything that I couldn't be the guy she needed right now, I still didn't know how to say the words.

To tell her I needed to be there for my family.

Yet, she was sitting there, with nothing but resignation in her sad expression.

"You don't need to do this, Cameron. I know what you came here to say, and it's okay."

I blinked, hardly able to believe my ears. "I— I don't understand. What exactly are you saying?"

"I would never ask you to choose between me and them. You need to be here, more than ever. I get it, and it's okay."

Relief slammed into me. She got it.

Fuck, she got it.

"Thank you." I went and sat beside her on the edge of the bed. "I need to do this, for Xander, for them." My voice shook as I tried to find the words. "She's terminal, Hailee. They can make her comfortable and give her meds to manage the symptoms, but there is no surgery this time or magic fix."

"Oh my god, Cameron." She threw her arms around me and I sank into her embrace. It had been the hardest thirty-six hours of my life. I'd spent all day with Xander trying to explain everything to him and then picking up the pieces of his meltdown as his developing brain tried to process things.

"I'm so sorry." Her tears splashed on my sweater.

I cupped Hailee's face, touching my head to hers. "Your mom said you were sick?"

"I'm okay now."

Our lips were so close I could almost taste her, but I didn't come here for this. I came to tell her I needed time and space to be with my family. But now I was here and she was clutching onto me as if I might disappear at any moment, I was overcome with the need to love her. To just *be* with her.

"Cameron?" Her eyes glittered with so much love it gutted me, and I knew if I asked it of her, she would give me whatever I needed.

"Come here." I tried to hold her tighter. I didn't want to be *that* guy, the guy who used sex as a goodbye, but I wanted it.

God, I wanted her.

Hailee made the decision though, sliding her mouth over mine.

"Hailee, wait..." I grabbed her shoulders, swallowing the ball of emotion lodged in my throat. "I'm not sure this is a good idea."

"I need this," she said, her hands trailing down my chest and tugging my sweater away from my body. "And I know you do too."

"You're sure?"

I was going straight to hell.

I was pretty sure Jason would drag me there anyway after I did this.

But I couldn't stop. Hailee was everything I'd ever wanted. She was strong and good and so fucking selfless, it was breathtaking.

She hadn't made me choose.

She'd given me a gift—she'd let me go.

Hailee climbed onto my lap, kissing me. Small uncertain kisses as my hands slid into her hair, so I could deepen the angle. She traced my lips with her fingers, her tongue. Teasing and tasting. Until the kiss took on a life of its own. Fierce and brutal, as we both fought our demons.

"Is this okay?" I murmured against her lips, as my hands began exploring her body, running them up and down her waist, tracing her soft curves.

She nodded, clawing at my sweater, until I pulled it off my body. Hailee painted letters of love over my skin, branding me with her touch. She felt good, too fucking good.

And you're going to give her up.

I forced down the thoughts. I only wanted to focus on this. Here. Now. On the way Hailee felt so perfect, the way her body fit against mine as if it was made for me, and me alone.

Her clothes went next, her jeans and t-shirt, her black cotton panties. Then my jeans and boxers. Until we were nothing but skin on skin, regrets and apologies.

"I love you, Cameron, so much," she whispered before kissing me deeply.

My dick ached for her, but I didn't want to rush this. I wanted to savor her, imprint this moment to my memory for when things got too tough and I needed to distract myself from the gaping hole in my chest.

I buried my hands deep in her hair, angling her face to mine as I captured her lips. Hot, needy kisses. "I will always love you," I barely whispered the words against the corner of her mouth.

Hailee rose up slightly, grasping my shaft in her hand before sinking down in one smooth motion. "Cam," she breathed, clutching onto my shoulders. "It feels—"

"I know," I groaned, rocking into her. My hand curved over her hip, guiding her movements. I wanted her slow and deep, fast and hard. I wanted her anyway I could get her. Because being like this with Hailee would never be enough... and yet, for now, it would have to be.

My chest tightened as she rode me. I memorized every roll of her hips, every breathy moan to fall from her lips. But I needed more. I needed every single thing she had to give.

Without warning, I flipped Hailee over and began thrusting into her. She raked her nails down my back, crying out as I went harder. "Oh God, Cam..." Sucking in a sharp breath, she held onto my shoulders as I chased that moment when everything else melted away and you were left with nothing but a feeling of complete ecstasy.

Hailee moaned again. "It's..."

Everything.

It was everything...

And it was goodbye.

Hailee

I woke up to an empty bed, but I hadn't expected Cameron to be here. We'd said all we needed to say last night, with every kiss and touch and whispered I-love-you.

I didn't doubt Cameron loved me; it was never about that. But I knew he couldn't be what he needed to be to his family while he felt tied to me.

So I set him free.

We hadn't discussed what would happen when I went back to Michigan. We hadn't discussed if we were on a break, or over, or going to try to do the long-distance thing.

We hadn't discussed anything.

But that told me all I needed to know.

Right now, Cameron's priority was his family, and I couldn't hate him for that.

No matter how much it hurt, I just couldn't.

"Sweetheart?" Mom's voice drifted through the door.

"Hey, Mom."

She peeked around the door. "How are you feeling this morning?"

"I'm okay."

"Did you and Cameron work through things?"

My cheeks heated. "Actually, I'm going to head back to Michigan later."

"Alone?" Confusion clouded her eyes.

"Cameron needs to be here."

"I know, sweetheart. I can't even imagine..." She perched on the edge of my desk. "But that sounds kind of final."

"We haven't worked out the details."

"And you're okay with this?"

I shrugged, dropping my gaze. "Cameron needs to be here for his family."

"Of course he does, but—"

"Mom, I appreciate your concern, I do. But it's done."

"You'll find your way back to one another. No amount of time or distance will ever change how that boy feels about you."

God, I wanted to believe her. But I also knew there was one thing that could change everything, and it was going to happen.

"Karen isn't going to get better, Mom." I couldn't hold the tears at bay any longer.

"Oh, sweetheart, I'm so, so sorry."

"Life is so unfair," I sobbed, falling into Mom's open arms.

"Ssh, sweetheart. I'm right here."

But as she said the words, I only cried harder, because one day soon, Cameron and Xander were going to have to say goodbye to their mom.

And Cameron would be left to pick up the pieces.

I FLEW BACK to Michigan after that. Mom and Kent gave me a ride to the airport, insisting that I call more often. They didn't like the idea of me being in Ann Arbor on my own, but there was something strangely comforting about returning to mine and Cameron's apartment.

It was so full of him. His Wolverine's hoodie on the coat rack, the sports column cuttings of all his mentions stuck to the noticeboard in the kitchen, right down to the lingering scent of his aftershave.

It hurt.

It hurt so much, but I wouldn't have wanted to be anywhere else.

Dropping my keys on the sideboard, I pulled out my cell phone and started a new message.

ME: Just got back to the apartment. Send my love to Xander, and your mom and dad xo

CAMERON: I will, and thank you Hailee, for everything.

THERE WAS STILL SO MUCH we needed to discuss, questions that needed answering. But they could wait.

They would have to.

My cell phone began vibrating and I hit answer.

"We need to talk."

"Hello to you too, Jason."

"What the fuck, Hailee? You were supposed to fight, not walk away."

"That's not... I didn't walk away." *I let him go.*

"Cameron is confused. He doesn't know what the fuck he wants right now. But I'm telling you: He. Needs. You."

"And I'm here, I am. I'm not going anywhere, Jason, but I'm not going to be an added burden either."

"I can't believe he let you leave." The fight left my stepbrother's voice.

"Yeah..." My heart ached as if it knew it was missing its other half.

"How are you holding up?"

"I'm okay. I just keep thinking nothing I'm feeling matters, not compared to..."

"Yeah," his voice sobered, "I know. I offered to drive to Rixon, but he wouldn't even entertain the idea."

"Cameron needs to do things his way," I said.

"And if his way isn't the right way?"

"Then we'll pick up the pieces."

"You'll get through this. It can't be the end, Sis. It just can't."

"Maybe," I said with little conviction.

"Just don't write him off, not yet."

"Jason, I would never do that." *I love him too damn much.*

"Do you need anything? I can drive up and—"

"No, I'm okay." I smiled. Jason was so different, and I was proud of the man he'd become. "Just take care of him, please."

"I will. He gets a couple of days and then I'm going down there."

"Good. He'll need someone to talk to."

"You're the best of us, Hailee, you know that, right?"

"Thank you." Emotion clogged my throat.

"I'll call you soon to check in."

"Okay, bye, Jas—" My stomach churned violently. "I need to go." I dropped the phone and raced through the apartment, crashing through the bathroom door just in time for my lunch to make a reappearance.

So much for a twenty-four-hour stomach flu.

26

Hailee

CAMERON DIDN'T RETURN to school. He quit the team and deferred his classes. Jason had driven up last weekend to collect some of his things and take them back to Rixon.

That had been hard.

But it was for the best.

Doctors couldn't give the Chase family a clear prognosis. But they had told them to treasure every moment which didn't sound good.

We'd talked a couple of times, but we didn't talk about us. Instead, I told Cameron all about my latest art project and he told me about his quest to make sure Xander knew how loved he was.

It was hard to stay mad at a guy who cared so much.

Devyn checked on me a lot, as did some of the other football girlfriends. But mostly, I preferred my own company. Besides, I'd been unable to shake whatever virus I'd picked up. I wasn't ill all the time, but I still didn't feel right. So much so, Mom had begged me to get some blood work done.

I was heading to get my results from the doctor's office before flying to Philadelphia to meet Felicity and Mya for some girls' time. The guys were in Rixon with Cam and Xander for the weekend, so Mya had invited us to hang out.

"Miss Raine?" The secretary said, and I nodded. "You can go straight in." She smiled.

"Thank you."

I made my way down the hall and knocked on the door.

"Come in."

"Hello."

"Hailee, take a seat." Dr. Jennifer said. "How are you feeling today?"

"Okay. I'm still a little lethargic though. And I had another bout of nausea the other day."

"I'm not surprised."

"Excuse me?"

"We ran a full blood work up. Everything came back fine."

My brows furrowed. "I'm sorry, I don't understand. I thought you just said—"

"You're pregnant, Hailee."

"P- pregnant?" It *whooshed* from my lips. "But I can't be."

"I have the results right here. Your levels put you at around nine weeks."

"But I didn't miss my period."

"It's rare but it happens. Do you experience light periods?"

"Usually, yes."

She made some notes. "Is it possible you missed your birth control?"

"No, I take it religiously."

"Again, it happens. Obviously, you don't need to take that anymore."

"You're sure I'm pregnant?"

"Hailee, I know this is a shock..." She wasn't wrong about that. Pregnancy was the last thing I'd expected to hear her say. It was so far down the list, I hadn't even contemplated it.

"Is the father on the scene?"

"It's complicated." My hands trembled as I tried to process what she was saying. "I'm sorry, when would I have conceived?"

"If the dates are correct, and sometimes they're a little out, it would put it at about seven weeks ago."

My hand instinctively went to my stomach. "I'm really pregnant?" Tears burned the backs of my eyes, but I didn't know if they were tears of joy or despair.

"You are. I suggest buying yourself a couple of home test kits. It might provide the visual proof you need." Her smile was reassuring but it did little to ease the storm raging inside me.

"Here." She pulled out a leaflet and pushed it across the desk. "This explains what happens next. If you have any questions, don't hesitate to call the office."

"I'm flying."

"Excuse me?"

"Today. I'm flying to Philadelphia to meet some girlfriends."

"You should be fine, but if you've been feeling nauseous then the altitude might not help. And no alcohol."

"Of course."

"I'm going to write you a script for some pre-natal vitamins, check your blood pressure, and then you can be on your way. Any questions?"

"I.... uh. No, I think that's everything."

It wasn't.

But I didn't know where the hell to start.

Dr. Jennifer took my blood pressure, handed me the script, and wished me well. I walked out of there in a complete trance, unable to think of anything else...

I was *pregnant*.

I BARELY REMEMBERED the flight to Philadelphia. I hadn't gotten sick, I'd just been stuck in a paralyzing state of disbelief. It wasn't until Felicity was pulling me into her arms in the arrivals lounge that I finally snapped out of it.

"Hailee, what is it? What's wrong?"

"I'm pregnant," I blurted out, a stream of big, ugly sobs following.

"Okay." Her eyes went wide as she dug out her cell. "Mya," she said. "Change of plan. We need to stop at the store for supplies then head straight to your apartment. I'll tell you when we're out of arrivals." Felicity hung up. "Come on, babe. It sounds like we have some catching up to do."

She didn't push for answers on the ride to Asher and Mya's apartment, and I was grateful. I still needed to assimilate my thoughts on everything. But when we pulled into their underground parking lot, I knew my reprieve was up.

I climbed out of the car and went around to the trunk to get my bag, but Flick beat me to it. "I can carry my bag," I protested.

"Hush, you've got to think for two now."

I shot her a disapproving look.

"Too soon?"

"What do you think?"

"I think you need to explain how you're pregnant when you told me you and Cameron were going through a dry spell?"

"Seriously, *that's* what you're choosing to focus on?"

"Fee, you're doing it again," Mya said.

"Sorry, I'm sorry, okay." She held up a hand. "I just... pregnant. She's freakin' pregnant."

"Yes, I got it the first time." Mya offered me an apologetic look. "How are you feeling, really?"

"Confused. Scared. Did I say confused?"

"It's okay, Hailee. You're going through something huge."

"Have you told Cam?" That was Felicity. I pressed my lips together, averting my gaze. "Hailee... you have to tell him."

"I can't, not yet."

He was dealing with something huge; he didn't need this to worry about.

"Girl," Mya reached for my hand. "He'd want to know."

"I need to process it first and then figure out what I'm going to do."

"What do you mean?" Felicity paled. "You're going to keep it, right?"

"I..." I couldn't answer that question. My heart said yes. But... *a baby*?

Cameron and I weren't even together. Well, at least, I didn't think we were.

God. Everything was such a mess.

"I'm still in college. I want to graduate." Guilt coiled around my heart.

The elevator doors pinged open and we all filed out, heading for Mya's apartment.

"You can't be more than, what, two months along?"

"The doctor thinks I'm nine weeks."

"So you're due when, June?" Felicity asked, doing the math.

"June second."

"Perfect. You can take finals, graduate, and then have the baby."

"And where we will live? What about my plans?"

Her expression fell. "It's not straightforward, but you'll figure it out. Besides, Cameron will step up."

"I think Cameron has enough on his plate." My heart clenched again. Finding out I was pregnant was supposed to be a happy occasion. It wasn't supposed to happen now, in the middle of all this.

She rolled her eyes. "You can't seriously be thinking about keeping this from him because of what's happening with his mom?"

I blinked away the fresh tears.

"That's all the more reason to tell him. God knows, that family needs some good news."

"I'll think about it. But please, don't tell Asher or Jason yet. I need time."

"Hailee—"

"No, Fee, I mean it. I told you in confidence. This is my business. Please respect that."

She let out a little huff, but nodded. "My lips are sealed."

"Good." Because this wasn't some salacious secret that would cause a scandal. It was the kind of secret that changed lives.

I knew Cameron deserved to know, but I'd walked away to unburden him. If I told him now, I'd only be adding more responsibility to his shoulders.

At least that's what I kept telling myself, as I followed my friends into Asher and Mya's apartment.

Cameron

"What will happen to me when Mom dies?" Xander's words were like a punch to the stomach. I hugged him tighter, running my nose over his hair as I tried to swallow the ball of emotion lodged in my throat.

"You'll have me and Dad."

"What about Hailee?"

Fuck. He was really hitting me where it hurt today.

"Hailee and I are..." The truth was, I didn't know what we were anymore.

We talked and texted occasionally, and she sent Xander these cute little care packages. But we didn't talk about the elephant in the room.

Us.

When I'd found out Mom was sick again, I hadn't turned to Hailee. I couldn't. Instead, I'd steeled myself to be there for my family. Hailee needed to graduate. She needed to chase *her* dreams, and figure out what *she* wanted.

I'd always imagined that our life would end up back in Rixon one day. But not like this. Not because Mom was… I still couldn't say it.

"Did she go back to Michigan because of me?"

I pushed Xander out of my arms and lowered my face to his. "Hailee loves you, squirt. She loves you so much. But I need to be here with you, and Mom and Dad. And Hailee's life is in Michigan right now."

"But after college, she'll come back, right?"

I couldn't answer him, because I didn't have one.

I hadn't asked anything of Hailee since she'd gone back to Michigan, and she'd given me the space I needed.

But nothing about it felt right. I missed her every second of every day. I missed her so much, my soul ached for her.

"Hey, boys," one of the nurses came out of Mom's room. "She's all yours."

"Thanks," I said, pulling Xander up with me.

"Don't get too rowdy, okay? She's tired."

"We'll behave." I gave the nurse a weak smile.

Xander hesitated when we reached her door, but I gave him a gentle nudge. He was doing better. Since I made the decision to stay in Rixon, my little brother no longer seemed so lost.

"There are my boys," Mom smiled, patting the bed.

"Go," I whispered to Xander, my heart swelling as I watched him fall into her arms and bury his face in her shoulder.

"Gosh, Xander, you get bigger every time I see you."

"Mom," he groaned, "It's been two days."

"Two days too many."

It was so good to see them together, even under the circumstances.

"How are you feeling?" I moved closer, leaning over my brother to press a kiss to her damp forehead.

"Okay." I heard the lie in her voice, but we didn't address it. We never did.

We'd made a promise—Mom, Dad, and I—that we needed to be strong for Xander. No matter how bad things got, we would shield him as much as possible.

"Are you hungry?" she asked Xander. "I heard they're doing tacos in the cafeteria today."

"I love tacos."

"I know you do, baby. You want to go with Dad and get some? He should be here any—"

"Did I hear someone say tacos?"

Mom chuckled and it was like music to my ears.

"Hey, Dad," Xander said.

"Hey, buddy. Shall we go feed you?"

"Don't be too long," Mom called after them. When they were gone, she patted the bed again. "Come closer, sweetheart."

"Hey, Mom."

"I wanted to talk to you about something," she said, and my brows furrowed. "I had a dream last night, and I woke up with the strangest feeling..." She took my hand in hers. "I know you want to be here, and I love you for it, I do. But I think you need to go and see Hailee—"

"Mom..."

"Just hear me out. You know I'm not one for superstition, but I can't shake the feeling she needs you."

"If you're trying to make me feel guiltier than I already do, you're doing a pretty good job of it." I gave her a tight smile.

"Oh, Cameron, my sweet boy." She pressed her hand against my cheek. "Hailee is your heart. You can't live without your heart, baby."

"But Mom, I can't go..." Tears burned my throat. "What if something happens—"

"Ssh." Her eyes fluttered closed. "All I want is for you and Xander to be happy. That's all any mother can wish for. And that girl is your key to happiness. You need to let her in, Cameron. Love is hard and messy, and God knows, it hurts sometimes. But the kind of love the two of you share is rare. And I can't explain it, but she needs you right now. I just know it."

"But you need me..." The dam broke and tears spilled freely down my cheeks.

"I'm not going anywhere yet, I promise. I need to make sure my boy pulls his head out of his butt and makes things right with his girl first."

"Okay," I breathed.

"Okay?"

"Yeah, Mom," I said, because how could I deny her?

How could I deny myself when all I wanted was to see Hailee, to know she was okay?

The answer was, I couldn't.

27

Hailee

I FELT LIKE CRAP.

Ever since finding out I was pregnant two weeks ago, it had been a constant cycle of sickness and lethargy. I'd missed a ton of classes, and spent most of my time camped out on the sofa watching daytime TV, sucking ice chips, and feeling sorry for myself.

Felicity and Mya were on my back to tell Cameron. According to my dates, I was almost entering the second trimester. I had a scan booked for next week.

I wanted to tell him. I did. So many times, I'd reached for my cell to call him. But every time, something stopped me.

Cameron was facing the biggest loss a child could have... the timing sucked.

Everything about it sucked.

Yet, I knew I had to tell him eventually.

I'd just got comfortable, ready for another episode of Friends, when the doorbell rang. That was odd. People usually buzzed to be let into the building.

Throwing the blanket off me, I padded across the apartment and checked the peephole. "Cameron?" His name spilled from my lips and I fumbled to open the door. "What are you doing here?"

"Hey." An uncertain smile tugged at the corner of his lips. "Can I come in?" he asked when I didn't reply.

"I... uh... this is your apartment too; you don't need an invitation."

Cameron was here.

Oh God.

I pulled my oversized cardigan around my body.

"Are you okay," he said, "you don't look so good?"

"I'm fine. What are you doing here?"

"I'm sorry to just show up, but my mom—"

"Is she okay? I mean, I know she's not okay. But did something—"

"Hailee, relax, she's okay, all things considered."

"That's good." I let out a small sigh of relief. "You didn't call to say you were coming?"

"Honestly?" He ran a hand down his handsome face. "I didn't know what to say."

"Oh."

This was so awkward, and I hated it. I hated that we'd become like strangers to one another.

"Do you want to sit?" I asked.

"Yeah, that would be good."

We moved into the living room. "Are you sure you're okay?" He eyed the glass of ice chips and the blanket.

"I haven't been feeling great."

"I didn't know."

"You've had bigger things on your mind. How's Xander?"

"He's good. Thank you for the care packages. He loved them. He misses you."

I gave him a small shrug. "It's the least I could do. Cameron, why are you here?" I blurted out.

"Sorry, I didn't mean—"

"That came out wrong. I'm happy to see you, I am. It's just you kind of caught me off guard."

"I miss you, Hailee. I miss you so fucking much. I wanted to call, but I was so scared you'd tell me not to come..."

"You thought I'd... Cameron, I'm right here. I've always been here. I've just been trying to give you space."

"I know you have." He reached for me, but thought better of it and thrust his hand under his thigh. It stung.

"My mom had a dream..."

"A dream?"

"I know it sounds crazy, but she got it into her head you needed me. She insisted I come to see you. Like got really weird about it."

"So, you're here because of your mom?"

"No, that's not... I know how it sounds, but I wanted to come. I've wanted to come ever since you left. But I couldn't leave them, and it wasn't fair to ask you to stay. Fuck..." Cameron's eyes shuttered as he inhaled a ragged breath. "Everything is so fucked-up."

Shuffling closer, I took his hand in mine, squeezing it gently. "It's okay. I understand."

"Do you?" His eyes slid to mine. "Because I don't. I don't understand anything anymore. But my mom said I needed to come, and it was like she was giving me permission... so here I am."

"Cameron..." I swallowed the words. It was like Karen was here, standing over us, watching as we tried to sort our shit out.

I knew if Cameron hadn't turned up here today, I probably wouldn't have told him yet. But could I really let him leave without giving him the truth?

"I don't understand either," I whispered. "But your mom was right."

"W- what do you mean?" His eyes were filled with trepidation.

"I'm pregnant."

The silence was deafening. My pulse hammered inside my chest, making me a little lightheaded.

"You're *pregnant*?"

I nodded. "Almost three months."

"But... how?"

"The doctor said it happens sometimes. I didn't miss a period, but I was sick when I came to Rixon with you, remember?"

"You knew and you didn't tell me?"

"I didn't think you'd be ready to hear it..." I still wasn't sure he was.

"The ice chips?"

"Morning sickness sucks." I went to pull my hand away, but Cameron caught it.

"A baby? We're having... *a baby*?" He swallowed, an awestruck expression falling over him.

It was too much, and tears sprang from my eyes as I nodded.

"I'm sorry." He dropped to his knees, moving between my legs. "I'm so fucking sorry. I should have been here. I should have been here with you."

"No." I brushed the hair from his eyes. "You needed to be with your family. I understand—"

"You're my family too, Hailee. I should never have pushed you away. I'm so sorry. She knew, my mom knew... how is that even possible?"

I didn't know, but I would be forever thankful to her.

"Maybe she just wants to make sure you're happy before she..."

Sadness washed over us both. "She said the same thing." Cameron curved his hand around the nape of my neck and touched his head to mine. "Can you forgive me?"

"There's nothing to forgive."

"I guess we have a lot to talk about," he said. "But first, I'd really like to kiss you."

I stared down at him, fighting a smile as I said, "What are you waiting for?"

Cameron

Six months later...

"I DON'T WANT TO," Hailee cried, pain filling her voice.

I squeezed her hand. "Just another big push, and he'll be here."

My son.

I was having a son.

To say the last six months had been a whirlwind was an understatement. After Mom had sent me to Michigan, Hailee and I started making plans for the future. We got to enjoy one last Christmas with my mom. It had been bittersweet, but we'd filled it with so much love and happiness and gifts, all the gifts, that it was hard to look back and be sad. Mom had gotten her wish. I was happy, Xander was doing better, and my son was about to make his grand entrance into the world.

"Okay, Hailee, he's almost here. I need you to push again, okay?"

"Cam, I can't do it." She turned into me and I kissed her damp forehead.

"You've got this, Hailee. One more push."

Her screams filled the room but then a different sound took over. A baby's cries.

"He's here," I choked out. "He's finally here."

It had been hard losing Mom three months ago. We'd all hoped she would make it to see the baby, but in the end it wasn't meant to be. I'd made a promise to her that he would know his Grandma Karen though. He would know of her love and strength and spirit.

Tears rolled down my cheeks as the nurses handed Hailee the bundle of blankets. "Oh God, Cam," she croaked. "Look at him."

I stroked a finger along his little face. "He's perfect."

"He really is."

As I watched Hailee watch our son, I was hit with such a sense of pride and love, I felt sure I would combust.

"Have you decided on a name?" I asked her, my voice shaky with emotion.

"Avery Chase, after your mom."

It had been her middle name.

"I love you," I said. "I love you both so much and I will spend my life loving you."

"We know." Hailee smiled, her eyes filled with so much happiness I just knew we were going to be okay.

Because if my mom had taught me anything, it was that life didn't always go to plan. We couldn't know what was around the corner, we could only live each moment as it came. And I intended on loving each and every moment for her.

For my son, and my family.

For the girl who had stolen my heart when I was just a boy.

I'd live it for them all.

Because I'd been taught once to play hard... fight hard... and ***love*** hard.

EPILOGUE

"IT'S OFFICIAL FOLKS. Fans everywhere will be mourning the loss of one of the greats today. Jason Ford, Heisman Trophy winner, American All-Star, and one of the NFL's top-rated quarterbacks of all-time is retiring. After six years with the Philadelphia Eagles, Ford suffered a string of injuries last season."

"Yeah, Dan, it's been a rocky year for the record-breaking QB. He enjoyed five years of success with the Eagles, including two super bowls, but last year he suffered that nasty shoulder cuff injury and things went downhill pretty quickly from there."

"But his high school team, the Rixon Raiders will be pretty excited to see the return of Ford as he joins them as assistant coach."

"That's right, Dan. Ford and his family are relocating back to Rixon. And who knows, maybe it won't be the end of his legacy."

Jason

There had once been a time when a three-year-old's birthday party would have sent me running for the hills. But when one of the birthday girls was your daughter, that wasn't really an option. I cut the engine, climbed out of my SUV, and set about emptying the trunk of all the balloons Fee and Hailee had sent me out to get.

Fuck knows why we needed more balloons. Cam's house was already full of the damn things. But I knew better than to argue with my wife *and* my sister.

Hands full, I trudged up the driveway, which was already full of cars, and let myself into the house. It sounded like a zoo, kids running and screaming, adults hovering on the fringes unsure whether to intervene or let them have at it.

God, I missed football.

At least back then, things were simple.

"Daddy, Daddy," Lily charged at my legs. "You got boons."

"Sure did, baby." I thrust the handful of balloons at the first person I saw and scooped up the birthday girl. "Are you enjoying your party?"

"Yes," she shrieked with glee. "I am free."

"Three, you're three, Lily."

"She's a handful, is what she is." Fee came over with our youngest, Poppy, asleep in her arms, and leaned in kissing Lily, and then my cheek. "Thank you."

"Anything for the birthday girls. This place is crazy." I eyed my wife discreetly. Three-year old's were cunning things, wily and intuitive. Cam kept telling me it was a girl thing, which meant I was shit out of luck since I had two daughters. At least he had Xander and Avery to balance things out.

Lucky fucker.

Guilt flashed through me. Cameron was lucky. He had a beautiful family, but it had come at a steep price. Three years after his mom had died, Clarke, his dad, had been killed in a traffic accident. He and my sister had become Xander's guardians after that, their family of three turning into four. Then Hailee found out she was pregnant again. Now they had their hands full trying to raise a teenager, a six-year-old, and a three-year-old.

But they made it look easy. Hailee loved being a mom and Cameron was so good with the kids, I was a tad jealous.

"There's my beautiful niece." Hailee approached us. "Where's my cuddle, Lil?"

"Auntie Ailee." Lily reached for my sister and I let her go.

"Where's Cam and Ash?" I asked her, hooking my arm around Fee's waist.

"The last time I saw Asher, he was trying to wrestle the twins upstairs for a diaper change."

"That I would pay to see."

"Babe," Fee warned, pressing her hand to my stomach. "He's trying his best. But twins are…" She shuddered.

"Yeah, I can't even imagine."

"Good, because I'm done. Two is more than enough for us." She grinned up at me and I captured her lips in a kiss.

"I'm going to find the men." In my experience, you needed to stick together at these things, otherwise the little monsters would divide and conquer.

I FOUND Cameron hiding in Hailee's studio. Ashleigh was asleep on his shoulder. "Hey," I whispered. "Too much for the birthday girl?"

Lily and Ashleigh were born only days apart, so we usually celebrated together.

"She just crashed like ten minutes ago. I don't want to disturb her."

"It's crazy out there."

"It's life." He took a long pull on his beer. "I can't believe they're three already." He gazed at his daughter.

"How did we end up here, man?"

"End up where?" Asher joined us.

"Here in a house full of screaming kids."

"Don't look at me," he said, perching against the sideboard. "I don't even know what day it is right now."

"You should just come home," Cam suggested. "Move back to Rixon and let your folks help out with the twins."

"We're thinking about it."

"Yeah?" I asked.

"Yeah. Mya's aunt is sick, and she wants to be closer to her. But we've got to think of the kids."

Mya and Asher had fostered six kids over the last few years. I didn't know how they did it, but they made it work.

"You can still foster in Rixon."

"We can, but you know how Mya feels about being in the city."

"It would be good to have you both back, the kids can grow up together..."

"Fuck, can you imagine?" I liked to live in denial about having daughters... daughters who would one day become *teenage girls*.

"Do you ever think it's karma for all the bad shit we did back in the day?" My eyes went to my niece still sleeping soundly on her daddy's shoulder.

"Karma?" Cam chuckled. "You think having daughters is karma?"

"I'm not ready for it."

"For what?"

"School..." My jaw clenched. "All those little punks thinking they can—"

"Jase, they're three."

"Yeah, and one day they'll be seventeen thinking they can tame the bad boy."

"You've really given this a lot of thought, haven't you?" Asher smirked, and I flipped him off.

"You're telling me you haven't thought about it? Remember what we were like in high school? What Hailee, Mya, and Fee were like." I glared at both of them and realization slowly dawned on their expressions.

"We're fucked," Cam said.

"Totally fucked." Asher ran a hand down his face.

"Welcome to my world," I grumbled.

There had once been a time I'd thought football was everything... but football was the dream. This right here, this was the life.

It was everything.

Every-fucking-thing.

THE FUTURE YOU MAKE

THE CABIN

CHAPTER ONE

Felicity

"BABE, WE'RE ALMOST THERE." Jason's voice lulled me from my dream.

"We're here?" I glanced out of the window but couldn't see much given the thicket. Huge, sprawling, snow-capped trees surrounded us, but our rental SUV made easy work of navigating the overgrown track.

"Are you sure this is the place?" I asked around a yawn.

Jase's hand slid over my thigh and squeezed, "Don't you trust me?"

I covered his hand with mine, loving how my engagement ring glinted in the dark. "You know I do. It just seems a little off the beaten track."

"Which is exactly why we're here. Just you, me, and an open fire."

"God, it sounds like heaven." I let out a contented sigh.

It had been a crazy couple of weeks. There had been the Heisman Trophy award ceremony weekend in New York. Jason had proposed, after which our families had insisted on throwing us a party, and then Christmas had come and gone. We'd barely had time to blink, so when Gio had mentioned his friend had a few cabins in Rhode Island, Jason asked if we could rent one for the weekend.

Just us, a cabin in the woods, and—

"Uh, babe, isn't that Gio's car?"

"Yeah." He frowned. "He said Nicco was meeting us here."

Nicco was Gio's friend who was gifting us the cabin for this weekend, since Gio said it was an engagement present.

"There's another car," I motioned to the truck.

"What the fuck is he up to?" Jason grumbled.

"I'm sure it's nothing." At least, I hoped it was because I really wanted to relax with my fiancée.

The car rolled to a stop, and Jason came around, helping me out. "Careful," he said, "the snow is pretty compacted."

"It's so beautiful out here." Even with the sun sinking into the horizon, you could see the cabin, hidden by a canopy of trees. An amber glow flickered in the window and fairy lights hung from the wooden wraparound porch.

"I'm so excited."

"Me too." Jason kissed me hard, letting his tongue tangle with mine. "This weekend is going to be perfect." Heat flared in his eyes making my tummy clench.

Even after all this time, I still couldn't believe I got to call this man—this strong, loyal, determined man—mine.

"There you are," Gio's deep voice filled the frigid air. "You made it okay then?"

"We did." Jason led us over to the cabin and the two of them fist bumped. "Wasn't expecting to see you here though." He quirked a brow.

"I wanted it to be a surprise, although I ended up with some clingers." He grimaced, something passing over his face. "I hope you don't mind."

"Actually, we—"

"Of course we don't." I hugged Gio, kissing his cheek. "We're just excited to be here." Jason shot me a bemused look, but I waved him off. "We have all weekend," I mouthed at him.

He rolled his eyes and went to the trunk to get our bags. Gio helped him and the three of us made our way up the wooden steps to the door.

"This is amazing." My eyes grew to saucers as I took in the huge, open-plan living room, the roaring fire, and open beams. There was a small tree glittering in the corner and garlands adorned the fireplace.

"I'm glad you think so." One of the most good-looking guys I'd ever seen stepped forward.

"Oh, hello," I stuttered, feeling my cheeks grow hot. "I'm Felicity."

"Nicco." He smiled warmly, and I swear my knees went weak.

So this was Nicco Marchetti, Gio's friend.

"This is my family's cabin."

"Well, it's really something. We appreciate you letting us stay here."

"Gio said you just got engaged?"

"We did." Jason stepped up to me, wrapping his arm around me in a total display of possessiveness.

Someone snickered, and my eyes found another Italian Adonis standing over by the kitchen area.

"Matteo." He smiled around a nod.

Oh boy, these guys had good Italian genes.

"You're so pretty," a girl peeked out from behind him. "I'm Alessia, Nicco's sister."

"It's nice to meet you."

"Congratulations. Can I see your ring?" She moved closer. She was also beautiful. Light to Nicco's dark, but you could see the resemblance.

"Sure." I thrust out my hand, more than happy to show it off.

"Wow, it's so beautiful. You guys are still in college?"

"We're sophomores, yeah."

"Nicco and Arianne just—"

"Sia." Nicco shook his head and she gave me an apologetic smile. "Sorry, I can get a little carried away with myself."

"It's okay."

"We weren't expecting the welcome party," Jason said.

"We had some business to take care of this way, so thought we'd make sure you were all settled in. The weather is forecasted to get worse, so I wanted to personally check you had everything you needed."

My brows furrowed. As far as I knew, Nicco was a sophomore like us. He seemed older somehow though, an air of command about him.

"Hello," another girl entered the room. "I'm Arianne."

Nicco welcomed her into his arms, gazing down at her with such love I felt it in my bones.

Wow.

They made a gorgeous couple.

She wrapped her arms around him and leaned her head on his shoulder. "Jason and Felicity, right?"

"It's nice to meet you," I replied.

"Gio has told us all about you. Congratulations on the engagement."

"Thank you."

"Why don't I show Jason where the emergency generator is—"

"Emergency generator?" My eyes widened.

"It's just a precaution." Nicco smiled, settling some of my nerves.

"Down, babe," Jase whispered against the shell of my ear, and I elbowed his ribs, my cheeks pinking.

I was only human, and Nicco was gorgeous. But Jason knew who I belonged to. I was wearing his ring for God's sake.

"How does hot cocoa by the fire sound?" Arianne asked me.

"That sounds pretty great actually."

Jason

"So, your family is in the cabin rental business?" I asked Nicco as we followed Matteo and Gio around back. The snow was already banking up, the icy wind like tiny blades across my skin, but I wasn't worried. If we got snowed in, it'd only give me an excuse to spend more time alone with Felicity.

Fuck knows we needed it after a busy couple of weeks. Everyone was excited about the engagement, but it had been a constant stream of drinks and dinners and celebrations. I was looking forward to spending some quality time with my girl.

Just the two of us with no interruptions.

"Cabin rental business," Matteo said with a hint of amusement. "Yeah, something like that."

"Matt," Nicco warned, and I felt like I was missing something.

"It's a nice place though, right?" Gio added.

"Yeah, it's something else. Thanks for hooking us up."

"It's all good. Nicco owed me a favor, right Nic?" He grinned at Nicco who rolled his eyes.

"Ignore them," he said. "This cabin is just one my family owns. We prefer to keep them for family and friends only."

"Well, thanks again." I gave him an appreciative nod, pulling the collar of my jacket tighter to give me some protection from the icy wind.

"Okay, so this is the generator. If power goes out, and it shouldn't, you'll need to come out here and manually start it." He motioned to the switch.

"Got it."

"We stocked the refrigerator and there's plenty of firewood, and I'm sure Fee will keep you warm." Gio smirked. I leveled him with a hard look.

"Joke," he murmured. "I'm joking. The snow is only supposed to last until the day after tomorrow, and they'll clear the main roads. You'll be good."

I really didn't care. In fact, getting snowed in for a few extra days sounded pretty damn good to me.

"Got any New Year's Eve plans?"

"We're heading to New York to celebrate with our friends." Asher and Mya were having a small thing at their place. Nothing crazy. Just the six of us.

"Nice," Matteo said. "We should think about making tracks soon." He and Nicco shared a look, and that strange sensation rippled through me again.

I didn't know much about Gio's friends, just that his sister Nora was best friends with Arianne and Nicco.

I figured they were good people to let us stay at the cabin for three nights, but I couldn't shake the feeling there was more to Nicco and Matteo than met the eye.

"Come on, my balls are freezing." Gio nudged my shoulder and we made our way back inside to the girls.

To my fiancée.

Fuck, saying that would never get old.

Felicity

"This is delicious, thank you so much." I took another sip of the hot cocoa.

"It's an old family recipe," Alessia said. "I left a tub here for you."

"Wow, thanks."

"We stocked the refrigerator too," Arianne added, "and the wine rack." She brushed some stray hairs away from her face and my eyes instantly found the wedding band on her finger.

"You're married?" I pressed my lips into a thin line and murmured, "Sorry, that sounded rude."

"It's okay." She gave me a warm smile. "We get that a lot."

"But you're so young."

She and Alessia shared a look, before she settled her warm gaze back on mine. "When you know, you know."

"Yeah, I get that." Things hadn't always been easy between Jason and I, but after the initial push and pull, I'd fallen hard and fast. I couldn't wait to be Mrs. Jason Ford. But we weren't in any hurry, not with two-and-a-half years of college left.

I was about to ask Arianne about the wedding when male laughter drifted down the hall.

"Comfortable?" Matteo's brow lifted as he glanced at Alessia who had curled into a ball in one of the armchairs by the fire.

"I love it out here," she sighed.

"Don't you get out here a lot?" I asked.

"Not as much as we'd like," Nicco replied. "Sia, let's go."

"Can't we stay just a little longer?" Her eyes flicked to mine and I was about to tell them it was okay, that they could stay, when Arianne stood.

"Nicco's right, we should leave Felicity and Jason to enjoy their stay."

"Spare keys are on the hook." Nicco pointed to a small hook by the door. "There are extra blankets in the cupboard in the bedroom. If you need anything else, we're only a thirty-minute ride away."

"I think we're set." Jason held out his hand. "Thanks again, we really appreciate it."

"Anytime." The two of them shook hands. Nicco broke away first, reaching for Arianne. It was fascinating to watch them together. He was clearly super protective of her, but not in an overt alpha way. It was subtle; in the way he held her close and slightly behind him, as if readying himself to become her human shield.

"It was nice to meet you both," she said. "Maybe we'll get to see you again before you leave."

"That would be nice," I said.

Jason caught my eye and frowned, and I could practically hear his thoughts. He didn't want visitors; he wanted the next three days to be about the two of us. Alone. Together in the middle of nowhere.

My skin turned hot just thinking about it.

"Fee, pleasure as always." Gio leaned in for a hug but I felt Jason move to my side.

He was such a caveman, but I couldn't deny it made my heart soar knowing how possessive he was.

"Thanks, Gio, for everything." I kissed his cheek. "Enjoy the rest of the holidays."

"Yeah." His expression turned tight but then he was gone, fist bumping Jason before moving to the door.

We watched as they filed out of the cabin and into the dark, snowy night. The second Jason closed the door, he slid the lock into place, and turned toward me.

"Thank fuck," he breathed. "I thought they were never going to leave."

"Jason! Don't be so rude. They wanted to make sure we had everything we needed."

"That's the thing though, babe..." He began prowling toward me with slow, sure strides. "I do."

CHAPTER TWO

Jason

I STARED down at Felicity and my heart beat wildly in my chest. Even after all this time, it was her.

It would always be her.

I hadn't proposed on a whim. It was something I'd been thinking about for a while. Then everything got kind of messed up at the beginning of the semester. Felicity was struggling with her classes, and I was feeling the pressure of leading the team. For a while there, we began to lose our way. But my faith in us, my bone deep love for her, never wavered. Even when she doubted our relationship, my belief only grew.

Felicity Giles was my endgame, and one day, in the not-so-distant future, she would be my wife. It didn't get much more fucking real than that.

"Jason?" She gazed up at me with love and devotion shining in her eyes, and it was like a bolt of lightning to the heart.

Every. Single. Time.

I sensed Felicity didn't realize it, but she'd saved me. Saved me from myself and a life of never being able to trust or open my heart up to anyone.

She did that.

"Fuck, I love you." I traced my fingers down her cheek, leaning down to brush my lips over hers.

She curled her hands into my sweater. "Jason," she whispered.

"Yeah, babe?"

"I love you."

"Yeah, I love you too. So fucking much."

"I'm glad everyone left." She peppered tiny kisses over my mouth and jaw.

"I was one second away from throwing them out." My quiet laughter filled the pockets of space between us.

"You're such a caveman."

"Does that mean it's time to throw you over my shoulder, take you to my cave, and have my wicked way with you?" Her breath caught, and I eased back to meet her hooded eyes. "Caveman fantasy, really?"

"Jase." She batted my chest, but I captured her wrist.

"Are you hungry?"

"Not for food." Her eyes flared.

"Thank fuck." I kissed Felicity hard, plunging my tongue into her mouth as I slid my hands to her thighs and hoisted her against my body.

"Do you know where the bedroom is?" she rasped between kisses.

"Who said anything about the bedroom?" I made my way over to the soft, faux-fur rug in front of the fire, carefully lowering myself to the floor. Felicity wrapped her body around mine, gripping my jaw between her slim fingers and kissed me as if she might never get to kiss me again.

On my knees, I gently laid her back and leaned over her.

"Smooth," she chuckled.

"I'm about to pull out all my best moves." I winked.

"You already put a ring on it, I think your moves were a resounding success." Felicity was a picture of happiness, her eyes sparkling and her smile infectious.

"God, I love you." I splayed my hand around her throat and looked down at her.

"Show me," she purred, the needy tone to her voice making my dick twitch.

I made quick work of stripping Felicity's clothes from her body, which was no easy feat considering how many layers she had on. But it was worth it, the red and black lacy bra and matching panties accentuated her curves.

"Look at you." It came out rough as I imagined all the things I wanted to do with her.

"Do you like it?" she asked around a coy smile, letting her fingers drop to the small bow between the valley of her breasts. "It's your post-Christmas present."

"Like it? I want to tear it from your body and—"

"Don't you dare, it cost me a small fortune."

"I'll resist, I promise."

But I couldn't resist sliding my hand up the inside of her thigh and rubbing her clit over the lace.

"God," she breathed.

"Not God, babe, your fiancé." I hooked the material aside and pushed two fingers deep inside her. Felicity writhed on the rug, one hand twisted into the thread and one clenched around my forearm.

"Does it feel good?" I curled my fingers and rubbed just how I knew she liked it.

"Yes... Jase, *yes...*" Her body began to tremble, but I needed more. I needed to taste her.

Yanking my fingers away, I sucked them clean before pulling off my jacket and sweater.

"Hurry," she whimpered. Desperate. Needy.

I unbuttoned my jeans and shuffled back, giving myself enough room to lower myself onto my elbows, running my nose along her panties. Inching them down her legs, I tasted her, groaning as she hit my tongue. "Best fucking meal I've ever tasted."

"Jason!"

I took another swipe, before tonguing her clit. "You were saying?" I chuckled, reveling in the string of cuss words falling from Fee's lips.

She tasted so fucking good, I didn't ever want to come up for air. I licked and teased, circled and sucked. I worked her with my fingers and tongue until she was a breathless mess screaming my name.

"God, Jase," she rasped, "that was..."

I moved up her body, kissing her deeply. "Just the beginning."

Felicity

Time stood still; it always did when Jason kissed me. He wasn't just highly skilled on the field, he was annoyingly good at everything he did—including sex.

I ran my fingers through his hair as his lips devoured mine. The crackle of the fire, the smoky scent in the air, even the soft fur beneath my body, all helped create this little slice of heaven we'd found ourselves in.

"Fuck, Felicity, I've missed this... us."

"I know exactly what you mean." Pressing my hand to his cheek, I leaned up, kissing him softly, tracing the shape of his lips with my own.

We'd spent time together since the engagement, but not like this. Not away from the fast pace of everyday life.

Jason eased back to remove his jeans. I marveled at his body, every dip and ridge, his perfect physical condition testament to his dedication to the game.

His body was a work of art, and I was the lucky girl who got to touch.

The *only* girl.

I reached for Jason, needing to feel him close, needing his weight pressing me into the rug and his hips pinning me in place.

I needed to feel owned by him—the man I'd one day call my husband.

"I need you," I whispered the second he kissed me.

"You have me, Fee, always." He snagged my left hand and brought it to his mouth. "One day, I'm going to stand in front of all our friends and families and declare you mine until death do us part. But until then, know you own me Felicity Giles, heart, body, and soul."

Jason slammed inside of me, so hard I cried out. My nails raked down his back as he sealed his promise over and over.

"Nothing," he kissed me, "*nothing* will ever feel as good as this. As good as you." He pulled my legs over his hips, changing the angle.

God, I could feel him everywhere.

"Jason..." I panted, feeling my world grow small. "It's... God..."

"You're mine," he growled, licking my throat, biting the skin there. "Mine, Fee."

"Always."

He slowed the pace, rocking into me with torturous restraint, dragging every ounce of pleasure from me as he pushed me toward the precipice of ecstasy.

"I'm so close," I cried.

"Come for me, babe, come all over my cock."

His dirty words sent me flying over the edge. I clenched around him, drowning in intense waves of pleasure.

"Fuck, babe... fuck..." Jason's body locked up and then he unraveled, jerking inside me. He dropped his brow to mine, brushing his nose down my cheek. "You are amazing."

"You aren't so bad yourself."

A smirk pulled at the corner of his mouth. "Something tells me I owe Gio big time for this."

Trailing a finger down his sweaty torso, I laughed softly. "We could've locked ourselves away in our apartment."

"It's not the same," he let out a small sigh. "There's always something. Ash, the team, Coach... our families."

"Yeah, I know what you mean."

"Here, it's like it's just us and nothing else can touch us. It's nice."

Jason's words touched something inside me. People underestimated how hard it was to be the best, to be loved and adored by thousands of football fans. Everything Jason did or said, every game he played, every practice and night out with the team, he was scrutinized.

And I was the girl by his side.

It wasn't always easy being in love with an athlete, taking a back seat to the devotion and dedication to their chosen sport. But Jason had proved to me time and time again that I was his priority.

Now I had the ring to prove it.

"I love you," I whispered.

And his response was the same as always.

"Not nearly as much as I love you."

Jason

After cleaning up, we raided the refrigerator and cooked spaghetti. Side by side, we worked together to slice the onions and peppers and dice the garlic. Nicco wasn't lying when he said they'd stocked up. There was everything we could need for at least three or four days. Including some whipped cream and chocolate sauce that I had big plans for later. It was probably meant for the tiramisu, but I knew it would taste better licked off Felicity's body.

"Hey, look at this," she said. She was rooting around in one of the drawers, looking for a pasta ladle.

"What is it?" I wiped my hand on a towel and joined her.

"An old photo, look. I think that's Nicco's great grandad and maybe his uncles."

It was a grainy black and white print, but the resemblance was obvious.

"Check out the Fedoras and suspenders." Holding my arm around Fee's waist, I pulled her back into my chest.

"They look like something out of a nineteen twenties mob film."

"Yeah, right," I chuckled, but something prickled up my spine.

No, they couldn't be.

Gio would have said something... he would—

Nah.

Nicco wasn't a mobster. The guy was too gracious and clearly loved up, if the way he gazed at Arianne was anything to go by.

"I don't know, they seemed kind of cagey."

"Who? Nicco and Matteo?" I brushed it off. "They were friendly enough."

"So, you don't think—"

"No, I don't." I pulled the photo from her fingers and shoved it back in the drawer. Felicity glanced up at me and I captured her lips in a bruising kiss.

"Dinner, we have to eat before we—"

I kissed her deeper, turning her into me. Without warning, I picked Felicity up and sat her on the counter, fitting myself between her legs.

"Jason, the sauce..."

"Can wait."

"You're insatiable."

"Never claimed to be anything else." My fingers went to the hem of the oversized shirt she'd pulled on after we'd taken a shower.

"But we just got cleaned up."

"And now I really, *really* want to dirty you up again." My fingers walked up the flat of her stomach and she sucked in a shaky breath.

"You're supposed to be feeding me." Felicity pouted.

"I'll feed you, I promise, once I've made you come all over my tongue." I pressed her back against the counter, laying her out before me. My heart pounded in my chest at the sight of her.

"Okay." It was breathless sigh. "But be quick. I don't want the spaghetti to burn."

Smirking against her thigh, I murmured, "Challenge accepted."

CHAPTER THREE

Felicity

I WOKE FIRST. Jason looked so peaceful, I didn't want to wake him. So I slipped out of bed, pulled on a big, chunky knit cardigan over my nightshirt, and went to make coffee. When it was ready, I nestled myself in one of the chairs near the window and watched the snow fall.

It was coming down fast, but everything looked so beautiful covered in white. The color of innocence and purity. It made me smile, imagining myself draped in white lace, standing under a snow-capped archway, saying my vows to a man who owned me in every possible way.

God, I loved Jason so much.

I wanted a life with him, a future. I wanted the big wedding and the white picket fence and a bunch of dark-haired, green-eyed babies running around.

I wanted it all.

A little sigh of contentment slipped from my lips, but it turned into something more when Jason cupped the back of my neck and tilted my head up to meet his. "Good morning," he rasped, his voice still thick with sleep.

"Good morning."

"How long have you been awake?"

"A little while. You were out for the count."

"You should have woken me," he breathed the words against my lips.

"It's okay, I was enjoying the view."

"I'm enjoying the view." His eyes went to where my nightshirt had fallen open.

"Pig." I smacked his chest.

"Temptress." He kissed me again, making my body stir to life.

God, would I ever get enough of him?

"Is there coffee?"

"Yeah, I just made a fresh pot." I watched Jason stalk over to the coffee machine. He was shirtless despite the cold air, but I wasn't complaining.

"I can feel your eyes on me, Giles."

"Fiancée perks," I teased.

He glanced back at me and winked. "Indeed." When he'd poured himself a coffee, he leaned against the counter and said, "What do you want to do today?"

"You mean apart from get naked and spend the day in front of the fire?" My brow arched.

"I didn't know if you'd want to explore? I saw a sled out back when Nicco showed me where the generator was."

"A sled?"

"Yeah, it could be fun."

"Are you going to pull me around like I'm the snow queen?"

He chuckled. "What will I get in return?"

"What do you want in return?"

Hunger flared in Jason's eyes as he raked his gaze over me. He stalked toward me, pulling me from the chair and lifting me up his body. Soft laughter spilled from my lips as I wound my legs around his waist.

"We need to shower," I protested.

"I'm going to dirty you up first, *then* we can shower."

My brow quirked. "Maybe you should dirty me up *in* the shower."

A slow grin spread over his face. "It's like you can read my mind."

"What about sledding?"

He nuzzled my neck, sucking the skin there gently. "It can wait."

Jason

Almost two hours later, we resurfaced. I couldn't get enough of Felicity. Her body, her soft curves, and her musical laughter. She was my addiction and after every high ended, I was desperate for another hit.

"Are you ready?" I called, pulling on my hat. It was freezing out, so we'd packed layers.

For as much as I wanted to stay in bed and discover all the ways I could make her cry my name, I also wanted us to have fun. Some good old-fashioned fun in the snow.

"Ready." She flounced into the living room. "Hmm, you look good in a hat."

"Babe, I always look good."

Felicity rolled her eyes, pulling on her thermal gloves. "Are we doing this, or what?"

"Oh, it's on."

Her smile grew and, hand in hand, we left the cabin.

"It's really coming down," I said, straining my eyes against the flurry. The wind whipped the snow around us, and I glanced back at the cabin. It was beginning to bank up against the porch. "I'll clear that off later."

"We'll be okay, right?" Felicity frowned.

"Yeah, the weather forecast said it's clearing into tomorrow." Hooking my arm around her waist, I pulled her back into my chest. "But would it really be so awful to be stranded here with me?"

"No." She smiled up at me. "But I don't want to miss New Year."

Shit. New Years.

"We'll make it, I promise."

"So where's this sled you speak of, because honestly, I'm tired just thinking about trying to find our way through that." Felicity tipped her head to the woods before us.

"Stay right here." I kissed her head before jogging around the side of the cabin and retrieving the sled. It was one of those proper wooden ones with metal plated runners and a curved back rest.

Felicity clapped her hands the second I came into view. "Now we're talking."

"Just go steady, we don't want no accidents."

"Jason," she huffed indignantly, "I am quite capable of getting onto—" Her foot slipped and she went backwards, landing on her ass with an *oomph.*

"You were saying?" I bit back a laugh, offering her my hand.

"It's very slippy." She huffed, slipping again.

"Here, let me." I scooped her up in my arms and gently lowered her to the sled. "Better?"

"Just when I think I can't love you anymore..." She rolled her eyes dramatically.

I grabbed the rope and tested the pull. The sled glided over the snow with ease.

"I could get used to this," Felicity called.

"Oh, really?" I arched a brow over my shoulder, smirking. "You'd better hold on then."

"Jason, no—"

Too late.

I took off running, pulling the sled behind me. Felicity's shrieks filled the air, but they had nothing on the rumble of my laughter.

Felicity

We spent all morning in the snow. I was cold and my boots and socks were damp, but I hadn't smiled so much in a long time. There was something about the snow that made you revert to being a kid.

We'd had snowball fights and made snow angels. Jason had pulled me through the woods, shaking the snowcapped trees over me as we went. We'd even made a snowman, complete with twig arms and stone eyes. By the time we finally made our way back to the cabin, my ribs ached from all the laughter.

"That was fun, we should do it again tomorrow," I said, trudging up the steps to the cabin. The snow was still coming thick and fast, but the wind had dropped a little.

"You go inside and get warm," Jason suggested, "and I'll clear the porch."

"I'll make some hot cocoa and see what there is for lunch."

"Sounds good." He kissed me before taking off in search of a snow shovel.

I pulled off my coat and hung it up before toeing off my boats and leaving them by the fire.

I was halfway through making us both a sandwich when Jason reappeared.

"Hello, snowman," I chuckled at the sight of him, snow clinging to his lashes and hair.

"It's coming down harder."

"Good job my plans for this afternoon included staying in then."

He shucked out of his coat and joined me at the breakfast counter. "And what exactly do your plans include?"

"I found some old board games." I smirked. "I thought I could whip your ass at Battleships."

"You want to play board games?" His eyes narrowed.

"What's wrong with playing board games?"

"Is there a pack of playing cards?"

"Playing cards?" My brow arched as I slid his cup of hot cocoa across the counter.

He smirked. "The only game I want to play, is one that ends up with you naked and underneath me."

"And we need playing cards for that?" My lips twitched.

Jason took a bite of his sandwich and grinned. "We do if we want to play Strip Poker."

Jason

Felicity's laughter was like music to my fucking ears. My arm shot out, pulling her toward me. I gripped her jaw and lowered my face to kiss her. "One day, I'm going to put a baby inside you." The words spilled out with warning, and I froze.

Had I really just fucking said that?

Felicity's brows furrowed. "Did you just say what I think you said?"

"I... uh..."

She chuckled again. "We've never talked about kids before."

"No, I guess we haven't." I ran a hand over my jaw. "But you want them, right?" Because now I'd said the words, all I could picture was a little kid with Felicity's big eyes and her big heart.

"Yeah, I mean... when we're older. *Much* older."

It was my turn to chuckle. "I love you, Felicity Giles. I love you so fucking much, I can't wait to make a life with you."

Her cheeks pinked under my intense regard. "What has gotten into you?" She batted my chest.

"What, a guy can't be happy?"

I'd never imagined myself wanting to settle down. Hell, I'd never imagined myself wifed up and playing house with a girl. But Felicity made me want things.

Scary as fuck things.

Going pro was still the dream, it always would be. Now that I'd won the Heisman Trophy, I had my sights set on the NFL draft. But lately—especially since putting a ring on her finger—I was thinking beyond that.

She narrowed her gaze. "Hmm, you seem, I don't know... different."

"It's you," I said with complete conviction. "It's all you."

Felicity

"Do you think we'll always be friends?" I asked Jason as he stroked my hair.

After lunch, and Jason's surprising confession, we'd climbed back into bed and spent the rest of the day there, tangled up in each other. We hadn't done this in forever. Life was always so busy with classes and my volunteering work, and with Jason practicing with the team. It was the perfect end to the year.

"Babe, you're wearing my ring, I should fucking hope so."

"Not us, silly. I mean with Cam and Hailee, and Asher and Mya."

"What kind of dumb question is that?" He grunted. "Of course we'll always be friends. We'll have kids and they'll have kids and they'll all grow up together."

"What if football takes us across country?"

"Then we come home after I'm done." He shrugged.

"You sound so sure of everything."

"Because I am, babe." Jason kissed my head, brushing his foot alongside mine. "Our life is going to be amazing, you'll see."

"I hope so." I couldn't imagine not having Hailee and Mya in my life. They were my ride or die friends, the way Cam and Asher were Jason's. The fact we all got on and were friends was an added bonus.

"I think Cam and Hailee will get pregnant first," I mused.

"What makes you say that?"

"Cameron wants to be there, back in Rixon. Don't you see it in his eyes?"

"Yeah, maybe."

"He's already counting down until the day they graduate and can move home." Part of me wondered if he'd even make it that long.

"I'm not so sure about Asher and Mya though," he said. "She loves the city."

"Yeah."

Silence settled over us. We still had time. We were only sophomores. But life was moving fast. Before we knew it, we would be seniors, counting down the days until graduation, and everything would change again.

As if he could sense my thoughts, Jason hugged me closer. "It doesn't matter, babe. Wherever we all land, we'll still be family. Always."

CHAPTER FOUR

Jason

THE NEXT MORNING, I woke first. But I didn't move. I was more than content watching Felicity sleep, thinking back on our conversation yesterday. I'd meant what I said, that it didn't matter where we went or how our lives moved in different directions, the six of us would always be tight. Cam and Asher were my guys. Even though I'd made new friends at Penn, they would never replace the bond I shared with my best friends.

Slipping out of bed, I pulled on a hoodie and went in search of coffee. Turning on the coffee machine, I went to start the fire next, adding a new pile of wood and lighting it. The flames crackled to life and I savored their warmth for second.

Satisfied with my handiwork, I made myself a cup of coffee next. The morning sun filtered in through the curtains, and mug in hand, I traipsed over to the window next, to see if the storm had passed.

"Fuck," I breathed. It had stopped snowing but there was at least another five or six inches, the snow drifts banked higher than the window ledge.

"Morning," Felicity's voice was thick with sleep.

I glanced back and smiled. "Morning."

"What's wrong?" She frowned.

"We might be snowed in after all." I'd joked about it, but I hadn't really imagined it would happen.

Joining me at the window, Felicity sucked in a shaky breath. "Wow, okay."

"Maybe it's not that bad out front." I moved to the door and pulled it open, my eyes going wide.

"Hmm, babe, what is that?" She joined me as I stared at the sheet of compacted snow blocking the door.

"Maybe it's the universe's way of saying we should stay here."

"You think?" Felicity wrapped her arms around my waist and rested her head on my shoulder. "You'll be able to clear it though, right?" She let out a strangled laugh.

"I'm not sure."

"Oh God. So we're actually snowed in?"

"Let me check the back door." I kissed her on the forehead before taking off down the hall. But it was no better.

"I'll have to call Gio," I said, joining her in the living room again. "Someone will have to come dig us out." I dug my phone out my pocket, but Felicity moved around me, covering my hand with hers.

"We have time." She smirked up at me. "There's that clawfoot tub in the master suite."

"Yeah?"

She grinned.

"I'd still better give him a heads up."

I typed out a quick text.

Me: We're snowed in.

He replied almost immediately.

Gio: Yeah, it's pretty bad out there. Nicco and Matteo are going to see if it thaws a little throughout the day. You good until then?

Me: Yeah, we're good.

Gio: I bet you are...

Me: Fuck off.

His reply was a laughing emoji.

Fucker.

"So, what's the verdict?"

"Nicco and Matteo are going to come up later if it doesn't start to thaw."

"Perfect." Fee went up on her tiptoes and kissed the corner of my mouth. "Then we'd better go make the most of it."

"Breakfast in bed?" I suggested.

"Sounds like Heaven."

Felicity

The snow didn't thaw. By lunchtime, the flurries started again. I sat by the window, watching the white blanket rise and rise.

"That was Gio," Jason said as he entered the room. "Nicco and Matteo should be here any—"

"I see them." I leaped up, and Jason chuckled.

"So eager to get out of here, or just that desperate to get a look at Nicco again?"

"What? No!" I blushed. "I didn't... I'm not..." God, why was it so hard to get out the words?

"Relax, I'm joking." Jason frowned. "Although I'm starting to question my manhood given how tongue-tied he's got you."

"You know it's you I love."

"Damn right." The corner of his mouth lifted into a knowing smirk.

"I don't want to leave," I said, wrapping my arms around his waist. "I just don't like the idea of not being able to get out."

"I could have always smashed a window." He shrugged.

"Behave." I went up on my tiptoes and kissed his stubbled jaw. "I like the scruff. You should keep it."

"Yeah?"

I nodded. "I can't stop thinking about that photo we found," I confessed. "I was thinking maybe you should ask—"

"No way. No fucking way. They are not mobsters." Jason rolled his eyes.

"Yeah, but there's something weird about—"

"Felicity, let it go. Nicco did a good thing letting us stay here."

"I know, I just—"

"Babe, drop it." He kissed me hard before moving to the window. "Okay, they're digging."

"God, I feel so bad. We should invite them to stay for dinner at least."

"Maybe we should leave early and check in at a hotel? Just in case."

I glanced around the cabin. It was so beautiful, but he was right. I didn't want to risk missing New Year's Eve with the guys.

"Yeah, maybe." My smile fell.

"It'll still be just the two of us. We don't have to leave for New York until the thirtieth.

"Okay."

"Hey," Jason came over to me. "I know you love it out here, but if the snow doesn't let up—"

"I know. It's just such an incredible place."

"Perhaps we can come again, in the summer?"

"I'd like that."

Jason grunted. "Although next time, I'll ask Matteo to meet us if you're going to get so hot and bothered every time Nicco is around."

"You're never going to let me live this down, are you?" I groaned.

"Nope."

Minutes passed, although it felt like a lifetime. Then there was an almighty bang on the door.

Jason went to open it. "Hey, guys. Sorry about this."

"Don't sweat it," Matteo said, stepping inside and shaking off the snow on his jacket. "The forecasters were wrong about this one."

"Are you both okay?" Nicco asked.

"We're good. Managed to get out and explore yesterday a bit, but both doors were completely blocked in this morning."

"Yeah, if the wind changes that can happen. We didn't think it would be an issue this time though."

"Can I get you both some hot cocoa?" I asked.

"Yeah, that sounds pretty great." Matteo made himself at home, dropping into one of the armchairs.

I set about making the hot cocoa from the batch of mixture Alessia had left behind. The guys were chatting about Jason's football career when I handed them their mugs.

"Heisman Trophy, that's pretty epic." Matteo grinned.

"You guys play?" Jason asked, and Matteo snickered.

"No, we don't really have time for sport."

My brows furrowed. That was… odd.

"That's cool. I forget sometimes that not everyone loves the game."

"Oh, I love the game," Matteo said. "I'm a huge Patriots fan,"

"See, babe, just regular guys." Jason winked at me.

Oh God, he didn't…

I scowled at him.

"I feel like we're missing something?" Nicco said.

"Oh, it's nothing." Jason looked far too smug, and I wanted to die. "Felicity found an old photograph and got it into her head that you guys might be mobsters or something." Laughter rumbled deep in his chest but nobody else joined him.

I was too busy shrinking into the couch.

"Mobsters, you say?" Matteo smirked. "That's a new one."

"Matt," Nicco warned. "Can you show me the photo?" he asked me, and I went to fetch it.

"Here."

"I had no idea this was here." He studied the photo. "That's my great grandfather and his brothers and cousins. I can see why you thought they might be mobsters. It's the Fedoras and suspenders isn't it?"

My cheeks pinked as he smiled at me.

"I... sorry. My brain runs away with me sometimes."

"It's okay. But I can assure you we're good people." Nicco winked.

"I told her it was nothing," Jason added with a little snort. "So do you think the snow is here to stay?"

"It's looking that way."

"I think we're going to drive to a hotel and stay there until it's time to head to New York. But we appreciate you letting us stay here."

"It's probably wise," Nicco said. "We can help you get packed up and make sure you get back to the main road safely."

"That would be great, thanks. Felicity?"

"Huh, yeah?" I blinked over at Jason who was frowning at me.

"If we get packed up, Nicco and Matteo will make sure we find the main road safely."

"Oh, that's nice, thank you." I smiled, barely hearing the words. Because my mind was still stuck on the idea that Nicco and Matteo were mobsters.

After all, he hadn't denied it.

But Jason was right—it wasn't possible.

Was it?

THE FIRST CHRISTMAS

Hailee

"Hailee, Sunshine, wake up."

My eyes drifted open to find Cameron's handsome face gazing down at me. "I fell asleep?" I croaked, my voice thick with sleep.

"Yeah. He's out cold too." His eyes dropped to the sleeping baby nestled in the crook of my arm.

Love radiated inside me as I watched Avery sleep. He was seven months old and growing too quickly.

"Where's Xander?" I asked.

"He's upstairs playing with his new game."

"Cam, I thought we agreed, no more gifts before Christmas."

"We did." Guilt flashed over his face. "But there was a sale at the store, and he gave me those puppy dog eyes and I just couldn't say no."

I reached up, curving my hand around Cameron's neck, and pulled his face down to mine. "You're a good man, Cam. The best big brother Xander could have." My lips brushed over his. "But you've got to stop spoiling him."

"I will... next year." He chuckled, deepening the kiss and curling his tongue around mine. Heat pooled in my stomach, desire rushing through my veins.

"God, I want you," I breathed.

"Tonight," his gaze darkened, "I promise."

"Tonight? It's Christmas Eve. You really think we'll get Xander settled and this one to sleep before midnight?"

"I hope so... it's been too long." He cupped my face and kissed me again.

Avery began to stir, and Cameron stood. "Want me to take him?"

"Could you? I need a girl's minute." I shifted forward slightly so he could slide Avery out of my arms and into his own.

"Hey there, buddy." Avery's eyes fluttered open, and he smiled up at his dad. The rush of love I felt whenever Cameron held our son was like nothing I'd ever felt before, and tears pricked the corners of my eyes as I watched them.

"It's your first Christmas, buddy," he cooed softly. "Are you excited?"

"Cameron, he's barely seven months old."

"I know." His warm gaze lifted to mine, making my heart squeeze.

It had been a whirlwind few months. We'd lost Karen at the beginning of the year, and I'd spent the last few months of college heavily pregnant and alone. Cameron needed to be with his family, and I wouldn't have wanted it any other way. But the second, my finals were done, he was right there to get me. We moved into his parents' house. Clark needed support with Xander, and I needed the father of my child. It was a lot—still was—but we made it work. Because family... family was everything.

We kept talking about getting our own place, but deep down, I knew Cameron wasn't ready to leave Xander and his dad, and I was okay with that.

"I'm going to take a shower and check in on Xander. If he gets hungry—"

"I got it. Go, you're starting to smell." Cameron's lip curved, and I gasped.

"I do not smell." Burying my nose in my tank top, I inhaled. "Okay, I smell a little." Avery-spittle wasn't exactly perfume of the month.

"I love you." Cameron smiled. "It won't always be like this, Sunshine."

"Home is wherever you are, you know that."

I left my boys on the couch while I went upstairs. Xander was quiet as I stood outside his door. He'd taken things the hardest losing Karen. He was getting there, but it was a slow process.

I'd been worried at first, that the baby would make him feel even more uncomfortable. But Xander loved Avery something fierce.

"Xan?" I knocked on the door, gently pushing it open.

Curled in a ball on the bed, he slept peacefully. I tiptoed over to him and pulled the cover over his body. There was a permanent ache in my chest knowing Xander had lost his mom. He was still a child, a boy. It's partly why Cameron and I had stayed here. He needed us. He needed Cameron. And whatever we decided going forward, it went without saying that we would include Xander in those plans.

Cameron had given up his dreams of going pro for his family and he'd never looked back, not once, and it only made me love him more.

"How's my little man?" Cameron pressed up behind me as I watched Avery in his crib. He slid his arms around my waist and let out a soft sigh.

We'd moved Avery into his own room a couple of months ago, but it had disrupted his sleep pattern. I was trying to persevere and not bring him back into our room, but it was hard.

"We've had a little talk and he says tonight is the night. It's Christmas Eve, Santa is coming," I chuckled, patting his little stomach, "and he needs to let Mommy and Daddy get some sleep. Isn't that right, baby?"

Avery gurgled, smirking up at us as if he was already planning to wake us at least four times during the night.

"I swear when he looks at me like that all I see is you, Hailee."

"Really? I don't see it."

"He's going to have me wrapped around his little finger in no time," Cameron added.

"I can't believe he's here, that it's our first Christmas together." It wasn't how I'd imagined my life going. I thought we'd graduate college and get jobs in the city. I thought I'd have my own gallery one day, spending my time covered in paint, lost in art. I'd imagined going to Cameron's games, soaking up life with an NFL player.

As if he could hear my thoughts, Cameron whispered, "Any regrets?"

I tilted my head to look into his eyes. "Not a single a one. I love you, Cameron. I love our life together. And I truly believe we're right where we're supposed to be."

Relief washed over him. "I'm so fucking relieved you said that. I keep thinking what if—"

"Don't." I slid a finger over his lips. "Don't do that. I love you. I love our boy and Xander. Even your dad. They're my family, Cameron. Nothing will ever compete with that."

Cameron

I swallowed thickly, her words touching something deep inside.

Fuck, I loved this woman.

I loved her compassion and heart. Her loyalty and humility.

After my mom died, Hailee had been my rock, still was. But more than that, she was there for my dad and Xander. Her unwavering love had gotten me through some of the darkest times of my life... but we'd made it.

I ran my nose along hers. "I love you, Hailee Raine. More than you will ever know." Kissing her softly, I pulled away. "Go. I'll see to the boys."

My heart swelled at just the mention of my son and brother. Xander was as much mine as Avery was. I couldn't really explain our bond, but I didn't need to. Hailee got it. Dad too. It's why we hadn't left and gotten a place of our own yet.

"You see to Avery, and I'll check in on Xander, okay?"

"Deal." I kissed the end of Hailee's nose as she slipped out from between me and the crib.

"Daddy needs you to do me a solid tonight," I whispered, letting Avery grip onto my finger. He cooed and kicked, smiling up at me in a way that completely melted my heart.

Fuck. This kid. He was every bit his mother and I wanted nothing more than to give him the world and then some.

I thought I loved Hailee immeasurably *before* Avery was born; but seeing her hold our son in her arms for the first time was like a lightning bolt to the chest, blowing my ribcage wide open and stuffing it with so much love that sometimes, when I watched them, I felt like I couldn't breathe.

Football.

The NFL.

Dreams of the Super Bowl.

None of it could compete with watching Hailee with my son.

"Santa's coming tonight, buddy. And I'd really like to make love to your mommy without being interrupted."

My dad had been invited to a work thing. He hadn't wanted to go, but we'd insisted. It had been almost a year since Mom passed. He needed to get back on the horse, and rumor had it that there was a woman he worked with who enjoyed his company. He'd be back later; much later, I hoped. Because I needed some quiet alone time with my girl, to feel her naked and soft beneath me.

My dick twitched in my sweatpants and I fought a smile. "Time for you to go to sleep, buddy. I'll see you in the morning hopefully. I love you, Avery." I smoothed my thumb over his chubby cheek before checking the baby monitor.

I'd barely reached Xander's room when I heard Hailee's voice.

"I think your mom is looking down on you right now, Xan, and thinking what an amazing kid you are."

"Do you think she misses me?"

"I think she misses you every second of every day."

I hesitated, my breath caught in my throat. Xander was doing better, but he didn't talk about Mom often. It was like this wall was between him and his feelings. We were all giving him time, so to hear him opening up to Hailee was the best fucking Christmas gift I could have asked for.

Creeping closer to the door, I peeked into the room. Xander was curled up against Hailee's side, his eyes closed and expression pensive as she stroked his hair.

"I miss her," he whispered, the words like a vise around my heart. "I really miss her."

"I know, Xan. We all do."

"Night, Hailee."

"Night, Xander. Merry Christmas, buddy."

"Merry Christmas." He rolled away from her, and she climbed gingerly off the bed, tucking the covers over his body.

I held back, waiting for her to leave his room.

"How much of that did you hear?" she asked, pulling his door closed.

"Enough." The word almost got stuck in my throat.

"He's going to be okay, Cam." Hailee gazed up at me and I knew she was right. We'd all lost so much when Mom died, but we all had so much to live for, so much to remember her by.

"Come on," I said, taking her hand. "I have something I want to give you."

My heart beat hard against my chest as I slipped out of the bathroom. Hailee was already in bed, sitting up against the headboard playing with her cell phone.

"Jason wanted a photo of Avery."

"I never thought I'd see the day he'd be a doting uncle." My lips curved.

"Yeah, something tells me we'll have to fight him for cuddles tomorrow."

After we opened presents in the morning, we were all heading over to the Bennet's for Christmas dinner. Jason and Felicity, and Asher and Mya were all in town for a few days. I was looking forward to seeing them. It had been a while since we were all in the same place.

"I can take him," I said.

Hailee's brow furrowed. "Are you okay? You seem a little nervous."

Fuck.

My fingers trembled as I ran a hand down my face. "Can you come over here?"

"Okay." Her frown deepened.

Hailee climbed off the bed and approached me. Without thinking, I dropped to one knee and stared up at her.

"Cameron... wh- what are you doing?"

"Hailee Raine," I took her hand in mine. "I had this whole speech planned. I was going to tell you about the moment I fell in love with you, reminisce about our life together, and all of the amazing things we've experienced. But honestly, watching you with Avery just now, and then Xander, I don't need to talk about the past. Because every time I watch you with our son and my brother, I fall in love with you all over again. But being the mother of my children isn't enough for me. I want you to be my wife. My other half. The better half of me. Will you marry me?"

"Oh my god," she breathed, tears dripping down her cheeks. "Yes! Yes, I'll marry you."

Hailee threw herself down onto the floor and wrapped her arms around me. I hadn't even managed to get the ring box out of my pocket, but it didn't matter.

"Do you have any idea how long I've waited to hear those words?" She eased back to look at me. "I want a life with you, Cameron. You and me and Avery and Xander."

"Yeah?"

"Yeah." She nodded.

"I didn't even show you the ring." I finally pulled the box out.

"It could be a candy ring and I'd still love it."

I flipped the lid and Hailee covered her mouth with her hand. "It's beautiful."

"Here." Plucking the princess-cut diamond ring out of the box, I slid it on her finger, feeling my chest tighten.

"It's a perfect fit." Hailee admired it. "I love it."

"And I love you, Mrs. Chase-to-be."

"God, I like the sound of that. Should we call everyone to tell them?"

"Tomorrow," I said gruffly. "Tomorrow we can tell them. Tonight, you're mine."

Hailee

Cameron scooped me up in his arms and carried me to our bedroom. The soft sound of laughter filled the room, as he lowered me to the floor.

"I want to worship every inch of your skin, Hailee." He cupped my face. "But honestly, I'm not sure I can wait to be deep inside you."

My core clenched at his words, at his hooded gaze, his eyes clouded with lust.

"So don't. I'm right here, Cam." Hooking my hands into my tank top, I pulled it over my head and dropped it on the floor. His mouth kicked up at the corner as his hungry eyes raked over my breasts.

My body had changed since giving birth, but Cameron never made me feel anything less than beautiful.

"So soft," he whispered, trailing his fingers over the curve of my skin. "But you have too many clothes on." Cameron slipped his hands into my lounge pants and panties and pushed them off my hips, letting the soft material pool at my feet. He lifted me with ease, lying me down on the bed and covering my body.

"This doesn't seem fair somehow." I curled my fingers into the hair at the nape of his neck.

"Give me a second." He dropped a kiss on the end of my nose and climbed off the bed to undress. My eyes feasted on his body. Cameron might not have played football anymore, but his physique was still impressive. Broad shoulders and cut abs pointed to a narrow waist. His muscles were defined and strong and I loved nothing more than feeling his weight pressed on top of me.

"How long do you think we have?" I asked around a knowing smile.

"Long enough." Cameron stroked a hand along my ankle and pulled me down the bed a little, fitting his body over mine. My legs hitched around his waist, anchoring us together as he kissed me. Our tongues tangled, slow and seductive as if they didn't want to rush. But it was Christmas Eve and we had a seven-month-old and an overexcited eight-year-old under the roof. Chances were, we didn't have the luxury of time.

As if he felt my urgency, Cameron slipped his hand between us and found my center. "So wet," he murmured against my lips, gently working two digits inside of me.

"Cam," I breathed as my body stretched around his fingers.

"Come for me, Hailee... come undone." He whispered the words against the corner of my mouth, his eyes fixed right on my face, watching as I hurtled toward the edge.

"It feels so good," I panted. "But I want you inside me, Cam."

"Fuck, yeah. Okay." Cameron hooked my thighs wider, then gently rocked into me, filling me. My breath caught as he pulled out slowly and pressed forward again, going deeper.

"Okay?" he asked, and I nodded.

"Don't stop."

Cameron made love to me in the dark, the room filled with our breathy moans and dirty promises. He felt so good, rocking into me, pushing me toward the edge. His pelvis bumped my clit with every roll, sending bolts of pleasure shooting through me.

"Do you have any idea how good you feel?" he groaned against my neck, licking and sucking the skin there as if he couldn't get enough.

I hugged him tighter, never wanting it to end, completely lost to the sensations flowing through my body.

"I love you, Hailee. So." Thrust. "Fucking." Thrust. "Much."

The wave of pleasure building inside me crested, crashing over me with such intensity I cried out. But Cameron was there to swallow my moans, his tongue lapping at my mouth as my body shuddered around him.

He kept rocking, harder... faster, his pace growing jerky until a low groan rumbled in his throat and he came hard inside me.

"Fuck," he rasped. "That was..."

"Yeah, I know." I touched the side of his face, smiling up at him.

"I can't wait to make you my wife, Hailee. To be tied to you in every single way possible. I can't—"

Avery's cries came through the baby monitor.

"So much for keeping his promise," Cameron muttered.

"It's a big step him being in his own room."

"I know. Stay. I'll get him." He kissed me softly.

"You're sure?"

"Yeah." Cameron climbed out of bed and pulled on his sweatpants. "I'll be right back."

"Take your time." I stretched my body, reveling in the delicious ache. "I'm not going anywhere."

Cameron

"You couldn't just give me an hour, could you, buddy?" I plucked Avery out of his crib and held him up. "You're supposed to be sleeping."

He smiled at me, softening my expression. "Cute kid, real cute." I chuckled. "You want to go see Mommy?"

He cooed, flapping his little hands in the air as I cuddled him into my chest. Hailee was insistent on trying to settle him back in his crib no matter what hour or how many times he had us up. But it was still relatively early, and the truth was, I missed the late-night cuddles with the three of us in bed.

"Your mommy's going to kick my ass," I said as we walked back to our bedroom.

Hailee was in bed, a sleep shirt pulled over her body. "Cameron, we agreed..."

"I know, but I told him our good news and he's excited."

She rolled her eyes, fighting a smile. "Ten minutes and not a minute longer." Hailee patted the space beside her, and I climbed in, nestling Avery in the crook of my arm.

"This... you and Avery... it's all I ever wanted, even if I didn't know it."

"You really mean that?" Hailee asked, looking at me through lowered lashes.

"I don't regret a single thing, Sunshine. I only wish Mom was here to see this. To see us. Boy, she'd love you." I gently rocked Avery in my arm.

"I like to think she's watching," Hailee said.

"Yeah, me too." My gaze lifted from my son to my girl... my fiancée.

Fuck, I would never tire of saying that. At least, not until she became my wife.

Just then, the door creaked open and Xander's face appeared. "I heard Avery. Is he okay?"

"He's fine, buddy," I said. "You wanna get up on here with us?"

"I... yeah." A big grin broke out over his face. "Okay." He ran and jumped onto the bed, tucking himself into my side.

Avery's overexcited giggles made us all laugh.

"He's so cool," Xander said, taking his nephew's hand in his. "I know I'm not his big brother, but I'll always look out for him." He looked up at me. "The way you always looked out for me."

Hailee caught my eye as I tried to swallow the ball of emotion lodged in my throat.

"I love you, Xan." I hugged my brother tighter while holding my son in my other arm.

"Whoa, wait, is that—" Xander grabbed Hailee's hand and tugged it across my body. "You're getting married?"

"Cameron just asked me."

"And you said yes?"

"I sure did, buddy."

"Holy crap, that's awesome! First I got Avery and now I'm getting a new sister." His grin was infectious. "This Christmas rocks."

"Yeah, it does." I grinned back, knowing that somewhere up there, Mom was looking down on us and smiling too.

"It totally does."

THE WEDDING

CHAPTER 1

Cameron

"IS HE OUT?" Warm hands slid around my waist and Hailee pressed herself against me as I watched Avery sleep.

"Yeah, I didn't even get to finish the story."

"He's had a busy day." She slipped around me.

"He's going to have an even busier day Saturday," I said.

"I can't wait to see him in his little tux."

"I can't wait to see you in your bridesmaid dress." Leaning down, I kissed Hailee. My wife. My best friend. My every-fucking-thing.

The last four years had been hard.

Mom had lost her battle with the brain tumor, right before Avery was born, and then Dad had died in a tragic accident before Christmas.

But we had so much to celebrate, to take comfort in. Avery was almost four and he brought so much joy to our lives.

"It's a good thing I'm not showing yet." Hailee took my hands in hers and laid them on her stomach, right where our second child was growing. "We're doing the right thing not telling them, aren't we?" she said.

"Yeah." I ran my nose along hers. "It's their big day, Sunshine. Let's not steal their thunder."

"Yeah, I guess. But it's hard keeping this from Fee. You know how intuitive she is. The second she sees I'm not drinking alcohol, she'll know."

"She'll be too busy soaking up everyone's attention."

"Fine. But if she asks, I'm not going to lie."

"Deal." I hooked my arm around her waist and pulled her closer, sealing my mouth over her soft lips.

God, I loved this woman.

Almost nine years together and my heart still beat wildly in my chest every time we kissed. I loved Hailee more with every passing year. After everything we'd been through—falling pregnant when we were still in college, my mom dying, helping raise my brother Xander, to being a young couple raising a son, and then being hit with my dad's sudden death—Hailee had been right there, standing by my side. Holding me up. She was my strength, my heart; she was the better half of my soul, and I was so fucking happy we were going to have another baby.

Even if I was a little bit terrified it meant we'd be raising an eleven-year-old, a four-year-old, and a newborn.

"Hmm," Hailee murmured against my lips, teasing me with her tongue. "We should probably make the most of him sleeping."

Xander was having a sleepover with Hailee's mom and stepdad.

"Yeah?" I eased back, gazing at her.

"Yeah. I need you, Cam."

"Come on." Grabbing her hand, I led her out of our son's room, and pulled the door closed.

The second I stepped into our bedroom, my eyes went to the pale-green silk bridesmaid dress hanging on the closet. I hadn't seen Hailee in it yet, but I knew she would look stunning.

"You know," I said, pulling her into my arms again. "That dress is bringing up all kinds of memories from our wedding."

"I'm surprised you can remember," she chuckled. "You were toasted by the end of the night."

"True." I trailed my lips over her jaw, along her neck and to her ear. "But I was still able to make you scream my name, Mrs. Chase."

Hailee's breath caught. "Maybe you should remind me."

Laughter rumbled in my chest as I buried my hands deep in her hair. "It would be my pleasure, Sunshine."

Slowly, I kissed her, tangling our tongues and nibbling her lips. Hailee melted against me as I moved her backward toward the bed.

"Be quick," she moaned, "in case he wakes."

"He's out for the count," I said, pulling away to yank my sweater over my head. Hailee's t-shirt went next. Then her pants and my jeans. I would have loved nothing more than to spend the entire night worshipping every inch of her skin, but when you were parents to a toddler every minute alone was a luxury.

And I didn't intend to waste a single second.

My hands painted a map over her body, studying every dip and curve, paying extra attention to her stomach, soft and round from her previous birth.

I'd known Hailee when she was just a girl, growing into herself. But now she was all woman, every blemish, scar and stretchmark a testament to the life we'd created together.

"Stop teasing me," she purred, arching into my touch as my fingers glided lower. "Cameron." Hailee grabbed my wrist and thrust my hand against her center, moaning softly.

"So impatient," I teased, fighting a smile.

Her eyes locked on mine, bright with lust. "He could wake any—"

"He won't." I pecked the end of her nose, lazily rubbing my fingers back and forth over her damp panties.

"Stop teasing me and just—" Hailee's words became garbled as I slipped two fingers into her underwear and pressed them inside her.

"You were saying?" I smirked.

Hailee dropped her head to my shoulder, breathing heavily as I worked her slowly, circling my thumb over her clit in perfect synchrony. After years of practice, I knew exactly what she liked, exactly how to touch her to get her to fall apart.

"God, Cam.... *God*!" she breathed against my collarbone, sending a shock to my dick. "It feels so good."

"Nothing compared to how it'll feel when I sink deep inside you."

Hailee lifted her face, gazing up at me with so much love and lust, I felt ten feet tall. "Show me," she purred.

"Come first." I curled my fingers deep inside, grazing her g-spot. She shattered in my arms, clutching onto my biceps and moaning my name.

Pushing her down gently on the bed, I shoved my boxer briefs down my hips and kicked them off. Hailee's hooded gaze immediately went to my dick: thick and long and more than ready to sink inside my wife.

My knees hit the mattress and I lifted her legs and curled them around my hips as I sank down and—

"Momma," Avery's small cries filtered down the hall.

"Jesus, kid, perfect fucking timing," I mumbled, dropping my head to Hailee's shoulder.

She chuckled, letting out a resigned sigh. "Let me get him settled and we'll pick right back up." She kissed me thoroughly, silently promising me of things to come.

But I knew our son, and once he got his momma in his bed, it was unlikely I'd see her again until the morning.

"I'll go," I said. "You get some sleep."

"Are you sure?"

"Yeah, you're growing our daughter. You need to get your rest." Clambering off the bed, I pulled on some shorts.

"Daughter, huh?" Hailee said. "And how do you know it's a girl?"

Pausing at the door, I glanced back with a smile. "Just a feeling."

Hailee

"I can't believe this is it," I said, accepting a glass of champagne from Mya.

We were having a pre-wedding pamper night at the hotel. Just me, Felicity, and Mya.

Best friends for the best part of nine years.

God, I couldn't imagine my life without these women. Next to Cameron, Avery, and Xander, they were the most important people in my life. And I couldn't wait to watch Felicity walk down the aisle to my stepbrother tomorrow.

"Did you feel this nervous?" she asked me.

"I barely remember it. Everything about that day is a blur." I just remembered feeling so happy, my cheeks hurt from all the smiling.

"Yeah, I know what you mean. I feel like I've waited my whole life for this day and now it's here, and I'm terrified."

"Fee, my brother loves you. You have nothing to worry about."

"Yeah, girl," Mya added. "You've managed eight-and-a-half years being Jason Ford's girlfriend, living life in the spotlight."

It was true. Jason was kind of a big deal after taking the NFL by storm fresh out of college. His career with the Philadelphia Eagles had gone from strength to strength. Like Mya and Asher, they lived in the city so all being together in one place at the same time was a rare thing these days.

Not this weekend though. This weekend, we would all be together to witness Felicity and Jason tie the knot, and it was set to be a big affair.

"I just... want everything to go smoothly."

"It will," I said, offering her a reassuring smile. "Cordelia has the day planned down to the second." The hotel's wedding coordinator made Monica Geller look disorganized.

"If in doubt," Mya added. "Drink." She thrust Fee's glass of champagne at her, but she held up a hand.

"I don't think that's a good idea. My stomach is so unsettled. The last thing I need is getting sick for my big day."

"You need to breathe." I sipped from my own glass, hoping neither of them would notice how I was barely drinking it. Cameron and I might have agreed to wait to tell anyone about the baby, but it was still hard keeping it from my best friends.

"I wonder what they're doing?" Fee said, letting out a weary sigh.

"Probably drinking beer and reminiscing about the good old days." I smiled.

"I swear to God, if Asher gets him drunk—"

"I already warned him." Mya smirked. "I told him I won't put out for a week, if he so much as thinks about getting Jase into any kind of trouble."

"A week?" I balked. "God, I've forgotten what it's like to have sex that regularly."

"Babe, you have a tiny human running you ragged. Not to mention Xander's mood swings. There's a lot going on."

"Avery's almost four. I thought it was supposed to get easier. My mom and Kent took Xander last night, but Avery interrupted us right before we got to the good stuff."

"That kid's so cute but a total cockblocker." Mya snorted, and I swatted her arm.

"I'm hoping we can enjoy the wedding reception." Mom and Kent had offered to keep the kids with them so we could relax. Kent's health wasn't so good lately, so it was doubtful he would be able to stay out that late anyway.

"Well, I for one, intend on seducing my man," Mya said. "It's been almost a year and he still hasn't managed to knock me up."

It was her attempt at a joke, but I saw the pain in her eyes. Mya and Ash had spent the last two years fostering kids, but we all knew how much she yearned for a child of her own.

"A year is nothing," I said around a reassuring smile.

"I know, but what if it becomes eighteen months or two years? I'm not getting any younger."

"You're twenty-six, babe. It's hardly ancient." Fee got up and headed for her kitchen. "Any requests while I'm up?"

"More champagne," Mya replied. "I might as well drink it if you won't. It's too good to waste."

I chuckled, taking another pretend sip of mine. "I'll go see if she wants a hand."

Mya waved me off, helping herself to another chocolate truffle, courtesy of Felicity's mom. She'd handmade the favors for tomorrow and had a bunch leftover. But I'd tried to resist. If I had any hopes of fitting in my dress tomorrow, I needed to refrain from gorging myself.

Entering the kitchen, I paused at the sight of Felicity bracing the counter, tears pricking the corners of her eyes.

"Fee, what is it? What's wrong?"

"Oh, babe, I'm a freaking mess." She sniffled, and I hurried over to her, discarding my glass and pulling her into my arms.

"It's okay to feel emotional; it's a big day."

"Yeah, I just didn't think it would affect me like this." She wiggled out of my hold and leaned over to grab some tissue paper, blotting her face. "I'm okay."

"Do you want to call Jase? I can cover for you if you need to—"

"No, I'm okay, I promise."

Taking her hand in mine, I squeezed gently. "You've got this, Felicity."

She gave me a weak smile. "I'm lucky to have you, Hailee. You're my best friend. I love you."

Emotion balled in my throat, and I swallowed over the lump stuck there. "Jeez, now you're making me cry. Come here."

We hugged again, holding on tight.

We'd come a long way since we were just two young girls struggling to find our place in the world.

A lot had changed.

College.

Living in different towns.

Babies.

Weddings.

But some things had stayed exactly the same.

Like our friendship—the extended family we'd made for ourselves. And the future we'd all share.

Together.

CHAPTER 2

Jason

I WAS GOING TO SUFFOCATE. My collar was too stiff, my tux jacket too tight, and I was pretty sure I was sweating to the point of dehydration.

"Relax, man," Asher said, smirking. "It's almost time."

Fuck.

I was going to puke. Not because I had second thoughts, no way, but because I was standing at the end of the aisle, surrounded by one-hundred and fifty of our closest friends and family.

We'd both wanted a small, intimate wedding originally, but it was hard to pull off when you were the star quarterback for the Philadelphia Eagles. I couldn't not share this day with the team who meant so much to me. We were family. Brothers. I didn't relish being the center of attention though—which was a weird fucking thing given my personal and professional life was often played out in the news.

Fee and I tried to live a relatively private life, but it wasn't always easy, and I was so fucking grateful that she'd stuck by me all these years as my football career took off.

"I think I see them." Cam nudged me, flicking his eyes to the double doors at the end of the room. Sure enough, I could just make out Hailee and Mya talking to Cordelia, the wedding planner. That woman scared me half to death, but she'd pulled off the wedding of Felicity's dreams. And part of me still couldn't believe that in less than an hour, we'd walk out of here as Mr. and Mrs. Ford.

Fuck, that sounded good.

Felicity was everything to me. When I'd entered the draft in senior year, she'd stood by my side and promised to follow me wherever I ended up. But I always knew I wanted to stay in Pennsylvania. It was home, and I couldn't imagine being too far away from our friends and families.

"You've got the rings?" I asked Cameron for the third time, and he nodded.

"In the same pocket they were the last time you asked," he chuckled.

"I could've watched them," Asher said. I gave him a pointed look, and he added, "Your confidence in me is astounding."

"Showtime," Cam whispered, and sure enough, the pianist started playing the opening notes to Elvis Presley's *Can't Help Falling in Love With You*. It filled the orangery, echoing off the glass ceilings and reverberating through me.

My skin vibrated, my heart crashing wildly against my chest as I stood there, poised to see my wife-to-be for the first time in her wedding dress. My stepsister appeared first, walking Avery down the aisle. He looked so fucking cute in his little tux, and I realized I wanted that. I wanted a kid with Felicity. I wanted to see her stomach grow round with my child. *Our* child. I swallowed over the lump in my throat, glancing at Cam as he watched Hailee and his son walk toward us.

Mya came next, holding Xander's hand. Asher sucked in a sharp breath at the sight of his fiancée, running a hand down his face.

"We're lucky bastards," he murmured under his breath, earning him a soft chuckle from the wedding officiant.

The bridal party reached us—Avery and Xander taking their places with Dad and Denise—and Hailee and Mya standing off to one side. The piano paused and the Master of Ceremonies said, "Please stand for the wedding march."

Blood roared in my ears as our guests stood just as Felicity appeared in the doorway on the arm of her father. Her dress was perfection: a second skin of lace and silk that molded to her curves and fell over her hips like an ivory waterfall. But she could have been wearing a burlap sack for all I cared because when her eyes met mine, everything else melted away.

I loved this woman. Unequivocally, irrevocably loved her. And she was giving me the greatest gift of all by becoming my wife today.

Tears pricked the corners of my eyes as she made a slow but steady walk down the aisle. When they reached us, her father kissed her cheek and took his seat beside her mom. I offered her my hand, needing to touch her, to ground myself.

"Hi," I said around a grin.

"Hi." Tears clung to her lashes.

"You look... fuck."

Laughter crinkled her eyes. "I feel... I don't know what I feel."

Unable to stop myself, I stepped closer. "Ready to become Mrs. Ford?"

An infectious smile spread across her face. "I was born ready."

"Right," the officiant said, "if we're ready to begin?"

We both nodded.

"Dearly beloved and honored guests, we are gathered together here to join Jason and Felicity in the union of marriage..." The words became white noise as I stared at Felicity—my heart, my reason, my every-fucking-thing.

It was hard to believe there was a time I hadn't wanted her. Hadn't wanted anyone. I was content focusing on football and my future. But Felicity changed all that.

She gently squeezed my hand and I blinked at the officiant.

"The bride and groom have each prepared vows that they will read now. Jason, if you'd like to go first." The officiant gave me a nod and I turned to Felicity, clearing my throat. This was it, my big moment. I'd played in front of ten of thousands of football fans, camera crews, and the nation... but nothing compared to this moment.

"If playing football has taught me anything, it's that to be the best, you have to play hard and fight hard." I inhaled a shaky breath. "But you, Felicity Charlotte Giles, you taught me to love hard.

"I can't promise you that life with me will always be easy. I can't promise that I won't screw up or make mistakes. But I can promise you that I will spend my life loving you the way you deserve to be loved. Because we're endgame, babe."

"Jason," her voice cracked as she looked up at me through her damp lashes.

"It's you and me, Giles." I leaned down, touching my head to hers, tradition be damned. "You and me and the rest of our lives together."

Felicity

I was married.

Married.

Mrs. Felicity Ford.

God, I still couldn't believe it.

"Congratulations," one of Jason's teammates pulled me into a bear hug, squeezing the life out of me.

"Get your hands off my wife, Tiny," Jason's gruff voice made my tummy clench.

"Relax, man. I'm just congratulating your beautiful bride." Jonas 'Tiny' Melvin planted a big wet kiss on my cheek. "I put a little something special in your card."

"Jonas," I said. "You didn't need to do that."

"Yeah, I did. Jase is one of the best men I know, and you both deserve it."

"Thank you."

The men did that guy-hug thing and Jonas left us to it. Jason curled his arm around my waist and pulled me close. "If someone had warned me that

I'd have to personally speak to every single wedding guest, I would have limited the list to twenty."

"The hard part is over." I smiled, running my hands up his chest, tugging his lapels. "We can relax now and enjoy the reception."

"I want to enjoy you." He kissed the corner of my mouth, and laughter spilled from my lips.

"Later. Everyone's watching us right now."

"And?" Jase pulled back to look me in the eye. "I think I'm allowed to kiss my wife on our wedding day." He smirked, capturing my mouth in a slow, bruising kiss.

"I'm pregnant," I blurted, my stomach sinking at how tense he went.

"P- pregnant?" The word formed on his tongue as if it was new and unfamiliar.

I nodded, tears glistening in my eyes. "I know we didn't plan on it—"

"We're having a baby?"

Another nod.

"Fuck, we're having a—"

"Ssh," I pulled him closer, wondering if I'd done the right thing telling him. But I needed him with me on this—I needed him to want it, the way I wanted it.

We'd talked about starting a family, in a few years when his career settled down a bit. But I'd been on medication the other month and I guess it had interfered with my birth control because my period never came and when I finally plucked up the courage to take the test, it was positive.

"Seriously? You did a test?"

"Three. All positive. I know the timing is—"

"You think I care about the timing?" he whispered, leaning in to envelop me away from the rest of the guests who were currently enjoying the free bar and entertainment.

"You're happy?"

"Happy? I want to grab the mic and announce to the entire room that I'm going be a daddy."

"Jason," I chuckled. "We can't tell anyone. It's early, and I don't want to jinx it."

"Of course not." He kissed me again. "I can tell Cam and Asher though, right?"

"Not yet. I haven't even told Hailee and Mya."

"You know, I thought this day was perfect. You, this dress," he ran his hand down the intricate beadwork along the curve of my spine. "Finally getting to call you my wife. But you just made all my dreams come true. A baby." His smile turned into a grin. "We're having a baby."

The awe in his voice stunned me. I hadn't known what Jason would make of us getting pregnant so young. He had a successful career with the Eagles, and I was busy working at a rescue center in the city. We had rich, full lives. A baby would upend that. But one look at his expression, and I knew I had nothing to worry about.

He wanted this.

Jason wanted this baby almost as much as I did.

"Promise me you won't tell anyone."

"Fuck, yeah. Okay." He hugged me tighter, peppering my face with tiny kisses.

To anyone watching, we probably looked like a newlywed couple unable to keep our hands off each other. I just hoped he could keep our secret past the groom's speech.

"Is that why you've felt off all week?" he asked.

"That and I was nervous about today."

"Having second thoughts, Mrs. Ford?"

"Even if I were," I said. "There's no escaping now."

He brushed his nose along mine and grinned again. "Damn right, there isn't."

"I'm so freaking drunk," Mya grabbed my hand and swung me around the dance floor for the third time. "Why aren't you drunk? It's your wedding. You should be ass-over-elbow drunk by now."

"Nobody wants to see the bride make a fool of herself."

"And you," she glanced at Hailee. "You're not drunk either."

"I didn't want to go crazy in case Avery plays up for my mom and Kent."

Mya stopped dancing, her eyes flicking from Hailee to me and back again. "What is—" She gasped, clapping a hand over her mouth. "You're both pregnant."

"What?" I balked. "No, I'm not."

"Me neither," Hailee added quickly. Too quickly.

"Oh my god... are you?" I blurted.

"Nope. No. I don't know—"

"You so are. You barely touched your wine at dinner. And last night you—"

Her expression dropped. "I wasn't supposed to steal your thunder. It's your special day."

"Are you freaking kidding me?" I threw my arms around her and hugged her tight, laughing. "I'm going to be an aunt again. Best wedding present ever."

She pulled back and smiled at me. "I'm so relieved you both know. It's been killing me holding it in."

"I guess I should fess up then," I said.

"Wait a minute," Hailee's eyes grew wide, "you mean..."

"Yup."

"Oh my god, this is amazing. We're going to be pregnant together."

"Mya?" I peeked over at her, my heart sinking at the trace of pain in her eyes.

She blinked, giving a little shake of her head. "I'm so happy for you both."

"It'll happen, babe," I said, squeezing her hand. "When the time is right, it'll happen."

"I know. And until then, I'll have two more babies to love on." She sounded sober all of a sudden and Hailee cast me a concerned look.

"Hey," Mya said. "Don't do that. Don't feel like you can't celebrate. This is good news, the best." She wrapped her arms around us both and pulled us closer. "Besides, I'm having all the fun trying."

"Lap it up," Hailee murmured. "Because after the baby comes, everything in that department becomes hard freaking work."

"Ahh, I can't believe this," I said, unable to fight the smile tugging at my lips. "Two more babies to add to our brood."

Hailee glanced over at the guys. They were standing at the bar, drinking and chatting. "How did Jason take it?"

"He was so excited. It was weird because I was expecting him to say it wasn't the right time."

"He adores Xander and Avery," Hailee mused.

"Yeah, I can't wait to see him with our little guy."

"Little guy?" Mya asked. "You already know the sex?"

"No, but I know he'll want a boy. He wouldn't know what to do with a daughter."

"You're right there." Hailee chuckled. "She'd have him wrapped around her little finger in no time."

Imagining him—my husband, my everything—with our baby... my heart was fit to burst.

I had everything I'd ever wanted.

The best friends a girl could want.

A husband who loved me.

And a future that I couldn't wait to live.

CHAPTER 3

Mya

"DANCE WITH ME," I grabbed Asher's hand and pulled him toward the dance floor.

"Babe, you're drunk, and it's late. I want to go up to our room and—"

"One dance." Batting my lashes at him, I swayed my hips to the sultry beat, not caring that the party was winding down.

And what a party it had been.

Everything about today was nothing short of perfect. Add in the fact that my best friends were both pregnant, and it was definitely a day to remember.

It didn't stop the gnawing ache in my stomach though. I was happy for them, so freaking happy, but I wanted that. I wanted a baby. I wanted in that damn club.

"One dance," Asher conceded, pulling me into his arms. "You, Mya Bennet are the most beautiful woman I've ever laid eyes on."

"Even when I'm butt drunk?"

"Even then." He kissed the end of my nose, twirling me to the music. Endorphins coursed through my veins, giving me a giddy high.

It felt like forever since I'd let my hair down. But there wasn't much time for yourself when you fostered kids requiring emergency placements. Our house was a revolving door of children with trauma and adolescents with attitude. I loved it though. Making a difference to their lives, playing a tiny part in shaping the adults they would one day become. For giving them a safe place full of love and comfort when they needed it most.

But for as much as I loved it, I yearned for a child of our own. We'd talked about it a lot over the last eighteen months, and we were both on the same page. Our bodies refused to cooperate though.

A whole year of raised hopes. I didn't even bother testing every month now, determined to let nature take its course. It was easier said than done though.

"Babe?" Asher nudged his cheek against mine. "What is it?"

"Hailee and Fee are both pregnant."

"They are?" He pulled back to look at me, and I nodded. "Shit, I had no idea."

"I figured it out earlier. But it's supposed to be a secret until they're further along and Hailee didn't want to overshadow the wedding."

"How did it make you feel hearing that?" His eyes glittered with concern, and I loved him all the more for it.

"I'm happy for them, of course I am. But I can't help but wonder if it will ever be us."

"It will," he said with utter conviction. "I know it will. I watch you with the kids who come into our home, and do you know what I see? Someone who is going to make a great mom. We have time, Mya. We have all the time in the world. And if things don't go the way we'd hoped, we'll figure it out."

"You're right. I'm being ridiculous." I tried to turn away from him, but Asher slid his fingers under my jaw.

"Your feelings are valid and it's okay to be happy for them and sad for us. But a year is nothing for a lot of couples."

"I know." Looping my arms around his neck, I leaned close, breathing Asher in. He was my anchor. My partner in crime. My best friend.

"We can practice," he breathed the words onto my lips. "Lots and lots of practice. How does that sound?"

I looked him in the eye and smiled. "I think I'm ready for you to take me to bed now."

"Fuck, babe, you feel... *fuuuck*." Asher rocked into me, his fingers clawing at my thighs as he rode my body into bliss.

"More," I cried, raking my fingernails down his broad shoulders. "More..."

I loved the feel of him hard and bare inside me. And being able to let loose and not worry about someone overhearing was only a bonus.

He pulled out, rocking back on his haunches. Grabbing my calves, he wound my legs around his waist before driving back into me slowly.

"Ahhhh." I fisted the sheets, the new angle so deep, so delicious I could barely breathe.

"I love watching your face as I fill you," he said, thickly.

"You're so dirty."

"Only for you." His deep chuckle melted me, and I lifted my gaze, locking eyes with him as he sank into me over and over. His thumb slipped between us, finding my clit.

"God, Ash, it's... *God...*"

All coherent thought evaporated as pleasure splashed inside me, and my legs began trembling.

"Give it to me," he rasped. "Give me everything."

I came apart, crying his name, silently praying that this was the time. That our bodies would do what they were damn supposed to and make a baby.

"Fuck, Mya... *fuck.*" Asher collapsed on top of me, a sweaty and sated mess. He kissed me long and hard, lazily tangling his tongue with mine, drawing out every last drop of pleasure.

His hand traced its way down to my stomach, resting there. "I feel like I gave my swimmers a fighting chance this time." Asher gave me a crooked grin.

"I hope so." *Because having a baby with you is all I want.* I swallowed the words.

"It'll happen, babe. If it's not this month, or the next, or the one after, it'll happen. And that baby—our baby—will be so freaking loved."

"I love you." I curved my hands over his shoulders and yanked him down to kiss him.

"Not as much as I love you, Mya."

Being pregnant was all I could think about.

But this man right here, he was enough.

And Asher was right.

Whatever the future brought, we'd figure it out together.

Always.

Asher

I watched Mya sleep. Watched her eyes flutter softly as she dreamed—dreams of me and the life we would have together, hopefully—and the gentle rise and fall of her chest.

I'd never loved another woman the way I loved her. Never would. She was my whole fucking world.

But I knew she was hurting, our prayers of getting pregnant still unanswered. It had only been a year, but every month that ticked by was another knock to her faith that everything would work out.

"I can feel you watching me," she murmured, brushing her nose along my arm.

"I like watching you sleep."

"What time is it?" One eye cracked open, that beautiful brown that melted me. She smiled at me.

"A little after nine. How's your head?"

"It feels like there's a brass band in there."

"That's what you get for unleashing your inner party girl." I smirked, brushing the wild curls away from her eyes.

"Uh. I didn't do anything embarrassing, did I?"

"You mean aside from dragging me to our room and doing that little striptease for me?"

"Ash." She swatted my chest, but I snagged her wrist, pulling her hand to my lips and kissing her knuckles.

"Do you have any idea how much I love you?"

"Hmm-mm." Mya snuggled closer as I traced my thumb over her wedding band.

It felt like a lifetime ago we'd gotten married in a small ceremony in my parents' backyard. They'd wanted us to have a big, lavish wedding, but it wasn't us. All we'd cared about was declaring our love and commitment in front of our closest friends and family.

"I'm going to get up and make myself a coffee. You want anything?" I asked her.

"No, I'm good, thank you."

"Okay. Sleep." I dropped a kiss on her head, untangling myself from her side. "I'll wake you up when we need to get ready to leave."

"Okay," she said around a sleepy yawn.

Throwing back the sheet, I climbed out of bed, but Mya grabbed me, pulling me back down to her. "Love you." She kissed me, then rolled over and went back to sleep.

"DIDN'T EXPECT to find you down here," I said to Jase and Cam as I joined them at their table.

"Hailee was up half the night with morning sickness."

"Shit, man, that's rough."

"What's your excuse?" I flicked my eyes to Jase, and he glowered at me.

"There was a couple above us going at it all damn night. I barely slept."

Cam and I exploded with laughter. "Shouldn't that have been you and your new wife?"

"Fuck off," Jase grumbled, nursing a strong mug of coffee.

"Yesterday was a good day," Cam added, "but I'm not cut out for long days of eating and drinking anymore."

"Having kids will do that to a guy," I said.

"Tell me about it." He ran a hand down his face. "How's Mya feeling... about everything."

"She's excited for you all, of course she is. But it's hard, you know? All she wants is to get pregnant."

"There's still time."

"I know and I truly believe it'll happen when the time's right." Because honestly, I didn't know what would happen if we couldn't conceive naturally.

If I couldn't give her the one thing she wanted most in the world.

"Well, until then, we'll have enough fucking kids between us for the two of you to pitch in with the babysitting." Jason managed a small grin.

"Sometimes, I can't believe this is our life. That we're this fucking lucky," I said.

"Yeah, I know exactly what you mean." Cam let out a steady breath. "It hasn't always been easy, but I wouldn't change it for the world."

"You're married, Jase. Married, with a kid on the way."

An awed expression washed over him as he stared at me. "Fuck, you're right. I'm screwed. Totally and utterly screwed.

Months later...

"Babe, I'm home," Mya's voice filtered down our hall. A second later, she appeared around the door. "What are you doing?"

"Just got done video calling with Jase."

"You saw Lily?"

"I did." I grinned. "She's getting so big. How was your day?"

"Actually, I need to talk to you."

"You do. What about?"

She pulled something out of her bag and came to sit on the couch with me, snuggling into my side. "It's probably easier to show you."

"What is this?" I asked as she pressed the envelope into my hand.

"Open it and see."

My brows furrowed. She was acting strange. But I wasn't opposed to a surprise or two. Perhaps it was tickets to a romantic night away, just the two of us in a hotel room.

Yeah, I could totally go for that.

But when I pulled out the grainy black and white image, I had the distinct feeling I was off the mark. "Mya, wh -what is this?"

"You know what it is." Her voice cracked, and my eyes lifted to look at her.

"We're...."

She nodded. "I went to the clinic today and they confirmed it. I'm about seven weeks along."

"But... how?"

"Well, you put the P in the V and sometimes it makes—

"We're having a baby?"

Her tentative smile turned into a huge grin. "We are."

"Fuck, okay. This is... wow."

After Jase and Fee's wedding we'd spent an intense six months trying to conceive. But it just hadn't happened, and by the time Jase's daughter, Lily, and Cam's daughter, Ashleigh, arrived, we'd decided to stop actively trying. It was consuming us, making us both stressed.

I guess the more relaxed approach worked.

"There's something else," Mya started, and my stomach twisted.

"Is everything okay? What did the doctor say? Is there—"

"Take a breath," she chuckled. "Everything is fine. But there's a tiny complication."

"Complication? Okay," I inhaled a deep breath. "Well, whatever it is, we'll handle it together."

"We kind of have no choice because it's... twins."

"Twins?" I gawked at her. "You mean there's more than one in there?" My eyes dropped to her flat stomach.

"Yeah," she said. "Two heartbeats, two babies."

"Okay."

"Asher?" Mya pressed her hand against my cheek. "Are you okay? You've gone as white as a sheet."

"I'm fine. Totally fine."

"Do you need a glass of water or something?"

I needed something all right.

I needed a minute to get my head around this.

Twins?

Fuck.

ABOUT THE AUTHOR

ANGSTY. EDGY. ADDICTIVE ROMANCE

Author of mature young adult and new adult novels, L A is happiest writing the kind of books she loves to read: addictive stories full of teenage angst, tension, twists and turns.

Home is a small town in the middle of England where she currently juggles being a full-time writer with being a mother/referee to two little people. In her spare time (and when she's not camped out in front of the laptop) you'll most likely find L A immersed in a book, escaping the chaos that is life.

L A loves connecting with readers.

The best places to find her are:
www.lacotton.com

www.ingramcontent.com/pod-product-compliance
Lightning Source LLC
Chambersburg PA
CBHW070838020826
48982CB00021B/1425/J
9781919637501